BARRY ONO

RUTH THE BETRAYER;

OR,

THE FEMALE SPY.

BY EDWARD ELLIS.

WITH FIFTY-ONE ILLUSTRATIONS.

BY W. H. THWAITES.

LONDON:
JOHN DICKS, 313, STRAND; AND ALL BOOKSELLERS.

INDEX TO THE ENGRAVINGS.

RUTH THE BETRAYER;

OR,

THE FEMALE SPY.

CHAPTER I.

MAN OR WOMAN.—A DELICATE QUESTION.—THE GALLANT ENTERPRISES OF CAPTAIN CHARLEY CROCKFORD.—A LADY QUITE CAPABLE OF DEFENDING HERSELF.—THE FEMALE DETECTIVE.—THE ENTERPRISE.—UPON THE TRACK OF THE DOOMED.—A THIRST FOR BLOOD.

"I TELL you it is a man!"

"And I tell you it is a woman!"

"Do you suppose I have no eyes?"

"And do you suppose I am blind?"

"I'll bet you a pair of ponies on it."

"How are we to decide?"

"Let's go and speak to him."

"To her, you mean."

These were two hot-headed young gentlemen, who, one summer's night, about a year or two ago, had been dining at the Guards' Club, in Pall Mall, and who afterwards, while standing smoking upon the steps, undecided whither they should go to knock out the evening, had got into this dispute about the sex of a mysterious individual who had just passed by, staring them hard in the face.

The person who had attracted their notice and given rise to this dispute, was seemingly a youth of eighteen or nineteen, clad in semi-nautical attire, something like a midshipman.

A very handsome youth it was, certainly, with a profusion of golden ringlets clustering round his face; with delicately-chiselled features, bright, white, even teeth, and big blue eyes, deep and expressive; by turns, full of fire and full of languor. If a boy, a very pretty one, surely; but very like a pretty woman in disguise, there was no denying.

Captain Crockford had wagered a pair of ponies that it was a female. He was certain of it, he said—he would stake his life on it. Anyhow, he had staked a pair of ponies, and as young Lord Windibank was of a contrary opinion, they determined upon pursuing the mysterious stranger, and having a good look at him.

There was not too much time to spare if they intended to catch him, for he was walking very fast, and they ran down the steps, and along the pavement, in the direction he had taken.

"We have missed *him!*"

"*She* has given us the slip."

"What has become of *him?*"

"I can't see *her* anywhere."

"Ah! there she goes."

Crockford had caught sight of the figure of which he was in pursuit.

It had crossed the road, and was making rapidly for the Haymarket. Crockford caught a glimpse of the gold lace upon the midshipman's cap, as it passed under a gas-lamp.

In another moment he was standing by the stranger's side, and leering with an impudent smile into his face.

The sailor boy stopped short, and drew himself up with an indignant ejaculation, making way for the other to pass.

But Crockford, instead of availing himself of the opportunity thus afforded him, stopped in front of the sailor, and barring the passage with his arms, burst into a loud, foolish laugh.

"Where are you going to, my pretty dear?"

The youth, if youth it was, stared at him indignantly, and his face flushed crimson.

"Let me pass," he said.

"No—no," replied the gallant Captain, insolently puffing the smoke of his cigar into the other's face. "Not until you have paid toll, my youthful mariner."

"Stand on one side, you drunken fool!" the sailor exclaimed, fiercely, and in a tone which, if feminine, was full of savage determination, and accompanied by an ominous compression of the lips, knitting of the brows, clenching of the teeth, and flashing of the eyes, seemed to indicate that it would not be very safe to provoke their owner much further.

But the Guardsman addressed had been partaking pretty freely of wine before leaving the dinner-table, and was not in a state to be too observant of trifling details.

In his eye there was nothing very terrible in the anger of this handsome stranger; and young Lord Windibank coming up at the moment, the Captain, wishing to distinguish himself before his friend, endeavoured to take the sailor round the waist.

But it was a very rash proceeding, for before he could accomplish his object, he had received a violent blow from the stranger's clenched fist, right in the face.

So well directed and telling a blow, that under it the Guardsman reeled back against a lamp-post and, losing his balance, fell heavily into the mud, where he lay ignominiously sprawling, wondering very much how he had got there.

Then, taking advantge of the momentary victory thus gained over one of his assailants, the sailor dealt another violent blow to Lord Windibank, which sent that nobleman's hat flying into the road, and taking to his heels, ran like a greyhound in the direction of Waterloo Place.

The young stranger's progress in this direction was, however, doomed to meet with fresh obstacles, for he had not gone half a dozen yards before he ran straight into the stomach of the foremost of a file of policemen, at that moment turning the corner from St. James's Square; and at the same time that he knocked the breath out of his body, knocked him backwards on to the top of the man behind him, who in his turn tripping up the other, and so on to the end of the file, the whole half-dozen fell in an undistinguishable heap against the shutters of the public-house at the corner of the street; while the sergeant, from the violence of the concussion, was precipitated, head first, into the jug and bottle department, to the dire confusion of a maid-servant with a quart pot and a pint and half of supper beer, at that instant in the act of issuing therefrom.

"Murder—murder!" cried Captain Crockford, from the gutter.

"Police!" shouted Lord Windibank, pursuing his hat.

"Take him up!" gasped the sergeant, when he had recovered sufficient breath to speak.

"Who did it?" asked the policeman, who had been at the other end of the file.

"This here young sailor," replied another policeman, seizing hold of the cause of the disaster, who was the only one unhurt.

"Take him up," said the sergeant. "I'll teach the young jackanapes better manners. Bring him this way, that I may look at him. What do you mean, you young vagabond, by upsetting the civil executive in that sort of way? I'll let you know what o'clock it is."

"I know the time pretty well as it is, Mr. Hardstaff," said the audacious young stranger, with a merry laugh. "I hope I haven't hurt you, sergeant. I did not mean to do it, upon my honour."

"Why, bless my stars!" the sergeant cried, in blank amazement. "You don't mean to say that's you, ma'am, do you?"

"Hush! yes. Who else should it be? Here, leave go of me, stupid!" (addressing one of the policeman.) "You're new in the force, I suppose, or you'd have known me. There, don't stare so—I'm one of you! Give your man the office, sergeant, to let me go."

"Leave go of the lady's wrist," said Mr. Hardstaff. "We won't take you up this time, ma'am, only I wish you'd try and turn the corner a little quieter the next time we meet. It rather takes the wind out of a fellow, does one of those headers in the waistcoat, and so I don't deceive you."

"It was an accident," said the female sailor—for a female it was, undoubtedly—"it was an accident," she said, laughing, "and I'm very sorry; but I was running for my life from two tipsy young Guardsmen, who would not leave me alone."

"Where are they?"

"I knocked one into the mud. I don't know whether he has got out yet. "Ah! there he is, and there's his friend. Just see if I have hurt them much; I haven't time to stop myself."

And so saying, the extraordinary young lady took to her heels, though, as before, Captain Crockford had caught a glimpse of her retreating form, and called to the policeman to stop her.

"Don't you see him?" he cried, impatiently, as none of the officers attempted to stir. "It's that sailor fellow I mean. Why don't you stop him?"

But the sergeant, to whom the officer was well known, coming up, touched his hat, and asked respectfully what was the matter.

"Why, that young vagabond," the Captain exclaimed, "struck me in the face, as you see. Look how he has cut my cheek. I shall have a black eye to a certainty."

"You don't mean that, Captain, said the policeman, unable in spite of all his efforts to refrain from a slight smile. "She hits uncommon hard, surely."

"*She!*" repeated the Captain. "Then it is a *she?* You hear that, Windibank? I've won my bet; and that's one consolation anyhow. Who is she, Hardstaff? Do you know her? Tell me all about her."

"Well, sir," said Hardstaff, with a grin, "we don't usually tell stories out of school, you know."

"Pooh, nonsense! Go on!"

"It would be revealing the secrets of the prison-house."

"What do you mean? Is she in the force?"

"Well, Captain, I should have thought you knew her, seeing how down you are to what's afloat. I should have fancied you knew most of the London celebrities."

"I don't know her; so come, who is she?"

"It's on the quiet that I tell you, now."

"You may depend upon me."

"Well, then," said the policeman, sinking his voice to a mysterious whisper, "she's a female detective—a sort of spy we use in the hanky-panky way when a man would be too clumsy."

"By Jove, I'd give a fiver to be introduced to her!"

"Well, I don't quite see my way to that," replied the policeman. "She's a very proud, haughty, cold-blooded sort of woman, I can tell you; and when she is off duty, lives in some magnificent house in the west—though where it is I cannot say exactly—and has her carriages and horses, and flunkeys in livery, and I don't know what all, besides."

"And her name?"

"She's got so many, you see; I don't know the one she has in private life."

"But the one you know her by!"

"Some call her Ruth Trail; some one thing, and some another; but most people call her RUTH, THE SPY."

But while these two were conversing, the subject of their conversation was making the best of her way in the direction of Bow Street.

Arriving there safely in rather less than a quarter of an hour, she ran lightly up the steps and nodding to a constable standing by the door, who obsequiously made room for her to pass, she entered, where the officer on duty was already at his post engaged in taking the night charges.

"Ah, Mrs. Trail!" said he, looking up, and touching his hat; "I was almost afraid that you were not coming."

"Why so?"

"It is so close upon the time you fixed to be here."

"You would not have me before my time, would you?"

"No, nor behind; though ladies usually are a little."

"I am not," the woman said, with something of contempt in her tone. "I am neither before my time or after it. I come to the minute. We will proceed to business, if you please."

There was an indescribable something about the woman's manner, degraded though she was by the hateful calling which she followed of spy and informer, that seemed sufficiently powerful to curb the tongues of the roughest, coarsest, and most lawless, and effectually to check any attempt at familiarity from those persons who might have thought that her temporary association with them, in moments like the present, placed them upon a footing of equality.

But although well known to almost every member of the police force in London, she was not, as Mr. Hardstaff's words would have led the Captain to believe, a female detective, employed by Government.

On the contrary, she was attached to a notorious Secret Intelligence Office, established by an ex-member of the police force, and her services were only rarely employed, as upon the present occasion, in connection with the regular police.

That she was employed in a matter of some considerable importance this evening was very evident, and that her presence was of very great consequence to the success of the undertaking, might have easily been surmised by the anxiety manifested by the policemen in plain clothes assembled there, who were to place themselves under her directions.

"Do you think it is time to start?" the inspector asked, in a deferential whisper.

"Yes. How many men am I to have?"

"Will four do?"

"Yes; if they are good ones."

"The best in the force."

"Are they armed?"

"Well."

"Then we will go at once."

There was a cab waiting outside the door of the police-station, and in this three policemen seated themselves; while the beautiful female spy went first to show the way in another cab, with a fourth policeman—a sergeant.

Then they turned the horses heads to the south, and crossing Waterloo Bridge, drove rapidly towards the Borough.

For some time after they had started, the woman sat perfectly motionless in one corner of the back seat, whilst the policeman occupied the furthest corner of the seat facing her, and silently pursued their ways without exchanging a word.

What thoughts were passing through her busy brain who can say?

The honest constable, eyeing her stealthily, could not have guessed at them, to save his life; and he was not trying to do so.

She had taken off her uniform cap, and the light from the lamps in the shop-windows they were passing by fell full upon her fair face and golden curls.

It was a lovely head thus lit up every now and then by a sudden blaze of light which encircled it like a glory, and then as suddenly lost again in the dim obscurity, only to be again revealed bright and beautiful as before.

It was the head of a woman of no more than twenty—a pink and white faced beauty, with delicately chiselled features, and a clear, open, frank, and honest face, over which, from time to time, there played a gentle smile of so much sweetness, one would scarce have believed that it could have had birth save in purity and innocence.

But, oh! who shall say what records of treachery and baseness were hidden beneath that fair, white bosom, which rose and fell as placidly as that of a sleeping babe?

Who shall say with what black crimes was she not familiar—had she not herself committed—was she not doomed yet to commit, before her allotted race was run, and the lovely head, with its lustrous orbs of blue, its crimson, pouting lips, and rich, soft, silken curls, should be in its last bed, beneath earth, and food for worms?

On, on the cab rattles merrily through the busy streets, alive with gay-hearted, careless holiday folks. The policeman nods and dozes, and the spy, still smiling sweetly to herself, closes her eyes, and dreams of vengeance and of death!

On, on! She is on thy track, wretched, doomed one!

The she leopard is on thy path!

See how parched are her lips—how hungry her eyes!

She is athirst for thy blood!

She is crouching for a spring, and will be on thee in another moment, rending thee limb from limb!

CHAPTER II.

A HORRIBLE NEIGHBOURHOOD.—THE SPY AND HER FOLLOWERS.—A GAME OF LIFE OR DEATH.—THE RUFFIAN IN HIS LAIR.—POCKET-PICKING EXTRAORDINARY.—A MOMENT OF BREATHLESS SUSPENSE.—THE ATTEMPTED MURDER.—A KNIFE AT HER THROAT, AND HELP OUT OF REACH.—THE PRISONER.—DEATH'S HEAD AND SKELETON KEY.—THE FURIOUS MOB.—MYSTERY, MYSTERY.

AT length, in a narrow, crooked, ill-lighted, ill-paved by-street, in a low and villanous neighbourhood, the cab abruptly stopped.

A hideous locality it was, reeking with disease and filth—densely crowded by a squalid, starving population, brutalized by work and want—steeped in sin, old in vice, savage, sodden, and joyless—at best, but one remove from beasts.

The first cab had stopped at a sign from the spy; and the cab behind following their example, the woman and the police all descended, and held a brief council of war in the shelter of a gloomy archway.

"Is it near here?" asked the sergeant.

"Close to," the spy answered.

"In this street?"

"No; the next. It would not have done to have brought the cab wheels nearer. He has ears like a fox."

"Will you lead the way?"

"Yes; you know what has been arranged."

"That you are to go in first, and give us the signal when all is ready."

"When I have secured his arms you mean?"

"You must make very sure of them," the sergeant said, with a countenance which was not altogether free from uneasiness; "or we shall not be able to bag our game alive."

"That's true enough," the woman said, with a sneering laugh. "He would not leave many of you alive to do it."

"Oh, if you come to that," retorted the sergeant, much nettled, "I'm not afraid of any man!"

"I don't suppose you are a coward, sergeant," said the fair spy; "or you would not have been chosen for this business. Give me your hand."

Then, as he did so, she held his hand for a moment in her own, looking him fixedly in the face with her bold, blue eyes.

"It doesn't tremble," said she. "You are the right sort, sergeant."

"No more does yours," said the man, with something of admiration in his tone and look. "There are not many of your sort, ma'am, who wouldn't tremble in your place, though, I reckon."

"You think so?" she cried, breaking into a low, musical laugh, though her face wore a strangely savage expression, much like that which might light up the face of an Indian warrior-woman at the sight of an enemy's scalp. "You think they'd scream and faint, do you? Ha, ha! I shouldn't at twice the danger. It is not the first time I have faced death, man! I have been much nearer to it than I shall go to-night, and I am going near enough, too! Come, we are wasting time. We shall catch the wolf in his den, if we go now. He is waiting for me, though he does not expect you. We shall astonish him, sha'n't we?"

Then, changing her tone to an impressive whisper, she said—

"Creep after me. Keep close, and keep your ears open. Then rush in the moment I give the signal, but do not show yourselves before the time, or your lives will answer for it! Come cautiously!"

And with these words she led the way down the street, creeping stealthily along in the shadow of the houses like a cat stealing upon its prey.

The two cabs remained where they had originally stopped at the woman's desire, to await their return.

When she had gone on a dozen yards or so, two of the policemen followed in her track. Then the other two followed them at an equal distance.

Proceeding with the greatest caution—a caution which; to those unacquainted with the wily character of the person to effect whose capture the party had been organized, might have seemed almost preposterous—the female spy turned the street corner, and led the way down another lane, more crooked, narrow, ill-lighted, and foul-smelling than this one.

At length she stopped about fifty yards down the street at the door of a miserable tenement, the broken windows, crazy shutters, and half-broken down door of which seemed to indicate that it was uninhabited. Going into the road, she took a long and careful survey of the outside, and, evidently satisfied with the result of her scrutiny, came back into the shadow of the wall, and beckoned to the foremost policeman to approach.

"Do you see the gateway?" she asked, in a low tone.

"Yes."

"Go through it; it leads into a sort of yard belonging to the public-house at the corner. You will find nobody about there to interfere with you. For the matter of that though, you know what to say to them if they do. It is best not to let the people about here know more than is necessary, or they might give the alarm. They are not too fond of your cloth in this neighbourhood."

"We had better wait until the street gets a little quieter, perhaps?"

"They are quiet enough now; there is scarcely

any one about. However, it is very likely that you may have to wait an hour or two before I can make all safe."

"But about this yard?"

"If you go down to the bottom and look to the left, you will see a faint light upon the third floor of this uninhabited house. That is his room. If you get over the wall you will be able to get in at the back kitchen window very easy in the way I explained to you. But for heaven's sake do not make any noise, or you will ruin all."

"And the other two?"

"Are to go through the public-house—only quietly, mind; Let them take the master on one side, and tell him what they want. Don't blurt it out before every one."

"No, ma'am, you may depend on us."

With this, she left them, and approaching the door of the dilapidated house I have before mentioned, she stooped down by the side of that door, and gently pulled the end of a wire which was so placed as to be only visible to those well acquainted with its whereabouts.

Then followed a faint tinkling within—so faint that it was scarcely audible even to the woman listening—and after a time a slight creaking upon the stairs, and a voice whispered, "Who's there?"

"All right," the woman answered. "Open the door."

"Is it you, Ruth?"

"Yes."

After a momentary pause, in which the person within was engaged in taking a survey of his visitor through a tiny hole in the panel, the door was cautiously opened, just sufficient for the woman to squeeze herself through the aperture, which was thus rendered narrow by means of a bar of wood ingeniously fixed into the wall of the passage against which the door opened, and which was so contrived to prevent the possibility of a rush being made into the house from without.

No sooner had she passed the threshold than the door was carefully closed again behind her, and chained and bolted.

"You're early, aren't you?" said a man's deep voice in the dark.

"Later than I thought I should be," returned the spy.

"Give me your hand, or you will tumble."

She held out her hand to him, and the man holding it in his, they groped their way up-stairs in the dark.

"It's ticklish work without a light," he muttered presently; "for the balustrade's broken down at one place; but it's not safe to flash a glim in the front of the house. Keep close to the wall."

"Take care of yourself," she replied; "I can feel my way."

They proceeded silently up the creaking stairs without exchanging another word until they arrived at a room on the third floor, the door of which he had left open.

It was miserably furnished, squalid and dirty, and a tallow candle burning, with a long wick, upon the mantel-piece, and stuck into the neck of a black bottle, which served as a candlestick, threw a sickly light upon the few crazy sticks which it contained, and upon the owner.

In one corner was a wretched truckle bed, the linen of which, tossed and tumbled in a heap, as they had been thrown when its late occupant got out of it, was filthily dirty. There was also a ricketty table, two chairs, decidedly upon their last legs, and an old deal box. A handful of hot cinders smouldered in the grate, over which a black pot was simmering. A black pipe lay on the mantel-piece, which the man had been recently smoking. He took it up now when he came in, and lighting it at the candle, sat and puffed for awhile in silence, thus giving his visitor an opportunity, if she had been so desirous, of studying his appearance.

However, it is questionable whether the result would have repaid any one for the trouble, for a more ill-looking, beetle-browed, black-muzzled ruffian it would have been difficult to imagine.

Bullet-headed, bull-necked, square, and thick-set, he evidently possessed a giant's strength, whilst the brutish wolf-like expression of the wretch's dirty begrimed countenance showed only too plainly that he was not a person who would scruple at the commission of any savage atrocity, were it his interest to commit it.

Perhaps the woman was thinking this as she seated herself upon the chair opposite to him, and regarded him for a few seconds attentively.

Perhaps the full terror of the situation in which she had placed herself now for the first time dawned upon her mind, for the slightest possible shiver ran through her frame as her eyes fell upon her companion's repulsive features, illuminated for a moment with an effect quite diabolical, as he stuck his nose almost into the candle while lighting his short pipe.

The idea flashed through her mind that she was now in this monster's power, and did he at that instant have a suspicion of any treachery on her part, he might murder her easily before any help could reach her.

Something, too, almost akin to pity for the brute she was about to deliver up to justice, came upon her as she sat watching him; but it did not long hold dominion over her, for in her breast lay smouldering a bitter, deadly hate, which a moment's reflection upon past events sufficed to fan up into a flame, and she could have seen him torn to pieces by wild horses before her eyes without an atom of compassion.

"No; he had defied her—he had thwarted her. He stood in her way—he was doomed; and she had set her fatal mark upon him, for the hulks.

"Well?" she said, breaking a somewhat lengthy silence.

"Well?" he repeated, looking at her.

"Have you nothing to say?"

"Have *you* nothing to say?"

"You are not prodigal of your welcomes."

"Humph!" said the man, with a grunt; "it's late in the day for us to begin to be civil to one another."

"Civility is never thrown away."

"So I've been told. I never found it bring in much, though." Then, after a pause, "As to having anything to say," he continued, "a poor devil cooped up in this rat's-hole of a place, without a blessed soul to see or speak to—without light, or air, or anything else that makes life worth having, don't find much to talk about. But you must have news."

"I have the news that the police are on your track, and are hunting for you high and low. There's scarcely a thieves' hiding-place in London they have not turned out looking for you."

"Ha, ha!" the man laughed; "I'm glad to hear it; it keeps 'em employed. What else do we pay taxes for?"

"They'll make you pay a tax, I expect, when they get hold of you!" the woman retorted.

"Get hold of me!" the man repeated, looking up at her suddenly and fiercely. "Not much chance of that, I suppose—is there?"

"How do I know?" his companion replied,

carelessly running her delicate white fingers through her golden locks.

"You wouldn't blab on me, I guess?" he said, eyeing her uneasily.

"I?" she answered, with a laugh. "What should I gain by it?"

"I don't exactly see that; I've acted fair enough by you, I'm sure. Except that you're hand and glove with those accursed police, I don't know why you should."

"Who else knows of your hiding-place?"

"No one," he answered. "Yes, though, they do, by the way!" he added, quickly.

"Who?" she asked.

"Skeleton Key."

She started at the name, and the colour faded from her cheeks.

"When did you see *him*?" she asked, with a slight tremour in her voice.

"To-night, about an hour ago."

"Have you been out, then?"

"No; he was here."

"Here?" she repeated, and her agitation grew more evident. "How did he come here?"

"He was here, hiding at this crib, once upon a time, some time ago—a long while ago; and he came to have a look at it, seeing it was in the state we left it then."

"Did he already know you were here?"

"No. He was rather surprised when he saw who it was. He had found the wire in the old place, you know, and gave it a pull on the spec'; and he was ready to drop when he heard my voice through the peep-hole. We were old pals, was the Skeleton and me. He says, says he, when he got the first sight of me, 'It's good for sore eyes, Jacob, this is!' We had not met for two years before—ever since he went across the herring-pond, in fact."

"He has returned from transportation, has he?"

"Yes; he had given them the double somehow. You didn't know him, did you?"

"No; I have heard of him, very often."

"Ah! he was an ornament to any society, was the Skeleton;—the sort of chap that would have stuck at nothing, from burking to baby's wizzens. A fellow after my own heart, he was."

"Ah!" said his companion, without much show of interest. "And so he isn't here now? He's not stopping with you?"

"I asked him to come and stop a bit with me if he could, and tell me a yarn or two to cheer me up. He can pull a rare one or two off, I can tell you. He told me a curious one, too, about an old mate of his—Jack something or other."

Again the colour forsook the woman's face. Again a tremour of agitation in her voice.

Luckily for her, however, her companion was too intent upon the lighting of his pipe, which somehow would not draw well, to notice it.

"Indeed!" she said, as he did not go on. "Jack something, was it?"

"I forget what," he said. "Jack Ruff—Riff—Raff—Rafferty; that was it—Jack Rafferty!"

The woman's face was deadly pale, and the hand with which she attempted to snuff the candle shook like a leaf.

Luckily for her again, she was standing with her back towards the ruffian smoking, and he could neither see her countenance, or notice the extreme agitation which seemed to shake her whole frame.

"To be sure!" he continued, puffing at his pipe; "Jack Rafferty was the name—a chap who got a sentence for life; but somehow they made out he was innocent, and got it knocked off, and he went into the bush."

"Yes, yes," she said, eagerly; "and was killed by the bushrangers."

"Who told you that?" asked the man, looking up surlily. "Did you know him? 'cos if you did, and know the story too, you'd better tell it."

"I don't know anything about him."

"Then what made you say so?"

"Because most people die in the bush, I suppose. At least, so I have heard. There, go on, if you have anything more to say."

She was dying to hear what he had to say, but was afraid of showing her anxiety, for fear that he might remain silent for the mere sake of annoying her.

After a pause, in which he appeared to be trying to make up his mind whether or not he should tell her at all, he went on.

"He didn't die in the bush, because he went to the diggins and dug up gold there by the pailful. He made his fortune, in fact!"

"Well?"

"And he's come over here to spend it, and—— What the blazes are you up to with that candle?"

This latter exclamation was caused by a sudden eclipse of the light, for the woman in her agitation had snuffed it out.

She lit it again, though, as rapidly as her trembling fingers would allow of, and sitting down in her chair, leant her head upon the table.

"What's the matter now?" the man asked, in astonishment.

"Oh, nothing," she replied. "I have not been well all day; I felt a little faint. Have you any water?"

"Well, we don't do much in that line here," he said, rising; "but I can get you some."

"Where is it?"

"Down stairs."

He was moving towards the door, but she stopped him suddenly.

"No, no!" she said, hastily. "It doesn't matter; don't trouble yourself; I'm better now; and I had forgotten I have some brandy in my pocket that I brought for you."

Then, as she spoke, she drew a pint bottle from a pocket in her pilot coat, and handed it to him.

He clutched at it eagerly, and, tilting himself back in his chair, let about half a quartern of the liquid trickle down his throat.

"That's prime!" he said, with a grunt of satisfaction, although the strength of the spirit had brought the tears into both eyes. "That's the right sort, that is! That didn't pay much duty, I reckon?"

"I believe not," said the woman. "Take some more of it, if you like it. I brought it here for you."

"Don't you want none?"

She just raised the bottle to her lips, but handed it back to him without tasting it.

"Now," said she, "I suppose it is time for me to go again. Can I do anything for you? Would you like your room tidied a little? Shall I make your bed for you?"

"Thank you," replied the man, gruffly; "you can if it amuses you. I'm not particular about that sort of thing myself."

She had been sitting in a chair between the table and the bed; and, while talking, before she had risen from her seat to snuff the candle, her hand had been resting upon the pillow on the bed, her fingers partly hidden beneath it.

The man, occupied, as we have seen, with his pipe, which obstinately refused to draw, did not pay any attention whatever to her movements, although the whole time she was busily engaged, for she was groping cautiously under the pillow for his revolver.

She knew that he usually kept it there. She had seen it in that place several times when she had formerly paid him a visit, but now it was gone.

"What had become of it?" she asked herself, her eyes the while wandering searchingly round the bare walls, upon the table, on the mantelpiece, and the box in the corner.

"It must be under the pillow," she thought; and for this reason she had proposed to make the bed, although her soul revolted from the idea of having to handle the black and filthy linen.

She, therefore, took off the pillow, turned down the sheet, and tumbled the clothes about it to look for it, but it was not there.

Then she hastily straightened them again, and threw the counterpane over all.

A thought had occurred to her.

When he came down to open the door for her, he had put it in his pocket. It was there now.

But which pocket?

"Your fire is going out," she said; and, rising from her chair, she made a feint of putting on some coals, so that she might touch his left breast-pocket to ascertain whether it was there.

In passing him she did so lightly and delicately, and found that it was.

Her fingers touched something hard and round. She grasped it. It was the barrel of his revolver.

But, now, how was she to get it?

She sat down again, and thought of half a dozen plans, all equally wild and improbable.

She could not remain much longer there inactive; but what could she do? She had all along calculated with the greatest confidence that it would be in the usual place. How could she possibly pick his pocket of it?

The ruffian, putting down his pipe, which he had smoked out, yawned prodigiously. Oh, if he would only go to sleep, she could easily manage.

But would he do so?

She was afraid that her talking might rouse him from his drowsiness, and yet she thought that if she sat there silently, he would think it very extraordinary. She was usually lively enough, and had lots to say for herself.

"When do you expect to see your friend again?" she asked.

"Who?"

"Skeleton Key."

"He'll perhaps be back to-night."

To-night! Then there was no time to lose. Every moment was of importance. The next might bring him.

"Shall you sit up for him?"

"Yes."

"You're sleepy?"

"I'm rather beat. There's nothing to keep me awake in this hole."

He was not very complimentary, this gentleman, but she cared very little about that. He opened his great mouth like a cavern, and yawned until the top of his head seemed to be in danger of falling off. Then he shut his eyes, and nodded.

The coal that she had thrown upon the fire made it blaze up fiercely, and the heat from it fell upon him where he sat. The room was already suffocatingly hot.

Would he be long before he went to sleep?

But she sat, and watched him with momentarily increasing impatience and anxiety. Supposing the other ruffian should return! Then the hope of capturing him quietly would be gone.

But she would not for the world have had the other man come and find her there, for reasons of her own.

Every second she expected to hear a tinkle of the bell.

If he came, then the man would go downstairs, and very probably meet the two policemen, who must by this time have got into the house.

Would he never go to sleep?

If he would doze off ever so slightly, she would make an attempt upon his pocket, she thought.

It would be a risk; but every moment now, until she had secured the revolver, she was risking her life with him.

Ah! he nodded again, and breathed a little more heavily than before.

She rose from her seat, as noiseless as a cat; approached him upon tip-toe, and leant over him.

Then, holding her breath, she began to feel for the weapon.

Yes, there it was, lying loosely in his pocket. It could be got out quite easily. Many a time she had been obliged to do more difficult tasks, and tasks requiring a much greater delicacy of touch; but it was the knowledge that discovery might end in death did he detect her and suspect her object, which made this moment seem to be the most trying and awful one that she had ever lived.

Gently propping up the bottom of the pocket with her left hand, she slipped her right into the pocket, and felt for the handle of the revolver.

Then, gliding her fingers noiselessly round it, so that she might be sure to draw it out without knocking against him or catching it in any way against the lining of the pocket, she drew it out.

Slowly, oh, how slowly—it seemed an age to her—slowly and cautiously, but safely; and at last, with a smile of triumph, she lifted up her hand clear from the coat.

"Thank heaven!" she muttered to herself, and she breathed again.

But at that moment, while she stood over him with the revolver in her hand, before she had time to draw back from the crouching position in which she had been obliged to stand, a loud noise below, upon the first floor, caused the ruffian suddenly to open his eyes.

It was the sound of smashing glass, and a heavy footfall upon the bare boards, which had startled him; and he opened his eyes, and glared wildly at the woman leaning over him.

Then, in an instant, from the horrified expression of her face, and from the weapon which she held in her hand, he read the whole story.

She was unarming him! The police were down below! He was betrayed!

But not taken yet, he thought! No; there was yet a chance for him.

He rose up to his feet with a bound and a snarl like that of an enraged tiger springing upon his prey.

"Traitress!" he yelled, and made a clutch at the weapon, determining that she should be the first victim.

But she was too quick for him.

Quick as lightning through her brain flashed the thoughts, "Are all the barrels loaded? Are there caps on? Shall I be able to hit him if I try?"

And then she determined not to risk any of these chances, but to put the revolver out of his reach; and as he sprang at it, she dashed it with all her might through the window into the yard below.

"Curse you!" he cried; "you shan't escape me. You were going to give me up, were you?"

"Yes," she retorted, with a flushed face and flashing eyes. And, placing a whistle which hung from her neck to her lips, she blew a shrill blast, and then sprang towards the door.

But this time he was before her.

He double-locked the door, and hastily fastened a bolt across it, which he kept there for the purpose, and then turned upon her.

She had no arms to use in her defence. She looked all round despairingly.

"Help! help!" she cried, at the top of her voice.

Would they never come up?

Upon the fire was the saucepan, the liquid contained in which was simmering when she came in, and which was boiling now; and she formed a desperate resolve.

As he approached, she seized the saucepan from the fire, and flung it at him with all the strength she was capable of.

The scalding liquor, boiling hot and greasy, flew into his face and made him stagger back with a frightful oath; and, in his agony, he covered his face with his hands.

Then, with a savage yell, like the howl of a wild beast, maddened and furious with pain, he made a rush at her.

Again she screamed with all her strength, and desperately sought to screen herself behind the table; but in a moment he had clutched her by the neckerchief and dragged her to the ground.

But, in her wild terror and hatred of this man, she struggled with a strength that she could hardly believe herself capable of, and gnashed her teeth fiercely, striving vainly to bite his hands.

The struggle, however, was not likely to be of long duration, for the man was powerful as a giant. With one hand he was able to hold her down upon the ground, and with the other he groped in his pockets for his knife.

But she heard steps upon the stairs. They were coming up.

Had they mistaken the room? Would they be in time?

"Help! help!" she shrieked, discordantly.

"They won't get here before I've settled you!" the ruffian said betwixt his teeth, with something almost like a laugh; and, as he spoke, he drew the knife from his pocket.

It was a large knife, with a long, bright, glittering, deadly blade, such as the rowdies use to whittle with or slit their neighbours' windpipes.

It did not, however, open with a spring in the usual way.

When he had got it from his pocket, he wanted to use his other hand.

This, though, he could not manage without loosening his hold on her; fearing to do this, he struggled vainly to drag it open with his teeth.

She lay there panting in his grasp, her eyes bloodshot, her apparel torn with the struggle, her breast heaving painfully.

A loud blow struck the panel of the door, and a policeman shouted to her to keep up for another moment.

Then shout followed shout, and blow followed blow, until the door was shivered to atoms.

The would-be murderer saw that he had not much more time to lose, and he left go of her to open his knife, determined to have her life before he made an effort to escape, even if it cost him his own.

But no sooner had he released his hold than, with all her remaining strength, she twisted herself with a violent jerk out of his grasp, almost overthrowing him in doing so.

Then, like a tigress, springing at his throat, she bore him to the ground, and strove to set her teeth in his throat and worry him like a dog.

He shook her off, however, and catching up the knife from the ground, on which it had fallen from his fingers, turned upon her and raised it in the air.

But a terrific smash at the door broke it down altogether, and the police poured into the room.

Relinquishing his design now that he saw his case was so desperate, the ruffian backed for a moment into a corner of the room, the better to make ready for a spring, and then dashed headlong at them, slashing and cutting at them with the fury of a wild beast; and over the bodies of those who fell bleeding and groaning beneath his murderous stabs, he rushed down stairs.

He had not quite escaped, though, yet; for his back being turned, the sergeant, who had been standing behind the rest and making ready for a blow at him, struck him now with his life preserver upon the back of the head with such stunning violence, that it brought him down to the ground like a pole-axe fells an ox.

Next moment, with the assistance of another policeman, who was not severely wounded, he had deprived the desperate savage of his knife, and had securely handcuffed him.

After which, they dragged him in a passive and half stupefied state down stairs, into the street.

A noisy, dirty, clamouring mob was assembled round the door, thrusting one another on one side, with every manifestation of eagerness.

The police brought down the prisoner. A thin, wiry-looking man, with a strongly-marked and remarkable face, which at first sight amazingly resembled a death's head, came forward to meet them, and said the cab was there.

"This way," he said: "it's waiting a stone's throw off."

But the crowd pressed upon them, and when they saw that Stone staggered, and looked weak and giddy from the effects of the blow he had received, and that his head was bloody, there arose a loud murmur of rage and resentment against the police, mingled with deep groans of sympathy for the wounded man.

"They've half murdered him," one said.

"They don't care," said another, "so as he lives long enough to be hanged."

"And where's the woman that split on him and gave him up?"

One shrill voice asked in the crowd, "Where's the spy?—where's the spy?"

And the cry was taken up, echoed from mouth to mouth, and swelled from a murmur into a savage howl.

"She ought to be torn to pieces," one wild-looking, bareheaded, drunken woman, foremost in the throng, was heard to say; and the suggestion seemed to meet with general approval.

"They're rough customers," the thin man with the death's head said, in a low voice. "If you leave the woman to them, they'll do her a mischief."

"We mustn't have that," rejoined the sergeant. "What's to be done?"

"It won't do to leave the prisoner here—he'll be rescued. Where are the other men?"

"I'm not quite sure the villain has not murdered them. He shot out right and left with his knife, in a way I never saw the like of."

"I'll tell you what," suggested Death's Head; "if you like, you and I, sergeant, can go on in the cab with the prisoner, and your mate here go back and look after the rest."

"That will be best," the sergeant said; and

acting upon Death's Head's suggestion, one of the policemen returned to the house, and the prisoner, having been assisted into the cab, the sergeant and the other man drove away with him towards the police-office, amidst the yells and hooting of the ruffianly populace.

The prisoner, at first leaning back in a corner of the back seat by the side of the sergeant, gave no other signs of life besides every now and then an occasional groan.

But after awhile he seemed slowly to revive, and stared about him in a stupid way at the policeman and his other companion.

At the latter, though, after a time, his stare became more fixed; and gradually as he stared a glimmering of intelligence came into his eyes.

But still he appeared bewildered, and his eyes travelled back to the policeman, whose uniform now showed a little through his unbuttoned overcoat, and then at the handcuffs upon his own wrists, finally reverting fixedly to the face of his opposite neighbour.

Did he know him, then? Yes. But he could not, for the life of him, connect his acquaintance with his present circumstances; for this man was none other than Skeleton Key!

"And he, too, has betrayed me!" thought the prisoner.

But a wink of intelligence and a significant leer, which Skeleton Key contrived to bestow upon him unseen by the policeman, changed his opinion.

"There is hope yet, perhaps," he thought. "He may be here to save me."

Some one, though, should have been at the place where they had just left, to save the woman whose treachery had placed Jacob Stone in the hands of the police from the fury of the mob; for by this time they had lashed themselves into a boiling rage against her, and were screaming for a bloody vengeance upon the black-hearted traitress and spy—for so they called her.

CHAPTER III.

THE SPY LEFT TO HER OWN DARK THOUGHTS.—THE HOWLING OF THE MOB WITHOUT.—ONE WAY OF ESCAPE.—THE ROOFS.—THE TRAP-DOOR.—FOILED.—DANGER ON EVERY SIDE.—THE PURSUERS CLOSE UPON HER.—THE STRATAGEM.—THE FATAL ACCIDENT.—"A SPY, A SPY!—DOWN WITH HER!"

WEAK from her recent almost superhuman exertions, and in the reaction succeeding them, prostrated mentally and physically, the Spy lay panting upon the bed in the room from which the man called Jacob Stone had made his escape a short time previously, and with her eyes closed and her hands pressed firmly to her fast throbbing heart, remained motionless and pale as death.

The groans of a dying man, lying across the threshold of the room, were unheeded by her, as were also the hoarse murmurings of the angry crowd without.

She lay there for quite ten minutes, without care or thought of anything occurring around her, only endeavouring by slow degrees to recover her usual calm and collected demeanour, which, in the horrible scene through which she had just passed, had almost entirely deserted her.

It was the entrance of the policeman, whom the sergeant had sent back to look after her and the wounded men, which at length aroused her.

She opened her eyes, and saw him standing by the side of the bed.

"Are you hurt?" he asked.

"No."

"Can I do anything for you?"

"No."

"What are you going to do?"

"I am going."

"I don't think that would be wise just yet, ma'am."

"Why not?"

"The people outside seem rather savage. This fellow Stone was rather a popular character, it appears."

"What of that?"

"They might do you an injury, I fear. It would be safest to wait a bit."

"I'm not afraid. When you are ready, we will go."

"I must look to my comrades here. One poor fellow seems at his last gasp, and the other is very badly cut."

He went, as he spoke, to raise the head of one of the fallen men: while she, stepping over the body of the other without much pity or compunction visible upon her pale but beautiful face, passed into the next room, and, with a great effort pushing up one of the crazy window sashes, which had warped and swollen in its frame, so as to require all her strength to move it, she gazed down upon the crowd below.

A hundred wild, haggard, and hideous faces were immediately turned upwards, and a loud yell broke from as many throats.

"Yah—ah! That's her! That's the woman that sold him! That's the female spy!"

She did not shrink back at once, and cower, and hide her head, as you might have thought that she would be likely to do, but stood smiling down at them.

"Poor fools!" she said, with a contemptuous glance at one woman in particular, who was screaming shrilly at her, and threatening her with her brawny fist. "Poor fools!" she muttered, as she turned away; "I like to see them fret and fume! What do they want to do with me, I wonder? I am not afraid of them!"

"It would be best not to aggravate them, though," said the policeman, who had overheard her words.

Then, after closing the window, he turned to her again.

"Take my advice, ma'am," he said, "and don't show yourself any more. They're dreadful spiteful at being kept away from you, to be sure. I give you my word of honour, I never knew a crowd look more like mischief; and they're a roughish set round this quarter to have anything to do with!"

They certainly appeared to be very eager to get at her, for the whole house at that moment seemed to be shaking with the violence of the blows which were being dealt upon the outer door, while the yelling and hooting had by this time grown almost deafening.

"There is a trap door," said the policeman, "which my two mates here came through: you had better go by that."

"The one on the roof?"

"Yes."

"Very well. I dare say I can manage; but what will become of you?"

"They won't hurt me. They're not so bitter against us, you know, for it's our regular profession."

The woman looked at him hard. She fancied that she noticed a faint indication of dislike and dread in the man's manner.

Had he a fear and horror of her? What did it matter if he had?

She smiled contemptuously, and turned upon her heel.

"You mean the trap over there, don't you?"

"Yes, over there in the corner. You can get through it easily by standing on the box. Stay, I will hold you a light."

"No need. I can manage very well. I have been up there before. I looked at it the last time I was here."

"You thought you might want it, perhaps?"

"I thought *you* might. Did I not tell you of it?"

"To be sure; I forgot."

"Did you leave the other trap open?"

"Yes. You can get down through the public-house."

"Very well."

She climbed upon a trunk overthrown in the corner, and by the aid of a piece of rope, which had seemingly been left hanging there on purpose to facilitate escape by the man who had lately made the house his hiding-place, she raised herself lightly through the trap, and in another moment stood safely upon the roof.

The yells of the mob outside in the street were now at their loudest, shrillest, and fiercest.

"Bring her out! bring her out!" they were shouting.

"Where is the she-devil who fattens upon men's blood?" one furious hag was shrieking.

"Let's get at her!" joined in a chorus of other hags. "Let's get at her! We'll spoil her beauty for her!"

The Spy looked down at them coolly from a safe place, where she could stand unseen behind a stack of chimneys.

"Ha, ha!" she laughed to herself. "Do your worst, and screech your loudest, you can't hurt me here!"

And saying this, she carefully shut down the trap behind her, after pulling up the rope, and heaped some heavy stones upon the outside, which were piled round about as though for the purpose for which she now used them.

When she had done this, she began, very cautiously and carefully, to ascend the slanting roof leading from the house which she was leaving to that next door, at a place where she could not be seen, while crossing the tilt of the roof, by the people in the street.

The roofs were very old, and in many places, where the tiles had been broken in, offered a very uncertain footing to the adventurous woman now scaling them with cat-like caution.

It was so very dark, too, that she could barely discern the objects at a couple of yards distance from her face; and as she groped her way upon her slippery path, she dreaded lest at any moment an uncertain step, or an incautious movement, might precipitate her below to certain death.

She crept on, however, and came at length in perfect safety to the trap-door of the house through which the police had ascended.

"Ah, there it is!" she exclaimed; "and not before it is time."

It seemed that there was very little time to spare, for, from the sound of angry voices in the direction from which she had come, and by a shuffling noise and a loud banging at the trap-door, which she had fastened down, she could tell that some of the people had got into the other house, and were striving hard to force their way out upon the roof.

With nervous haste she applied herself to the task of opening the trap-door leading down into the public-house.

With all her strength she endeavoured to raise it.

But it was fast.

"They left it open, he said," she thought to herself. "Is this the right door? Yes, it must be! But it is so horribly dark there is no telling where one is!"

The spraining, and bumping, and shuffling of the other door showed that those imprisoned within were making desperate and determined attempts to get out.

"They'll have to push pretty hard, though," the Spy said to herself, with a chuckle, and she knelt down and applied herself earnestly to her task.

"It cannot be fastened," she thought. "There is some trick about lifting it up, I suppose; or it has stuck fast somehow. I wish there was a little more light."

But it was fastened sure enough, for the wiry individual with the death's-head had bolted it after the policemen when he had shown them the way to the roof.

While she was striving to open the door, she all at once stopped suddenly, for she heard voices underneath.

"Take care how you come," one said.

"Lead on, then," said another.

"Can you find the bolt?"

No: show us a light."

Then she heard the rusty bolt turning in its socket, and the hard breathing of the man within struggling with it.

"Do you suppose she's up here?" one of the voices resumed.

"There is not a doubt of it," the other replied.

"Unless she has got away."

"How could she? There's nowhere to get to!"

The bolt had been drawn back by this time, and the trap-door opened outwards.

The first inclination of the Spy was to stamp in the upturned face of the first man who made his appearance at the opening; but a moment's thought convinced her of the folly of such an act. No: a better plan suggested itself to her quick intelligence.

The first man put out his hand, holding the candle high in the air: she instantly blew out the light, and sprang back nimbly before they could catch sight of her, and creeping round behind a stack of chimneys close to the spot, she managed to jam herself into a narrow place, where the obscurity was so intense, that from a very little distance it was impossible to discern the faintest outline of her form.

"Drat the wind!" the man exclaimed: "the candle is out already."

"Never mind: go on."

"Easy behind, there: I'm not a cat."

The men scrambled up with a good deal of difficulty, puffing and blowing considerably with their exertions.

"It's as dark as pitch. I can't see anything."

"Don't go that way, man, or you'll break your neck!"

"I'll tell you what it is."

"What what is?"

"What my opinion is."

"Well, what is that?"

"That we'd be a precious deal safer where we came from. We shall never catch her!"

"Don't let us give it up, though, before we have looked."

"I don't see anything of her."

"She's somewhere hereabouts, though, depend upon it, dodging us behind the chimneys."

As luck would have it, the men chose the opposite side of the stack of chimneys to that on which the spy was concealed, and they scrambled up the roof with a great deal of shuffling and scraping, calling to one another loudly the while to hold up and keep steady, and look out where they were going to.

All at once they heard a noise behind them—a sudden crash.

"What's that?"

"The roof given way."

"No; it was the trap."

One of the men slid down to it again.

"Hallo!" he shouted.

"What's the matter, now?"

"Somebody has bolted it inside. Hallo, there! No larks, if you please!"

But the person inside made no reply; but leaving him to kick and bellow to his heart's content, ran rapidly down stairs.

It was the Spy who had played them the trick—who had taken advantage of this opportunity offered her, and who was now using her best efforts to effect her escape.

Would she be able to get away, though? It was yet uncertain. Would they recognise her if she went out into the street? Would they recognise her at the bar below, and give her up to the fury of the mob?

She was at a loss to understand how all the

outcry had arisen. Who could have got up the cry against her? How had the story of her treachery become known? Who had pointed her out when she was at the window? All that was a mystery to her which she could not fathom.

The only way she could possibly account for it, was that one of the policemen had been chatting incautiously at the bar of the public-house, or that this man Skeleton Key was in the crowd, and had seen her, and pointed her out.

But how could he do so? Did he know her? She had never met him, that she knew of; although she had so often heard him spoken of by——

By whom?

What was there in the thought which flashed upon her now, that turned her suddenly faint, and sick with terror—that caused her limbs to shake and totter under her—the cold perspiration to break out upon her forehead, and her very blood to curdle in her veins?

It was the same dread horror which had seized upon her a while ago, when talking with Jacob Stone; when Stone had spoken of a man who was a friend of Skeleton Key, and who had returned from transportation, with a free pardon and enormous wealth.

The weakness which, at this mysterious and terrible dread of a nameless something she dare scarcely explain to herself, had overcome her, obliged her to pause for a few moments and rest before proceeding any further.

She, however, recovered her wonted strength, composure, and presence of mind very rapidly, and descended the remainder of the stairs.

She took the precaution of fastening a comforter which she wore over the lower part of her face, and pulling down the peak of her cap to conceal her features as much as possible.

Then she pushed boldly into the crowd thronging the bar.

Everybody was eagerly discussing the same topic Some speculating what would be done to Stone; others wondering what could have become of the woman who had given him up, and whether they would be able to catch her.

Holding down her head, and looking neither to the right nor the left, the Spy forced her way through the throng; and availing herself of the door being opened at that moment to allow some one else to go out, followed in their wake, and found herself unquestioned in the street.

The crowd, which by this time was very large, blocked up the road before the house, and was so deeply interested in watching the movements of some of the persons upon the roofs, that they had not much time to notice her, and probably would not have done so had not she, in her haste, run violently against a group of ragged women standing close to the door of the public-house, out of which she just made her escape; at the same time that she herself staggered back with the violence of the concussion. She almost knocked one old woman on to her face.

The whole party turned upon her angrily.

"Now then, you fool, where are you running to? What do you want? Who are you?" were the exclamations which greeted her upon all sides.

And then followed a cry of astonishment.

"Why, it's a woman!"

And then a cry of recognition at the sight of the midshipman's cap.

"It is the Spy!"

"The Spy! — the Spy!" a score of voices echoed.

"Down with her!—down with her!"

Casting a wild and terrified glance around upon the savage faces glaring after her, she turned and fled.

Scattering the crowd to the right and then to the left as she struck out at those who would have attempted to stop her, she rushed madly on the the mob howling at her heels.

Where could she hope to go? How far could she run? How long last out?

She dashed down the first narrow turning she came to, trusting to heaven that it would not prove to be a blind alley, or a no thoroughfare.

Clinching her teeth together, breathless, panting, half fainting, she tore along, her assailants rapidly gaining upon her.

"Stop her!—stop her! Down with her! A spy!—a spy!"

CHAPTER IV.

HUNTED DOWN.—IN THE HANDS OF THE FURIOUS MOB.—A CRITICAL MOMENT.—THE STALWART STRANGER —WHO ARE YOU?—A TOUGH CUSTOMER —THE SPY DENOUNCED.—WHAT MADE HER TREMBLE?—AGAIN THE SECRET AND MYSTERIOUS DREAD.—THE TERROR OF FIVE YEARS PAST.—DAWNING MEMORY.—THE RECOGNITION.—THE ESCAPE.—THE PURSUIT.—THE STRANGER VOWS TO BE AVENGED UPON THE BLACK-HEARTED TRAITRESS.

It was done.

Some one, a burly ruffian of villanous aspect, had sprung out from a doorway and caught her in his arms.

A moment afterwards she was down on the ground, surrounded—hemmed in—howled over—dragged hither and thither, and threatened by a dozen savage voices.

"What will you do with her?" the ruffian asked who had dragged her down. "What has she done?"

"She is an informer in the pay of the police. She has just given up a man to them, and it's not the first by a score or more. She lives by men's blood. There's nothing that is too bad for her."

This, and much more, was hoarsely bawled in answer to the man's question, and a rush was made by those behind to get at her.

"What are you going to do to her?" the man asked again, still keeping between the angry crowd and their would-be victim, and holding her back, as it seemed to be making their rage more furious, like one might excite a terrier with the sight of a rat.

"Let the women settle her!" decided some one else, creating himself a judge. "Give her up to the women—they'll manage her."

"Yes—give her up to us!" screamed a chorus of vindictive hags, who, with blood-shot eyes, ragged apparel, bare heads, and dishevelled hair, were no bad impersonations of the furies. "Give her up to us; we'll spoil her beauty!"

Whether or not the Spy's lot was to have been delivered up to the fate which awaited her at the hands of these wretches, it is impossible to say, for at that moment help arrived. A stalwart and manly form burst its way through the crowd, and what appeared to be a foreign-looking man, with a wide-awake and a huge beard, stood amongst them, and swinging round a heavy stick which he held in his hand, bade the mob stand back and give the captive a little air.

"What are you up to all of you?" he demanded indignantly! "There's pretty near enough of you to one, I should think. Call yourselves Englishmen do you, you pack of yelping hounds? And you women, eh? You ought to be ashamed of yourselves. You're all of you old and ugly enough to know better, curse me if you're not! Stand back, I say; or if you don't, by G—— I'll split a few of your skulls to begin with, and let the rest have something for themselves, when I get my wind a bit."

There was something so determined and resolute in this man's manner, that no one felt inclined to trifle with him, and a tolerable distance was cleared round the fallen woman in an inconceivably short space of time.

But having fallen back out of the reach of the stranger's cudgel, they began to growl among themselves, and to ask each other whether they were to stand his interference, and what right he had to rob them of their prey.

The burly ruffian who had assisted in her capture was among the loudest and most indignant.

"Who do you call yourself?" he demanded, fiercely. "Who are you, to come interfering with what don't concern you?"

"Don't trouble yourself about who I am, friend," replied the stalwart stranger. "It don't matter twopence, that I can see, to you or anybody else, who I am or where I've come from. It's quite enough that I have come in time to prevent you walloping this poor lad, which is what I mean to prevent; and if there's anybody as don't believe it, let em try it on, and see how I shall serve them."

"You talk very big, my fine fellow," retorted the burly one."

"No bigger than I act!"

"Don't it strike you that you might as well have asked what the party had done that we was chivying, before you made yourself into her champion?"

"*Her* champion!" repeated the stranger, in astonishment.

"Yes; it's a woman."

"A woman!"

He stooped down over the prostrate form in blank amazement, and gently raised her in his arms.

She had not fainted. She was perfectly sensible and conscious of all that was passing around her; only that she felt giddy, and weak, and out of breath.

She was trembling violently.

Was it through fear of the angry mob surrounding her?—through terror lest her deliverer should again hand her over to their fury! Was it the anticipation of the fate which awaited her at their hands?

No!—a hundred times, no! No such thoughts had occurred to her.

No such fears agitated her.

The conscience of this bold, bad woman was not to be daunted by the danger threatening her.

She had fled from them, it is true, for she saw at once that it was hopeless to attempt to make a stand and fight against them. She knew that now they had got her in their clutches, they would beat and maltreat her—disfigure—lame her, perhaps; and her heart was full of baffled rage, and hate, and scorn, and loathing for her would be tormentors.

They had caught her—they had got her down. They might beat her into the dust—they might trample her under feet, and tread the life out of her body — but she would not beg them for mercy.

Like a hunted cat, she felt more rage than fear; and she made up her mind that while she had strength left she would tear, and claw, and bite at all that came within her reach, until they overcame her by superior force and battered out her senses.

No, it was not this present fear of death at her pursuers' hands which seemed to threaten her.

Something else alarmed her. Something—what it was she could not tell herself—had brought back the recollection of that awful dread which had already twice before that night overtaken and overcome her.

Was it fancy? Was it some stray voice in the crowd which had recalled the terrible memories of past times?

Something like that voice—his voice—the voice which had cursed her from the felon's dock!

The voice which had vowed a terrible vengeance against her!

Vowed to have her life, and sworn to live, through no matter what hardships and misery, to carry out his threat!

That voice which, sleeping or waking, had haunted her these five years past—which had awakened her in her sleep, and make her start up erect and shivering with fright—the deadly dew of agonized fear upon her white and clammy face —wake up in the dead of the night to shiver, and scream, and cry aloud for help!

Was it the terror which was realised at last; and had he come back to make good those parting words which she had treasured up and pondered on these five years past.

The stranger raised her in his arms, and looked down into her face.

She lay there passively, with trembling like a leaf.

She lay there, with her mouth a little open and her eyes wildly dilated.

It was very dark at the spot where they were standing, and he carried her up the court ten yards or so towards the entrance, where a gas-lamp stood, under which he stopped again and looked down at her.

"It is a woman," he said, half aloud, but more to himself than any one else.

Then turning to some one standing close at hand —"What has she done?" he asked.

"She is a spy in the pay of the police!" the crowd chorused eagerly—and began to recapitulate all that they had been told, and all that they had themselves invented about her during the last hour.

But the stranger heeded them not, and listened not to what they said.

At the word "spy" he had started violently, and the colour had forsaken his face.

"A spy! a spy! an informer in the pay of the police!" he repeated again and again, as though he were incapable of attaching any meaning to the words.

And his eyes remained riveted upon the face which, frozen as it were into a look of intense dread and horror, lay there turned up towards him.

He looked at her searchingly and doubtingly, as if a dim recollection of something long gone by were shaping itself into recognition.

Suddenly another change stole over his features.

His teeth were set.

His breath came quickly.

He loosened his hold of her, and she shook off the snake-like fascination which up to now seemed to have held her spell-bound to the spot, and with a wild and piercing shriek she twisted herself out of his grasp and fled precipitately.

Some of the mob would have joined in the pursuit, but the stranger, recovering from the astonishment into which he had at first been thrown by the movement on her part, stopped them as they were rushing past him.

"Leave her to me!" he roared in a voice of thunder. "Leave her to me, curse you! It is I who have to settle with her! I have a hundred times more cause for anger than you can have. Leave her to me, and keep back where you are. For as there is a God above us, I'll brain the first man who lays a hand upon her!"

Then, throwing a scowling glance around, full of deadly menace, upon the crowd of ragged creatures hemming him in, he also took to his heels and plunged into the darkness, in pursuit of the Female Spy.

But the darkness had swallowed her up, and he ran on and on down one court and up another, through endless mazes of intricate lanes and alleys, without success.

She had escaped him!

At length, completely worn out and exhausted with fatigue, he sat down upon the stone-work at the botttom of some railings surrounding a small, stived up, and crowded church-yard; so full of graves and gravestones, and choked up with rank herbage, that it seemed as though it would have been impossible, had there existed such a desire, to find room for another occupant.

Here he sat a long while in silent meditation, after he had recovered his breath, nursing his own evil thoughts.

The street was lonely and desolate. Day was fast beginning to break, and the city seemed to him to be supernaturally still.

He rose at last, and going slowly round to the church-yard gate, hung on to it with his hands, and leaning his head against it, gazed wistfully through the bars upon this grim receptacle of the forgotten dead.

The tears trickled slowly from his eyes down his brown and furrowed cheeks.

"I thought she had been dead!" he muttered to himself. "I thought she had been dead! Would to God it had been the case, or that we had never met! Would to God that she had been lain years ago beneath the cold earth, and that my vow had been buried with it! But it was not to be! We were to meet! It was the will of heaven, and my vengeance must be carried out as I at first intended. She has given me the slip this once, but we shall meet again—we shall meet again as sure as death; and then——"

He sank down before the gate upon his bended knees, and stretched his hands, locked in each other, towards the sky

Then, there, bareheaded, unseen by every eye but ONE, he swore an awful oath of a black and bloody vengeance, to be wreaked upon the head of the fiend in angel's form who had betrayed him, doomed him to perpetual chains and slavery, and falsely sworn away his freedom.

* * * * * * *

Meanwhile the object of his promised revenge had safely reached the police-office in a cab, which she had taken a short distance from the place where she had escaped from the stranger's hands, upon finding that she was not pursued.

She had by this time almost entirely recovered from the agitation consequent upon the trial she had recently passed through.

She now walked up the steps of the police-office with an easy, jaunty air, as though she had but returned from taking a quiet stroll, and nothing whatever of an extraordinary character had occurred to her.

But upon entering the room from which she had originally started at an earlier period of the evening, a startling sight awaited her, and one which brought back all the old dread and terror which she had but just succeeded in shaking off.

CHAPTER V.

DEATH'S HEAD, SERGEANT SCRUFF, AND THEIR PRISONER.—THE STRUGGLE IN THE CAB—THE GAG.—THE CABMAN'S FATE.—MORE ENEMIES AT LARGE.—THE SPY AT HOME.—THE GILDED SALOON.—THE DEADLY WEAPON IN THE LADY'S BOSOM.

THE sergeant of police, the man with the death's head, and Jacob Stone the prisoner, proceeded upon their way in the cab, as I have described.

For some time they were perfectly silent, each occupied by his own reflections.

The sergeant was thinking how fortunate he was not to be one of the wounded, and what credit he would get among his fellows for having captured so notorious and desperate a ruffian as the Jacob Stone.

He was also thinking that, all things considered, perhaps the business being all so nicely finished was not a very disagreeable circumstance to reflect upon.

"Because," the sergeant argued with himself, smiling to himself as he did so,—"because a skinfull of whole bones ain't no particular drawback to nobody."

Then another pleasant thought occurred to him.

"I shall probably be promoted. It's certain I shall be complimented by the bench."

And he began to think of his probable rise in the world and altered fortunes, and of the dash that Mrs. Sergeant Scruff (his name was Scruff, you may perhaps have noticed it in the newspapers, where usually he is spoken of as "that active and zealous officer") would make at Camberwell Church on Sunday next, in a bran new silk gown, and a bonnet of the latest fashion and loudest colours.

The prisoner, with his handcuffs resting on his knees, leant sullenly back in his corner of the cab, and stared in a dreamy way out of the window at nothing particular.

The blow which he had received upon the back of his head had stunned and confused him.

The events of the last half-hour had passed dimly before him like those of some distant period, and he strove in vain to recall certain details which, in spite of all his efforts, he could not remember.

But what think you were the thoughts of the third occupant of the cab?

Of the thin wiry man? Of the man whose face was gaunt and fleshless, like that of a death's head, the eyes sunken and the teeth grinning white whenever he opened the great slit across his jaws which served him for a mouth?

What think you were the thoughts of this strange ally of the police, whom we already know to have been a friend of the ruffian now in custody?

What was he there to do? What was he pordering upon? For he was pondering about something, and he was getting ready to act, as we shall shortly see.

"You've made a good ketch this time, haven't you, sergeant, by our friend here?" said Death's Head, at last, breaking a long silence.

"Pretty middling," replied Sergeant Scruff, cheerfully.

"To be sure," said Death's Head, showing every tooth in both jaws by an extensive and amiable grin. "I thought he was a bit of a prize."

"He's not a bad 'un as times go," responded Scruff.

"So I should say, sir," said Death's Head; "and if I might make so bold, what was our friend's little game?"

"His game?"

"Yes; what has he been up to?"

"What hasn't he been up to? That's the question. There's scarcely a law to break but he hasn't broken it. He's a out-and-out incorrigible —A 1, and no mistake about it."

"You—don't—say—so?"

"By Sir Peter, I do, though!" replied Mr. Scruff, swearing by the name of a departed magistrate who was in his time the terror of itinerant salesmen. "But it's all up with him this journey."

"What, it's to be a lifer, is it?"

"It's to be a case of a hornpipe upon air. He'll be hanged to a dead certainty."

"Oh, he's gone as far as that, has he?"

"Yes; he's kicked a little over the traces, has our friend," said the Sergeant, facetiously. "He couldn't keep his hands off knives and pistols. If he'd only kept to picking and stealing, he might have gone on very well; but he always would be a deuced deal too fast, and see what's come of it."

The sergeant looked hard at his prisoner, and shook his head despondingly and sighed.

The man with the death's-head eyed him keenly; and the prisoner, staring at him sullenly and dreamily, scarce knowing whom he was staring at, saw—or dreamt that he saw—him wink.

"I think I brought your two men pretty safely over the roofs, didn't I, sergeant?" Death's Head continued; "though I must say that it was rayther green of them to be chattering there before the bar about what they were going to do. If they hadn't happened to drop into my hands, they might have come across some one who would have sold them as clean as a whistle; and then what would have become of them? Our friend here would never have been grabbed, the whole affair would have gone to the winds, and Mr. Jacob Stone been as free as air——"

"Hullo!" cried the sergeant, with a start. "Mr. who?"

"What?"

"Who told you his name was Jacob Stone?"

"Why—why," stammered the other, "I didn't say it was."

"Yes, you did."

"Then you must have told me."

"No, I didn't, I'll take my oath!"

"How could I have known it, then?"

"I don't know," said the sergeant, suspiciously; "but it strikes me——Here, cabby!"

He had risen from his seat, and was trying to get hold of the check-string.

"What are you going to do?" asked Death's Head, quickly.

"Never you mind," replied the other, and called again, "Here, cabby!"

But before the policeman could repeat the cry, the other had fastened upon him like a tiger, and, pushing him back into his seat, clutched his throat with his two hands, and did his best to throttle him.

"Don't speak a word!" Death's Head whispered between his teeth. "Don't speak a word or breathe a syllable, or I'll murder you!"

But the policeman struggled with him fiercely.

"Jacob! Jacob, you idiot!" cried the sergeant's assailant. "Help me, man, can't you? Batter in his skull with your handcuffs! Knock his teeth down his throat! Smash his face in if he won't hold his noise!"

The other ruffian, seeming at length to understand how matters stood and what was wanted of him, rose to his feet and staggered round to the other's side.

"Lay hold of his throat!" said Death's Head; "and pinch your hardest, while I feel in my pocket for a gag!"

"We shall murder him—shan't we?" muttered Stone, gruffly.

"What odds?" the other replied. "I don't care, if you don't!"

He found the gag after a little trouble, and they forced it into the policeman's mouth.

Then they securely bound his hands and feet with pocket and neck handkerchiefs, which they took from their own pockets and those of their victim.

Then Death's Head felt in the policeman's pocket for the key of the handcuffs securing Stone's wrists, and, having found it, unlocked them.

"We'll leave him now," said Death's Head. "I think he'll come to."

"He looks bad."

"Yes; it's nearly a case with him. See, this is a nice quiet street."

Death's Head undid the window and looked out. He could see no one about.

"This will do," said he.

"How will you manage the cabman?" asked the other.

"You shall see. I will call him to the window; when his head is near enough, you get him by the throat and pull it in. Then I'll settle him."

He put his head out of the window after he had said this, and called to the coachman to stop.

"What is it?" the cabman asked.

"Come down; we want to speak to you."

Death's Head clutched a life preserver which he had taken from the policeman's pocket, in his hand, and kept it out of sight.

The cabman stopped his horse, descended from the box, and unsuspectingly approached the door.

When he got close enough, Stone seized him by the neckerchief, and dragged him suddenly forward. The man, astounded, uttered a curse, and strove to free himself; but next moment he received a stunning, crashing blow upon the forehead, and then, in rapid succession, another and another, each more violent than the last, until the fearful instrument with which the murderer dealt them was soaked in his victim's blood.

Then they flung the body out into the road, and, stepping out of the cab themselves, looked round eagerly to see that the coast was clear, and took to their heels as fast as they could run.

* * * * *

It was not the sight of the cabman's dead body

and of the senseless form of Sergeant Scruff, lying in the room at Bow Street, which had alarmed the Spy.

But it was the dread intelligence that Jacob Stone was free.

It was the thought that there were, at that moment, two men alive, and at liberty in London, who bore her a deadly spite, and had sworn to have her life.

She called a cab, and ordered the man to take her to Knightsbridge. She discharged him at Hyde Park Corner, and walking down Grosvenor Place, turned down one of the streets to the left, and with a latch-key let herself into the side door of a handsomo mansion, the windows of which were brilliantly illuminated.

She went straight up a narrow staircase, the door of which she carefully bolted behind her, and arriving at the top, opened a door, and entered a dark room, again closing and bolting the door.

She groped her way to a corner, which she seemed to know well, and very rapidly found and lighted a match. By its aid she lit a gas-lamp close at hand, and casting a scared glance round her, sank exhausted into a chair.

She was in a splendidly-furnished bed-room, fitted up in a most luxuriant fashion, with high mirrors in richly carved and golden frames upon every side, and of every shape; soft arm-chairs and couches; a dainty bed, with curtains of lace, and quilt of embroidered satin; and a number of beautiful pictures, statues, and works of art, tastefully disposed.

Here, having stript herself of the disguise she had worn, and locked it up in a box, she put on a rich dressing-gown, and rang a bell.

In a few moments it was answered by a French maid, who asked respectfully what she wanted.

"Dress me," said the Spy. "Is anybody here to-night?"

"A good many, madam."

"Thank God for that!" muttered the other woman. "Anything to banish for awhile the horrors of this night."

"You've bruised your face, madam. Can I do anything for it?"

"Nothing, thank you."

In a short time the toilet was completed, and in a rich, full robe of black velvet, that swept in a long train on the ground behind her—with diamond bracelets sparkling upon her plump, white, polished arms, and round her throat, and on her snowy bosom, she looked supremely beautiful.

She cast one glance at herself in the glass, and tossing back her golden curls with a saucy smile, she left the room, and descended a broad staircase in an opposite direction to that by which she had entered the bed-room.

A quarter of an hour hence she was the merriest of a merry supper-party. Peals of laughter, flashing eyes, sly glances full of devilry, full bumpers of champagne!—a merry supper-party, made up of rich and vicious young men of fashion—hawk-eyed, hook-nosed foreign noblemen—knaves and dupes—pigeons and decoys—and richly-dressed and beautiful women, whose trade was plunder, and whoso smiles were ruin.

This was the society that nightly frequented the gilded saloons of a famous woman of fashion—Mrs. Belinda Belvidere, who was the widow of a general, was enormously rich, and gave the best supper-parties in London.

And Belinda Belvidere was—the Spy! And—the Spy was this woman of fashion; and it was at her own house to-night that she quaffed champagne, and joked, and laughed, and looked in her dazzling, queenly beauty as unlikely a person to be an informer upon, and associate with, low thieves, coiners, burglars, and murderers, as you could well have fixed upon.

But for all that, it was the truth. And in the bosom of her velvet dress, close to her snowy bosom, nestling warmly, was a tiny pistol, which, with her own fair fingers, she had an hour ago loaded and placed there, and with which in future she had vowed never to part company.

"No," she said; "let either of them come. They shall find me prepared. Sleeping or waking, I will never part with it. Heaven knows how soon it may be needed!"

CHAPTER VI.

CONTAINING A FULL, TRUE, AND PARTICULAR ACCOUNT OF THE REASONS WHY CADBURY KID DID NOT MAKE AWAY WITH HIMSELF; AND DETAILING THE MOST EXTRAORDINARY AND HITHERTO UNPARALLELED ADVENTURES WHICH BEFEL HIM IN HIS ATTEMPTS TO PUT AN END TO HIS MISERABLE EXISTENCE.

WHILE the wild, gay, and lawless guests at Mrs. Belvidere's Belgravian mansion were giving themselves up to the full and unbridled enjoyment of the present hour—alike careless and forgetful of the morrow—some strange and startling occurrences were taking place in another part of London, which bore so strong an influence over the life of the mysterious woman whose story I am writing, that before proceeding any further with her adventures I must relate them.

Allow me then, first of all, to present to you a high-born, well-bred, well-educated, and handsome man, in the prime of life, and possessing an amiable and lovely young wife who dotes on him, but who was so sick of his miserable existence that he had firmly made up his mind to blow his brains out.

Imagine a meanly-furnished room upon the third floor of a house in a narrow, squalid street in Lambeth.

A candle with a long wick, burning upon the table, threw a dim and quivering light upon a rosy face of surpassing loveliness, belonging to a young girl scarcely nineteen, who, half-hiding her smooth white brow and clustering ringlets of chesnut hair under her bare, rounded arm, like a bird nestling under its own wing, dreamt placidly of happy days gone by and a bright future never to be realised.

Seated by the bedside was the man I have described—pale, serious, and silent, fixedly contemplating the beautiful face of the sleeping girl, his own as white and motionless as that of a statue.

There was something in the gaze of this man which showed that his mind was dwelling upon no frivolous topic—that something of deep and thrilling interest to himself, and to her whom he loved so dearly, was working in his excited and agitated brain.

Yes; he was thinking of death!

Of his own death—of his own death by his own hand—how, where, and when it was to be effected.

That he would kill himself he had decided long ago.

Many days before this he had well weighed and

considered the question. Yes, he must die! He *would* die!

It was not fear which stayed him from the immediate perpetration of the act, but it was the sight of that beautiful and innocent face, sleeping there so happily, which had unmanned him.

He was going to leave her whom he loved so tenderly and well; and it was on her account that he was about to commit suicide—for her sake he was about to blast his future hopes—to damn his soul to all eternity!

In spite of himself—in spite of all his courage, fortitude, and fixed determination, the tears rose to his eye and slowly traced their course down his hollow cheeks, while his breast heaved convulsively with the violent emotions which seemed almost to tear him to pieces.

Suddenly a neighbouring church clock struck one.

The man rose to his feet with a deep sigh, and approaching a table, on which were a quantity of writing materials, very cautiously, so that the noise of his movements should not disturb his sleeping wife, he seated himself, and spreading a sheet of letter paper before him, dipped a pen in the ink and began to write.

But for a moment he paused again to contemplate the round, rosy face, and tangled mass of dark and glossy curls; then sighing again more deeply than before, he went on with his work.

"At the moment that I take up my pen to write to you, dearest Alice, you are sleeping peacefully, little dreaming that I am awake and watching you. You are dreaming of happiness, poor angel! for you are smiling in your sleep. The Almighty guarding your slumbers mercifully debars you from a knowledge of the mental agony I endnre.

"Dearest Alice, as I look upon you, I feel that a long course of joyous years are yet awaiting you.

"Mourn not then upon my account. Forget

me—forgive me! Remember me not with horror and abhorrence for the crime I am about to commit. I am committing it for your sake, and because I love you too much to stand in the way of your happiness.

"You know that I have always loved you, Alice; that since our wedding-day my every thought and care has been for you. God knows that the great love I have borne for you has nerved me to efforts of which I should have been utterly incapable. You know all this, because I have told it to you all over again and again a hundred times and more; and you know, too, that in spite of all my labours, all my efforts, all my prayers for strength and for success, that I have failed—wretchedly, bitterly failed in all that I have striven to do, and that I am a beggar.

"You have told me, dearest, that you loved me more in my poverty than in my wealth—that you would always be true to me—that you would always keep with me through all my trials and troubles—that your place was at my side—that my griefs were yours, and that your love would never weaken. But, Alice, it must last no longer!

"Alice, I am sick of my life, and I am resolved to die—by my own hand!

"You gave up home and friends to wed a poor man. Your love was great your conduct noble—but I was a villain to take you. When your guardian, forseeing that I should throughout my life be never better than I am, a poor, half-starved, struggling, unsuccessful wretch, forbade you to fulfil the promise you had given me, you still persisted in it, and marrying against his consent, forfeited the fortune which would otherwise have been yours.

"Would to God that, before you had made that sacrifice, I had done then what I have made up my mind to do now.

"When I am dead, Alice, your guardian will receive you again. You will again be restored to the position in society which you forfeited on my account. You will have wealth and a happy home. You will say good bye to all the mean and sordid penury to which my accursed folly has introduced you. Often I have feared that you must have hated me for it; but now I am about to make the only atonement I can for what I have done, and rid the world of one who has no place in it.

"Tremble not for me, dearest; pity me not. Death—what is it? A brief pang, a momentary struggle, and all is over. I am not going to die a death of lingering torture, of weary, restless, slowly devouring disease. I shall not suffer much. It will be but a moment's work, and the impediment to your happiness will be removed for ever.

"They will abuse me when I am dead—they, the friends of my prosperity. They will say that I was extravagant, profligate, and vicious; that I was a worthless cur, and died a cur's death. But you, Alice—you will think kindly of me when I am gone, if ever you think of me at all. Sometimes a recollection of the happy days—oh, how long ago, how long ago they will seem to you!—may come across you! You will shed a tear then to my memory, dearest Alice — a tear to the memory of the poor-spirited, broken-hearted man, whose greatest act in life was to love you; whose worst crime was to marry you.

"But I must end my letter here, for time presses; before the day breaks I must die!

"Oh, how tranquilly you sleep, sweet wife! How beautiful you look! How like what you were the first day that we met! Do you recollect in the bright garden at your guardian's house, how you were gathering violets? There are violets here now, upon the table. They have the same perfume—and it recals to me the happy times gone by—the same sweet perfume that I smelt that day, when first I saw and loved you; but still they seem to smell, too, of the grave—the grave that is yet undug—into which, in a few short hours hence, they will fling my dishonoured body—at dead of night, perhaps, and in unhallowed ground!

"When you read this letter, I shall have ceased to live. You will not try to learn any tidings of me, dearest. You will not go to claim my corpse, if you should learn that it has been found, for I would not have a frightful impression of me left upon your mind.

"Farewell, dearest, for ever! We may meet hereafter. Heaven knows!—heaven forgive me!

"ERNEST TREVELLYAN."

When he had finished writing, the young man rose to his feet, and cautiously opening a drawer of an old secretary standing in a corner of the room, took from it a pair of pistols.

He charged them, put a bullet into each, put on caps, and half cocked them.

Gently as this was done, the slight noise disturbed the sleeper. Trevellyan trembled violently, and hastily hid the deadly weapons behind him.

But it was only a passing dream which had disturbed her, it appeared; for her pretty head, having half turned over, arranged itself comfortably upon her arm, and she slept soundly as before.

"I would like to kiss her for the last time," the man said to himself, and he approached the bed on tip-toe.

But at the moment that he was going to press his lips upon her forehead, he arrested himself in the act, and contented himself by regarding her long and fixedly.

There was in her sleep so much calm and serenity, that for a minute Trevellyan began to doubt the poignancy of his past griefs, and to forget his horrible project. What was he going to do?—was it real?—was it necessary? Could they not live happily, after all?

But casting his eyes round the wretched room, the miseries of his frightful position came back upon him fresh as ever, and full of agonizing grief, he tore himself away.

"It must be done!—it must be done!" he said.

He put the pistols carefully away in his pockets, and put on his hat. Then he noiselessly drew up the blind, and placed the candle in such a position that he could see it from the street.

He fancied that this would be a consolation to him; but upon reflection, it occurred to him that Alice might wake up, and be alarmed by seeing the candle in that position, and read the letter before the morning, and so he blew the light out, and crept out of the room in the dark.

He opened the door, and closed it again, with the greatest caution; and listening a moment with his ear to the keyhole to her undisturbed and regular breathing, he went on tip-toe down stairs, and let himself out into the street.

A clock struck two.

"Come, come!" he said. "I have no time to lose. I must kill myself before daybreak, and I have yet got to find a place."

He looked up at the home he had just quitted,

and at the window of the room where she slept. He heaved a sigh, and clenched his teeth.

"Courage, courage!" he whispered to himself. "It will soon be over, and she will be happy!"

He walked on in the direction of Westminster Bridge.

Arrived in the middle of it, he stopped for a moment and looked down in the black and silent water beneath him, running quickly out towards the open sea.

There was nobody about at the time to speak to or interfere with him. The bridge was almost deserted. Why should he not drown himself?

For a very good reason, because he knew how to swim.

He watched the lights twinkling on either side of the dark waters, and in the far distance crossing Waterloo Bridge.

He listened to the rumbling of carriages afar off, and to the faint splashing of the water below against the arches of the bridge, until at length a clock, chiming the quarter, aroused him from his reverie, and sent him on again at a more rapid pace. Very soon he reached Birdcage Walk, and then having looked round him cautiously to see that he was not observed, he climbed over the gate at the corner into the enclosure of St. James's Park, and pursued his course along the left hand bank of the ornamental water.

He walked along silently and cautiously, keeping as much as possible in the shadow of the trees, lest any wondering policeman might chance to catch a sight of him through the railings, and demand to know what he was about.

He had not gone very far before he noticed on his left a thick mass of shrubs and bushes surrounding a large tree, the spreading branches of which threw a dark shadow, in some places at least a dozen yards from its trunk.

Just such a place he had pictured to himself in his dreams—just such a place had he determined, to select. The bushes were high, the tree large the branches overhanging, the grass at its foot, which was to serve him as a couch, was soft as velvet.

In the east he could see the first faint indications of coming day; the moment for the execution of his project had arrived, and he hesitated no longer.

There was no reason why he should.

He drew the pistols from his pocket, and drew back the triggers with a sardonic smile, which would have been the making of many a melodramatic actor.

He placed the barrel of one of the pistols against his forehead, and murmured, "God bless you, Alice!"

Then turned his eyes appealingly towards heaven.

But between him and heaven there was an opaque body which intercepted the light.

It was not a branch of the tree, but something on a branch; and it was a man lying on his stomach, with his head through the noose of a rope, and his mouth and eyes very wide open.

Not by any means because he was choking, but simply because he was very much astonished, and not a little frightened, at what was going on underneath.

It was evident that this place, which had so taken Trevellyan's fancy, had also taken the fancy of some other murderously inclined individual; and the suicidal stranger had already gone up aloft with the intention of hanging himself, when Trevellyan sat down upon the grass at the foot of the tree, with the intention of blowing out the small quantity of brains which he possessed.

Trevellyan lowered his pistol, and stared hard at the stranger.

The stranger, who was already staring very hard indeed, continued to do so without winking.

"Hillоa, you up there!" said Trevellyan; "what are you about?"

"It strikes me," said the man with the rope, "that I am about pretty well the same sort of job that you are."

"I came here," said Trevellyan, pointing to his pistols, "to blow out my brains in peace. Will you have the kindness to go and hang yourself somewhere else?"

"I have taken a good deal of trouble, sir, to fasten this rope," said the other, showing Trevellyan how it was firmly knotted to a branch over his head. "I came here to hang myself, as you see, and I came here first; therefore I will trouble you to follow your own advice, and go and blow out your brains at some other part of the enclosure."

"What you say is perfectly just," said Trevellyan, rising to his feet, and making the stranger a low bow; "only it is rather annoying, for I shall not easily be able to find another place so well suited to the purpose."

"That's true," said the man with the rope. "I don't think it is badly chosen. Have you long had your eye upon it?"

"No; chance brought me here this morning."

"Oh! that's quite another affair. I had fixed upon it for weeks past. Every time when I have taken a walk in this direction, to get an appetite for my dinner, I have said to myself, 'When the time comes, that shall be the place—that is where I shall hang myself.'"

"I see, sir, that you are quite at home; and so I shall leave you, with a sincere apology for my intrusion."

"Stop a minute!" said the man with the rope.

Trevellyan, who was walking away, turned round, and came back.

"You came here to kill yourself?"

"Yes; and as you came here with the same intention, I shall take my departure, so that we may not interrupt each other any longer."

"But stop," said the other: "since we have both come here with the same intention, and fate has thrown us together, I do not see why we should not kill ourselves in company. There is some consolation in knowing you are not the only person dying."

"As you choose sir!" replied Trevellyan; "and if you would prefer it, I will lend you one of my pistols. It seems to me that hanging is a very vulgar sort of death."

"No, thank you," replied the other. "I have reflected upon the subject some time, and have determined to hang myself."

Trevellyan bowed slightly, and discontinued the conversation. He again cocked his pistol.

"Has it occurred to you," said the party up the tree, altering his position and sitting astride on the branch,—"has it occurred to you that what we are about to do is very awful?"

"Well! yes," replied Trevellyan; "and the very cool way you go about it strikes me as being, to say the least, extremely remarkable."

"I'm used to it, sir!" replied the man up the tree.

"How so? You don't mean to say that you've done it before."

"Yes, I do—three times!"

"Three times?"

"Exactly!"

"But you're alive now, are you not?"

"I'm ashamed to say I am."

"To tell the truth," said Trevellyan, "you show a perservance worthy of a better cause; and you must have suffered a great deal to have made up your mind so determinedly to go to the next world!"

"Suffered! you may well say so," exclaimed the man with the rope. "So as no other man alive ever suffered before."

"Not more than I have!" said Trevellyan with a sigh.

"Not more than you, you think?"

"It is not likely."

"Isn't it?"

"No!"

"Pray, sir, were you born on a Friday?"

"I haven't the least idea."

"I was," said the other, lying down again upon his stomach, and again putting his head through the noose. "I was born on a Friday, and to that circumstance I attribute all my misfortunes."

"Humph!" grunted Trevellyan, in a contemptuous tone. "Suicide seems in your case to be a sort of monomania."

"Indeed! I can see that you are no better than the rest."

"Well! but what a reason you give for taking away your life. Is it sensible?"

"It is, very probably, more sensible than yours!" retorted the man with the rope, in an angry tone.

"Who says so?"

"I do!"

"You shall prove your words, sir, or——"

"Or what?"

"I'll knock you off that tree!"

"I don't care if you do. You will see me throw myself off, if you stop long enough!"

"By the way," said Trevellyan, "I think it is rather ridiculous for us to quarrel in our position. I beg your pardon."

"It is granted, sir! But I still maintain that I am the most miserable wretch in the world."

"Why! what has happened to you?"

"What has happened? What has not happened to me which should not have happened? When I was a baby I had every possible malady which can befall a miserable infant: croop, hooping cough, scarlet fever, and measles—none of them missed me. Each tooth I cut was a little martyrdom. I fell down double the number of times that other children did, and I hit myself twice as hard, and hurt myself twice as much."

"You had a bad time of it, sir!"

"When I was at school, I was a fag, and a dunce, and I never did anything that was not found out, and for which I was not flogged; and I very seldom recollect anybody else ever doing anything, either, that I was not wrongfully accused of, and thrashed for accordingly."

"You seem to have been a victim!"

"I have always been one. I never knew a father or mother. I have reason to believe that I am a member, though unacknowledged, of the aristocracy. When I was at school, in a mysterious way, a lawyer used to call and pay for my schooling. Since I have left school, he has, from time to time, supplied me with funds, for I have never been able, in spite of all my efforts, to earn my own living."

"No more have I."

"In my case it is not extraordinary, for, as I told you, I was born on a Friday—and, worse than that, a Friday in July."

"Are they more particularly unlucky about that time, sir?"

"Yes. Have you never read 'Zadkiel's Almanack?'"

"No."

"Have you ever read 'Jenkinson's Book of Fate; or, Ninety Nativities for a Halfpenny?'"

"I can't say I have."

"Well, then, I'll tell you what Jenkinson says about persons who are born in July. 'In July,' says Jenkinson, 'Mars enters the sign Aries, his domal dignity. He who is born between the 5th and 25th of the month will be brave, bold, magnanimous, benevolent, eloquent. His noble soul will be accessible to sweet emotions of compassion and brotherly love. He will be witty and sarcastic. He will be passionately fond of the other sex.'"

"That doesn't seem to me to be a bad sort of destiny."

"Wait a minute! Says Jenkinson—'His children will be his consolation and happiness. Riches and honours will come to seek him, but not until he has sought them long and patiently. Let him fear the sea and the fire, wild beasts and fire-arms. *He will have large calves.*'"

Trevellyan naturally at this point cast his eyes upon his friend's legs, and never in his life did he recollect to have seen so pitiful a pair of drumsticks.

The other noticed the movement.

"Yes," he said with a deep sigh. "This one mistake of Jenkinson's is one of the causes of my death."

"How so?" asked Trevellyan in amazement.

"It is the only error the prophet has made," replied the man in the tree. "The rest is extraordinarily exact. I am brave, and eloquent, and noble-souled, and all the rest of it. I am passionately fond of the other sex—but I have not got any calves. I never had. I never could get them. They never came, and their absence was the cause of my first real sorrow."

"But people don't have calves like they have courage, by strength of will. I doubt even whether they can be brought on like whiskers by any outward application?"

"No more than one can purchase courage like one may purchase calves."

"False calves, you mean?"

"Exactly. You may divine the rest. I could not tranquilly lie here and recount the fearful story of my shame and humiliation. Imagine a fancy ball and a fancy dress; a young man with legs like walking-sticks obliged to put on tights; a spiteful pleasantry invented by a fiendish younger brother; paper flags stuck upon pins, and stuck into the false calves of that young man without his knowing it. Fancy him figuring in a quadrille before his beloved, who is choking with laughter in a pocket handkerchief. Do you know on what day that awful event occurred to me?"

"No."

"On a Friday!"

"You don't mean to say so. But still I don't think that's enough to kill yourself for?"

"I'm not going to: that's only one of a hundred of the reasons."

"Let us have one of the other ninety-nine, then?"

"The second is the affair of the eye-tooth."

"The eye-tooth?"

"Ah, it interests you. We have plenty of time

yet: take a seat, and I rather fancy that I shall astonish you."

CHAPTER VII.

A CONTINUATION OF THE FOREGOING, BUT INTRODUCING A MURDER AS WELL AS A SUICIDE.

"I DON'T know that I can well be astonished at anything else in this world," said Trevellyan; "but anyhow, if you won't be very long, I should like to hear how anything about an eye-tooth could cause a man to want to hang himself."

"I'll tell you. About a year ago I fell in love with the most lovely of her sex, and I had reason to believe that she loved me in return, and I was very wretched."

"What the deuce had you to be wretched about? Why could you not marry her?"

"Because she already happened to be somebody else's wife."

"Oh!" said Trevellyan.

"It was a mad passion," said the man up the tree; "but do what I would I could not conquer it, or summon up sufficient courage to fly the scene of temptation. She was the wife of a general, but I never saw him, for he was always abroad, while she lived here in a splendid home in Belgravia. I met her first of all riding in Hyde Park, and I was introduced by a friend, and was afterwards frequently a guest at her table.

"For a long while I do not think that she thought that I loved her, but it was unmistakable. So great was the influence which she had over me, that I started, and trembled, and blushed at the sound of her voice.

"The first day that I dined at her house, fate seemed to have set its veto against my love. We were thirteen at table, and it was a Friday. Somebody there remarked it; and everybody, except myself, treated it as a joke and laughed at the observation. But I trembled so violently, that my fork rattled against my teeth, and I spilt my wine down the neck of the lady sitting next to me. Directly after the cloth was removed, I made some excuse and got away; but throughout the night I found it impossible to go to sleep, and next day I was very ill. I was so near death, indeed, it is a miracle that I ever got over it However, I did; and here I am, going to hang myself to-day. Well, time wore on, and I thought at last that she knew my secret. We were frequently together. We rode together in the Park—together we went to the hunting-field. We met frequently at the same parties and balls—at the opera and at the theatre. She seemed to be far from displeased at my presence, although her conduct was not always the same.

"We never spoke of our love until one day. One day I made my usual morning call, and going up into the drawing-room, as accident would have it, unannounced, I found her in tears.

"You can imagine what fear oppressed me at the sight.

"I made sure that her husband had returned home at last, or was going to do so.

"Her handkerchief covered all the lower part of her face. When she caught sight of me she wept even more copiously than before. I ran towards her, and threw myself upon my knees, at her feet, for my first idea was that the horrible thought of our approaching separation pained her, and I asked her in an agony of fear if such were the case.

"But she said no.

"I must own that as her husband's return was the only evil I feared, when I heard that it was not this at which she wept, I was very much comforted. I even reflected with a fiendish pleasure, which I found it impossible to repress, that, perhaps, some misfortune might have happened to the General himself—that he might be dead, and that we were free.

"But such was not the case.

"What was it then? I racked my brains in vain to conceive the cause of her tears. To everything that I said she only shook her head, weeping more and more, as though to say, 'It is not that! it is not that!'

"I held her hand in mine, and covered it with kisses. 'Speak—speak, beauteous Belinda!' I cried passionately. 'Is there anything in the world that I can do to assuage the pangs of your grief?'

"'Cadbury!' she softly murmured—(Cadbury is my Christian name—my other is Kid)—'Cadbury,' she murmured gently, whilst her soft hair swept my burning brow,—'do you love me?'

"It was the first time that the word love had ever passed between us, and now it came from her mouth—from the mouth of my Belinda!

"Heaven seemed opening to my rapturous sight.

"I replied with passionate energy, 'I would die for you!'

"'And you would love me in spite of everything?' she asked.

"'What do you mean?' I inquired.

"'I mean in spite of any misfortune that might befal me.'

"'Belinda,' I said, 'my life is yours, and no human power, if you say the word, shall separate us!'

"'Look, then,' said she, taking her handkerchief from her mouth.

"And she showed me her white and glittering teeth. One of the eye-teeth had been broken.

"'And you thought,' cried I, 'that such a trifle as that would cause me to cease to love you?'

"But she began to cry harder than ever.

"'Believe me—believe me,' I exclaimed, 'I love you now more than ever I did—now that you have suffered this dreadful pain. But we must hide this quickly. Your lady friends will only be too happy to hear of it. Let us conceal it from them. And if there were no more pearls in the world, we would find a tooth to replace it.'

"She was not consoled, though she was calmer.

"'A false tooth!' she exclaimed; 'and in front too! Heaven has punished me! I have so often ridiculed other women who have had bad teeth Oh, I shall be ridiculous in everybody's eyes!'

"'There is no time to lose,' said I. 'You must go to your dentist's at once.'

"'But if he betrays me—if any one I know should come in when I am there?'

"'It is not likely. But to avoid that, go to mine.'

"'Is he a good man?'

"'One of the best in the profession.'

"'Cadbury—Cadbury,' she gently murmured. 'And you love me still?'

"'Oh, Belinda!' cried I, and again covered her hand with kisses.

"'Leave me now, dear Cadbury,' she said, rising, and ringing the bell for the footman. 'Where does your dentist live?' she asked.

"I told her his name and address, and she quitted the room. I said that I would accompany her, but no sooner had the door closed than a great and glorious idea occurred to me.

"I uttered a cry of joy, and rushed frantically from the house, and to the nearest cabstand.

"I drove to the dentist's.

"He was in, and alone.

"I seized him by the arm, and dragged him out of his consulting room into the back parlour.

"He stared, as well he might, and no doubt thought that I had gone mad.

"But I reassured him upon that point.

"'What is the matter?' he asked.

"'Is it true,' I asked him, 'that when a person breaks a tooth, if it is taken out, and at the same instant another tooth belonging to somebody else is put into the cavity, this new tooth will take root and remain as firm as the original one, and as though it had grown there?'

"'Such a thing has been done,' said the dentist, 'but I believe only in the case of eye-teeth.'

"'The very thing!' I screamed with joy; and, springing at him, I hugged him to my heart.

"'Don't you think you had better take some soda-water?' said he, for he thought I was tipsy.

"'No, no!' said I; 'will you listen to me?'

"'With pleasure.'

"I looked round me anxiously, to see whether we were observed.

"'No one is listening,' said he. 'What have you to say?'

"'I will tell you. A lady who has had the misfortune to break one of her teeth this morning will call upon you in about half an hour's time. You will ask her in here. I will be in the little room beyond. When you have pulled out the stump of her broken tooth you will come to me, and pull a similar tooth out of my head, and put it into the cavity in her jaw.'

"The dentist stared at me as though I were a lunatic.

"'You're mad!' said he.

"'Yes, sir, mad with love.'

"'It's a great sacrifice you are making.'

"'It is not a hundredth part of what she merits.'

"'Very well; you know best,' said the dentist, with a vulgar grin.

"'Please to do what I tell you, then.'

"'You won't take my advice?'

"'No, sir,' replied I with dignity.

"'I ought to warn you of one thing, though.'

"'What's that?'

"'That it will hurt you horribly.'

"I laughed a withering laugh of scorn."

At this point of the narrative Trevellyan could not refrain from a little snigger, but he disguised it as much as possible by a profuse use of his pocket handerchief.

The man up the tree regarded him for a moment suspiciously: but Trevellyan, observing it, became suddenly as serious as a judge, and his companion continued his story.

"Just at this moment," said he, "the bell rang, and I rushed into the inner room to which I have already alluded.

"Five awful minutes—the dentist came! He had the weapon in his hand.

"'Well?' said I.

"'She is here,' said he.

"I took my seat in an arm-chair, and opened my mouth.

"'Pull away,' I said, in hollow tones.

"'You really mean it?'

"'You see I do.'

"'You will never reproach me for having done it?'

"'Never!'

"'Pull as gently as you can, though; and keep it a profound secret from the lady whose head you are going to put the tooth into."

"'You may rely upon me,' the dentist said; and smiling a horrible smile, he left the room.

"An instant afterwards I heard a shrill scream, which made my blood run cold.

"'Poor suffering angel!' I murmured.

"The dentist returned.

"'Are you ready?' said he.

"I opened my mouth as wide as I could.

"He rattled the pincers against my tooth, then stopped.

"'Tell me once more,' said he, 'that you want it done.'

"'Yes,' said I, closing my eyes. 'Go it!'

"He did.

"In one second the tooth was out. I will do him the justice to say that he was clever.

"But during that moment what I suffered I can never describe. It was something awful!

"I had never had a tooth taken out since I was a little boy, and I had no notion what it was like.

"You atrocious miscreant!" I screamed.

"But he put his hand before my mouth.

"'Hush!' said he; 'you forget.'

"'Do I?' said I. 'I don't think I ever shall.'

"But recollecting how unjust was my conduct, I shook his hand warmly, and begged his pardon. The pain was in a measure subsiding, and I began to reflect that though the pang had been severe, the reward would be great. My tooth had been torn out, it is true; but where had it gone? Into the mouth of my Belinda!

"When he had left the room, I went to a side-table and filled a glass from a decanter of water standing there to rinse my mouth, and in some measure stay the pain. Then I looked at myself in the mirror.

"I won't deny that when I saw the vacant space in my jaw, I felt inclined to burst out crying.

"Then a shudder ran through my whole frame.

"'Merciful powers!' I exclaimed; 'he has made a mistake!'

"It seemed to me, as well as I could remember, that it was the left eye-tooth that Belinda had broken: the dentist had pulled out the one on the right.

"Presently, I heard the shop-door go, and the dentist returned to me. I looked at him with anxiety; but his face was quite calm.

"'Well?' said I.

"'Well,' he repeated; 'if she has the courage to stop for two days without eating, or talking, or agitating her jaw, the tooth will take root, and all will be well.'

"'Do you mean it?'

"'I have every hope."

"'And what explanation did you make about having another tooth so handy?'

"'I told her that there happened to be a young chimney-sweep in the house at the time, who was willing, for a crown, to have a tooth taken out.'

"'That was very clever; and she agreed?'

"'Without a murmur!'

"'What did she say?'

"'She said, "Poor little wretch! He must be either very foolish, or very much in want of five shillings!"'

"'Oh!'

"'And she took a couple of sovereigns out of her purse, and asked me to give one of them to the sweep; so if you will allow me——'

"'Nonsense!'

"'Well, you have earned it, I am sure. You ought to have it.'

"'How do you make that out? I have to pay you for your trouble! By the way, it was the right tooth, wasn't it?'

"'Yes.'

"'That's most extraordinary!'

"'What is?'

"'Why, I thought it was the left tooth she had lost!'

"'No; you are mistaken. However, your tooth seemed to have been made exactly for her; she has a really splendid set.'

"'She has, indeed.'

"'And what hair!'

"'Ah! what hair!"

"'Like a raven's wing.'

"'Like a what?' I exclaimed.

"'As black as jet.'

"'Black?'

"'Yes.'

"'Why, it's yellow!'

"'Yellow! You're dreaming!'

"'Good heavens!' I exclaimed, while my blood seemed to curdle in my veins; 'what have you been doing?'

"A broad grin, which, I suppose, he could not suppress, stole over the dentist's face. He left the room, but returned almost immediately with a card.

"'She's left this,' he said. 'I am to send something to her for her gum.'

"I snatched it from his hand, and read—'Miss Penelope Higginbottom, No. 7, Talboy Place, Highbury.'

"I almost fell to the ground.

"'*You've given my tooth to the wrong woman!*'

"'Well, we can't get it back now, I suppose; unless you go and ask her for it.'

"I heeded him not. Prostrate with grief, doubled up with pain, I had not the pluck to answer his jibes.

"At that moment there came another ring at the bell.

"The dentist went back into the other room, and returned again to me after a few moments' delay.

"'This time,' said he, 'we have got the right lady.'

"I only groaned in reply.

"'Yes,' he continued; 'you are quite right: it is the tooth on the left side she wants!'

"'Oh, lord!—oh, lord!'

"'Well, if you don't think it is she, you had better look through the keyhole!'

"I dragged myself towards the door and looked.

"Yes, it was Belinda—my own beautiful, blue-eyed, yellow-haired Belinda!—pale from what she had suffered, and the thought of what was yet to come.

"'Have you said anything to her about it?' I asked.

"'No; I thought it best to consult you first. I thought that after what you had suffered——'

"'I will suffer it again. That miserable impostor—that Higgingbottom, who deceived us, sha'l not deter me from doing what I had intended.'

"'Then I'll go and tell her my tale of the sweep.'

"'Go!'

"I need not again go through the details I have already described. Imagine the scream of Belinda; followed by the howl of her adorer.

"Five minutes afterwards, the beautiful Mrs. Belvidere departed with my tooth in her mouth, and left me groaning.

"It was my turn now to require the aid of the dentist to stop the gaps which the devotion of my love had created in my agonized jaw. But as, unfortunately, I could find nobody who would in like manner sacrifice his teeth for me, as I had done for those two young ladies, I was obliged to put up with two horrible contrivances fixed into my head with a spring, and threatening every moment to jump out of my mouth like a couple of young frogs.

"I went away with them, disfigured for life—unable to laugh or eat; but I had one consolation: I thought of my Belinda.

"For a whole week I suffered so intensely from the swollen state of my gums, and found so much inconvenience from and difficulty in accustoming myself to the use of my false teeth, that I thought it best to keep my room. I, therefore, wrote to Mrs. Belvidere, and explained my absence by saying that the sight of the dreadful accident which had befallen her had had such an effect upon me that a severe illness had resulted from it.

"Next day, I received a letter—such a letter as only a woman can write—four pages, crossed, and nothing in them; though it was full of love, and consolation, and pity, half expressed. There were, however, two sentences which atoned for all the shortcomings in the rest of the letter. They were, 'Come if you can to-morrow evening. *I shall be alone.*'

"I need not say that I went. I dressed myself with the greatest care; indeed, I was so long about it, that my servant came to tell me that my cabriolet was waiting at the door before I was ready. I, therefore, finished my toilet as quickly as possible, and hurried down stairs.

"Just, however, as I was stepping into the carriage, the postman came to my door with a letter for me. My servant brought it to the carriage, and I opened it; but seeing that it was only a tradesman's bill, I put it into my pocket without reading it, and drove away as fast as I could.

"When I arrived at Mrs. Belvidere's house, I can hardly tell you how disappointed I was, upon being shown into the drawing-room, to find half a dozen ladies there assembled, besides the one I had come to see.

"I sat down stupidly enough among them, and all the pretty speeches I had prepared by the way died out of my recollection. I talked about I don't know what, to I don't know whom. Most of the time my eyes were fixed upon my Belinda's teeth. How white, and regular, and beautiful they were—yes, and there was mine among them.

"I don't know how long I had been there before somebody began to talk about a quotation from Shakspere, and a dispute arose upon the subject. Mrs. Belvidere asked me if I would be kind enough to get the book from the next room.

"I went for it; and on my return found everybody tittering—at what I could not imagine; but everybody was staring at me very hard. Mrs. Belvidere induced me to take a seat where the light fell full upon my face; and she found a pretext for coming close to me, and looking at me eagerly.

"I began to tremble for my teeth, and to twist my mouth into odd shapes, while I talked to conceal the gold plate, which I was afraid was visible. At last she induced me to rise from my seat to show me something in the book; but as I was getting up, she stretched out the book towards my face. I started back, and involuntarily put my hand up to my mouth.

"Then she burst out laughing, and, followed by all the ladies, left the room.

"You can imagine my stupefaction. I stood for a moment staring after them, like a man in a dream. Then my eyes fell on a piece of paper lying on the table. I took it up, for my name attracted my attention.

"Good heavens! it was the bill of that accursed dentist for my two false teeth.

"Where had it come from? How did it get there? Ah! a thought occurred to me. It was the letter which I had put unopened into my pocket when I was getting into my cabriolet. I felt in my pocket. My supposition was correct.

"What do you suppose I could do after this? Could I explain the circumstances? Who would believe me? If the bill had been for one tooth alone, I could have told Belinda, and taxed her with her cruelty in laughing at me; but two—oh! it was not at all probable she could believe that anybody had been such a fool as I had.

"I left the house, and did not come back for a fortnight. But I wrote her wild and passionate letters, to which I got no reply. Then, unable to stop away any longer, I returned, and knocking at the door, timidly inquired after her.

"She had gone out of town.

"Where to?

"To Paris, to meet the General.

"That was the last cruel blow.

"I made up my mind to kill myself, and bought a pistol.

"I did not, however, exactly know how they should be loaded, and I was obliged to ask my servant. The villain somehow suspected my design, and he loaded me one without a bullet.

"The sound of the report brought him running into the room, with the landlord and all the other lodgers in the house at his heels.

"'I thought as much,' said my valet.

"'Mad!' said the landlord.

"'As a March hare!' said a doctor, who came to look at me; and they shaved my head, and put me into a straight-waistcoat.

"For a month they watched me, and for a month my valet has never let me get out of his sight. We often came for a walk this way; and that is how I came to choose this tree.

"Next night I gave him the slip, and here I am! And now, I think, we had better not waste any more time, but polish ourselves off at once."

"Poor maniac!" said Trevellyan to himself, as he cocked his pistol.

"Are you ready?" asked Cadbury Kid, adjusting his noose.

"Quite!" replied his companion, pointing the pistol at his head.

But at this moment they heard a noise behind them, and a man made his appearance at an opening in the bushes.

At the sight of him, Cadbury uttered a cry of alarm.

"It's my valet," he said.

"Oh! there you are, are you?" responded the new comer. "So I've found you at last—and only just in time!"

"Hold him back!" shouted Cadbury, in great excitement; "hold him back, only for half a minute!"

The valet, however, rushed towards him.

Trevellyan threw himself between the two.

Cadbury by this time had got all ready for a spring from the branch.

"In the name of mercy!" cried the valet, "let me get at him! Do you not see what the poor creature is doing?"

"He's hanging himself," replied Trevellyan, coolly.

"But help me—help me to prevent him from committing such a crime!"

"Help you?"

"Yes—yes!"

"Ha! ha!" laughed Cadbury, from the tree; "why, he is come here for the very same purpose!"

"Thank heaven, then, that I am in time to save you both!" cried the valet, with enthusiasm.

"I beg your pardon, sir!" said Trevellyan haughtily. "Have the kindness not to interfere with my affairs. As for my friend there, you can do as you think fit."

"No, no!" cried Cadbury; "hold him tight for half a minute longer!"

"You pair of wretched idiots!" cried the valet, and he made a clutch at Trevellyan's pistol. "Do not you know that you are both going to damn your souls?"

"Amen!" said Cadbury, pitching himself off the branch.

The valet, at the sight of his unfortunate master, struggling frantically in the air, uttered a terrible cry, and used all his efforts to shake Trevellyan off.

A fearful struggle ensued, in which one of the pistols went off.

At the same instant, Trevellyan felt the fingers which grasped his arm relax their hold.

The valet started back, reeled, and fell, bathed in his own blood!

Trevellyan looked at him in terror!

The ball had struck him in the face!

It was frightfully disfigured!

He was dead!

The wretched murderer turned towards the hanging man, who still seemed to retain a little consciousness, and appeared to be staring at the horrible scene with eyes which were bursting from their sockets.

An overwhelming fear and horror seized upon Trevellyan. His wits deserted him. He rushed wildly from the spot, and vaulted the railings into Birdcage Walk.

At the moment he alighted in the road, he saw a carriage approaching rapidly.

"I have killed a man," he said. "There is more reason than ever why I should kill myself."

He placed this time, without any obstacle, the barrel of the pistol against his heart, which throbbed violently.

He drew the trigger!

Then fell back with a shrill cry of agony, and the blood trickled down his breast!

CHAPTER VIII.

NEXT MORNING—THE TENDER-HEARTED ALICE.—SUSPENSE, ANXIETY, TERROR!—THE BLOW FALLS AT LAST.—A FOOTSTEP ON THE STAIRS.—THE WICKED OLD MAN.—SCHEMES AND PLOTS.—IN A VILLAIN'S POWER.—"SHE IS MINE! SHE IS MINE!"

BUT we must go back now to the beautiful girl whom Trevellyan had left in the midst of a gentle, peaceful slumber, when he set forth, as we

have seen, upon this fool's errand, bent upon steeping his hands in his own blood.

'She slept on, poor creature, little dreaming of the fearful letter waiting for her upon the table, ready to strike misery into her innermost soul, when she should unsuspectingly take it up from the spot where Trevellyan had placed it in such a position as was likely soon to catch her eye, and where it lay looking as pure, and innocent, and harmless a piece of paper as you can well conceive.

Yes!—she slept on, in happy ignorance.

Twice or thrice she might have turned over restlessly when her slumbers were momentarily disturbed by some passing dream, like a fleeting cloud passing over and obscuring the summer's sky; and then she might have stretched forth her arms, as though she would have nestled closer to her husband for protection from some impending danger.

And then she might have turned away again, and sighed, or tossed her pretty ringlets fretfully upon the pillow, in vexation at not finding him; but she never thoroughly awoke until several hours after daybreak.

Then she turned round towards the wall to look for him—she had been lying with her face towards the window—and not seeing him by her side, turned back.

For several minutes, having just awaked from her sleep, and still feeling drowsy and confused, she could not exactly account for his absence.

When, however, she came to reflect, she came to the conclusion that he must have gone out to buy something for their breakfast; or had he gone to take the work which he had been engaged upon overnight, to the newspaper office?

He was, or tried to be, an author, and toiled laboriously, though with very little success, as he said himself, to earn a scanty livelihood.

More than once, when she had gone to bed, she had left him at work; and waking next morning, had found him still at his labours. Or sometimes he had fallen asleep, completely prostrated with fatigue, with his head upon the table.

She turned over again towards the wall, to look at the other pillow.

It lay there, perfectly smooth and uncrumpled.

No head had pressed it that night!

Had he not been to bed, then, at all? Most probably not.

"Poor fellow! poor fellow!" she murmured—and the tears rose to her eyes. "He has been working like this, and I have been sleeping here so comfortable, and never caring for him the least bit in the world. Oh, I am a nasty, selfish little wretch! I am! I am!"

But she was not, though; and one of the best and truest hearted women that ever lived, for ever reproaching herself with faults that she did not possess, and believing herself incapable of the dear, kind actions, and tender cares and sacrifices, which quite unconsciously, and in her own blind goodness, she was guilty of, every day of her life.

She did not know all this, I say, and continued to upbraid herself, and to call herself all sorts of dreadful names, and to wring her pretty little hands, and bury her head under the clothes, sobbing wofully.

Until all at once it occurred to her that she was an incorrigibly selfish little creature to be there in bed, instead of getting up and doing something to make herself useful.

And so up she jumped directly.

She was always very busy in a morning—much busier than the busiest bee.

Generally, if he were lying in bed asleep, she would creep out—oh, so gently!—and set about lighting the fire, boiling the kettle, and spreading out the two odd cups and cracked saucers, and the one or two other dilapidated pieces of crockery-ware which constituted their breakfast service.

She rarely felt light-hearted the first thing in the morning, when she awoke from dreams of peace and plenty, to look round upon the squalid misery surrounding her; and this particular morning she even felt more sad than usual.

But she thought to herself—"He has gone out, and will be back shortly. I will get everything all ready for him—the tea made and the toast buttered—and directly I hear his step outside I will pretend to be singing, as though I were the happiest little woman in the world. And so I ought to be if I were not a nasty, discontented little wretch, for there never was any other woman, I am certain sure, who had a husband who loved her a half quarter as much as mine does me."

And she began to bustle about twice as much at usual, to conquer, if possible, a very strong inclination to burst out crying, which somehow or other she felt was creeping over her.

It was this reason too, perhaps, which prompted her to begin to sing like a little thrush, although as yet she had heard no footstep approaching, and to sing very loudly, and for the most part very sweetly, although, now and then, the emotion which she was struggling so very hard to get the better of, somehow or other, in a most inexplicable fashion, got the better of her instead.

He was a very long time coming, she could not help thinking now and then when she paused for a moment in her work, only, however, to go on again with renewed vigour.

She lighted the fire first, and having watched it burn up for a minute or two, set on the tea-kettle with not too much water, so that it would not be a great while boiling.

Then she opened the window, and carefully inspected a flower-pot containing a small crop of mignonette — about a sprig and a-half—for a couple of minutes.

Then reproaching herself for this dreadful waste of time, made a rush at the wonderful crockery I have described, laid it out with strict regard to angles; and the kettle having boiled up by the time she had put the bed straight and brushed up the hearth, she made the tea and set the tea-pot on the hob to draw.

But why did not he come?

She bustled about the room, and set things straight, generally dusting some of them twice over in excess of zeal, and at last, having done all that she could do, and put some more water in the kettle to boil for a second cup, she sat down to do a little needlework.

But why did he not come?

She had been up an hour—a full hour by this time. What could have become of him? Where had he gone to?

You are wondering, perhaps, how it is that she did not see the fatal letter.

But it is very easily explained. The wives of men who do much pen-work are the very last persons in the world to interest themselves with pens and ink and paper.

Therefore, although this busy little woman had had a sharp eye to everything else in the apartment, it never for a moment occurred to her that there could be anything among the writing materials lying upon one corner of the table which could possibly interest her.

She had raised them from the place where they lay, and put them down upon the top of the old-fashioned secretary, but without taking any particular notice of them, or reading the name upon a folded piece of paper which he had left for her.

It must be confessed, too, that his writing was at all times extremely difficult to decipher, and that on this occasion it had been accidentally blotted and smeared so as to be scarcely legible.

She sat down, as I have said, to her needlework, and waited.

At the moment that she took her seat a clock without struck nine. She worked on and on until the same clock struck ten.

Two hours gone! Why did he not come back?

She began to grow very anxious. Her anxiety increased every minute, until she found it utterly impossible to sit there any longer.

She took to walking about the room, pacing it from side to side; but its size scarcely permitted of any one taking much exercise in it, and she desisted, from fatigue.

The slightest sound upon the staircase took her with a palpitating heart to the head of the stairs, to see if it were the long expected truant returned at last.

But, alas! he came not.

Many a time she looked out of the window, and strained her eyes in the hope that she would see him in the far distance hurrying homeward.

She now began to be seriously alarmed. This absence must mean something. But what?

At last, without any particular reason for doing so, but more because she could not keep at the same occupation for two consecutive minutes together, she went and looked over his papers.

And then her eyes for the first time fell upon the letter.

With a terrible dread of some great misfortune about to happen to her, although she could not imagine what, she opened the paper and read.

She read and read. At each word the poor distracted woman passed her hand across her eyes, as though a shadow got between them and the paper.

She pressed her hand upon her head, as though she felt that something was giving way—that some cord was snapping in her brain—that she was going mad.

Her sobs choked her. She suffered too much for her agony to find vent in tears; hers was a grief too deep—too heartrending!

When she had completed reading the strange, wild letter which we already know the contents of, she stood a moment, perfectly silent and motionless, as though she had been a statue.

Then, clutching her hair with both hands, she fell down upon her knees upon the floor as though the blow had felled her, and her long pent-up anguish found vent in words.

"Oh, heaven!—oh, heaven! what have I done to deserve this dreadful fate?"

And then the intensity of her suffering being more than her frail strength was equal to, her senses entirely deserted her, and she sank down at full length in a swoon.

But she had not lain there thus very long when there came a stealthy footstep on the stairs, and a few moments afterwards a hand was laid upon the handle of the door without.

Was it Trevellyan returned at last? Had it been, the poor girl lying prone and senseless upon the floor could not have risen to have welcomed him.

But this was no welcome guest, although, alas! no stranger.

Whoever it was, after he had turned the handle round again, and hesitated for a moment, he knocked upon the panel with his knuckles.

Tap!

But he received no reply.

Tap, tap!

Still all was silent within.

Tap, tap, tap! this time much louder and with a good deal of impatience.

"I could have sworn I heard somebody moving inside," a voice said without, as though the person upon the landing was thinking to himself aloud. "It's very singular."

Then there were several more taps; and then, the handle of the door turning slowly, the door was very cautiously opened.

After a moment's pause, an ugly head was poked in, and a pair of remarkably wicked-looking eyes peered at the form of the fainting girl in great astonishment.

It was the head of an old man which was thus intruded; and if one is to believe in what physiognomists tell us, it must have been the head of a very wicked old man, for he was villanously ugly, and his yellow and wrinkled countenance bore an expression of such wickedness and cunning, that any honest person, however unprejudiced, must almost at first sight have felt a sort of dislike for, and distrust of him before he opened his mouth.

And when he talked he had an oily, wheedling manner, and a sneering, sniggering laugh, which was extremely hateful.

But at this present moment he was only very much astonished at the sight of the prostrate form of the beautiful girl at his feet.

He stood looking at her for full a couple of minutes, contemplating her with a malicious and satyr-like glare in his ugly eyes, which rendered him ten times more hideous than he ordinarily was.

"What is the matter now, I wonder?" he said to himself at last. "She's not dead, I suppose."

He took her hand in his.

"No," he continued, "it's quite warm. She's a beautiful creature, even with her eyes shut, though eyes are everything to most faces. She's very lovely, lying quiet like that; although I like to see her animated, myself—when her spirit is up—when she's suffering under a sense of wrong—he! he! he!—when she's in a passion with me—that's how I like to see her best. He! he! he! he!"

He chuckled like an ugly old goblin, croaking in his devilish merriment like some old raven hoarse with fog.

It was not long, though, before his eyes alighted upon the open letter which lay upon the floor by the girl's side, and he instantly left off chuckling to pick it up.

"What's this, I wonder?" said he.

And he turned it over.

"It's what caused her to faint, no doubt. Who's it from, I wonder?"

There was no particular occasion why he should continue wondering for any great length of time, he seemed to think, for he immediately, and with the greatest possible coolness, began to read the paper to satisfy himself.

He was a most unscrupulous old man; and besides, he felt a natural curiosity to learn as much as possible about everybody else's affairs

Indeed it was his trade—as we shall see, before very long.

He read the letter very carefully, grumbling a little now and then, when he had more difficulty than usual in deciphering a sentence, owing to Trevellyan's peculiar handwriting, and occasionally uttering an ejaculation of surprise—though very mild surprise, for he was not a man to be easily surprised by anything.

He was a hoary-headed old sinner, and from his cradle upwards had been nothing else but a scoundrel; and he was familiar with every named and nameless crime. What could he be surprised at?

Indeed, he was extremely amused by the letter he was reading — this grey-headed, wrinkled, ghoul-faced old wretch!—and when he concluded its perusal he chuckled hideously.

But he paused, too, when he had finished reading, and after giving way to his diabolical mirth for a moment or two, became suddenly silent and thoughtful.

"Let me see—let me see!" he muttered to himself. "What is best to be done?—what is best to be done?"

He scraped his chin with his hand, glaring down the while upon the pale and beautiful face before him.

"I wish I could employ Ruth in this business," he said. "She'd worm out of her all I want to know in as many minutes as it may take me hours. I must know who these rich friends of hers are, and take steps to prevent her seeking shelter with them. This guardian's mind must be poisoned, to begin with. That won't be very difficult, though, I expect, if he has come into possession of her money through this absurd marriage. He! he! I'll manage him, I've no doubt. But his name! Well, there's only one way: I must turn out all the place, I suppose, and overhaul her papers."

He looked round the room with a searching and practised eye, to discover the most likely spots for the objects in which he was in want, to be concealed.

"But that must be done another time," he muttered. "Another time will be soon enough."

His eyes reverted to the letter in his hand, and

he looked long and thoughtfully at it and at the girl.

All at once an idea seemed to strike him.

A perfectly fiendish expression stole over his face, and all the worst and most debasing passions of human nature seemed to be typified in his revolting countenance.

"I have it! I have it! I have it!" he cried in an ecstacy. "I'll keep the letter. She's in my power! It shall be the instrument of her destruction if she defies me any longer. He! he! he! he! Proud Alice Trevellyan, we shall see now whether I am any longer to be loathed and despised. We shall see."

He put the letter carefully into his bosom as he spoke.

Then he moved towards the door.

"She must not see me here," he said, "or that will spoil all. I must be off and bide my time."

He paused, though, on his way out, and looked at her again.

She lay there, looking very innocent and beautiful—a beauty which was almost child-like—with her rosy cheeks and pouting lips, and her glossy curls half concealing her fair and polished brow.

He looked at her a moment in silent and intense admiration. Then, going back to the spot where she lay, on tip-toe, stooped down, and kissed her lips

But she sighed, and moved her head as though consciousness were returning; and rising hastily to his feet, he crept noiselessly from the room.

And on his way down stairs, he chuckled as before, and muttered to himself, with a hellish triumph lighting up his features, "*She is mine! she is mine!*"

CHAPTER IX.

ALICE SEARCHES FOR THE BODY.—COMPLICATION—CONFUSION—MYSTERY.—THE PLOT THICKENS, AND THE WICKED TRIUMPH.

BUT scarcely had the old wretch quitted the room when Alice opened her eyes.

She turned them wearily and wonderingly around.

It seemed to her that she had been dreaming an awful dream, and that on waking she had seen a devil's face grinning at her.

Then she pressed her hands to her aching head—and slowly the recollection of her awful sorrow came back upon her as fresh as ever.

She rose hastily to her feet, and looked round for the terrible letter which had caused her so much misery; but it was nowhere to be found.

For a moment she began to doubt whether or not she had been dreaming.

Had she really read a letter? Had he written to her at all? If so, what had become of the paper?

But a moment's reflection perfectly convinced her that the letter had been no dream.

No, no—far from that. She could distinctly recollect almost every word that was in it.

Each word, as she read it, had seemed to eat its way, like so much molten lead, into her very soul.

No, alas! it was too true.

Suddenly she thought of the pistols. No doubt it was with them that he had killed himself. Of course it must be; for only three days before Trevellyan had sent her to take them out of pledge, where they were at that time, and had told her that his reason for doing so was that he intended to sell them to somebody for double the amount.

She went hastily to look in the place where they were usually kept, and opening the drawer, could not refrain from an exclamation of horror.

They were gone!

She did not pause another moment. Heaven only knows what wild scheme was in her head. She scarcely knew herself; but she caught up her bonnet and shawl, and flew from the house, and along the streets, like one possessed.

She was going to look for his body.

Where?

She did not know. But she must find it. She felt sure she must find it. She felt sure that heaven would guide her steps to the spot where lay all that remained of him whom in life she had almost worshipped.

There was something so wild and frantic in the face of this poor, distracted creature, that the persons in the streets whom she met moved out of her way, and stared back after her, saying to themselves, "She is mad! she is mad!"

But she knew not that she attracted any attention, and ran on and on until fatigue compelled her to lessen her speed.

Then she paused, and tried to consider calmly what she should do.

It then occurred to her that she had better at once make application to the nearest police office, that being the place where she was most likely to obtain the information of which she was in search.

She stopped still suddenly, and looked round to see where she was.

She had been walking on at random, never heeding where her steps were leading her. She found that she had somehow made a kind of half circle, and was now close to the spot from which she had started. Where should she go?

A wild hope seized her, and her heart bounded furiously within her poor aching breast.

Perhaps he had returned home!

Yes, yes! She felt sure that he had. It was, after all, only a joke which he had played upon her, and she would find him at home when she returned.

He would ask her forgiveness for the pain which he had caused her; and she would forgive him—oh, how willingly, heaven knows!

Upon the basement floor of the house where she had lodgings, there was a shoemaker's shop belonging to the landlord, and in which he sat almost all day long, hard at work, but with his face towards the street door, so that he could hardly help noticing any person who went in or out of the passage leading to the stairs.

"Good morning, Mr. Jones," she said to him.

"Good morning, ma'am! I hope I see you well."

"Quite well, I thank you. You're very busy at work, I see, as usual."

"I haven't stirred off this here stool this last three hours."

"Have you—have you seen my husband come in lately, Mr. Jones?"

"No—I can't say that I have."

A dead weight fell upon her heart. But still she hoped on.

"Perhaps you haven't noticed?"

"I can't see how I could miss him; but he may have come in, for all that."

"Yes, he may have come in."

"I hope he's quite well, ma'am?"

"Yes, yes, thank you. I hope so!" she added with a sigh, as she turned away.

"What's she mean by 'hope he is?'" said Mr. Jones to himself, looking a little puzzled. "I hope there's nothing wrong. Perhaps he's cut and run; and there's a week's rent owing to-morrow. Who am I to look to for it, I wonder? She's a nice little woman as ever breathed: but I can't let her have the loan of my rooms for nothing. No, that's quite another pair of shoes!"

Poor Alice pressed her hand to her head, on which the cold perspiration stood in great drops.

One of the greatest tortures that can be suffered by those who hope against hope, is to hear an indifferent person respond to their eager, half-despairing questions with careless indifference. She turned away, and went slowly up stairs.

"Perhaps I shall find him there," she softly whispered to herself. "Perhaps I shall find him there, waiting for me. God grant I may! God grant I may!"

As she drew near to the door, her heart throbbed, so that she could scarcely gather breath. She stood with the handle of the door in her hand, and listened intently.

But a death-like silence reigned within.

No he could not be there, unless——

A shuddering horror stole over her—unless his spirit had returned—unless there were waiting for her some hideously disfigured, mangled, and bloody semblance of him whom she had loved and lost, propped up, rigid and ghastly, in his customary chair, ready to welcome her!

The frantic terror which seized upon her at the bare thought, caused her to rush forward into the room, determined to know the worst at once, without any further suspense, and meet the phantom face to face, if phantom there awaited her.

But the room was empty, cold, and silent.

The fire had gone out. Never before had the hearth seemed to her to wear an aspect so mournful and desolate as it did now.

She did not remain long. Wearily she retraced her steps.

At the shop she paused again, and addressed Mr. Jones, who was still busy at work, but who looked up as she approached.

"Nobody has left any letter for me this morning—have they, Mr. Jones?"

"Not with me."

"And no message?"

"None."

"It is too true, then," she said with a sigh; and she went out again into the streets, and began to wander on, scarcely knowing whither.

But in wandering without purpose, she found herself at last in the neighbourhood of a police-station, and she went in to make some inquiries.

"Can you tell me, if you please," she asked of a policeman whom she first saw when she entered the door,—"can you tell me whether anybody has been found dead this morning, or during last night?"

"Found dead?" said the policeman, looking very much surprised. "What! have you been a-killing of any one?"

"No, no! I want to know whether any of your division have found the body of a suicide; or has information of such a discovery been brought to the office?"

"No," said the policeman; "I don't know that there has. Stop, though, by the way! Wasn't you saying something about a case in the Park, Mr. Scruff?"

"Certainly I was," replied another policeman, who had a bandage over his face, and looked a good deal bruised and scratched. "Who wants to know? Do you, miss?"

"Yes," replied Alice, faintly.

"A young man he was?"

Alice nodded her head. She could not speak.

"Blew his brains out, didn't he?"

She reeled back, and would have fallen had not the wall behind propped her up. Mr. Scruff stepped forward to help her.

"Is it any one you know, my dear?" he asked gently. "Come, come, don't cry like that! You know that's very foolish. What is it all about, my dear? Here—take a little drop of water, and be as calm as you can."

"It is my poor husband!" she cried in an agony of grief, wringing her hands. "It is my poor dear Earnest, and I have killed him!"

"Hush, hush!" exclaimed Mr. Scruff hastily. "Mind what you're saying, you know. It all goes down in evidence. If you have anything to say, say it, only don't criminate yourself."

Then Alice, endeavouring to be calm, told the policemen all that she knew,—the inspector on duty, as she spoke, taking notes of her statement.

When she had concluded, it was suggested that the best thing that could be done was for her to go at once before the sitting magistrate, and inform him of the circumstances.

Other important matters were just then occupying the attention of his worship, and she was obliged to wait some little time.

At last her turn came. Mr. Scruff stepped forward, and in that confidential tone for which he is celebrated, opened the case in a stage whisper.

"Oh! ah! yes! To be sure! Certainly!" said his worship, staring hard at the pretty woman through his spectacles. "And so you know the deceased, Miss—ah!—What's-your-name."

"I am his wife, sir."

"Oh! ah! yes! Oh, his wife, eh? Put that down, Mr. Quildriver. And what's your name, pray?"

"Alice Trevellyan."

"A very fine name indeed! And where do you live?"

"At No. 27, Canterbury Street, Lambeth."

"Ah! not a very fine address. And your husband's name?"

"Ernest Trevellyan."

"He lives with you?"

"Yes, sir."

"And his occupation?"

"A writer for the press."

"Humph! Very queer persons some of these press gentlemen. Queer lot—very queer lot! Rather a bad lot. And pray what do you know of this affair?"

"I did not dream until this morning that he had any such intention."

"Stop a minute. We don't want any dreams, if you please. We have to deal with realities, if you please, Mrs. Trevellyan. What do you know about this suicide? Come, out with it?"

But here what strength she had hitherto possessed seemed to desert her. A deadly pallor stole over her face, and she seemed as though she were about to fall.

"What's the matter now?" asked his worship.

"She's rather faint sir, I think," said Mr. Scruff. "Shall I give her a chair."

"Humph! Ah! yes. Now, ma'am, when you're ready!"

She was accommodated with a chair, and preently recovered sufficiently for the examination to be proceeded with.

"Had you any reason to believe before to-day that the deceased was about to commit suicide?"

"No, sir."

"And what caused you to think so to-day?"

"When I awoke this morning, I found a letter lying upon the table waiting for me, which he had written."

"Had he not been at home, then, all night?"

"Yes—no—I don't know, sir."

"How do you mean, you don't know?"

"I left him writing when I went to bed. I fancied he came to bed too in about an hour's time, but I was half asleep, and cannot be certain."

"And what time did you get up this morning?"

"At eight o'clock."

The magistrate looked at his watch. "It now wants a quarter to two," said he. "What have you been doing in the meantime?"

"I did not see the letter at first; and I was waiting for him to come home."

The magistrate considered for a minute or two.

"Do you mean that you waited for him to come home after you read the letter?"

"No, sir—before."

"Show me the letter."

"I have not got it."

"Where is it?"

"I don't know."

"You don't know?"

"I think I left it at home. I could not find it when I came to look for it after I came to myself; for I had fainted when I first read it."

"What did it say?"

"It said that he was going to kill himself, because he would not stand in the way of my happiness."

"Oh!" said the magistrate. "What did he mean by that?"

"He meant that he would not keep me poor."

"That's strange. Would you have gained by his death, then?"

"Yes."

"Oh!"

The magistrate leant over to his clerk.

"Let me look at what you have written, Mr. Quildriver."

Then he carefully re-read all that had been deposed to by Alice Trevellyan.

When he had done so, and before he could resume the examination, the poor girl, who hitherto had had no opportunity allowed her of asking any questions, entreated the magistrate to tell her what had been done with her husband's body.

"He has been taken to the Charing Cross Hospital."

"Oh, sir!" she cried; "will you allow me to go and see him? I beseech you to allow me to go!"

"There is plenty of time yet," replied the magistrate. "As soon as I have concluded my examination you shall be taken there and confronted with him."

"Is he, then, not dead?" she almost shrieked.

"Not yet."

"Thank heaven! Thank heaven!"

"But there is no hope."

She sank back in her chair speechless.

"I shall not detain you much longer," said the magistrate, in a gentler tone. "Do you know this pistol?"

She looked at it. She knew it well.

"Yes, yes!" she cried, a shudder running through her whole frame. "It is one of those which I took out of pledge three days ago."

"Indeed!" said the magistrate. "Have you got that down, Mr. Quildriver? Why did you do so, Mrs. Trevellyan?"

But before she had time to make any reply, a policeman entered the court, and whispered a message to his worship.

The magistrate looked grave and thoughtful.

"I am sorry to tell you, young lady," said he, "that your husband is no more. He died half an hour ago."

Alice staggered under the shock; but she exclaimed, frantically and beseechingly, "Oh, let me go, sir—let me go to him!"

"You can go," replied the magistrate; "but it must be in the care of a policeman. I am sorry to inform you that you must consider yourself in custody on the charge of wilful murder."

Alice looked at him with a wild, half-crazed expression.

"Wilful murder!" she repeated. "The murder of whom?"

"Of your husband, Ernest Trevellyan."

One wild, piercing shriek she gave, and she fell senseless to the ground.

One wild, piercing shriek, which thrilled through the hearts of the trembling auditory.

A shriek which spoke of an agonized soul—of blasted happiness—of blighted hopes—of a broken heart!

They carried her away, white and motionless as a corpse.

Many pitying glances followed her—many tearful eyes were turned towards her. The women in court murmured among themselves, and some expressed their sympathy in sobs.

"She never did it; I am sure she never did it!" some were heard to say.

"She is innocence in every look and gesture."

"Well, if she is, she'll clear herself."

"That doesn't follow; there have been plenty of innocent people hanged before now," said some one.

"Ah! you're right. Some of the circumstances are rather suspicious."

"*Rather?* Very, you mean."

"That tale about the letter?"

"Yes."

"And the pistol?"

"To be sure!"

"And she as good as owned she wanted to get rid of him."

"She said he stood in her way."

"Ah! you may depend upon it she's not quite so innocent as she looks. It's a bad world this, and full of wickedness."

And thus the people in the court talked the matter over.

One man there, who had been a witness of the proceedings, evidently did not sympathise in the least with the sufferings of the accused; although he might, had he chosen to have done so, perhaps have been able to throw a good deal of light upon what now seemed dark and mysterious.

This was a sinister-looking old man, with a hooked nose, straggling grey hair, evil eyes, and a devil's grin upon his lips.

"He! he!" he chuckled to himself. "So far, so good. Nothing could have been better. The plot thickens. She will be mine yet, for none but I can save her. I triumph! I triumph!"

CHAPTER X.

THE BOUDOIR OF A BEAUTY.—AWAKENING TO A NEW EXISTENCE.—A STRANGE WAY OF COMING INTO ONE'S PROPERTY.—RUTH TO THE RESCUE.—WHERE DOES SHE GET HER MONEY?—MORE MYSTERY.—IN THE MESHES OF THE SPY.—A SLAVE FOR LIFE.

I MUST leave poor Alice to her fate for a page or so, that I may explain what became of Trevellyan's body, and who picked it up, and how Ruth the Spy came to be mixed up in the business.

How shall I begin?

"Where you left off," says the reader.

No—stop a minute. I am telling the story, and I have a right to begin where I choose; and I choose to begin somewhere else—in a bedroom.

And what a bedroom! Upon the floor, a thick, soft Turkey carpet—so soft and so thick that your feet positively sunk into it, like walking in wet sand.

A ceiling covered with the most delicate white and pink fluted satin, studded with glittering silver stars, from the centre of which hung a lamp of coloured glass, supported by a silver Cupid.

The walls were hung with an arabesque pattern in pale pink silk damask.

There were two doorways, partly veiled by richly embroidered curtains, with a ground of deep crimson velvet. There were several tables, in mother of pearl, and ebony, and ivory, crowded with costly knicknacks of almost fabulous value.

Upon the walls, hung in richly gilt frames, were priceless oil paintings—tiny master-pieces by the most eminent painters—depicting various love-passages between satyrs and nymphs.

There was a little piano, richly inlaid with ebony and marqueterie work.

The windows were hung with curtains of pink silk and lace, and the window was of stained glass—gorgeously dazzling when the sun's rays fell upon it; and between the windows, or perhaps in the place where a third window had originally been, there was a little conservatory crowded with plants and flowers of the brightest colours, in the midst of which played a fountain of scented water, exhaling a sweet, delicious perfume.

And on the table again there was a splendid vase in Sevres porcelain, filled with the rarest exotics.

As for the bed itself, it was a perfect marvel of splendour. The bedstead of rosewood elaborately carved, and in places thickly gilt; the sheets of the daintiest, snowiest white; the curtains of white brocaded satin, lined with pink; the counterpane of quilted pink satin, worked with gold.

And please to imagine stretched upon this bed, in this room, Ernest Trevellyan.

"Hallo!" says the reader; "what on earth is this about? Do you mean to say he is not dead, and lying in Charing Cross Hospital? What is he doing here, in the name of all that is wonderful? and who does this splendid bed-room belong to?"

This bed-room, if you please, belonged to a lady known in certain circles as the fascinating widow of a general—Mrs. Belinda Belvidere, in fact; if you like it better, Mrs. Ruth Trail; or, to be still more explicit, Ruth the Spy.

Yes—this is her room; the room to which we have already introduced the reader; the room which she entered by a back door and a secret staircase, upon the night when she betrayed Jacob Stone into the hands of the police.

And here, upon the evening of the day on which he had made so determined an attempt upon his life, Trevellyan opened his eyes and looked round him in blank amazement.

"Where am I?" thought he.

And then he repeated aloud, "Where am I?"

But no one answered him.

A profound silence reigned in the apartment, alone broken by the faint murmur of the tiny fountain in the little conservatory.

"Am I in fairy-land?" Trevellyan asked himself.

And well he might.

There was a little silver bell lying on the bed close to his hand, and upon which his fingers rested.

He rang it, and as though by magic, a servant in dark, quiet livery stood by his bedside.

Trevellyan lay staring at him. He was an elderly man, with white hair and peculiarly gentle-looking blue eyes.

He spoke in a low, deferential tone, and inquired whether Trevellyan wanted him.

"Yes," replied the other. "Where am I?"

"In London."

"At whose house?"

"At your own."

"How long have I been here?"

"Twelve hours."

"I did not kill myself, then?"

"Not quite, sir, I believe."

"And I am all right again?"

"Not quite, sir, I believe."

"This is a very beautiful house. Have I any servants?"

"I am one, sir."

"Give me my clothes, then."

"I don't think it would be any good, sir."

"Why?"

"Because you are not able to get up, sir."

"What will prevent me?"

"Your want of strength, sir."

"Pooh!"

"Try."

Trevellyan made a desperate effort to carry out what he had proposed. That is to say, in his mind he struggled very hard to get out of bed, just like you struggle sometimes when half awake in a morning, without in reality making the least movement.

He struggled thus, endeavouring to free himself from the mountain which pressed upon him and kept him down.

"I can't do it," he murmured presently. "Never mind; bring me the pen and ink."

"I'm afraid that won't be much use either, sir."

"Why?"

"You won't be able to move your hand, sir."

"No more I can. But I say! You can move?"

"Yes, sir."

"And you can take a message for me?"

"Certainly, sir."

"Directly?"

"This instant, if you choose."

"But while you are gone, suppose I should want anything?"

"You will ring, sir!"

"Have I two servants, then?"

"You have half a dozen, sir."

"Ah!" said Trevellyan, with a deep sigh. "I suppose I shall understand better presently, but I feel a little confused—my head is giddy. I want you to go—to go—I wanted you to go somewhere—yes—yes—I want you to go——"

He would have told the servant to go at once, and tell his wife that he was yet alive.

But he had already talked much too long for the weak state in which he was. He had considerably over-taxed his strength.

A sudden giddiness seized upon him—a hopeless confusion in his ideas; his head remained as it were glued to the pillow—his eyes closed, and his breath came short and quick.

Fever had seized upon him, and his wits wandered.

But while he is thus in the land of dreams, I really must explain how it was that he came to find himself in the safe keeping of the mysterious mistress of that Begravian mansion.

You may recollect that at the moment that Trevellyan discharged the pistol, a carriage was rapidly approaching him.

Had he not heard the carriage coming, it is very probable that he would have been still more deliberate in his movements, and have taken a rather better aim, and then there would have been an end to his adventures as far as this story is concerned.

But he was in such a hurry. He was not only afraid that they might prevent him from shooting himself, but even that they might arrest him for the murder of Cadbury's valet, and he rather hurried the business.

You may wonder, perhaps, why he should have cared whether or not they took him into custody for murder. If he were tried, found guilty, and hanged, surely that was exactly what ought to have suited him?

He was eager to die, and here was a capital chance of being done for professionally by the master of his craft.

But not at all. He wanted to die, it is true, but in a *gentlemanly* way. As you may remember, he had designated hanging a vulgar kind of death, and the idea of dying by the hands of a common hangman!

It was monstrous!

He would rather have lived!

He had, then, hastily pulled the trigger, received the ball in his breast, and fallen with a shrill cry, insensible upon the ground.

At the sound of the shot, the horses in the carriage had been seized with a sudden fright, and began to rear, plunge, and kick furiously.

Then the carriage window was lowered, and a beautiful woman's head put out.

"Stop! stop!" cried the owner of the head, who was none other than Ruth the Spy. "Stop! stop! What was that?"

"A pistol shot, I think, ma'am," replied the coachman from the box.

Ruth alighted from the carriage, and went direct to the spot where Trevellyan was lying. An instant afterwards the coachman heard her calling to him for help.

The coachman having managed to subdue in some measure the restlessness of his horses, drew the carriage alongside of the pathway where Trevellyan lay stretched, insensible.

"It's a man who has shot himself," said Ruth.

"Or been shot by somebody else, ma'am, perhaps."

"No! Here is the pistol lying by his side."

"What shall we do, ma'am? Shall I call the police?"

"No, no! Hold your tongue! I am thinking." She remained for a moment perfectly silent.

Then looking up, she said, "Do you hear any one coming?"

"I think I heard somebody running in the distance."

"Quick, then! Get off the box for a moment and help me——"

"To do what, ma'am?" asked the coachman, alighting.

"To put this man into the carriage."

"Where are you going to take him to, ma'am?"

"Home."

"What! a dead body?"

"He is not dead. Come, make haste."

The coachman was very much astonished, but he knew his mistress too well to show it, or to cross her in any little freak or fancy that she might conceive.

He therefore lifted Trevellyan up in his arms, and placed him very carefully indeed, in a reclining position, upon one of the seats of the carriage.

"Now," said Mrs. Belvidere, "drive home as soon as you can."

While they were upon the way, Ruth occupied herself in stanching, as much as possible, the flow of blood.

Arrived at her own house, she looked about up and down the street, whether there was any one likely to observe them; but at that early hour there was scarcely any one awake, and that particular place was entirely deserted.

Having ascertained this fact, she alighted at the door which I have already alluded to; and opening it with a key she carried, she told the coachman to lift up the insensible man, bring him into the lobby, and place him as comfortably as possible upon the stairs.

This done, she told the coachman that she had no further need for his services.

"But mind," said she, "that what has occurred to-night you must keep a profound secret, and tell to no one. There is something for your trouble. Take care, now! Nobody but you can give information of this. If you do, you quit my service. You know best whether it is worth your while to do so."

"You may depend upon me, madam," said the coachman; "I am not such a fool."

Then, when the door had been closed upon him, and he had mounted to his seat, he shook his head in a doubtful way, and frowned, and shook his head again.

"She's a most extraordinary woman!" he said to himself. "She's a regular puzzle! What does she do? How does she live? How's it all managed? What's it all mean? Blessed if I know! Blessed if I can find out! There never was such another place for wages, though, or for living. She must have a gold mine somewhere, and digs it out by the barrow-full. She throws it away as though she did."

And as he spoke he turned over the two bright shining sovereigns which Ruth had given him, and put them away in his trousers pocket with a smirk of satisfaction.

Ruth mounted to her room, and shortly summoned to her aid the elderly servant whom Trevellyan spoke to when he came to himself. With his assistance the wounded man was taken upstairs and put to bed in Mrs. Belvidere's room; it being thought, for certain reasons, that this would be the best course. The wound was found not to be very serious, although Trevellyan had suffered greatly from loss of blood; and the elderly servant having carefully dressed it, the patient was left to his care whilst Mrs. Belvidere sought a few hours' rest upon a sofa in an adjoining room.

Next day, when Trevellyan awoke calm, re-

freshed from a long sleep, he found Ruth bending over him.

Her golden hair almost sweeping his cheek—her deep blue eyes fixed upon his.

"Well," said she, "are you better?"

"Much better," replied Trevellyan; "thanks to you, madam—for you must be my kind benefactress. This is your house, is it not?"

"Yes."

"And you found me——"

"Where you fell—in Birdcage Walk."

"I should have died had it not been for you. But what made you bring me here to this beautiful place? It was very kind of you."

"Do you think it beautiful?"

"It is like a palace."

"And would you like to live here always?"

"I—I cannot. I have a home already."

"What made you try to kill yourself? You intended to leave it, then, I suppose?"

"Yes."

"Then, what makes you want to go back now? Don't you think they will be able to get on without you?"

"Yes—yes! It had been much better if I had killed myself!"

"What, for Alice's sake?"

"Alice! Do you, then, know——"

"I only know what you have said in your sleep. You said that it was for Alice's happiness that you were going to kill yourself."

"True—true," said Trevellyan, with a groan; "and I am yet alive!"

"No."

"No?"

"You are dead to her."

"Dead to her! How can that be?"

"Have you not written to her to say that you were going to commit suicide?"

"Yes."

"And won't she believe that you have done so?"

"Yes; I suppose so."

"Then why need you ever let her know the contrary? You can make her happy, if your absence will have that effect, without dying yourself."

"But she may find out that I am still alive!"

"Who from?"

"From—from——"

"From me, you mean. Fear not; your secret is safe with me. Come, what say you? I can put money and happiness within your reach, upon one condition."

"And that——"

"That you swear upon your soul to do my bidding!"

"But—but what am I to do?"

"To do all that I tell you!"

"And if I refuse——"

"I will ring the bell, send for the police, and give you into custody!"

"For trying to kill myself?"

"No—for murder!"

Trevellyan fell back, trembling upon the pillow, trembling violently.

It was true, then! He had murdered a man, and his secret was known!

He was still alive, and the scaffold was waiting for him!

CHAPTER XI.

THE FASCINATION OF THE SERPENT.—THE FALSE HEART. — THE WICKED OLD MAN AGAIN. — HATCHING PLOTS — THE SECRET STAIRCASE — AT DEAD OF NIGHT.—THE ASSASSIN'S KNIFE.

TREVELLYAN cast a terrified and appealing look upon the mysterious woman standing by the bedside.

She appeared to him perfectly queenlike in her superb beauty. Her splendid golden hair hung in thick masses, soft and silky, upon her snow-white shoulders.

She wore a rich dress of black velvet, and her bare arms and neck were ornamented with long strings of pearls wrapped round and round in the form of necklace and bracelets

He thought that he had never in all his life gazed upon so magnificent a creature.

His wildest dreams of the perfection of female loveliness fell far short of this woman, with her classic features, her proud, bold, flashing eyes, her faultlessly modeled arms, and her firm white bosom, voluptuously developed.

But yet there was, he could not help fancying, hidden beneath this love-inspiring beauty, a something false, hollow, snake-like, satanic!

Something to be feared and dreaded—something to fall back from, shuddering—to make his flesh creep—though he knew not what it was.

It seemed as though hers was the beauty of a serpent, which, while it dazed and fascinated him, lured him on to certain death.

Her lovely blue eyes were fixed upon him, and seemed to burn their way into his innermost soul.

Her wicked glittering eyes met his, and he weakly shuddered and cowered beneath her gaze.

He was in the meshes of the Spy.

He was her slave from that time and for ever.

His life was in her keeping.

His fate was in her hands—those small, soft, plump, white, and pretty hands, which had so cruel and deadly a grip when they closed on their victim's throat, as they closed now upon the wrist of the wounded man.

He felt the corpse-like chill of her lithe and slender fingers, covered with gorgeous rings, studded with diamonds, now tighten and tighten, like the folds of a snake slowly creeping round the doomed one's body, to crush its bones and flesh to pulp, and he felt that her piercing eyes were on him still, and shivered feebly like a fascinated bird.

He felt a tress of her soft golden hair again sweep his feverish cheek—he felt her soft, scented breath upon his cheek.

"Trevellyan," she said, in a low, melodious whisper, which thrilled through his whole frame like an electric shock,—"do you wish to return?"

"No—no," he answered, faintly.

"Then you will stop with me?"

"Yes—yes."

"Then you will be true to me, and faithful to your trust?"

"Yes—yes."

"You will do what I bid you?"

"Yes."

"If it is even murder?"

"If it is even murder!"

"And you can give up Alice and poverty for my sake?"

"Yes."

"And can you love me?"

The question was asked in the gentlest, the most loving, the most tender of tones.

The bright eyes drew nearer.

The golden hair crept round his neck.

The serpent's breath was hot upon his face.

Oh, he was mad! he was blind! His illness had turned his brain. He had no power of reason left, or how could he have forgotten his lost love—his vows of eternal devotion—the sweet, noble-hearted, pure and loving wife, whom only two days ago he was willing to lay down his life to serve?

He has sworn now that he will be this woman's slave. Now she has asked him if he could love her!

It seemed to him so deep, so powerful, so passionate was the new love with which she had inspired him, that the old was poor, paltry, and insignificant.

"I shall love you till my death!" he cried.

He would have risen to press his burning lips upon the angel's face overhanging him—to kiss those sweet lips, smiling there so bewitchingly—but the exertion was too much for him.

The sudden movement loosened the bandages upon his wound the blood gushed forth afresh, and he sank back, with a hollow groan, insensible.

For a moment the Spy stood looking down upon him, and the angelic smile, fading from her face, gave place to one of such devilish malignity that it was like nothing human, save the smile of that horrible old man into whose power the wife of the false-hearted Trevellyan had fallen.

"Yes," she said, with a bitter sneer, "he will be an easy tool. He is dead to all the world, and he shall remain so until—until the time comes when I have no further occasion for his services, and then—ha! ha!—he can go after the rest!"

But the blood welling from his wound began to come through the bandages with a broad crimson stain.

The Spy hastily rang a bell, and the elderly servant made his appearance

"Look to him," she said, "or he will bleed to death. You must not let him die—yet!"

"Bless me!" the servant said, "his wound's broke out as bad as ever. I must have fresh bandages."

"Do what you choose, but do it well. You can manage without me, I daresay. I cannot help you, or I may stain my dress"

And casting a glance at her toilet, in the mirror upon her dressing-table, she left the room, humming an air from the last new opera.

A servant met her on the stairs, and said that somebody wished to speak to her.

"Who is it?" she asked.

"Who is it?" inquired Mrs. Belvidere.

"It is Mr. Earthworm, ma'am."

"Indeed! Tell him that I will be down in a moment, and ask him to be kind enough to wait for me."

And so saying, Ruth hastily entered a bedroom, upon the same floor of which, if one might judge by certain articles of her clothing scattered about, was the apartment where she had been dressing just before she went into her own bedroom to pay a visit to the wounded man.

She went straight to the glass, and took a much more lengthened and anxious survey of herself than she had done just now, when she left the other room.

Whoever this visitor, with the curious name, might be, it was evident that he was somebody whom the Spy considered it well worth her while to put on her best appearance to meet.

Not, however, that much change in her toilet was requisite — for, as it was, she looked extremely beautiful in her velvet and jewels,—but she essayed several fresh ornaments, and tried on a variety of shawls and scarfs;—at last, determining upon going to see her visitor just as she had originally intended to have gone down stairs, had she not changed her mind, as we have seen, upon her way.

In the passage below, she again met the servant.

"Where is the gentleman?"

"He is in the drawing-room."

"Is he alone?"

"Yes, ma'am."

She entered smiling, and walked forward, with her pretty hands and white arms extended, to meet an elderly gentleman, who stepped forward from the window at which he had been amusing himself by contemplating a fallen cab-horse, and came towards her.

"Well, Ruth!"

"Well, sir; this is a very great act of condescension."

"What is?"

"Your coming to see me."

"Don't I often come?"

"Heigho! You call it often?"

"'Gad! it's often enough for you, I expect. You can't love the sight of me so very much as all that!"

"You are a wicked man to talk so, when you know very well that I quite worship you."

"Ah! so I'm told."

"And you don't believe it?"

"I believe in nothing. I cut credulity with my wisdom teeth. Here; sit down. You're looking very pretty to-day, Ruth."

"Don't I always, sir?"

"Is that colour natural?"

"Try."

And she held her peachy cheek towards him, with a merry laugh.

But the visitor resisted the temptation of kissing it, if that was what she meant, and smiled grimly.

"It looks so," he said "They get these things up wonderful, nowadays."

"Why, you monster! you know it is real! Upon my soul——"

"What's that? Pooh! There, don't excite yourself! I've come to talk about business. Listen seriously, if you can; and don't make eyes at me."

He, surely, was not a very likely person for anybody to "make eyes" at, unless something was to be got by so doing—for he was, without exception, the ugliest old man you could have met with in a long summer's day.

He was yellow and wrinkled; and thin, and pinched, and haggard.

He was——But I have already described him; for he was that same wicked old man who had secreted the letter which Trevellyan wrote to his wife previous to setting out upon that murderous journey, with the result of which we are already acquainted.

Yes; it was the same mysterious old man, who was as wicked as he was ugly, and who, to judge by his conduct, was quite at home in this Belgrave mansion, and upon tolerably intimate terms with its mistress.

"What have you got to talk about?" she asked, seriously.

"I'll tell you. About this man, Stone."

"Yes; what of him?"

"The police have not been able to catch him yet; nor the other, either; and I know for a fact that they have turned out all the likely places. It is not so very wonderful the police should blunder; but how I have been defeated, too, seems to me to be rather extraordinary.

"Oh! for heaven's sake, do not leave a stone unturned! Search night and day, until you find them."

"Why, what makes you so vitally interested?"

"What makes me interested!" replied the woman, bitterly. "Because I love my life, that's all."

"But it is not so bad as that."

"What do you mean?"

"They won't hurt you."

"They'd murder me, if they could."

"Yes; but you see they daren't show up; that's where it is. Besides, Stone doesn't know of Rosamond's Bower, does he?"

"I don't know," replied the Spy, rising to her feet, and pacing the floor uneasily. "He said he had found me out. I told you so. That was one of his threats; and one of the reasons why I thought he had better be put out of the way. I wish I had done it in the manner I thought at first"

"What, killed him?"

"Ay; why not?" she responded, looking at him with flashing eyes and compressing her lips. "I was not afraid; and I should have done so if you had let me"

"You would have done, probably as I told you. You are much too impetuous. There's no good comes of spilling blood. It's silly, and makes a mess. Besides, what's the good of taking the trouble, when Mr. Calcraft is paid to do the business for you?"

"But you see it has not been done."

"Not as yet; but we shall have them safe enough, never fear."

"Would to heaven we had them now!"

"They are as good as taken. The dogs are waiting at the mouth of every hole, and as soon as the rats show their noses, they'll worry the life out of them to a dead certainty."

"Oh, if I could only think so!"

"Why should you not? Why, Ruth, I never saw you show the white feather before. This Stone is not the first by many a one who has owed you a spite, and would like the wringing of that pretty white neck of yours. You've been at it all your life—you know you have, you deceitful slut."

"Peace! peace!" she cried angrily. "Choose another subject for your conversation. You know that I do not like this one."

"Ha, ha! I suppose not; but that reminds me. What was the name of that young fellow long a ago, to whom you acted so—so unkindly shall we call it?"

The colour, real or false, had all disappeared from the Spy's cheeks, and she turned upon him now a face as white as death.

"Who do you mean?" she asked in a hollow tone.

"You know him—Jack!"

She gave a sudden start, and almost a scream; and then made a clutch at her throat, as though to silence herself.

Earthworm eyed her narrowly.

"You know it, then?" said he.

"Knew what?"

"That he has come back?"

"Ye—es."

"Where did you see him?"

"I met him when I was running away from the crowd. He rescued me."

"That was kind of him, too."

"He did not recognise me at the time."

"Ah! that accounts for it. And did he recognise you afterwards?"

"Yes."

"Did he seem glad to see you?"

She made no answer. After a moment or two she asked, "How did you know that he was here?"

"I know everything, don't I?"

"Yes, yes. Where did you see him?"

"He came to see me."

"Where?"

"At my Secret Information Office, to be sure."

"What for?"

"Don't be frightened; it was not to ask me to find you. If it had been, I should not have given you up. It was for me to set a watch upon some young swell, and that's what I have come here for. You know him, I think."

"Who is he?"

"He's a captain in the Guards. They call him Captain Charley. Crockford his proper name is. He's a dreadful rip, I believe, and over head and heels in debt. He plays a good deal, I am told."

"Yes."

"Has he been here?"

"Yes."

"Often?"

"Several times."

"And made love to you?"

"Not particularly. He has suffered severely at our tables. By the way, I met him, too, the other night."

"How was that?"

"He tried to stop me in the street. He caught sight of me in my sailor's dress, and thought I was a woman."

"Did he find out who you were?"

"No. I think not, though it was a wonde He found out I wouldn't stand his nonsense, for knocked him over into the mud, for interferin with me. But about Rafferty?"

"I don't know much more about him than I have told you. For some reason or other, h wants that Crockford watched. I know very litt about the man myself, but I thought you could te me, and then I should flash my knowledge whe he comes to-morrow."

"Is he coming to-morrow?"

"Yes."

"When?"

"At ten in the morning, precisely."

"I should like to see him."

"You can do that easily."

"Unseen by him?"

"Yes."

"And you must find out where he lives."

"I will try."

"You must set some one to follow him."

"As you like. What are you going to do t him?"

"Nothing."

"Oh, very well! I don't want to find out you secrets, only don't let him find out this place, an be more careful with the people you employ in th smashing trade; so that we shan't have the sam trouble with them that we had with Stone. We' better give up the bad money business altogethe and try something else. We can't run this ris you know, very long, without coming to grief. should not like to see you get into trouble wit the police, because, although they love you dearl they might act ungratefully to you, in spite o all past services. Human nature is very desp cable."

"And you, too—how would you fare?" sh asked, with a sickly smile.

"To be sure!" said he, with a devilish grin. " should probably die of a broken heart, if I had t lose you."

If there were ever two faces which resemble one another, the faces of this man and woman d now.

And yet how could that be?—for one was th perfection of female loveliness, and the other th most hideously ugly?

How it was I cannot tell, but they did. Upo both faces for one brief moment there dwelt a loo of fiendish malignity, malice, hate, defiance—tw sneering, smiling faces, which must have bee such as his Satanic Majesty would see did he loo into a looking-glass.

But this expression did not last long.

Ruth broke into a short laugh and turned upo her heel.

The old man blew his nose and chuckled.

"Come," said Ruth, after short pause—"sha we go up-stairs? I want to show you the man wrote to you about."

"What, the fresh victim?"

"Yes. One of the best we have ever had."

"You met him the other night, did you not?"

"Yes. After I had been to tell you abo Stone's escape, when I was coming back throug Birdcage Walk, I heard the report of the pisto and found him lying upon the pavement.

"He was going to kill himself, was he not?"

"Yes. He was tired of his life, and it struc me at the time that he was exactly the sort o person we wanted."

"You were right," said the old man; "and yo say that you have got some hold upon him, do you?"

"I have a threat of the gallows hanging over him."

"That ought to be sufficient; but, whatever you do, do not let him get the upper hand, or have any chance of threatening you. We must not have another affair like this of Stone's for some time to come."

"You may trust me for that," said Ruth. "Very few of them have had the better of me, as yet."

She smiled as she spoke, a dark and bitter smile, fraught with terrible memories of vengeance in times gone by, and led the way to the room where the unconscious victim lay sleeping.

The old man advanced towards the bed, and leaning over the sleeper, regarded him silently and attentively for some moments. When he drew back again, and turned his head towards his companion, he was chuckling at some unspoken thoughts.

"What is it?" asked Ruth, with a slight manifestation of impatience.

"Nothing," replied the old man. "Did you say that he was married?"

"Yes."

"And his wife's name?"

"Alice."

The old man coloured slightly, but made no further remarks; only he chuckled to himself a good deal, as though at a joke of more than ordinary humour.

Ruth regarded him with a puzzled expression, but refrained from making any remarks upon the singularity of his conduct; only she watched him narrowly as he walked away rubbing his hands together, and chattering and chuckling like some malicious old ape.

"So, so!" he muttered; "she is in my power, and he is in hers! What a complication! I could never have hoped for anything so lucky. He cannot help but be our tool, and she is mine! —mine, without hope of escape!—mine, body and soul!"

But seeing that Ruth had her eyes fixed upon him with an intensity of gaze which seemed as though she were striving to read his innermost thoughts, he turned to her and said, "Let us go down stairs again. I want to speak to you about this Crockford. We must arrange some plan for your meeting him, and bringing him here. The day after to-morrow is the day of the great review at Aldershott. I believe he will be there. You are going down, are you not, with the Prince?"

"Yes."

"You can ask the Captain to join you at lunch."

"If the Prince does not object."

"Oh, he won't. I dare say. Tell him Crockford is a relation—a relation of your husband's family," said the old man, with a diabolical chuckle.

They quitted the room together, talking earnestly, and again left Trevellyan to the care of the respectable man-servant, who moved noiselessly about the room, arranging such things as he thought might be required for the invalid's comfort during the night.

This respectable serving-man intended to sit up with the invalid, and he had lighted a small fire to boil a little kettle, which might have been intended to make the sick man a cup of tea, should he require one; but which, as he did not require one—or as the respectable serving-man seemed to have made up his mind that he did not—boiled instead some hot water for a stiff and comfortable glass of grog for the respectable man's own private drinking; for the night, although it was midsummer, was none of the warmest.

He sat down in the chair when he had arranged everything to his satisfaction, and taking a book off a shelf containing Mrs. Belvidere's favourite authors, began to read and to sip his grog, and to feel as though, after all, sitting up and taking care of anybody under such circumstances was not so very uncomfortable a process.

It was, when he began his vigil, about nine o'clock in the evening; and the time passed so quickly until about eleven, that he had no idea it was so late, until he accidentally glanced at the face of the clock upon the mantel-piece.

"Bless me!" said he; "how quickly the time has gone! By the way, I'm getting rather peckish."

He had provided for this emergency, and had a very tempting *paté* upon a side table, to which he helped himself very liberally, washing it down with a couple of glasses of choice Madeira. Then he came back to his seat again before the fire, threw on some more coals, and settled himself down nice and comfortable for a good long read.

"The back of this chair is rather hard for one's head," said the respectable man, presently. "I wish I had a pillow."

And he fidgetted about for a few minutes.

"I really do wish I'd got a pillow," he repeated. "And I will have a pillow!" he said decisively; and without more ado, he rose, and helped himself to that which supported Trevellyan's head, leaving him, instead, the bolster. Then he settled himself down again to his book.

But somehow or other either the book, or the fire, or the *paté*, or the Madeira had a very somnolent effect upon the respectable serving-man, and in spite of all his efforts, he could not for the life of him contrive to keep his eyes open.

He intended to have taken forty winks when he began—no more and no less; but he took, instead, eighty, and a hundred and sixty, and three hundred and twenty for that matter. Indeed, he did not know how many he had took, for he lost count altogether after a bit, and snored away unconciously for hours.

Until, at last, he awoke with a start, and looked about him in terror.

How lonely and ghostly the room seemed to look! The fire was out—the candle had burnt down very low into the socket. He felt very chilly and wretched. The breathing of the sick man was so very low, that at first the watcher feared that it had ceased altogether, and that he was dead; and trembling violently, he approached the bed on tip-toe to ascertain the truth.

But no; he was only sleeping.

The servant hesitated what he should do.

The invalid seemed to be sleeping very comfortably. Would he require anything until the morning? It was very questionable. But then Mrs. Belvidere had strictly ordered the servant to sit up with him. He could not light the fire, for he had no wood or paper. How could he sit in the cold? He had nothing to wrap himself up in, or he might have had a very comfortable nap on the sofa.

After a slight hesitation, he determined to go to his own room, which was at some distance off, being two floors above, and get some blankets to cover himself with.

Acting upon this notion as soon as he had conceived it, he took the candlestick in his hand and left the sick man's chamber, carefully closing the door behind him

It was about two o'clock—about a quarter of an

hour before daylight—and a profound stillness reigned without in the deserted streets.

At very rare intervals the heavy boots of a policeman prowling mournfully past upon his lonely beat became faintly audible; but these slight interruptions of the otherwise unbroken silence only caused it to appear more heavy and oppressive.

The whole city seemed hushed in slumber. Surely no one save the guardians of the peace were awake and about! But stay; crime, which never sleeps, was stealing along with stealthy steps, and creeping with upraised dagger nearer and nearer its victim's throat.

Yes, murder and theft were abroad; the wicked were awake: and innocence, in its blissful slumber, lay in dire peril from the assassin's knife.

Tick! tick! tick! tick!

Could it have been the clock upon the chimney-piece?

Tick! tick!

Could it have been a death-watch in the wall?

Tick! tick! Crick! crick!

No, it was neither of these.

It was a remarkable sound, quite unlike either of these noises. It was a scratching, grinding, rasping sound.

It was either a file or a saw. Yes, somebody was breaking into the house below.

The respectable man-servant had gone upon his errand in search of bed-clothes. Trevellyan was left alone. His fever had passed away. He had just awakened, much refreshed, from a long slumber, but was devoured by thirst.

He stretched forth his hand for the bell, but it had been removed. He strove to raise himself, but sank back with a deep sigh. The effort was too much for him.

Then he began to frame his lips into the necessary form for calling out for help, and in a drowsy, dreamy way was trying to make up his mind what he should call; and while so engaged quite forgot what he was going to do, and fell into a half-torpid state, unmindful of anything save one particular noise which he heard, and for which he could not possibly account.

Tick! tick! tick! tick!

Where was the noise? he wondered—and what did it mean? Not that he was particularly interested by it; only somehow it seemed to jar upon his nerves.

It was so persistent and so monotonously regular; and yet it stopped every now and then for a moment, so it was unlike a clock. What could it be?

Nothing he could think of—unless, as I have said, somebody breaking into the house.

He was in a curious frame of mind, and he was not at first inclined to be much alarmed by the idea of burglars.

Was it his house they were breaking into? Yes, he had been told so. Still, he thought if they would only take what they wanted, and go away again quietly, he would not so much mind—only he could not be disturbed; and if he could only have something to drink, he could go to sleep again quite contentedly, if all the burglars in London were helping themselves to his property.

What a strange feeling was this which seemed to overpower him, to weigh him down, to keep him helpless and incapable of motion, as though a ton of iron rested upon his breast!

Presently, however, the feeling of careless indifference changed in some measure to anxiety. Perhaps this was when he became more awake, and when the sounds which had at first attracted his notice grew more audible.

He began, now, to listen to the "tick, ticking" below with a curious sort of interest, not unmixed with fear.

Presently he raised his head from the pillow, and strained every nerve in terrified anxiety.

The sound grew louder and louder.

Then suddenly ceased.

Then there was a shuffling sound, and a creaking sound, and a heavy, muffled tread upon the stairs.

The listener turned his head upon the pillow, and strove to ascertain from what quarter the sound proceeded.

It was not from the side where lay the staircase up which the respectable-looking, grey-headed, smooth-spoken, serving-man had come, when Trevellyan had first rung the bell. No; the sound appeared to come from the wall just behind the head of the bed. After all, he fancied, it might perhaps be in the next house.

But it was not. Trevellyan was unacquainted with the existence of the secret staircase.

It was through the door communicating therewith from the street without that the burglars, if burglars they were, had forced an entrance.

Slowly and cautiously the footsteps advanced up-stairs.

Trevellyan listened more and more intently.

Not a limb did he move. He held his breath. The cold perspiration started forth upon his forehead.

Every nerve in his body seemed to be quivering, every muscle drawn out painfully.

The footsteps neared the door leading into the bedroom. The handle slowly turned. The door opened a chink.

Trevellyan, as he lay, could not see it, but he heard a faint creak of the hinges, and he heard a faint rustle of the velvet curtain.

He lay as motionless as death, and strained his ears and his eyes.

His heart seemed to him to thump audibly within his breast.

Then came a footstep within the door, and a deathlike silence, and for a moment the throbbing of his heart appeared to stop altogether.

There was not now the faintest sound audible within or without.

Trevellyan felt as though he would go mad if this suspense and anxiety had to be endured much longer.

What was it? Who was it? What did they want? Had they come to harm him?

A sudden and awful dread took possession of him. Perhaps these were the police who had effected an entrance. He would be dragged to prison and to the scaffold!

But now came a faint sound, like the opening of a cigar-case, or the noise of a light book being drawn off a shelf; and then a bright, sun-shaped light started forth upon the wall opposite to him, and began to travel rapidly round the room towards the spot where lay the sick man's head.

But just before it reached him, he had the presence of mind to shut his eyes—not screw them tightly, but close them as though in sleep.

In a moment afterwards the light fell upon the lids, and danced off again almost instantaneously.

But Trevellyan still kept his eyes closed, and held his breath, and listened intently.

There was a low whispering in the room.

"Are we right, Jacob?"

"Quite right; this is her room."

"She's in bed, isn't she?"

"Yes."

"Asleep?"

"Sound as a rock."

"Be cautious, for heaven's sake!"

"Never fear."

"You keep the doorway open. It will be over in a moment."

Trevellyan could not catch these words; for the two men who had entered the room—burglars or murderers, or whatever they might be—spoke in the lowest possible whisper—a whisper which at the distance of a few feet, was perfectly inaudible.

But he could make out this much—that they were consulting together; and then he heard a sharp click, which vibrated through his whole frame; for he felt instinctively that it came from some instrument of death—a pistol, perhaps, which was being cocked, or a knife which was being opened!

Trevellyan decided in favour of the latter supposition, and he was right.

A moment afterwards the sun-shaped light began to dance again upon the wall, and crept round to the spot where lay his head.

Then came a slow and cautious, almost inaudible tread—a tread which, save to one listening with tightly-strung nerves, throbbing heart, and bursting brain, as listened this sick man, momentarily expecting death, would have been quite so.

The assassin was stealing upon him!

Yes, the assassin! Trevellyan, half-fainting from fright, with wide open, staring eyes, saw him coming through the gloom of the bedchamber, deep as it was, and saw him creeping—creeping—creeping!

Saw the dark lantern in one hand, and in the other the deadly weapon glittering!

The long, cold, bright, murderous blade raised in the air, ready to bury itself in his heart!

The would-be assassin crept nearer and nearer. He took a deadly aim—judging of the position of the supposed sleeper in the bed by the hasty survey that he had already taken by the aid of his lantern.

Cautiously, noiselessly, he crept forward, holding himself in readiness to strike the blow.

Then, when he had reached the distance which he judged to be requisite, he suddenly threw the light full upon the face of the inmate of the bed, and the same instant raised his knife in the air.

Next moment it would have descended with a deadly aim. Next moment Trevellyan's life's blood would have oozed out beneath the murderous stab; but, with the knife upraised, the would-be murderer uttered an exclamation of astonishment and alarm.

At the same moment, with a mighty effort, Trevellyan raised himself; and though his tongue hitherto had cloven to the roof of his mouth, the spell was broken, and he uttered a long, loud, piercing shriek, and struggled into a sitting posture, stretching forth his arms to ward off the blow.

"Strike, man—strike!" cried a hoarse voice behind the bed.

It was that of the other assassin; but the man who had been upon the point of striking, stood motionless, with wide opened eyes and mouth.

"Perdition seize me!" he muttered betwixt his teeth, and turned to fly.

"What are you doing? Are you mad?" cried the other.

"No, no; let's go!"

"Go! What, without doing it?"

"Yes—come along! I hear footsteps!"

"Lend me the knife, if you are afraid, man! I'll settle her with a stab!"

"Come away, I say! It is a mistake!"

"A mistake?"

"Yes. It is not the woman, after all!"

At that moment Trevellyan again uttered a piercing cry for help

"A thousand curses seize him!" cried Jacob Stone, for he was the man with tho knife. "I'm a good mind to settle him, whoever it is!"

"If he does not hold his noise, I will," said Skeleton Key.

And he made a movement towards the bed.

"Are we going without any swag," he asked, "after all our trouble?"

"Yes, yes, we must! Here is some one coming! Fly!"

But before they had time to leave the room, the door was flung open, and the grey-headed servant, with a candle in his hand and looking wild and terrified, came running in out of breath.

CHAPTER XII.

CAPTAIN CHARLEY IN THE PARK.—THE BEAUTIFUL LADY IN THE CARRIAGE—THE WAGER—THE CAPTAIN'S OUTRAGEOUS IMPUDENCE, AND ITS RESULT.

DURING the height of a London season, when the *elite* of the aristocracy, and a fair sprinkling of the snobocracy, were enjoying equestrian exercises in Rotten Row, Lord Windibank and his intimate friend Captain Charley Crockford entered the ride.

His lordship was about three-and-twenty, of a fair complexion, with light hair, and eyes of an undecided hue. He might have passed for good-looking, had it not been for an expression about the mouth which suggested that this youthful patrician was not blessed with a greater amount of intellect than it was absolutely necessary for him to possess to enable him to get through his duties as an officer of the Guards, in one of which distinguished regiments he held a commission

His companion, Captain Charley Crockford, who belonged to the same regiment as his lordship, was a tall and elegant man, a perfect Adonis in appearance, and a great contrast to the young lord at his side. Being about the same age, the two young men had left Eton within a short time of each other, and entered the Guards almost on the same day.

Unlike school friendships, which, as a rule, are anything but lasting, theirs had continued as warm as ever for some years past; and Crockford, although immeasurably superior to his lordship in an intellectual point of view, good-naturedly gave him his society, and tolerated his vagaries, in return for which Lord Windibank felt a sincere regard for handsome Charley, and was never very happy when long away from him.

On this occasion they were taking their daily ride, and had passed several times up and down Rotten Row, where Charley elicited his usual share of admiration from many a bright-eyed maiden—and, it must be owned, not a few flattering comments from even married ladies, who failed not to notice to their husbands the beautiful horse he rode—at the same time. may be, inwardly admiring the handsome face of its rider, though, you may be sure, without mentioning this interesting fact to their beloved spouses.

Many a bright glance fell upon him as he rode by these admiring maids and matrons, with the matchless ease and grace of an Oriental.

Not only a favourite with the fair sex, Charley Crockford was beloved by all who knew him; in which category I mean to include not only friends and acquaintances, but even unpaid tailors. All these felt the irresistible influence of an undefinable something about this young man, which went straight to the heart, and insensibly prejudiced them in his favour. In fact, everybody who knew him loved handsome Charley.

Although idolized by the set in which he moved, courted and admired on every hand, however strange it may appear, Charley Crockford was not happy.

With him there existed a restless longing for excitement — a ceaseless seeking for something new. He was, according to his own account, the most wretched young fellow under the sun.

"What do you say to a stroll, Windibank? I'm rather tired of riding," said Charley to his friend, after they had been for some time in the Park.

"Wherever you like, my dear fellow," returned his lordship.

"And send our Rosinantes home by your servant?"

"As you please," acquiesced my lord.

And acting upon Crockford's suggestion, the two young men alighted, and their steeds were handed over to the care of Lord Windibank's groom; but they had been lounging about for a very little while, when Charley began to feel just as tired of walking as he had been of riding, and, betaking himself to a seat, began, as was his wont, to growl at the monotony of their existence.

"By Jove! nothing would please me better than a war," said he. "There would be some excitement in that; but here—bah!—one day is a facsimile of the other, and I'm tired of my life"

"As for being tired of my life, I don't feel that, exactly," replied Windibank; "but I must admit the life we lead is very monotonous, although I shouldn't wish to exchange it for the trenches. Why not try matrimony, for a change? There's Lady——"

"Nonsense! It might do very well for you—become an M.P., and have a large family—but not for me: I'm not a marrying man," replied Charley, cutting at his boot in a decisive manner with his whip.

"After all," he resumed, after a pause, "I don't think there are many women worth loving, to say nothing of marrying them."

"I don't agree with you on that point at all. Even in the short time we have been seated here I have seen plenty of pretty women pass."

"Oh! so have I, but——"

"But what?"

"A greater number than it would take to gratify a hundred hearts such as yours, my lord."

"And yours?"

"Oh! I'm different."

"How are you different?"

"I'm insensible to the tender passion."

"'He laughs at scars, who ne'er has felt a wound,' my gallant Captain."

"'Who ne'er has felt a wound;' but I have—and what is more, have made many a fair one share my feelings."

"Upon my word, you are the coolest hand I ever met with! Your assurance is——"

"Stop, my good fellow; you know I'm not given to boasting."

"No, you are not; but, by Jupiter! that speech of yours was a deuced good imitation of it."

"I did not intend it as such, although I'm tolerably successful with the dear creatures."

"There you are again!"

"Well?"

"You'll get snubbed by one of these dear creatures, as you call them, one of these days."

"I don't anticipate anything of the sort, I assure you."

"Vain boaster!"

"Not at all, my lord; you judge by yourself. Come, now, do you feel inclined to lose five pounds?"

"How?"

"By a bet."

"On what?"

"The first pretty woman that we see pass in a carriage by herself shall be the subject of it."

"But how?—I don't understand."

"I will take my seat by her side, and kiss her hand before we get out of the Park!"

"What! a lady who is a stranger to you?"

"Of course."

"And a real lady?"

"You shall choose which."

"In the height of a London season, and in broad daylight? Ha! ha!"

"Will you bet?"

"It's absurd, Charley."

"That's my business. Do you bet?"

"I should not like to rob you."

"Your remark is decidedly absurd, when you know that neither you nor any one else would ever bet if they intended to lose."

"But your proposal is preposterous."

"That's your idea."

"And your own, I should fancy."

"Yes, I'm so anxious to lose five pounds," said Charley, sneeringly.

"Well, come now, Charley, your word of honour will be quite sufficient. I'll take this bet, just for the fun of the thing; and I'll give you a whitebait dinner, at Greenwich, with the money."

"Softly, my friend; there's just a possibility that I may win it."

"A *possibility*, I allow, and that's all."

"I'm glad you admit even that much. I thought you knew me better than to fancy that I should undertake anything that offered no chance of success."

"But, my dear fellow, what you propose doing is a most unheard of thing."

"Then there's novelty in it."

"Rather too much novelty you will find, I should say. It might go down with a pretty horsebreaker—but with a lady, by Jove! it's a frightful risk!"

"You think so?"

"I do, Crockford, and should advise you not to try it."

"You've accepted my bet, and I mean to win it."

"Hang the bet! I don't care about that!"

"But I do, though, I can tell you!"

"I see you are determined!"

"Of course!"

"Then look out for a pretty woman, and a pretty hand——"

"You may depend upon that," returned Charley, who had not the slightest idea of wasting a kiss upon an ugly one if he could help it.

"I very much doubt your seeing a pretty woman enjoying her drive alone."

"Why so?"

"Oh! it's a thing you don't often see, for if they are pretty, they have generally some cavalier with them."

"Not always."

At this moment a very elegant carriage approached, and in it, reclining with the air of a sultana, was a most lovely creature, magnificently attired.

Charley rose from his seat, and turning to Windibank, who was nearly lost in admiration at the sight of her, asked him if he thought she would do to bet upon.

"I never saw such a splendid woman before," replied his lordship.

"Is that the one you choose, then?"

"Yes—no. But, my dear fellow——"

"Answer quickly—is she your choice?"

"Well, then—yes."

"Well, then—here goes!"

Lord Windibank opened his eyes and mouth in blank astonishment. What on earth was this audacious Captain going to do?

His desire for information on that point, however, was very speedily gratified.

The Captain left his friend's side, and ducking suddenly under the rail dividing the road from the path where they stood, in another moment was standing by the side of the open barouche containing the lady.

Then, with the agility of an ape, and with one single bound, he seated himself opposite to her in the carriage.

At that instant there was a block among the vehicles in front, and the coachman and footman by his side were so much occupied by the plunging and rearing of their own and the other horses around them, that they did not notice the action. And from the same reason, extraordinary as it may appear, the attention of the occupants of the other carriages in their immediate neighbourhood being similarly engaged, this bold and impudent act was quite unnoticed by all save the lady herself.

She made a hasty movement as though to ward off an expected blow; but without uttering a single word, stared at the intruder in blank amazement.

In the most courteous manner, however, Captain Charley saluted her, although she seemed to be so thoroughly amazed and dumbfounded by the appearance of the strange gentleman, as not to be able to move a limb or utter a cry.

"Doubtless your ladyship wishes to know who I am, where I come from, and where I am going," said Charley, who had glanced at the coronet on the panel of the carriage, and thus guessed at its occupant's rank.

"I have not the honour of your acquaintance, sir," gasped the lady; "and this audacious——"

"Ah!" began Charley, "when you know why I——"

"Get down instantly, sir, or I will order my people——"

"Think of the scandal——"

"Sir!"

"Think of the scandal if you oblige me to get down, for I swear I will not do so willingly!"

As he said this, Charley cast a glance of admiration on the beautiful woman before him. She in her turn could not refrain from throwing a curious glance upon the handsome face and stylish dress of her eccentric companion, and this very curiosity aided Charley immensely.

Whilst her ladyship was looking at her *vis-à-vis*, a very pretty landau, which, with the pretty ladies inside, had the appearance of a basket of flowers, passed by them, and the ladies who were seated in it recognising Charley, saluted him with almost a familiar smile.

Her ladyship, who had seen all this, felt more curious than ever, and by this time had relinquished the thought of making the mysterious stranger alight.

"Now, sir," said she, "explain yourself!"

"I will not tell your ladyship that I have mistaken your ladyship's carriage for that of some other person. I have the honour to be near you because I wished to be so. An ordinary person would not fail to excuse his conduct by saying that he thought he knew you—had met you at some place at which he had never been—or give some such reason for springing into your carriage in such an unceremonious manner; but I candidly confess that I have never seen you before."

"I will not listen to such impertinence, sir; and beg you will leave my carriage instantly!"

"If you order me," said Charley, "I will throw myself out; but I repeat, take care. There would be as much scandal caused by my doing so, as if I had thrown myself from your bed-room window."

The lady winced a little at this remark, for she saw the force of it, but still preserved her temper wonderfully, and in a calm manner again desired Charley to alight.

"Shall I throw myself out?" said he with his peculiar smile.

"Certainly not," replied the lady; "my servant will open the door."

"I could not think of such a thing. If I go out, it must be in the way I have named."

"Well; I am not responsible for the follies of a madman."

"A madman, madam!"

"I said so."

"Your ladyship is mistaken."

"A very pardonable mistake. But now, sir, in a few minutes we shall leave the Park, and you can then alight without compromising yourself."

Till now, the lady's face had been hidden by her parasol, which she had kept provokingly before it but as she said these last words, she removed it and looked at Charley with a slight smile.

"Can it be possible?" he exclaimed, with true emotion, or an admirable imitation of it.

"I comprehend you, sir, less and less."

"Until now," said Charley in a faltering voice, "I could not see your face. When your parasol fell on your lap, the sight of so much loveliness perfectly dazzled me."

"You are very flattering!" said the lady, contemptuously.

"Your ladyship is mistaken. You are beautiful, and I only pay a just tribute to your charms. When I entered your carriage my heart was untouched; but now——"

"Really, sir, your behaviour——"

"Oh! pardon me—pardon me, madam! Believe me or not, your image will be indelibly stamped upon my heart until the day of my death."

"Ridiculous!"

They were going in the direction of the Park gates, and as they came in sight of the Wellington Statue, Charley seized her hand.

The lady's eyes flashed fire, but although she slightly resisted, she did not altogether draw it away.

"We separate, never to meet again!" he said, in hollow tones. "Never!"

He still retained her hand, and her ladyship, seeming to have noticed it at this moment only, looked at him with a surprised and severe air, but made a very slight movement to withdraw her fingers from his grasp.

"You are beautiful, and I love you!. Pardon me, and forget my presumption."

Saying this, he raised the lady's hand, and slightly touched it with his lips.

"In truth, sir," the lady cried angrily, "I know not how this will end. You ought to know that——"

"I only know that between your bracelet and glove there was a place for my lips."

The lady seemed perfectly bewildered at his impudence, and did not finish her remark, so that Charley had an opportunity of continuing.

"Happy is the one who has the right to love you!" said he.

"It is a right I accord to every one, on the condition that they say nothing to me about it."

"Then I may love you?"

"On the condition I have named."

"But may I see you again?"

"Never!" said the lovely creature in an imperious tone, passing her parasol over her face. "You must alight here."

"Already?"

"You take your folly seriously."

"I shall never forget you."

"A melancholy pleasure—a remembrance more sad than sweet—but whose very sadness is an attraction. Is that what you mean?"

Charley did not reply to this, and the lady continued.

"Take my advice, young gentleman. You have committed an act which, had I resented, might have placed you in a very unpleasant position. Let that pass. It is over and forgotten; but do not attempt to carry this pleasantry any further. We must never meet again."

This was said with some little emotion, and she held out her hand to Charley, and told the coachman to stop.

The young man seized the hand thus offered him, and again pressed it to his lips.

The footman came to open the door, eyeing the Captain with considerable astonishment, and inquired where they should drive to.

"Anywhere. Straight on."

Charley had jumped down and turned round, looking at her ladyship with a supplicatingly resigned air.

"Adieu!" she cried; "and should you see the dear Duchess, tell her that she must come and see me."

Charley scarcely heard the last words.

"What the deuce did she say about the Duchess? Ah! I see what she meant!" said he, as the thought flashed across him that she had only spoken thus to hide his folly from her servants.

He stood watching the carriage and its lovely occupant until both were lost in the maze of vehicles in Piccadilly. Then he slowly retraced his footsteps to the spot where he had desired Windibank to await his return.

"What does it matter?" said he to himself. "She without doubt comes here every day; and besides, she will come again, if only from curiosity. Then I have won my bet; and what is more, had a charming ride, for the short time it lasted. I really could love that woman!"

He rejoined Windibank with the most triumphant air imaginable.

Occupied as he was in seizing a favourable opportunity for jumping into the carriage, he remarked that Windibank was much struck by the coat of arms on the panels and the liveries of the servants.

"What shall I tell him?" said Charley to himself. "He will know her again. I do not even remember what she said at the last words of my adventure. And should I gain any praise from him? Better to go a little further in the affair before saying anything."

"Well, Charley?" said his lordship.

"Well?"

"What news?"

"What news, eh?"

"Yes. Have you won?"

"No."

"Ha, ha! I told you you wouldn't."

"Yes; but then you always were so clever, Windy—were not you? Let us go and have dinner at the club."

CHAPTER XIII.

THE MYSTERIES OF THE CONVENT OF SAINT SOREBONES WITH THE BLEEDING BACK.

"By the way, Windibank," said Captain Charley, "now I come to think of it, I hardly know whether I shall have time to dine with you, after all."

"Why not, pray?"

"Because I have just recollected that I have got an appointment."

"With a man?"

"No."

"Won't she wait?"

"I don't know, I am sure."

"Well, try her, then. If she doesn't, I am sure she is not worth your bothering yourself about. I can't bear those women myself who require such a deal of dancing about after them. It isn't business."

"And dinner is?"

"Most decidedly."

"My lord, those opinions do you credit A commission of lunacy would bring you in sane to a dead certainty, if they only heard you express them. Let us to dinner, then! It is just six; we shall dine at seven. My appointment is at half-past eight. If we do not sit too long at table, I daresay I shall be in good time, after all. Come along, then."

They strolled into Piccadilly, hailed a Hansom cab, and told the driver to take them to Pall Mall, where, at their club, they were, in less than an hour from the time they left the Park, seated at table before a very dainty little repast; for Captain Crockford was a good liver, and loved a good dinner as much, or more, perhaps, than a pretty woman. It may have been upon this account, indeed, that the dinner lasted rather longer than the gentlemen had originally intended; and even when the Captain at last consulted his watch, and found that it only wanted ten minutes of the time which had been fixed for the rendezvous to which he was about to repair, he yet dawdled over his wine, and seemed almost inclined to break his word with the expectant fair one, and not go at all.

However, at length he summoned up the necessary amount of resolution required to make a movement and got up from the table.

"Hallo!" said his lordship—"are you off?"

"Yes."

"In real earnest?"

The Captain made no reply, but began to prepare himself for the road.

"By the way," said Windibank, presently, "who is your friend, if it is a fair question, and where are you going to meet her?"

"She is a little governess in a Papist family, and lives about two miles from Charing Cross, in a suburb where all the families are either Roman Catholics or play-actors; and I am going to meet her at a Roman Catholic Chapel, of all places in the world—the Church of St. Sorebones with the Bleeding Back, if you ever heard of such a name."

"I can't say that I ever did, or ever wanted to. But I wish you luck, and I hope you're not too late."

"It's a close shave if I'm not," said Captain Charley; and apparently determined not to waste any more time in talk, he hurried out into Pall Mall, called a cab, and drove away to the place of rendezvous.

Most Londoners must know by name that famous chapel which I have thought it best to designate Saint Sorebones with the Bleeding Back. Those in the habit of passing daily through the broad and generally crowded thoroughfare in which it is situated, must have noticed a tall brick building, of sombre and threatening exterior, surrounded by a high wall of red brick, over the top of which peep the heads of five smoke-stained, leafless trees, which even in midsummer are blessed with but a very scanty crop of foliage.

Most persons casting a cursory glance upon the forbidding exterior of the gloomy edifice would suppose it to be a private mansion, or probably the property of some eccentric person who coveted science and seclusion, and are determined, as far as lay in their power, to block out all sight and sound of the busy traffic hard by.

It is probable they might suppose it to be the

dwelling of some miserly person living in great dread of thieves, for those of the upper windows which can be seen from the road are closely barred and shuttered. Perhaps some might suppose that the house was uninhabited, for all looks dark and desolate. At night there are never any lights seen glimmering in the windows; by day, rarely is a living soul seen to pass in or out of the great black gates, studded with rusty nails, and apparently sunk deep and fixed immoveably in the grass-grown path leading up to them.

But the house is not uninhabited; on the contrary, it contains at the least from fifty to sixty souls.

Fifty or sixty women are immured within its walls. Many young, many beautiful, many rich, many who have been worshipped by fond, loving hearts, to whom they are now as good as dead.

Yes, for this house is a convent—the Convent of Saint Sorebones with the Bleeding Back.

"And are there convents in London?" perhaps an unsophisticated reader may inquire, with surprise. As well may he ask whether there exist crimes which never see the daylight; hidden vices of black enormity, which lie hidden in dark holes and corners, and are never discovered.

Yes, there are convents in London, and there is the convent of Saint Sorebones, although its name is not Sorebones, but something else; and the black walls of that austere and gloomy mansion, standing apart from the busy life of the crowded London street, hide mysteries and sorrows, follies, vices, and crimes, black and unpardonable, from which it will be my duty to tear aside the veil and fearlessly expose, whatever may come of the wrath and resentment of the wrong-doers.

By the side of the brick wall to which I have alluded, there is a high, square-shaped building, having somewhat of the outward appearance of a Dissenting chapel; and this is the Church of Saint Sorebones, to which Captain Charley bent his steps after he had discharged his cab.

It was now at least half an hour after the time which had been agreed upon between the Captain and his Papistical fair one, when Crockford flung away his three-parts smoked cigar, and entered the sacred edifice.

He passed through a heavy wooden door, which swang to and closed with a heavy bang that echoed loudly through the building.

Then he opened a green baize-covered door beyond, and entered the church.

The interior seemed at first sight to be quite deserted, and the greater portion of it in almost total darkness; but when his eyes became more accustomed to the obscurity, he was able to make out the figures of saints, of large oil paintings, and the shrine of the Virgin, round which three or four tall candles glimmered faintly, shedding a dim and flickering light around upon the objects in its immediate vicinity, and upon the form of the Virgin standing out from the deep shadow, ghostly white.

So profound was the silence which reigned around, that the light tread of the Captain's polished leather boots upon the flagstones of the aisle seemed to find echo in the wooden galleries above full of dark shadows, heaped up into fantastic shapes, like huge goblins crouching together and hatching mischief in every dark hole and corner. It seemed to Crockford that his very breathing became unusually loud and audible, and that the very rustle of his clothes was fraught with quite an unusual noise.

He advanced further into the dim obscurity, straining his eyes to the utmost to discern the objects surrounding him.

"I'm too late, I suppose," said he, "or too early. I should think my little charmer has not come yet, or else she has gone. Yes, she must have left in disgust. The evening service is over, I suppose. Well! heigho! that comes of stopping to eat one's dinner. One ought not to have a stomach, to be a lover. What an extraordinary place this is!"

It was an extraordinary place, indeed; and the unusual sight would have been one naturally likely to excite his curiosity had he come prepared for it, but he had never been inside the building before; for the young lady, when he met her, was coming out, and the Captain at any time was not a very great church goer, and was not therefore ever likely to attend places of worship belonging to other faiths than his own—if faith his could be called who was professedly a Protestant, but practised nothing.

But the change from the daylight and bustle without to the intense gloom within was almost stupifying.

He walked slowly down the aisle, looking to the right and to the left, and finding at almost every step some new object to excite his curiosity and astonishment.

He was wondering where on earth were the persons who had charge of the church, and how it was that the edifice was thus left deserted, when, all at once, it seemed to him that he heard a low murmuring voice close at his elbow.

He started violently in spite of himself, for the sound came so suddenly and unexpectedly upon him, that it took him by surprise before he could find his courage.

He stood still, and listened.

The sound seemed to be close to him, I say, but the cause of it was invisible.

In vain he endeavoured to pierce the darkness shrouding the surrounding objects: he could see nothing.

It must have been fancy, he thought.

But now, a low, plaintive, wailing sound again smote his ear.

The sound of a beseeching murmuring—plaintive, passionate. Yes, the voice of a woman praying!

And as he stood and listened intently, holding his breath, he could recognise stray words and broken sentences poured forth in deep despairing entreaty.

"Oh, God—oh, God—forgive—forgive! Lord God, have pity! Lord God, have mercy!"

The voice ceased suddenly; and Crockford, with a feeling of dread which was almost akin to superstitious awe, stepped forward cautiously in the direction from which he had supposed the sound to proceed.

After a few steps he paused again; and, with his hand resting upon a rail which surrounded the Virgin's shrine, he listened intently.

But all was now still.

So still, that it seemed like the silence of the tomb.

But he was about to raise his hand again, and move away, when a passionate burst of sobbing caused him to throw a surprised and half-terrified glance into the darkest corner of the alcove in which the figure stood; and there his eyes encountered a sight which, for the moment, transfixed him with terror and made his blood run cold.

There, faintly discernible in the reflected light

of the white figure, was a white human face, upturned and quivering as though in agony.

What was it? Who was it? Was it the face of a living person, or of a corpse?

He stood motionless and speechless—quite incapable of forming any conjecture upon the subject; but, as he gazed, it began to rise before him, until it stood at least seven feet from the ground, and then a dark substance veiled it from his sight; and as he still stood, watching in awe-struck silence, he heard a rustling sound creeping out towards him from the darkness, and a sombre figure, with bent head, and covered by a black cloak and hood, slowly descended the steps from the feet of the Virgin, and sweeping by him so closely that he felt the cold draught caused by its passage through the air, proceeded noiselessly down the aisle, and, while he seemed yet to have his eyes fixed upon it, disappeared.

"Good heavens!" the Captain exclaimed, beneath his breath, and wiping away the perspiration which had gathered thickly upon his forehead. "What, in the name of all that is incomprehensible, could that have been?"

What, indeed? He was no coward, this gay young rake, and had but little fear of aught earthly; but the strangeness of the place and of the apparition had dazed and bewildered him.

In spite of himself, a sick faintness had crept over him, which with great difficulty he managed to shake off.

"By Jove!" he said, suddenly. "What a fool I am! It was a nun—a live nun, by all that is glorious! and not a dead ghost. It was a nun, I'll swear; and I will follow her if I meet all the terrors of the Inquisition by the way! Why, what a fool I am!" he continued, trying his best to laugh and treat the matter lightly. "Is not this London, and the nineteenth century? And are not the police within call? Yes; I will follow her, and see if she is young and pretty. Some nuns are pretty—or, anyhow, I have read as much in story books."

But the first thing to be done, before he could follow her, was to find out where she had gone to.

She had disappeared in a most mysterious and spectre-like fashion.

It seemed as though she had gone straight through the wall, without leaving any opening behind her; but such a proceeding struck him as not being very probable, and so he advanced to the gloomy corner into which she had vanished, and began to grope about in the darkness for some signs of a doorway.

"If she *has* gone through the wall," said he, "there must be a place for me to go through, also."

In the gallant Captain's composition impudence had not been omitted, whatever other virtues or vices might have been left out.

It naturally occurred to him that if he were to force an entrance into the convent and be discovered, and somebody should desire to know what his business was there, he would have some difficulty in accounting for his presence; but the thought did not deter him from making the attempt to find the doorway.

He did not even take the trouble to consider what he should say.

"Something will turn up," he thought to himself. "I shall think of something when the time comes. What does it matter?—they can't eat me—so here goes!"

He had, to some extent, by this time mastered the superstitious feelings of dread to which he had recently been a prey, and comforted himself with the reflection that these were not, in England at least, the days of the Inquisition, and that the metropolitan police was an institution there was not much chance of getting over.

Crockford felt very carefully round the walls in the corner where the nun had disappeared. A heavy curtain hung over and hid it, but this he pulled on one side, and feeling certain that there must be an opening somewhere, passed his fingers gently along over the oaken panels in search of some crack or crevice.

At last, to his great joy, he discovered one—gave a pull and a push, and succeeded in opening a door.

Then he looked eagerly through the aperture into a long, narrow, stone passage, dimly lighted by a swinging lamp.

He listened intently for a moment.

All was as silent as death.

"Now for it!" said the Captain to himself; and with a heart which fluttered a little in spite of his efforts to be calm, the Captain stepped across the threshold, and advanced cautiously into the convent.

The place had a strange, earthy, unwholesome smell, like a vault beneath a church containing the bodies of the dead.

"It is a grave," he said to himself—"a great grave, where they bury living, breathing women, instead of corpses."

Traversing the passage, which was of considerable length, he came to a large, square, vaulted chamber, from which opened four doors, each bearing over it the name of a saint, painted in long, thin, white letters upon a black ground.

Crockford tried the first of these doors, but found that it was locked. He tried the next, with the same result.

"Here is an end to my journey, I suppose," said he, as he approached the third.

He essayed this door with increasing anxiety; for at that moment he fancied he heard footsteps in the chapel approaching the door by which he had entered the passage.

If any one belonging to the convent were coming towards him from that direction, and he could not hide himself, there must at once be an end to the expedition; for what explanation could he offer were he discovered trespassing there without permission? The consequences would, without doubt, prove to be extremely disagreeable.

But then, you may say, how was it that he persisted in such extraordinary conduct? If you had asked the Captain himself, I do not think that he would have been able to have offered you a satisfactory reply. All he could have said, or would have said, would have been that he had made up his mind to discover some of the mysteries of St. Sorebones' Convent, if mysteries existed; and that he was willing to run any amount of risks to do so.

He therefore struggled vigorously with the stiff, rusty lock of the third door, but without success.

The door at the far end of the passage was now opened, and, as he had expected, some one made their appearance.

In the semi-obscurity he could not very readily discern whether the figure was male or female; and, indeed, he did not stay to look, but at once turned his attention to the fourth and last door.

He got hold of the door with both hands, and shook it vigorously—pulled it and pushed it.

The steps approached nearer!

One more effort—a despairing and desperate one, and the difficulty was overcome. The door yielded suddenly, he passed hastily through, and closed it behind him.

He found himself at the top of a flight of stone steps leading to another passage, vaulted like that which he had just left, but still more dimly lighted.

He walked down this until he reached a heavy door, studded with nails; and finding it open he peeped in with some slight feeling of uneasiness.

It was a square-shaped room—narrow, but lofty; and was faintly lighted by a small window, strongly guarded by massive iron bars. The last dying flicker of daylight which struggled through, now revealed the bare walls and the bare floor, cold and damp.

But the object upon which the adventurer's eyes were first turned, and upon which they immediately became riveted in astonishment and alarm, was a large coarsely painted red, wooden cross, and dangling from it some drapery, blood-stained.

By the side of this instrument of torture or terror, lay a whip, with several lashes, and a coil of rope, and upon the floor at the foot of the cross there were large black stains; but whether or not these were also stains of blood, it was too dark for the Captain to see.

But what he had seen seemed to him so mysterious, so inexplicable, barbarous and dreadful, that he left the room again shocked and confounded, and quite incapable of forming any rational guess as to what these evidences of brutal fanaticism, of torture inflicted, or martydom endured, or merely ghastly mockery and mummery, could signify.

What did it mean? What horrors—what infamies were here perpetrated?

Unable to solve the difficult riddle, Captain Crockford determined to pursue his voyage of discovery in another direction. Close to the door of the room which he had just quitted there was a flight of stone steps, and up this he mounted, always walking as noiselessly as possible, for fear that he might come upon some of the inhabitants of the convent unawares, in which case he hoped to be able to retrace his steps without being discovered.

But that he should meet some one very shortly he felt convinced, and he therefore determined to make as much haste as possible, and see all he could before the fatal moment arrived.

"Though how on earth it is I have met nobody yet," he said to himself, "is more than I can imagine. They must be assembled at evening prayers or at supper. Well, never mind; only if I could have dropped across a solitary one, I don't know that it would have been altogether unsatisfactory—supposing, that is, that she had been young and pretty."

Having reached the top of the flight of steps, he found himself now in another passage, much like those he had already passed through, except that upon one side of it opened a number of small doors, on which were painted white numbers.

The door of the first one which he tried, and which was numbered XXV, was pulled to, but not fastened, and he entered upon tip-toe.

It was a small cell, very similar to that which he had seen in prisons, only that the life of the inmate seemed to be much harder and more painful than that endured by any felon in an English gaol.

The cell was about eight feet long and seven feet wide. There was a bed—if bed it could be called—composed of four planks, covered by a small quantity of loose straw and a thin blanket.

There were a wooden crucifix, a stone pitcher and basin, and a little vessel of tin containing holy water.

There was also a scourge.

Doubtless, also, the fair occupant of this little chamber wore a horse-hair shirt next to her skin—and otherwise mortified the flesh, to keep it in subjection to the spirit.

Upon a shelf there were two or three little books, bound in black, and evidently religious works. And there was a square volume, with brass clasps, locked up, in which it would seem that somebody had been very recently writing.

"What is it, I wonder?" Crockford said to himself, when his eyes alighted upon this book, which lay upon the outside of the bed.

Nobody was there to see him.

The Captain was devoured by curiosity. He advanced into the cell, and took the volume in his hand.

Upon the outside was printed the word "Journal."

"By Jove!" exclaimed the Captain, in a delighted whisper, "I must have it, if I'm hanged for the robbery. What a prize! It will beat any work that was ever written!"

And so saying, this unprincipled young gentleman thrust the book into his breast pocket.

But hardly had he done so, when another object attracted his attention.

This was a round case lying upon the blanket, which had been covered by the book he had just removed.

"A looking-glass, by all that's feminine!" said the Captain, with a chuckle. "Some of these young ladies, after all——"

But it was not what he supposed: on the contrary, the case contained a large brooch, in which were some locks of hair of different shades.

Through the tiny window there struggled a faint light between the bars. With the greatest difficulty he managed to discover that there were four names engraved upon tiny scrolls of gold twisted round the hair. With some difficulty he deciphered the words. They were, however, these:—

"FLORENCE.

"CECILY.

"ALICE.

"RUTH.

"*May God preserve and unite my children in this life and the life hereafter!*"

All at once, he was disturbed by a faint rustle at his elbow.

He turned round with a sudden start.

There was a door on one side of the cell leading into a second cell beyond.

This door was open, and a nun stood upon the threshold.

Her face was unveiled and deadly pale.

Her eyes were red, as though with weeping. She seemed worn and weary by recent violent emotion; and now her features had a wild and terrific expression as they fell upon the unexpected sight of a stranger in her cell—and this stranger a gay and handsome man.

The Captain, at first almost as much startled as the lady herself, stood staring at her, quite unable to find a word to say in explanation of his conduct.

But yet, in his confusion, he noticed all that I have described in the lady's appearance.

And he noticed, too, that she was very beautiful.

And a thought struck him, that somewhere in his life he had seen her face before, or one very much like it; but where it was he could not imagine. They had met before, or he had met some one the very counterpart of her. But where?—where?

He had not much time to consider the question now, for he felt that he must give some explanation of his conduct.

The nun was at first too terrified at the sudden apparition to say anything; but at last she found the use of her tongue, and asked in trembling accents, "Who are you, sir? What—what is the cause of this visit?"

What, indeed? Captain Charley found it extremely difficult to reply; however, his only course was to brazen it out. He must say something—in fact, he must keep on talking, and trust to some idea coming into his head which would help him out of his difficulty..

"How can I hope that you will pardon me?" he said. "How can I hope for your forgiveness? But I was forced to act as I have done. It is my destiny!"

The nun lowered her veil, and replied coldly, "I do not comprehend you, sir."

"Oh, how can I hope that you would?" replied the Captain, speaking as though he were deeply agitated. "And. by Jove!" he muttered beneath his breath, "I am not far wrong there, for I haven't the remotest idea what I'm driving at."

Just then, a bell within the convent began to toll.

"What is that?" asked Crockford.

"I think that is the bell to warn us that the hour for retiring to rest has arrived. You must leave my cell, sir, immediately!"

"Oh, madam, you surely would not drive me out into the passages, where I shall run the risk of being discovered and ignominiously expelled from the building?"

"But cannot you go the way you came, sir? I do not understand what you mean, or what has brought you here."

"Need you ask?" the Captain cried, seizing her hand, which she strove in vain to wrest from the tight grasp of his fingers. "Are you blind as well as deaf to my love?"

"Love!" repeated the nun in a frightened voice, struggling more than ever to free herself from him "Do you wish to insult me, sir? I can in no other way construe your meaning."

"Oh, yes!" cried the handsome though unprincipled profligate, addressing her. "Oh, yes! it is an insult and a crime for me to love you; but how can I help myself, however I struggle against my fate? No; if I must meet death for your sake, I will meet it gladly; for what is there in the world without you worth living for?"

"But, sir," cried the nun, agitated and confused, "how is it possible that you can love me as you say?—for, to the best of my knowledge, I have never seen you before. Where have you seen me? How could you have conceived a passion such as you describe for the inmate of a place like this, where we are dead to all the world?"

"Ah, dead indeed!" cried Crockford: "it is a living tomb! But why should you thus immure yourself? Has the world no attractions for one so young and beautiful? Is it not sinful—is it not monstrous that so lovely a flower should be shut up in this odious place, away from the joyous sunshine and the free air of heaven?"

The nun was silent, and she turned away her head, while her breast appeared to heave convulsively, as though with strong emotions with difficulty suppressed.

The *roue* regarded her with a wicked smile.

"She is very beautiful," he thought. "I have nothing particular to do She must be very sick of this place, or very soon will be with a little persuasion. It is a great shame, perhaps, but I don't see why I shouldn't."

He did not pursue his reflections any further; or the nun, having at length succeeded in freeing herself from his grasp, made towards the door as though she would have escaped.

The Captain, however, was too quick for her; he threw himself in the way, and barred the passage.

"Oh, sir!" she exclaimed, in a supplicating tone, and the tears, though unseen by her tormentor, starting to her eyes. "Allow me to go! In mercy's name do not detain me!"

"Where would you go?"

"I do not know; but I cannot stay here. I must not listen to what you say."

"Why?"

"Why? because your words are perdition. I have no right to hear them. I must not hear them. Oh, what evil power has sent you to tempt me! Go—go, for heaven's sake—go and leave me!"

"Never!"

"But you are mad. If you are found here, I shall be ruined and disgraced."

"If I go, will you promise me one thing?"

"What is it? Oh, I cannot! What is it?"

"That you will see me again?"

"Where?"

"Here—or outside—which you like."

"It is impossible. You cannot, must not return here, or I am lost You know not the awful punishment which is visited upon those of the sisterhood who are frail and sinful—who, in the slightest degree, break the solemn vows which they have taken. No, you must never return here again."

"Then you can meet me without the walls"

"No—no; I never go abroad."

"Have you taken the veil?"

"No, not yet; but—but I am going to do so in a few days."

"Listen to me!" the Captain said, seizing her hand again, and drawing her towards him, in spite of her struggles, murmuring burning words of love in deep, impassioned thrilling tones into the beautiful woman's ear, while she, shivering with terror, strove vainly to escape from him. "Listen to me! I love you madly and desperately, and all the powers of heaven and earth shall not separate us Say that you will meet me again, or I will kill myself here in your cell, and they shall find my dead body lying upon your bed when they break in at the sound of your shrieks."

"Oh, no! For heaven's sake, do not talk like that! Oh! have mercy upon me! Heaven give me strength, and teach me what I can do."

"Heaven will only teach you, dearest," the Captain whispered, "that one so loved and so loveable was never created to live in a vile dungeon like this."

The nun sobbed.

"Come," continued the tempter in persuasive accents,—"come, tell me that you do not hate me."

"I hate no one. But, oh, leave me, while I have yet strength! Would you damn my soul? Have pity if you are strong."

"Have pity, sweet angel?" he said, encircling her waist with his arm, and gently pressing her to his breast, while his eyes looked down lovingly into the moist, tearful, and beautiful face, which she strove to hide with her hands, for her veil had fallen to the ground. "Have pity, my poor lamb? Do you think that I, who love you so dearly, would harm a hair of your loved head?"

And as he spoke, he pressed his burning lips upon her brow; while she, weak with weeping, and overcome with agitation and terror, blended with some strange mysterious emotion, which made her heart beat violently for some cause quite unknown to her, strove feebly to disengage herself from his embrace.

But at that moment there was heard the sound of many footsteps in the passage without, and a loud knock came at the door.

"Oh, heaven!" the nun muttered, with something between a cry and a groan. "We are discovered! I am ruined—I am ruined!"

"Be brave!" whispered Crockford. "Be brave, dearest! Say, where can I hide?"

And he looked inquiringly round the room.

Again there came a knock at the door; this time, louder than the last.

"There—there!" whispered the nun, pushing him towards the door leading to the inner room.

The Captain walked towards it on tip-toe, and hastily hid himself.

Then the nun, replacing her veil and trembling violently, opened the outer door in answer to a third summons, louder and more imperious than the others.

CHAPTER XIV.

THE LADY SUPERIOR.—THE CAPTAIN LEFT IN THE DARK. — MORE ADVENTURES — MORE DANGERS — MORE MYSTERIES — THE SECRET TRIBUNAL — PEEPING TOM — THE SKYLIGHT.— THE BEAUTIFUL MAIDEN HELPLESS IN THE HANDS OF HER TORMENTORS — THE SCOURGE.

"I THOUGHT that you were asleep, daughter," said a stern female voice, which sounded harsh and unpleasant to the Captain, listening in anxiety in the next room. "You were a long while making up your mind to open the door."

"I—I—did not hear you at first, mother."

"Were you dreaming, child?"

"No, no; I was not asleep."

"I thought that you were, and that you were talking in your dreams."

The young nun was silent, and the old woman eyed her suspiciously.

From the place where the Captain was standing, he could see the face of the elder woman, which was turned towards him.

It wore, a sour, savage, and malicious expression.

"I am very glad I don't live here, if that old woman is the mistress," said the Captain to himself, with a chuckle. "She leads them a life of it, I warrant me."

She was the Lady Superior, and a very severe woman, the bare sight of whom struck terror into the hearts of the more timid of the nuns, and who was feared and dreaded by the boldest. It required a very bold spirit indeed to be able to tell this woman a falsehood, and look her the while straight in the face.

The young nun cowered and shrank back beneath the piercing eyes, full of distrust and suspicion, fixed upon her so sternly; but luckily for her, the thick veil she wore hid her confusion in some measure, and after a few moments of intense scrutiny, the Superior, to her great relief, averted her gaze.

"I came to find you, daughter, because you had complained of indisposition; and although, as you know, it is against our rules for any nun to absent herself from the supper-table, unless she is positively too unwell to leave her bed, yet I allowed you to do so, as, as yet, you are only a novice. As, however, you are not as ill as I expected, I must insist on you attending prayers."

"Yes, dear mother, I will do so willingly; but —but——"

"But what?"

"I am really very ill, and I trust that you will not compel me—that you will allow me to——"

"To do what, Cecily? What means this strange hesitation and confusion? I do not understand you?"

"I would have said that you would allow me, good mother, to absent myself from that which is to come afterwards."

"What, from witnessing the punishment of Sister Agatha?"

"Yes."

"It is impossible. You must attend."

"Oh, mother, I beseech you!"

"What reason have you to assign for such a desire?"

"It is because—because I feel weak and faint, and I am afraid that I shall not be able to endure the sight."

The old woman's brow darkened.

"What!" she said, angrily stamping her foot, "do you mean to say that that lost and wretched creature has not justly merited the punishment which is about to be meted out to her?"

"No, no!" stammered Celily, in a faint voice; "but—but—I am afraid that I have not got the strength——"

"Peace, child!" exclaimed the Lady Superior, imperiously. "Let me have no more of this, but follow me at once."

"At once?"

"Yes; at once."

"Is it time?"

"It is quite time for you to come. Besides, you shall stand next to me, so that I can look to you."

"Oh, mother—mother! if you would but permit me to remain here!"

"I will not! The punishment of this girl is to be an example to you all—to be a warning to those frail and wavering sisters who have not yet succeeded in getting the flesh into subjection to the will. Come, I say, and instantly wipe away those tears, which you should be ashamed to shed for such a cause. Come at once."

The nun saw that it was useless to attempt to delay the departure any longer. Indeed, she was fearful lest the Captain, hidden in the next room, might make some noise by which he would be discovered; and she felt a sense of immense relief when the Superior led the way through the outer door into the passage.

But when they had proceeded a few yards further on, the Superior stopped, and turned round.

"Cecily," she said, "you have not locked your door. Go back and do it."

It was a rule when any nun left her cell, she should lock the door and bring the key away with her. Cecily retraced her steps, without making any reply, and turned the key in the lock.

She would have unlocked it again before taking out the key, but the Superior's eyes were fixed upon her.

"I will come back if I can steal away for a moment," thought the nun to herself—"let him out, and implore him to go."

The Captain within heard the door close with a bang, and the key turn in the lock; and at that moment it would have amused you not a little to have seen the wofully stupid expression upon the Captain's handsome face

"This is a pretty kettle of fish!" said he. "Here am I locked up in a nun's bed-room, and can't go if I wanted! Dash it, I say! By Jove! it's getting rather too hot, this! What will be the end of it? How precious gloomy it is! I wish there was a candle; I don't care about being here by myself in the dark. This is rather slow. If the nun was here it would be different."

It was, in truth, "slow" enough; and rather ghostly, had the captive been at all superstitious—which, by the way, he was not.

No; he cared very little about the gloominess of the cell—the grim obscurity, in which everything seemed to take fantastic and frightful shapes—and the intense silence, which was almost overpowering.

He did not care at all about these things; only being a very restless and used-up gentleman, he could not bare to spend twenty minutes by himself with no other companionship but his own thoughts.

"If I could only have smoked a cigar," he thought, "it wouldn't be so bad; but that's against the rules. Hang it! if I only had a bit of string, I could amuse myself playing scratch-cradle; only it is hardly worth while taking the trouble to pull out my boot-lace."

After this, he sat silent for some time, listening.

Then he got tired of that, and hummed all the tunes he knew.

Then he thought he would amuse himself by burning a fusee; but he refrained, from the same reason which had prevented him from lighting his cigar.

"This is deuced slow," said he, at the end of the next ten minutes.

Then he began to wonder. He wondered how long he was likely to be left there, and how he should effect his escape from the convent, and who this sister Agatha was who was going to be punished, and what they were going to do with her?

"I'd give my right hand if I could only see the operation," said he.

And the thought of the room which he had discovered on the floor beneath flashed across his mind.

The red cross! The scourge! The bloody linen!

"I will see it," said he; and, full of this determination, he advanced towards the outer door.

"If I could only force back the bolt!" he thought; and he felt in his pocket for his knife.

But just at that instant a key was put in the lock outside, and the door opened.

He had not time to get back to his hiding-place, but he stood up close to the wall behind the door—as close as he could possibly get—and he gave himself up for lost.

But the person entering was without a light; and presently he heard a low, soft, musical voice, which he easily recognised.

It was the voice of the nun.

"Where are you?" it said. "Come—come quickly! Now is the time to escape!"

"I am here, dearest Cecily!" the Captain replied, coming forward.

"Give me your hand."

He gave it her, and pressed the cold trembling little fingers in his warm grasp.

"What am I to do?" he asked.

"To fly at once," she said, in an agitated tone—"to fly while there is time! Do not linger!"

"What! am I to go without a parting word of kindness?"

"No! Good bye! God bless and preserve you!"

"Good bye; but we shan't meet again, Cecily!"

"Yes—perhaps! Good bye!"

She would have left him then, but he caught her in his arms and pressed his lips to hers.

Then, freeing herself with a violent struggle, she broke away from him and ran down the passage.

He looked after her for a moment, and then looked to the right and left, in uncertainty.

"Which is the way, I wonder?" said he. "The way I came, I suppose; but I don't believe that I shall find it again!"

He made a step or two in that direction; then suddenly retraced his steps.

"By Jove!" he exclaimed; "now I am out of the cell, I won't go until I have seen this punishment, whatever it is!"

At that moment a bell began to toll solemnly, as though for the burial of the dead.

"I cannot wander about like this," he thought to himself, as he fancied he heard footsteps coming that way.

Then he remembered that he had seen a large black cloak, such as the nuns wear over their dresses when out of doors, hanging up in the inner cell He determined at once to put it on.

"I shall pass muster in this dark place, perhaps. Who knows? I can only be killed once, thank goodness, if it's a killing matter. In for a penny, or in for a pound, is my motto. I might as well be hung for a sheep as a lamb."

The tolling of the bell continued; and while the audacious Captain was attiring himself in the cell, the door of which the nun in her confusion had left unlocked, he heard footsteps continually hurrying past the door, and all going in one direction

He was not very long dressing himself, and then, pulling the hood over his face, he did look something like a nun, only he made a very tall one.

He listened to hear whether any one was coming before he opened the door, and peeped out to see whether the coast was clear.

Then, everything being to his satisfaction, he stepped across the threshold, and taking the direction which those had done who went before him, advanced cautiously; though he could not, in spite of the risk and darkness by which he was surrounded, refrain from chuckling quietly to himself as he thought of the extraordinary astonishment the description of these adventures would create when related over a cigar in the smoking-room of the Guards' Club.

The bell continued to toll, but the sound of hurrying footsteps had ceased. Crockford walked forward in the direction from which the sound of the bell proceeded. He descended a flight of steps, and traversed a long, dimly-lighted, and damp passage upon a level with the mysterious room that he had previously explored.

The bell ceased. He paused and listened.

Then the Captain heard a low, monotonous murmur of female voices, as though they were muttering prayers; and then the first words of a hymn suddenly burst forth, loud, thrilling and melodious.

Guided by this sound, the Captain directed his steps towards the room in which he had seen the cross and bloody cloths. The windings of the passages were so intricate, and there were so many doors all looking so much alike, that had not the voices led him to the spot, it would have been almost impossible for him to him to have found the room again.

But he found it now. He felt certain that this was the door when he arrived before it. Bending down, he peeped through the keyhole, and could just catch a glimpse of the red wood of the cross.

Yes, this was the room. He was certain of it now. But what were they doing, or going to do? His curiosity seemed momentarily to increase, until it became almost intolerable.

He was determined to see what was passing inside the room—let it cost him what it might. But how was it to be managed? It was an utter impossibility to see through the keyhole; and as I say, he meant to see somehow.

All at once, he recollected the two high windows lighting the room. Where did they look out upon? He would endeavour to get round upon the outside.

With this intent, he left the spot, and kept along the passage, looking eagerly upon every side in the hope of discovering some door opening into a back-yard or area.

His search was fruitless: however, in the course of it, he came to another flight of steps, which he ascended.

Then he began to try every door he came to; and in those which were open, he examined the windows, but they were all fast and strongly barred

At length, however, trying one of the doors in a despairing sort of way, and without at all expecting that anything would result from it, he was astonished to see a light inside the room, instead of the darkness which he had found in every other.

Yes, in the room there was a subdued yellow light. It did not come from a light in the room itself, but from a window in the floor. At first sight, Crockford imagined that it was caused by a reflection from the window; but looking a second time, he discovered, to his surprise, that there was a sort of skylight in the floor, lighting the room below.

At the same moment the sound of a number of female voices singing together the "Miserere," in slow and solemn cadence reached his ear.

The sound came from below. He was, then, in a room over the mysterious torture-room; and the skylight, which somehow he had never noticed when in the torture-room, would afford him a view of the proceedings beneath.

Scarcely able to repress an exclamation of triumph at the fortunate chance which had led him to the spot, he approached the skylight on tiptoe, and kneeling down, rubbed a small place upon the dim and dust-covered glass, and peered eagerly into the room beneath.

Almost all the nuns in the convent, as well as he was able to judge, must have been assembled there.

There were between fifty and sixty. They were all dressed in deep black. They stood in a half-circle, and many of those in the front row held lighted tapers in their hands, while some held books; and one, a stout woman, standing in the middle, and a little apart from the rest, held a whip in her hand which had several lashes like a cat-o'-nine tails.

As Crockford stooped down to look into the room, the singing suddenly ceased, and the nuns' heads all turned in the direction of the door.

A death-like silence reigned throughout the apartment.

They were evidently expecting some one to come; and at that moment the door opened, and four nuns entered, leading, or rather dragging, some person with them.

It was a woman that they were bringing thus; two women supporting her at the sides, one supporting her back, and another leading the way, holding the end of a rope, the other end of which was round the victim's throat.

When they had brought her thus into the middle of the room, obedient to an imperious gesture from the Superior—for such she was who was holding the scourge—the nuns fell back from the person they were supporting, and she sank down trembling and sobbing at the Superior's feet, and with hands clasped and upturned tearful face, seemed to beseech her mercy.

The Captain looked down in wonder and pity upon the fair suppliant.

She was a young creature, over whose head, at the utmost, eighteen summers had barely passed. In spite of her deadly pallor, and the traces of recent suffering upon her face, she was very lovely, and the outlines of her faultlessly chiselled, yet voluptuously rounded form were plainly visible through the scanty clothing which she wore.

Her whole garb consisted of a haircloth, or a sort of very coarse chemise, which, fastened loosely at her neck, descended almost to her feet, but which the poor creature seemed obliged to hold to keep it upon her at all.

Her head was uncovered, her arms and feet were perfectly bare, and her long raven tresses hung in rich luxuriance over her naked shoulders almost to her knees.

"Mercy, mother! Mercy! mercy!" the sobbing girl exclaimed.

But the Superior repulsed her harshly.

"Wretch!" she replied, "you have deserved your fate! Prepare yourself."

"Mercy! mercy!"

"You shall have no mercy from me."

"Spare me—spare me!"

"Prepare yourself."

The poor girl covered her face with her hand, and sobbed bitterly.

"Strip her!" cried the Superior, savagely.

The young girl struggled desperately in the hands of the nuns who now surrounded her, and prepared to execute the Superior's orders.

But she struggled in vain;—for, in spite of her shrieks, and sobs, and prayers, and entreaties, they overcome her, and held her powerless in their arms, as though she were an infant.

Then these hard-hearted monsters prepared to strip her!

CHAPTER XV.

THE DEATH STRUGGLE.—JACOB STONE CHOKING. — THE MURDERED SERVANT. — A GHASTLY BURDEN.—THE SCREAMS OF THE WOMEN.—THE MYSTERIOUS PERFUME. — THE OPIATE. — THE UNEASY CONSCIENCE.—SPURNING THE DEAD. —COMING TO LIFE. —WHICH WAY OUT?—A CLOSE SHAVE FOR IT.—THE CELLAR.—THE BURST PIPE —THE DEADLY GAS.

THE reader may remember that I left Jacob Stone and his companion, Skeleton Key, escaping from the room in which Trevellyan was lying sick in bed.

The respectable servant man, attracted by Trevellyan's screams for help, came rushing down the stairs, from the room to which he had been for his clothes, and entered the apartment just as the two ruffians were making up their minds to silence the sick man with a stab from one of their knives.

So unexpected was the sight of the two robbers or would-be assassins, whichever they were, that the servant's eyes no sooner fell upon them than he staggered back, and seemed as though he would have made his escape again if possible.

But, the robbers turning to fly, he plucked up courage, and rushing towards the fire-place, seized the poker, and dealt a desperate blow at Stone's head.

The ruffian ducking to avoid it, took a deadly aim at his assailant with his knife; but the weapon which the servant wielded missing its aim, struck the knife instead, and knocked it from his hand.

Then they closed with a desperate struggle, in which neither uttered a cry, or made any unnecessary noise, both fighting furiously to gain the mastery.

In the meantime, Skeleton Key, instead of assisting his companion, as might have been supposed, was busily employed cramming his pockets with such valuable articles as he could find lying about on the tables close to his reach.

To have seen the cool, collected, and matter-of-fact way in which he performed the robbery, nobody would have imagined that at a yard or two's distance two men were fighting the fight of life and death.

The only thought which occupied this robber

was to get as many things as he possibly could; and making sure that escape was close at hand by the secret staircase, and that Stone would be more than a match for the man with whom he was struggling, he proceeded coolly to cram the various articles into his pockets, without disturbing himself in the least about his companion and the servant.

But all at once he fancied that he heard footsteps upon the floor above.

Somebody was alarmed.

Skeleton Key stepped hastily towards the door and listened. He heard a door open above.

There was no time to lose. They must escape.

"Can't you manage him?" Skeleton Key inquired — bringing forward a dark lantern to see which was which, for the candle that the servant had brought into the room had been overthrown and extinguished.

All was in darkness, save where the dark lantern threw a round spot of light.

But as he advanced with the lantern towards the struggling men, the servant, who was the uppermost, struck it a violent blow, and sent it flying to the other end of the room, extinguishing it by the fall, and all was now in perfect darkness.

"What are you doing, Stone?" Skeleton Key inquired.

"Pull him off!" cried Stone, panting with exhaustion, and out of breath. "Pull him off!"

Skeleton Key, instead, stooped and groped about upon the floor for a fallen knife, which, however, he could not find; and groping still, his fingers came at last in contact with the poker with which the servant man had armed himself, and then passing his hand over the uppermost of the two combatants, he felt for the position of his head, and prepared to take an aim.

"Quick, quick!" cried Stone, in choking accents.

The ruffian's strength was entirely failing him. He had ceased to struggle. A rattling sound became audible in his throat.

The servant had wrenched Stone's handkerchief tightly round his neck, and he was thrusting his knuckles in under the other's ear.

Stone felt his brain going round. The blood seemed to have mounted to his head, and threatened to burst out from mouth, and nose, and ears.

And while the servant held him thus, he too had been groping on the ground for the knife.

He had found it now; he had it in his hand; he was preparing to strike.

But at that moment, and just at the instant when Stone's senses seemed to be upon the point of deserting him altogether, he fancied he heard the sound of a heavy blow.

A dreadful, sickening sound—the sound of the iron poker falling with a heavy crash upon the shrinking flesh of the man above him, who instantaneously relaxing his hold, fell over upon one side, with a deep groan, and lay motionless.

Then Skeleton Key, catching hold of his friend by the collar, used his utmost endeavours to raise him into a sitting posture.

But Stone was a large, powerful, and heavy man, and the task was too much for his strength.

"Come, come—bear up!" he cried. "You are not hurt. Come, come—we must be off. All the house is waking up."

What he said seemed to be true, for as he spoke the sound of a watchman's rattle was heard upon the floor above, and the loud shrieking of women's voices.

"Help! help! help! help!"

Although Skeleton Key had some vague notion that there ought to be honour among thieves, and that one thief ought not to leave another when in trouble, still his friendship for Jacob Stone was not sufficiently great, he thought, to justify him in risking his own life, and the chance of coming into the hands of Jack Ketch by waiting any longer, and so he turned to fly.

He rushed down the staircase, through the door, which they had left ajar after effecting their entrance; and finding no one about to bar the passage or interfere with his progress, he sped on at his utmost speed up the street, in the direction of the Green Park.

Stone, left to himself, lay for several moments perfectly motionless—unable to move a limb, to raise hand or foot, or to do anything to effect his escape.

There was no other noise in the room that he could hear, save a faint groaning from the wounded man lying by his side, and the rustling of the curtain against which he lay, and in which the poor wretch's limbs were twisted convulsively in the throes of agony.

Of the man upon the bed he heard nothing.

Probably he had fainted with fright, at the right of the assassin overhanging him with an upraised knife.

Presently Stone felt that the wounded man was endeavouring to get upon his feet, by supporting himself upon his body.

Then in the faint grey light which stole through the open door behind, he saw rise before him a dark and bloody figure.

A mangled and horribly wounded, scarcely human object, which, reeling, and staggering, and stumbling in its weakness, crawled like a crushed and lacerated toad, upon the breast of the prostrate man.

A faint light coming through the open door behind, revealed to Stone's eyes the repulsive spectacle of the servant with whom he had been fighting, the lower part of his face shattered and smashed, and covered with blood.

His protruding eyes rolling hideously, sightlessly, in the pains of death!

His hand still clutching the knife, with which, even in the last gasp of life, he sought to effect the other's murder.

He seemed, in his pain, to be almost bereft of sight; but with one bloody hand he felt along Stone's body, seeking a vital part.

With the other, he feebly endeavoured to plunge in the knife.

And while doing so, he was staggering and rolling, and shaking his gory, mangled head, in a manner horrible to contemplate.

But still striking and striking, he all at once lost his balance, and fell forward exhausted on his would-be victim.

Stone endeavoured in vain to thrust him off; the weight of the dying man kept him down, and held him powerless.

With a few more struggles, growing fainter and fainter, and more painful and weak, the old man at length gave up the ghost.

Then, almost stifled by the weight of the horrible burden, and overcome with the exhaustion consequent upon his own struggles, Stone relapsed into a dreamy, helpless state, closely bordering upon insensibility.

But by this time the loud screams for help in the room above had brought several policemen to the spot; for it happened that the sergeant and five or six policemen were at that moment passing by at the end of the street, upon their way round to relieve the men from their various beats.

And seeing the door of the staircase open, they began to troop up into the room, where lay Jacob Stone, Trevellyan, and the dead body.

The ladies whose screams had attracted the attention of the police were three of those whom the reader may recollect having met before, at the supper-party, at Ruth's house, upon that eventful night when she betrayed Jacob Stone, and escaped from the fury of the mob.

They were three of the bewitching syrens who lured the young men of fashion and wealth to the gaming-table in Ruth's drawing-room, and whose bright eyes probably attracted a larger amount of their attention than the cards, upon which they were squandering pocketsful of bright sovereigns.

It was not the habit of these ladies to live in the house, but three of them were at this time on a visit to Ruth, and were awakened and alarmed, as we have seen, by the cries of Trevellyan, and the sounds of scuffling in the room below.

Their first act upon awakening was to hastily bury their heads under the bed-clothes, as the notion of danger dawned upon them.

Their second was to fly in a body to the window, fling it up, and scream with all the strength of their voices for assistance; and when they saw it come in the shape of four energetic policemen, running with all their might, and storming the back staircase like a second Redan, they grew a little bolder, and keeping in a body, crossed the landing, and knocked at the door of a room which was occupied by the lady of the house during the temporary monopoly of her own by Ernest Trevellyan.

They had to knock a long while, however—for the door was locked upon the inside—before they could awaken Mrs. Belvidere.

"How sound she sleeps!" said one.

"Perhaps she isn't there."

"Yes, she must be; the door is locked."

"I hope she is not ill, or—or——"

The speaker did not conclude the sentence. The frightened expression of her face, and the frightened expression upon the faces of the other two, seemed to indicate that the same dread was felt by all.

Again, and again, they knocked, and knocked.

Again, and again.

At last a faint voice, scarcely audible to those listening attentively without, asked in faltering accents, "Who is there?"

The ladies outside told her in frightened whispers that something dreadful was happening; that thieves had broken into the house; that there was a scuffle down below, and the sound of groans.

Scarcely had they finished these communications, when a step was heard upon the floor of the room, and in another moment the door was opened. Then, as they stood there silently in the darkness whilst Ruth struck a match and lighted a wax candle upon the mantel-shelf, they became aware of a certain curiously powerful odour in the room, something resembling the smell of almonds.

But they were too much terrified and confused by the exciting incidents which had just occurred to notice particularly the other facts about the room and its occupants, which at another tim , in all probability, had deeply excited their curiosity.

At other times they might have noticed that the curious odour was strongest about that part of the room where stood the bed; that it hung about the person of Ruth herself; that it was in her dress; that upon a pedestal by the bedside stood a wine-glass and a tiny vial, and that upon the vial was written "Poison."

Was it thus that this woman, whose life and every action seemed shrouded in such inscrutable mystery—upon whose soul weighed a thousand crimes, foully black and damnable—sought to quiet her conscience, and lull to rest the ever-present dread of that terrible something which seemed for ever hanging over her.

They might have noticed, too, that as she dressed herself she was compelled from time to time to press her hand upon her forehead, as though it throbbed with pain; and she was obliged also to steady herself now and then by clutching at the back of a chair, as though giddiness and weakness had come over her.

But she dressed rapidly, in spite of these drawbacks, and in a very short time came out upon the staircase, and prepared to descend to the floor below.

"Where—where are you going?" the three ladies cried, in alarmed voices.

"To see what is the matter."

"But you will be hurt!"

"Nonsense! we are more likely to be hurt if we stop here quietly till they come up and cut our throats. Besides, you do not suppose, surely, that I am going to have my house robbed without making an effort to prevent it?"

They saw that it was useless making any effort to prevent her going down stairs, for that she was determined to do so. They followed, therefore, in the rear, keeping close together, and looking very much scared.

Ruth proceeded at once to the room where Trevellyan lay. She found the apartment full of policemen, who were examining the body, and wondering among themselves how it had all come about, and how three men should be found lying in the same room, all covered with blood, and all apparently dead.

Ruth turned with a slight shudder from the revolting spectacle which the corpse of her servant presented, and bent her eyes upon the blood-stained form and features of the ruffian, Jacob Stone, who lay upon his back in a pool of gore.

With an almost imperceptible start—a start which was unnoticed by the policemen around her—she recognised him.

She recognised the man who had attempted to take her life—who had no doubt come there that night with the same fell purpose.

Yes, there lay the wretch whom she had betrayed to the police—whom she had so bitterly hated and so profoundly dreaded.

There he lay, dead, and harmless.

A huge, ugly, blood-stained corpse.

"Is he quite dead?" she inquired of one of the policemen.

"Yes," the man replied; "he's dead enough."

A malignant smile of triumph for a moment distorted the delicately chiselled features of Ruth's lovely face. As she stood by the side of the body she kicked the head contemptuously with the toe of the tiny blue satin boot which she wore.

Had not a feeling of shame deterred her, she would have liked to have set her foot upon that hated face, and stamped out the features until they were unrecognisable.

She laughed a soft, low, devilish laugh, which was inaudible to those around, and of which there was no other outward indication than a slight tremble of her plump, white shoulders, and a more than usually rapid movement within the bosom of her dress.

"Are you the lady of the house, ma'am?" one of the policemen inquired.

"Yes."

"Do you know any of these persons who are wounded?"

"That one," said she, pointing to the servant, "was my steward; this man" (pointing to Jacob, Stone) "seems to be a robber."

"The gentleman in bed has been wounded, also, though he seems to be still alive."

"He has not been wounded by the robber," replied Mrs. Belvidere: "he has been hurt by an accident, and his wound occurred several days ago. But do you suppose that there was only one burglar?"

"We saw no one come out of the house," the policeman replied. "Perhaps these ladies did?"

But the ladies said they did not.

"Do you think the house has been robbed, ma'am."

Ruth looked about the room, examining the different tables.

"I miss a hundred pounds worth of things at least," she cried presently.

"There must have been another man then, for this one has got nothing about him."

"Yes," said Ruth, picking up something from the floor: "here is a man's cap, and yonder is an old white hat. Evidently there were two of them."

One of the policemen bent down over Stone, and looked at him very hard.

"Hallo!" he said.

"What is it?" another asked.

"Do you know who this is?"

"No."

"It's Jacob Stone, for a penny!"

"What, the Smasher?"

"Yes."

Ruth remained silent, not choosing to exhibit any knowledge upon the subject.

A brief consultation was now held, as to what should be done. And it was determined that two of the policemen should go to the bottom of the secret staircase, and keep guard; that two others should guard the front door; and the rest should go round the house, and carefully examine all the rooms. And at the same time Ruth rang the bell violently, to summon her domestics—who hitherto, either owing to their not having heard the noise, or to their having heard it, and in consequence having locked themselves up in their rooms in terror—to come down stairs and lend what assistance they could.

Ruth, with the rest, left the room for a short time; Trevellyan and the bodies of the other two men were left unguarded.

But scarcely had they quitted the apartments, when Jacob Stone began to show signs of returning consciousness, for he was not dead, as the policemen had supposed, but only in a swoon.

Slowly he opened his eyes, and looked around. The two candles had been left burning upon the table, and the objects in the room were all distinctly visible; and as he awoke from the torpor, his eyes were set upon the ghastly figure of the murdered servant, which was propped up against the wall, right in front of him.

His first feeling was that of intense terror at this dreadful sight, but his next was a hope that escape was possible. Of course, he did not know that so many police were in the house, and that the means of exit were guarded by them; but he clearly remembered that just before his senses had deserted him, the body of the servant had lain across his breast. Now it was removed. Somebody, therefore, must have had a hand in the matter.

He rose with some difficulty to his feet, and walking upon tiptoe to the door leading to the secret staircase, peeped down to see whether the coast was clear.

A step or two down the staircase, and a glance over the banisters, showed him how matters stood.

The police were waiting for him there.

Escape in that direction was cut off without hope.

The only way then lay by the other door, and he felt that no time was to be lost.

Stealing out on tiptoe in this direction, as he had done in the other, he listened intently for any sound in the house, which might indicate the whereabouts of his enemies. He heard footsteps above, the rustling of women's dresses, and the sound of men's voices.

Without pausing to consider, he crept down stairs.

The bottom of the house was plunged in profound darkness; day had began to break, but no ray of light as yet had forced a passage through the coloured glass fan-light over the street-door.

He hoped to be able to escape by the area: he intended to hide, until things grew quieter, in one of the cellars.

The great difficulty was, how to get there. But it was not impossible.

The carpets upon the stairs were very thick. He would take off his boots, and creep down as noiselessly as possible.

As he had no time to spare, he took out his penknife, and cut his boot-laces instead of undoing them in the usual way.

Then he began to creep down stairs as cautiously as an Indian creeping upon his prey.

A step at a time he descended, holding his breath—carrying his boots in his hand—expecting every moment to find himself face to face with one of the policemen.

When he got down to the flight leading to the street door, he could hear the men talking in a whisper upon the door-mat.

Fortunately for him, they were so interested in the subject of their conversation, that they did not pay any attention to an occasional creak upon the stairs, which it was impossible, with all his caution, to prevent.

The staircase was quite dark, and he managed to come down it unseen. He managed to creep round the bannister, and make his way down the passage towards the flight leading to the kitchen.

Feeling in the darkness with his hand upon the wall, he came to a cupboard, which at first he mistook for a door. But he passed it, and continued to descend the steps.

But he had not gone far, however, when he heard voices below.

Some of the police had been examining the kitchen and other offices, and were about to return again to the ground floor.

Even now they were upon the stairs, and Jacob Stone turned to fly.

He clenched his teeth. The perspiration burst out upon his forehead. He gave himself up for lost.

But a sudden thought occurred to him: he would hide in the cupboard. There was just a faint chance that they might already have examined this, and would pass it by.

In an instant he had carried his purpose into

execution, had pulled the door to, and concealed himself.

He griped at the inside of the door with his nails, determining to do his best to resist its being opened, but the police passed by without trying it.

He heard their footsteps retreating in the distance, and breathed again freely.

When they had ascended to the floor above, he opened the door and descended to the floor below.

The door leading to the area, however, he found was double locked; but a coal cellar within the door was open, and into this he crept, closing the door after him.

"Curse them, I'm free for a little while here," the ruffian muttered. "When they have done their hue and cry, I shall be able to come out quietly and walk my chalks."

He leant against the wall, and began to put on his boots.

"I wish I had something to sit down on, though," he said to himself. "How frightfully dark it is, too! It almost makes me think I'm blind. How horribly close it is! I'd give the world for a breath of air. What the devil has made the door stick fast?"

Whatever it was, it had stuck fast, and in spite of all his efforts, he could not get it open.

To enable him to have a better purchase, he grasped firmly, with both hands, a leaden pipe, which jutted out from the wall, by the side of the door, and then planting his foot against the door, pulled and pushed with all his might.

But the effect was very different to that which he expected. For, instead of the door bursting open, it only creaked, and the pipe giving way with a snap, Mr. Stone was sent violently backwards among the small coal, where he lay almost senseless.

Getting up, however, with his face very dirty, and the back of his head very sore, he gave vent to his ill-humour in a volley of deep and terrific curses.

Who was to know that the pipe was going to break so easily?

"What is it, and what has made the door stick fast?"

He began to push and strain again with all his might, but without success.

He was afraid of making a noise, for fear of attracting attention to his place of concealment.

After a time, fatigued by his exertions, and their want of success, he sat down upon the coals, quite out of breath.

But all at once he began to cough. He began to feel suffocated.

He gasped for air.

What was it that choked and stifled him?

A moment's reflection convinced him of the horrible truth.

He had broken the gas-pipe.

The gas was pouring into the cellar.

He was shut up there, without any chance of escape.

Without air—without ventilation!

To a dead certainty, in the course of another quarter of an hour, the deadly gas would overcome, and kill him, if he did not call for assistance.

And if he called for assistance, almost certain death awaited him at the hands of the police.

Yes, he felt that he was doomed.

The thought occurred to him that he might perhaps prevent any more gas coming into the cellar, by stopping up the hole with his pocket handkerchief.

But there were two holes. The first he found after a little trouble, and plugged up roughly in this manner. But the second baffled all his efforts to discover it. He felt, at first, slowly and cautiously, then wildly, eagerly, frantically, over the walls, but he could find nothing.

Meanwhile, the gas continued to pour into the cellar.

His breathing grew every moment more difficult, more painful, more laboured.

He began to grow faint, sick, and giddy.

He felt that he was getting light-headed.

And he felt that he was doomed.

CHAPTER XVI.

THE SEARCH.—SQUABBLES AMONG THE X'S.—RUTH'S FURY.—THE TRAP IN THE PAVEMENT.—THE RUFFIAN FOILED.—WHAT WILL BE THE END?

MEANWHILE, the police were instituting a vigorous search in the upper part of the house, in the hope of finding the hardened ruffian at that moment choking in the cellar.

No hole or corner did they leave unvisited.

They searched in all the cupboards, in all the closets, in the wardrobes, in the linen chest, among the lumber in the cock-loft, and under the bed.

But they could not find him.

"He ain't by no means sich a small 'un," said one policeman to another.

"Right you are," the other made answer: "he's not the kind of figure for a pill-box."

"One thing's certain," said a third.

"And what's that, Jack?"

"That wherever he is, it must be a tidy big place."

"That's very sure. If he has crept into a hat-box, he must have left his legs sticking out at the top."

"But where's he got to, then?"

"He could only have gone one way," said a policeman who had formed one of the exploring expedition down stairs.

"And that must be upwards."

"Well, but look here!" said a policeman who had been left on guard upon the secret staircase. "If you can't find him?"

"Well, that proves nothing."

"It seems to me it proves that he can't be there; consequently, he must be down below."

"What's the good of talking like a fool? He's not below. How could he have gone down without us seeing him?"

"Well, he must have passed you."

"But he didn't."

"Where is he, then?"

"You know as much as I do, I suppose."

"How can I know?"

"You know, if you let him pass down *your* staircase."

"Let him pass me, indeed!"

"Did you?"

"Of course I didn't. Do you take me for a fool."

"If I took you at all, I should be obliged to."

The dispute began to get very warm. X 20 was for pulling X 25's nose; X 30 joining in, got at loggerheads with X 31; and the remainder of the X's present were all at sixes and sevens.

It was a most provoking thing, they all agreed, that this vagabond, Stone, should have been allowed to slip through their fingers, when they had him so nicely.

Who was it that had said he was dead? What wiseacre was it?

Nobody could say, or would say, but they all agreed that he was a wretched idiot; forgetting that they had all an opportunity of judging for themselves, if they had only chosen to have taken the trouble.

There was a heavy price set upon Jacob Stone's head, and this they had missed if they could not find him.

Where was he to be found? They set about their search again with renewed vigour, though without any very great hope of discovering its object.

But while they were rummaging about in every hole and corner, grumbling at their ill-luck, in allowing so valuable a prize to slip through their fingers, Ruth, a prey to various and conflicting emotions, was angrily pacing the floor of one of the lower rooms, looking out on to the streets. A policeman was with her, and he was explaining in a very abject and apologetic tone what had occurred upstairs, and how the bird had taken its flight.

"How the dickens it happened" said the man, "is more than I can tell."

"Do you suppose he has got out of the house?"

"I've no doubt of it, ma'am."

"And none of you saw him?"

"No, ma'am. Worse luck!"

The fair beauty's eyes flashed indignant fire, she clenched her small hand, and stamped her feet in a fury.

"Don't think that you will hear the last of this very soon," she cried. "You shall smart for it, I promise you."

"I hope you won't get us into trouble, ma'am."

"Indeed I shall, or it will not be my fault!"

"I'm sure we couldn't help him getting away. We all thought he was dead."

"It's most extraordinary!"

The lady paced the floor, seemingly in a greater passion than before.

"It is scandalous! It is outrageous! It is disgraceful!"

"Perhaps he isn't gone yet. We may find him," the policeman said humbly.

"Go and find him then, you fool, and don't stand staring there!"

And, with a stamp of her foot, and a wave of her hand, she dismissed the sergeant of the X division, looking very sheepish.

He had escaped her vengeance again, this powerful, revengeful, dare-devil ruffian, who feared neither God nor man.

Again he had escaped her. Again he was at large.

Again was she in dread of his murderous knife overhanging her.

But this dread, after all, was weak and puny in comparison with the awful, agonizing, benumbing, paralysing terror which she had of that other man who had returned from transportation—that Jack Rafferty, to whom there have been so many allusions during the few chapters already written of this eventful history.

As for this man Stone, she would soon dispose of him, she thought, when she got him again into her clutches.

"To think that I should let the wretch escape me this time!" she muttered between her teeth. "When his body was beneath my feet, why did I not trample out his heart—why did I not smash his skull in with my heel? To think that I should have allowed him to lie there unharmed, and to get up, and creep away, and come again, perhaps, another time and murder me!"

She fancied at that moment that she heard a slight noise behind her in the room, and she turned round with a sudden start expecting to see Stone creeping upon her.

But it was nothing; and she turned back again to the window where she had been standing, and leaning her head upon her hands, a deep sigh, half of weariness, and half of relief, escaped from her troubled bosom.

"I am a fool," she said, "to start like this at shadows, like a school-girl. I must be growing a coward. Since I saw that man, and knew that he had returned, I have not felt a bit like my own self. Oh, how long is this to last? What will be the end?"

While she was speaking, she was looking out of the window upon the pavement in front of the house, in an abstracted, absent, thoughtful way, half unconscious of outward objects. But something now attracted her attention, and caused her gaze to grow fixed and earnest.

It was not a very important object, surely, which had engrossed her attention? What was it?

Nothing more than a slight motion of the circular iron plate in the middle of the pavement, placed there for the purpose of allowing the coals to be put down into the cellar.

A very slight movement—a trembling of the plate, and nothing more.

But she watched it intently.

Before long it began to bob up and down a little more, just like the lid of a kettle might do when the water was boiling fiercely underneath it.

Then it cocked up on one side about six inches.

A minute afterwards, it rose several inches higher, and at the aperture appeared for a moment a human face.

If Ruth had been inclined to be at all superstitious, she might have thought that it was a ghost; for it was very white, like ghosts are supposed to be; and it was rising up just in the way that ghosts do in the theatre; and, besides, the face was the face of a man, whom the last time she had seen him she had supposed to be dead.

And surely now he must have been rising from the grave.

But not being at all superstitious, she was not too frightened to stare at it very hard, and to remark upon the appearance which it presented.

If it were a ghost, one thing was evident—it had been rolling among the coals.

It had also hit itself a hard knock upon the nose which was a little bloody and a good deal swollen.

If it were a ghost, it was none other than the ghost of Jacob Stone; and a moment's reflection convinced her that it was no ghost at all, but Jacob Stone himself, in the flesh.

Without wasting any more time in staring at the apparition, she ran out into the passage, called loudly to the police to come to her help, and opening the street door with great caution, so as to make as little noise as possible, she stole down the steps towards the unconscious Jacob.

Jacob it was, who half suffocated with the poisonous gas, had managed after a series of desperate efforts to raise the iron lid upon the roof of the cellar, and thus obtain a mouthful of fresh air.

There he stood, supporting himself as well as he could upon some large lumps of coal, clinging to the mouth of the aperture with his hands, and gasping like a stranded fish for breath.

The gas every moment seemed to grow more dense. At the top of the cellar it was thicker than down below.

At the aperture where he stood it was pouring out in such an opaque volume, that he could scarcely find a sufficient quantity of pure air to breathe to keep life in him.

He knew very well that he was risking detection by keeping the trap open; but to shut it, it was death.

What could he do? He pulled it down for a moment, but he was compelled directly to open it again.

At one of these moments, when he was hesitating whether he should not at once call for help, and give himself up, or whether he should shut down the trap again, and choke quietly, without making any further effort, Ruth saw him, and stole upon him as I have described.

She flung back the lid of the cellar all of a sudden, and as rapidly dragging forth the pistol which she always carried loaded in her bosom, she clapped the muzzle against his head.

He made a start, and a faint struggle to disengage himself from her grap, but she twisted her left hand in the hair of his head, and held him fast.

"So," she said, "I have you again, have I, Jacob Stone! This time you shall not escape so easily."

"What do you want with me?—curse you!" the ruffian muttered between his teeth. "Why do you want to hunt me down? What have I done to you?"

"Nothing, Jacob," the woman replied with a bitter smile—"nothing; because you could not. But no thanks are owing to you. What did you come here for."

"I came here to cut your throat," the man replied doggedly; "and I wish I had."

"But you have not, Jacob! And I must teach you not to play at such a dangerous game in future."

"If I live, I will do it yet," growled Stone.

"Then it would be my wisest course to blow your brains out now that I have you in my power."

The ruffian's case was so desperate, that its very desperation gave him courage.

"Why don't you?" he said. "What prevents you."

"Only this, Jacob," she replied—"that you are too great a scoundrel to cheat Jack Ketch of, and I think you will suffer more if I let you die in the usual way. Those are my only reasons."

This conversation occupied a much shorter space of time than it will probably suffice for the reader to peruse it.

By the time that it had reached the point at which I have paused, the policemen whom she had summoned to her aid came flocking to the spot.

Two of them, at her directions, waited above in the street, while the rest went down below to the cellar, intending to rush in upon and secure the robber.

Stone having raised himself a little more through the aperture, had completely blocked up the space through which the gas had hitherto been escaping. The consequence was, that the cellar below was full to suffocation.

The policemen making a rush into it, staggered back in a heap, all but choked, coughing and retching violently.

At the same instant, Stone, with a furious wrench of his body, managed to disengage himself from Ruth's grasp; and finding himself for a moment free, and his assailants in a state of hopeless collapse, he made a rush headlong out at them, in the vain hope that he might be able to effect his escape even now; and perhaps he might have been able to do so had it not been for his implacable enemy above.

He had scrambled half-way out of the area by grasping the rails above, and in another instant would have been safe upon the pavement out of the reach of the policemen below, and ready to struggle with the two waiting for him at the top.

But perhaps he might have managed these two, for they were weak, under-sized men in comparison to him.

Ruth, however, was a more formidable obstacle in the way of his liberty.

As he rose up to the railings, and his face came upon a level with the pavement, she pointed a pistol at his head.

"Leave go!" she said quietly.

And as he persisted in climbing, she placed the pistol against the back of his right hand, and with a diabolical cruelty, which scarcely another woman in the world would have been capable of, she drew the trigger and shattered his knuckles.

With a scream of pain and a frightful imprecation, the man released his hold, and fell down below a dead weight.

A moment afterwards he was handcuffed and a prisoner.

They bore him off triumphant, and with great rejoicing, to the nearest police station; and Ruth returned to the house, and summoning one of the frightened domestics, ordered breakfast to be prepared directly.

"So much for Stone!" she said, as she sipped her coffee and nibbled her buttered toast. "This time I hope to see him hanged without any more trouble."

She felt quite secure now. There was no more fear, upon the ruffian's account at least. She had done with him.

Ah, vain thought! Vain hope! One danger departed but gives place to another!

One victim put away, another rises in his place.

It was lucky that she could so easily forget a terror when it had passed. It was lucky that she had no thought of the awful future in store for her.

Oh, if she had had, would not her reason have given way? Would she not then and there have committed self-murder? Could she have borne the misery in store for her.

But it was far distant yet.

Yet was there happiness, boundless wealth, almost unlimited power, to be grasped by her. Yet was that angel's face, which masked a devil's heart, to lure fresh victims to her net—make fresh captives, and bring more babbling dotards, with sacks of gold, and honours and titles, to her feet, beseeching her to give them her love.

Her love!

What did she know of love, this sweet-faced fiend?

This woman without a heart?

CHAPTER XVII.

AGATHA IN THE HANDS OF THE TORMENTORS.—A SCENE OF HORROR—THE FEMALE MONSTER.—THE FAINTING NUN—THE BROKEN SKYLIGHT.

Panting, palpitating, breathless!

Flushed, scratched, beaten, and bruised!

Divested of even the scanty clothing which she had worn, cowering in terror, shrinking in shame, the poor, ill-used nun struggled in the hands of the merciless wretches who held her captive.

"Strip her!" shrieked the fat old beldame, furious at the long-protracted delay. "What are you waiting for? Strip her!"

The myrmidons of this savage and brutal old woman were already using their utmost efforts to carry out her directions.

The passionate, half-despairing, madly desperate efforts of the poor, sobbing, outraged girl grew every moment more weak and futile.

At last, in a half-unconscious and entirely helpless state, she suffered them to drag from her white, soft, delicate body the coarse chemise which she wore; and, fastening it round her waist with a knot, they raised her arms in the air, and attached one hand to either extremity of the cross-beam of the sacred symbol which these arch-fiends had converted into an instrument of torture.

When they had thus fastened her very tightly, which they did by means of some strong, thin twine, that cut into the poor creature's flesh almost to the bone, so that she groaned bitterly more than once during the process of the operation, and bade them, in a weak and wavering voice, to deal gently with her, the Superior bade the nuns who had bound their victim to stand on one side, and herself approaching Sister Agatha, called upon her by name.

The wretched girl, however, was so much exhausted by the recent struggle in which she had been engaged, and. perhaps, also from the effects of recent privations, ill-usage, starvation, and blows, even, which she had suffered at the hands of her tormentors, that she was quite incapable of making any reply.

She rolled her eyes, however, as though in great pain, threw a piteous glance towards the Superior, and inarticulately murmured a prayer for mercy.

But the prayer reached her not.

The piteous and appealing glance of the sufferer's soft grey eyes fell unheeded upon this heart of stone.

Frowning menacingly, the Superior again called her by name.

"Sister Agatha," she said, "have you any justification to offer for your infamous and disgraceful conduct?"

But Agatha made no reply.

"Before inflicting the punishment which you have so justly merited—which is but light and trifling in comparison to the black enormity of your monstrous turpitude—I wish to afford you every opportunity of making any explanation, if you have any explanation to make."

Still Agatha was silent.

"In the first place," continued the Superior, "did you not, of your own free will, enter this convent, and take the veil and vows of righteousness and chastity?"

"No, no!" replied the girl with sudden vehemence; "I was forced into it; I was compelled to do it. I never wished to come. I never wished to be confined in this hateful place, and subject to your hateful laws."

The face of the Superior Abbess grew dark and lowering.

She clenched her hand — she set her teeth. Her eyes glowed like those of an angry tigress. She shook her fist in the face of the shrinking girl; and it appeared as though shame alone prevented her from flying upon and violently assaulting her unfortunate victim.

"You lie!—you lie!" she shrieked passionately. "You know you lie, you false, white-hearted wretch!"

"I speak the truth," retorted the young nun. "You know I speak the truth!"

"I know that what you say is an infamous falsehood; and that you know it yourself. But let that pass. We will now proceed to the next question. Have you not broken the vows which you have taken? Have you not listened to a declaration of love from one without these walls? Have you not disgracefully encouraged the same, and brought shame and discredit upon this holy institution?"

The nun was silent; but her breathing seemed to grow each moment more and more laboured and painful.

"You know this that I have said to be true," the Abbess continued, triumphantly. "You know that you have listened to the temptations which some miscreant, thirsty for the damnation of your soul, has polluted this sacred building by breaking within its hitherto unsullied walls. You know this, and more. You know that the result of your crime has been to sully the pure fame of all the sisterhood; and that, at the hands of all, you deserve the punishment which is about to be meted out to you."

Here the Abbess paused for a moment, to allow the words which she had uttered to have full effect upon her hearers—not only the woman to whom they were specially addressed, but the other nuns, for whose benefit they were quite as much intended, perhaps, as for the culprit herself.

After a moment's silence she proceeded, in slow and impressive tones, calculated to strike awe and terror into the hearts of the poor, weak, misguided disciples of the black and idolatrous faith professed by the inmates of this dreadful place

"There is only one way, as you know, by which you can hope to escape the punishment you so justly deserve, and that is by naming this monster who has profaned the sanctity of these walls."

Again she paused, and looked expectantly towards the woman tied to the cross, perhaps thinking that she would speak, but Agatha was silent.

"The honour of this establishment you will be able to preserve if you at once give up this man's name. We have agents in London, in Paris, indeed all over the world, who are willing and eager to serve us in any way that may be suggested to them. As I have told you before, if you deliver up this man's name the secret can yet be preserved, for it shall die with him."

Still no answer was extracted from the culprit.

"Do not think that by this obstinacy you will do him any good. That he shall be found out I am determined; and if you will not confess the truth by fair means, it shall be wrung from you, if necessary, by the most excruciating torture."

The poor girl upon the cross sobbed convulsively, but yet offered no word of explanation.

"Sister Agatha," the old woman continued, "the time is growing short. Have you anything to divulge? Will you comply with my request?"

The nun ceased sobbing, and was silent.

"Are you still obstinately bent upon your own destruction?"

No reply.

"Do you intend to give up this man's name?"

The nun, clearing her throat, now for the first time since her vehement outburst broke silence, and said, "If I comply with your request, what will be the result?"

"That his death will take the place of yours."

"If I give you his name, then, I shall destroy him?"

"Assuredly. Pray have you any love for this man who has brought disgrace, and ruin, and misery upon you?"

Agatha's bosom heaved violently again, but she made no reply to the question.

She murmured to herself, however, although in a voice which was audible to the Abbess and to those standing around, "If I do not betray him, no other can. His secret is with me alone, and no mortal power shall wring the secret from my bosom."

"Poor fool!" the Abbess cried, contemplatively. "If your flesh, in doing so, is torn from your back, yet shall the secret be torn from your obstinate spirit. For the last time, I ask you to give up his name."

"And for the last time, then, I refuse to comply with your request, and defy you all to do your worst."

"Enough of this!" cried the Abbess, impatiently. "Get ready the scourge."

A thrill of terror ran through the hearts of all present when they saw that the obstinacy of this unrepentant sister rendered the punishment inevitable.

Even the boldest among the women turned pale, while many shrank back, trying to get as much as possible out of sight, and to hide the horrible spectacle which they expected to be coming from their eyes.

The scourge was, as I have said, a species of cat-o' nine-tails, such as is used, to the disgrace of this Christian country, to flog soldiers and sailors.

But it was, if possible, a more terrible instrument of torture, for at the end of each thong was a piece of catgut, artfully knotted and twisted, so as to give the sufferer an almost incredible amount of agony at each stroke. The thongs were so stiff and sharp that a cut from them resembled a blow from so many pieces of thick twisted wire or whalebone.

It was a devilish instrument, which none but a fiend in human form could have conceived.

When one of the nuns, who had assisted to bring her into the room, and who was a brawny and muscular woman, tucked up her sleeve, and, baring her arm to the shoulder, took the scourge in her right hand, another thrill of horror ran through the group of spectators.

Crockford could not help fancying that it was somewhat of an impolitic proceeding on the part of the savage old hag at the head of this extraordinary community to indulge in such an exhibition of severity, however great the offence of the culprit might have been; for were not all these women capable of revolting against such treatment if they thought fit? and if they rose up in a body and usurped the authority of the Superior, what was then to become of the entire institution? Would it not be at once abolished, broken-up, and done for?

But the Captain, living in an entirely different world, and having no experience of the strangely exceptional life which he now saw for the first time, and which was for the greater part entirely incomprehensible to him, and as confused and reasonless as the events in a disordered nightmare, could not believe that such a state of priest-ridden, helpless, and terrified ignorance was possible.

The Abbess, however, was much better acquainted than was the gallant Captain with the style of intellect with which she had to deal; and she knew that if the scene which was about to be enacted should deter one noviciate from entering the order—and that, however, was extremely improbable, for the poor creatures, when once inside those terrible walls, rarely, if ever, again effected their deliverance—it would have a beneficial effect upon the rest, and would tend in future to keep them in subjection, and cause them to stand in a wholesome dread of her authority.

Therefore, without any further delay, she gave directions for the punishment to proceed at once.

The woman with the whip stepped back for two or three paces, and, separating the thongs with her fingers, swung it round in the orthodox style, and allowed it to descend upon the bare back of her victim with such violence and effect as to cause a hollow groan or half-suppressed shriek of agony to escape from the sufferer's breast.

But this was all. No word did she utter, no complaint did she make; the wales which the blow had caused to rise up instantly upon her soft, white, delicate flesh, stood out livid and purple.

The woman wielding the lash separated the thongs as she had done before.

As she had done before, she again stepped back a foot or two, and again, with all her strength, brought down the whip upon the unfortunate girl's bare back.

Again a half-stifled sob escaped the sufferer's bosom, and that was all.

Once more the woman went through the same process, and once more with the same result.

Half-a-dozen of these fearful blows followed in rapid succession. The sufferer's back by this time was quite covered by the blue and livid wales inflicted by the instrument of torture.

The flesh seemed to be swollen, inflamed, and puffed out with blood in many places, as though upon the point of bursting out bleeding.

As the blows continued to descend, the skin peeled away here and there, and the blood trickled down on to the coarse cloth garment which she wore.

Before long her poor lacerated back seemed naught else but a hideous mass of bruises.

One frightful wound, from which the blood was streaming in torrents at each stroke.

For a long while the sufferer held out heroically under the excruciating torture which was being inflicted upon her without complaint, and alone testifying to a sense of its severity by an occasional groan or sob which burst from her lips, in spite of all her efforts to repress them wrung from her by the intolerable agony she suffered.

But at length the torture became too much for human endurance—she could bear it no longer.

One more ferocious blow than the rest, which by its violence almost cut a piece of flesh out of her quivering back, dragged a shriek of agony from her lips, which thrilled through the hearts of all who heard it, save the female monster who had ordered the infliction of this punishment.

"Mercy—mercy—mercy!" shrieked the tortured girl. "Mercy—mercy!"

"Will you give up the name?"

Agatha groaned and sobbed, but made no reply.

"Will you give up the name?" repeated the Abbess.

"No, I cannot—I dare not!"

"Proceed with the punishment."

"Mercy—mercy!"

"There is no mercy, wretch," replied the Abbess, "while you are obstinate."

Again the woman with the whip persevered in her cruelty.

A piercing shriek burst from the tortured girl as the thongs cut into her flesh.

She writhed and twisted frantically upon the cross, until the twine fastening her wrists penetrated to the very bone.

"Oh," have mercy!" she shrieked; "I cannot bear it any longer."

"Will you give up the name?"

"Oh! you are murdering me—you are murdering me! I feel that I am dying!"

"Proceed with the punishment!"

But at this moment there was a commotion among the shivering and terrified nuns assembled in the room.

One of them had fallen, fainting, to the ground.

It was Cecily.

They raised her in their arms, by the Abbess's direction, and carried her from the room.

Then they were about to proceed with the torture, when some one called the Abbess's attention to the condition of the victim.

Agatha, too, had swooned away.

"She is dead!" said one.

"Not she!" replied the hard-hearted Superior, contemptuously. "I will soon bring her round again."

So saying, the monster took up a bucket of cold water which stood in the corner of the room, and flung it over the fainting girl.

It had the desired effect, for the sufferer's eyes

again opened, and a hollow moan showed that life was not yet extinct. But could she endure it much longer?

Was the torture to continue?

Most probably it would have done, had not at this critical juncture a most unexpected event occurred to interrupt the enactment of further cruelty.

Crockford, who hitherto had been kneeling upon the floor of the room above, with his eye to the small place which he had cleared for that purpose upon the glass, had been by turns an amused and a horrified spectator of the scene which I have described.

He had been looking through the small peephole silently and attentively, too much occupied by what was occurring below to heed anything which might be occurring in the room itself in which he was.

Suddenly, without any notice whatever, a great weight descended upon his back.

Somebody had crept into the room, probably for the same purpose which had brought him thither, and not observing that anybody was there already, had stumbled over the Captain's leg, and come down heavily upon the Captain's shoulder.

Whatever had been the cause, the effect was this:—

The Captain's weight broke through the framework of the skylight, and although the other party, whoever he was, was able to save himself in time, the Captain was less fortunate.

To the astonishment and terror of the women assembled below, he came down all at once like a thunder-bolt among them.

CHAPTER XVIII.

CAPTAIN CHARLEY CROCKFORD ASTONISHES THE LADY SUPERIOR OF ST. SOREBONES' CONVENT.

The reader can imagine as well, or better than I can describe, the panic which was created by the Captain's sudden and unexpected appearance among the ladies of the convent.

At first, the greater part of them were inclined to think that there was something supernatural about this extraordinary visitation from above—that he was some avenging angel fallen among them; and they fled shrieking on all sides, in the greatest possible terror.

I do not know, however, whether these notions were shared by the Superior; in fact, I am inclined to think they were not, although at first she was quite as much terrified as the rest.

I am inclined to think, however, that she dreaded a visit from the legal authorities, and imagined then that some energetic policemen had adopted these means of bursting bodily into the secrets and mysteries of St. Sorebones' Convent.

When the Captain came down through the trap with a terrific crash, sending the bucket flying to the other end of the room—knocking down the cross and the woman fastened to it—and sending the nuns flying upon all sides in the wildest confusion, his first appearance was greeted with a piercing shriek, and the ladies, young and old, fled towards the door in terrified disorder.

However, once arrived among them, he took no further steps towards establishing his character as something to be frightened of.

On the contrary, he lay flat on his back, perfectly motionless and apparently insensible. The fact was, that in coming down he had hit his head a violent knock against the cross-beam of the dreadful instrument to which Agatha was attached, and the blow had half stunned him.

Had it not been, perhaps, for his fortunately hitting against the cross in his way down, he would in all probability have been killed by the blow. But as it was, it had only the effect of depriving him of all power of reflection or motion for some minutes to come.

During this brief period, the Superior, who had not fled from the room like the rest, was able to take a more comprehensive glance than they had done of the exterior of this bold intruder, and form some notion as to who he was, and what motive had brought him there.

At the same time she could not help puzzling her head with another question, which was, how on earth had he got in?

Until now she had always believed that the strictest possible watch was kept upon the door leading from the church to the convent, and that it was always kept locked, except when being used as a means of ingress or egress by the Lady Superior, the attendant priest, and the chosen few among the sisters of the order who were allowed to go outside the walls.

The other door, which led to the outer gate I have already described, had long ago been locked up, and was never used by any one but herself, upon any occasion whatever: the Lady Superior guarding the key with a jealous watchfulness, suggestive of a miser tending his hoard of gold; for with this in her possession, she felt certain that those in her charge were safe.

The person who had the care of the other door—the door leading to the chapel, through which Captain Charley Crockford had effected an entrance—was an almost stone-deaf, very infirm, and half-blind old man, who had long been in the Superior's service, and whom she believed she could place the most implicit confidence in.

Where, then, had this person entered the convent? How had he done it? Who was he? Where did he come from?

All these questions she asked herself, as she scrutinized the stranger's appearance.

He was a gentleman, that was very sure. Evidently a young man of fashion—of wealth—of position. Was he the seducer of this Sister Agatha, whose cruel punishment she had been superintending?

The thought no sooner occurred to her, than another followed it. This was that she must have a private interview with him, learn all she positively could from him, and then dispose of him in the best way that should present itself.

All these reflections, which have taken me so long to describe, scarcely occupied as many moments as I have devoted lines to them in passing through the Abbess's brain.

By the time that one of the terrified sisters had plucked up courage to peep into the room again, she had formed a resolve, and was ready to put it into immediate execution.

By this time, also, Crockford had begun to show signs of returning consciousness.

No time was to be lost.

"Here—quick!" exclaimed the Lady Superior. "Bring in Jane and Martha, to help you to carry this man to my cell."

The nuns, though somewhat astonished, perhaps, at the destination which the handsome stranger was to be transported to, were not in the habit of questioning their Superior's orders in any way whatever; and, therefore, with as much expedition as possible, set about doing what had been desired of them.

Crockford, still feeling very giddy and confused from the effects of the tremendous thump which he had given himself, had, however, sufficiently recovered to know what they were doing to him, although he felt very curiously careless and indifferent about the result.

He felt himself being raised from the ground, and carried out into the passage and up the stairs.

"What are they going to do with me?" he presently gave himself the trouble to think. "Perhaps they are going to throw me out into the street, like an old pair of shoes; or they are going, perhaps, to give me in charge, though that is not likely. Most probably they are going to lock me up: I don't care much about that; and as long as they do not use that precious cat-o'-nine-tails, which I shall take good care they don't, they may amuse themselves with me any way they think fit."

He was a most accommodating young gentleman, as you see. To tell the truth, he possessed the courage of a lion, as well as the impudence of a Crockford, which is the greatest height of impudence I can think of.

He was not at all terrified by the position in which he found himself, and was inclined to look upon his imprisonment in this nunnery as one of the best bits of fun he ever had in all his life.

"The only thing I wish about it," thought he to himself, "is that they would keep me here as a boarder, on condition that I did not split upon any of their secrets. It strikes me I might suggest several improvements in their domestic arrangements, if they were not unreasonable. The first thing I should do away with would be the flogging system—unless, indeed, I gave that old woman a dozen, just by way of letting her have a notion of what it tastes like. And with respect to the pretty ones, like Miss Cecily, I should——"

But before he had time to come to a thorough understanding as to the course of conduct to be pursued in these instances, the nuns carrying him had reached the door of the Superior's apartment, which one of the women opened with a key the the Superior had given to her. They bore him in, and laid him down upon the bed.

After which, they immediately quitted the apartment, and left him to his own reflections.

But he did not think it necessary to retain a recumbent position any longer. Rising to his feet, he asked himself seriously what he was going to do.

The door was locked upon him. He was a prisoner, whether he liked it or not. What sort of a place had they put him into?

By this time he had grown so used to helping himself to what did not belong to him, and making himself at home with the property of the convent, that he now, in the most matter-of-fact, cool, and unhesitating style, began to feel about the mantelpiece, on the table, and the chairs, and even in a cupboard, the door of which he found to be unlocked, for some lucifer matches.

With the same good fortune which had hitherto, with the notable exception of that tumble through the skylight, attended all his proceedings since he entered the building, he was not long before he discovered the object of which he was in search.

And he boldly struck a light.

With its aid, he discovered a small lamp standing upon the table, and this he lighted.

He was, then, in the Superior's cell. It was a better and more comfortable one considerably than that occupied by Sister Cecily.

"The old woman looks after herself," said Crockford aloud, "and I don't blame her." One might lead a very jolly life at this place, perhaps if one were a Lady Abbess."

He was looking in the cupboard.

"She seems to have some very good things here to eat," said the Captain reflectively. "I wonder what this tipple is?"

As he said this, he took out a black bottle, and without any hesitation whatever, helped himself to a glassful.

"Not bad" said the Captain, smacking his lips. "I begin to have a respect for that old woman, in spite of her bad qualities. This wine is"—(here he took another glassful)—"A 1."

Since he had been in the convent he had committed so many depredations of various sorts, that he had become by this time quite careless and hardened; and he helped himself to a third glass of wine with as much coolness as though the wine were his own, and he were at his own table.

Then, reflecting that he had now no more occasion for concealment, he opened his cigar-case, took out a cigar, lit it, leant back in his chair, and began to smoke.

"Gad! how I shall astonish the old woman!" said he to himself, with a chuckle. "I wonder whether she particularly objects to tobacco!"

If he thought she did, he was a very inconsiderate fellow, for instead of putting out his "weed" he went on puffing, if possible, harder than ever.

While thus engaged, the door opened, and the Lady Abbess entered the room.

Captain Crockford, after retaining his position for just one moment to give the lady an opportunity of observing how perfectly at his ease he had been during her absence, rose to his feet with a low bow as she entered, and stood waiting for her to open the conversation, at the same time extinguishing his cigar by pressing it against the mantelpiece.

"Well, sir?" said the Abbess, after eyeing him for a few moments in silence, an action which the impudent Captain also imitated,—"well, sir?"

"Madam!" replied the Captain, with another low bow and an affectation of humility and respect, which was not a little insulting.

"To what am I indebted for this honour, sir?" asked the Abbess, with a frown.

"Curiosity, madam," replied the Captain,—"curiosity, in a great measure; and something of a stronger motive, perhaps."

"How did you gain admittance to this building?" asked the Abbess.

"Through a door."

"Who opened it for you?"

"I opened it myself."

"That is impossible."

"I never contradict a lady. What made you ask me?

"Did you find a door open?"

"Yes. I am not a housebreaker."

"I am sure I don't know what else you call yourself. What brought you here?"

"I have already endeavoured to explain."

"You looked through that skylight some time before you fell through it into the room—did you not?"

"I did."

"And you saw——"

"A sight which disgraced humanity."

"It was the just punishment of an abominable and unpardonable sin."

"You speak very harshly."

"You think so, because the victim of your treachery was the person punished."

"My victim!" exclaimed the Captain, in blank astonishment.

"Do you deny it?"

"Deny what?"

"That that unhappy and misguided girl was your victim?"

"Well, not that I know of," replied the Captain, with a smile.

And he was thinking to himself while he spoke, "What the deuce can she be driving at? What does she mean by my victim? Ah! to be sure."

And the reccollection of what he had heard in the torture-chamber flashed across his mind.

The nun who had been so cruelly flogged was accused of carrying on some secret intrigue which had brought disgrace and discredit on the convent.

The Abbess thought, then, that he was Agatha's lover.

"By Jove!" said he to himself, "she must not think that; she'll be having me murdered, perhaps. Who knows? This is such an extraordinary sort of place, there is no knowing what they mayn't do."

"My dear madam" he cried earnestly, "at once dispel such a notion from your mind! I assure you that you are mistaken."

"Don't tell me, sir! Do you suppose that I am to believe your statement just because you make it? If you did not come here to see that miserable wretch who has so basely betrayed her order, what other cause brought you within these walls?"

"Madam, if I only dared——"

"You have dared a great deal as it is. How is it that your courage forsakes you all at once?"

"I have not courage enough to tell you what I want."

"What have you to tell me, pray?"

"It was to tell it to you that I came to the convent to night."

"Impossible! Do you mean to pretend that your object in coming here was to obtain an interview with me?"

"I came for that purpose alone."

"I do not believe you."

"Why?"

"Because if you had wished to see me, you had only to ask for me at the door."

The Captain was just about to reply that he would have done so had he known her name, but he checked himself. He did not think it good policy to appear too ignorant. Presently, perhaps, he might learn a little better how matters stood, and be able to act upon the knowledge. As yet, he did not know exactly who the woman was to whom he was speaking.

In that mysterious room down, stairs, and in Cecily's cell, she appeared to be a person in authority, but he had heard nothing which positively proved to him that she was the head of the convent. He therefore hesitated what to say. However he said at last, "I should have asked for you at the door if there had been any one to ask."

"There was the porter."

"There was no porter."

"Which door did you come in at?"

"The door leading from the chapel."

"How did you find it?"

"It was open."

The Abbess looked at him for a moment fixedly.

"He is speaking the truth, I believe," she muttered to herself.

Then she added aloud, "And what did you want to say to me?"

A most audacious idea had occurred to the gallant Captain.

There was only one way of accounting for his presence, it seemed to him. He was a devout disciple of the popular doctrine that "there is nothing like cheek," and he determined to make a bold stroke.

It might not succeed. Indeed, in all probability it would not. "But," said he to himself, "here goes!"

And he flung himself upon his knees before the astonished Abbess, who, raising her hands in alarm, opened her mouth and eyes to their widest, and staggered back against the wall.

"What are you doing that for, sir?" she gasped out. "What do you mean?"

"Oh, madam!" cried the impudent Captain, in a tone of voice which was intended to show the intensity of his feelings,—"oh, madam! need I tell you? Need I use words to reveal my secret? Need I say that it was because I loved you?"

The old lady stared at him in the wildest amazement.

She would hardly have been more surprised if the moon had tumbled through the ceiling and flown back again up the chimney.

She stood perfectly silent. Her lips opened and shut a little, and her nostrils twitched after the style of a fish which has risen to the surface of the water, taking large mouthfuls of wind.

But she said nothing.

Who, if not my lady readers, can tell what feelings were agitating her gentle breast?

She was a murderous, cruel-hearted woman, as you know; but she was a woman! And because one woman has no feeling for another of her own sex, it does not prove that she should not be susceptible to the tenderest feelings of pity when a gentleman is concerned.

And here was one who said he loved her!

When I tell you that she was a great, fat woman, with a pointed nose, little, twinkling, ill-tempered eyes, and a large, thin-lipped mouth, and that she was much nearer fifty than forty, you may be inclined to think that the idea of handsome Captain Charley's plumping down upon his knees at her feet, and professing love, and adoration, and all that sort of thing, was extremely ridiculous; but then, you see, you and I were not born foolish like other people are.

I give you my word of honour, as a story-teller, she did not think it the least bit in the world ridiculous.

I should very much like to know the lady who, in her heart of hearts, thought that anybody was talking absurdity when they said that they loved her; although, I have no doubt, hundreds of thousands of ladies have told their lovers so over and over again.

The agitation of the Abbess was so manifest, and her confusion so great, that Captain Charley inwardly chuckled with fiendish delight.

"Its most suprising how quietly the old girl takes it!" thought he. "Well, as the proverb says, 'faint heart ne'er won fair lady!'"

And he made a clutch at the Abbess's hand, and covered it with passionate kisses.

He felt the hand tremble in his, and with a

voice of deep emotion, the Abbess at length gave utterance to the feelings which oppressed her.

"Sir!" she cried, "I cannot believe you. You have chosen this line of conduct—you have determined upon making this dreadful, this unpardonable declaration in the hope of concealing the real motive which caused you to pay a visit to this convent."

"Oh, madam, I assure you — I swear to you——"

"Hush! I command you! If there be really any truth in what you say—if you have formed this—this rash, this—this mad attachment—the very thought of which is madness—I conjure you to abandon it at once and for ever! Oh, let me beg of you, let me entreat you to fly while there is yet time, and put the width of the world between yourself and its miserable object!"

"The old girl's growing poetical!" thought the good-looking scamp; and then, striking his breast with his closed fist, he cried, dramatically, "No, madam, no! No, adored object of my fondest hopes; my love for you is too great, too deep, too powerful to be thus easily extinguished and destroyed!"

"What would you have me say? Your words terrify me!"

"Is there no hope?"

"None, none! You know not what you ask. Our very oath and vow forbid that we should love one of the other sex; and of all others, I, to whom the rest are taught to look to as an example—to take as a pattern. No, it is impossible!—it is horrible! Fly at once! Come; I will conduct you to the door of the convent, and allow you to depart free, if you will promise never again to venture within these walls, and to banish at once from your mind every notion of this—this boyish folly and weakness!"

As she spoke thus it was very evident to see that she was violently agitated, that she was struggling with herself.

It seemed to him, from the convulsive heaving of her bosom, and the soft languor of her eyes, at that moment, that this woman could be beautiful.

That she could be passionate.

That her heart could throb with love; that she could be a woman!

He knew, too, how the struggles of Sister Cecily, at first fierce, angry, and scornful, had changed at last to almost tenderness.

It is true that he had no very strong desire for the love of this woman, but then it occurred to Captain Charley, that if there were no other point in the amour, it would be a something to talk about.

It was not everybody in the world who could say that they had carried on an intrigue with an Abbess, and above all with the Abbess of the Convent of Saint Sorebones with the Bleeding Back.

And so, instead of being easily repulsed, he poured forth the wildest and most extravagant vows and protestations.

He endeavoured to seize her in his arms.

The Abbess, uttering a stifled shriek, strove to free herself from his embrace, striving her hardest at the same time to look angry and resentful at his audacity; but somehow he could not help fancying that she was not quite as angry as she pretended to be.

Fortunately, perhaps, for the credit of the convent there came a tap at the door.

The Abbess, with a stronger effort than she had hitherto made, tore herself from his grasp.

Both the Captain and the Abbess stood still and listened.

"Confound the place!" Captain Charley thought to himself. "There's always somebody knocking at the door it seems to me."

He was not very much vexed though. He did not seem to take the interruption very much to heart.

"After all," thought he, "there's nothing particular lost by the interview being cut a little shorter. If it was only Cecily, now, or that unfortunate Agatha. I somehow don't seem to care much about the old lady; and I suppose I should have been obliged to have given her a kiss if I'd gone on telling her I loved her so much longer."

The Abbess turned round, and motioned to him to be silent, and to stand in such a position that when the door was opened, the person outside could not see him, for she thought it best to lead them to believe that the Captain was still lying upon the bed, in a state of insensibility.

But, as she was moving towards the door, she saw something glittering upon the ground.

It had fallen from the Captain's pocket, during the recent struggle; and as she picked it up, and restored it to him, she took an eager look at it.

It was the brooch which he had found in Cecily's cell, and, in his confusion, he had put it into his pocket.

However, although he was by no means anxious to have this trinket back again, unless it was for the purpose of restoring it, as soon as possible, to its owner, he felt anxiously in his pocket to see whether the journal was there all safe and sound, and found much to his delight that it was.

Being occupied with the thought I have described, he had not noticed a great and ominous change which had stolen over the face of the Abbess.

As her eyes fell upon the brooch, a deadly paler took the place of the rosy blushes which a few moments back had suffused her plump cheeks.

Her brows knitted. Her eyes wore the savage and tiger-like expression which they had worn awhile ago, when superintending the cruel castigation of the wretched Agatha. She looked at the Captain for a moment sternly, and without quavering; then dropped her eyes again, and moved towards the door, in answer to another knock.

"He has lied—he has lied to me, and he shall die!" she muttered betwixt her clenched teeth.

The Abbess had recognised the brooch as Sister Cecily's property. She had often seen it in Cecily's cell.

He then had come to the convent to see Cecily, the Abbess thought; and this love which he had just been professing was, after all, but makebelief.

The passions agitating the breast of this revengeful woman, under the sense of outrage and insult under which she suffered, were truly terrible; but she kept them hidden in her bosom; and when she reached the door, there was no trace of agitation visible upon her white and motionless features.

The nun who had used the scourge was standing outside.

"Well?" said the Abbess, seeing that she did not speak.

"I am sorry to disturb you."

"What do you mean?" asked the Abbess, angrily.

"I—I," stammered the other,—"I thought that you might be questioning the strange gentleman about the cause of——"

"No—no. He is yet insensible. What have you to say?"

"I came to tell you about Sister Agatha."

"Well?"

"We have taken her down from the cross."

"Well?"

"And bathed and bandaged her wounds."

"Well?"

"And we have administered all the usual restoratives, but——"

"Well?"

"She seems to be sinking fast, and—and we are afraid she will die."

The Abbess was silent for a moment, and seemed to be in deep thought, with her eyes bent upon the ground.

Then looking up suddenly she said, "Wait a moment; I will come with you."

And she was turning again to re-enter the cell when the nun stopped her.

"I—I have not told you the worst yet," said the nun, with a slight tremble in her voice, as though even now she were afraid of revealing that which she had hitherto kept back.

"What is the worst, then?" asked the other, angrily. "Speak at once!"

"Well, then, she—she ——"

"Who?"

"Agatha."

"What of her?"

"She is a mother!"

The Abbess started as though she had been bitten by a serpent.

"Do—do you mean that a child has been born?"

"Yes."

"And alive?"

"And alive!"

"The wretch!"

A dark cloud crossed the Superior's brow, and

her eyes seemed filled with passionate vindictiveness.

"Go back to her cell," she said, "and I will come to you. Keep the cries of the—the child as quiet as possible. Do not allow anybody to hear them if you can help it. Who knows already?"

"Only Mary and I."

"That is well. *Only you and I need know the rest.*"

There was some awful import hidden in these words, which seemed to make the listener's blood run cold.

She shuddered violently.

The Superior continued.

"Send Mary away," she said; "we cannot trust her. Go!—I will be with you, shortly."

And so saying, the Abbess returned to her cell.

But as she entered the door, the evil expression which her face had worn a few moments ago had faded away from it, and she met the handsome Captain with a winning smile.

"You must remain here no longer," she said, in a whisper; "I will conduct you to the door."

"You would never be so cruel as to banish me thus?"

"Yes—yes. You must go now. We may meet another time."

"Oh, but this parting is hard to bear!"

"You will get over it."

"You do not believe me!"

"No—would that I could."

"Not if I swear?"

"Do you swear?"

"Yes; and kiss the book."

And as he spoke, he pressed his lips to hers.

Then she turned from him, to take a key from a side cupboard.

There was a looking-glass on the wall, just by it, and she looked in it half-unconsciously, as she opened the cupboard door.

She was thinking at the time, Is this man sincere? How shall I treat him? Shall I do as I intended, or shall I let him go safely?

Oh! if the Captain had only known that his life was hanging as it were upon a thread—that the woman was debating with herself whether or not she should put him to death—it is probable that he would have been a little more serious than he was.

Only to think what might not have happened to him, if he had only been serious just at that particular moment, and there had no happened to be a looking-glass in the wall just in the place that I have described.

But so it was to be.

Yes, that little looking-glass, eight inches by six, was the cause of a score of marvellous, thrilling, horrible, and ridiculous adventures, which it will be my duty to describe, if the gentle reader will kindly follow me.

That looking-glass was the cause of all, and for this reason.

When the Abbess looked into it, much to her amazement, she saw—what, think you? Nothing more nor less than that audacious, deceitful, shameful, story-telling, palavering, good-looking, good-for-nothing making a grimace behind her back!

There was no doubt of it—there could be no doubt.

At first she almost hoped there was—and she looked her hardest in the glass to make sure; but there was no mistake about it.

That double-faced villain was making a grimace behind her back, and a gesture indicative of disgust; and he was actually wiping his mouth where her lips had touched his!

Oh, who shall say what a fury filled the woman's heart at this sight?

Her mind was made up at once.

He should die, as she had at first determined!

She took a key from the cupboard, and lit a lamp, and then bade him follow her, with a winning smile—a smile which would have been worthy of Ruth herself, that blackest of black traitresses.

They said little upon the way, because she enjoined him to be silent, and to tread lightly.

She led the way down stairs, towards the torture-room, but passing this, led on up a long, narrow passage, until she arrived at a door, which she unlocked, and they descended some steps leading to what appeared to be another passage below. But arriving here, they found it to be a small, square, red-tile paved cellar, from which one other door opened.

"Where are we going?" asked Crockford, in wonderment at the long journey.

"I am going to show you the secret way out," she replied.

"Indeed!"

His eyes sparkled at the news.

"It will be the secret way in again, too," he thought.

She felt in her pocket for a small key, and opened the door I have mentioned; but in doing so, either accidentally or purposely, put out the light.

For an instant they stood motionless; a death-like silence reigned around, except that Crockford fancied he heard a faint trickling sound, like running water, a long distance off.

What was it?

"How provoking!" the Abbess muttered. "However, you can find the way in the dark. This is the door. Go straight on, and keep to the right."

"It's precious dark," said the Captain. "Where does it lead to?"

"To a lane at the back of the convent."

"I don't see any sky."

"You will in a moment. Come, good night."

"Good night, and pleasant dreams."

"They will be of you."

He stepped forward in the direction she gently pushed him.

But scarcely had he passed the threshold of the door when he felt the floor giving way beneath him.

He would have sprung back, but suddenly the door was slammed upon him.

Next moment a grating on which he stood, and which had been swaying to and fro, twisted round, and he was precipitated headlong into a black and yawning abyss, full of thick and filthy water, slime, and mud.

He uttered a loud yell for help as he fell, but no one heeded him.

And then the horrible liquid closed over his head.

He had been betrayed; and the murderess above gave vent to a low laugh of savage joy.

"So perish all who would know the secrets of our faith!" she said, as she retraced her steps towards her cell.

But at that moment, almost before the sound of Crockford's voice had died away, another shriek was heard coming from the interior of the convent.

A loud, piercing shriek—full of despair and agony!

CHAPTER XIX.

THE BEAUTY'S TOILET.—AN UGLY FACE.—IS HE A SPY?—THE MYSTERIES OF EARTHWORM'S OFFICE.—THE IMPISH CLERK.—TEMPTATION.—PEEPING AND PRYING.—THE LETTER.—THE CHEQUE-BOOK.—THE MEDITATED THEFT.—THE SPECTRE.

WHEN Mrs. Belvidere had finished her breakfast, she lay down upon the sofa for an hour or so, to rest herself after the fatigues and anxiety which she had suffered that morning; and, presently, when she felt herself equal to the task, proceeded to make her morning toilet.

It was an elaborate one, and one which I will describe, as an example to those young ladies who are terrified at the notion of cold water and coarse towels.

She first of all began by taking a shower-bath of icy-cold water, at the bare mention of which I know many a strong man's teeth would chatter.

Then, after rubbing herself with a rough sack-cloth towel until her delicate white flesh blushed crimson with the friction, she went through the most arduous scourings and scrubbings with the coarsest yellow kitchen soap, and, to crown all, immersed herself completely in a bath of tepid, soft, and highly-perfumed rose-water.

Then, rising, like a second Venus from the sea, and daintily drying herself upon the softest linen cloths, which, with their elaborate fringes and red borders, looked more like pocket-handkerchiefs, or tiny d'oyleys for knicknack tables, than things to wipe oneself upon, she began to dress herself, with the aid of her maid, in the snow-white, scented, and warmed linen and costly articles of female dress prepared for her.

Her toilet was superb.

After her magnificent golden hair had been disposed in the form of a diadem, in which shape it seemed like a glory round her lovely head, she put on a dress of violet moire silk, so rich and stiff that it seemed capable of standing by itself upon the floor without her form being in it to support it.

The corsage was high, but plainly showed the form of her voluptuously rounded bosom, slightly pointed at the waist, and fastened up the front by small black velvet buttons.

There was a little turn-down collar of black velvet, and under it was passed a black velvet neck-tie, fastened with a brooch made out of three golden guineas over-laying one another. Her sleeves were loose at the ends, with broad mousquetaire cuffs trimmed with three rows of black velvet, beneath which she wore a tiny plain cuff, like a man's, with golden-guinea studs.

Her bonnet was of violet velvet, with a bavolet of white blonde covered with black lace; a small plume composed of two feathers, the one white and the other black, fixed in front of the bonnet by a coquile of black lace; quillings of black blonde on the forehead and white at the sides, and strings of broad violet ribbon with black velvet edgings.

The most delicate violet kid boots, to match the dress, and the tightest-fitting of violet kid gloves.

Then, pink silk stockings, and yards upon yards of white drapery, a foot deep in embroidery and open-work.

A shawl which cost a hundred guineas.

That was the way she was dressed.

It was her notion of simple morning costume, and except that she knew as well as any body, and a great deal better, that she was an angel of loveliness, and that she knew how to attire herself to the greatest advantage, I do not believe that she thought there was anything very unusual in the costly magnificence of her toilet.

But she was splendid.

As she swept along in her regal, queenly beauty, people turned eagerly round to look after her; and beggars flocked around her carriage and whined piteously, in the hope of coming in for some of the silver pieces which they felt must be as plentiful in this wonderfully attired beauty's pockets, as shells are upon the sea-shore.

Some of the beggars, particularly the children, were so dazzled by the blaze of her charms and beauty, that they could not find their tongues to beg for what they would have had her give to them, but stood round about her carriage, with mouth and eyes wide open, staring in stupified admiration at the glorious vision before them, until the carriage moving on again, they were obliged to fly in all directions, like a covey of startled birds, to save themselves from death by the cruel wheels which threatened to slaughter them like another Juggernaut.

She had ordered out her carriage with the intention of driving to the office of Mr. Eneas Earthworm, with whom the reader may remember she had an appointment; but as she drove towards her destination, she saw by a church clock that she passed upon the way, that she had yet some time to spare, and she told the driver to stop at Covent Garden Market, where she thought she would amuse herself by purchasing some flowers.

The man drew up at the entrance by St. Paul's, and the footman got down from the box and assisted her to alight.

It was a very handsome brougham, drawn by two very handsome grey horses; the liveries and appointments were of the very best; there was a coronet upon the panel, and inside, filling the whole vehicle with her ample skirts, this beautiful lady, her fair hair glittering golden in the sunlight as she leant forward her pink and white face towards the window to give her orders.

It was no wonder that there should be a larger crowd than usual assemble to see her alight, or that the people standing round should hustle one another rudely, in their anxiety to get a front place.

And this popularity delighted her. She felt as much pleasure in the homage of the unwashed, expressed in a loud murmur of coarse admiration, as she would have done in the most refined and polished flatteries in her Majesty's drawing-room.

She alighted, with a proud, triumphant smile upon her crimson lips, and a sparkle of delight in her dark blue eyes; and the small, neatly-booted feet, visible for a moment as she descended the step, trod proudly and almost defiantly as they carried their fair mistress towards the arcade.

But in the sweeping glance which she took of the faces in the little crowd, she noticed one particularly; perhaps because it stood out from the rest by reason of its superlative ugliness, and by the extreme singularity of its shape—for it was horribly gaunt and fleshless, like a death's head, and from the hollow cheeks the sunken eyes glared out in a ghost-like fashion, which even in broad daylight, and a crowded street, was rather terrifying.

But though she noticed it in passing, the sight of it inspired no fear within her own breast; for I need hardly tell the reader, by this time, that she was anything but the timidest of womankind, and she only muttered to herself, as she glanced towards him, with a pretty little shiver of her plump shoulders, "What a horribly ugly wretch! However could they have allowed him to grow up so? He ought to have been put an end to long ago. Such frights as those should be put out of the world as soon as they come into it. I'd have had him suffocated if I had had anything to do with him."

With which amiable thought, the beautiful lady began to smell, and admire, and delicately handle the beautiful bouquets, which a florist at her approach hastened to show to her.

When she had selected the largest and best nosegay in the shop, she retraced her steps towards the carriage, holding it to her face, as she walked along, inhaling the odour of the choice flowers, and almost concealing her own pretty features among the rosebuds, lilies, and camillas.

But peeping out over the laced border of the bouquet, she saw again that ugly face which she had noticed a few minutes before, staring intently at her round one of the pillars, with a sort of a half-leer upon his features, which, if possible, increased their natural ugliness.

She gazed upon him for a moment in intense surprise, and then in some alarm; and the colour faded suddenly from her hitherto rosy cheeks, just for all the world as though the roses in her hand had absorbed their colour like a sponge sucks up water.

What was he staring at her for? she asked herself; but a glance at him satisfied her that he was unknown to her, and so it mattered very little what was his motive.

She always of late, however, since he—that Rafferty, of whom so much has been said—had returned to England, started and shivered at the sight of any stranger regarding her earnestly; and although she dismissed the idea as rapidly almost as it was conceived, she could not help fancying for a moment that this ugly man, whose eyes were fixed upon her, was somehow or other connected with this dreaded person, whose deadly vengeance she knew was overhanging her.

"Pooh! pooh!" she muttered to herself, as she stepped back into her brougham, and bade the driver to take her at once to Bedford Row. "He most likely wanted to rob me. He took a fancy to my gold watch-chain most, I dare say. I don't suppose that there is very much harm in him, after all, although he is such an ugly monster; but I'd have had him smothered, though, for all that, if I'd had my way. The sight of him, I declare, has taken all the perfume from the flowers."

She leant back in the carriage, and drove along with her eyes shut, dreamily occupied with a score of castles which she was building. She felt very happy this morning in the bright sunshine, and the sparkling of her eyes reflected but dimly the joyous thoughts which thrilled through her brain.

She had no occasion to be so very happy, one might have thought, after the horrible scene which had just occurred at her house. But the recollection of the murder of her servant, and the perils which she had herself run from the assassin's knife, were all submerged in the one happy thought that Jacob Stone was now safe in prison, and that there was sufficient against him to hang him in front of Newgate, and so rid the world and her of his dangerous presence in future.

"Yes, he must be hanged," she said to herself. "It will be better that he should be hanged. There is no safety in transportation; they come back again; and when one thinks that they are firmly chained and fettered a thousand miles away, they are at one's elbow. No!—no mortal power shall save him this time. But who would try to save him?—who would petition for mercy on behalf of such a wretch? I am sure that he has done enough to merit hanging half a dozen times; and I will take care that there is no lack of evidence, if hard swearing can do him any harm."

By this time they had reached the house in Bedford Row where Mr. Earthworm had his office; and, descending from her carriage, she rang the bell of a door upon which Earthworm's name was printed in thick black letters upon a highly-polished brass plate, that bore also in small capitals, and under the name, the words "secret agent."

The door was promptly opened by a light-haired, red-eyed, blinking boy, who expressed, by a faint grin upon his weasened, colourless face, that he recognised her.

She stooped down, and, laying her finger upon her lips to warn him to be silent, whispered in his ear, "Who is inside?"

"Nobody, ma'am," replied the boy.

"Who is expected?"

"A gentleman, at ten."

"Of the name of Rafferty?"

"Of the name of Rafferty."

"It wants five minutes to ten now—does it not?"

"Six minutes."

"Go out, and send away my carriage; and tell my people to come back in a couple of hours' time, and to wait six doors off till they are called. When do you expect your master?"

"He will be here before the other."

"Give me warning as soon as either of them come. I do not want the stranger to see me."

The boy left the office to give her directions to the coachman, and Ruth entered a sitting-room in which it was Earthworm's habit to receive his clients.

It was a curious place, furnished with a vast number of strange and awe-inspiring objects, well calculated to impose upon the credulity of the weak-minded persons upon whom Earthworm practised his deceitful arts.

There were a large number of books arranged along some shelves, the greater part of them having reference to criminal jurisprudence; but there were also ten thick volumes labelled alphabetically, and entitled ominously, "Suspicious."

That these books contained biographical sketches of a number of unconvicted rogues and vagabonds in all classes of life, was a thought which most probably occurred to a great number of clients of an imaginative turn; but those who were not imaginative were yet not a little curious about the contents of these curiously named volumes; and had they not been under lock and key, there is very little doubt that they would have been frequently visited by those persons who found themselves alone, and supposed themselves to be unwatched, in the mysterious apartment.

There were also several other things in the room calculated to attract a stranger's attention.

There were two ugly plaster casts, one upon each side of the mantel-piece, representing persons with the most revolting style of features, and bearing these inscriptions:—

"J. R., hanged 3rd of March, 1837."

"H. R, strangled by self, 3rd of August, 1845."

Between these pleasant memorials there was a dreary oil-painting, the subject of which, at first sight, was extremely difficult to decipher; but which proved, upon investigation, to represent the interior of the Old Bailey Session House during a trial; and underneath this, hanging upon a nail in the wall, was an instrument of an almost incomprehensible nature to those unacquainted with the "housebreaking craft," but which was what is commonly known among "cracksmen" as a "jemmy."

Upon a table lay a litter of books and papers, and among these, as though they had been left there accidentally, a pair of handcuffs.

All these objects, curious as they might have appeared to a stranger, were yet familiar enough to the incomprehensible being who now regarded them; and she gave but a careless glance at the various objects as she took a seat in an easy chair, and smiled to herself at a thought which crossed her busy brain.

"He's a clever fellow," she said to herself—"a very clever fellow; but what's the good of it all? What is the good of so much ingenuity to make so little? I hardly think that he is rich, although he has spent a good deal upon me. Not lately, though. His devotion has cooled a little; but that's my fault perhaps. He's very jealous, and wants a great deal of attention, like all old men; and he's full of whims and fancies. But, bah! I don't want him for a lover. I'd rather his attachment was platonic. I'd rather have him as a friend or an acquaintance: he might do me many a good service if he liked. And so he will when he has the chance, I make no doubt; for I think he loves me, after all, although he doesn't go crazy about me like he used to do. I'm glad of it. I'm tired of him. I wish I had all his money, and he was dead and buried twenty feet deep."

With that she went to the looking-glass, and arranged her silky, golden tresses to the best advantage, examined her bouquet, read the titles of the books on the bookshelves, and thus passed passed away five or six minutes.

At the end of this time, however, she began to grow rather impatient, and consulting her watch, remembered that the last time she had looked at it it had stopped, and she called out to the clerk in the outer office to tell her what time it was.

"Five minutes past ten," he said.

"What makes them both so late?" she asked herself. "What can have happened? Perhaps they won't come. But then Earthworm is sure to be here, I should think."

To beguile her time she took another survey of the contents of the apartment, examined the gloomy picture over the mantel-piece, took down the "jemmy" and looked at it, scratched the nose of one of the plaster casts with a hair-pin, and tried on one of the handcuffs: they were a large size, and went on very easily, so she put on both to try the effect.

"They are too big for me. I wonder whether they make them my size?—though of course they do, for I have seen children handcuffed before now; and I, too—but that was years ago. Ah! how many years ago? It was when I was a poor little houseless, homeless, friendless vagabond. I wonder what has become of all those I knew then? I hear nothing of them. They may be dead. Well, I don't care; dead or alive, it matters very little, that I can see, as long as they don't pester me. There's only one of them whose burial I should like to be at, and he is alive—as yet—and will be here, I suppose, in a few minutes."

But a few minutes passed away without any appearance of the expected visitor, and the lady's patience soon became exhausted again.

She went into the outer office to inquire the time of the small, blinking boy; and she found him busily engaged in the rather brutal pastime of stringing live flies upon a piece of thread like beads.

"What are you doing that for?" she asked, in disgust.

"Eh?" said the boy, looking up and blinking at her.

"What are you torturing those flies for?" she asked.

"Torturing 'em?"

"Yes."

"To make 'em fiz," replied the young gentleman, continuing his pastime with deliberate coolness.

"Don't do it," she said.

"Why not?"

"Because I tell you."

"Are they yours?"

"Put them down."

"I'll give them to you when I have threaded them all;" and the young gentleman proceeded as before.

But Mrs. Belvidere, aggravated by his opposition, put a stop to the amusing pastime, by suddenly delivering upon one of his great red ears such a sounding thwack, that he blinked and winked for full three minutes afterwards, in pain and amazement.

When, however, he recovered his breath, he threw himself into an attitude of resistance, and made as though he would have struck at her, a course which so exasperated the lady, that she immediately boxed his other ear harder than she had boxed the first; and seizing hold of him suddenly by the coat collar, shook him until the teeth chattered in his head like castanets, and then flung him to the other side of the room.

"You horrid little wretch, I'll teach you to mind what I say," she said. "I should think no more of wringing your neck and killing you, than you do one of those flies. Don't scowl at me like that, because I shall give you worse than you've had if you do. Come here."

"I shan't," replied the boy, doggedly.

"Come here," repeated Ruth, with a stamp of the foot, "or it will be the worse for you."

"You ain't my mistress, are you?" said the boy, with a whine.

"You see that I am, and mean to be. Come here this moment."

The lad evidently thought it best to obey the commands of this imperious beauty, and he came shambling up, rubbing his knuckles in the corners of his eyes, and sniffing piteously.

As he approached, she stretched out her hand, and he dodged suddenly back, as though expecting another of those sounding cuffs upon the ears, which that pretty little red-gloved hand could so well administer when occasion required. But her intention this time was not to box him, only to catch hold of him by the cuff and draw him nearer to her.

"Don't shrink like that," said she in reference to the backward motion which I have described, "I'm not going to hurt you."

He seemed by no means too confident of this; but he stood still, nevertheless, and regarded her out of the corner of his eyes in a sly, sneaking, half-frightened fashion, which was peculiarly his own; and she in her turn regarded him attentively.

He was not a prepossessing-looking boy, this young clerk of Mr. Earthworm's.

He was a pale, unwholesome-looking lad, with

a face, in many places, covered with blotches; and his great red ears stood out prominently on each side of his head, like handles to a jar.

He was dressed in a very worn and threadbare suit, which had more than once been darned and patched, and which was several sizes too small for him. Some of the buttons were wanting; and this deficiency had been atoned for by pieces of red tape and pins, and little bits of string, and even something seemed to have been done with gum and sealing-wax.

He did not appear to have any very heavy official duties to perform in Mr. Earthworm's employment, for upon his desk there lay only a sheet of clean blotting-paper and an unused pen; and it was very certain that he had a good deal of spare time upon his hands.

But being of an ingenious turn of mind, as may be seen from this little episode of the flies, the time did not hang very heavily.

Upon the edge of his desk, for instance, he had manufactured a very clever kind of musical instrument, out of broken steel pens, upon which he was wont to play a variety of street-melodies, remarkable for their simplicity.

He had also cut his name in every variety of type upon the desk; and he had very nearly got a brick out of the wall at the back of it, in a dark corner, where this amateur masonary would not be likely to attract the attention of Mr. Earthworm.

As this young clerk was very short-sighted, and as he was devoured by an intense anxiety to know how the day was going—although, as a rule, when he was left to his own devices, it went fast enough—he had contrived a way of obtaining a view of the clock in a neighbouring public-house, by fixing a broken bit of eye-glass into a corner of the window, with a frame-work of sealing-wax; and through this he took observations when he required to know what was the hour.

Upon the other side of the window there was another very clever device for ascertaining who was coming up the door-steps, which was managed by means of a piece of broken looking-glass, and was resorted to very frequently, when he heard any noise without, to guard against surprise from his equally artful employer, who in his leisure moments very frequently amused himself by setting traps for the clerk, and bowling him out, if possible, in some juvenile peccadillo.

Ruth sat watching him attentively for some moments, and studying the workings of his interesting countenance; and if she secretly felt any admiration for the preternatural shrewdness, craftiness, and impish ingenuity of this young clerkly goblin, she certainly did not allow the same to be visible upon her face; indeed, her features expressed a very strong dislike for the young gentleman. She, however, spoke to him in a kind tone.

"How do you like your place here?" she asked.

The clerk looked at her distrustfully.

"Very much, ma'am," he replied with a grin.

"And your master?"

"I'm very fond of him."

"You are a double-faced, deceitful, hang-dog-looking little wretch. Can you tell a lie?"

"What's that, ma am?"

"You would know, if it were worth your while, I suppose?"

"I dare say, ma'am. A poor boy can't starve; any I may have to learn it before I can get my next place."

"You'd have to learn it before you came into my service; and to do it well."

"I could learn anythink of you, ma'am, if you'd be so kind as to teach me. I wish you would take me into your service."

"Why so?"

"Because I'd like you to be my misses."

"Why so?"

"Because I should be so proud of having such a pretty one!"

Ruth looked at him for a moment attentively, and then smiled slightly, and rose from her seat.

"We shall see," she said, and turned upon her heel.

Then turning round again and confronting him, she asked suddenly, "What is the most money you ever had at the same time in your life?"

"Half a bull, a bob, two joeys, and a tanner," said the boy thoughtfully, after a brief mental calculation.

"Four and twopence," said Mrs. Belvidere, who seemed perfectly conversant with the low slang terms which he had used. "How did you come by that?—stole it?"

"Had some of it gave me, and earned the rest, except one joey, which I fun' permiscus."

"You never had as much as this?" said she, opening her purse and displaying before the boy's eager eyes three or four sovereigns, lying, bright and glittering, in their crimson silk nest.

"Never a hundredth part of it!" he cried, excitedly. "Oh, my eye, how lovely they do look!"

"They look well, do they not?" said she.

"When shall I ever earn anythink like 'em? But I never shall."

"Why not?"

"A poor boy can't get on in this world by only working hard and being honest."

"That's not the way you'll get on, my fine gentleman," said the lady, with a sweet smile. "You will never have a quarter of this money if you wait until you've earned it in the way you are doing."

"How then, ma'am?"

"It is other people's sovereigns you must have the fingering of, if you are ever to hope to have the fingering of any at all. I could tell you your fortune without any cards. There are only two roads for you to choose from, and they both lead to the same point."

"What point is that, ma'am?" asked the boy, rather uneasily.

"Newgate," she answered, with a laugh. "There's 'prison' written in your face; perhaps the gallows also. It's only for yourself to say whether you will hang on miserably for a few years, and put off doing what at last they will hang you by the heels for; or whether you will choose a short life and a merry one, like a boy of spirit."

The lad listened to her attentively while she talked, and, young as he was, he seemed to understand the purport of every word she uttered.

"What shall I do, ma'am, to earn some money?" he asked, presently.

"I don't know," she replied. "How am I to tell?"

"But—but I thought, from what you said, you might be going, perhaps, to—to——"

"To what?"

"To perpose something."

"Not I. I don't feel any interest in you or your career. What time is it?"

"It's half-past ten," replied the boy, after looking through the window.

"I wish I had not sent away my carriage," she said to herself, as she moved towards the inner room. "But I suppose I had better wait now I have waited so long."

She passed through the apartment in which she had been sitting just before her interview with the young clerk, and trying the handle of a door at the far end of it, she discovered, apparently somewhat to her surprise, that it was unlocked; and she crossed the threshold, after throwing a backward glance upon the outer office, where the boy still stood staring after her.

Scarcely, however, had she entered the room when a thought seemed to occur to her, and she retraced her steps, at the same time opening her purse.

When she reached the office again, she, in the boy's sight, took out one of the brightest of the gold coins and contemplated him thoughtfully, holding it meanwhile in her hand.

The boy's eyes opened to their widest, and his fingers itched to be handling the tempting coin which every moment he expected was about to become his property. He was, however, doomed to disappointment, for she seemed to alter her intention, whatever it had been, and replaced the money in the purse from which she had taken it.

"No," she said aloud, and as though talking to herself; "I will try him first."

"Ma'am?" said the boy, in a doleful tone.

"Can you tell when your master is near the door?" she asked.

She knew of the existence of the apparatus which I have described, but she affected an ignorance of its existence, for reasons of her own.

"Yes, ma'am, I can tell when he is coming."

"Be careful to look out for him, then; and when he comes——Can you whistle?"

"Yes, ma'am."

"Whistle your loudest, then, so that I may hear you in the next room."

"Yes, ma'am."

"If you don't make a fool of yourself I may give you something for your trouble; but it depends upon your conduct."

She left him with these words, and returned to the inner room, and, opening the door, passed into what was Mr. Earthworm's *sanctum sanctorum*.

"What a fool I was," she muttered to herself, "not to try the door before! But who was to imagine that he had left it unlocked? Besides, he was likely to come back any minute. I have never known him break his appointment, unless there was some very strong reason for doing so. Perhaps he has seen Rafferty somewhere else. He may not come back now at all—anyhow, not for a long time; so while I have the chance, I will look over his papers. I can't help finding something that he would not like me to know—and anything I find will be useful. Perhaps, even, I may get hold of something that will put him into my power. Heaven grant that I may! If I could only get enough money out of him to be able to leave this life for good—to go away from this hateful city—to have done with it all—to rest—heigho! But that is impossible!"

She had been turning over a vast number of papers which lay littered upon the table, as she muttered these broken sentences to herself, reading the labels upon documents tied together in bundles, and opening letters and scanning their contents, and examining the bills and receipts upon a file.

There was a pocket-book lying upon the table, and this she hastily glanced through; but she could see nothing which she deemed worthy of her attention, except one paper very much crumpled, and directed upon the outside with the simple word "Alice."

She opened this out of curiosity, and not because she at all expected to find it to be a document of any value. And when she saw the exceedingly crabbed and illegible style in which the letter was written, she was about to throw it down in disgust, had not the signature caught her eye, and caused her to look at it again more attentively.

"Ernest Trevellyan!" she muttered. "How extraordinary! What does Earthworm know about him, I wonder? Where did he get this letter? He must have stolen it from my house yesterday. But still I am almost certain that I did not see it among Trevellyan's papers: no, I am certain I did not; and I am equally certain that I missed nothing when I looked over his pockets. How ever did Earthworm get it?"

She began to read the letter without troubling herself any more with conjectures; and as she read, her astonishment increased more and more.

The difficulty in deciphering the writing caused her only hastily to skim over its contents; but she put it away in her pocket, intending as soon as she got home to read it all through again very carefully, and see to what purpose the information which it contained could be turned, and then continued her search among the other papers.

As she turned them over, she at last discovered something half hidden in a heap of old letters which made her suddenly pause and change colour.

The object which caused this agitation was an oblong book in a cardboard cover, containing a number of pages of a dull, greenish-grey tint, with some printing upon each.

Only a glance it required to satisfy her what was the nature of the prize she had found.

It was a blank cheque-book.

For a minute or two she stood perfectly motionless with the book in her hand. Then, as she turned over some difficult questions in her mind, she allowed the leaves of the book to flutter through her fingers.

The sound fell upon her ears like music—like the trickling of spring water upon the ears of one who is parched with thirst, and hot and weary—like the rustle of crisp bank-notes affects a miser.

"I said I did not think he was rich," she repeated to herself;—"but how rich? He has a couple of thousands, perhaps, safe at his banker's; and one thousand—only one thousand would do for me; would take me far away—put me out of reach of all pursuit. I could go with it to some far distant spot—to the New World—to somewhere where I could find rest and peace!"

How the leaves rustled! How inviting they looked! There they were, all ready to be torn out, and to be filled up with any amounts she thought fit!

Why should I not?"

Why indeed? Such a chance might never come again.

She was alone and unobserved.

Who could say that she did it?

"I have only to imitate his writing—and that is easy enough; then not fill them up for too large amounts, and use them cautiously."

Her lips were compressed, her brows knitted. Something in her eye spoke of determination—courage—recklessness, even.

She was resolved upon effecting her object.

The outer office was so still that she could not be quite certain whether the young clerk was still there where she had left him, or whether he had gone out into the street. She advanced to the door upon tip-toe, passed through it, crossed the outer room, and looked through the half-open door leading into the office.

The boy was there.

Upon the watch for the return of his master, apparently; for he stood at the window with his nose squeezed against the glass.

"I'll do it!" she muttered, and returned upon tip-toe to the inner room.

Her skirt in passing out had drawn the door to a little; and in opening it again, although it had shown no signs of such a weakness before, it most unaccountably creaked.

She pushed it open again, though with the greatest caution, and, in passing over the threshold, threw a backward glance towards the spot where the boy stood.

Earthworm's private apartment was plunged into a state of semi-obscurity, owing to the fact of a dirty blind, brown with age, being drawn down over the window, which only received its light from an extremely narrow court at the back of the house, the opposite wall of which was not more than a couple of yards distant from the glass.

It was not, therefore, very easy to discern the objects in the room, more particularly when entering hastily from the brighter light of the outer room.

Entering thus, Ruth advanced towards the table where she had left the cheque-book.

There it lay.

She stretched forth her hand, and clutched it.

But, in doing so, she raised her eyes, and at the same moment, uttering a faint scream, let the book fall again upon the table.

What was it? Could it be real? Was it a ghost?

Whatever it was, human or superhuman, it bore the semblance of an old man—an old man with a sallow, wrinkled, hideous face, and two piercing eyes, which leered at her with a sinister and lowering expression, full of devilish malignity.

There it sat, upon the opposite side of the table, in an arm-chair, which, upon quitting the apartment, she could have taken her oath she left vacant.

There it sat, motionless as death—silent as the tomb—with its eyes fixed on her ashy face and trembling, bloodless lips.

CHAPTER XX.

ALICE IN PRISON.—THE VISIT OF THE TEMPTER.—THE VILE PROPOSITION.—DEATH OR DISHONOUR?—THE HEROIC GIRL—THE PRAYER TO HEAVEN.—THE BAFFLED MISCREANT.—WILL VICE OR VIRTUE BE TRIUMPHANT?

"I WANT to see one of your prisoners."

"Which prisoner?"

"Alice Wentworth."

"Number 26. Here's the ticket."

"I'm not going to talk through the grating, you know. I've a special order to go into the cell."

"Oh! where is it?"

"Here."

"Humph! Ha! It's all regular enough, as far as I can see. Only I've no authority in the matter. My mission's only to give you this 'ere tin ticket. You take it across the courtyard there, and up them steps, and show it to the other warder. Then show him the letter. I expect you'll have to see the Governor."

The other warder was of a similar opinion; but as the Governor was not in the building, the bearer of the "order," or "pass" which was signed by one of the magistrates, was after some hesitation allowed to enter the cell containing the unfortunate prisoner whom he desired to see.

It was the same horrible old man with whom we have already had to deal upon several occasions: old Eneas Earthworm, the spy—informer—sham detective, and what not—who was paying a visit to Alice Trevellyan, in her prison.

Poor Alice! only a few days have elapsed since she was incarcerated; but this short confinement had sufficed to banish the roses from her cheeks—to dim her once roguish, merry eyes, and waste her plump little figure.

She had suffered—suffered deeply.

Sleepless nights had she passed; weeping far into the dead silence of the night—weeping unheard and alone—unseen by any eye but ONE, which watches at all times the sorrows of the friendless, hopeless and sore afflicted; the motherless orphan, the deserted babe, the lonely widow, the broken-hearted parent sobbing at the bedside of the loved one passed away!

Yes, she had suffered. She who had known so much suffering during her husband's life, had borne more anguish and misery since his death than she believed to exist in the world.

To have lost him, was that not enough?

But at the same time to be accused of his murder—the murder of him whom she had doted upon—whom in life she had almost worshipped and idolized—a hair of whose head she would not have harmed!—oh, it was too much—too much!

She had left home and happiness—had given up friends and connexions, wealth and position, for his sake, and had not regretted them, for she loved him more than all.

And to think that she should be accused of his murder!

She could not bear it—no, she would go mad! She felt that the agony she had borne during the last few days was too much for her, and that her mind would soon give way.

She would go mad, and then there would be no occasion for the hangman's office—no occasion to avenge the loved one's death. She would go mad, and die, and be buried within the precincts of the mad-house, and there would be an end to her sufferings here, and a great and glorious future to look forward too, when she would meet him again—meet him in the realms of holy love and peace.

But we who know that Trevellyan was not dead, but safe in the keeping of Ruth, the Spy,—does it not make our blood boil to think that the black-hearted traitor could forget this innocent, suffering angel, and that his heart already belonged to Ruth, and his soul was damned by his blind, infatuated passion?

"Is this the cell?" asked Earthworm when the warder stopped in front of a door on which was a number corresponding to that upon the tin ticket the first gaoler had given to him.

"Yes."

"Let me go in by myself."

"There you are, then. I must lock the door again."

"Do as you please."

"You must not be long."

"I won't tire you with waiting."

The gaoler opened the door, obedient to the old man's directions, as noiselessly as passible, and Earthworm entered the cell.

He entered so quietly—for he had at all times a stealthy, cat-like tread, and a creeping, sneaking motion in walking—that the inmate of the cell did not hear his approach, and remained occupied in the same way that she had been before he came for several moments after he had crossed the threshold.

She was upon her knees, praying, with her face turned towards the window.

Earthworm held up his hand, and motioned to the gaolor not to shut the door, and not to make any noise to disturb her; and they both stood for awhile looking at the beautiful face upturned towards heaven, with a gentle, supplicating look upon it like that which might have been found upon the face of some suffering angel.

Surely it was a sight to move the stoniest heart to pity, one would have thought; but the hoary-headed old wretch who contemplated her was no way affected by the sad picture of beauty and innocence in distress which this fair creature afforded him.

His only thought was how she was to be got into his power, and whether she was worth the trouble and time which must necessarily be expended in the achievement of his object.

"Yes," he muttered to himself—"she is most beautiful. She is too fine a prize to be allowed to slip through my fingers. She shall be mine, though all the powers in hell were opposed to me!"

The door slamming to suddenly aroused the kneeling girl from her devotions, and she turned with a frightened look towards the spot where the stranger with evil eyes and satanic smile stood watching her.

For a moment or two after she had risen from

her knees she did not readily recognise her visitor; but as he moved forward from the shadow in which at first he had been standing, she was able to see his face, and, with an exclamation of dread and terror, shrank back.

"You here?" she muttered in a low tone, speaking, however, more to herself than to him.

Then stood perfectly still, waiting for him to address her.

The old man moved forward a few steps, and, folding his arms, again contemplated his victim with a look of satyr-like triumph.

"Well," he said at last—"are you tired of your imprisonment?"

The poor girl looked at him in astonishment, but made no reply, for she could not understand what he meant.

"Has your lawyer been to see you?" he asked.

"No," she answered. "I have no lawyer."

"Are you going to conduct the case yourself, then?"

"I do not understand what you mean. I have no one to help or assist me; but I am innocent. God is my witness that I am innocent; and every day I pray to heaven to be delivered from the dangers surrounding me and the suspicions hanging over me. Heaven, I feel certain, will hear my prayer!"

"I'm glad you think so," said the old wretch, with a fiendish chuckle. "It's more than I do."

"But surely I cannot be condemned upon the evidence which has been brought forward against me? My innocence must be proved sooner or later."

"I don't see that at all," observed the old man, quietly helping himself at the same time to a pinch of snuff "The case seems to me to be very black—very black indeed."

"But you, sir, know that I am not guilty; you will tell me what I ought to do—how I ought to act. You have come here to save me: is it not so?"

"It is," replied Earthworm. "I have come with that purpose—upon certain conditions."

Alice looked at him anxiously. She sought to read the meaning of his words in his face, but that was impossible.

He took his seat upon the small wooden bench which stood on one side of the cell, and helped himself to another large pinch of snuff.

"There is only one way that you can escape. The case is black against you now—it will grow blacker still presently—there is only one person who can save you!"

"And that is——"

"Myself!"

Alice threw herself upon her knees at the old man's feet, and clasped his hand in hers.

"And you say that you have come here for that purpose?" she cried. "Bless you—bless you for your goodness! How shall I ever repay you for such kindness?"

"I have not saved you yet, please to remember," said Earthworm, with an ugly grin. "I spoke about some conditions, if you recollect."

"Yes, yes," she replied, eagerly—"what are they? Let me hear them."

"It is not the first time that we have talked together, my dear. Do you recollect the subject of our conversation the last time we talked together?"

A change came over Alice's face.

A deep blush mantled her cheeks.

She rose hastily to her feet, and endeavoured to free her hand from his, though ineffectually, for he tightened his hold upon her when he saw her intention.

"Do you recollect what I proposed to you then?" he asked.

"Do you suppose that I can ever forget it?" she retorted—"do you think it possible that even years can wipe away the remembrance of the shame and humiliation which I suffered—which I still suffer, when I think that I could have submitted to listen to the propositions of unpardonable sin, ruin, degradation, and dishonour, which you had the audacity to make to me, thinking, because I was poor and in distress, you could insult me with impunity?"

The old man regarded her with a faint smile and a look of intense admiration, for it seemed to him that in her rage and indignation at his atrocious conduct, she looked far more beautiful than she had done before.

Alice, however, unmindful of his look, and without noticing the expression of his face, twisted her hands from his grasp, and turning her back upon him, hid her face and wept.

"Oh, why did you come here, if you had nothing better to say than to remind me of that which I would fain forget for ever, and bury in oblivion?"

"It was for that very purpose that I came here," replied the old man. "Do not take such a high hand in the matter, but be sensible and listen to reason. I told you, long ago, that I had taken a fancy to you, and that I intended that you should be mine. You were miserably poor; your husband was a penniless, struggling, starving simpleton, incapable of providing for you in the way that you deserved—incapable, even, of purchasing you sufficient food. I told you that if you gave him up—as any woman with any sense and spirit would have done—that I would surround you with luxuries, and load you with riches. But you refused."

"Yes," replied Alice, with a look of unutterable scorn and contempt, "I did refuse; and in the same position I would reject again, with the same scorn, so monstrous a proposition!"

"Unfortunately, though, Mrs. Trevellyan, your position is entirely altered. Having murdered the husband whom you affected to be so devotedly attached to, and whose honour you were so mighty particular about, you would not now, I imagine, be very sorry to leave this cell for the position which I then offered you."

"If there were no other way to save my life—if the gallows at this moment waited for me, I would refuse again!"

"Pooh! You know that you are talking nonsense; you fancy that you may yet escape! You have the bad taste not to care about me, and you hope to get off without my assistance!"

"I hope that heaven will assist me, and that I may be proved innocent!"

"But you shan't be, while I am alive to prevent it!"

"What do you know against me, then? What can you prove?" she asked, in desperation.

"I know something in your favour. It lies in my power to save you! I have the letter in my possession which Trevellyan wrote to you before he went out to commit suicide!"

"But you will not suppress it, surely? You cannot threaten to do me such an awful injustice?"

"Indeed! Why not?"

"It would be murder! My death would lie at your door! No, no! Say that you will spare me! What have I done to you that you should treat me thus?"

"I have no more time to waste," replied Earthworm, rising from the seat with a gesture of impatience. "If you consent to my wishes, you shall be saved: if not, you shall die!"

"But you cannot, you dare not suppress that letter!" cried Alice, with sudden energy. "I will compel you to appear as a witness! I know that I can do so! You shall be put into the witness-box and examined upon your oath, and then you will be obliged to tell the truth!"

The old man laughed ironically.

"Who says so?" he asked, sarcastically. "What difference do you suppose an oath or two will make to me? It is my trade, woman! Yours will not be the first life by many that I have sworn away; and if you do not consent, there is no power in the world to save you!"

"Monster!"

Earthworm looked at his watch.

"I must go now," he said. "What do you say—yes or no?"

Alice sank upon her knees upon the ground, and hid her face in her hands, sobbing violently.

"Heaven give me strength!" she prayed. "Heaven direct me! What shall I do? what shall I do?"

"Consent!"

"Never—never!"

"Is that your final decision? Will you be mine?"

"No; a thousand times, no!"

"Then perish, fool! Your own folly is your executioner!"

She still remained in the same attitude—her face covered with her hands.

Still remained sobbing violently.

A shudder ran through her delicate frame at the sound of the savage whisper which her tempter and tormenter hissed into her ear; but she affected not to hear him, made no reply, and allowed him to pass out of the cell without endeavouring to stay his progress.

He stopped, though, at the door, and looked back at her, and the expression of malignant hate which a moment before had rested upon his features, again gave place to the hideous leer which so frequently distorted them.

"She is a deal of trouble," he said to himself, "but she is worth it. Let her lie here a little longer. She will tire of these stone walls before long, and I am in no hurry. I can bide my time. She shall be mine or Jack Ketch's! I don't think she can hold out for ever. We shall see."

CHAPTER XXI.

EARTHWORM'S RETURN.—JACK RAFFERTY'S MYSTERIOUS COMMUNICATION.—THE SECRET DOOR.—RUTH SURPRISED—THE DEADLY RESOLVE.

THESE occurrences which I have just been relating occurred upon the morning of the day when Ruth paid the visit to Earthworm's office—the account of which is to be found in the nineteenth chapter.

When Earthworm left the prison, he had plenty of time to get to his office before the hour which he had fixed for an interview with Rafferty, and he walked leisurely along the streets, preferring to go upon foot to spending his money in taking a cab—for he was an extraordinary mixture of contradiction, this old man; and though he would not have scrupled to have wasted several guineas in a momentary gratification of any desire that might seize him, at other times he grudged the outlay of a penny, and would suffer an extraordinary amount of pain and inconvenience rather than stretch his purse-strings.

He was plodding along, therefore, and was close to home, when Ruth's carriage passed by, almost scraping the edge of the pavement where he stood.

The fair inmate, however, did not notice him, for she was too much occupied with her own thoughts. She was leaning back luxuriantly upon the soft cushion, smiling sweetly to herself.

The old man looked at her hard.

"She's very beautiful," he said to himself. "And she's very like—extraordinary like the other one. What spirits and pluck they have both got; though Ruth is the boldest, as she well may be, seeing what bringings up she has had. What a wonderful career! Why, her life up to now would fill a dozen volumes brim full of villany, and treachery, and crime, and horror! But she has not done yet, nor nearly, unless I nip her in the bud, or she does any foolish act and gets herself into trouble! There is no knowing what she may do! She's capable of doing such great things, and yet descends to do such paltry ones!"

While he was thinking thus, and was walking towards the door of his house, a cab suddenly drew up by his side, and a man riding in it called out to him by name.

"Mr. Earthworm!"

The old man turned round quickly.

A handsome, manly face, bronzed by exposure to sun and air, and wearing a huge brown beard, presented itself at the cab window.

"I was going to your house," said the owner of this face, "to ask you whether you would be in in about an hour's time, or whether you would appoint any other time for us to talk over that business together. I cannot wait now—I must go on into the City. I suppose you could not manage to ride there with me; if so, we might talk by the way?"

Earthworm hesitated for a moment, and then accepted the offer, and they rode off together.

"Have you learnt anything about Captain Crockford?" asked Rafferty.

"A little."

"Can you put your hand on him?"

"Whenever I choose."

"Well, then, we can go to business at once."

"I am only waiting for your instructions."

"Before giving them, I will tell you what the mystery is concerning the Captain, which I hinted at when I saw you last. You say that he moves in the highest and best society, that he belongs to one of the wealthiest and noblest of English families, and that his father is a peer and high up in the Government. Where do you think I learnt the secret about this young swell that I am going to tell you of?"

"I have no idea."

"You know that I am a convict, and have returned with a ticket of leave?"

"Yes; I know that."

"Out then in a trackless swamp in the country where they sent me to, from a miserable fragment of humanity, stricken down with ague, half starved to death, all covered with bruises and sores, and eaten up with half a dozen diseases, I learnt that which affects the honour and position of one of the best families in England. With his last dying breath he gasped out the story that I must tell to you. It is not very long, but it's rather astonishing, as you will find. Will you listen?"

"I am all attention."

* * * * *

At least an hour after the time he had appointed for Ruth to meet him at his office, Eneas Earthworm bent his steps towards the house in Bedford Row, where his famous scheme of secret inquiry was prosecuted. It struck the old man as he approached the door, that as Ruth had been left to her own devices for a considerable length of time, there was a faint possibility of a chance that she might have got at some sort of mischief.

"I wonder how she's occupying her time?" he thought. "I'll just creep in quietly by the back way, and see what she is about. No good, I'll be bound. Though, for that matter, she can't do much harm, as nothing is left about within her reach. Only I know what she is; for ever trying to find something out. There's no keeping a secret from her without the help of one of Chubb's locks. I'll just go in and see what she is doing."

Running out of Bedford Row, on the right hand side going towards the Foundling, there is a narrow street, and out of this runs a mews, down which Mr. Earthworm now directed his steps.

About half-way down it he came to a court or blind alley, one side of which was composed of a high dead wall, and which contained only three or four mean-looking houses, and a couple of workshops.

It also contained a quiet-looking, dark green door, deeply sunk into an old-fashioned portico, and bearing the appearance of having been nailed up long ago, and left unused.

It was a door, however, which Mr. Earthworm upon many occasions availed himself of. Very frequently at night, and sometimes also in the daytime, the old man would creep in and out at this entrance to fetch things away from his private room, or even to sit there and work when strangers were occupying the waiting-room that I have already described, without their for a moment suspecting that he was so near.

He, however, adopted the greatest caution in using this means of egress and ingress, and hitherto succeeded in doing so without his sharp-witted clerk ever discovering that there was another way of entering the office except the usual one through the street door, although he had been in Earthworm's employ for at least six months.

Old Earthworm sneaked cautiously down the court, peeping round upon all sides to see whether any one was observing him.

But no, the coast was clear.

He arrived at the door, and peeped round more cautiously than before.

Not a soul could he see.

Still peering and peeping, he slipped the key into the lock, turned it round, and pushed the door gently open with his left hand.

Then dived suddenly into the dark passage yawning for him.

Arrived here, he cautiously and noiselessly closed the door behind him, and walking upon tiptoe along a dark and narrow passage, climbed up some stairs, and groped about for some time upon the wall to get hold of the handle of a lock.

When turning this, he paused and listened eagerly, for he fancied that he heard the sound of some movement within.

He strained his ears to catch the sound, and a cunning smile lighted up his small grey eyes.

"It's as I thought!" he said; "she's got in here. I must have left the door open, then, as I supposed I did. She's turning my papers over."

This was clear enough. Where he stood he could distinctly hear the papers rustling.

The old man felt half inclined to fling open the door and rush in upon her, but he thought better of this the next minute, and listened, and cautiously turned the handle of the door, biding his time in his usual stealthy, cat-like fashion of proceeding; without making much more noise than would have been caused by a feather falling to the ground, Earthworm turned the handle, and pushed the door open two or three inches.

However the sudden rustling of a silk dress alarmed him, and caused him hastily to pull the door to again.

The rustling ceased, and with it a hasty footfall upon the floor. The lady, if it was Ruth, had left the room.

Earthworm listened with all his might and main, then pushed open the door, and entered the apartment.

The room was empty. Ruth had gone back, as we have seen, to look after the boy in the outer office.

As we have seen, she returned with a stealthy tread, intent upon appropriating to her own use some of the blank leaves of the cheque-book.

She came in hurriedly, breathless, white with fright—dreading exposure and shame, but still intent upon committing the felonious act.

She made a clutch at the cheque-book as she entered, raised it in her hand, took two or three of the leaves in her fingers, and was about to tear them out, when she all at once became aware that a pair of evil eyes were fixed upon her.

The old man had crept into the room, and seated himself in an arm-chair by the side of the table; and here he sat, with his hat a little on one side, his long, lean hand covering his mouth, and a cunning smile in his eyes, which was dreadful to look at.

He looked so horrible an object, when she came upon him unawares, that she started back with a suppressed scream, and in her agitation violently clutched the back of a chair which stood near her, letting the cheque-book fall upon the floor.

She thought he was a ghost, and her blood froze in her veins.

She opened and shut her eyes, and stared at him.

He sat there so motionless, that at first she almost fancied that she did not see Earthworm in the flesh, but that it was a spectral illusion.

At last the power of speech, of which she had at first been entirely bereft, returned to her, and she stammered, "Is—is it you?"

"Who else should it be?" said Earthworm. "You didn't expect me just this minute, did you? I've interrupted you, I fear!"

"Interrupted me in what?"

"You've dropped something, haven't you?" asked Earthworm, with a smile.

And as she made no reply, he stooped down and picked up the cheque-book, and laid it upon the table.

"I shouldn't have believed it," Earthworm continued, presently, after a brief pause, in which he occupied himself in turning over the leaves of the book, and ascertaining that nothing had been torn out.

They were all right, however.

Presently he said, "It's very weak of you, this is! Very weak, indeed! How did you suppose that you could manage it without being nobbled? How did you suppose that you were going to best me? I should have thought that you would have known better."

"You have done nothing very wonderful by coming in at the moment I was turning that over," Ruth replied with a sneer. "What did you suppose that I wanted to do with it?"

"It was very easy to see what you intended to do," replied Earthworm.

"Do you think I wanted to steal them?"

"If you did not, I do not exactly know what you could have wanted."

"It does not occur to you," replied Ruth, "that I might want to see how you spent your money."

"I don't believe it."

He laughed insultingly, as he put the book away in his pocket.

"It doesn't much matter what your reason was," he said, "since you did not do any harm. Only it would have been a pity if you had done anything to get yourself into trouble. You are so impetuous and headstrong, and you will do such things. It is most providential that you have got an easy-minded person like I am to deal with, or there is really no knowing what would come to you. Are you in want of money?"

"I always am."

"That is extraordinary, too. The Prince is very liberal, is he not?"

"Yes, he is liberal enough; but I can spend more than he can give me."

"Well, how on earth you do it I cannot imagine. However, I suppose you want a little loan of me?"

"Yes. I want you to lend me twenty pounds, if you will not give them to me."

"It's just as good as giving it you, you know that very well. However, we will go through the usual form. Here's a bill stamp; just sign this, and you shall have the money."

The old man scribbled hastily across the paper as he spoke, and then handed it to her for her signature.

She barely glanced at it before writing her name, but, handing it back to him, said, "I should like the money in gold, if you can give it me."

"I haven't got it."

"Nonsense; you always keep some by you, I know."

"I've only a pound or two, and I want to use it. You must take a cheque."

"I must have some gold," persisted Ruth.

"Well, well!" Earthworm answered, after grumbling a little to himself; "I'll see what I can do."

And he rose from his seat, and approached an old-fashioned secretaire in a corner of the room. He opened a drawer in this, and discovered a number of small drawers within, the handle of one of which he pulled.

Something made it stick, and he gave it a sharp jerk; then it opened suddenly, and, contrary to Earthworm's desire, emitted a loud chink, which told plainly that there were more sovereigns in it than he had owned to possessing.

He sat in front of the secretaire, with his back towards her, and he spread out his hand to hide the gold from her sight, and pushed the drawer back again into its place.

He did not look round, because he felt somewhat confused at the mischance; and for a moment or two he was fumbling, as it were, in his mind for some excuse for not giving her the money in the form which she desired.

A thought was also passing through the brain of the woman—a terrible thought.

"How much money has he got here, I wonder? Could I, as he sits, stab him to the heart? Would the boy in the outer office hear the struggle? Could I not prevent his crying out? If I do it, what is to be done with his body?"

This much passed rapidly through her brain; and, as she thought, she felt in the bosom of her dress for a dagger-knife which she had got concealed there in company with a tiny pistol.

She had half drawn it forth—she had half unsheathed it. She was about to strike, or to choose the place where the blow was to be struck, when the old man turned suddenly round upon her.

In spite of herself, she changed colour.

His eye fell upon the position of her hand.

He put out his own, and clutched it tightly upon her fingers.

Then forcibly drew forth her hand, and disclosed the dagger in it.

The expression of their two faces at that moment would have been a study for a painter.

"What would you do?" he asked fiercely.

"Nothing," she replied, doggedly.

"Is it war between us?"

She made no answer.

"What interest have you in my death? Is that what you are aiming at?"

"Not I," she answered, contemptuously. "If I had wished to have taken your life I could have done so. I had no such intention."

"Let us understand one another. I pay you well for all you do for me. Is it not better that we should be friends?"

"It is all I wish for. Give me the money, and let me go."

"Here are ten pounds and a cheque."

She took them, and moved towards the door.

"What a fool I've been!" she thought to herself! "How came I to let him catch me? When he caught me there was time to do it then. It would have been my best plan to do it. There is nobody but the boy in the outer office. What of him? I could silence him easily; if by no other means, in the same way that I silence this hateful wretch. How I loathe him! How I detest him! If I do not do it now I may never have so good an opportunity."

CHAPTER XXII.

THE SHRIEK OF AGONY.—THE ABBESS GOES BACK TO FRESH CRIMES. — AGATHA'S CELL. — THE SLAUGHTERED BABE.—THE FURIOUS MOTHER — THE THREAT OF VENGEANCE.—A NOISE OUTSIDE THE DOOR. — THE ACCOMPLICE. — WHAT HORROR IS COMING NOW?

A SHRIEK!

A loud and piercing shriek!

A loud, heartrending wail, thrilling and tremulous—the utterance of a tortured soul!

The language of intense pain, physical or mental—a cry torn from the sufferer in terror or in agony!

A sound to make the heart beat faster, the teeth clatter, the blood curdle!

Such a sound saluted the ears of the Abbess, and she slowly retraced her steps from the vault into which she had so artfully betrayed the gallant and too credulous Captain Crockford.

She left the vault and ascended the stairs down

which she had brought him, but she directed her course to an opposite part of the building to that in which her own cell was situated.

Upon her way she passed the door of the cell of Sister Cecily.

She knocked at it with her knuckles, and one of the elderly nuns—the one who has already been alluded to as Mary—opened to her.

"What are you doing here?" asked the Lady Superior.

"Sister Cecily is very ill. She has fainted several times since we brought her back to her cell. The sight of Sister Agatha's chastisement has been too much for her."

The Abbess regarded the speaker angrily. "A poor milksop!" she exclaimed. "They are all alike. Everybody to-night seems to be trying their hardest to cause me some annoyance."

And, with these words, she pursued her way along the passage, muttering to herself.

"I was a fool," she thought, "to allow her to be present! How could I have done so? Perhaps it may have disgusted her with the place. She may want to go; and, as yet, we have not secured her. Bah! I was an idiot to act in such a way! It cannot be helped, though; I must be more cautious in future."

She proceeded now to the cell containing Sister Agatha. Upon the way, at her approach, several doors were hastily closed; and the nuns peeping out from them ran in and hid themselves like so many frightened rabbits.

They had been brought out by the sound of Agatha's shriek—for it was her shriek which the Abbess heard, and which, at the beginning of this chapter, I described.

With a feeling of anxiety which it was impossible to repress, and with a flutter of the heart which she could not control, the Abbess opened the door.

Within the room a sight awaited her but little calculated to restore her ruffled equanimity.

In one corner of the cell, upon a pallet-bed, pale and motionless, lay stretched the victim of the brutal outrage of which Captain Crockford had been a horrified witness.

The nun Martha was leaning over her with an expression of terror upon her hard features, and with her hand pressed upon the heart of the senseless woman.

"What is it?" the Abbess exclaimed, as she entered the cell,—"what is it? Whose cry was that?"

"It was hers," replied the nun, pointing to Agatha. "I—I am afraid that—that—that——"

"That what, woman?"

"That she is dead."

The Abbess, with a face almost as ashy as that of the insensible woman, approached the bed and bent over the prostrate figure.

Then she, too, placed her hand upon Agatha's heart.

But it beat not.

Not a throb.

The sufferer's hands, too, were icy cold, and there was a blue tint about her face, and a fixed rigidity, such as is seen rarely but upon the face of the dead.

Was she then dead?

The Abbess asked herself the question with fear and trembling, for if her suspicions were correct, the matter must be hushed up immediately without loss of time, and with the greatest secrecy.

While she was hesitating what steps she should first take, a sound upon the other side of the cell suddenly caused her to start and turn round in that direction.

It was a small, weak, though shrill cry.

The voice of a new-born babe.

A dark and angry cloud passed over the Abbess's face.

"It still lives, then?" she said.

The nun looked towards her in astonishment and uneasily.

"Yes," she replied. "I told you that it did."

"It must be got rid of."

"When?"

"Now—immediately."

"How?"

"We will strangle it."

The nun instinctively shrank back from the speaker, as she uttered these words, with horror and loathing.

But the Abbess heeded her not.

She went to a workbox, standing upon a side-table, and after rummaging for a few minutes among its contents, discovered a strong piece of string.

In this she made a slip-knot; and taking the child from a basket in which it had been placed, wrapped carelessly round by a piece of blanket, she passed the string over its head and round its throat.

The nun looked on in speechless horror.

"Come here, will you?" exclaimed the Abbess, turning upon her quickly. "I want you to hold the child, or to pull the cord."

The other woman remained motionless where she was, and made no reply.

"Don't you hear me speak?"

"I—I cannot do it."

"Why not, you fool? What is there to be afraid of?"

"I am not afraid, but I have not the heart to commit such an atrocity. I cannot look down upon that innocent, sweet babe, and take away its life."

"Don't talk like an idiot," the Abbess exclaimed, angrily. "I don't want to hear your sentimentalities"

"I could sooner help to murder a grown-up person, than I could assist in the assassination of that poor helpless babe."

"You may have to do both, perhaps, before we have settled this business. There, do not put me out of patience by talking such twaddle. Do you think that this child has any sense or feeling. I would ring the life out of a dozen such, without a shudder or the faintest feeling of remorse. Do you suppose that it has any soul to lose? Do you still hesitate? Come, I command you. Hold the child, or pull the string, without needing any more asking."

But still the nun hesitated. The Abbess fixed her eyes upon her, with a look of intense passion, which seemed to warn her that any further delay would be dangerous.

"Do you intend to do what I bid you?" the Superior inquired.

Evidently the nun was in the Abbess's power, for she resisted no longer.

Slowly and reluctantly she approached, but she did approach, nevertheless. She allowed the other to place the unresisting infant in her hands, and while she held it, the Abbess prepared to execute her diabolical purpose.

With her left hand she pressed upon the child's face, with the right she tightened the cord.

The babe opened its eyes, which a moment

before had been closed, and gave vent to a low, plaintive cry.

Next moment the cord tightened upon its throat.

Its poor little face grew swollen and black.

Its eyes stared piteously, as it seemed, into its murderess's face.

A few brief seconds, and all was over. It was dead; and the Abbess laid it back in the basket from which she had taken it.

At that moment the mother recovered from the trance into which she had fallen—for it was but a trance—and looked up and round wildly and distractedly.

"My—my child!" she cried,—"what have you done with my child?"

At the instant that she spoke, the body of the babe was yet in the hands of the murderess. She was in the very act of laying it down.

She started up, as though she had heard a voice from the grave.

"My child—my child!" repeated the mother: "give me back my child!"

"Peace, woman!" cried the Abbess.

But Agatha again repeated the request.

"What have you done with it? You shall not harm it. Where is it?"

"Peace!" reiterated the Superior. "Peace, I say! It is dead!"

"Dead—dead! Then you have slain it!"

"It was born dead!"

"You lie! Monster—fiend—murderess! You have slain both mother and child! Your soul is dyed with a hundred crimes! Eternal torments await you in the next world. You know that, and in this you hope to escape. But it shall not be so. I will denounce you. While I have life and breath left I will summon help, and give you over into the hands of justice. It is not possible that such horrors can be committed in the very heart of London, and with such impunity. No; your career has come to an end. Your moments are numbered."

Then she began to scream at the top of her voice.

"Help—help—help! Murder—murder! Help—help!"

The shrieks grew every moment more loud and fierce.

"Murder—help—murder—help!"

The Superior, furious with rage, and trembling lest these violent cries should alarm all the inmates of the nunnery, and even perhaps the people out of doors, sprang upon the woman lying on the bed, and grasping her by the throat, did her best to strangle her, as just now she had strangled the child.

But with a strength and energy which one would scarcely have believed that the dying woman was capable of, Agatha struggled and fought, and the Abbess found it impossible to hold her down.

There was only one way of silencing her.

Her shrieks continued loud and piercing. In the distance might be heard the door in the corridor opening.

The Abbess felt that if she did not at once put a stop to the disturbance, there was no knowing what evil results might not arise from it.

The Abbess seized her victim by the throat with her left hand, then doubling her right fist, struck at her repeatedly and violently.

The victim slowly sank under the blows.

With a hollow groan she again became insensible.

The Abbess desisted from her violence when she saw there was no more occasion for it, and paused for a moment to get her breath.

Just then she heard a sound outside the door, which seemed like that of a light footstep retreating.

The Lady Superior advanced hastily, and threw it open.

Upon the outside, in the passage, stood a short man, with a swarthy, dark complexion, and black, beetling brows almost meeting across his forehead.

"You here?" exclaimed the Abbess, furiously. "What do you want? What are you prying about for? How dare you come into these passages?"

"I came to see what was the matter," the man replied; "to tell you that the noise could be heard in the chapel—out in the street, perhaps. I came to warn you that we should have the police in if this went on much longer."

"The sounds cannot be heard outside," said the Abbess. "That is impossible! Are any of the nuns listening? Have you seen any out of their doors?"

"I have seen none."

"Come, then, into the cell," said the Abbess, after a moment's hesitation, in which she seemed to be turning over some thoughts in her mind. "Come, then; I want your assistance."

He entered after her, and closed the door.

"You see that woman?" said the Abbess, pointing to Agatha's prostrate form on the bed.

"Yes; it is one you have been flogging."

"How did you know that?"

"I should have had to have been much deafer than I am if I had not heard her screams."

"She has brought ruin and disgrace upon the building; or if she has not already, she will do so. She must be silenced, now and for ever!"

"Killed?"

The woman nodded her head.

The man stepped towards the basket where reposed the dead body of the slaughtered babe.

"You have already put the child out of the way?" said the man.

"It is dead."

"Murdered!"

He pointed as he spoke to the string which was round the little innocent's throat.

"I have not brought you in here to chatter about that," replied the Abbess; "but to act. Have you sufficient courage?"

"I have courage for anything," answered the man, "providing that it is made worth my while."

"It shall be, if you do not shrink from what I bid you do."

"I will not stick at a trifle," the man said, with a horrible leer.

To judge from his face—from its black and lowering expression—from the sinister look in his deep-set eyes—from the villanous shape of his head—from his long, picking-and-stealing, cruel hands, with their bony fingers, like claws—one could easily have supposed him to be capable of almost any atrocity.

His face seemed to indicate the existence, in his horrible nature, of every base and degrading passion—cowardice, cruelty, and lust.

"Raise her in your arms," said the Abbess.

The man, who seemed to be possessed of almost superhuman strength, raised Agatha from the bed.

She lay, a dead weight in his arms.

Heavy and cold, her joints stiff, her limbs rigid.

"Bring her this way," said the Abbess.

Then, opening the door of the cell, she peered out into the passage, and listened.

All was still.

The Abbess walked on first, carrying a lamp.

The man followed next, carrying the body of the insensible victim.

Martha followed last, carrying the body of the dead child, wrapped up in the blanket.

Without exchanging a word, they proceeded noiselessly towards the vault.

What fresh horror—what fresh crime—was about to be perpetrated?

Were they unseen—unnoticed—save by the Eye which sees all, the good and the bad?

We shall see.

I fancy that, if we could pierce the gloom behind them in the dimly-lighted vaulted passage, we should see Sister Cecily creeping after them, holding her breath, and straining her eyes to watch their movements.

CHAPTER XXIII.

DOWN IN THE SEWERS. — A VOYAGE OF DISCOVERY.—A QUIET CIGAR.—A STRANGE POSITION FOR A MAN OF PROPERTY TO BE PLACED IN. — THE CELLAR. — THE BATH. — THE SURPRISE.

And were Agatha's piercing shrieks heard by Captain Crockford as he fell through the trap?

How had he fared down there in the dark sewer? What had become of him?

Was he dead?

No, life was not yet extinct, although the gallant Charley was as nearly dead as anybody can be who has yet remaining in his body the faintest spark of vitality.

He was not dead, but he was next door to it.

He was pretty nearly choked.

His mouth was full of mud, his ears were full of mud, his nose was full of mud.

He was plastered over, caked, coated with the filthy black slime of the atrocious hole into which he had been thrown.

He was unable to cry out or to look about him—to use his tongue or his eyes.

For some time after he had fallen into the horrible mess he thought himself dead, although the spirit of self-preservation had caused him to scramble to his feet, after he had been soused heels over head into the dark mucky water, and to assume an upright position, supporting himself by the wall, with his head and shoulders out of the liquid.

But he gave himself up for lost.

It was impossible that he could live long here.

A stifling and noxious aroma rose from the filth in which he wallowed.

He felt faint, and giddy, and sick.

By some miracle, he had not been killed by the fall. He had not struck his head in the descent and knocked himself senseless, or he would, without doubt, by this time have been suffocated or poisoned in the foul abominations.

Great God, he thought, in agonizing terror, was he doomed to remain in this monstrous place?

Was he to sink down presently, overcome by the strength of the exhalations, and die?

The idea was too horrible.

It almost sent him mad.

The cold perspiration broke out upon his face. His knees knocked together. His hair bristled up upon his head.

He shrieked aloud again and again for help.

But the trap was closed above his head. The door was shut. After that, the door of the cellar was also closed. There was no chance of his cries being heard, and even if they were, who would hear them?

Only the woman who had betrayed him: none other. Then it was not very likely that she would take pity upon him. No; if she heard his cry, it was much more likely that she would resort to some means of instantly depriving him of life.

His chance, then, for living was to remain still.

But what a chance was that! What was he to do, then? To hold out for a short time until the aroma overcome his strength; or until otherwise, from sheer fatigue, he succumbed, and sunk down into the filth?

But suddenly he determined to wade about cautiously and grope in the darkness, to see whether he could not find some outlet from this horrible spot.

Where was he? The thought occurred to him that he was in all probability in a sewer. There was then, it was only reasonable to suppose, some kind of outlet.

The only question was, would the outlet be large enough for him to creep through?

He felt but little hope! He might have fallen into a square hole, encompassed by walls upon every side. It was quite likely enough; only a faint ray—ever such a faint ray of hope he certainly did feel; and without loss of time he began his investigations, and cautiously stepped out from the place where he had hitherto been standing, feeling round with the greatest care for the wall.

He was not long before he discovered that the spot where he stood was deeper than the rest.

The floor was upon the slant, and as he crept cautiously forward, he gradually came out an inch at a time, until at length he stood in a place where the water barely reached above his knees.

The vault or sewer, or whatever it was, seemed to him to be of great size. Perhaps the darkness which encompassed him made it appear larger than it was, although at the same time it had that effect which doubtless the reader has observed when groping his way in the dark, of making the walls seem close upon him.

Where were they, though?

He crept on and on, with his hands outstretched.

At length he reached some obstacle. It was brickwork, cold and slimy to the touch.

He kept his hand upon it, however, and slowly worked his way along.

After walking for about ten or twelve yards, he came to a corner. Passing this, he continued on for about four yards, carefully feeling the wall, and very carefully patting the ground with his foot, lest he might unexpectedly pop into some deep hole. Then he came to another corner.

He was now walking in the direction from which he had started. He walked on, ten yards, twenty yards, and came all at once unexpectedly to a standstill.

There was a wall in front of him.

He went round the corner and groped about, almost in despair.

He had felt round three of the walls; if there

was no opening in this, the fourth, all hope was gone.

Ah, he had found it!

There was an aperture—a sort of tunnel—running out of the cellar in which he had been thrown.

This passage, however, was very narrow, and the ceiling very low. He had to walk in a stooping position, or his head would have touched the top.

The water was high in it; and, by stooping, he therefore brought his face nearer to the filthy fluid.

He hesitated, for a moment, whether he should proceed further. But what else could he do?

He must go. His great fear was that the passage would grow narrower and narrower, and the ceiling lower. In time, he might come to a part where the water filled it entirely.

Such a thought was too horrible to dwell upon,

and, determined not to do so, he plunged boldly forward.

But, as he progressed, to his indescribable relief, he found that the air grew purer.

Soon he came to a turning, and he found himself in what is termed a "main."

He might, if he had been learned in sewerography, have known this by the increased coldness and current of the air, and a loud, gurgling sound, as though of running water.

The stream of water began to press rather heavily against the back of the Captain's legs, and the bottom of the tunnel was in many places very rugged and uneven, whilst in others it was extremely slippery.

It was with the greatest difficulty that he contrived to maintain his footing, but he managed to do so by walking very slowly, and keeping one hand always upon the wall.

As he pursued his journey, the road became

more and more broken and uneven, and its course more angular and winding.

When he had gone a little way further, he saw, at some distance ahead of him, a faint light.

"What is it?" he asked himself; and his heart began to go pit-a-pat, with the hope of liberty.

But liberty was not coming quite so soon.

After he had plodded on for another fifty yards, bumping up against the sides of the passage, and stumbling at every step, he came at last to a spot where there was a small grating overhead.

Here was liberty at last, he thought.

Above his head must be a street; somebody must be passing by, and he would call out to them.

He stood still under the grating and listened, but all above was still.

"Hilloa!" he shouted

What an echo his voice had!

"Hilloa! hilloa!" half a dozen goblin voices seemed to answer far away in the distance among the intricacies of the winding, passages, but not the faintest sound replied to him from above.

He was not to be daunted, though, and soon began to shout again.

Where on earth could the grating be situated? thought he. Anyhow, it must be in a place far removed from human life. Perhaps it was in the middle of a park.

However, it occured to him that there must be another grating not very far off, and in the hope that the next one he came to might be in a thoroughfare, he walked on again.

He had made one discovery, and that was that this sewer in which he was walking must be an old one, which had been disused for some years, and probably the present active channels had been constructed in another direction. As he walked on, the stream got more and more shallow, and before very long he came to a place where there was no water at all. Upon his read to this spot he had crossed several other branched passages down which the stream ran pretty briskly, and which were, no doubt, the sewers at present in use.

One cannot blame his taste in choosing the dryest passages he could find; for we must bear in mind that Captain Charley had been brought up as a Guardsman, and not as a mudlark.

It might be a pastime to a dirty little boy to walk up to his waist in mud and filth; but Captain Crockford never recollected in the whole course of his life to have felt so dirty and miserable.

The sewer which he chose, therefore, was the dryest that he could find, and he was enabled to see it was dry by the light from another grating which by this time he had come to.

He had hallooed out again as he did before, and with the same effect, and now he wandered on again.

As he progressed, he noticed how old the brickwork was, and how in many places it had fallen down, so that it left nothing at the sides in many instances but the bare earth. Now and then he got a glimmer of light through a grating, which enabled him to see these things, but generally he was groping his way in pitchy darkness.

Whenever he came to a grating, he bawled out as he had done before, but nobody on any occasion took any notice of him.

"Well," said he to himself, upon one of these occasions, when he had shouted himself hoarse, "this is a cheerful sort of game for a young gentleman of property. There's no doubt about it that I shall see life. The only question is, whether I shan't see death, too, before I've done. Anyhow, I shall have a cigar first."

He felt in his pocket, which he found full of mud, and presently brought out what had once been a beautiful silk case, richly embroidered, completely caked with dirt.

But the cigars inside were all right, and so were some matches in a little tin box.

"These sewers go much better with a little tobacco," said the Captain to himself. "It's upon the same principle that they smoke in the hospitals."

Then leaning against the wall, he burst out laughing.

"By Jove!" he said, "if anybody was to tell our fellows where I was this minute, how they would stare! I can imagine them. 'Where's Crockford?' says one. 'Taking a stroll up Fleet Ditch,' says another. 'What's he doing there?' says the first. 'Having a quiet weed,' says the second. 'Where's he been to?' 'To see a Lady Abbess, and she has let him out at the back door.'"

Captain Crockford walked on again, puffing at his cigar, and wondering how many miles he would have to travel before he came to a place where there was an opening through which he could make himself heard. He came, however, upon a sudden and abrupt descent, which was not a constructed decline, but a hole caused by a slip of the ground. Overhead there was a grating and by its light he could see the position of affairs and he could see upon the other side of the hole through an opening in the brickwork, something that looked uncommonly like a cellar.

"That's my way out," said the Captain, "but to go, I shall have have to climb on my hands and knees. Hang me if I think a man of property ever spent such an evening as this is! However, here goes"

In another minute, Captain Charley Crockford, of her Majesty's Guards, was creeping about on all-fours, looking uncommonly like an old buck-rat.

The worst of it was, though, that after he had wriggled himself up two or three yards, he found he had blocked the light out with his own body, and now he had not the slightest notion which way he ought to turn.

He found himself, presently, in a passage running in two slanting directions, right and left. He tried the right, and was stopped by a barrier of earth, which appeared to have fallen in some time or other, when they were doing something to the road above, and had blocked up the way.

Turning round, though with a good deal of difficulty, for there was but very little room, he crawled on to the point from which he had set off, and then crawled to the left.

For some distance he travelled up a slight incline. Then, having reached the top, he began to travel down another incline, at the end of which he found himself in the cellar that he fancied he had caught a glimpse of in the distance.

He entered it through a small arched doorway, and opposite to him he could see another arched doorway, for the obscurity in this cellar was not so intense as in the passages; and after so much groping about in the dark, the Captain was able to make a very great deal out of a little light.

He crossed over to the other doorway, the door of which was very old and tottering, and he was able easily to pull it open. Passing through, he found himself at the bottom of a winding flight of narrow steps, and proceeding up them he found himself in a brick vault or room, upon one side of which was a thick partition of oak, containing, in the middle, something that looked like a door.

Across this was an iron bar, and in the middle was a large iron handle.

The Captain, without having any idea what would be the result of such an act laid hold of the handle, and hung on to it with all his might.

Very much to his astonishment, he found that it moved under the pressure, and that the handle and the bar sliding along, a door opened in front of him, and he looked upon what appeared to be a large cupboard.

Stepping into this without any hesitation, the Captain felt round the sides, and presently pushed open the door, passed through it, and found himself in a room evidently belonging to a large house or mansion.

And what sort of room was it? In the name of everything that was wonderful—a bath-room!

"If this is'nt like the Arabian Nights' entertainments," said the Captain, "I should like to know what is. If anybody had told me they had done anything like this, I should have told them it was a lie; and if I had read it in a book I shouldn't have believed it; but, though I know it is true, I expect I shall not find anybody to believe me when I tell him. Now look at this," continued Captain Charley; "if there was anything in the world which I wanted, it was a bath; and here it is provided for me. By jingo!"

The reason for this last exclamation was that the Captain had discovered that the large tin bath in the middle of the room contained water, and something more extraordinary.

And what was that?

I will tell you.

The water was warm.

"If this isn't providence," said the Captain, "it's—— Soap?"

Yes; there was soap—the best brown Windsor; and there were towels—very thin ones with fringes, and very thick ones with borders, rough ones and soft ones. There were flesh-brushes, too, and there was a bottle of scent. The preparations were elaborate, almost magnificent.

"If ever I have a wash in my life," said the Captain, "I'll have one now. I will, if I die for it!"

I have told you already that that Captain was the cheekiest young fellow in Christendom, but you who have read the preceding chapters know that as well as I do.

He had made up his mind to have a good wash. It seemed to him that if he were to live another hour he must have a good wash. He felt quite certain that if he had had a hundred pounds in his pocket, and a good wash would cost a hundred pounds, he would have had it.

"I don't care what the deuce happens to me after I have washed myself," said the Captain—and he began to wrench away at one of his soaked boots.

Captain Charley was one of those persons who never looked forward. His motto was "Sufficient for the minute is the evil thereof."

He took off his clothes without the vaguest idea how he should get them on again.

He took them off with a feeling of intense satisfaction, flung the filthy things on one side, and hopped into the warm water.

I don't suppose there ever was a young duckling in the world who made half as much of a puddle as the Captain did of that tin bath.

As far as the size permitted, he took any number of headers, like any number of Mileses after any number of Colleen Bawns. He waded, and paddled, and floundered, and splashed to his heart's content; and at last, when he thought that he had enjoyed himself sufficiently, and was something like himself again, he stepped out upon dry land, and with the coolness of the coolest of cucumbers used up all the towels.

But when he was dry, and when he began to feel just a little bit cool, the gallant Captain began to think what he should do next.

He could not go back into the muddy clothes, that was certain.

It was equally certain that he could not go about as he was. A costume, or rather the want of it, which might be considered full dress in the Cannibal Islands would not do at all in London, where peg-tops were the fashion.

He had half a mind to make himself a costume *a la* Leotard, with the towels.

"But they are so precious wet," said he. "This is growing awkward, and it's deuced chilly. I shall have to go back into the bath again. Why couldn't they leave a kettle or something with some more hot water?"

Just at this moment his eye fell upon a cupboard. He skipped across the room towards it.

He opened the door.

Wonder upon wonders!

There were some clothes.

Only, when he came to examine them, he found that they belonged to a footman—to a dreadfully gaudily-dressed footman—a footman in the habit of wearing the brightest of plush unmentionables!

It was a horribly absurd livery, but it was better than nothing at all, he thought; so he dressed himself as far as he could.

The suit was not quite complete, for there were no shoes nor stockings, and he had no shirt except that one which was already wet through.

He dressed himself, then, as well as he could, and he emptied the contents of his other pockets into those he had on;—his cigar-case, his money, Cecily's diary, the brooch, and all his other treasures.

Then he walked towards the door of the apartment, which before getting into the bath he had taken the precaution to bolt.

He unbolted it, and was opening it to look out into the passage, when he heard somebody coming.

With the agility of a monkey the Captain skipped over the bath, sprang through the sliding panel into the outer cellar, and pushed it to after him.

CHAPTER XXIV.

THE DISCOVERY. — ASTONISHMENT. — THE LADY AND HER HUSBAND.— THE SEARCH.—SUSPICION. —THE GUILTY WIFE.—THE MAN IN THE BOX. —HORROR! HORROR!

He had hardly reached the other side of the door and closed it upon him, when some person, in heavy creaking boots, entered the bath-room.

The person, whoever he was, appeared to have advanced into the middle of the room with large strides, then came to a sudden halt, and stood stock still.

The Captain listened intently.

What could have happened? What was going

on inside? He could easily imagine. The person, whoever he was, had discovered the muddy clothes and dirty water, and the Captain pictured to himself the look of blank astonishment which was probably worn by the face of the spectator of these very unexpected sights.

But the silence was a long one. What on earth could the gentleman inside be doing? Had he noticed anything, or had he not?

The Captain's doubts were however very rapidly dispersed by a terrific volley of oaths and imprecations, which burst forth from the inside of the room.

"Here! I say! Here! I say! Halloa! D—n it all, James! what have you been about? You atrocious scoundrel, what do you mean by this? Come here, or I'll break your neck when I catch you!"

The person of the name of James, apparently not desirous of having his neck broken, came running in to see what was the matter.

"Look here, sir," cried the voice which had just spoken, and which belonged to James's master; "what does this mean?"

But James seemed too much astonished to reply.

"Well, I'm blest!" he said at last.

"What does it mean?" repeated his master.

"Well, I'm blowed!"

"Do you mean to tell me?"

"I can't, my lord!"

"Don't say you can't, you booby! but answer me at once. Who the devil has been washing here?"

"He's a dirty devil, at any rate!" said James, venturing on a joke.

"Don't grin at me!" roared his master; "or I'll hold your head in the bath till I've drowned you!"

A sound of scuffling followed this, and Captain Crockford came to the conclusion that his lordship was endeavouring to give James the ducking.

James was heard to choke and to gurgle, and to make all kinds of strange noises, and at last to scream out for mercy in terrified treble.

"It ain't me, sir, that's done it!" expostulated James. "I will take my oath, my lord, that less than fifteen minutes ago I got the water ready for you, and left everything right and proper; and who the dickens has been washing theirselves since is more than I can imagine. But whoever he is, he has been a black one; and by the look of his clothes, he seems as if he had been rolling about in the mud. I should say it was a scavenger."

The Captain, on the other side of the door, shook his fist, and in imagination punched James's head.

"What's become of him?" asked his lordship.

"I can't imagine, my lord."

"He's not at the bottom of the bath, is he?"

"The water's anything but transparent, but still he can't be there without his toes sticking up."

"Where is he, then?"

"He seems to have bolted, my lord."

"Where to?"

"Ah, that's the question!"

"If he's bolted, as you call it, he's bolted in a state of nature, I suppose, and that's not likely."

"My lord, I've got an idea."

"Where?"

"I mean to say I know what's become of him."

"What is that?"

"He's—he's—he's in the cupboard!"

"To be sure he is!" his lordship acquiesced.

Then, in a commanding voice, he cried out, "Come out, you vagabond, whoever you are!"

But the vagabond did not seem to care about it.

"It will be the worse for you, if you don't do as you are bid," continued his lordship. "I know where you are, and it's no good your trying to hide yourself."

"Perhaps he's rather bashful, my lord?"

"What should he be bashful about?"

"Perhaps, my lord, it's because he has left his things outside."

"Come out of that, you scoundrel!" his lordship continued, "or I will send for the police!"

But still the scoundrel hung back, and his lordship, out of patience, went to the cupboard and threw open the door.

Nothing was there but a row of empty pegs.

"Where's he got to?"

"He must have got somewhere in the house."

"We will go and find him, then."

With this intention, his lordship and the servant quited the bath-room; and Captain Crockford, with a feeling of intense satisfaction, heard their retreating footsteps.

"So far, so good," said he to himself. "They don't seem to know that there's this way out. It's a sort of secret passage, I suppose. I'm not very likely to be discovered if they don't happen to see the marks of my footsteps upon the floor, coming from the room. And by Jove! if they have the police in, that's exactly what they will do."

The Captain began to reflect.

He was in a dreadful fix—there was no doubt about that; but what could be done?

He did not want to go down the sewers again; he had had quite enough of that.

Even supposing he could screw up his courage sufficiently to go down into the mud once more, it was very questionable whether he would be able to find a way to an opening. See what a trouble he had had to find this!

No, it could not be done. Liberty lay upon that side of the door which was nearest to the house, not upon the side towards the sewers. It was true that if he went into the house, he was going, so to speak, into the lion's mouth, but it was the only way. If he waited a while, perhaps after they had searched the house, and found nobody, the excitement would die out, and he would be able to creep quietly away without being discovered.

Bnt then the worst of it was, if he did wait, the darkness would be fading away, and the daylight coming; and then how could he hope to be able to get through the house into the street?

And when in the street, how could he hope to get home in such a frightful masquerade dress as that which he was wearing.

"What the deuce am I to do?" he asked himself again and again. And eventually he decided upon a bold stroke.

He had gone through so much during the night,—had run through so many dangers, and had had so many wonderful escapes—that it had given him a courage—indeed, I might almost say a recklessness—which, under ordinary circumstances, he would probably never have arrived at.

He made up his mind to make a plunge for it, and the next minute pushed open the sliding panel.

All was still in the house. His lordship and James must by this time have completed their search in the lower part of the mansion, and gone up-stairs to look in the upper storeys.

Not having on any boots, the Captain was able to walk very quietly up-stairs, and in a very few moments he had reached the street door; he pulled down the chain, and endeavoured to open it.

But it was locked.

At the moment that he was wondering what he should do next, or whither he should bend his steps, he heard the furious shaking of a door upon the second floor, and the voice of his lordship calling out to be let in.

"Florence! Florence! Florence!"

There was silence for a moment, and then the door rattled again louder than before, and his lordship again called, "Florence! Florence! Florence!"

Then a louder shaking and clattering.

Then the lord's voice again.

"Florence! Florence! why don't you answer? I hear somebody moving in your room. There are robbers in the house! Why don't you answer? What has happened? Open the door, and let me in."

The door was opened now, and a woman's voice, which, at the very first word that she uttered, struck the Captain as being familiar to him, although he did not recollect where he had heard it before, said, with some indignation in its tone, "What is the meaning of this outcry? Has your lordship taken leave of your senses? What does it all mean?"

The lord, instead of answering, pushed rudely past the speaker into the room, holding the light high above his head. James and several other servants, who had been alarmed by the noise, crowded round the doorway, and looked in with faces full of surprise and alarm.

The lady, as far as the Captain could judge by the tone of her voice, had become very indignant.

"This outrage surpasses all," he heard her say. "How dare you intrude into my apartment, with a troop of lacqueys at your back? What do you expect to find here?"

"I tell you that there is somebody in the house," answered the lord; "and that I heard footsteps in your room. Did you hear anybody?"

"I heard nobody," replied the lady. "I was walking across the room myself. When you knocked, I was dressing myself. Did you expect me to open the door in my night-dress?"

"But I heard voices before I knocked. Were you up then?"

"I tell you there was nobody in the room. Look for yourself. I have no patience with such drunken stupidity. Do what you choose—insult me as you like! It is in your power—I expect nothing else at your hands."

"I'll take an oath I know that voice!" said Captain Crockford to himself. "Who the plague can she be, and what's all this row about? This is a night of discoveries; and if I'm hanged for it, as I believe I have previously remarked upon more than one occasion this evening, I'll see her face!"

The way that this was to be done was only by going up-stairs. Passing along the passage, he brushed his head against a cloak hanging on one of the pegs. Without any hesitation he appropriated it.

"If I am caught," thought he, "it will cover this cursed livery, and I shan't disgrace myself quite so much."

He walked cautiously up-stairs upon the points of his toes.

The crowd of footmen looking in at the doorway had all their faces turned towards the room. He passed them by without being observed.

A little further on he saw a door open, and a dark room within.

Holding his breath, he made for it.

He reached it in safety, pushed the door to a little behind him, and stood still.

Not for long, though.

Before him he saw a window, with the blind partly drawn up, and a gas-lamp shining without, and upon the other side of it a balcony.

"If the blind is only up at the other window," said he to himself, "I'm all right."

He crossed the room, opened the window with great caution, but rapidly, and stepped out upon the balcony.

The blind *was* up at the other window, and next moment the Captain (was there ever such an impertinent Captain in the world?) was peeping round the corner, into the room, and squeezing his nose flat against the glass.

The lady, in her dressing-gown, and with a shawl wrapped round her, stood with her face turned towards the window.

The light shone upon her features.

The Captain recognised her with a start.

It was the same lady into whose carriage he had jumped, in the Park, that very afternoon; or rather, the afternoon of the preceding day, for it was now past one o'clock in the morning.

As the Captain, after awhile, was able to discern the other objects in the room, he saw, in the distance, the faces of the footmen staring in at the door; and standing by the lady was a tall, dark, and rather handsome middle-aged man.

This was, no doubt, the person who had entered the bath-room, and whom James had addressed as "my lord."

At the moment that the Captain looked into the room, his lordship was pointing to a cupboard, with his eyes turned with an appealing sort of expression towards the lady, as though he were asking her what it contained.

The lady replied to him, however, only with a contemptuous gesture, and turned away her head.

Then the lord, with a muttered oath, stepped towards the cupboard and flung open the door. There were some dresses hanging up inside, but nothing else.

He turned them over and over, and with another oath strode back into the middle of the room again.

"Are you satisfied?" she asked.

"No," he answered, abruptly. "I am certain that I heard somebody."

The lady turned round towards the servants.

"Go away," she cried, with an angry wave of her hand,—"go away, and shut the door."

The crowd of lacqueys retreated in some confusion.

When they were gone, the lady faced the lord, and said, with a frown and an imperious glance with her dark, glittering eyes, "Be kind enough to explain yourself. What do you mean, and what do you want?"

"Look here!" he answered, in a low, savage tone betwixt his clenched teeth. "Now we have no listeners, I will tell you. You say that when I knocked at the door you were moving about, and that it was you whom I heard. Who was with you?"

She looked at him with an expression of unutterable scorn.

"No one," she answered shortly.

"You lie!" said the lord, fiercely. "I will take my oath that I heard you speaking to some one."

"You did not."

"I say, I did."

"In that case, the person must be still in the room."

"I believe the person is."

"Find him, then."

She turned away, having said this as though all her interest in the matter had ceased.

She walked to the other end of the room, and sat down on a sofa. Her husband took a glance round, and wandered in an undecided way between the cupboard and the window, approaching which latter so nearly that the Captain drew back as though he had been touched, and gasped for breath.

After taking a turn or two he paused, and appeared to hesitate.

Perhaps he was ashamed of having done what he had—of having made this scene—of having doubted, or appeared to doubt, the good faith of his wife.

But this was not the first time, by many, that he had doubted her; it was not the first time that they had quarrelled. He had never, perhaps, acted with such violence, and outraged decency to such an extent; but never before had he had such a good opportunity.

Coming up-stairs, unsuspectingly, in search of the supposed thief, he had suddenly been arrested by the sound of voices in the lady's room. He had listened attentively, and it seemed to him that he could distinctly recognise the sound of a man's voice. It would be a difficult task to give any notion in words of the varied and conflicting emotions which the sound had caused him.

Nothing in the world was there he longed for so much as a separation from his wife.

But this could not be obtained without some improper act on her part. Hitherto he had been unable to discover the slightest impropriety; and now that he had discovered that of which he was in search, he was furious.

It had occurred to him that if he could discover the hidden lover, whoever he was, he would wreak his vengeance upon him; and at the same time, through his instrumentality, he would be able to obtain the long looked-for and long desired divorce.

He rushed into the room, as we have seen, and looked round expecting to find him.

But he was not there.

As the furious husband paced to and fro, feeling in his own mind that he was a dupe, though unable to prove it, he scrutinized every likely hiding-place, hesitating which to look at, for fear that he should make some stupid mistake. But there was really no place where he could be hidden.

No! Nowhere!

It was ridiculous to think that he had got up the chimney.

There was scarcely room to squeeze a bolster under the bed, which was made of richly-carved oak, and fashioned so as to almost lie upon the ground.

It was equally certain that he was not inside the bed. His lordship could see that at a glance.

Then there was no other place in the room where he could be, unless it were inside the sofa on which the lady sat, which was a kind of ottoman couch.

But his lordship's mind did not dwell long upon the probability; because it seemed to him that anybody hiding inside, in the very limited space there was, would hardly have escaped from being choked, packed as they must be like a sardine in a box, and tightly shut in without a breath of air.

"No; he could not be there," his lordship thought; and after fidgeting about for some time, and looking, it must be owned, extremely sheepish, he strode towards the door.

Turning upon the threshold, he glanced back at his wife's face.

It wore a smile of triumph which was to the last degree exasperating.

The husband strode back into the room, and advanced within a yard to the place where she sat.

"I cannot find you out this time," said he, fiercely; "but I am as certain that you are guilty as that there is a heaven above us, and it only requires time and patience to effect the rest."

She made no reply, unless it was a low, scoffing laugh; and with an angry gesture and an ominous frown, the husband flung out of the room, banging the door to after him, and was presently heard descending the stairs, accompanied by his lacqueys.

"I'm quite as certain as the governor is," said Captain Crockford to himself, "that there is somebody in the room. If I were inside, I'd bet a shilling I could find out where he was."

The Captain, however, not being inside, could only squeeze his nose against the glass, in the hope of presently seeing something, and of finding something out.

"He is as blind as a bat, and as stupid as an owl," continued the Captain, "or he would have thought of looking outside on the balcony, and then what would have become of me I cannot imagine. However, he did not look, and didn't seem to think of it; and so I argue from that that he most likely passed over several very likely hiding-places inside the room. Ah!"

The exclamation to which he gave utterance in an almost audible tone was caused by the sight of something occurring within the room.

It was this.

No sooner had the sound of the footsteps died away, than the lady rose from her seat, glided towards the door, and listened.

All was quiet in the house.

She opened the door very cautiously, and listened again.

Apparently satisfied with the result, she shut the door, and returned into the room with a bright smile upon her face; and although the Captain was unable to hear the words she uttered, it was evident to him that she called somebody by name.

As it appeared that the person she called did not make any reply, she called again. She only spoke in a whisper, but it was a loud whisper; and the Captain, straining his ears so as to catch the sound, fancied that he heard the word "Jack."

Whoever and wherever Jack was, he made no answer.

A dark shade passed over the lady's face.

She hastily double-locked the door behind her, and hurriedly advancing across the room, approached the sofa upon which she had been sitting.

The Captain screwed his eye round the corner, so as to get a good view of what was going on to happen.

The lady dropped down upon her knees by the side of the couch, and raised the lid of the ottoman, or seat of the couch, with both hands, and looked inside.

"John! John!" she whispered anxiously.

There was no answer.

"Jack," she continued, "what makes you lie there? He is gone—we are safe! Speak!—speak!"

But all was silent.

She laid her hands upon the face of somebody lying curled up inside the ottoman, and endeavoured to arouse them.

But in vain.

The form which she touched lay passive and immoveable, and stirred not in spite of all her efforts.

"What is the matter?" she cried, in an agitated whisper,—"what is the matter? Why don't you speak to me? You are trying to frighten me. Oh, look at me! Speak—only one word! Oh, my God! what does it mean?"

She stooped more than ever over the ottoman, and with a desperate effort raised up the body of a man from the inside.

She raised him up—shook him, rubbed his face and hands, sprinkled his pallid brow with some cold water, and applied a scent-bottle to his nose—all in vain.

Her efforts were fruitless. She could not rouse him from his stupor.

With frantic energy she strove to raise him from the box. When, however, she relinquished her hold of him he fell back a dead weight, as a corpse would fall.

An awful dread seized upon her and distorted her whole face.

It was a corpse which she was looking at!

She had smothered him!

He was dead!

With a frantic effort—with the strength of a mad woman—mad with grief, terror, and despair—she raised him in her arms, and dragged him out of the box.

She carried him towards the window.

She tore the window open, heedless of the noise she made.

The Captain stepped back, wondering what was going to occur next.

She laid the body down upon the window-sill in such a way that the cold night-breeze would blow upon his face.

It was the face of a corpse.

The body laid in the position that she had placed it—in a position which was horribly grotesque and ghastly.

She fell upon her knees beside it, and tore her hair and beat her face with her hands.

"He is dead—dead—dead!"

Oh, horror! horror!

Her lover was a corpse!

CHAPTER XXV.

CROCKFORD TO THE RESCUE—THE RETURN TO LIFE.—THE LADY AND HER LOVER.—THE ALARM.—THE CAPTAIN IN A WORSE FIX THAN EVER.—A PRISONER IN THE BOX.

But she could not realize the fact of his being dead.

It seemed impossible.

How could he be dead, when only a short time ago he had been alive and well?

He had gone into the box with a smile and with a joke, and laughed as he pulled down the lid.

And now he was dead—dead!

It was incredible.

She called him by every loving name that her lips could frame.

Again and again she passionately kissed his cold white face.

"Speak—speak! oh, my love, speak to me! Why do you not answer? You are not dead!—say that you are not dead!"

A thousand silly words she uttered, knowing not what she said.

She called to him again, and again, and again.

Oh, why would he not answer her?

She spoke in a hoarse, agonized whisper.

She dare not speak out loud, because she feared that she might be overheard.

Captain Crockford, unable to utter a word—unable to move—unable to stir hand or foot—stood listening to what she said, and thinking what he could do to help her.

All at once the lady looked up with dilated eyes and a stony expression of face, and saw a dark figure standing betwixt her and the gas-lamp in the street.

She sprang to her feet with a half-suppressed cry.

She thought that it was her husband.

Captain Crockford placed his finger upon his lip to betoken silence, and whispered in a low tone, "Do not be alarmed! Do you not recognise me? I am a friend."

She stared at him very hard, but without any sign of recognition.

"You do not remember me?" he repeated. "It was I who got into your carriage this afternoon in the Park. Do you recollect now?"

"Yes, yes—I recollect. What do you want with me? Who are you?"

"I am a friend; I only want to assist you."

"What brought you here?"

"Accident. I had no idea that you lived here until I recognised you through the window. You will not send me away when I can be of any service to you—will you?"

"What service can you be?"

"I do not know. Perhaps I can do something towards restoring this gentleman to life."

And without waiting for her consent, the Captain stooped down over the man's body, and anxiously inspected the cold, white immoveable face.

"Have you a small looking-glass?" he asked.

"Yes."

"Give it to me."

He held it close over the man's lips.

Presently he raised it again. The surface of the glass was dull.

Crockford uttered a joyful exclamation.

"By heaven!" he exclaimed, "there is life in him yet. He is not dead."

She had been regarding him with a stony indifference—with an expression of despair upon her face.

She had no hope of his recovery. She thought him dead.

But now she suddenly awoke from her mental stupor to a wild exultation and delight.

"He might be saved."

The Captain commenced applying the remedies which he thought proper for the occasion. He tore open the neck of the insensible man's shirt. Then he took a bottle of scent from off the dressing-table, poured some into his hand, and flung it into the man's face.

The stranger sighed deeply, and slowly opened his eyes.

But only for a moment.

With another sigh, deeper even than the last, he rolled his eyes wearily from one side to the other, and closed them again.

Then relapsed into unconsciousness.

Captain Crockford had an opportunity of observing the stranger while he thus lay insensible, the moon shining full upon his face.

He had a stalwart and manly form, and boldly chiselled features, on which there was an expression of great gentleness; although certain lines about the corners of the mouth, and a wrinkle between the eyebrows, seemed to indicate that his character was not without firmness, and that he could at times be determined and even brutal.

He wore a great brown beard, which gave him the appearance, at first sight, of a foreigner; although when you came to look at him you could not deny that his was an entirely English physiognomy.

"He isn't a gentleman," thought Crockford, as he looked at the senseless man; "but he's a good-looking fellow. Not quite my style, but still not a bad style. It rather shows a want of taste in her ladyship, to my thinking; but there's no accounting for women's fancies"

"Do you think he will recover?" the lady whispered presently.

"Oh, yes; he will be all right directly. There is nothing much the matter with him, only he wants a little air and something reviving. I wish there was a little brandy here."

"Will eau-de-Cologne do?"

"Yes. Have you any?"

"Here is some."

She handed him a bottle as she spoke, and the Captain poured a few drops of it into the mouth of the insensible man.

The effect was quite as much as could have been expected: more so, perhaps. With a shiver, he opened his eyes again, and raised himself upon one elbow, and looked round.

"Are you better now?" the lady inquired, advancing towards and bending over him.

Captain Crockford discreetly retired to the background while they spoke together.

"I am much better. I know not what folly of mine made me go off in this way. But there was not a breath of air in that box. I should have been smothered, to a dead certainty, in a few more minutes."

"Noble heart! and you would rather have died than have cried out for assistance!"

"There is not much merit in that, perhaps."

"Why?"

"How do you know that I wasn't afraid to call out? Perhaps I thought that I should be killed if I was found there by your husband."

"No, no! I am sure it was not that."

The lover smiled.

"Well, supposing that it wasn't that reason which kept me quiet, (for I must say that there's hardly a man alive—at least, I've never seen him—that I'm afraid of); yet it isn't the sort of position one would like to be caught in by a rival, all of a bunch like a trussed fowl, with one's toes cocked up in the air. No, he would certainly have rather had me at a disadvantage."

"Oh, no! I am sure that it was not for that reason that you forbore from crying out. Do not underrate your own generosity. It was your fears for my safety which kept you silent, though in torture. You would have died rather than have betrayed me."

"Well, perhaps so. You know that I would give my life for you if it would do you any good. To save yours, I'd give half-a-dozen if I had them."

"I'm sure that you would, Jack."

"That does not say much, though, perhaps. I fancy I can recollect the time when I was rather eager, than not, to throw my life away. Heigho!"

The stranger sighed deeply at the recollection of some past events—some painful thought—some painful memory of times gone by.

Rousing himself, however, with a strong effort, he chanced to cast his eyes towards the spot where Captain Crockford was standing.

With an exclamation of surprise, he started to his feet.

Then rushing upon him suddenly, thrust the Captain back against the wall, half-throttling him in his violence.

"Now then! now then!" gasped Crockford. "What the devil are you about now? What do you want? Hands off!"

"Who are you?—who are you? What do you want here?"

"I don't want anything here, particularly, except to get away if I could manage it. But please to keep your hands off my throat all the same. I don't want strangling, at any rate!"

"Who are you?" again repeated the other, furiously.

As the Captain was by no means deficient in personal courage, and was not wanting in obstinacy, it is very probable that he would not have rendered any explanation until he was half-strangled or half-jellified by the stranger's strong fists, had not the lady come in now with an explanation, and endeavoured to appease both parties.

"I do not know who this gentleman is," she said, "but he wishes to prove himself our friend, and he has done a considerable service to me and to you in helping to restore you to consciousness. There is no occasion, therefore, for you to quarrel, nor is there time to waste in idle words. Let us hold a council as to what is to be done."

"What is to be done?"

"You must leave here, directly."

"Yes, I must leave here, it is true. Is the coast clear?"

The Captain walked to the door of the room and listened.

"All seems still," he said.

"Look from the window."

Obedient to her direction, Captain Crockford stepped through the window on to the balcony, and looked out on to the street.

All was quiet; the street-door was shut.

No one seemed to be looking out of the other windows. The front of the house appeared dark and silent.

"I can easily descend into the street," said the stranger, "if you think that I had better go now."

"Yes, yes—at once!"

"But I fear to leave you to the mercy of that man—your husband."

"There is nothing to fear."

"Do not you think that he suspects that some one is concealed here? Do not you think that when I am gone he may return and attempt some violence?"

"No, no! nothing of the sort is to be dreaded. He would not attempt to ill-use me."

"And you wish me to go?"

"Yes, yes—I hear footsteps! We shall meet

again soon—at some future time—when I trust all suspicion will have been removed."

The stranger made no further reply, but assuming a great coat and hat which belonged to him, and which had been concealed at the bottom of the cupboard, stepped out upon the balcony.

Captain Crockford assisted him to descend, saying that he would follow immediately afterwards.

"I will explain how I came to be here," said the Captain, "when we have a little breathing time."

The stranger bowed stiffly.

But when he had reached the ground, and Crockford was going to follow, the lady detained him for a moment.

"Circumstances have placed me in your power, sir, but I feel confident that my secret will be kept safely—that in the hands of a man of honour there is no fear of its being divulged."

"You may rely upon me, my lady," replied Crockford, though in a chilling tone, for he was not over-delighted by the incidents which I have just related, as you, reader, may suppose. Having formed some sort of attachment for the lady himself—or having conceived a kind of passion for her—or, any how, having set his mind upon her conquest, it was desperately aggravating to be a witness of what he had seen—to find out that the lady had another lover, and to be obliged to help his own rival to escape!

"It is deuced hard," he said to himself; "but it's like my luck."

"I have not the pleasure of knowing your name," the lady said; "but I am, indeed, extremely thankful, and greatly indebted to you for the kindness you have shown. It is not likely that we shall meet again——"

"I think you said as much, my lady, when we met last."

"Yes, it is indeed extraordinary that we should

meet here again as we do. I am quite at a loss to account for your presence."

"The story is a most romantic one, if your ladyship would allow me to recount it."

"Indeed, sir, I am dying with curiosity to hear the particulars; but at the present moment——"

As she spoke, a low whistle was heard. It came from the lover on the pavement below, who, impatient, as he well might be, at Crockford's delay, was thus summoning him.

"You must be gone at once," said the lady, pushing him gently towards the window.

"Yes, I must reserve my explanation."

"You must forego it, I fear."

Again there was a whistle below.

"Go—go!" cried the lady. "How imprudent of him to make that noise! We shall be discovered."

Crockford was moving towards the window, when all at once they heard a window in front of the house open.

Then they heard the sound of the lover's footsteps retreating hastily. It was, of course, the wisest thing that he could do; for his presence would serve only to compromise the lady whom he wished to screen.

But the person who had opened the window above began to shout loudly for the police.

"What is to be done," whispered Crockford, anxiously.

"You cannot go now by the front."

"What am I to do?"

"Can't you—can't you go where you came from?"

"No, hang me if I can!"

"Do you think you can escape by the stairs?"

"No. Listen! There are steps upon the landing outside."

"Can you let yourself down from the balcony by the rope which that gentleman used."

"Not while they are looking out of the window above. That would be a mad act."

"What on earth, then, do you propose?"

"There is only one thing for it?"

"And that is?"

"And that is——"

"What?"

"For me to stop here."

"Here?"

"Yes."

"Impossible!"

"But it is more possible than anywhere else."

"But, sir, if you are found, I shall be ruined."

"I mustn't be found, though."

"Where can I hide you?"

"Anywhere you choose, except in that box."

"There is no other place. Hush!"

There was a loud knock at the door, and the husband's voice was heard calling, "Let me in!"

"Yes, in a moment," replied the wife Then she added to Crockford, "Quick! quick! You must get in. It's your only chance."

"It's a poor chance, too," said Crockford, with a long face. "I shall be smothered."

"Not if you keep the lid open a chink."

"Here goes, then; but for heaven's sake don't let anybody sit down on it"

"No, no; there is no fear."

"That's easy talking," thought the Captain, to himself, as he stepped into the box. "I stand about as much chance of coming out alive as a man does who heads a forlorn hope."

The lady advanced to the door. The Captain laid himself down in the box, and screwed himself round in an extremely uncomfortable position.

He pulled-to the lid upon him, but did not quite shut it.

"If nobody pushes it down," thought he, "I shall be all right, except that——Oh, Lord! what a frightful cramp I have got already in my left leg!"

The pain that this caused him sufficiently occupied his thoughts for a moment or two; but another dreadful idea very shortly occurred to him.

"It's to her interest to get rid of me," thought he. "Haven't I played the spy upon her? Do I not know a secret that she would like to be buried in a grave? It's quite likely enough she may kill me herself, if this cursed cramp doesn't."

By this time the husband had entered the room. He threw an eager glance around. It was evident to the trembling wife that his suspicions were not lulled to rest. On the contrary, they appeared to be stronger than ever.

There was upon his face a savage determination, which seemed to say, "This time I will not be thwarted."

CHAPTER XXVI.

THREE COMPANIONS IN CRIME. — THE VAULT BENEATH THE NUNNERY. — A SCOUNDREL'S SCRUPLES.—THE VIAL OF POISON.—THE MURDERESS.—THE VILLANOUS PROPOSITION.—THE BURIAL OF THE BODIES.—HIDING THE TRACES OF THE DEED OF DARKNESS.—NEXT DAY—CURIOSITY AMONG THE NUNS.—THE RETURN TO LIFE.—THE LIVING TOMB.

But, even at the chance of suffocating him, we must leave our gallant Captain shut up in the box while we return for a few moments to the nunnery, and see what is being done to Agatha, who, curiously enough, stands in a similar peril.

The Lady Abbess directed the man who was carrying the unfortunate nun to descend the stairs into the cellars. Not into the cellar from which the Captain had been thrown a little while ago into the sewers, but another one on a level with it, and to arrive at which they were obliged to pass through two heavy, strong-made doors, thickly studded with huge nails, and apparently coated with iron, which had rusted and corroded with the damp.

When they had passed through these formidable portals, and stood for a moment silent and motionless upon the floor of the vault, not a sound could they hear—not the slightest noise reached them from the other parts of the convent.

It was a dreary spot—a gloomy vault, which seemed more like some noisome dungeon, such as one might have found under the dreaded Inquisition, but which here, in what is facetiously termed merry England—in the heart of civilization—under the eye of the all-seeing, all-knowing police, appeared perfectly incredible.

But, as I have said before, in this description I have drawn very little upon fancy; and there are, alas! but too many persons alive at the present moment who could more than corroborate the truth of my descriptions of the dreadful scenes which I have been telling you of, and the still more dreadful things which are yet to come.

There are moments, indeed, in which I almost feel inclined to lay down the pen and abandon at once and for ever the resolve I had formed of exposing the secret crimes and infamies which have hitherto, from some reason or other that find it impossible even to guess at, been shrouded with so much secrecy.

But, no!—having once begun, I feel that I cannot go back; and, whatever may be the consequences, I will, in spite of threat and intimidation, tell the awful truth.

But I interrupt the narrative.

Having carefully fastened the door behind them, the Abbess motioned to the man to lay Agatha upon the floor of the vault, and to lay the body of the dead child by her side.

At this point, Martha, the nun, who was leaning against the wall, and pressing her hand upon her side, with a deadly paleness upon her face which seemed to indicate that she was almost upon the point of fainting away, asked in a weak and feeble voice to be allowed to go back to her cell.

"Why?" asked the Abbess, shortly.

"I—I do not feel that I have strength to stop."

"Why?"

The nun hesitated.

"What are you going to do with her?"

"Whatever we are going to do, it is necessary that you be a witness, and that you render us some assistance."

"I—I cannot do that."

"Oh, you have scruples of conscience, perhaps. Do not think, though, to escape that way. You shall render yourself an accomplice, if it is only by the fact of your being present."

The nun felt herself perfectly powerless in the hands of the Abbess. It was useless to struggle—useless to resist. She resigned herself to her fate.

"What are we to do with her?" asked the man when the Abbess turned towards him.

"Bury her."

"Bury her?"

"Yes."

"What, alive?"

"Why not? It will kill her, won't it? We might as well smother her in that way as dispose of her in any other."

The man stood for a moment speechless, as though with horror. The cool way in which the woman made this revolting proposition terrified him, ruffian as he was.

He stared at her in amazement, scarcely crediting his own ears.

"Well, well," she answered, "you are very nice all at once. What do you propose yourself?"

"I hardly fancy, by the look of her," said the man, stooping over Agatha's prostrate form, "that she has many hours' life in her. If she were left to herself she would die of her own accord."

"What reason, then, for these nice scruples? It is only anticipating her death by an hour or two."

"Perhaps it doesn't matter much as far as you are concerned," replied the man, surlily; "for you'd have murdered her any way. But it would make all the difference to me."

"Dolt! Is your soul so bloodless? Have you not already crimes sufficiently damning to answer for? Will you, think you, escape the fate in store for you, whether you do that murder or not?"

"There," growled the man, "I don't want to argue about it. You mean to pay me for this job, I reckon."

"You know very well that you will have no cause to grumble if you do as I bid you."

"What am I to do?"

"Look over there."

She pointed as she spoke to a corner where a heap of earth was thrown up, and beyond it what appeared to be a hole in the floor.

"Yes," said the man, "I know that. There is a coffin inside, you know, which was to have been used for that other job"

"We will put her in it."

"Not without killing her first, if it's only a knock on the head," the man grumbled. "I don't like doing it—upon my soul, I don't."

She responded with a gesture of impatience.

"Will this please you?" she said. And as she spoke she stooped down over the body of the young nun, and taking a small phial from her pocket, held it to her lips.

"What is it?" asked the man, bending anxiously forward.

The Abbess, by way of reply, held up the small bottle, and her accomplice read the word "poison" upon its label.

He nodded his head in approval, and she, opening the girl's lips, poured the contents of the phial into her mouth.

Then, pushing back her head, allowed the liquid to run down her throat.

Scarcely had it done so than a very visible change took place in the face of the victim.

It had before been very white and motionless—white as marble, and almost as still.

But now a dark shade stole upwards from the neck towards the eyes, which, slightly opened, appeared to glaze. It was a greyish tinge which thus crept upwards, and might be likened, without much exaggeration, to the approach of twilight coming over the surface of untrodden snow.

The sufferer breathed a faint sigh, but so faint that it was hardly audible, and then was perfectly motionless.

The Abbess, Martha, and their male companion stood leaning over her, watching her intently.

"She is gone," said the man, in a whisper scarcely above his breath.

"Yes," rejoined the Abbess, in a hollow tone; "she is dead."

The nun made no remark, but walking, or rather staggering back for a yard or two, clung to the wall for support.

"What was the stuff?" asked the man, as he took the bottle in his fingers and was about to smell it.

"Take care," rejoined the Abbess, coolly; "it was prussic acid."

The man, with a fearful oath, flung the bottle from him, and dashed it to a thousand atoms on the floor.

Then, in obedience to the Abbess's order, he raised the body of the young nun in his arms, and bore it towards the grave.

In it, as he had said, there was a coffin—a roughly-made deal coffin.

In this he laid her, and the body of the dead child was placed at her feet.

An old battered shovel was lying by the side of the heap of earth which had been thrown out of the cavity. With it he shovelled in the mould, trampling it down as he went on. Previously, however, I should have said, he fixed a lid upon the coffin, or rather box, containing the body, but only secured it with a couple of nails which were sticking loosely in the lid, which he hammered down as well as he could with the shovel.

There was more earth, though, he found, than the hole would contain after the coffin had been put into it, and the surplus mould he piled up in a heap in a corner of the cellar.

When he had put in what he deemed to be sufficient to allow for what he was going to do, he laid the bricks that had been displaced from the floor as well as he could manage it in the order in which they had originally been.

He placed them and replaced them, arranged them and altered them again, until he had got them to his liking; then he patted them all carefully down, scattered some loose soil over them to fill up the cracks, and stamped and trampled upon them until they were all jammed firmly into their places. Then, at the Abbess's direction, he fetched a basket from another cellar, put into it the loose mould, and carefully brushed up all the particles of earth lying about, so that when he had finished it would have been extremely difficult with a minute examination to have discovered that the floor had been disturbed.

Indeed, as the three paused and stood on the threshold of the door and looked back into the dreary vault, so damp, mildewed, airless, and foul-smelling, it appeared as though it had never been visited by light or life for at least a quarter of a century.

No stranger, surely, coming into it would for a moment have suspected that beneath its floor lay concealed so horrible an evidence of crime. No stranger would have supposed that there was anything about the place more than the ordinary run of cellars. But to those three upon whose souls the weight of the horrible crime just committed lay yet heavily, one oblong spot upon the floor stood out conspicuous from the rest.

The spot where the body was buried.

They went away, however, closing the door carefully after them; and while Martha retired to her own cell the man followed the Abbess to her apartment, there to receive the reward she had promised him.

Daylight was breaking by this time.

All the inmates of the convent save those who had been engaged in this deed of darkness appeared to be at rest.

In a short time they also had sought their couches, perchance to slumber soundly, as are supposed to slumber the innocent and good; perchance to toss wearily to and fro, and long for the repose and unconsciousness that was denied them.

Many hours passed thus, and in course of time the inmates of the nunnery rose from their beds and commenced their usual occupations for the day. It is not likely that there was one among them all to whose recollection the dreadful scene in the torture chamber did not recur over and over again.

They were forbidden to visit each other in their cells; but during the morning many inquiries were made respecting Agatha of those elderly nuns who had assisted in the flogging, and who were to some extent privileged persons in this curious establishment.

A report was circulated that Agatha had left the nunnery.

Where she had gone to nobody could tell; but nobody could dispute that she had gone.

During the afternoon the Abbess herself entered into a circumstantial account respecting her departure, which in every respect appeared so truthful, that not the faintest suspicion of foul play remained upon any of the listeners' minds

The day passed away in the customary manner, and no hing of an unusual character occurred.

The Abbess took an opportunity of saying a few words concerning the harsh treatment which Agatha had received, and without entering particularly into the circumstance connected with the crime for which she had been punished, she contrived in a great measure to justify the severity of the flagellation, and she finished her oration by appealing to heaven for protection and strength to resist such temptations as this wicked and faithless sister had fallen a prey to.

Night came at last, and the convent was again hushed in sleep.

And Agatha, housed in her grave, how fared she?

Poor sufferer, though she might have been guilty she had been severely punished — perhaps too severely.

But now it was all over, and there she lay cold and dead—food for worms.

But stay; what have I to tell? Are not her sufferings finished yet? Is she not dead?

No; horrible to relate, twenty-four hours after they had laid her in her coffin, she opened her eyes with a faint sigh, and found herself, as it appeared, pinioned and in utter darkness.

CHAPTER XXVII.

BURIED ALIVE.—THE UNUTTERABLE HORROR OF AGATHA'S DOOM.—DESPAIR.—FRENZY.—MADNESS.—DEATH.

Her first sensation was merely one of astonishment. She was as though she had been suddenly aroused out of a deep sleep, and was not yet thoroughly awake.

She found, however, that she had no room to stir; and though she struggled to get up into a sitting posture, she could not do so. She found that she had scarcely any covering upon her, and her feet felt icy cold.

Her feet touched something colder than they were; and then she drew them back, in horror, as far as possible from the object, for she knew that it was her dead child.

All at once the full terror of her situation flashed upon her mind.

She had been buried alive, and her dead child buried with her.

The poison, which had been administered to her by the Abbess, was, of course, not of that kind the murderess had asserted. Whatever kind it was, it is to be supposed that she administered too strong a dose, and had thus counteracted the effect which would otherwise have ensued.

The result had been that the victim had swooned only, and had, after a short trance, returned to a consciousness of her situation. She was a living inmate of a tomb!

Her horrible doom, she felt, was inevitable. She lay for a time paralysed with terror.

A clammy moistness burst forth from every pore of her body.

There was no possibility of a hope of her escape; and she resigned herself, or rather resolved to resign herself, to her fate, and lie there quietly and wait for death.

It was very terrible. It seemed to her to require more courage to meet death in this sluggish, helpless form, than it would in a more dangerous and terrible shape where there was more excitement. She thought, even, that more lively pain would make it easier to endure. But to lie thus and wait for it was something too fearful.

How long would it be coming? Could she endure the suspense?

She began to pray to God to grant her strength and fortitude to bear such a death without repining, and with as much calmness as she then left.

For she tried to persuade herself that she was quite calm.

But if there existed any tranquillity it much resembled the dead lull which sometimes comes before the storm.

It was a tranquillity of despair, presently to change into a hurricane of passionate agony.

With all the power of her mind she strove to keep her heart at rest—to stifle the mad longings for longer life—the wild hopes of escape which her reason told her could never be realized.

She began to endeavour to remember how long it was possible for a person to live without food. She had heard of people living a week.

Gracious God, a week in a coffin!

But that was ridiculous; she would not die of starvation in that way. No; she knew what would be the cause of her death. It would be suffocation!

The comparative calm, which hitherto she had been able to maintain, now soon deserted her.

She began to fancy that already she felt a difficulty in breathing. She gasped for breath.

Then she strove hard to get a mouthful of air; and presently she began to fancy that there existed a much greater freedom of respiration than she had at first supposed; this gave her the notion that perhaps she had not yet been buried. She fancied that she might be lying screwed down in her coffin, but had not yet been put into the earth.

As soon as she was put into the ground suffocation would ensue to a dead certainty. Extraordinary as it may appear, though she had a few moments before shuddered to think she was going to die the slow death of starvation, she now began to look upon this death, which would almost be instantaneous, with a great deal more horror than she had done upon the other.

But the thought that she might not have yet been interred, filled her heart with false hopes; and she strove her hardest to make herself heard, by calling at the top of her voice and hammering against the sides of the coffin.

She screamed herself hoarse, and knocked her knuckles sore without any effect.

Again and again she screamed. Again and again she beat at the coffin's side.

A solemn silence reigned all around her.

An unbroken pitchy darkness.

She began now to sob and tremble with mental agony.

She shrieked with horror.

She plunged her nails into her very flesh. She strove to tear out the wooden sides of the coffin.

The blood flowed from her wounds.

At length, completely spent with the violence of her exertions and emotion, she lay inanimate and motionless, like something dead.

After a while she began to call aloud again.

Again and again she repeated the name of the man whom she loved—from whom had resulted all her misery, suffering, torture.

She prayed long and fervently. She prayed and wept. She blasphemed even, for she knew not what she said or did.

A long period of insensibility followed. She might have fallen asleep. She had horrible dreams—dreams full of frightful phantoms and hideous spectres mouthing at her horribly.

She awoke after a while in a cold perspiration and gasping for breath.

Deep and palpable darkness and unbroken silence reigned around.

She was still in the coffin, buried, and without hope.

She began, before very long, to renew her vain efforts to attract attention.

She screamed and knocked as before.

After a time she discovered that she could, with a great deal of difficulty, move over on one side and on to her face. Then she strained her utmost to force up the coffin lid, but as she could not do it she imagined that it must be screwed down very tightly, for she still was possessed with the idea that she had not been buried, but was only screwed down in the coffin and lying in the cell ready for interment.

These struggles for liberty were utterly fruitless, and only wearied her out, without doing the least good. There was nothing for her to do but to lie down again and rest, if *rest* it could be called, which was merely a change from intense physical agony to mental agony the most excruciating.

Every recurrence of these wild and fruitless strivings after freedom left her more weak and exhausted than ever, but still she would persist in them.

While she lay passive she wept unceasingly, for she thought with a bitter heartrending grief of a world she had left behind. She thought of all the happy days she had spent—of all the happy days she might hope to spend yet, if she could only be spared to live a few years longer.

A few years! She would be content with a few months, a few weeks, a few days, a few hours, even.

When she thought of the bright blue sky, the warm sunshine, the sweet flowers, the fresh air in the world without, the recollection of them drove her almost mad.

She began to ask herself what crimes she had been guilty of, that so horrible a fate should be hers.

She had been guilty—very guilty. But still others had been as much guilty as she, and died at least easily in their beds.

She gasped for breath.

If they did not come soon to look at her she thought she must be suffocated. She knew that they would come. She felt certain that they would come to move the coffin, and then she made up her mind to scream out to them for assistance. But if they did not come soon she must die.

The terror of her situation seemed to increase. Every limb and joint were aching. The soreness of her bones was extremely painful; sometimes she endeavoured to move her feet a few inches, or to bend her knees, but the change of position which she was able to make was so very slight that there was scarcely any relief to be found in doing so.

The wearisomeness of this awful restraint became at length intolerable.

She was in a burning fever.

Her temples throbbed—her brain whirled.

She was choking with thirst—her tongue was dry and swollen.

To describe the unspeakable frenzy and anguish of this miserable woman's situation would be impossible.

The torture, mental and physical, which she endured, was terrific.

At last the climax came. There is a point at which endurance finds its limit.

Something in her brain seemed to crack like a thread.

She went raving mad, and so lost all consciousness of her suffering.

The air grew thicker and thicker.

Black in the face, with all her features dreadfully distorted, she gave up the ghost. After what wearying, sickening, heart-breaking misery, who shall say?

The day broke again, the sun shone again, the world laughed and made merry. Not a soul in the busy, bustling streets without had a thought for the miserable sinner who had died the horrible death I have described.

Thus we see that many of our poor suffering brothers and sisters are ruined, break their hearts, die in agony, and what not, while you and I are eating our dinner, or smoking our pipes, or having a social glass together; and perhaps it is quite as well that we know nothing of them, or they might seriously interfere with our digestion and enjoyments.

CHAPTER XXVIII.

DEADLY PLOTS AND PLANS OF MURDER—THE SYREN'S WILES.—THE AMOROUS OLD MAN.—THE WINE.—THE KISS OF JUDAS.—THE INTERRUPTION.—THE LONELY HOUSE.—THE WELL HOLE.—TREACHERY.—THE FAIR-FACED FIEND.—THE SCREAMS FOR HELP.—FOILED AGAIN.—THE VOW OF VENGEANCE.

ALTHOUGH Ruth had made up her mind that this would be a good opportunity to murder the old man, still she did not exactly see how it was to be managed.

We left her, you may perhaps remember, in the act of quitting Eneas Earthworm's private apartments, just after he had caught her feeling in her bosom for a knife to stab him with when his back was turned.

This little incident, it cannot be denied, had greatly diminished the old man's confidence in the trustworthiness of his beautiful though dangerous companion.

To be sure, he was not quite certain that it had been her intention to take his life, but circumstances were certainly against her. If she had not intended to stab him, what else was she doing there behind his back, with that vengeful expression of face, glaring at him murderously? But hitherto they had been such good friends, or had appeared outwardly to be on such cordial terms with one another, that he could not for the life of him believe that she had intended to act so treacherously. No, surely not.

She on her side saw well enough that he suspected her of being capable, at any moment, of renewing her murderous attempt. It would be a difficult matter to catch him again unawares.

She thought this, and she thought also that it would be much easier at some future time to effect her purpose; but in spite of her reason urging her to make the delay, she was resolved to make the attempt at once.

A line of action presented itself to her ever quick and ready mind, and she returned hastily into the room, closed the door after her, and took her seat opposite to the old man at the table.

He seemed scarcely to relish this approach, and drew back a little, watching her warily.

"You thought, just now," said she, "that I was going to try and kill you."

"I did," he replied, curtly.

"You did?"

"Yes."

"You were right."

The old man backed his chair a little.

"Is she mad?" he was thinking to himself.

She watched him in silence for a moment, then bent her eyes upon the table, and he saw that her lips quivered, and two tears trickled down her cheeks.

"What's the matter now?" thought the old man to himself: "this is something quite new. I never saw her cry before. What's it about, I wonder? She's going mad, decidedly."

It was quite sure that she was crying this time, or making belief to cry.

She covered her face with her hands, and broke into sobs and loud lamentations.

"What is the matter?" asked the old man presently, when this had gone on for several minutes. "What is the matter with you? What has gone wrong? Are not you well? What have I done to you?"

"Oh, don't talk to me, you horrid monster," replied the sensitive young lady. "You know very well what you have done. You want to break my heart, you do. I wish I had killed you."

"Don't talk such nonsense," said the old man impatiently. "I didn't think you could have been so silly, Ruth."

"Why not? Am not I a woman?"

"I don't understand you."

"You won't understand, you mean."

"What are you driving at?"

"You love somebody else."

"Stuff! You won't break your heart about that. You know that very well. You are not such a delicate plant as all that comes to; and if you ever loved me at all, I am certain you have got over it by this time. Why, bah! how many scores of times have you told other people that you loved them. You know very well that you can fall in love whenever you choose, at a minute's notice, and have done often enough when I have told you to do so. Are not the prisons and hulks full of objects of your adoration? It has been the worst possible thing that could have happened, my dear Mrs. Belvidere, your unfortunately taking a fancy to them. Of course, they fell in love with you; I don't deny that for a moment. I don't see well how they could help it. You are beautiful enough to send a whole Jesuit college frantic. St. Antony would have had no chance with you. I believe in my heart you would be too much for the Pope. But as for your being in love yourself, I tell you candidly I don't believe it."

"Well, if you don't, it's because you don't believe in anything in this world that is beautiful and good."

"You're fishing for a compliment, Miss Ruthie: you want me to say that you are beautiful and good. And so you are—at least, as far as the beauty goes; but as for the goodness, I don't think I can say very much for it."

Ruth tossed her head contemptuously.

"You've always been a dreadful slut, it seems to me. I did not know you when you were a baby, but I fancy you were a vixen, and caused your mamma and nurse a great deal of trouble."

"You think so?"

"From my experience of you, from the first day I had the happiness of making your acquaintance, I have had plenty of opportunities of observing your little peculiarities; and I must say that I have fancied you showed signs of being, as I observed before, an out and out slut."

"I have learnt very little good of you."

"You knew a thing or two before I met you

I should imagine. I should very much like to read your biography, if you would only take the trouble to sit down and write it."

"Pooh! I have not yet arrived at the most interesting chapter in it; when I do, perhaps it will be worth reading."

"As far as it has gone, however, it wouldn't make such a bad book. Let me see; it opens in Ratcliff Highway, does it not?—where you lived with your very respectable papa and mamma; something in the public line, I believe?"

They were not my father and mother, as I have told you before."

"You mean to say, I suppose, that they only took care of you, and that you are the disowned child of noble parents?"

"And suppose I am?"

"Suppose you are, and suppose they own you some day or other, you will be fortunate. In the meantime, though, I don't see any particular pull in it. Do you know what has become of the old people who brought you up?"

"I neither know nor care."

"That sounds affectionate."

"If it does, I did not try to make it so. There was no love lost between us: they never did anything to cause me to love them. They were cruel wretches, both of them. They half-starved me, and beat me, and left me almost to perish with want. They used to let me run about the streets in old tattered boots that let in the wet, and thin ragged clothes that let in the cold. They treated me worse than they treated their dog. The man often beat me till the blood came. The woman locked me up in the coal-cellar, swarming with black-beetles, until I screamed myself into fits with fright. I don't believe that they were my father and mother; but if they were, I hate them, and I should rejoice if I heard of their death."

"Well, if they acted as you describe, I don't wonder at your not feeling any extraordinary amount of affection for them. But still, you know, I don't believe you are one of the affectionate sort, Ruthie. Come now, you never loved anybody, did you?"

"Yes, I did, and I do. I love you."

"I don't believe it."

"What must I do to make you believe it?"

She drew her chair closely to him as she spoke.

She laid her hand upon his, and looked straight into his eyes in a strangely languid, amorous, and fascinating way.

He could not help thinking that she was very very beautiful. He could not help thinking that it would be a happy thing to be loved by such a woman, were love in such a woman possible.

There was something bewitching in her that he had never found in any one else. A year or two ago, when he had first met her, he had fallen madly in love with her. He would have given the world to possess her, had it been his to give. It had not required quite so large a sacrifice, although the price was heavy. She had long maintained a hold over his affection, and might have prolonged her reign still further had she chosen. But she, of her own free will, had neglected to exercise her wiles, and smiles, and captivating graces. She had, indeed, chosen to bestow her heart and herself elsewhere.

Therefore, was it that old Eneas Earthworm had seen very little of her lately, and the love passages between them grew more and more rare. But it was decidedly all Ruth's fault, for if the old gentleman had a weak point, it lay in his love for the ladies; and of all the ladies he had ever met with, Ruth was the one he could have loved the most, if she had only allowed him to do so.

Never before had he thought her to be so beautiful as she was that morning, attired with the most luxuriant elegance, wearing the daintiest gloves, the most becoming of bonnets, leaning over him in such a way that he could perceive the delicate scent from her hair, which mingled with the other delicious odours of the flowers in the bouquet which she held in her hand, and the choice perfume which she wore in the bosom of her dress, and all combined to captivate his senses and get the better of his reason.

He was thinking to himself as he looked at her, "Is she not much handsomer than that little girl I have been seeing in the prison? Would it not be better to have this woman's love than the other's? How happy I could be if she only would behave well! But she won't, and it's no use hoping for it! She was trying to murder me a little while ago! She says that it was through jealousy. Can I believe her? Can I believe anything she says?"

He thought that he could not, when he came to reflect upon it; but, after all, what did it matter? If she said that she adored him, and she made believe to do so, what else did he require? He was an unreasonable old man, and he allowed himself not to be satisfied with love upon the terms offered to him.

He got up from his seat, and going to a little cupboard in one corner of the room, brought out a bottle and two glasses.

"Will you have some?" he asked.

"What is it?"

"Sparkling Moselle."

"The wine of all others that I love!" she answered. "Fill me a bumper!"

He cut the wire, and the cork flew out with a report like a little pistol.

Then he filled up two glasses, handed her one, and took the other himself, chinked them together, and drank off the bubbling liquor.

"What do you think of it?" he asked.

"Beautiful!"

"Some more?"

"If you please."

He filled the bumpers again, and again she quaffed the contents.

"You were jealous of me," said the old man with a chuckle—"or jealous of some imaginary sweetheart of mine!"

"It is not imaginary. You know very well that you have forgotten me altogether, and are carrying on an amour with some one else!"

"Nonsense! I never saw any one who could beat you for good looks; I never cared for anybody half so much. If I feel inclined sometimes to go after some fresh beauty, and meet you by the way, I see at once how plain they are in comparison, and how worthless as compared to you!"

"Oh, if I could believe you!" she said, in a low, deep tone, which seemed to be tremulous with passionate emotions, and she leant forward, so that a stray tress of her golden hair swept against his cheek; then, approaching her pink and white face still nearer to him, her moistened lips were glued to his.

The old man took her eagerly in his arms.

But at that moment the bony knuckles of the office-boy rapped against the panels of the door.

With a muttered curse, Earthworm strode across the room, and opened the door a few inches.

"What is it?" he asked.

The boy started back at the sight of him. Not knowing of the secret entrance at the back, as I have explained, he was astonished beyond belief at finding his master face to face with him. He had come to knock at the door to apprise Ruth of the arrival of visitors, and he had never for a moment anticipated meeting with old Earthworm.

Earthworm himself would probably upon any other occasion have hesitated before showing himself, for fear that it might lead the sharp-witted clerk to discover the existence of the back entrance to the office. But the wine, or the love-making, or something or other, had put him off his guard to some extent, and caused him to make this little mistake.

"A gentleman to see you," said the boy, when he had recovered from his astonishment.

"Let him sit down in the waiting-room."

"But there are two ladies as well, sir!"

"What ladies?"

"The ones that were here yesterday."

"What—about the divorce case?"

"Yes, sir. Lady Florence Darcy is one of them."

"Ah! I want to see them, then, particularly. You must send the gentleman away. Who is he, by the by?"

"He is the gentleman that you said was going to come this morning."

"Perdition seize it! how awkwardly everything happens! He must not go away, either. Here, bring him into this room, and show the ladies into the waiting-room. But tell neither of them I am here. You can say I'm expected, if you like, but I've not come yet."

"Very well, sir."

The sharp boy retired, and the old man closed the door.

"Come away from here," said Earthworm to Ruth; "I do not wish you to meet the people who are coming in. Be quick!"

He led her away as he spoke by the secret door which he had entered a little while ago, and conducted her across a dark passage and up a flight of stairs."

"Where are you taking me?" she asked.

"I have a private room up here," he said. "Nobody will disturb us: I want to talk to you about something."

He held her hand in his, and pulled her on eagerly.

She held back, however, and looked round with some curiosity.

"It is a strange old place, this," she said, "and it smells as though the sun and air never came into it!"

"Not too much of it," he answered.

"Do you keep a servant?"

"Not exactly. There is an old woman who comes in and does for me after a fashion."

"Is she here now?"

"No. She only comes in the morning."

"Then we are here alone!" she said, in a low tone, speaking more to herself than to him.

"Yes," he answered, in a thick whisper, encircling her waist with his arm. "Do we want any other company?"

They were at that moment passing a door that stood a little ajar. Within seemed very dark and gloomy.

"What is in there?" she asked, peeping in.

"Nothing—nothing," he replied; "it is only a well!"

"A well!"

"Yes. Who on earth contrived it, and what it is for, I cannot conceive; but it is a well with near fifteen feet of water!"

"Fifteen feet of water!" she repeated softly to herself.

"Yes, yes," the old man said, impatiently, endeavouring to draw her away. "There's nothing to look at! Come along! Why, how you tremble!"

"It—it is a cold!"

Then, turning round her head, she held up her face for him to kiss.

"I should like to look at the well," she said.

"Well, look, then, if it interests you."

"I dare not go with myself. Come with me."

With a gesture of impatience, the old man took her hand and led the way.

"Be careful—be careful," he said. "See where the hole is: close at our feet!"

"How black and dark it looks!"

"Yes, black and dark enough Once down there, it would be all over with us!"

She stood a little between him and the door, and spoke over his shoulder.

"Look, look," she said, pointing; "see what is glistening there!"

He could see nothing, but stooped to look into the chasm.

Suddenly, she flung all her weight upon his back, and sent him sprawling headlong into the black abyss.

He uttered a piercing scream; and, as he fell clutched at the edge of the trap.

Clinging to this with frantic energy, he screamed again with all his might.

She stood a moment confused at the ill-success of her attempt.

But her hesitation was only momentary.

Then she began to fumble in the bosom of her dress for the dagger-knife.

"I will stab him in the face!" she thought.

But she could not find the object of her search and the piercing screams of the terror-stricken wretch rang through the house.

She heard a door opening down stairs, and a heavy footstep in the passage.

There was only one way that occurred to her of finishing her victim.

She clung on to the side of the wall as well as she could to reach him, and stamped with her heels upon his fingers.

She scraped the skin off his knuckles—almost smashed them with her vengeful stamps, but he still clung in mad despair to the edge of the trap.

And his piercing shrieks for assistance grew louder and louder.

There were footsteps upon the stairs without.

There was no more time to spare, and she turned and fled.

But before she went, she had the presence of mind to pull down her veil.

Outside, she met a man with a large beard, coming running up the stairs three steps at a time.

"What is it? what is it?" he gasped.

She pointed to the door.

"In there," she cried. "Quick, quick!" and ran past him down the stairs.

The new comer—Jack Rafferty—without recognising her, rushed forward in the direction indicated.

He found the old man clinging and screaming.

Clinging frantically.

His strength deserting him.

His face a picture of horror.

But when Earthworm saw him, he called out

furiously, "Where is she gone? Stop her! Bring her back!"

Then, as Rafferty made a step back towards the door, the old man screamed to him to return.

"Curse her, let her go, I can't hold on any longer. Pull me out first."

Jack Rafferty stooped over the well, and with a tremendous jerk landed the old man safely by his side.

"What's all this about?" Rafferty asked. "Did she throw you in? Who is she?"

"Curse her!" the old man answered, licking his bruised knuckles; "she's tried to murder me twice withan an hour."

"She must be a devil."

"She is a fiend incarnate. But I will have her blood. Why, you ought to know her; you owe her a grudge."

"What do you mean?"

"Why, it's the woman who got you lagged."

"Ruth Trail?"

"Yes."

Rafferty waited for no more, but ran down stairs.

He found the door of Earthworm's private room closed.

Then he struggled to force it open. It was locked on the inside.

At the most trying junctures the Spy always had her wits about her. You would have had almost as much difficulty in catching her sleeping as you would have had to have caught the proverbially wide-awake weasel.

Therefore she did not run through the door, and leave it wide open after her, like many foolish women would have done; but she turned to lock it, knowing that by doing so she would gain at least three or four minutes' start upon her pursuer.

She gained more than that, for the passage

being very dark, he for a long while was unable to find the place where the door was situated; and when he had found it, it resisted all his efforts to force it open.

The old man having recovered in some measure from his fright, came running down stairs, but he also failed in opening the door, for he had left the key inside when he took Ruth through a while ago.

Earthworm, however, suggested running out by the back door, and Rafferty, without waiting to ask any questions, ran out into the mews, but taking a wrong turning, got far away from the street which he intended to reach, and so was full ten minutes longer than he need have been in getting round to the front door.

There was no sign of her.

He looked up and down the street, crossed over to the other side of the way, and returned again; then went into the office, and inquired of the sharp lad there, how long it was since Ruth had gone through?

"Ever so long ago," replied the boy.

"Did you see which way she went?"

"Up the street."

"Which do you call up?"

"That way" (with a wave of the hand).

"Was she running?"

"She went in her carriage."

Rafferty recollected that he had seen a brougham standing by the side of the pavement at the street corner.

He muttered a curse as he turned away upon his heel.

"Missed her again," he said gloomily. "How often is this to occur? When shall I next come across her?"

But it occurred to him that he might as well interrogate the boy.

"Do you know where she lives?"

"No," he answered.

"Does she come here often."

"No."

There was no getting anything out of this young gentleman.

But Earthworm could tell him all about it; and he walked into the office. It was some time before he could see the old man, and when he did, a great change appeared to have come over his sentiments with respect to the treacherous Ruth. He would not now afford any information respecting her He said that he did not know where she lived. She came there now and then about some business. She was somehow or other, he believed, connected with the police. But he did not know much about her. He hardly could say how he came to learn that she was the woman who had years ago betrayed Rafferty to justice The only thing that Rafferty could get out of him, after an immensity of badgering, was a promise that he would make it his business to discover her whereabouts.

Cursing the old man in his heart, Rafferty at last left the office—determined, however, that he would leave no stone unturned in endeavouring to find out the Spy's hiding-place.

It would be comparatively easy, he thought. If she kept an equipage like that, she most likely had a house and servants: if she went into society, she would probably be met with in the Park.

He was sure to find her somewhere or other.

This London of ours, though, is a good large place—a tremendous bottle of hay for a human needle to get lost in. He might look high and low, and look all through his life—without being able to come upon her hiding place; for do not we hear every day of criminals eluding the lynx's eyes of the law—giving the double to the "downiest" of detectives?—and I have been told of cases where very artful thieves, playing at hide and seek with the civil executive, have taken lodgings in the house of the very detective who has had "the office" to catch him.

But do not think, though, that pretty Mrs. Belvidere has got away scot free. As far as Jack Rafferty was concerned, she was safe enough; but at the moment she stepped into her brougham, a very ragged, ill-favoured individual, who was apparently taking a very great interest in a remote chimney-pot, accidentally observed her out of the corner of his sinister eye.

When the carriage drove away, this gentleman followed behind some distance at a sharp trot, utterly heedless of the mud and puddles he ran through.

After a little time, he came up to the cab-stand, and shouted for a cab; indeed, he sprang into a Hansom standing in front of the rank, and bade the driver set off immediately; but the man was so tardy in his movements, and had so many arrangements to make before starting, that the shabby gentleman, fearful of losing sight of the object of his pursuit, jumped out again and took to his heels, greatly to cabby's astonishment, and ran on again as fast as he could.

Fortunately, however, just when his breath was beginning to fail him, and he was panting fearfully in a dreadful state of exhaustion, he came up with a cab travelling in the same direction, and, flinging himself into it with a sigh of relief, bade the driver to follow the carriage rattling on ahead.

Half across London they journeyed thus.

Ruth, reclining gracefully among the soft cushions, arranged her crumpled bonnet-strings, and replaced the violet kid gloves, which she had damaged in her struggle with the old man, by another pair which she took from her pocket.

She smiled to herself, too, as she was thus occupied—smiled because she was safe for the moment. She felt a little uneasy, though. Earthworm was a very dangerous enemy. It would have been much better to have remained friends with him, as she had not succeeded in killing him. If she could only have managed that, it would have been most satisfactory; but she had not.

"What will he do, I wonder? He dare not betray me to the authorities. If he tried that, I could retaliate upon him—I could transport him easily—I might hang him, perhaps! I wish to heaven I could!"

While she was buttoning her pretty kid glove round her delicate white wrist, she was thinking how her friend Earthworm's business would be settled. You would never have thought, to look at that lovely face—so placid in its beauty—so calm—so full of innocence, gentleness, and purity—a very angel's face it was—that such horrible thoughts could be running through its owner's head—that such a fiendish nature could have existed in so fair a form.

But there is very little exaggeration in the picture I am drawing; and if you happen to know any of the oldest hands at Scotland Yard, go down and ask them if they ever heard of Ruth; and if they say they did not, ask them whether there was not once—and a good deal less than a hundred years ago—a certain fair-haired damsel whose name began with G——, and who had so much influence with a certain member of the Cabinet, that she did not go to the hulks, as every one expected, when she was tried for the great B——d diamond robbery, but was sent abroad instead as the wife of a consul, created for the emergency, and so put out of harm's way.

Ruth's carriage, meanwhile, bore her along, and in course of time landed her in safety before the portals of her mansion in Belgravia.

She had by this time quite recovered from the agitation caused by the recent startling events that had occurred; and, alighting from the brougham with the assistance of her officious footman, she was bestowing a threepenny-piece upon a ragged beggar-woman who accosted her, with one of those heavenly smiles she had so many of, when her eyes alighted upon an extremely ill-looking face peering at her through a cab window, which had just drawn up about half a dozen yards from the spot where Ruth's carriage stood.

With a start and an exclamation of fright which she could not repress, she recognised the man whom she had before noticed watching her in Covent Garden.

The man had evidently followed her.

For what purpose?

Was it to find out where she lived? It must be that; and her ready wit suggested a plan for thwarting him.

Having walked up to the door before the idea occurred to her, she came down the steps again, after giving an order to her servant, and drove away towards Piccadilly.

"I will puzzle him if he follows me," she thought to herself. "He will have to keep his eyes fixed well upon me if he does not want me to give him the slip."

The shabby man did look a little confounded when the horses' heads were turned again in the direction from which they had just come.

But he evidently strove to make the best of it.

"It will be a precious stiff fare I shall have to pay," said he to himself; "but now I've begun the job I'll go through with it; and if I don't run the she-fox to earth, my name is not Skeleton Key!"

Ruth rode on in front, trying to conjecture who this person could be who was so indefatigable in her pursuit. Who could he be employed by? Was he an agent of Jack Rafferty?

Ruth heaved a deep sigh.

"This life will kill me," she said to herself. "It cannot last much longer. I seem to be beset on all sides. Rafferty—Stone—Earthworm,—all my enemies are thirsting for my life! If I could only realize a sufficient sum of money, I would leave London to-day. Yes; it shall be done—I will make an effort. If this goes on much longer, supposing I don't get murdered, I shall grow grey, or turn ugly at the very least. To-morrow I shall see the Prince at Aldershott, and then I shall know what can be done. If I am spared my life, I will leave London in three days from now."

Three days!

Not a very long time to pass; but what terrible events—what strange adventures was this woman doomed to experience before their expiration!

CHAPTER XXIX.

THE GUILTY WIFE AND THE SUSPICIOUS HUSBAND.—THE CAPTAIN CAUGHT.—THE CHALLENGE.—THE CHOICE OF PISTOLS.—THE DISCOVERY.

We left Captain Crockford shut up in a box, and with your leave, we will go back to him.

He, however, has not shared the fate of poor Agatha, because he hit upon a very ingenious scheme of avoiding suffocation; and that was this.

He very cautiously raised the lid without making any noise, and then slipped the journal which he had taken from Sister Cecily's cell between the lid and the side of the box, in such a way that it propped the former up, and admitted sufficient air for him to breathe.

The lord who had entered the room had paused in the middle of it, and, while he was talking to his wife, was casting a lynx's eye over the objects within the range of his sight, and endeavouring to discover something which might justify his suspicions and his somewhat extraordinary behaviour.

"To what am I indebted for this further outrage?" the lady presently inquired, her eyes flashing indignant fire as she spoke.

The husband did not answer for a moment, and his wife continued: "Pray have you found any more thieves in the house, or have you heard any more whispering in my room?"

"I have come here," his lordship replied, "for the purpose of having a few moments' conversation with you about what has occurred to-night."

He had not come for any such reason; but he felt a necessity for accounting for his presence in some way or another. For it seemed to him that a bad excuse was better than none.

The fact was, that he had been listening on the stairs, and had made certain this time that he heard voices in the lady's room.

As he had caught nobody, he felt somewhat embarrassed; and, to hide his confusion, he began to work himself up into a passion.

"You cannot suppose that we can any longer go on as we have been doing," he said, "after what has happened to-night?"

"To what do you allude?"

"To this indecent scene—this scandal!"

"The scandal of whose making?"

"It does not matter at all who has made it! You, in the first instance, were the cause!"

"How so?"

"You had somebody concealed in your room."

"Had I?"

"You know you had!"

"Can you prove it?"

"Unfortunately, I cannot; but I am morally certain of the fact."

"You have done very little good for yourself, then, it seems to me, by the scene you have made."

"One thing, at any rate, I will make sure of."

"And what is that?"

"You shall leave my house."

"What a punishment!" she said, with a scoffing laugh. "Perhaps you would like to push me out into the street! Believe me, my lord, I thoroughly give you credit for being ruffian enough to resort to any violence! I wonder you don't strike me! Why don't you kick and trample on me, like the costermongers do with their wives? I give you full permission to do so; only allow me, in the first place, to ring the bell for the servants. Whatever we do ought to be before witnesses, or it will do neither of us any good."

The husband moved towards the window.

It still stood open, though only five or six inches; and his lordship noticed this circumstance to be rather a suspicious one.

He pushed the window wide open, and looked out upon the balcony.

The lady's face turned pale, and she held her breath, and listened, for the thought of the rope occurred to her.

Would he find it?

Yes, he had!

He made a loud exclamation, and uttered a curse.

"So!" he cried, rushing back into the room, and shaking his fist at her—"so!" he cried, in a furious passion, "what I said, then, was true! You are guilty, and your lover has made his escape!"

Then, drawing a pistol from his breast, he cocked it, and continued, with a savage imprecation.

"By heavens! if I had come a moment sooner, he should not have gone alive! And you, wretch, who have brought shame and dishonour upon my house and name, why should I not take your worthless life? Why should I stay my hand? Am I not justified in killing you?"

He made a spring forward, and grasped her by the cloak.

But she rapidly loosened it from her shoulder, and thus slipped out of his clutches.

Then, in the twinkling of an eye, seizing a small decanter of water which stood upon a table close at hand, with all her might she smashed it at his head, fled rapidly from the room, and locked the door after her.

The bottle struck him on the breast, and knocked him flat on his back.

He lay there gasping for breath, soaked to the skin, and looking very foolish, but without attempting to get upon his feet again.

He lay like this for five minutes.

Captain Crockford, hearing the crash and the fall, and no sound following them, came to the conclusion that if he was not dead, he must be knocked senseless.

Therefore, he raised the lid of the box, sat up, and looked at him.

His lordship, still upon his back, rolled his eyes slowly round the room, until they settled in blank astonishment on Captain Crockford's face.

Then his lordship slowly assumed a sitting posture, and with his hands resting upon his knees, and his legs tucked up in the attitude of a tailor upon his shop-board, he sat staring at Crockford.

The Captain, taken by surprise, was unable to pop back into the box, and, therefore, continued to stare with all his might and main. Upon the other hand, with all his main and might, his lordship stared at the Captain.

"Hallo!" the lord gasped, at length, when he had sufficiently recovered from his astonishment as to be able to use his tongue.

And the Captain involuntarily echoed—

"Hallo!"

As he spoke, Crockford rose up from the inside of the box, and enveloped in the long black cloak, owing to the bottom of the box being raised about half a foot from the ground, appeared to be of a preternatural height.

His lordship, absurd as the notion may appear, could not help fancying for a moment or two that it was a ghost, for he made quite certain that the lover had made his escape by the rope hanging from the balcony.

He had seen Jack running down the street, and had sent one of the servants full cry after him. He had made sure that this was the lover.

Then again he had been a little confused by hearing whispers in the room; but when he came into the room and discovered the rope, he made sure that he had been mistaken.

But if the lover had escaped—and certainly the person who had ran away must have been a lover—who the deuce was this party in the box?

The idea of two lovers was ridiculous and improbable. But who the deuce was he?

"I'll have his blood, whoever he is," thought the lord to himself, as he rose to his feet.

Then the recollection of the bath, the dirty clothes, and the rest of the wonderful events down stairs occurring to him, he made up his mind that there had been a thief in the house, and that the thief had run away, and that this gentleman was the lover.

Boiling over with passion, he still contrived, by almost superhuman efforts, to appear calm.

"What explanation have you to offer, sir?" he asked.

"None, sir!" replied the Captain, coolly. "I could not give you the briefest account of the circumstances which have led to my present situation under anything short of a couple of hours' steady talking."

"You can spare your breath, sir," replied his lordship, with a wave of the hand.

"Perhaps it would be as well," replied the Captain.

"There is only one course open to you——"

"Certainly; I will therefore wish you good morning."

"Do not think to play the fool with me, sir," cried his lordship, purple in the face with indignation.

"I don't feel much inclined to play at anything," said the Captain. "What the dickens do you want?"

"If you are a gentleman, you do not require to be told. Take one of these pistols."

"This is rather hard," thought the Captain to himself; "but I suppose I must be a victim again, as usual."

"I can assure your lordship," Crockford however managed to say, "that you are labouring under a great mistake."

"A mistake!" cried his lordship, contemptuously; "how can there be any mistake?"

"But I tell you there is."

"Pooh! nonsense! This is only the prevarication of cowardice."

"Oh, well, if you come to that," said the Captain, savagely, "I'd fight half a dozen of you; so let's go at it, for I want to go home to bed."

"Choose your weapon," said his lordship, sternly.

Crockford took one of the pistols in his hand, and drew back the hammer.

"Have you got such a thing as a cap?" said he, with a smile.

Then, before the other answered, he began to unscrew the barrel.

"It isn't loaded," said Crockford.

The lord turned a fierce look upon him in answer to the slight sneer which he noticed upon the Captain's face.

"This one is charged," said he. "I took them

both up from my dressing table, without knowing whether they were loaded or not."

"But we shall want two if we are to fight a duel, shall we not? Have you got such a thing as a bullet and a bit of powder?"

"You seem to be inclined to treat this affair as a joke."

"D—n me!" said the Captain; "I suppose I am at liberty to treat it how I like? If it amuses me to be murdered, you have nothing to grumble about!"

The lord suppressed an angry exclamation to which he was about to give vent.

"I'll make him suffer for this presently," he thought.

"Well," said Crockford, "how is it going to be? Let us begin."

"We have only one pistol."

"What do you propose, then?"

"I will cover them both with a cloth, and then you shall choose."

"Very well."

"Are you satisfied with this arrangement?"

"As for being satisfied, as you seem to be bent upon having my life, I shall feel extreme satisfaction, if I chance upon the loaded pistol, in shooting you instead; otherwise——But we are wasting time."

His lordship laid the pistols upon a table and covered them over with a shawl which the lady had worn, turning his back towards the Captain as he did so.

But Crockford did not appear to be so violently interested in the operation, but was humming a tune the while as he sat upon a sofa.

When the pistols were arranged, he came forward, put his hand under the shawl, and chose the first he touched.

He looked eagerly for the cap.

He had chosen the right one: it was loaded.

The Captain could not forbear smiling.

"You have brought it on yourself," said he. "It would have been much better for you to have let me said good morning to you when I wanted to."

"Please to spare me any unnecessary pleasantry, and take your aim."

His lordship folded his arms, and stood immoveable upon the other side of the table.

The Captain upon his side raised the pistol. The table was so small that he could easily have placed the barrel against the other's forehead.

But instead of doing so, he crossed the room and took up his position in a corner, as far as possible from the man whom he was going to fire at.

"That sort of thing is all very well in America," said Crockford; "but there is no occasion for us to be so murderous. Besides, for the matter of that, I could hit you at double the distance."

"Fire at once, then, without any more talk. And take an aim at a place where you can kill me without unnecessary torture. Shoot me through the head."

"I am at liberty to shoot you where I like!" said the Captain; "and I am going to break your arm!"

The lord ground his teeth with rage, but said nothing.

"I have a fancy for the left one," said the Captain, "if you will be so obliging as to hold it out, as I shall then avoid hitting you in the body."

"Fire at once, sir, without more buffoonery!"

"Come, now," said Crockford, "I'll make you a sporting bet. What odds will you give me I don't break the bone to a nicety eight inches from the shoulder?"

"Fire at once, sir, or by ——"

But just as the Captain raised his pistol, the fastening of his cloak came undone, and it dropped off on to the floor, disclosing his gaudy livery. The lord sprang up in the air as though he had been shot.

"Stop, stop!" he shouted. "You atrocious miscreant—you impudent scoundrel—you low, menial vagabond, what the devil do you mean? Do you suppose I am going to fight with a footman? You wretched knave, how dare you have the insolence to attempt such a thing? By the Lord above us, I will have you horse-whipped within an inch of your life!"

CHAPTER XXX.

WHAT IS TO BE DONE WITH HIS WIFE'S LOVER?—GET OUT OF MY HOUSE, SIR!—"LEND ME YOUR BOOTS."—THE STRUGGLE.

"You had better keep a civil tongue in your head, at any rate," retorted Crockford, fiercely, "or else it may be worse for you! I did not ask you to fight me, did I?"

"You had no business to accept the challenge!"

"Come, I like that; it strikes me it was a case of Hobson's choice!"

"Don't bandy words with me, you low brute, but leave the house at once, or I shall throw you out of the window!"

"Come, I say," retorted Crockford, "mine's a pretty good temper, as tempers go; but hang me, if I put up with much more of this! Who do you suppose you are talking to?"

"Get out of the house!"

"Don't make a fool of yourself. How am I to do it?"

"The way you came!"

"Not if I know it!"

"Go some way, and quickly, for I shall not be able long to control my passion!"

"As to that, you may let it loose as soon as you choose. I'll tell you what it is! If I was not sorry for the position in which I found you, and did not make allowances for your blunders, I should throw *you* out of the window, or blow your brains out, or wring your neck! But, on the contrary, willing to oblige you, I ask you simply how am I to go?"

"Go down by the rope from the balcony, you scoundrel!"

"Don't you see I haven't got any shoes and stockings on!"

The lord almost foamed at the mouth.

"Where are they?" he asked.

"I haven't the remotest idea!"

"You know where you pulled them off!"

"Yes; down in your bath-room!"

"This is too much!" replied his lordship to himself more than to the other. "You cannot fetch them!" said he. "You must go without!"

"Don't talk nonsense!" said the Captain, wrapping himself up in his cloak. "How can I do that?"

"What do you propose, then?" asked his lordship, in a despairing voice; and he muttered to himself, "Great heavens! where will this scene of humiliation cease?"

"What I propose is that you should lend me a pair!" said the Captain.

"I have got none here."

"You have got some on, haven't you?"

"You are the most impudent blackguard I ever met with!"

"Egad! you'd be, too, if you'd gone through what I have during the night!"

"Wretch! there must be an end to this! I can bear it no longer!"

As he spoke, he sprang forward and endeavoured to clutch Crockford by the throat.

As, however, the Captain had on no collar, the other's fingers slipped from his bare neck, and Crockford struck him a blow in the face, which sent him staggering back upon the table.

The lord then strove to get hold of the pistol which the Captain had laid down there, but this Crockford prevented.

Next moment they were locked in each other's arms and struggling desperately, though neither cried out, for fear of raising an alarm.

The Captain was the strongest man, and the handiest with his fists, so that the other soon became weak and powerless from the violent blows which he had received "in chancery;" but, in spite of the severity of his punishment, the lord managed to retain hold of the skirts of the other's garments, which he could not shake off.

The Captain's only aim was to get out of the window: for he meant to get through the other window into the next room, and so down through the house.

The lord hung on to him like grim death.

Crockford grew savage.

At last, he got his antagonist in his arms, and flung him heavily into the box.

Then he struggled desperately to tuck in his legs.

But it was no easy job, for his lordship plunged out right and left with all his remaining strength, more than once sending the Captain sprawling upon his back.

By this time there were voices upon the stairs, and a loud hammering at the door.

"If I could only get his boots off, they should be mine. But, damn it, they are Balmorals!"

At length, with a tremendous effort, the Captain contrived to cram the lord's last leg into the couch, and slam down the lid, doubling the unhappy nobleman up like a Jack-in-the-box.

Then, without waiting to see what would be the result, Crockford leaped out of the window and sprang along the balcony.

To his horror, he discovered that the other window he intended to get in at was fastened and shuttered.

Escape was cut off in that direction.

What was to become of him?

CHAPTER XXXI.

FRANTIC ATTEMPTS AT ESCAPE.—PERILS AND DANGERS.—CAPTAIN CHARLEY TURNED THIEF.—THE CHASE IN THE DARK.

The Captain could hear a loud battering at the bedroom door.

Then followed a tremendous crash.

The lock had been broken open, and his lordship's lacqueys and retainers had burst into the apartment.

"It's one consolation to think that they'll find him before he is suffocated—that is, if he only kicks at the lid; though, to be sure, I am not over certain that he's got a kick left in him. I've half-murdered him, I expect. Anyhow, I suppose I had better make myself scarce. But how?"

He could not well afford to waste any more time over this window. There was no getting it open.

He could hear the footsteps of the people in the bedroom, and dreading lest at any moment some one of them might come out on to the balcony, he being unable and unwilling to go down into the street—for to have got to the rope he would have been obliged to pass the open bedroom window, and without his boots the drop which it was necessary to make would have been extremely painful—he resolved upon climbing over from that balcony into the next.

When he came to try, he found that this was not very difficult. The next balcony was little more than half a yard distant, and he was easily able to step across.

In the next balcony he hoped to find one of the windows open. It was summer time, and servants are sometimes careless. It was not unreasonable to suppose that they might have neglected to fasten the windows before going to bed. But there was no such luck.

He tried the same experiment with the next balcony, but with the same result.

This was the last house so built. The next one had not a balcony to the second floor.

What should he do? It occurred to him that it would not be impossible to descend to the floor beneath by one of the iron pillars which, at the corner, connected the balcony he was on with the one under it.

The worst of it was that gymnastics with bare feet was extremely painful, and several times he managed to strike one of his big toes in an extremely painful manner against some projecting piece of iron-work.

But this was not a time to be squeamish; and without more ado, he made up his mind to attempt the perilous descent. It was not so very difficult a task, he found, when he came to try it; and, excepting that at one time he was dangling in the air much after the fashion of a Cupid in flight, and lounging out wildly his bare legs in search of a safe landing-place, nothing very disagreeable resulted from his efforts, only that he landed upon the balcony below, considerably blown, and a good deal bruised about the knees and knuckles.

Unfortunately, he found that the windows below were fastened quite as tightly as those above, and all that he could do was to see how he could get on to the balcony of the next house.

This house was a large hotel, and had been built at a different time to the edifice upon a portion of which he was standing.

He had to perform that wonderful feat which, I believe, acrobatic people term doing "the splits;" that is, laying hold of the balcony he stepped from, he spread out his right leg, until he was expanded like a pair of compasses; and then it required an act of balancement which Blondin himself would scarcely have sneered at to support his equilibrium and catch hold of the opposite rail. It was a dreadful moment, when hesitation was almost certain death; for the least slip would have precipitated him backwards on to the area spikes—dashed him backwards upon the flag-stones nearly twenty feet below—broken his spine—in all probability, killed him.

To think of this was to tremble—to tremble was

almost to fall. But how could he help thinking of it as he groped wildly, striving to reach the opposite rail, but unable to do so?

How could it be managed? He had fast hold on one side, and he could easily have gone back, but it was impossible to lay hold of the second without leaving go the first.

If he let go the first, and gave a sudden lurch forward, he might be able to manage it.

Otherwise there was an end to his hopes.

"By heavens, I'll venture!" said the Captain, whose impiety the danger could not extinguish.

Then summoning up all his resolution, and setting his teeth, Crockford left go with his left hand, and threw himself forward.

Through all his life afterwards—through the many dangers which he met with, never did he pass such another moment—never was a moment fraught with such intense anxiety, concentrated danger, flesh-creeping terror, as that one when he thus made this wild and desperate effort after liberty.

He could not tell how on earth he managed—how it all came about—how he got over it at last, and came out with his life safely upon the other side. But he did.

At the moment that he threw himself forward, his left foot slipped a little. He felt himself going back.

He clutched wildly at the wall.

He closed his fingers round a nail sticking out of the brick-work.

Steadied himself for one moment by it while he threw himself forward.

Steadied himself for one instant only with its aid before its frail support failing him, it dropped out from the mortar.

Then, with a frantic energy, he sprang out, and clutched the opposite rail.

Then, before he could get his breath, and make up his mind whether or not he had really escaped with life, he found himself upon the opposite balcony leaning against the wall, with his hand pressed upon his heart.

That danger, at least, was over.

But then arose a loud hullabaloo. His lordship and the lacqueys were calling a thousand murders

Had they seen him? No; he thought not. He began eagerly to try the windows.

Thank heaven! one was unfastened. With a sigh of relief, he passed in, and closed the window after him.

It was a sitting-room where he found himself. Somebody had been having supper there over night, and the things lay scattered upon the table. His eyes fell upon a decanter, with about a glass full of wine in it, to which he helped himself.

"They'll lay it to the waiter, perhaps," said he. "Poor devil! I'm sorry for him, but I cannot help it. I wonder whether I shall ever be a thief by profession," he continued, as he helped himself to a ham sandwich. "Hang me, if I should be surprised at anything, if I had one or two more of these evenings to go through."

The light from the gas-lamp in the street shining through the window on to the table, enabled the Captain to faintly discern the objects lying there, but all the rest of the room was in darkness.

He groped his way across it with some difficulty, giving his shins some ugly raps by the way, and came presently to the door.

He paused, though, and cautiously descended the stairs.

He hoped to get out at the street door, but again a disappointment awaited him.

In the hall, to his horror, he found a light burning, and a fat porter watching in a large chair, where it was his habit to pass the night.

A very fat porter, indeed; incapable, perhaps, of violently resisting a desperate man. A paunchy person, indeed, whom a good one from the shoulder in the wind would double up to all eternity, but still, though very fat, unfortunately so very wide awake, that Crockford did not like to face him.

"For if I were to kill him," thought the Captain to himself (he had got into the most extraordinary ways of thinking this night, as though there existed in the world no policemen, magistrates, Jack Ketch, and the rest of them)—"for if I were to kill him, I might not get out then. Who knows but that there may be two or three more fat ones within call? Who knows but that he may have a bony, muscular wife within earshot, who would rush out at me, all legs and arms, after I'd settled the old man's business, and hang on to me till the peelers came?"

Uncertain what to do, the Captain sat down upon the stairs, to reflect a little.

But his reflections came to nothing.

Although the staircase at the spot where he was sitting was dark enough, up above, on the second floor, there was a light; and, being of a rather venturesome disposition, and moreover of an inquiring mind, the gallant Captain thought he would go up and look what was to be seen above.

He found a long passage, dimly lighted, into which opened a number of doors, evidently the doors of bedrooms, for upon the mat in front of most of them stood the boots or shoes of the owners.

Captain Crockford examined them with some curiosity.

"I'm rather in want of something of this sort myself," said he, "and I don't think I could have got a better selection by going to a shoe-shop The only thing is, will any of them fit me?"

The fit was certainly the only difficulty, for the choice of kind was most extensive.

There was every sort almost that could be mentioned. First of all came a pair of polished leather Wellingtons; next door to them a pair of strong shooting boots; then came a pair of Balmorals; then a pair of Bluchers, a good deal trodden down upon one side; then two pairs of ladies' boots; then a lady and gentleman's; then a number of boots of all shapes and descriptions.

As the Captain picked them up, one by one, to examine them, in his progress up the passage, he made his observations upon them as he went along.

"This pair belongs to some young man from the country, I should think. These polished ones have got too strong soles to be dress boots; they're the property of some commercial gent, I should fancy—the traveller for a Manchester warehouse, or something of that sort. I fancy these precious old Bluchers are worn by some old gentleman who could buy me up a dozen times over. He's had them soled once or twice, by the look of them, already, and the heels are scandalous. Nobody but a millionaire would think of wearing such; it is your penniless ones who are so particular about their get-up. When I come into my peerage I shall go in rags."

Perhaps, he thought that his dress at the present moment was not much better than that. However rich he was, he could not very well go worse than barefoot. He must have a pair of shoes.

"It's deuced cold," he said to himself, by way of excuse, "for a fellow to paddle about with his bare toes who hasn't been accustomed to it."

He began to try on the shooting-boots.

"They are a mile too large," said he, "and a pound too heavy. I should stamp about in them like an elephant. This infernal bagman has a ridiculous small foot, or else it's such an extraordinary shape, I cannot get his boot on. I won't have the old man's Bluchers at any price. And what are these? Two ladies' boots! I wonder whether they are mother and daughter, or sisters, for they seem to be both of the same pattern, though one of the ladies treads more heavily than the other. I should say that's the mother—or unless it's a fat sister. But that does not follow, either; for though she's fat, she might not be heavy on the heel. However, I don't see what it matters to me, for I can't wear either. And so to the next. This is evidently a case. There's a rakish air about those high heels there's no mistaking; and they have got red boot-laces, too. The gentleman's seem about my size, and so I shall take the liberty."

The Captain finding he could put the boots on, leant up against the wall and did so.

The effect was striking, because the boots, being half-Wellingtons, and the plush breeches rather short, there was an interval of bare legs between. But the Captain did not trouble himself about that, but set out upon a further voyage of discovery.

"By Jove!" said he to himself, "if I could only find a room empty, I would go to bed and spend the remainder of this awful night. Then, in the morning, I'd ring the bell, and swear somebody has stolen my clothes. I have read somewhere about somebody doing it before, and I'll try it, if it ends in transportation for life."

Poor Captain! he little imagined what agony this unfortunate idea would cost him.

He went quietly up the passage, trying the doors upon either side.

Unfortunately, however, they were all locked.

"There's an end to that," thought he.

But then the idea occurred to him, why not try the floor above?

He, therefore, went to the floor above, and in the same way proceeded down a passage, which he found there similar to that on the floor below, and at last, to his great joy, he discovered a door, unlocked, at the furthermost end.

The light was at the other end of the passage. He peeped into the room, but the objects within were veiled in obscurity. He could just make out that there was a bed; but he thought that he would like to have a better look at it before venturing in to take his rest.

This could be easily done. He took a piece of paper from his pocket, screwed it up, and retraced his steps towards the lamp; but before leaving the door, almost unconsciously, he pulled it to.

He approached the lamp, and tried to stick in the end of the twisted paper, but the lamp was built upon some ingenious plan which prevented him doing so. Neither could he, for the life of him, make out how it was opened; but he began fumbling about with a little knob, which he supposed was the handle, until, suddenly, he extinguished the light.

"Curse it!" said the Captain. "Everything is alike. However, I'll go to bed in the dark."

He felt his way as well as he could until he got to the corner where he supposed the door was.

But everybody knows who has tried what groping about in a strange place is in pitchy darkness.

He came to the place where he supposed he had left the door, but when he tried, to his horror and amazement, found it locked. Then he tried another and another.

At last, he discovered one that he could open. This must be the one, and he entered joyfully.

The first thing he did was to pull off his boots again, and put them outside the door.

Then he took off his coat and laid it on a chair.

Just at this moment, when he was about further to undress himself, he was suddenly startled by a noise in the room.

It was a gurgling, clucking sound, something like the running down of an old cuckoo clock, but he took it to be somebody choking in their sleep.

With a sensation of despair he spread out his hands to ascertain the truth, and laid it upon a bald head, lying upon the pillow.

It would be difficult to describe the Captain's feelings; but the most prominent one was the awful sense of injury in being done out of his bed.

He paused for a moment to consider.

The occupant of the bed showed signs of waking up.

The Captain thought it extremely probable that he should be discovered. It was next to impossible to get out of the room without making a noise.

The Captain was desperate.

He formed a terrible resolution.

"I'll have 'em, if I die for it," said he to himself.

Next moment he clutched the bed-clothes, and fled.

The bald-headed gentleman, in the condition of a new-born babe, uttered a savage howl, and followed in pursuit.

With one bound he sprang into the middle of the floor. The Captain, by this time, was in the passage. Hugging his trophy like grim death, he fled wildly, scarcely touching the ground.

The Bald-headed came pounding heavily along in the rear.

The Captain reached the staircase, tripped over the first step, and tumbled on his nose. But reckless of all bruises, he scrambled on to his feet again, and ascended three steps at a time.

The Bald-headed reached the stairs in like manner, stumbled down in like manner, but could not get up again, and lay there groaning.

The Captain pursued his mad career, running up one passage and down another, still believing himself pursued.

The building was a large and rambling one, and he very shortly lost himself in its intricacies.

At last, however, he found himself at the door of a little attic, which was empty.

He entered, bolted the door behind him, wrapped himself in the bed-clothes in a corner, and hugged himself together.

"Men sleep the night before their execution," I am told, thought Crockford; "but then, what's a simple execution in comparison to what I've got to look forward to? I can't conceive what will become of me, but I feel certain that it will be something awful. I dare say I shall be disgraced for life. However, whatever is coming, I'll have forty winks."

And so he took them.

CHAPTER XXXIII.

SECRETS OF RUTH'S MANSION IN BELGRAVIA REVEALED.—THE CORONER'S INQUEST.

THERE were very few persons, with any pretension to being called men about town, who did not know, at least by sight, the beautiful and stylish woman who drove a pony phaeton in the Park, and who rejoiced in the euphonious cognomen of Belinda Belvidere.

She was the lucky widow of an old general, who had died and left a "pot" of money behind him.

So people said, and our pretty friend was envied by many a proud and virtuous lady, who affected to despise the gay widow's face and fortune. Mrs. Belvidere did not move in the highest circles of society. She was never seen talking to a lady.

When her carriage made its appearance in the "drive," it was beset by heavy swells, who lounged round it, and leant against it, and egled pretty Mrs. Belvidere through the window. Live lords were anxious for her smiles, and the male aristocracy generally lavished every attention upon her, while their wives, and mothers, and sisters, and daughters looked evilly on, and wondered what on earth people could see in such a mincing, grimacing, vulgar, and conceited creature, rouged up to the very eyes.

It was generally allowed, both by men and women, that Mrs. Belvidere was no better than she ought to be; and we, who are acquainted with her in the character of Ruth Trail, have very good cause to suppose she was not. But I have no occasion to tell you that she was artful. Whatever improprieties she might be guilty of, they were most artfully concealed; and although everybody suspected her, and, indeed, recounted stories of her profligacies, nobody could bring forward any proofs.

A chosen few went to her mansion in Belgravia, and were acquainted with something of its inner mysteries. They had been presented, perhaps, at some of the wild and reckless orgies which were there of such frequent occurrence. They had seen and assisted in some of the revels where wine had flooded the table, women had gone crazy drunk, and the entertainment had subsided from frantic hilarity into bestial debauch.

Ruth had been present upon these occasions over and over again—had been as loud as any in her laugh—as lawless in her talk; but she had somehow or other always disappeared towards the close of the saturnial, and nobody could say what had become of her.

A great many people had a shrewd suspicion what sort of an establishment this was that she presided over, and how it was supported.

In it resided, beside its beautiful mistress, five or six women, all of a different style of loveliness—all extremely lady-like and polished in their manners, except, as we have seen, when they got tipsy at the supper party—and all alike fascinating and bewitching.

Their toilets were superb. They wore the richest brocades and the costliest velvets—they were in the highest degree of perfection powdered and rouged. Nothing was wanting which art could supply, and here nature also had been prodigal of her favours.

Who could be surprised if the simple youth was dazzled by the charms of the syrens? Who could resist the influence of their big and beautiful eyes, by turns bright and flashing, and languid and lascivious?

Their scented hair—their moist red lips and pearly teeth—their fair white necks, swelling bosoms, and voluptuous forms!

It is no invention of mine, but a real fact, that in London there are several houses of the same description; and the way that they are supported, and the victims lured into the meshes of the beautiful bloodsuckers inhabiting them, is this.

Certain young men of fashion, who have outrun the bailiff—got into difficulty—perhaps, in their folly, committed some criminal act,—fall into the power of such a man as Earthworm, and become his tools.

They are then made into what is called "decoy ducks;" they are obliged to keep ever on the watch when in society; and when they come across any young man first commencing life, and whom they deem fit for the purpose, some evening, after plying him with wine, they take him to a *soiree* at Mrs. Belvidere's, or at Mrs. B—gue's, or Mrs. S—ma—t's, and, led on to play, it very rarely happened that he departed without leaving behind him all his available gold, and very often an I O U or two, which he was astonished next day to see the largeness of.

Very often it happened that some gentleman made the acquaintance of another gentleman at the house of a mutual friend, and accepted a cast in the new acquaintance's cabriolet. Instead of going home, however, it somehow or other happened that they went to one of these houses, and that next day, when the gentleman who had accepted the lift woke up with a splitting headache, he found that he had been "cleaned out," and he only remembers sufficient to recollect that he got dreadfully tipsy at some strange house, and would play at cards, in spite of all that the rest of the company could do to prevent him.

But it is a very curious fact that he has rarely, if ever, been able to recognise the person who took him to this unknown mansion; and never, under any circumstances, is he able to discover where the mansion itself was situated.

It was far from agreeable to the inmates of Mrs. Belvidere's establishment that a coroner's inquest should be held therein, but it could not be helped. The policeman had given information of the death of the old servant, whom the reader may recollect was murdered by Skeleton Key, and there was no chance of escaping the disagreeable investigation.

It was disagreeable enough to all the ladies, but more particularly so to Ruth, owing to her connexion with the police being known to a large number of the force.

She saw no way of getting out of it, however; and she foresaw that the publicity of the business must inevitably lead to her house being known—to her hiding-place being discovered, and the veil which she had so carefully spread over her private life being torn roughly from it. Hitherto she had contrived to baffle all the attempts of the police to discover what became of her at those times when she was not employed in her detective duties.

She rarely, if ever, performed them in female attire, and never under any circumstances without making some very material alterations in her personal appearance; so that, although some of the policemen meeting her afterwards, in the Park, or at the Opera, or catching sight of her in the street, had fancied that there was something of a likeness between the beautiful Mrs. Belvidere, in her melting loveliness, and the bold, blue-eyed Ruth, in her audacious, half defiant beauty, none of them could suppose it possible that they could be one and the same person; and when some one had hazarded the suggestion, he was pooh-poohed and laughed down by his associates, who felt certain that wherever Ruth got to when she took off her official clothes she did not go into society, and play the fine lady.

Thus, for more than eighteen months past this extraordinary woman had played two parts with the greatest success; and whenever there was any business requiring more than usual delicacy, artfulness, and cunning, Ruth's assistance was obtained; and among the London detectives, and even among higher personages still, she had acquired a startling notoriety as the heroine of many dramas, full of black treachery, lying, and meannesses innumerable, in some measure relieved by acts of daring, which proved that this woman could be as brave as she was cunning, cruel, and licentious.

There was no escape, she saw full well; the whole secret of the house must be dragged to light.

What could be done? She had made up her mind, though, what course to pursue. She would leave London immediately—immediately she had obtained a sum of money, which she hoped to be able to wheedle out of the foreign nobleman to whom she had alluded in her conversation with Earthworm, and who contributed rather largely to the gratification of Mrs. Belvidere's extravagant caprices.

I have been obliged to enter somewhat lengthily into these matters, to render the position of our heroine intelligible; but I will now go back to the place where I left her, and follow her adventures.

She was driving back into town in her carriage, for the sole purpose of mystifying Skeleton Key, who was pursuing her for the purpose of discovering where she lived.

That Skeleton Key should be following her for this purpose may at first appear somewhat extraordinary to the reader, who knows that he accompanied Jacob Stone to Ruth's house, with the intention of assisting in the Spy's assassination.

But I must mention here that Skeleton Key was perfectly innocent of the knowledge of the lady whom he was pursuing being the Spy herself. The reason which prompted him to track Ruth to her hiding-place will be duly explained when the time arrives: it will then be found that he was hunting down this woman for a certain reason, without for a moment suspecting that she was the Ruth Trail, *alias* Belinda Belvidere, who had caused the incarceration of his accomplice, Jacob Stone.

Although he had many times been upon the point of meeting her, and, indeed, had it not been for a very fortunate chance, would have assisted in her murder, he was totally unacquainted with the face of the woman whom Stone had such bitter cause for hating, and he was tracking her, not in the character of Ruth Trail, or Belinda Belvidere, but a third person, a character which this versatile lady had also assumed.

He thought it was rather a curious coincidence that she should call at Mrs. Belvidere's house: but the little trick she had practised of speaking to the servant at the door, and returning to her carriage again without entering the house, had completely deceived him.

He never for a moment supposed that she could live there, and he was determined to find out where she did live, whatever trouble it might cause him.

She, too, without knowing what reason prompted him thus to follow her, felt certain that his object was to discover her address, and she was quite as determined that he should not do it.

It was then a trial of skill between two practised players.

He was determined to run her to earth.

She was determined to give him the double.

Gentle reader, did you ever try to dodge a bailiff?

Did you ever try to mystify some one equally polite and persevering in their attendance upon you?

As I feel certain that I only number among my readers ladies and gentlemen of the strictest honour, such a question is an idle and almost impertinent one.

But supposing anybody did wish to perform such a trick, they might perhaps take a lesson from my heroine.

This is the extremely clever trick she played upon her pursuer.

CHAPTER XXXIV

WHICH EXHIBITS ANOTHER EXAMPLE OF THE ARTFULNESS OF PRETTY MRS. RUTH.

As she rode along, Ruth asked herself what she was going to do.

How was she to escape? It was not so very easy. She thought first of one plan, and then of another. She had an idea of going into Her Majesty's Theatre, where there was a morning concert in course of progress. The price of admission would be rather too much for her follower, she thought; but then, when she came to reflect, she saw that this place was anything but a good one, because the man would, in all probability, wait outside the door till she came out, so that she would spend her money, fatigue herself with sitting out what she did not care about hearing, and, after all, be in no better position than she was at that moment.

The carriage continued its course down Piccadilly; and Ruth pursued her meditations with the same unsatisfactory result.

She looked despairingly out at the window, in hopes that the objects passing by on the other side would suggest some plan; but they suggested nothing.

Ruth leaned back, and bit her lips with vexation, tapping her small kid boot the while impatiently upon the carriage-floor.

Suddenly, however, she uttered an exclamation of delight.

"I have it—I have it!" she cried. She looked through the glass at the back of the carriage, and saw that the cab containing Skeleton Key was still following her, and that Skeleton Key's head was thrust through the window.

They had by this time passed St. James's Church.

Ruth stopped the coachman, and bade him turn back again, and take her to Cork Street.

When Ruth's brougham turned up Bond Street, Skeleton Key's cab followed at a short distance behind.

Ruth was taken to the Burlington Hotel, where the carriage stopped.

The idea which had occurred to Ruth was this. The Burlington Hotel has two entrances; one is in Burlington Street, the other in Cork Street. She was acquainted with the people staying in the house. She would make up some plausible tale for calling upon them. She would go in at the Cork Street entrance, dismiss her carriage, leave Skeleton Key waiting at the door, and quietly make her exit by Burlington Street.

This was the plan of action she suggested to herself; but there were difficulties.

She alighted from her carriage, and sent it away. So far, so good.

Then she entered the hotel door.

"Is Lord Norton at home?" asked Ruth, mentioning the name of her friend, a certain fast old gentleman, who was a frequent visitor at her supper parties.

"No, madam," replied the servant who opened the door.

Ruth had made sure that she would find him at this period of the day, and for a moment she felt embarrassed—but only for a moment.

Glancing round at the sound of wheels, she saw that Skeleton Key's cab had stopped two or three doors down the street, and that he was watching the door through which she entered the hotel.

"He has not beaten me yet," she thought to herself

Then she continued to the servant, "I should like to write his lordship a letter. Will you show me to a room where I can do so?"

The man, who appeared to be a novice, stood staring at her, uncertain how to act.

"I don't think it would be any good, ma'am," said he, with a slight grin.

"What do you mean?" asked Ruth, indignantly.

"His lordship, ma'am——"

"Well?"

"Isn't here now."

"You can give him the letter when he returns."

"He has gone away."

"What do you mean?"

"He left for the country last night."

Ruth was staggered. What could she do? Anything but return into Cork Street. But this man was such a fool, she could not do anything with him.

"Can I see the landlord?"

He was ill in bed, the man said. Ruth persisted in seeing somebody.

Presently the head-waiter made his appearance, and Ruth held him as long as possible in conversation, concerning the departure of Lord Norton. Fifty questions did she ask, to most of which the man could make no reply; but this did not concern her much, for she consoled herself by thinking that she was tiring out the person watching for her, and convincing him, perhaps, that she lived there, which might also induce him to give up further chase.

Presently, however, the head-waiter began to show signs of impatience. A bell was ringing loudly, and more than once he had been apprised that his presence was looked for in another part of the building.

At last Ruth saw that she could detain him no longer, and must take her departure.

She asked then, as naturally as she could, whether he would allow her to go out at the other door, as she wished to make a call in Burlington Street.

He was extremely sorry, he said, but they were repairing the floor of the passage, and it would be impossible for her to get past without injuring her dress.

She would have told him that her dress was not of the slightest consequence, in comparison to her desire to go that way; but this fresh obstacle deprived her of the power of speech for some moments.

At length, though, she summoned up sufficient presence of mind to say, "If it is nothing very dreadful, I will run all risks."

"I am afraid you won't be able," the man said, eager to get rid of her; "but you shall see."

And he led the way. There was no very great difficulty to surmount, as it turned out; and Ruth was stepping eagerly forward, when, to her horror, she saw the driver of Skeleton Key's cab slowly driving past the door.

Ruth stepped back.

"Thank you," said she; "I will go the other way." And she beat a hasty retreat.

"Could he have suspected her trick?" she thought to herself. "It's most extraordinary. Anyhow, he is thwarted."

And she stepped out into Cork Street, with a chuckle.

But very soon the smile faded from her lips; for there, upon the other side of the way, stood Skeleton Key, waiting for her.

She carefully avoided meeting his eyes, and hurried rapidly onwards, scarcely knowing whither she went.

This persecution was becoming intolerable. If she were to get rid of him, it must be by exercising her wits to a better account. He evidently was as cunning as she was; so she thought. However, it is but fair to state that when Skeleton Key had paid the cabman and dismissed him, the latter had wandered round the corner and up Burlington Street, without having the remotest notion that there were two entrances to the hotel, and without any intention of spying Ruth's movements; so if Ruth had gone out at the other door she would have been safe, and would have escaped altogether from her pursuer.

And now the game of "diamond cut diamond" began in downright earnest.

Ruth set off as fast as she could walk, quite undecided what she was going to do, but still hoping that something would turn up as she went along—that some means of escape would suggest itself to her.

She walked hastily down the Burlington Arcade.

When she got almost to the bottom she paused suddenly, for she heard steps close behind her.

She paused, with the intention of bringing the affair to a crisis, for she was determined to appeal to the beadle of the Arcade for protection, if the stranger persisted in dogging her footsteps.

"I will say that he has been annoying me," she thought, and then the beadle, or some policeman, will see that it does not continue any longer.

She was delighted with this notion, and there is very little doubt would soon have put it into execution had the stranger allowed her only the opportunity; but when she paused and turned round and faced him, Skeleton Key slunk back under her fierce gaze, and making way for her, wandered off upon one side, and affected to be deeply interested in a shop window.

Ruth inwardly rejoiced. She had cowed him, she thought, and now would be able to proceed unmolested.

She walked on towards the gate opening into Piccadilly, keeping her eyes, however, steadily fixed upon the seedy man, so that whenever she turned, as she did once or twice to see what he was doing, he turned back again very quickly, and went on staring into the window as though his life depended upon it.

Just now a Chelsea omnibus approached on its way to the City.

It stopped in front of the Arcade, and one person alighted.

Two ladies at the same moment hailed the conductor, but the man shook his head, saying that there was only room for one.

A thought struck Ruth. At that moment the stranger's face was turned the other way; she could escape, but it must be done without loss of time

She tripped lightly down the steps, and next moment was inside the vehicle. It drove on rapidly, and she congratulated herself upon having given her pursuer the slip.

But still she did not feel altogether at her ease, because she expected every moment he would come running after the omnibus.

"But if he does," she said to herself presently, "what does it matter? He will not be able to ride, for the man said there was only room for one, and thank God, I occupy that place."

She began to breathe as freely as the tightly packed parcel of eleven fat passengers would allow of.

The interior of the vehicle was stiflingly hot, and Ruth longed impatiently for escape. But she could not get out yet—not, at least, until she reached the Regent Circus or the Haymarket; for who knows, he might be following her again in the cab, or he might be running after the omnibus on foot? Anyway, it would be better for her to go some little distance in the vehicle before she alighted

No sooner, however, did she reach the Haymarket, than she called to the conductor to stop.

Before this, she had several times looked out of

the window to see whether she could get a glimpse of her pursuer. No; no one was to be seen. She had escaped him, she felt certain. Therefore she got out of the omnibus, feeling quite secure.

As she walked from the Haymarket in the direction of Her Majesty's Theatre, she chanced to glance back at the occupant of a Hansom cab passing rapidly by, she saw, to her astonishment and vexation, that the omnibus in which she had been travelling had stopped again, and from its roof was descending her unconquerable pursuer.

"How on earth was this?" she asked herself. The omnibus had not stopped in its progress from the spot where she got up, to that at which she had alighted.

The way that she could account for it was that he must have run after the conveyance, and climbed up at the back without her observing him, which, in the position she occupied, was not impossible.

But this was very vexing. What was she to do?

She looked round again, and saw that he had turned round, and was in the act of paying the conductor. Down a by-street on the right there was a Punch show. She walked rapidly down, and plunged into the crowd gathered together in the enjoyment of that celebrated drama.

Had she escaped him now? She stood motionless there, afraid to look round, but hoping that the danger was past.

A low chuckle at her elbow startled her. She turned quickly. The everlasting follower was there again.

This was becoming unbearable. She was about to inquire of him fiercely what his conduct might signify, when she saw that his eyes were not fixed upon her, but upon the puppet. No; he was not taking the slightest notice of her, but was laughing immoderately at the antics of Mr. Punch.

But, in spite of that, she knew very well that this was only a ruse on his part, and that he was dogging her as before.

She did not know what to do. She could do nothing only pursue her course, and, if possible, run him out.

She entered one of the *cafés*, and ordered a cup of coffee. Before she was served, her persecutor had entered, and took his seat upon the opposite side of the room.

As soon as her coffee was brought, she paid for it; and then, while the waiter was still there, left the shop, hoping that he might be detained to pay for his score before he could follow her. But this hope again was a faint one; he had soon conquered the difficulty, great or small, and she had not gone a hundred paces from the shop before she became aware that the man was again upon her track.

She walked on now as fast as she could, thinking that her only course would be to hire a cab and drive about until she had finally wearied him out; for, from the appearance of the stranger's exterior, it was not unnatural to suppose that he could not be overstocked with capital.

She therefore called a Hansom, and bade the driver take her Citywards.

But when she reached Hungerford Market, a better idea occurred to her, and, alighting from the cab, she descended the steps on the right-hand side of the market, and took her way rapidly towards the river. Here she hailed a boat, and bade the waterman row her towards Westminster. She had not yet quite tired out her tormentor; indeed, she did not expect to get rid of him so easily. Presently she saw him sitting quite easily in another boat, which was following in her wake.

But her plan was now to be put into operation.

"Which is the landing-place near here that is the least used?" she asked the man.

He considered a minute, and then replied, "Whitehall Stairs."

"Are there any boats there?" she asked.

"You very seldom ever sees one," he replied.

"Row me there, then," she said.

When he had done so she landed, telling him first, however, to wait for her return, and should another boat stop there presently, to be sure and send it away out into the middle of the stream.

When she got upon shore she walked quickly along for some little distance, and then pausing, watched the seedy man with considerable anxiety land and pay his waterman, evidently dismissing him. She watched a little longer, and saw the man row back into the middle of the stream.

Then she allowed the man to run up the steps and pass her, she meanwhile managing to escape his notice by drawing back under the shadow of the wall.

"Now for it!" she cried aloud, when he had passed by.

And she rushed rapidly down the steps again and jumped lightly into her own boat.

Next moment the boat had run out into the middle of the river, and next moment, again, was the seedy man gesticulating wildly and frantically from the shore.

But it was useless.

No boat was within hail, and Ruth was carried away in triumph.

The seedy man was left cursing and swearing.

Pretty Mistress Ruth waved him an adieu, and the notes of her silvery voice, as she laughed out merrily, were borne to him upon the breeze.

CHAPTER XXXV.

CECILY PLAYS THE SPY.—PRAYERS AND SOBS.—THE NUN'S SECRET.—WHAT IS IT?—THE STOLEN DIARY.—SHAME.—A MAIDEN'S BLUSHES.—THE ATTEMPTED ESCAPE.—CAUGHT IN THE ACT.—THE POWER OF A VILLAIN.

WHEN the Abbess and her villanous male companion were employed in effecting the interment of the unhappy Agatha, they weakly imagined that no other eyes were watching them than those of the shrinking and trembling Martha, who was too much horrified and terrified by the atrocity they were perpetrating to render them any assistance.

But other eyes than hers were fixed upon them.

Other eyes were watching in silent fright and horror the abominable deed which these black-hearted wretches supposed they were perpetrating in secrecy and security.

A pale-faced woman, shivering miserably, scarcely able to stand, her teeth chattering in her head, her knees knocking together under her, watched their proceedings in an agony of dread and apprehension.

Dread and apprehension lest at any moment they might come out upon her, discover and punish her. Yet she lacked the courage and strength of mind necessary to tear herself away.

This spy upon their actions was Sister Cecily.

She it was whose tender heart, yearning with

sympathy, pity, and loving-kindness towards the poor tortured woman Agatha, was stealing out from her cell, bent upon paying a visit to that of her suffering sister, saw the Abbess and her male companion and the nun Martha conveying the body of the dead child and its unhappy mother towards the vault where they were afterwards buried.

Cecily, taking care to keep at a safe distance, followed them along the passages, down the steps, towards the cellars.

When they at last arrived at that vault where they found the grave, and closed the door behind them, she remained outside and watched their movements through the key-hole with dilated eyes and palpitating heart.

She heard all they said, or almost all, losing only a stray word, here and there, of no great consequence, and she saw all that they did.

She saw them give Agatha the draught, which the nun supposed to be poison, and which the Abbess said was so; although, as it afterwards transpired, this monster in human form knew perfectly well that it was only a sleeping potion, and that if the miserable nun were not dying then from the effects of the torture and sufferings she had so lately endured, she would come to herself again after a few hours' sleep, and find herself buried alive in her coffin, there to die of suffocation or fright, as the case might be.

Cecily, almost fainting, watched the horrible scene to its close; saw the body placed in the coffin, the earth shovelled in upon it and trampled down, and the bricks arranged over the top

Then, when the man came out of the cellar, as the reader may remember he had occasion to do when he fetched the basket, she fled precipitately.

She ran along a passage, branching out to the right from the door of the vault where the body was buried, and she hid herself round an angle of the wall until the man had found what he wanted in another vault close at hand, and had gone back to resume his frightful occupation.

For a long while she remained there in such a state of helpless terror that she was unable to move hand or foot, or to decide how she ought to act.

Not until the Abbess and her companions in crime had quitted the vault, where lay buried the body of their victim, and had slowly retraced their steps up-stairs, did she venture out of her hiding-place.

Even then she felt so sick, and giddy, so frightened and helpless, that she could form no plan as to her future course of action. She could not help thinking, though, that her wisest and safest plan would have been to have turned the key in the lock (the key was outside), and so confine the murderers with the evidence of their guilt. But this opportunity she had let slip, and now it was too late.

She never for a moment suspected that the miserable Agatha had been interred alive, or she would have endeavoured, with the best means that lay in her power, to have effected her escape —to have rescued her from her fearful doom.

Now, the only course that was open to her was to make her escape herself. That she must do, and at once.

It was impossible to remain under the roof any longer where such fearful crimes were perpetrated. She must escape at all risks.

Even at the peril of her life she must escape.

But when she grew a little calmer, and had, in some measure, recovered from the terror under which she had been suffering, she thought that perhaps, it would not be so very difficult to manage this. The murderers, it was to be supposed, would very shortly retire to their slumbers. Then she could creep out unobserved.

She determined to set about it at once; and the first thing to be done was to go back to her cell and make up a bundle of all the little treasures which she was desirous of taking with her.

When the echo of the murderers' footsteps had died away she followed in their wake, ascended to the ground floor, and gained her own cell, fortunately, unobserved.

But here, having bolted the door, she remained for some time totally incapable of any further exertion.

She rested her aching head upon her hard pillow, and for several minutes remained in a kind of torpor.

Starting up from this, however, at last, she covered her face with her hands, and burst into a violent fit of sobbing.

Then fell upon her knees and lifted her voice on high, praying with passionate fervour.

As she had prayed in the gloomy chapel early in the evening, when Crockford was so startled by the sound of her voice, now did she pray in her cell.

In the same heartrending accents did she beseech the Almighty's aid to strengthen her against temptation.

In the same bitterly reproachful, almost abject prostration, did she now pray for forgiveness for some crime which she had been guilty of, and forgiveness for which, to judge from her agony and despair, she appeared to think was almost hopeless.

But what crime could this be? What sin could one so young and so beautiful have been guilty of?

Here, within these gloomy walls, away from temptation, jealously guarded and watched, and kept a close prisoner, what fault could she have committed?

One almost felt inclined to believe that it was some fanciful fault which this poor young innocent creature accused herself of. But still her misery, her mental agony, her wild supplication and despairing sobs were too vehement, too heart-rending, to have only a frivolous motive for their utterance.

What was this mystery? Time must show.

She rose at length to her feet, spent and exhausted with her emotion, and began her work of packing.

She had very soon got together the few effects which she required, with but two exceptions.

Two objects were missing. Two objects, the most important of all.

One was a brooch. The other a volume containing her diary.

She could not believe at first that they were really missing, and again and again turned over and over all the articles in her little bundle to make quite sure she had not overlooked them. Usually she kept them both with a little purse of sovereigns, her sole earthly wealth, except what was in possession of the Superior of the Convent.

Never before that day had she failed to lock up these treasures—the diary and brooch—when she had done with them; but this day had been a day of so much anxiety, emotion, and excitement, that she had put them down somewhere or other out of the usual course, and had overlooked them.

The question now was, where had she put them?

Everything in the cell did she turn over—every hole and corner did she visit.

Nothing escaped her; but after more than an hour spent thus, she was obliged to give the search up in despair.

To her great terror and inexpressible grief, she was obliged to come at last to the conclusion that they had been stolen.

First of all, with respect to the brooch. It was the only relic which she possessed belonging to her deceased mother; the much-prized memorial of a parent whose love she had never known—the only thing remaining to her upon earth to remind her that she had kith or kin.

It was a treasure which she valued next to her life, and now it was gone—gone for ever.

And then the diary; she turned hot and cold with fear and apprehension when she thought that it might perhaps have fallen into the hands of the Lady Superior.

For all the wealth of the Indies—for all the happiness in the world, she would not have such a thing occur.

To remain any longer under the roof, if the Abbess had read the contents of the book, was quite impossible.

Its pages contained an account of that scene for which she had just been asking God's forgiveness.

The awful fate of Agatha was fresh in her memory, and she trembled as she thought of it. No, she could remain no longer under that roof; instant escape would perhaps alone preserve her life.

Suddenly, however, another thought occurred to her, and struck her motionless, as though it had been a stroke of lightning.

"Gracious heavens," she exclaimed, "can it be possible? Can *he* have taken it? Can *he* be in possession of my secret?"

She had recollected that Crockford had been some time alone in the cell, and it was he whom she alluded to.

The thought that he was the thief—that he had taken possession of her journal—that he would be able to read all which was there written, and which was intended to have met no human eye save her own—that her innermost soul would be laid bare to him, filled her with unutterable terror and shame.

Scarlet blushes mantled her burning cheeks.

She trembled like a leaf.

"Oh! anything, anything, would be better than that," she said. "I am certain that he is a wild, fast young man; that his principles are anything but honourable where women are concerned. Who knows but that he may read my diary up to his companions? It will be made the subject of their wicked jokes, sneers, and ridicules. Oh! I shall die for shame at the thought."

And a still more disagreeable consequence now occurred to her.

It would so place her in his power, that, if he were the libertine she supposed him to be, he might oblige her to comply with any terms he chose to propose, in the hope of keeping her secret inviolate.

In any case, and into whosoever's hand the book might have fallen, it was certain that she must escape, and that she must waste no more time in consideration.

She gathered up her bundle, and noiselessly opening the door of her cell, stole upon tiptoe along the passage.

To reach the door of the chapel by which she intended to make her exit, she was obliged to pass the door of the Superior's apartments. When she reached it, she placed her ear against the key-hole, and listened intently; and by the regular breathing of the Abbess, she knew that she was sleeping.

"All is safe," she muttered to herself, and pursued her way.

The key of the door leading into the chapel was kept in the room of the porter, a half-blind, half-deaf, infirm old man, in whom the Abbess placed the greatest confidence, and whom she thought she might possibly rob of his charge without awakening him. Anyhow, she was going to make the attempt.

When she reached the door of his room, she opened it cautiously, and entered without making any more noise by her footfalls than if her feet had been feathers. She crept towards that part of the room where she knew the old man was in the habit of keeping the key hung upon a nail.

She found the nail, but the key had been removed. The discovery startled her not a little, but when she reflected upon the circumstance, she was even more alarmed. The key had been removed, there was very little doubt, by the man who had assisted in the burial of poor Agatha. He had taken it to let himself out. Was he coming back again? Had he only taken it to unlock the door?

She stood there in the gloom of the apartment, listening intently for the sound of his returning footsteps without, which she momentarily dreaded and expected.

But it came not; and presently she ventured out again into the passage. A vague hope filled her breast. The door might have been left open. The key might be in.

The key *was* there. Her heart fluttered at the sight; and she advanced eagerly and laid her hand upon the handle.

But as she did so, she heard a noise upon the other side.

A stealthy footstep—a hand upon the lock without.

Then the door opened before she could escape.

Before she had time to step away from it, the door opened a quarter of a yard, and the villanous countenance of the man who had assisted in the burial was thrust in at the aperture.

The face, at the sight of her, expressed great astonishment and considerable alarm.

Then, after a prolonged stare, these emotions gave place to others.

An ugly leer spread slowly over the man's face; and, stepping within the door, he grasped her wrist with his long bony fingers, and held her as though in a vice.

She shrank back from him, and seemed as though she was about to utter a scream.

"Hush!" he hissed into her ear. "What are you about? What do you want to do?"

She did not cry out, as she was at first about to do, but, setting her teeth and summoning together all the strength she was capable of, struggled with him silently.

Struggled, but without avail, for he retained his hold upon her without exertion.

At length she paused for want of breath, and he looked down upon her with a sarcastic grin.

"You pretty fool!" said he; "you're weak as water! What are you trying to do?"

CHAPTER XXXVI.

SISTER CECILY AND THE PRIEST.—THE STRUGGLE FOR FREEDOM.

THIS man who had thus placed himself between her and liberty, was the priest who attended upon the convent.

When he was assisting the Abbess in that work of horror in the cellar, he was not attired in his usual priestly dress; but now he wore the long skirts, the peculiar-shaped hat, the white band, and the rest of the ecclesiastical toilet.

In the common dress which he had worn before he had looked nothing but a swarthy, ill-favoured ruffian; but in this black dress, his long, lank figure had something horribly mean and cringing about it.

Something serpent-like, reptile-like, and creeping in its motion.

Nobody looking at him from behind could possibly have expected to have seen anything but a mean and sneaking expression of face in the owner of such a form; and surely it is very rarely that so despicable a countenance could have been met with.

"What are you trying to do?" the man asked. "Do you want to run away?"

"Yes," she replied, desperately. "Let me pass!"

"Likely," observed the priest. "What next?"

"Let me pass!" she repeated.

"Why do you want to go, my poor child?" he inquired, with a tone of affected pity.

"I do want to go—and I will go!"

"Will is a strong word!"

"I will!"

"You can't do anything without me, you know. It depends upon me whether or not I should take you back to the Lady Abbess. What would become of you then?"

"I won't be taken back, and I'll shriek for help until somebody comes to my assistance from out of doors!"

"Bah!—bah! That's very childish! Nobody would hear you out of doors: if you shrieked ever so, it would be only tiring yourself for no purpose."

"I can try it, anyhow."

"No, no—you won't be so silly; you will come back to your cell, like a good girl, and not oblige me to use force."

"You shall kill me first!"

"I couldn't have the heart to hurt so pretty a creature! I do not want to cause you any pain. What have you got to complain about? Perhaps I can help you in some way. Come back, now, quietly to your cell, and tell me all about it."

What could she do? To struggle with him was worse than useless. To hope to make him let her go she could not. The only plan was to pretend to give up the idea, and take the next opportunity.

While she was thinking thus, he all the while maintained a light hold upon her wrist.

All the while he was looking down into her face, apparently trying to read her secret thoughts.

"Will you listen to reason?" he asked.

She made no reply.

"Will you listen to reason?" he repeated. "Will you leave off being so foolish?"

Still silence.

"I tell you I want to be your friend. Come back with me quietly to your cell, and I will not give the alarm."

"And if I do not?"

"I will at once alarm the Abbess, and then——"

"And then?"

"You know the fate of Sister Agatha."

Cecily shuddered.

"Come, then"

As she spoke, he drew her along the passage.

She followed him mechanically, walking with a heavy, listless tread, trailing her feet after her. He noticed this presently, and whispered to her to tread lightly.

They were passing the Abbess's door at the time, and Cecily noticed, with surprise, that he trembled slightly, and that his countenance expressed great fear.

He drew her on eagerly, and they soon arrived at the nun's cell, the door of which she had left open behind her.

"Is this it?" he asked.

"Yes."

He pushed it open, and she entered first. He followed quickly after her, and locked the door behind him.

There was something, though, in the eagerness of his manner, in the action itself, and in the expression of the priest's face, which filled Cecily with a vague alarm.

What did his conduct mean? She trembled as he approached her, and recoiled from him in terror.

He took her hand in his, and seated himself by her side upon the bundle of straw which served her as a bed.

"Listen to me, Sister Cecily," the priest said in a low, thick whisper, while his eyes had a strange wolfish glare in them, which made her shiver and flush deeply beneath his devouring gaze. "I do not wish to get you into trouble. I could not bear to think that I had been instrumental in you being punished for your attempt at escape, like was our unfortunate Sister Agatha, a few hours ago. Now whether I shall inform upon you or not all depends upon you."

"Upon me?"

"Yes; it is for you to say whether you would rather have me for an enemy or for—for—a lover?"

She gave a violent start, although his words were more than half expected by her.

She endeavoured to disengage herself from the encircling arm which he stole round her waist.

She pushed back the hideous face which he thrust close to hers.

Wrestled with the hand which strove to violate the sanctity of her pure bosom, heaving with deep indignation, intense loathing, and suffocating sobs.

But his strength was gigantic. She was like a child in his arms.

Her struggles were without avail.

With loosened hair, flushed face, and disordered apparel, she struggled madly in the monster's arms.

His hot and hateful breath upon her face, his dry lips glued to hers so red and moist.

His lustful eyes eyes glaring into her shrinking orbs of liquid blue, distressed and terrified, languid and weary.

She felt her last remaining strength fast falling away, and soon nothing could save her from the clutches of this odious wretch.

But in her desperate striving to free herself from the priest's embraces, her hand fell upon some sharp pointed weapon in her own pocket.

It was a pair of scissors.

She dragged them forth, and with a desperate effort tore her arm for a moment from his hold, and then stabbed the ruffian in the face.

He started back from her with a sharp cry of agony, and staggered away a yard or two, the blood streaming down from a deep wound in his forehead.

Then, before he could recover himself, she bounded past him, and catching up her bundle by the way, and locking the door of the cell from the outside, fled panting down the passage.

In a moment afterwards she had gained the chapel door, had passed it, and locked it behind her.

And now she found herself unmolested in the chapel.

The outer door of the chapel leading to the street was always kept locked; but she calculated upon being able to get through a certain window that she had observed about four feet from the ground.

This was not such a very easy matter, she found, for it would have been difficult even to one more used to gymnastics than she was.

It was higher from the ground than she had supposed it to be, and it was extremely narrow.

Having got as far as this, however, she did not feel inclined to be beaten easily; and she began to look about for some means of escape.

There was a bench standing not far from the window, and she drew it towards it; then mounting upon this, she pushed up the sash and looked out previous to taking a leap.

She saw how it was to be done: she must stand up upon the window seat and jump out. To endeavour to slide out or to let herself down gently would be almost impracticable; she would to a certainty catch her dress upon some of the iron work of the window, and hang suspended, a prisoner upon the very threshold of liberty.

Therefore she determined to make a spring, and though it was quite five feet from the ground upon the outside, yet as there was some grass to alight upon she thought that she might easily do it. At any rate, she would try.

First of all, she must throw out her bundle. She tossed it lightly on to the ground, and stepped upon the window ledge.

But as she stood there in that position, and just upon the point of taking a spring, she heard some one coming round the corner.

She started back in a fright, for she dreaded that it might be the priest who had somehow or other, by some inexplicable means, managed to escape from the cell in which she had locked him up, and had got round the outside of the convent by the other door in time to intercept her progress.

But this, to her intense relief, proved not to be the case, for the person who now made his appearance was not her late tormentor, nor did he in any respect resemble him.

It was, on the contrary, a youth of about eighteen, dressed in a worn suit of corduroy, greasy and patched in many places, whose cap was cocked very much upon one side of his head, and who was chewing the stem of a short, black pipe, which, however, was not lighted.

When Cecily's eyes first rested upon him, this young man was coming round the corner rather cautiously, not to say in a sneaking fashion, and at first catching sight of the nun he made a start backwards, and appeared to be upon the point of making a bolt of it.

At the same time he let fall some object which he held in one hand. This appeared to be, as well as Cecily could make out, a piece of lead piping, and she innocently supposed the gentleman in corduroy was employed in making some repairs in the roof of the convent. It is my opinion, however, that he was engaged in stealing some lead, for the purpose of selling it again for a few pence to a marine store dealer.

The man, I say, was just upon the point of running away, but when he came to take a longer look at her, and saw that she appeared to be almost, if not more, frightened than he was, and when he caught sight of the bundle lying upon the grass, he changed his mind, and appeared to form a different determination.

"Halloa!" said he; "what's up now?"

She did not understand what he meant, and made no answer.

The young man approached nearer, and took up the bundle.

"What's this?" he asked. "Swag?"

She still remained silent.

"It ain't heavy," he observed, weighing the bundle in his hands. "Couldn't you have got nothing else—no ornaments, nor saints, nor nothing?"

Cecily began to comprehend him. To her horror, she perceived that he supposed that she had been robbing the church, and that her bundle contained the spoil.

"Can't I come in, and have a bagful?" the young man suggested. "There must be some plate, and some candlesticks, and things. There allers is, in these 'ere chapels! Why didn't you grab none? Get back again, and help us up."

"No, no!" she said, in horror. "No, no—you mistake; there is nothing inside to take—nothing worth taking!"

"Not after you have had the picking of them, perhaps!"

"No, no—I have not taken anything. I am running away. Will you help me?"

On hearing this, the young man's expression changed.

"What's these 'ere?" he asked.

"They are my clothes."

"There's other things besides clothes! You've been collaring a little something besides, I expect!"

"No, no, I have not! There is only my property—my necklaces, my money, and other things belonging to me."

At the words "necklaces and money," the young man's eyes brightened considerably, and he handled the bundle more affectionately. Indeed, after feeling it over for a moment or two, he put it under his arm.

"And so you're a bolting, are you?" said he playfully. "What games have you been up to, I wonder?"

"I have been doing nothing, but I am afraid to stop. I am afraid that they will treat me cruelly."

"Go on with you!" said the young man. "I know what you nuns is! There's rare carrying on among you, on the quiet! You're going to bolt off with some young feller or other, I'll bet a halfpenny!"

"No, no, indeed I am not; and if you'll assist me——"

"I don't see why I should at all! What am I to get by it?"

"I shall be most grateful to you."

"That ain't filling! What'll you stand?"

"I do not understand you."

"That's the old kid, that is! You don't want to!"

"If there is anything that I can give you——"

"Well, that's more reasonable! But what have you got besides what's in the bundle?"

"Nothing: all my money's there."

"Ah!" said the young man, with a broad grin, "then it will be handier if I help myself!"

Cecily regarded him in terror. What was he going to do?

He was opening the bundle.

"Stop, stop!" she cried. "How dare you? Would you rob me?"

"What do you mean by rob? Did not you say I might have it?"

"No, you know I did not. Put it down, or I will scream for assistance!"

"Not so green! Why should you scream? You'll get ketched yourself if you do!"

"Wretch, it is all I have in the world!"

"It's a precious sight more than I have, anyhow!"

"You would not have the heart to take it!"

"I should be a precious fool if I didn't!"

She saw that he meant what he said. There was no way of preserving her property unless she jumped down and struggled with him for it. But, as I have said, the leap was an awkward one for a lady to take. Most likely she would stumble. To slide out was worse. But to stop where she was, and hesitate any longer, was to tamely submit to be robbed.

When she was making up her mind to risk all, and make a spring, the young man stopped in his occupation of unfastening a knot, and listened to what he seemed to think was the sound of approaching footsteps.

For a moment, Cecily hoped that his fears might

be founded on truth, that some one was coming; but instantly afterwards came the reflection, if any one came she would be discovered in what must appear a very suspicious position. If it were a policeman, she might be taken into custody; i' it were some one from the convent, a worse fate awaited her.

Whoever it was, the young man seemed in no humour to wait for them, and catching up the bundle under his arm, ran off as fast as his legs could carry him in an opposite direction.

Without waiting another moment, Cecily gathered her skirts about her and sprang from the window.

She alighted safely upon her feet, and followed in pursuit of the thief as quickly as she was able; but she was not able to compete with him, for by this time he was scaling a wall, and in a minute afterwards was in the streets.

It required all her strength, and it sorely bruised her hands and strained her wrists in the process, to drag open the heavy gates, the rusty bolts of which refused for a long time to come forth from their sockets.

When at last she conquered the difficulty, and had also got out into the open street, he was nowhere to be seen.

Day was beginning to break, but the morning was dark and foggy, and it was difficult to make out the nature of any object at twenty yards distance.

He was gone. She was robbed.

There was no hope of recovering her property.

But for a long while she could not believe this to be the case; but in a despairing sort of way, and sobbing as she went, she hurried on up one street and down another, until at length, worn out with anxiety and fatigue, she sank down upon a doorstep, covered her face with her hands, and sobbed as though her heart were breaking.

How long she sat thus it is difficult to say; she could scarcely tell herself: she felt very languid and weary, and quite unable to make any exertion.

She had had the presence of mind before quitting her cell upon the first occasion, before she met with the priest, to put on a large black cloak, which to some extent concealed the singularity of the costume she wore underneath, and she had removed the remarkable head-dress which it was the habit of the nuns to wear. Being only a noviciate, she had not been shorn of her flowing locks, so that there was nothing unsightly in the appearance of her head when this covering was removed. Upon the contrary, it was a very beautiful head, with soft, silky tresses, black as the raven's wing.

Some of her hair during her rapid course had fallen from the handkerchief loosely bound round it.

This, and her crouching position as she sat huddled up half-fainting upon the doorstep, attracted the notice of a policeman who came by upon his beat, stamping his feet upon the pavement to keep them warm; for he found the morning raw and chilly, and he was half wishing that a "case" would turn up to put a little life into him.

He was looking out, was this worthy man, for a stray Italian boy with white mice or guinea pigs, whom he might have the pleasure of waking up with his toe, or of rousing by a sharp pull of the ear, or of suddenly saluting with a shower of buffets, as it is the custom sometimes of the police (the very bad ones—I mean in the double Z division) to do when they can find a little boy to be kicked and cuffed with impunity.

"If I come across one of them chaps," said this policeman to himself, "I'll make him tingle."

The worthy guardian of the peace went on to say, in the words of the ancient Robert Ridley that he would make his eyeballs jingle, and he was further expressing himself poetically and menacingly when his gaze alighted upon the form of Cecily crouching in the doorway.

"Ah! it's one of them women," said the officer; "she'll do as well."

And he set his teeth and quickened his pace, eager to carry out his little plan of persecution.

"One of them!" Whom did he mean? One of those unhappy beings who wander homeless and friendless through the streets of our mighty Babylon. A class in which there exists more misery and wretchedness of every description than among any other order: misery of the mind, and of the heart, and of the body; remorse, disease, hunger, the disgust of self, enmity with the world, memory's agony and futurity's despair, extinction of hope here and hereafter, and horror and anguish in the very fire of passion.

One of these it was, he thought, and so a being whom he could ill-use with impunity—whom he could ill-treat without any fear of disagreeable consequences—for who in the world is there to befriend such as these?

The policeman laid his hand upon her shoulder and shook her roughly.

"Now, then!" he said; "what are you doing here?"

She looked up at him in a vacant and appealing sort of way, as though she did not understand what he said.

Thinking, perhaps, that a good shaking might be beneficial to her under the circumstances, he proceeded to give her a shaking to the best of his ability.

She was too weak to make much resistance, and too terrified by his violence to know what she ought to do, but she indignantly freed herself of his hold on her, and rose to her feet.

"This won't do, you know," said he, "and so you needn't try it on. I should advise you not to try it on. You may take my word for it that you'll get yourself into trouble if you do, and so just leave it off."

Cecily endeavoured to walk away, to get out of his reach. But she was weak and feeble. She had not proceeded more than a dozen yards before a sudden helplessness and languor crept over her.

She tottered and would have fallen had she not caught at a lamp-post for support.

The policeman eyed her fixedly. When he saw this movement a grim smile crept over his face.

"Oh that's it, is it?" said he to himself.

He had made up his mind at once. There could only be one way of accounting for this unsteady gait.

The woman must be intoxicated; that was the only solution which the worthy constable was capable of. And upon this supposition he argued further—"If she is intoxicated, she ought to be locked up. If I lock her up, I shall make a case out of her. If I make a case out of her, it will be a trifle in my pocket. If by any chance she doesn't happen to be tipsy, as I suppose she is, it will still be a trifle in my pocket. Anyhow, here goes!"

He, therefore, pursued the shrinking girl, and again seizing her by the arm, pushed her roughly forward.

"Move on!" he said; "I've warned you once,

and if you don't take notice of what I say, it will be the worse for you."

"Oh, sir!" Cecily replied, "I am afraid I cannot walk much further. I feel very ill, and I have nowhere to apply to for shelter. What am I to do?"

"How am I to know what you are to do?" asked the policeman gruffly. "I must say it is like your impertinence to put such a question to an officer of the peace."

"But you are the right person to apply to, I should think!" Cecily said.

"Don't argue with me!" the man rejoined. "If I'd my way, I'd stick the lot of you into the stocks! Whatever they have done away with whipping at the cart's tail for, is more than I can understand! Come, move on, I tell you!"

"Oh, sir, where am I to go to? where can I find a night's lodging?"

"You know where, well enough! You'd have no trouble in finding one if you wanted to, I'll be bound!"

"Indeed I do not!"

"Then I'll find you one at the police-station!"

Having delayed thus long in the execution of what he facetiously termed his duty, the policeman seized the unfortunate girl by the shoulder, and half pushed and half dragged her along with him.

She was so utterly confounded and amazed by this savage and unprovoked assault, and so wholly incapable of accounting for it, that for some time she offered no resistance to his violence, but suffered him to drag her on in silence down a dark quiet by-street, which probably led towards the police-station.

However, she did not appear to go quite fast enough to please the policeman, for he growled deep curses betwixt his teeth, and the expression of his face betokened an amount of half smothered ferocity which terrified her; and, seeing it, she began to struggle to free herself from his grasp.

"Come on!" he growled, fiercer than ever.

"Release me!"

"Come on, I say!"

"Release me!"

"It will be worse for you a good deal if you give me any more of your nonsense! As it is, I'll get you twenty-eight days hard labour! I think that'll take a little of the bounce out of you; and if it doesn't, I can accommodate you next time with a little more! Curse your squeaking! Come on!"

But though she scarcely understood the meaning of his words, both by reason of her inexperience and the giddy weakness which oppressed her and rendered her half unconscious of what was going on around her, she understood sufficiently well to make out that he was dragging her to prison, and was going to prefer some false charge against her, which she, in her friendless and unprotected state, would be wholly unable to refute; and the dread attendant upon this knowledge caused her to struggle with increased violence and to utter a piercing shriek for help.

"Help! help! help!"

Her cries echoed through the lonely street, and were borne far away upon the still morning air.

The policeman grew every moment more angry. He fancied that he could hear footsteps approaching in the distance, and a door opening in the same street.

Assistance was, perhaps, close at hand. Some one might interfere with him.

He grew furious at the thought; for there is nothing so likely to increase a bully's cruelty as interference.

By this time he had made up his mind that, cost him what it would, he would take her into custody.

She shrieked and struggled more than ever.

He found that her strength was growing too much for him unaided, and her cries were bringing spectators to the spot.

There was only one way of conquering her.

Before any one came—before there were any spectators—it must be done.

He raised his fist, and struck her a heavy blow upon the side of the head.

It was, perhaps, a heavier blow than he at first intended; for he was so carried away by his fury, that he scarcely knew what he did.

It was a cruel, crushing blow, which felled her to the earth.

With a piercing cry she sank down insensible.

On the spot where she fell, she lay motionless.

The policeman, with his fist yet raised in the air, stood over her. But the next moment he himself had received a heavy blow, which sent him staggering half a dozen yards forward, until he dropped down upon his hands and knees half-stunned.

CHAPTER XXXVII.

THE POLICEMAN'S VICTIM.—A WHOLESALE SCRIMMAGE.—THE RESCUE.—A HOT-BED OF CRIME.—THE CELEBRATED DUMB FORTUNE TELLER.

The person who had thus come to the rescue of the policeman's victim was a tall, strongly-built man, with a bronzed face and a huge beard. His hat he wore carelessly upon one side of his head, and he was smoking a cigar; his left hand he had not removed from his trousers' pocket; and when he had dealt the constable the staggering blow, which had sent him down upon his hands and knees, the stranger put the other hand, with which he had dealt it, back into its place in his other pocket for a moment, as though the habit of lounging thus was so habitual with him, that it was impossible otherwise to dispose of his hands when not actively employed. But it was only for an instant that he kept them there; and then advancing towards Cecily's inanimate form, he raised it in his arms.

But scarcely had he done so, and his eyes had rested upon the pale features of the fainting girl, than he uttered a loud exclamation of astonishment, and gave a great start, as though something in the features before him astounded and horrified him.

For more than a minute his eyes were fixed upon the cold, white face before him, his own features rigid and motionless, and his eyes dilated to the uttermost.

At last his emotion found utterance in words, and his bloodless quivering lips muttered almost inaudibly.

"What mystery is this?" he said. "It is, and yet it is not. Could any one in the world believe that such a likeness could exist? I myself would never have believed it, had I been told. I could not believe it now, if I had not seen the other living likeness of her so lately. Is it fate that has thrown me in with this woman, the very counterpart of the one I am seeking; and if so, for what reason?"

The policeman by this time had scrambled to his feet, rubbing the back of his head; and now taking his rattle from his pocket, began to ply it with all his might.

This aroused the stranger from his reverie to a sense of danger.

"Now, then," said he impatiently; "what are you doing that for?"

But the policeman, instead of replying, worked away harder than ever at his rattle. Footsteps were rapidly approaching; in another moment, three or four more policemen made their appearance at the end of the street; and they ran forward, and without a word, surrounded the pugilistic stranger.

"Hold him!" cried the constable, who had been knocked down, and who, for a very good reason, did not wish to put himself forward too conspicuously; "hold him!" cried he. "Knock him down! Take him up! He has been trying to murder me!"

"Stand back!" shouted the stranger, at the same time throwing himself into an attitude, which in a man of his proportions was so very threatening, that the policemen felt a little uncertain as to which of them ought to rush in first. "Hold! The first man who lays a hand upon me shall smart for it. That scoundrel was ill-using this poor girl in the most ruffianly way, when I came up; and if I had not come in time, there's no knowing whether he would not have killed her."

"Its a lie!" cried the policeman from the back; "the woman fell down and hit her head. She's blind drunk besides, and that's her flash cove. It's a made up a thing between them, and he's trying to rescue her from me when I have her in custody."

"We'll see whether your tale or mine will be believed," said the stranger. "Here, some of you, help to carry this poor girl. You need not mind me; I'll come of my own accord."

But this arrangement was not deemed quite satisfactory.

The policemen whispered among themselves. Their testimony would have more weight if it were brought forward against a person in their custody. It would not be wise policy to allow this person to walk of his own free-will to the police station, and prefer a charge against a member of the force.

They therefore, after a momentary consideration, made a general rush upon him, and endeavoured to pin him against some area railings close to which he was at the moment standing.

A moment before, the stranger had placed the senseless form of Cecily upon a doorstep close at hand, so as to have his hands at liberty in case of emergency.

There is very little doubt that had any one of the policemen attempted to tackle the stranger alone, he would have found him much more than a match; but this general rush was overpowering from its weight. Five policemen converting themselves into living battering-rams, and simultaneously going full-butt into a man's stomach, was enough to knock the wind out of the biggest giant alive.

They knocked the stranger, gasping, backwards. At the same time, they knocked open the area gate against which he leant.

The stranger and the five policemen shot through the aperture, and alighted in a confused mass upon the lid of a large water-butt with a violence which carried all before it.

In the natural course of events, carrying the water-butt with other things, the policemen found themselves in a moment completely saturated, and after a desperate struggle to gain an upright position, and shake off the, as it were, drowning grasp which their companions had made upon them, they scrambled to their feet again like so many drowned rats, and began to look for their prisoner.

But the stranger, being the first one to fall through the gate, had fallen free of the rest, for he had fallen close down by the side of the wall, and they had shot over him.

Consequently, while they were struggling in a confused mass, apparently all legs and arms without heads or bodies, their would-be prisoner had scrambled out, and climbed up again into the street, shutting the area gate behind him.

And now he paused for a moment, uncertain whether he should carry the girl away with him, or whether it would be best to leave her. If he left her, would she not be certain to meet with ill-usage at the policemen's hands?—but if he took her, would it not impede his flight?—and certainly, as soon as they had scrambled out, they would give him a stiff run for it. But before he could make up his mind what he was going to do, one of the policemen began to climb out of the area by the aid of a cellar door, and shouted to his fellows to come on.

But his progress was speedily cut short by a tremendous bonneter dealt him by the man with the beard, which sent him head-over-heels backwards on to his companions. Again they all rolled about in company with the over-turned water-butt in the most pitiable plight.

By this time the awful disturbance which these tumbles had occasioned caused numerous windows to be opened up and down the street, and any amount of sleepy-looking heads, with or without night-caps, frilled and plain, to be thrust forth in search of information with respect to the cause of the rumpus.

The inmates of the house itself were all aroused; and an elderly spinster lady, who was its proprietor, springing out of bed, and flinging open the window, emptied the contents of the first vessel which came to hand upon the heads of the unfortunate constables struggling confused below—a politeness to which they responded with a loud yell of indignation.

Profiting by the momentary panic which succeeded, the stranger turned to fly, and reluctantly determined to leave Cecily where she was, for he saw that to attempt to rescue her also would only be to make certain of the capture of both. He took to his heels, and very soon put a couple of hundred yards between himself and his pursuers.

A general rush was made after him as soon as the drenched constables succeeded in escaping from their present dangerous quarters; but by this time he had turned a corner of the street and engulfed himself in a labyrinth of narrow lanes and alleys, where all hope of finding him was soon abandoned.

Meanwhile, poor Cecily was left in the power of the police. Having lost their would-be captive, they turned upon the unfortunate girl with a determination to make her suffer for the misdeeds of her would-be liberator.

But just at the moment that they were about to drag her away, a new friend happily appeared upon the scene. This was a stout, fussy little man, who came from one of the houses opposite, and who professed to have been a witness of all that had occurred.

"Stop! stop! stop!" cried the little man in an authoritative tone. "What are you about? What are you going to do? Why are you ill-using that young woman?"

"What do you say?" asked one of the policemen, turning round upon him fiercely, for he did not relish the interruption. "Do you want a night's lodging, too?"

"I don't want any insolence!" said the little man, backed up by the presence of several of his neighbours; "and I shan't put up with it!"

"You'd better take yourself off, then!"

"I shall stop here as long as I choose!"

"Move on!"

"I shan't!"

"You shall!"

"I've a right to be here!"

"You have not!"

"It is my street!"

"That's got nothing to do with it!"

The little man was getting extremely irrate; but perhaps bearing in mind the melancholy fate which generally befalls all those who are rash enough to take the law in their own hands or kick against it, he would in all probability have subsided into quiescence after a little more grumbling, and have taken himself off as desired, only, most unfortunately, his better half, a large woman with a great frilled night-cap and a broad check dressing-gown, rushed frantically upon the scene, and clasping her arms round the little man's waist as though he required as much holding in as a fiery racer, screamed pathetically, "Don't, Johnny dear—don't! Don't hit him, for my sake! You'll only get hurt—I am sure you will; for you know you can't fight." It might have been true enough, and probably was; but who could have borne the loud derisive giggle which the remark called forth?

The little man turned purple. He might not have had any more strength than a moderate-sized bluebottle; but what little he had he determined to exhaust upon this occasion in the defence of the cause he had somewhat rashly espoused. If it had not been for the giggles of the spectators and of the ill-timed interference of his better half, the little man might easily have got out of the mess he had got into by his ill-advised attack, but now there was nothing left for him but to put a bold face upon the matter.

"You go in again, my dear," said he, "and I will show these fellows who they have to deal with."

It would be tedious to narrate particularly all that was said upon either side upon the occasion. But the result which should be arrived at, without any of the bystanders exactly understanding how, was the forcible abduction of the fussy little gentleman, who was carried away between four policemen, kicking violently and vowing vengeance, only to be locked up the remainder of the night in company with a drunken sweep and a couple of pickpockets, and next day to be fined heavily and severely reprimanded for assaulting the police in the execution of their duty.

But this diversion in favour of the luckless little man had the effect of causing Cecily's deliverance.

Whilst the dispute was at its hottest, and blows instead of words were being freely exchanged between the combatants, a woman, who had been one of the spectators of the scene almost from its commencement, suddenly laid her hand upon Cecily's shoulder, and shaking her roughly, though not unkindly, whispered eagerly in her ears, "Now is the time, why don't you go?"

But the girl scarcely understood what she said. Again the other strove to arouse her from her torpor.

"Come, come!" she said; "no one is looking at you. Escape!"

The last word alone fell upon Cecily's ear; or, at least, I should say the last word alone she understood.

She rose to her feet at the sound, and exerting all the power at her command, assisted by her friend and another woman, who helped to cover her retreat, she quietly slipped out of the crowd at the back of the policemen, who were at that moment very busily engaged struggling and fighting with the little gentleman who had questioned their authority.

Rapidly turning the corner of the street, the women supported Cecily upon either side, and urged her into a run.

Then plunging into the same labyrinth of narrow lanes and alleys in which the stranger with the beard had dived a while ago, they hurried her on, down one turning and up another, and through a number of dark, squalid courts and filthy by-streets, all apparently in the last stage of decay, until they stopped at length at a lonely spot, which appeared to be something between a deserted brick-field and a very undesirable bit of ground, which its owners were anxious, though unable, to dispose of for building purposes.

Under a ruined archway, which seemed to have been built to support a road above it, the women stopped and rested their companion, in a sitting posture, upon a heap of bricks, which had been roughly fashioned into the semblance of an arm-chair.

"Well," said one of them speaking to her companion, "we are safe."

"It was a close shave for it."

"The Bobbies were so bent upon locking up that poor little man, they had no eyes for anything else."

"What has she done, do you think?"

"You'd better ask her."

"I think she's fainted. Here, my dear, hold up. What's the matter with you?"

But Cecily made no reply. The excitement of the scenes through which she had just passed, and the exertions which she had been obliged to make, and to which she was so unaccustomed, were too much for a frame already weakened by illness, and she had now swooned away; and to the repeated questions as to how she felt, what was the matter with her, and what could they do for her, she made no reply; and such remedies as they were able to apply, in the hopes of restoring her to consciousness, proved fruitless.

The two women consulted together.

"What's to be done with her?"

"We'd better have left her where she was."

"Much better there than here, for she'd have had a night's lodging; and they'd have taken care of her perhaps the next day, if she hasn't done anything very bad, and she is really ill."

"There's no doubt about her being ill, and we ought to get her a bed somewhere if we could."

"We can't get her a bed, though, without any money, and I suppose you've none?"

"I've about twopence, and I want it myself."

"I've nothing at all; but if we had another penny we might have got her a bed at old Crozier's. He'd let her sit by the fire, I dare say, if we give him the twopence; and that'll be better, poor thing, than shivering out here in the cold and damp."

"How you talk! I want the money myself, I tell you, and I am not going to spend it. You've got so very liberal all at once with other people's twopences. If it was your own it would be different."

"Don't put yourself out about it," said the other woman impatiently; "perhaps she has got some money in her own pocket. We'll look."

They stooped down over Cecily's prostrate form, and one of them raised the cloak which hitherto had effectually concealed the nun's dress that she wore. Upon catching sight of it the women both uttered an exclamation of astonishment.

"What do you call that?"

"It's a fancy dress, I should think. Perhaps she's been to a masquerade?"

"Nonsense! She's a nun, and she must have escaped out of a convent."

"What convent? I don't think it's at all likely. Perhaps it's a reformatory."

"Well, let's feel in her pocket."

They felt there, but did not find anything of any great value.

The only articles which her pockets contained were a Mass-book and some beads.

Neither of these was deemed to be of sufficient value to be converted into a night's lodging. But one of the women, after some argument, proposed that they should take her to the house of the Crozier already mentioned, and endeavour to work upon his charitable feelings, and induce him to take the homeless wanderer in for the night.

"One thing's sure," the kindest-hearted of the women said; "if she's left here, she'll die, to a certainty; and then her death will be, in a manner of speaking, on our hands."

"For goodness sake, then," said the other, "let's take her to Crozier's."

They raised her from the spot where they had placed her, and supported her, as well as they could, back by the way they had come, to a vile alley, almost more villanous in aspect than any of the others they had passed through.

It was truly a frightful place—an ill-smelling, evil-looking pestiferous quarter;—a place capable of inspiring even the bravest heart with fear.

Very clearly the inhabitants of this vile slum were far from respectable. At this late—or, rather, early hour—when day was dawning, several of the windows were lit up, and some of the doors stood partly open, showing lights within.

Sounds of loud and boisterous revelry in many cases emanated therefrom; whilst here and there the sounds of contention, drunken brawling, and deadly strife were plainly audible.

Down one reeking alley, of a most cut-throat aspect, issued a fearful din of curses, cries, and groans; and more than once, as the women walked along, a woman's piercing shriek—a heartrending wail, full of intense bitterness and anguish, was wafted towards them on the damp and chilly morning air.

However fear-inspiring, though, this neighbourhood might be to strangers, these two women appeared to be perfectly well acquainted with its peculiarities, and the many strange noises which greeted them on every side they treated with indifference, and continued their course, chatting to one another about their own private affairs, which, by the way, I do not think possessed sufficient interest to warrant me repeating them for the edification of my readers.

The low threepenny lodging-house to which they were bending their steps was situated down a dark, unwholesome-looking yard, leading out of the noisome spot where they were at present walking.

At the corner of this yard, and at the top of a flight of half a dozen steps, which led down into it, stood a dilapidated shop and house, which, although propped up in several places by large beams, threatened every moment to fall over upon the houses opposite. Indeed, this grimy edifice gave one very much the notion that it was taking a nap, and had nodded its head towards its knees in such a way that nothing but the vigorous jerk backwards would save its equilibrium.

There was a good deal of ornament about the front of the shop, and a number of bills stuck up upon its shutters, most of which were ornamented with glaring cartoons, although, in the uncertain light which prevailed in this very unenticing neighbourhood, it would have been a matter of considerable difficulty to have discovered what they were about.

With the aid of daylight, though, it would have been seen that they bore reference to the trade in rags and bottles, bones, and kitchen-stuff carried on by the enterprising tradesmen who resided there.

According to these announcements, this was the shop where the highest price was given for every imaginable kind of objectionable articles. Just exactly what you and I would have been most desirous of getting rid of, Mr. Garbidge was eager to buy.

Every kind of revolting dirt seemed to be eagerly accumulated by this most acquisitive of tradesmen.

Nothing came wrong to him, and he bought eagerly all kinds of odds and ends which persons unaccustomed to such dealing would have supposed to be utterly worthless.

Something, though, more remarkable than Mr. Garbidge's stock-in-trade, or his highly-coloured pictures of harlequins, columbines, clowns, and pantaloons, lords and ladies, and profusely decorated military officers, all somehow or other deeply interested in the sale of kitchen-stuff, to which I desire to call the reader's attention.

This was a small board—a black ground with white letters, over the private door of the house, and which contained this legend:—

"JOHN JEER,
"The Dumb Astrologer."

The reason that I call the reader's attention to this announcement, is because it was to it that one of the women directed the notice of the other, at the same time saying, "That's where the man lives I told you of. It's where Sal went the other day, when she wanted to buy some of that stuff."

"Did he sell any?"

"He wanted too much for it: besides, she was frightened at him, and at what he said."

"But he don't talk, does he? I thought he was deaf and dumb."

"He don't talk in the regular way, but he does somehow with his fingers; and Sal says he swears awful."

But just at this moment the companion motioned to the speaker to be silent, and pointed to the door which had led to the conversation.

It had just opened, and from it came two persons—one, a stout, elderly woman, rather showily dressed, but somewhat dowdy in appearance; the other, a short, dark man, with long black hair, hanging wildly about his face, and almost covering his eyes.

"That's him," said one of the women in a whisper; "but who's the other?"

"It's Mother Raddle, as I live. Where the dickens can they be going to at this time?"

"Come back into the shade here, where they can't see you, and we will watch them."

This plan, however, was frustrated, for the man catching sight of them, in the act of drawing back into the shadow of a doorway, nudged his companion to indicate their whereabouts by a jerk of his thumb.

The woman turned hastily round to look at them, and her face exhibited signs of recognition.

"Who's that?" she said. "Ah, to be sure, I thought I knew you! It's Nancy, isn't it?"

"Yes," one of the women replied.

"And who's that with you?"

"It's a friend of mine."

"And the other one?"

"A poor young thing, who has been taken very poorly in the street, and would have been in the police's hands by this time, and locked up, most likely, if I hadn't just chanced to have come across her at the right time."

And Miss Nancy proceeded to narrate the circumstances connected with Cecily's escape, with which the reader is already acquainted.

While she was speaking, the woman who had made the inquiry was eagerly examining the face of the half-insensible girl.

"Bring her out under the lamp," said she presently; and when this had been done, she continued her scrutiny with increased earnestness.

"She's very beautiful," the elderly woman remarked, "or would be, if she wasn't quite so pale and ill. I wonder what's the matter with her? I suppose it's nothing so very serious, but she wants a little rest and quietness. Where are you going to take her?"

"We were all going to ask old Crozier if he'd let her rest a bit in his kitchen, by the side of his fire."

"The place is almost sure to be full, and I don't think it's any good your going. But I'll tell you what."

"What?"

"Mr. Jeer here, perhaps, can take her in for a night or so. Mr. Garbidge is away, and he's got a room to spare."

The two younger women looked at one another at hearing this proposition in rather an uncertain way, as though they were not quite sure whether it was the best thing that they could do for their unfortunate charge. Indeed, it was not, by any means, the place or the guardianship which they would have chosen; but being somewhat desirous of getting Cecily off their hands, they at length accepted, and helped to convey her into the house.

Before doing so, the elderly woman explained, by means of signs, to her male companion, what was desired. He nodded his head. An ape-like grin which illuminated his dark and sinister face, might have implied either a welcome to the wanderer, or foreboded some coming "evil." He nodded his head, though, several times with great rapidity, and limping back towards his house, for he was lame of one leg, and hopped about with a bird-like motion, that was anything but graceful, he opened the door.

Then they carried Cecily into the house.

One of the women remained outside, but the one called Nancy went in to assist in carrying the insensible girl.

She did not go further than the passage; for the man, making an impatient gesture, or rather a gesture of warning to his female companion, she, Mother Raddle, stopped Nancy as she was about to ascend the stairs, and told her that that would do.

"We'll take every care of her," said Mrs. Raddle, with a grin, elbowing the other towards the door.

"I'll call in in the morning," said Nancy, "to see how she is."

"As you choose; but there's no particular occasion. She'll be quite safe where she is."

"Anyhow, I'll call in."

"As you please."

Nancy had no other course open to her than to retire; and she went out slowly by the street door, which was closed upon her immediately by Mrs. Raddle.

The two women stood silently upon the pavement outside the house, with their eyes turned towards the windows.

All was silent within—silent and dark. They expected to have heard some sound—to have seen a light in one of the front rooms, either upon the first or second floors: but they heard and saw nothing.

"I don't know that she would have come to any particular good in old Mother Raddle's den."

"You're right there. It's rather a bad day for anybody who falls into that old lady's clutches."

"Though it was better that she should be there than with that horrid man. He is a perfect monster."

"You were going to tell me about him if they hadn't come up just at that minute."

"I will tell you now. I suppose it's no good waiting any longer."

"They seemed to be going out somewhere. Perhaps now they have changed their minds. I don't think we shall do any good by stopping; but I shall certainly come round in the morning. Let's go now."

"Do you think they will harm her?"

"I would not trust them."

"But do you know, I think you are prejudiced against Mr. Jeer. He is not, perhaps, as bad as you suppose."

"Isn't he? Well, I should not like to trust him. Haven't you heard of poor young girls being kidnapped into that house?"

"Well, I think I have, but I can't quite remember."

"Don't you recollect the inquest upon that poor creature who died there about a month ago?"

"No. What was that?"

"Well, they did say——"

Here the girl glanced round her cautiously. Then whispered.

"They did say——"

"What?"

"It is almost too frightful for even such women as we are to talk about!"

"Nonsense! I'm dying to learn the particulars!"

"I hardly like to relate them."

"Is it something so very awful?"

"It is, indeed!"

"Why you quite terrify me! I never dreamt he was such a wretch!"

"There is nothing you can say of him bad enough! Have you not read about him in the newspapers?"

"I read something about a seduction."

"Under circumstances of great atrocity, was it not?"

"It was very bad, I believe. But he was acquitted. But come, let me have your story."

"It will make your blood run cold, but you shall hear it!"

CHAPTER XXXVIII.

CERTAIN AWFUL OCCURRENCES WHICH BEFEL THE CAPTAIN—SHOWING HOW HE GOT OUT OF THE FRYING PAN INTO THE FIRE.

BUT instead of terrifying the reader with this tale of the dumb astrologer's depravity and atrocity, I will reserve it for a page or two; and though I reluctantly leave Sister Cecily in about the very worst hands that she could possibly have fallen into, I must necessarily do so for a short time while I go back to Captain Crockford.

As the Captain lay coiled up in a corner of the attic in a very uncomfortable attitude, his sleep was disturbed by a variety of very uncomfortable dreams.

He dreamt, at one time, that he was down the sewers again, and that he was condemned to live there for the rest of his life, never coming up except on Christmas Day and the Queen's birthday; and that he was obliged to gain a scanty supply of food by watching at the grating for any chance morsels that might be thrown down to him.

Then he dreamt that he had gone into the boot and shoe line; and then that he had somehow or other put a boot on over his head in a way that it threw him into a perspiration to comprehend, although he knew to his sorrow that the result of the act caused him the greatest distress. Then, again, he did not exactly know why, but he had to get the boot off before the husband of the lady, into whose house he had intruded, came in and caught him; and to get it off without cutting off his leg or his head, (he could not make out which it could be), was impossible.

Then the next cause of distress was that he desired to hide himself in a box, and couldn't, owing to it being several sizes too small for him; and, at last, when he did manage to get all the rest of him in, he could not manage to get in the foot, with the boot on.

Lastly, he dreamt that he had taken the veil, and was one of a hundred virgins in a convent where everybody wore plush unmentionables, and then he woke up, and looked about him.

He was not in a convent, or down a sewer, but he could almost have wished that he could have been in either place rather than where he was.

At first he was by no means sure of the reality of the scene to which he opened his eyes.

He was in a garret, perfectly destitute of furniture. He was wrapped up in a blanket, a sheet, and a counterpane. He had on no other clothes of any kind except a waistcoat and a pair of bright yellow plush breeches.

He remembered that he was in a hotel. How long he had been there, or what time of day it was, he had not the least idea.

What he should do next was a question which caused him to tremble when he asked it of himself; but it was very sure that he couldn't stop there for ever, and if he did not make up his mind to commit suicide he must make up his mind to face the inhabitants of the hotel.

He might, he thought, possibly escape out of the window, and over the roof. But where to? What was the good of running fresh risk? No, he had better open the door and descend the stairs.

"My plan will be," said he to himself, "to find some bed-room, get into bed, ring the bell, and ask to see the landlord. Then, I can make some kind of explanation, the Lord only knows what, and ask him to send to my house for some clothes and money."

He was inclined at first to wrap himself up in the counterpane, by way of a cloak; but then, when he came to think of it, he did not like to do so, because it would connect him with the bed-clothes robbery, if the counterpane were found in the room to which he was going.

This, however, could not be avoided, for it was impossible for him to walk about with nothing on but that absurd waistcoat, and that ridiculous pair of breeches. And he folded the counterpane over across his breast and over one shoulder as gracefully as he could, after the fashion of a bandit's cloak at a theatre.

Then he opened the door, and, with his heart in his mouth, set off upon his travels.

There was no room upon the floor upon which the attic was situated in which he thought it advisable to take refuge, and there was no room provided with a bell.

He, therefore, cautiously descended to the floor below, but when he arrived upon the bottom step but two he stood still suddenly, with an expression of terror upon his face, and his heart palpitated more than ever.

Close by him, just round the bend of the stairs, at most not half a dozen yards off, there was a woman employed in scouring the floor.

Where he stood he could not see her, but he heard the sound of the brush, and he heard the sound of her voice, as she softly sang to herself a hymn tune.

The Captain peeped round the corner with the greatest caution.

"If she has only got her head turned the other way," he thought, "I may get past her."

No such luck!

Her face was turned towards him. Luckily, however, she was not looking up. Her eyes were bent upon the floor, which she was busy scrubbing.

"I shall never get past," said he. "What's to be done?"

He sat down upon the steps to think about it, at the same time silently rubbing his knees, for they did not feel over-warm.

She was scrubbing away with all her might, and making a great noise. He felt certain that she would not have heard his footfall if she did not happen to look up. But then she was almost certain to look up, because she paused every minute or so to plunge the scrubbing brush into the pail; and then it was her custom, as far as he could judge by the stealthy glances he had cast at her, to look all round in a meditative sort of way and rest for a moment or two after her labour.

If he could calculate well and make a sudden plunge past her just at the very moment after she had dipped the scrubbing brush, he would be able, perhaps, to get up the passage and into one of the bed-rooms before she raised her head.

But that depended upon two things. First of all, that the stairs did not creak as he came down. Secondly, that one of the bed-room doors chanced to be open.

He crept down upon the points of his toes until he got to the bottom step, keeping all the while close to the wall, so that, in the position in which the woman knelt, she was unable to see him.

Then he waited until the time when she should dip the scrubbing brush again.

The reader, I feel quite sure, will be inclined to think that I am departing from the strict truth when I say that the servant, instead of dipping her brush immediately, as she had always done before, took it into her head to sit down and rest awhile; and the unfortunate Captain, balancing himself on one leg, and waiting until it should please her to resume her work, endured a perfect agony.

She did resume it, however, at last; and he stepped down into the passage. In holding his breath he bit his lips almost till the blood came. He did not look round at her; he hardly dare do so; but he went on tip-toe up the passage until he reached the first door. He tried it—without success. The second also. Then the third.

Muttering a deep curse, he moved on to the next.

But as he placed his hand upon the handle, an exclamation behind him caused him suddenly to pause, and his heart to go pit-a-pat with apprehension.

He was afraid to turn round. He could not see who had spoken, but he knew very well who it was.

"Lauks-a-mercy!" some one said; "who on earth is that?"

The Captain twisted round.

"It's all right, my good girl," he said.

The girl, who was a rather elderly maiden, between forty and fifty, stared with all her might and looked very much horrified.

"Oh! I shall scream," she said, however, more to herself than to the Captain.

"For God's sake, don't!" replied Crockford, "there isn't the least occasion for it."

"Oh! I must."

"But I don't see why," persisted the Captain, endeavouring to reason, and at the same time approaching a little nearer.

This was the worst thing he could do, for the elderly maiden's alarm became intense.

"I shall faint!" she said, apparently addressing the pail, or the scrubbing brush.

"Don't do that," said the Captain, persuasively; "there's no good in fainting. What is there to faint about?"

"Good ivans!" exclaimed the ancient maiden; "he hasn't got no things on!"

"I assure you, miss, it isn't my fault that I am not more suitably attired; but as far as I go I am quite correct."

"Don't come any nearer me, or I shall squeal!"

"For goodness sake don't; you'll alarm all the house."

"What are your intentions, horrible man?"

"They are honourable, upon my soul they are!" gasped the Captain.

"I don't believe you."

"If you will only allow me to tell you a half quarter of what I have suffered since this time yesterday."

"I won't listen to you!"

"But look here."

"I won't!"

"I assure you, upon my honour——"

"Go away!"

The Captain all this while was trying one door after another to find one that was open, but unsuccessfully.

At last, in desperation, he turned round and again addressed the antique vestal.

"I haven't got any money in my pocket," said he; "but I will stand five pounds willingly if you can get me out of this scrape."

"What do you want me to do?"

"I want you to hide me somewhere, and send to my lodgings for my clothes."

"But where do you suppose I can hide you?"

"How the deuce am I to know? You've got a room somewhere, I suppose? Suppose you lock me up in it?"

"Good ivans! Does the man suppose I am going to conceal him in my apartment?"

"Well, you know, there is five pounds hanging to it, if that's any object?"

"I can't do it—it's impossible! It's more than my place is worth!"

"But look here! you know," the Captain persevered; "nobody need knew anything about it."

"But, good ivans! isn't there my conscience?"

"Bother your conscience!—isn't there five pounds?"

"Five pounds!" repeated the maiden, contemptuously.

"Hang her impudence!" said the Captain, to himself. "It's about a year's wages, in the regular course of business!" Then he added, "How much would you like, if you please? Whatever you do, don't be afraid to open your mouth!"

The ancient maiden paused to consider awhile.

"Where's the money?" said she.

"Well," said the Captain, with some hesitation, "I haven't got it here. I want you to send for it with my clothes."

This proposition was not at first very favourably received. The ancient maiden, although a stickler for propriety, had yet a keen eye for the main chance. She wanted the money down. She did not believe in the Captain's possessing the private resources he professed to have at his command. He might certainly have another suit of clothes; but she did not put too much faith in his promise for five pounds.

But the Captain, I have already told you, had a persuasive tongue. He was a universal favourite with the ladies. However prejudiced they might be against him at first, they eventually believed him. Or, if they did not believe him, they did what he asked them to do, which was all he could reasonably have desired.

It is not therefore to be supposed that this poor faded damsel, this scrubber of floors and scourer of passages, could resist his fascinations. Besides, after all, he did not ask so very much of her. He wished only to be concealed for a short time, until she could despatch a messenger for some suitable apparel.

With what appeared to him to be a preposterous amount of giggling, and blushing, and maidenly objections, she led the way at last to a dingy little attic, situated not very far from that in which he had passed a portion of the night.

Into this she stowed him, with the strictest injunctions not to meddle with anything that the room contained, and on no account to look into the drawers and cupboards.

"You may depend upon me," said the Captain, intending to make a general tour of inspection as soon as the door was shut.

"For ivan's sake, don't make a noise."

"I'll hold my breath," said the Captain with a facetiously serious air.

The maiden then retired, and he was left to himself.

For a time all was silent, but not, however, for very long. He heard a sound of voices disputing loudly upon the floor below.

"I tell you it is ridiculous," he heard somebody say.

"I tell you it isn't."

"Do you take me for a fool, sir?"

"What else do you suppose I take you for?"

"You're a fellow!"

"You're another!"

"Am I?"

"Yes!"

"Indeed!"

"Oh!"

"Oh!"

The Captain began to get very much interested in this conversation, and he would have liked to have heard a little more of it, but unfortunately the ancient maiden, when she left him, had locked the door after her, and although he placed his ear close to the key-hole, he could not hear very much of what was going on.

A word or two here and there he caught, and the words which I have repeated, which happened to be spoken in a very loud and excited tone. But after these, several sentences were mumbled, of which he could make nothing at all. After that, one of the voices loudly exclaimed—"The person to whom the coats belong must be one of your servants, or anyhow must be somebody stopping in the house, and I insist upon an examination being made."

The Captain began to feel very uneasy. What coat were they talking about? It could be none other than that dreadful livery he had left in the bed-room, from which he had taken the blanket, sheet, and counterpane.

"I assure you, sir," the other voice continued, "that we shall not do any good in searching the house. I do not see what we can expect to find.

The livery does not belong to me, as I have told you already, and I have no livery servant at present stopping in my hotel. Nor, indeed, have I had for some time—several months at least."

"I don't know anything about that, but it's very sure that the person who stole my bedclothes was the owner of the coat, and I feel convinced that it was somebody in the house."

"But where do you suppose they got the coat from? I never saw any livery like it, and I don't think that it's at all likely that either of my servants or any of the guests could have had it in their possession. Anyhow, from the articles that were in the pockets, one would suppose that the owner of the coat would have come forward and claimed it. That brooch alone must be worth several pounds."

"Yes, I should think it was."

"It almost proves that it couldn't have belonged to a servant."

"I'll be hanged if I can tell who it could have belonged to."

"Well, I've told you several times that there's only one way of finding out."

"And what's that?"

"It is to search all the rooms, to see if we cannot find some trace of the robber."

"What do you hope to find, though?"

"Well, it can't be very unreasonable to expect to find the trousers and waistcoat."

"I haven't much hopes of our doing so."

"Anyhow, we shall find the bedclothes that were taken from my room; and if we had only looked last night when I wanted to, I'll stake my life we should have found the man who took them."

"We could not very well disturb everybody in the house, as I told you. However, come on now, and if we do find the man he shall smart for what he's done. I'll promise that."

The Captain felt anything but comfortable as he listened to this conversation.

He heard the footsteps of the talkers approaching in his direction, and presently he heard a door open in the same passage which contained the room in which he was concealed.

"It will be my turn, shortly," he thought. "Whatever shall I do? When they find this door locked they'll suspect there is somebody concealed inside. If the door wasn't locked I should have a better chance, for I might hide myself under the bed. But, as it is, they're sure to have the door broken open, if they can't get in any other way, and there is no escape for me. I am regularly in a corner."

The Captain heard the footsteps drawing nearer. They were now in the next room but one. In a minute or two more he expected them to be trying the handle of the door.

"Where can I get to?" he asked himself. "There are bars across the window. The chimney seems to be dreadfully small. And even if it was a regular size, I don't think I could climb up it. Besides, I suppose there is a chimney-pot on the top, and though I've gone through a good deal, I don't think I could go through that."

But he fancied he heard voices in the passage. Something must be done, and very shortly. An idea occurred to him. Although it was the most extraordinary and reckless proceeding, he had no alternative left, and must resort to it.

Upon the pillow of the bed there was a nightgown rolled up, and inside it a night-cap, with a large frill.

They belonged to the elderly virgin whose bedroom it was.

"If they come in I'll be ready for them," said the Captain, and proceeded to put on these articles of lady's apparel.

"I don't think these moustaches and whiskers do very well; they don't look quite feminine enough. However, the hair's all right," (he wore it parted down the middle), "and I must keep myself covered over."

Then, having put on the night-cap to his satisfaction, and tied the strings under his chin, he stepped into bed.

A minute afterwards, some one tried the door handle.

Then shook the lock, knocked at the panel, and called out, "Is anybody inside?"

"Could they have heard me?" thought the Captain; but he said nothing, and kept quite still.

"This is where the clothes are, I'll wager a pound," observed a voice outside.

"What's to be done?"

"Break the door open."

"No, don't do that; one of the keys of the other rooms will most likely fit it."

This statement proved to be correct. The Captain waited some time with great anxiety, and then the door was opened; and the landlord, a tall, thin man, and the guest, a short, stout man, thrust their heads in and looked around.

The Captain's back was turned towards them, the clothes were pulled up to his chin, and the frill of his cap was just visible.

As they entered, he snored.

The short man, who was in front, started back at the sound, and bumped his head up against the long man, who, in his turn, bumped his own head so sharply against the wall, that for a moment he saw several beds and any number of sparks.

Then both gentlemen beat a hasty retreat out into the passage.

"I say," said the long man, "there's somebody there."

"Where?" said the short man, who had not time to catch more than a very fleeting sight of the occupant of the room.

"In the bed."

"What is it?"

"I'm not quite sure, but by the frill on the night-cap——"

"Let's look again."

Both the short and long peeped in at the doorway. The Captain's broad shoulders looked broader than usual, in the position in which he was lying.

"It's a woman," said the long man; "though I don't know who; but who ever she is, she's a wopper."

"A remarkable fine woman," said the little man; "five foot six, I should think."

"Five foot six! Six or seven foot, you mean. She's a regular giantess."

The Captain, exploding with an internal laughter, made a clucking sound in his throat. Both gentlemen again beat a hasty retreat.

Outside the door they held a consultation.

What was going to be done next?

"That can't be the owner of the coat," said one.

"It is to be hoped she don't wear the rest of the livery, at any rate," said the other.

"But what puzzles me," the landlord continued, "is, who she can be for me not to know her."

"Don't you know whose room it is?"

"It's one of the housemaid's, but she's not at all that sort of build. Indeed, she's rather inclined to be spiky."

"What do you say," said the little man, "to waking her up?"

The landlord hardly approved of the notion, but he, nevertheless, assented to it, after a little hesitation; and together they then approached the door and put their heads inside the room. The delicate object of their curiosity, however, thinking they were gone, had popped up his head to look after them, holding the clothes up to his nose.

The two gentlemen were again upon the point of flight, but somehow they had so blocked themselves up in the door that they could not get out again in a moment, without tumbling over one another; and as the lady's eyes were fixed upon them, they thought it best, under the circumstances, to stay where they were. At least, that is to say, they hardly knew what to do, and stood panic-stricken.

The fair creature in the frill cap uttered a slight scream.

"Oh, gracious ivans!" cried a shrill, small voice from under the bed-clothes, "what do you want here? Go away this moment, do, or I shall scream!"

"I beg your pardon, ma'am," said the little man. "This gentleman here, the landlord, did not know that this room was occupied, and we came up to look—that is, to see if we couldn't——But it's quite a mistake, and I'm sure we're very sorry."

"Go away, you horrible monsters. I think you are both tipsy, or worse."

"Certainly, ma'am, we're going," said the landlord; "but might I venture to inquire, as the master of this house, who you might happen to be, and how you came to be sleeping here? For certainly it will be a great weight off my mind if I only knew."

"You'll know soon enough, if you're not both off in another minute!" said the party in the frilled cap, getting very excited, and looking as if she were not inclined to stand much more nonsense.

"I only asked a civil question," said the landlord.

"I don't want any more of your questions," said the one in the frill cap. "Go about your business. How dare you come into a lady's bedroom? You ought to be ashamed of yourselves. But I know you both. You won't hear the last of this for some time to come, I can promise you!" and the lady began to scream hysterically.

"Don't do that!" cried the little man. "We will go directly. I am sure, if you only knew our motives——"

"I know your motives well enough, without your telling me. Oh, dear—oh, dear! Why doesn't somebody come up-stairs? And there's no bell in the room! Oh, dear—oh, dear! I'm ruined—I'm ruined!"

"No you're not, my dear madam," said the little man, in an entreating tone. "For heaven's sake be calm, or you will disturb all the house! We shall have everybody coming up the stairs to see what's the matter!"

"What do I care?" cried the excited female. "Let them come up as soon as they like! I only wish they would! I wish half a dozen policemen would come with them, and I would soon see whether a poor, lonely, unprotected woman was to be outraged in this manner!"

The little man would have continued further to expostulate and reason with the indignant lady, but that she would listen to him no longer.

All she would do was to lie upon her back, kicking and screaming hysterically.

The little man looked at the large man, and both their faces were pale with fright.

"What's to be done?" said the little man to the large man.

"I haven't the remotest idea," replied the large to the little.

"I'll tell you what, then."

"What?"

"We have no time to lose, and we had better——"

"Better what?"

"Better hook it!"

There were to be heard at that moment footsteps upon the stairs. Alarmed by the Captain's cries, some of the waiters, housemaids, &c., were coming up to see what was the matter.

The suggestion of hooking it was the best that could be adopted under the circumstances, and hook it accordingly they did in the direction of the second floor.

No sooner was the Captain assured of their retreat than he sprang out of bed again, and bolted the door upon the inside.

Then, as there was no other course left for him, he made up his mind to climb up the chimney.

It isn't the easiest thing in the world to climb up a chimney. The great drawback to chimney climbing probably appears to most people to be the unpleasantly dirty nature of the journey, but the amount of gymnastics required is very considerable.

The Captain found it much more difficult than he expected, although he expected to find it difficult enough.

Luckily it was a good large chimney, but the amount of puffing and blowing the poor Captain expended upon his journey was wonderful to listen to. He scrambled, and pushed, and shoved, clutched and kicked, wedging himself occasionally in such a position that he could scarcely extricate himself again. He managed at length, more dead than alive, to poke his head out at the top, which fortunately was not ornamented with a chimney-pot, as he had dreaded.

With his head poked out and his mouth wide open, the Captain gulped down huge mouthfuls of air.

But after he had rested himself a little, he felt that it was necessary he should be getting on, and so he pulled himself through, and sat down upon the roof.

"By Jove," said the Captain to himself, bursting out laughing, "I might just as well have taken off that young lady's night-gown. I'm afraid it will take a good deal of soap to get it anything like white again. However, such as it is, here it is. I have been unfortunately, during the last day and night, driven to the commission of various thefts, but I won't have this night-gown upon my soul or the night-cap either; so here goes!"

And having rolled them up, he dropped the night-cap and night-gown down the chimney, into the room. After that, he looked round to see where he could drop himself.

It must not be into the street, was very sure; that was rather too deep a drop to be taken by any one not wearing wings. The roof of the hotel and the roof of the next house only were accessible to him, owing to the fact of these two houses being much higher than the houses on either side.

Over the roofs, therefore, of the hotel and the house next to it, the Captain wandered inquiringly, trying all the trap-doors and peeping about, in the hope of finding some means of escape.

None other, however, were visible, and he sat down at last upon the parapet with a very rueful expression of countenance, and asked himself, with a bitter curse, what good he had done by climbing up so high, and why he had not given himself into custody long ago, without taking so much trouble.

It seemed to him that he had been getting into a worse fix every change he had made, and now he was worse off than ever. Surely nothing worse was coming! We shall see.

The trap-doors were all fastened. The only way off the roof—that is to say, the only way with life and without wings—was down another chimney.

Not down the chimney he had come up, of course. Down one of the chimneys of the next house, if possible. The only difficulty was to find a chimney large enough, for a glance at those around showed him that he had been very fortunate in finding a chimney in the first instance, which admitted of the passage of his body through it.

He found one at length, and without considering or caring very much what was going to happen to him, he poked his legs in, stuck out his knees and his elbows, and began to scramble down.

If he had found it difficult to scramble up, he did not find the descent any easier. Quite the contrary. He felt himself choking. He was cramped and pinched, and all his limbs were aching.

Once or twice he got wedged up in such a way that he made sure he had stuck fast for ever, and the cold perspiration of terror burst out upon his forehead.

Extricating himself after a frantic struggle upon the last of these occasions, he straightened his legs too rapidly, and shot down the chimney like a pea out of a popgun.

Shock!

He had stopped suddenly as he had fallen. All the sense was shaken out of him. He felt as though every bone in his body had broken in half.

"Where was he?" he asked himself. He had stuck fast, and jammed himself tight in the chimney, and if he could judge by the distance, he seemed to have fallen not far from the bottom.

He began to make a tremendous effort to free himself, but he could not do so.

At last, finding how useless were his struggles, he abandoned them for a moment to get a little breath.

While thus quiet, he heard a voice which sounded close to his feet, and which asked, in stentorian tones, whether he knew where he was coming to.

The Captain bawled out at the top of his voice, in reply, that he neither knew nor cared.

"Then why don't you go back," said the person, "and knock at the door in the regular way?"

"I'm stuck fast," said the Captain, "and I shall be choked in a few minutes, if you don't help me!"

"How the deuce can I help you?"

"Pull my legs!"

Next moment the Captain felt two hands clutching his ankles, and he received a couple of tremendous jerks, which made his joints crack in a dreadful manner.

"Hilloa!" said the voice below.

"What is it?"

"I shall pull them off."

"Never mind."

"All right!"

More jerks, more joint-crackings, a good deal of agony upon the Captain's part, and a good deal of puffing and blowing upon the part of the person pulling.

"I say," called the voice presently; "I don't see why I should help you into my room, when I don't know who you are. Who are you?"

"I'm an officer and a gentleman, and I'll explain everything, as soon as I get out of this cursed hole."

"Well, I don't know what your head's like, but your legs and feet don't look very gentlemanly. If you had not told me otherwise, I should have taken you to be a footman."

"The mistake is very natural, but those trousers don't belong to me; and as I said before, I'll explain everything as soon as I am able to empty the soot out of my mouth."

"If you're a gentleman, perhaps you have got a card? Pass it down to me."

"I haven't got one, but I will tell you everything if you will only help me out. Just another pull, and I shall be clear."

"I think I'm acting very foolishly, but here goes!"

A tremendous deal of pulling and puffing ensued, and then, at last, to his inexpressible relief, but not without a vast amount of anguish, he was dragged with a jerk into the room, and found himself face to face with his deliverer.

As soon as he had rubbed sufficient soot out of his eyes to be able to see anything at all, he saw a very extraordinary-looking gentleman standing before him.

He was a young gentleman, with wild-looking eyes, and long, wild, wiry-looking hair. He wore a magnificent dressing-gown—magnificent as regarded the material of which it was made, but the pattern was ridiculously gaudy.

It had a crimson ground, and upon it were large yellow flowers, the size and shape of marigolds. Nobody, the Captain thought, could ever so have dressed themselves out of a farce; but evidently this young gentleman, whoever he was, was a young man of property, for the apartment was magnificently furnished.

The Captain made the gentleman a low bow, and expressed his thanks for the service which had just been rendered him.

"How do you find yourself?" said the gentleman: "you look black in the face, but you are not choking now so much as you were."

"Thanks to your kindness, I have escaped with my life. Allow me to introduce myself. I am Captain Charles Crockford, of Her Majesty's Foot Guards."

"I am delighted to make your acquaintance. My name, sir, is Cadbury Kid. I'm not anything particular, except the most unfortunate devil on the face of the earth; for which, however, I cannot tell you the reason."

"I don't think you can say you are more unfortunate than I am," retorted the Captain. "If you had gone through what I have during the last twenty-four hours, you'd tell another story."

"Have you gone through much, then?"

"Yes. I have had almost everything occur to me of a disagreeable character which could possibly occur to anybody under the circumstances."

"And you've got safely through it?"

"Yes."

"Then I don't call you unfortunate."

"If I were not unfortunate I should never have got into such scrapes."

"You are not half so unfortunate as I am, I'm certain of that."

"So you think. Egad! I wouldn't mind changing places with you?"

"Will you change places with me?"

"What do you mean?"

"What I say."

"I don't understand you."

"It's easy enough to understand. Put on my dressing gown, and pretend you are me when somebody knocks at the door."

"What's the good of talking nonsense? They'll know it isn't you."

"No, they won't; the person who will knock has never seen me."

"Well!" thought the Captain, "if I'm not dreaming, I'm in Bedlam. Bedlam, though, is better than where I have come from, so I'll let things take their course."

The young gentleman by this time had taken off his dressing-gown, and thrust it on to the Captain.

"Had I not better wash my face and hands?" Crockford asked.

"By no means; it will be a better disguise."

"What are you going to do, then?"

"I am going up."

"Up where?"

"Up the chimney!"

The Captain opened his mouth as wide as he could open it.

"This is a maniac," thought the Captain to himself; but he had no more time allowed him for thinking. The young gentleman had begun to climb up the chimney.

The Captain, in blank amazement, watched one leg disappear after another.

Then he fell back into a chair, and burst into a roar of laughter.

In this he was interrupted by a loud knocking at the door.

"Now for it!" said the Captain. "In the name of any number of Hanwells, what's coming next?"

CHAPTER XXXIX.

THE ONE-EYED MAN—A CHASE ROUND A TABLE.—THE GAG.—THE CAPTAIN'S SUFFERINGS, INSTEAD OF BEING OVER, SEEM ONLY JUST TO HAVE COMMENCED.—THE JOURNEY IN THE CAB—A PRISONER IN DOCTOR THROTTLEMANN'S ASYLUM FOR INCORRIGIBLE LUNATICS.

For some time the Captain hesitated whether or not he should remain silent, or whether he should tell the person knocking at the door to come in. After some consideration, not having arrived at any conclusion, he decided upon remaining silent.

The party outside acted in the opposite manner. He beat the devil's tattoo; and finding that it did no good, and that the door was locked upon the inside, he placed his foot against one of the lower panels, butted his head against one of the upper panels, and sent the door open with a loud crash.

The Captain awaited the appearance of this energetic intruder with some apprehension.

The exterior of the party who now showed himself was not calculated to reassure him

He was a very tall man—considerably over six foot, and stout in proportion. He wore a short velveteen coat, a pair of corduroy trousers, and an old, battered white hat, with a black band.

In his left hand coat pocket he carried a short stick. This short stick had a large knob, very suggestive of cracks on the head. It stuck out of his pocket in a conspicuous fashion, and he kept one hand upon it as though he expected that it would very shortly be called into requisition.

He was an extremely unpleasant-looking man in all respects.

His mouth was a large one, and had the expression of a bull-dog.

His eye was a villanous one, but it is a question which is not easily decided whether his expression would have been more or less villanous if he had had the regular number of eyes, like other people, and had not worn over one of them a black patch.

This pleasing individual, having entered the room, pushed the door to behind him, and brought his one available eye to bear upon the Captain.

"Well, young fellow," said he, "so you are up to your larks, are you!"

"Up to what larks?" asked the Captain.

The one-eyed man fixed him with his solitary optic, but made no answer. Only, after a pause of a minute or two, he continued reflectively, "Up to your larks again, are you?"

"Who are you?" asked the Captain; "and, as I said before, what larks?"

"You know me; and you know what I mean. What the dickens have you been up to?"

"Up to?"

"What have you been doing to your face? Are you thinking of becoming a nigger wocalist? P'raps you're going to cut out Mr. Mackney?"

"If you've got any business here, perhaps you will be kind enough to say what it is, and then take yourself off."

The man looked rather hurt at being thus addressed.

"Just look here, you know," said he: "your wally said I wasn't to leave you, and I was a fool to allow myself to be sent out of the room by you for a few minutes; and you see how you go and take advantage of my absence. Why, you ain't fit to be left a minute by yourself! Look at the condition you are in! It's my opinion you have been trying to get up the chimney."

"Look here, my good man!" said the Captain very seriously, for he began to feel very uncomfortable as a thought occurred to him; "look here my good man! Who do you take me for?"

"Hold your nonsense! Who do you suppose I take you for?"

"Never mind what I suppose; answer my question."

"You're Mr. Kid, ain't you?"

"No."

"What do you say?"

"I said no."

The one-eyed gentleman regarded the Captain attentively, with his head a little on one side.

"No?" he repeated. "Then who the dickens are you?"

"My name is Crockford," answered the Captain, "if you want to know. And perhaps you will be kind enough to tell me what your business is with me."

"Now look here!" retorted the one-eyed man. "If you fancy that by coming any of that nonsense you will get out of coming with me, you're very much mistaken."

"But I tell you that you're mistaken. I am not the person you suppose."

"You've been changed by magic then, perhaps. I left you here ten minutes ago when I went down for a cab, and when I come back again you pretend you are not the same person. Now do you suppose that I'm a fool, or do you suppose that I'm blind, or what do you suppose?"

"I don't care about troubling myself to suppose anything," retorted the Captain savagely; "but I tell you my name is Crockford, and that I'm not Mr. Kid."

"Now look here! Whoever you are, it don't matter a button. You are coming along with me, and you had better come quietly, without any nonsense."

"Where am I to come to?"

"Oh, not to any place where we shall hurt you. You needn't be afraid."

"I am not afraid; only I don't mean to come."

"We'll see that."

"Yes, we will."

No more was said upon either side. The one-eyed, keeping his one eye fixed upon the Captain, turned up his coat-sleeve.

The Captain returning the stare with interest, rose from his seat, and walked round to the other side of a large table, which stood in the middle of the room.

Then they began to dodge one another without saying a word, or without changing countenance.

Round the table went the Captain, and after him followed the one-eyed man, every now and then stretching out one of his long arms, and endeavouring to make a clutch at the other's collar.

There is no knowing how long this sort of amusement would have continued, had not the Captain at last caught his dressing-gown upon an arm-chair, and dragging it over, pulled it after him half round the room until he had blocked himself up in a corner, and the one-eyed man made a plunge at him and pinned him against the wall.

"I've got you at last!" said he; and the Captain was too much out of breath to contradict, even if he had been so disposed. But as his captor became more and more rough in his treatment of him, he presently, when he had got his wind a little, began to bawl with all his might for help.

The one-eyed man, however, by this time had contrived to throw the Captain upon his back and to plant his knees upon the Captain's breast.

He was evidently accustomed to struggles of this character, for although the Captain was by no means deficient in physical strength, the other very easily managed to pinion his arms and fasten them to his sides with a strap that he took from his pocket.

Then, as quick as lightning, he opened the Captain's mouth by a sharp wrench of his jaw, and inserted therein one of those horrid wooden instruments called gags.

The Captain was therefore unable to call for help. He was unable also to describe his situation to a small crowd of men and women whom the noise had attracted to the scene of the struggle, and who were to be seen staring in at the doorway, with terrified faces.

"Lend a hand here," said the one-eyed man, and two men stepped forward to assist him. They holding the Captain's legs, the one-eyed took off the strap which confined the Captain's arms, and substituted in its place a complication of straps and canvass, which Crockford felt instinctively was a strait-waistcoat.

This one-eyed man was, as he had supposed all along, a lunatic keeper. He (the Captain) had been taken for a lunatic. What was going to be done with him?

He tried to speak, but he could not.

They carried him down the stairs, and forced him into a cab that was waiting at the door, he, all the while, as helpless as a child.

The keeper then called out a direction to the cabman. The Captain shuddered when he heard it, for it was to a madhouse that they were going.

"I wish I was up the chimney again," thought the Captain to himself, "or down the sewer, or in the vault, or in the box. I'm hang'd if I don't think I've got out of the frying-pan into the fire; though, after all, of course they won't keep me locked up when they find out that I am not a lunatic, and not the person they suppose. The only difficulty is how I'm to convince them of the mistake. I wonder whether this infernal scoundrel is going to take the gag out of my mouth. This strait-waistcoat will be the death of me if he don't loosen it a little!"

Poor Captain! he rolled his eyes and groaned, and regarded the one-eyed keeper with a piteous expression.

This gentleman's heart, however, was not to be softened.

"You'd better be quiet," said he, "or I'll give you something that'll make you!"

The Captain groaned.

"You don't know when you are comfortable, you don't. Just you wait till you get to the guv'nor's, and then you'll get it pretty hot."

The Captain not being able to speak, was not able to tell him that, in his opinion, he was getting it "pretty hot" as it was, and so he only groaned again, and looked more piteous than before.

"You'd better take care what you are up to!" said the one-eyed man: "you are rather restive just now, but we shall give you the cold water cure when we get you to the guv'nor's; and when you've had your head shaved, perhaps you will be a little more reasonable."

The Captain shuddered at these dreadful words.

How did he know but that they might shave his head and cut off his moustaches and whiskers before he could convince them that he was the wrong man?

This time he groaned louder than ever.

"Oh, dear! oh, dear!" he thought, "what will become of me? If they disfigure me in that sort of way, and just at the beginning of the season, too, when I've got engagements for every night in the week to dinner parties and balls! I wouldn't have it happen for a hundred pounds if I could help it."

The one-eyed man seemed as though he understood what was passing in the other's mind, and he said with a fiendish chuckle, "You'll look very different when you've been cropped. You won't know yourself hardly."

The cab, after jolting along upon its way for three-quarters of an hour, drew up suddenly in front of a large, bare, red-bricked house, surrounded by a high wall and a pair of strong wooden gates, painted green.

This was the private madhouse of the celebrated Dr. Throttlemann.

The Captain knew it well, and the Doctor's reputation was also well known to him.

There had been some very ugly stories from time to time in the newspapers concerning the treatment of the patients under the Doctor's care. Stories about ice-baths, rope-ends, strait-waistcoats, un-

merciful floggings, and ticklings with straws upon the soles of the patients' naked feet.

"By the Lord Harry, I'm in for it!" thought the Captain.

The cabman rang the great bell at the gate, the harsh clanking of which sounded like a knell upon the Captain's heart.

A man answered the summons, whom Croskford also took to be a keeper. If anything, he was uglier than the one-eyed man.

The Captain groaned at the sight of him.

With the assistance of this pleasing individual, the one-eyed man carried the Captain into the house. The great gate banged to behind them, shutting out life, and light, and hope.

They bore him into the gloomy house, and locked the door after them.

"It's all over with me," thought the Captain. "Nothing but an earthquake could do me any good in this awful place."

CHAPTER XL.

A PRISONER IN NEWGATE.—THE FRIENDLESS MAIDEN.—A CONSCIENTIOUS LAWYER.—MRS. HUDSON'S SYMPATHY.—AN OLD GENTLEMAN WHO WAS HENPECKED.—A GENTEEL ROW BETWEEN TWO LADIES.—NO HOPE—NO FRIEND.—THE PRAYERS OF THE CONDEMNED.—AGAIN THE TEMPTER.

Gentle reader, come with me to prison.

A dark and gloomy prison, where is incarcerated a poor young creature, a victim of perfidy, treachery, and false swearing.

Innocent, yet deemed guilty by all.

Innocent, and unable to prove it. Unable to pierce the hard hearts of her judges with one solitary ray of pity.

There are not many persons, I believe, who

can pass by the dark and dismal entrance of Newgate prison, without something approaching to a shudder passing over their frames.

A great many persons stay for a while, out of curiosity, and regard with a kind of frightened awe the strong, rough, massive masonry, the prodigiously thick walls, the curiously narrow doorway, and the door itself jet black, coffin colour, studded with nails and bristling with twisted spikes.

The exterior of this prison very frequently presents an appearance of extreme liveliness and bustle. The street is very frequently crowded with waggons and light carts—with a number of different vehicles just arrived fresh from the country; the healthy appearance of their drivers contrasting strangely with the sallow, sickly faces of the denizens of the reeking courts and alleys round about; and their open, honest countenances presenting a still greater contrast to the dark and lowering prison walls, frowning menacingly down upon them.

Many of these gentle-hearted, soft-headed, happy yokels, gazing upwards in silly wonder at the huge monster's face, think nothing about the load of crime and misery enclosed within the smoke-stained walls. Of a warm summer's afternoon, when Giles, lolling upon his load of clover, lazily flicks at the impudent flies with his whip, thinking, may be, of Moggy and the cow and the coming drinking time at "whoame," how different is the scene to that presented by the same place one of those awful Monday mornings, at eight, when some shivering wretch is dragged out, hooted at, yelled at, execrated and cursed, and launched headlong, more like a dog than a human being, into the presence of his Maker, by way of a moral lesson to the ruffians and blackguards there assembled.

In this prison we again find the unfortunate Alice Trevellyan, who, after being remanded several times, has now been sent to Newgate to await her trial.

She has suffered much since we saw her last. Her cheeks are paler even than they were upon the occasion that Eneas Earthworm paid her a visit.

Deadly pale are they, and bearing upon them the traces of bitter anguish and deep sorrow.

Much had she suffered — much and deeply. Long had she prayed for assistance from the Divine Power; fervently had she implored the protection of heaven against her persecutors; but as yet protection had not reached her.

She had yet to suffer—suffer bitterly and long.

Not until she had been in the prison for some time did she think of applying for professional assistance. For a long time she hoped that her innocence would assert itself triumphantly, and that she would not require any aid But very soon she found that this hope was fallacious.

Every fresh examination before the magistrate proved that some secret and insidious power was at work to effect her ruin.

Some snake-like power coiling round and round about her, drawing nearer and nearer, and narrowing the compass each moment, threatening to crush her in its folds.

The unfortunate girl at length consulted the matron upon the course she ought to pursue.

The innocence of her looks, and her language, elicited the woman's sympathy—or at least such a sentiment as must stand in the place of sympathy in a bosom incapable of any very affectionate demonstrations.

The woman, after humming and hawing for some time, feeling apparently undecided whether or not she should mix herself up in the matter, and take any trouble in what did not really concern her, recommended a lawyer of her acquaintance, whose name was Block.

This gentleman, who in other cases probably proved himself very efficient, distinguished himself from the very first, in poor Alice's cause, by a series of blunders of the most exasperating nature.

From the very first, this Mr. Block appeared to be so impressed with an inward conviction of his client's guilt, that perhaps, being a man strong in conscientious motives, he could not bring himself to devote his energies in behalf of an unworthy person.

As the day fixed for the trial approached, he appeared to grow more and more despondent.

He came and went in extremely doleful fashion, shook his head mournfully, and sighed deeply, and looked as though he would willingly have given a trifle to get the disagreeable business off his hands.

One day, when Mrs. Trevellyan had had an interview with him, and he had been more despondent, if possible, than he was the last time, she inquired the cause of it.

"Is our case really so bad?" she asked.

For some time he would make no reply.

Alice, however, could read his answer in the dark cloud overshadowing his averted face.

"Yes," she said, "I can see that it is. But surely I shall not be condemned when I am innocent? God is my witness that I am guiltless"

The lawyer made no answer.

"Do you think, sir, that I shall be convicted?"

"It is impossible to say."

"But what is your opinion?"

"Our case is a bad one."

He would say nothing more, and he left her, after a silence of a few moments, saying that he would call again next day, if anything of importance transpired.

When the matron came to Alice's cell, she found her plunged in grief, upon her knees, with her head buried in her hands, sobbing bitterly.

"What is the matter?" asked the matron.

"Oh, madam, I have no one to protect me, no one to help me, no one to assist me. My lawyer despairs of my case. I have no hope, now, of being proved innocent."

"What has he said to you to-day?"

"Alas! he has said nothing, or very little; but I can tell by his manner that he has no hope whatever that he will gain the cause for me."

"I can't understand it, replied the matron. "He is a most able man, I'm sure, and one whom I myself would employ in such a case before all others. I really don't know what to say about it."

"Oh, dear—oh, dear! I am very unfortunate! I who, in my dear husband's life, was the happiest woman in the world, am surely now the most wretched!"

And poor Alice sank down upon her knees and wept bitterly.

"There, there!" cried the matron, whom the sight affected to some extent. "Bear up, my dear creature—bear up as well as you can, and I will see Mr. Block myself, and have a long conversation with him"

Next day, she took an early opportunity of putting her project into execution.

She had an interview with the lawyer, and, after a great deal of trouble and no small amount of fencing backwards and forwards, and beating about the bush—for Mr. Block was very much afraid of displeasing his friend, and for a long while evaded all her questions, and artfully wandered away from the point to which she endeavoured to bring him—she extracted from him the fact that he thought the prisoner to be guilty, and that she had not a shadow of a ghost of a chance of escape.

The matron, however, did not share in this view of the business, although it must be owned that her sympathy for Alice to some extent abated.

But when she came again into the unfortunate prisoner's presence—when she again gazed into those pure and truthful orbs, and listened to that voice so touching and tender, so fraught with conviction, for any but the most hardened, callous, and obdurate, she could not help believing that the tale the poor girl told was the true one, and that she was the victim of circumstantial evidence—of machination—of atrocious villany.

She, however, was most eager that Alice should have every possible assistance to prove the innocence which she so strongly asserted.

"Have you no friend to whom you can apply?" the matron inquired.

Alice replied in the negative.

"No relations, however distant, who could be persuaded to take an interest in your welfare?"

"I fear not. I am, I believe, an orphan. My parents and my sisters are dead. I am alone in the world, without friends or relations."

"You can mention nobody, then, to whom you could apply?"

"No one."

"Your case is indeed hard."

"My guardian, I think, I have spoken to you about?"

"No, I do not remember—at least, tell me again."

"He was very much opposed to my marriage with Trevellyan. He forbade my husband the house. I eloped with him, and owing to my having married without my guardian's consent, the fortune which I should otherwise have possessed became his property."

"Then your guardian is still alive?"

"Yes; but I do not think that he could be induced by any amount of persuasion to stretch forth his hand to save me."

"Anyhow, I will try him. Where does he live?"

Alice gave her friend the name and address of the gentleman, and the matron promised without loss of time to seek him out, and endeavour to persuade him to bestir himself in favour of the unhappy girl who otherwise there was every reason to suppose would finish her life shamefully upon the scaffold.

Mr. Jonas Starkey lived at No. 5, Mornington Crescent.

He was an elderly gentleman, who had recently married his housekeeper. He lived without seeing much company, drinking his bottle of wine at dinner, and his stiff glass of grog the last thing at night, having the gout every now and then, and being perpetually very much under the thumb of Mrs. Starkey.

To everybody else but Mrs. S. he was decidedly a very irascible old gentleman, and the matron happened to come upon him at a very unfortunate moment.

He was not only very much under the thumb of Mrs. S. that morning—in fact, not alone under the thumb, but, I may say, under the entire fist of the good lady; but he had also got an uncommon twinge of the gout to contend with, which was gradually worrying him into a state of intense crossness with himself and everybody and everything else—except, of course, the aforesaid Mrs. S., whom it was not very wise to be at variance with; or, rather, it was wisest to take the slap on the head she gave you, and smile as though you rather liked it.

The matron gave her name, and was announced.

"Mrs. Hudson."

"Who does she want to see, Mary Ann?" asked the lady of the house snappishly.

"I think Mary Ann said it was me, my dear," replied Mr. Starkey meekly.

"What does she want to say to you, I should like to know? I shall go and see her."

"Perhaps she had better come in, my dear?"

"No, she shan't do any such thing. Ask her what she is, Mary Ann, and where she comes from?"

Mary Ann departed, made the inquiry, and returned again.

She was giggling at something.

"What now?" asked Mrs. Starkey angrily.

"Oh, if you please, mum——"

"Don't stand grinning there, Mary Ann. I'm surprised at you. But I suppose I can be insulted with impunity in my own house when I have such a—such a thing for a husband."

"My dear, I can't help the girl grinning, can I?"

"You can't help? No, I should like to know what you could help! And I should like to know what good you're of! I never found it out."

There is no knowing how long the dispute might have raged upon this delicate subject had not Mary Ann providentally come to the rescue.

Suppressing her mirth for the present, she said, "If you please, mum, the lady said she has come from Newgate."

"Gracious heavens! From Newgate? What next?"

Mr. Starkey also looked astonished.

"What can the woman want?"

"Don't you think, my dear——" began Mr. Starkey timidly.

"Don't I think what, sir? Do you suppose that I am going to receive into my house a lot of your cast-off mistresses?"

"My what?" asked Mr. Starkey, aghast.

"Your good-for-nothings, who have just finished their oakum picking!"

Mr. Starkey sank back into his chair with a groan, and gave up the dispute.

If it had depended upon him he probably would not have seen the matron at all. But luckily Mrs S. was devoured by curiosity to learn what errand could have brought Mrs. Hudson to the house; and so, after fretting and fuming a little while in silence, she bade Mary Ann admit the visitor immediately.

Mrs Hudson entered the room shortly afterwards. She bowed stiffly to the master of the house—more stiffly to the mistress—then drew herself up, and waited to be questioned.

Mr. Starkey hesitated for a moment or two, fearful that any course of conduct he might pursue would only lead to the same result—namely, another row with Mrs. S.

However, at length he asked diffidently, "To what am I indebted for the honour of this visit?"

"I have the honour of speaking to Mr. Starkey, I believe?"

"That is my name, madam."

"The business about which I desire to see you is of a private nature."

"If you mean that you want to go out of the room, ma'am, you're very much mistaken if you suppose I should allow it."

This was what Mrs. Starkey broke in with, looking as fierce as a turkey-cock.

Mrs. Hudson looked at her in astonishment, but made no reply.

Mr. Starkey blushed a deeper red than the highest coloured beet-root.

"I—I—I——" said he, in a mildly expostulating way.

"Sir!" exclaimed his better half, indignantly.

Mrs. Hudson endeavoured to set matters straight, seeing how they stood.

"If the lady desires to be present, I see no objection, sir, supposing that you have none. The lady is, I suppose, your—your——"

"I'm his wedded wife, if you mean that, ma'am," cried Mrs. Starkey, scarlet with indignation.

"Then there can be no objection," continued the matron, affecting not to notice the other's anger.

After a brief pause, she continued: "You were, I believe, the guardian, before her marriage, of a young lady named Alice Graham, since the wife of Mr. Ernest Trevellyan?"

Mr. Starkey changed colour, bit his lips, and answered, "I was."

"That unfortunate young lady is now confined in Newgate, awaiting her trial, and charged with the murder of her husband."

"Yes, I've read the circumstances in the newspaper."

"The poor young creature is quite without friends, and without means. I am a matron in that prison, and I have had many opportunities of observing her conduct, and I have frequently conversed with her upon the circumstances of her case."

Mrs. Hudson paused here a moment, as though for some question to be put to her.

"Well?" said Mr. Starkey, at last; and she continued.

"From what I have seen of her, and from the many opportunities which I have had of observing other prisoners under like circumstances, I have come to the conclusion that she is innocent."

Again she paused.

Again Mr. Starkey said, "Well?"

Again she continued.

"Hearing from her that you were the only person in the wide world to whom she could appeal to exert themselves to rescue her from the melancholy position in which she is placed, I came at once to beseech you to exert yourself in her behalf."

"What would you have me do?"

"There are many ways which a gentleman, with means at his command, can befriend a prisoner in like case. If I might suggest the employment of counsel."

Mr. Starkey seemed to hesitate. Perhaps if he had been alone he might have listened and yielded to the appeal which was being made to him. But now the dread of Mrs. Starkey's anger held him back, and he mumbled out after awhile—

"I really do not think that I should be justified in incurring a large expense in behalf of a person who has proved herself so—so utterly unworthy of—of my—so to speak—that is, I mean to say——"

It is quite uncertain what he would have said only Mrs. Starkey broke in here with a burst of excited eloquence which bore all before it.

"The very idea! The insolence—the assurance—the presumption. A worthless beggar like that! an ungrateful wretch, who could run away and marry the first scamp who asked her!—who is accused, and in my opinion very justly, of the murder of this scamp! No, ma'am, as long as I have a voice in this house, and pray heaven that may be for some time to come yet, Mr. Starkey shall do nothing to assist that unworthy person, either by word or by deed."

Mrs. Hudson vouchsafed no reply to these observations, but looking towards Mr. Starkey, said, "What is your answer, sir?"

"You—you ——" stammered the old gentleman, —you—you have ——"

"Got it!" added Mrs. Starkey.

"And this is what I am to tell Mrs. Trevellyan?"

"Yes, it is," said Mrs. Starkey.

"Is that your answer, sir?"

"Yes—yes; that's my answer."

"Well, sir," cried Mrs. Hudson, bouncing off a seat which she had taken, and sweeping indignantly towards the door with a contemptuous toss of the head, intended for both lady and gentleman,—"well, sir, I must say I'm surprised at you, and ashamed of you! And as for you, ma'am, if I did not consider you a great deal beneath me, I should tell you what I thought of you; but, as it is, I shall wish you good morning."

And before Mrs. Starkey could spring forward, which she was going to do, probably with the intention of setting her mark upon Mrs. Hudson's countenance, the latter slammed the door in her face, and beat a hasty retreat into the street.

She could do nothing more. The worthy matron sorrowfully retraced her steps to the gloomy prison, where Alice anxiously awaited her arrival, hoping that she would bring with her a favourable account of the expedition.

When Mrs. Hudson communicated the unsatisfactory tidings of which she was the bearer, poor Alice sunk down overcome with the weight of her misfortune.

"Oh, dear madam!" she cried, suddenly seizing her kind friend by the hand, and turning upon her an intensely beseeching look,—"do you think that all hope is over for me? What do you think will be my fate?"

"My poor dear, everything seems against us. Nobody will assist us. I should be acting wickedly did I do other than bid you prepare for the worst."

Alice trembled violently, and her fingers tightened upon her friend's hand, which she held in hers.

"I fear that you will be convicted," said Mrs. Hudson.

"And if convicted," said Alice, "I—I——"

"We will hope for the best. I cannot believe it possible that the full sentence will be carried into effect."

"And if not—if the sentence is commuted, what have I to hope for but perpetual imprisonment?"

Mrs Hudson made no answer, but caught the young girl to her heart.

"My poor dear, I feel as confident in your innocence as there is a heaven above; and we can only pray that you may have justice done you"

There, then, in that prison cell, the matron and the captive sank down upon their knees, and in an outburst of fervid devotion, besought the aid of heaven.

Long did they pray. Long did they remain there upon their knees, mingling their prayers and tears.

Would she be proved guilty? We shall see.

The day fixed for the trial opened with a dark and gloomy morning, in which there was not one ray of sunshine to brighten the dull face of nature.

The aspect of the day could be taken as an omen of the fate which awaited the unhappy prisoner. It was indeed a forlorn one.

With a heart as heavy as lead, Alice rose from her couch, and, as was her custom, spent an hour in prayer.

She was resigned and calm.

She was determined to meet her fate with fortitude.

The hour at which it was supposed that her trial would come on was noon.

She was to leave her cell at ten o'clock.

At nine, a visitor was announced. It was a very unusual thing for any visitor to have an interview with a prisoner in his or her cell. It is customary for the solicitor to see his client in a room with glass sides, so that a warder in attendance can see all that takes place between them, without, however, being able to hear what they say.

This visitor must have been a person of some consequence; anyhow, a person who was able to command admittance to the place from which the public were excluded.

Alice was sitting, plunged in a deep and mournful reverie, when the announcement of a visitor caused her to raise her head with some astonishment.

The matron, after admitting the visitor, shut the door upon him, and retired.

Alice looked up—uttered a half suppressed shriek—started back, and clutched at the wall, as though for support.

Eneas Earthworm stood before her.

The old sardonic smile was upon his face.

"I've come again," he said.

"God protect me!" muttered the girl to herself, as she covered her face with her hands, and trembled like a leaf.

"I will protect you, if you will allow me," said Earthworm, with a grin; and he advanced and took her hand in his.

But she struggled, and made as though she would have cried for help.

"Hold your silly tongue," said the old man. "I can save you yet, if you are not going to be an idiot."

CHAPTER XLI.

THE CAPTAIN IN THE LUNATIC ASYLUM — THE MECHANICAL CHAIR.—THE SOUNDS OF VIOLENCE SHRIEKS AND BLOWS.—THE HOUSEMAID.—A RUN FOR IT.—FREE ONCE MORE.—FATE!

POOR Captain! He made no resistance as they carried him into the lunatic asylum.

Perhaps he thought that his struggles would be useless. He knew very well, or at least he supposed, that shrieks must be frequently heard coming from this dreadful lunatic asylum, and that his cries would sound as much like a lunatic's as any other.

Besides, his reason told him that if he remained perfectly quiet and acted like a rational person, he would be all the more likely to impress his keepers with a notion of his sanity.

They carried him into the house, down a passage, and into a large, barely-furnished room, which seemed to be used as a kind of receiving-room. In it was a large arm-chair, into which they thrust the new arrival.

It was a curious kind of chair, with a contrivance upon each arm and at the back, just behind the occupier's neck, of a very uncommon character.

This contrivance was something in the form of a dog's collar, which closed round the arms and neck of the party sitting down, and held them as though in a vice. It was no good then to kick and squeal, because the chair was a heavy one, and unless you carried the chair with you it was impossible to move from your place.

Into this chair, as I have said, they thrust the Captain, and the clasps closing upon his wrists and his neck, he was held fast and was perfectly helpless.

The men began to consult together, paying no respect whatever to the presence of the Captain; indeed, treating him as though he had been an inanimate piece of furniture—the chintz cover of the chair, or something of that sort.

"Is the guv'nor at home, Bill?" asked the man with the one eye.

"No; he's out."

"How long will he be, do you think?"

"He might be only an hour," he said; "but perhaps he won't be back till this evening."

"Hum! hah! what's to be done with the new subject?"

"I don't know, I am sure. We can't very well put him anywhere till the guv'nor comes back."

"Why not?"

"Why, you know, if we do, it's sure to be the wrong place, and there's sure to be a row about it. There allers is."

"You're about right there. But what are we to do with him?"

"Leave him where he is; he'll be comfortable enough till the guv'nor comes in."

"Shall I?" thought the Captain. But he forebore making any remark, lest greater evil should befall him.

I ought to have told you, but I forgot it at the moment, that the gag had been removed from the Captain's mouth, and his arms had been unbound, before he was brought into the lunatic asylum.

He said nothing, though, determined to reserve all his eloquence until the arrival of the doctor, whom he trusted with less difficulty to convince of his sanity.

After a little more conversation, chiefly relating, however, to their own affairs, the keepers retired from the room; the one-eyed gentleman, however, taking the liberty, before he followed them, of shaking his fist in the Captain's face, and threatening, in not the mildest possible manner, that he would have much pleasure in knocking Mr. Crockford's head off if he came "any of his infernal nonsense."

The men then left the room, the door was shut after them, and the Captain was left to himself.

"This is a nice look-out!" said he to himself, after a brief pause. "How long shall I be left here, I wonder? What am I to do if I want to use my pocket-handkerchief?"

He began to have a cramping pain in all his joints, and he felt generally very uncomfortable.

"I've heard of a chair like this in the 'Mysteries of the Court,' but at the time I didn't believe in it. They would be capital things at a dentist's; but they are deuced uncomfortable if you have to sit in them very long at a time."

The time that Captain Charley was to be doomed thus to be held a prisoner appeared to be very uncertain. Half an hour passed by, but nobody came into the room to set him at liberty. An hour passed, and still he was a captive. He went to sleep for a short time, and woke up again to find himself very cold and cramped, and as tightly fastened up as ever.

"I'd give a trifle to be out of this," he thought. "It's deucedly provoking. By rights, I ought to have been at Aldershott, where my governor was to be to-day. I shall offend him, and be cut off my quarter's allowance. That's just my luck!"

At last he came to the conclusion that the best thing he could do would be to bawl out with all his strength, and try if he could not attract the attention of some of the keepers; then, when they came, endeavour to bribe them to let him go; or, anyhow, to send to his chambers and ascertain whether what he said was not correct.

"They can't be such fools," he argued to himself, "as to refuse to do what I ask them; because, of course, when the doctor comes, he will find out that I am not the party they suppose; and then they will have to give up all hope of getting anything out of me. At least, I should suppose they would not try to keep me here when they find out that I am not the madman."

Acting upon this idea, he spent no more time in consideration, but bawled out at the top of his voice for some one to come to him.

The person who answered the shout was the individual with one eye.

"So you are at it, are you?" said this gentleman, in whose hand Crockford, with some uneasiness, observed a thick stick. "What do you want now?"

"I want to speak to you," said the Captain, in as pleasant a tone as he could assume.

"What do you want, I say?"

"I want to know whether a five pound note would be of any service to you?"

"As much service to me, I reckon, as to anybody else. Where is it?"

"I haven't got it here ——"

"Oh, that's your game!"

"But it's easily come-atable."

"Where is it, and what do you want doing for it?"

"I want you to send to my valet to my rooms in Piccadilly. Tell him to come here, and bring my clothes, so that I may dress myself and go home."

"But you know very well that your home is not in Piccadilly any more than mine is: and your valet ain't likely to send you any clothes, because he must know very well that you don't know how to use them."

"I tell you I'm not the person you imagine!"

"Yes, you've told me that before; at the same time, I mean to stick to you."

"Now, don't go away like that, if you please, but listen to what I've got to say. Have you ever seen the Mr. Kid that you think I am?"

"Yes, I saw him for a minute or two."

"There!—then you own yourself that you don't know him well! Do you know his face?"

"I know your face is his, if you mean that?"

"There, that is what I deny. How can you recognise my face with an inch of soot upon it? Let me wash it first, and see if you are not mistaken."

"Well, I must say, you stick to it hard enough to make one almost doubt one's senses. But you shall have your face washed if you like, so as I may have a good look at you."

"That is all I wish for."

"You shall have your wish."

To gratify it, the keeper left the room in search of water and towel.

Presently he returned with them, and releasing the Captain from his bondage, he allowed him an opportunity of cleansing his face from the mass of soot with which it was thickly coated.

While Crockford was thus occupied, however, a sudden noise within the house attracted the keeper's attention, and took him outside the door into the passage to listen.

The sound was a combination of shrieking and sobbing, with some other noise which seemed like the heavy thuds of a stick upon a human body.

When the door was opened, the sounds grew louder—the blows were apparently dealt with greater violence—the sobbing was more violent and most passionate.

Muttering a deep curse, the keeper slammed to the door, and strode away down the passage and up-stairs, stamping heavily upon each step as he went.

Crockford paused for a minute or two in the middle of his wash to wonder whom it could be that was thus being ill-used, and then went on drying himself.

Although the door was shut, he could yet distinctly hear the same sounds of punishment and of agony which had attracted the notice of the keeper; but when he had dried himself, and gone to the door in the hope of hearing a little more, he found that the door had been locked, and he had been made a prisoner.

He listened at the keyhole intently, straining his ears to catch the sounds, which only reached him imperfectly, but gradually they died away; and then, after standing there listening for a short time, he resumed his seat in the chair, taking care, however, to avoid the clasps which had before held him so uncomfortably tight.

Time wore slowly away. He heard nothing more of the sounds to which a short time ago he had been listening.

All was still within the house.

The keeper did not return.

How could he account for this? He did not endeavour to do so, but as patiently as he could he sat and waited.

At last he heard a door open up-stairs, and a sound of heavy footsteps descending.

He expected that this was the keeper, and that he would come into the room—but it was not the case.

The footsteps passed by, and went out at the street door. Immediately afterwards other footsteps followed, and he heard voices talking in an excited tone.

And then a loud slamming of the door, and then all was still.

Crockford was at a loss to understand what was the meaning of these proceedings; and although he endeavoured to console himself with the reflection that it did not very materially concern him, he felt anything but comfortable.

All the stories of cruelty which he had heard came fresh upon him. Frightful stories some of them, the recollection of which was enough to make his blood run cold.

Stories of brutal violence, fiendish cruelty, and demoniacal ingenuity displayed in the infliction of torture.

He had heard of a patient who had been tied down and driven to madness, like the unhappy prisoners were in the back days of the Inquisition, by the constant trickling of a drop of water upon their bare heads.

Worse than that, how they had been tied down helpless, whilst some devilish monster had irritated the soles of their bare feet with a straw or feather, and they had laughed and screamed their senses away, and become no better than babbling idiots.

Many such stories as these he had read of, or had been told about, from time to time; and, though the time had been when he would have laughed at them as silly fancies, yet he could not, now he was in a lunatic asylum and a prisoner, altogether treat them with contempt.

As the time wore away, without anybody coming, he began to grow very impatient. He had quite made up his mind that the one-eyed man would have given him his liberty when he found that he, the Captain, was not the Mr. Cadbury Kid he had been taken for.

Most likely this would have been the case, because the keeper had seen Mr. Kid; and although it was only for a short time, he was nevertheless conversant with that young gentleman's physiognomy.

The fact was this: the keeper had been sent for that morning to take charge of Mr. Kid, and had arrived at his house only a few minutes before the Captain down the chimney.

Mr. Kid, having certain suspicions of the character of the keeper, was not a little alarmed when that gentleman made his appearance at the foot of the bed, before he, Mr. Kid, had risen from his couch, and with great artfulness he contrived to induce the one-eyed individual to go down stairs into the street to call a cab, while he dressed himself.

It was just at the moment, that having hastily completed his toilet, Mr. Kid was asking himself what was to be done next, that the Captain made his appearance down the chimney.

Thus it was that the keeper, although he certainly had seen Mr. Kid, was not very well acquainted with his personal appearance; and so, as the Captain had unfortunately been disguised in soot, the keeper, never dreaming that Mr. Kid could have escaped him, never for a moment suspected that he had not got that eccentric young gentleman in his custody; and, naturally enough, imagined that it was one of those artful ruses so common to lunatics, to pretend to be somebody else.

After Crockford had waited a long while, hoping that the one-eyed man would return, he began to hammer at the door and shout.

He found that this was of no particular use, and desisted again.

But while he was pausing, intending, perhaps, very shortly to resume, he heard a rustle in the passage without.

He stooped and peeped through the key-hole.

Outside, in the passage, he was able to discern a female form.

He was uncertain whether or not he ought to call out, but he was relieved from any lengthy consideration upon the subject, by the woman's advancing towards the door; and suddenly opening it, she stood face to face with him upon the threshold.

By her dress and appearance the Captain judged her to be a housemaid.

She was very much astonished to see him; and uttering an exclamation of surprise and terror, made a step backwards, as though she would have beaten a hasty retreat.

"Who are you?" she exclaimed. "What are you doing in this room?"

"I have been shut in by accident. Show me the way out"

"No, no; stop where you are. If you attempt to come out, I'll call to one of the keepers."

She hastily retreated in the direction of the foot of the stairs, and in all probability would have carried her threat into execution, only the Captain, driven to desperation at the thought of all he had suffered and all that he would have to suffer, at once making a bold stroke for liberty, rushed at her and dragged her back.

"Hush, for your life!" he muttered, in a low tone. "If you make any alarm, you will pay for it dearly."

"If you don't keep your hands off me, I'll scream."

"If you do, I'll strangle you."

He looked so savage, that she was terrified and silent.

Nobody seemed to be stirring below stairs. He was in hopes of effecting his escape without attracting any notice, and the only drawback lay in the clothes which he wore. But he must not stick at trifles. Clutching the girl tightly by the wrist, he led her towards the street door. Until he had passed this he did not think it safe to release her.

She submitted to be dragged towards it, fearing to resist him; and holding her with his left hand, with his right he undid the bolts.

Then having opened the door, and still threatening her with his vengeance, he dragged her down the steps and across the yard to the outer gate.

All this while he had heard no one. No one had appeared to interrupt their progress.

He easily opened the outer gate, and then releasing his hold of the woman, he sprang through it and bounded up the street.

Not very far had he gone, however, before her piercing shrieks had brought some of the inmates of the asylum to the window, and a loud shout of "Stop him!" was raised by the keepers.

At the same time, the well known figure of the one-eyed man progressed towards the flying Captain from the other end of the street.

Catching sight of him, Crockford redoubled his pace. A loud shout of "Stop thief!" greeted him.

He rushed on wildly; he looked an extraordinary figure—he knew that, well enough—but he was now determined on only one thing, and that was to make his escape.

On he panted, the skirts of his dressing-gown flying in the wind, his bare legs and plush breeches giving him a most ridiculous appearance.

The crowd joining in the pursuit evidently thought so, too; for some of the tag, rag, and bobtail could scarcely run for laughing.

"Stop thief! stop thief!" echoed upon every side.

He rushed on frantically, but his pursuers gained rapidly upon him.

At length, rushing round a corner, Crockford ran violently against somebody coming in the opposite direction, and they rolled together in the mud.

Then the pursuers rushed up, and Crockford

was laid hold of by at least half a dozen busybodies.

Then the one-eyed keeper, coming up, claimed him as his prisoner.

"What has he done?" asked a policeman, who formed one of the crowd.

"He's a lunatic," said the keeper.

"I swear I am not!" cried Crockford.

"He's just escaped from the asylum."

"I was taken there by force, to day, in a mistake for another person; and I demand protection from your hands," he said, addressing the policeman.

Certainly, the Captain looked very mad indeed, in his extraordinary costume; but when the keeper came to look at him, he now saw, for the first time, that he really was not the Mr. Kid whom he had supposed him to be.

He opened his eyes and mouth in astonishment, and was uncertain how to act.

While thus hesitating, too, the policeman came to the rescue.

"I beg pardon, Captain," said he, touching his hat, and saluting Crockford, with a broad grin,—"I beg pardon if I've made a mistake, but I ought to know you, sir."

"Of course you know me," said Crockford, intensely delighted, for he recognised one of the men to whom he had spoken that night when Ruth had knocked him down, in Pall Mall; "I know you well enough, and I wish to heaven you would help me out of this mess."

"To be sure, sir," replied the man. Then turning to the keeper he said, "Here, you know, this gentleman don't want any of your nonsense; he's no more a lunatic than I am. Just please to take yourself off."

"I don't want to annoy the gentleman; only, as he got off my patient, and I shall get into a good deal of trouble by it, and lose my berth perhaps, I think the least that he can do is to stand something handsome"

Meanwhile, without taking any notice of the complaints of the keeper, the policeman had called a cab, and put the Captain inside, driving back the grinning crowd which pressed eagerly upon him from all sides.

"Where to, sir?" asked the policeman.

The Captain gave his address, and the cab started.

The mob cheered the departure, cheered the cab up the street and out of sight.

Some of the ragged little boys ran after him, bellowing at the top of their voices.

The Captain was, however, by no means anxious that this popularity should be prolonged: he pulled down the cab blinds, and shrank into the corner of the carriage out of sight; first, however, having told the cabman to drive his fastest.

They were not long before they arrived at Crockford's room in Piccadilly, and having directed the driver to knock at the door, he waited anxiously until it was opened before he made a plunge out of the vehicle into the house.

You can easily suppose that he was by no means anxious to be seen frisking about upon the sunny side of Piccadilly in the broad daylight, in that ridiculous dressing-gown, those absurd plush breeches, and those poor bare legs of his.

As it was, unfortunately, by some great ill-luck, the Dowager Lady B——, and her four daughters, chanced to be coming up the street, and catching sight of the Captain's extraordinary figure, they stood stock still, raising their hands and eyes in amazement.

"Gracious goodness!" cried the dowager.

"Goodness gracious!" cried the young ladies.

"What is it?"

"Who is it?"

"Can it be possible?"

"Never!"

"But it is!"

"He must be mad—or tipsy! What on earth does it mean? What an extraordinary proceeding!"

I don't know that the Captain's valet was more impressed by the sanity of his master than were the Dowager and her daughters.

He decidedly thought that his master was out of his mind. He was well accustomed to the Captain's vagaries. He was accustomed also to the Captain's stopping out all night—to even more prolonged absences, for that matter.

But during the time he had been in Crockford's service, he certainly had never known him return home in plush breeches.

Neither had he ever known him to return home without a shirt, or without shoes or stockings.

But he was the best bred of valets, and he forebore from making any remarks, or even of smiling. He assisted at his master's toilet, handed the clothes as they were required, with the grimmest possible countenance, but he offered no remark.

The Captain was, however, too much occupied by his own thoughts to have noticed the valet's demeanour, however curious it might have been. He was mentally thinking, thanking heaven for his happy deliverance, and vowing to himself never in his life to get into such a series of scrapes again.

"It was all owing to my curiosity," said he to himself. "What the deuce made me want to go and look into that stupid nunnery? It was all owing to one false step. If I hadn't gone through that door—if I hadn't followed that nun, I should have been all right; but what I regret the most of all, is having left behind me that diary and brooch."

He straightway fell to thinking how he should redeem possession of them.

But he could not afford to spend much time in reflection, for the day was rapidly passing away, and he had a long journey to make.

He was going, as the reader may remember, to Aldershott, where he expected to meet his father, from whom he was in hopes of getting a little pocket-money; for the Captain at this time—or, indeed, at any other time, for that matter—happened to be what he termed "uncommonly hard up"

When he was dressed he sent for a cab, and waited in the hall until it arrived, uneasily watching the minute hand of the small Geneva. He then set off to the railway station.

He was not a believer in omens. If he had spilt the salt at dinner, I do not suppose that he would have taken the trouble to throw a pinch over his shoulder. If a cinder had flown out of the fire at him, I don't think he would have searched for it in anxiety to discover whether it was shaped like a purse or a coffin.

He did not believe in dreams, and he did not care a bit what he dreamt about. No amount of black thoughts frightened him; and whatever was the subject of his nightmare, at daylight he dispersed their terrors effectually.

No, he did not believe in omens.

If he had, perhaps, the fact of the cab's breaking down upon the way to the station might have deterred him from his journey. Or the fact of his

having missed the train when he arrived there. Or, last of all, the extraordinary trouble which befel him, after all.

This was, that he lost his ticket after he had purchased it, and was upon the point of losing the second train in consequence.

Surely, fate was against the journey. Why did he persist in making it?

He was by no means in the humour for it. He was dead beat. Nothing in the world would have afforded him so much pleasure as going home and going to bed.

He felt as though he could have slept for a week.

But he determined to go. He must have the money. He could not do without it. Nothing in the world would keep him away.

I cannot say that I believe in mesmerism, and yet I think there must have been something like mesmerism at work in this case.

What was it that drew him on? If mesmerism were not at work, it must have been fate which dragged him onwards towards his doom.

Dragged him on to the strange destiny which awaited him.

Dragged him on as though against himself, against his will.

As the train left the station, and rushed through the steep cuttings into the open country, a wind sprung up, the sky appeared suddenly overcast, the face of nature darkened, and a storm seemed to be brewing.

Surely, there were very poor hopes of a day's pleasure. It would have been better for him to have stayed in town. If he had only known what a strange fate awaited him—what misery, what sorrow, what grief—he would never have gone.

But he was suspicious of no danger, and he went like a lamb to the slaughter.

The train bore him rapidly along, and he dozed happily in a corner of the carriage, little thinking what was coming.

Hitherto the Captain's adventures had been rather of a facetious character. The adventures which are now about to befal him will be stranger than those which I have already recorded. Some of them are very terrible—some of them very horrible.

Decidedly, if he had known that by stopping away from Aldershott he would have escaped from all this, he would have stopped away.

His fate awaited him. His fate in the form of a beautiful woman. In the form of Ruth the Betrayer!

Poor Captain! what was going to befal him?

CHAPTER XLII.

A TALE OF HORROR.—THE ORPHAN CHILD IN THE CLUTCHES OF THE DUMB ASTROLOGER.—THE DRUG.—THE VICTIM.—DEATH AND DISHONOUR.

The day had broken with a misty drizzle; and even now, although it was at least a couple of hours old, looked anything but promising.

I must take the reader back to a horrible neighbourhood, where he may recollect I left the unfortunate Cicely in the hands of a very suspicious couple, residing at the rag and bottle shop, whilst two houseless wanderers crouching in the doorway opposite were silently watching the exterior of the house, in which she had found the questionable refuge; and in a low tone that would scarcely have been audible at the distance of half a dozen feet, earnestly conversing upon the subject of the dumb astrologer's unenviable reputation.

As yet, none of the inhabitants of that vile locality had risen from their slumber to commence another day. Here and there might have been heard the faint sound of revelry, where some dissipated wretches had prolonged their godless orgies beyond daybreak into another day, but these gradually became rarer and rarer.

Every now and then some staggering sot, issuing forth from one of these dens of infamy, came rolling, and lurching, and staggering down the court, mumbling to himself, perhaps, or droning over the words of some Bacchanalian ditty, until he turned the corner, and was lost to sight and hearing.

At length the last of these had passed. The last light burning in the houses where the merry-making had been was extinguished, and all was still.

The two women not having any home to go to, had determined to sit in the doorway, where they were, to a great extent, sheltered from the wind and rain, and watching to see whether Mrs. Raddle and the dumb astrologer would come out again from the house.

And while they watched they were busily engaged in conversation. One of them was relating to the other the circumstances attending the mysterious affair, to which it may be remembered she had alluded, connected with the death of a young woman in the astrologer's house—a death which was accompanied by circumstances of a painful and suspicious character.

The wind howling mournfully round the house, formed an accompaniment of a thrilling and plaintive character, strangely appropriate to the nature of the story.

The woman telling it spoke in a subdued voice, and with an earnest and solemn expression.

The listener's face expressed the deep interest which she felt in the narrative.

"What was it?" one had asked.

"I will tell you," the other replied; and the story which she told was this:—

"About five months ago, according to the man's account, he wrote his story down, and they could only cross-examine him with a deaf and dumb alphabet—talking on their fingers, that is;—about five months ago, one night as he was coming home he found her sitting outside the gates of a workhouse, very cold and wretched, faint and ill; and out of compassion he brought her home, and gave her a night's lodging.

"Finding that she had quarrelled with her friends, and was in search of some employment, he offered to give her a situation in the house."

"It isn't his house, is it?"

"No—it belongs to the rag and bottle man; but he rents all the upper portion. Mr. Garbidge sleeps in the back of the shop upon a bundle of rags and rubbish, I believe."

"The deaf and dumb man lives up-stairs, then?"

"Yes. He wants all the rest of the house for the exercise of his profession."

"How is that?"

"To see his clients in, you know. Bless you, there are lots of ladies—ladies in carriages—who come to see him about their nativities."

"Their what?"

"Their nativities! To have their fortunes told, you know."

"Why you don't mean to say that they believe such a pack of rubbish? I should have thought poor people without any education might have done so, but not people in a better class of life."

"Why, bless you! they are every bit as stupid in some things as the others. Look at the spirit-rapping and table-turning! Why, it is only the educated classes, as they please to call themselves, that put any faith in such humbug as that. But as I was telling you——"

"Yes—about the girl."

"She was a relation of Mr. Jeer, the astrologer—his sister's daughter; and she had been searching in vain for him for several days, having come up to London for that purpose upon her mother's death; and she had expended her last shilling, and pawned her last available article of wearing apparel, when she met him. She thought that Providence had sent him to her rescue. Poor thing! it would have been better had she died of cold and starvation in the street before she had fallen into the monster's clutches!"

"Go on," said the other woman, seeing that her companion hesitated. "Your story interests me deeply."

"He took her, as I have told you, into his service, and she was to be cook and housemaid. As far as the first office went, it was almost a sinecure, for he was a miserly wretch, and scarcely partook of any more food than was absolutely necessary to keep body and soul together. Indeed, before she had come he had been his own cook and housemaid, and the whole house was filthily dirty—as dirty as his own person and linen—which you can judge for yourself."

"He is a most disgusting object, truly."

"Her duties were very light; they consisted for the most part in opening the door to the visitors, and as sometimes a whole day might elapse without any one calling, you can easily imagine that her duties were light enough. Indeed, it was this circumstance which caused her first of all to be weary."

"How was that?"

"It turned out afterwards. At least, I have it from the person herself, although the facts of the case were not stated as they ought to have been at the Coroner's inquest. But the poor girl told a woman in the neighbourhood, who told me. She said that the girl began to be a little uneasy sometimes when she asked herself why Mr. Jeer should keep her there unemployed. It was time that she was his wife—that she had some claim upon his generosity; but then he might have found her a situation somewhere, she thought, instead of keeping her in his own house, where he had really nothing for her to do."

"Still I see nothing so very suspicious in that."

"No, nothing that need have alarmed her, I think. But besides this, she began to notice that there was something in the man's manner which was very odd and unpleasant. He was entitled from his relationship to be to a certain extent affectionate. He embraced her every morning and evening, and blessed her, and patted her on the head and chucked her under the chin. She did not relish these fondlings over much, but she could not help herself."

"She did not know his character, either?"

"Well, not at first; but her friend—the woman, that is from whom I have these particulars—put her a little upon her guard when she told her of the dumb man's conduct, and warned her to be careful. You may be sure she was very anxious and uneasy about it, though she tried to think that her fears were altogether without foundation, and that she was frightening herself without cause. But to think this very long was impossible. His attentions soon became far too open, too unmistakable. You may conceive her terror and horror when, at length, one day when they were alone and no help at hand, he threw off the cloak which had hitherto covered his unbridled licentiousness, and made open love to her of the most dishonourable kind, accompanied by the basest and meanest threats of consequences which would ensue did she not yield to his hateful wishes."

"Poor girl, what did she do?"

"She defended herself upon this occasion so well, and the sight of her anger, her shame, her grief, and her disgust at his conduct, perhaps had the effect of cooling his transports, for he desisted from his odious love-making, and left her in peace without further molestation."

"Why did she not go then, at once?"

"I will tell you. When this occurred, it was about nine o'clock in the evening. She usually went to bed about half-past ten. She sought her room now, earlier than usual, determining, when the house was still, and he was asleep, to creep noiselessly down to the street door, let herself out, and make her escape. She listened, in the greatest anxiety, for the sound of his footsteps in one of the upper rooms to cease, as then she might conclude that he had gone to bed; but he was moving about for hours. At length, all became still. She listened with all her ears. Had he, at last, lain down to go to sleep? No. She heard the door opened very cautiously, and then a creaking footstep upon the stairs. She hastily blew out the light, and listened more intently than ever. She held her breath. Her heart throbbed violently. The footsteps approached nearer and nearer. At last a hand was laid upon the handle of the door. But the door was locked."

"He might have supposed that."

"I should have thought so; but he tried it several times. She could hear him rattling with the lock—hear him breathing, almost. She stood erect, and listened, clutching in her hand a sharp knife that she had brought with her into her bedroom, and which she intended to defend, while she had life, what she deemed of greater value than existence itself—her honour and purity!"

"Did he insult her?"

"No. Upon this occasion he did not; for when she called out, presently, 'Who's there?' he beat a retreat without making any reply, and she heard no more of him that night. Next day he apologized in the humblest possible manner for what had occurred the day before. He said that he had been mad, or drunk—that he would never more offend in like manner—and besought her forgiveness upon his knees, even calling the spirit of his dead sister to witness to the truth of his oath in a manner which, to the trembling and horrified girl, was hideously appalling and repugnant."

"What did she say?"

"What could she? Only that she wished to leave the house. She besought him to let her go. He entreated her to stay. She persisted. He became violent. At length he swore that she should not quit the house, and he locked the doors, and kept the keys in his pocket. She was now a prisoner, and was jealously watched by him at every turn, so that she found that any chance of getting away was quite hopeless."

"I should hardly have thought that."

"No; not to you or me. I think it would be next to impossible to lock us up in that fashion. But, you know, this was a poor, helpless, silly country girl, quite ignorant of the world—a mere child, in fact, as well in years as in understanding."

"And she could not get away?"

"No. Only upon one occasion did she contrive to tell the woman I have mentioned something of what had happened. She was speaking to her for a few moments one night, but the astrologer caught her, and dragged her in, threatening her in the most fearful manner."

"How did he treat her—cruelly?"

"During the time that she was kept thus, a captive, he was alternately harsh and affectionate. Now and then he returned to the vile propositions which he had made to her, and, with the most insidious and artful arguments, endeavoured to overcome her scruples. But she had been brought up in the fear of God by a tender and loving mother, and his honied words and alluring promises fell upon a deaf ear. At length, it appears that he grew savage, and determined upon possessing her; and he told her one night, after a more than usually daring attack upon his part, and fierce resistance upon hers, that no power in heaven or hell should save her from him. From that time, I believe, the atrocious miscreant had determined upon her death."

"What did he do now?"

"Curiously enough, a great change for the better took place in his outward manner, but this was only to conceal the black and bloody thoughts which filled his heart. His manner changed so much, that she was, to a great extent, thrown off her guard, and thought that he might have been moved to pity by her many tears, prayers, and entreaties when she had besought him, over and over again, upon her bended knees, to spare her upon account of her helpless and orphan state—upon account of the poor dead mother whom she had lost, and whom he professed to have loved. Alas! he was now to be feared more than ever. One evening—it was Sunday—a hot, sultry day, with scarcely a breath of air stirring, and hardly a murmur reaching her from the court without. She had felt very ill during the morning and afternoon, and only when the evening was far advanced, quitted her own apartment. It was only late in the evening that she felt sufficiently strong to go down stairs. And then it was more because she felt that a cup of tea might do her good, and she was not very anxious that the astrologer should mix it for her."

"How was that?"

"She feared him so much even yet, and she dreaded lest he might put some drug into it."

"Well?"

"Well, she came down as I say, and she found the man at tea. He invited her to take tea with him, and she consented after some slight hesitation. The exertion of coming down stairs, however, had deprived her of almost all the little remaining strength she possessed, and she sank into a chair by the side of the table with a deep sigh, which she found herself utterly incapable of repressing. He looked up at her anxiously, and inquired in his language, and with a look full of compassion and sympathy, whether she felt very ill, and gently upbraided her for leaving her room in her present state of health without assistance, and begged of her to allow him to summon medical aid."

"She ought to have agreed to that."

"Yes, it would have been a wise plan. However, she did not think so at the time. Her great fear seemed to be that he should discover how weak and helpless she was, and that his black heart should suggest to him the awful wickedness of taking advantage of it to effect her ruin."

"Poor creature, what a terrible position to be placed in!"

"Yes, indeed, her situation was truly awful. Brought up with the severest principles, with the profoundest horror of vice, the dread of dishonour was more terrible to this poor creature than would have been the thoughts of ten thousand deaths. But she was young, and guileless, and innocent. Even her experience of the baseness and treachery of the vile man into whose power she had fallen did not render her entirely suspicious of the truth of his professions of sympathy. She thought, or rather she hoped—hoped with all her heart and soul, that his sentiments had altered, and that now he intended to treat her with the consideration and kindness which she was entitled to at his hands as the child of his dead sister. He kindly arranged a pillow for her upon the chair on which she sat, and fetching a teacup and saucer from the next room, poured her out a cup of tea, and sat down opposite to her while she drank it, helping himself at the same time to another cupful from the same pot."

"From the same pot?"

"Yes, this she noticed; and before she ventured to drink her own, waited anxiously to see whether he drank his. He did so, and she was satisfied. When she had finished her cup there came a ring at the bell, and he left the room, closing the door after him. An hour or so might have gone by while she sat there alone, half dozing in her chair. Now and then a slight noise in the court outside would alarm her, but then again all was oppressively silent within and without. She strove for a long while to struggle against the absorbing sensation of mingled melancholy and terror that seemed to have seized upon her. She never, in her life, had felt anything like the sensation which now oppressed her. She felt as though a cold death-hand were laid upon her heart. Dim forebodings, an indescribable, indefinite, fluttering, aching dread of coming danger, seized upon her. An overwhelming sense of something awful—she knew not what—took possession of her senses, and kept her in speechless terror. Never before had she experienced anything like the sensation which now oppressed her mentally and physically. At last, she could bear it no longer. She felt her senses leaving her; she felt her limbs numbing, and an icy chill creeping over her. A strong, unaccountable desire seized upon her to write down her feelings. She staggered as well as she was able from the room up to her own apartment. Here, finding pen and ink, she, with some difficulty, sat down to her task."

"But how do you know all this?" asked the other woman, who hitherto had been listening eagerly.

"She wrote down what I have told you," said her companion, "in the words that I have related it, or in very similar ones; and she had reached the point in her narrative where she had reached her room and sat down to write. Then her strength seemed suddenly to have failed her. The words are scrawled and blotted, and almost illegible. Only there could be made out, '*I have been drugged*,' and then '*it is that man*,' and '*God have mercy*——.' After this the letter finished. My informant some time after, when she and some other neighbours came into the house, found it lying on the floor."

"Well, well! And what happened to the girl?" asked the other woman, anxiously.

"Late that night, aroused by loud cries, some other neighbours came rushing into the dumb man's house. They found him wringing his hands in the passage, his face expressing consternation and terror. Following him to one of the upper rooms (the girl's bedroom), to their intense horror, they discovered the unfortunate creature stretched upon the floor, with her throat cut in a frightful manner, and life quite extinct."

"She had been murdered?"

"Yes, barbarously and brutally."

"And by whom?"

"It was supposed by some robber, for the room had clearly been broken into and robbed. The only thing against this idea was that the doctor who examined the body asserted it his opinion that the wound in her throat had been made after death, and that she had died from the effects of an over-dose of laudanum."

"But what was said at the inquest?"

"Nothing transpired to throw any suspicion upon the astrologer. The doctor, in the most extraordinary way, disappeared, and did not give his evidence, nor has he since been heard of."

"And the woman who read the paper, and knew the facts you have told me of?"

"Said nothing. Why, it is impossible to say."

"It is altogether a strange story; but you might come forward."

"It is nothing to me."

"But you think the dumb man killed her?"

"I am certain he did. The doctor also affirmed that she had been cruelly abused. The hellish monster has another crime besides murder to answer for."

"But surely, in the cause of our common

humanity, you will make an effort to bring this villain to justice?"

"In good time, perhaps, I may, but at present I dare not. Let us say no more upon the subject."

CHAPTER XLIII.

THE DUMB ASTROLOGER'S DEN.—MRS. RADDLE'S JEALOUSY.—THE MYSTERIOUS CONVERSATION.—THE LIKENESS.—THE FRIENDLESS MAIDEN.—WHAT WILL BE HER FATE?—ALONE WITH THE MONSTER.

THE dumb astrologer and Mrs. Raddle bore the inanimate form of Cecily into one of the up-stairs rooms

It was a room at the back of the house, and this circumstance may have accounted for the fact of the two women watching in the doorway opposite not having seen a light appear at any of the windows.

However, for that matter, it would have been difficult for them to have seen a light even had they been watching the back instead of the front of the house, for the whole dreary building was plunged in the densest obscurity.

An impenetrable cloud of mystery seemed to hang over it.

By night, and very often by day also, all the shutters in the house were carefully closed. Then, upon the inside, the blinds were drawn down before them, and the curtains pinned across them. Thus not the faintest glimmer of light was visible from without.

Mr. Jeer's trade was a dark one, and his residence was even darker. The neighbours regarded it with timid dread, and approached it very shyly, believing for the most part that deeds of a fearful character were hourly occurring within its precincts, and that its owner had sold his soul to the devil

The little boys in the court, and in the neighbouring courts and lanes and alleys, occupied themselves at intervals throughout the day in endeavouring to peep into the house through the key-hole of the private door.

Though this was very unsatisfactory, after all, because the passage within was pitch dark, and there was a great perverseness among the inquiring youths, which caused them to be perpetually quarrelling about their turns, and dragging one another away at the most critical and trying moment.

Another great drawback to this amusement lay in the excessive artfulness and intense ferocity of the dumb astrologer himself.

He would lay in waiting for them patiently two or three hours at a stretch, rush out upon them, and beat them so unmercifully with a stick, that boys who were unlucky enough to fall into his clutches had been known to go limping for a week afterwards.

The consequence of these repeated sallies, and of many false alarms when the dumb astrologer was supposed to be coming, but in reality when he was not, was that flights of terrified boys were repeatedly scudding round the corners of the adjoining streets in wild confusion, and at the top of their speed, very much to the discomfort of unsuspecting elderly persons coming in an opposite direction, who were wont to be butted at suddenly in the pit of the stomach, and sent gasping, more dead than alive, on to the broad of their backs.

When Mrs. Raddle had seen the young woman who had proffered her assistance safely out of the house, she closed the door upon her, and returned to the apartment to which she and Mr. Jeer had carried Cecily.

The poor girl had been placed upon a mattress in one corner of the room, which, stuck upon a ricketty and top-sided contrivance of a very tumble-down character, and covered by a ragged quilt full of patches and darns, was facetiously termed a bed.

When the woman returned, she found the astrologer standing by the side of the fainting girl, and, shading his eyes with his hands, peering down at her earnestly.

The light from the candle which he held, fell full upon her face; and it was, indeed, very beautiful, in spite of its ashy paleness, and a certain worn and ancient expression, a look full of pain and fatigue, which its features wore.

It was a face which any one might well have contemplated, for the sake of its beauty alone; and, perhaps, there was a little jealous suspicion of Mr. Jeer's purpose expressed in Mrs. Raddle's face, as she entered the room.

"What now?" she asked, sharply. "What have you got to stare at her for?"

The man, without altering his position, continued to gaze at Cecily's face for some moments, silently.

Then, turning round, he uttered a number of strange sounds, accompanied by a great deal of gesticulation and pantomime. An extraordinary kind of gibberish it was, and quite unlike any language, ancient or modern; and in which the same words, or, more properly, noises, were repeated over and over again, in a most confusing manner.

There did not appear to be any novelty, though, in this curious mode of conversing, as far as Mrs. Raddle was concerned, for she answered him immediately—repeating, however, now and then, something which he was supposed to have said, but the sense of which she had not, perhaps, caught very readily.

As an attempt, upon my part, to reproduce the sounds the man uttered would but fatigue the reader unnecessarily, I will take the liberty of translating Mr. Jeer's choking and gurgling into plain English.

"Look here," he said; "do you know this face?"

"Know it! How am—how can I know it?"

"Haven't you seen something very like it?"

"Perhaps I have; but I don't take very much interest in the faces of a pack of girls."

"I thought that you would have remembered it, as there is more reasons than one why you should."

"I do not. Tell me what it is."

"No. We will wait awhile. I will tell you presently, when Skeleton Key arrives."

"As you please," replied the woman, a little surlily.

She spoke no more upon the subject, and went to the other end of the room, where, from a cupboard she took out a black bottle and a glass, taking with her, at the same time, a candle.

The astrologer moved away from the side of the bed, and, seating himself in a chair in front of the fireplace, in which there smouldered a few live cinders, began to stir them up with a piece of wood, which served in lieu of a poker.

After a while, he looked up, and, glancing towards his companion, appeared as though he waited for her to speak to him. But she affected not to notice the expression of his face, or the direction of his eyes.

Filling the glass with the liquor which she took from the bottle, Mrs Raddle approached the fainting girl, and poured a small quantity out, and put it to her lips.

Cecily moved her head uneasily, and with an expression of pain, but did not move her eyes.

"I tell you what," said Mrs. Raddle, after a short pause; "if we only take care what we are about, we may make a good penny by her."

"It was very lucky that we met with her."

"It was lucky that I suggested bringing her here. If we keep her quiet for a while, I've no doubt we shall come across some of my old friends."

"You'll never be able to open your house again. That's blown for ever."

"I'm not so sure of that," replied the woman. "I have friends enough to help me out of any scrape, if they would only come forward."

"But then they don't like, and it is very natural, for they have all reputations to lose, and wouldn't like to be mixed up in such a business."

"They wouldn't have to come before the public to help me. They know what to do without that, and how to work the oracle."

"You have got clients of all kinds, haven't you—some of them tremendous swells?"

"Pretty well, I think. There are some lords in the Cabinet, and Judge Black Stock, and the Bishop of Jericho."

"But as I told you, I think your best plan is to remain quiet for a little while."

"Yes, and for that reason I think it will be best to keep this girl here for the present, until I find some new place, which won't be long first, most likely."

Cecily lay still insensible, heeding not this strange conversation which was taking place in her hearing, and which, had she been able to penetrate its meaning, obscured by the unintelligible jargon of the astrologer, and the ambiguous terms in which the woman expressed herself, was calculated to have filled her with dread of coming evil.

The dumb astrologer relapsed into silence, and sat smoking a pipe, puffing the smoke up the chimney.

The woman was engaged in carefully turning out Cecily's pockets, and examining the make and texture of her dress, with some appearance of curiosity. Suddenly she paused, and said, "What time is it? We ought to have gone on to my house. It is too late now, I think."

"I think it is," said the astrologer, looking at his watch; "and I expect Skeleton Key will be here every moment."

"We will wait till he has been, then, before we go; but I think we might as well go, whether it's too late or not, just to see how they are getting on."

At that moment was heard a loud whistle at the back of the house.

The dumb astrologer rose to his feet, and took the light in his hand.

"There he is," said Mr. Jeer.

He went down stairs, and presently returned with the new comer, who was the goblin-like visaged individual to whom I have already introduced the reader.

"I have been expecting you for a long time," said Mrs. Raddle. "Have you got any information?"

"Nothing very wonderful, perhaps, but still something. I have found out that her name is Darcy. She gave me the slip this time, when I was following her, but I hope to be more fortunate upon the next occasion."

"I thought you had given up the business altogether," said Mrs. Raddle.

"Not quite, but I've been in great difficulties since"

"What has been the matter?"

"Everything, pretty near. You know that party who used to be a friend of Jacob Stone's."

"Who's that?"

"That mysterious lady who used to take all the money of him, when he was in the smashing line."

"To be sure; she was almost his only customer."

"Yes, I think so. What was her name?"

"Mrs. Trail, was it not? Certainly, I had forgotten. She calls herself something else, though, it seems, and lives in a swell house in Belgravia."

"Well, what of her?"

"You know, I suppose, that she was something in the informing way—in with the police, I mean?"

"Yes—I had heard so."

"Well, she took it into her head, for some reason or other, to split upon poor Jacob, and she put the police upon him—indeed, she helped to nab him herself"

"The deuce she did!"

"She gave him up to them in the artfullest way you can conceive; and I only managed to rescue him by running my own neck into the noose. However, we both got off clear, and Jacob proposed paying her out."

"I should think so!"

"With that idea, we went together to this Mrs. Ruth's house, and got in by the back door. The consequence was that Jacob contrived to get himself lagged, and if I hadn't given them leg-bail myself, I should have been had too."

Skeleton Key then entered into a lengthy description of the circumstances which had occurred at Ruth's house upon the night that Jacob and he broke into it in the way I have already related. When he had done, the conversation again turned upon the subject about which they had been previously speaking. The two men and the woman were in earnest conversation; and for a time the girl whom they had brought into the house, and who lay there still and motionless in a corner of the room, was quite forgotten.

Still and motionless she lay, to all appearances insensible; yet in reality she was not so, but earnestly attentive to the words which were being spoken within her hearing.

She listened to them with intense and breathless attention. Every word she sucked in. Many of the sentences which, at the first moment of hearing them almost, were entirely incomprehensible to her understanding, she repeated over and over again, until she arrived at some kind of solution of the mystery which at first enshrouded them.

Since she had lain there, a great change had taken place in her.

She had no strength—indeed, she felt herself weaker than ever; but the confused mist which had hitherto been hanging over her understanding cleared rapidly away; and, though she was barely strong enough to open her eyes, and far less to speak, to take part in any conversation, or even to express herself lengthily, she was still able to watch the people into whose company she had fallen, and to wonder to herself who and what they could be.

It required a person of a very hopeful and sanguine disposition, and of a very charitable nature, to suppose that they were anything but respectable, and that the business which now occupied them was not of a sinister and doubtful kind.

They sat close together, with their heads almost touching each other, muttering and mumbling in an under-tone, which was scarcely audible to the girl who was listening attentively to it.

As well as she could make out from their indistinct mumblings, they were talking about this same Lady Darcy—for it seemed that she was a lady of title who formed the subject of their conversation; and Mrs. Raddle and the dumb astrologer were consulting with Skeleton Key upon the best means to be adopted for the discovery of her place of residence.

The conversation ran thus:—

"How was it you discovered her name?" Mrs. Raddle asked.

"By something she had in her pocket—a card-case."

"How did you see that?"

"I picked her pocket in the crowd."

The two others laughed.

"We mustn't let her slip next time, when we get hold of her!"

"She won't slip out of my fingers, I'll take my oath of it," said Skeleton Key; "if ever again I clap my paw on her!"

"You're quite sure you'd know her again?"

"Quite sure."

"Look there, then!"

It was the dumb astrologer who spoke, or rather gurgled and spluttered out some strange sounds, apparently, however, intelligible to the person he addressed.

As he spoke, he twisted round sharply, and with his long, lean fore-finger, indicated the form of the recumbent girl upon the bed.

Cecily instinctively closed her eyes, and pretended to be unconscious.

Skeleton Key, taking the light in his hand, and approaching the bed, stood gazing upon her in the same attitude which the dumb astrologer had assumed a short time previously.

But scarcely had he well seen the face before him, when he uttered a loud exclamation of astonishment, and almost let fall the candle.

"Good heavens!" he exclaimed; "it is she!"

"No," said the other, "it is not; but still it is extraordinary like."

"Wonderful!" said Skeleton Key, drawing a long breath, as he moved away from the bed.

Some more conversation ensued, but it was in so low a tone that Cecily was unable to catch a word of it. Then the three wretches quitted the room together, closing the door to after them.

Cecily listened to the sound of their footsteps down the stairs, to the heavy closing of the street door, and their footsteps in the street.

When these, after a time, had died away, all was still save the pattering of the rain against the window panes, and the melancholy howling of the wind as it rushed through the keyhole and the crack under the door.

This was all she heard—no other sound reached her. As she lay upon the bed in the dark, she trembled violently, and her heart throbbed with anticipation of something dreadful about to happen, though she could not say what.

She felt, though, that she was in danger here—that she must have fallen into bad hands.

She must escape. When? Now!

But when she strove to raise herself from the bed, she found that her strength was unequal to the task.

After struggling vainly for a few moments, she sank back, half-fainting, upon the bed, and lay there perfectly motionless, like a corpse.

How long she remained thus she could not tell, but it seemed to her that it must have been a long while.

She was aroused at length by the sound of the door closing below.

The sound of a person ascending the stairs was next audible It was only one person.

Then the door opened, and the dumb astrologer entered alone

Cecily instinctively shrank back at the sight of him.

She would, if she could, have sprung off the couch on which she lay at full length; but she was weak and powerless.

He closed the door carefully behind him, and it was with speechless terror that she saw him turn the key.

Then he advanced towards her, and fixed his eyes upon her face—his fox-like eyes, shadowed by overhanging, bushy eyebrows.

He fixed his eyes upon the shrinking maiden's face, across which a crimson blush spread rapidly beneath the lustful gaze of this hideously deformed monster of depravity.

CHAPTER XLIV.

THE MORALITY OF ALDERSHOTT.—THE BEAUTIFUL LADY.—WHO AND WHAT IS SHE?—CAPTAIN CHARLEY'S MEMORY FAILS HIM.—CHAMPAGNE.—AN UNPLEASANT MEETING—THE PRINCE—ONE LOVER TOO MANY.

EVERYBODY, I am sure, has heard enough from time to time about the immorality of the life of the private soldiers in Aldershott Camp.

But I doubt whether, if an examination were instituted, the life of the officers and gentlemen would be found very much purer.

It is so easy to accuse poor people of being vicious, though I am not aware that their betters afford them a very praiseworthy example. If you had been down at the Camp upon the day of a certain review, to which I am about to take you, I think you would have been of the same opinion.

Among the assemblage of fair creatures there brought together to witness the coming sight, how many were there belonging to that class which, though a blot on our increasing civilisation, appears to be a certain attendant thereon. The handsomest equipages, the showiest toilettes, the most splendid liveries, all belong to the rich courtezans who batten upon the favours of the wealthy young officers whose vicious tastes lead them to prefer such society to the more virtuous.

It was a sight to cause sorrow and alarm in any thinking mind to see the daring and shameless way in which vice and licentiousness were unblushingly paraded in this place.

Heedless of the frowns or sneers or the averted glances of the more virtuous portion of the community, the dashing occupants of the barouches, britzkas, and phaetons paraded their diamonds and finery, laughing noisily, and passing disparaging remarks in the loudest tone of voice upon their humbler attired, though more virtuous, sisters;

while even the almost ragged, utterly lost, and hopelessly seedy strumpets of the private soldiery appeared to hold a higher position in the social scale, among the profligate and immoral young men of fashion, than the chaste daughters of respectable tradesmen and modestly attired wives and daughters of honest artisans.

But as this book is not intended to be a series of sermons upon public morals, but a romance founded upon scenes and characters taken from real life, I will proceed with my story, after this short digression, which the reader is perfectly at liberty to skip without the fear of offending me.

It was a splendid summer's morning, the birds were singing, the trees were in full leaf—all nature seemed smiling and glad. A momentary dulness, which at one time had threatened the pleasure-seekers with a heavy shower of rain, cleared away again, and all was once more bright and hopeful.

A great crowd was assembled to see the review which was about to take place; and the proceedings would occur immediately upon the arrival of the Commander-in-Chief. Something, however, delayed him. Some unforeseen event had caused him to be behind his time; and many anxious eyes were turned in the direction in which it was known he must approach the scene.

At length, close upon the outside of the crowd, was heard in the distance a loud clatter of wheels—a great cloud of dust is seen—everybody made sure that the great man had arrived.

The carriage approached nearer; but it was not until turning the corner of the road—until it had dashed impetuously in among them, scattering the crowd to the right and left, and narrowly escaping the destruction of those who were rash enough to come within reach of the high-blooded and prancing horses, that they saw that its occupant was not the person whom they expected.

Instead of the grey-headed and grim old warrior, the hero of many a hard-fought battle, it was a young and beautiful woman, attired with a most costly and magnificent dress, absolutely dazzling in the sunlike glory of her loveliness.

Yes, she was truly splendid. One could see at a glance that she was one of those happy beings whose lot it was only to enjoy wealth and happiness, to be fed, and clothed, and worked for by an inferior race of male mortals—to live only to be loved.

But I, who knew her well, and who am here to write her history, knew the reverse—for she was Ruth.

It appeared to those who saw her upon this happy day, when she appeared all life and spirit, happiness—thoughtlessness, and gaiety, that for her the world was a great pleasure-garden—that nature was bound over to keep a smiling face for her sake, and that nothing must ever go wrong to vex her.

The awe-struck and admiring throng gazed in rapture upon her angel face, her fairy-like elegance, the costly taste displayed in her toilet, the grand voluptuousness of her faultless form, and the matchless grace of her easy attitude.

To see her thus, it would almost have been utterly impossible to have believed that she could have been the heroine of the many stories of darkness, treachery, villany, and baseness, which were told of her—that she could have done that I have already described.

But if this were difficult to realize, how much more so would it have been to imagine that which is yet to come—to picture this fair creature so bright and beautiful in the awful scenes through which she will have to pass?

Could any one believe that those splendid habiliments are to be changed for rags and filth?

That instead of the luxuries which now surrounded her, she will be skulking away, hiding for her life in a dark cell!

Among thieves and outcasts of the lowest grade!

That heavy chains will fetter her wrists and ankles—that she will lie pinioned and manacled in a noisome dungeon, forgotten, despised, hopeless, and helpless, and awaiting a shameless death before the eyes of a brutal, jeering, and unsympathising mob! Yes, dread even such a fate as this, less than that which might await her did she fall into the hands of this same populace, thirsting for her destruction—longing to wash their murderous hands in the heart's blood of this arch traitress and betrayer.

But we must not anticipate the end. All this, and worse even, shall she certainly pass through, but not yet.

Deeply shall she sink, though high shall she rise again.

Misery, grief, and degradation await her. Agony, mental, and physical. Great shall be her sufferings, stupendous her triumphs. And the end of all shall be something so unlike all that you can possibly expect, knowing her now so little as you do, that you must even wait patiently until I arrive at it by a slow and tortuous, though a necessary course.

She seemed this particular day to have thoroughly made up her mind that she would enjoy herself and be happy, whatever fate might be in store for her to-morrow; and she came among the crowd with her gallant steeds and splendid equipage, looking so beautiful and good, that a little army of hungry ragamuffins immediately surrounded the vehicle upon it stopping, and vociferously begged for alms; a course of proceeding, however, which resulted unhappily for them in the coachman laying about their backs and shoulders the sharp tingling thong of his coach whip, until they howled piteously for quarter, rubbing themselves at the same time with such wry faces that the pretty lady laughed merrily at the sight of them, and complacently begged the coachman to lay it on harder.

"But who was she?" everybody asked.

A few of the men knew her, and they were questioned eagerly by those less fortunate persons in their company who did not enjoy the same advantages.

More than one general officer raised his hat as she passed by; a great lord, who happened to be present, bowed low to her when she looked at him; but nobody approached her carriage—nobody appeared to be upon terms of sufficient intimacy to enter into conversation with the beauty.

"By Jove!" said Lord Windibank, "she's heavenly. And what a turn-out! Do you know who she is, Charley?"

"Who who is?" asked Crockford, who was giving a sketch of some of his recent events to a small, but greatly astonished, group of brother officers, who interrupted him every now and then by loud "Oh's!" and hearty bursts of laughter. "Who who is?" he asked, feeling rather vexed at this interruption to his narrative. "What are you bothering about now?"

"Why, look there!" said Windibank; "did you ever see such an almighty stunner? But who is she? Do you know her?"

"Yes, I know her," answered Crockford, turning again to his companions, and resuming the story where he had left off. "As I was telling you——"

But his lordship was not so easily to be put off.

"Don't you see she's beckoning to you?"

"Who's beckoning?"

"The lady in the carriage."

"What lady?"

"What lady? Why the deuce don't you look? ou said you knew her just now. If you don't, what's the good of telling any lies about it?"

The Captain turned round, and, fixing his eye-glass in his eye—for he was rather short-sighted—stared fixedly at Mrs. Belvidere.

She had at the time her face partly turned away, for she was speaking to one of her footmen; but when she turned again, he uttered an exclamation of astonishment, and hastily advanced towards the carriage.

But when he did so, just before he reached it, he stood still again, and, with another exclamation, appeared as though he were about to retrace his steps.

After all, it was not the person he had supposed. Whom had he supposed it to be?

While he stood hesitating, Ruth looked at him and beckoned. With a face indicative of surprise, he obeyed the summons and approached.

"You don't remember me, Mr. Crockford?"

The Captain regarded the speaker with attention, and answered, after a slight hesitation—

"It is extraordinary, madam! I feel certain that I do know you; yet at the same time I see that you are not the person whom I supposed you to be. There is some difference, though what it is I cannot describe. In fact, I am in a perfect maze."

"You are a most inconstant person, or you would remember me without any difficulty. I thought that I had made more impression upon you than I seem to have done. At least, I was vain enough so to think to myself."

The Captain continued to gaze at her with the same intensity of regard. For the life of him he could not call to mind where he had seen this face, which was so familiar to him.

It was not the face which he at first supposed. He felt certain of this, as he turned to look at her; for, among many other points of resemblance in which they differed, he saw that this lady had very light hair, while the other one had very dark.

He would have been almost led to suppose that he had not known this lady at all, and that her likeness to the one for whom he had taken her was a mere accidental circumstance.

She seemed to know him; that was the most confusing part. What could be the meaning of it all?

"And so, sir, you mean to tell me that you have forgotten who I am?"

"Upon my word, madam, I own it with shame and humiliation, that I have not the least idea; something in your appearance has undergone such a change since I last had the pleasure of seeing you."

It was now Ruth's turn to blush.

The last occasion in which they had met she was dressed as a sailor, and had knocked him over into the mud in Pall Mall upon the evening when we first had the pleasure of making her acquaintance.

But she did not suppose that he alluded to that circumstance, and she very easily recovered her self-possession. Indeed, blushing was a weakness she was not much given to. The Captain, however, attributed it to a very different cause. He thought that she was offended at his rudeness, and the idea did not at all tend to set him at his ease.

"I am so altered, you say?"

"Yes—that is—I mean——"

"I am grown so old and ugly. That is what everybody tells me."

"I can scarcely believe that," said Crockford.

"But is not your forgetfulness a proof of it?"

"No, I do not see that. Indeed, if you had not mentioned my name, I should almost have thought that you had been mistaken in me: in fact, now, I believe you take me for my elder brother."

"Oh, no, I don't! At least, I believe I have the pleasure of speaking to Captain Charley Crockford."

"I have the misfortune to be that individual."

"Why is it a misfortune?"

"Firstly, because I am a younger son, with nothing to live upon, and no particular expectations; and secondly, because it appears to me that at some time or other I must have missed the opportunity of improving the acquaintance of the most beautiful of her sex."

"Meaning me?"

"As a matter of course."

"That is too pretty a compliment to go unrewarded. What reward can I give you? Will you have some lunch?"

"There is something substantial about that, and I accept it with pleasure."

Ruth gave orders to her servants to lay out a cold collation upon the opposite seat of the carriage, at the same time motioning the Captain to take a seat beside her.

"If I might only venture to ask the name of the lady who is of such a forgiving disposition, and so bountiful a nature?"

"You won't receive any information upon that head, sir, I assure you. Your having so easily forgotten me, is a very poor encouragement for me to repeat it."

"In that case, generous, beautiful, but mysterious unknown, I drink to you with my eyes."

He also used his lips in this process, and took a long draught of champagne to the honour of his hostess.

The little lunch spread out before them was of the most delicate description: chicken, paté de foi gras, Strasbourg pie, and a variety of other dainties, accompanied by the choicest fruits and the rarest wines, whilst the manner in which this little repast was served up, and the silver appointments, in the form of forks and spoons and cruet-stands, were so many unmistakable signs of wealth and luxury upon the part of their owner.

"I wonder who the deuce she is," thought Charley Crockford to himself. "She's got lots of tin, it is quite evident; and she's a swell of the first water. But, however I could have seen such a beautiful woman before, and have forgotten her, is astonishing."

But as he was very hungry, and as the delicacies displayed before him were extraordinarily tempting, he made the best use of his time with his knife and fork, instead of troubling his head unnecessarily in respect to his hostess's identity.

It was very certain, whoever she was, that she was a most accomplished woman, and a most agreeable talker. As they sat trifling with their dessert, they chatted about the review and the company attending it, the people in town, the celebrities of the season, the prima donnas at the rival operas, the last new ballet dancers, and the latest divorce case.

Thus their conversation ran on very pleasantly, until Crockford chanced to make some remark about a certain Italian prince who was at that time one of the notables upon town, celebrated for his lavish expenditure and combative propensities.

"Do you know him?" asked Ruth.

"I know him well enough by sight: almost everybody about town does the same. I know one or two fellows who have been out with him. I owe him a grudge myself, but we have never chanced to be thrown into each other's company."

"It is very curious," said Ruth, "but I expected to have met him here."

"Indeed! Have you not seen him, then?"

"No, he has not come."

"Not come?"

"No."

"But excuse me, I think you are mistaken."

"How do you mean? One of his servants met me upon the way here, with a message from the Prince to say that he would not be able to come."

"That is indeed very curious, for just before you came on to the ground I passed him."

"But then I am afraid, Mr. Crockford, that your knowledge of faces cannot be relied upon."

"If you do not believe me," said the Captain, "judge for yourself;" and as he spoke, he pointed to a horseman in the distance.

Ruth looked in the direction indicated, and turned deadly pale.

The Captain, in amazement, asked her what was the matter, and endeavoured to take her hand.

But she freed herself almost roughly from his grasp; and though it did not tremble in the least, he fancied that it seemed deadly cold.

Then she sat back pale and motionless, with her

eyes fixed upon the face of this foreign nobleman, seemingly anxious to shun observation, but unable to withdraw her eyes from his face.

And you may readily suppose that her feelings were not the most enviable.

Here was a man, the most jealous, exacting, and suspicious, and the most revengeful, passionate, and violent. He was the source of almost all her income It was from him that she hoped to have got a sum of money sufficient to fly the country, and escape from the mob of enemies and the crowd of dangers surrounding her. Had she supposed there was any chance of meeting with him at the place, she would not have asked Crockford into her carriage.

Everybody knew Captain Charley and his dreadful reputation.

He was almost the last person in the world that she would have had the Prince find her in company with.

But there he was, and there was no getting rid of him.

And now, the Prince having turned his head caught sight of her, and approached the carriage.

Ruth clenched her little fist, and prepared to meet the storm.

There was no doubt that a storm was coming.

She could read it in the Prince's lowering brow, flushed cheeks, and sparkling eyes.

CHAPTER XLV.

THE PRINCE IN A PASSION.—RUTH PLAYFUL, AND THE CAPTAIN INDIGNANT.—CARRYING A JOKE TOO FAR.—THE RUNAWAY POSTBOY.—A FORCED ELOPEMENT.—MAKING LOVE, TO PASS THE TIME AWAY.—THE FOREST.—THE HORSEMAN.

Yes, the gentleman's face indicated mischief.

There was, to say the best of it, upon the gentleman's brow a very savage scowl.

There was in the gentleman's eyes a very sinister glare, and about his mouth a certain twitching which seemed to say that, if he had been a dog, instead of a well-bred gentleman, he would have liked to bite.

In spite of all these unpleasant signs, however, the Prince was sufficiently master of his emotions to dispel the cloud from his face; and though there was still a slight trembling about the lips, and an unusual pallor about the cheeks, he came forward smiling, then took off his hat, and bowed low to the lady.

Captain Charley looked very hard at him.

The Prince looked at the Captain with an angry glare. They both looked as though they could have eaten each other, but neither made any remark.

"How do you do, my dear Prince?" said the lady, with an amiable smile. "I am very glad to see you."

"Are you?" said the Prince, quietly.

"How well you're looking! Do keep your horse quiet, though; I think your spur must be pricking him. You will frighten my horses if you don't mind, and you know how restive they are."

Oh, how evil his eyes looked! His lips were ashy white.

I don't think, either, he took her advice about the spur. He must have plunged it even deeper than before into the horse's flank, for it began to rear and plunge furiously.

When the horse was again a little quiet, Mrs. Belvidere continued, with even a more pleasant smile, almost, than her features had hitherto worn.

"I waited for you some time," said she.

"That was very kind of you. Did you wait long?"

"No, not very long."

"I thought not."

"No, I never wait long for anybody. I waited more than a minute, though."

The Prince bowed low.

"You were too good. I am deeply indebted to you."

His face was livid with passion; but he managed to keep an appearance of tolerable calmness, in spite of the furnace raging within.

But the provoking coolness of Mrs. Belvidere was more than flesh and blood could endure. She began to laugh and chat with her other companion, and appeared almost to forget that there was a third person in the company. The Prince, with something that sounded very much like a muttered curse, dashed his spurs into his horse, and galloped away to the other end of the field.

"His Highness seems a little put out," observed Captain Charley, with a grin.

He thought all this was rather good fun, although he did not exactly understand what the connexion could be between the Prince and this lady. And "who was this lady?" he asked himself again and again. He could not tell. Decidedly he had seen her before; but, for the life of him, he could not think where, or under what circumstances.

Meanwhile, the Prince at the other end of the field had been joined by his groom, and they were engaged in earnest conversation. Presently the Captain saw that he had dismounted, and was coming towards the carriage on foot.

"I wonder what's going to happen now," said Crockford to himself. And he could not help feeling some slight internal emotion, so determined and savage was the expression of his Highness's countenance as he advanced.

He said nothing, though, upon the subject; but curled his moustache, looked as pleasant as he could, and waited.

The Prince approached the carriage, and addressing Ruth in a low voice, said, "Will you oblige me with a few moments' conversation, madam?"

"I am quite at your service, Prince," she answered. "We are listening to you."

The Prince could not help making a slight grimace; but he continued, in the same courteous tone as before, "It is to you alone, madam, that I wish to speak. Presently I shall have a few words to say to your companion. I shall not ask for your presence then."

The Captain twisted his moustache, and addressed the other with the greatest possible coolness—outwardly so.

"I should think," said he, "that you don't require to be told that I shan't be likely to take it into my head to get out of the carriage, so as to afford you an opportunity of intruding your company where it is not required. It's very easy to see, I should imagine, that I am very comfortable where I am; and I should suppose, from your position on the outside, that you have a very lively appreciation of the great disadvantage you unfortunately happen to be placed at."

How pleasantly the pretty, fair lady smiled upon them as they talked. You might have thought that they were acting a little play for her special amusement. You really never could have supposed that she knew very well that blows and bloodshed must inevitably result from it.

"You surely are not serious?"

She knew they were.

"You surely are not serious?" she repeated, with such a pretty pretence of being afraid they would hurt one another.

"No, madam," said the Prince, calmly. "Do not be alarmed. I never lose my temper in company, and I never quarrel about such trifles." Then he added, in a stern tone, and with an imperious glance, "At another time I can say what I have to say to you. I shall remember it."

"In that case, I'm glad you are going to keep it in your own possession," said the lady, "if it is worth anything; for I have such a shocking bad memory myself, I should be sure to have forgotten all about it in half an hour's time."

The Prince did not condescend to make any reply, but he turned upon his heel and walked away.

Without turning his head again, he proceeded towards his groom, who was standing holding his horse at the other end of the meadow.

Talking with the groom, was one of the postilions of Mrs. Belvidere's carriage.

To both of these men the Marquis appeared to give some orders. Then he turned round his horse's head, and galloped across the field in the opposite direction to London.

Ruth watched him depart, and laughed as though it were a capital joke.

"He's mad," said she; and then turning to the Captain, requested him to fill her a glass of champagne.

She had recovered entirely by this time from the terror in which the appearance of the Prince had at first thrown her. She very easily made up her mind when in a dilemma what would be the best course to pursue. She knew very well that the Prince would be offended when he found her in company with the Captain: but she would not have made affairs any better if she had got rid of Crockford; and she had also some idea that she might get something out of him.

No, she thought it would be wisest to risk the Prince's anger. Nothing so dreadful could come of it; at most, probably only a little quarrel, which the Prince might patch up again with a little present—a present of the sum of money which she was so much in want of.

Ruth and the Captain, drinking their champagne, did not notice that the postilion had remounted his horse.

Then he began cracking his whip, and the carriage dashed off through the crowd.

"What is he doing?" cried Ruth, rising in her seat. "Stop him."

But it was not so easily done as suggested.

"Stop!" cried the Captain.

"Stop!" cried Ruth.

The postilion made no reply; but thrashing his horses vigorously, they broke into a gallop, and dashed into the open country.

Captain Charley, standing up in the carriage, shook his fist, stamped his feet, and bawled with all the strength of his lungs to the postilion to pull up his horses.

The man seemed to be deaf. He did not pay the slightest attention.

The horses now were tearing along full gallop.

"What shall we do?" asked Crockford of Ruth.

"I haven't the least idea," she replied.

"We ought to stop him. But how? Shall I throw a bottle at him?"

"For heaven's sake, don't; you may kill him."

"What's it matter?"

"Certainly it doesn't matter much," said Ruth; "only what's to become of the horses? He'll upset us."

"To be sure; but then what are we to do?"

"Let's sit down and take things quietly."

"I'm sure I am quite agreeable," said the Captain; "with so beautiful a carriage, such a beautiful road, and such a beautiful travelling companion, I'm sure I should be the last person in the world to wish to bring the journey to a close."

"If you have no appointment to call you away, and I am not trespassing upon your time, I am very thankful for your company."

"They are first-rate horses. What a tremendous pace they are going at!"

"I hope they are not running away."

"By Jove! what shall I do? Shall I jump out into the road? If I do, I shall most likely lose my footing, and get left behind. If I throw myself among the branches of one of the trees by the road-side, I shall get stuck fast, like Absalom, and get hung up by my whiskers."

"If you will take my advice you will sit down instead, and make love to me. That's the best thing you can do. Suppose you'd run away with me, or I had run away with you, or that we had run away together."

"So we have. If I could only believe that we were really lovers——"

"Well, what prevents you?"

"Nothing that I know of, except that I suppose that you do not care twopence for me. That may exceed the value you set upon me, but I'd love you with all the devotion——"

"With all the fiddle-sticks! Everybody has heard of Captain Crockford and his love-affairs. You're a dreadful man, now! Are not you? By the way, who was that lady I saw you riding with in the Park, the other day? I could not catch a sight of her face, but you seemed to be deeply engrossed in each other's conversation. It was a beautiful carriage, too, with splendid appointments."

"What day do you mean?" asked Crockford, eagerly.

"Why, when I come to think of it, it was yesterday."

"Yesterday! So it was; yet it almost seems like a month ago."

"Poor fellow! does the time pass so slowly when you are separated from her?"

"Not at all; a great many things have happened to me since, which I may, some time or other, describe to you, if you will give me a patient hearing."

"And about this lady?"

"Yes; I was going to tell you. I made a bet with a friend of mine who was with me at the time, that I would make the acquaintance of the first lady who came by in her carriage, that I would take a ride with her, and kiss her, before we came to the gate."

"What! supposing you did not know her?"

"Of course; that was part of the wager."

"You must have a tolerable amount of impudence."

"Pretty well, I believe, as times go."

"And, pray, what was the end of the adventure? What did she say to you?"

"I can scarcely recollect all that was said, but I shall always remember the adventure as one of the pleasantest in my life."

"And this ride—shall you forget that?"

"Never!" said Crockford, pressing her hand to his lips."

For a few moments they rode on silently. Suddenly Ruth said, "Look, Mr. Crockford! Where are we going?" "We have quitted the high road."

What he said was perfectly correct. They had passed through an open gate, and were now crossing a broad common, thickly studded with furze. Avoiding this, however, the postilion rattled along at a brisk pace, until at length they reached a small, but thick wood, and, dashing into this at a spot where there was a kind of path formed by nature, and free from tree or shrub, the horses were brought to a sudden halt.

Ruth sprang upright in the carriage.

"Well," said she, addressing the postboy, "have you taken us to our journey's end? What next?"

The man grinned and touched his hat, but was silent.

Ruth was about to make some further remark, with increasing indignation, when her eyes all at once alighted upon a horseman slowly approaching them through the trees.

With an exclamation of surprise, she recognised the Prince.

CHAPTER XLVI.

TRICKS UPON TRAVELLERS — THE LONG FOOTMAN.—THE LEAP.—RUTH'S HEART.—THE OLD WOMAN.—THE RUFFIAN.

THE Prince took off his hat, and bowed to the lady and gentleman with an ironical smile.

"I hope you liked the ride," said he. "Is it not extraordinary that I should have met you?"

Crockford, with a savage frown, made as though he would have sprung out of the carriage on to the ground, but the Prince stopped him.

"One moment, if you please."

"It doesn't please me," replied the Captain. "What do you mean by this trick? What are you going to do? Both this lady and myself are anxious to return to London to-night, and I will thank you to allow us to do so without any further delay. As to you and I, we, at some future time, will have a few words to say together."

"You won't go back to London to-night, either of you!"

"Indeed!—why?"

"Simply because you have no horses!"

"What do you mean, sir?"

"I mean that I want my horses!"

"Your horses?"

"Yes; the lady understands perfectly, though you may not. The carriage is hers—the horses and postilions belong to me!"

"Is this true?" asked Crockford of Ruth.

Ruth blushed a little, but answered in the affirmative; and the Prince, without taking any more notice of the Captain, turned his horse's head, and rode away a few yards from the carriage.

While, however, this conversation had been going on, the postilion had very quietly detached the horses from the vehicle, without either the Captain or Ruth having noticed the circumstance. By this time he had mounted upon the back of one, and was trotting very quietly away, leading the other horse by the bridle.

"Very well," said Crockford, white with passion, as he leapt down upon the ground. "It is then, sir, for you and I to try which is the best man! As this seems such a deep-laid plot, you surely have not forgotten to bring your pistols with you?"

"We will manage all that another time," replied the Prince, smiling. "At present, I prefer to leave you where you are, in the lurch! You are not more than four miles from a town, if you only walk in the right direction. There are a few roadside inns, and a village or two, at a little distance; but I do not think that you will be able to get any conveyance nearer than the town to which I have alluded."

Crockford gnashed his teeth, but was silent.

"It is rather far," continued his Highness, with another smile; "but in the company of the beauteous Belinda, the path will seem strewn with roses. Farewell, and *bon voyage!*"

So saying, the Prince spurred his horse, and galloped away, laughing heartily.

The Captain was livid with rage.

He stamped and swore.

He shook his fist. He rushed after the Prince, and ran himself out of breath Then he came back, panting.

But, as he drew near to Ruth, he burst into a loud roar of laughter.

Ruth, who was sitting very still, and looking very solemn, asked, rather angrily, what was the matter.

Crockford tried to answer, but could not. He could only point to the carriage behind Ruth's back. Ruth turned round, and, in spite of her feelings of pique and indignation, could not refrain from a smile.

For there, bolt upright, as stiff as a ramrod, with a face as solemn as a judge, stood Ruth's footman, who had been a silent spectator of the foregoing scene.

Truly the expression of the worthy creature was wonderful to contemplate.

There he stood like a statue. Like a stoop, if you like it better; or like Lot's wife when she was turned into salt. During the altercation he had said no word. He had been afraid to speak or move a finger.

He did not want to offend his mistress, and he dare not offend the Prince.

Poor fellow, he thought it quite likely that one of the gentlemen, either the Prince or the Captain, would turn round upon and kick him, when they found that they could not kick each other.

Therefore was it that he kept quite still and held his tongue.

"Now then, big man," said Ruth in a mocking tone, addressing the stately flunkey who, was a good deal over six feet high, and who, with his powdered hair and cocked hat, looked perfectly gigantic. "Now then, big man, where is your comrade?"

"Left behind, ma'am," replied the footman.

"And what are you doing there, pray?"

The man looked sheepish, but made no reply.

"I think you'd better get hold of the pole and pull the carriage," said Ruth, laughing merrily. "Or, stay!" she added after a pause, in which she seemed internally to enjoy the long footman's discomfiture. "If you open the carriage door and let down the steps, I think I had better walk."

The Captain held out his hand, and assisted her to alight.

"Which way, madam?"

"Which you like. All roads lead to Rome, if you would like to go there."

"No, not to day. I should very much like, though, to come across one of those famous castles one reads of in fairy tale books, where invisible hands would lay for us a dinner of roasted larks plovers' eggs, champagne and strawberry ices."

"Well, perhaps we shall—who knows?"

"I like this walk," said Ruth.

"Yes," said Crockford, "though I am afraid it will tear your satin boots."

"Oh, never mind my boots, you careful creature, but go and gather me those violets"

The Captain did as he was bid, and returning with the flowers, arranged them in the bosom of his companion's dress.

In doing so he could feel her heart beating beneath his hand, which lightly touched the voluptuous contour of her graceful form.

Then his eyes looked down into hers, and hers looked up into his, and a curious thrill of ecstacy seemed to quiver through his frame, and draw him towards her. Was he too in the folds of the snake?

Another victim?

They walked on silently for some little time, the long footman preceding them some little distance in advance.

They followed the course of a small stream through the wood which serpentined gracefully among the trees. Presently, at a spot where the foliage was at its thickest, they came to a sudden halt.

It was because they found the long footman had pulled up short, and was contemplating the water with a meditative expression of countenance.

"Now, then!" said the Captain impatiently, "what has happened."

"We shall have to go back, sir."

"Why?"

"You see, sir, this ditch turns round here in a sort of loop, and goes back almost to where we started from."

"Why, my fine fellow, can't you jump over a drop of water like that? I'm ashamed of you, really."

"I'm not a good hand at jumping, sir."

"Try."

"But what'll you and missus do, sir, even if I manage it?"

"To be sure!" said Ruth; "what am I to do?"

Crockford made no reply. He raised Ruth in his arms, and sprang lightly over the stream, alighting safely upon the other side.

The long footman, who had gone a dozen yards off, in the hope of finding a narrower spot, looked at the feat with his mouth wide open, too much astonished to make any remark.

But Crockford noticed that Ruth's face was pale, and she seemed deeply moved with some secret emotion.

"You are afraid," he said, gently.

"Yes," she replied, in a tone of deep feeling, regarding him with her great blue eyes full of tenderness,—"yes, I am afraid."

"But the danger is past."

"That danger," said she—"the danger of the little ditch. But it was not that I was afraid of."

"What then?"

"I am afraid to tell you."

"Do tell me!"

"I was afraid of loving you!"

The sun was setting over the distant hills, tinging them with a roseate hue.

"We must get on quicker," said Ruth, "or it will be dark before we get out of these fields."

She took his arm now, and they doubled their pace. Presently, the long footman called to them.

In the distance he could discern a small cottage, he said. Should they go towards it, and inquire the way? It was agreed that they should, and thither they bent their steps.

When they approached the door, they found an old woman sitting spinning in the porch, and she rose and dropped a curtsey to them, as they came forward towards the house.

"Could you tell me, my good woman," the Captain asked, "where we should be likely to get some kind of conveyance to take us to London?"

The old lady considered a while.

"Jarvis lets out traps," said she.

"Does he?" said the Captain. "And where bouts does he hang out himself?"

"He lives over yonder, at Woodbrook."

"How far is that?"

"Less than a couple of miles."

Ruth heaved a little sigh.

"I shall never be able to walk so far," she said.

"What is to be done?"

"Suppose Joseph goes?"

"Who's Joseph?"

"This," pointing to the long footman.

"Oh!" said Crockford—"that!"

"Yes, he can fetch one for us."

The long footman looked a little glum at this, but he nevertheless took himself off in the direction indicated by the old lady. When he was out of sight, Ruth asked permission to sit down and rest inside the cottage, and the old woman picked a tiny bouquet out of her garden, and presented it to the lady.

But the time soon began to hang rather heavily upon their hands. The twilight was stealing towards them over the hill-tops and up the valley.

"I wonder when ever we shall get home?" said Ruth.

"How far is it to London?" asked Crockford of the old woman.

"A goodish step," she replied, after due reflection.

"How far is that?"

"Fifty miles, perhaps."

"Good heavens!" ejaculated both the Captain and Ruth simultaneously. "We can't go to-night!"

And they felt inclined to give the old woman a good shaking for not having mentioned the distance sooner.

But what was to be done?

"The railway is the quickest way," said the old woman presently.

"How far is that off?" asked Crockford.

"About a mile to the station."

He felt as though he could have sworn a good round oath, but he refrained from doing so, as he desired a little more information.

"Have you any idea when the trains go?" he asked.

"I think there is one at half-past eight"

Ruth looked at her watch.

"It is five minutes past now; but I am fast, I think. We may catch it."

They decided at once upon the course to pursue. They gave the woman five shillings, and desired her, when the footman returned, to tell him to pay the man for his carriage, and then go back and look after the other carriage he had left in the wood. This he was to put up somewhere, and telegraph to London for further orders.

Having thus settled matters as well as they could, they inquired the way to the railway, and set off at once.

But they seemed to be doomed to meet with adventures; and now one befel them which, perhaps, at first the reader might suppose it is not necessary to relate, though it will be found, when the story is further advanced, that it considerably influenced the fortunes and the future of the two persons concerned in it.

It was this.

The road pointed out to them by the old woman lay across a field. There was a stile to climb, and the Captain, going first, lightly vaulted over it on to the grass upon the other side. But he did not alight only upon the grass, for he also came down upon something lying upon it, and this smashed under his feet.

The Captain looked down in surprise, and his astonishment was not diminished at finding that he was standing upon the crown of a man's hat, which he had crushed as flat as a shut up gibus.

Casting his eyes a little further, he saw, at half a foot's distance from it, a man's head.

"Thank God I did not come down on that!" thought the Captain; and he was going to mutter some apology, when the owner of the head, a burly ruffian, with a dirty and brutal-looking face, sprang to his feet, and demanded fiercely what he meant by his behaviour.

"It was an accident," said the Captain. "I'm very sorry, I'm sure, but I'll pay you for it readily."

"Yes, there's no mistake about that," growled the man.

"How much do you want?" said Crockford, without noticing his insulting tone. "Will that do?" and he handed him half a sovereign.

The man tossed it over, and put it in his pocket, growling to himself. It seemed as though he would rather have had a row than had the money, but he could not well say anything, and he stuck the battered hat on his head.

Crockford advanced towards Ruth, and was going to assist her over the stile, when the man stepped forward, and made as though he would have crossed it before her.

"Now, then!" said the Captain, wrathfully; "allow the lady to go first, if you please."

The man took no notice. To allow him to pass, Ruth would have been obliged to descend again from the step on to which she had mounted.

"There's room enough," growled the man, elbowing her slightly.

Crockford, furious, was about to strike him, when, to his amazement, Ruth herself seized the ruffian by the neckerchief, and, with a sudden jerk and push, sent him flying backwards into the ditch.

"By Jove!" thought the Captain, "what a strength she has in the wrist!"

Then he helped her hastily across the stile, and turning to the fallen man, prepared for the attack which he supposed would be made upon him.

But the man lay motionless.

He appeared to be stunned. Crockford thought he was half drunk, perhaps. He looked like it.

Anyhow, as he did not come forward, there was no reason why they should wait for him; and they hurried on, fearful lest they should lose the train.

They crossed the field and entered a lane beyond, without the man's coming after them; and taking no more heed of the circumstance, except to laugh at it, pursued their way.

But this was not the last they were to see of him, as time will show.

Little dreamt they, also, what scenes of horror they would soon encounter, as they walked on arm-in-arm, like two lovers as they were.

"I like this Crockford," thought Ruth to herself. "I don't think I ever met a man I cared so much for."

"She's the sweetest woman, by Jove, I ever clapped eyes on!" thought Captain Charley. "And what pluck she has!"

They had need of pluck before long, as we shall see.

On they went, little dreaming what was in store for them, or that they were both going so near to death.

CHAPTER XLVII.

LOST AMONG THE LANES.—THE STORM.—THE LONELY HOUSE ON THE MOOR.—SIGNS OF DANGER.—FALLEN AMONG THIEVES.—VILLANY.—TREACHERY.—TERROR.

THEY walked together down the road for some distance without making any observation; each being too deeply occupied with his or her reflections.

They had not, however, proceeded very far before they came to a place where two roads branched off, one to the left and the other to the right.

Between them was a finger-post. The Captain stood still before it and looked up.

He could make nothing of it, however, without the aid of his eye-glass. Using his eye-glass, it was still an unfathomable enigma; and after staring at it very hard for a few minutes, he summoned his fair companion to his aid.

She, in her turn, used her own eyes and her eye-glass, with the same result.

"Can you make it out?" asked Charley.

"Not a word of it. Can you?"

"Not a letter."

"Well, I won't go as far as that, because I fancy I can just discern something faintly resembling a capital T turned upside down."

"Well, it's a useful sort of finger-post, I must say. What on earth are we to do?"

"But don't you know which way you were told to go?"

"I can't be quite certain. I think, though, they said keep to the right."

"Was it the right? I thought it was the left."

They argued the matter together for a few minutes rather warmly: one persisting upon the right, and the other being just as positive upon the left.

It was very awkward. How could it be decided? No way suggested itself to the disputants except turning upon their steps, and going back to the house to re-inquire of the person who had directed them. This idea, however, was finally rejected; and Captain Charley very gallantly deferring to the lady, they set off at a brisk pace.

There was every reason why they should not lose more time than was positively necessary upon the road. The evening, which for some time had been close and murky, as though it portended a coming storm, now momentarily became more and more threatening.

Scarcely a breath of air was stirring. The air seemed to be so thick and heavy, one might almost have fancied that it could have been cut assunder with a knife.

"I wonder whether the station is much farther off?" said Ruth, presently, with a faint sigh; and at the same time she stepped to press her hand upon her brow.

"Not far," said Crockford, "if we have taken the right road."

"Thank God for that!" said Ruth.

"Are you ill?" asked her companion, anxiously, noticing an unwonted pallor on the lady's cheek.

"No, no!" replied Ruth, with an accent of intense weariness. "It is nothing. I am a little tired, that is all. It will pass off directly."

"Will you rest for a while?"

"No, thank you. We had better get on, if we can, as quickly as possible, before the rain comes down."

"But you seem scarcely able to stand."

"It is very foolish of me. I am not usually so childish. I scarcely seem to be like my own self, though, to-day. The excitement of the scene I have just gone through—I don't know what it is, in fact; but I do feel very ill."

"I am sure you do, dearest! Lean upon my arm, and I will assist you; or, if you will stop here, I will run on foot, and try to find out whether or not we are on the right road; because, perhaps, you may be walking now in the wrong direction, and fatiguing yourself without any necessity."

"No, no; I will not leave you. We will go together."

Again they continued upon their way, silently, as at first. Another turn of the road, however, brought them to a place where two more roads branched off, as before.

This time, though, there was no finger-post.

"Well, it's no loss," observed Crockford, with a smile, "supposing all the finger-posts in this part of the country are the same pattern as the last."

"But what on earth shall we do?"

"We can only keep on walking. Which way do you propose?"

"I have no choice."

"Well, we'll keep to the left, I think, as we began with it."

They therefore proceeded, taking the road to the left.

"I wish, though, we could see some one, to tell us something about the place we're in," said Crockford. "I can't see anything of the station."

"Look!" said Ruth, pointing across the fields to the extreme right. "Don't you see a light there?"

"Yes."

"Perhaps that is the railway."

"We'll go to it."

They were standing at that moment close to a stile that led into some fields, upon the other side of which the light that Ruth had spoken about was shining. Crockford assisted Ruth to climb over, and they set off across the fields.

By this time darkness had set in; and after proceeding for some short time, when they came to look back, they could not discern the objects even at a distance of a dozen yards. Curiously enough, too, the light by which they had been steering their course became suddenly extinguished.

"Halloa!" said Crockford, pausing abruptly. "Where are we?"

"We must have come wrong."

"We certainly have."

"I hope we shall not lose ourselves."

"I am afraid we have done so already."

"Oh, dear! what will become of us?"

Just then the storm, which had been long threatening, burst forth with tremendous violence.

The rain positively poured down upon them. They had got to a place which was flat and open. No trees could they see upon any side to afford them the slightest shelter. Indeed, it was impossible to see much further than the ends of their noses, so dark was it; but they, nevertheless, ran on as quickly as they could, Crockford insisting upon taking off his coat to wrap round Ruth's shoulders and protect her in some measure from the violence of the storm.

All at once they came up to, and almost ran full tilt against, a wall.

"What's this?" said Crockford, in amazement.

And looking up, they found, to their inconceivable delight, that it was a house.

It was a large house, too, but the night had been so dark they had not been able to see it.

"I hope it is an inn," said Ruth; and they proceeded round the wall in the hope of coming to the street door.

If it were an inn, it was not one apparently much frequented. As well as they could judge, it stood upon a bleak and open spot, far away from any other houses.

There were no lights in the windows.

All was still as death within and without. Save and except the splashing of the rain upon the earth, no other sound could they hear.

Presently, though, they came to what appeared to be the principal entrance. It was a strong door, shuttered and closed.

Over it, however, there hung something betwixt them and the sky. They looked up at it inquisitively. It was a sign-board, swinging mournfully to and fro with a low, creaking sound.

"It is an inn, then?"

"Yes, it seems so."

"Though, whether or not it is inhabited is another question."

"How can we tell?"

"I will knock."

It was Crockford who spoke; and he began to hammer away at the door with his knuckles.

But without causing any effect. No one replied to the summons—no one took any notice of him, although the noise he made was, in his opinion, quite loud enough to have been heard in any of top rooms, or at the back of the house, had the inhabitants been there.

"If anybody does live there," said he, presently desisting when his knuckles were sore, "they are either asleep or dead."

Just then, a bell-handle, projecting from the wall, attracted Ruth's notice. She pointed it out to her companion.

"Perhaps that may rouse them!" said the Captain; and catching hold of the bell with both his hands, he began to tug away with all his might.

The noise was like that which might be supposed to be caused by the bell of a monastery being rung upon an alarm of fire or some other dire calamity having befallen its monks. It clanged and clattered discordantly. The sound of it might have been heard nearly a mile off across the bleak, swampy, flat country. As its echoes died away the two travellers stood wistfully watching the door, in the hope of its being opened; and at they stood and waited, they crept as close at possible under the shadow of the porch, which, although it afforded them a poor shelter from the pitiless storm, was still, in want of a better, not to be despised.

At last, to the unspeakable satisfaction of the listeners, they heard a faint sound of footsteps within.

The footsteps appeared to be coming down stairs

They approached the door, and then stopped suddenly.

At this, the Captain losing his patience, began to drum with his fists upon the door panels.

When he was still again, they could distinctly hear fresh footsteps pattering, and then whispering within.

"I don't very much like the look of this," said Crockford to his companion; "but we must not turn tail now."

"No, no!" said Ruth; "we cannot face the storm we have come through."

Again they listened, and again the sounds of whisperings saluted their ears.

This time an angry altercation in a low tone of voice appeared to be going on within. There were the voices of a man and a woman. The man appeared to be insisting, the woman resisting.

Then came the sound of a blow, and a half suppressed shriek.

The Captain began to hammer again, and in the middle of his tattoo the door was thrown suddenly open.

The person who had opened it threw back the door wide, and stood upon the threshold, shading a candle which he held with his hand from his face.

It perhaps would have been no particular drawback had he been able so effectually to shade it that it could not have been seen at all, for truly it was not a face at all likely to entice a wayfarer into the establishment. There was a remarkably bad look about the mouth—a very bad look indeed—which, however, was surpassed in ugliness by the expression of the eyes.

The owner of this unpleasant physiognomy was a short thick-set man, apparently past the prime of life, and dressed in an old smock-frock, with a wide-awake thrust low down over his forehead.

As he stood for almost a minute without saying a word of invitation to the travellers, but instead, staring very hard at Ruth's face and figure, Crockford asked sharply whether they were right in supposing that they had come to an inn.

"Yes, this is an inn," replied the man surlily.

"Can we have accommodation here for the night?"

"If you choose, you can."

"Well, suppose you get out of the way, then, and let us come in," said Crockford impatiently.

The man moved slowly upon one side, and admitted the travellers into a large, bare, half-furnished apartment, which, from a few coarse benches and a deal table standing in the middle of it, and one or two empty beer jugs littered about, appeared to be used as the common tap-room upon those remote occasions when anybody came to their house to drink; for from the forlorn and forsaken appearance of the premises, both within and without, it was not unreasonable to suppose that the business done there was of the smallest.

The aspect of this dreary room, so chill and cold and forlorn-looking, caused a shiver to run through Ruth's frame; and for the first time since the idea had been formed by the travellers of remaining at this inn for the night, a half regret took possession of her, and a misgiving of she scarcely knew what, passed through her mind.

But, after all, what was there to be afraid of? Nothing as yet of a very alarming character had transpired.

True, it was a large, lonely house.

True, there was an ugly and ill-favoured landlord.

True, there had been a good deal of whispering within before admission could be obtained.

But all these things put together did not amount to much. Besides, it was very sure they could not go out again into the rain.

"I am very wet and chilly," said Ruth, shivering again, but this time from the cold: "have you not got a fire somewhere, landlord, where we can warm ourselves and dry our clothes?"

"The fire's out."

"Have one lighted for us, then, if you please," said Crockford. "I should have thought that you would have kept one burning such a night as this."

"I didn't expect any one would come out such a night as this."

"Have you no neighbours?"

"Not less than a mile off."

"Ah, that's a long way for this weather. But I should have thought that you would have kept a fire upon your own account."

"I had something else to do. I was busy down in the cellar when you came."

"That accounts for your not hearing us, perhaps. We had been hammering for half an hour before you came."

The man did not appear at all anxious to prolong the conversation. He appeared to be of a very taciturn nature, although it must be allowed that during the last few minutes, since he had had on opportunity of studying the exterior of his guests, his manner had become rather more polite, and he appeared, after a fashion, to be desirous of making them comfortable.

Turning round, now, he addressed some person standing immediately behind him, and whom Crockford hitherto had not noticed.

Ruth, however, had been observing her attentively.

There was something in her face—for the person alluded to was a female—which must have struck even a casual stranger.

There was a certain fixedness about her features, and a ghastly pallor upon her cheeks.

She certainly was beautiful, although her beauty was, to a great extent, faded. Her figure was slight, and appeared to be wasted by illness.

The hand which she reached forth to take a light from the hand of her male companion was so frail and attenuated that, coming before the candle, it was quite transparent.

"Light the fire," said the man, gruffly, "in the Blue Room."

Then turning to Crockford, he said, "Would you like some supper?"

"If you have got any in the house," said the Captain, with a slightly contemptuous smile.

"What would you like?"

"What have you got?"

"What you choose."

"We are not particular," said Crockford; "but if we were, I don't suppose that your assortment is very extensive. However, get us what you can—something hot, I think."

The man considered a little, and hem'd and ha'd a good deal, and at last promised to make them some tea and toast.

The travellers, however, were more desirous of warming themselves by the fire and drying their clothes, than of settling upon what kind of refreshments they would take afterwards; and Crockford asked whether they could not at once proceed to the apartment which was being prepared for them

The landlord appeared to object to this, and delayed an unnecessary length of time in preparing some candles to take up before them to light the way.

Before he was ready, the girl come back to say that "the fire was lighted."

What was it that made Ruth look towards her with an anxious expression of alarm and dread, throwing upon her face a glance of piercing scrutiny?

When the girl had taken the light from the man a little while ago, she had contrived to exchange a rapid glance of deep though unfathomable meaning with Mrs. Belvidere.

For one brief moment, when she had got an opportunity of doing so, unobserved by the landlord, she had telegraphed to Ruth that some danger was abroad.

Ruth fancied that this was the meaning of the sign which was made to her; but she could not conceive how she was to benefit by it, or what course she ought to pursue.

Now, again, as she made her appearance at the foot of the stairs, she contrived to throw the same appealing, warning look towards Ruth, and for a moment to gesticulate earnestly, though what she intended to convey by this motion was impossible to tell.

Then, as the man looked towards her, her face suddenly changed again to the fixed and motionless attitude which it usually wore. Observing it attentively, Ruth began to understand the meaning of a certain painful expression which had settled upon it long ago.

It was the impress of some strong emotion at some former time—the trace of some great terror through which she had passed.

Some awful terror—terror unspeakable and overwhelming.

A fearful dread, never to be overcome or effaced from the mind of the woman who had felt it.

As Ruth looked at her, though, a suspicion passed through her mind.

"Is she mad?" Ruth asked herself.

Mad! If anybody was mad it was Ruth, who did not take the warning that was now offered to her.

Another moment, and it was too late!

CHAPTER XLVIII.

THE STRANGE CONDUCT OF THE LANDLORD.—THE BLUE ROOM—THE STORM CONTINUES—A HAND UPON THE DOOR.—THE STRANGE GIRL AGAIN.—THE INTERRUPTION.—MYSTERY.

THE landlord, taking up the candles in front of his guests, led the way ceremoniously to the apartment which he had designated "Blue"

As well as the guests could perceive, there was, however, nothing in the colour of the wall paper, the painting, or the appointments of the room to warrant the bestowal of such a title.

It was a large, gloomy, windy place, however, which the two tallow candles that he set down upon the table were quite incapable of lighting up.

When the landlord had put down the lights he withdrew, and left the travellers to themselves while he went down stairs to look after the supper.

As soon as the sound of his footsteps had died away in the lower regions, Ruth addressed her companion.

"What do you think of this house?"

"It's a curious place."

"Yes. I wish we were out of it."

"Why?"

"I don't know. I think there is danger in it."

"What, do you suppose it is one of those wonderful inns we read of in old romances, where the beds sink down into a pit, and the travellers are robbed and murdered, and never heard of any more?"

"I don't see why such things should not exist."

"No; no more do I. Only I am pretty sure they do not."

"Do you think all murders are found out?"

"Very few are not, I should say."

Ruth seemed as though she were inclined to impart to the Captain some private experiences to the contrary; but she refrained from doing so upon consideration. She rose instead, and began to examine the apartment.

It was extremely large. It appeared, indeed, to be much better adapted for public meetings than for private parties. There were several doors in it, most of which, however, were locked; and the remainder opening into bare rooms, unfurnished, or on to the great bare staircase.

There was hardly any furniture in the room: decidedly nothing unnecessary. There was a scrap of carpet in the middle, upon which the table stood. There were half a dozen chairs placed at long distances, a small sideboard, fender and fire-irons, and a hearth rug, and that was all.

Ruth sat down opposite to Crockford on one side of the fire-place, and dried her boots as well as she could.

The wind without howled, and whined, and surged mournfully.

The rain beat heavily against the window panes.

Within the house all was unnaturally still and quiet. If the landlord and the strange female who had so excited Ruth's curiosity were below, they must have been sitting still, or were perhaps in some distant part of the building, for their movements were quite inaudible.

Very shortly, however, the landlord and the woman made their appearance, the latter carrying a tray on which was a tea-pot, some tea-things, and a dish containing ham and eggs; and having set these down, the couple retired again, and left the guests to themselves.

Ruth sat down to pour out the tea, and the Captain very gallantly carved the ham and assisted his fair companion to a couple of poached eggs. The hot tea, too, in a great measure dispelled the dull feeling of discomfort, which for some time past had caused Ruth to maintain a gloomy, thoughtful silence, and which had even such an effect upon the amorous Captain himself, that for the last twenty minutes, at least, he had not attempted any compliment, or ventured upon one languishing glance at his fair companion.

Reviving, however. under the influence of the beverage which "cheers, but not inebriates," he pressed Ruth's hand twice whilst taking his teacup from her, expressed devoted attachment for life between two mouthfuls of bread and butter, and told her he loved her between a couple of gulps of hot tea.

He was a great lover of the ladies, was Captain Charley, as I have already intimated, and a great *roue* and rake; and he was by this time beginning to bless the lucky chance which had thrown this lovely woman into his way.

He thanked Providence, too, that it was a wet night, and that they had lost the train. And although he was not quite sure that his companion would be an easy conquest, for he was still quite unable to remember where he had seen her before, or by her manners, appearance, and conversation to judge what was the station in life which she might occupy; yet he had great confidence in his winning tongue and seductive fascinations, which had been, alas! ere this, the ruin of many a maid, wife, and widow.

The tea progressed, and the gentleman's attentions grew more and more pointed, and his meaning more apparent; but though the lady suffered his attentions with but a small show of prudery or resistance, it was impossible to say whether or not she would yield to the fascinations of the lady-killer any further than submitting to a rather warm flirtation over the tea-cups.

"It still rains," said Ruth, rising to her feet, pushing away her cup, and turning round to the fire; "will it never leave off?"

"I shouldn't care if it didn't," replied the Captain.

"Why, pray?"

"Is not my motive evident? Because it keeps you here a prisoner with me."

"But you would soon grow tired of my company, if you were obliged to be here. You can't think how ill-tempered I become when I am bored!"

"I hope you are not bored yet?"

"Not at all. I am very happy, all things considered——"

"Meaning that you would have preferred another cavalier."

"No, I should not. But I should prefer a better inn—a little more comfortable, if possible. I never saw such a great wilderness of a place. By the way, I hope that our bedrooms are a little better furnished."

"You speak in the plural?"

"Of course I do, sir! What do you mean?"

"I only meant——Hush! See!"

The Captain paused, and became silent. His eyes were fixed upon the door.

Ruth looked at the alarmed and eager expression of his face with amazement, and then followed the direction of his eyes.

It was at the door that he was looking—and she looked at it, too.

"What is it?" she whispered in a low tone.

"Look!" he replied—"it is moving!"

"What?"

"The handle!"

"What is moving it?"

"Hush! Speak softly; some one is opening the door from the outside. Let us talk as before."

And then, in a louder tone, he resumed the conversation, and began to chat upon some indifferent subject, scarcely knowing, though, what he said, so anxiously was he observing the movements of the door-handle.

It turned slowly—slowly.

Then the door was pushed open with a faint creak.

The Captain gently motioned to Ruth to turn her head away from it. Then, shading his face with his hand in such a manner that the person without could not, when they looked in at the door, tell whether or not he was looking in that direction, he watched eagerly.

The door opened very, very slowly—as though the person entering the room were fearful of making the least noise—very, very slowly and cautiously.

At length, when the aperture was sufficiently large, a head was thrust in, and as suddenly withdrawn again.

Then thrust in once more.

It was the head of the beautiful girl. Her face wore an anxious and terrified expression.

She advanced into the room upon tip-toe, and approached Ruth. The Captain, quite unable to understand what could be her reason for this mysterious behaviour, started suddenly to his feet, and intercepted her progress.

She sprang back, alarmed by the unexpected movement, and uttered a slight scream.

Next moment, though, she recovered her self-possession, and laying her finger upon her lip, anxiously motioned to Crockford to be silent.

"Whist!" she said between her teeth, looking in a wild scared way towards the door "Whist!"

"What is it?" Crockford asked, in profound astonishment.

Ruth had risin to her feet, and she also was regarding the excited girl in dumb amazement.

"Oh, madam," said the girl, "I must speak to you! I must say what I have to say, though he would kill me if he knew."

"Who would kill you?" asked Ruth.

"*He* would," said the girl, pointing with her finger in the direction of the lower part of the house.

"What, the landlord?"

"Yes—yes. You will not betray me?"

"No, my good girl. What have you to say?"

The girl advanced closely to Ruth, and approached her lips to Ruth's ear.

The other woman bent down her head, and waited in anxious expectation of hearing what the girl had to say.

But at the moment that she seemed about to speak, a sudden noise below attracted her attention.

A grating noise, as though the bolts of the outer door were being drawn, either in or out of the sockets.

With a shiver which shook her whole frame, and an expression of intense dread and terror upon her ashy face, she stole from the room towards the landing, and stood there listening to the sounds below.

CHAPTER XLIX.

THE PLOT THICKENS.—THE DANGER INCREASES.—ANOTHER RUFFIAN APPEARS—THE WARNING.—THE BEDROOM.—WAITING FOR DEATH—THE EVIL MOMENT ARRIVED.

THE Captain and Ruth waited anxiously for the girl to return.

But she came not.

Presently the door was pulled gently to again.

They listened intently for the sound of her retreating footsteps upon the stairs; but they heard nothing.

If she had gone down stairs again, she must have made the descent with a step noiseless as the approach of death.

At length Ruth turned towards her companion. Her face was as white as death. She mutely inquired his opinion of what had transpired by the expression of her eyes.

The Captain, though, seemed completely puzzled. He pursed up his lips, and shook his head.

"Well?" said Ruth, interrogatively.

"Mad!" replied the Captain.

"I don't think so."

"What do you think, then?"

"I think there is danger in this house. I think we would be better out of it, if we could get away."

The Captain, though, had his reasons for wishing to prolong their stay.

"Listen!—how awfully it is raining!" he said. "We can never face such a storm as that!"

"Oh, dear! will it never hold up? Perhaps they may have some kind of conveyance, though. I wish we had inquired at first. Will you inquire, now? Perhaps we might be able to get on to the railway station, or to some other inn."

"My dear, I really do not think that there is any cause for alarm. Believe me, you do our host a great injustice. He is a surly country bumpkin, but nothing more. Besides, remember this is England, and not the dark ages. You don't suppose that anything dreadful could happen——"

Just then he fancied, though, that he heard a cautious step outside the door; and into his head, at the same moment, came rushing the recollection of the scenes in the convent, through which he had so recently passed.

If such things could occur in the heart of the most civilised city in the universe, why should not robbery and murder take place here at this wild, forsaken spot?

He did not feel over comfortable for a minute or two, but then he was a plucky, courageous fellow, and not easily daunted.

"I'll tell you what!" said he very suddenly. "I will go down stairs, and have a look around me, and report thereon; and if I see my way clear, we'll get off."

He took one of the candles, and walked towards the door. Throwing it open suddenly, he looked sharply round.

But he could see no one. Had he found anybody

lurking about, he certainly would have dreaded foul play.

There was nobody, however, and he began to think again that their suspicions were unfounded.

"You won't mind being left by yourself for a moment or two?"

"No, no; do not be long."

The Captain descended the stairs as quietly as he could. The slightest noise, however, that he could not avoid making, brought the landlord out at the bottom of the staircase.

"Did you want anything, sir?" he asked.

"Yes," said Crockford; "I want to ask you if you have a time table of the railway."

"No, sir, I have not."

"Do you know anything about the time the trains go?"

"No, sir; we never have occasion to know anything about 'em here. I ain't much of a traveller."

"Pray have you any conveyance?"

"No, sir—none."

"Does anything pass your house?"

"To-morrow morning a cart will be by early, and call here. I can send on for a carriage for you then."

"Thank you. How far is the railway from here?"

"Two miles."

Crockford was silent for a minute. During the pause, he heard the wind roaring without, and the rain beating upon the outer door.

It was absurd to think of going away at such a time, or of facing such weather as this.

"Thank you," he said; "we won't sit up late Bring up a glass of brandy and water, and a glass of port wine negus, hot."

The man had no wine to make the negus. He would bring the spirits, though, in a few moments.

While they had been talking, Crockford had been looking round inquiringly, endeavouring to find out as much as possible about the house.

There was really nothing, however, of a suspicious character visible, and he turned upon his heel, and retraced his steps.

He could hear some one moving in an inner room upon the ground floor—a room which might have been the bar parlour, if an inn of such a primitive character, and so badly furnished and fitted up as this one appeared to be, could have such an office.

The person he supposed to be the girl who had been up to speak to them, because he fancied he could discern the rustle of a dress, and that when he was speaking the noise ceased, as though she had paused to listen to what he said.

Crockford retraced his steps, however, greatly relieved in his mind with respect to the character of the house and the landlord.

He was an ill-shaped, ill-looking, ungainly lout, that was sure enough.

But he was no worse, the Captain felt convinced, and he laughed at himself for having been persuaded by the fears of his fair friend a few moments ago, to feel any fear himself.

"Besides, hang it all," Crockford thought, "he's only one man, after all; and I don't think I can recollect having met with any one man yet whom I was very much afraid of!"

He walked up-stairs very briskly, and hummed a tune softly to himself.

He had closed the door of the room where he had left Ruth; and when he got upon the same landing again, just for a moment, he did not recollect which door it was.

By some fatality he opened the wrong one.

He opened the door of a room next to the one where Ruth and he had been sitting.

He opened it quickly, and made a step forward, and he found himself face to face with another man.

Struck dumb with the astonishment which so unexpected an event called forth, he stood stock still, and examined the face of the person he had thus suddenly come upon.

He had seen the face before; where, he could not remember.

The man was in the same way attentively examining the Captain's countenance, and probably in the same way endeavouring to recollect where they had met before.

All at once, he appeared to recollect; and pulling a battered hat, which he wore, down upon his brow, went slouching past.

The movement attracted the Captain's attention. It was the man whose hat he had jumped upon early in the evening, when he was getting over the stile.

The man made no remark, neither did the Captain. The latter, full of misgivings and forebodings of evil, returned to the room where Ruth was waiting for him.

"Did you hear any movement outside the door while I have been away?"

"Yes," she answered, eagerly; "I thought I heard a footstep. I have been listening. I feel very uneasy."

"Perhaps, after all, we should be better out of the place. But what can we do? Listen to the rain!"

"Never mind the rain. Let us brave it, and escape!"

"No, no!" replied Crockford. "We cannot do that. What is to become of us out on that wild, desolate moor? I hardly think that the landlord would be a very desirable guide. We must stop now. But we will be watchful."

"Have you, then, seen or heard anything to cause you to be uneasy?"

Crockford made no reply.

He, certainly, if he could have seen his way clear, would have changed his quarters. But he thought that there was no way of doing so without exciting the suspicions of the landlord.

If his suspicions were aroused, they could expect nothing else but that an attack would be made upon them at once.

Why should they hesitate? If they had any pluck, they need not wait until the Captain was asleep. Two men to one were formidable odds, when the two were armed and the one was not.

Even suppose he and Ruth could get safely out of the house, the Captain thought, would they not stand a good chance of being waylaid and robbed —perhaps murdered—outside?

When he came to think of it, would it not be safer to stay where they were? for, if robbery only was intended, the landlord might be chary of committing it, should there be any risk of the guests tracing it to him.

Crockford, though, deemed it wisest not to say anything about the man he had met and recognised. He did not know what stuff Ruth was made of, and he was afraid of alarming her. Turning to her, however, he said abruptly, "Are you as timid as most ladies?"

"No," replied Ruth, with something of her old dare-devil smile and laugh. "I am not timid at all." And that was true enough in a general way; only, at the same time, upon this occasion, her courage had a little failed her, for she had no notion of being quietly murdered in an out-of-the-way spot like this, and never heard of again. It was very different if it had been in some bold adventure, where there was a great stake to gain. That would have kept her courage up to the sticking place but there was no such incentive now.

"I rely upon you for assistance," said Crockford, with a smile, "should we require it."

Just then the landlord came up to the room, bringing the brandy. He had brought two glasses. He placed them on the table.

"Did you order these?" asked Ruth, when the man had left the room.

"No; I only ordered one; but try and sip a little of the other—it will keep your courage up."

"My courage will do without. Do not be afraid of me; and I would advise——"

She was going to warn him not to drink the spirit himself, only at that moment the door opened again, and the girl appeared upon the threshold, holding a light.

Ruth looked eagerly towards her, expecting that this time she would make the communication which, upon the previous occasion, had been interrupted; but she saw, much to her disappointment, that the landlord had accompanied the girl, and was standing close behind her in the doorway.

The girl had brought the bed-candles, and had come with the intention of showing the travellers to their sleeping apartment. Advancing into the room with her eyes downcast, she contrived to get close to Ruth's side with a pretext of stirring the fire.

Ruth was standing on one side of the fire-place, with her face towards the door and her back towards the grate. Her left hand was hanging down listlessly by her side.

As the girl stooped by her side, Ruth felt something tickling her palm.

Her first inclination was to twitch her hand away; but suddenly she thought the girl must be endeavouring to attract her attention, and presently she felt the girl's fingers closing upon hers.

She had forced something into Ruth's hand, and had gently shut her fingers upon it to prevent it from falling.

It was a piece of paper.

When she had done this, the girl left the fire and went again to the door. There she stood holding the bed-candles, ready to light the way up-stairs.

"Are you ready, madam?" she asked.

"Are the rooms ready?"

"The room is," said the landlord; "there's only one."

The landlord very naturally, after what had occurred, had taken his guests as man and wife.

Ruth was going to protest loudly against the arrangement that was being forced upon her so systematically, only something in the expression of th Captain's face, half a frown and half a nod, caused her to swerve from her determination.

There was a warning in it, and a beseeching prayer to her not to offer any obstacle to some plan of action which he might have formed. Therefore, without another word, she followed the Captain to a room upon the floor above.

The landlord, before leaving the apartment where they had been sitting, took up one of the glasses of brandy and water.

"I am sorry, madam, that I was not able to make any negus," he said with a smile and a sort of rough attempt at a bow. "But it's such an out-of-the way place, this; and we're such uncouth folks—so little used to ladies and ladies' ways. But you won't find this too strong, madam, and rather palatable."

He placed the glass, as he spoke, into the hands of the girl.

"Carry that up-stairs for the lady," said he.

Ruth thanked him, and they proceeded up-stairs. The girl opened the door of a bedroom, merely furnished with a small scrap of carpet and bare boards—a dreadful poverty-stricken place. Putting down the light upon the table, she withdrew again with another meaning glance at Ruth, and saying "Good night!" aloud, shut the door.

All this while the landlord upon the landing without seemed to be keeping watch upon all three, and never for a moment withdrew his eyes from his female companion, whose every movement he watched with a fox-like look of cunning.

When the door was shut and the footsteps without had died away, Ruth turned to her companion with something like a blush upon her handsome face.

"Well, sir!" she exclaimed, rather angrily; "this is a pretty situation you have placed me in! It is well contrived——"

"My dear madam, accept my humblest excuses and grant me your patience; but listen to what I have to say. We must not separate."

"Indeed, sir!"

"You mistake my meaning. I would say that our safety in this house depends upon our putting our wits together, and uniting our strength and our tactics."

"Have you any cause for fresh alarm?"

"Yes—yes. There is another man besides the landlord in the house—a man I don't like the look of at all; and whose presence here at this moment, I cannot help thinking, does not argue much for the honesty of the landlord."

And then he briefly told her how he had met the man when he had accidentally opened the room door in looking for the sitting-room. To this he also added the information that he had seen him on the landing just now, when they came out of the room below, hiding away in a dark corner, screening himself as much as possible from the sight of Ruth and her companion, but still apparently anxious to see the lady's face—perhaps, Crockford thought, with the desire of ascertaining whether she was really the woman who had knocked him backwards into the ditch that evening in crossing the fields.

Ruth listened attentively and silently.

"Well?" said Crockford.

"It looks bad, I think."

"Very bad."

"There's danger?"

"There's no denying it. But I do not think you are the sort to be frightened by trifles."

"No, you may depend upon me."

As she spoke, she suddenly recollected the morsel of paper, which as yet she had not read, and which she still held crumpled up tightly in the palm of her hand.

"The girl gave me this," she said.

Then she opened the paper, and spread it out close to the candle. It was written in a sprawling hand, and had apparently been effected in a great hurry, perhaps in the dark.

The words it contained were these:—

"BEWARE! DO NOT SLEEP! DO NOT DRINK! FOR YOUR LIFE!"

She read the sentences over twice, and looked up to the Captain, with a pale face. The Captain's face, looking down upon her, was pale also.

He was holding his head in his hands. His eyes were wide open — dilated, staring. He looked panic-stricken.

"By heavens!" he exclaimed.

"What's the matter?" she asked, in alarm.

"I—I—have been drugged!" he said. "That cursed drink—the brandy and water——"

"Did you drink it?"

"Every drop!"

Ruth looked at him aghast. Then she turned, and took up the glass of spirits and water other from the table.

Crockford fetched a glass from the wash-hand stand, and very gently poured the contents of the other glass into it. When he had poured out the last drops there was a small quantity of white sediment at the bottom.

He tasted a tiny particle with his finger. It was not sugar, as he had supposed it to be. It was bitter.

He put down the glass with a muttered curse, inaudible, though deep.

"What is to be done?" he cried.

Next moment he was clutching his head, through which rushed a violent pain, as though his skull were actually coming in half—splitting asunder.

Ruth asked him, anxiously, what was the matter. But he made no reply.

He reeled backwards for a yard or two, and would have fallen to the ground, had not the bed chanced to have been there to catch him.

"Are you suffering?" she asked.

"Yes—yes!"

"Is it the drug?"

"I suppose so. My head is splitting!"

"What can be done?" she asked herself, aloud, searching her brain vainly for some cure which she fancied she had, at some remote period or other, been acquainted with, but which now had slipped her memory.

Then, going to the water jug, she dipped a towel into it, and, approaching Crockford, who was lying upon his back on the bed, with his arms hanging down listlessly by his sides, and his head thrown very far back, she began to bathe his throbbing temples.

The action of the cold water had a soothing and refreshing effect.

Presently he heaved a long-drawn, deep sigh of heartfelt relief.

Then he suddenly opened his eyes, and looked languidly around.

"How do you feel now?" she asked.

"I am more than half stupefied," he replied, speaking with evident pain and labour; "but I shall be better presently."

Even as he spoke, though, his eyes closed again wearily, and he appeared to sleep.

Ruth flung more and more cold water upon his head and face.

Again and again she called him by name.

She shook him violently until he opened his eyes.

"Arouse yourself—arouse yourself! Bear up! Keep awake! For heaven's sake, try to bear up!"

She stopped to listen

"I hear them outside!" she continued, in a terrified whisper. "Bear up, for heaven's sake! They think, no doubt, that the drug has had time to operate! They are going to attack us! Bear up a little while longer! If you can bear up for a short time, we may be able to combat them!"

She dragged him into a sitting posture as she spoke.

She searched in the fireplace, and, to her great joy, found a poker—not a very formidable weapon, but still something not to be despised.

Getting the Captain into an upright position, and making him, to the best of her power, conscious of the situation, she thrust the poker into his hand, while she herself listened at the door.

She listened intently, with a throbbing heart.

Yes; she distinctly heard footsteps without.

They were stealthy footsteps, stealing upwards, thief-like, towards the door.

The assassins thought that the drug had had time to operate.

They expected that their two victims would be asleep.

Asleep, and ready for the knife!

CHAPTER L.

LISTENING AND WAITING.—THE STRATAGEM.—THE MURDERERS AT THE DOOR.—THE BOLT.—THE SPY IN AMBUSH.—THE FINGERS.—THE KNIFE FALLS.

But while Ruth was straining every nerve in her endeavour to hear what was passing without, she was aroused by a deep sigh from her companion, and the sound of his heavy fall upon the bed.

Overcome by the potion, he had again relapsed into insensibility.

Luckily, the poker, falling from his hand, slipped down to the ground noiselessly, and those without could not have heard it.

She considered for a few moments, and rapidly decided upon what would be the best course to pursue. She had bolted the door as well as she was able. To be sure, the fastening was anything but secure; but she did not think it at all probable that any attempt would be made to enter the room before she and her companion were supposed to be asleep.

The landlord expected by this time, no doubt, that she had drunk up her dose. He knew that the Captain had finished his, for he, Crockford, had drunk it up before his eyes.

She presently knew, by the sound outside, that the person, whoever it was, who had come upstairs, was standing close outside the door.

She began to talk for their edification, as though she were addressing the Captain.

"There!—don't you be in such a dreadful hurry!" she said. "I am sure it is like your rudeness to go to bed first in that unceremonious way, and leave me to put out the light! But I shan't be very long. Though, by the way, I don't think I shall put out the light at all, for I like to have one burning. There!—don't you fret now! I have only got to say my prayers, and drink my grog, and I shall come to bed too!"

She thought it best to allude to the grog. That might make them wait a little longer.

"By the way," she said, after a pause, "I forgot to ask the landlord to call us early in the morning. You know we must go by the first train. I think I shall go and tell him now. There is no bell in the room; but I will go and call him at the top of the stairs."

As she said this, she began to rattle the door-handle violently.

In this there was a great deal of artfulness, as I will show you presently.

Her motives were these.

First of all, she was not quite certain whether or not the listeners were still outside; for some time they had been perfectly silent. Perhaps they had gone? Or perhaps it was, after all, only fancy on her part, and they had not been there at all?

But the rattling of the door-handle set the matter at rest at once.

She immediately heard a great shuffling without, and retreating steps upon the stairs.

There had been a listener, and he was stealing away as cautiously and as noiselessly as possible.

This was exactly what she desired.

It was necessary that she should have a little breathing time. Now she had got it, what use should she make of it?

She had no one but herself to look to—that was certain. The poor Captain was as good as no Captain at all—or, at best, a dead Captain. There he lay, like a log, in a state of stupefaction.

The potion had done its work. He was drugged—senseless—helpless—entirely at the mercy of the wretches into whose clutches they had fallen.

While the coast was clear, she must prepare for the attack, which, she doubted not, was near at hand.

To commence with, she threw off her shawl and bonnet, and dispensed with all those articles of wearing apparel which she considered would prove impediments in the way of a struggle.

Then, before going any further, she raised the Captain in her arms, and, with a display of strength which seemed almost incredible in so delicately formed a creature, and one who might naturally be supposed to have had her system weakened by the enervating dissipations of fashionable gaiety, she lifted him from the ground.

She placed his apparently lifeless body upon the bed, and covered the counterpane over it in such a way that he appeared to have gone to sleep in the usual fashion, and without his coat, boots, &c.

Then she put the bolster in bed, on the other side, sticking the clothes up with it in a great lump; and this was supposed to represent her fair self.

Her reason for doing so was to make the people, when they came up-stairs again to peep through the keyhole, think that they had both gone to sleep.

She knew, or at least fancied, that from the key-hole any one outside could command a view of the bed.

When her preparations were complete, she crouched down upon the other side of the door, behind a chair upon which she had arranged her dress and shawl, so as to form a kind of screen.

Then she drew from her breast that pretty dagger knife which she carried; and also placing that pretty pocket pistol in such a position that she could get at it easily in case of need, she knelt down, and waited something in the position that a tiger might wait, making ready for its victim and a spring.

All was still without.

The house was perfectly quiet.

Not a soul stirring. No one upon the stairs.

The light gleamed faintly upon the listener's white face, and glistened a little upon the bright blade of the poniard.

The rain had abated somewhat. Now it came down with a faint pit-a-pat upon the window-panes, but only when driven by the violence of the wind, still careering in fitful gusts over the wild, bleak marsh land.

The suspense of waiting was most terrible to endure.

Scarcely another woman, I think, could have been found capable of living through it. The anxiety and the dread of the situation were perfectly terrific.

When would they come? How would they come? How many of them? And for what purpose?

Did they mean murder as well as robbery? And if so, how could she, alone and unaided, hope to combat them?

She trusted to find an ally in the girl who had so strangely and mysteriously endeavoured to warn her of the danger that she and her companion were running in this nest of robbers. But she did not think it at all probable that the girl would dare openly to render her any aid; and without she did, what assistance could she possibly be at this dreadful extremity?

She waited and listened. Still no one approached. She could easily understand this: they were determined to allow sufficient time to elapse before they made the attack, for their victims to go to sleep.

At last it came.

Creak! creak!

They were on the stairs.

They! Yes, there were two of them; and they came up upon tip-toe.

When they got to the door, they also paused and listened.

One of them, Ruth judged, was stooping down and looking through the key-hole.

She kept as still as death, holding her breath until the veins swelled in her throat.

Those without were quiet enough, but not so quiet as she was.

She heard them breathing.

Then she heard a whispered conference.

"Are they asleep?"

"I think so."

"Is the light burning?"

"Yes."

"Can you see the bed?"

"Yes."

"Which is outside?"

"He is."

"We'll settle him first, then."

Ruth could not refrain from a slight chuckle. "There's something here," she said to herself, as she felt the edge of the sharp dagger-knife, "that may spoil your calculations."

There was a slight pause and an entire silence without, and then the handle of the door began to turn.

It turned round twice, once over and once under, as though the person turning it had fancied the first time that he had made a mistake and turned the wrong way.

Then the door was pressed upwards a little, and shaken gently.

"It's bolted," said one voice.

"But the bolt does not catch."

"Yes it does. Try."

Some one else began to shake the door a little more roughly, but still not sufficiently to shake it loose from the bolt.

"Curse it!" one of the voices muttered; "why didn't you look to this before? We shall wake them."

"No, we shan't; no fear of that. Lift the door up from the bottom."

The door fitted very badly. There was a considerable space between it and the floor—sufficient for anybody to thrust their fingers through.

Eight fingers presently made their appearance. grasping at the bottom of the door preparatory to raising it up.

Ruth, clenching her teeth, crept forward.

Steadying herself with her left hand against the wall, she raised the knife.

Then brought it down with a crushing, grinding clash upon the fingers of the hand next to her.

Next moment, a howl of agony without rent the air.

Next moment, her glittering blade, crimson with the robber's blood, was raised again, ready to plunge into her other foe.

CHAPTER LI.

WHAT BEFEL CECILY IN THE HOUSE OF THE DUMB ASTROLOGER.—SUSPICIONS.—ALARM AND DREAD. —A FEMALE FIEND. —THE FEARFUL PROPOSAL.—THE ATTEMPTED ESCAPE

The worst of this story, or the worst of any story, I suppose, with a lot of characters in it, is, that while the narrator is faithfully following the fortunes of one individual, and helping him through his scrapes, another, whom of necessity he's been obliged to leave up to his neck in the mire, languishes there a most unreasonable time, much to his own disgust, and, perhaps, to the disgust also of the reader who has been kind enough to feel an interest in him.

Let me see, now, who must I go back to? If I only had the reader here to ask his advice, I would most willingly give the preference to the character he selected. But, unfortunately, being deprived of that advantage, I must pick upon a character myself.

I think, for the purposes of my story, it is necessary that I should return to Cecily for a short time; although Jacob Stone, Alice, Lady Florence Darcy, and the celebrated Mr. Cadbury Kid, all have claims upon my consideration, and with whose adventures I hope before long to cause you no small amount of astonishment.

Yes, decidedly the best part is coming, if you will only be patient; but in the meantime I cannot afford to talk any longer, but must follow the thread of my story.

The dumb astrologer, whom you may recollect had returned alone to the house, and had cautiously entered the room where Cecily lay asleep, stood gazing at her silently for some moments, rubbing his chin with his hand, with a sawing movement, and biting his lip.

Her heart beating fast with fright, she watched his movements, though with half-closed eyes, feigning to be asleep.

He appeared to be anxious to know whether this sleep was feigned or real, and he rattled the handle of the door once or twice, watching her the while to see if she moved; then he approached the bedside, and stood watching her.

Once or twice he made a rapid movement across her face with his long, thin hands.

She kept her eyes shut, though, and did not flinch.

After a bit, he withdrew to the other end of the room, and searching among a heap of rubbish in the corner, drew forth something which appeared to be a small bag.

It must have contained money, from the chinking sound which it emitted. It was to secure this treasure, which he had deemed it unsafe to leave in her company unprotected, he had come back. She felt a sense of intense relief on discovering this to be his motive for his return.

Other and worse fears had beset her, though she was happily ignorant of the fact which the conversation I have recorded between the two women in the street has put the reader in possession of.

She did not know what a monster of iniquity was this man into whose clutches she had fallen.

The knowledge, alas! will soon come. She will not have long to wait before she has reason to repent bitterly that she attracted the notice of that good Mrs. Raddle, who, with such a purely Christian-like spirit, had insisted on her being provided with a night's lodging.

The dumb man put away the clinking bag into a pocket in the breast of his coat. When he had done so, he turned, as though he were about to leave the room, and he walked towards the door without looking at the bed; but just when he reached it, casting his eyes back towards Cecily's face, he noticed, with a start, that her eyes were fixed upon him.

He noticed it with a start and a half-scream, and he sprang forward towards the bed, gesticulating wildly.

Cecily, raising herself upon her elbow, spread out her hands in terror, to ward off the blow which she dreaded was coming, uttering a faint cry for help.

The man stood over her, with his fist clenched and his eyes glaring savagely, his jaws working, and some jabbering, incomprehensible sounds issuing from his mouth, of which she could make no meaning, but which were, undoubtedly, furious threats of vengeance.

What did he mean? What was she to say or do to appease him?

He pointed to the corner from which he had taken the bag of money, and to the bag itself in his breast-pocket.

Did he mean to imply that she had robbed him, or was he entreating her to be silent?

Before she could decide which motive it was that prompted this strange conduct, a ring came at the bell below.

The dumb man ran from her to the window, and threw up the sash. When he had looked out he came rushing back again, gesticulating more wildly than before.

Then he left the room, and descended the stairs hastily.

Cecily, listening, heard a woman's voice below, talking angrily.

She recognised it to be Mrs. Raddle, the woman who had assisted the dumb astrologer in bringing her thither.

"What made you come back?" she cried, in a shrill tone. "You said you were not coming back here."

"And you did not believe me?"

"No, I didn't."

"Much good your suspicion has done you! What have you got from it?"

"I've got a lesson from it, anyhow. I have learnt that you are a liar!"

"That was worth the trouble: I could have told you so without your coming back all this way to get the proof! You are not much better yourself, I believe!"

The woman made no reply, but pushed past him into the house. Cecily listening, heard the sound of her footsteps coming up-stairs.

"And what have you found out, after all?" the man continued. "What do you suppose I came back for?"

"I know well enough."

"What do you know?"

"It was on account of that pale-faced chit of a girl!"

The man burst out laughing.

"To be sure it was," said he; "though I didn't think of it before. I did not think that you was so sharp. I must be very careful in future."

"Don't laugh at me, you ugly wretch!"

"Not too ugly to be jealous of, though! It is quite gratifying, I assure you. You can't think how it has pleased me! I was silly enough to think you didn't care about me, when all the while you are actually dying for love of me! It really is very gratifying!"

Then the man cackled like an old gander, and the woman burst into a torrent of abusive epithets, each worse than the last, though each apparently afforded more and more gratification to the pleasing individual to whom they were addressed.

Cecily listened to this conversation with the greatest anxiety, although the greater part of it was perfectly unintelligible to her, owing to it being delivered in the apeish dialect of the dumb man—a language not very easily to be understood by anybody who had not spent a considerable length of time in his company.

She could make out, though, that this woman, Mrs Raddle, was to some extent jealous of her; and the knowledge of this fact caused her considerable gratification, because, as she had not the slightest desire in the world to become the woman's rival, she thought that Mrs. Raddle's jealousy would prove one of the most formidable obstacles to the dumb astrologer's gallantry that could be desired.

The man and woman came up into the room, and the latter, finding that Cicely was awake, inquired, with a greater show of kindness in her voice than the other had expected, how she found herself.

Cecily thanked ner. She was "very well," she said; "at least, she was much better."

The woman asked her whether she should get her anything, and proposed a cup of tea. Whilst she was making it, and getting a tea-cup ready, and the sugar and milk from a cupboard, she managed to keep a very sharp eye upon the girl and the astrologer.

Two or three times, when she fancied that she noticed an exchange of glances of intelligence, she would turn round with a start, and a flushed up, angry face, hoping to catch them in the act; but every time she did so, it turned out, greatly to the good lady's discomfiture, to be a false alarm; and, though the man took pretty good care upon these occasions not to let Mrs. Raddle see him, he, upon each occasion, relapsed into a paroxysm of exciting chuckles at the glorious thought that she was sold again, and very savage.

Poor Cecily, lying upon the bed, watched this pantomime with much apprehension, and but little appreciation of its humour.

She asked herself why she had been brought here, and how long she was to stop.

The bare idea of remaining long with these wretches was abhorrent to her soul.

She was resolved, though, not to remain a moment longer in the house than she was actually obliged to do. She felt weak and ill now, but that would not last long—she made up her mind to that. In the course of the day she would be able to leave the house—in about an hour or two, at most.

The jealousy of this woman she felt thankful for; but very soon she hoped to be out of the clutches of both; for she could not help thinking—although, certainly, she had no proof in either word or action upon the part of the woman, and not a great deal either on the part of the man—that they could be keeping her there for no good object.

Strange was it that she should have fancied that the woman's jealousy would be her protection. Alas! had she only known what an awful tragedy would accrue from it—what shame and misery, and peril to life and soul, that circumstance would cause her, she would not have hesitated, I really and truly believe, with her own hands, to have taken her own life, had there been no other means of escape, than to have remained any longer in this den of infamy.

As soon as the tea was prepared, the man took himself off, either leaving the house or going to some distant portion of it, and the woman and Cecily were left by themselves. The former having helped herself to a cup of tea, into which she had, however, poured a wine-glass full of liquid from some bottle, by way of a relish, began to nod in her chair, every now and then butting with her head in the direction of the grate, and recovering herself as though by magic, only in the very nick of time, and when her case seemed altogether hopeless.

Cecily lay watching her in a dreamy, drowsy way, intending every moment to arouse herself from the dull torpor which oppressed her, and to tell the woman that she felt strong enough now to continue her journey, and that she was very much obliged for the hospitality which had been shown to her.

But it was most curious she could not for the life of her rouse herself sufficiently to do so. Once or twice she made an effort. Once or twice she half uttered a phrase, but the words seemed to stick in her throat; then again closing her eyes, she almost dozed off to sleep, lying in a half-confused state of semi-consciousness, in which she fancied absurdly enough that she had already spoken to the woman and told her that she wanted to go.

Then she dreamt that she had gone, and that she was out in the street, and walking away as fast as possible; only that, somehow or other, she could not tell why, she could not for the life of her get rid of the companionship of this woman and her hideous dumb companion, who, together, persistently pursued her and kept pace with her, in spite of all her efforts to get rid of them and shake them off.

At length this dreamy, confused feeling, and a dull singing in the head which had accompanied it, gave place to total unconsciousness, and she fell fast asleep.

How long her slumbers lasted she could form no notion, but a considerable time must have elapsed; for looking towards the window, she saw that the panes were quite black—that it was night without. She awoke wearily, and with a burning thirst.

She fancied at first that she must have been asleep for five or six hours—indeed, that she had slept from breakfast time until tea-time; but certain circumstances led her to believe that her stay had been much longer.

One circumstance was, a complete change of dress upon the part of Mrs. Raddle. Another was, an alteration in the pattern of the wall-paper. A third, a change in the position of the bed.

But there, at the tea-table by the side of the fire, sat Mrs. Raddle, and the dumb astrologer, and the man with the death's head, whom we know as Skeleton Key; and they sat there chatting together just as though they had never parted.

Cecily listened to their conversation: they were not speaking in a low tone, and she caught every word they said.

"And so you followed her?" said Mrs. Raddle.

"Followed her? I should think I did. I never had such a dance in my life before She led me half over London."

"She did it on purpose!"

"There's no doubt of that, though at first I didn't suspect it. However, when I did, I stuck to it all the same, for I'd made up my mind to run her to earth!"

"But you didn't?"

"No, she managed at last to put the neatest conceivable plant upon me. I never came across anything to equal it out of a story book. It was like one of those dodges that you read of the Indians being up to."

"Whatever was it?"

"She took a boat, you know, after she had danced me up in every other kind of vehicle till I'd hardly a mag left. I'm hanged if I was not afraid at one time she would take a special train all by herself and leave me hopelessly in the lurch, for she seemed to have her pockets full of money."

"Well, what did she do?"

"She took a boat, I say, and rowed straight off to a precious place where scarcely anybody ever lands at. Here she gets out and sends her boat away, and then hurries off up a narrow lane I was a good bit behind. 'By Jove! said I to myself, 'she's given me the slip now;' and I told the man to pull like blazes. She was out of sight when I got to the shore, and I was kept some little time there by the fool of a boatman, who thought I wanted to bolt and bilk him. However, I threw him some money, the last I had, and left him grumbling while I ran after her. Up the lane I ran as fast as my legs could carry me, but I could not see a sight of her."

"What had become of her?"

"I could not make out at first, though I found out a little too late the artful trick she had played me. She had just quietly hidden herself behind a wall, in a corner where, running by, I did not notice her. Then, when I had got past, and was half-way up to the end of the lane, she plunged out and bolted down to the boat again. In half a jiffy she was out in the middle of the river. I was not long in going after her, I can promise you, but it was no good. The wooden-headed fool who had brought me had rowed out into the middle of the stream. I stamped and swore, and roared to him to come back; and I offered him a tidy price for doing so, but she offered him double to stay where he was, and so we hammered away like they do at an auction, she outbidding me at every bid."

"But you had no money in your pocket, you said!"

"No, that was what made me so precious liberal. I shouldn't have given it him, of course, but it was a consolation to me under the circumstances to think I had put her to a great expense, and so I bawled out pounds as though they were pennies."

"She got away, however. She deserved to do so, in my opinion."

"So she did in mine. She was the artfullest party I ever came across. And how she learned it all—and her a lady of title, too—beats me entirely."

"It does seem strange."

"Her husband, Lord whatever his name is, must have picked her up in some rum place or other. I don't believe she's what you call a regular bred-and-born lady."

"Well, perhaps you've had better opportunities of judging what are the habits of the best society," said Mrs. Raddle, with a sneer; "but I saw nothing amiss with her."

"She's as beautiful as an angel, anyhow; and her hair—by Jove, it's just like so much yellow floss silk!"

The dumb astrologer and Mrs. Raddle happened both to have their cups up to their lips, as though they were at the point of drinking.

They both put down their cups without carrying out their original intention.

"What did you say?" asked Mrs Raddle.

The dumb man grunted, and spluttered something which might be supposed to be the same interrogatory, his way of putting it. Skeleton Key stared at them hard and leisurely, emptied his mouth of the bread and butter with which it was filled, disposed of it in gulps, but said nothing.

"What did you say?" repeated Mrs. Raddle, in great excitement. "Are you deaf?"

"Are *you* silly?" retorted the other. "Didn't you hear what I said?"

"You said something about her hair being yellow."

"Well, what of that?"

"Why, it isn't."

"Isn't what?"

"Isn't yellow?"

"Is it green, then? What the blazes are you talking about?"

"It's black. Or if not black, it is very dark brown—only a shade or so off black."

"Don't talk to me. I'd opportunity enough to see it. I tell you, the lady I followed had yellow hair!"

"Well, then, you followed the wrong woman."

"But that's impossible!"

"But it's the fact. Her hair could not have changed colour, as both the astrologer and I saw her, and we know her hair was dark. And so it is very clear that you have been wasting your time upon a wrong scent."

"Now, look here!" retorted Skeleton Key, indignantly. "Didn't I see her with you? Didn't you keep her talking while I had a good stare at her? It's true I didn't look so very particular at the colour of her hair; but, hang it! I saw her face plain enough, and I could swear to it in a thousand."

"Well, I can't understand how you could be mistaken!"

"But I wasn't! Besides, didn't you give me the photograph visiting-card, or whatever it is, that he had left behind. Well, I looked at that when I first came across my lady in Covent Garden Market, and I was quite sure I was right."

"But the photograph hasn't got light hair."

"No; but those kind of pictures always come out darker than the people really are that they are taken from. Everybody knows that."

"Anyhow, by some wonderful chance, there is some other woman exactly like her, except the colour of the hair. And that accounts for her doing all the queer things you say. If you had followed the real lady, she would never have been up to them."

"Anyhow, it's no good talking about it any more We must wait till next time."

"I wish something else would look up, that's all I have to say. Things are going on dreadfully bad. My trade is knocked up for good and all. The police have seized every bit of furniture there was to take after the landlord had walked the bulk of 'em off for his rent while I was in limbo."

"You've got no trace, either, of the girls that took your money, too."

"Not the slightest. No, we're regularly stumped up. The smashing trade has gone to the dogs since Stone has been in quod."

"The governor, here, can't do anything in that way, can he?"

"He can only make shillings, and what's the good of that? The risk is so precious great, and the gains so precious small. No, the fortune-telling is the best game left; and that's bad enough since that affair of the girl that Jeer, here, murdered."

The dumb man mumbled something in dissent.

"Don't talk to me!" retorted the woman. "Do you suppose I'm a fool? I know you did it, you wretch, and what you did it for; and I'd have murdered you instead, if I'd not been laid up by the heels. Why, if I hadn't myself silenced that woman who got the girl's letter, you'd have been scragged by now. But let that pass. What I was saying was, that something must turn up. If this other girl we've got here don't kick the bucket, or lose her good looks altogether, we might earn an honest penny by her with some of my old customers; or if we find out where that other lady lives, we must get a little money out of her. So, the next time, don't you run after the wrong one."

The man roared out indignantly.

"I tell you I wasn't mistaken, and I could not be mistaken. There could not be another woman with such a likeness to her, and still not be the same; and so—Good heavens!"

He started up with this exclamation, with his eyes fixed upon the bed.

The dumb man also sprang to his feet in terror, though he knew not at what. The woman, who had her back turned towards the bed, let fall the cup and saucer she was holding from her hand, and sprang forward, to the imminent danger of upsetting everything, and demolishing all the crockery.

"What, in the name of mercy, is the matter with you?" she cried.

"I don't know," replied Skeleton Key, sitting down and wiping the perspiration off his face. "I thought it was the lady herself, or her ghost!"

"What was?"

"The girl there sitting up in bed. Hang me, how like she is, too! I don't know, after all, but what I might have been mistaken in the other one."

But Mrs. Raddle was not listening to him. She had risen from her seat at the first alarm, and got as far off the bed as possible. Now she came back again, and approached the girl's side.

When Skeleton Key had first looked at her, Cecily was sitting up in bed, her face blanched with terror, her eyes dilated, her heart throbbing.

What horrors was she hearing? Who were these monsters talking together? Into what den of infamy had she fallen?

All this she asked herself, and whether it was not, after all, a frightful dream, and not the reality.

But no, she was awake. Her brain, even distorted by fever, could not have conjured up such horrors. She could not have imagined such wretches as these to be in existence.

When Mrs. Raddle came to her side she had sank back exhausted upon the pillow. Her eyes were again closed, and a deadly pallor had overspread her fair features.

The woman laid her hand upon Cecily's shoulder, and the poor girl, with a shudder of intense horror and abhorrence, opened her eyes again.

"Well, child," said Mrs. Raddle, in a kind tone of voice, "how do you feel now? Are you better? How long have you been awake?"

"Only a few moments," replied the girl, faintly. "I am very thirsty and hot. I want something to drink."

"I'll give you something," said Mrs. Raddle. "You're burning hot and feverish. Did our talking disturb you?"

"No, ma'am."

"Perhaps you did not hear us?"

"Yes, I heard you."

"Did you hear what we said?" the woman asked, affecting a tone of indifference.

Cecily blushed slightly, and feigned to rub her eyes to hide her confusion.

"I did not hear what you were talking about," she answered, with a great effort, turning away her head.

"Lucky for her!" muttered Skeleton Key. "Devilish stupid, though, for us to go prating before her! Do you think she did twig anything? I am blessed if I know what we said; but I suppose it was something we might as well have kept to ourselves."

"There's no harm done," said the woman; "only we'll say no more. She hasn't heard much, bless you! Her wits were wool-gathering. The fever's on her still."

They mumbled to themselves for a short time, and then took themselves off, leaving the girl to her reflections.

They were not pleasant thoughts which poor Cecily had to keep her company. "What was she to do?" she asked herself. She was quite helpless in these people's hands—as helpless as a babe.

What was the fate reserved for her? She was in ignorance of the truth, but yet she could form a shrewd guess, and she shuddered at the frightful thought.

This woman Raddle, as well as she could understand, must have been recently the keeper of some infamous house, and for that offence had been committed to prison. To one of her customers, as the vile creature termed those lawless profligates, those grey-headed, infamous men who patronised her den of depravity, she was to sell Cecily, if they would purchase her. Sell her, as the poor, miserable quadroon girls are sold abroad, to infamy and dishonour.

And these vile companions of hers, they would undoubtedly aid and abet her. Skeleton Key was evidently an unscrupulous scoundrel. His face was an index to his character.

The other—that deformed and stricken object, revolting alike morally and physically—he would help her also: unless, indeed—and the thought was more frightful than any other—he should take a fancy to her himself, and should deem the gratification of his own unlawful desires worthy the sacrifice of the gain which he might otherwise hope to obtain from the revolting commerce his paramour had proposed.

One man was a murderer. They were all passers of base coin—all scoundrels and thieves. Cecily looked in vain for some quarter in which there might be a faint spark of hope But it was clear that there was no hope beneath that roof.

She must escape. Yes, she must escape, and at once!

But when she strove to rise from the bed, she found that her strength was so small—that she was so wretchedly weak, and so reduced by her late illness, that all movement was impossible

She could just raise herself upon her elbows, and that was all. With a low moan of pain and misery, she sank back upon the bed again, and very shortly afterwards relapsed into insensibility.

All that night, and throughout the whole of the coming day, Cecily was still a prisoner upon the weary couch; and, though she was burning with a mad desire to be up and stirring, she would not have been able to have stood upright had she risen from her bed.

Upon reflection, also, she deemed it wisest not even to appear to be so far recovered as she was. She felt that she would soon now recover her strength. The strength of her will must overcome her illness.

She was determined to be well, and to act, and nothing should keep her back. It is not the first case of strength of will triumphing over bodily weakness. She grew hourly stronger as her determination to get the better of her illness strengthened within her breast. Upon the third day after the little tea-party which had taken place, and at which had passed the conversation she had been the unwilling listener to, she determined upon making an attempt at escape.

The dumb astrologer and the woman Raddle had left the house early in the afternoon; and, from what Mrs. Raddle had said upon going out, Cecily deemed it more than probable that they intended to remain away until late.

Before going out, however, they had double locked the door at the bottom of the house.

"If any one rings," said Mrs. Raddle, "you must let them ring. Take no notice of them."

"Must not I answer the door?"

"No; there is no occasion I have taken in some milk for some tea, and you need not answer the man if he calls."

"Very well, ma'am," replied Cecily.

"You're not well enough yet to run up and down stairs," explained Mrs. Raddle; "and you had better sit quite quiet. I shan't be long away."

But, although she said this, Cecily did not believe her. She thought that the woman's reason for telling her so was to keep her out of mischief. Perhaps Mrs. Raddle was afraid that if Cecily thought she had been left quite to herself, and there was no fear of interruptions, she would be making a voyage of discovery among the up-and-down-stair rooms.

Several times before, Cecily had noticed that both the man and woman were very much afraid that she should see what they had stowed away in the other apartments—supposing that they had anything; or that she should find out the mysteries of the house—supposing there were any.

Mr. Garbidge, the rag and bottle merchant, was at that time away from home, and the shop was shut up. She was alone in the house, and its secrets, did any secrets exist, at her mercy.

She did not, however, feel any desire to find the secrets out; her only wish was to escape. Her own desire was liberty, and that she was determined upon obtaining at any risk.

As soon as they were gone, and the door well closed upon them, she made up her mind to make the attempt.

CHAPTER LII.

IN THE ARMS OF A SKELETON.

It was not until close upon three o'clock that the astrologer and his female companion finally left the house.

Even then it seemed doubtful whether or not they had gone for good; for, after they had been away almost a quarter of an hour, they returned hurriedly, and the man came up-stairs with so little noise, that Cecily was not aware of his approach until he was at the room door.

Fortunately, Cecily had not as yet stirred from her place, the arm-chair in which she had been sitting when they left her. Perhaps he had returned in the hope of discovering whether she had been at any tricks or not. If that was the case, he was disappointed.

He had come back, he said, to get something he had forgotten; and in corroboration of this statement, took from the mantel-piece an envelope lying there, with an address upon it, and took himself off.

She waited until she heard the last of him, going slowly down stairs, dragging his feet after him, with a shambling, creeping gait, that was peculiar to him; and she listened to him, when he got into the court outside, speaking to Mrs. Raddle, as they walked away together.

When the sound of their voices was no longer audible, she still waited patiently, and listened. Perhaps they would come back again — come back upon her again unawares, just as she was trying the street door, or opening one of the windows in the lower part of the house.

Her heart jumped at the thought of it. When the man had come back before, he had, as near as possible, caught her. She was just in the act of rising from her chair, when she heard a creak upon the stairs. In another moment, had she not chanced to hear him, she would have been out upon the landing.

She made up her mind to let a whole hour elapse before she took any decisive steps. And with an amount of determination which the reader, if not placed in similar circumstances, will find it difficult to understand, she carried out her resolve.

She waited with all the patience at her command, until a neighbouring clock apprised her that the weary time had gone by, and that now she could act.

She opened her room door, descended the stairs, and went straight to the street door. As she had supposed, she found it locked. She also found that it was impossible to open it from the inside, without she had some instrument to force back the bolt, and this was not at her command.

She now bethought her of the other street door, leading out to an alley at the back of the house. She found this equally impracticable.

The door leading from the passage into the shop also baffled her efforts, and all the windows at the lower part of the house which she could gain access to—these being only one in a small room on the ground-floor, and another in the back kitchen—were shuttered up, and the shutters not bolted in the usual way, but nailed.

Indeed, there were no weak places in Mr. Garbidge's house. It was not difficult to see that it had been thus fortified and secured to guard against a sudden attack from without—an event which, knowing the desperate life they, its inmates, led, Cecily deemed to be by no means improbable.

Unfortunately for her, the fact of the house being difficult to break into, also rendered it difficult to break out of.

After pulling and dragging at the shutters, and shaking violently at the doors, she saw how hopeless it was to struggle with these formidable obstacles without the aid of tools; and, thoroughly exhausted, she retraced her steps up-stairs, in the hope of finding something that would assist her in one of the rooms above.

These rooms were all locked, like those below; but she found one door which was not quite so strong as the others; and that, she thought, she might be able to force open.

It was the door of a room upon the first floor, and the aparment in question she had heard the astrologer designate his consulting-room.

She grasped the door-handle with both hands, and shook the door violently, then threw herself against it with all her force. It creaked very much, and groaned not a little. One more effort would do it.

Collecting all her strength, she threw herself

against the panel. With a crash, the door flew open, and she found herself in a mysteriously gloomy apartment.

The sudden giving way of the door had caused her to stagger forward, and she was obliged to clutch at the door-post to save herself from falling.

Before she had time to discern any of the objects which the room contained, even as they were in the dim obscurity reigning around, she was startled by a growl and a sharp cry, and something black flew past her on to the staircase, and fled precipitously. For a few seconds she was so petrified by this unexpected event, that she could not reasonably account for it; but she at last concluded that the mysterious cause of her alarm must have been a black cat, which the astrologer probably kept as a part of his fortune-telling stock in trade, but of the existence of which she had hitherto been unconscious.

She advanced into the room, and as her eyes had nearly become accustomed to the dim obscurity, she was able to make out something of its furniture.

It was curiously fitted. The walls were hung with dark green curtains; and here and there, through apertures, grim oil-paintings of men's heads, yellow and faded, and ghastly in their effect, peeped out, and at first sight appeared as though they were live figures, half hiding behind the curtain and staring silently at her.

The window was covered by several folds of green muslin, carefully nailed to the wood-work, and stretched tightly across the paint, so that only a very subdued light penetrated into the apartment.

There were here two or three black stuff covered chairs, there was a small black table standing in the middle of the room, and from the ceiling over it hung a curious old-fashioned lamp.

This was all.

When Cecily had noted all these things, however, she could not help feeling a little disappointed in finding there was nothing more wonderful. As soon as these things were well noticed, and had been casually examined, there was nothing more to look at; and seeing that there was little hope of finding any weapon here to aid her in her escape, she was about to leave the room again, when she fancied that she noticed a slight opening at the other end of the apartment in the green curtain.

She walked towards it, and pulled the curtain upon one side.

It had concealed the entrance into an inner room.

She looked in as well as she could, but the most profound darkness reigned within.

She walked through the doorway and turned her eyes slowly round, expecting to find a faint glimmer somewhere, which would indicate the existence of a window.

In this, however, she failed, and after a little consideration hurried up to her bedroom to get a candle.

She returned immediately with it, and passed quickly through the outer room into this inner apartment.

In it she found an arm-chair, and a small table before it. Upon this, an open book, slate, pen and ink, and one or two cards, painted over with some cabalistic signs of a totally incomprehensible character.

Upon the slate there was some writing. Cecily took it up and read it:—

"The object of your love is not indifferent to you, although led away by another. You love an enemy, whom you think to be a friend. Come here again to-morrow night at the same time, and bring as much as you brought to-night."

This was written in a vile hand, and some portions very vilely spelt. It was evidently some of the dumb astrologer's handiwork he had thus been imposing upon some silly woman who had been consulting him about her love affairs.

The book lying open upon the table also concontained a variety of memoranda in the same handwriting. They were chiefly addresses of persons who had consulted him about their destinies. Cecily turned over the leaves with some little curiosity, to see what sort of persons they could be who could come to consult, and noticed with astonishment several addresses in well-to-do and even fashionable parts of London, which proved that their owners must have belonged to good society, although they could yet be silly and wicked enough to come there and consult this cunning and vile man, who fattened upon their superstition.

When she had looked through a few leaves, however, Cicely recollected that she had not much time to spare, and that she must be stirring, there was nothing here that would aid her escape, and she had found nothing to repay her for the time she had wasted already.

There was a cupboard or a door leading to some other room, and Cicely passed her hand over it, endeavouring to find out how it could be fastened. There was something like a button in the middle of one of the panels, and pressing this, the door suddenly flew open with a creak.

But Cecily uttered a faint scream, and endeavoured to spring upon one side—endeavoured, however, too late; for what she had wished to avoid had come upon her too rapidly for her to escape from it.

She uttered a faint scream, and shivered throughout her frame with intense horror.

As she touched the spring of the door, it opened. At the door a white, grisly, grinning death's-head was suddenly protruded.

Then a long, thin, bony arm stretched out.

Long, thin, bony fingers closed upon her. The arm encircled her waist with a grip she could not shake off.

She found herself in the arms of a hideous skeleton.

In her alarm and horror at so unexpected an event, she let fall the candle, and the room was plunged into darkness.

In the dark she struggled frantically, and strove to free herself from the embraces of the ghastly object which held her prisoner.

But in vain.

CHAPTER LIII.

THE SKELETON IN BED—THE RUSTLING CURTAIN—A NOISE BELOW.—IS SHE CAUGHT?—THE OTHER PRISONER.—A FEARFUL OBJECT.—THE ROPE.—THE STRUGGLE.—LOST! LOST!

It was a wonder that the horror of the situation did not turn her brain.

Such a fright as this has, before now, been known to drive a person mad.

There is a well-authenticated story of some foolish people having once played a practical "joke," as they termed it, upon a young lady, who slept alone in a remote wing of an old rambling country house. She had often boasted that nothing in the world could frighten her, and so they one night put a skeleton into her bed.

When she retired for the night, they followed her stealthily up-stairs, and listened outside the door. At the first sight of the horrible bed-fellow they had prepared for her, when she opened the curtains, and saw it lying there, with its head upon the pillow and its lean arm and bony fingers lying outside upon the coverlid, she uttered a loud scream, then remained perfectly silent.

They waited outside, chuckling to themselves, expecting, perhaps, that the poor frightened maiden would rush out in her undressed state, regardless of naught but the terror of the ghost she had left behind her.

But nothing of the sort occurred; and the practical jokers felt not a little disappointed.

The silence continued. They listened and wondered.

At last a sound reached them, though, which filled them with astonishment. They heard her laugh!

They went away on tip-toe, feeling rather small. After all, they had not frightened her, and she had only laughed at their poor bogey.

But next morning the young lady did not come down at her usual time. Some one went up-stairs to call her.

They knocked, but received no answer. They listened. Again that strange sound, so unexpected—the sound of laughter!

Again they knocked, and called loudly to her by name, but without eliciting any reply.

But she was inside—they knew that. They heard her laugh. At length somebody suggested breaking open the door. It was done, and they burst in a body into the room.

What a dreadful sight met their eyes! There she sat upon the bed, the wreck of her former self, her hair snow white—it had turned so in a single night—and her wits gone for ever.

She was an idiot, and there she sat, babbling idiotically, playing with the skeleton's bones.

For some time Cecily battled with the strange captor, without being able to free herself from its grip. It seemed as though the more she pulled, the tighter its hold upon her became.

The skeleton's bones, in fact, were very strongly attached together by wires, and it was also strongly fixed by its feet upon the springs which had enabled it to jump out upon her from its box; and in her wild, hot terror, wrestling frantically, she could not help thinking that the skeleton was pulling against her; and as in the struggle its bones rattled noisily, she thought that it was moving of its own accord, and this notion filled her with an intense terror, which it is impossible to describe.

But when at length, for want of strength or breath, or both, she paused for a moment, and stood still, she found that the skeleton was perfectly still also.

Then she thought to herself how silly she was to be terrified by such an absurd "bogey" as this, and she set about releasing herself with some degree of calmness. It was the fingers of the skeleton, being twisted in the trimmings upon the back of her dress, which had held her prisoner. She would free herself, though, now she was more calm and collected.

It only required a little patience and a little coolness.

After all, what was there to be afraid of? If it had been broad daylight, there would surely have been nothing so very terrible in the adventure. And now she knew what it was that held her, why should she be afraid? Now, if it had been a live man, the case would have been very different; but to be afraid of a lot of old bones, why, it was absurd.

Thus was it that Cecily reasoned, or tried to reason, with herself, as she strove to free herself from the ghastly embrace of the grim object holding her back.

At length she effected her purpose, though not without a great deal of trouble, for the skeleton's fingers had become curiously twisted and entwined in her dress.

At last, though, and with a sense of relief which it would be difficult for a strong, hardy man to realize, Cecily found herself free, and turned to fly from the room.

But suddenly she stood stock still, and listened.

Her heart seemed to have risen up into her throat. A cold perspiration burst out at every pore.

What was it she heard? For a moment she could not believe it, and then she felt certain of the fact. Yes; there was something moving in the room.

There was a faint, rustling sound—a faint rustling of the black drapery with which the room was hung.

She strained her eyes to their utmost, and strove to pierce through the deep obscurity which enveloped all the objects around. Her eyes had, by this time, become, to some small extent, accustomed to the darkness, and she fancied that it was less opaque at the particular point from which the sound emanated than at any other.

Unable to endure that suspense any longer, at last she made a spring forward, and tore the curtains upon one side.

Then, with a sigh of relief, which burst from her palpitating breast, and a flood of happy tears, she found herself, not in the presence of any fresh terror, but before an open window, through which a flood of light poured in upon her, and a soft breeze played refreshingly upon her feverish cheeks

The air coming through a narrow aperture, and cautiously guarded by iron bars, had caused the curtain to rustle in the way described.

But the sight of the light, and the pleasant sensation of the cool air upon her aching forehead, gladdened her heart, and revived her drooping spirits. Then she began to think whether she would not be able to make her escape in a way which she had not hitherto thought of.

The plan had not before occurred to her. But why should she not lower herself through the window into the yard below?

This window looked out upon the back yard, a grim and dingy, deadly-lively spot, in which a smoke-dried tree kept guard over the dilapidated water-butt.

There was a high wall round the yard, but there was a door which opened out into a lane beyond; and she thought it very probable she would be able to make her exit by its means.

But then there was a drawback, as far as this window was concerned, and that was not a small one. The window was very narrow, and it was strongly guarded by iron bars. But then she thought she might escape through some other window, which she might be lucky enough to find, not quite so well protected.

The way that the descent must be made must be by aid of the sheets of her bed, and to get them was her first care. Then they must be twisted into a rope.

She did not delay any longer in considering the question. There was no time to waste, for the dumb astrologer and Mrs. Raddle might return; and though it is true that neither of them had as yet said anything which she could justly construe into a refusal on their part to allow her to leave the house, yet she felt quite confident that they would prevent her doing so. Yes, she was to all intents and purposes their prisoner, and they were keeping her there, and had doomed her, did she not effect her escape, to a fate at the bare thought of which her blood ran cold, and her spirit revolted.

Leaving the room with only a shuddering glance backwards at the death's head dimly seen in the uncertain light in which the greater part of the apartment was plunged, she hurried out on to the staircase and began to ascend to stairs.

With her foot upon the first step, she paused again in alarm at another sound which suddenly fell upon her ear.

This time it was not a sound emanating from the astrologer's mysterious room. It was a noise in the lower part of the house.

It was a noise caused by somebody shaking a door.

At first she stood panic-stricken. She made sure that the man and woman had returned. If so, all would be discovered. Then what would be her fate?

She did not know whether she ought to run back up-stairs, or whether it would be best to remain where she was.

She had no idea what course it would be best to pursue. She only knew that she must pursue some course, and that it would not do to remain idle.

At length she made up her mind the best plan would be to go down stairs, and to make a sudden rush out directly the door was opened.

Then she might get past them into the street. Anyhow, she would be able to appeal to the passers-by—to scream out for help if they wanted to force her back again.

She descended a flight of stairs with this intention, biting her lips and clenching her hands—summoning all the fortitude she was capable of for the coming struggle.

When, however, she reached the passage below, which she did before the noise ceased, she found that it came from a door leading to the kitchen, and not from the street door, which she had expected at first.

Still, that might be the way they would return. There might be an entrance in that direction which she was not aware of.

She came close up to the door, and waited in anxiety for it to be opened.

But the sound suddenly ceased, and then a low moaning sound was heard—a strange wailing, inconceivably melancholy and plaintive.

Cecily could not help thinking at first that it was some dog that had been shut down below, and was trying to make its escape. Clearly enough it was neither the astrologer nor Mrs. Raddle; and this idea lent her courage.

On her side, she also shook the door, and called out, thinking she was speaking to some dumb animal in distress, "Poor thing, what is it?"

The wailing sound immediately ceased, and all was quiet upon the other side.

Cecily shook the door again. Then she heard hasty steps retreating.

She continued, however, to speak in a soothing tone, as though it was some pet animal she was addressing. The sound of the footsteps again drew near.

There was a rustling, curious noise upon the other side of the door, which she could not comprehend.

Suddenly a voice said, "Who's there? Who are you?"

She started back as though something had struck her, and stood speechless, terrified, by the unexpected event.

"Who are you?" the voice again repeated, but in no angry accents. "Are you a friend?"

Cecily hesitated what to say. A friend of whom? Who was this person who inquired?

"Yes," she said, at length. "Who are you?"

"Are you come to deliver me from this horrible place?" continued the voice. "Oh, if you have any pity, do not desert me!"

"What are you doing in there?" asked Cecily. "Are you a prisoner?"

"I am indeed; and a most unhappy one," replied the unknown speaker. "Are you a prisoner also?"

"Indeed I am," said Cecily, whose sympathy had been greatly awakened by the question. "But how can I assist you? I am every bit as helpless as you are."

"We can assist each other," replied the voice on the other side of the door, "if you are willing."

"I am willing enough, if you will tell me how?"

"The first thing to do is to get this door open."

"How can we manage that?"

"We will manage it, if you will push while I pull."

"Pull, then!"

The person on the other side of the door began to pull with all the strength of which she was capable. Cecily knew, of course, she was a female by the voice; knew also that she was exerting all her strength, by the sound of her breathing; and she fancied that the unknown woman must be very weak, because the door seemed to be old and crazy, and almost falling off its hinges; yet, when Cecily paused for a moment, and did not add her strength to the other's efforts, no effect seemed to be caused by the struggles upon the inside.

At last, however, somehow or other, between the two, it was done, and the door flew open.

The darkness was so great within the doorway upon the stairs leading to the kitchen, that Cecily could not at first distinguish the outline of the form of the woman standing there.

Presently, however, she walked, or rather crept, out into the broader light.

Cecily looked at her for a moment in silent amazement.

Then she uttered an exclamation of horror.

The sight which met her eyes was certainly frightful enough to warrant it. It was a sight revolting and sickening in the extreme.

No language could describe the horrible state to which neglect had reduced the miserable creature before her.

She had scarcely a rag of clothing left to cover her lean and emaciated body, reduced to skin and bones.

Her hair was matted and tangled out of all kind of form, and looked more like a mass of weeds than anything else. Her face, almost entirely fleshless, looked horribly gaunt, and, with the dirt upon it, appeared like the face of a baboon. There was nothing human in its aspect.

Underneath the eyes, which were deep and sunken, were black and blue rims, appearing to be the discolouration caused by blows at some distant period.

Her arms, which were bare beyond the elbow, were only two bones dreadful to look at, and the sharp elbows seemed actually to be breaking through the skin. The long, thin, bony, claw-like hands, with very little more covering to them than the hands of the skeleton up-stairs, were garnished by horrible nails resembling the talons of a bird of prey.

As the wretched object stood there crouching and blinking in the light—which, dim as it was, for twilight was coming rapidly on, appeared to be too much for her feeble sight,—Cecily saw that the rags that she wore had the appearance of being damp and mildewed, and it was perfectly plain to see that her wretched, burst boots and ragged stockings were soaking wet.

As she stood there crouching, a sudden fit of coughing attacked her, which appeared to almost tear her chest to pieces with its violence.

It was, indeed, a graveyard cough—a cough fearful to listen to.

"Where have you been?" Cicely asked at length. "What makes you in this dreadful condition?"

The melancholy creature she addressed shivered and hugged her rags together. She spoke in a hoarse, faint, whispering voice.

"I have been down there!" she said, pointing in the direction of the kitchen.

"Have you been a prisoner?" asked Cecily.

"Yes, I have been locked up in the cellar. But I have undone the door and got out at last."

"How long have you been there?"

"Oh, a long while—a very long while!"

"Who has locked you up? How did it come about?"

"He wanted to keep me there. He wanted to kill me. It was the only way, he thought, of shutting my mouth."

"Of shutting your mouth?"

"Yes; he was afraid of his life that I should tell what I knew. And I will tell it yet—perhaps before I have done. I could hang him if I choose, and if I had the chance!"

Cecily thought that her mind was wandering; she could not understand the meaning of the other's words. What was it she was saying?

The woman was silent for a time, for another violent fit of coughing seized upon her, which seemed to paralyze her energies; but after a while, though, she said eagerly, stretching out her arm and clutching at Cecily's skirt, "Come, come! let us go; we have no time to spare if we are to make our escape."

Cecily asked her how she proposed getting away. "Was there not some outlet from below?"

"No!" the woman said; "there was not: but could they not force one of the upper doors?"

There was little chance of that, Cecily thought; and with no more strength than the poor woman seemed to possess, escape in such a way was an impossibility.

"Come, come!" repeated the other again, pulling at her. "Come, come! we must away; there is danger, there is death in this awful place. It will not be the first murder that has been committed in this den of robbers!"

"What do you mean?"

"Have you not heard of that poor girl who died there lately?"

"Yes, I heard something, but I forget what. Tell me about it."

Then the woman narrated in a few words, and as briefly as she could, the chief facts respecting the horrible death of the astrologer's niece, that have been already communicated to the reader.

The woman also informed Cecily that she was the person to whom the astrologer's niece had spoken about the treatment she had received shortly before her death, and she had also picked up the letter which the unfortunate victim had written immediately before her murder.

For these reasons was it that she was now a prisoner in the astrologer's house, and she had been kept in a damp and noisome cellar, with scarcely a ray of light, and scarcely a morsel of food, for three long, weary weeks.

Cecily hearkened in mute horror. She could scarcely believe her ears. Still, what she said she could scarcely help believing. It was very frightful; and whatever came of it, Cecily felt that an attempt must be made immediately to escape from this dreadful house and from the clutches of the wretches who lived in it.

Without consulting the unknown woman, whom she felt certain would not be able to render any assistance, Cecily lead the way up-stairs again to her own apartments.

There she took the sheets off the bed, and, cutting them down the middle, twisted them as well as she could into something resembling a rope. With this she intended to make a descent from the window.

It was a great height; but only from this window was there any chance of getting out, for this was the only window not protected by bars.

She fastened one end of the rope to the leg of the bedstead; then passed the other out of the window.

The twilight, by this time, had given place to darkness. The lamps in the street without shone brightly. In the streets beyond, in the far distance, they were still visible, faintly twinkling like so many stars, standing out from the surrounding blackness.

Cecily got upon the window seat, and looked down into the yard below. The distance, seen from above, was appalling. The undertaking too, to one unaccustomed to such feats, was fraught with peril and danger, but she was a courageous girl, and not easily daunted.

Besides, this was the only way to escape, and to escape she was determined.

The poor woman, who had been watching her intently, though evidently without understanding what was going to happen next, while Cecily cut up the sheets, twisted them into a rope, and tested their strength by tugging at them several times with all her might, now that she saw her mount upon the window seat and prepare to descend, ran forward and clung to Cecily's skirt.

"You will not leave me?" she cried. "Oh, say that you will not leave me?"

"No; I do not intend to forsake you. Do not be afraid!"

"But you are going away? What is to become of me?"

"You shall come, too."

"But how?"

"In the same way."

"Oh, no—no! I dare not! I will not! I would rather stop!"

"What do you mean? Do you think you would not be able to hold fast enough?"

"I don't know—I don't know!" cried the miserable woman, wringing her hands, and whimpering in her terror and despair. "I am afraid!"

"What are you afraid of?" cried Cecily, impatiently.

"Oh, suppose the rope should break?"

"Well, if it did, you would not likely be killed."

"Oh, dear! oh, dear!"

"But, if you remain here, what will become of you, do you think?"

"Oh, I do not know—I do not know! Oh, dear! oh, dear!"

"Will you not also be killed? Which death do you think is preferable? Besides, there is not much risk in this. Come! I am certain this rope will bear us."

"Oh, no—no! I dare not! I will not! I would rather stay!"

Cecily saw that there was but little to be done with her. The poor creature's brain had evidently been turned by the sufferings which she had lately endured in her incarceration.

What could be done? There was nothing for it but to leave her.

But even this course was not easily taken; for, as Cecily was preparing to descend, the other rushing forward, clung to her frantically, and held her fast.

Cecily endeavoured, though fruitlessly, to shake her off.

"You shall not go!" the other cried. "You shall not leave me!"

"Take away your hands!" cried Cecily, angrily. "What do you mean?"

CHAPTER LIV.

THE ASSASSINS IN THE DARK.—THE ATTACK.—THE DEADLY STRUGGLE.—THE DEATH.—THE ROBBER'S WIFE.—THE DAWN OF LOVE.—ONE MORE EFFORT FOR FREEDOM.

WHEN I left Ruth, I left her lying in wait for the attack of the robbers.

To have seen her crouching there, with firmly set lips, and flashing eyes, and cheeks and forehead flushed with vengeful hate, one would not much have relished being waited for in like fashion by so beautiful and terrible a foe.

She crouched there like a tigress or like a cat. Every muscle strung, as it were, ready for the fatal spring.

Her fingers nervously grasping the handle of the glittering knife, with which she longed to deal a death-blow to her adversary.

Even now there were blood-drops upon its long, sharp, cruel blade, the record of one vengeful slash already inflicted.

She waited there for a short time after she had maimed the hand of one of the robbers, in momentary expectation of a furious attack being made upon her. But it was not yet to come.

After the first wild, uncontrollable shriek of agony, which the intensity of the pain had wrung from the breast of the suffering wretch, no cry was made.

Ruth heard the sound of the retreating footsteps, and could hear some other sound which appeared like stifled sobs and half-smothered groans, but evidently the sufferer was making fearful efforts to drown the sounds of his misery.

He would return soon, she thought; or, if he were disabled, the others would come, and she must prepare for them.

The first thing she did was to blow out the light. She could manage then better in the dark; and she reasoned, very knowingly, that an unseen assailant is the most terrible.

She took her pocket handkerchief, and holding her dagger in her hand, bound them firmly together in such a way that even a violent blow could not make her loosen her hold very readily.

She had seen this mode adopted abroad in Mexico, where they sometimes fight with the stiletto or bowie knives.

When she had made these preparations, she also got her pistol all ready, cocked it, and put it back into her bosom,—arranging it in such a way that it could not very easily get shaken, so as to discharge it; but fixing it in such a manner that, in an instant, she could make use of it.

When she had done all this, she was ready for the attack, and crouching as before in a corner close to the door, waited very patiently.

She had to wait a long while, though, before there was any sign of renewal of hostilities.

The house was very still—so still that she could hear the pattering of the rain-drops falling upon the window, and the faint creaking of the signboard without; and it appeared to her, in the heavy and oppressive silence, that these small noises were unusually loud, and seemed almost as though they were beating like small hammers upon her brain.

At length, in about twenty minutes' time, perhaps, from the date of the last attack, a very slight sound without, upon the staircase, caused her eagerly to twist her head round in that direction, and hearken with an earnest intensity.

It was a sound of breathing.

Some one was listening at the key-hole.

Ruth raised her pocket-pistol, and for a second or two hesitated whether she should not fire through upon them. But she thought that it might be the beautiful girl who some time ago had endeavoured to warn her, and who had now, perhaps, come back with the intention of helping her.

If it were the girl, though, she would make some sign without, to let her presence be known.

Ruth waited for a short time, but no such sign was made; and presently she heard a slight scratching and picking noise outside, which, from the direction from which it came, she felt sure was caused by one of the men endeavouring to force back the bolt from the outside, with the blade of a knife.

The noise continued very steadily for a long time; but there was no whispering, and no other noise of any kind; and this circumstance led Ruth to believe that this time she would only have one foe to encounter.

For one foe she was well prepared; and she waited with all the patience she had at her command, until he should present himself.

Very slowly and cautiously did the would-be assassin ply his knife until the bolt was shot back. Then there was a pause, and then the door opened, and the man crept very cautiously into the room, apparently dreading an attack from some hidden enemy, and, probably, making ready to repel it.

There was a very faint light struggling in round one corner of the blind—far too faint to have been of any service to the man now making his entrance, but still of use to the woman lying in wait. It showed her some indication of the outline of his lusty form, and gave her some notion, though a very indefinite one, regarding the direction of his eyes. She felt somehow that his gaze was fixed upon her—that he was about to make a spring in her direction.

But this was fancy. The assassin could not see an inch before his nose. He was glaring fiercely round him in the pitchy darkness, but all was black and unfathomable.

He scarcely moved—he listened intently. From what had happened to his companion, he could scarcely believe that the travellers slept; yet for a very long time had he been listening outside, upon the staircase, in the hope of hearing some noise, however low, which, if they were awake, might indicate their wakefulness; and as he had heard nothing, he hardly knew what to believe.

As all was so still, he could not help thinking that the drug must have had its effect, and that his two foes were under its stupefying influence.

If he could only have been certain, he, of course, would have advanced rapidly enough; but in the pitchy darkness he could judge nothing.

He might be facing his foes, or standing with his back to them—it was impossible to tell; and the man hesitated whether to go backwards or forwards would be safest.

"Why the devil did I not bring up the dark lantern?" the man muttered between his teeth.

After a pause of the most complete silence on both sides, the man decided that the drug must have operated, and that they were asleep.

Then he crept forward towards the bed, with an axe, which he grasped in his right hand, uplifted in the air.

The moment that he moved in that direction, however, the Spy, lying in wait for him, moved forward also, and prepared to deal a fatal blow.

The man heard her coming, and half twisted

round, so that her knife entered deeply into his right shoulder instead of through his back, into his heart as it otherwise would have done.

He staggered back a pace or two, with his mouth agape, and, in falling, clutched at the window-blind, which he tore away from the roller as he fell.

The moon's light, thus admitted, fell upon the man's face blanched with pain, but with a brow black and heavy with scowling hate.

As he fell, the dagger was knocked out of Ruth's hand, in spite of the caution which she had taken to guard against such an accident.

The man, although severely wounded, was not deprived of his strength; and though the axe had fallen from his right hand, rendered helpless by the wound he had received in the arm, he strove to gain possession with his left.

But Ruth seeing his object, sprang upon him as quick as lightning.

She leaped upon him with more of the savage ferocity of a wild cat, than the enmity of a human being.

With both her hands, and with all the power of her wrists—so powerful, as we well know—she grasped the man's throat, as once she had grasped the throat of Jacob Stone, in giving him up to the police.

Then she grasped the axe which he was striving to get hold of, and tore it from his fingers.

In the struggle, she bore her foe down to the ground, clinging to him all the while; then, with the weapon which she had wrested from him, she dealt him a shower of savage blows, in furious haste.

Yet another and another blow did she deal him. The axe had entered his brain. The very handle was bloody; but she seemed, as it were, unconscious that her work of vengeance was complete.

The axe slipped at last from her fingers, and, in feeling for it again upon the ground, her hands came in contact with the knife which she had let fall.

She caught it up, and though her victim lay there still enough, and dead enough, with his hideously gashed face and shattered skull, she drove the reeking blade again and again into the victim's breast, until want of breath alone compelled her to desist from the ferocious slaughter.

She rose up to her feet and made towards the door.

But at that moment a light was seen approaching, and the door being flung wide open, the landlord, with one hand bound up, and his face ghastly white and blood-stained, rushed into the room, holding a crow-bar in the other hand, which was not disabled.

The noise he had heard had apprized him that his companion was getting decidedly the worst of it; but when he came to see the dreadful sight which awaited him, he started back in horror.

Only for a moment, though, and then he rushed forward upon Ruth.

But she had time to save herself from the blow which he would have dealt her; and, drawing the pistol from her breast, she fired upon him as he approached.

She could not take a very good aim, for she was trembling violently from the effects of the deadly struggle in which she had been engaged; but the shot nevertheless took effect in the lower part of the ruffian's jaw, and, with a howl, he fell backwards into the passage.

The light which had illuminated this dreadful scene was held by the beautiful and mysterious girl about whom we have heard so much. She stood there in dumb terror, clutching a candlestick in her hand, unable to speak or act.

Ruth, without heeding in the slightest the mutilated body of the robber she had killed, and the recumbent form of the landlord, writhing and groaning upon the floor upon the spot where he had fallen when the bullet had laid him low, rushed eagerly up to the terrified girl, and bade her tell her whether there were any more people below, and to employ her assistance in helping them, the Captain and herself, to escape.

But the girl, somewhat to Ruth's amazement, made no reply; shook off her grasp with a kind of horrified shiver, and approaching the landlord's prostrate body, knelt over him and wrung her hands, apparently in bitter grief.

"Oh, you have killed him!" she said; "you have killed him! What shall I do?"

"You need not grieve about him," said Ruth; "he is not worthy of it. You know he would have taken our lives if he could have done so. As it is, I think he has killed my friend."

But the girl, still stooping over the man's body, and striving to stanch the flow of blood from his wound, made no reply.

"Come, come!" said Ruth, again appealing to her; "what makes you stop there by his side? What was he to you?"

"What was he to me?" the girl replied, almost fiercely. "He was my husband!"

"He ill-used you, though!"

"But I loved him!"

"He is not dead now," said Ruth. "Assist us to escape, and we will see what can be done for him."

But the girl still remaining in a half state of stupor, without paying any attention to this appeal, Ruth left her, taking the light in her hand, to go to the bedside and look at the insensible Captain.

He lay there very white and motionless. Save that he was not disfigured by the mark of gore, he looked as dead as the ruffian who had fallen beneath Ruth's murderous axe.

She laid her hand upon his heart and felt for its throbbings, but his heart was quite motionless.

How fixed and leaden in its hue was his cold, handsome face!

His cheeks seemed sunken; and his lips had a blueish tinge upon them, something like the bloom upon a plum.

She raised his head upon her arm, and looked down anxiously into his still, white face; and as she looked long and earnestly, some new sensation—a sensation of pity, or even of something stronger—agitated her breast.

Never before, since the old, old times when she was young and innocent, and happy (great God! how long ago it seemed), had she ever felt like this to any human creature.

She knelt down at the bedside, and she laid her pretty pink and white cheek against his cheek so cold and rigid; and her features, which only a short time since had been convulsed by hate and passion, and that thirst for blood which at times held possession of her with a wolfish rapacity and longing, relaxed into a soft womanly look, full of deep sympathy and love.

Love!—yes, it was love!

What other passion in the world were strong enough to conquer her rebellious nature—to cause her to forget herself, as now she did?

Those who knew this woman when plying her

abhorrent trade of informer and spy, would not, could not have believed her to be she who grovelled there now upon her knees by the bedside, with her cheeks moist with burning tears, sobbing upon the icy hand of the man she loved, imploring him in piteous accents to live for her sake, and not to die yet, so young and so handsome, and when she had learnt to love him.

When she had learnt, for the first time in her life, that she had a heart.

Yes, she loved him. A strange and mysterious, invisible, unaccountable change in her whole nature had somehow been wrought during the last few hours.

Some secret and unseen subtle influence had been at work within her.

What was it? She could not tell; but there was some change now in all her thoughts upon, and views of, life.

The first indication of the arrival of these new sentiments she remembered was when her companion had caught her up, all blushing and palpitating, in his arms, and sprung with her across the brook.

She had never yet in all her experience come across a man so brave, so light-hearted, so gay and joyous as this Captain Charley.

He was the spoilt child of fashion—a rollicking, jovial spirit, whose face was scarcely ever overclouded for two consecutive minutes by a thought of care.

"Ah!" she reflected to herself with bitter heart-burnings, and vain regrets for what was past and gone, never to return,—"if I could have known such a man once! If I could have had the chance to meet with such a one! If he had loved me."

Then she fell to thinking how different would have been her lot. She might then have been a beloved wife and a happy mother.

Existence would then for her have had an aim and object, instead of being as it was, a desert and a blank.

Upon her knees by the bedside she raised her voice on high, and clasping her hands in supplication to the heaven she had so often and so grossly profaned, poured forth frantic prayers and lamentations over the body of him whom she supposed to be dead.

He was not dead, or nearly at death's door. He was only stupefied and insensible, from the effe s of the narcotic which had been administered to him.

There was really no occasion for fear; but she loved, and she feared for the object of her love; and fear took the place of reason in the heart of the terrified creature.

If she had used her reason, she would have known that, could it have been so, it would have been better that the Captain had never awakened from his sleep.

It would have been better for them to have parted at once. For what good could possibly come of their loving one another?

They belonged to different stations in life. He would never marry her. If he made her his mistress—and to that, if she might remain with him, she would have consented, perhaps, without much difficulty—would he not some day or other leave her to get married? And then——

And then? Here was a pretty to do! She was tearing her heart to pieces at the notion of what would probably never occur, for it was much more than probable that she never would be his mistress.

Besides, had not she only a moment ago been beating her head and tearing her hair, bemoaning his untimely death?

Was he dead?

"Oh, dear love, look up! Look up at me! Open your eyes, and speak to me! Only one word! For the love of God, only one little word!"

But he lay silent.

"Only one little word!" she pleaded—"ever so little a one, to prove to me that you are living still!"

She sobbed herself quite out of breath, at last. She might have fainted, or fallen asleep In either case, she became, for a short time, insensible.

When she awoke again, day was breaking, with a dull, leaden hue, upon the bed and its silent occupant—upon her own fair form, lying half-naked, and with tangled hair and bare bosom, by its side—and upon a hideous mass of blood and bruises, which had been a man some time or other.

It was the corpse of the ruffian whom she had murdered, lying exactly in the spot where it had lain when she looked upon it last.

Ruth regarded the horrible object with a shudder. Then she turned her eyes towards the doorway, where the other man had fallen.

She started in alarm when she saw that he was gone. The girl had gone also.

There was a great stain of blood upon the floor.

Had the man died? and had the girl removed the body?

Or had he recovered, and had she helped him away?

It was curious, Ruth thought, that she had not heard them leave the room. The man must have been dead, she thought, or she would have heard the noise. It was while she was weeping over the Captain's body that the landlord's wife had drawn away the corpse.

But while Ruth was thinking of the matter, in a dreamy kind of way, she thought all at once that she heard the sound of voices in the room beneath.

They were gruff voices, talking angrily in low savage tones, above which some voice arose now and then, and she could catch a few of the words which were uttered.

"She killed them, did she?"

"The woman up-stairs!"

"Perhaps it was the man!"

"Do you think the man is dead, then?"

"We will settle her soon!"

There seemed to be a general movement towards the door. But suddenly the door was banged to, and a loud voice bade them stop.

Ruth rose to her feet and gasped. What should she do?

While she was hesitating, though, an event occurred which caused her to alter all the plans she was before maturing. The sound of the door slamming to heavily below, aroused the Captain from his torpor.

He sprang into a sitting posture on the bed, and opened his eyes.

But then the violent pain in his head overcame him again, and he sank back wearily.

Ruth took his hand into her hands, and kissed him in wild delight.

"Are you better, dear?" she asked anxiously. "Can you move?"

"I—I am afraid not!"

"Try—try, for my sake!"

"My head aches horribly!"

"Shall I assist you?"

"Mayn't I lie here awhile to rest?"

"No, no, dear—there is no time! There is danger in every moment lost! Come, come! a little courage, and a little effort!"

The Captain struggled into a sitting posture, and rose painfully from the bed.

"What am I to do? Where are we going?"

"We must fly! We must fly at once, or we shall be murdered!"

He seemed yet more than half-stupefied, but he put his hand into the one which she held out to him.

Ruth then took up her bonnet and shawl, and bidding her companion walk as noiselessly as possible, led the way from the room.

The voices were distinctly audible below, engaged in an angry dispute, in which the voice of the woman appeared to be urging some course of action which was not popular with the rest.

The daylight streamed into the passage where Ruth and Crockford stood. Ruth saw that there was a staircase at either end. The one leading in the opposite direction to that in which they had come up when they came to bed, they now descended.

At the bottom of the stairs they came to a door strongly bolted.

With a slight effort, however, Ruth withdrew the bolts.

The door opened. They passed through, and found themselves in the open air. In a back yard they were standing. The gate was open. Beyond was a meadow, and in the distance, about a hundred yards off, a small wood, or thicket.

"If we can get there!" whispered Ruth.

"Yes," said her companion; "let us try."

"Can you make an effort?"

"Yes."

"Have you strength enough to run?"

"Plenty!"

"Thank God for that, then! We may escape yet."

"Which way?" he said.

"To the wood."

"Shall we be safe there, do you think?"

"Yes—yes; if we can only manage to reach it without being seen."

"Come along, then!"

They started, hand-in-hand, without further parley, and set off at their utmost speed.

CHAPTER LV.

A NEST OF ROBBERS.—THE BACK STAIRCASE.—THE FLIGHT.—THE WOOD.—THE AMBUSH.—ANOTHER LIFE IS SACRIFICED.—A RUN FOR IT.—THE STOLEN HORSE.—A HARD GALLOP.—THE BLOODHOUNDS ON THEIR TRACK.

I AM very much averse to the introduction of long descriptions into a story-book. You would not thank me if I went in largely for landscapes, or was particular in telling you what clothes all my characters wear every time they come on to the scene for the purpose of making a few observations. Explanation, likewise, I endeavour to avoid as much as possible; and if sometimes I by chance leave some trifling incident unexplained, you must kindly bear with me, reader, for it is because I am afraid that I should weary you by dwelling too long upon one subject, and I am eager to get on to the next

A few words, though, upon this occasion—only very few.

This inn into which the ill-luck of Ruth and her military cavalier had guided their steps was the rendezvous of a gang of desperate ruffians, half poachers and half smugglers, who carried on their nefarious practices in the neighbourhood, and lived a rollicking life, in defiance of the local police, who occasionally, in a sleepy sort of fashion, endeavoured to rout them out of their stronghold, but who were invariably worsted and sent to the right-about after some well-meant but extremely feeble attempts to put them down.

Whether or not they had often resorted to the amicable practice of knifing the guests at the "White Horse" is questionable. In the evidence which was subsequently brought forward in the trial of one of the miscreants, which may yet be fresh in the readers' minds (for the existence of this murder a matter of history), it is very certain that a case was clearly proved against them, but how many such cases there had been which had not been discovered it is impossible even to conjecture.

Upon this occasion the band had arrived from an exploring expedition in the neighbourhood about daylight, and had found the landlord's ill-used wife mourning over the body of her ruffian husband, which she had carried down, as best she could, into the sitting-room, and upon which she lay stretched in a perfect paroxysm of grief, heedless of all external objects, and deaf to every attempted consolation or eager question.

Only at last was it, when a suggestion of vengeance was made to her, that she recovered at all from the state of abject apathy into which she had fallen under the weight of her woe.

Then throwing off the shrinking timidity which had seemed hitherto a part of herself, she had sworn that no harm should befall her husband's murderers. "No," she cried, "blood enough has been spilt; no more shall come of it. Let them escape. He has been a bad, wicked man, and has used me harshly, although I could love him still were he alive. Nay, I would willingly lay down my life now, could I restore his, but that is impossible. He brought this fate upon himself. God has guided the hand of man; and so surely as any among you attempt to shed more blood, shall you perish in like manner! Let them escape!"

But this reasoning was not popular with the gang: they wanted to have vengeance upon the slayers of their comrade. "Where were they? Let them be delivered up."

Now it was that the woman threw herself betwixt them and the door, and refused to allow any of the ruffians to pass by; and while they were arguing the point, it was that the two adventurers were beating a retreat.

You may be sure that one poor, weak woman was not very long able to hold at bay half a dozen strong men. Very soon they had forced her from the position she occupied, and were pouring up the stairs in a body to the bed-room which the fugitives had just deserted.

Pell-mell they rushed into the room where they expected to find their victims, and exclamations of astonishment and baffled rage soon apprized the woman below that they had met with some rebuff.

What it was, though, she did not at first understand. However, after a few moments' pause, a loud shout arose, and the body of ruffians came trampling out into the passage, and bawling to her, "Where are they? Which room?"

"The room where the body is!" she answered.

That was the room which they had entered. There was the body, sure enough; but what had become of the fugitives?

"They must be there!" the woman cried up from the bottom of the stairs.

"They are not, you fool! Come up yourself, and see!"

"Thank heaven, they are gone!" the woman muttered to herself, and she mentally offered up a prayer of thanksgiving for their deliverance.

Meanwhile, the robbers were ransacking the house from top to bottom, muttering fierce threats of vengeance as they went.

The fugitives made the best of their way to the wood, in the dark intricacies of which they had plunged eagerly, hoping to escape observation.

It was not a very large wood, this, although its foliage was very thick, and upon the other side the country was bleak and open. Therefore did they deem it prudent to lie for awhile in ambush, because if the robbers came to look out through the windows, they would infallibly have been seen out in the open.

It would be best, at any rate for a little while, to remain perfectly quiet where they were, before they made any attempt of escaping to a further distance. Presently, when the robbers had looked, and had come to the conclusion, as they possibly might do, and as the fugitives sincerely hoped that they would, that they (the runaways) had managed to clear off, and were beyond all hopes of pursuit.

Thus it was that they kept perfectly quiet; and the Captain, resting on a mossy bank, Ruth spied through the trees, and took observation of the movements of the enemy. As she had good eyes, she could see, now and then, the faces of one or the other of the robbers at the window.

Presently, the whole party came out upon the roof of the house—a flat roof—and appeared to be taking observations of the surrounding country.

They looked to the right and the left, and appeared to enter into argument, and discuss in turn each proposition made by any of the party.

At last, as by one consent, the general attention was centred upon the wood.

When, at first, she saw their eyes all fixed that way, poor Ruth came shrinking back from the point of observation, fearing that they had seen her, but then she came to the conclusion that this was not the case.

They came down from the roof in a body, descending, as they had ascended, by a trap-door in the housetop, and in a few minutes afterwards, a door leading into the yard being opened, they came pouring out.

Ruth and her companion watched their movements in deep silence, and with intense anxiety.

"Back—back!" whispered Crockford, laying his hand upon the arm of his companion, and drawing her under the shadow of the tree; "if they are coming after us, this will be a pretty place to be caught in! We can be murdered here very quietly, and our bodies buried, where there would never be any chance of their being found again."

"We can fight for it," said Ruth.

The Captain, though, appeared rather doubtful about this. "We have no arms," he said.

"Yes," answered Ruth; "here are a knife and a pistol."

"Give them me."

"What, both?"

"Do you know how to use them, then?"

Ruth smiled.

"Ask that dead body in the sleeping-room," she answered, grimly, as she handed Crockford the pistol, and a charge, which she had also got in her pocket.

The Captain betook himself to the occupation of loading; while she, clutching the handle of the dagger-knife, crept forward again to her hiding-place, and watched.

They were coming her way. They would soon be there. Not all the gang had set out in their pursuit. Some had remained at the inn. Three men there were on foot, and one riding upon a shaggy colt.

Crockford and Ruth had chosen a spot where the briars and thickly-set bushes completely concealed them from view; and although the party in pursuit came within half a dozen yards of the spot where they were hidden, they did not perceive the fugitives.

As they passed by, the fugitives could hear what they said.

"We will turn them out of their hiding place, I'll warrant me!" said one.

"It's very sure," said another, "that they cannot be at any very great distance."

"No, they must be hereabouts—somewhere close at hand."

"If they have got beyond the wood, we should have seen them upon the other side, out in the open country; unless they happen to be under the shade of the trees, having just got through the wood."

"That is not likely, though. You may take your oath they are hiding here a few yards off!"

"If we alight on them, they mustn't get off scot-free, that's very sure. They've got secrets that'll string up the whole lot of us!"

The speakers passed away, and entered the wood a very short distance from the spot where Ruth and Crockford were hiding.

It would be difficult to describe their feelings as they gazed upon the savage countenances of those lawless ruffians bent upon their destruction.

It was a breathless moment.

The robbers were still muttering among themselves, but their words were no longer audible; the only clue that the fugitives possessed to their intentions being in their angry gestures, and occasionally an extra loud curse which escaped them in the fury of their disappointment.

"We are certain to be found," whispered Ruth, almost beneath her breath. "Do you see what has become of them?"

"They have divided, I think. The man on horseback is left outside."

"I don't see the others, though. Yes, here are two coming towards us!"

The fugitives crept closer, and nothing more was said.

Two of the robbers were advancing in their direction; and they passed by, scrutinizing the bushes upon either side, within a few feet of the spot where they were hiding.

Both Ruth and Crockford kept their eyes riveted upon them. But a new cause of alarm arose. They heard some one passing behind them.

The rustling of leaves, and the snapping of twigs, gave fearful evidence of the proximity of the third man.

Just when they got to the exact spot where the fugitives intervened between the one man and the two men on the other side, as fate would have it, they stopped to talk. The conversation which ensued, therefore, passed directly over the heads of the lady and gentleman lying concealed.

Nothing, indeed, sheltered them but the

branches and leaves of shrubs, so frail and pliant that every current of air passing through them caused them slightly to yield and flutter, and a stronger gust of wind than usual was liable to blow them upon one side, and expose the fugitives to view.

Fortunately, however, the two men were standing on a piece of high ground, and the line of their sight carried their eyes right over the bushes that concealed Crockford and Ruth, to the spot where the third man stood; and as they were staring at one another's faces, instead of on the thick mass of foliage intervening, they, for the moment, escaped notice.

The conversation which took place was conducted earnestly, but in a low tone of voice, as though they were anxious, if possible, to prevent any listeners from hearing, should any be concealed in the immediate neighbourhood.

"They are gone to the other end of the wood, one said.

"There's no chance of finding them about here, even if they were here, the branches are so precious thick."

"All this while they are getting out at the other end."

"Shall we go back, then?"

"Yes."

The two men began to move away, and the other very shortly followed in their wake: when, however, he had gone a few paces, he stopped suddenly, and stood quite still.

Crockford and Ruth listened. The party of two had ceased talking, and they could hear their retreating footsteps and their slow and guarded movements, as they pushed the bushes aside in their wary progress.

It was evident that they had passed by the

cover, but the third man still remained, scanning the bushes around with savage, glaring eyes.

"Had he seen them?" they asked themselves in terror. He might have fancied that he had, but it was only fancy; for, after a pause of one or two minutes, he began also to slowly walk away, step by step, as a person might do who was searching for some object fallen upon the ground.

When he had got to a distance of six yards or more, Crockford could not refrain from exchanging a smile of triumph with his companion, but their rejoicing was premature.

The third man, just as he was disappearing from sight round the trunk of a huge tree, which concealed the two men, appeared to hesitate, and returned upon his steps.

When he had advanced about six feet nearer, he stood still again; and the fixedness of his attitude, and the intensity of his gaze, betrayed at once the awful truth that he had discovered something about the bushes to arouse his suspicions. If he had called to his companions, and they had all come forward in a body, the fugitives must have been discovered directly; but fortunately for them, some unexplained motive prompted the man to return alone.

Without recalling the others, therefore, he retraced his steps, and his companions walked away in an opposite direction. He very cautiously approached the bushes, upon which his eyes seemed to be riveted, as though by some kind of fascination.

He had caught sight of something glittering among the leaves; and this, to tell the truth, was the reason which caused him to return. It was a scrap of ribbon, embroidered with gold thread, which had somehow become detached from the lady's dress, and he did not think that it was in any way connected with the fugitives after whom they were searching.

He thought it was some kind of prize—something worth having—and he did not feel at all inclined to share it with his companions.

But as he drew near he could not help thinking that perhaps he might be advancing upon an ambush, and he began to hesitate and quaver.

But the hesitation was only momentary, and he advanced again.

He drew nearer and nearer. He could not be quite sure what the object was.

But he could not leave it in doubt.

By this time his companions were far away; and after a little more hesitation he walked hastily forward, and pushed the boughs upon one side, to get hold of the glittering object.

In doing so, he had advanced a step within the hiding-place, and he was standing less than a foot off the two fugitives before he perceived them at all.

They were crouching there like breathless statues—their eyes fixed upon him.

He had only time, however, to utter a low exclamation of terror, before the dagger-knife which Ruth held was plunged deep into his breast.

At the same moment she had grasped him with the other hand by the handkerchief, and twisted it round so as to prevent him uttering any exclamation.

The robber fell backwards, with a low groan and a gurgling sound in his throat, and then lay perfectly still.

Crockford stood for a moment, horrified into silence, although he could not help admiring the extraordinary courage and presence of mind of his companion; for this wholesale shedding of blood was something so out of all experience, that he was half terrified by the presence of its perpetrator, although it was certainly done for his preservation.

Next moment, though, while he was still aghast at what he had just witnessed, Ruth pulled him by the arm, and whispered hoarsely, "Now is the time, if we are to go!"

They could hear the voices of the other two men quite at the other end of the wood, shouting to the man who had just been killed, to follow them. Only the man upon the colt remained, but they did not know whereabouts he had taken up his station.

They did not bend their steps towards that side of the wood which faced the inn from which they had escaped; nor did they, of course, go towards the one where the two men were looking for them. But they made for the open country, upon one side.

Pushing through the briars and brambles with as little noise as possible, but still losing no more time than they could help, they very soon broke through to an opening.

Here, as they left the shade of the trees, they came suddenly out upon the man on the colt, who was sitting with his back turned towards them.

He did not turn round at their approach. He was busy lighting his pipe, and, though he heard the branches cracking, he supposed that the noise was caused by one of his companions.

"Stand still for a moment," whispered Crockford. "Lend me your shawl. I think I can settle him!"

He took the shawl as he spoke, and stole up behind the robber. Then, with a turn of the hand, he muffled the robber's head in it, and adroitly jerked him out of the saddle on to the grass, where he lay struggling and groaning, being badly hurt by the fall.

"Now for it!" said Crockford; "we'll have his horse!"

The Captain's strength seemed by this time to have revived, and his courage and spirits returned.

He took Ruth in his arms, and placed her on the saddle; then jumped up himself behind her.

The man smothered in the shawl bellowed "Murder!" with all the strength of his lungs; but, without heeding him, Crockford struck his heels into the horse's sides, and scattered the dust as he broke into a gallop.

But just as they quitted the wood, the two men, aroused by their comrade's cries, came running up, brandishing their bludgeons and vowing vengeance.

They were not twenty feet away when the Captain and his companion started. They were, however, forty feet distant in another minute.

The two men, pausing for a moment to tug the shawl off their companion's head, came roaring after them.

They were swift runners, and the colt went at a good round pace. Which was going to beat?

Crockford held on as a grip like that of grim death. It was difficult, though, to keep on the saddle himself, and hold his companion on also; but he managed it somehow, and a hundred yards were passed over in half a dozen seconds.

The pursuers made desperate efforts to gain upon the pursued. The pursued redoubled their exertions to get ahead of them.

The Captain clenched his teeth, and griped the horse's sides with his knees. Ruth's pale face bespoke determination and courage, but she trembled slightly.

"Bear up!—bear up!" whispered Crockford. "Are you afraid?"

"No!" she replied, grasping his hand. "We shall beat them yet!"

CHAPTER LVI.

A HARD RUN FOR IT.—OUT OF BREATH.—THE SHOT.—THE CATASTROPHE.—UP AGAIN.—DODGING A PISTOL.—FREE ONCE MORE.—ANOTHER ADVENTURE MORE WONDERFUL THAN THE LAST IS PROMISING.

THE pursurers were beginning to get out of breath.

They were beginning to curse.

The Captain caught a sound of their imprecations, and chuckled to himself. "We shall beat them!" he thought, and drummed the sides of the horse harder than ever with his heels.

Presently they arrived at a little hill, and up this the horse strained and panted with its heavy load. The two pursuers, however, panted worse when they came to it.

One was at least half a dozen yards behind the other, who was losing ground every minute. The foremost was a wiry, muscular fellow, without a superfluous ounce of fat on his ribs: the other was of a fuller habit of body, perhaps a little paunchy, but a good tough subject, too; and they both stuck to it manfully.

Down the hill upon the other side went the colt and its riders full pelt. The two pursuers thought they would never with life have reached the summit, but they did somehow, and turned the corner, and came down, too, with all their might and main.

But there was only a short spell of level ground, and then came another hill. This beat the fat man altogether. He gave it up, squatted down, wiped his head, and whined. The other stuck to it still.

He stuck to it in such right good earnest that Crockford, glancing back over his shoulder at him, began almost to despair of shaking him off. And the colt, too, was beginning to blow.

The riders, however, had less confidence in their chance of escape than their pursuer, for the latter all at once lost heart and gave up the chase. But as he did so he drew a pistol from his pocket, took aim, and fired!

Ruth and Crockford simultaneously uttered a sharp cry of dismay.

Next moment, they and the colt were rolling together upon the ground.

I hardly know whether the man who fired the pistol, or the lady and gentleman who tumbled, were the most astonished.

The pursuer, however, began to bawl out lustily to his companion to come on, and help to wreak vengeance upon those who had given them so much trouble.

The fat man, though he had scarcely a gasp of breath left in his body, rose to his feet and came staggering onward. The other man bounded forward like a stag.

But he did not bound far, for suddenly, at the top of the hill, up popped Crockford with a pistol in his hand.

The sight of this weapon was too much for master thief.

He instantly dropped down flat upon his stomach behind a small stone-heap, which providentially lay there.

He bobbed up his head next minute, but bobbed it down again the next, for there was Crockford still with the pistol, and its muzzle was pointed right at him.

"Stop where you are!" shouted the Captain, and the thief obeyed.

Meanwhile, Ruth having risen unhurt to her feet, endeavoured to assist the horse out of its difficulties. She found, to her surprise, that it had not been wounded. Just at the moment that the man had fired at them, the colt had stumbled over a loose sod, and came down sprawling to the earth.

The ball therefore had gone over their heads, and left them unharmed, except a few slight bruises.

"Mount the horse, and be off," cried Crockford.

"And you?" returned his companion—"what will you do?"

"Don't fear for me," he replied—"I will be after you directly. Only you clear the top of this hill, out of harm's way; then wait for me on the other side."

Ruth did what she was told, and Crockford remained behind.

"Move but a step nearer, either of you," he bawled out, "and I'll blow your brains out!"

With that, he began to walk backwards towards the top of the hill, keeping the muzzle of his weapon, however, always directed towards them.

Both the robbers were of opinion that the Captain's aim was a bad one, and that the pistol would not carry as far as from where he stood to where they were. Each of them wondered why the other did not summon up the necessary pluck to go forward like a man; only neither liked to do it himself, because, you see, there was a slight risk, after all. He might be a good aim, and the pistol might carry as far.

Therefore they let him go; and when he had reached the top of the hill, he set off down the other side as fast as ever his legs would carry him.

Ruth was waiting for him about twenty yards off, and he leaped on the colt behind her.

Then they set off at full gallop across the country.

The men did not quite give up the chase yet. They struggled on for some short time longer: but a man is no match for a horse; and so, at length, they, in the natural course of things, broke down, and away went the colt and its riders, leaving the pursuers in despair and out of breath.

"Thank God for that!" ejaculated Crockford at length, as he looked back upon his foes, now two tiny black specks in the extreme distance. "We have got rid of them at last."

"I wonder what fresh dangers are going to befall us?" said Ruth.

"That's more than I can guess at," rejoined her companion. "So many wonderful things have happened lately, perhaps something more wonderful still is reserved for us."

"Perhaps so."

"This is a lonely spot, though, is it not? I think I see something like a house yonder through the trees. Let us make for it."

"Hark! what is that? Don't you hear a voice calling to us?"

"By Jove! I hope it is not those fellows again! Where's my pistol?"

"No, it is the opposite direction. There is an old man yonder, waving his hand and shouting."

"Ah! I see him! What does he want, I wonder?"

"He seems to want us."

"So he does. I told you something wonderful was about to occur. I wonder what it will be."

Something very wonderful it was, too, which I will describe to you.

CHAPTER LVII.

THE LITTLE OLD GENTLEMAN.—A MYSTERIOUS REQUEST.—THE OLD MANOR HOUSE.—A RECOLLECTION OF RUTH'S CHILDHOOD.—WHAT WAS IT THAT RECALLED IT?—THE STRANGE MEETING.—THE RECOGNITION.—A CONNECTING LINK TO BE EXPLAINED.—UPON THE THRESHOLD OF THE CHAMBER OF DEATH.

THEIR pursuers had by this time disappeared altogether. They had most likely given up the chase as a bad job, and taken themselves off to the place from which they came.

Nobody was to be seen upon any side but the old man approaching them at a trot across the meadows.

There could, therefore, be very little doubt about the old man's intending the loud "Hilloa, there!" to which he gave utterance as he approached, to be addressed to them.

"Hilloa, there! Hilloa! hilloa!"

Crockford pulled the bridle, and bawled also in return.

"Hilloa!"

"Stop!" shouted the old man.

"What do you want?" responded Crockford.

"Wait till I get up to you," bawled the old man.

"He talks as though he were monarch of all he surveyed," said Ruth, laughing; "but I suppose we had better wait."

"Yes, we will wait."

The old man, seeing that they had stopped, came forward at a more leisurely pace, for until now he had been running at the top of his speed; but he was panting and breathless when he reached them, for all that, and as red in the face as pickled cabbage.

"Oh! oh! oh!" said he.

"What is it?" asked Crockford.

"Oh! oh! oh!"

"What is it?" repeated the other, with gathering impatience. "Can't you speak?"

"You wouldn't be able to speak much plainer if you had been running like I have," retorted the old man. "Can't you wait a moment, till I get my wind a bit?"

Crockford saw that it was no good trying to hurry him. The old man sat down upon a large stone which lay close handy, and wiped his head round and round.

He was a small, dried-up little old man; so very dry, and so much like parchment, that it was a matter for surprise that he could perspire so profusely.

He certainly did perspire, though. There was no mistake about that. And he sat there upon the stone, almost doubled up, and gasping like a fish.

When his breath began to return, though, a little, he said, in an apologetic tone, "I'm not used to running; but I had no time to lose. I'm glad I caught you."

"What do you want with us?" asked Crockford.

"I want you to go with me," replied the little man.

"Go with you!" repeated Crockford. "Why?"

"I want you to be a witness to the execution of an instrument."

And saying so, the little man rose to his feet, and began to retrace his steps in the direction from which he had come, at the same time intimating, by an impatient gesture to the strange lady and gentleman, that they must follow him. Crockford looked at Ruth with an inquiring smile, as though asking her advice. She also smiled and nodded, and without more to do they both followed silently at the old gentleman's heels, Ruth sitting upon the horse, and Crockford walking by its side, and leading it by the bridle.

All at once the old gentleman stopped, took a spectacle-case from his pocket, took out a pair of spectacles, put them astride upon his nose, and stared hard at the Captain.

"What now?" asked Crockford, returning the stare with interest.

"I beg your pardon," said he; "but you're of age, are you not?"

"Yes, why?"

"Only you could not have signed if you had not been."

"I am not quite so sure that I can sign, as it is."

"Why not; can't you write?"

"Yes; I can write well enough for that, I dare say."

"Well, then, what do you mean?"

"I mean that I should like to know what you want me to do."

"To sign your name."

"To what?"

"To a will."

"A will!" said Crockford, looking round him in amazement. "Why, who has made a will? and why do you want me to witness it?"

"I want you," replied the other, tartly, "because I can't get anybody else."

"That's candid. But, my good sir, if I may make the inquiry, how far have you come to look for me? You look as though you had run a mile."

"It is not far short of one, either. See how out of breath I am! I saw you out of the window, and I said to myself, 'If I run straight out I shall catch him as he passes by on the top of the meadow.'—for that was the direction you were going in. And I did catch you, you see, and here you are!"

"What window do you allude to?"

"That one with diamond panes in the gable end of the old house you see there, peeping out from the trees."

"And is that where the person is who wants to make the will?"

"Yes, and if we don't make haste he may die before we get to him."

Crockford drew back, and appeared to hesitate about proceeding further.

"Now, then!" cried the little man, tugging at his arm, and endeavouring to pull him along. "What are you waiting for now?"

"Well, you see, I don't much care about these sorts of jobs," said Crockford. "I would rather you found somebody else to be a witness."

"But I can't, young man," retorted the old gentleman. "I could not get anybody else, I tell you, or I should not have run after you."

"But, if my eyes do not deceive me, the house is a large and handsome one. It is quite a chateau—a hall—the residence of some wealthy country gentlemen, very evidently."

"Well?"

"Well, then, there must be servants. Why did you not select one of them?"

"There is only one servant, and she is a legatee; consequently, she could not sign."

"Do you mean to say that in a mansion like that there is only one servant kept?"

"I do."

"And were there no other persons in the house besides the dying man, yourself, and the servant?"

"I did not say that. There was also the daughter of the gentleman who wishes to make the will; but the same reason which precludes the servant from being a witness, also applies to the daughter."

"Well, I don't like the job—that's all. I don't like wills. I am of opinion that money should go into the proper channel. How do I know but that I may be assisting some malicious old wretch in robbing his family of what, in the natural course of events, would have been theirs?"

"What does that matter to you?" asked the old gentleman, petulantly. "What does that matter to me or you, sir? For goodness sake, do come before it is too late!"

"Well, I don't like it, you know!"

"But the testator is in the possession of all his faculties, sir! Come, come! I am sure, when you reflect, you will see how groundless are your objections."

Perhaps Crockford thought so himself, for he now followed the old man without further comment.

By this time they had reached a spot from which, peeping upwards between the knolled trunks of some leafy elms, they could see a quaint old manor house standing upon a little eminence beyond, in the middle of what had been, at some time or other, a well-kept lawn, but which now was a neglected wilderness of rank weeds and rubbish.

It was a curiously-fashioned and quaint old edifice—a strange jumble of gable ends, pointed roofs, diamond-paned windows, overhanging eaves, and toppling stacks of chimneys. It was surrounded, and almost buried, by bushes and shrubs which quite obscured the lower portion of the building; and a small forest of oaks and elms at the back, coming between the house and the rising sun, so cut off from it all light and life, that it lay there in a cold, leaden stillness almost resembling twilight; and there was about the whole scene an air of such intense melancholy and gloom, that Crockford, advancing towards it, and regarding its exterior with silent curiosity, could not, somehow, banish from his mind an indescribable trembling and dread, such as, in scenes of real danger, he was quite incapable of feeling.

And Ruth, also, what thoughts were passing through her ever busy brain! Her face was pale, and her lips bloodless, while her eyes wandered uneasily around, with a painful expression, like that of the half-returning memory of an unhappy past.

"What is the matter, dearest?" whispered Crockford, gently, looking down towards her.

"Nothing—nothing!" she replied, with a slight start and a sigh. "Only this place — somehow——"

"What is it? Shall we go any further?"

"Yes, yes; I should like to do so, above all things. I was only thinking how like it was——"

"Yes?" said Crockford, seeing that she hesitated.

"How like it was to something I have seen in my dreams—or, I mean, that I used to see in my dreams when I was young and—and—happy!"

Crockford looked at his companion in astonishment. He did not quite comprehend what she said. She was a puzzle to him in many respects, but a very amusing puzzle, and a fascinating puzzle, and one that he had in this short space learnt to love.

Poor fool!—he had much better have lain down in his grave to die, before he had conceived so mad a passion; for nothing but misery, grief, crime, and eternal damnation here and hereafter, could possibly come of it!

"How slow you walk," the old gentleman cried, testily. "You will be too late now. I believe nothing else."

He led them round the bushes into a deserted court-yard, where the grass grew up between the cracks in the green flag-stones.

The side of the house looking on to this yard was dark and dismal as a prison. The windows looking out upon the yard were closely barred and covered with rusty wirework.

In some places, the panes had been broken and stuffed with rags. In some places, they were patched with brown paper.

The aspect of the whole place betokened misery, ruin, and neglect. Over all these was an air of indescribable melancholy and wretchedness, oppressive to the spirit of the two strangers gazing upon it.

A door leading into the house stood open, and through the deep gloom they could perceive the indication of the staircase of black wood. But only the first two or three steps were faintly visible; all else was enveloped in profound darkness.

Not a living soul was to be seen. Not a sound reached them.

They had left the horse tied to the branch of a tree just outside the shrubbery; and as they walked over the soft mossy grass, their footsteps had no sound.

They could not help thinking, so deep was the silence, and so oppressive the gloom of the whole scene, that the man to whose bedside they were about to repair was dead, and that his spirit might perchance meet them upon the threshold of that dark doorway.

Such a thought as this was passing through the brain of Ruth as she drew near, and she could not refrain from starting backwards and uttering a slight scream of terror at the sight of something white gliding down the stairs towards them.

"What is it?" asked Crockford, who had not noticed the object which had attracted her attention, and he followed the direction of her eyes.

But it was now his turn to regard the apparition in speechless consternation.

Was it the ghost of the dead man that they saw?

No; if ghost at all, it was the ghost of a young and beautiful woman, but pale as death, and wan and anxious, as though with long watching, anxiety, and grief.

He knew the face in a moment. It was familiar to him as his own, but he regarded it with a most unutterable amazement; and as he looked at it he seemed to grow even more and more astonished.

Then his eyes, slowly revolving, fixed themselves upon the beautiful face of his companion.

He started, and muttered to himself inaudibly. His lips framed themselves into words but half uttered; uttered too lowly to reach the ears of the woman by his side.

"Strange, strange," he muttered—"strange that they should be so alike! Strange that I should meet them both; strange that I should love them both; but strangest of all that we three should meet here together to-night in this place!"

The little old gentleman had gone forward to the door, and was speaking to the lady standing there.

He was explaining, probably, where he had met Crockford and Ruth, and for what purpose he had brought them thither.

The lady turned her eyes upon Ruth with a cold, proud stare, at once haughty and repelling.

Then she looked from her to Crockford.

But as their eyes met she started violently, and a deep blush suffused her pale face.

She, too, had recognised him—recognised him with shame and terror.

It was Lady Florence Darcy.

The lady in whose carriage Crockford had ridden in the Park, and of whose amour he had been an unwilling witness when he had seen her lover concealed, and half smothered in the box.

There was no time for either party to make a remark; no time for them to do aught but exchange a hasty glance of intelligence.

The little gentleman had stepped across the threshold of the door, and beckoned Ruth and her companion eagerly forward.

The Lady Darcy rapidly ascended the stairs before him, and noiselessly glided away up a dark corridor.

Ruth and Crockford entered the house. The little gentleman closed the door behind them, and as he did so, shut out what little light there was in that dreary place.

Then the three began to ascend the stairs in the dark, with palpitating hearts, and an anticipation of some coming evil, though of what nature they could form no notion.

As they reached the corridor, gloomy and close-smelling as had been the staircase preceding it, they perceived in the distance a small light glimmering.

It came through the chink of a half-closed door.

As they drew near, they heard a hollow, moaning sound within.

CHAPTER LVIII.

THE MISER'S DWELLING.—THE PROGRESS OF THE UNACCOUNTABLE MALADY.—IS IT DISEASE OR THE HAND OF THE SECRET POISONER?—THE DOCTOR PUZZLED.—ALONE WITH THE SICK MAN.—IN THE DEAD OF THE NIGHT.—A BEDROOM SCENE.

But before we enter the chamber where lies the dying man, in company with Ruth and Crockford, we must go back a few hours in our story, and see what is occurring in the same room upon the previous evening.

It wanted about ten minutes of ten o'clock. It was a raw, bleak night, as we already know, and the rain was pouring in torrents and unremittingly, except for a moment or two now and then, when the wind tore madly round the house, shaking the doors and windows, and threatening to bring the crazy stacks of chimneys tottering in confusion through the roof.

It was a small, low-browed room in which lay the dying man, wainscoted with black highly-polished oak, decorated with grotesque mullions and quaintly-carved cornices.

Massive beams of black oak stretched across the low, smoke-stained ceiling; and the walls, slanting a little towards the roof, gave the room the appearance of a cabin on board a ship. At the same time, it also lent to the place an appearance of ponderous strength and solidity, like one might have expected to find, perhaps, in a clumsy old fortress.

The room was dimly lighted by a long-wicked tallow candle, which, hanging over very much on one side, flared and guttered in what appeared to be a gold candelabrum, standing upon a bare deal table.

In the middle of the apartment was a richly-carved and massive bedstead, the head of which rose like a kind of canopy, and touched the ceiling, ending in pinnacles of curiously-carved mahogany, from which descended a huge heavy mass of thick, dusty drapery.

On the floor, by the side of the bed, there was a large black box, strongly clamped, and apparently fastened by three locks. Upon the top of this stood a number of physic bottles, of all shapes and sizes.

On the floor, upon the other side of the bed, was a quantity of old, dusty papers, some upon files and some packed into ungainly parcels, and fastened with scraps of faded red tape.

There were several quaintly-carved chairs and tables standing about, and there were one or two beautiful mirrors, costly though old-fashioned, but almost entirely hidden from view by the thick layer of dust which covered them and every other object in the apartment.

The floor was naked and covered with dust. Some old sacks were lying about, and a quantity of straw. The was even an old battered shovel in one corner, leaning up against one of the richly-carved mirrors.

The panes of the windows were like those in the windows down below, broken and patched up with rags and paper; and the wind and rain in some places penetrated into the miserable apartment.

Nothing could well have been more sordidly wretched than was this place. No one looking at it could have doubted that it was the abode of some despicably penurious and avaricious wretch, who hoarded his wealth for the mere sake of hoarding it, without any other aim or object.

In the bed, in dirty sheets, and covered by a ragged and patched counterpane, lay an old man.

The light fell full upon his face. It was an old, withered, and meagre face, dark and swarthy.

A few grey hairs straggled from beneath his filthy night-cap, and lay upon the black and grimy pillow, and the lower part of his face was covered by a grizzled but scanty beard.

The old man's cheeks were hollow and pinched. His eyes were deep sunk in his head, and his whole countenance bore the traces of long and intense suffering.

His bare arm, which lay upon the coverlid, was wasted to a shadow. Evidently his had been a long and wearisome illness. Even now the old man seemed to be suffering intensely, for he rolled his head slowly from side to side, groaning dismally.

The room was, as I have said, very dark and gloomy. Two persons besides the old man occupied it. One was an elderly gentleman, with grey hair and a gentle, though not over-intelligent, face. The other was Lady Florence Darcy.

In the lightest part of the room sat the old gentleman, with the light playing full upon his face.

In the darkest part of the room, with her face carefully excluded from the light, the lady sat.

They were talking together in a low tone. The substance of their conversation was as follows.

"Doctor," the lady said, "you promised when last you were here to tell me candidly what you thought of my poor father's case. Will you tell me now?"

The doctor was silent for a moment or two. He passed his hand over his chin carefully and slowly, in a rasping sort of way, very much as though he was shaving himself.

"Mr .Hawkestone's case is positively the most unexplainable that ever came under my professional observation."

"But do you think that he gets any better?"

"To speak candidly, I don't think he does."

"Do you think that the medicine you give him has any beneficial effect?"

"As yet, I don't think it has had."

"And supposing he had had no medicine at all, do you think that his case would have been worse?"

Privately, the doctor thought it would not, and that the physic had been so much harmless wash, doing neither good nor harm. But this was an opinion that he thought it best to keep to himself, and so he hemmed, ha'd, and frowned, and shook his head.

"Most decidedly," said he, "he would have been a good deal worse; if he had not had the physic, there is no knowing what would have become of him."

"But he grows no better, you say, and you cannot account for it!"

"To be candid, my lady, I cannot. The medicine I have given him has kept life in him. I am convinced of that; but at the point where he ought to have begun to get better and regain his health, he has, contrary to all my experience, done exactly the opposite."

"But tell me, doctor, what complaint do you think he is suffering from?"

"That, madam, I own, puzzles me. It has the symptoms of no complaint that has hitherto come within my observation; and, for that reason, I have so frequently urged the employment of other doctors besides myself."

"Pray what conclusion have you come to with respect to the symptoms? Is there any peculiarity in them?"

"That is exactly where the difficulty lies. There is nothing peculiar about the symptoms."

"Nothing peculiar?"

"Nothing but a wasting away of the vital energy; a fading away, as it were—a running out of the sands of life. There is no disease. All the organs appear to be healthy. Your father is not in years an old man. It is not time for him to die, according to the natural course of things; but die he surely will, if there is not very shortly a great change for the better."

"Has it ever occurred to you that my poor father is suffering from atrophy?"

"This is not a case of atrophy. In atrophy, it is the flesh which wastes away, but this is different. Here it is the vital principle which appears to be going. It is unaccountable."

"Then," said the lady in a hollow tone, "you cannot save him?"

"I did not say," replied the doctor, "that there was no hope, because as long as there is life there is hope; but you must prepare for the worst. I will not deceive you—you must prepare for the worst."

"Alas! I feared that you would tell me this. And nothing can be done?"

"Other medical aid can be summoned, as I have said before; although I must own that I have little faith in any good arising from such a course. Still it would be a satisfaction to you, my lady!"

"No, doctor, I have every confidence in you, and I am sure my father would not consent to such a course. Still it shall be done. Whether he consents or not, a consultation shall take place."

There was a long pause of several minutes' duration after she had uttered these words. The doctor broke the silence.

"I scarcely know, my lady, whether I am justified in expressing an opinion—or rather, I should say, of putting a silly idea which I have had into words."

"Speak, doctor! What is it?"

The doctor sunk his voice.

"Have you ever heard of those mysterious poisons supposed to have existed in the dark ages?"

It was so dark where the lady sat, that it was quite impossible for the doctor to see the expression of her face. Indeed, he was not looking in her direction. Had he been looking, and had he been able to pierce the obscurity enveloping her, he would perhaps have been rather surprised.

He might have seen the colour fade suddenly from her cheeks—from her lips, even.

He might have seen her start and shiver. It was a violent fit of trembling, which, for a moment, seemed to convulse her whole frame.

He noticed nothing of this, however, for he was too busy with the theory upon which he was speculating.

"You've read of these poisons, my lady, I have no doubt; and though one knows very well that it is all wretched absurdity, one cannot help wondering at the amount of invention which has been expended upon the description of their effects—how the victim of one of these deadly drugs lingers for weeks, months, years—even dying slowly—almost imperceptibly—dying by inches;—how the malady, leaving no scar, blights, as it were, the victim, and withers him slowly. Now, if it were not too absurd—but it is——"

"What is?" asked the lady, in a hard voice, and with a queer, choking sound in her throat.

"My dear lady, nothing—nothing! I beg a thousand pardons; but the thought somehow occurred to me."

"My poor father's illness reminded you of some of the symptoms of one of these mysterious poisons?"

"No, no! I did not mean to say that At least, to some extent, it is correct. But, my lady, I hope you will excuse me!" cried the doctor, in great confusion.

"I am not at all offended," said Lady Darcy. "I am only anxious to have your true opinion—that you should speak to me without reserve."

"Well, then, my lady, what I intended to say was, that if we lived now in the middle ages, instead of in an age of enlightenment, so mysterious and inexplicable is the malady of Mr. Hawkstone, that the ignorant and superstitious would be inclined to attribute it to the fearful results of one of those drugs said to be known to the Borgias."

"But modern science has overthrown the belief in these poisons?"

"Yes—yes, my dear lady; science has utterly routed such nonsensical ideas. All belief in the deadly properties of the perfumed gloves of the Florentines—of the wine of Cyprus—is certainly exploded. You might as well say that some malicious wretch had fashioned your father's likeness in wax, and was slowly melting it before fire!"

"Alas, yes!" said Lady Darcy, with a deep sigh. "I fear that these speculations are but idle ones."

"Preposterous, my dear lady — preposterous; and I was very wrong to mention such absurdities."

"And you think, then, that nothing can be done?"

"I don't say that; I only am of opinion that continuing the course of medicine we are at present pursuing would be fruitless. I would advise having a consultation upon Mr. Hawkstone's case without loss of time."

"It shall take place as soon as ever it can be managed. Might I so far trespass upon your kindness as to request that you would summon the doctors to your aid?"

"Certainly, my lady. When shall I appoint?"

"As soon as ever you please—as soon as possible."

"To-morrow?"

"Yes."

"It shall be done. And now, my lady, allow me to say good night. I have a long ride before me, and the storm appears to get worse instead of better."

And, thus saying, the doctor took his departure, and was presently heard clattering over the stones down the road at the back of the house.

Lady Darcy sat perfectly still, listening to the sound of his horse's hoofs as they gradually died away in the extreme distance.

Then she heard a door closing in the lower part of the house, and the sound of footsteps. Then another door closing, and then all was still.

Still she sat perfectly silent for a few moments more Then she rose cautiously, and taking up the candle, passed it twice or thrice across the eyes of the sleeper.

The old man was sleeping soundly now, and his plaintive moaning had ceased.

When she had assured herself of the soundness of his slumbers, she carefully drew the curtain upon one side of the bed; and then, returning to a small table which stood in a corner, behind the curtain, where it was impossible for the old man, unless he rose up in bed, to notice her actions, she carefully unlocked a small workbox, standing among a heap of scattered papers.

Taking out the odds and ends of rags and cottons which filled it, she presently came to a small screwed-up packet at the bottom.

Unrolling this carefully, she disclosed a small bottle, in which appeared only to remain a drop or two of some transparent liquid.

She took out the little phial, and placed it upon the table. Then going, she fetched from the box upon the other side of the bed, a physic bottle, and poured some of its contents into a wineglass.

Upon the physic in the wine-glass she cautiously, and with a hand that trembled not in the least, dropped one drop from the phial.

The light shone full upon her face, which wore a deadly pallor, fell full upon her bloodless lips, and shone brightly through the clear and richly-tinted medicine the glass contained.

Slowly the drop of the colourless drug mingled with the other, and the faintest discolouration took place; but so trifling, that it would have required a careful comparison of the contents of the glass with the contents of the bottle, to have discovered that any change had taken place in its appearance.

She still held the small phial to the edge of the wine-glass, to allow, probably, of what slight moisture might yet adhere to the phial's mouth to trickle down into the medicine; and, as she did so, she regarded the operation with an earnest intentness, which blinded and deafened her to what was occurring within the room.

The old man had again awakened from his restless sleep.

He began slowly to open and shut his dry, parched lips—to roll his hot, swollen tongue, and to gasp for breath.

Then he weakly stretched forth his long, lean fingers, and grasped the bed-curtain.

His lips formed themselves into the words "Florence," and "water," but no sound issued from his throat.

A sigh, which was so soft and low as to be quite inaudible to his daughter, escaped his labouring breast.

He turned his eyes wearily round the room, searching for her.

There was a light shining through the curtains.

He drew them back a little more.

He struggled into a sitting posture, and looked at her.

He regarded her long and silently, with eager, searching eyes; but his eyes were weak and failing, and the figure before him was bleared and shapeless.

His daughter meanwhile concluded the process upon which she was engaged, re-corked the small phial, and put it away in her breast.

Having done so, she rose up and turned towards the bed.

Then, with a stifled scream, stood rigidly transfixed by the sight of the old man's eyes fixed upon her.

CHAPTER LIX.

A STARTLING SITUATION.—DOES HE SUSPECT?—THE EFFECTS OF THE DRUG—NIGHT.—THE CAPTAIN AND THE LADIES.—THE MISER'S NAME.—RUTH'S STRANGE CONDUCT.—AN INTERRUPTION.—A SURPRISE.—ANOTHER MYSTERY.

She was too much horrified for a moment or two to make any remark.

Her teeth chattered in her head, and her cold, trembling fingers could scarce close upon the wine-glass.

A grey, leaden hue stole over her features, which became of a sudden fixed as though they had turned into stone. One might have fancied that she had been suddenly frozen stiff with terror.

The old man, upon his side, kept his eyes fixed upon her with an intensity which was unaccountable, unless he suspected her of foul play.

And was there foul play? was there base and hideous treachery at work?

Was she plotting the perpetration of a crime, at once revolting, unnatural, unpardonable, damnable?

By the black and lowering cloud which overshadowed the woman's brow, and the gleam of savage ferocity which lit up her eyes for a moment, as she stood staring at him, one might almost have thought that she meditated taking a

spring upon, and strangling, the poor, feeble old man where he lay.

And such, horrible as it is to relate, were the actual thoughts which at the moment flitted through the woman's brain.

"If he has found me out," she was saying to herself,—"if the game is played to the end—if I am at my last card, there is nothing else left for it—I must finish him now, at any risk. And it is so, I can see. He suspects me—he knows all. He must die!"

Another moment would have decided his fate; another moment, and the murderess's fingers would have closed upon the old man's throat; but he stayed her hand all at once, by what he said—he stayed her hand, and saved his own life.

"Florence," the old man babbled weakly, "I am very thirsty; give me something to drink."

The fixed earnestness of her face gradually relaxed.

He had not seen her, then. It would have been impossible for him to have feigned ignorance of the knowledge of her fell purpose, had he detected it.

No; the fixedness of his regard she could now account for.

His eyes were glazing—his sight was failing him. He had been staring at, without seeing her.

She came towards him with the physic in her hand.

"Here is your draught," she said.

"I am very thirsty," said the old man. "Have you anything for me to drink?"

"Take your draught first."

"Is not it too soon?"

"It is the right time."

The old man stretched forth his trembling hand. The lady bent down over him, and guided the glass to his lips.

She was careful that he did not spill a drop, and held the glass to his lips, although, with a gesture of disgust, he strove to push it from him.

"You must finish it," she said.

"It does me no good."

"It will do."

He groaned peevishly as he drained the glass. Then she handed him a tumbler of lemonade, which he greedily swallowed.

When he had finished, she took the glass from him, and set it down upon the box by the side of the bed.

The old man, when he had done, lay back with a weary sigh.

"How do you feel to-night?" asked Lady Darcy, presently.

"Very weak—very weak!" he murmured,—"very weak and ailing. I shan't last long."

"No," muttered the woman to herself, with a bitter smile; "I could tell him that!"

He rolled his head to and fro upon the pillow, sighing plaintively, half in weariness, half in pain, until at length, apparently worn out by this continual motion, he heaved a deep sigh and lay perfectly still.

Lady Darcy watched him for a while in silence, then drawing the candle to her side upon the table, sat down in an arm-chair, wrapped herself up as comfortably as possible in a thick cloak, and, taking up a book, began to read.

Thus an hour passed.

An old-fashioned timepiece standing over the fireplace ticked noisily; the rain pattered against the panes of the window; every now and then the wind shook the window-frame, or shrieked shrilly through the keyhole, or through the chinks in the door.

No other noise disturbed the death-like silence of the sick room.

Lady Darcy read on at her book, heedless of these sounds and of all outward things, wrapt in the interest of the romance she was perusing.

A faint cry from the dying man suddenly aroused her.

She started to her feet, and went to the bedside.

"What is it?"

She spoke in a low tone, and her face wore a terrified expression. Perhaps she thought that the end had already come.

"Oh, dear! oh, dear!" the old man sighed; "I cannot rest—I cannot sleep! I am very, very bad to-night!"

"Are you worse?"

"Yes, much worse!"

She looked at him with an uneasy expression.

"How do you feel?" she asked presently. "You must try to bear up, you know. The lawyer will be here soon!"

"I will—I will if I can, for your sake! But I feel an icy chill, as it were, stealing up to my heart. My feet are as cold as stones!"

She hastily heaped upon the bed a quantity of old clothes lying strewed about the room, and she put on to them the cloak in which she herself had been wrapped up a few minutes ago.

The old man, whose teeth had been chattering, as it were, with cold, expressed himself more at his ease; and she left his bedside, where she had been standing, anxiously watching the changes in his countenance, to walk to and fro in the room.

As she paced the apartment from wall to wall, she muttered to herself inaudibly, frowning as she did so, and biting her lips.

"I am a fool," she muttered—"a fool and an idot! I thought that I had gone too far! But if I had, it would not have been my fault. The directions were, the whole contents of the phial a drop at a time. And I have followed out the directions to the letter. The dumb man told me that the patient would retain the use of his faculties sufficiently to do what he was bid, until the last. After he has signed the will, I am to give the last drop. Then—then all will be over!"

The old man lay still and motionless. So still was he, that more than once she paused in her walk, to approach the bedside and scan his wan, worn features.

"Was he dead?" she asked herself as she looked at him.

No, his eyes were closed. His breast rose and fell almost imperceptibly, but still with a steady and regular motion.

He breathed very softly, almost inaudibly; but he did breathe, and he slept.

Again she paced the room from end to end.

Once or twice she approached the window and listened, or opened the door, fancying that she heard a noise below.

"What can detain him?" she said to herself. "What can make him so long? A miserable, drivelling idiot! it must be this storm which keeps him away."

To and fro—to and fro she paced like a tiger in its cage; and the hour-hand upon the timepiece slowly crept round the dial, and the night passed thus.

* * * * *

Mr. Jefferson, a lawyer, from a neighbouring town, made his appearance about daybreak.

Some other business had detained him. He was profuse in his apologies; but he really could not come any sooner, he assured her ladyship.

He had not been in bed all night. He had not had a moment's rest. He was nearly worn to death. But he had obeyed her commands, and here he was, willing to do her bidding.

What she required of him was, to add a codicil to a will already made, securing the property which her father had left her, from her husband, Lord Darcy.

It was necessary, the lawyer said, that there should be two witnesses to the signature. He himself would do for one, but there must be another.

An ancient, half deaf, and almost entirely idiotic woman, who had served Mr. Hawkstone for servant during the last forty years or more, was suggested by Lady Darcy; but the lawyer thought that, perhaps, if it were possible, it would be more satisfactory to have the will witnessed by a stranger, an uninterested person.

He ought to have brought his clerk with him, but he had forgotten to do so. He owned his error, and said that he would do all in his power to remedy the omission, but how was it to be accomplished?

While he was puzzling his head for some means of doing so, accidentally looking out of the window, he saw in the distance a horse galloping towards the house, on the back of which were two well-dressed persons—a lady and gentleman.

If he rushed out at once, and ran with all his might across the fields, he thought he might be able to intercept them on their course, and then he must press them into the service.

Of this he was determined: if he only caught them, he swore they should come. And, as the reader knows already, he was as good as his word.

He caught them, and brought them.

There was every reason, too, for his anxiety in hurrying the witnesses into the chamber of death; for when he left the house, he left the old man in a most precarious state.

He was going rapidly.

Indeed, the lawyer had great fears lest Mr. Hawkstone should not last out until he returned.

So very weak and feeble had the old man become within the last few hours, and so evident was it that he was approaching the end, that Mr. Jefferson feared that he would not be able to hold a pen to make the necessary signature, or that his wits might have deserted him before the moment came.

Arriving at the house, as we have seen, he found Lady Darcy waiting for them.

Her eagerness for their arrival was, however, ten times as great as was his anxiety that they should arrive in time.

Every moment now was precious. Unless the will were attested, her property would pass into the hands of the husband whom she hated.

She would still be dependent upon him.

Still at his mercy. Still obliged to endure his hateful presence.

But a few brief lines, a scratch or two of the pen, and all this would be altered. She would be rich, powerful, and able to free herself from bondage. For she could purchase a divorce—or rather, I should say, she could purchase witnesses, and bribe her husband to give his consent to a course which he had hitherto strenuously opposed.

When Crockford and Ruth entered the room, they found Lady Darcy seated by the bedside, holding the hand of her dying father in her own.

Mr. Jefferson murmured two or three words of introduction, as he brought the witnesses into the room. Then he placed a chair for Ruth, and indicated another where Crockford might seat himself.

"I did not, by the way, inquire what your name was, sir?" said the little lawyer, looking up from the document which he had begun to peruse, which was the will they were shortly about to witness.

"An introduction is unnecessary," here broke in Lady Darcy. "I have already the pleasure of this gentleman's acquaintance."

"And the lady," said the lawyer, "is doubtless——"

He was not quite sure *what*, when he had got thus far.

There was indeed considerable doubts upon the subject in more minds than his.

Who was she? Lady Darcy was asking herself.

Who was she? the Captain would have had as much difficulty in replying as any one else. The worst of it was, too, he did not know who she wanted him to say she was. Unless she spoke herself, he knew no more than Adam what she would have liked him to have said.

He was not particularly anxious to say that she was his wife, in the presence of Lady Darcy, to whom, only a little while ago, he had been making violent love.

But if it would have pleased Ruth for him to have said so, he certainly would. Then came the question, though, would it please her?

It was questionable. He was in doubt, and he did the only thing he could do. That was—nothing.

Ruth also was perplexed. She was doubting whether or not she should own to her name of Belvidere. What would Crockford think of her when he found out who and what she was? Would he loathe and despise her? Should she give a false name? If she did, would he not find her out? She was silent, not knowing what to say.

The lawyer, after pausing for a moment, expecting some one to reply, concentrated his attention upon the document before him, and was silent.

After a few moments he looked up and said, "Is he ready, my lady?"

"I think so."

"It would be best for us not to delay any longer."

"I am desirous that we should not."

Lady Darcy bent over the dying man, and whispered in his ear.

"Father—father! the will is prepared. Have you strength enough to hold the pen?"

"Father! father!" repeated Lady Darcy. "Remember, it is for my sake! You will make an effort, won't you?"

But the old man still remained passive and motionless.

"Mr. Hawkstone is very weak," the lawyer whispered to Crockford. "He has sunk rapidly during the last few hours. I fear that he will now only just have strength sufficient to execute this deed before he sinks altogether."

"Is he rich?" whispered Crockford.

"Enormously. He has accumulated thousands upon thousands. He is, to tell the truth" (here the lawyer whispered lower than before) "extremely *near*."

"What did you say his name was?"

"Mr. Martin Hawkstone."

"What?"

It was Ruth who spoke. She had hissed out the word in strangely excited tones, and with a wild look on her face.

"I beg your pardon," said the lawyer, not having caught what she said.

"Repeat the name again," cried Ruth, grasping his arm.

"The name?"

"Yes, the name of the man there who is dying."

"Certainly, my dear madam; only a little lower, pray. That is his daughter. Think of her feelings! I am afraid——"

"Will you speak?"

"Yes, yes; only, I beg of you——"

"Speak, I say!"

"Certainly. You want to know his name?"

"I do! Cannot you understand English, dolt?"

The lawyer looked as though he were about to make an indignant rejoinder, and he probably would have done so, only just at this moment Lady Darcy called to him.

"My father will sign now," she said. "Bring the will here."

"Certainly," replied the lawyer, hurrying towards the bed.

"Stop!" cried Ruth, seizing his arm.

"My dear madam!" expostulated the little lawyer, aghast at her violence.

"Tell me his name, I say?"

"Well, I will. His name is Martin Hawkstone, if you must know; though I must observe that your manner of asking is very far from——"

"Quick—quick!" interrupted Lady Darcy. "Put the pen into his hand."

Mr. Jefferson did so.

"I must read it first," said he.

"No there is no occasion; you have already read it to him."

"To be sure! Try and sign here, sir. Your cross will do, if you cannot manage your signature."

The dying man grasped the pen as well as his weakness would allow, but he had not sufficient strength to make a mark.

"Shall I guide his hand?" asked Lady Darcy, eagerly.

And without waiting for a reply, she took her father's trembling fingers in hers.

But it was not an easy matter to do what she proposed.

His hand was cold and stiff. His fingers refused to close upon the pen. His arm, too, was stiff, and difficult to move. His hand lay a dead weight upon the paper.

Crockford was looking on, deeply interested by this strange scene. Mr. Jefferson had approached the bedside. He, too, was watching intently the movements of her ladyship. Perhaps some vague doubts as to the strict legality of these proceedings may have crossed the lawyer's mind, as they crossed Crockford's; for the latter could not help noticing that Mr. Jefferson appeared to be endeavouring to block out the view as much as possible from the strangers, by the interposition of his own diminutive carcass between them and the dying man.

He might have thought to himself that the dying man appeared hardly to be sufficiently in possession of his faculties to warrant these strangers in being witnesses to his signature to so important a document as that to which it was now about to be attached.

If his intention was to make himself into a sort of screen, as I have said, it was, however, speedily frustrated. Suddenly there came a great tug at his coat-tails.

Ruth it was who pulled them.

"I want to speak to you."

"Yes, madam, in a moment."

"In a moment won't do."

"But, my dear madam——"

"I want to speak to you now."

Lady Darcy had just succeeded in holding her father's hand in such a way that she could guide the pen. She found then, though, that the pen had no ink in it, and would not mark. Remedying this, with a low-toned ejaculation of impatience, she again adjusted his fingers.

The lawyer looked on at these arrangements with evident anxiety. Another moment would complete the business. But an awful change seemed to be coming over the dying man's face.

A dull, leaden hue—something like the approach of twilight—seemed creeping over it. Was he at his last moments?

But another moment would settle all, if there were no interruption.

Should he step forward and assist her ladyship? That would be the best course to pursue. There was no time to lose—no time to waste in hesitation He would do it.

He was moving forward, when Ruth spoke to him. He impatiently disengaged his coat-tail from her grasp

"Bother the woman!" he inwardly ejaculated. "What does she want, plaguing me at such a moment?"

But he could not shake her off so easily as he supposed. He shook his coat-tail from her grasp, but now her fingers closed tight upon his arm.

He strove to free himself, but could not.

Then turning angrily upon her, with a face as red as a turkey-cock with suppressed indignation, he was about to ask what she wanted, and how she dared thus to act at such a moment, in so very unseemly a fashion, only something in her face rather frightened him, and silenced him most effectually.

"Wha-a-at——" he began.

"Out of the way!" she exclaimed; and with one of those twists of that powerful wrist of hers, sent the man of law spinning.

Then she stepped forward to the bed, and laid her hand upon the paper, on the spot where, in another moment, the old man's signature would have been affixed.

Lady Darcy, drawing herself up to her full height, regarded the other woman with an expression of mingled surprise, hatred, and contempt.

Ruth, upon her side, returned the contempt and hatred with interest.

So strong were the emotions which agitated the breast of Lady Darcy, however, that for some time she was literally dumb, and unable to give utterance to a single word.

When at length her speech returned to her, she asked, indignantly and almost fiercely, "What is the meaning of this outrage?"

"I hope that I can convince you, madam," replied Ruth, "that it is not an outrage, and that I am only acting as I have a perfect right to do!"

"Indeed! I am anxious to hear an explanation which will satisfactorily account for conduct which, I own, at present appears to me to be most extraordinary."

"I will endeavour to render myself intelligible."

But here the lawyer broke in.

"My dear lady—your father—will your ladyship look at him? He—he is sinking fast!"

A most alarming change had come over the face of the dying man. Was it not the shadow of death?

Lady Darcy bent over him in great anxiety, and laid her hand upon his heart.

It beat feebly. There was still life, but no time could be lost.

"Father—dear father," she whispered, "do you know me?"

His lips moved, but he uttered no sound.

"Will you sign the will?"

Again a movement of the lips; but words, if he intended to utter them, were inaudible.

"Madam," said Lady Darcy, "your interruption is most ill-timed. If my father is to sign this will, he must do so immediately. The least delay may be fatal."

"Fatal to your interests," said Ruth

Lady Darcy stared at her with a deep frown, and a look of surprise.

"What do you mean?" she asked.

"I mean that the signature of that will must be delayed for a few moments."

"A few moments will be too late."

"Even at the risk of its not being signed at all, it must be delayed."

"Mr. Jefferson!" cried Lady Darcy furiously, losing all command of herself in her rage and anxiety for the safety of the fortune which seemed to be slipping through her fingers.

"Mr. Jefferson!"

"Yes, my lady."

"Do you know this—this person?"

"No; I—I——" stammered the lawyer, almost at his wits' end.

"Why did you bring her here?"

"I—I——"

"Will you, sir," she said to Crockford, "witness my father's signature, and kindly prevent this—your companion from interfering in what does not concern her?"

"Crockford," cried Ruth, laying her hand upon his breast, "you shall not witness this deed. I forbid it!"

"But, my dear lady," expostulated the Captain, "will you explain? I am at a loss to conceive what you mean!"

"I mean that this will is a fraud, and shall not be executed!"

"A fraud!" cried the lawyer, in astonishment. "What are you talking about?"

"You say," said Ruth, "that it is the will of Martin Hawkstone?"

"Yes."

"And it is made in favour of one of his children only?"

"Certainly it is, as only one is at present alive."

"It is false!" cried Ruth; "and you know it! And she" (pointing to Lady Darcy)—"she is the fortunate daughter, I suppose?"

"She is Lady Florence Darcy, the eldest and only surviving daughter."

"It is false. I say!" cried Ruth; "and she knows also that what I say is true!"

If a deadly pallor, overspreading her features, and a violent tremor, agitating her whole frame, could be taken as a proof of Lady Darcy's knowledge of the truth of the statement Ruth was making, there was proof enough. But she managed to stammer out, though almost in an inaudible tone, "It is false! You lie!"

"I do not!" cried Ruth loudly, dragging the will from the other's fingers, which had closed eagerly upon it.

"I speak the truth," cried Ruth; "and I call heaven to witness that what I say is true! The four daughters of Martin Hawkstone are at this moment alive!"

But scarcely had she uttered the words, when the old man, as though electrified, struggled suddenly into a sitting posture, and with wildly-dilated eyes, and a face quivering with intense emotion, cried out, "Where are they? Bring them to me! Give me my children!"

"Hush, dear father!" interposed Lady Darcy; "do not agitate yourself. This woman is an impostor, and your children are all dead except me. I, dear father, am your only child!"

"I will clearly prove the contrary," said Ruth, with unnatural calmness.

"What does she say?" asked the old man, whose consciousness seemed restored as though by a miracle. "Let me hear what she says."

"My dear father," cried Lady Darcy, "she is an impostor! She is mad! She does it only to pain you, and annoy me!"

The old man gently pressed his daughter's hand.

"Yes, yes," he said; "you are my only child, dear, and you shall be my heiress! My other children are dead!"

"They are not!" cried Ruth.

"Where are they, then?"

"I will tell you."

"Yes—tell me."

"Not before these people. I must tell you alone."

"That you never shall!" retorted Lady Darcy. "Father, dear, you must not listen to her! You would not send me away?"

"No, no!" said the old man, in a weak voice, and as though his strength were again leaving him, and his senses gradually subsiding into the torpid state from which they had just been temporarily aroused. "No, no, dearest; we will not separate!"

"And you will die without granting my request?" said Ruth.

"What have you to say?"

"I have that to say, the knowledge of which may save your immortal soul from everlasting torment!"

"Florence, Florence! I must hear her!"

"No, father!"

"Refuse me at your peril!"

"Do not listen, father!"

"My child, I must! Leave us together for awhile."

The passion of Lady Darcy had by this time reached its climax. She vehemently declared her intention not to quit the apartment under any pretence whatever; and so great was her rage against Ruth, that had not Jefferson and Crockford interfered, she would probably have even resorted to violence, in her endeavours to tear the woman from the bedside of her dying father.

But as Ruth firmly held her ground against them all, and as the old man persisted in his intention of giving her a private interview, there was nothing for it at last but to allow the interview to take place.

Indeed, the lawyer, seizing an opportunity, took Lady Darcy upon one side, and, in a low whisper, but with great earnestness, entreated Lady Darcy to allow it to take place.

"It will look, my dear lady—you will excuse me, as I speak only in your cause, and you must attribute any rudeness on my part only to zeal in your behalf—it will look, I was going to say, very bad if you do not allow this woman access to your father at this moment; and as there is a witness, also, I should strongly advise your allowing her to speak to Mr. Hawkstone."

"Well, the interview shall be a short one."

"Decidedly—it must be very brief. The state that your father is in is sufficient reason for its being of short duration."

"And it is positively necessary?"

"Yes."

"Well, then, she can talk to him for a few minutes."

"For a few minutes we will leave them alone, my lady."

So saying, Mr. Jefferson led the way from the room followed by Crockford and her ladyship.

Ruth was left alone with Martin Hawkstone.

The first thing she did was to lock the door. Then she approached the bed, took up the will, and read it carefully through, the old man watching her the while silently in a kind of dreamy state of half-consciousness.

Ruth looked at him attentively.

"Can you hear me?" she asked.

He nodded.

"Can you understand what I say?"

He nodded again.

"So far, so good!" she muttered. "He has got sense enough left, perhaps, for the purpose. We shall see! At the worst, if he has not strength to execute another will, if I destroy this, it will answer the purpose."

As she spoke, she approached the door, and listened intently.

Perhaps some one outside might be playing the eavesdropper, she thought; but she could not hear the slightest sound.

No; she was alone—unwatched.

No one was there to hear what passed between her and the dying man.

CHAPTER LX.

THE BRUTALITY OF MRS RADDLE.—THE TORTURE OF THE POOR PRISONER.—THE DUMB MAN'S VILLANY.—A CAREER OF CRIME.—THE MAN-MONSTER MEDITATES THE PERPETRATION OF A FRESH ENORMITY.

When Cecily had slid down the rope into the yard, that was by no means the end of her difficulties

She was very far from having escaped when she found herself in the back yard.

For there she found herself encompassed by a high wall. It was true that there was a door leading out into a court beyond.

To it she flew with frantic haste directly she found her feet resting safely upon the ground.

At the same moment she heard voices in the room above, from which she had just descended. The voice of the woman Raddle, asking, in discordant, savage tones, what was the meaning of the window being open, and why the other captive was up there in Cecily's room, and what had become of Cecily? And she also could distinguish the outlandish gibberish of the dumb man as he jabbered, shaking his fist in impotent fury.

Cecily rushed wildly to the door, and tore at the handle.

But it was fast. The dumb astrologer had locked it before he went out, or it was fastened in some artful way, the secret of which was unknown to the terrified girl, who now battled with the obstinate lock, desperately.

Her efforts were fruitless; and at length, finding that in struggling thus she but exhausted herself needlessly and threw away her strength, she desisted, and stood still, panting something like a poor terrified cur might do when chased into a corner by savage dogs—turns round, and weakly strives to face the foe in its mad desperation.

She turned now because she heard the backdoor of the house slam to with violence, and next moment the dumb man and his female companion rushed out.

The former was first.

Cecily regarded him with mingled terror and hatred. She felt a strong inclination to fly before his fury, and would have done so, there is little doubt, only there was no place to fly to.

Driven up into a corner, then, there was no other course left to the poor half-frenzied girl than to turn round and face her foes.

But what would her woman's strength avail against the ferocity of these monsters?

Ah! a thought occurred to her. Thank heaven for a weapon which lay at her feet!

It was a rude weapon, though, you will say, and perhaps not a very formidable one.

It was a brickbat.

She caught it up, though, as her eyes gleamed fiercely.

As the man came forward, mouthing horribly at her, she flung it at him.

It struck him, not upon the head, though, at which she had aimed it, but upon his shoulder.

The force of the blow, though it was only wielded by a frail girl but lately risen from a sick bed, was sufficient to bring him to the earth.

The wretch swung heavily round with the force of the concussion.

Then fell flat upon his back.

But the advantage which she gained by this bold stroke was only momentary.

In a second afterwards, the dumb man sprang upon his feet.

Then, with a howl like that of a wild beast, he rushed upon her, and clutched her by the throat.

She shrieked with all her strength, and struggled with all her might; but he still held her tightly in his grasp.

His fingers pressed deeply into her throat. He well-nigh strangled her.

Indeed, there is small reason to believe that he would have done otherwise, had not his female companion come opportunely to the poor girl's rescue, and dragged the savage monster away; overcoming him, at last, by clutching his hair, and twisting it brutally by handfuls out of his head, before she could make him release his hold.

He left go at last, with a series of snappings, and snarlings, and grunts, and gurgles, which, had he been endowed with the power of speech, would probably have been replaced by a volley of oaths and imprecations; and, transferring his grasp from the girl's throat to her waist, carried her, in spite of her furious struggles, back into the house.

Upon the way she would have shrieked out for help, in the hope of attracting the notice of some of the neighbours; but her intention in this respect was probably anticipated by Mother Raddle, who effectually prevented its execution by holding her hand upon the girl's mouth, and pinching her nostrils together, at the risk of suffocating her, until the man had carried her back into the house.

Then when the door was closed upon her, Mrs. Raddle probably deemed such a precaution superfluous, and released her hold.

The dumb man, clutching her roughly in his arms, carried the poor girl panting and sobbing up the stairs, and never paused until he reached the room in which she had so long been kept a prisoner.

Here, placing her upon the bed, he retreated to the door, and placing his back against it, folded his arms, and contemplated her with a look of savage fury, not, however, altogether unmixed with admiration.

There was little admiration, though, in the expression with which Mrs. Raddle regarded her prisoner.

Shaking her fist in the girl's face, she shrieked out at the top of her shrill voice, "I'll teach you, minx—I'll teach you to play these delights! What do you mean by it? Are you mad? Why do you want to run away, you fool? What have you been about? You have been ransacking the house!"

The last few words seemed to arouse the anger of the dumb man, which had lain for a moment or two dormant. Evidently there was more offence in this crime of searching the house than in aught else that Cecily had done.

Evidently there were secrets in the house that the dumb man and his companion dreaded should be revealed. And this, after what she had seen, Cecily could readily believe.

As the terrified girl made no reply, the dumb man urged Mrs. Raddle, in his own peculiar tongue, to question her more closely.

"Where have you been?" she asked. "What have you been looking at? How did you get into the rooms? Has this fool been helping you?"

As she spoke, she turned round upon the miserable object in the shape of a woman, whom Cecily had assisted to escape from the lower regions.

"What are you doing there?" screamed Mrs. Raddle, brandishing her fist at her.

The object was cowering in a corner of the room, squatting upon the floor, and nursing her knees.

"What are you doing there?" screamed Mrs. Raddle.

The miserable woman hid her head, and rocked herself, and moaned.

"Get up, you fool, or I will kick you!"

But the poor creature's wits appeared entirely to have deserted her. Probably she did not comprehend what was said to her. Cecily thought that she was too frightened to understand.

Whatever the cause was, however, which prevented her replying to Mrs. Raddle's imperious demands, her silence enraged the questioner to an alarming extent

Making a spring upon her wretched victim, as a cat springs upon a mouse, she clutched her by the hair, and showered down upon her n ck and shoulders, upon her head, and even upon her upturned face, a score of violent blows, which caused the tortured woman to scream in agony, while, with the other hand, Mrs Raddle almost wrenched the hair out of her head.

Cecily, horrified by the spectacle, sprang from the bed, and made as though she would have attempted to rescue the poor creature from the clutches of her tormenter.

But the dumb man intercepted her, and held her back.

She could not understand the meaning of his jargon; but if she had been able to, she would have heard that he advised her to let well alone, and thank her stars that she was not the person ill-treated.

Meanwhile the monster continued her brutality, beating the wretched, half-witted creature about the head and face until she was a mass of black and blue bruises, and the blood was pouring from her wounds.

Then dragging her across the floor by the hair of her head, despite her shrieks and agonizing prayers for mercy, Mrs. Raddle flung her out upon the landing, and with her foot spurned her down the stairs.

"Back—back to your cellar!" she cried, fiercely. "Quicker; or I'll murder you, if I have to use my hands again!"

It is a matter of great uncertainty what amount of ill-treatment the amiable lady considered requisite to kill a person outright; but it is very sure that the same quantity already administered, if repeated at that time, would have sent its unhappy recipient straightway to a better world.

As it was, by the time that she had dragged and kicked the poor victim to the bottom of the house, and flung her all in a heap into the damp and noisome cellar from which she had made her escape, the wretched woman was in a state of insensibility.

To revive her from this, Mrs. Raddle drew a couple of pails of cold water and dashed it over her prostrate form, lying at length, moaning and shivering, stretched upon the cellar floor, her teeth chattering in her head, and scarcely a spark of life visible in her ghastly features, bruised and blood-stained, and her poor body wasted, disfigured, and discoloured by ill-usage, want, and neglect.

It was not safe to beat the creature any more. Another half-dozen blows would have made a murder of it.

Mrs. Raddle thought this; and, though it might not have been from any fear of the consequences which would ensue upon such an event, she perhaps refrained from further violence on this occasion, so that she might wreak her vengeance upon her victim at some future time. For if she had killed her outright now, there would have been an end to all torturing for ever and ever.

It was then, perhaps the fact of her being obliged to desist from the fiendish cruelty she now was practising, that caused Mrs. Raddle to return up-stairs with her thirst for vengeance still unquenched.

She was indeed in a towering passion, and, like a wild beast that had smelt blood, rapacious for more.

Upon the way she stopped to examine the broken lock of the door of the room Cecily had entered; and, pushing through into the room beyond, was soon heard screaming at the top of her voice for the dumb man to come down and look at the awful scene of destruction.

The tables and chairs upset—the skeleton overthrown, and broken by the fall.

"Come down—come down, Jeer!" she cried. "Look what the cat has been doing! Here's pretty havoc! Everything upset and broken!"

The man ran down stairs upon hearing this, and Cecily could hear his voice also raised in anger, as though he were vowing vengeance against her. The two held a long conversation together in excited tones; but, although they both appeared to be angry, it was evident to Cecily, from the disjointed sentences of the woman's which occasionally reached her, that the dumb man was suggesting that what vengeance was to be taken should be taken upon the poor creature down stairs; and he made it appear, for some reason which Cecily for the life of her could not fathom, that it would not be to their interest to hurt their younger prisoner.

Although Mrs. Raddle eventually appeared to coincide with his opinion upon this subject, it was not, however, without a severe struggle; and when she came back into the room where Cecily was, she could not refrain from shaking her fist in the face of the trembling and shrinking girl, and deluging her with a torrent of the vilest and filthiest abuse, which filled the listener's soul with horror, and made her more than ever hate and despise this disgrace to her sex and humanity.

"If it was not for spoiling your beauty, I'd tear your eyes out!" Mrs. Raddle concluded by saying, apparently using a very strong effort to restrain herself from the temptation of so doing.

"You may kill me, if you choose, madam," Cecily answered, at last, through her tears; "but I will not stop under your roof any longer alive!"

"You talk like a fool!" retorted Mrs. Raddle; "but you shall stop! You may take your oath it will be a long while before you get another such a chance as you have missed! You shall be moved into another room, where the window is strongly barred, and there is no chance of your being able to attract anybody's notice outside! But you are a fool, I tell you! You might have been comfortable enough, if you had chosen, where you are!"

By this time Mrs. Raddle, quite worn out and exhausted by her recent exertions, had sunk into a chair, and was wiping her perspiring face upon her shawl. During her abuse of Cecily, the dumb astrologer had busied himself in opening a cupboard, and producing therefrom a black bottle and two small glasses, from one of which he solicited her to take a "drop of gin."

Mrs. Raddle, with a grunt and a mumbled remark about her companion's having already had quite as much as was good for him, accepted the proffered liquor and drained the glass.

It was then for the first time—for she had hitherto been much too terrified to notice anything particular in the bearing of her gaolers—Cecily saw that the man was decidedly the worse for liquor

The woman also had had something to drink a little stronger than water. She was very much flushed and rather excited.

That might have been caused by the violent exercise she had been taking, you will say; but still Cecily attributed some of the strangeness of her voice and manner to an over indulgence in alcoholic stimulants.

But, in the man's case, there was no doubt about it. His dearest friend and greatest admirer must have owned that Mr. Jeer was drunk.

He was not savage drunk, or gloomy drunk—he was rather sociably inclined, and rather jocular, and rather amatory.

Although he was, without exception, the ugliest monster of the man species to be met with in a circuit of five miles from the place of his dwelling—and that is saying a great deal, too, for he lived in the vilest neighbourhood, peopled by the most squalid, and emaciated, and famine-stricken wretches,—he, nevertheless, laboured under the delusion that he could be very agreeable to the ladies when he thought fit

I suppose it would take a long time before anybody could come to the conclusion that their company was unbearable—that their personal appearance was revolting.

It is very certain that this knowledge was denied to the afflicted and misshapen monster in question. To some extent, it is probable that his mistress, Mrs. Raddle, thought him companionable, and was, in a measure, blind to his atrocious ugliness.

Besides the vanity of the wretch, though, he was endowed with the vilest and basest passions.

He was, in his heart, a *debauchee* and voluptuary, such as there exist, happily, but very few men resembling.

Had he only been decent-looking—had his ugliness been only passable—had he possessed the power of speech to plead his cause—there is little doubt that this villain's life would have been one long career of gross sensual indulgence, and his crimes would have been as numerous as already they were black and damnable.

Practising upon the credulity of those poor, simple girls who came to him to consult him respecting their future destiny, he had contrived, after worming out their secrets, to get many of them into his power.

Then their ruin quickly ensued, and the particulars of his atrocious villany were never made public, as he had so worked upon their minds, and excited their fears, with picturing to them what would be their fate if they betrayed their seducer, both here and hereafter, that his counsels were kept secret. Impunity lending him courage, he was urged on by his vile passions to perpetrate outrage upon outrage, and to systematically plan the ruin of every unfortunate creature who was unhappy enough to set foot in his den.

From the first had the dumb man conceived an overpowering passion for the poor nun who dwelt beneath his roof; and from the first day that she passed the fatal threshold of his house, he had sworn that she should be his.

Although bent upon her destruction, the disgraceful woman, his companion, was far from imagining that the dumb man entertained any nefarious intentions with respect to their beautiful lodger other than those which they had planned together.

The terrible woman had profanely termed the advent of the poor innocent creature "a godsend"

She had made up her mind to make a little fortune by the hideous plan which she had proposed, and with which the reader is already acquainted.

But she never dreamt that the dumb man's lust would prove an obstacle to the realization of her hopes of gain.

A horrible woman—perfectly unwomanly—unsexed—unnatural.—the only passions left in her were intense avarice, sensuality, and jealousy; for she could be jealous even of such a hideous abortion as Jeer, the dumb man, when she was too much provoked.

Not long ago she had been sent to prison for keeping a house of bad character; and while in confinement, the murder of the poor girl, which I have described in a former chapter, took place in the dumb man's house.

Although Jeer was not indicted for the murder, and in the course of the investigations no suspicion alighted upon the miscreant,—yet all those who knew his character, and among others the woman Raddle, were morally convinced of his being the guilty party; and his mistress was furious at the thought that while she had been safely incarcerated, and was languishing in gaol because she had been robbed of all her savings, this man, who pretended to be bitterly grieved by her position, and only anxious for her freedom, should be thus employed while she was safe out of the way

He had asserted over and over again, and had sworn to the truth of his statements, that he had left no stone unturned in endeavouring to discover who was the thief who had robbed his late mistress, and in obtaining sufficient money to release her from prison; and although she had no positive proof, she felt certain in her heart it was a lie.

She had strong reasons for suspecting that the dumb man knew more about the robbery of her money than he chose to say; and we, who remember how, upon the first night that Cecily had passed beneath his roof, he had returned clandestinely to the house, and taken away with him a bag of money, may be inclined to be of the same opinion.

She found out also that somebody had been round to the most wealthy of her patrons, and solicited their pecuniary assistance. She had desired the dumb man to go on her behalf. He had done so, and had told her that the result had been unsatisfactory. But she had since ascertained that somebody had solicited assistance from these gentlemen, and that it had been given.

Had the dumb man then appropriated the money to his own use? Or was she to believe the explanation that he made—namely, that some one had been beforehand with him, and that the same person who had stolen her money, which she kept locked up in her bedroom, had also gone round and obtained money from all her patrons; and that, consequently, the patrons, disgusted at a second attempt to fleece them, had refused to render any further assistance?

This was the explanation that the dumb man

offered; and as she could not positively prove it to be false, she was fain to believe it, or pretend to believe it, though in her heart she mistrusted him greatly.

Since she had been out of prison, though, she had watched him narrowly: she had not, however, been able to discover anything in his conduct to warrant her suspicions, but she watched still.

If he were the thief who had taken her long-hoarded treasure, and consequently allowed her to lie in prison for a whole year, and at the same time allowed her furniture to be seized, and sold for rent in default of payment, he must, indeed, be a heartless scoundrel; and if she ever traced this villany to him, she swore that it would be atoned for by a bloody vengeance.

She had forgiven, or had affected to forgive, his conduct with respect to the poor murdered and outraged girl; but the very next time when she should prove his unfaithfulness, she swore that he should suffer bitterly.

But I need not delay the course of the narrative any longer, having now explained all that *is* necessary upon the occasion. Only, first, I ought to say that the dumb man's passion for Cecily was the cause of his being less angry about her late escapades than he would otherwise have been. He was not savagely drunk, as I have said; but, on the contrary, rather amorous.

The two wretches sat down by the side of the grate; and the dumb man having kindled a small fire with the aid of a few sticks, boiled some water, and made some grog.

Then he lit a pipe, and appeared to intend to make himself comfortable.

The woman, though, would not join in these innocent festivities. She held herself aloof, and sat silent and glum.

"Well, old girl," said Mr. Jeer, pleasantly; "what's the matter?"

She looked at him angrily, but made no reply.

"Don't be down in the mouth, old lady!"

"I suppose it pleases you," she replied, snappishly, "to see everything going to rack and ruin?"

"I don't think there's any great harm done," he replied.

"What do you mean?"

"What I say."

"Isn't the skeleton broken to bits?"

"Not quite."

"It can never be mended again."

"I think it can."

"It will cost an awful lot of money."

"Not an awful lot."

Mrs. Raddle made a gesture of impatience, and turned up her nose in contempt.

"You're drunk," said she. "You'll think differently when you get sober."

The dumb man chuckled.

"Not at all," said he. "I'm only good company. Here, you take a glass too, and try and be a little sociable."

He pushed the glass towards her, and poured in a large quantity of spirits.

"Drink!" said he.

"I don't want any."

"Oh, yes, you do!"

"I can't drink no more."

"Take just a little drop."

Any third person, unacquainted with the peculiarities of his dialect, would have supposed that the dumb man was choking himself with his grog, instead of conversing affably.

His gruntings and gurgling, however, appeared to possess a persuasive power sufficient to overcome the scruples of the gentle female to whom they were addressed.

After a little more resistance, growing more and more feeble every moment, she gave in, and took very kindly to the grog.

Another good stiff tumbler the dumb man mixed her after she had got through the one that he had last prepared; and then, as the spirits were running rather low, he put the bottle into his pocket, and betook himself to an adjacent public-house, to get a fresh supply.

Before he left the room, Mrs. Raddle had lit a cigar; and with one foot upon the hob, and the other on the fender, lolled back, with the air of an overgrown and rather blowsy sultana—alternately puffing at her weed and sipping at her grog.

The dumb man, as he stood in the shade at the back of the room, fixing his hat firmly upon his head, leered at her coolly.

Then his eyes turned round slowly to where Cecily lay upon the bed, her fair head resting upon her naked arm, worn out and fatigued by weeping.

It was an uncommonly ugly leer with which he regarded both the women; and as Cecily hastily averted her eyes beneath the bold lasciviousness of his glance, she shuddered involuntarily.

What mischief was he going to be about now? she asked herself.

What fresh enormity was he contemplating?

The smile left his ugly face, and a dark and ominous frown replaced it.

Some scheme of villany he contemplated. She watched him in a flutter of terror as he left the room, wondering what it could be.

Alas! but too soon was the doomed to learn the truth

CHAPTER LXI.

MRS. RADDLE COMES TO GRIEF.—CECILY MAKES ANOTHER ATTEMPT AT ESCAPE.—AGAIN IS SHE FOILED. — THE PLACARD — THE REWARD.—WHAT FATE IS IN STORE FOR HER?

The dumb man was much longer gone than would have seemed to be necessary, had he only have been going to a neighbouring public-house for the sake of replenishing the bottle

Mrs. Raddle drank up all her grog, finished her cigar, and began to grow rather impatient.

"What makes the fool so long?" she muttered to herself.

There was no doubt about her being the worse for liquor. She was much more intoxicated than the dumb man had been some time ago. While he had been getting sober, it would seem she had been gradually fuddling herself.

When she was left alone, and after she had finished her cigar and grog, she took it into her head that she would have liked to have had a cup of tea.

That would set her right. She felt sure of it. The only drawback, though, was who was to make it.

She dropped her foot from the hob, and the other foot from the fender, and made an effort to rise. But it was fruitless.

Mrs. Raddle only discovered at this juncture how very tipsy she was. She had some idea that she had taken rather more to drink than was good for her; but she did not imagine before she came to try to stand, how very unsteady she was upon her legs.

The little tea-canister containing the tea was upon a side-table about two yards off the spot where she stood.

She drew herself up, and frowned at it with determination.

She swayed to and fro unsteadily, holding on by the mantelpiece.

Then she made up her mind for a plunge, and took it.

Only she had not calculated the distance very well. And she had quite omitted to notice that between her and the side-table upon which the tea-cannister stood, there happened to be another small table, holding the glasses Mrs. Raddle and Mr. Jeer had been drinking out of, as also a few dirty plates and a jug of water.

Catching her foot in this table's leg upon the way, she sent it over with a loud crash, smashing all the objects standing upon it, and tripping herself up afterwards, rolled sprawling among the ruins.

Such a very melancholy object did she look, with her bonnet smashed over her eyes by the fall, and her petticoats very much tumbled, that Cecily could not, in spite of the terrors of her situation, refrain from a smile at the good lady's expense.

Mrs. Raddle, though, was far from smiling. She groaned and grunted a good deal, and struggled frantically to get upon her legs

But in endeavouring to do so, she pulled over the coal-scuttle upon top of her, and then smeared her face with her black hands She had such an absurd appearance under these unfortunate circumstances, that Cecily laughed outright.

Mrs. Raddle looked at her indignantly.

"Well, I'm sure!" said she.

Cecily tried to be serious, but could not refrain from a slight titter.

"I don't know what you've got to laugh at, miss, I'm sure!"

"I beg your pardon!" said Cecily. "I'm very sorry!"

"If you are sorry, why don't you come and help me, then?"

Cecily rose and lent her assistance to the other woman to rise from the ruins. It was a stiff struggle, and Mrs. Raddle was no small weight; but Cecily did manage, after a good deal of trouble, to get the lady up and into a chair.

There she sat panting for a few minutes, and then turning to Cecily in an appealing way, said, "Make us a sup of tea, dear!"

The girl felt but very little inclination to do what she was told—or, indeed, to raise her hand in any service for these wretches whose prisoner she was; but when she came to consider it, she thought that it would be much wiser to endeavour to conciliate this woman.

Who could tell?—perhaps, if she used the proper arguments, she might gain Mrs. Raddle's sympathies.

She might make a friend of her enemy.

How? Ah, who could tell? It was extremely difficult to say how she was to begin.

She had a vague idea that she might have got this woman's assistance, if not her good-will, by disclosing her suspicions—for she had suspicions—that the dumb man was enamoured of her.

If Mrs. Raddle thought that her lover was false to her, would she not be likely to help her to get away, even though, by so doing, she should lose a little money by it?

But, then, Cecily dreaded the woman's jealous fury. The little insight she had had just now into the fiendishness of her character, when she attacked and unmercifully beat the poor, wretched woman who had made her escape from the cellar.

No; she thought the matter over for some time, but she thought she had better delay the attempt for awhile.

Meanwhile, she made the tea, poured out a cup, and handed it to Mrs. Raddle.

Mrs. Raddle drank it up, and then, turning her eyes slowly upon her companion, said, "Have some yourself."

"No, thank you."

"Why not?"

"I don't want any."

"What makes you so unsociable?"

"I am not."

"Ain't you? Take some tea, then."

Cecily, thus urged, helped herself to half a cup, and sipped at it.

"I wonder at you," said Mrs. Raddle, shaking her head, and biting her teaspoon in a thoughtful sort of way—"I do wonder at you."

Cecily made no remark.

"If I was in your place, I should be thankful," continued Mrs Raddle,—"I should be grateful to them as had taken me out of the streets when I was at death's door, and been the saving of my life. I should be grateful, I should."

"I am," said Cecily, abruptly.

"Oh, are you? You don't look like it."

"Yes, I do."

"Well, you don't act like it, anyhow."

"Why?"

"Well, you wouldn't have run away if you was grateful; or, rather, you wouldn't have tried to run away. However, one thing's very clear."

Mrs. Raddle paused here, and shook her head, and frowned. Cecily looked towards her, in apprehension.

"Yes; you'll get into a worse box than this, depend upon it."

"If I want to go away, why do you wish to keep me?" Cecily asked.

"Keep you?"

"Yes; why do you lock me up here, a prisoner?"

"Who is locking you up?"

"What's the good of wasting words about it?" cried Cecily, impatiently. "What's the good of beating about the bush? You know I am a prisoner!"

"No, I don't."

"Am I not?"

"Not that I know of."

"Am I at liberty to go when I choose?"

"I suppose so."

"Then what made you lock me up when you went out?"

"I did not lock you up."

"Indeed!"

"No, it was the woman you talked to—that idiot down in the kitchen."

"Indeed!"

Cecily was silent for a while.

"Am I to understand," she asked, presently, "that I am at liberty to go when I choose?"

"Why not?"

"Very well, then; I choose to go now."

Mrs. Raddle made no remark, and Cecily, walking to the other end of the room, put on her cloak, which lay there, where she had thrown it off, upon the bed.

Would she be allowed thus peacefully to depart? she wondered.

If she could get away before the dumb man came back, all would be well.

She walked towards the door, and stood for half a moment with the door-handle in her hand, eyeing her companion.

Mrs. Raddle sat there, half asleep, nodding, with her chin upon her breast. She was far too tipsy to see or care what the other was doing.

There could not have possibly existed a more favourable opportunity for making her escape, supposing the dumb man did not return.

Without addressing any further conversation to Mrs. Raddles, and walking as noiselessly as she could, Cecily cautiously opened the door, and stepped out upon the landing.

But it was only to start back with a half-suppressed scream of terror, for she found herself immediately face to face with the dumb man.

There he stood, just outside the door. He had been listening, no doubt.

By the unpleasant leer of triumph and malice upon his face, she knew that he had heard all.

Her hopes of escape vanished into thin air, and she felt sick with fright at the sight of him.

"Well?" said he, with a kind of chuckle, addressing her in his strange tongue.

She did not understand what he was saying, although by a gesture he seemed to be inquiring whither she was bound.

She thought it best to pretend not to be frightened of him, or to suppose that he wished to prevent her passing; and so, without looking at his face, she made an attempt to get by him and go down stairs.

The attempt, however, was unsuccessful.

Scarcely had she moved half a yard away, when she felt herself clutched by the arm.

She turned her eyes upon him with an expression of indignant astonishment, to which he responded by jerking his left thumb over his shoulder in the direction of the door out of which she had just come.

She looked at him angrily, and a deep blush mantled upon her pale cheek.

"Take your hands off, sir!" she cried.

He tightened his hold of her.

"Let me pass!"

He laughed.

"Let me pass!" she repeated, stamping her foot passionately, and struggling to free herself from his hold on her.

But he was not so easily shaken off. His tenacity strongly resembled that of a bull-dog.

When she found how useless were her efforts, and stood trembling and panting in a state of exhaustion, he placed himself in such a position upon the stairs that she could not pass by him, and dragged out from his pocket a dirty, greasy, little pocket-book.

Then, with an end of pencil, scribbled upon the top of a blank leaf.

Cecily looked at the words he had written. It was that same handwriting that was in the book down stairs.

The words were—

"Be reasonable."

She read the words, but made no reply. The dumb man wrote again.

"Do not oblige me to use force."

She looked at them with contempt, but spoke not.

"Go back into the room again," he wrote: "I want to speak to you."

"I want to go," she retorted: "I don't want to have anything to say to you."

"Be reasonable, I tell you," he wrote, "and go back. When you have heard what I have to say, you shall go if you like."

"You promise this?" she asked.

"I swear it," he wrote.

True, his oath was not worth much, but what could she do. She was in his power—at his mercy.

Without attempting any further resistance, she followed the dumb man submissively.

He motioned to her to sit down by the tea-table.

Then, with a smile of contempt at the drunken woman snoring in a chair, with her head thrown back, at the evident risk of dislocation to her neck, he took a seat opposite to her, and turning over his book to a new leaf, began to write very systematically.

He wrote with singular rapidity; and though it was a bad hand, and the spelling was nothing to boast about, Cecily very easily understood what he intended to say.

Thus it was, then, he writing and she talking, they carried on their conversation.

"Would you like to leave this house?" he wrote.

"You know I would," she replied.

"Where do you mean to go to?"

"That is my business!"

"Have you any friends in London?"

"That is my business!"

"Are you going back to the place you came from?"

"Yes."

"I don't believe you!"

Cecily started, and looked at him in astonishment.

"What do you mean?" she asked.

"The place you came from is worse than this!"

"It must be bad, then!"

"It is."

"What do you know about it, pray?"

"Everything!"

"Indeed!" she said, with a sneer. "Allow me to say I don't believe that."

"Will you believe you own eyes?"

"Not when I look at your writing."

"Will you believe print?"

"They print lies sometimes."

"These are not lies."

As he spoke, he drew a printed paper from his pocket, and unfolded it.

Cecily read:—

"Absconded or enticed away, a young lady of weak intellect——"

Then followed an exact description of her dress and personal appearance as she was when she made her escape from the convent.

Cecily read the words with increasing terror at every fresh line.

When she came to the last—offering a reward of fifty pounds to any one who would bring information of her whereabouts to the lady abbess—her fright had reached its climax

The sum was small enough, to be sure; but from her small experience of him, she could believe that the wretch before her would be capable of any atrocity for the sake of such a reward.

Besides, there was no earthly reason why he should not earn the money by giving her up.

He intended to do so, she felt sure. What other intentions could he have? What else could he mean to be her lot?

Poor Cecily! she did not know what an atrocious monster she had to deal with.

She dreamt not of the fate in store for her.

CHAPTER LXII.

A NIGHT OF HORROR.

THE dumb man could see the effect that the sight of this placard had had upon his fair companion.

He watched her with an inward chuckle of intense satisfaction.

When she had read every word which the bill contained, she folded it up, and returned it to him without saying anything.

She did not look at his face, because she did not wish him to see how agitated she was.

Poor girl! he could see that well enough, as it was.

Inwardly did the monster rejoice at her confusion, and at the mental anguish which he well knew she was suffering.

At length, Cecily raised her eyes to his face.

"Do you mean to gain this reward?" she asked, abruptly.

"No," he wrote down immediately.

She was astonished, and, for a few moments, silent.

Then she said, suddenly, "Why?"

The man looked at her, very much surprised. Then he wrote down, "Because I am in no want of money. I have got enough, without earning more by such baseness."

She looked at him very hard. Could she believe him?

Surely she knew enough of him to know that he was thoroughly unscrupulous and vicious.

She believed him also to be a rank hypocrite.

"Tell me," she said, "why you want to keep me here? What do you hope to make out of me, that you do not give me up at once, and receive the reward of fifty pounds?"

The dumb man looked at her eagerly. A sudden flush came into his face, which, dying away again as rapidly, left his cadaverous countenance more ghastly than ever.

It seemed as though he were about to make some declaration—some confession; but in the very act of doing so, he hesitated, changed his mind, and wrote, "I'll tell you another time. Be under no apprehension, however. You are quite safe here. No one shall hurt you; and to-morrow morning, when my wife recovers herself a bit, she shall tell you exactly what we want. It is nothing to grumble at. It will put money in your pocket, and ours. So no more upon the subject to-night. Have some tea."

She shook her head.

"Make some for me, then, if you please."

She went to the fireplace, and put on the kettle, without making any remark. As she raised it in her hand, however, she felt that it was nearly empty.

The jug from which the kettle had been filled before was overthrown, and lay broken upon the floor.

"There is no water," she said.

Now, she knew very well that, upon the landing outside, there stood a great stone pitcher, containing a large quantity of water; but she did not like to quit the room for the purpose of fetching any, because she was fearful of exciting a suspicion in his mind that she was about to make another attempt at escape.

And her reason for wishing to dispel such a thought from his mind was because she really did mean to make the attempt.

Tha tnight she would try again—she had sworn it to herself.

She would make another attempt, if she died for it.

It was the dumb man's policy, also, to make her believe that he was not afraid of her making an attempt at escape.

He desired to establish her confidence—to make her feel at home.

Therefore was it that he pointed to the teapot, and then made a motion with his hand in the direction of the door.

While she was yet hesitating—feeling uncertain whether or not he intended to signify that she should go out and fetch the water—he t rned away his head again, and affected to be deeply engrossed in burning up of two or three sticks which he had placed in the grate.

He was, apparently, paying no further attention to her movements.

She hesitated no longer, but went out on to the landing, and filled the teapot from the earthen pitcher.

She was not long gone from the room; and when she returned, she found the dumb man in exactly the same position he had occupied when she went away.

Indeed, he was so intent upon the occupation in which he was engaged, that he appeared not to hear her approach until she was standing close by his side.

Then he sprang up suddenly, and, taking up the teapot and the little tea-canister containing the tea, he dropped into the former two or three teaspoonfuls of tea.

Cecily made a motion as though she would have stayed his hand.

"Won't you throw out the tea-leaves first?" she said.

He shook his head, and smiled, as though he would have said, "It does not signify."

She, meanwhile, put on the tea-kettle, and watched it until it boiled. Then he held the teapot whilst she poured in the water—holding the teapot in such a position, though, that, had she endeavoured to do so, she could not very well have seen down to the bottom, which lay in deep shadow.

When these preparations were over, he motioned to her to take a seat at the table, and to fill him a cup, and take one herself.

She felt dreadfully fatigued and weary, weak and faint.

Why should she not partake of this refreshment? She had refrained from doing so just now, when Mrs. Raddle had wanted her, because her soul revolted at the notion of sitting down at the same table with such wretches.

But it was a hard struggle to resist from taking what she knew must do her good—or rather, what she thought must do her good.

And she asked herself why should she so hesitate? I should say, though, that she had no suspicion of foul play. Even if she had had, and had reflected upon the reasonableness of such a feeling, she would most likely have decided that there was no cause for fear in the present instance.

Poor Cecily, although she knew this dumb man to be a most unmitigated ruffian, she did not know what a wily, crafty devil he was, and how his every act was the result of deep cunning and craftiness.

Just now, when she had gone out upon the landing, what think you had he done?

Quick as lightning, he sprang up from his seat before the fire, tore a small paper from his pocket, and tilted the contents into the teapot, hastily stirring round the leaves at the bottom with a teaspoon.

Then, with stealthy rapidity, he resumed his place by the fire; and Cecily returning to the room, found him, as I have already said, just as she had left him when she left the room.

She sat down, therefore, all unconscious of what had occurred, and after she had helped him to a cup, filled one for herself.

Hers she drank off at once; and when she had finished the cup, looked into the teapot to see whether there was any more left. There was some; but she paused before she filled up her cup, to ask him whether he required any more.

He had not drank his yet. He was filling, or pretending to fill, a pipe with tobacco from his pouch.

"Are not you going to drink your tea?" she asked, when she had waited a few minutes rather impatiently.

He nodded. It appeared as though his mind was occupied by some subject foreign to the question. He rose from the table without drinking his tea, and left the room.

I need not tell the reader that this was a scheme of his to induce her to drink her share of the drugged liquid. He himself did not intend to taste it; and when the door was closed between him and his intended victim, a smile of fiendish triumph flitted across his hideous face, and he broke into a low chuckle of delight, frightful to listen to.

"She is mine!" he muttered to himself. "No power on earth can save her! Ha! ha! She is mine—she is mine!"

But there was yet an obstacle to the perpetration of the monstrous outrage which this wretch had in contemplation.

The poor unsuspecting victim was drugged, and would soon be powerless in his grasp.

But there was another formidable obstacle to be removed.

And that was Mrs. Raddle.

He had left her, when he left the room, fast asleep, and incapably drunk, to all appearance.

But he had some experience of the good lady's intemperate habits, and he knew that she had a wonderful knack of pulling herself together, as it were, and getting all right again at a moment's notice.

Besides, even if she were as incapable as he supposed her to be, he wished to get rid of her out of the room.

He had gone away from the tea-table only so that Cecily might have an opportunity of drinking some of the tea before she noticed that he shirked it himself. He could not very well have sat opposite to her, and defrained from drinking; and so he had come away, intending to allow some time to elapse before he returned to the room.

He went down to the street door, and waited impatiently until he thought half an hour had gone by. Then he prepared to ascend the stairs again.

As he placed his foot upon the first step, however, he heard the sound of a door closing above.

As he gradually ascended the stairs, he heard the rustling of a dress upon the stairs above him.

Somebody was descending slowly, a step at a time.

At first, he thought that it was Cecily making another attempt to leave the house; but when he came to listen more attentively to the heavy, trailing step, and the loud, panting breathing, he knew that it was Mrs. Raddle, who, having recovered to some extent from the effects of her intoxication, was coming down to bed.

"So much the better," he thought. "If she goes to bed, and goes to sleep, it is exactly what I want her to do."

And he stood up close against the wall, so as to allow her to pass him in the darkness.

But, unfortunately, Mrs. Raddle made a false step as she approached the landing upon which he stood, and lurched up against him. Then, to steady herself from falling, she clutched hold of him, and held him tight.

The dumb man ground his teeth with rage, but he said nothing. He waited for her to speak. He had not long to wait.

"Who is it?" she hiccupped.

"Who should it be?"

"Oh, it's you, dear, is it? It's bed-time, isn't it?"

"I don't know."

"I'm going to bed."

"Go, then."

"Are not you coming?"

"Not yet."

"Why?"

"Oh, because it's not time yet."

"It's getting late."

"Well, I've something else to do."

"Do it to-morrow, then."

"No, I can't. Besides I've got to go out. I expect to see Skeleton Key—I've some business to talk to him about. There! good night!"

He pushed her away impatiently, and turned to go up-stairs.

She stopped him.

"Why are you going up-stairs?"

"I've left my hat."

He passed her without any further remark, and walked slowly up-stairs; but to his surprise, and somewhat to his mortification, he noticed that she had not moved.

When he reached the landing on which was the door of Cecily's room, he listened.

Not a sound could he hear from below.

Mrs. Raddle must have been standing in exactly the same place that he left her.

Was she watching him?

Was she suspicious?

Was she jealous?

"Curse her!" growled the dumb man between his teeth "I must put her off the scent. I must get her quiet, or there'll be a nice row in the house."

Then, as he did not require his hat, and had only made a feint of going for it, he turned back again and descended the stairs. As he expected, he found Mrs. Raddle waiting for him; and when she heard him coming, she turned round and walked slowly down to her bed-room upon the floor below.

The dumb man entered the room with her, and lighted a candle, which, in her very shaky state, she was unable to do. When he had done so, while Mrs. Raddle was making her arrangements for the night, he lit his pipe, and thrusting a cap on to his head, threw up the window, leant out, smoked, and stared at the moon.

* * * * *

Shortly after Mrs. Raddle, having awakened from her slumber, had staggered out of the room, Cecily began to be first conscious of a gradually increasing drowsiness stealing over her.

She thought very little of it at first; indeed, she, to some extent, encouraged the feeling. She thought that she would lie down upon the outside of the bed, and take a few minutes' rest.

If she could sleep for half an hour, she thought, then she would be better capable of meeting the fatigue and exertion which, if she carried out her scheme of escape, undoubtedly awaited her.

But suddenly a horrible thought flashed across her mind.

Flashed across her mind like an electric shock. She started to her feet, and uttered a sharp cry of terror.

All at once, the idea that she had been drugged occurred to her; for the awful fate of the poor girl who had been murdered in the house came fresh to her recollection.

The horror of the situation far exceeded that of Captain Crockford's; but I fancy that she would have given a trifle to have had his experience of the effects of a sleeping-draught—supposing that this which she had taken was of a like character.

What was she to do? At any cost, she must keep awake. She must find some means of conquering the drug. She must—she would keep awake.

But, curiously enough, she found that her fright had effectually dispelled all sleep from her eyes. She was awake, as wide awake as ever she had been in all her life, and her brain was as clear as possible.

After all, then, no drug had been administered to her, or was it that as yet it had not had sufficient time to operate, for now there was a violent throbbing in her forehead?

There was, she remembered, a cruet containing about half a pint of vinegar in a cupboard in the room.

She had heard Mrs. Raddle, a day or two before, talking about the effect that a large draught of vinegar had upon a person who was intoxicated. She said that she had known a man to sober himself almost instantaneously by these means.

Might not vinegar, Cecily thought, have a similar effect upon her? Might not it cause her to keep awake, if she had really taken any drug? Might it not act as an antidote?

She fetched the cruet from the cupboard, poured out its contents, and drank them off without any hesitation.

A violent pain in the head immediately succeeded it, and a feeling of great sickness; but very shortly both these disagreeable sensations passed away, and she felt herself in a strange state of excited wakefulness.

She felt certain that some evil was going to befal her. She was positive that some foul play was intended. She knew into what hands she had fallen.

She must be prepared.

She looked round the room in search of some weapon with which she could defend herself; but there was nothing that she could see.

There was no knife in the room. There was not even a poker, for Mr. Jeer was in the habit of poking the fire with a piece of wood, when it required stirring.

While she was still thinking how she could best defend herself, in case of attack, she heard a step upon the stairs.

She listened, and she fancied that it was Mrs. Raddle's foot. What should she do? She would pretend to be asleep

She hastily threw herself upon her bed; but as she did so, she bethought herself of her scissors.

Drawing them from their case, she clutched them in her hand, kept her eyes fixed upon the door, and waited.

She heard a hand upon the door-handle. The door opened slowly. An ugly head was thrust in.

It was that of the dumb man.

Although the room was almost dark—for the only light in it was thrown by the faint flickering flames of the dying fire—she could yet discern objects with sufficient distinctness to see that it was the ugly head of Mr. Jeer which had been intruded, and which remained there stationary, cocked a little upon one side, as though its owner were listening for the sound of her breathing.

So intently did she stare at it in her terror, that she almost persuaded herself that she could see his eyes moving in her direction.

She fancied more than once that they glittered in the fire-light, though this must have been pure imagination, for his face, turned from the fire towards her, was in deep shadow.

He stood motionless. He listened intently.

She held her breath. Her blood seemed to curdle. Her heart almost ceased beating.

"She is asleep," the wretch muttered to himself. "The potion has done its work. She is mine!"

Upon tiptoe he crept towards her. The darkness served to conceal the wolfish savagery of his revolting features.

Noiselessly as an assassin might approach his victim, he drew nearer to the couch upon which poor Cecily, sick and faint with fright, lay palpitating.

Next moment, when the pollution of his lips would have sullied her fair cheek, she sprang to her feet, and dashed him fiercely back.

He was so terrified, this cowardly, sneaking hound, by the suddenness of the action, that he slunk from her and cowered in fear, incapable for some moments of speech or action.

Taking advantage of his panic-stricken state, she made a spring past him towards the door.

But as he saw her slipping thus from his clutches, the dumb man's presence of mind suddenly returned to him.

He jumped after her, and, just as she was about to cross the threshold, seized her in his arms.

She uttered no cry, for she required all her strength for the struggle which she felt was to come.

She clung to the door-post frantically, and held on to it with a persistency which, in so young, beautiful, and, apparently, frail a creature, appeared absolutely miraculous.

Her resistance at first astounded, then infuriated, her lawless assailant.

But it caused him only to redouble his efforts to overcome her struggles to thwart him.

The monster's strength was next to superhuman,—she was no more than a child in his arms,—and as he grasped her round the waist, the contact of her soft, voluptuous form but contributed to set his already heated blood boiling tumultuously in his veins.

Then, unable to brook any further delay, and heedless of the pain which his violence might cause her, he roughly grasped her, and dragged her with a sudden wrench from the door, to which she frantically clung.

Poor Cecily! she felt that her efforts would avail her nought in the hands of this brute.

Her struggles would be as useless as her prayers.

In an instant, a hundred remembrances and thoughts, and a hundred wild and agonizing appeals, rushed in frightful chaos through her brain.

Then, in wildest terror, did Cecily utter shriek after shriek, as she yet wrestled desperately though unavailingly, in the arms of the hellish monster, bent upon the accomplishment of her ruin.

Oh, for some ministering angel of mercy to protect her innocence and beauty!

Oh, for some brave champion, with iron arm and lion's heart, to beat, and batter, and crush into the dirt the cowardly hound abusing her!

If there exists in the world one who loves this fair girl, so cruelly ill-treated, and about to be so brutally and foully wronged, come—come at once to her help! Save her while there is yet time Save her from ruin—from death—from worse than death!

And was there such a one in the world, who loved her, and would risk his own body to save her from so horrid a fate? Who knows? What was the meaning of those prayers and lamentations in the chapel that night, when Crockford found her upon her knees, praying before the altar What confessions did the diary which he had taken from her cell, contain? If we only knew these things, we might perhaps know where to turn in search of a champion for the poor girl, who is now struggling in this ruffian's arms.

Alas! no such champion is at hand. Poor Cecily art thou, then, defenceless?

Her strength has deserted her; she must succumb, unless some timely succour arrives.

But no, thank God! she was not altogether without hope. She had yet a friend, though in a quarter where it was least expected.

For at the very moment when the poor girl's strength and senses were on the point of deserting her, Mrs. Raddle, her face crimson with gin and indignation, burst into the room.

There was very little light in the room, as I have said, and it was difficult to discern the objects which the room contained, but perhaps she had had some suspicions of the dumb man's intentions. Anyhow, Mrs. Raddle did not require to take a second glance to convince herself of the atrocious object which had brought the villain to the spot.

With a half-scream of rage, she fell upon him with the fury of a wild cat.

Grasping the wretch by the hair of his head, she shook him to and fro until he howled with agony, the intensity of the pain depriving him of all power of resistance.

Then, when she had dragged several handfuls of hair and whiskers from his head and face, she twisted her left hand in his neckerchief so as to half throttle him, at the same time banging him in the face with her right fist clenched.

The dumb man, who as yet had not been able to rise from a kneeling position, into which the first violent shock of her unexpected attack had flung him, staggered back bloody and half stunned.

But no sooner had she quitted her hold of him, and desisted from her attack through sheer exhaustion, than he sprang to his feet.

With a savage growl, and gnashing his teeth like some wild beast, he set upon her.

She fell beneath his blows as a bullock falls beneath the butcher's pole-axe.

She fell, bleeding and breathless, with a deep groan.

The stunning strokes of his iron fist, which gashed her face and bruised her bosom, were, one would have thought, a sufficient vengeance for the ill-treatment she, in her furious jealousy, had bestowed upon him.

But it was not with a man she had to deal. It was not with a human creature, endowed with human passions. It was with a brute beast—a hideous mixture of hyena, gorilla, and goat.

A vengeful, brutish, lustful, bloodthirsty monster, capable of any atrocity in its mad passion.

As his hand rested upon the ground, where it fell as he stooped over his victim with the intention of strangling her as she lay, he felt something cold beneath his fingers.

It was a pair of scissors.

Not such a formidable weapon, you may think; but still, in this man's hands, an instrument of death.

Full of passion and hatred, half wild with the pain which he suffered from the excoriations on his face and head, he plunged the sharp-pointed scissors again and again into his victim's breast, until he had stabbed her through the heart.

Then leaping to his feet, he spurned the body from him, and turned towards the girl.

But Cecily, who, during this frightful scene, terror had rendered speechless and motionless, rushed from him in affright, and rent the air with her piercing shrieks for assistance.

"Curse you!" screamed the ruffian in his devilish gibberish. "You, at least, shall not escape me! Though I have to murder you also, you shall not thwart my desire!"

She understood not the words he uttered, or endeavoured to utter, but she could not doubt what were his intentions.

Her ruin was certain; her cold-blooded and brutal murder more than probable.

Great God! was there no escape for her?

Again and again she shrieked in frenzied accents.

The dumb man took her again in his arms, and dashed her with violence to the ground.

But again was there an interruption to his hellish purpose.

A loud thundering at the outer door seemed to threaten the smashing in of the panels.

At the same time, the bell wire was pulled so fiercely that it broke with a loud twang.

With a savage howl of fury, the disappointed miscreant released his victim.

Blinded as he was by his passion, he knew that it would be worse than madness to remain here any longer under the circumstances.

But to relinquish this fair creature now, after the risks that he had run to obtain possession of her, goaded him to a fury which well-nigh deprived him of reason.

Thwarted in the accomplishment of his fiendish purpose, he would fain have murdered the poor girl out of pure spite.

He had flung from him the scissors with which he had murdered his mistress; or with them he might also have taken the life of the intended victim of his brutal lust.

But there was no time to look for them—no time for anything; there was not a moment to lose.

In answer to Cecily's piercing shrieks, the sound of loud voices shouting reached them from the street without.

The smashing of woodwork, too, announced that the door below had either given way, or was just upon the point of so doing, beneath the violence of the attack the mob without were making upon it.

That there was a mob besieging the house, and that an angry mob, there could be little doubt.

The shouts of the infuriated populace smote upon the shrinking wretch's ear as he rushed wildly down stairs.

The girl's piercing shrieks had ceased when she saw that help was at hand, and her assailant was beating a retreat; and this the mob took as a sign of some calamity having befallen her.

She was dead, perhaps—perhaps they would be too late; and, urged on by this thought, the would-be rescuers redoubled their efforts; and at length, beneath a shower of blows, smashed in the door-panels, and rushed in a body into the house.

CHAPTER LXIII.

A POPULATION OF RUFFIANS.—THE INIQUITY OF THE PUBLIC-HOUSE.—THE SURLY LANDLORD.—THE RED-HEADED YOUNG LADY.—RAFFERTY UPON THE WATCH.

I HAVE told you that Mr. Jeer's neighbourhood was none of the choicest.

It was, perhaps, all things considered, as undesirable a locality to pitch upon for a place of residence as any in London.

Thieves and strumpets, for the most part, composed its population.

Brawls were of hourly occurrence—robberies happened every day—and a murder every now and then—that is to say, once or twice a week.

When women fought with one another—tore one another's hair out in handfuls—and endeavoured to tear out one another's eyes— the bruta

spectacle only created a little amusement for the bystanders.

When husbands kicked and trampled upon their wives—or when children were unmercifully flogged within an inch of their lives—no particular excitement was caused by these events; nobody felt any pity for the sufferers—and nobody, for a moment, ever dreamt of interfering.

It was supposed to be a matter of course, in Mr. Jeer's neighbourhood, that somebody should be always beating and ill-treating somebody else; and nobody cared a button how much anybody was beaten or ill-treated, as long as they themselves were not the recipient of the kicks and cuffs.

If anybody was awakened in the night by hearing a piercing scream, coming in her anguish from some poor suffering woman, ten to one the person who heard the cry for mercy or help, as the case might be, grówled at being disturbed; and, turning round upon his other side, pulled the bed-

clothes over his head, grunted, and dropped off to sleep again.

You wonder then, perhaps, how it was that the neighbours, upon this occasion, should have so far gone out of their way as to think of breaking into the dumb astrologer's house, in the hope of rescuing the female in distress, whose piercing shrieks had rent the air, and startled the drowsy loafers and idlers in the court below.

It was no feeling of humanity, it must be owned, which now had prompted this attempt at rescue, but the hope of gain.

A man, a stranger, a foreign-looking man, with a large beard, had been passing by the house, either by accident or design, at the very moment that Cecily had descended, as we have seen, by the aid of the sheets, formed into a rope, from one of the second floor windows.

The circumstance very naturally striking this stranger as remarkable, he had hung about the spot for some time, in the hope of seeing or hearing something else of a like wonderful character.

Presently, he had heard Mr. Jeer's uncouth jabbering in the back yard, and Mrs. Raddle's shrill cries; then Cecily's faint prayers for help; and then peeping through a crevice in the door leading into the back garden from the lane without, through which Cecily had hoped to be able to make her escape, he had seen the dumb man carrying the poor girl, struggling vainly, into the house.

He had been passing by in the lane at the back of the house when first he had caught sight of Cecily descending from the window; and after the back door had shut to upon the girl and her captors, he betook himself into a miserable little public-house, opposite the door before mentioned, and ordered a glass of ale, with the intention of questioning the landlord upon the character of the inhabitants of the house in question.

He found the public-house inside to be a sodden, dirty, close-smelling place—a beer-shop of the very lowest description.

The bar was deserted, and there was no sign of customers in the house, with the exception of two most villanous-looking wretches, in sordid, greasy attire, who, with their heads close together, muttered and mumbled over a pewter pot, in a dark corner of a dingy little tap-room, leading out of the bar, on the right hand side.

When the stranger entered the house, a dog, behind the bar, tied up to the leg of a table, began to bark furiously; and this aroused a red-faced, filthily dirty-looking man, in short sleeves, who had gone to sleep, stretched full length upon a bench.

He was the landlord, it appeared, for he came forward, after staring at the stranger for some moments in a drunken, stupid fashion, and asked what he wanted.

"Glass of stout!"

The landlord drew some horrible black mixture into a glass, and handed it to him; then leant upon his elbows on the counter, and stared the stranger full in the face.

The stranger, though, was not a man to be easily stared out of countenance.

His was an open, good-humoured face, bronzed by travel and exposure to sun and wind.

He had bold eyes, too, that looked at one so steadily, you could scarcely have believed it possible to have caused them to wink. They were bold eyes, it is certain, and belonged not to a coward.

"Your health!" said the stranger, nodding to the landlord in return for the stare.

"Yours!" growled the man, with a bearish politeness, taking a gulp at the contents of a pot by his side.

"You are quiet here," observed the stranger, looking round him.

"Want to be," retorted the landlord.

"That's all right."

"It is."

"Customers are no object to you, I suppose?"

"I didn't ask *you* to come!"

"You don't want me to go, do you?"

"You can, if you choose!"

"I don't!"

"Don't put yourself out on my account."

"As long as you don't put me out, there's no fear of that!" said the stranger, smiling.

There was no spoiling his good humour.

It was proof against the landlord's surliness; and the latter had presently to unbend a little, and enter into affable conversation—or rather, as near an approach to it as he was capable of.

The stranger then, in a chatty way, asked him a variety of questions, and endeavoured to elicit as much information as possible concerning the dumb man's house and its inmates.

The landlord, though, was anything but communicative.

He knew nothing about his neighbours, he said, and he did not want to know anything. If they left him alone, he left them alone, &c.

He had no more to say, and took to puffing of his pipe, as a hint that he did not mean to enter into further particulars.

A red-headed young woman, in a dirty cotton frock, and a pair of shoes much too large for her, and trodden down at heel, whose face was brazen and bloated, and whose bosom was rather more exposed than was consistent with the strictest propriety, came in with a jug to fetch some cooper for her Benjamin, as she was kind enough to explain; and she, hearing one of the stranger's questions, volunteered the required information, with more that was not asked for, concerning herself and her private affairs.

She described more graphically than truthfully the murder of the dumb man's niece, and the circumstances attending it, and expatiated lengthily upon the dumb man's peculiarities.

He was supposed to have sold himself to the Evil One, she said, and he was supposed to be a miser, and enormously rich.

That was why his house had been broken into when the poor girl was murdered.

She knew Mrs. Raddle. She was the dumb man's mistress, and she had kept a bad house in the neighbourhood, which had been cleared out by the police not long ago.

She did not know anything about a girl being in the house, she said at first; but upon reflection, she remembered hearing Mrs. Raddle relate at the bar of a gin-palace hard by, a few nights ago, that she had residing with her at the dumb man's, a female relative, who was not quite right in her head.

No doubt Mrs. Raddle's object in making this statement was to prevent anybody's believing what Cecily should say to them, did she find an opportunity of communicating with the neighbours through the windows; unless, indeed, which is more likely, it was the poor wretch down-stairs, locked up in the coal cellar, whom the dumb man and his mistress seemed bent upon torturing to death, that they intended to pass off as a lunatic.

When he had learnt all there was to learn—or, more properly speaking, all the information the young lady was capable of imparting—the stranger swallowed the remainder of the murky compound in his glass, and left the house.

As he did so, a piercing shriek for help reached his ears.

Again and again was it repeated.

Then it died away suddenly, and all became silent within the house from which it had emanated, the house occupied by the dumb man and his mistress.

Whatever might have been the occupation or class in life of the man with the beard, he was evidently a most eccentric character.

I do not intend to make any mystery out of the matter. He was our old friend Jack Rafferty. He was lounging about this villanous neighbourhood for a purpose which I will hereafter explain more fully, but which I may now simply attribute to a fancy he had for seeing "life" and low company;

and his curiosity having been excited by the strange behaviour of Cecily before described, he had made up his mind to watch the house.

CHAPTER LXIV.

THE TWOPENNY CONCERT, AND ITS PATRONS.—A HOT BED OF JUVENILE VICE—THE YOUNG PICKPOCKETS AND THEIR FEMALE COMPANIONS.—THE SINGERS ON THE PLATFORM.—THE DANCING WOMAN.—HER CAREER.—HER DEPRAVITY.—A TERRIBLE PICTURE FROM LIFE—JACK RAFFERTY MEETS A YOUNG FRIEND AND AN OLD ACQUAINTANCE—A BATTLE OF SHARP WITS—THE MAN OF THE WORLD AND THE ARTFUL DODGER.—AN INTERRUPTION.—AN ALARM.—A WOMAN'S SHRIEK.

LEAVING the little beer-shop and its unsociable landlord, Jack Rafferty followed round the wall of the back yard of the dumb man's house, and presently came out in the court in which the front door and the shop were situated.

In the court he found there was another public-house, of a larger size than the one he had just left; indeed, this partook more of the character of a gin-palace, and upon the first floor of which, according to a gaudily-painted placard, nightly occurred a "grand concert and ball."

As well as he could judge by a most demoniacal howling and stamping of feet upon the first floor, the concert was then taking place; and having watched the opposite house for some time through the window of the gin-palace, without anything having occurred which in the slightest degree compensated him for the waste of time spent in this curious occupation, he bethought him that a little recreation would be advisable, and having paid his twopence at the pay-place, walked upstairs, and joined in the festivities.

It was a long, low-ceilinged room in which he found himself, at the end of which was a platform raised about a yard from the floor, where there was a piano and a small space for the performers to sing and dance upon.

The remainder of the apartment was filled with rude benches and tables, all very narrow, and placed as closely together as possible, so as to squeeze a very large number of spectators into a very small quantity of room—an arrangement which, as respected the impurity of the atmosphere, was as undesirable as could well be conceived.

The company assembled, numbering in all probably seventy or eighty persons, were composed for the most part of boys and girls—and, indeed, children of tender years.

Wretched young thieves, lads with hang-dog faces and wisps of hair tortured into the corners of their eyes, were to be seen associating with, and treating to gin and beer, with the air of men of forty, little strumpets not more than twelve years old, whose faces already bore the evidences of profligacy and intemperance, and whose language and behaviour were revoltingly indecent.

There were also some older females present, who appeared so anxious of cultivating the acquaintance and gaining the notice of some smartly-dressed young prigs, that one might suppose these youths to be in possession of considerable wealth.

There were, however, no middle-aged or even full-grown men in the room, with the exception of one or two old men, hoary-headed wretches, whose faces were enough to hang them without further evidence; and who were there not only to pander to the vices of the miserable thief-boys, and to lavish their vile caresses upon the child-wantons accompanying them, but they had evidently got under their especial charge a number of more youthful and inexperienced thieves, whom they had seduced from the paths of virtue, and had brought to mix with this evil company, and to corrupt by the example set before them.

Jack Rafferty, with mingled sensations of pity and disgust, contemplated the youthful profligacy around him; and, as he drank some gin-and-water in a corner of the room, where he was removed as much as possible from the company, he watched for the performance to commence—for, at the time, the stage was deserted, and the piano without a performer.

Before long, however, a Jewish-looking gentleman, with a quantity of greasy ringlets, took his place at the instrument, and began a vigorous assault on the keys, whilst, at the same time, he favoured the company with some doggrel rhymes upon the events of the day, in none of which was there an approach to wit or humour, although his audience were sufficiently indulgent to applaud the singer at the end of every verse; and, once or twice, when some grossly indecent allusion touched their fancies, a loud shout of delight greeted his efforts to amuse them.

After this, a young gentleman, attired in a convict's dress, sung a song descriptive of life on "the mill," with an imitation of working that instrument of punishment, which was rapturously received by the company, some portion of which could probably say from experience how successful was the imitation.

When this singer had responded to a treble encore, and had made a short but pithy speech, in acknowledgment of his patrons' approbation, saying, merely, with a tug at his forelock, "Gents, you does me proud!" the piano was pushed a little further back, and a man and woman made their appearance, and then bowed, amidst great applause.

They were evidently popular favourites, and they danced as well as sung, both performances apparently affording the company the liveliest satisfaction.

These performers were dressed in juvenile costume, as a charity boy and girl, though they had reversed the order of things by the man dressing as a girl, and the woman as a boy.

The former was a blue-muzzled wretch, with strongly-marked features, which, in the attire he had chosen, rendered him perfectly revolting; while the woman, who was fair, fat, and forty, at the very mildest calculation, was so very voluptuously developed, that, in the close-fitting and almost transparent dress which she had chosen, a very scrupulous person might have been inclined to accuse the costume of indecency.

But if the scantiness of the woman's attire were calculated to call up a blush of shame to every modest cheek, her language and gestures were in the highest degree objectionable; and Rafferty could not help feeling some disgust for a woman who, old enough to be the mother of two-thirds of the boys and girls present, could lend herself to such a revolting display, for the purpose of pandering to the worst passions of humanity, and earning her bread by so degrading and horrible an expedient.

Did she ever feel any remorse for the lawless life she led, he wondered.

In the midst of an obscene jest or allusion, when

in the act of outraging decency by her lascivious gestures, or striving to inflame the passions of some successful young thief in the audience by the bold sensuality of her glances—for she was base enough to ply another and more horrible trade when her performances had concluded upon the stage—in the midst of all this, he asked himself, did any thought of her own childhood ever occur to her?

Did she remember temptations and seductions applied to herself by wretches equally vile and debased as she was now?

Were monsters then ever lying in wait to lure her from the path of virtue—to reap a harvest from her shame, and ruin, and disgrace?

Alas, no! he learnt afterwards that this woman had not been like many of those around her, doomed from her cradle to a life of infamous profligacy.

She had been well educated, was the daughter of a clergyman, and had of her own free-will deserted her home and friends; and without the excuse of necessity, but led on by the strength of her passions, and the corrupt blackness of her heart, she plunged into a life of sin and infamy, happily as rare as it was incredibly sickening in its revolting atrocity. This is no fancy sketch, and this shameless woman is at the present moment alive, and in London, performing, as I have described, to an audience of juvenile thieves and prostitutes, and perfectly revelling in the consciousness of the indescribably disgusting and degrading avocation she pursues from choice, and not from necessity—a systematic corruption of truth and innocence.

But while Rafferty was somewhat mournfully pondering upon the hideousness of this spectacle of bloated vice, and wondering at the inexperience of the passions that could be excited by the lavish display of this revolting strumpet's faded charms and huge, hulking, overgrown carcass, he was suddenly aroused by hearing his name pronounced in a loud tone.

He turned round in angry astonishment in the direction from which the sound had proceeded, and stared hard at, without recognising the speaker.

Then his eyes wandered inquiringly round upon the faces of those sitting in the immediate vicinity, fancying that he might have been mistaken in supposing that it was the person he had first thought who had addressed him.

But he knew none of the faces of the others, and his eyes again returned to the boy whom he had at first looked at.

He was a pale, unwholesome-looking youth, with a face which was in many places covered with blotches, and he had an immense pair of red ears stretching out on each side of his bullet head, and looking like the handles of a jar.

Jack Rafferty stared at him for a long time silently.

"Have I ever seen that boy's ugly mug before?" he said to himself.

Somehow, he thought he had. But where?

"He's as ill-looking a young vagabond as ever I clapped eyes upon!" thought Rafferty.

And so he was; although, by the way, he was very smartly dressed.

He had on a bran new hat, very hard and shiny; a crimson velvet waistcoat, with gold sprigs; a bright blue scarf, with a magnificent penny diamond pin; and a pair of large check trousers, a good deal after the style of the Ethiopian serenaders who perform in the streets.

But who was he?

"You don't seem to remember me!" observed this young gentleman.

"No!" replied Rafferty.

"But I remember you!" said the young gentleman, with an affable smile.

"Indeed!"

"My memory is better than yours, you see!"

"Ah!"

"I shouldn't have thought to have met you here, though!"

"Indeed!"

"Are you a reg'lar?"

"A what?"

"Do you often come here, I mean?"

"No; God forbid!"

"Why? I don't see it in that light! It's a very good entertainment!"

"Perhaps so!"

"That party now on the stage: she's a fine figure of a woman, sir! Don't you think so? Plenty of her, sir! Crummy, sir—eh? Crummy and scrumptious! She's very fond of me; and the passion's reciprocal!"

Rafferty regarded his companion with a bland smile.

He was not more than fourteen, at the outside; and he was small for his age.

He had not a particle of moustache, nor the faintest indication of coming whiskers.

"Why, you precious young shrimp!" cried Jack Rafferty, bursting into a hoarse laugh, "what woman is going to fall in love with you, do you suppose?"

"You needn't be personal, Mr. Rafferty!"

"You've got my name very pat, young man; where did you learn it?"

"Where do you suppose?"

"I want to know, confound you! Here, sit down, and tell me."

And as he spoke, Rafferty made a clutch at his young friend's collar, and brought him down upon a chair between them, with a bump which knocked the youth's hat off his head on to his nose end.

"Now, then," said the young gentleman; "say what you like, but keep your hands off!"

"Then tell me what I want to know!"

"What's that?"

"You know well enough."

"No, I don't."

"Well, I shall make you know, if you give me much more of your nonsense."

Perhaps the young gentleman thought Jack Rafferty's face showed certain indications of its owner having a hasty temper. It would not be wise, he thought, may be, to excite him too much; and so, refraining from some pleasantries that he seemed upon the point of indulging in, he said, in a conciliatory tone, "I didn't go for to offend you. It's not what I was trying at. I'll tell you where we met, with pleasure."

"Do so, then, without any more palaver!"

"It was at Eneas Earthworm's."

Rafferty stared at the boy intently.

Then all at once he recollected his face. It was the same young gentleman who had had a conversation with Ruth—the young man whose ingenious contrivances for ascertaining the approach of his master, and other little dodges of a like character, had so tickled the fancy of the eccentric and unscrupulous woman.

Rafferty was pleased at the meeting. He would be able, he thought, if he cultivated the young gentleman's acquaintance, to learn some particulars about Ruth which might lead to the discovery of her dwelling-place.

The boy, when last Rafferty had questioned him, had professed entire ignorance upon the subject; but Rafferty strongly suspected that he knew a good deal, if he only chose to impart his information to another.

Would he do so? Well, under the influence of spirituous refreshment, he might be induced to become more communicative.

Rafferty determined to exert himself to the utmost to gain his young friend's confidence, and he strove his utmost to render himself an agreeable companion, and by his off-hand, free-and-easy air to banish from the young clerk's mind any suspicion that he feared might there be lurking of the harmlessness of his intentions with respect to the female spy, supposing that the clerk should be so enlisted in her interest that his loyalty was proof against the temptations to be brought to bear upon it.

But curious to say, although Rafferty was working his hardest to be sociable and agreeable, his manners were anything but what he intended them to be. Before he knew who the boy was—or rather, before he had made up his mind to worm out of him the information he desired—his manners had been easy and jocular enough, if, perhaps, a trifle rough and uncouth; but now the fixed purpose which possessed him had cast a sullen and constrained air over his whole bearing.

A kind of gloomy, concentrated ferocity was visible in his knitted brows, tightly clenched teeth, and doubled fists.

His young companion eyed him askance.

"What is he up to?" he mentally asked himself. "What's he going to be after? What's his particular little game?"

Then, after due reflection, with an inward chuckle, he added, "Whatever it is, he won't get much change out of me. Not if I know it! Oh, no—not at all! Thank you, not so green! Not quite! Certainly not, if you've no objection!"

But Rafferty was thinking otherwise.

"The young cub knows all about her, I'll take my dying oath of it; and he shall tell me what he knows, or I'll wring his infernal young neck for him!"

It was a curious contest these two engaged upon, and it would, indeed, have been very difficult to foretel the result, or to calculate with any degree of certainty upon the probable winner.

One was a man of the world—a man who had faced danger a hundred times—who a hundred times had risked his life, and looked death straight in the face.

A wild and dangerous life had he led, and often enough had he been called upon to pit his shrewd common sense against the wiles and machinations of his enemies.

The stealthy, treacherous Indian—the calculating, long-headed Yankee—the brutally ignorant and savage negroes—all these had he in his time successfully combated.

More than that, he had often enough given the double to the most knowing of police officers, and "put a plant" upon the very artfullest of detectives.

But now he had to deal with a London boy—a cunning, dodging, impish young scamp—reared under the tender care of a low, pettifogging attorney, and nurtured in the streets.

He was a different customer to deal with, this young vagabond, it was very certain; but Rafferty had made up his mind to master him, and so he squared his elbows upon the table, and prepared to open the game, as though he were beginning a game of chess with some one whom he hoped to beat, but, at the same time, was more than half afraid he might get the better of him instead.

"Well, young gentleman!" said Rafferty.

But just at that moment he paused and listened.

"What was that?" he exclaimed.

"What was what?" asked the boy, in astonishment.

"Did you not hear?"

"No!"

"Hush, then—listen! There it is again!"

This time, the sound that had alarmed Rafferty was audible to both.

It was a woman's shriek.

Evidently the cry of some one in suffering, or in intense fear.

The shriek of a persecuted female in distress.

CHAPTER LXV.

THE MOB BREAK INTO THE HOUSE—THE DUMB MAN DRIVEN INTO A CORNER.—ONE CHANCE LEFT FOR LIFE.

Rafferty hesitated not a moment.

At once the thought flashed through his brain that it must be the voice of the woman he had seen attempting to escape from the astrologer's house.

They were beating her—ill-using her—murdering her, perhaps.

Abandoning his purpose of pumping his young friend until a more favourable opportunity, he sprang from his seat, and calling upon him to follow, made for the door.

Then together they descended the stairs, four steps at a time.

In another moment, they found themselves in the street.

Outside the public-house, the little crowd of ragged vagabonds and squalid, dowdy females there assembled were staring up at the house opposite.

Rafferty saw by the direction of their eyes that his supposition was correct. The shriek he had heard had come from the dumb man's home.

He, however, deemed it best to make an inquiry before taking any energetic steps towards effecting a rescue.

"Did you hear a scream?" he asked of a man standing near to him.

The man addressed looked him up and down.

Rafferty repeated his question, "Did you hear a scream?"

"Ah, I heard it!"

"It was a woman's voice, was it not?"

"It sounded like one."

"Didn't she cry out 'Murder?'"

"I did not listen to what she said."

"But you must have heard. They may be killing her."

"I should think they had killed her, as she's left off bawling.

"Well, d—n me, if you don't take it coolly!"

"How would you have me take it?"

"I'd have you do something to help her, if you call yourself a man."

"I don't see that at all. She's nothing to do with me."

"And so you'd let her be butchered — perhaps within fifty yards of the place where you stand—without troubling yourself to lift your voice, or raise your finger?"

"I shouldn't be surprised if I did."

Rafferty turned away with an expression of disgust, and appealed to some others of the men standing round.

But the same spirit seemed to animate them all. No appeal to their manly sympathies had any effect upon them.

If he were to arouse them to action, it must not be thus.

They cared nothing for suffering virtue in distress Indeed, they did not care a button about virtue in any shape. Vice would probably have had a better chance with them.

But Jack Rafferty could easily see what would be the best course to adopt, and he acted upon it accordingly.

At the moment that he had made up his mind upon the point, another loud and piercing shriek rent the air.

Then, again, another and another.

"Do you hear that?" he cried. "Who will help me to smash down the door?"

Nobody responded.

Then Rafferty added, "I'll give a pound to the first who gets into the house!"

And scarcely were the words uttered, than the whole company of roughs made a simultaneous plunge forward in the direction indicated.

"Five shillings for a pickaxe!" shouted Rafferty,—"five shillings for a pickaxe! Half a sovereign for a pickaxe! A sovereign to the man who brings me a pickaxe!"

He had not got long to wait. The offered bribe had a magical effect upon these ruffians, whom no appeal to their sense of justice would have aroused.

A pickaxe was handed over the people's heads until it reached him; then Rafferty, waving back the people pressing upon him on either side, grasped the weapon with both hands, swept it round his head, and brought it down with a thundering crash upon one of the panels.

The door, however, was made of good stiff wood, and resisted the attack successfully.

Once more he raised the pickaxe, and once more brought it down with a crash that echoed loudly throughout the house, and seemed to shake it to its foundation.

At the same moment, as though responsive to the blow, a loud shriek rent the air.

Rafferty shouted loudly in reply, and then exerted his lungs to the utmost in urging on the mob at his back.

Again and again, with deafening reports like the crash of artillery, the blows fell upon the door, which creaked and groaned ominously beneath the assault upon its venerable timbers.

And it was not long before the blows began to take effect. The hinges, sprained to their utmost, began to bend and twist. The panels, belaboured by furious blows, which became every moment more and more violent, splintered and split, and at length fell out upon the floor inside the house.

At length a sufficient aperture had been made for an entrance to be effected.

Rafferty squeezed himself through, shouting to the others to follow.

Almost simultaneously, however, an entrance had been forced through the door of the shop, and the mob burst tumultuously into the house in two angry and turbulent streams.

The dumb man was upon the stairs, between the second and third floors, when he heard the sound of the voices below.

A loud and savage shout greeted him, above which the voice of Jack Rafferty was plainly audible, urging on the rest.

"Secure the dumb man!" he cried. "Take him, dead or alive!"

The dumb man paused for a moment to listen, in astonishment.

What was the meaning of the words? Why should he be marked out? Who was this man who would hound him down like a mad dog?

He leant over the banisters to look.

Although he had not a moment to throw away if he must secure his safety, yet he could not restrain the strong curiosity he felt to know who it was thus bent upon his destruction.

The voice was unknown to him.

When he saw the face, it was equally strange to him.

But he took a long and earnest look at it.

"I shall know it again!" he muttered; "and if we meet again, by heaven! he will not get off as easily as I am doing now!"

He, too, was not making his escape with the facility that he had anticipated.

He thought to have got out of the house by the back door; but now the passage was crammed with men, and exit that way was impossible.

How then? He bethought him instantly of the window out of which Cecily had let herself down into the yard.

"If that old idiot, Raddle, didn't take away the ropes, I'm all right."

Unfortunately for him, however, the ropes were gone.

He had locked the room-door behind him.

That would keep out his pursuers for a moment or two, perhaps.

But it would only be for a moment or two.

He could not hope for a long delay. Even now they were scrambling up the stairs—scores of them crowding upon one another, murmuring savagely as they came along.

"I should not like to fall into their hands," he said to himself. "They'd tear me to pieces—they would, by heavens!"

He did not fancy this treatment, however. He was desperately afraid of a mob. You may say, perhaps, that he had also cause to fear the law, and that, if he had been caught, they might have stretched his neck for him before the Old Bailey, upon account of the murder he had just committed.

But that was not what he was most afraid of.

He might get off; he might escape somehow—he did not pause to think how: by some quibble of the law, perhaps—or by some false swearing upon the part of some of his friends, if he made it worth their while to do a little quiet perjury for him; and he could make it worth their while, if he chose.

But he feared the mob. There was no law respected by a savage mob. He might be lynched—they might take his life. Did he not deserve it? And would they not be rather more brutal about it than a professional Jack Ketch?

Trembling in all his limbs, with a face as white as a sheet, and the cold sweat of deadly fear hanging in great drops thick upon his brow, the dumb man advanced towards the window, and groped about in the dark upon the floor, in the hope that he might find the twisted sheets lying there.

In the corners of the room, too, he searched then, all over the floor, groping about upon his hands and knees.

The longer he searched and the nearer became

the footsteps without, the more frantic did he grow.

Upon all fours he ran about all over the room, more like a monkey than a man.

Had anybody been there to have seen the frantic antics of the poor scared wretch, they would nearly have cracked their sides a laughing.

Although it was nevertheless an ugly spectacle to look at, and one you might perchance have felt more inclined to cry than laugh at.

At last he gave up the search.

Somebody was trying the door. In another moment he knew the lock would be broken open.

He rushed madly at the window, flung up the sash, and crept through.

What was he to do? He could not jump, of course.

It was a fearful height from the ground. Beneath, a stone-yard to catch him when he fell, and to dash out his brains.

But by the side of the window there was a water-pipe, and he had thought of that before.

He would go down by it somehow.

There was scarcely any room for him to grasp at it. He could only get in his fingers between the pipe and the wall.

He clutched at it, though, with both hands, and he began to slide down.

When he had travelled downward about a couple of yards, he heard the door in the room he had just quitted open with a great smash, and then the sound of many feet trampling upon the bare boards of the floor.

Directly afterwards some one came to the window, and shading his eyes, looked out.

Three or four other men's heads filled up the background.

The dumb man remained perfectly still, balancing himself as well as he could with his toes just resting on a projecting ledge below him.

His fingers ached so as they had never ached before.

He could not cling much longer. He must fall if he had to bear this strain for any time.

But he dare not continue his descent while they were at the window.

He must remain quiet, and suffer in silence.

"God! how it hurts," he muttered to himself with a faint groan of anguish.

Those above were talking.

"I see no one."

"Some one must have got out of this window."

"But why?"

"Because I heard the window open."

"Because it was your fancy."

"I saw the girl escaping from here."

"But the rope has been taken away since."

"Yes, it has gone, certainly."

"You were mistaken, I tell you; we are losing time."

"Come on, then!"

Those at the window retreated now.

The dumb man breathed freely again, and muttered half aloud, "Thank God!"

"What's that?" a voice cried suddenly.

The dumb man looked up sharply.

To his horror, he saw that one man had been left behind.

He was leaning on his elbows upon the window-sill.

He had been straining his eyes to see whether there was any object moving in the yard below, and the half-uttered ejaculation of the dumb man had caught his ears.

"Who's there?" he cried.

The dumb man remained as quiet as he could.

But he had slightly shifted the position of one of his feet before he was aware of the other's close proximity.

The mortar breaking away and falling down below, caused the man at the window to look in his direction.

He saw him directly, and shouted to him to stop.

But it was not very probable his order would be obeyed. The dumb man, on the contrary, continued to scramble down as quickly as he could.

It was a wonder that he did not fall, so rapidly did he slide down the pipe.

He clung on tightly with his hands. He could not touch it with his feet. He could find no place for his toes.

But he clung on tightly with his hands. His knuckles were bruised and bleeding, but he would not relax his hold.

All at once, his legs felt strangely cold.

A few inches more, the cold seemed to mount higher, until it reached his body.

Then he felt the ground beneath his feet.

But at the same moment he comprehended the position in which he had placed himself.

He had come down into the water-butt.

CHAPTER LXVI.

CECILY AND THE POLICEMAN.—THE FALSE ACCUSATION.—THE GIRL'S DESPAIR.—CIRCUMSTANTIAL EVIDENCE.—THE SCISSORS.—THE SELF-ACCUSED.—THE PRIEST.—THE SWOON.

MEANWHILE the mob had gone crowding up-stairs, and had burst open the door of the room where the dumb man had left Cecily and the body of his victim.

They found the dead body of the murdered woman, lying weltering in her gore.

Over it they found Cecily standing, horrified—her attire torn and disordered, her hands bloody.

A policeman had joined with the crowd, and he aided the party which had forced its way up-stairs into this room.

He now rushed forward, and apparently comprehending the whole scene at a glance, clutched Cecily by the wrist.

Holding her tightly with one hand, he groped in his coat-tail pocket with the other.

At the same time he shouted loudly to the eager and half-terrified mob, swarming into the room, and crowding the landing and staircase without.

"Keep back!" he cried. "Please to keep back! Will you keep back? In the name of her Majesty the Queen, I command you to keep back!"

Awed by his authoritative tones, the mob did fall back a little, and stared at him open-mouthed.

The policeman then still feeling in his pockets, eventually produced the object of his search.

This was a pair of handcuffs.

When he had found them, quick as thought, he slipped them upon Cecily's wrists.

The girl started at the contact of the cold iron, and made a gesture as though she would have wrenched them off again.

"Oh, no!" the policeman remarked, quickly. "They're tight enough—you needn't waste your strength. Come, come, be quiet, my dear, and we'll use you well!"

"What do you want with me?" exclaimed the girl, looking round upon the faces crowding towards her, with a shuddering horror. "What do you want with me?"

"We want to lock you up, to begin with," replied the constable. "After that, I can't say what; but we shall learn all in good time, I have no doubt."

"But why?—why? What have I done?"

"I arrest you for murder!" answered the policeman, sternly; "the murder of the woman here at our feet. If you haven't done it, why, this is not the time to prove it. You can do that elsewhere."

He had stooped down just now, before he said this, and laid his hand upon the dead woman's heart.

She was dead enough. He could tell that in a moment.

But he turned to one of the persons standing by, and said, "Go, and fetch a doctor!"

Then he said to the rest, "You must clear the room, if you please!"—though the request would not have been complied with, very probably, only that another policeman had just made his appearance, and, at a hint from his companion, he began to push the people roughly out of the apartment, and jostle them down the stairs.

For several moments after the man had put on the handcuffs, and formally taken her into custody, Cecily remained silent and motionless.

It was as though the words he had uttered had deprived her of her senses.

Petrified her, as it were.

"Murder!" she repeated to herself, at length, in a faint whisper, gradually waxing louder and louder, until it almost approached a scream,—"murder!—murder! Oh, heaven! he accuses me of murder!"

The policeman, perhaps dreading, from his experience of the conduct of other female prisoners, that Cecily was about to become hysterical, endeavoured, in a rough, though kind, sort of way, to offer her some consolation.

"Look here! You know," He said, "there's no occasion to make a row about it!—there's no good comes of making a row about it!"

But she appeared not to heed him—not to hear him.

"Be a plucky girl," said he. "I'm sure you've got some courage in you, if you like. Don't let 'em see you're down-hearted; it'll make 'em think you're guilty."

"But I am not guilty. By heaven, I swear that I am innocent! It was not I who did the murder——"

"There, there! I don't want to hear anything about it. Whatever you say will be took down, and go against you."

"But I only want to say the truth. I want to tell you——"

"You'll hold your tongue, if you take my advice."

"And be dragged to prison without saying a word in my own defence?"

"You'll have plenty of opportunity to say what you like, presently; only, not now. This isn't the right place."

"But surely you will let me——"

"No, I won't!"

"But you are letting the real murderer escape!"

"Hold your noise!"

"He will have got away while you are wasting your time with me!"

"Come, come! I say, do be reasonable"

Cecily burst into a violent flood of tears.

"Oh, why am I treated so? What have I done, that I should suffer in this way? I am doomed to death. There is no hope for me; and he, the wretch who has caused all my misery, will escape scot free! Oh! this is too much—this is too hard to bear!"

The policeman, somehow, could not help thinking, as he listened to her frenzied ejaculations, that there might be some truth in these wild words which she uttered.

While he was wasting time securing her, the real murderer might perhaps be making his escape.

If he ran in the right direction, he might catch him yet.

He did not like to question the girl, because he was fearful lest she might commit herself by what she said. Still, she must be questioned; because, unless she were, he might be blundering all this time in the dark.

"Who do you say did it?" he asked.

"Her husband."

"Whose husband?"

"The dead woman's!"

"What's his name?"

"I don't know."

"But you knew them both, I should have thought. Don't you live here?"

"I have been here for some time—at least ten days."

"Then how is it you don't know their names?"

"I have been ill. I have been out of my mind—delirious."

"Were you and the deceased good friends!"

"No—she was jealous of me, and hated me"

"Come—come!" said the policeman, "that will do! I don't want to hear any more."

It seemed to him that every word she uttered tended only to make the case worse, and the evidence stronger against her.

Had he been alone with her he might have questioned her more; but his companion had now returned, and he knew very well that if he were inclined to keep the particulars of the conversation to himself, the other policeman would not.

Therefore he prevented her from saying any more.

The doctor who had been summoned had also arrived.

He examined the body, and pronounced the woman to be dead.

"She has been stabbed by some sharp instrument—a stiletto, perhaps—though the wound is a curious shape. I hardly know what it could be caused by."

The second policeman just at that moment stooped to pick up something from the floor.

"What is it?" asked the other constable.

"A pair of scissors."

"Ah!" cried the doctor. "Are they bloody?"

"Yes."

"The wounds have been caused by them."

"I will take charge of them," said the policeman who had picked them up, preparing to wrap them in a piece of paper.

"They are remarkable scissors," said the doctor; "foreign-looking things. I've seen scissors like those abroad, if I remember right—in a convent."

"There is some word carved on one, only can't read it."

"Let me look."

"What is it?"

"It is a name, I think."

"Can you read it?"

"Yes, in a minute. I must wipe it first, though."

"What is it?"

"C-e-c-i-l-y. Cecily!"

"Who is that, I wonder—the dead woman?"

"No," said Cecily—"it is my name."

"Do these scissors belong to you?"

"Yes."

"Well, we must be going, if we're not going to stop here all night!" cried the first policeman, angry at the foolish conduct of his prisoner in volunteering this information. "Come on, will you?"

"Can you walk?" they asked Cecily.

"Yes," she replied.

"We will get a cab below."

"You keep back the crowd. I can take care of her."

One policeman went in front to clear the way The other followed, leading Cecily.

At the street door, though, they found more members of the force, and they surrounded the prisoner.

A cab was easily procured, and they got her into this without much difficulty.

But just as they were about to drive away, a man who had been in the mob, catching a sight of her face, cried to them, in an excited tone, to stop

"What is it?" asked one of the policemen, angrily.

"I know that woman," the man replied. "What are you going to do with her?"

"We are going to take her to the station-house."

"What for? What has she done?"

"Murder!"

"But she is mad! Who says she has committed murder? Was it her own statement?"

"No; we have proofs."

"I must come with you. I can give information about her."

"Who is she?"

"She has escaped from the Convent of Saint Serebones."

"Do you come from there?"

"I am the father confessor attached to that convent."

"You had better come with us, then."

"Yes, if you will give me a seat. I am well known to Mr. ——, the magistrate. This is my card. I am Father Drake."

They opened the cab door for the reverend gentleman, and he stepped into the vehicle.

At the sight of him, Cecily gave a slight scream, and fell backwards.

It was the man who had assisted in the interment of the wretched nun that night in the convent.

The nun who had been so brutally flogged—who had been delivered of a still-born child, and the same night buried alive—the Sister Agatha.

It was also the same wretch in whose arms she had struggled—who had surprised her attempting an escape from the convent—who had brought her back to the cell, and there, taking advantage of her helplessness, and the absence of all succour, had endeavoured to violate her chastity, though, as the reader may remember, happily without success.

What did this wretch want here now? she asked herself.

What fresh evil was about to befall her?

"She knows you," said one of the policemen.

"Oh, yes!"

"Look, though!" cried another, — "look at her!"

"What is the matter?"

"She has fainted."

It was true. Her senses had deserted her, and she lay like one that is dead in the policeman's arms, who strove to raise her from the position into which she had fallen.

CHAPTER LXVII.

WHAT HAD BECOME OF THE LEADER?—THE INDIGNATION OF THE POPULACE.—VOWS OF VENGEANCE.—THE DUMB MAN IN THE WATER BUTT.—THROWING STONES.—ONE FOR HIS NOB. —AN AWFUL PREDICAMENT.—A DIVE AND A DISCOVERY.

WHILE the excitement attendant upon the seizure of Cecily continued, nobody troubled their heads about what had become of Jack Rafferty.

Presently, though, the excitement began to abate, the cab had driven away, and the police had locked the door, and the mob were getting elbowed and bustled out into the street.

Then some one asked some one else whether he had any idea what had become of the gentleman with the beard, who, a short time since had been so energetic in his attempts to force an entrance into the dwelling-house of Mr. Jeer, the dumb astrologer.

Some one having set the question going, somebody asked everybody else, and seemed very much surprised indeed that nobody volunteered any information.

A perfect Babel of tongues reiterated the inquiries, and everybody asked—

"Where is he?"

"What has become of him?"

"Where has he hidden himself?"

"Does anybody know who he is?"

"Does anybody know where he came from?"

Then a wise man said—

"Does anybody know where he's gone to? That's what we want to know, I suppose."

But that was exactly what they could not learn.

"He never came into the house," said one.

"Yes, he did," said another.

"I'll take my oath he came up-stairs just before me."

It's rather a sell for me," observed a third with a very long face, "because he promised to give me a pound for the loan of my pick-axe."

"He offered me something, too, which I suppose I shan't get."

"Well, I wouldn't have worked quite so hard if I had thought this was all I was to have."

"No, you're right there, Bill; no more should I."

"There might have been a score of women bellowing, 'fore I should have moved."

"All the women in creation yallowing out, wouldn't have made me stump."

"They might have done what the blazes they chose to 'em, for me!"

"Same here, Bill."

Thus the amiable gentlemen conversed. Fortunately for poor Cicely, everybody in the world had not been of the same opinion with respect to the fair sex.

Perhaps, though, they were not really as bad, these men, as they themselves tried to make out. They were wearied, dead beat, out of breath, blown and "precious dry," and there was no one, after all their hard work, to reward them with even as much as half a pint of beer.

It was enough, I should hope, to make anybody savage; and these sold ones grew the more savage and revengeful-minded the longer they brooded over their wrong.

"If ever I come across him ——"

"If ever I clap eyes on him ——"

"I'll teach him to play the fool with me again and no mistake!"

"He won't do it twice with me, when I have the squaring of accounts with him!"

"I'll mug him!"

"I'll smash him!"

"I'll dust his jacket for him!"

"I'll warm his hide!"

They certainly would have done their best to pay Jack Rafferty out for what they considered to be the trick that he had played them. However, he was not the sort of person to be easily frightened.

I am not quite sure that he would not have burst out laughing if he had heard them.

As it was, though, he was otherwise occupied.

The person who had staid behind at the window, when the rest had gone back into the house to explore the interior, was Jack Rafferty.

He had detected some one in the dark, climbing down the water-pipe.

Some dusky object he could just make out against the house side.

It was too dark to distinguish anything with any degree of certainty, but he could make out something very much like a dusky human form, sliding down the wall.

Rafferty did not know of the existence of the water-pipe, and so he supposed that it was down a rope that the dumb man was slowly working himself, as cautiously and noiselessly as possible.

Once he fancied that through the darkness he saw something white gleam for an instant.

And this he took to be the dumb man's face.

Presently, the figure working down and down into the darkness was at length swallowed up altogether; and Rafferty, staring down with all his might and main, could see no more of it.

There was such a fearful uproar going on within, that it was impossible to hear any sound down in the yard below.

Therefore, Rafferty could not hear the faint splash of the water in the water-butt.

It was so dark, too, that he could not distinguish the shape of the butt itself; and so it seemed to him, at first, that the dumb man must have sunk into the earth.

Now Rafferty, although he had not the slightest proof in support of his theory, felt as certain as though he had been able to minutely examine his countenance that this person thus stealing away was the dumb man; or, at least, as he did not know the dumb man to swear to, he made certain that he was the man he had seen carrying Cecily back a prisoner into the house, after she had made an attempt to escape, by letting herself down out of the window.

I say he was certain of this, but had he not been so he would have felt pretty sure, and with cause, too, that the person who was endeavouring to effect his escape had been somehow connected with the piercing cries for help which had led to the forcible entry being made into the dumb man's house.

Jack, thinking he had descended by a rope, leant out of the window as far as he could consistently with the preservation of his balance, and groped about upon the surface of the wall to find it.

But he could not.

His hand came into contact with the pipe, but it never occurred to him that anybody would have dreamt of going down the house-side with such a frail support.

You see, his case was not quite so desperate as the dumb man's had been.

It was not a matter of life or death with him.

Therefore he gave up all idea of following by the window, supposing that the ground must be a good distance off; and without stopping to waste any more time in considering what he could *not* do, he set about finding out what he could.

He rushed pell-mell down stairs, thrusting the people out of his way with very little ceremony.

He reached the back door, dragged open the bolts; it was unlocked, and he burst through into the yard.

Arrived here, he found himself in company with the water-butt.

But as well as he could see, with no living creature.

There were lights, though, at the moment, through the windows above, in the house which he had just quitted.

He looked round him, and could see no one.

There was, indeed, nowhere where anybody could hide—nothing that would afford any shelter—nothing that anybody could get behind.

"I have it!" said Rafferty, suddenly.

Which meant that he had not got *him*.

"He's gone through the door!"

The dumb man, shivering up to his waist in cold water, devoutly wished that he had.

Jack Rafferty, however, to make sure that what he supposed was really the case, went to the door in question and tried it.

It was bolted on the inside.

That was conclusive, then, to Rafferty's mind.

The dumb man had not escaped that way, or else how could he have bolted the door to again behind him, and upon the other side?

Rafferty, thinking the matter over, unbolted the door, and pulled it open. Then leaving it so, returned to the examination of the house.

There was only one door into the house—the door out of which he had come himself.

There was no chance, therefore, of him having got back into the house by some other entrance.

There were two windows, but they were closely barred. Entrance by them was impossible.

There was no trap-door in the ground.

There was no way that he could have hidden himself, except one.

And that one seemed preposterously improbable; but still there was, somehow, a probability, though preposterous.

Perhaps he was in the water-butt.

It was rather awkward to climb up to it.

Jack Rafferty looked at it from several points of view, and it appeared every way equally impracticable.

It stood in a very ricketty position. There seemed to be no ledge upon which to place his foot, to enable him to get up, and look in at the top.

"I'll try, without," said Rafferty to himself.

To do this, he picked up a stone about two inches long, and chucked it in at the top of the butt.

He did this to hear whether there was any splash. If there was a splash, it was only reasonable to suppose that there was nobody in it.

He did not throw the stone with any violence, it is true; but it nevertheless fell down with an unconscionable hard knock upon the bare head of the dumb man.

From the dumb man's head it fell, then, with a dull splash into the water.

Jack Rafferty listened, but could not make quite sure of the state of the case.

Clearly the stone had not fallen straight into the water. It had come in contact with some other object. Not exactly a soft object, but had hit upon something, Rafferty thought.

To make sure, Rafferty took up another stone, and threw it again.

Chock!

With a hollow sound, it came down upon the dumb man's head.

The victim ground his teeth, and muttered curses beneath his breath.

Another stone came presently, and hit him so hard, he groaned aloud in spite of himself.

Rafferty caught the sound, and climbed up, as well as he could, to look in.

The dumb man heard him coming, and shivered with terror and cold.

There was only one way of hiding himself, but it was a way he did not relish.

However, he must do it. At least, he would try it.

He was wet through as high as his arm-pits. There could be no great harm in getting a little wetter.

He held his breath and dived.

Just as Rafferty poked his nose in at the top, the dumb man's head disappeared under the water.

Rafferty stood staring in at the top, amazed at finding nothing.

"What the deuce did the stones hit against?"

He continued to stare at the surface of the water.

Meanwhile, the dumb man, running very short of breath, found it to be a perfect impossibility to remain any longer under water.

What was the good of dying under the surface, hiding from death?

He could stop no longer; and, snorting like a sea-horse, he popped up his head.

Rafferty gazed upon the unexpected apparition in blank amazement.

The dumb man panted, and stared at him.

At the same moment, a man, in one of the rooms in the house, threw open the window, and waved to and fro a burning torch.

The light of the torch lit up the yard as though it had been broad day.

CHAPTER LXVIII.

A STRUGGLE.—A RUN FOR IT.—AN AWKWARD TUMBLE.—THE DARK ALLEY.—THE SEARCH.—THE AMBUSCADE.—THE MURDEROUS ATTACK.—PLUNDERED AND STRIPPED.

THE dumb man saw that he was discovered. He did not require to have very good eyes for that.

He was discovered—he must escape. Rafferty stretched out his arm and clutched him by the collar. The dumb man tried to dive again, and pull the other head first into the water. Rafferty, on the contrary, used all his strength to pull the dumb man out.

A desperate struggle ensued, with the result which may be anticipated.

The water-butt was overthrown.

The dumb man and Rafferty, tightly locked in each other's arms, came with a crash to the ground.

The man above with the torch withdrew again just as he saw the butt fall, and left the yard in perfect darkness.

Unfortunately Rafferty's head came down with a crash upon the stones, and for a moment knocked him silly.

Taking advantage of his helplessness, the dumb man instantly sprang to his feet.

Then fled precipitately.

The door, as I said, had been left open. Rafferty had done so inadvertently. The dumb man took advantage of it.

By the time that Rafferty had sufficiently recovered his senses to be able to be quite certain which was his head and which was his feet, the dumb man was out in the lane.

Then Rafferty, pulling himself together, rushed after him.

The dumb man had not a start of more than half a dozen yards, but it was just enough to enable him to get round the corner into the next lane before Rafferty could get outside the door leading out of the back yard.

I say he had got round the corner, but I should have said very nearly. His head and body and one leg were already out of sight. Only one foot and a few inches of ankle remained. Unfortunately for the dumb man, Jack Rafferty's eye fell on them as he plunged out of the doorway headlong.

"Stop thief!" roared Jack, and followed at the top of his speed.

"Stop thief!—stop thief!"

The dumb man bounded on ahead like an antelope.

To have seen the miserable, deformed, serpentiny, corkscrewed gait of this unsightly object upon most occasions, no one would have believed it possible that he could be capable of running so straight, and making such progress: but he did.

He flew onwards like a hare.

The neighbourhood, too, was not unlike a rabbit warren. It was so full of dark courts and winding alleys, and narrow, crooked lanes—a perfect labyrinth of tangled byways, down which surely none but old inhabitants could find their way with any certainty.

There were so many hiding-places, too, so provokingly inviting, Jack felt certain that if he once lost sight of the game, he might as well give up the chase as a bad job.

"Stop thief!" he roared, with all the strength of his lungs. "Stop thief!—stop thief!"

He might just as well have saved his breath, for any good it did.

"Stop thief!" indeed Why did he want to stop all the neighbourhood? When he called out thief, he could not very well do so without being unpleasantly personal to some of the residents.

"Stop thief!" Why should they stop him? They went upon the principle—and it was not a bad one to go upon, either—that they should do unto their neighbours as they would that their neighbours should do unto them. Now if they had committed a theft, of course they would not have had their neighbours stop them, when they were in the act of bolting from justice; and so they looked on now, with their hands in their pockets, and felt inclined, if they stirred in the matter at all, to put all the impediments they could in the way of the pursuer, and help the pursued to the utmost that lay in their power.

Round the corner rushed the dumb man, caring little what he ran against, or whom he upset. After him came Rafferty, equally regardless of all the obstacles which chance had thrown in his path.

Up one street and down another.

Down one street and up another.

On they went!

On, on!

Helter skelter!

The dumb man could not have held his breath much longer, and was beginning to pant furiously. Rafferty held steadily on.

Jack would have caught the dumb man to a certainty, only, turning the corner of a dark cutthroat alley, he caught his foot upon a projecting doorstep and went sprawling.

He hit his head a terrible blow upon the pavement, instantly raising up a great lump with the bruise.

When he staggered to his feet again, and could see anything but sparks and rainbows, the dumb man had disappeared.

But he felt sure that he must have gone down the alley, although he could see and hear nothing of him.

The alley was down an archway, and it was evidently a "no thoroughfare."

Rafferty ran down it. He found that there was no outlet. The dumb man, then, must have sought refuge in one of the houses.

The question was, which.

There was no garden or area before any of them They were all mean one-storied tenements. He walked quietly up one side and down the other, the whole length of the street, feeling the doors and listening.

It was a strangely deserted spot, strangely quiet, and horribly gloomy.

Not a light could he see, not a sound could he hear.

When he reached the end of the alley, though, he paused, and listened. The door of a house he had just passed he heard creak slightly.

He sprang to it, and threw himself with all his weight against it.

Next moment he found himself full length upon the passage within.

Then, before he could recover his feet, he had received a violent and stunning blow upon the back of his head.

He had some vague idea that he was immediately afterwards seized by several pairs of hands, and gagged and tightly bound.

Then that he was raised from the ground, and carried into some other room.

But at this juncture his senses deserted him, and he became perfectly unconscious.

Meanwhile his body, in the hands of his unseen assailants, was rapidly plundered, and stripped stark naked.

CHAPTER LXIX.

JACK RAFFERTY, IN THE CELLAR, OVERHEARS A STRANGE CONVERSATION BETWEEN THREE SCOUNDRELS.—A DIABOLICAL PLOT.—A SCHEME OF WHOLESALE BLOODSHED —A REVOLTING PICTURE OF MORAL DEPRAVITY.

He awoke to find himself stark naked.

He awoke shivering with cold.

He found himself lying upon the damp floor of what appeared to be a cellar, and he lay there striving to recollect where he was, and under what circumstances he had arrived at this horrible place, without being able to recall to his mind any of the incidents which had led to his incarceration.

Was he incarcerated? Where was he? Buried alive, perhaps. He strove to get upon his feet, but he found that he was tightly bound hand and foot.

He was bound, too, with unnecessary tightness, for the cords cut into his flesh.

A gag had been forced into his mouth, which caused him great pain: and his head was aching violently, from the effects of the blow he had received in the unlucky tumble at the top of the alley.

After struggling vainly for a moment or two, he sank back upon the cold, wet stones.

As he did so, some noxious animal, a toad or a lizard perhaps, crawled over one of his hands.

He flung it from him with an expression of intense disgust.

"Good God," he said to himself, with a deep groan, "how long am I to be here? What is going to be done to me? What is to be my fate?"

As he lay stretched upon the ground, exhausted with his futile efforts to free himself, he became conscious that at the other end of the cellar there was a tiny aperture in the wall, through which the light was visible.

He raised his head a few inches from the floor, and listened intently.

He could hear the sound of voices, although he could not make out what was being said.

But he found that he could drag or wriggle himself worm-like across the floor; and steering in the direction of the light, he worked himself laboriously onwards.

When he got just underneath the opening, he raised himself into a sitting posture against the wall. Then, after a great deal of trouble and considerable pain, he managed to get upon his feet. Then he brought his head close to the hole, and with a little twisting and straining of his eyes and neck, he contrived to look into a room beyond where the light came from.

Three men were seated there, round a fire-place, in the grate of which was a small handful of red coals.

The man upon the other side of the room, with his face towards Rafferty, was the dumb man.

The other two were unknown to him, though known to the reader.

They were Jacob Stone and Skeleton Key.

Upon the table there was a black bottle, into the end of which a lighted candle had been stuck.

There was also another black bottle, probably containing some gin. There was a broken wineglass to drink out of, and some tobacco in a paper. The three appeared to be having a kind of carouse, and two were laughing heartily at something the third was reading.

The person reading was Skeleton Key, and Jack Rafferty saw in his hand some dark object, which he presently recognised, with a savage curse, to be his own pocket-book, the contents of which the ruffians were very coolly overhauling.

"Go on," he heard one say—"Jacob Stone. "Go on, Skeleton. What's she say next?"

"She seems to be very fond of him," said Skeleton Key, who appeared to be reading a letter.

"She's a nob in her way, too, I take it. Anyhow, she expresses herself beautiful, don't she?"

"I'm no judge," grunted Stone.

"Ain't you never had no love-letters, Jacob?"

"Go on. What's she say next?"

"That's all she does say. She's wrote to him to make a assignation."

"A what?"

"A assignation, Jacob. Ain't you never made none?"

"Blowed if I know! I don't know when I do make 'em."

"What do you mean?"

"What do you mean? Why don't you talk English?"

"So I am, Jack."

"Well, I'm hanged if I can understand you, then. I suppose you've been overhauling the dictionary, and picking out all the hard words. But then you allus was a scolard. That's how it was as you got sent across the herrin'-pond the first time, through writing somebody else's name in a mistake for your own."

"Never mind, Jacob; let bygones be bygones; you don't want me to remind you of your early indiscretions. I dare say it wouldn't please you if I were to go out of my way to remind you how I have seen you wollopped in Tothill Fields when you first started in the profession! I don't want to hurt your feelings, and so I shall not revert to the unpleasant circumstance."

"Come, then, look here; suppose you drop it!" growled Jacob, savagely.

"Suppose you do ditto, Jacob!"

"Well, then?"

"Well, then?"

Jacob growled a little bit after this, and then said, "Go on with the letter."

"I have finished it."

"Ain't the portrait inside that she talks about sending him."

"No, he's taken that out, bless you, and had it framed, to hang up in the best parlour, over the piano."

"I am sorry for that; I should have liked to have a look at her. What's she call herself?"

"Ah! by the way, I didn't read the name. Here it is, though! Florence Darcy."

"It's rather green of her to write it full, though, ain't it? If her husband should have dropped across it, there would have been a nice kettle of fish to fry, wouldn't there?"

"I say, Jacob," said Skeleton Key, suddenly, "do you think Florence Darcy can be the wife of Lord Darcy?"

"What, the Secretary of State, do you mean?"

"To be sure."

"I was thinking as much myself. Somehow, I didn't like to say so, for it didn't seem at all likely."

"If we had only got her portrait here we could settle it easy enough; for I've seen her many a time sitting in the Park, and I'd know her anywhere."

While Stone was speaking, the other man was occupied in silently turning over the contents of the pocket-book.

There were a great number of papers, letters, memoranda, &c., to which he appeared to attach no value whatever, and which, greatly to Rafferty's indignation, he saw him coolly thrust into the fire, after he had perused them. Presently, though, he came to a piece of printed paper, which he unfolded carefully, and spread out before him.

"By heaven!" he ejaculated, "it's a ticket of leave!"

"A what?" cried Jacob, leaning over his shoulder and reading eagerly. "So it is, and do you see the name?"

"I see it plainly enough—it is my old pal, Jack Rafferty! Only to think of him coming this game! It's wonderful! and if she should only prove to be some nob, and we could find out who, she would be worth a small fortune to us, bribing us to keep it dark. If we could only contrive to get hold of her picture, we should——Why, here it is, by God!"

He jerked a photograph out of a little paper case, in one of the compartments of the pocket-book. But when his eyes fell upon the face of the lady's portrait in his hand, an extraordinary change came over his own countenance.

Stone, who noticed it, asked with astonishment, "What was the matter?" at the same time snatching away the picture from the other's hands.

Stone's face in its turn underwent a wonderful change. He had recognised the lady. He had recognised her to be the wife of the Secretary of State, and he was not a little astonished at the discovery, although he had anticipated as much a short time before.

But being certain of the fact, he was now asking himself whether or not he ought to acquaint his companion with the fact. If Skeleton Key did not know that this lady was in a position which would secure him many little pecuniary helps, why should he inform him? What was enough for one, would be nothing if divided between two.

Then the Skeleton was such a mercenary wretch—such a grasping, avaricious wretch, he would be sure to be spoiling the game by his cupidity.

But while these thoughts were running quickly through Stone's brains, others, far different in their nature, were agitating those of the man called Skeleton Key.

The latter had recognised in the portrait before him the counterpart of another portrait which he had in his own pocket.

It was the portrait of the lady in whose search he had passed many days lately.

It was the same lady for whom he had mistaken Ruth upon that morning when, the reader may remember, he had met the spy in Covent Garden, and dodged her half over London, and had last been foiled by Ruth's trick with the ferry boat.

Skeleton Key was thinking to himself, "How shall I make the best thing out of this? Shall I let either of these men into the secret?"

But while he was hesitating, the dumb man looked over his shoulder, and called out in his peculiar language, "I know her! It is the woman!"

"Yes!" said Skeleton Key, seeing that he could not deceive him.

Then Jacob Stone demanding an explanation, he was informed at some length how the lady in question had been to see the dumb astrologer first of all for the purpose, either real or nominal, of having her nativity cast, and secondly to purchase a certain noxious drug.

"What for?" asked Stone; "to put a kid out of the way?"

"Not at all! It was to practise on a full-grown person!"

"The devil!"

"You may well say that. I can understand what you mean by a *beautiful fiend*, when I look at that lady! Sometimes there was a sort of expression about her eyes which I can compare to nothing but forked lightnings!"

Here the dumb man broke in with his strangle gabble.

"What's he say?" asked Stone.

"Why," replied the Skeleton, who understood Mr. Jeer's peculiar lingo, "he says that I followed the wrong woman."

"What's he mean?"

"Why, it appears that I followed some lady who bore a most extraordinary likeness to Lady Darcy in every other respect but the colour of her hair; and as I had only a photograph to guide me about her likeness, I could not tell very well whether the lady I was to follow had light hair or dark."

"But were they so very much alike? I shouldn't think it was possible?"

"But it was, I assure you. Besides, for the matter of that, there was a girl that Mr Jeer, here, and Mrs. Raddle picked up one night out of the streets, who was also the very counterpart of the other two!"

"Well, that's a rum go, I must say!"

"Do you know, Stone," said the Skeleton, after a brief pause, in which he seemed to have been cogitating profoundly,—"do you know, I can't help thinking, after all, that the party that I followed was somehow connected with that Ruth Trail that we were going to put out of the way the night you were lagged!"

"What makes you think that?"

"Why, because she seemed just such another woman. At one time I half thought it was her, for she called in the very next street—the house round the corner."

"What, the first door round the corner?"

"Yes"

"Why, that is her house."

"How do you mean?"

"There are two doors. We went in at the back door."

"By Jove, then, it might have been Ruth herself!"

"If it wasn't, it was uncommonly like her tricks."

"What sort of a woman is this Ruth?"

Stone described her, and Jack Rafferty, listening in rapt attention, sucked in every word, and with bent head and eager eyes, trembled with intense anxiety for him to mention the name of the street where the woman in whose pursuit he had so long been engaged had her abode.

But he waited in vain.

Presently, after they had been speculating upon the probability of the woman the Skeleton had followed being Ruth, the Spy, their thoughts again reverted to their prisoner.

"It's devilish lucky he ran after you, Jeer," said Stone; "and it's a most extraordinary chance that has thrown him into our clutches. Only I tell you one thing!"

"What's that?"

"We mustn't let him die in the cellar."

"He's pretty well a croker by this time, I should think."

"Oh, no! He's only had a little knock on the head. But that infernal damp cellar will polish him off, if we don't look out."

"Do you think there's anything to be gained by keeping him alive?"

"Why, yes, I do. He's awfully rich, isn't he?"

"I think so."

"Well, then, we'll keep him alive till we find out where he keeps his money, and till we've got it all out of him."

"Perhaps that will be the wisest plan."

"To be sure it will. Let's go and look at him."

CHAPTER LXX.

THE CONVERSATION CONTINUED.—FRESH REVELATIONS.—FRESH HORRORS.

RAFFERTY, dreading lest they should immediately descend into the cellar, limped back to the place from which he had come with all the haste of which, in his confused and crippled state, he was capable of, and again resumed his recumbent posture.

But after he had lain there for some time in great dread and eager expectation, he found that his captors had changed their minds with respect to him, and for the present, at least, did not intend to pay him a visit.

But he was unwilling to miss the conversation which was going on in the next room, and every word of which seemed, somehow or other, strangely connected with the subject which had for many, many weeks past occupied his thoughts upon every occasion that he was alone, and over which, through long sleepless nights, he had silently brooded, nursing, as it were, his hate and vengeance in his heart, until it grew, thus fostered, to a monstrous size, and crowded out all better feelings from his soul.

When he had remained for a short time upon the ground, he felt that he could no longer resist the great temptation which beset him to again approach the hole in the wall.

He crept towards it in the laboriously slow and painful mode of progression which the tightness of his bonds compelled him to adopt.

But he reached it as before, and looked through the opening.

The men were seated in the same position as when he had left them.

They were conversing now in low and guarded tones, and he had to strain his sense of hearing to the utmost to catch the words which they uttered.

That the subject under discussion was an interesting one none could doubt who gazed upon the eager faces of the villanous trio; though, from the low chuckles and grins of delight, it would have been difficult for any one unacquainted with the depths of depravity to which these hideous monsters of iniquity had descended, to believe that they could thus be hatching a scheme of bloodshed and atrocity which has rarely found a parallel in the annals of the blackest crime.

"But do you think it can be worked?" asked the Skeleton, after Stone had been giving a long muttered explanation in too low a voice for Rafferty to hear what he said.

"Worked? To be sure I do!" replied the other.

"How did you get hold of it, Stone? You don't mean to say that it is a scheme of your own concocting?"

"I can't take the credit for it, Jacob. Besides, if it was only an idea of mine that hadn't been worked out, I should hardly like suggesting it, you know; because I should know that you would think there was a precious sight too much risk about it."

"There is a goodish bit, it seems to me."

"Perhaps so; only, as I tell you, it has been carried on safely for these ever so many years, and is likely to be carried on much longer."

"But that's abroad, isn't it?"

"Yes, in France; only there's no earthly reason why it shouldn't take place in London."

"Who put you up to it? You haven't told us yet"

"It's no secret," replied Stone. "One of the chaps in the Jug told me all about it. He was a foreigner—a Greek sailor, I think—in for ripping up a mate of his in a row down Shadwell way."

"Had he done it?"

"No; it was a man he worked with. They had been in the galleys together, and had escaped together. This man proposed it to him, but he would not go in for it at the time, and the other chap tried it by himself. Then afterwards, when he found out how well it worked, he wanted to join very badly, and his friend wouldn't let him."

"Did the foreigner propose starting it with you?"

"Yes; only I don't take the foreigners very kindly. I didn't much like the notion of being mixed up with him. You see, he knew next to nothing of London, and there was no particular pull about his partnership. If we had been working together in his own country it would have been different; only here, it seemed to me, he would have been rather a drawback than otherwise."

"Yes; you were quite right."

"I think so. I turned him up, anyhow. Then you know, we were to have escaped together, if things had gone on as they ought to have done; only, as things turned out, they nabbed him scaling the wall, while I got off scot free, and cut my lucky."

"He cooked the turnkey's goose, didn't he?"

"Yes; and they'll scrag him for it, to a certainty."

"Poor devil! that's a bad job for him. Here's his health!"

And the Skeleton drank deeply, and laughed loudly at his own delicate humour.

"But, I say," he observed, presently; "tell us about this plot of yours over again. I'm not quite up in it."

"It's as simple as A B C, and a precious sight simpler. What we've got to do is to open a kind of office, in some nice quiet part of London—just such a place as this, for instance, where nobody is likely to interfere with us much, or trouble their heads what we're up to. Then we stick some notices in the paper, you know, that you and Mr. Jeer can manufacture between you, and we pretend there's a lot of capital places for domestic servants to be heard of at our place, with heaps of advantages, high wages, and all that."

"Yes; I understand."

"Well, then the servant girls comes in shoals, and we picks out those that have saved up a bit of money, and got a good stock of clothes."

"How will you know that?"

"We shall know it easy enough. They'll be proud to tell us."

"Well?"

"Well, then I'll work it next so that they bring their clothes and money, or banking-books, to our office."

"How's that to be done?"

"Very easily. We appoint a time for the steward or butler at the place they're going to, to meet them. You're the butler, if you like, or I could be him. Then we tell them to bring their things, and we will take them to the new place."

"Well?"

"Well, when they do bring them, the rest is easily managed. We very quietly cut their throats for them, or knock them on the head, and collar all they've brought in the way of valuables. Besides, if they're pretty ones——"

Here the ruffian proposed new and still more horrible atrocities to be perpetrated by himself and two ruffianly associates, with the particulars of which, however, I must refrain from sullying my pages.

The dumb man and the Skeleton burst into a loud shout of brutish laughter, and loudly applauded the suggestion by hammering with the heels of their heavy boots upon the floor.

"Bravo!—bravo!" bawled the latter. "That'll suit Mr. Jeer, here, to a T—won't it, old flick?"—and he hit the dumb man a sounding thwack upon the back, which was pretty nearly hard enough to dislocate his spine.

"I'm not quite sure, though, after all," observed the Skeleton, "that there is not an awful amount of danger about this scheme of yours."

"What makes you think that?"

"Why, when these girls keep on disappearing in this sort of way, won't there be an inquiry about them?"

"Well?"

"Well, if there is, the affair will get blown, and we shall have our windpipes stretched! That's what will come of it, I suppose."

"I don't see that at all."

"But if there's an inquiry, they'll find the whole thing out!"

"No, they won't!"

"The relations and friends of the girls will trace them to our place!"

"We can very easily choose from among the many that come to us girls who are friendless, and who are not likely to have any inquiries made about them."

"Yes, we can, easily. The girls will tell us all about their private affairs. You know how they talk, these servant girls. They'll tell us everything we ask them."

"Perhaps you're right."

"And suppose there are any inquiries?"

"If there are, they can come to nothing. Suppose the girls are traced here—what of that? We know nothing of them. They are gone on with the steward and butler, or what not, and we have never seen them before or since. They can't make much of that, can they?"

"Not much, I should think."

"If they think that there has been foul play, we laugh at the idea at first; and then, if they persist in it, we offer all the assistance in our power to find out the parties who have got hold of the poor things!"

"To be sure!"

"The end of it is, that they give up the search as a bad job, and all the bother finishes!"

"Well, it does seem a good plan. Anyhow, one thing's certain!"

"What's that?"

"That there's a tidy lot of swag hanging to it!"

"I tell you what!" said Stone, emphatically; "it's the best plan that has ever been hit upon yet; and if we are only able to work it for a year, our fortunes will be made!"

The three scoundrels still continued upon the same subject for some time to come. Before long, they had settled a plan of action, and arranged upon the preliminary steps which ought to be taken.

The more they talked, too, the more elated they became with hopes of future success. To hear the monsters plotting and planning the bloodthirsty work they intended to perpetrate, one could scarcely have believed in the reality of the hideous scene.

Some impious person might have wondered why the Divine wrath did not interfere with their murderous machinations; and then, before the deed of horror which they contemplated had been perpetrated, send death to silence them, and defeat their ends now and for ever.

But heaven willed it otherwise.

The wretches were allowed yet for a short time to continue their devilish plots. They were even allowed to put them into practice; and the reader will see ere long how the scene I have described came in the end to have an influence upon the fortunes of more than one person in this our history, and ruled the destiny of those whom one would least have thought likely to be brought in contact with these professional murderers.

But presently, in the middle of this interesting conversation, the dumb man suggested that they had better go and look after Jack Rafferty, upon whom the tightness of the cords and the dampness of the cellar might have a very detrimental effect, if suffered to continue much longer.

"The question is," said Stone, "whether it will be best to keep him alive, on the chance of making something out of him presently, or——"

"Or what?"

"Or to put him quietly out of the way, now, without any more trouble!"

"Well," said the Skeleton, "I'm in favour of allowing the poor wretch a few hours' respite."

"If it's only to be a few hours, well and good."

"It's not to be long, of course."

"We're going to cook his goose eventually, ain't we?"

"Certainly we are!"

"Well, let's go and look at him, anyhow. We can easily knock him on the head, if it's necessary!"

With this consolatory thought, which was perfectly audible to the unfortunate listener, they prepared to descend into the cellar.

Rafferty, in the slow and laboriously painful way in which he had been obliged to move before, now limped away to the other end of the cellar, and extended himself at full length.

He had scarcely time, however, to gain this position when the door opened.

Stone advanced first, holding high in the ir the candle in the bottle.

The other two followed immediately behind him.

Rafferty eyed their approach with a quaking at the heart, but with knitted brow and set teeth, and no signs of fear or weakness visible on his resolute features.

"They have come to murder me perhaps," he thought. "They will find that, at any rate, I can die game."

And he met their eyes firmly and defiantly.

CHAPTER LXXI.

WHAT HAPPENED IN THE CHAMBER OF DEATH.

THE interest of my story compels me most reluctantly to desert Jack Rafferty at this momentous juncture, and return to Ruth, whom I left, the reader will probably remember, alone with the dying miser in his bedroom in the quaint old manor house, whither chance had so strangely guided her footsteps, and those of her companion, Captain Crockford.

Having got rid of the lawyer, and the Captain,

and Lady Florence, the first thing that Ruth did was to lock the door; and having also ascertained for a certainty that no one was outside on the landing, listening to what might pass in the room between her and the dying man, she advanced to the bed-side, and stood for some time silently contemplating the features of Mr. Hawkstone, lying grey and death-like upon the pillow.

For some time she said no word—she moved not; she appeared scarcely to breathe, so intently did she regard the pallid features of the dying man.

He, conscious of her scrutiny, seemed to quail under it.

Surely he must have had some crime lying heavily upon his soul which he dreaded that she had come to speak to him about.

He seemed to know that she was there to threaten him, but he had not the strength, either moral or physical, to combat with her.

He lay there, groaning softly to himself, and shaking in every limb.

Then, as the silence, still continuing, became at length more than he could possibly endure, he gasped out, in so low a voice as to be almost inaudible, "What have you got to say to me? What is it you want to speak to me about?"

She made no answer at first, but drawing a chair close up to the bed-side, rested her hand upon the counterpane, and regarded him from a shorter distance with increasing earnestness.

"Speak to me!" he cried, at last, somewhat between a scream and a groan. "What have you got to say?"

"Have you no idea?" she asked, at last. "Does not your heart tell you who it is that comes here to seek at your hands justice and retribution?"

"Justice and retribution?" he muttered.

"Yes," she continued. "Does no sin weigh heavily upon your soul on this your death-bed,—"no sin for which you seek forgiveness?"

"No!" the old man replied, rolling his head to and fro upon the pillow as though in impatience and anger,—"no; I do not understand you!"

"And you do not know what is the subject about which I have come to converse with you?"

"No!"

"Is there no one of whom you can think whom you have wronged?"

"No."

"Your memory fails you."

"Tell me what you have to say," the old man cried, impatiently. "If you have anything to say, say it! If you have come here to threaten me, and try to extort some money from me, you have miscalculated your powers, and you know not with whom you have to deal. I am not so easily mastered as you think. I am dying, I know, but I am not dead yet. I have strength left, and the use of my faculties, and I am not going to be bullied—I am not going to be bullied!"

He tried to speak in a resolute tone, but his voice was weak and wavering.

"You know very well," said Ruth, "that what you are saying is false. You know very well that, as you lie there, your memory carries you back to one whom you bitterly wronged, and betrayed, and deserted."

"Who do you mean?" faltered the old man.

"Ask your conscience," retorted Ruth. "Do not you remember, perfectly, the incident to which I allude, or were the crimes of your youth so numerous that you do not know which of them I am referring to?"

"I don't know which."

"Well, then, I am speaking of your wife."

The old man was silent. He knew well enough that this was the subject upon which she was about to speak to him. He waited tremblingly for her to continue.

Ruth saw what effect her words had had. Presently she resumed.

"It is of your wife that I am come to speak to you. Did not your heart tell you so? Did not my face tell you that she would be the subject of our conversation?"

"How could I tell by your face?"

"Can you not tell by the likeness? Do you not know who I am?"

"My eyes are dim. I cannot see you."

"Cannot you now?"

"No."

"Now—now?"

"I cannot see you, however close you are."

"Is not the sound of my voice familiar to you?"

"I have heard a voice like it before."

"Yes; your wife's."

"What do you mean?"

"I mean that I am——"

There was a faint sound, Ruth fancied, upon the landing without, and she thought that some one might be listening.

She therefore stooped her head over that of the dying man, and, bringing down her lips close to his ear, whispered a few words.

The effect that these words had upon the old man was very powerful.

He trembled violently.

He made as though he would have pushed her away from him.

But she moved not from her seat; and, sinking her voice to a low tone, which was almost a whisper, but which was perfectly audible, she continued,—"Yes; heaven it must have been that guided my steps hither at this moment—that brought me to your bedside in time to see you before you died!"

The old man groaned.

"As I came through the court-yard, do you know," said Ruth, in a deeply thoughtful tone, as though she were talking to herself,—"something came upon me—some feeling, for which I could not account, crept over my senses. Everything, although I cannot say that it appeared in any way familiar to me, strangely reminded me of something that had been once—long ago—though I knew not what!"

The old man turned uneasily upon his restless bed, but made no answer.

Ruth continued,—"Yes, if there be a heaven above, to rule our destinies and guide us through the thorny and crooked paths of life, that heaven was watching over me then, and sent me hither, to save you from the perpetration of further evil."

"I do not understand you," the old man cried, chafing furiously beneath the powerful eyes fixed so pitilessly upon him.

"Have you provided for your children?" asked Ruth.

"I have only one child," the old man replied heavily, "and I have provided for her well."

"You mean for Lady Florence Darcy?"

"Yes."

"And your other three daughters?"

"I have none other!"

"Are they dead?"

"I don't know anything about them!"

"Yes, you do!"

"What do I know?"

"You know that they are alive!"

"If they are, it does not matter to me! They are no longer children of mine! I have discarded them!"

"Why have you done so?"

"Because of their mother's crime!"

"What crime?" asked Ruth, indignantly. "You know well that what you state is false! You know that she was guiltless of the sin you attributed to her!"

"It is a lie!"

"You know well that you persecuted your poor wife—that you ill-used her—that you even subjected her to your brutal violence! You know that it was her lot to suffer from the very first day that she was unfortunate enough to fall beneath your baneful influence! You know all this, I say!"

"I know nothing at all!" cried the old man

"You have forgotten it, perhaps!" said Ruth, sternly. "I will refresh your memory!"

CHAPTER LXXII.

THE HISTORY OF AN ILL-USED WOMAN.

THIS was the story that she told him.

Long ago, down in the mining districts, there lived a family who had worked in the pits for generations—or so it was supposed. They had not any of them much book-learning to boast of. There were few family records existing. What they knew of their ancestors, they knew from hearsay; and it was generally understood among the Hardwicks that the family had worked in the pits for generations.

A horribly hard life it was.

They worked long, weary hours, in cold and darkness. Wet through, half-naked, frequently covered with bruises and sores, the poor, fagged-out wretches struggled through a horrible existence, the heart-breaking toil of which was but relieved by brutal excess, gross obscenity, and savage deeds of wanton cruelty.

It was a scene of unbelievable horror which existed in those days in the bosom of the earth.

A perfect pandemonium underground, in which men and women, sunk far beneath the level of the brute, held hellish revels, blasphemed and cursed, fought, and slew one another, and committed a thousand hideous crimes which never saw the light, and passed unpunished upon earth, only, perchance, to meet with a more awful visitation of divine wrath hereafter.

A poor little child of twelve years old—a poor little half-starved, hardly-used, naked, shivering wretch—born, in the coal-pit, of a mother who died in giving birth to this unfortunate, is the heroine of the story.

Her name was Ruth.

She was a miserable, wretched little child from the very beginning,

Nobody had a kind word for her. Many had much foul abuse, and not a few blows to bestow on her frail little body.

Her father had hated her mother bitterly. It was from the results of the ruffian's violence that the poor woman died, after a premature labour also brought on by his brutality.

The little child she left behind her might, for all its father cared about it, have died of cold and starvation as soon as it came into the world; but a woman working in the pit, who had lost her own child, took compassion on it, and suckled it for awhile.

It had not too much care bestowed upon it, you may be certain. It was brought up chiefly upon kicks and cuffs, and grew to be a very ragged, dirty, shock-headed little girl; a young savage, knowing no God; a hard-mouthed little heathen, leading the life of a dog.

The duty of this miserable little child was to drag along a cart, containing from one to five hundred-weight of coal, a distance of near upon a couple of hundred yards along narrow, low-ceilinged passages.

She was stripped naked to the waist. She wore a kind of belt round her waist, and to it was fastened a chain, which, passing between her legs, was fastened to the cart.

She wore coarse canvas trousers; a candle was fastened to her head to light the way; then she crawled along upon all-fours in the wet and filth, dragging her weary load after her.

It was the life of a beast of burden—not a human creature—but she lived through it. Very often there were frightful accidents. Huge masses of coal fell down and maimed these miserable children.

Sometimes they fell down the shaft. Sometimes they were drowned by the water breaking suddenly in upon them from the old working.

Sometimes they were run over and crushed to death, or frightfully maimed.

Sometimes they were killed by choke-damp.

If they escaped all these evils, they were likely enough to be murdered by their brutal taskmasters, who beat them upon all occasions, with and without cause, and frequently tortured the unhappy children by way of pastime.

It is not to be wondered at, then, that they grew up little devils, some of these children.

The boys and girls herding together indiscriminately, all virtue and modesty was, alas! next to impossible in this hideous haunt of wickedness. Religious instruction was a thing unknown. Right and wrong were but names. It was a horrible life, and it is not very surprising, surely, that Ruth Hardwick grew up a young she-devil, corrupt in heart, unclean in body, utterly shameless and lost.

A frightful accident, by which many lives were sacrificed, called public attention to this particular pit A number of gentlemen descended after the danger was over, to inquire how the accident had occurred; and the state, moral and physical, of the unhappy miners became the subject of a little pity, and a great deal of curiosity.

Some of the gentlemen were very affable and condescending, and questioned the men and women they met with at considerable length. Some provided beer, and some distributed halfpence. There was a celebrated London author among the company, and he took down their statements, and afterwards dressed them up a little for the newspapers.

The boys and girls were delighted with the novelty of the proceedings, and were only too eager to be questioned.

During their explanations, a party of gentlemen came upon an assemblage of those ragged and forlorn creatures, all huddled up in a heap, trying to keep themselves warm.

They all—boys and girls—were dressed alike; all naked to the waist, and wearing rough canvas trousers.

It was next to impossible to distinguish between the sexes; and the gentlemen stared very hard at them, uncertain whether to address one standing a little apart from the rest as "Here, boy," or, "I say, my good girl."

But when the light of the torches, which some of the party carried, came to fall full upon the figure of this child, it turned out to be Ruth.

"It is a girl, I do believe!" one of the gentlemen said, after a long and scrutinizing glance at the plump and comely figure of the little maiden, which, disfigured by dirt and grime though it was, was not entirely destitute of a graceful roundness in its budding charms.

So the gentlemen seemed to think; for they surrounded her, and hemmed her in, and appeared to take a mighty interest in her.

She was by no means bashful, this young slut; and with her hands in her pockets, laughed and chatted with them, as careless of the scantiness of her clothing as though she had been brought up as an artist's model at the school of the Royal Academy, and accustomed to a public display of her figure to a room full of young men.

She laughed and talked as much at her ease as any of those who addressed her; and the fearlessness of her language and premature sharpness of her wits pleased them so much, that one proposed taking her away from the mine, and educating her at his own expense, for the purpose, as he said, of getting her on in life.

Any one, to be told of this, would have thought it a token of the goodness of his heart; would have attributed the action to his charitableness, his benevolence, his philanthropy. But it was due to no such kindly motive.

He was not a charitable man, or a benevolent or philanthropic person.

By no means.

He was a hard-hearted, grinding, and exacting task-master.

A cold-blooded, avaricious man, incapable of one kindly sentiment.

The motive which actuated him was the basest and worst. He had taken a fancy for this poor lost child, and he had determined upon making her his mistress.

Had this been America—had he been a slave-owner, and she his slave, there would have been but little difficulty about putting his vile scheme into execution.

Had he been bent upon her ruin, or the ruin of any other poor friendless child among his slaves, he would have singled her out and taken her away then and there.

But this is a land of liberty, and one cannot trample down the poor—openly.

Therefore he went cautiously to work. He thought, to begin with, he would take her out of the pit, have her suitably attired, educate her a little, civilize her a little, make her companionable, and then ruin her soul and body, and blast her happiness and future hopes.

That was what he proposed to himself very calmly, as he took a pinch of snuff, and he determined to carry out his plan at once.

He had her taken from the pit, and sent her for a time to school. She stayed there, perhaps, a little more than eighteen months, before he sent for her home. Indeed, he had almost forgotten her existence, for he had plenty of other matters to occupy his attention.

When he saw her, though, he was for a moment dumbfounded by the improvement that this shore time had effected in her appearance. When he had first met her, her young charms were, as we have seen, almost entirely obscured by grime and coal dust. She appeared to him now to be perfectly beautiful.

Her beauty, too, had something about it so delicate, so refined, it would have been impossible for any one unacquainted with the fact to have dreamt for a moment that her origin had been so humble a one, and that she had been reared in such a frightful place.

The progress that she had made in her education—the manners that she had acquired—the ease and elegance of her carriage, all caused him the profoundest astonishment.

He could not believe at first that it was the same girl he had taken out of the pit.

He even asked her her name.

But she told him, with a smile and a blush, she was the same Ruth Hardwick; and she kissed his hand, and expressed her deep gratitude for his kindness to her.

What could have made him thus befriend a poor girl like she was? What was there about her—what claim had she on his kindness? Oh, he was too good! She would always love him—like a father.

He didn't at all mind her loving him, but did not much care about filial affection.

She looked up to him, her beautiful blue orbs brimming over with tears of joy.

He looked down upon her with a satyr-like grin; and as he feasted his eyes upon her youthful form, swelling gracefully into a soft voluptuousness of contour, his black soul revelled secretly in a thousand carnal delights his depraved imagination conjured up.

From the very first night that the young and unsuspecting girl took up her abode beneath his roof, this man set out, systematically, and in cold blood, to deprave her mind and seduce her from the paths of virtue.

With the most devilish ingenuity he strove to effect her ruin.

Strange as it may appear, after the horrible childhood she had passed through, he found her virtue unconquerable.

I have said that she was not virtuous when first he saw her—I have said so because that was the accusation levelled against her by her enemies.

It was said that her subsequent modesty, reserve, religion, and conscientious scruples, were only shams and tricks, and that she was acting a part.

Perhaps she was. Anyhow, she could not be blamed, surely, for refusing to sin again, even though she had sinned before.

The man persevered in his villanous scheme. He took her with him to London. He allowed her to taste all the happiness, all the joy that wealth can alone procure. Then he told her one day plumply that she could only enjoy the continuance of such a life at one price—the price of her dishonour!

It was a devilish thing, surely, to do this.

He chose his time well, with an ingenuity quite satanic.

It was one night at the Opera, when they sat together in a box, she attired with a luxuriant splendour to which he had gradually been accustoming her.

As they sat, she gracefully reclining upon the soft velvet-covered cushions, he leaning over her, his arm resting upon the back of her arm-chair, he pointed out to her the gay throng hemming them in, as it were, upon every side.

"Is it not a glorious sight?" he asked.

"It is, indeed," she answered, with a faint sigh.

The man looked at her searchingly beneath his bushy eyebrows.

"What makes you sigh?" he said.

"Did I sigh?"

"Yes."

"I was not aware that I did so."

"But you are aware what thought it was, passing across your mind at that moment, called it forth?"

"No," she said; but presently sighed again.

"Are you not happy, Ruth?"

She looked up at him quickly.

A crimson flush mantled her soft, peachy cheeks.

He could see tears glistening upon the long, drooping lashes which half-concealed her splendid eyes.

He took her hand in his. It trembled like a bird.

"Are you not happy, Ruth?" he said again, seeing that she made no reply to his question

"Oh, can you ask me?" she answered in a choking voice, in which was visible the deepest emotion. "You know that I am happy—very, very happy—and very grateful to you for your great goodness to me!"

"And this life that you have lately been leading pleases you?"

She was silent.

"You can hardly believe in the existence of such misery as that I took you from," he said. "You could not go back to it now, Ruth, could you? What would you do, do you think?"

"I should die!"

"Yes, you are unfit for such a life now, my pretty Ruth. You are very different now to what you were. And even if you had remained the same that you were then, you probably would not have lived very long the horrible life that is led there in that hell upon earth!"

The girl shuddered at the recollection of those bygone horrors, and hid her pale face in her hands.

"Oh, no, no!" she said; "I could never live such a life again—never again! Oh, God bless you, dearest friend, for rescuing me from such awful misery!"

"Do not be alarmed," he said; "there is not the faintest chance of your ever going back: that is, if you only do what any reasonable woman would do in your place."

These were curious words. She pondered over them silently, but could not fathom their meaning. Neither did he offer any explanation.

Just at that moment the curtain drew up again, and as he appeared to be engrossed with the performance upon the stage, she was not able to resume the conversation.

But she could not much longer endure this state of suspense, and before the evening was over she found out a method of leading the conversation round again to the desired place. She asked him then what career he intended for her—how she was to live—what she was to do.

She owned that many times, when she had thought about the vague future in store for her, she had, in spite of all her efforts to the contrary, been borne down by an overwhelming melancholy and foreboding of coming evil.

Then did her companion cautiously set about unfolding his plans to the amazed and horrified girl.

He began by asking her that evening, as they drove home together, whether she could love him.

Love him! There was no necessity for such a question. He could see plainly enough that her heart was already his.

Perhaps, however, she was not so sure of the state of his feelings regarding herself, for she seemed overcome, almost terrified, as it appeared, when first he declared his passion for her.

The strength of her emotions overcame her; she sank back half-fainting upon the cushions of the carriage, gently murmuring his name.

With frenzied eagerness he took the inanimate form of the fair young creature in his arms, and passionately pressed his burning lips upon her lovely face; and, as he muttered a hundred endearing words, showered kisses upon her soft cheeks, and mouth, and fair, white neck.

But, perhaps, when the uncontrollable strength of his devouring passions would have carried him beyond the bounds of reason, the carriage stopped before the door of the house where they lived, and the footman, hastily descending from the box, let down the steps in a great hurry, and compelled his master to accept of his assistance in conveying the insensible young lady to her own room, where the housekeeper applied the necessary restoratives.

When she recovered, the poor girl could scarcely believe in the truth of what had taken place.

He loved her. What happiness! He, of all men in the world! He, the cleverest, the kindest, the best!

She never for a moment dreamt what sort of love it was which he offered her.

She thought that he intended her to be his wife.

She had no idea that he only meant her to be his mistress.

Such was, however, the case; and such she soon learned, to her shame and sorrow.

Her dishonour was to be the price of the love of ease which he proposed to her.

She was to barter that which was dearer to her than life for this wealth and luxury. She was to lead a life of shame and infamy. She was to imperil her immortal soul.

The man who proposed this to her saw no great sacrifice upon her part.

He proposed it cautiously, it is true He broke it to her with as much delicacy as the case allowed of.

She was greatly agitated when she heard him; but he felt in his own mind so certain of her acceptance of his terms, that he was in no great hurry for a reply. He told her, therefore, to take time, and consider of his proposal.

He reasoned to himself, "The girl is not a fool. She will see the advantages of the offer. Let her think it over a little, and she will see what luck she's in."

He, therefore, went and smoked a cigar, and gave her a couple of hours to think the matter over.

Then he sent for her down to his study.

She did not come herself; but her maid brought him a note.

He was very much astonished at this line of conduct; but he did not allow his astonishment to be noticed by the servant. He had a wonderful command over his feelings, and he waited very patiently until she had left the room before he attempted to unfold the paper.

"What the deuce does this mean?" he muttered to himself as he adjusted his double eye-glass.

Then he read the letter through carefully.

"Damnation!"

He sprang up in an awful passion as he reached the last word.

Then rang the bell furiously.

The maid answered it.

"Where's your mistress?"

"Gone out, sir."

"Gone out?"

"Yes, sir."

"When did she go?"

"Five minutes before you rang the bell, sir."

"Where is she gone?"

"I don't know, sir."

"Didn't she say?"

"No, sir."

"What did she say, you fool?"

"She told me to give you that letter."

"Was that all?"

"Yes."

"Go to the devil, then!"

When the servant had closed the door, he stamped to and fro from one end of the apartment to the other like an enraged tiger.

He gnashed his teeth; he clenched his fists; he tore one or two small handfuls of hair out of his head; and he swore until he was black in the face.

"The infamous hussy!"

"The outrageous slut!"

"The insolent baggage!"

Each sentence louder than the last; and each accompanied by a string of oaths that any costermonger might reasonably have felt proud of.

"I'll make her suffer for this!" he cried, buttoning up his coat, with the intention of immediately rushing in pursuit.

But the reflection that he had not the vaguest notion where he ought to go to, restrained him.

"Curse her!" he cried, with a stamp of his foot. "She shall repent this, bitterly! Let her go! I don't care. I won't take any trouble to follow her. I shall hear of her, somehow, before long; I have no doubt of that. And when I do, by ——"

But here he paused again, and changed his mind.

"I will follow her!" he said. "She shan't get away! I'll hunt her down! I will, by heaven! She shall be mine, in spite of all the world!"

But you are wondering what was the meaning of all this. Astonishing as it may appear, the girl had rejected the offer he had made her, and had fled from his protection.

CHAPTER LXXIII.

THE CONTINUATION OF RUTH'S NARRATIVE.

He was determined to possess her.

The thought of the money that he had blindly lavished, in the hope of dazzling and bewildering her, as it were, into sin, made him furious when it recurred to him.

He called himself all the asses and dolts upon the face of the earth, for having allowed her thus to escape out of his clutches.

If he only caught her again, it should not be so.

Bah! The idea of a chit of a girl treating him thus—snapping her fingers at his love, throwing up this splendid chance he had offered her!

It was outrageous!—it was monstrous!—it was positively incredible!

However, he determined not to be foiled. When he found her, she should be his—ay, were he even obliged to resort to brute strength to obtain her.

He straightway set about taking the necessary steps to find her. He had plenty of money at his command; and, with money, there are few difficulties which cannot be overcome.

He set about finding her with the aid of the police.

He lavished his gold on every side, and he was finally successful.

He found that she was living as a governess in a quiet family in Thurlow Square.

He ascertained what were the hours when she was accustomed to go out, and whether she ever went alone.

After ceaseless watching, his infamous agents were rewarded by success.

It was not, however, without a considerable amount of time having been expended for information, that it was discovered, considerably to the discomfort of the conspirators, that Ruth was not in the habit of leaving her employer's house, except it were in company with her employer's children.

Then only for an hour or two in the morning, when they usually walked about in the garden in the middle of the square, very rarely venturing beyond its precincts, and then only going into Kensington Gardens, or Hyde Park.

At either place she was quite unapproachable.

The conspirators were obliged to wait with what patience they could muster.

The head conspirator had no patience at all. His indignation burst forth at every fresh delay; he overwhelmed his agents with virulent abuse, and accused them of defrauding him of his money under false pretences; called them thieves and liars, and vowed fearful vows of vengeance against both them and her.

At length, however, when the uncontrollable strength of his passion, by this time increased into a species of frenzied madness, perfectly unrestrained by the dictates of reason, was urging him on to the commission of some wild, lawless act, that would have placed him most likely in the hands of the authorities, fate threw the poor girl into his clutches.

One night, for some reason or other, which the wretches did not trouble themselves to ascertain the truth of, but which was doubtless simple and innocent enough, Ruth came out by herself alone, and hurried away rapidly down the street.

It was in the hope of such an occurrence that they had been waiting for more than a fortnight past, keeping a cab hanging about in the close vicinity of the house.

She hurried away from the door, and crossed the road towards the railings of the enclosure.

The men watching for her, when they had made certain who it was, lost no time in effecting her capture.

The square was at that time almost entirely deserted.

No help was at hand.

Suddenly, she was seized in a pair of strong arms. Something was flung over her head, so as to muffle her cries and to blind her to the way she was being taken.

Then she was lifted off her feet and carried forcibly away into the cab.

In vain she strove to free herself from the grasp of her captors.

In vain she struggled to make her voice heard.

She was powerless. She was like a baby in

their hands; and once inside the cab, all hope of rescue seemed departed for ever.

When they had got her safely into the interior of the vehicle, they closed the windows and drew down the blinds.

Then, in spite of her sobs and prayers, and passionate supplications and entreaties, they securely fastened her, hand and foot, and threatened her with instant death did she utter one single word, with an attempt at obtaining a rescue, either during their journey or when they reached their destination.

They travelled on for what seemed to the poor, terrified girl the greater part of two hours.

During the whole time, her captors kept down the blinds of the cab, and, save now and then, when one raised a corner of either of the blinds to peep out at the road, she obtained not a glimpse of the neighbourhood through which they were journeying.

Occasionally, however, she could see lights flitting past the side of the cab. Now and then she heard a buzzing sound, added to the noise of many wheels, in close proximity, and then she knew that they must be in some crowded thoroughfare.

Once, by the cab stopping, and by a stray word or two that she heard, she knew that they were passing through a turnpike gate.

After a time, the sound that the wheels made upon the road became more subdued, and she judged, from this circumstance, that they had left the streets, and were upon some country road.

All without was now very dark. They must be passing between hedges at times, she fancied, for what little glimmer of light there otherwise was, was blotted out by some opaque object.

The two men who rode with her in the vehicle had lighted their pipes. They smoked the vilest tobacco, and the fumes from the noxious weed were almost suffocating.

She sat there, though, for a long while, suffering a perfect martyrdom, until, at length, unable any longer to bear it, she begged to be allowed to have one of the windows open a little while.

"What for?" one man asked, gruffly.

"The smoke chokes me."

"Ha! ha! ha!" laughed the person addressed by way of reply.

"What does she say?" asked the other.

"She says the smoke chokes her."

"Does she, Jack? Poor thing!"

And they both burst out laughing.

"Sorry for her," said one, lighting up a fresh pipe.

"Extremely grieved at being disagreeable, miss," said the other.

And having thus spoken with mock politness, the two vagabonds nudged one another in the ribs, chuckled immensely at their own facetiousness, and went on smoking harder than ever.

The unfortunate girl bore it as long as possible.

She felt giddy and sick. She gasped for breath.

But she suffered in silence, preferring rather to have died than to have again appealed to the sympathies of her ruffianly captors.

But the misery she suffered became intolerable.

She could bear it no longer.

She felt her head spinning round, and her senses deserting her.

Gradually she began to slide down, as it were, from the seat Her head fell over on one side.

She fainted.

It is impossible to say whether or not in this helpless condition the unfortunate girl would not have been subjected to some shameful indignity by the wretches who had taken her prisoner, had not the cab by this time arrived at its destination.

"She's swooned," one of the men said.

"Yes," replied the other, raising her up from recumbent position.

"She's a good-looking wench, isn't she?"

"She's what I call a screamer."

"It wouldn't be a bad thing to be the governor, eh?"

"It would be worth a year of one's life!"

"Gad! I think so myself."

"Do you mean it?"

"By the Lord Harry, I do!"

"Then what do you say to——"

"To what?"

"You won't blab if you don't fancy the idea?"

"Not I."

"Honour bright?"

"I'll take my Bible oath——"

"Well, then, what do you say to disappointing the governor?"

"What do you mean?"

"Why, now we've bagged the bird, why should we give it up, if we'd rather keep it ourselves?"

"But there's no point in keeping it, when there's some one else wants it, and will give double the price it's worth."

"Couldn't we sell it to him when the gloss has come off it's pretty feathers?"

"He wouldn't care for buying it then, may be."

"Wouldn't he?"

"I'm afraid not."

"He'd never know anything about it unless we told him."

"Well, we shouldn't be likely to do that."

"Not very, Bill."

"What do you say, then?"

"There's our mate outside."

"What of him?"

"He'll want to go snacks."

"There's no objection to that."

"Very well, then; let's stop the cab."

"Yes, we must be close there by this time; and if we are to do what we say, we mustn't lose more time about it."

But at this moment the cab stopped itself.

The man who was going to call out to the driver had some difficulty in opening the window.

The fainting girl had slid down, as has been said, and the man who had raised her in his arms had placed her inanimate form in such a position that it blocked up the passage of the door.

The delay caused by having to raise her again from this posture, and place her so as to allow him to get by, enabled the driver to get off his box.

By the time that the cab door was opened, the driver had rung the bell at a gate before which the vehicle had stopped.

He rung with a loud jangling noise, which brought, with but a brief delay, somebody out of the lodge to see who was there.

The two conspirators inside the cab muttered curses loud and deep.

Their diabolical plot had failed.

There was no time now to do anything else but to carry out the plans already formed.

It was an old man who answered the bell—a very aged and decrepit individual, who seemed more than half blind, and three parts silly.

Anyhow, he stood a long while scratching his head with one hand, while with the other he held a lantern he carried, close up to the face of the driver; meanwhile staring at the amiable physiognomy thus illuminated with a vacantly idiotic expression of countenance, indicative of very limited intellectual capacity on the part of the starer.

"Don't you know me, stupid?" asked the driver.

"To be sure I do!" responded the old man, presently, with a faint smile of recognition. "I've been waiting for you ever so long — ever so many weeks."

"Is the master in?"

"Yes, I think so."

"Open the gate, then."

The gate was opened accordingly, and the cab proceeded slowly up a long carriage drive, until it came suddenly round the corner upon a quaint Elizabethan mansion, perfectly dark and apparently tenantless.

Here the driver, again descending from the box, applied himself vigorously to ringing the door-bell.

For a long while, however, without causing any visible effect.

Tinkle, tinkle, tinkle.

Jangle, jangle, jangle.

It seemed as though they were trying to raise the dead to life, rather than to awaken a sleeping person.

It was not much more than ten o'clock, but people in the country go to bed early, and the first sleep is usually a sound one.

At length, when the patience of the driver and his two companions was well-nigh exhausted, the door opened, and he whom they had several times, during the conversation upon the road, alluded to as "the governor," made his appearance.

He explained that the old woman, his housekeeper, and the only other person in the house, was stone deaf, and that they might have rang for hours before they could have aroused her from her heavy slumbers.

He himself had been at a distant part of the rambling wilderness of a mansion, for such it was, and he had not heard them at first.

"Well," said he, changing the subject presently, as his eyes alighted, for the first time, upon the cab which had drawn up at some little distance under the shadow of the trees,—"what news have you brought?"

"The best!"

"What do you mean?"

"We have brought something besides news this time."

"You don't mean to say——"

"Yes, we do."

"You have brought the girl?"

"Yes."

"That's lucky! I should have gone away tomorrow. I was weary of waiting in this dreary hole."

The men assisted their employer to take the girl from the cab, and they carried her up-stairs into a room which had apparently been prepared for the purpose, in a distant wing of the building.

There having safely deposited her, the master accompanied his myrmidons down to the door again, paid them the price of their crime, saw them get into their cab and drive away, and stood at the door listening to the sound of the wheels until they died away in the far distance.

Then, with a smile of devilish triumph, he turned, to ascend the stairs to the room containing his helpless victim.

CHAPTER LXXIV.

RUTH'S STORY, CONTINUED.

He paused upon the first step, to gloat his depraved mind upon the victory in store for him.

At last he had been successful!

He had lavished much money, and wasted much time, in obtaining his object; but at length it was obtained, and now he could triumph.

Had it cost him double the money—had he been obliged to waste as much more time as he had already wasted, he would not have hesitated about pursuing the course which he had begun.

No! He had determined that this girl should be his.

He had sworn a fearful oath that he would accomplish his fell purpose; and had it cost him the whole of his fortune—had he been obliged to waste upon the attainment of this end the very last penny he possessed in the world, he would not have hesitated for a moment, but still have pursued the same course.

He was a hard man—a hard, unsentimental, middle-aged man, who had lived until he was forty years old before he had ever conceived any serious passion for living woman.

As often happens with love, when it comes on late in life, it was ten times more powerful than it would have been had it happened twenty years ago.

It had more influence over him, and tempted him to the perpetration of what a short time ago he would have laughed at in others as the grossest of absurdities.

Yes, he loved this woman with a mad, sensual love, which consumed him like a furnace raging in his breast.

As he ascended the stairs, he pictured to himself the hellish delights which he anticipated in triumphing over the honour of this poor defenceless girl.

He thought with unholy rapture of the lovely form, the budding charms, the soft, voluptuous contours of the fair young creature, who had fallen into his clutches.

The anticipation of the triumph which awaited him, sent his blood boiling through his veins, and he rushed madly up the stairs, and flung open the door of the room where he had left the poor girl.

Only to find her gone.

Or so he thought, at first; for, casting his eyes upon the bed where he had left her lying senseless, he saw her not.

With a savage curse, he rushed towards the window, thinking that she might have escaped that way.

But the window was fast.

She had gone by the door, and was somewhere hidden in the house.

He caught up a candle, which he had left upon the table, and rushed out upon the stairs, in pursuit.

It was true she had fled, but not very far.

Released from the suffocating atmosphere of the cab, she had quickly recovered from her fainting fit.

When left alone upon the bed, her senses were not long in returning to her.

She stared in terror round upon the decorations of the room.

It was a large apartment, furnished with rich luxuriance.

It was evidently the property of a rich man.

For what purpose could she have been brought thither?

Into whose hands could she have fallen?

She gazed round upon the decorations of the room with increasing fright and horror, when she discovered their character.

There were many large oil-paintings, exquisitely finished, but all of a character which outraged decency, and were calculated to call up a blush to the cheek of even the most abandoned.

She could no longer doubt with what infamous object she had been kidnapped.

That she had fallen into the hands of some wealthy profligate, or was a prisoner in the abode of some female monster, who made a living out of others' ruin, she felt very certain; and now, or never, was the time to make an effort to escape.

She struggled furiously with her bonds.

The villains had not secured her very effectually. She was not long before she had contrived to free her hands.

When she had done so, the rest was easy.

Therefore, although the master had not been absent from the room more than seven or eight minutes, when he returned she had quitted the apartment, and was flying wildly up-stairs.

Unfortunately for her, the house was in darkness. She had not taken a candle with her, and she could not find the way.

She ran up the stairs, and found herself at the top of a couple of flights upon the landing above.

Here she hoped to discover the door of some room open, and she thought that she would lock herself in the room, and call frantically for help.

But she could find no door, and while she was searching in desperate haste, the man came upstairs again, discovered her flight, and pursued her at once.

The light he carried illuminated the passage and the stairs beyond. For the latter she made at the top of her speed.

He catching sight of her skirt, rushed in pursuit.

In another moment he had overtaken her.

She crouched down in a corner close to the wall, overcome by an overwhelming terror she could not struggle against.

He stooped over her, holding aloft the candle he carried, and with a slight scream she recognised him.

She had never for a moment imagined who it was that had been instrumental in effecting her abduction.

Many and various thoughts had crossed her mind—many evils she had pictured to herself, but not this one.

Now she knew that her case was indeed a bad one.

A man who had not hesitated to commit such a breach of the peace, who had conceived so bold and lawless an act, was not likely to hesitate at any other outrage.

But she thought if there were one way by which she might escape from the terrible fate that she dreaded was in store for her, it was by boldly facing and defying this man in whose clutches she found herself.

Therefore she drew herself up to her full height, the first alarm over, and with fiercely flashing eyes bade him tell her what he wanted, and why he had brought her there.

"Don't you know me, Ruth?" he asked, with a smile.

"I do," she replied coldly.

"You do?"

"Yes."

"And still you ask why it was I brought you hither! Oh, Ruth, you know it was because I loved you!"

"Loved me!" she repeated, with a bitterly scornful accent—"loved me!"

"You know I do," he said. "Had I not, should I have done all that I have done to get you here?"

"And now, what would you do?"

"I would have your love in return."

"You think that your conduct is likely to make me love you?"

"What else would it do?"

"More likely it would make me hate you."

"And you do hate me?"

"Yes."

"Look here, Ruth," the man said, in a hoarse and passionate whisper: "it matters very little what are your feelings towards me. I have sworn to possess you, and, by the heaven above us, I will make good my oath!"

"No," she cried, repulsing him as he strove to take her in his arms; "while I have life, you shall not!"

"We shall see!"

He stooped over her, and encircled her with his strong arms.

Then, in spite of her frantic efforts to prevent him, he raised her from the ground.

The candlestick he had placed upon the ground: in the struggle, it was hurled down the stairs.

The light was extinguished, and the candlestick went bumping down the stairs, one at a time.

She was in hopes that the noise would have alarmed the servants, if there were any in the house, and that they might come to her rescue.

But the deaf old woman slept on, unconscious of the exciting scene occurring within the house, where she supposed her master was comfortably snoring away the hours, as she was herself.

Besides, the old woman's bedroom was at a distant part of the house; and, even had she not been as deaf as she was, she was so very far removed from the scene of the conflict, that in all probability she would not have heard the noise.

The poor girl began to fear that any efforts she might make to obtain assistance would be fruitless.

Probably, she was alone in the house with the villain, but she would try.

Then, summoning all her remaining strength for the effort, she shrieked shrilly for help.

The man, however, irritated by her resistance, clutched her more tightly, and dragged her from her hold of the banisters, at which she had made a grasp, hoping to be able to keep her ground.

"Help! help! help!"

It was useless. No one came.

He dragged her more violently, and her fingers relaxed their hold.

"Help! help! help!"

He did not try to stay her from screaming, because he well knew that her cries were inaudible to the only person within call; and even had they not been so, it was not very likely that the poor, feeble old creature could have helped her.

"Help! help! help!"

Her cries grew fainter.

"Help! help!"

She was hoarse with screaming. She could only weep now, and struggle weakly in the arms of the hard-hearted scoundrel.

He bore her easily down the stairs, and back into the room from which, a few moments before, she had wildly rushed.

She was almost exhausted now; but when he left go of her for a moment, while he made fast the door, she sprang from his side and rushed to the window.

It was strongly bolted. There was no escape that way.

She caught the bell-pulls, and dragged at them till they came off in her hand.

Her captor laughed grimly, knowing well that no human aid could come to her. Then, having fastened the door, he strode across the room towards the spot where she was standing.

But she fled at his approach.

There was a large table in the middle of the room, and he chased her unsuccessfully for a moment or two, until, with an oath, he thrust the table back into a corner of the room, and obliged her to come out from her temporary shelter.

It was sheer madness in her to hope to escape from the despoiler.

She knew there was no escape; and yet, like a timid, panting fawn, she flew round the room, screaming, and bent upon only yielding at the last extremity.

And when the last extremity came, and the poor girl, bruised and panting, sank down to the ground unable to do more, there surely was something in the beseeching pity of those gentle eyes—something in the mute agony of that girlish face, which might have turned the demon from his devilish purpose.

But, alas! it was not so.

The sight of her helplessness, her weakness, but added to his enjoyment, and strengthened his determination.

"She shall be mine!" he muttered to himself. "I have sworn that she shall be mine!"

Her hair hung in luxuriant masses upon her bare shoulders, from which, in the furious struggle, her apparel had been rudely dragged away, as though it had been so much tissue paper.

Her heaving bosom, exposed to view, was white as the driven snow.

The excitement of the chase had lent to her soft peachy cheeks a rosy hue, which at other times was the only charm wanted to render her beauty perfect.

She was, indeed, lovely!

Her face and figure, faultless in the semi-nudity to which his ruffian violence had reduced her, she was a sight to tempt the good Saint Anthony himself.

But to the unscrupulous wretch, in whose Tarquin-like embrace she feebly battled, half-delirious as he was with desire, the blaze of her charms was perfectly maddening.

In vain she prayed upon her knees that he would spare her—that he would take her life, rather. Prayers, tears, and entreaties were thrown away upon him.

He had determined upon the perpetration of this monstrous crime, and she was helpless and powerless, at his mercy.

CHAPTER LXXV.

RUTH'S STORY CONCLUDED.

This poor woman's enemies asserted that none of these things really occurred in the way that has been related.

Her enemies said that she was a designing, shameless creature.

That even while in the mine, and at that tender age, she led an immoral life, and was as depraved in body as in mind. They said that she affected a virtue that she never felt, and that she beguiled the man who ruined her by syren's wiles; and that at length, having got him quite in her power, she forced him into a hateful union, which formed the misery of all his after-life.

He married her, it is true; but that she urged him to do so, is utterly false.

This man, who had behaved so basely and brutally towards her, in reality loved her—loved her not alone with a sensual and debasing passion, but with a deep affection and devotion, which manifested itself hereafter in a desire to make her his wife.

He could find no one whom he could compare to her. No other woman whom he met with in any class of society afforded him such happiness. By her side, the charms of all rivals faded into insignificance.

Therefore he determined upon marrying her, and carried his determination into effect.

They lived happily together for about five years; and during that time the young wife had blessed her husband with four beautiful little girls, all extraordinarily like their lovely mother in the style of face and general resemblance, although the colour of their hair and eyes were dissimilar.

After the first child was born, however, an event occurred which cast a shadow over the young wife's future life, and soon dashed all her dreams of happiness to the earth.

This event was the arrival of a young man in the house, as private secretary to her husband.

He was a handsome, clever young man, to whom her husband had taken a great fancy. He was under some obligations to the father of this young secretary, and was, therefore, anxious to treat the son with every possible kindness.

He gave him, therefore, a very handsome salary; he took him into the house, and behaved to him in every respect just as though the young man had been a member of the family.

As well as he could judge, there was no reason why he should have repented of the kindness thus shown to the young gentleman.

He was extremely assiduous to his duties. He possessed intellectual capacities far beyond the common order. He proved of the very greatest possible use to his employer, who was anxious to obtain a seat in Parliament. When this object was attained, in return for the exertions that the young man had made, his employer increased his salary; and he even went so far as to offer to obtain for him a more lucrative appointment elsewhere, which, although it would be, undoubtedly, to the young man's advantage, would be rather a loss to him individually, as he would thereby lose his services.

But he was quite convinced that Mr. Herbert was one of the worthiest of young men, and did there require to be any further proof of the undoubted truth of the fact, it must have been found when the young secretary refused to leave his employer, or to avail himself of any of the offers which his employer's kindness suggested.

"I shall ever feel deeply grateful for the interest which you have exhibited for my welfare," said the secretary; "but I think that the increase of salary, which you have been generous enough to make for me, has more than compensated for the trifling services which I have been able to render you!"

There was, perhaps, a little too much humility about the wording of this speech, and about the tone in which it was delivered, and the low, deferential bow which accompanied it, to please a fastidious taste.

But the employer found no fault with it, and he shook the young man warmly by the hand, and thanked him again and again for his generous self-sacrifice; resolving, though, in his own mind that it should not go unrewarded.

Meanwhile, the very humble and most deserving young man had also arrived at a similar resolution.

He had no intention of going unrewarded.

He had set a price upon his services. He had determined upon a reward.

That reward was no less than the love of his master's wife.

It was a most infamous scheme.

He had not the faintest excuse for thinking that she loved him. Indeed, he had positive proof to the contrary. He knew that upon several occasions she had manifested a decided distaste for his society.

But he was by no means dispirited by these tokens of her disapproval. He forced his company upon her at all times and places. He pursued her unremittingly, and in spite of all rebuffs, determined upon effecting her ruin.

She knew that her husband esteemed Mr. Herbert's services very highly, and that he was anxious to make his home happy to the young man who had exerted himself so much in his behalf.

For that reason, she exerted herself to the utmost to show that she also was grateful to him.

But she could never like him. There was something, she fancied, so deceitful and underhand in his manner. That he was in his heart a traitor and a villain she had no doubt, yet she never dreamt what was the truth.

When at last she discovered his secret, she was overwhelmed with confusion and terror.

What could she do? To whom could she appeal?

Decidedly the best and wisest course would have been to have told her husband all about it, and to have appealed to him for protection; but she thought that she must have been mistaken, that she had misunderstood Herbert's words, and placed a wrong construction upon his behavour.

Very soon, though, when, growing bolder, he told her that he loved her, and implored her to fly with him, she saw that there could be no mistake; that he was, indeed, a double-faced villain, as she had supposed him to be, and that she stood in a position of great danger.

She dreaded to appeal to her husband for his protection, because she thought that he would imagine her to be prejudiced against Mr. Herbert. Several times before, when she had intimated that she doubted the sincerity of the secretary's professions, in various matters of business, her husband had become very angry, and had called her words folly.

Now, she thought, if she told him of the insult that had been offered to her, he would not believe that she was blameless.

She hesitated, therefore, allowed the opportunity to escape, and was lost.

The longer she delayed making the confession, of course, the more difficult did it become.

Once having permitted him to talk to her with impunity of his unlawful love, she rendered him more daring for the future, until it became at last a continual struggle between the young wife and the tempter.

She was not, however, one very likely to fall an easy victim to his wiles.

Basely betrayed and brutally outraged as she had been, by the man whom she now called lord and master, it is not to be expected that she could esteem or love him greatly after what had occurred.

But she had married him, and she had sworn to be faithful to him; and she determined, with her life, to keep her vow.

Her husband was an obstinate, violent man, and she knew that he was almost impervious to reason when he lost his temper.

He was also of an extremely jealous disposition, and she dreaded the outburst of wrath which she knew must accompany the discovery of Herbert's treachery and its object.

One night the husband received a letter summoning him immediately to town (they were living then in the country), and he refused to take his wife with him, as he said that the fatigue would be too much for her, and that he would return again by the first train in the morning.

"I will leave you in charge of Mr. Herbert," he said. "You could not be in better hands, my dear."

She shuddered when she heard him, but made no reply.

"You look poorly, Ruth," said her husband, anxiously. "Go to bed early, my dear, and take care of yourself."

He wished her good-bye, and departed almost immediately afterwards.

She was left there alone in the house, with only the servants and the children, and the man who would have effected her ruin.

The station where the husband was to meet the express train that was to bear him to London was distant not much more than a mile from the house, so that altogether a storm was evidently brewing, and would burst forth with violence at no very distant period. The wife was in great hopes of the dog-cart arriving at its destination before the rain came on.

The storm was coming on when the husband left the house.

Already there had been several vivid flashes of lightning, illuminating the surrounding country with a ghastly glare

About five minutes after the door had closed upon her husband, the house was shaken almost to its foundation with a terrible peal of thunder, that rattled and clattered among the window frames as though the house was soon to be shaken about their ears.

The young wife ordered the blinds to be drawn down, and the windows closed, and she sat in her own room, endeavouring to while away the time by the perusal of some favourite work of fiction, determined that, if possible, she would avoid any conversation with Mr. Herbert.

While thus engaged, and just before she thought of retiring to rest for the night, which was, however, at a very early hour, the servant came to tell her that Mr. Herbert would be very glad of a few moments' conversation with her, should she be disengaged.

She sent her compliments in reply, and said that she was indisposed.

Shortly afterwards, her maid came to inquire whether she could be of any assistance in preparing her for her couch.

The mistress replied in the negative, and the maid, having arranged certain articles of apparel upon the chairs and the bed, prepared to leave the room.

As she laid her hand upon the door-handle, her mistress called to her.

"Mary!"

"Yes, madam."

"It is very warm here, is it not?"

"It is very warm, ma'am."

"Are the windows shut?"

"Yes, ma'am, you told me to shut them."

"Open one again."

The servant approached one of the windows, and began to undo the fastening of the shutters.

"Not that one," she said. "Open the one that leads on to the balcony."

This balcony communicated with Mr. Herbert's bedroom. This fact, and the whole of the dialogue just recorded, was remembered presently, and a construction placed upon it most infamous to the poor lady, as will be presently seen.

The young wife sat alone reading for a long time, in the position in which her maid had left her when she quitted the apartment.

The rain by this time had ceased. The air coming through the open casement, laden with the odour of the sweet honeysuckle which clustered thickly round about the window and verandah outside, was delightfully refreshing.

Scarcely a sound was audible in the quiet country, until at length a distant church clock chimed the hour of twelve, and startled her from a reverie into which she had fallen unconsciously, allowing her book to lie unheeded upon her lap.

She rose at the sound, and laid aside her book.

Then commenced her toilet for the night.

It was, indeed, a beautiful sight to see this lovely creature in the rich luxuriance of voluptuous *neglige*, when, unfastening the loose wrapper which she wore, she allowed it to slide gently downwards from her white and rounded shoulders over her taper waist and her splendidly-modelled form, till it reached the carpet, and lay wreathed around her feet.

As she stood before the glass, she raised her white arms in the air, let loose her golden ringlets, and tossing back her head with the proud motion of an Arab steed, let the silky locks fall like water upon her snowy neck, burying the swelling globes of purest alabaster in the flood.

Well might she have been tempted to regard herself complacently as she stood there in her queenly beauty, the magnificent charms of her faultless form exposed with all the fearless abandonment of unsuspecting innocence.

Well did she know that she was lovely. It would have been necessary for her to have lost the use of her eyes and of her senses not to have known that she was one of the most perfectly formed and intoxicatingly lovely of human creatures.

Perhaps, when she reflected upon the amount of temptation, she was almost inclined to look somewhat leniently upon the sins of those who desired to possess that fair person.

She was thinking then, in rather a tender mood, upon the misplaced love of this young secretary, and the pain that it would be to him to find his case was so hopeless, if he really loved her, when she was disturbed by a slight noise in the room behind her.

She turned hastily round, and uttered an exclamation of terror.

She looked in the direction of the open window.

A dark object stood betwixt her and the moonlight; and, although the lights upon the dressing-table brightly illuminated her own figure, that of the intruder was enveloped in obscurity.

Her first thought was that her husband had returned, and that he had entered the apartment by the door, without her having heard his approach.

But the next moment she recollected that, just before commencing her toilet, she had, as was her custom, locked the bedroom door.

A second glance, too, at the intruder, assured her that it was not her husband who had returned.

The person who stood there had come by the window, and he was none other than the Mr. Herbert who had vowed that she should be his.

Two thoughts immediately rushed through the brain of the terrified woman.

Two emotions agitated her breast.

The first was one of confusion and shame at the undressed state in which the young man had found her, and to remedy which, with a woman's instinct, she caught at the hangings of the bed, and twisting them round her, strove as much as lay in her power to screen herself from the gaze of the lawless eyes which were fixed in passionate desire upon her.

The second emotion was one of overwhelming terror, as the thought occurred to her that she was locked in the room with this man, and at his mercy.

Her presence of mind for a brief period deserted her, though not for long.

She summoned all her courage and resolution to her aid, and turned upon him with flashing eyes.

She said nothing, but looked sternly at him, and the young man cowered beneath her indignant glance.

He hesitated, and trembled slightly, apparently half-inclined to beat a hasty retreat, evidently very much ashamed of himself, and at a loss to know how to act, and in what way he ought to proceed, to keep the advantage which he had gained.

"Ruth!" he said at last, in a trembling voice.

But she made no reply, and looked as though she had not heard him.

"Ruth!"

Still no answer, although he spoke in an appealing, supplicating tone, which thrilled distinctly to the furthermost limits of the apartment.

"Ruth!"

"What do you want?" she inquired, suddenly and harshly. "What are you doing here? How dare you enter this apartment?"

"Oh, forgive me!" the young man exclaimed, clasping his hands together, and flinging himself upon his knees before her,—"forgive me, dearest, most beautiful of women! My love was too strong for me. I have striven in vain to wrestle with it. Oh, forgive me, and have pity on me!"

"What do you mean?" she asked, coldly.

"Oh, Ruth, look not at me thus! Your eyes kill me! Oh, be human! Grant me a little of that love, of which you are so prodigal with him who values it so little. Dearest Ruth, frown not upon my suit; despise me not for thus humiliating myself before you! Ruth, I love you more than my life, and without you I shall die!"

"Die, then!" she answered, fiercely. "What are your life and love to me?"

She said these words so bitterly, vindictively even, that the young man shrank back from her.

But the contemptible position which he had assumed there, grovelling at her feet, seemed all at once to occur to him, and he appeared to make up his mind to adopt different tactics.

Springing to his feet, he caught her fair form in his arms, and as he pressed her heaving bosom to his heart, in spite of her angry struggles, covered her blushing cheeks with burning kisses.

But while she was wrestling with him, they were suddenly alarmed by a noise at the window.

The young man desisted from his violence, and moved hastily in that direction.

With a couple of strides he reached the balcony. There he found himself face to face with a man.

Her husband!

This very unexpected appearance was to be accounted for in this manner. The husband had proceeded by the train to the next station on the way to town, when he suddenly discovered that he had left at home some papers which were positively necessary in the business that he was about to transact. He thought at first of telegraphing for them to be sent after him, but he had the key of the secretary in which they were kept, and he did not like the idea of his private papers being overlooked.

He therefore determined upon returning himself. He came back by the next train, having had to wait some length of time for it.

Arriving at home, he proceeded at once to Herbert's room.

Having knocked, and received no answer, he entered, and found the room empty, but the light burning upon the table.

Supposing that Herbert was smoking upon the balcony, which it was his habit to do, the husband went out in search of him.

Then he saw that there was a light in his wife's room, and that the window was open.

And he heard voices murmuring—one, a man's.

With a beating heart he drew near. At that moment his wife was struggling in the treacherous villain's arms.

The husband's fury grew beyond all control, and he was about to rush in upon them, when Herbert turned and met him.

They stood there silently. No words were required.

The husband motioned with his hand for him to stand upon one side.

He seemed as though he had the greatest difficulty in restraining himself from seizing the villain by the throat, and hurling him over the balcony upon the flags beneath.

But he had reserved some other fate for him, and he did restrain himself, and pass him by.

But the wife, seeing her husband, sprang forward with a joyful cry.

"Thank God for this!" she said. "Thank God, you are returned!"

Then she would have flown into his arms.

But, as she advanced, with one cruel blow he struck her senseless at his feet.

Then seizing a box from a side-table, containing his pistols, he followed Herbert to his room.

"There is only one way of settling this matter," said the husband: "we must fight!"

"Willingly," replied the other. "When?"

"Now!"

"Where?"

"Here!"

"The whole house will be alarmed; let us go out into the park. It is beautifully light—as light as day."

They proceeded, without another word, out of the house and down the avenue, to a spot which the husband selected.

Then, having loaded the pistols and taken their positions, at a signal which they had previously agreed upon, they fired.

The lover fell beneath his antagonist's shot, and rolled over upon his face, groaning horribly, and bleeding at the mouth.

The husband stooped over him, to ascertain what injury he had sustained, and whether the wound was likely to prove fatal; and, while thus engaged, a white figure burst through the trees, and stood before them.

It was the wife.

Pale and terror-stricken, but with a face which bore the marks of the savage blow he had dealt her, the poor woman had come to see what harm had befallen her husband, and to endeavour, if possible, to prevent the shedding of blood.

But her husband met her with a scornful laugh.

"Look!" said he, pointing to the prostrate form of the man upon the grass—"there he is!"

"Dead?"

"No, but he soon will be. You are just in time to see him breathe his last."

"Oh, heaven! how horrible!" exclaimed the wife. "How he has been punished!"

"And you," retorted the husband, fiercely—"what fate do you deserve?"

"Oh, husband!" she cried, beseechingly, "you do not believe me guilty—surely you do not believe me guilty?"

"What else am I to believe, after what I saw?"

"You are mistaken—indeed, you are mistaken!"

"Pooh! What do you take me for? Do you suppose I am so easily gulled?"

The wife covered her face with her hands, and sobbed violently.

Presently, though, she drew herself up erect.

"I swear that what I say is true!" she cried, vehemently. "That wretch forced his way into my apartment, and had it not been for your timely intervention, I should have fallen a victim to his violence."

"And it was not at your invitation that he came?"

"No, by heaven, it was not!"

"Oh, if I could believe this!" said the husband, evidently more than half convinced already.

But at that moment the dying man struggled up into a half-sitting posture, and beckoned to him to draw near.

The husband approached reluctantly, and bent over him with an expression of hatred and disgust.

"I want to speak to you," said the dying man. "My time is growing very short, and I have a confession to make before I die."

The husband impatiently motioned to him to proceed.

"I cannot die in peace," said Herbert, in a choking voice, "without begging for your forgiveness! I have been an ungrateful wretch! I have bitten the hand that fed me!"

"Speak!" cried the husband, impatiently. "Tell me at once, is what my wife says true—is all the blame on your side?"

The dying man was silent for a time, for he seemed to be suffering excruciating agony.

When he was able to speak again, he resumed.

"Alas! I cannot die with a lie upon my lips!" gasped the wounded man. "Why must you ask me?"

"Answer me at once!" cried the husband, fiercely.

"We were both to blame," said the other,—"both equally culpable! But, oh, forgive her! Do not wreak your vengeance upon her also! Let this deed that has been done atone for the sin of both!"

The wife, who had listened to these words, paralyzed with horror at the atrocious wickedness of the wretch who could thus die with so black a falsehood upon his lips, now sprang forward.

"It is false!" she cried,—"it is false! He does this to be avenged upon me! Oh, man! if you have any pity in your soul, unsay the words that you have said, and clear me from this imputation before my husband, here, as I am clear before heaven!"

But the dying man, meeting her gaze with a smile of bitter hatred and intense triumph, was silent.

"Is this true that you are saying?" asked the husband, sternly. "Surely you would not go to your God with such an awful lie upon your lips—if it is a lie?"

"It is the truth!" replied the other. "I swear it is the truth—upon my soul!"

Then, rolling over upon his face again, another paroxysm seemed to seize him; and in a few moments more he was a corpse.

* * * * *

Little more of this terrible story now remains to be told.

Nothing more, save that the wife was driven from her husband's house, a ruined and disgraced woman.

Nothing, but that the father disowned his three youngest children, acknowledging only Florence, the eldest, whom he brought up in the expectation of being his heiress

Nothing more need be told about the mother, who died shortly afterwards of a broken heart

Of her children, however, more must be told hereafter.

"And that is all the tale," said Ruth, when she had concluded the narrative which I have told in different words above,—"that is all the tale. You were the husband, and my poor mother the wife!"

CHAPTER LXXVI.

FATHER AND DAUGHTER.—THE OLD MAN REPENTS.—ROBBING THE DEAD.—THE DOOR BURST OPEN.—THE THIEF DETECTED.

WHEN Ruth had concluded her story, a silence ensued which endured for some moments.

The old man was the first to break it.

He rolled to and fro uneasily upon his bed, waving his right hand feebly, as though he would by these means repel the facts that the woman stated.

Or perhaps it was a method which he adopted to express his dissatisfaction and disbelief of what she stated.

"No, no!" he said, impatiently—"no—no!"

"What do you mean?" she asked, abruptly.

"It is not true!" he replied. "What you state has no foundation in truth!"

"What have I said that is untrue?"

"All of it!"

"You lie, old man!" Ruth cried with vehemence. "I wonder that you dare do such an act of foul injustice to the memory of the woman you have so shamefully wronged!"

"What wrong was there in what I did? I made her ample reparation afterwards."

"What do you mean?"

"Married her."

"Yes, yes; I know that. But that was not the part of the story to which I was alluding."

"To which, then?"

"To your conduct after Herbert's death."

"What would you have had me do?"

"What did you do?"

"I allowed her sufficient to live upon, and money to educate her children."

"Your children!"

"Her children, and——"

"*Your* children, I say!"

"And to bring them up to some useful employment."

"And they were to work for their bread, whilst the fourth child was reared in affluence?"

"The fourth child I believe to be my own."

"As they all were. I swear before heaven that my poor mother was innocent!"

"Well, well! perhaps she was."

"What! And you coolly say that, and then make a will by which you leave your other three children paupers?"

"If she wanted money, why did she not apply to me? She refused to accept what I offered."

"It was natural enough, when you so falsely accused her—it was natural enough that she should have preferred rather to starve than to taste the bread that you bestowed upon her."

"She was wrong."

"Wrong?"

"Yes."

"Why so?" asked Ruth, with a scornful accent.

"Because she ought to have considered her children."

"Did you consider them?"

"I tell you I allowed her sufficient to educate them, and bring them up properly."

"A miserable pittance!"

"It was quite sufficient for the purpose."

Ruth laughed scornfully.

"When I found her once in great distress and very ill, I offered to take the children from her, and release her of the burden of their support; but she refused. I brought the children down here. They were about seven or eight years of age at that time. I hired a governess, and would have educated them here, if she had been willing."

"But she was not?"

"No. She stole the children away, and I heard no more of them!"

"You made no inquiries, perhaps?"

"Not I! Why should I? I had done all I could, and what I had done was thrown away."

"My mother refused to live with you?"

"Yes; I asked her to do so, but she refused to be forgiven."

"Why should she be forgiven, when she had done no wrong?"

"Well, well!" cried the old man impatiently; "I can't argue the matter now. I thought that the children were dead, or I should have done something for them."

At that moment there came a loud knocking at the door.

Those without were tired of waiting, and demanded admittance.

Ruth bent over the old man, and took his hand in hers.

"Father," she whispered, "they are not all dead, for I am living. Heaven has sent me here at this time with a good purpose!"

"My eyes are very dim," the old man said in a faint voice; "I cannot see your face distinctly. Draw up the blind, and let in more light."

Ruth rose hastily to obey him.

The knocking at the door, which had ceased for a moment, was again resumed.

Lady Florence's voice was heard.

"Open instantly!" she said. "I must come in to my father. You shall remain alone with him no longer!"

"Another five minutes, and I will let you in," replied Ruth.

"Open directly!" said the other.

"Three minutes more!"

"No, no!—open at once!"

"Yes—in a minute!"

"Open, I say!"

Ruth made no answer, but returned to the bed.

"Open, I say!" cried the lady outside.

But the other did not respond.

She well knew that if she allowed this opportunity to escape her, she would not again be able to hold any communication with the dying man.

"I will break open the door!" cried the enraged lady without.

But the door was an extremely solid one, strongly barred and protected upon the inside.

Ruth fancied that it would be a very difficult matter to force an entrance, and it was an operation that would require a considerable length of time to effect.

She, therefore, sat down again by the old man's side with the utmost deliberation, and resumed the conversation where she had broken it off.

"Can you see me now, dearest father?" she asked in gentle accents.

The old man strained his eyes, and raised himself up as much as he was able, to get a better view of her.

But his efforts were fruitless.

"No, no!" he said; "I cannot see you. All is confusion! My sight is gone!"

"Poor father! But does not my voice remind you of my mother?"

"Yes, yes—it does."

"You thought so when first you heard it?"

"I thought I knew the voice."

"But you cannot see me?"

"No, no! But are you like your mother also in your face, as you are in your voice?"

"I am very much like a picture that I have of her."

"Is your hair light-coloured?"

"Yes, and my eyes are blue."

"Are you handsome, child?"

"So I am told."

"Handsomer than Florence?"

"I think so."

"But why did you not come before? Where are your sisters?"

"I know nothing of them; and they, too, do not know where to find you. It was chance which guided my steps to-day."

"But it is too late now to change my will. I feel that I am going fast. I could not hold out as long."

"Let me feel your pulse, father. Yes, it is very weak. There is no time to be lost!"

As she spoke, she approached the table, and, taking up a pen, began to write upon a piece of paper.

"If he can sign this," she muttered, "all will be well."

But the old man began to exhibit some very alarming signs of approaching dissolution.

A greenish-greyish shade seemed to have passed over his face.

His features appeared to have become all at once rigid and fixed.

He laboured with his breath.

Ruth regarded him with terror.

"Perhaps it is even now too late," she muttered; and at the same time she plied her pen with even greater rapidity than before.

In a few moments she had completed her task.

Then she approached the bed, and looked at the old man eagerly.

But when her eyes fell upon him she started back in terror, and uttered a faint scream.

He lay perfectly motionless.

Was he asleep?

No! This must be the sleep of death!

She laid her hand upon his heart. It had ceased to beat.

She listened for his breath.

Not the slightest indication of it was audible.

He must be dead!

She flung the paper upon which she had been writing upon the floor, and, with a passionate ejaculation, stamped her heel upon it.

"Thwarted!" she exclaimed. "Thwarted at last! Fool that I was to delay it so long! What is to be done?"

She cast her eyes rapidly round the room as she spoke.

"There must be money here!" she said aloud. "He keeps some of it in one of those boxes here, I'll wager my life!"

But Lady Florence, who had gone away from the door to obtain assistance, for the purpose of breaking it open, returned now with the lawyer, and a labouring man who had chanced to make his appearance upon the high road.

"Open the door!" cried her ladyship in a loud voice.

But Ruth returned no answer.

"Open the door—open the door!"

"Where does he keep his money?" Ruth thought. "Which of the boxes? It must be one!"

"Open the door!" cried the lady's voice without, and then she was heard to give an order to the labourer to commence breaking it open.

Ruth went to the boxes in turn, and tried the lids.

There were two of them, one standing upon each side of the bed.

Both were locked.

"Which shall I try?" Ruth asked herself. "There isn't time to try both"

There was not much time, certainly. Loud blows fell upon the panels.

Ruth hesitated for a moment, and soon decided.

The one with the physic bottles must be the box containing the money. Now for the key!

She went at once to the bed, and groped eagerly under the pillow.

As she expected, the key was there.

"Now for it!" said she—and she ran round to the box.

With one sweep of the hand, she flung all the bottles and glasses which stood upon the box-lid on to the ground.

They fell with a loud crash, which caused the blows without to be repeated with increased violence.

Ruth flung up the lid.

She saw within a couple of bags.

She raised one.

It was heavy.

She hastily undid the string at the top, which was lightly fastened.

She saw the glittering gold.

"Now for it!" she cried. "Where can I conceal it? How can I carry it?"

But at that moment the door burst open, and Lady Florence rushed into the room.

CHAPTER LXXVII.

RUTH'S PERPLEXITIES.—THE STRUGGLE BETWEEN THE SISTERS.—A PAINFUL SCENE.

Ruth had determined that she would, if possible, have made off with money.

The reader may perhaps suppose that her motive for this proceeding was merely that which prompts the generality of dishonest persons to appropriate to themselves the goods and chattels appertaining to their neighbours.

But such was not exactly the state of the case in this instance.

It must be remembered that upon her own showing—and upon this occasion, although the lady's veracity as a general rule was far from being reliable, we must take it for granted that what she said was true—she was entitled to a share of the property of the deceased, who was, when living, undoubtedly possessed of immense wealth.

Under these circumstances, you might suppose that she need not have sought to commit this crime, but could have put in her claim in the regular way, and would then, in all probability, have obtained a very handsome fortune.

But if by the commission of this theft she knew for a positive certainty that she would forfeit all hope of sharing in her father's money, and that the share thus forfeited would have greatly ex-

ceeded the sum that she was stealing, yet she would have stolen it still could she have effected her purpose.

This may appear to be at first very contradictory.

But it is easily explained.

I have already said that she was most anxious to escape from England.

At any price, it was necessary that she should leave London in the course of a few days.

She wanted to go back to it to fetch away a number of articles which belonged to her, and which were lying at the house in Belgravia.

She had hesitated more than once whether or not she should go back at all.

She knew that her life was in danger every moment that she passed in the same city that contained so many of her enemies.

But she could not quite summon up sufficient resolution to sacrifice her dresses and trinkets.

No. 30.—Ruth.

It is in the same way that we hear of persons, when their house is on fire, going back again and again through the flames, hoping to be spared until they shall have been able to rescue first this or that valued article, until at last the roof falls down upon and crushes them, or the walls topple over and bury them beneath, or the staircase gives way and cuts them off from liberty and life.

Thus this woman, who possessed a strength of mind and character and reasoning power of a very high and unusual order, was about to sacrifice herself for the sake of a few jewels and some pretty frocks, which she might surely have dispensed with under the circumstances.

It was, however, to enable her to leave England as soon as possible that she wished to appropriate this money.

Even if she got no more from any other source, there was sufficient here to enable her to live at her ease for some considerable time.

It depended upon herself, and whether she was careful and economical. Who knows? she might make it last for several years.

And then she was young and very beautiful; and youth and beauty have their value in the money market.

She had hoped to have been able to have induced her lover, the Prince, to have advanced a sum sufficiently large to have enabled her to leave England and live abroad.

But that very unfortunate circumstance of Captain Charley Crockford's having been discovered taking his lunch so very coolly in the lady's carriage entirely spoilt her game.

Not only had she lost the Prince as a powerful friend, but she had made him a bitter enemy.

She knew his character well enough.

He was proud, and passionate, and revengeful.

He stood very much upon his dignity, and when that dignity was ruffled, there was scarcely anything that was too mean or too cruel for him to resort to, with the intention of thereby wreaking his vengeance upon those who had offended him.

She had no hope of obtaining help from him, and she thought of him now as only another reason why she should fly from London.

Yes, she must escape.

Oh, how she longed for liberty—for the free open air—for change of scene!

She must get away from all this horrible life.

She had thought so much during the last few days, that she felt confident the excitement and anxiety she must have suffered must have had a detrimental effect upon her beauty.

She thought with terror that if this lasted much longer she might become prematurely grey. She might grow old long before her proper time; her roses fade, her bright white teeth discolour, her plump cheeks grow thin, her fair bosom wither, and her milk white flesh grow wrinkled.

She might, in short, become ugly.

Then what would become of her?

While she was beautiful she was powerful.

Her beauty gone, there would be nothing left her but death, she thought.

She could not bear to live if she were ugly, she had often said to herself.

No; if it came to that she would commit suicide.

But I left her some time since, with the gold in her hand, thinking how she was to conceal it and get it clear out of the house.

At the moment that she stood with the bag of gold in her hand, and just as she was about to conceal it hastily under her shawl, the door burst open.

It was Lady Florence who entered.

At the first glance, she saw the position in which affairs were standing.

She saw that the woman before her had broken into the old man's strong box.

She saw also that the old man was lying back upon the bed, apparently dead.

She scarce paused for a moment to dwell upon these details.

Then she rushed forward, and laid hold of the would be thief.

At the same moment she uttered a loud cry for help.

As, however, Crockford and the lawyer below thought that, as yet, she had not been able to force an entrance into the bedroom, and was merely crying out in a state of hysterical excitement, the result of baffled rage, they did not come up-stairs directly.

The labourer also contented himself with staring in at the door with a face which expressed the blankest terror and amazement.

Lady Florence, therefore, was left alone, unassisted, to struggle with the robber.

In another moment after her ladyship was convinced of Ruth's treachery, the two women were locked in each other's arms.

Ruth, grasping the bag which contained the gold, endeavoured to retain possession of it.

Lady Florence, clinging to her sister with one arm round her waist, strove with the other to tear the bag from her grasp.

Yes; they were sisters, and yet were thus opposed to each other in bitter strife.

There could be no doubt of their relationship. The resemblance between them was striking.

They had both the same expression of face, the same coloured eyes, the same class of features.

Both possessed the same exquisite style of beauty, and the same faultless symmetry of form.

Only one difference was there between them: Lady Florence's hair was black as the raven's wing, while that of Ruth resembled so much floss silk, the brightest and most beautiful golden locks.

They formed a beautiful sight, although a sad one, thus flushed, and angry, and contending.

Had one not known them to be sisters, and blushed to see them thus opposed to one another in a deadly feud, it would have been almost impossible to have regretted that this struggle should take place, as it had afforded an opportunity of seeing these fair creatures under circumstances which tended materially to enhance their natural loveliness.

The exertion had heightened their colour. Their cheeks glowed with burning blushes, which also suffused their swan-like necks; and, in the case of Lady Florence, whose dress had become slightly disordered about the throat, covered her fair bosom with a rosy tint.

It does not, you will say, in these days of crinoline, tend to the increase of gracefulness, for ladies to romp and gambol.

It is almost indispensable that their movements should be slow, gliding, and swan-like, if they want to look to advantage; for hasty movements are nearly certain to result in a disarrangement of drapery the very reverse of elegant, and which the more scrupulous might be inclined to term, and not without reason, shamefully indecent.

But at the time of which I write, steel petticoats had not yet been introduced The fulness of Ruth's dress, which surrounded her like a sea, undulating gracefully with every motion of her body, was caused by a number of under petticoats, which nearly rivalled those of a ballet dancer.

Thus, then, as the two beautiful women, struggling fiercely for the mastery, strove each to obtain her object, they fell into attitudes which displayed the splendid modelling of their forms, their garments clinging to their shape, while the unwonted exercise lent, as I have said, a new charm to their beauty, which made it perfectly dazzling.

But the combatants had no such thoughts as these.

They would not, at this moment, have been at all likely to notice each other's beauty, even had they been able to do so under more favourable circumstances; but it is very difficult to perceive any beauty in those whom we dislike.

They knew not that they were sisters, it is true; but had they known it, I do not think that they would have been any more likely to love each other.

No! they hated each other, to commence with; hated each other with a woman's hate, which is much more powerful than a man's, and much more easily provoked.

They struggled desperately on, and for some time it would have been extremely difficult to have hazarded a guess at the probable termination of the contest.

But, before long, it became evident that Ruth was the strongest of the two, and that she would soon be the master.

Before long, she had shaken off the other's hold, and flung her violently back.

Then, had there been no other obstacle to her escape, she was at liberty to fly, as far as Lady Florence's opposition was concerned.

But even if she had got past the labouring man keeping guard, as it were, upon the stairs, and waiting only to receive orders before he rushed in and secured her, she could not possibly have hoped to have got off with her booty without the interference of the doctor, and perhaps, also, of Captain Crockford, for she was not certain that he would side with her, as he seemed to have been previously acquainted with Lady Florence.

For a moment, though, she thought that she would make the attempt, and was moving towards the door, resolved to buy the aid of the working man by a handful of sovereigns scattered upon the stairs, which she felt pretty certain he would stop and pocket, rather than lose the opportunity by running after her.

Full of this idea, therefore, she was turning to fly, when an object met her gaze which filled her with sudden horror.

In the bed before her, her father was sitting up.

His arms were stretched out towards her, and his empty fingers grasped the air.

His eyeballs were dilated;—his lower jaw had dropped.

He looked hideously ghastly.

Ruth uttered an exclamation of fear, and stood stock still, gazing at him with wide-opened eyes, and parted lips.

Was it her father returned to life? Was it his spirit come to rebuke her?

But then reason came to her aid, and she knew that she had been mistaken just now when she thought that he was dead.

It is difficult to say whether the old man had sufficient sense left to know what was passing in the room, or whether he still retained enough of his weakened power of vision to be able to see who were the persons struggling at the other end of the room.

But he comprehended enough to know that something was wrong, and he had strength enough left to scream out for assistance.

"Help! help! help! help!"

Then Lady Florence added her cries to those of her father, until the building echoed with their voices.

The rustic, who hitherto had held himself aloof from the scene of action, now began to think that it was perhaps time that he interfered.

He therefore threw himself between Ruth and the door, and spread out his arms to prevent her passing by.

Whether or not she would have attempted to do so is uncertain, had she not heard steps approaching up the stairs

Next moment the little lawyer rushed into the room, followed by Captain Crockford

Ruth saw now plainly enough that the game was up.

She therefore took a seat, and hastily laid the money down by the side of her upon a small table.

But the sack which contained it being extremely heavy, overweighted the table, and falling to the ground with a crash, the string fastening the top of the sack gave way, and the sovereigns were scattered far and wide upon the floor.

"Heyday!" cried the little lawyer; "what's all this noise about?"

"That woman—she—she has been trying to rob my father!" gasped Lady Florence.

"You don't mean that, surely!" exclaimed the little man.

"Send for the police!" continued her ladyship; "and secure her!"

The little man looked slightly embarrassed.

He did not see his way very clearly. Ruth was such a very beautiful lady, magnificently attired, and he did not dare to lay his hand upon her.

There was, to tell the truth, something very wicked about the beautiful lady's eyes, which terrified him not a little.

"I shouldn't like to offend her," thought the little man to himself.

Then he added aloud, "I trust that we shall be able to manage matters satisfactorily."

"The woman is mad!" said Ruth, disdainfully.

"Ma'am?" said the lawyer.

"She speaks about my robbing her father, and wants you to send for the constables! Perhaps it may surprise her to hear that I have as much right in this house as she has!"

The little man looked astonished.

Lady Florence smiled contemptuously, but was silent.

"Her ladyship," said the little man, with a half bow, and a wave of his hand towards Lady Florence, "is, as you are not, perhaps, aware, madam, the only surviving daughter of this gentleman" (with a bow towards the bed).

"I was not aware of it," replied Ruth coldly.

"It is, however, the fact!"

"Indeed?"

"Yes, madam!"

"I beg to differ with you!"

"I beg your pardon, madam!"

"I say, I beg to differ with you!"

The little man looked flabbergasted.

Lady Florence also appeared not a little astonished by the words which she had just heard.

For the first time, a suspicion of the truth began to dawn upon her mind. Hitherto, she had not had any idea that Ruth herself was one of Hardcastle's children.

She only thought that she was somebody who knew them, and who spoke on their behalf.

"Do you profess a relationship to my father?" she inquired.

"Yes," replied Ruth.

"You are——"

"His daughter!"

"It is false!" cried Lady Florence, fiercely.

It was now the other one's turn to respond with a smile of contemptuous pity.

"It is hardly possible that I should make this statement, if it were easily to be refuted. I shall, no doubt, be able to substantiate my claim when the time comes. Until then, you are at liberty to be of what opinion you choose."

Lady Florence was silent.

She had turned deadly pale, and she trembled visibly.

Terrible thoughts were passing through her

brain. She was reflecting upon the fearful crime she had been committing, and inwardly cursing herself for having thus damned her soul to no end—without any gain, without any profit.

For, after all, this woman might overthrow all the work that she had done.

After all, Ruth might obtain the property, to gain which she had dyed her hands with a parent's blood.

But suddenly a hope arose in her breast.

The will—what had become of the will?

Had it been altered? It had been originally made in favour of Lady Florence.

Had the old man, while she was absent from the room, altered it in favour of Ruth? Had Ruth induced him so to do?

Lady Florence looked round eagerly in search of the document.

It had been left in the room. It lay at that moment upon the floor, close by the bed-side.

The little man perceived it also, and went forward to pick it up.

When he had raised it from the ground, he began very deliberately to unfold it.

But Lady Florence, boiling over with impatience, attempted to snatch it from his hand.

"Hollo!" cried the little man, astonished.

"Give it to me!" she said.

"Give it you, my lady?"

"Yes!"—with a stamp of the foot.

"Certainly, my lady!"

He was folding it neatly previous to handing it to her with a low bow, but she jerked it fiercely out of his hand.

Then she eagerly turned over the leaves.

She looked with anxiety to see whether there had not been some alteration effected therein during the interview between Ruth and her father.

But the will was exactly as it had been when she left the room.

The codicil to which the old man was about to affix his signature when Ruth's interruption prevented him putting that design into execution, was there as it had stood, yet unsigned.

The thought that her object was yet unattained caused her a feeling of uneasiness and disappointment, and she reflected inwardly what steps she ought to take.

As matters now stood, her father had elected her as his sole heir, but the property left to her was subject to her husband's control.

But even this arrangement she thought would be preferable to a division of the property between herself and Ruth.

However, she would make one attempt. Perhaps her father would yet sign in her favour.

And while this thought was passing through her mind, a slight movement on the old man's part, which was something akin to beckoning with his lean hand, seemed to indicate that he desired her presence by the bed side.

She approached him hastily, and leant over him, holding her head close to his lips to hear what he wanted to say.

"Give me a pen," she heard him whisper, faintly.

"Yes, father," she answered: "you are going to secure the property to me, are you not, dear father?"

He muttered something inaudibly.

"You are going to sign the codicil in my favour?"

"No."

She shrank back.

"What did you say, father?"

"A new will," the old man muttered in a low tone,—"I will make a new will, while I have yet strength."

A lowering frown darkened the daughter's brow, but she moved not, and made no attempt to do his bidding.

"Quick—quick!" he continued; "my time is short!"

"It shall be shorter!" she muttered, betwixt her clenched teeth.

CHAPTER LXVIII.

THE MURDER

Those at the other end of the room could not hear what the old man said, for he spoke in the faintest whisper.

Now, however, they came crouching round the bed.

Ruth, in her turn, leant over the bed, and tried to catch the scarcely audible sounds issuing from her father's lips.

"Give me my physic," he said,—"the reviving draught."

Ruth repeated aloud what he had said.

"Where is it?" she asked.

"I will get it," answered Lady Florence.

Then she went to a distant table, to fetch a bottle and glass.

She stopped at the table to pour out the draught.

Her back was towards the bed, and towards the persons standing clustered round it.

There were none of them observing her; and even if they had been doing so, it would have been impossible for them to have seen exactly what she did.

Beyond the fact of her back acting as a screen to her actions, the corner where the table stood was enveloped in deep obscurity by a thick red curtain, which blocked out such faint light as in other places managed to struggle through the dull diamond-shaped panes.

Had they been able to watch her movements narrowly, to what opinion would they have arrived, think you?

Without seeing her movements—seeing only her face, her lowering brow, her clenched teeth, her wicked eyes—there could have remained no doubt upon the observer's mind that that woman meant mischief—that she was employed on some deed of darkness.

And that deed was murder!

Let us watch her.

From her breast she drew forth a tiny phial—the same from which she had poured a few drops upon the previous night.

It may be remembered that there was only one dose left in it: that dose she now poured into a wine glass, into which she had previously emptied the contents of a physic bottle.

With the wine glass containing the deadly poison, then, she approached the bed.

The old man lay there pale and silent, apparently unconscious.

The murderess bent over him, and placed the glass to his lips.

It contained scarcely more than one table spoonful: she held his head, however, in such a position that the liquid must run down his throat.

Then she tilted the glass.

The deadly liquid trickled slowly over his lips.

A slight gulping motion showed that he had swallowed the fatal dose.

Then the glazed pupils of his eyes began to dilate, and beads of cold perspiration began to gather upon his forehead, and stream slowly down his face.

It was the death-sweat.

Then a faint, bluish, greenish tint was visible upon his cheeks.

His lips parted, and he uttered a low wailing sound, and uttered some words which were inaudible.

The strange blue tint spread now all over his face, and more particularly under his eyes, where the colour deepened.

The lips kept muttering for some little time yet, and then their motion began to slacken.

The muscles of his face appeared to have lost all their strength, and they began to stiffen and grow rigid.

The body was perfectly motionless, and the lips were stilled. What life there was left in the old man, appeared to exist only in his eyes.

But momentarily it faded and paled.

The light slowly passed away, and the glazed eye-balls gleamed sightlessly.

Suddenly the jaws fell open, and there was a low rattle in the throat.

He was dead.

With a stifled scream, the murderess dropped down upon her knees before the bed, and clutched convulsively her throbbing brow betwixt her icy hands.

Then her figure slowly drooped, and she slipped down shapelessly upon the floor.

Crockford bent forward, and raised her in his arms.

She had fainted.

CHAPTER LXIX.

THE LAWYER AND RUTH.—A FATHER'S WILL.—A SISTER'S HATE.—ANOTHER ENEMY.

The lawyer covered the face of the dead man with a sheet.

Then he drew down the window-blinds, and darkened the room.

Meanwhile Crockford had raised Lady Florence in his arms, and borne her from the apartment where death now reigned alone and silently.

Ruth was the last to quit the room, and she pulled the broken door to as well as she was able.

Crockford looked at her curiously. Her face was very pale, but there was no sign of emotion visible thereon.

"She is a strange woman," he muttered to himself; and he inwardly resolved that he would be careful how he fell into her power.

Poor fool! he was already her slave, did she choose to exert her influence over him.

The three went down stairs, and the men assisted Lady Florence into a room upon the floor below, which had, during his life, served the miser in some sort as a drawing-room and reception-room, did he chance to be obliged to receive any visitor upon matters of business.

There they placed the fainting woman upon a sofa, and, opening the window, allowed the fresh morning air to play upon her face.

Slowly her senses began to return, and she bade them leave her awhile to herself.

Obeying her wishes, the two men approached Ruth, who had lent no assistance to her sister, but sat apart at the other end of the room.

The little man thought that he was called upon to make some remark; and as Crockford did not appear disposed to do so, he broke the silence himself with a little cough, and murmured gently, for Ruth's edification, "A very sad business this, madam!"

She, however, took no notice of him.

"A very sad business!" he repeated.

"What is?"

"I said it was a sad business."

"I heard you. What do you mean?"

The little man subsided, and felt very much smaller than usual.

"This—the death of your father, I alluded to."

"Oh!"

The little man gasped again, and resolved to have no more to say to so very extraordinary a young lady.

As he was moving away, however, she called to him.

"What are the first steps that will be taken about his property?" she asked.

The lawyer explained that Lady Florence would admister to his will.

"Why Lady Florence?"

"Because she is the heiress."

"But am not I entitled?"

"Entitled, madam!—to what?"

"To a share of my father's property?"

"No; I am afraid not, madam!"

"Why not?"

"Because her ladyship is his sole heiress."

"But I am also his daughter—and I have proofs."

The lawyer smiled. After the insolent way in which Ruth had treated him, he was not sorry to have it in his power to retaliate mildly.

"It is not a question of your relationship to the deceased," said he; "but as the will was made in her favour——"

Ruth sprang suddenly to her feet, and confronted him fiercely.

"What do you mean?"

"The will having been made in Lady Florence Darcy's favour——"

"But it was not executed. He died before he had affixed his signature."

"To the codicil!"

"To the will!"

"No, madam. The will had been already properly executed in favour of Lady Florence. It was only to a codicil written this morning that his signature was required."

Ruth made no answer, but the expression of her face for a moment was perfectly terrible.

"Fool that I was!" she thought to herself. "The will was lying there all the time that I was alone with him. Why did I not destroy it? Why did I not add a few words of my own?—that would have been better. I could easily have imitated his signature when I had one there to copy from. I was a fool!—a fool!"

A score of mad schemes passed through her brain, all alike impracticable.

In vain she strove to think of some course of conduct which, under the circumstances that had aroused it, would be best for her to adopt.

But she could think of none. She could decide upon nothing.

One thing only was clearly comprehensible to her aching brain.

And that was, that she had lost her chance of becoming rich.

She had lost her chance of obtaining sufficient money to escape from her enemies.

She was still in their power, and she must try some other plan to obtain her end.

But what plan? Where must she look for help—to whom must she turn?

Accidentally she turned her eyes upon Captain Crockford.

He was sitting at some short distance from the spot where she herself was seated.

She watched him narrowly.

His eyes were bent upon the face of Lady Florence, who lay languidly stretched upon the sofa, her handkerchief pressed to her lips. By the expression of his countenance she fancied somehow that he was considering which of the two sisters was most desirable—which pleased him most—which was most beautiful.

Such thoughts as these must have been passing through his mind, for presently he glanced furtively towards Ruth, as though he was making some comparison.

"He is my only chance," thought Ruth. "Has he any money, I wonder?"

He had almost said that he had not when they were talking together. He had bewailed his lot as a younger brother. Perhaps he was poor, and unable even to obtain the loan of a sum large enough for her purpose.

But still she fancied, too, that his name must be good among money-lenders.

She was acquainted with a certain Israelite, who advanced money at a ruinous discount.

This man was in the habit of frequenting the gambling-house at which we have seen Ruth was one of the reigning goddesses.

Upon several occasions Mr. Levi had, in a roundabout way, suggested to her that could she recommend to him any young men of good family who wanted to raise money upon their personal security, did he approve of them, he would pay her a liberal per centage for the introduction.

At the time she had treated this suggestion with great contempt. Now she began seriously to consider its feasibility.

"Yes," she thought, "I will try him."

And then she reflected that if she must retain her influence over the young man, she must not allow him any longer to remain here, in this dangerous proximity to Lady Florence.

She therefore rose to her feet, and approaching him, said, "We will depart, if you will kindly escort me, Captain Crockford."

He rose in some confusion, and bowing, said that he was ready

Ruth then left the apartment, and Captain Charley, after a few words of polite condolence addressed to Lady Florence, prepared to follow her.

"Are you going?" asked her ladyship.

"Yes, I am going with—with your ladyship's sister."

"My sister!" repeated the other, with an awful emphasis upon the word.

The Captain retired in confusion. Not her sister? The resemblance between them was most extraordinary. The most casual observer could not have failed to detect it.

The fickle Captain paused for a moment, and tried to consider which sister he admired the most.

She upon the stairs called to him, however.

The hand of Lady Florence yet rested in his. He bowed his head to kiss it, and as he raised his eyes again, fancied he saw a tear trembling upon her silken eyelash.

He fancied, too, that her hand trembled slightly.

"How beautiful she is!" the Captain thought. "How loveable! I scarcely know which to choose. If I could have them both——"

Again Ruth called him, and he hastily departed.

In a few moments afterwards they were upon their way to town.

Lady Florence, gazing after them from the window at which she sat, saw them pass slowly through the trees.

Ruth was leaning upon her companion's arm.

She was looking up into his face, and smiling upon him with her sweetest smiles.

He was stooping down towards her, and listening intently to the honied words that she poured into his ears

"She is beautiful!" Lady Florence muttered to herself. "I wonder what she is, and where she lives. Whatever she may be, it would have been much better for her that she had not crossed my path. In two things has she come between me and my desire. With my father she strove to thwart me; and with this handsome Captain, too, who, were it not for her, would love me, and whom I, too, love a little."

She looked out of the window after the retreating figures just disappearing among the trees.

At that moment Ruth looked back and laughed merrily at something that the Captain had said.

Lady Florence hastily closed the window.

"How I hate her!" she said, beneath her breath—"how I hate her!"

Then she added, aloud, seeing that the lawyer's eyes were fixed upon her, "That woman said she was my father's daughter, did she not?"

"Yes, my lady."

"Did you hear her laughing just now?"

"Yes, my lady."

"What did you think of it?"

"I thought that it was very shocking, my lady."

"Horribly unnatural, I call it!" exclaimed Lady Florence. "She might act the character better I should think. She might pretend to feel what she does not—at any rate, if she would have us believe her story!"

Lady Florence walked away as she said this. The doctor looked after her with a half-puzzled expression, and something like a smile flitted across his lips.

"They're neither of them as affectionate as I could wish, if they were daughters of mine," he said to himself.

* * * * *

And thus we see how Ruth had made another enemy—another enemy, bent upon her destruction.

How many more are there to come? How is it all to end?

Surely the avenger is upon the track of this most beautiful, but most detestable of women!

Yes, her doom is sealed!

She has returned to the capital—returned to the place where there are others plotting her downfall and destruction.

Her fate is sealed; and soon will come shame and misery!

Read on.

CHAPTER LXX.

SHOWS HOW A CERTAIN PRETTY YOUNG LADY FOUND IT EXTREMELY DIFFICULT TO RAISE THE WIND, AND TO WHAT SUBTERFUGES SHE RESORTED, AND WITH WHAT RESULT.

SOLOMON LEVI lived in a handsome villa in St John's Wood, when he lived in town, upon which occasions he had a curious fancy for calling himself Mr. Montague,—a name to which he had certainly as much right as the very beautiful young lady, so expensively attired in such rich velvets and sumptuous silks, who was by turns termed Mrs. Montague and Mrs. Levi, according to the fancy of the Jewish gentlemen who visited the money-lender and his mistress.

When in the country, he lived at a very handsomely-furnished villa in Cliftonville, Brighton, and drove in his four-in-hand. That was where the legitimate Mrs. Levi resided, and the young Levis, six in number, and all strongly developed nasally.

His place of business, however, was in the Adelphi, where, for some reason or other best known to himself, he went by the name of Solomon.

When he sometimes referred to a mysterious friend of his, residing in the City, whom he had, according to his own account, to borrow all his money of, and who was the most remorseless of creditors when a defaulter was concerned, he spoke of him as Levi.

This naturally caused those who were acquainted with Mr. Levi's proper name to fancy that the friend in the City could be none other than his "noble self."

In appearance, he was fat, sallow, greasy, and be-ringleted.

He wore a good deal of jewellery and smoked expensive cigars. He was a connoisseur of old paintings, choice wines, and fine women.

To him went Ruth two days after the events which have been described. She called upon him about ten o'clock. He was at home, and glad to see her.

She was ushered through a dingy little outer office, where, behind a grating strongly resembling a dilapidated meat screen, a mouldy little old man was writing with a loudly-chirping pen, into the presence of the great Solomon.

At the time that she entered he was standing with his back towards her, looking over some papers in a cupboard; and although there could be no possible doubt about his having heard her enter the room, he continued to lean over his papers, mumbling to himself as though he were unconscious of her presence.

Ruth, having paused for about a couple of minutes upon the spot where she had first stopped upon entering the room, and the position growing rather irksome, she took a chair, making, in so doing, a prodigious rustling of silk.

Still the Jew took no notice of her.

"What does the old fool mean?" she asked herself. "Is he deaf?"

After a pause of another minute, during which the lady was gradually working herself up into a fury, she gave a loud stamp of her foot.

No notice was taken of the circumstance.

Another, louder.

Same result.

Ruth could and would bear with this conduct no longer.

"Mr. Levi!" she cried.

Mr. Levi turned round sharply.

"Mr. Levi, are you going to attend to me, or are you not?"

"My dear madam," said the Jew, "I had not the remotest idea that you were there!"

"Do you mean to say you did not know it?" she cried in great wrath, knitting her brow and biting her pretty red lips.

The Jewish gentleman was, according to his account, quite astonished to see her.

"You knew I was here, I suppose?" replied Mrs. Belvidere, curtly.

"No, no, my dear madam, I assure you!"

"Your clerk brought my name in!"

"I think not!"

"My card is here, anyhow!"

"Ah, to be sure; and I mistook you for somebody else!"

"But you heard me come into the room!"

"No!"

"You must be deaf, then!"

"I am a little hard of hearing."

"A little, you call it? You're either as deaf as a post, or you did it on purpose!"

"Oh, my dear lady, you don't think it possible, do you?"

"Think what possible?"

"That I should behave so rudely, knowingly!"

"I daresay you would, if you could get anything by it."

"But what could I get?"

"You'll get nothing from me."

"Indeed! To what, then, am I indebted for the honour of this visit?"

Ruth bit her lip, and her face flushed crimson.

She would dearly have liked to have quitted the house then, and for ever.

But she could not afford to do it.

"I must eat humble pie," she thought. "Curse him!"

Then she added aloud, "I have not come to ask a favour; I am here upon a matter of business. The favour is mutual. We may each gain by the transaction."

"That is delightful news!" the Jew said, seating himself before her, and rubbing his hands together as though in delighted expectation of a great treat in store for him. "Things are so very queer at this moment, my dear madam. Trade is so very bad; business is so very flat; and there is absolutely no money to be had anywhere."

Ruth's heart, for a moment, sank within her. But she knew a little of this class of gentry, and she knew what their word was worth.

They are always very short of cash, of course, when cash is wanted; and so it is quite natural that the scarcity should account for an increase in the rate of interest.

Therefore, when she came to give the matter a moment's consideration, she smiled to herself.

"Is money so very scarce with you, then, Mr. Solomon?"

"Frightfully scarce! I haven't seen the sight of it for ever so long."

"Dear me! that's a pity! I have come at an unfortunate moment, I suppose! I will wish you good morning!"

"Where are you going, my dear young lady?"

"It's no good stopping here, is it?"

"Who says so?"

"You did!"

"I did?"

"Didn't you?"

"Well, not that I know of."

"You said you had no money!"

"Well, but then, of course, you know when one says that one hasn't got any money, that means—you understand—that one hasn't got much to spare."

"To be sure! but, as I want a good bit, I had better go somewhere else. Good day to you!"

She rose from her chair and approached the door with a very fair pretence of really meaning what she said.

The Jewish gentleman was quite deceived by the manœuvre, and ran forward to stop her.

"Look here, Mrs. Belvidere, if *you* please! Let's come to business!"

"That's what I want," retorted Ruth, abruptly, and in quite a different tone to that which at first she had adopted

"Very well, then, madam!"

"Very well, then, sir, without a further waste of words than is necessary, if I give you a gentleman's acceptance for five hundred pounds, what will you give me for it?"

"That depends——"

"Upon what?"

"Upon who the young man is, of course."

"His name is a good one, as you will find."

"To be sure!"

"If it had not been so, I should not have proposed it."

"Certainly!"

"He is the son of a peer."

"That's very good!"

"He will, at the death of his brother, who is in very delicate health, succeed to the title and estates."

"And he is called?"

"The Honourable Captain Crockford."

"Ha! ha! ha!"

"What now?"

"My dear Mrs. Belvidere!"

"What do you mean?"

"I really shouldn't have thought it of you."

"What are you laughing at?"

"At the idea of your bringing such a name as Charley's.'

"Do you know him?"

"Reyther! He's up to his eyes in jobs of this sort"

"What of that? He'll pay when he comes into his money."

"Ah! if he doesn't die first."

"Not much chance of that!"

"I don't know. He lives hard. Wine and women, and all that sort of thing, play the deuce with any man."

"You've stood it pretty well, Mr. Solomon."

"Bah!" said the Jew, colouring a little. "I've never been fast."

"Oh, no!—to be sure Everybody knows your reputation!"

"Get along with you! You've been misinformed."

"Oh, Mr. Solomon, you know you are a shocking creature, and that we poor women haven't a chance with you!"

And as she said this she sighed and looked languishing

"You're not afraid of me?" asked Mr. Solomon, taking her hand.

"Yes, I am, you naughty man!"

"But I wouldn't harm you for the world!"

"That's what you told all your other poor victims!"

"Victims, indeed! You talk of victims, who have crushed so many beneath your chariot-wheels—me among the number!"

"What! do you love me very much?"

"Upon my soul, I adore you!"

"If I could only believe you!" she said, looking fixedly into his eyes as he approached his face to hers until it was so near that her sweet breath fanned his cheek—"if I could only believe you!"

"If you would only believe me, I'd give—I'd give——"

"What will you give me for Crockford's acceptance?" she asked, with a laugh, as she rose to her feet.

The Jew was confused for a second time, and bowled over by her tricks

"Damn me!" he couldn't help exclaiming, "you're a devilish clever woman!"

"I need be!" she returned, with something savage in her tone. "I have no one to lend me a helping hand. I have risen by my own acts from the gutter. I shall rise higher yet, as you will see, and I shall not forget the friends that I may have made upon the road."

But the Jew did not seem to be quite as much impressed by the promise He thought more of a single sparrow in the hand, than a whole forest full of uncaught canaries. So says he—

"I'm obliged to you, I'm sure!"—and then began to whistle.

"I want to know, however," she remarked, after a pause, "what you will give me for Crockford's acceptance?"

"It's no good to me."

"What will you give?"

"It's no good to me, I say!"

"It must be worth something!"

"It isn't to me!"

"Than we can do nothing together?"

"I'm afraid not!"

"Good morning!"

"I'll tell you what I'll take!"

"What's that?" she asked, facing round quickly.

"I'll take the elder brother's signature."

"Who says you wouldn't?" retorted Ruth, indignantly. "You'd only be too glad to get it, I expect, if it were offered to you."

"The younger's is no use to me!"

"It must have it's price. However great the risk is, it must be worth buying at some price however small."

"I can name none!"

"Then we can do no business!"

"Bring me my lord's name!"

"How can I do that?"

"Look here!" said the Jew, sinking his voice almost to a whisper—"I'll tell you."

Then he went to the door very cautiously, turned the handle noiselessly, and flung the door open suddenly.

No one was there.

"I thought one of them clerks might be listening," he explained, as he returned to the room.

Then, seating himself by Ruth's side, he continued.

"I'll tell you how it can be done. The elder brother's very ailing, you say?"

"Yes."

"And nearly off the hooks?"

"Yes."

"You're very pretty."

"Well?"

"You can make the Captain do what you like."

"I don't know."

"I think you can."

"Well?"

"Get him to sign himself 'Etherington.'"

"What! forge his brother's name?"

"It isn't forgery—at least, not exactly. He will be Etherington when the other dies."

"It seems like forgery to me."

"It's the only way he'll get the money."

"He won't do it."

"Propose it."

"I dare not. He would refuse."

"Try him."

"No; it is impossible."

"Oh, very well; you know best. It isn't I who wants the tin. Do just what you like. I hope you will excuse me staying with you any longer. I've got some particular business to transact in the City."

As he spoke, he began to button up his coat, as though he were getting ready to go out.

Ruth held a consultation with herself.

She must have the money. By hook or by

crook, she must have the money. But how could she hope to obtain it in the way suggested?

No; it was impossible!

But, ah! a thought struck her.

She turned quickly towards the Jew, who was sidling in the direction of the door.

"Well," said she, "suppose I bring you his signature to-morrow?"

The Jew looked at her very hard under his bushy eyebrows.

Ruth blushed.

Then the Jew grinned.

"I think I would rather the Captain signed in my presence," said he, "if you have no objection!"

She made no reply to this; but turned upon her heel, and quitted the room.

An obsequious Jew boy bounded off his stool, in the outer office, to open the door for her.

As she passed out, she noticed him leering and grimacing behind her back to another Jew boy with an eye-glass; and turning upon him suddenly, with the rage of a tigress, she boxed his ears till they blushed blood-red.

Then she stepped across the threshold, and sauntered down the street, with a placid smile such as angel might have worn returning from a work of heavenly mercy.

CHAPTER LXXI.

SHOWS HOW A CERTAIN VERY NAUGHTY YOUNG LADY MAKES UP HER MIND TO TURN OVER A NEW LEAF, AND ACT PROPRIETY.

But though to all outward appearances she was perfectly calm and tranquil, there was a furnace raging within her which scorched her very soul, and dried her heart's-blood with its remorseless flames.

As she walked away from the money-lender's, she rapidly turned over in her mind every possible way that was left to her for obtaining money.

Money she must have, and a considerable sum—enough to escape with from this, to her, hideous city, fraught with so many dangers.

And how this money was to be obtained, she knew not.

A strange conflict was taking place in the brain of this extraordinary woman. She was asking herself whether or not she would sacrifice her life for love?

Her love! the reader may say, with an ejaculation of astonishment.

Has not this woman hitherto been depicted as one totally incapable of the feelings of love or mercy?

But she was yet human.

A woman is not human unless she loves; and this most cold-blooded and heartless of beautiful fiends was human in this respect.

At length, a vulnerable place had been discovered in her hard, cruel heart. Her weakness had been laid bare

She loved; and Crockford was the object of her passion.

And now, ten times more bitterly than ever they had done, did his misfortunes afflict her.

Just when life began to have a new charm for her, it was going to be snatched away. For might he not at any moment fall a victim beneath the assassin's knife?

And London, which a month ago, had she then had the good fortune to make this young man's acquaintance, would have been a paradise, she must now fly for dear life.

Hitherto had she pursued her nefarious career with impunity; hitherto, though stained by countless crimes, she successfully battled with her enemies.

Hitherto she had triumphed; but surely, now, her time had come!

Retributive justice was on her track! She was doomed.

Vainly had she striven to cast from her all traces of the hateful life she had led.

She longed to be able to begin existence afresh—to forget the crimes, the horrors of the past, and live, in her new-found love, a purer and better life.

But it was not to be.

She had tried very hard. When she returned to town, it was with the idea that she would obtain possession of her jewels and valuables from the house in Belgravia, and as soon as possible convert them into money.

This idea, however, she had soon forsaken.

As she approached the scene of her past wickedness, her heart failed her.

Why should she go there? she asked herself. No; she would not. She was mad to think of it. It would be better to sacrifice the property she had there, than to run the dangers which she must run, did she return to that hated home.

It was rather a severe struggle which she had with herself upon this subject, but in the end she triumphed over her weakness most successfully, and came off victorious.

She determined upon sacrificing her silks, and velvets, and diamonds—all the property she had left in the gambling-house,—and seeking instead a refuge in a distant part of the town, where she would be unknown, and where she could pursue her amour with Crockford uninterrupted until the time arrived when she must quit London.

There were several difficulties about this course which must be overcome, but they were overcome in the end, as many great difficulties had been also when this artful woman's wits had been brought to bear upon them.

The first was about the place where she was to live.

The neighbourhood she had soon decided upon. She chose Brixton.

Brixton was the very best place she could think of. Perhaps it is not very far distant from Belgravia, but who among the Belgravians were in the habit of going there?

The upper ten ignored the plebeian locality. They were acquainted with its whereabouts, and spoke of it, when they spoke of it at all, as "somewhere over the water."

When I say plebeian, though, I only mean plebian in comparison to Belgravia. There could not very well be a more genteel and respectable locality for its class. Ruth had at first had some idea of settling in St. John's Wood, but what would a man about town like Charley Crockford think of a lady who lived in that gay quarter alone?

No, she must go to Brixton; and there was some chance of her being able to pass herself off as an honest woman.

She hoped to be able to make Crockford believe in her virtue and chastity.

She was going to pass herself off as a widow who had lived all her life abroad. How could he tell that what she said was not true?

He had met her, as I have already told you, a long while ago in the gaming-house, and every now and then a suspicion flitted across his mind that he knew her face well, and had somewhere or other seen her before.

But, in spite of all his efforts, he could not for the life of him recall to mind where or under what circumstances the meeting had taken place.

She could read in his face the thoughts which more than once had passed through his mind, and she saw that his efforts to remember her were unsuccessful.

The fact is, that upon the nights that Crockford had seen Ruth at the gambling-house he had been taken there after dining and drinking rather freely, and he had at the time but a very indistinct notion of what he saw and did; and thus was it that he could not remember where the glorious vision of Ruth's countenance had before appeared to him, and he made up his mind that he must have met her somewhere or other out in society.

He had some misgivings, though, about her respectablity.

That was why he adopted such a free-and easy style towards her at their first interview; but gradually, as he came to know her better, he began to change his opinion.

What earthly reason had he, he asked himself, for believing that she was not what she pretended to be.

She dressed with the very best taste; her manners and choice of language were faultless; she appeared to be perfectly conversant with the usages of the polite world. She was undoubtedly a lady.

But then, again, if she were, how did she come to know the Prince, who had such an awful character as a rake, debauchee, gambler, and everything else that is vile and villanous?

She explained. He had paid his addresses to her, and she was not aware what a horrible character the man had until Crockford informed her.

Now she would never speak to him again.

Captain Charley did his best to find out all about her, but could find out nothing.

She lived in handsome apartments, in a quiet street in Brixton, and the people of the house, when questioned, could, or would, tell nothing about her.

When Crockford and Ruth returned to London, the latter, after much persuasion, had informed the Captain that she would be at the Opera that evening, and that if he wanted to see her he must come there.

He pressed for her address; but at the time she would not tell him.

Simply because she did not know it herself, and intended to employ her day in finding some apartments. Having found them, she took the landlady into her confidence to a certain extent; and having very easily won the old lady's heart, persuaded her to enter into a little plot for entrapping the Captain into wedlock.

Thus did it happen that when Crockford endeavoured to pump the landlady and her servant, he only learnt what Ruth had told them to tell him—namely, that she was a most respectable widow lady, who had lived a long while abroad, and whose name was "Beresford."

Well, the Captain thought, she might be respectable, and she might not. He was not a marrying man—he had no idea of marrying her. Any other sacrifice in the world he would gladly make, to obtain possession of her; and even that, if no other would do.

In fact, by slow degrees our handsome profligate began to lose his heart to the beautiful syren, and soon he was as much in love with her as man ever was with woman.

Thus passed away some days, and Crockford came every day to visit her, and found her every day more lovely and loveable.

Every day, though, Ruth grew more and more desperate about money.

For the present, she managed to get on very well, and keep up appearances as a rich widow, by pawning and selling such jewels as she had in her possession upon the day of the review.

But soon these would be exhausted; and what then?

One pet thought she cherished, and the more she brooded on it, the more did she come to look upon it as a necessity of her very existence.

And that was, that Crockford should accompany her abroad as her husband.

But how was it to be managed?

CHAPTER LXXII.

SHOWS HOW A WICKED RAKE FELL IN LOVE IN EARNEST, AFTER HAVING ALL HIS LIFE ONLY PLAYED WITH THE TENDER PASSION; AND HOW THE SYREN RESOLVED UPON WORKING HIS DESTRUCTION.

Yes, for the first time in his life, Charley Crockford was really and truly in love.

A hundred times before, he had fancied himself to be consumed by the tender passion; but always, in a very short space of time, had he discovered that his heart was but slightly touched by these passing amours.

He had all his life been engaged in amours and intrigues. He had made the pursuit of women his sole occupation.

Very creditable, was it not?—but by no means an unusual occurrence with idle young men of fashion.

To be quoted as a rake and a seducer was his end and aim; and the more broken hearts and ruined homes he had laid at his door, the more he was flattered.

Not that he was really the vicious, callous wretch he would have liked you to believe him to be.

On the contrary, his seductions were not quite so terrible as he would have had you to suppose. Very often he was more the seduced than the seducer; and it could never be said of him that he deserted his victims.

Indeed, so many calls were there upon the Captain's purse, to all of which he honourably responded, that he had contrived thereby to exhaust two very handsome fortunes; and it was upon that account that we find him now so very hard up, and his credit so very bad among the bill discounters.

But, in all these affairs of the heart in which he had been engaged, he had, after all, only been playing at being in love. Now he was in love truly.

There could be no doubt of it. He was positive of the fact.

Long days he could have passed, lying at the feet of the lovely creature who had so captivated him.

He felt half stupefied and wholly fascinated by her smiles.

He dragged himself away from her house every night with the greatest difficulty, and not before she had several times plainly told him to go.

When he got home he was unable to sleep.

Two or three times he had hinted at the possibility of a *liaison*, but she had become so indignant that he had never dared openly to approach the subject again.

"Will nothing but marriage satisfy her?" he asked himself. "If not, by heavens, I must marry her!"

The worst of it was, that, supposing she should turn out to be an improper person, and his brother should discover the marriage, he was quite capable of leaving his money, at his death, to somebody else, and which it was in his power to do, if he chose.

"What wretched folly it is of her to be such a prude!" he said to himself sometimes. "Is she not her own mistress? Apparently she has nobody that she need care about I feel certain she loves me, too! And yet she won't make a sacrifice!"

His case soon became very desperate.

His passion overcame every other calculation.

His love for Ruth was the sole thought which occupied him from morning to night.

Once or twice, going home of a night from the bower of the beloved one, he determined to shake off the snake-like influence which she seemed to have obtained over him.

He plunged into a vortex of dissipation. He gave himself up to the wildest excesses.

He frequented the haunts of vice, and passed the night in drunken and licentious revels. But these efforts to banish from his mind the goddess who had taken possession of his heart, were unavailing.

Next day he loved her more than ever.

He looked back with disgust upon the companions of his debauchery. The frail beauties who had lavished their meretricious embraces upon him, he recollected only with horror and loathing when he came again into the presence of the beautiful woman whom he loved.

All night long would Crockford toss in feverish unrest upon his sleepless couch.

One vision haunting all his dreams, one thought agitating his heart.

Wild and frantic ideas overcame him: voluptuous scenes, in which Ruth was ever the heroine, were conjured up by his excited brain.

The world appeared to be lit up to glorious day by this woman's eyes. Her graceful form, robed in gauzy garments of spotless whiteness, soft and clinging, and half transparent, floated before him in a hazy cloud, accompanied by dulcet strains of the most ravishing melody.

Often he dreamt that she was about to fall into his arms—that she smiled upon him—that she promised to yield to his desire.

He was intoxicated by anticipation. He was at last about to consummate all earthly bliss by calling this treasure his!

But he would awake cold and shivering, to find himself alone.

He would leap from his wearisome couch, and pace the room with angry strides, like some baffled Tarquin disturbed upon the eve of the perpetration of his treacherous deed.

Sometimes, as soon as it was daylight, he would spring upon his horse, and gallop out into the country, endeavouring to abate the madness of the fever which consumed him.

Mr. Spinks, the valet, coming in several hours afterwards with the shaving water, would be astonished to find the room empty; and he and Fanny the housemaid would compare notes upon the state of wild disorder in which they found the furniture and the Captain's wearing apparel scattered about, and the tumbled state of the forsaken couch

And Mr. Spinks would wonder, with a wink, what could ail the governor.

And Miss Fanny, with a blush, would say that she had no idea

Hard galloping is perhaps not a bad remedy for some kinds of fever, and Charley Crockford drove the spurs into his horse's flanks, and sped along as hard as the horse could go.

The clear fresh air, when he had got out of the streets, revived him.

Overhead, morning unfolded itself from blossom to bud, and from bud to flower. The trees were bathed in deliciously varying hues of light.

The open fields spread out before him fresh and green. The dew drops sparkled in the sun.

Sometimes he would ride on for an hour or two.

Then, suddenly, he would turn his horse's head towards Brixton, and return home as fast as his horse could bring him.

Perhaps he found Ruth at breakfast, and perhaps she had not yet come down stairs; and he could picture her at the toilet in the sanctity of her chamber, fresh as the morning dew, rising from her bath with her golden hair flowing upon her white shoulders.

Generally, though, he found her in a little conservatory, tending her flowers, and waiting for him.

She was, when seen thus, wondrously fair.

The roses on her cheeks, and the sparkling clearness of her dark blue eyes, seemed almost to bear witness to her health and virtue.

Her flaxen curls, like rippling waves, flowed in a torrent down her back to her waist.

Her white arms were bare; and under the light wrapper that she wore, he could see her breast heaving with a gentle motion, and he could, as she reclined upon a couch and he sat at her feet, trace a faint indication of the rounded form of her sweet person, which it draped gracefully without concealing.

Even thus early in the day he was desperately in love with her; and as the hours wore on, he grew more and more intoxicated by her bright eyes, and charms, and graces.

One night he had dined with her, and had stayed later than usual, and he accidentally discovered that the landlady and the servant had retired to rest, and that he was alone with the object of his passion.

No one was likely to disturb him, he thought.

Was she not now in his power?

Should he not profit by this opportunity? Such another chance might never again occur.

Summoning all his courage to his side, he vehemently poured forth vows and entreaties.

At first she laughed at him.

He grew more excited and more daring.

He would at last have endeavoured to profit by her helplessness to obtain by force the return to his love, which she refused.

But when he would have taken her in his arms, she swiftly unsheathed a dagger from her breast, and threatened him with his life.

So that the Captain was fain at length to take his departure rather sheepishly, and to apologize next day in a letter for his disgraceful conduct.

When he had gone away that night, Ruth, left alone with her own thoughts, formed a resolve.

"He shall sign a bill for me, in the way that the Jew suggested," she said. "He shall forge his brother's name. He will then be more than ever in my power, and I can see a way that I can compel him to fly with me from this hateful country."

Next morning, at an early hour, before the Captain paid his usual visit, she went to the Adelphi in search of Solomon Levi.

CHAPTER LXXIII.

THE JEW IN HIS DEN.—THE ISRAELITE AND THE BETRAYER—SCHEMES AND PLOTS—THE ARRIVAL OF A VISITOR—RUTH'S DILEMMA.—THE VISITING CARD—THE DISCOVERY.—COMPLICATION.—VENGEANCE.

Solomon Levi was at home, and, as upon the former occasion, glad to see her.

She found him as she had found him before, busy among the papers at his cupboard.

But this time she did not feel inclined to wait his pleasure.

On the contrary, she advanced straight towards him, and jerked him round by the arm.

In doing so she caused him to scatter his papers, and he was wroth.

"Now, then!" he said peevishly, as he scrambled about the floor, picking them up—"now, then! What did you do that for?"

"Just to make you attend."

"Vell, I'm sure!"

"You were so deaf the last time I came, I thought that you should not be this time, if I could help it!"

"I'm obliged to you!"

"You're welcome!"

The Jew was inclined to be rather crusty at first, but somehow or other, in a way known only to herself, but by a species of enchantment which she had never found to fail, she brought him back to his good humour.

Presently his brow cleared again, and a complacent grin spread over his sallow features

"I could love that woman," he thought, "only it would be too expensive!"

He asked her to take a chair quite politely, and pressed her to partake of a glass of wine.

"You've come about that little affair?" he said.

"Yes."

"Have you done anything in it?"

"No."

"No?"

"Not yet."

"I should have thought you might have managed it by now!"

"I haven't tried"

"Ah, that accounts for it, then! Whatever you tried to do I am sure you could accomplish!"

"You think so?"

"I do, on my soul! There's a coaxing way about you. You'd twist any man round your little finger if you wanted to."

"Could I twist you?"

"Gad! I should be deucedly afraid to let you try. I've no doubt you could, though I'm not a lady's man."

"No, you're not over polite."

"You're alluding to my having made you stand waiting for me a few minutes yesterday morning?"

"Yes."

"Then I can easily explain my conduct."

"Do so."

"I did not know who it was, and we always act like that to strange clients. It makes them think that what they have come to ask for is a greater favour than it really is. Don't you see, it put them somewhat at a disadvantage?"

"I see," she replied, thoughtfully. "Perhaps you intended it to have the same effect with me?"

"My dear lady, can you suppose——"

"Let's come to business!"

"With all my heart. What have you to propose?"

"About this bill, then. You will not be content without Crockford signs in your presence?"

"Well, no—I am afraid that that is indispensable. Not that for a moment I suppose——"

"Yes that will do," she interrupted imperiously. "Don't put yourself out of the way. It shall be as you wish."

"And when will you bring him?"

"Where?"

"Here, at my office."

"I am not going to bring him at all."

"I don't understand."

"He will sign it at my house."

"Oh, very well; I will wait upon you whenever it is convenient, and you can introduce me to him."

"You are not going to be introduced to him at all."

"But if he is going to sign in my presence!"

"He will not see you!"

"Not see me?"

"No, you will be concealed at the time, and will be able to observe him unobserved."

The Jew stared at her in astonishment.

"Well," said he, after a pause, "I'm agreeable that way if you like it, only I don't quite understand——"

"I see no necessity for your understanding more than I choose to tell you. You want the signature to the bill. That is all, I believe?"

"Yes, if I see him write it."

"You shall!"

"And when is this to be?"

"To-night!"

"At what time?"

"At eleven."

"Eleven! That is late"

"I cannot fix an earlier time. Is it worth your while to take a little trouble in the matter?"

"Yes, if you like; I don't mind trouble, for that matter. I will come when you choose"

"Come to my house, then, at ten to-night. Here is my address" (writing it, as she spoke, upon a card.) "You shall see the bill signed to-night, and you must have the money ready for me to-morrow, when I come for it."

"It's a bargain. How much will the bill be for?"

"I want a thousand pounds. How much must he draw it for?"

"A thousand pounds!" exclaimed the Jew, in astonishment. "You talked of five hundred the other day."

"I want a thousand now. Can you do it? Yes or no?"

"Well, well! don't be so hasty. Yes, I daresay I can manage it. I'll let you have five hundred to-morrow, anyhow."

"No; I must have it all—at once."

"I can't do it."

"Then the affair falls to the ground."

"Well, then, there! you shall have the money. There's no refusing you anything."

"How much must he draw for?"

"Two thousand!"

"Nonsense!"

"I won't take less!"

"You'll take twelve hundred!"

"No, I won't!"

"Yes, you will!"

"I'll be damned if I do!"

"It'll be the same if you don't!"

"Ha! ha!" laughed the Jew. "Never saw such a woman in all my born days! Well, then, fifteen hundred. Come, what do you say to that?"

"That will do," replied the other, wearily; and as the Jew walked away to his cupboard she muttered to herself, "He could have had what he chose. After all, a pound is the same as a penny, when neither is to be repaid."

The Jew meanwhile had been searching among the papers in his cupboard.

Shortly he returned with an oblong slip of

paper in his hand, which he laid upon the table, while he consulted his pocket-book.

"That will do," he said. "That is the proper stamp Now be careful. He is to sign this paper. A smaller stamp will be of no value whatever, so be careful not to lose it, if you please."

"I will take care."

"You ought to pay me for it by rights, but you shall owe it me, for the sake of your pretty eyes. You're a downright beauty, you are, by the Lord!"

Ruth smiled and turned towards the door.

The Jew stepped forward, opened the room-door for her, and was conducting her down the passage, when a knock at the street-door caused him to pause.

"Perhaps you had better wait a moment," he said—and, as he spoke, he opened the door of his own room, and allowed her to pass in.

She had not, however, time to disappear before the street-door opened, for one of the Jew clerks had happened to come in from an errand at the moment, and had admitted the visitor with his key.

As the visitor entered he called to Levi, and Ruth, with a violent palpitation at her heart, recognised the voice.

It belonged to the Prince.

"Levi," said he, "I want to have a little chat with you. But you—you're engaged, I see."

"Oh, no!" replied Levi, who was anxious to speak to the Prince about some business. "Will you step into my office for one moment?"

Then, as the Prince entered, he motioned to Ruth that the coast was clear, and that she could now make her escape.

Ruth hesitated, however, for an instant.

She was uncertain what to do. Should she beg of the Jew to keep her visit a secret from the Prince?

If she did, would not the Jew be the more likely to tell him?—or, if he did not tell him, would he not trade upon the secret of her hiding-place, and endeavour, thereby, to extort from her some bribe, to keep the secret from the Prince?

She decided, at last, that she would trust to chance. Levi knew of her connexion with the Prince, and, for his own sake, she fancied that he might be inclined to keep the fact of her visit a secret.

She drew down her veil, and, having hastily requested the Jew to be sure to be at her house at the time she had appointed, hurried rapidly away.

The Jew watched her depart, and then invited the Prince into his private room.

For a few minutes they were engaged in an earnest conversation, upon a matter of business which, however, as it does not in any way relate to the story I am telling, I need not bore the reader with the particulars of.

When this matter was discussed, the Prince was rising to go, but the Jew stopped him.

"How are things going on in Belgravia?" he asked, casually. "All right?"

"All right, I believe."

"The ladies are all well, I trust?"

"I believe so."

"Mrs. Belvidere, particularly?"

The Jew saw that something was wrong, by his companion's manner, which had changed very much since the conversation had taken this turn.

"I suppose that Mrs Belvidere is still the reigning deity amidst that galaxy of female loveliness?"

"She is not there any longer."

"Not there any longer!" exclaimed the Jew, in amazement. "Why, she never said——"

"Said what?" asked the Prince.

"Nothing!"

"When did you see her last?"

"Oh, not long ago! But, tell me, what has made her leave our company?"

"Her reasons are best known to herself. I am not acquainted with them."

"And where has she gone?"

"I do not know."

"You do not know?"

"No."

"Perhaps you do not care?"

"Perhaps not much. Nevertheless, I am just this much anxious. I will give——"

"Well?" said the Jew, seeing that he paused.

"I will give fifty pounds to find out where she—where she——Where the devil did you get this from?"

The Prince, as he had been speaking, had chanced to take up a card, which the Jew had left lying upon the table.

He had been almost unconsciously reading an address written upon it; and, as he looked at it, it struck him that somewhere or other he had seen the writing before. But whose writing, and where?

He twisted the card over carelessly, and started suddenly, at seeing that it had been written upon one of his own visiting cards.

Hastily he turned it back, and recognised immediately the handwriting.

It was Ruth's.

It was a card which she had taken unthinkingly from her card-case, and had written her address upon, when she gave it to the Jew.

He carelessly had laid it down upon the table while he went to look for the bill stamp, and had forgotten to take it up again.

"What's the matter?" he asked.

"Where did you get this address?" asked the Prince eagerly.

"Bless me, it's of no moment to you, I am sure!" said the Jew.

"Yes, it is!" replied the other, warmly. "Whose address is it?"

"It's the address of the lady who was here just now."

"Good heavens! Then it was she!—it was Ruth! Where is she?"

"Ruth!" gasped the Jew; "What do you mean? How do you know?"

"See here!"

Then the Prince turned over the card which he still held in his hand, and showed his own name upon the other side.

The Jew stared at it, and scratched his head and grinned.

"What makes you think it is Ruth?"

"I am certain it is; I know her writing; and ——But I can go and see for myself now I know her address."

"Stop! stop!" cried the other. "What a state of excitement you are in!—how you tremble! What are you going to do?"

The Prince paused, and drew himself up to his full height.

"Nothing," he replied; "at least, not yet."

"Not till to-morrow, at any rate?"

"Why to-morrow?"

"Because she is going to put a little money in my way to-night. After she has done so, I don't care a curse what becomes of her!"

"You will warn her against me?"

"No. Why should I?"

"Promise me you will not Here, I will pay you for your silence."

"I'm much obliged to you!"

"You will not mar my scheme?"

"No, if you don't spoil mine. By twelve to-night I shall have no further use for her."

"At one, then, she is mine; and then vengeance!—vengeance!"

CHAPTER LXXIV.

A VERY SHORT CHAPTER, BUT WHICH IT IS NECESSARY SHOULD BE READ CAREFULLY.

Upon the evening of the same day when occurred the events I have just described, two men met at the bar of a low public-house in the neighbourhood of Drury Lane, and after exchanging a "Good evening," and How d'ye do?" asked one another what they were going to drink.

This matter having been settled, they retired to a dark corner, and began to talk in a low tone earnestly.

One was evidently a foreigner, although he spoke English fluently.

The other was a John Bull.

They had both the air of determined, resolute men. They had both something peculiar in their carriage—something slouching, indescribable.

One was Sergeant Cop, of her Majesty's detective police.

The other was a Frenchman, a spy and an informer, and an agent of the secret police of Paris.

"How goes it, Mr. Cop?" asked Monsieur.

"Same as usual," responded the Englishman.

That was the way they began.

"Have you any news, Mr. Cop?"

"Not a blessed scrap!"

"Why, how is that? Have you given the job up?"

"Not exactly. As long as I am paid I shall work"

"But you get no nearer the end!"

"That's not my fault, is it? I've searched high and low. There's not a likely or an unlikely place that I haven't looked for her—and I haven't found her. But, as I said at first, it's been a tough job I said it would be, and it has."

"Well, I allow we ain't often set to catch such a tartar. She was in our line herself, you told me."

"She was the artfullest hand that I ever came across. She'd have given the double to Old Nick himself!"

"She's given it to us."

"You're right there; and she'll give it us a good bit longer, or I'm much mistaken."

"You are much mistaken, then, Mr. Cop."

"What do you mean?"

"I mean that we've found her."

"Found her! Where?"

"At Brixton."

"Where—in the gaol?"

"No; in a villa, under the name of Beresford, pretending to be a widow, and keeping company with Captain Charley Crockford."

Mr. Cop opened his eyes and mouth as wide as he could, and said, "Oh!"

When he had recovered a little from the astonishment which the information seemed to have caused him, he asked rather glumly, "Who found her?"

"The Prince himself."

"The deuce he did! That's awkward!"

It was very awkward, for these two men had been receiving a couple of guineas each every day, for a fortnight past, during which time the Prince had been paying them to use their best efforts to discover Ruth's biding-place.

Regularly every day they had pocketed the money, and slouched about and looked uncommonly knowing, but had discovered nothing.

The Prince, at the onset, had even suggested that they should watch Crockford; and Mr. Cop had made some sort of show of doing so, bu nothing had come of it.

"It seems to me," said Mr. Cop, "that the game is up."

"As far as you are concerned, there's no doubt about it."

"Well, I am very sorry for it. I am sorry we are going to part company."

"So am I, for we have spent some very pleasant evenings together over this little job."

"When are you going to make the seizure?"

"To-night."

"Am I wanted?"

"Yes, we want your assistance until we get her into the boat. Then we can manage by ourselves."

"What time are you going to take her."

"Not until past midnight."

"That's making it late."

"We've two reasons for doing so."

"What are they?"

"The first is, that we want to conduct the business as quietly as possible, when there is no chance of a crowd."

"And the second?"

"Is that we want to catch her when Crockford is not with her, for he has supper there sometimes, and stops rather late."

"And so, to make sure he won't be there, you wait until she has gone to bed?"

"Yes."

"Well, it strikes me that that is just the time that he is likely——You know best, though, I suppose. Where am I to meet you?"

"I am going now to see the Prince, to receive his instructions. Come with me."

"Lead the way."

As they quitted the house, Mr. Cop heaved a sigh.

"I am rather sorry for her," said he. "I suppose she'll get it rather hot when you get her in your clutches."

"Very hot indeed when she reaches her journey's end."

"Will you take her away directly?"

"Yes; the boat is lying waiting for us now!"

"You manage these little jobs well in France!"

"We do, Mr. Cop! We manage them without any fuss or bother. We lay our hand upon the party we want, and we walk them off. We lock them up, we lop off their head, and there is an end of it, and nobody interferes!"

"God grant that I may never be 'wanted!'"

"God grant you may not, or it may go as hard with you as with the woman we are about to take—this Mrs. Trail, *alias* Mrs. Belvidere, *alias* Mrs. Beresford, *alias* Ruth Hardwicke, *alias* Ruth the Betrayer, *alias* the Female Spy!"

CHAPTER LXXV.

NIGHT IN BRIXTON—MARY ANNE, AND THE SUPPER BEER.—THE STRANGE MAN KEEPING WATCH—A POLICEMAN BENT UPON DISTINGUISHING HIMSELF.—THE SUPPOSED BURGLARS.—A SCUFFLE.—THE DISCLOSURE—RATHER HUMILIATING FOR THE "GENTLEMAN IN BLUE."

NIGHT!

Night in a genteel suburb of London. A very different kind of night to that which we find in the busy East-end, teeming with life—noisy, bustling, crowding, ever restless, and busy

A very quiet night, indeed, it was, this summer's evening, in North Brixton.

The neighbouring church clocks had just struck nine, and the "supper beer" was going his rounds, wakening the distant echoes with "sounds melodious."

Behind the illuminated blinds of the well-to-do houses, the outline of Mary Anne, the housemaid, might have been seen passing to and fro, like a figure in a fantoccini-show, whilst engaged in laying the cloth for supper.

Presently, perhaps, Mary Anne might also have been observed upon her way to the fishmonger's, round the corner, from which she would shortly return, laden with three dozen of the best natives, or an extra-sized crab, warranted fresh-boiled that morning; or, should her master and mistress be in a humbler sphere of life, and bent upon a more economical style of refreshment, a quarter of a pound of the best brisket, and two ounces of ham, by way of relish.

Then, at the street corner, may be encountered, boldly facing the north-east hurricane, which, lying in wait for that coy maiden, with devilish cunning and villanous intent, seizes her in its rough embraces, and shamefully tumbles her white petticoats and virgin frock of cleanly-washed cotton, with its rough gambelling, sending her, blushing and palpitating, on her way, embarrassed almost beyond all power of endurance—between her fears for the well-being of the articles of refection she carried, and her sense of outraged propriety with respect to the unseemly display of her shapely legs and snow-white cotton stockings.

"It's rather windy, ain't it?" the potboy says, who meets Miss Mary Anne round the corner, and tumbles up against her, with profuse apologies—"it's rather windy, ain't it?"

"It's dreadful!" says Mary Anne, still struggling with her petticoats. "I never see the like!"

"Nor me, neither!" says the potboy; and they are blown away in different directions—she with the supper, and he with the beer.

"It *is* uncommon rough!" says the old lady with the trotters, who sits just outside the door of the somebody's Head, and whose wares she fancies must have been blown away by the wind—for, when she went inside the bar just now, for half a minute, to see what time it was, she found two of the finest missing.

Unless those boys, who had been playing round the corner all the evening, and who curiously enough disappeared simultaneously with the trotters, could have had any hand in their abduction.

But that couldn't be, surely; for they were such very innocent-looking boys; and one, to look at them, could not have believed that butter would have melted in their mouths, let alone trotters.

But then boys are naturally bad, and so "shocking artful."

A rough night it was, indeed; and what was only a boisterous, petticoat rumpling, and trotter-abducting wind in North Brixton, was an awful hurricane out at sea.

A fearful wind, fraught with death and terror.

A wind for sailors' wives and children to lie in bed, and listen to with quaking hearts.

A wind bearing in its breath a warning of death and desolation, shipwreck and disaster, fatherless babes and weeping widows!

A dreadful night, surely, even at North Brixton, at which the interest of our story keeps us. Thank goodness, though, there is no pressing necessity for its keeping us kicking our heels in the cold at the street corner, as it has kept a certain mysterious individual for a good hour past.

Let us take a look at him

He was rather a stout party—decidedly a Jewish party, too—with a good deal of nose, for a middling sized man.

He was buttoned up very tightly, in a thick great-coat, and he wore his collar turned up, and carried his hands deeply buried in his trousers' pockets, and he looked as if he felt the cold severely.

Anyhow, he said he did.

He said that it was awfully cold—abominably, infernally cold; and he used the very worst language about the matter.

"It's like my damned luck, this is!" said the Jewish gentleman, as he stamped up and down, endeavouring to keep his toes warm, without being very successful. "How long am I to wait, I should like to know?"

But after he had been stamping to and fro for an hour, he was still stamping, still cursing his luck and the weather, and still waiting for somebody or something that did not turn up

"The worst of it is, you know," said the Jewish gentleman, apparently taking himself into his own confidence, and confiding in himself in a deeply injured tone,—"the worst of it is, that I can't as much as go and get a little sup of something warm."

Driven to desperation, he had partaken of a half-pint of bitter ale some short time ago, when the potboy, drifting, tray in hand, before the north-east hurricane, had swept round the corner upon him, and nearly knocked him backwards.

But it was bad beer, and left a disagreeable taste behind it; and it was not a cheering beverage, for it left him feeling very cold, and he was obliged to stamp about harder than ever to warm himself.

Then he thought that perhaps a cigar might comfort him a little, if he could get a light; but the three or four persons who passed by, either had not got one, or would not give one if they had; and after sucking the end of his weed for some time, until it began to unroll, and was otherwise very much damaged, he put it back into his case, and stamped and cursed more than ever.

He found it precious dull, too, for it was a very long sort of road where he was standing—a broad road, lined upon either side with handsome villa residences.

There were no shops, and the nearest public-house was a long way off, round that corner to which allusion has several times been made during the course of this description.

He walked about in front of one particular house, and appeared to be waiting for a signal.

But the signal was such a long while coming,

that he got out of all patience waiting for it; and after he had exhausted a five minutes' flirtation with Mary Anne, and a slight chaff with the pot-boy, he found the time began to hang very heavily upon his hands.

He began to fancy, too, that people noticed his staying in the same place so long, and looked upon him with an eye of suspicion.

One old gentleman, whose railings he had been leaning against unthinkingly, evidently considered him to be a very questionable character, for he had come out of his house, and eyeing the Jewish gentleman with great severity, locked his garden gate, as though to guard against the possibility of the Jewish gentleman's walking into the garden, and off with the plants.

The policeman, too, was not prepossessed in his favour; and the old gentleman and he thus conversed upon the subject.

"I say, policeman!"

"Yes, sir."

"Do you see that strange-looking person standing over there by the lamp-post?"

"Yes, sir."

"A very strange-looking person, I think, policeman!"

"A rum 'un, sir, I should say!"

"Bless me, do you think so?"

"I do, sir."

"What do you think of him, policeman?"

"I don't think much of him, sir."

"Bless me! I wish you'd keep your eye on him?"

"I've had my eye on him for some time, sir!"

"You'll keep a sharp look-out?"

"Trust me for that, sir!"

"That's right. I shall depend upon you;—and I say, policeman!"

"Yes, sir."

"Here's a shilling for you!"

"Thank you, sir."

And the policeman departed, very well satisfied with himself and the shilling.

In about half an hour's time, the old gentleman and the policeman, still keeping a sharp look-out, held another conference at the former's garden-gate.

"What's become of that party, policeman?"

"He's here still, sir."

"Where?"

"On the other side of the road, over there, in the shadow of that garden wall."

"Ah, to be sure! But he's not alone!"

"No: there's two others with him!"

"What sort of persons?"

"Rum 'uns, sir, both of 'em!"

"I hope you're keeping your eye on them, policeman!"

"I haven't had it off yet, sir!"

"That's right, for there's no knowing what they may be up to! We may all be murdered in our beds if we don't look out! Thank heavens! I have a capital blunderbuss, and a watchman's rattle, and a sword-stick, and I don't think much harm can come to me if I only happen to be awake at the time they are trying to force an entry! But, for goodness sake, keep an eye on them!"

"You may depend upon me, sir!"

After another five minutes, another interview took place between the same parties.

"Well, policeman?"

"Well, sir?"

"What's going on now?"

"One of 'em's gone into a house, and the other two's waiting outside!"

"Gone into a house! Good gracious! Has he picked the lock of the door?"

"No."

"Has he cut a pane out of the window?"

"No."

"What then, in the name of goodness?"

"He's been let in by the servant!"

"The infamous hussy!"

"You may well say that, sir!"

"What do you think is their intention, policeman?"

"Burglarious, sir, I should say; but I'll keep my eye on them!"

"What do you mean to do?"

"I shall be relieved in a few minutes; then I and my mate will try and collar the two waiting outside!"

"That will be the best plan!"

That was the plan which the sagacious protector of the public peace thought it wisest to adopt; but at the same time another thought struck him.

Perhaps this was an opportunity for distinguishing himself. It was an opportunity he had been longing for ever since he had been in the force.

Should he allow it to slip through his fingers?

Should he allow these burglars to slip through his fingers also?

Would it not be best to pounce upon them, and, single-handed, bear them off in triumph?

Would not that be the shortest road to promotion? Was not that the way to become a sergeant or an inspector?—to be spoken of with praise by his worship at Bow Street, and quoted in the newspapers?

Should he be able to do it? It was worth trying. He would try.

Summoning up his courage for a great effort, he approached the two men standing upon the other side of the road in the shadow of some trees in the spot which he had pointed out to the old gentleman.

The two suspicious parties had got their heads very close together, and were, at the moment that he approached them, staring earnestly through an opening in the bushes towards one of the villas.

It was the villa into which their companion had gained admittance a short time before by the aid of the servant-girl.

They were watching and talking together in tones sufficiently loud for the policeman to catch the words which they uttered.

He listened.

"What a long while he's gone!" said one man to the other.

"I wonder how long he's going to be?" observed the other.

"Is he to give us notice?"

"He said so."

"I wish he'd do it, then. I'm tired of waiting."

"We mustn't go in till he does."

"Well, the job's safe, anyhow, and the swag is certain; so we'd better wait patiently."

"What's he say about 'swag?'" the policeman asked himself. He could just catch a word here and there, and what he made out convinced him that he had to deal with burglars.

The two men did not notice him coming, being too intent upon watching the house through the trees.

The policeman crept behind them.

Then made a sudden spring, and collared them both.

The next minute the three were rolling in the mud.

But they shook off his hold without much trouble, and soon were on their legs again.

He also resumed an upright position as soon as he could get his breath.

Then all three contemplated each other, with expressions of astonishment upon the part of the two supposed burglars, and hesitation upon the part of the policeman.

"Hollo!" said he, "what are you up to?"

"What are *you* up to?" retorted one of the men.

"Yes," said the other, speaking with a foreign accent; "what's your little game?"

"I'll precious soon show you!" said the policeman, making as though he would have collared them again.

But one of the men waved him off impatiently.

"Don't make a fool of yourself!" said he.

"A fool of myself!" gasped the policeman.

"You're young in the service, ain't you?"

"What's that to you?"

"Everything. You're green, I see."

"I'll let you know who and what I am directly!"

"And I'll let you know also, sawny! I'm Inspector Cop."

"And I'm Fisk, of the Imperial Police of Paris."

"The deuce you are!"

As they spoke, the two men threw open their over-coats, and disclosed uniforms below.

"Why didn't you speak at once?" said the disappointed policeman.

"Why didn't you give us the chance?" said Mr. Cop. And then he added, "You take my advice, my lad: you mind your business, and we'll mind ours. Good night to you!"

CHAPTER LXXVI.

VENUS.

LEAVING the detective officers watching the outside of the house, allow me to introduce you, gentle reader, to the interior.

Come with me.

Into an apartment upon the first floor, splendidly furnished, partly as a drawing-room, partly as a boudoir—a sumptuous apartment, illuminated by near upon fifty candles of rose-coloured wax, which shed a soft, deliciously warm light upon the objects which the room contained.

Vases full of rare hot-house flowers stood upon the side tables and upon the mantelpiece. Upon a table in the middle of the room were spread several dishes loaded with luscious grapes and peaches, whilst a couple of bottles of champagne stood in ice by the side of the table, for use should they be required.

At the time that I would have had you enter the room, it contained but one person—that person, a woman.

There are many vaunted types of female loveliness. Some go in ecstacies over the tinted Venus; some are in raptures with that of Titian; many believe that in nature there exists nothing to compare with their painted or sculptured *beau ideal*.

But those who had gazed upon the fair creature which that room contained must have had a curious taste, or have been predisposed to make objections, who would not have owned right off that there was loveliness transcendant, dazzling, unapproachable—the loveliness of a real living and breathing, beautiful woman.

It was Ruth, at all times beautiful; but never upon any former occasion, probably, had her loveliness so asserted itself as it did upon this.

All the artifices of the toilet had been employed to heighten the effect of that beauty which nature had bestowed upon her in a form the very rarest, most delicate and bewitching.

She sat, or rather reclined, at full length upon a kind of divan of crimson velvet, beautifully soft and easy, like a bed of down.

She was clothed in a flowing robe of some material, the texture of which resembled the finest web—a material which you could have imagined it would have been possible to blow away with a breath, but which yet was not quite transparent.

Not quite, but almost so. The voluptuous form which it enclosed was hidden as if it were in water, and deep down beneath a gauzy cloud the figure of the reposing beauty could be dimly discovered, lying in a graceful attitude of dreamy languor, beautiful beyond description.

Her fairy flaxen hair, twisted into a hundred curls, covered her lovely head, and flowed upon her bare bosom, her swan-like throat, so snowy white, and round, and polished.

Upon her neck she wore a necklace of glittering diamonds, and diamonds were on her wrists.

In her hair was twisted a garland of real flowers.

Her tiny feet would have been naked, had it not been for slippers of rose-coloured satin, embroidered with gold, which were so wonderfully fragile and delicate, one felt that a teaspoonful of water would ruin them for ever.

Have I more to describe? Can I say more than I have said? She was beautiful beyond description.

The sight of her, lying there, languid and dreamy, surrounded by flowers, jewels, velvet, fruits, wine—every luxury, apparently, which one is accustomed to meet with in the most extravagant flights of the poet's imagination, who tells us of the loves of the gods—was sufficient almost to turn any ordinary person's head, and make them believe that they were dreaming, and instead of North Brixton, that by accident they had got into paradise.

Such an idea probably entered the head of the Jewish gentlemen, when, after kicking his heels for almost an hour and a half out in the cold and wind, he was summoned into the house by a maidservant, and ushered into the warm and scented apartment, which contained the lady he had come to see.

Mr. Solomon Levi opened his eyes and stared, but he was a great deal too much astonished to say anything.

The girl left the room, and closed the door behind her.

Mr. Levi still continued staring.

After a while, appearing to get rather dazzled by the vision before him, he rubbed his eyes very hard, and stared again.

Ruth broke into a merry laugh.

"Well, Mr. Levi?" she cried.

"Well!" he uttered with difficulty.

"Don't you know me?"

"What, you are real, then?"

"What did you think I was?"

"I thought you were waxwork; I thought you were supernatural—a spirit—a vision—I don't know what. I never knew anything so beautiful."

"You're joking!"

"Upon my soul I'm not!" the Jew cried with energy, drawing nearer towards her as he spoke. "If all the wealth of Peru were mine, and by parting with it I could purchase so priceless a treasure as your love——"

The lady looked at him a moment steadily, as though she were turning over some scheme in her mind; but she dismissed it with a slight gesture of impatience, at the same time rising from the couch, just as the Jewish gentleman was about passionately to press one of her fair, plump white hands to his lips, in token of his devotion or attention, which she rewarded by a tingling slap on the cheek.

"Come, come!" she said; "I did not ask you to come here to make love to me!"

"No, but now I have come, will you be so cruel?"

"Silence! we understand one another. You love your gold more than you love me, Mr. Solomon. Don't be so deceitful!"

"How can you say so?"

"Silence, I say! Have you got the thousand pounds."

"Yes."

"Where is it?"

"At my office."

"Ready for me to-morrow?"

"If you get the bill signed."

"Very well."

"And I must see it done."

"You shall."

"Where am I to be?"

"Do you see that curtain in the corner of the room?"

"Yes, what of it?"

"It conceals a closet. Inside there you shall hide yours lf."

"Can I see there?"

"I have had it arranged on purpose. In the door there is a peep-hole, as you will discover when you are inside. We have no more time to waste. Come, and I will show you to your hiding-place.

"Is Crockford here?"

"Yes, he is down stairs, and will be here immediately. Quick—in with you!"

She held open the door of the cupboard as she spoke, and the Jewish gentleman, very much annoyed and bewildered, stepped forward as directed.

"I shan't be shut up very long, shall I?" said he.

But the next moment the door was shut on him.

He looked round eagerly, and found, as she had said, a round hole in the door.

To this he applied his eye, and waited in intense anxiety for what was to come next.

CHAPTER LXXVII.

THE JEWISH GENTLEMAN IN THE CUPBOARD.—PEEPING TOM IS BAFFLED.—ANXIETY.—MYSTERY.—A GLEAM OF LIGHT.—THE SIGNATURE.—THE SYREN'S WILES.

THE Jewish gentleman was extremely anxious to see and hear all that went on within the apartment.

When the door was closed upon him, he was, at first, almost inclined to think that some sort of sell had been practised upon him by the beautiful, but artful, young lady who had lured him into his hiding-place.

But when, after some little trouble, he discovered the hole in the door which she had spoken of, a great weight was lifted off his mind.

Instantly he applied his eye to the orifice.

He was compelled to assume a most uncomfortable position to bring his eye down to its level; but he cared nothing for discomfort.

The curiosity he felt to see and hear all that passed, would have caused him to have borne a very large amount of misery without repining.

He therefore screwed himself into a crab-like attitude, and applied his eye to the hole.

"The devil take her!" he muttered.

There was a glimmer of light upon the other side, but he could see nothing.

The curtain which had partly concealed the door from his view when he was in the room, covered the hole in the panel.

"She did it on purpose!" he muttered to himself, with an oath. "However, she shan't play the fool with me, I can tell her that! She won't have a halfpenny of the money, unless I see the Captain write the signature!"

He was just upon the point of calling out to Ruth, to tell her that he could not see, when he heard the room door slam.

Rapidly placing his ear where a moment before he had had his eye, he listened intently.

With great difficulty he caught the words uttered within the room.

It was the lady's maid, who had, apparently, answered her mistress's summons.

"You rang, ma'am?"

"Yes."

"Captain Brown is still down stairs?"

"Yes, ma'am."

"What is he doing?"

"He is smoking in the dining-room."

"Has he asked for me?"

"Yes, ma'am."

"Often?"

"Twice."

"Did he wonder why I detained him below so long?"

"He asked what you were doing."

"Of course you said nothing about my visitor?"

"Not a word, ma'am."

"Does he seem impatient?"

"I think he does, ma'am, rather so."

"Tell him I shall be glad to see him, then And, Mary——"

"Yes, ma'am?"

"Do not disturb us until I ring."

"No, ma'am."

"You understand, under no pretext whatever.'

"Certainly, ma'am, by no means."

The servant left the room, and the door slammed as before.

Ruth was left alone.

The Jewish gentleman determined to profit by the chance, while he had the opportunity of so doing.

He therefore began to hammer with his feet against the door, calling out at the same time.

"Hallo!—hallo! I say!—I say! I want to speak to you!"

Almost instantaneously the curtain was snatched from before the door, and the light shone in upon his eyes.

Then a voice, which was anything but silvery and musical, demanded—

"What now?"

"I can't see!"

"What?"

"The curtain has fallen down in front of me."

"Well?"

"I can't see what is doing in the room."

"I don't intend that you should."

"But, I say, you know——"

"Well?"

"If I don't see the signature——"

"You shall."

"But I must see it written——"

"You shall."

"Oh, very well; in that case——"

"Have you any more to say?"

"No, as long as it's all right."

"Hold your tongue, then, you fool, or you will suffer for it."

She dropped the curtain with these words, and left the Jewish gentleman to his reflections.

It was a most provoking proceeding upon the lady's part, thus to leave him in the dark. He could not help thinking that; and the epithets he bestowed upon Mrs. Ruth for so doing, were the reverse of flattering.

"But," thought he to himself, "if I can't see, I can hear;" and he applied his ear to the orifice, and listened with all his might and main.

Presently, he heard the door open and shut gently, and he heard a voice say, "Oh, my love, how heavenly beautiful your are!"

The voice was Crockford's, although the tone in which the words were uttered was extremely low, and he could barely hear it.

What Ruth said in reply was perfectly inaudible, and then followed a silence of several minutes, which the Jewish gentleman filled up with muttered curses.

Just now, when the servant had come into the room, it was with extreme difficulty that he had been able to catch the words which had passed between her and Ruth; but now he could hear absolutely nothing.

Then, perhaps, she might have conversed in a louder tone of voice; and lovers' vows are usually uttered in an undertone, except it is upon the stage.

The Jewish gentleman, however, could not help thinking that Ruth must have drawn the curtain more than ever over the outside of the door, so as to drown all sounds.

He very soon worked himself into a fever of anxiety, and began to feel half smothered for want of air.

"Curse her!" he muttered between his teeth, as he wiped great drops of perspiration off his brow. "I'll pay her out for this some day!"

The conversation in the room was continued in a low tone—so low that it was impossible for him to catch a word.

An endless time, which was wearying beyond belief, elapsed without his hearing a syllable that passed.

Then there was some movement in the room—a noise as though a table were being wheeled across the floor close to the door of the cupboard.

He listened eagerly.

A voice spoke close to him.

It was the voice of Ruth, speaking in persuasive accents, though in a light and playful tone, as though she were requesting some trifling favour of her lover.

Suddenly the light streamed in again brightly at the hole in the panel.

As quick as thought the Jewish gentleman applied his eye. Before him he saw Crockford writing at a table. Over Crockford leant the beautiful syren, who, whilst one of her snow-white arms rested upon her lover's neck, and her hand gently caressed his curls, contrived with the other hand to hold back the curtain in such a way that the Jew could obtain a full view of all that passed.

Crockford was writing hastily across a blank piece of paper, which, by its oblong shape, he knew to be the bill-form that he had supplied to Ruth.

"You know, dearest," Crockford said, as he finished and handed it to her, "you must not let this go out of your hands, or—or there will be the deuce to pay."

"My darling, I would not do so for the world!"

"I am sure of that. And stop! Let me sign it."

"Have you not done so?"

"No, but I will do."

"With the name of Etherington, you know."

Crockford dipped his pen in the ink, and appeared to hesitate.

"My name won't do, you say?" he said.

"No, love," she answered. "I explained my reasons."

"To be sure! Only, for God's sake, be careful! What I am doing is forgery!"

"Oh, the idea!"

"It is the case, though. If that paper leaves your hands, I am ruined!"

"Can you not trust me?"

She leant over him as she spoke, and her red, moist lips glued themselves to his—her soft yellow hair smothered his hot face—her languid eyes gazed into his, full of pent-up passion and half-smothered desire.

"I'd trust you with my life!" he said, and scribbled across the paper.

Then the curtain fell.

CHAPTER LXXVIII.

THE JEW OUTWITTED.—VIOLENCE.—THE THEFT. —THE DOOR IS LOCKED.—THE GARDEN.—THE LEAP.—THE CHASM.—THE FALLEN CANDLE.— FIRE! FIRE!—THE RESCUE.—THE MYSTERIOUS DISAPPEARANCE.

For some length of time the Jewish gentleman waited in feverish anxiety to know what was going to be the issue of this strange scene.

But time wore on, and he heard no more and saw no more of Crockford or his betrayer.

"Damn her!" muttered Levi. "What new game is this?"

He grew very impatient, and had some idea of kicking the door open, but he was afraid of the consequences which might befall him did he incur the Captain's wrath.

However, at last, flesh and blood could bear the suspense no longer, and he was about to resort to violent measures, when suddenly the door opened, and Ruth stood before him.

The room was almost in darkness. The lights were all extinguished. The moon, struggling in through the curtains, which half obscured the window, alone illuminated the apartment, which looked sombre and shabby.

"Are you satisfied?" asked Ruth, in a hoarse whisper. "You saw it done."

"Yes! yes! Where is it?"

"Where is what?"

"The bill?"

"What do you want with it?"

"Give it me, and I will have the money ready for you when you call in the morning."

The woman responded with a low laugh.

"Do you take me for a fool?" she said. I will bring the bill with me to-morrow."

"That will not do. I will have it to-night."

"Why?"

"Why! Because—because you will be—that is, I must have it, I tell you!"

"You haven't told me why."

"No? Well, it is necessary I should show it to the party who is going to advance the money. He won't let me have the money without he sees the bill first."

"He shall see it to-morrow. We will go there together."

"I have to see him to-night. He won't be there to-morrow."

"To-night! It is a very strange time! You must make an appointment with him for me."

"It can't be done. You can't have the money without you do as I say."

"Then I'll go without it. Look here, Mr. Levy, you understand me—I am not to be cheated. When you give me the money, I will give up the bill. Not before!"

The Jew gnashed his teeth with rage.

Was he thus going to be foiled by this cunning woman?

"No, by God!" he muttered to himself. "I will have it, by fair means or foul."

Of course he meant foul. But how was he to obtain his end? Suddenly an idea struck him.

"Have you got it here?" he asked, calmly.

"Yes," she replied, with some hesitation.

"I should just like to look at it."

"Why?"

"Only to see that it's all correct and formal. What the devil else should I want it for?"

"Mind, you shan't take it."

"Don't frighten yourself! If it's all correct, it's worth the money I said I'd give for it, and I'll see what can be done without taking it away. Perhaps I may be able to work the oracle for you, though I promise nothing."

She stood still a minute, as though reflecting upon what he said.

He could not see her face, but he fancied that this was how she must be occupied.

He fancied, too, that her piercing eyes must be fixed upon him in the darkness.

He could not see them, but he seemed to feel them.

Presently she moved away from the spot where they were standing, and crossed the room.

He stood still, listening, and heard her strike a match.

Then she returned, holding a lighted taper in one hand, and the bill in the other.

She held the latter tightly between her fingers, and held it in such a position that he could read what was written upon it.

He read. The words were what they should have been. There was no flaw in the document.

The Jew had intended to have snatched it from between her fingers. He saw that this would have been impossible without destroying the paper.

What could he do? There was but one course left.

All at once, without any warning, as she bent her head over the paper, he struck her a fearful blow with his clenched fist upon the forehead.

It fell upon her like a stone.

The next moment he had seized the precious document and thrust it into his breast. Then he rushed precipitately down stairs.

The street door was locked, and the key removed. Ruth had ordered that it should be so, and that, when she rang, the girl was to let him out at the back.

Finding egress by the front impossible, he made his way down the passage, and searched for the back door.

He was not long in finding it; and, to his great relief, he found it open; for he dreaded every moment that Ruth would recover her senses, and scream to the Captain for help, and that he should be pursued, and the forged bill wrenched from his grasp.

He dragged open the door, however, and got safely into the back garden.

His object now was to make his way round to the front; but he found the gate which divided the front and back gardens locked, or bolted, in a way that defied all his efforts to force it open.

"I'll get out, somehow, though!" he said; and, trampling over the flower-beds, he scrambled on to the top of the wall which ran along at the bottom of the garden.

Upon the garden side, it was not more than five feet from the ground, and he easily managed to gain the top. When there, he prepared to spring down to the ground.

But just at that instant the moon hid itself behind a cloud, and prevented him from seeing what lay in front of him.

He would have hesitated about taking a leap into an unknown country, but he fancied that he heard one of the upper windows open suddenly.

If he waited for the moon to come out again, he thought, he would surely be detected.

Perhaps the Captain might fire at him. It would not do to risk it. No, he would jump down into the road, which, he supposed, lay before him; and then as quickly as possible make his way round to the front, where the detectives were anxiously expecting his return.

Without further delay, then, he took a spring—into eternity!

Unhappy wretch! Had he waited for the moonlight, he would have seen that a deep excavation had been made immediately below him, preparatory to laying the foundation of a villa similar to the one which he had just quitted.

Into this yawning chasm he fell, unthinkingly.

His head was dashed with violence against some brick-work at its bottom. His brains lay scattered upon the ground, and he was a frightfully mangled morsel of humanity, when the bricklayers came to find his corpse next morning, stiff and dead.

* * * * *

Meanwhile, Ruth lay senseless upon the floor of the apartment where he had left her.

Thus for a long while she lay undisturbed, and the wax taper which she had lighted, thrown to the ground by her fall, rolled away beneath the muslin curtains of the window.

* * * * *

"Fire!"

The sky is lurid red.

The eager mob, shouting, rushing, scrambling, rush pell mell onward in the direction where the heavens are reddest, and where the fiery monster surely rages.

"Fire! fire!"

The whole firmament seems to quiver in the blood colour. The housetops glitter, and the chimney-pots stand out, lowering and black, assuming shapes half goblin-like, half human.

"Fire! fire!"

Men out of breath, but still running eagerly, ask one another where it is.

"In the Strand!"

"No, in Lambeth!"

"Further than that! It is the Victoria Theatre!"

"Further than that still! It is the Surrey Theatre!"

"Further still! It is Mr. Spurgeon's Tabernacle!"

"No, it is further still! It is out Brixton way!"

Many gave up running, and walked fast, to rest themselves. Some gave it up altogether, but their places were quickly filled by hundreds of others, and on the mob rushes pell mell as before.

Still on—still on—still with the same cry.

"Fire! fire! fire!"

"There's the engines!"

Yes, there they go, at a furious gallop. There they go, with a roar and a clatter, and a yell and a cheer.

Lights gleam from the firemen's helmets. The horses smoke. It rushes swiftly through the air with a rumbling like cannon, and is gone.

"Fire! fire!"

At last the house is reached. That is it—a detached villa in North Brixton.

That quiet, genteel suburb was surely never so crowded before!

The whole road is blocked up by a pushing, shouting, eagerly-excited mob.

The red-hot sparks rose up in columns, and the flames tinged and reddened the thick, black smoke.

The shouts of the populace respond to the roar of the hungry flames.

Through the mob comes soon the snorting

horses and the clattering engine; but they come not in time.

The house is doomed. The devouring monster has got too firm a hold upon it.

Red flames burst forth from its glassy window frames. Flames leap out from holes in the roof.

The house is a raging furnace.

Then suddenly there is an awful crash—a momentary lull of the flames—then a blaze, fiercer and stronger than ever—and a fountain of red-hot sparks rush up into the air, and drift away in volumes of smoke.

The roof has fallen with a deafening roar, and the house is gutted.

But where are the inmates? Who is saved? Where are they all? Is any one missing?

All have left the house. That is very certain.

The landlady and the servant were the first to escape.

Then a gentleman—a Captain of the name of Brown, as it was reported.

Then it had been discovered that a lady had been left behind.

And the Captain had entered the house again, and at the risk of his life had rescued her—carrying her down the ladder of the fire escape in his arms, insensible.

He had left her in the safe keeping of some kind persons, who had come forward to assist him—one was a policeman, the other a foreigner; and he had returned to the fire, to see whether he could be of any assistance to the firemen.

Presently he had returned to inquire about Ruth, whom he had only quitted for a few moments with the greatest reluctance.

But she was gone!

Who had seen her go? Where had she gone to?

Nobody could tell him. She had gone—that was all he could learn. She had gone with the policeman and the foreign gentleman in a cab, and she had left no message for him.

It was most unaccountable.

CHAPTER LXXIX.

THE ABDUCTION—THE TRANCE.—THE PRINCE'S REVENGE.

SLOWLY had Ruth's senses returned, when she heard a well-known voice calling her by name.

Faintly she answered him; but she had not sufficient strength to raise herself from the floor to which the ruffian had felled her. She had just sufficient sense left to know that the Captain raised her in his strong arms, and bore her through the window, through the fire and smoke, down to the earth below, where a score of arms were stretched eagerly out to help her.

Then she felt the cool air fanning her cheek and her aching head, and her scattered senses began slowly to return.

She heard Crockford ask some one to take care of her, and she heard some one say she was perfectly safe.

She looked at the faces round her; but they were all the faces of strangers.

She asked for the landlady, and she was told that she should be taken to her.

Presently she found herself in a cab, and a strange man holding her in his arms—a man in a policeman's uniform.

Some vague terror seized her now; and she struggled and strove to cry for help, but was prevented from doing so.

There was also a foreigner in the cab—a stranger likewise—and he it was who pressed a silk pocket-handkerchief over her nose and mouth.

Then she gasped for breath, and tasted a strange sweet taste.

She was breathing chloroform.

All afterwards was a blank.

Powerless and passive in their arms, they bore her along. The nerves of feeling still acted feebly to the weary and feebly-acting brain.

But the power of motion had deserted her.

She knew not whither she was bound. She knew not how long the journey lasted, or when she reached her journey's end.

She was dimly conscious of outward objects, but she could not open her eyes. She could hear voices faintly, but she could not understand what was said.

She was dimly conscious of dark shapes moving round her. She fancied that she was raised from the ground, and carried some distance, muffled in a cloak; and she thought of the abduction of her mother, and wondered really what would become of her, without feeling very much interested in her own fate.

Hands, she fancied, were placed upon her forehead and mouth, and her own hands were fastened together by something cold, which felt a little like bracelets of jet, but which she presently knew to be handcuffs.

After a time, she felt that she was being rocked to and fro gently, and she guessed that she was in a boat.

Then she was being raised again in a man's arms. She was being borne up the side of a vessel.

Then she was being carried down into a cabin.

Then she was at rest.

Time passed on.

Her head throbbed—her eyes were heavy; she could not raise the lids.

Her eyes were closed—her teeth tight-set; she could not open her mouth.

All at once, something cold was dashed into her face. The dead weight which oppressed her vanished. The muscles of her mouth relaxed.

She slowly recovered her senses. She shook off the lethargy, and opened her eyes.

Opened her eyes to find herself in the small cabin of a ship, lying handcuffed and half undressed upon a sofa.

Opened her eyes to see a scowling face looking down upon her, and recognised with a shudder and a half scream, the Prince, to whom she had been false.

He it was, then, who had caused her to be brought hither.

For what purpose?

He it was into whose power she had fallen.

What did he want with her, if it were not revenge?

"You know me?" the Prince said, hissing the words at her betwixt his teeth.

She made no answer.

"You know me?" he repeated.

"Yes," she replied, with her old scorn and daredevil courage—"of course I do!"

"Do you not think it strange that we should meet here, in such a place?"

"Not I! I do not think about it."

"Have you no interest in what shall befall you?"

"What are you going to do with me?" she asked, fiercely.

"You know that you played me false!"

"Well?"

"I swore to be revenged!"

"Well?"

"I intend to keep my oath!"

"What do you mean to do?"

"I mean to have your life."

"Would you murder me?" she asked, with a half-shriek, struggling meanwhile into a sitting posture.

The Prince smiled.

"No," he replied, "I am not an assassin. There are others who will do the work for me—they are the instruments of my vengeance."

As he spoke, he turned upon his heel and left the cabin, taking the light with him.

The wretched woman, left to herself in the pitchy darkness, felt all her courage deserting her, and with chattering teeth awaited her murderer's approach.

CHAPTER LXXX.

THE STORM.—THE PRISONER.—FEVER AND DELIRIUM—ESCAPE IMPOSSIBLE.—THE DESPERATE RESOLVE.—THE VOYAGE OF DISCOVERY.

With all her timbers straining, and creaking, and cracking as she wallowed in the deep trough of the sea.

Rolling and heaving, heaving and rolling, upon the ridges of a tumbling ground swell.

With loud flapping canvass and disordered rigging, tossing to and fro, like a nut-shell upon the surging billows, the gallant little cutter Swallow held upon her way, and struggled manfully for France.

The night was dark and lowering, and it was also a threatening night to those who were weatherwise, and whose path lay over the deep, deep sea.

There was scarcely a breath stirring—the sky above was black and starless. A close and torpid atmosphere seemed to brood over the whispering waters, ever restlessly rolling.

Upon the south-eastern horizon there was a narrow streak of dull red light stretched right across the heavens. In the centre of this the moon appeared, half-veiled by flowing masses of spreading and shifting vapour.

On board the ship there reigned an unbroken silence.

The steersman, who, as a rule, has not very much to do during a calm, was seated on the taffrail, smoking a pipe, and swinging his legs in tune to a drinking chorus which he sang to himself beneath his breath.

He seemed to be a very careless and rather roystering dog, and one not easily to be alarmed, and yet there is no denying that every now and then his eyes wandered in the direction of the narrow streak of light in the south-eastern sky, and he seemed to regard that portion of the heavens with an expression of face in which there was a boding anxiety which it was difficult to conceal.

He was a foreign-looking man, this steersman, swarthy and black-muzzled.

A jovial-looking fellow, as I have said; and yet he had a certain lowering expression about the brows, a hardness in the eyes, and wrinkles near the mouth, which indicated that he could at times, if it suited him, be savage and cruel.

One could not help comparing him to the bandits and bravos that one meets with at the Opera or the theatre, as willing to bathe their hands in blood as wine.

To him presently another man ascended from the little companion ladder leading to the cabin below.

A few steps brought him to the side of the steersman, who rose to his feet at his approach, and leant upon the tiller to talk to him.

The new-comer was none other than the French policeman who had assisted Mr. Cop in kidnapping Ruth.

This was the vessel on board which Ruth had been taken.

There were, besides the two men now talking together, two others, the captain and the mate. These and the prisoner composed the whole number of persons on the boat.

"What do you think of the night?" asked the policeman of his companion, addressing him in French.

"Don't overmuch like it," the other replied.

"Squally, you think?" inquired the policeman.

"Looks roughish."

"We can bear a bit of knocking about, though."

"Who can? Do you mean us or the boat?"

"Both."

"We can do with a little of that sort of thing, as far as we go; but the boat——"

"What about the boat?"

"Well, it ain't the strongest vessel in the world."

"Will it hold out against a stiffish gale, do you think?"

"Oh, I think we're safe enough."

"Well, that's a consolation."

The policeman looked abroad on all sides.

Turning his face towards the west, he could see before him a steady and bright light, and upon one side of it, a great distance off, a ruddy light. A little to the left of this were three lights in a triangular shape. At the back of this, very high up, were two other lights, very bright ones. And from behind these a last light, red and bleared.

From all these lights sailors are able to learn the mysteries of the pilotage of the English Channel, and by their position at any time to determine the position of the vessel.

One of the lights he knew to be burning in the market-place of Calais; one burnt on Cape Grinez; one showed the position of the South Foreland; one was the harbour-light of Dover; the last was on the light-ship at the Goodwin Sands.

The person observing these things, however, was profoundly ignorant of their meaning; and I don't believe that he was very anxious to learn it—an opinion which perhaps the reader may also entertain, and so we'll drop the subject.

But meanwhile the storm which threatened was brewing.

A deep, hoarse roar—the sound of wind and water—the gathering, combing, and breaking of the crested waves and sweeping of the currents of air, was audible above the flapping of the sails and the creaking of the timbers of the ship.

"The wind's getting up, isn't it?" asked the policeman.

"We shall have it directly."

"How long first, do you think?"

"About half a minute. Stand steady; its here!"

A damp draught of air rushed by the vessel, swelling out the canvass suddenly, and swaying the ship heavily over on one side with its strength.

But recovering after the first shock, the cutter rose briskly from the encounter; and flinging back, as it were, with a toss of her head, the water that deluged her decks, rushed rapidly onwards, ploughing the green waves with her sharp, wedge-like bows, and bearing off in the direction of the lurid light which marked the position of the town of Calais.

What the steersman had predicted came true before very long.

In half an hour's time, at the utmost, a storm broke over the little vessel.

The Swallow was plunging from sea to sea, dipping her bows into the falling masses of briny water, often with violent shocks which caused her to shiver to her foundation, and driven onwards in her wild course by a rent and flapping mainsail, diminished to one half of its size by a little jib and three reefs, the former of which was for the most part forced into the ocean, and housed again and again by the frothing waves.

Overhead, all was dark and lowering, but the sparkling foam as each wave combed, curled, and burst, lit up the sea around the vessel's sides for a distance of at least twenty feet.

The howling wind came heavy and wet with the driving froth and water gathered in its progress from the water's surface.

By this time the captain and the mate had made their appearance, and the former stood by the side of the latter, anxiously watching the run of the seas, occasionally with a motion of his hand directing when the steersman should ease off the cutter's bow as each rising mass of water went frothing past her cutwater.

All this time the woman confined below lay

prone upon the sofa, unable to rise to her feet, so weak and ailing did she feel.

Her head ached intolerably, and a devouring thirst had taken possession of her; which, in-increased by the fever that consumed her, caused her to be half delirious

It was a curious state of mind which she was in.

The unbridled storm raging around the ship appeared to find something like an inward echo in the deep recesses of her agitated soul.

A strong prognostication of evil forced itself upon her mind that an awful change in her life was about to take place.

She felt that she was about to sink very low.

She had often enough before been in straightened circumstances, had faced poverty and penury, had tasted danger in many and dreadful shapes.

But now a presentiment took possession of her that the stirring epoch of her existence was at hand—a presentiment that intensified upon her momentarily.

Then, as the hurricane howled fiercely without, and the wet sails surged and battled against the strained cordage, and the struggling ship wallowed and staggered with roaring plunges deep into the fastly coming waves, her excited brain made from the jangling uproar a sort of overture to the unknown and awful drama in which she was shortly doomed to act a part.

"What was I brought here for?" she asked herself. "How is it all to end? What are they going to do with me?"

She lay there perfectly motionless, twisting and turning these questions over in her mind.

Why was she there? What were they going to do with her?

She was in the hands of the police—the French police. But why?

Of what crime had she been accused? As yet, of none.

Had her arrest been a legal one? Certainly not.

She knew well enough that she had committed many crimes that would justify her committal to gaol; but they were the laws of England which she had broken—not those of a foreign country.

Then the ominous threats of the Prince recurred to her mind

He had threatened to have her life. She knew well that the Italian's threat would, if it were possible, be carried out. She knew well that he had money and power, and that he could readily procure instruments to carry out his deadly vengeance.

But why had she been brought out upon this voyage?

If they had determined upon her death, why had she not been killed in London?

The deed might have been easily enough committed. There are foul crimes every day perpetrated, which never see the light.

"No" she thought. "Some devilishly-contrived and horrible revenge the Italian was going to wreak upon her, the details of which, to those unacquainted with what a vengeful Italian's mind is capable of conceiving, would appear wild and improbable."

She lay thus pondering silently for a long time, listening to the storm raging without, and longing, though without knowing how to satisfy the desire, for some cold water to slake her intolerable thirst.

Gradually, however, the sensation of heat—hard, dry, fever heat—reached its height.

The sick woman feebly moved her limbs, and writhed under the torment.

That great channel of nervous power, the spine, was at length affected. All at once, what appeared like a stream of liquid fire appeared to run downwards from the brain, and enveloped her whole frame.

Every nerve and muscle appeared to be quivering and tingling.

At length she could bear her restlessness no longer.

At one spring the sufferer started from the sofa, uttering a low, husky cry, and stretching forth her fettered hands, her eyes dilated.

But the pain in her head was so intense, and her weakness was so great, that she sank down again exhausted, and remained motionless for several minutes.

Then, again shaking off, as well as she could, the languor and lethargy which pressed upon her, she rose once more to her feet, resolved upon some immediate course of action.

But what? Where should she go? What could she do?

A score of questions flashed confusedly through her aching and bewildered brain.

As yet, however, she could not reason. Her mind was a chaos of tumultuous emotions.

A sensation of intense fear, however, had the mastery over every other.

What horrors had she not to look for from the hands of her captors! Certain death, and, in all probability, brutal outrage, awaited her.

Flight—instant, swift, and hidden flight was her only resource.

Flight anywhere—flight far away. There was no safety for her until miles and miles of sea were placed between her and her enemies.

But at the moment she had forgotten that she was on shipboard—that escape was impossible.

Yes, impossible!

She paced the cabin eagerly, but with stealthy footsteps.

She gazed out from the port-holes through the bleared glass.

There was a black gulf of unknown depth beneath, and a raging sea, which lashed furiously against the vessel's side.

She listened.

She could hear the tramping to and fro of the men upon the deck.

No one but herself seemed to be below.

She advanced cautiously to the door, and tried it. It opened easily, and she stepped out upon the landing.

A dim light burned in the other cabin—a cabin, the door of which was opposite to the one she had just left.

Entering this, she glanced eagerly round, wondering to whom it belonged

There were papers on the table, scattered about, and some books. A gun was reared up in one corner, and she raised it in her hands, and would have ascertained whether it was loaded, only the handcuffs she wore crippled her.

She must get them off They were not very tight Before she could do anything else this must be effected.

She sat down upon a seat, and commenced resolutely wrenching and dragging, squeezing her fingers together in the hope of getting them into a sufficiently small compass to pass through the iron that encircled her wrists.

While thus engaged, however, she heard a heavy footstep fall on the stairs.

There was not time to get back unobserved into the cabin which she had just left.

In one corner of the cabin where she was there was a dark cupboard.

Into this she crept as noiselessly as possible, pulling the door to after her, and waiting anxiously to see what course events were going to take.

CHAPTER LXXXI.

A HORRIBLE PLOT. — THE PRINCE'S PLAN OF VENGEANCE DISCLOSED. — THE MEDITATED MURDER.

SHE had hardly hidden herself before two men entered the cabin.

One was the captain of the cutter, the other the police officer.

Entering the cabin, the captain called upon the other to be seated, and, at the same time, pushed a bottle and glass towards him, which he took out of a small chest, fastened to the wall.

"Take a drink," said the captain.

"Thank you. I want something a bit cheering."

"You don't seem a very good sailor."

"No," replied the other, with a motion of disgust. "It plays the devil with me. Is the weather mending, do you think?"

"Yes. The worst part is over. I'm afraid the wind will fall directly."

"I hope to heaven it may."

"I'll tell you why it shouldn't, though. I've a scheme to propose."

"Let's have a drop more brandy. Thank you. What is your scheme?"

"Not a bad one, I think."

"Let us hear it."

"Well, this money that the Prince has given us to pay for the lady here——"

"To pay the governor of the prison we are to take her to."

"Exactly."

"Well?"

"Suppose we were to keep the money ourselves?"

"Yes; but we shall have to pay the man at the prison before he will take her in."

"Suppose we don't try him?"

"I don't understand."

"Suppose she never gets as far as France?"

"Where is she to get to?"

"To the bottom of the sea!"

The other man was silent. He regarded his companion with deep attention, and his face grew a shade paler.

Then sinking his voice to a low, hissing whisper—

"Is it murder?" he said.

"If you like to call it so."

"But the consequences?"

"No harm can come to us if we manage matters properly."

"Is everybody on board safe, do you think?"

"No."

"Which would be against us?"

"The steersman."

"How should we manage, then?"

"We mustn't let him know."

"How can we help it?"

"Easily enough, as I'll show you. I'll give him a good dose of spirits presently—half stupefy him."

"Well?"

"Then get him to turn in for awile. I'll tell him that I am sure he must be tired."

"Well?"

"When he's asleep, we'll get her upon deck, and throw her overboard. It's easily done."

"Stifle her screams?"

"Yes— she shan't have much chance of making a noise."

"He wouldn't join us in the scheme, you think?" said the policeman presently, after a little hesitation.

"He is a complete tool of the Prince's. He belongs to him, body and soul."

"What sort of explanation can we make afterwards?"

"As to how it occurred?"

"Yes."

"I keep a log, you know."

"I suppose so."

"In it I enter an account of everything that occurs upon each voyage. In it I shall enter the particulars of this accident."

"This accident?"

"The accidental drowning of our prisoner."

"Ha, ha!"

"You and the mate shall sign it. That will be proof enough for the Prince."

"Well, if he ever found out the truth, he wouldn't so much care."

"We won't let him find it out, though, if we can help it. Whether he cares or not, it would put us into his power."

"Anyhow, his object is to get rid of the woman, if I understand him rightly."

"Yes; but I'll tell you what strikes me."

"What's that?"

"That he'd think drowning—if I may say so——"

"What?"

"Too easy a death for her."

"What the devil does he mean to do, then?"

"Lock her up for life."

"I know that, of course; and I know the prison well enough. I've been locked up there myself."

"Did you like it?"

"There was nothing so very bad about it. She'd be much better locked up there than sunk to the bottom of the sea, I should think, if we only gave her the chance."

"I think not."

"Why not?"

"There are some awful cells or dungeons there, I'm told, where poor wretches are stowed away, out of sight and mind, and die, after years and years of misery."

"They say there are. Now I come to think of it, when I was caged there I heard talk of them."

"And she will be shut up there, will she?"

"Ay, till she dies."

"Poor creature! It will be a mercy to her to drop her in the water."

"Ha, ha!"

"Ho, ho!"

"When's it to be?"

"As soon as we can get the steersman off to sleep."

"Come on, then—let's lose no time."

"It should be over before the morning."

"In less than an hour it will be all finished."

"Come along, then!"

"Lead the way!"

They each took another deep draught from the bottle, and then left the cabin, without exchanging any more words upon the subject.

The listener, with a throbbing heart, heard their retreating footsteps

Then stole out from her hiding-place.

CHAPTER LXXXII.

A SCENE OF HORROR.

LEFT to herself, she began to tear and drag fiercely at her fetters.

Her hands, with the efforts she had been making, were hot and swollen.

There was some cold water in a basin, and into this she plunged her hands. She found that this method was a good one. With a few more arduous struggles, in which she hurt herself dreadfully, she was free.

She had hurt herself badly in the process, and was suffering such pain that she was obliged to sit down and rest herself for a moment or two.

Not for long. There was no time to waste. What should she do next.

Her plans were already formed. She would make a struggle, and, if possible, sell her life dearly.

As soon as she had recovered herself sufficiently, she returned to the gun which she had been examining when she was interrupted.

Taking out the ramrod, she drove it down the barrel.

Ah! It was loaded!

She uttered a joyful exclamation at the discovery; but, next moment, her heart sank low again.

There was no cap upon the nipple.

She searched hastily round the room.

There were two pistols hanging up. One of these, when she tried it, she found to be loaded.

But neither had caps.

Again she resumed her search.

She opened the box from which she had seen the man take out the bottle There was nothing there.

She searched through a chest of drawers There was nothing there.

She began to grow desperate. Her own little pocket-pistol and her poniard had been taken away from her.

She was quite defenceless.

But the thought of her helplessness made her desperate, and, strange to say, instead of depriving her of all courage, made her doubly courageous

All at once, while she was engaged feeling in one of the drawers, she again heard footsteps on the stairs.

Next moment she had jumped back into the cupboard.

A moment afterwards the door opened, and the captain and steersman entered together.

The captain was speaking at the time in a jovial voice.

"You don't feel tired, old fellow?" said he. "Don't tell me, Jacques! You must be. Turn in and rest yourself."

"I'm not tired, I tell you."

"You must be."

"Well, I'll go to bed presently, when the wind goes down"

"The wind has gone down sufficiently already Here, man! have a drink, and go to your berth."

The steersman made no reply, and the captain went to his chest, and brought out a bottle and something in a paper.

The chest was close to the cupboard, and Ruth could hear him muttering between his teeth, probably vowing vengeance against his companion for causing him so much trouble.

When he had found what he wanted, he tilted a little of the powder into a glass, and handed it, filled up with spirits, to the steersman.

The latter gulped it down at a draught.

Ruth watched him drink it in great anxiety

She felt half inclined to make some sign to warn him against doing so, but there were two reasons which occurred to her why she should not follow such a course.

One was. that the surprise which he might feel at discovering her hiding-place might cause him to cry out and betray her to his companion.

Then, again, how did she know that he would side with her?

Probably, he would not do so, for had not the captain said just now that he was devoted to the service of the Prince, and that it would be difficult to corrupt him?

The blood rushed from her heart to her head as she thought what a risk she might have run had she yielded to the first impulse that came over her.

Next moment she found that she had acted rightly in remaining silent. Next moment she could fully appreciate the danger which she had escaped.

The steersman spoke.

Having drank up the spirits which the captain had handed to him, and made an abortive effort to light his pipe, he yawned prodigiously.

"I'll take your advice," said he; "I'll turn in for a while."

"That's right; I'm sure you must need it."

"You won't want me on deck?"

"No more to-night."

"The wind is dropping."

"Rapidly. There's no more occasion for you to remain up any longer. Besides, we can call you if we want you."

"All right, then."

"You'll turn in?"

"Ay. Good night——But, I say!"

"Yes."

"What about the Englishwoman?"

"Well, what about her?"

"She's all safe, I suppose."

"Safe enough, you needn't fear. Where could she get to?"

"Not far, I expect. I'll just have a peep at her, though."

"Do so."

Ruth shivered from head to foot.

Were they going? She would be found out to a certainty—she would be lost!

There was no escape for her; she had no weapon at hand with which to defend herself.

All these thoughts rushed quickly through her brain. In one moment she seemed to live a day.

To suffer the agony of a lifetime!

The next words, however, brought relief.

"She's right enough, poor thing!" the steersman said. "There's no good in disturbing her; let her rest while she can"

"Ah! let her rest while she can," replied the captain.

"We must take care no harm comes to her, that's all."

"Yes, we must look after her."

"I'd rather lose my left hand than that we should not deliver her up safely."

"So would I."

"Good night to you, then. I've come on awfully sleepy; I don't know how it is."

"You're tired!"

"I didn't feel so a few minutes ago."

"It's the warm cabin, perhaps, after being out in the cold."

"I shouldn't wonder. How tremendously sleepy I do feel!"

"Turn in, then, without so much jaw!"

"All right, old fellow! What makes you in such a precious hurry?"

"I'm in no hurry," replied the captain, who scowled so that by the expression of his countenance one could easily have believed that he would gladly have assisted at the other's funeral;—"I'm in no hurry," said the captain; "only you're precious slow."

"Well, I'm off!"

"At last!"

"Eh? did you speak?"

"No."

It was Ruth from whom the ejaculation had involuntarily escaped, without her being conscious of having spoken.

"I thought you said something," the steersman remarked, pausing to listen, with his head a little on one side.

"I said nothing. The brandy has got in your head."

"No, it is because I am sleepy. I am awfully sleepy."

He stood there, opening his huge jaws and yawning prodigiously. The fatigue of this scene to the woman, holding her breath and listening in a tremble, was terrible.

Would he never go to sleep? Would the other never go up the ladder again on to the deck?

Would she never be left to herself?

She began to fear that one of the other men might come down.

She had calculated, by the conversation which had taken place between the captain and the policeman, how many there were on board, and a desperately wild idea had come into her head.

To carry out her plans she must have arms, and she could only find them if left to herself.

If she could not provide herself with some weapon before they returned, she would surely be killed.

"Oh, heaven!" she muttered; "will they never go—will they never go?"

Presently, however, she heard the captain's footsteps ascending the stairs. Then she heard the other man tumbling heavily into his berth.

Two bangs, like small cannon going off, indicated that he had taken off his boots, and let them fall, with a crash, to the ground.

Ruth staid no longer in her place of concealment. She felt that the time had now come for her to take active measures.

She immediately resumed the search which had been interrupted by the captain and his companion.

This time she was more successful. In a drawer of the table she discovered a knife—a long-bladed glittering knife, sharp as a razor, and with a double edge like a dagger. With it she could either cut or stab.

With a smile of triumph she placed it in the bosom of her dress, and looked around to see what else she could find.

Perhaps by a diligent search, she thought, she would come across some percussion caps; then the pistols, at present useless, would be of service to her.

But she could see none. While she was yet looking for them, she again heard footsteps upon the stairs.

"If it is only one of them," she muttered to herself, "I am all right."

It turned out to be the captain.

He paused for a moment opposite the berth in the passage outside the door, where the steersman was sleeping, as Ruth supposed, for the purpose of ascertaining that he was fast asleep.

But soon she saw that he had been otherwise engaged.

He entered the cabin with a couple of pistols—one in each hand.

"That's all right," he muttered to himself. "He's a queer customer, and if he had been rusty he might have given us an ounce of lead."

"He has been taking away the man's pistols," Ruth said to herself.

"Now then," muttered the captain, "where's my log?"

He opened the table drawer, and began to rummage about the papers which it contained.

He had his back turned towards Ruth. He was in a stooping position—the position which was best suited for her purpose.

As he stood there, all unconscious of the fate that awaited him, she drew the knife from her bosom and stole up behind him

She crept forward noiselessly.

She was not in the least hurry. She made her calculations, and deliberated where the thrust should be made.

Then being ready, she raised the knife.

It fell.

With a groan, the captain dropped, face downwards, upon the table, his blood gushing out in torrents upon the papers which littered it.

But Ruth clutched him by the collar, and dragging him backwards, flung his body heavily down upon the ground.

He was already dead Her knife had entered between his ribs, and pierced his heart.

"It's all over with him!" she said to herself, with a fiendish chuckle. "I've turned the tables upon you, old fellow! It was not badly done, I swear! A doctor couldn't have picked out the place much more neatly!"

She hesitated what she should do next; but, after a moment's reflection, she had decided upon a course.

She swept all the papers off the table which the dead man's blood had stained.

Then it occurred to her that if the corpse remained in the same position, it could easily be seen by any person entering the cabin.

If it was seen, and the person seeing it was alarmed by the sight, he might call to another for assistance.

She would, perhaps, have to deal with two. They might even arouse the steersman, who, at present, seemed to be sleeping soundly.

She must not risk this, she thought. What, then, should she do?

Her object was to get each of her enemies, one at a time, into the cabin, so that she might despatch them in the same way that she had done the Captain.

The best plan for effecting her purpose seemed to her to be the one which she adopted now, without any more hesitation.

She exerted all her strength, and taking the corpse in her arms, raised it into an arm-chair, standing at one end of the table.

Having got him there, she forced down his head—resting upon his arms—in a position which made it appear as though he had fallen asleep, with his head on the table.

The limbs, as yet, were not stiff, and she was able to place the body in the way she chose.

The task, indeed, was much more easily managed than might have been supposed, and was not, in the excitement and terror of the moment, so horribly revolting as it appears to one who reads of the handling of this dead body, sitting at home by their fire-side, removed from all danger and fright.

But even under the exceptional circumstances of this case, and of this woman to whom the shedding of human blood was not the greatest novelty, there was something frightful in the act which she was performing, that made her flesh creep, and caused a feeling of sickening loathing to take possession of her.

She paused not, however, to argue with herself, or allowed the feeling of terror to gain a stronger hold upon her nerves.

Working with feverish energy and haste, she was not long before she had fixed the body in the position which she thought was the most likely to lead the person entering the cabin into the belief that the dead man was taking a nap. She had soon finished her work.

When all was arranged, there was nothing left for her to do but to wait for the next victim to come down stairs.

She went to the door, and waited and listened for some moments without any interruption.

She heard the steady pacing to and fro upon the deck overhead of a man walking up and down, apparently the whole length of the vessel.

Some one to whom he occasionally addressed a few words of conversation in a loud tone of voice, remained stationary. He was, although Ruth was not aware of the fact, standing at the wheel; and had taken the place of the steersman, who had been persuaded by the captain to "turn in" for awhile.

After stamping past two or three times, the person walking about stood still just at the head of the cabin stairs, and appeared to be listening.

Ruth remained perfectly motionless, and in her turn listened.

Presently the man spoke.

"Captain!" he said.

Ruth held her breath.

"Captain!" he called again.

He paused awhile and listened.

"Captain!" he cried, for the third time; "why don't you answer?"

Why did he not answer? She trembled at the question, and her blood turned cold in her veins.

"Captain!" the man said above; "why don't you speak? Come up-stairs a minute. I want you."

She stood perfectly still with her eyes fixed upon the ladder, and her back turned to the cabin.

All at once she heard a movement behind her.

A rustling sound, which made her hair bristle upon her head with fright.

She sprang round instantly, expecting to find the dead body having recovered its strength of motion, creeping upon her from the back.

But no—the body was still where she had left it.

What had caused the noise, then, that she had heard?

Ah! great heavens!

The body was there where she had left it, but it was moving.

Was it about to rise?

A second glance, however, told the truth—it had not been securely fixed in its place.

It was slipping down to the ground.

As it looked, it slipped and slipped slowly.

Then of a sudden, fell with a dead, heavy sound upon the cabin floor.

As it did so, and while she was yet pressing her hand upon her heart to stop its throbbings, the man's voice above again attracted her attention. He was again talking to the man at the wheel, and was calling to him loudly.

Where she stood she could both hear what he said and what the other one replied.

"I can make him hear," said the man at the top of the stairs.

She knew by his voice that he was the police-officer.

"What is he about, I wonder?" said the other.

"I can't imagine, unless he has fallen asleep."

"He said you were to wait for him, didn't he?"

"Yes—but he is so long."

"It's very funny. Bawl to him again—louder!"

"Captain! captain!"

"Go down to him. He's as deaf as a beetle when he likes."

The police-officer waited no longer, but began slowly to descend the stairs.

Ruth rushed into the cabin, and prepared for his approach.

CHAPTER LXXXIII.

THE POLICE-OFFICER IS VERY CAUTIOUS, BUT NEVERTHELESS FALLS INTO THE TRAP.—THE DEATH STRUGGLE.—THE PRAYER FOR MERCY. —THE DISGUISE.

THE police-officer descended the cabin stairs, whistling the last popular street melody, and, to all appearances, little dreaming what danger was in store for him.

It must be owned, though, that he was not in reality as much at his ease he would have wished people to suppose.

The fact is, he was a bit of a coward; indeed, a very great coward; and the captain's not having made any reply to his call caused him considerable uneasiness.

Not that he would have confessed as much had he been questioned. But in his heart, he, figuratively speaking, shook in his shoes.

He could not have told you exactly what he dreaded, but he did dread something; and though he whistled very loudly, he came down the stairs very slowly, and he looked before him, and behind him, and upon either side of him, with the utmost care and precaution.

Indeed, had he known the truth, and expected that round some dark corner an assassin was waiting ready to rush out upon and slay him, he could not have taken more care to avoid surprise and be upon his guard.

One step at a time he came.

"What's he up to?" the police-officer asked himself. "What's he up to? Is he acting fairly? Is it fair play he means? Is he working on the square? What's his little game?"

Thus ruminating, he reached the last of the stairs, and came along the passage past the berth where the steersman snored happily, unconscious of the tragedy which had been enacted at so short a distance from his place of repose.

He paused for a moment when he got thus far, and listened.

Ruth held her breath, tightened her grasp upon the knife, and waited for him.

He seemed more reassured at hearing all was quiet, though she could see by the expression of his face, upon which a ray of light from the lamp in the cabin fell full, that he was not altogether without a lurking apprehension of danger.

"Captain!" he said again, in a loud whisper.

And then he came forward on tiptoe.

Arriving at the cabin door, he poked his head into the room and peered round inquisitively.

Unless he was going to advance further within the cabin, he could not see the dead body.

A box under the table hid it completely from his sight, at the spot where he stood.

A few feet further on, though, he would come within full view of it.

Ruth hesitated, and asked herself whether she should allow him to come thus far.

If he caught sight of it he might cry out. That was to be dreaded; but then, again, if he did not come a little further in, she could not get a good thrust at him.

As he stood now, she could only have plunged the dagger into his left ear.

She therefore allowed him to come creeping in. He came in like a sneaking police spy, as he was, twisting his closely cropped ferret's head to the right and to the left, and prying with all his eyes.

Advancing head first, he got his head and shoulders and his body, to the waist, all round the door post, before his legs left the passage.

When he had got thus far, he dragged his legs after him, and now stood about half a yard from the door.

His eyes were fixed upon the dead man's feet, lying towards him.

In a moment he bounded back towards the stairs.

Ruth flung herself in the way, clutching at him with her left hand, and striking with the right.

She must have exerted enormous strength, or the little man was miserably weak, for she dragged him backwards off his feet, and sent him sprawling to the ground.

In doing so, too, she jerked him with her left hand from the spot at which her right was aiming. The consequence of which was, that instead of plunging the dagger deep into the unfortunate little victim's body, she drove it into the wooden panel, composing the cabin wall.

There it quivered, deeply embedded in the wood.

She almost lost her balance at the moment, and striving to drag out the knife again found that it was impossible.

But there was no time to waste upon that.

The little man was scrambling to his feet.

Turning round, she sprang upon him like a tigress, and dashed him backwards.

The force of the fall brought his cropped head with a frightful crash against the leg of the table.

The blow might truly have been said to have knocked him silly.

He lay there, bleeding like a pig, rolling his eyes, and lolling his tongue at her.

Something he managed to mutter inarticulately, as she clutched at his neckerchief, but whether it was a curse or a prayer for mercy it was impossible to tell.

She knelt upon his breast and grasped his neckerchief, probably with the intention of strangling him.

But the little man wore some paltry contrivance in the way of a stock, with a large made bow in front, and a button to fasten it round his neck behind.

As she grasped at it and gave it a fierce wrench, it gave way with a crack and came off in her hand.

The little man then recovering his presence of mind and what strength he had, began to struggle to get up.

But she held him down, pressing her knee upon his chest, and griping his throat with one hand, while with the other she strove to get hold of a pistol hanging upon a nail above her head.

The little man was in a state of the most abject terror.

Poor wretch! he could not doubt for a moment that she intended to murder him.

Had not the fiendish expression of rage and hate which lit up her handsome devil's face been of itself sufficient warning of the fate in store for him, the dead body of the murdered captain afforded a ghastly proof of her ferocity.

He had recovered the power of speech by now, and he managed to gasp out betwixt his chattering teeth a prayer for mercy.

"Mercy—mercy!"

Mercy, indeed! He might as well have prayed to a stone.

There was no mercy for him in that stern, rigid brow, in those hard, cold eyes—those bright teeth, tightly set and rigid.

No; there was no hope for him there.

But he saw it not. He thought there was a chance. That if he made no resistance, and appealed to her for pity, she might spare him.

Poor fool! it would have been a thousand times better had he, while he had strength left, screamed loudly for help.

Instead of screaming, he only groaned and whimpered.

"Mercy! mercy! Good lady, you wouldn't, surely, take my life? Why should you take my life? What have I done to you?"

She did not answer him. She appeared not to hear him, or to notice him.

She was full of her fell purpose.

She grasped him tightly with one hand, and with the other reached the deadly weapon from its nail.

"Mercy! mercy!" he cried, in an agony of terror. "Oh, spare me!—spare me! Oh, God of heaven! what would you do to me?"

She had got the pistol down now.

"Oh, spare me! I never wronged you! Why should you murder me? You won't murder me? I'm sure you won't; you couldn't have the heart to murder me in cold blood like this?"

But in the midst of his whinings, and groanings, and beseechings, the butt-end of the pistol fell with a blinding smash upon his brow.

She struck him with it a stunning blow, as one might have struck an ox.

A fearful smashing blow.

Again and again the weapon fell, until the end was reddened with the victim's blood.

For a while he wriggled and writhed beneath her grasp like a bruised worm.

But soon his strength was exhausted.

Soon he was stunned and motionless.

Still, though, she battered furiously at the poor wretch's skull, until the bone was fractured beneath the murderous strokes which her fair, white arm dealt upon it with a giant's strength and a savage's fury.

But even she at last was satisfied with the deed of blood.

She was satisfied that she had slain him, and she rose, as it were, sated from the hideously defaced and mangled stem of humanity over which she had been bending, and turned to think what should be done next.

Two men yet remained on board.

Two more murders yet remained to be committed.

How was she now to proceed? Should she wait here in the cabin with the bodies of her victims until the other victims came to share their fates?

She did not in the least hesitate about shedding more blood, but she did not wish to shed blood in a way which she herself would have called unnecessary. She, however, could not quite decide which of the two men remaining on board she ought to kill, if she were able to kill either.

The man in the berth would very easily have been settled.

He was asleep. It would only have required a thrust of the knife, and all would have been settled.

But, then, she asked herself, would such a course have been the wisest to take under the circumstances?

The man in the berth was devoted to the Prince's service. Would he aid her to escape, or would he give her up to the prison to which she was being taken?

She might make better terms, perhaps, with the man upon deck.

He was not devoted to the service of the Prince. She might make terms with him.

She might offer him all the money, a share of which only he was to have had, if the plan of her murder had been carried out.

Would he not agree eagerly to these terms?

But then, again, could she trust this desperate ruffian? No, it would be weak to do so.

Of course he would take all the money, and then what guarantee had she for his good faith? Would he not afterwards betray her to the authorities?

No, she thought, she would be safer in the hands of the other man.

Perhaps she had better kill both? But no, that would not do very well, because in that case who was to steer the ship?

Somebody must steer the ship. The storm had not yet altogether ceased, although to a great extent it had abated its fury.

She stood thinking of all these things, and turning over her various plans and schemes of action, and listening to the wind which swept through the rigging overhead with a shrilly scream, as though it were some huge bird of prey which had sniffed afar the blood of the murdered men, and hovered round and about, eager to feast upon their mangled corses.

And, as though to add a greater semblance to this fancy, the wet sail flapped heavily to and fro like wings.

But she heeded little this or any other sound save the regular breathing of the sleeping man in his berth, and the voice of the man upon deck, which occasionally reached her when the wind brought in her direction stray snatches of the sea song he was chanting.

She was not long before she had settled, to her own satisfaction, that the man upon deck should be the victim, and she straightway set about her preparations.

In rummaging about for the percussion caps she had seen a quantity of male attire in one of the chests in the cabin.

This she intended at once to dress herself in.

Firstly, because in men's clothes she was able to move about, and, if necessary, struggle with more ease.

Secondly, she would be able, dressed as a man, to approach the sailor on the deck, and to get close to him before he would recognise her, or be able to distinguish her from his companions.

Having selected a pilot coat, a blue shirt, and a pair of coarse serge trousers, which she thought would suit her, she at once began to divest herself of the articles of female clothing which she wore.

Ruthlessly breaking away button-holes and laces, and demolishing hooks and eyelet-holes with a wrench, she stripped herself, with the exception of her fine linen chemise, which she retained to save her soft flesh as much as possible from the scouring of the blue shirt, a garment that was of the coarsest.

It was not by many the first time that she had assumed man's attire, as any one might easily have told if they had seen her now rapidly dressing herself in this sailor costume.

When she had finished, she looked a very pretty sailor lad, with her yellow curly hair, and her bold dark eyes—only, perhaps, she was a trifle too white and delicate-looking.

She did not want to look quite so young, though, and she thrust the Captain's hat over her eyes, turned her coat-collar up to hide as much as possible of the lower portion of her face, and swaddling a large woollen comforter under her neck, prepared to ascend the stairs.

Before going, though, it occurred to her that it would be as well, if possible, to have other arms about her besides the long knife which by this time she had withdrawn from the wall.

It very naturally occurred to her that the most likely place to find the caps would be in the captain's pocket.

It is true that the job of searching for them was a very horrible one, but it was most important.

She thought that it should be performed.

She bent down, therefore, and hastily rummaged through her pockets.

She was not long before she found them.

Then taking down one of the pistols from the wall, she placed a cap upon the nipple, and put the weapon into one of the side pockets of her pilot coat. In the same way she did with another pistol; and then concealing the sharp knife in her breast, she took her way up-stairs.

Most likely the man upon deck had not any arms about him. She would be able to take him at a great disadvantage.

But she must not stay to consider about what she should do. Everything depended upon the rapidity and decision of her movements.

Coming upon deck, she easily discerned the figure of a man standing at the wheel.

Him she approached, with her hands in her pockets, walking as steadily as she could; for the boat, during the last few minutes, seemed to have begun to roll and pitch with the violence that it had done a short time ago.

—

CHAPTER LXXXIV.

THE SAILOR AND HIS SONG.—THE SUDDEN DEATH—THE WAVES WASH AWAY ALL TRACES OF THE CRIME.—MORE PLOTS AND PLANS.—DANGER FROM WITHOUT.—AN UNEXPECTED ENEMY.—THE VESSEL BOARDED.—RUTH A PRISONER.

THE man on the deck, quite unconscious of the danger approaching him, was singing a song in what would have been a very loud tone of voice, had not the wind been so strong that it carried all his top notes away, quite out of hearing.

As it was, he managed to make himself heard every now and then, when he bellowed extra loud.

He was not a Frenchman, like the rest of the crew; and he was singing an English song, not very remarkable for sense or tune, but, as I have said, a good loud one, full of flourishes.

"'Oh, I wish I was along of my Sue—
I do.
I wish I was along of my Sue.'"

I wonder where the poor old girl is?" said he to himself. "It's four year and more since I left her to go privateering. Perhaps she is married to some one else by this time, and given me up for lost.

"'Oh, I wish I was along of my Sue—
I do.
Instead of sailing away on the waters blue,
Sailing away on the waters blue,
All the wide world through.
I do.'

Perhaps she's dead!" said he "Poor thing! Well, if she is, I don't know that I should exactly like to join her! Not yet a while, anyhow! Just when there's a chance of coming into a little sum of money! But there ain't much chance of my dying, I fancy! I'm hearty enough, and strong enough! No, no! There's many a year afore me yet, I'll wager a crown!"

But while he was talking thus, Death was creeping towards him, slowly but steadily.

Looking from the sea to the deck, all at once he saw a dark figure before him, with a young, white face that was unknown to him.

"Oh, Lord!" he said. "What's that?"

He leant forward to get a better view of the woman's face, for he could not quite make up his mind whether or not it was human or superhuman.

Ruth, taking advantage of his bewilderment, drew one of the pistols from her pocket, clapped it against his forehead, and fired.

The man sprang up in the air, and fell backwards against the vessel's side.

Here he swayed to and fro heavily for several minutes, and then rolled backwards into the sea.

The dumb waters instantly closed over his head, and the body drifted away out of sight.

Ruth stood for an instant gazing in the direction in which he had gone, as if spell-bound.

With such rapidity had the deed been done, and so completely had all traces of the man been swallowed up in the dark abyss, that for a moment, until reason came to her aid, she could scarcely believe that what had occurred had really taken place, and that she had not been dreaming.

But, looking to the spot where the man had been standing, she saw the blood-stain upon the deck.

There could, then, be no doubt on her mind that the deed had really been done.

Strange to say, though, next moment, a wave, dashing over the vessel's side, washed away all trace of it.

Ruth stood gazing at the place where the blood had been an instant before; and, as she did, a thought struck her, upon which she determined at once to act.

She resolved upon going down again into the cabin, and, if possible, drag the bodies of the now dead men up upon deck.

Then to fling them overboard, and to wash away all traces of the blood.

If she could do this, she thought, when the other man awoke, she would possess a great advantage over him by his being in ignorance of the way in which his companions had been disposed of.

This was a very wonderful idea, to be sure; and there is no knowing what other wonderful schemes her fertile brain would have hit upon, only that we sometimes, as the reader may be aware, reckon without our hosts

While she was deciding how very cleverly she was going to act, she quite forgot that the boat had no one to look after it, and that the storm was increasing.

Also, she quite forgot that there was a possibility of danger from without, as well as within, the vessel.

Just as she was placing her foot upon the first step of the companion-ladder, a loud voice from the water saluted her ear.

At first she fancied that it came from the man whom she had shot, and who had fallen into the water.

But turning in the direction from which the sound proceeded, she saw the dusky outline of a long boat upon the water.

A loud voice again hailed her.

"Who are you?" it said, in French.

She did not understand what she ought to do. She had a vague idea that these were revenue officers who were calling to her, and that she ought to say something in reply. But what?

She had not the remotest notion what it was customary to answer under these circumstances.

Again the voice shouted to her.

She made no answer.

Next moment she heard something strike the boat's side.

She drew forth her other pistol, undecided what to do.

She had some idea of firing upon the first person who should make their appearance upon the deck; but this notion she rapidly abandoned when she saw one dark form after another coming over the vessel's side, to the number of six.

While she was yet hesitating what she ought to do, she was surrounded.

Dark-visaged men, mostly with beards, all wearing half-military costume, all evidently Frenchmen, Custom House or police officers.

"Who are you?" one asked.

"English," Ruth replied, abruptly.

The other looked at her hard, and held a lantern to her face, while another rapidly knocked off her hat, and took up a handful of her golden curls.

"You're a woman?" said he who had first spoken.

"Yes."

"What are you doing here?"

"Nothing."

"What have you got on board?"

"I have got nothing."

"You're smugglers?"

"I am not a smuggler."

"Is any one below?"

She hesitated, thinking that, perhaps, she might be able to get rid of them again, if she answered boldly.

"No," she said.

But then she reflected that if they went down stairs her denial would go against her, and she said, "Yes."

"No—yes!" repeated the man. "Which do you mean?"

Then he left her in charge of two of his companions while he descended below.

Ruth made no objection; she offered no remark.

Hitherto, the desperation of her case had lent her courage.

Slowly, now, it was deserting her.

Her presence of mind, too, was leaving her.

She felt confused and giddy.

She knew not where she was, or who was speaking to her.

Presently she heard a loud shout of "Murder" below in the cabin; and then heavy footsteps came trampling up the stairs again.

Again a lantern was thrust into her face; and the man who had before interrogated her, resumed his questions.

"There are men below, dead! Who killed them?"

"I did!"

"We heard a pistol-shot just now: who fired it?"

"I did."

"Why did you do so?"

She made no reply; she strove to think what she ought to say, or how she ought to act.

She was quite confused, and hardly understood what they said to her, answering all at random.

The man repeated his question; but she heeded him not.

Again he asked, "Did you fire it as a signal of distress?"

"No."

"Why did you fire it?"

"At a man."

"One of the men below?"

"No."

"Another man?"

"Yes."

"Where is he?"

"In the sea!"

"Did you kill him?"

"I don't know."

"Did you wound him?"

"I tried to kill him"

"Where did you hit him?"

"In the head."

"And he fell into the sea?"

"Yes."

"There isn't much doubt what's become of him, then," said the Frenchman to one of his companions, with a grim smile.

"No," replied the other. "A man, with a hole in his head, floundering about in a sea like this——"

"Is pretty sure to go——"

"Where do you say, Mr. Pierre?"

"There's only one way he could go."

"And that is——"

"The way the stones go!"

"To the bottom?"

"Just so."

She heard them jabbering thus: the words indistinctly reached her ears; but she heeded them not.

She struggled in vain to contend against the fast-increasing giddiness which seemed stealing over her.

But her efforts were fruitless.

She reeled, and staggered back, and would have fallen to the ground, had not some of the men standing round her started forward to catch her in their arms.

"What's the matter with her?" one asked.

"She's as heavy as if she were dead!"

"Has she fainted?"

"I think so. What can we do to bring her round?"

"Leave her alone, man. She'll come round of her own accord. Women are always fainting, and always get over it."

"It don't hurt them, you think?"

"Hurt 'em? Bah! They rather like it, if anything!"

"Lend us a hand with her, then. Is she to come down to the boat?"

"To be sure she is! She's got to go before the tribunal, my friend! She's too rare a bird to let slip through our fingers!"

"It'll go hard with her—won't it?"

"Egad, there's every reason to believe that it will! Three men polished off in a night! Why, she's a first-class criminal!"

"She'll lose her head, I reckon?"

"There's little doubt about that, I should say."

"And the other man down below?"

"An accomplice, I take it."

"Does he confess?"

"No. He says he doesn't understand. He pretends to be drunk."

"Ah!—that's to gain time."

"Yes; an old dodge."

"Oh, we'll bring him to his senses, too, before we have done with him!"

"I hope so. We shall have to grease the guillotine knife for both of them, I expect?"

"For the woman, at any rate. And I'm sorry."

"Why?"

"She's very beautiful, isn't she? As beautiful as any angel?"

"Ay; or a devil!—one or the other!"

They carried Ruth, in a state of insensibility, into the boat which they had fastened alongside.

The steersman was also brought down, and placed by her side, securely handcuffed.

CHAPTER LXXXV.

A WEARY DREAM.—RUTH'S GAOLERS.—THE COURT-HOUSE.—THE EXCITEMENT OF THE POPULACE.—THE EXAMINATION.—RUTH'S STRANGE MANNER.—IS SHE MAD?—HER STORY IS NOT BELIEVED.—THE ARRIVAL OF THE PRINCE.

A WEARY, confused dream followed, in which the phantoms conjured up in her imagination were so confused and mixed up with the actual scenes acting around her, that she found it perfectly impossible to separate the real from the ideal.

When her senses returned sufficiently for her to be able to form a vague notion of what was taking place around her, she found herself in a dark, damp, uncomfortable cell or dungeon, lighted by a grating high up against the ceiling, miserably wet and cold, and her head and limbs aching most painfully.

Without, and at no great distance from the door, she heard a loud, but confused, murmur of voices, occasionally interrupted by shrill cries of "Silence!" and "Make room there!" with other orders of a like character,—leading her to believe that the place of her confinement, wherever it was, could not be at any very great distance from the court-house.

She was lying upon her back on the floor of the cell, which was dirty and wet, and she wore the sailor's dress which she had worn when she left the vessel.

It was broad daylight, and if she could judge by a solitary streak of sunshine which came very narrow and dusty into the cell through the narrow grating already mentioned, it was a sunny day, as well.

While she was lying there, staring at the sunshine, a clock struck not far off, and she counted the strokes—twelve.

It was noon, then. But whether it was noon the day of the storm, or the day after, she could form no notion.

While she was ruminating upon the subject, the door of the cell opened, and two persons entered.

One was a man, by his dress, evidently a gaoler; the other, one of those women who are employed in prisons to search female prisoners.

They stooped over her, and looked at her hard in the face, Ruth returning their stare in a dreaming fashion, without speaking.

"Well," said the man, at last, "how do you find yourself?"

"I want some water."

"You can't have any now," the woman answered gruffly. "Get up, if you can. You've got to go into court."

"I can't get up."

"You must try."

"I can't."

"You will be carried if you don't, so I tell you."

"Very well."

"Very well; I warn you, that's all. We don't want to treat you ill if you don't oblige us to do so. Try and be reasonable."

"I only asked for some water."

"You shan't have it, then—there!"

Ruth frowned at her, and clenched her fist for a moment.

Then closed her eyes again, and tried to forget that she was thirsty.

Presently, however, the man and woman began to shake her.

"Get up, I say!—get up, will you? Don't you hear?"

"I don't want to get up. Leave me alone, can't you? Be quiet!"

"That's a good one," the man said to the woman. "Leave her alone, when his worship is waiting to see her. She's a cool one, this Englishwoman, isn't she?"

Ruth felt sick and faint.

The old woman seemed to her to smell intolerably of garlic. There was an odour of stale snuff about the man that was absolutely suffocating.

The prisoner rolled her head from side to side, and strove weakly to push them away from her.

Why were they hanging over her? What did they want.

She felt dreadfully ill. Her head was splitting with pain; she could not for the life of her understand what was the meaning of the scene then being enacted before her.

Why did they want to move her?—why could she not be left there in peace?—what had she done, that she should be used thus?

"Come, come, get up!" the old woman said.

"You'd better arouse yourself," the man added, "unless you want us to handle you roughly."

Then, as she made no answer to either of their suggestions, they began to pull at her, in not the very gentlest fashion.

Ruth groaned aloud.

"Oh, for heaven's sake!" she muttered, "leave me here to die!"

"What does she say?" the man asked the woman.

"She's talking some sort of gibberish," the other replied.

Ruth had spoken in English, and what she had said was unintelligible to the French people.

However, had they been able to understand her prayer, it is not very likely that they would have paid much attention to it.

It never seemed to occur to them that the reason she did not obey their bidding, and at once get up upon her feet, was because she was too ill to do so.

They thought she was obstinate, and treated her accordingly.

It is a very common thing to see thieves, particularly young ones, when they don't want to go along with the policeman, throw themselves on their backs, and kick up their heels, so that the only way left for the constable is to drag them by the collar, or get the aid of a brother officer, to bear them bodily away to the lock-up.

The worthy gaolers thought that it was much the same sort of case with the prisoner, and they stood upon no ceremony with her.

In spite of her groans, they raised her upon her feet; and as she would not or could not walk without assistance, they propped her up under the arms, and helped her out of the cell.

They took her down a short passage, and across a small hall, where a number of soldiers and police officers were lounging about.

Then through folding doors, into the court itself.

A busy scene it was.

Lawyers, judges, barristers, with curious caps and strange-looking gowns; a goodly show of soldiers and police, and then at the back, a great crowd of people dressed in gay colours, all with very red or very brown faces, most of the men in blue blouses, and the women in white caps, high-crowned, and spotless white.

Such a gabble of tongues too, as she showed herself, and such pointing of fingers in her direction.

"There she is!"

"That's she?"

"That's the woman!"

"Did she kill half a dozen men, do you say?"

"Ay, and double the number of women!"

"Oh, the wretch!—oh, the monster!"

"She looks like it, too, doesn't she?"

"That she does!"

"One could tell at a glance that she was a murderess!"

"Silence in the court!" roared the usher.

And then everybody began to tell everybody else to be silent and to hold their tongues, and to listen to the wonders that were going to be told.

But greatly to everybody's disappointment, the judge ordered the court to be cleared, being resolved to open the proceedings privately.

Then Ruth, staring languidly about her, without understanding what was going on, or that the court-house was cleared of all but half a dozen gentleman in gowns, and black, curiously-shaped hats, after listening for some time, confusedly, to a drowsy voice talking French, became conscious that the judge was addressing her personally, and that she was under examination.

Then summoning her fastly scattering senses to her aid, she contrived to hear and understand most of what he said to her, and to reply to him as well as it lay in her power to do.

"Your name?"

"Ruth Belvidere."

"Your trade, or occupation?"

"Have none."

"How do you live?"

"How I can."

"Do you live by your wits?"

"I have done."

"Do you now?"

"Not while I am staying in your prisons. I have no occasion to do so. When I am free again I may."

"Take care what you're about, prisoner," the judge said; "your manner is very objectionable. You seem not to understand that you are here charged with an awful crime, and that your life hangs upon a thread. Take care, I say, for all your answers will be taken down, and at a future time used in evidence against you!"

She looked at him with a stupid stare, as one might have done who was intoxicated by wine, and broke out into a wild and silly laugh.

The judge seemed stupefied, and the other people in the court whispered together.

Was she drunk or mad?

The question was quickly echoed from mouth to mouth.

Was the woman mad?

It was impossible otherwise to account for her conduct—for her language—for the wildness of her looks.

There was a haggard, stony glare about her eyes.

Her hair was tumbled and matted—her shirt disordered at the neck.

She gave her answers in a half-savage, half-jeering and defiant tone, as though she looked upon the whole business as a capital joke.

The judge appeared to think that it was almost useless to continue the examination; however, after consulting for some short time with a person who seemed to act as his clerk, he resumed his questions.

"What were you doing on board the vessel where you were taken prisoner?"

"I was a prisoner."

"Do you mean that you were a prisoner before you were taken into custody by the officers of this court?"

"Yes."

"Why were you?"

"I do not know any more than you."

"How long had you been on board?"

"I do not know."

"Who took you on board?"

"I do not know."

"Did you kill the two men whose bodies were found in the cabin?"

"Yes."

"Why?"

"Because they were going to kill me."

"What reason had they for killing you?"

"I do not understand their reason."

"And do you mean to say you can give no clue to your mysterious confinement on board this ship, for your story as yet is most unintelligible and improbable?"

"I can only give one explanation."

"And that is?"

"That I had mortally offended a Prince. That he had sworn to have my life. That he had had me conveyed away in this manner, and that he intended a worse fate than death for me, in the end, though what I know not."

The judge eyed her incredulously, as though he thought this explanation more improbable than the story that had preceded it.

"And the name of the Prince?" he asked, with a slight smile.

"He is the Prince——"

But ere she could utter the name, the door of the court was thrown open, and a tall, stately-looking man strode into the midst of the assembly.

It was the Prince himself.

CHAPTER LXXXVI.

SHOWS HOW A FEMALE PRISONER IN THE INFIRMARY OF THE PRISON OF SAINT LAZARUS DESIRED TO SEE HER OWN FACE IN THE LOOKING-GLASS, AND WHAT SHE SAID AND DID WHEN HER WISH WAS GRATIFIED.

INSENSIBILITY must have stolen upon her again about this juncture; for all that followed was a blank.

Whether she remained in a state of unconsciousness for an hour, or a day, or a week, she could not tell.

Her mind, as well as her strength, would seem to have abandoned her; for she could remember or understand nothing of what had occurred.

At last a faint streak of sunlight, pouring down upon her bed, as it had poured down into the cell through the grating overhead on the morning that they had brought her into the court-house, was the first event that her weak reasoning powers seemed capable of grappling with.

She was in bed; and when she tried to rise, she found she was too weak to stir.

The sun came through a narrow window, with diamond-shaped panes, surrounded by white curtains, very clean and neat.

There were two flower-pots upon the window-ledge, and in them two little rose trees basking in the sun. Beyond she caught a glimpse of the sky—clear, blue, and cloudless; and she lay a long while, dreamily gazing into the azure depths, without another thought or care in the world.

But some slight noise in the room caused her to turn her head slowly in the other direction, and she gazed wonderingly upon the scene which met her eyes.

She was lying upon a small iron bedstead, surmounted by a white canopy, and it was one bed of about fifty which lined the sides of a long, narrow apartment.

Above each bed was a small, black board, with a number painted upon it in white figures.

The bed opposite to that upon which she lay was No. 25; and Ruth could see, by a kind of hill which the bed-clothes formed in the centre, that it was occupied.

As she lay there she began to speculate dreamily as to who the occupant of the opposite bed could be, and what was the matter with her, and whether she had been as long in bed as she (Ruth) had been.

"I wonder how long I have been ill?" Ruth thought; "and I wonder where I am?"

She looked again at the row of beds upon the other side of the room, and at the white numbers upon the black boards.

It was not very difficult, surely, to guess the kind of place.

"It is a hospital," she said.

The words, though faintly spoken, were spoken aloud.

The sound of her voice, though scarcely audible, reached the ears of an attendant.

A woman dressed in the garb of a nun—a middle-aged woman, hard-featured, and forbidding in aspect, approached the bedside.

"Did you call?" she asked.

"No; but I want to know——"

The nun interrupted her to take a seat by the bedside, and to take Ruth's hand in hers to feel her pulse.

"You are better to-day," the nun said.

"Have I—have I been ill?"

"Yes."

"Very ill?"

"Yes."

"Long?"

"Four weeks."

"Four weeks!" repeated Ruth to herself, in astonishment. "Four weeks! that is a long time."

Then, as the nun seemed upon the point of walking away, Ruth called her back to ask another question.

"What is this place?"

"The infirmary"

"Is it a hospital?"

"It is the infirmary attached to the prison."

"What prison?"

"The prison of Saint Lazarus."

Ruth ruminated silently for some time upon the information she had received. Then, as the nun was still there, she again sought for information.

"If you please——"

"What is it? You mustn't keep talking."

"I only want to ask one question."

"What is it, then?"

"Am I a prisoner?"

"Yes."

"Of what am I accused?"

"I can answer no more questions."

The nun going away, Ruth was left to herself, and consequently compelled to remain silent. But her curiosity to know more kept her restless and uncomfortable.

She waited for a long and weary time, hoping that the nun, or somebody else whom she could question, would come near her, but she waited in vain.

She waited, watching the streak of sunshine, until it faded away, giving place to a dull, leaden hue very sad and depressing.

After a long while, she waited until she wearied herself out and fell asleep.

When she awoke, the woman to whom she had spoken was standing by the bedside with some tea in her hand.

Ruth, with the nun's assistance, raised herself a little upon the pillow.

In doing this, the strings of the nightcap which Ruth wore were pulled very tight, and she had to beg of the nun to loosen them for her.

The woman did so, but in the operation one of the strings came off.

The woman therefore took away the nightcap, and said that she would bring her another.

Ruth, left to herself, passed her thin, wasted hand over her brow and on to her head.

What had happened to her?

For a moment all the blood seemed to rush in a stream from her heart to her face, and suffused her cheeks and forehead with crimson blushes.

What, in the name of heaven, had befallen her?

She passed her hand over her head, and the expression of blank dismay which at the same time passed over her features absolutely distorted them out of all likeness to her own self.

What had happened to her?

She understood it at last, but only very slowly did the truth dawn upon her confused brains, weakened as they were by the ravages of the sickness from which she was recovering by slow degrees.

She had had her head shaved!

She screamed out as much with rage as fright when she found out the dreadful truth.

The nun came running back to the bedside to see what was the matter, and she found Ruth clasping her head betwixt her hands, with a horror-stricken look upon her pallid face.

"What is it?" the nun asked. "What has happened to you?"

She could not enter into the other's feelings.

"Have you exerted yourself too much in sitting up? Do you feel any worse?"

"No, no!"

"What is it, then?"

"Oh, my God!"

"What can I do for you?"

"Nothing! Yes, you can, though!"

"What is it?"

"Give me the looking-glass."

"There is none," the woman replied.

"No looking-glass?" Ruth cried, in astonishment. "No looking-glass? Ridiculous! There must be a looking-glass! A hospital for women, and no looking-glass! It is impossible!"

But the nun replied with a smile which was rather sarcastic—

"There are no looking-glasses in prison."

Ruth flung herself back upon her pillow, angrily tearing at the counterpane with her fingers.

"I want a glass!" she said, pettishly. "I must have a glass!"

"You can't."

"I will! I will!"

"Here, don't be silly, child!" the nun observed. "Take some of this tea, and lie quiet. You are not strong enough to get into these tantrums without doing yourself some harm."

"I don't care what harm I do myself! I don't care if I kill myself! I will have a glass!"

"Drink your tea."

"I won't have any tea—I don't care for any tea! I wish I was dead!"

The nun walked away, and left her without any further remark.

Ruth rolled about from side to side, and sobbed passionately.

No one who could see her thus acting like some spoilt child, could have believed that it was the same woman whose dare-devil courage and iron will had carried her scatheless through such hairbreadth dangers, such incredible perils, such scenes of horror.

There she lay, whimpering like some poor baby puling for pap.

Nothing at all like what she was. Nothing but the ghost of her old self—a wreck to look upon!

How had she fallen? How had sickness brought her down?

Her sole desire at this moment was to get the loan of a looking-glass for a few moments.

Nothing in the wide world did she long for half as much as to look at herself in a looking-glass.

As the man obstinately refused to gratify her, she as obstinately refused to take any nourishment or any physic.

Her illness, therefore, gained upon her rapidly.

All the worst symptoms returned.

When the doctor came his rounds in the evening, he found her in a burning fever and delirious, babbling about ball dresses, and *cheval* glasses, and mirrors.

"What's she say?" the doctor asked the nurse, for he did not understand English.

"She wanted a looking-glass, poor vain creature. I believe it has made her ill because I would not give her one."

"You should have done so."

"I had not got one."

"You ladies don't use them in the convent?"

"No."

"And there are none here?"

"None."

"Bless me! Well, I'll send for one from my lodgings."

"And if she asks again, I am to give it to her?"

"Certainly, poor thing! if it pleases her, though she's not much to look at, is she?"

"Not now!"

"She was very beautiful, I am told?"

"Before she came here. As beautiful as an angel!"

"Dreadfully altered now, isn't she?"

"She is, indeed!"

"Upon my word, I hardly know whether it is best to let her know how the fever's spoilt her beauty!"

"I do not think it is wise."

"Only that if we don't, she'll go on longing to see herself, and picturing herself worse than she is, perhaps."

"Perhaps!"

"Well, there, then! Let her have the glass!"

"As you please, sir!"

When Ruth again recovered from the attack of illness which had come back upon her, her desire to see her face remained unchanged.

In great fear lest her prayer might be refused, she begged of the nun to obtain for her that which she so longed for—a looking-glass.

To her unutterable joy the woman brought her a small one, and laid it on the bed.

Ruth, starting up in bed, clutched it eagerly in both hands, and gazed upon the reflection of herself which it afforded.

The nun made a hasty movement forward, as though she would have snatched the glass out of Ruth's hands, so terrible a change came over the other's face at the sight of herself.

The nun seemed to dread some fearful outbreak.

There was, however, nothing of the kind; and the nun, after watching her for a few moments, stepped back again, and heaved a sigh of relief.

There had been a dreadful change in the sick woman's face when she first caught sight of herself—a contraction of the brow, a dilation of the eye, and a quivering of the lip, which seemed to foretel a violent outburst of passion.

All these signs of emotion had died away.

After awhile, Ruth laid the looking-glass gently down, and turned her eyes inquiringly towards the nun's face.

"Have I been very ill? What has been the matter with me?"

"You have had brain fever!"

"A very bad attack, you said?"

"Yes; very bad."

"It has changed me very much."

"Don't fret about it, my dear. You will recover your good looks when you get well again."

"I look very old."

"You have suffered much."

"You were obliged to cut my hair off, and disfigure me in this way?"

"Yes; we were obliged to do so."

"Take the glass away; I do not require it any more."

The nun did as she was bidden, wondering much that the other was so calm.

An hour afterwards she heard a loud sound of agonized sobbing.

"What is the matter?" she asked.

"But Ruth made no answer.

The nun bent over her. Her eyes were closed. She was sobbing in her sleep.

CHAPTER LXXXVII.

RUTH'S FAREWELL TO THE NUN, AND THE INFIRMARY.—UPON THE THRESHOLD OF THE PRISON.

A WEEK passed away.

A week passed slowly, without any incident having occurred which is worthy of note.

Ruth grew slowly better. She was able at the end of four days to sit up a little by the side of the open window, through which the sunlight had come streaming on to her bed.

On the sixth day two police-officers, attended by a man, who looked something like a lawyer, and carried a roll of papers under his arm, came into the room and asked the nurse several questions concerning her.

"How is No. 12?" the lawyer-looking man asked.

"Better," the nurse replied.

"Well enough to be moved?"

"When?"

"To-morrow?"

"Not before three days, the doctor says."

"Very well, in three days I will send for her."

When they were gone, Ruth asked the nurse what they were going to do with her.

"You are going into the prison," the nurse said.

"Am I going to be tried?"

"I don't know."

"Have I been tried?"

"I can answer no questions."

It was always thus that the nurse replied when Ruth tried to question her upon the subject.

She saw that it was useless endeavouring to find out anything about it.

All she could do was to wait, and time would show her what she desired to know.

Upon the day that had been fixed for her removal, two police-officers again made their appearance, and told the nurse that they had come to take Ruth away.

The nun said that she would be ready directly; and she brought to her, and laid open upon the bed, a bundle which one of the officers had brought to her, and which contained a dress of coarse blue serge, a white nightcap, a pair of coarse blue woollen stockings, a couple of coarse chemises, a flannel petticoat, and a pair of list slippers.

"What am I to do with these?" asked Ruth, eyeing these articles of female apparel with disgust.

"It is the prison dress."

"Well?"

"Put it on."

"Why can't I wear what I have?"

"Because it is against the rules. You must leave these clothes here."

She had been wearing a dressing-gown, and soft under-clothing, which had been supplied to her in the infirmary.

She felt very indignant at what she thought was a great degradation; but there was no help for it, she thought: and so she stripped, and dressed in the prison clothes.

"How frightful I must look!" she thought.

Presently, when she was dressed, the nun came and kissed her cheek, wishing her "Good-bye!"

"Here is something for you," she said, putting something into Ruth's hand.

"What is it?"

The other squeezed Ruth's fingers to upon the top of whatever it was.

"Never mind," she said; "you can look presently. Don't show it to the men!"

"It's money?" said Ruth, turning it over in her fingers. "Is it yours?"

"No, it is yours!"

"But who gave it to me?"

"The Prince!"

"I shall not require it—shall I?"

"Indeed, you will!"

"Good-bye, then!"

"Good-bye," the nun said, "and God forgive you!"

"Forgive me for what?" the other asked, fiercely; but the nun made no reply.

"Good-bye!" said Ruth. "You have been kind to me. You wish me well?"

"I do—indeed, I do! I will pray for you."

"I hope your prayers will do me good, but I don't believe in prayers."

Much of her old spirit had returned with her returning health.

She stepped out proudly, in spite of the hideous disfigurement of the dress she wore.

Next moment the infirmary door had closed on her, and she was on her way to the prison.

To the prison!

And what else? God only knew!

CHAPTER LXXXVIII.

THE PRISON OF SAINT LAZARUS RECEIVES ANOTHER INMATE.

The police-officers led her through several passages, until they arrived at a great black door studded with nails.

At this they rang a bell. It was answered by a man with an enormous bunch of keys hanging to his girdle, who said, eyeing Ruth like an ogre, "Who's this?"

"It is the woman I told you of," said one of the police-officers.

"Oh!"

"Are you prepared for her?"

"Quite. Follow me."

The man with the keys led the way, Ruth followed, and the police-officers brought up the rear.

They took her up a narrow, winding staircase opening into a gallery. Along this gallery they proceeded, then through another gallery, separated from the first by a door which the man with the keys unlocked with much apparent difficulty.

At the end of this he came to a long, low-ceilinged, narrow room—a kind of attic, very dark, and only half-lighted by a tiny window in the roof

Ruth looked round the low walls anxiously, for she supposed that this was the place where she was going to be locked up, but it turned out not to be the case.

With one of the large keys the gaoler opened a thick iron-bound door, about three feet high, in the centre of which there was a small square hole, with cross-bars protecting it.

Then turning to Ruth, he said, as though he were addressing a dog—

"Go in."

"In there?"

"Yes."

With some difficulty she crept through the narrow opening.

He immediately closed the door and locked it upon her; and she heard him putting up a heavy chain, and driving rusty bolts grinding into their sockets.

When he had made the door sufficiently secure to suit his fancy, he called to her through the trap.

"What do you want to eat?"

"I don't want anything yet," she replied.

"Very well. Remember I asked you, that's all."

She wondered what he wanted, and was going to ask him, but he slammed to a little trap over the opening in the door, and went stamping heavily away down the passage.

She listened to the sound of his retreating footsteps, and the footsteps of the other man in his company, and when all was still, she walked over to the window, rested her elbows upon its sill, and began to think upon the peculiarity of her position.

The window was not very large. It was about a foot and a half square, and crossed by four bars of iron, each about an inch thick.

Between these the light entered in small streaks, but was prevented from entering freely from the window by a large and cumbersome beam, which crossed the ceiling just in front of it, and to a great extent blocked out the rays of light which would otherwise have made an entry between the bars.

The cell itself was not more than five feet and a half high, and about six feet and a half square.

In one side there was a kind of recess, in which a bed might have stood. But there was no bed, neither was there a table or a chair, or any other article of furniture. Indeed, the only things which the room contained was an earthenware pan for slops, and a rough deal shelf fastened to the wall, about a yard and a half from the ground.

When she had walked all round the room several times—an occupation, by the by, which did not require a great deal of time, or cause her to take a great deal of exercise—she looked about, wondering what she was to do for a seat; and not being able to make up her mind to sit on the floor, she returned to the window-sill again, rested upon her elbows, as before, and stared through the iron bars.

After all, near the window was the best part of the room.

It was about noon, and as well as she could judge by the glimpse of a roof she obtained with difficulty from her window, the room where she was was situated directly under the roof of the prison.

Yes, it was intolerably hot The sun seemed to pour down full upon the ceiling. When she left the window for a minute or two, she gasped for air.

"What a horrible place!" Ruth exclaimed aloud. "How long do they intend to keep me locked up in this dog's kennel?"

It was so very hot that she felt she could not breathe anywhere but at the window. Even there the heat was overpowering; and she shut her eyes, and dozed for a moment or two.

A scratching noise close to her awakened her.

She started up, and stared through the bars in the direction from which the sound came.

A grey-headed old rat was peeping in at her from the outside, and he walked very leisurely away when he saw her, seemingly not at all frightened at her proximity.

Ruth turned from the window with a shudder. She had always entertained a great dread and detestation for those animals. Were there many of them, she wondered, and would they come, when it grew dark, in swarms, and clamber over her when she slept?

Outside the window there was a gutter, upon which they walked. Placing her face close to the bars, she could, with an effort, see twenty yards or more down the gutter. Doing so, she saw a couple more rats, as grey as the last, disporting themselves in the sun.

"Frightful!" she exclaimed; and, with a gesture of disgust, retired from the window.

But the heat was so great that it was almost next to an impossibility to breathe anywhere except close to the window. Here, therefore, she took up her position again, and waited almost for a couple of hours, wondering when somebody would come to visit her cell, and fully determined, as soon as she saw any one, to complain bitterly of the horrible place in which they had put her, and beg to be moved, or to see some of the prison authorities, that she might expostulate with them upon the indignities which she had been obliged to submit to.

For full two hours she remained at the window, however, without anybody coming near her.

Two hours again, at the end of that.

She began to grow very impatient—very angry—very much exasperated.

The afternoon began to wear away, and she would have been more impatient and exasperated still, only that she felt certain in her own mind that somebody would visit her before the close of day.

But when the daylight waned away and night set in, she became furious.

" Is nobody going to bring me anything to eat and drink ?" she screamed at the door.

Then after more weary waiting—

" I want my bed! Help!—help!—help! Will nobody come to me?"

But nobody came.

Her rage now knew no bounds.

She stamped and screamed with rage.

She might as well have saved her breath and her feet.

Nobody took the slightest notice of her.

Round and round the cell she went. She beat the walls, and shook the door, and yelled through the window, without any result.

At length, quite exhausted with this exercise, she lay down full length upon the floor, reckless of rats, and all else in the world—tired to death—dead beat.

It was perfectly dark now, and the prison was awfully silent.

Did they intend to leave her thus to die? That must be the course they had adopted.

She was to be starved to death.

Very well! Only, in the meantime, she must go to sleep.

When she had rested herself a while she would try and think how she could escape.

She went to sleep, and dreamt that she had awakened again to find the door open, and that she had run away at full speed across the open country.

She awoke, however, as she had gone to sleep, in her hot, stifling cell.

She awoke as she had gone to sleep, in the pitchy darkness.

She stretched out her hand to raise herself from the ground, and laid it——

"God of heaven!"

On what had she laid it? Upon another hand, as cold as ice. The hand of a corpse!

She was so terrified for a moment or two that she could not believe her senses.

Then, when she began to reflect, she thought that she could hit upon the solution of the horrible mystery.

They had put a dead body into the cell with her.

They had done so to prepare her for the fate which was probably in store for her, and to increase, as much as possible, the terrors of her already terrible situation.

Then, again, she thought that perhaps she might be mistaken, and she stretched out her hand again, fancying that the cold, clammy hand that she caught hold of when first she awoke might have been the result of a nightmare.

But stretching out her hand again, she came in contact with the cold and horrible object.

Her fright the second time was perhaps worse than the first, and she started to her feet with a piercing scream.

It was with difficulty that she could stand for a moment or two, because she was so cramped and numbed by lying on her side on the hard boards.

And the pain she suffered, to some extent, quelled her fears.

After a while, indeed, they gave way altogether to a feeling of intense rage and indignation when she thought that she should be treated so—that she should be, in spite of herself, dragged down to the lowest depths of misery and degradation.

Thinking thus, all her fright evaporated. She only desired now to be sure that it was a dead body, and whose dead body it was.

She, therefore, stooped down, and approached the spot where she had felt the cold hand.

She could not find it.

She felt slowly and carefully, at first.

Then more rapidly, and in some agitation.

She felt rapidly all round the cell, at the window, and about the door.

Again and again she retraced her steps.

Sometimes she struck her head against the wall, and sometimes severely hurt her fingers.

But nothing could she find.

Then, when she felt quite certain that the object which she had laid hold of, the cold, dead hand, was no longer in the cell, her terror returned tenfold.

An awful supernatural dread came over her, and she crept into a corner, and screeched herself hoarse.

No one came to help her, and she screamed out at intervals for almost an hour.

Then fatigue and fright overcame her, and she fainted clean away, falling down upon her face upon the floor.

And there she lay, immoveably, until daybreak.

CHAPTER LXXXIX.

THE BEGINNING OF THE LIVING DEATH.

Until two hours after daybreak.

Until about six o'clock in the morning.

Then, recovering her senses slowly, she sat up and listened.

She heard footsteps approaching her cell, along the attic without.

Then the bolts and bars were withdrawn, and the rusty key ground round in the lock.

After that, the door was flung open, and the gaoler poked in his ugly head.

"Well?" he said, with a grunt.

"Well?" she replied.

"Are you inclined to talk about your victuals, to-day?" he asked, with a coarse laugh.

She felt in an awful passion; but she smothered her rage as well as she could.

Was she not altogether at the wretch's mercy?

Surely now or never was the time when humble pie should be eaten.

"I should feel much obliged to you," she said, "if you will let me have something."

"I've no objection," said the man.

"What can I have?"

"Have you any money?"

"Yes—a little."

"You can buy what you like."

Ruth said that she would like some tea and bread and butter.

"You'd better get all you want for the day," said the man. "I can't keep on dancing up-stairs every five minutes!"

"How long am I to stay here?"

"Some time, I expect. But you'll know that before long, I daresay. Anyhow, it will be a week——"

"A week? Good heavens!"

"What are you squalling out about? Why, a week's nothing!"

"I can never endure it!"

"Not endure a week, you think?"

"No!"

"I think differently."

"How do you know?"

"Well, I ought to. I've looked after the prisoners in Saint Lazarus's for a good long while—thirty year, off and on. Some were here when I came. I've seen lots in and out; and a great many, when they came at first, were very bad about it, and abused the lodging, and the living, dreadfully!"

"I should think they did!"

"But, bless you, in time they took to it more kindly!"

"Grew to like it, perhaps?"

"Yes, I suppose so. They seemed quite fond of it before they died!"

"Do many die here?" asked Ruth, with a shudder.

"Yes," replied the man, shortly; "an awful lot!"

"How is that?"

"Well, you see, it's not healthy," said the man,

with his head on one side, and smiling, as though he rather liked the subject. "It really isn't healthy; and cholera and typhus thin us dreadfully!"

"Frightful!"

"Well, perhaps so. However, if I had my choice, I would much rather die here than go out one way."

"What way is that?"

"By the little gate."

"The little gate?"

"The little black gate!"

Ruth looked at him for an explanation.

"What do you mean?" she asked, seeing that he wanted to be pressed a little.

"Well," said he, "I mean the gate they go through to the guillotine. or worse!"

"Worse!" exclaimed Ruth. "What do you mean by worse?"

"The galleys!"

'Is that worse than death, then?"

'The lord save us both from it, say I! But I can't stop talking here; I've lots more lodgers to look after. I shall say good-bye to you for the present. What do you want? and where's your money?"

Ruth told him what she wanted, at the same time consulting him about the price of the different articles

"You'll want a bed," said he, "and a chair, and table."

"I suppose so."

"I lend them out on hire."

"Very well."

"Pay me first."

"How much?"

He named a price, and she gave him the money for the use of the furniture and the articles she had mentioned—some tea, sugar and milk, bread and butter, cold meat, thin soup, and potatoes. She had spent close upon fifteen shillings in English money.

"What shall I do when all my capital is expended?" she thought to herself

But nothing was to be gained by anticipating evil. She had better wait until the evil day arrived.

In the meantime the gaoler departed, and in about an hour returned with a mattress and a blanket, a dreadfully ricketty table, and a still more ricketty stool, and a basket containing the eatables.

"You can't have any knife and fork," said he, "because they're not allowed. You'll find it awkward perhaps at first, but you'll get into it, I daresay."

"I daresay I shall!"

She thought it best to appear not to care for his rough jokes, and to be rather pleased than otherwise at his unpleasant pleasantries.

"There's a spoon, anyhow!" he remarked.

"That's a comfort!" said she.

"I hope your tea isn't all spoilt. It's awkward to carry."

"It will do very well."

"It slopped over on to the bread."

"Never mind."

"Now I've forgotten the sugar!"

"I'll do without it."

When he had taken the eatables out of the basket and arranged them on the table, he said, "You had better tell me what you want to-morrow. I can only come up once a day. Tell me what you would like now, and give me the money."

"Am I to stop in this cell without any candle?"

"Why not?"

"Because—because—I am frightened."

"What of?"

She was ashamed to tell him about the *dead hand.*

"Of the rats!" said she.

"The rats! Bah! They won't hurt you."

He went away after this, and closed the door.

When she had heard his footsteps dwindle away in the far distance, she thought she would try and eat something.

She, therefore, placed the ricketty table as near as she could to the window, and sat down to her meal.

She, however, felt too sick and ill to touch anything, except a few spoonfuls of tea.

She had a splitting headache, and she ached in every limb.

She thought she would lie down for a short time, and retired to her mattress, after she had in vain endeavoured to gulp down a morsel of bread and butter.

The whole day passed away in a kind of reckless feverish sleep.

In the afternoon she was awakened by a noise at the window, and opening her eyes, saw two huge rats on the table among the eatables, endeavouring between them to drag away the loaf of bread, which was, however, too large to be got betwixt the iron bars of the air-hole.

To frighten them away, she flung one of her list slippers at them, but they did not appear to be much terrified by it, and retreating leisurely into the gutter, peeped round the bars at her, as though they were taking her measure.

Presently they came back, and carried away the cold meat, and the greater part of the butter.

This was very frightful, but it was nothing to the awful dread of the dead hand.

She could scarcely shut her eyes when it grew dark, expecting that it would be laid upon her face.

She dare not stretch out her hand, for fear that she should get hold of it again.

There were more reasons than one why a prisoner should not have slept in that dreadful cell.

First of all, let us suppose it was haunted

Secondly, it was swarming with rats.

Thirdly, it was stifling hot.

Fourthly, it abounded in a certain loathsome insect, which is generally associated in our minds with cheap lodgings in Margate, furniture shops in the Gray's Inn Road, and second-hand beds at a pawnbroker's.

Somehow or other, though how she scarcely could tell, the night passed away, and morning came again without any fresh visitation from the ghost.

She felt rather better next day, but very weary and languid; and the heat was so intolerable, she suffered continually from a distracting headache.

She, therefore, kept on her bed most of the day, and slept away as much time as possible.

The day was got through somehow thus.

Then night came again, and more dread of the ghost, which, however, did not put in an appearance.

Two or three days passed away in nearly the same fashion.

She ate very little, and slept a great deal; and wondered what was going to be the end of it all.

Sometimes she grew impatient; and when the gaoler came to bring her food in the morning, questioned him eagerly.

"When am I going to be tried?"

"I don't know," he always said.

Then, as she persisted in making the inquiry, he asked, one day, "What makes you think you're going to be tried at all?"

"Am not I?"

"I don't see why you should!"

"But I am not to be kept here a prisoner, all my life, without being told of what I am accused?"

"Don't you know?"

"No."

"Can't you guess?"

"I am. perhaps, accused of murder; but I am innocent At the most, it was manslaughter. I did it in defence of my life. I could prove it, if I had the opportunity."

"Ah!" said the gaoler, with a grin. "We're all innocent according to our own account!"

One day, when she told him she insisted upon seeing the Governor of the prison, and that she would not thus tamely submit to being buried alive, without knowing the why or the wherefore, he said—

"You take my advice, and don't be troublesome. You're better off here, perhaps, than you might be in another cell."

"Why should I be in any cell at all? What have I done? Why am I not free?"

"To be sure!" said the gaoler. "That's the question."

"Are there people in this country," she asked him, "who have the power to lock up their fellow-creatures for years, without any trial or any legal proceedings in public?"

"To be sure there are!" said the gaoler.

"Then I suppose that is my case?"

"Yes."

"Shall I ever be free?"

"It is impossible to say."

She had no patience to talk to the wretch, who yawned as he spoke, and appeared to feel not the slightest interest in the world what became of her.

She therefore refrained from talking to him upon the subject, and stifled her curiosity, although it was a bitterly hard task.

There was one subject, however, in which the gaoler took a very great interest, although he took none in his prisoner's welfare, and that was her money.

One morning he asked for the cash, as usual, to go upon his marketing.

"What do you want?" said Ruth.

"The money!" said the gaoler, rather astonished.

Ruth burst out laughing.

"What are you grinning at?"

She laughed louder.

"Now then," said he, "if you want your dinner, you'd better give me the money!"

"Suppose I haven't got any?"

"Haven't got any!"

"No!"

"What's become of it?"

"You ought to know best."

"Why should I know?"

"You spent it."

"All?"

"Every penny!"

"Haven't you got any more?"

"Not a farthing."

"Where am I to go for some for you?"

"I don't know."

"What do you mean by that?"

"What I say."

"Can't you tell me the name of some one who would advance you any?"

"Not a soul."

It was, as the saying is, as good as a play to see the gaoler's countenance when he received this information.

Ruth could not help bursting out laughing, he looked so dreadfully woe-begone.

"Oh, very well!" he cried at last, in a great rage. "It's you that will suffer, and not me."

He went away saying this, and banged the door to with a crash.

Ruth heard his retreating footsteps across the passage, and then heard him halt and turn round again.

In a minute afterwards, he popped his head in at the door.

"What do you suppose I am to do, then?" he asked.

"What about?" she inquired carelessly.

"What about? What we've been talking about, to be sure!"

"I have not the remotest idea."

"Oh, very well!" said he, and stamped away again.

Ruth wondered what was going to happen. She could not think it possible that he was going to leave her there to starve; but it seemed rather like it.

The usual time for bringing her food had long passed, and she began to grow hungry, she grew anxious.

At last, however, she heard footsteps approaching.

This time, there were more than one person coming to see her. She rose up as the door opened, and, to her surprise, found herself in the presence of a couple of police-officers, the gaoler, and the same lawyer-looking man who had come to see her in the infirmary.

This man was the Governor of the prison.

He asked her whether she had any complaint to make; and when she said she had, and was going to make it, he called to one of the police-officers to bring him the ink.

The man addressed approached with a low bow, and displayed a small ink-bottle, suspended to his button-hole.

Into this the Governor, taking a quill-pen from behind his ear, dipped it, and began to enter Ruth's remarks into a large book, being most particular in each case to have her exact words.

As follows:—

"Have you anything to complain of?"

"Yes."

"What is it?"

"A great deal. The food, and the bed, and the cell, are——"

"One at a time, if you please. What have you got to say against the cell?"

"That it is not fit for a human creature to live in; and——"

"Stop a minute; I must put that down first. That's it. Now, why?"

"Because it is so small."

"Small, eh? Seems lofty and wide."

"I wish you had to spend a month's holiday in it, that's all!"

"Prisoner! Respect, if you please"

"Certainly."

"Have you any other complaint to make? You mentioned the food."

"Yes."

"Do you complain of that also?"

"I have none to complain of."

"Have you no food, do you mean?"

"I have had none to-day."

"That must be looked to. And, now, the bed: isn't that satisfactory?"

"It's disgusting!"

"And the water?"

"Atrocious!"

"Is there anything else wrong?"

"The rats annoy me."

"Anything else? I've got the rats down."

"Well," said Ruth, who could not refrain from laughing, "if you have, I wish you'd get the fleas down, too; there are a good many of them."

The Governor having entered all her complaints, said that he would do all he could for her, but he would not promise too much.

It was lucky that he did not, perhaps, as he never performed any of his promises.

That afternoon, however, a supply of food was brought to her of rather coarser quality than she had been accustomed to; and she was informed by her gaoler that she was now upon the living of the prison, but if, at any time, she could get any more money, she would be allowed, as before, to purchase luxuries.

"Luxuries!" she repeated, with an accent of contempt

"Well, luxuries compared to this stuff," said the gaoler.

And certainly he was not far wrong. Such frugal fare she had never partaken of before, although she had had some extensive experience of poor living in England.

"Never mind!" she muttered betwixt her teeth; "they shall not beat me to the dust. No, no! by heaven, I will triumph yet!"

But as yet the triumph was distant.

Owing to the awful heat of the prison-house, and the inanition caused by the miserable quality of the food she was obliged to partake of, she was confined to her bed, and unable even to creep from one end to the other of her narrow cell.

It was, perhaps, the hottest month in the year when Ruth was locked up in this hateful prison. The rays of the broiling sun at noonday fell almost perpendicularly on to the leaden roof above the cell, making it almost as hot as a furnace.

Again she had a fever.

For ten days she suffered the most excruciating agony, begging every day to be allowed to see the doctor, but the gaoler, who thought that she was only shamming, refused her request.

She gave up asking at last—gave up eating and drinking—speaking, moving, even.

One morning the gaoler was in great fright, for he thought she was dead, and he ran down stairs fit to break his neck, leaving the door wide open behind him.

Now was the time for her to have made her escape, you may say.

The poor creature had not the strength to raise a finger.

She was wasted to a mere skeleton!

She was horribly emaciated!

She was but the ghost of what she had been. Bah! she was not handsome enough to have been her own ghost!

Poor wretch! Could such an awful change have been possible? There were absolutely no good looks left about her.

She was brown and wrinkled. Her hair had fallen off. She was a bag of bones—a scarecrow!

Could anybody possibly fall lower than this? Could there be any greater punishment for her who, but a few months ago, in the full blaze and glory of her voluptuous beauty, had scorned and loathed mankind?

What a frightful end to such a life!

To such a sinful life! Oh, reader! you, who know so much, yet know not a half of the iniquities this woman had been guilty of! You know not the history of her youth—her childhood—her girlhood — her seduction and prostitution, and all the nameless horrors of the career she was now closing upon the hideous bed in this prison of Saint Lazarus.

Closing, did I say? Am I not too hasty?

Tossing in feverish restlessness upon her couch, the sick woman rolled to and fro, ever repeating 'twixt her teeth one form of words—one sentence only—a defiance which she seemed to fling in the face of her enemies—her misfortunes—her Creator!

"I will not die—I will not die—I will not die!"

"Poor devil!" the prison doctor said. "I wouldn't give a penny for her life."

CHAPTER XC.

SHOWING HOW A DROWNING SOUL CLUTCHED AT A STRAW.—HOW RUTH FORMED A GREAT PROJECT, AND SET ABOUT PUTTING IT INTO EXECUTION.

BUT she did not die that time.

Perhaps nobody was more surprised than the doctor was himself when he found that his messes did her good, and that she recovered.

After an illness of a month's duration, she was able to totter about a little without help. She was then allowed, every day for a couple of hours, to take a little relaxation—that is to say, a walk in the garret; and the food which was supplied to her was slightly improved in quality.

The enormous boon which the walk in the garret was to the poor woman can hardly be believed by those who all their lives have been at liberty to roam wherever they listed without any restraint

But the increased freedom she thus obtained caused her to sigh for more.

She determined upon making her escape

How, was a question rather difficult to answer.

The way was by no means clear, although that there was a way she felt pretty certain.

As for any hope of liberation in a legitimate manner, it was quite hopeless

She had long ago given it up.

"Have you heard when my trial is coming on?" she asked the gaoler sometimes.

"Don't be impatient," he would make answer.

"What do you think is a reasonable limit to patience?"

"It hasn't come yet."

"I think it has. Am I to remain here all my life?"

"Ask the Governor."

Whenever she saw the Governor she did put the question, but without receiving any satisfactory reply.

At last, one day, having been badgered, virtually, into a corner, he said, "I have no orders for your release."

"Have you any orders for my detention?"

"I have not received any order about you since you were committed to my safe keeping, when you were directed to be locked up in this cell."

"For how long?"

"At the pleasure of the authorities."

"Write to them, or let me write, and ask what is their intention concerning me?"

"I don't know whom to address."

"The person who signed the warrant of committal."

"The Prince——"

"What, my lover?"

The Governor opened wide his eyes.

"Was he your lover, madam?"

"Yes," she answered, haughtily. "I was better-looking then."

"You were very beautiful when you came here."

"I am not now, I know."

"You have had bad health."

"Well, well, I do not want to speak about that!" she cried fiercely. "About this man: let me write to him."

"Write to his Highness?"

"Yes."

"It would be useless."

"Why useless?"

"He never changes his will for prayers or entreaties. All Europe knows his character."

"How do you mean by 'All Europe?' Has he grown famous lately?"

The Governor looked at the gaoler, and then they both laughed.

"I forgot," said he. "You don't read the newspapers. There has been a great deal doing in the world since you were locked up here. His Highness is very popular, just now, in this country, and has great influence."

"Were he in ever so exalted a position," said Ruth fiercely, "I could drag him to the dust were I only free!"

"You are not free, though!" said the Governor, with a smile.

And the gaoler grinned from ear to ear.

Ruth made no further observations. But she had formed a great resolve.

She would be free.

She had an end and an aim in life.

She would be free—and when free she would rise again in the world. Not to the old position—far, far beyond that did her ambition lead her.

If she were only at liberty she could see her way clearly.

Now she would require patience—patience and a picklock.

Next morning she got one tiny step nearer freedom.

Only a very tiny step.

But still a step.

The two hours that were allowed to Ruth for exercise were not two consecutive hours. One hour was in the morning, the other in the evening.

During both, the gaoler remained seated, and kept a pretty sharp look-out upon his prisoner's actions.

But she managed sometimes, when he was not looking, to tarry round about, and examine carefully a small heap of rubbish in one corner of the garret.

She was afraid of standing there long, or of touching the rubbish with her hands; but she managed sometimes to kick against it, as though by accident and scatter a few of the fragments.

She was in hopes, some day or other, of finding there a sharp nail, or some such weapon, for she had read *Jack Sheppard* and *Baron Trenck*, and she had great hopes, if she only got a chance of making a hole for herself, to lead her to liberty.

One day her heart jumped up into her mouth, at the sight of something.

An iron bolt a foot long, and as thick as an ordinary man's thumb.

It happened that that day the gaoler was remarkably chatty; and as, when he talked to her, he always stared right at her, she was unable to take advantage of the discovery.

Therefore, after passing it to and fro at least a dozen times in her promenade, she was compelled to leave it behind, when the time came for her to retire to her cell.

"I'll get it next day, though," said she to herself, as she heard the key turn upon her.

She was not, however, to be quite as lucky as she thought. There were more difficulties to be overcome yet than she at first supposed; and she had supposed that there would be a great many, I can assure you.

Next morning the gaoler came to her cell as usual.

"What do you think?" said he.

"What?"

"Good news for you."

She thought she was going to be set free, and sprang eagerly to her feet, her eyes almost starting from her head.

But the gaoler motioned her to be seated.

"No; not quite as good as that," said he. "We are not going to lose you yet, only we're going to treat you a little better."

"What are you going to do with me?"

"Well, the Governor thinks you ought to have fresh air."

"You don't say so?"

"That was my remark."

"And am I to go out of doors?"

"Yes; a walk on the leads."

"I am not to walk in the garret any more, then?"

"No; you'll go out on the roof instead."

Ruth felt ready to choke with mortification.

"Why, what's the matter?" cried the gaoler.

"Nothing."

"I'm sure there is."

"There is not."

"You don't look pleased."

"I am."

"You have a strange way of showing it, then!"

"You took me by surprise."

She followed the gaoler across the garret and along a passage, and down a flight of steps, and up some more, until they came out at last upon a flat part of the roof of the prison.

It was quite a journey to get to it, but it was very delightful when she did get there.

The sensation of again breathing the fresh air of heaven, excepting when filtered through iron bars, had such an effect upon her that she burst into tears.

She looked up at the clear blue sky in rapture.

Never in her life before had she seen a sight, she thought, half as beautiful; and yet it was a dull, cloudy morning.

The delight of her new walk almost made her forget the disappointment she had experienced at not being able to get the iron bar.

"But I will have it some time!" she said to herself.

Every day, now, she was brought out here to walk.

It was the event of her life.

The only thing worth living for, except that hope of freedom which she cherished within her bosom.

There was not an extensive view from this part of the roof, for the squared yard where she walked was surrounded by a wall seven feet high. The place had been constructed on purpose for a promenade for prisoners, and nothing could be seen from it but the sky above.

At first, she had had some idea that perhaps she might find some way of making her escape over the roof, but she soon gave up this idea as absurd.

No, the only way would be a way she had already thought of.

"I must have that bolt," said she, "and I will have it to-morrow!"

CHAPTER XCI.

IN WHICH THE RAT SHARPENS ITS TEETH.

NOTHING particular happened "to-morrow," when it did come.

Nor on the next day, nor the next.

But the time did come at last, as you shall see.

Some of my readers, may be, have, while perusing these last few chapters of the story of RUTH THE BETRAYER, thought it rather odd that this female prisoner should have had a male attendant.

There appears, upon the face of it, some impropriety.

But then, you know, I am not writing of England, but of France, where some things, according to Sterne's Quotations, are managed better.

There are some very curious things happen in that country. I can, from my own private experience, take my oath, and I am told by those *who know*, that there are far more curious things yet happening every day in sly holes and corners, out of sight, but "by order."

I don't suppose that, if you were to get a list of the prisons of France, and were to be able to compare the accurate description of any one of them with the description of this one which it pleases me to call Saint Lazarus, that you would find out exactly which one I meant; for although in the main I have kept to the truth, there are obvious reasons why I should endeavour to disguise facts a little.

But there is such a prison, believe me; and God grant, gentle reader, that yours and mine have never the ill-luck to come within its four high walls.

A frightful prison.

A hotbed of loathsome vice and sickening disease, dirt, and pestilence, and death.

There are prisoners of all ages: the young and innocent and the old and hardened huddle together indiscriminately.

There is all remaining innocence and virtue blasted; and often enough has such a thing been known as for the warders and gaolers, profiting by the helplessness of the poor unfortunates under their charge, to brutally ill-use them.

At others, to escape from cruelty and persecution, and to curry favour with their ruffianly attendants, the unfortunate women, and even children, have willingly offered themselves up to the shrine of their seducers' vile passions.

Was it to be wondered at if such an unscrupulous woman as Ruth, unrestrained by any moral teachings, utterly lost to all sense of virtue and purity, —a scheming, heartless, shameless woman—should have been led to calculate how far she could gain by bartering her self-respect, were her gaoler susceptible to her allurements?

She was not *quite* as handsome as she used to be.

I have told you that before.

But those promenades upon the roof had really a magical effect upon her personal appearance.

After the first two or three days the roses began slowly to steal back into her face.

She could see herself that she was growing better-looking. She could see it two ways.

And how do you suppose? I told you that looking-glasses were forbidden fruit in St. Lazarus's infirmary. In the prison they were things unheard of. I don't think even the gaolers had any, for those who did not wear their beards in wild luxuriance, went to a barber's in the town.

But you do not surely suppose, then, an inventive female prisoner would not get over such a trifling difficulty. She fell back upon the usages of the ancients, and returned to metal as a mirror.

She found a brass button lying on the garret floor, and brightened it up until she could see her face in it.

It distorted her features, slightly, it is true, and made her nose a very preminent feature, but it was better than nothing.

In the same way female prisoners make up for the want of pomatum by skimming their broth, and using the grease for their hair, and many other equally ingenious and nasty contrivances.

One way that Ruth saw that she was improving in her personal appearance was by the aid of her button.

The other was by the aid of her gaoler's face, which also served her, in some sort, as a reflector.

Thus, one day:—

"I tell you what!" said he, after having taken a remarkably long, open-mouthed stare at her.

"What?" she asked.

"This fresh air——"

"Well?"

She pretended not to know what he was driving at.

"This fresh air, I say, or the sun, or something or other——"

"What do you mean?"

"Well, I mean that it's doing you a power of good."

"I feel better."

"You look better, too!"

"Am I changed?"

"I'll be hanged if I ever saw such an alteration! Why, I'll take my oath you're absolutely——"

He very probably would have grown complimentary, only, as usually happens in these cases, an interruption occurred just at this juncture, and the conversation was broken off short.

The prison-bell beginning to ding-dong loudly at this minute, the gaoler was obliged to go to his duty elsewhere, and he hurried his prisoner back to her cell without saying another word.

When left to herself, Ruth sat down to consider seriously what was the best game to play.

There was no chance of being able to corrupt the gaoler so far as to induce him to unlock the prison gates for her.

He would not do that. It was not at all likely.

How could he do so without suspicion alighting upon him?

Then he would lose his situation. No, that was out of the question.

Might he not, however, be induced to procure her the means of escape? Might he not obtain for her some tools?

It would be difficult to induce him to do so, but it might be done, she thought.

There were, then, only two ways to bribe him.

The first way was with money. She might have persuaded him had she thought of it when she had any money left.

But now, that chance was gone.

The other means only remained, and that she must try.

That other means my reader can easily imagine, without any unnecessary explanation on my part. At least, I hope so.

Profiting by her returning good looks, Mrs. Ruth began to cast sheep's eyes at her gaoler.

But she had some doubts in her mind as to whether or not she would be successful. When in the full glory of her charms she had never failed; but then, it is true, she had always practised upon willing subjects.

She had her doubts about this old gentleman.

He was an old gentleman; a very cold and passionless old man, as well as she could judge.

His only weakness seemed to be snuff.

The blandishments of the fair sex, as a general rule, were thrown away upon him. He was up to snuff, in one sense, certainly, but that was all that you could say about him.

He was inclined to be a little complimentary, it is true; but this had only happened once.

No, she would have hard work with him; but she intended that if he would not make love to her, she would make love to him.

Therefore, from the day when the gaoler had broken the ice, she brought such a battery of charms and graces to bear upon him, that the old man was staggered, and knocked, as the saying is, right out of time.

She asked him if he were married.

"Not such a fool!" said he.

She asked him to tell her his love affairs.

"Got none!" he answered, gruffly.

"Do not any of the prisoners ever fall in love with you?" she asked.

"With who?"

"With you, you naughty man."

"Why should they? It's not likely."

"Don't you think it's possible?"

"No."

"Has it never happened?"

"No."

"Suppose it did?"

"I can't suppose it."

"But do suppose it, for the sake of argument."

"Well?"

"What would you do?"

"Leave 'em to get over it again."

"What a monster!"

"I know that; that's what I want to be!"

"Oh, no, you don't; you're only putting it on."

"I'll be hanged if I am!"

"You are. Do you ever read story-books, pray?"

"I never read anything."

"You never heard, then, perhaps, of the Beauty and the Beast?"

"No: what did they do?"

"The Beauty fell in love with the Beast!"

"And what did the Beast do?"

"Love her in return."

"Then he was a stupid beast."

"Was he?"

"Yes."

"You're incorrigible."

"You don't seem to be able to believe it."

He was not a very promising subject to exercise upon. If Saint Anthony had been of the same temperament, he probably would not have fallen.

But, lord! when a woman regularly sets her cap at a man, he must fall a victim, sooner or later—particularly when he is obliged to spend two hours a-day in her company.

In the end, there is no doubt—particularly as her good looks were now returning more and more every day, slowly, but surely—that he would have been at her feet eventually, only something unfortunate occurred.

Just as her influence over him was beginning to be indisputable, and he had in a clumsy, bear-like fashion, upon several occasions made advances of a tender nature to his fair charge, the whole courtship was knocked on the head.

One day, by order of the Governor, another female prisoner was ordered to share that prison with her.

Good-bye to love-making!

The gaoler withdrew into himself like a snail withdraws into its shell.

Even had he not been a very bashful old gentleman, there was little chance of exchanging fly glances and tender words in the presence of this other prisoner.

She was a middle-aged and repulsive-looking woman, who, from the very first moment of their meeting, hated Ruth as cordially as Ruth hated her.

"If I were to attempt an escape now, that woman would betray me," Ruth thought to herself.

Then she reviewed all her chances and opportunities.

"My case now is worse than ever," she said. "I am wasting, and I have wasted, valuable time. I had even forgotten that bar."

She resolved she would not lose the first opportunity of securing it.

"It may be useful, though at present I don't know how," she thought.

She was growing desperate.

But, as heretofore, difficulties only lent her strength and courage.

Obstacles sharpened her wits.

She meditated long and deeply, and formed her resolves. Often in the dead of the night she lay awake and thought while the other prisoner slept.

In the stillness of the night, when the gaolers thought all safe and sound, and that the locks and bars held their charges secure, the rat was on the alert. One human rat was wakeful, and was sharpening its teeth.

CHAPTER XCII.

THE WORK COMMENCED.

It was the custom in Saint Lazarus's Gaol to provide the female prisoners with needlework, which was allotted out to them once a-week; and collected once a-week, when finished.

Ruth, however, for some reason or other, had not much work given her to do. She was rather clever, too, with her needle, and she did not take long to get through what she had given to her.

She therefore had a good deal of time hanging on her hands.

Before the other prisoner arrived, being of an imaginative turn, Mrs. Ruth amused herself by composing verses, and these she scratched with a pin upon her prison walls.

But all at once she took to another amusement of a very different character.

She took a great fancy for playing at ball.

She made a ball of a piece of rag tied tightl, together with waxed thread. It was very hard and rebounded when thrown against the wall.

The other prisoner, seeing her play with it, thought her childish, and called her a great fool Ruth saw that she required exercise, and saw that playing at ball developed the muscles

The other prisoner laughed contemptuously and refused to join in the sport.

Perhaps she might see nothing very curious in this fancy of Ruth's, knowing what an eccentric young female she was: but a reflective mind might, perhaps, have arrived at the conclusion that there was something curious in the fact that the time she selected every day for taking this exercise was that which the gaoler chose for coming to take the women out for a walk on the roof.

By these means, it often occurred that when he came for them Miss Ruth would throw her ball at him, and would go gambolling out into the garret like a young lamb, very much to the old gaoler's disgust.

Whenever she played this way, too, she contrived, somehow, to throw the ball near the heap.

I have said it rebounded. Very often it hit the heap, and flew off again.

For a long while she could not manage to throw it past where she wanted.

But at last she did.

The ball fell on the bolt.

With her back towards the gaoler, she picked up both.

The bolt she concealed in her breast; the ball she brought back in her hand, looking as innocent the while as a sucking baby.

A day or two afterwards, playing round the

rubbish, she managed to pick up and secrete a small piece of black marble, which was also lying there.

She had a use for this, and she set about turning it to account immediately.

Now when the other prisoner slept, the rat was busy sharpening—sharpening—sharpening.

She discovered, to her great joy, that she could use the piece of marble to grind the bolt to a point.

It only required patience and elbow-grease.

It was a long and weary job, but it could and should be accomplished.

Of that she was resolved.

It was, indeed, a difficult and tedious process. But she was not easily overcome by difficulties, and had the process been still more tedious than it was, she would not have hesitated about commencing it.

Owing to the presence of the other prisoner in her cell, the difficulty was greatly increased; for she was only able to rub the bolt in the dark.

She was obliged to wait patiently until the woman went to sleep, and sometimes she was obliged to wait a very long time, for the other complained of the heat, and was extremely restless and wakeful.

But when at last, by her regular breathing, Ruth knew that she was in the arms of Morpheus, she began to rub.

To do this, she was forced to sit up in bed and hold the little marble slab between her knees, steadying it with her left hand.

Then with her right she ground away perseveringly.

At first she had nothing to moisten the stone but saliva, but after the first two nights she saved some of the fat from the prison broth, then she got on quicker.

But it was an awfully wearisome job; and many and many a time, unseen there save by the eye of God, the wretched woman shed tears of angry sorrow over her work; and as daylight dawned, lying down perfectly dead beat, she almost resolved upon giving up her scheme altogether.

But when by stealth next morning she examined her work, and saw what progress she had made, she gained fresh courage, and resolved to renew her efforts again.

It took a whole week of nights to file the bolt to a point, but it was done.

It was, to look upon, a very creditable piece of workmanship, but the suffering it had caused its maker was scarcely credible.

Her right hand was so stiffened by the constant motion, and her arm also, that she could scarcely move it.

The inside of the left hand, owing to the hardness of the stone, the constant friction, and the occasional wounds caused by the accidental slipping of the weapon being sharpened, had become horribly swollen and bruised.

The result of all this was that she could barely wield her needle and thread; and though she had such a small quantity of work allotted to her, she nevertheless found it impossible to get it done in the time.

This, naturally enough, caused surprise, for before, her work had always been completed, and had always been well done.

Now it was never done when asked for, and what little she had finished was disgracefully executed.

To account for this falling off, Ruth pleaded ill-health, and fortunately for her the excuse was accepted without much trouble.

But she was careless about their opinion, so great was her joy at the thought that she had so well performed the first step in her laborious undertaking.

The bolt she had filed down to six pyramidal facets, terminating in a point extremely sharp, and each facet about two inches long.

It was really a formidable weapon, and one well suited to her purpose, which was to pick a hole through the floor of her cell.

She had not lost an opportunity, you may be sure, in obtaining information, when information was to be obtained, concerning the internal economy of Saint Lazarus's.

She had discovered, by dint of much circumlocution and round-about interrogation, that directly underneath the cell she occupied was situated a large hall, which was occasionally, though rarely, used as a chamber of justice.

Through the floor, then, she thought, lay the road to freedom.

The place must be shut up and empty at night.

When she had removed the planks above, she could easily break a way through the laths and plaister, and let herself down somehow by the aid of her blanket.

That was her idea, but nothing could be done until she was again alone.

In the meantime, having sharpened her spike, she kept it next to her skin night and day for fear of discovery.

The piece of marble, when she had done with it, she flung out of the window one night into the gutter, where the rats gathered round it and held councils of war, not knowing exactly what its mission might be in their territories.

When was she to get rid of her fellow-prisoner? The days passed slowly by. Weeks were succeeded by months, and still her undesired companionship had to be endured.

The autumn gave place to winter. The nights began to grow long. The weariness of the long hours of darkness spent in that prison cell were unendurable

Would this woman never go? Would she never be rid of her? Why had she come there to thwart the darling scheme of her heart?

There were times when Ruth, driven to a pitch of frenzy by disappointment, felt almost inclined to take her fellow-prisoner's life.

But that was not the way to effect her own liberation. She had sense enough, even in her blindest passion, to know that.

But if she had only looked at the matter in the proper light, she would, perhaps, have been inclined to think that this delay, wearisome as it was, was nevertheless, for the best.

The cold in the cell at the top of the prison was most intense.

It was every bit as bad to bear with as had been the suffocating summer heat, for the exposed position of the room caused the extreme of every weather to be acutely felt by its unfortunate inmates.

One day in spring, Ruth's fellow-prisoner was removed quite as unexpectedly as she had come; and now she was at liberty to set about her work.

It was twilight when the woman was taken away; and Ruth determined upon commencing next day, but it was then too dark to make sure of the exact spot to begin upon.

That night the ghost of the dead hand was revived.

She was so full of her plans for the morrow and so violently excited with the thoughts which crowded upon her, called up by the near approach of the time when she was to begin the great work, that when she lay down in bed she could not for the life of her obtain a wink of sleep.

After rolling and tossing to and fro until she was nearly distracted, she rose from her bed, and dragged the mattress from its usual place into the middle of the floor.

Unnaturally-warm weather had set in during the last two or three days, and she felt half-suffocated this evening in her then feverish and restless state.

She thought that the alteration in the position of the bed, and the fact that in the new place she could obtain much more air than in the old, would enable her to fall off to sleep.

But even here, under these more advantageous circumstances, she could not obtain the slumber which she so coveted; and it was not until she had tossed about for some hours longer that, at length, perfectly worn out, she dropped off to sleep.

She awoke with the cramp.

She had rolled off the mattress on to the hard boards, and she was lying on one arm, in which she had such an intense pain, caused by the pressure of her whole weight upon it, that it had awakened her.

To raise herself up, she stretched out the other arm, and laid her hand upon the floor, meaning to lean upon it to lift herself.

But laying it on the floor, she at the same time laid it upon something else.

That something was a hand.

A cold, lifeless hand.

In a moment, the recollection of the fright that she had had upon the first night that she came into the prison rushed through her mind.

She trembled violently, and perspired profusely.

But she had yet courage enough, and enough strength of mind remaining, to retain her hold of the ghost, if ghost it was.

Grasping it tightly, she struggled to obtain an upright position.

But, curious to relate, in trying to get up, she seemed to pull herself down.

She struggled harder, with less success.

Then, unable to stir, she was obliged to remain seated, and reflect.

She dragged the hand towards her, and burst out laughing.

It was not a laugh of terror, mind you—it was not an idiotic and hysterical giggle, brought on by excess of fright.

It was a good, honest laugh of enjoyment of a droll joke.

The hand she had seized was her own!

Her other hand!

She had lain upon it and stopped the circulation of the blood, so that it had no feeling left.

What an absurd ghost, was it not? And the last ghost, although she never could be quite certain of the fact, she in her heart felt pretty sure was much of the same family.

CHAPTER XCIII.

THE WOODPECKER.

Next morning, Ruth examined her cell more carefully than she had ever done before, and determined in what part of it she would commence operations.

The place she chose was the corner under her bed.

It was dark there, and less likely to attract the gaoler's notice; but even then she must take a great many precautions.

The worst part of the business was that every other morning the gaoler carefully swept the floor. The reason he did this was because Ruth had complained so bitterly to the Governor of the enormous quantity of fleas infesting the prison, which by these means were, she thought, to some extent kept under.

Now she resolved on not having the floor swept at all.

And how to have this alteration made without exciting the gaoler's suspicions was more than she could tell.

When she told him to leave off sweeping he was astonished.

"Why?" he asked promptly.

"I don't like it."

"That's no reason!"

"Yes, it is, quite sufficient!"

"You made fuss enough until you got it done."

"Now I want it left off."

"Why?"

"Because I do!"

He took the broom away that day without any further argument, but next morning, as though nothing had happened, he began again.

"I asked you to desist," she said.

"Why?" he asked.

"Because it annoys me."

"Why?"

"It hurts my lungs."

"What does?"

"The dust."

"You've been a long while finding it out."

"What of that? I have found it out now. Will you be kind enough to leave off?"

"Oh, it's nothing to me, only I think the place ought to be swept."

He, however, desisted after a little grumbling, and brought in a can of water, with which he began to sprinkle the floor.

"What's that for?" she asked.

"To lay the dust."

"I can't endure the damp."

The gaoler therefore put away the water-can, and contented himself by grumbling.

He did not either sweep or water the floor for five or six days after this; but at the end of that time one morning he came in, and insisted on moving out the bed and all the furniture which she collected in the garret, and cleaning the place well out.

She saw at once that he did this because he suspected she was up to some trick, and she inwardly thanked God that she had not yet begun to make the hole.

But she was nevertheless determined that the annoyance caused by the gaoler's officiousness should cease at once.

She consequently scratched her hand, and making it bleed profusely over her pocket-handkerchief and the breast of her night-dress, she remained in bed until the gaoler had come in the morning, and on his appearance was groaning pitifully.

"What is the matter?"

"Oh! oh! oh!"

"Are you ill?"

"Oh! oh!"

"Shall I go for the doctor?"

"Oh! oh!"

The gaoler, in a mortal fright, fetched the surgeon.

"What is it?" he asked, after looking at Ruth's tongue and feeling her pulse.

"I said how it would be," cried Ruth, between her fits of groaning. "I shall die—I am sure I shall!"

"But what's the matter with you?"

"I have burst a blood-vessel!"

"Indeed!"

"Yes; and"—pointing to the gaoler—"he is the cause of it!"

"What have you been doing to the prisoner?" asked the surgeon, severely.

"I don't know anything about her or her blood-vessels either!" growled the old man, in a pet

"You know it's your fault!"

"How is it my fault, pray?"

"Because you would sweep the floor."

She then gave a heartrending account of the sufferings she had endured recently, owing to the fine dust settling down her throat upon her lungs; and the surgeon, perhaps because the prisoner exerted the full power of her languishing eyes, or because he really believed her, agreed that, under the circumstances, sweeping the floor was an extremely dangerous proceeding, and that he must at once desist.

The surgeon then wrote down a prescription, which the gaoler was to get made up, and took his departure, not, however, without expressing, as far as his looks went, a considerable amount of interest in the comely features and beautifully-modelled form of his patient, which the scant covering of the prison bed but poorly concealed.

"An Englishwoman, is she?" said he to the gaoler, as they walked away.

"Yes," grunted the other.

"What's she in for?"

"In by order."

"Corrected by the secret police?"

"Yes."

"Dear me! I should like to know a little about her. She is the same woman who was so ill in the infirmary about nine months ago?"

"Yes."

"She's picked up her looks since then. And she has been ill since."

"Ah! she's always got something the matter with her, according to her account. They're all alike, these women!—a pack of good-for-nothings!"

"Ha! ha! You're too hard on them!"

"I'd be harder if I had my way! I don't see any need of 'em, myself!"

"You don't think them superior creatures, then?"

"Superior fiddlesticks!"

"That's a remarkable woman, though, mind you. If ever she gets a chance, I'll warrant she'll make a way in the world!"

"She won't get a chance, I expect!"

"Why?"

"Because she's here for life!"

"Poor thing! I'm sorry for her! I wish she wasn't! I could take quite an interest in that woman, if she wasn't a prisoner."

Ruth had made a friend in this most friendless of places, it seemed. Would she ever have occasion for his services? We shall see.

When the gaoler related the particulars of this conversation, she asked whereabouts in the town he lived, for the gaoler said that he lived without the prison walls, and took a mental note of the address.

She still waited for a day or two after the doctor had called upon her, to see whether the gaoler would attempt any more of his sweepings.

He, however, when she asked him, assured her that he did not want her death laid at his door; and that, if she chose, she might sit up to her knees in dust for all that he cared; and that he would never lay hand to broom again.

She then requested him to allow her to keep the broom in her cell, so that she could sweep what she required herself.

To this he consented.

Then she set to work.

Having found that the gaoler was most regular in the times he called on her, she chose a time for beginning her work directly after he had been in the morning.

It was her intention, as I have already described, to make a hole through the floor into the room below.

At night, then, she intended to descend; and when there, if she found the door of the room locked, she would be pretty sure of finding some place in which she could hide until it was opened.

Then, with her spike, she would be a match for any single, unarmed gaoler.

Most likely, however, the flooring was very thick.

It had the appearance of being so.

She might have to take up several planks, or hack away through layer after layer of hard woodwork.

In such a case it would, perhaps, be the work of weeks; and it was for this reason that she had acted that little farce about the dust, and the cough, and the broken blood-vessel.

She did not want her handiwork discovered during its progress, which might be a very tedious one.

Well, to begin work at last!

She, first of all, moved the bed into the middle of the room.

She then lay down upon her stomach, and, taking the spike in her hand, began to chip at the woodwork of the floor.

She saw directly that it would be a long job.

She could not raise the wood up a large piece at a time, it was nailed down so securely.

She was obliged to wriggle it away in tiny pieces, at first, no longer than a peppercorn, but, in time, a little bigger.

For several hours, the first day, she was chipping away with a noise very much like a woodpecker; and when she had done, she had only made a little hole, about half a foot in circumference.

When she had done, awfully fatigued, she replaced her bed, and, lying down on it, fell fast asleep.

There was a good deal of difficulty she found about disposing of her chips; but she managed at last to get rid of them, by putting them, one or two at a time, into a paper funnel, and blowing them out of the window with all her might, so that they might go over the parapet, upon which had they unfortunately lodged, they might have caused some suspicion.

Next day, when she began work again, having made a hole through the topmost board, which was nearly three inches thick, she came to another, which she found to be about the same thickness.

Being terribly afraid that somebody might be sent to share her imprisonment with her, she worked laboriously all day long, except at such times as she expected a visit from the gaoler, or when sheer fatigue compelled her for a long period to relinquish her toil.

She worked and worked with a per istence which would have been almost impossible under any other circumstances.

But it was the hope of freedom which was urging her on to fresh exertions

In a really incredibly small space of time, considering the difficulties with which she had to contend, the paucity of tools, the limited and cramped space to which her efforts were necessari y confined—for she must not, you may be very sure, make a hole in the floor too large for the bed easily to cover, — in really an incredibly small space of time she had wormed her way through the three layers of planks which formed the upper part of the partition betwixt her cell and the room beneath.

Arrived at this point, she encountered a formidable difficulty.

The first part of the work having been accomplished with comparative ease, the tremendous obstacle which now blocked up the way caused her at first to give herself up as lost.

The obstacle was a layer of small pieces of flint and other ex rem ly hard stone cemented together in one solid mass, like so much iron.

It may have been put there, perhaps, with the idea of making the prison more secure; but I believe that the builder of St. Lazarus's prison intended to render the ateful edifice fire-proof.

What was to be done? All her efforts were unavailing w en she strove to break through the composi ion with the weapon which she had hitherto so successfully wielded.

She was quite at a standstill.

It was useless to struggle any longer against her fate, and she pulled the bed back over the hole that she awhile ago had fondly hoped was to lead her by a short road to liberty.

For a couple of days she made no further efforts to escape.

She was quite disheartened. She gave the affair up as a bad job

She was desperate.

But at the end of that time something occurred that again raised her hopes.

She was talking to her gaoler about indifferent matters, and he turned the conversation, rather to her dismay, upon prison-breakers.

"There was a bit of a stir to-day," he said.

"What was it?"

"Only a fo l trying to get away."

"Get away?" she gasped, turning pale in spite of herself. "Trying to escape?"

"Yes. Poor wretch!"

"Was he—was he caught?"

"Ah, he was caught!"

"What will he be done to?" she asked, in a tremble.

"Done to?"

"Yes."

"Oh, nothing more will be done to him."

She looked at him in terror.

"Are not the prisoners punished, then, if they attempt to break out of prison?"

"I should rather think they were."

"Well, then?"

"Well?"

"This prisoner?"

"They won't do any more to him, I tell you."

"Why?"

"Because he's dead!"

"Did he—did they——"

"Ah, they killed him, if you mean that! He was in the hall, you know, and saw the gates open for a moment, and, like an idiot as he was, made a bolt at them."

"Well?—well?" said Ruth, in great anxiety.

"T e sentinel on guard shot him down, like a pig"

"Killed him?"

"Dead as a herring!"

"Poor fellow!"

"Nonsense! Why was he such a fool?"

"One would risk a great deal for liberty, sometimes!"

"Well, don't *you* try it, that's all!"

"I? Not likely!"

"You'd never do it, you know! There is only one way——"

"What's that?" she asked, trying to appear careless of his answer, but trembling so that she could hardly stand.

"That's by bribing the turnkeys!"

Her heart sank within her.

"Oh, that's the only way?"

"Yes; and I'm not to be corrupted."

"If you're throwing out a mild hint for my benefit, sir, I beg to assure you that I haven't the remotest idea of trying!"

"Oh, haven't you?"

"No!"

"Well, I don't suppose you have, for that matter. There! — don't take offence—I didn't mean to give any, I'm sure; only, I was saying, that's the only way to escape out of this place!"

"There's nothing to be done in the way of breaking through the walls with a pickaxe, is there?"

"Where are you going to get your pickaxe in the first place? And talk about breaking through walls, bless you, it's not to be done! Ridiculous!"

"You think so?"

"Don't you?"

"Me? I know nothing about it? You know best!"

"Well, I say it's impossible? Nobody has, as yet, at any rate. Why, when I was at school, I learnt a pack of lies about some chap or other—Hannibal, I think his name was—who made a hole through the Alps by softening them with vinegar! It's just as likely to do that, I should say, as to bore a hole through these walls!"

"To be sure!"

"I'll tell you what!" said the gaoler, before he locked her up in her cell again,—"I tell you what!"

"Well, what?"

"I'll tell you what you should do, if ever you try it!"

"Try what?"

"Breaking out of prison!"

"But I don't want to!"

"Well, but if you did!"

"Well, if I did?"

"I'll tell you what you'd better do!"

"Tell me, then?"

"Try vinegar!"

He said it quite seriously, and looked quite serious, until he had closed the door.

But when the door was shut, she could hear him roaring with laughter outside.

Ruth sat and meditated for a while.

"I will try vinegar!" said she; and she did so at once.

The surgeon had sent her a bottle of "Condy's Patent Concentrated Vinegar," which has more than ten times the strength of vinegar of the ordinary kind in use, and which, being the very best, and by far the cheapest, that can be purchased, is used in all hospitals, prisons, and Government institutions in France and England.

A pint bottle had been sent to her by the surgeon, as she complained bitterly of headache; and she had been instructed to dilute the vinegar very much with water before using it. The consequence was, that although she had used several quarts at the ordinary strength, she had still a large quantity remaining in a concentrated form, and she determined to apply it to the cement.

"There must be some truth in what Livy says," thought Ruth, recalling the gaoler's anecdote. "Anyhow, I'll try!"

She therefore removed the bed, and poured the whole remaining contents of the bottle upon the cement.

Then she covered up the place again for that day.

Next morning, when she examined her work, she did not, of course, expect to find the stone was pulp, but she hoped that the strong vinegar would have some effect upon it.

Such proved to be the case; the surface was decidedly softened.

She renewed her work with as much energy as ever, and before night had destroyed the hitherto formidable barrier of stonework

She came now to another plank; but this, she expected, was the last; and she was prepared for it.

There were yet almost two hours more of daylight; and although she was terribly wearied, she determined not to give in until it was too dark to see any longer.

The hole she had made was, as I have told you, very narrow; and it was extremely difficult, now she had got down so far, to chip away the woodwork; but she maged to do it with much patience and labour.

Lying upon the floor, straining every nerve and muscle, with her face smeared with dust and perspiration, and her fingers cut and bloody, she was struggling on, when all at once, with such a feeling of dread as never in her life before had she experienced, she heard the sound of voices in the attic outside the door.

How, in the name of Mr Woodin, she contrived to drag the bed over the hole, and throw herself upon it, before the gaoler opened the door, is more than I can say; and it was probably more than she could have said either.

But she did it, and lay there, panting, when the gaoler popped in his head.

"I've brought you another lodger," said he. "Here's a young lady come to stay with you."

She heard this much, and fainted.

CHAPTER XCIV.

THE CRUELLEST BLOW OF ALL.

It would but weary the reader beyond all power of endurance, did I dwell upon the sufferings which the wretched prisoner endured, mentally and physically, in the company of the person who had been put into her cell

She, like the last, was a person she could not confide in.

Indeed, she had been placed there only because the remainder of the gaol was full; and the term of her imprisonment she had great hopes of getting shortened, through some influence she meant to bring to bear upon the prison authorities from without.

Therefore it would not have been worth the other woman's while to risk her chance of liberty by helping Ruth; and Ruth did not betray her secret.

To keep the secret, though, was extremely difficult. How could it be otherwise?

When even the other woman approached the bed, Ruth was in a fever of anxiety. Then again she was continually complaining about the dirt and fleas, and was most eager to have the floor swept.

She only remained one week, but the week seemed months long.

Directly she had gone, Ruth returned to her work.

How many toilers are there who slave and slave unseen, unknown, and break their hearts at last with grief and disappointment, within the very sight of the goal they have struggled so desperately, yet so unavailingly, to reach.

She had now come down to the lath and plaster. She was almost in the room, you will say. Not quite.

She pierced a tiny hole, and looked down

Yes, there was the room, sure enough. So far so good. Only——

Only she had made the hole in such *a way that a beam below crossed it*

To see the poor heart-broken creature sobbing over this fresh disappointment would have moved a stone to pity.

She conquered her grief somehow, though, and set to work again as hard as ever.

She was now compelled to enlarge the top of the opening, for as it was, the beam below rendered the passage too small for the body to go through.

She managed to make the opening in such a way that it was still concealed by the bed, and now at last her work was finished.

It would only be the work of a few minutes to break through the laths and plaster. She had a large quantity of calico by her, on which she was engaged in shirt-making

Everything now was prepared, and that night the attempt should be made.

Before night came, one of the most awful disappointments befel her which it is almost possible to conceive.

As she was sitting in a reverie, wondering where she should be that time next day, the gaoler made his appearance.

It was the time for her to go out on the roof, and she rose to accompany him.

"Not just yet," said he. "What do you think?"

"Think?" she repeated.

"I have some fine news for you."

"For me?" she repeated, turning pale.

"First rate news! Wonderful news! Glorious news!"

"Am I," she gasped, leaning against the wall for support,—"am I to be set at liberty?"

"Well, not quite as good as that, either."

"Speak, then! In heaven's name, what is it?"

"You're going——"

"Going—oh, heaven! going——"

"Going into another room—ever so much larger and more airy."

She fell back upon the bed as though she had been shot.

"What now?" cried the gaoler, in amazement. "What on earth is the matter with you? I never did see such a woman!"

"I don't want to move," said she.

"Eh?"—and the gaoler thought he could not have understood aright. "Don't want to move."

"No."

"You never get a chance of tasting anything too strong for you, or I should be inclined to suppose that you had taken a drop too much."

Ruth made no reply.

"You must be mad!" said he,—"you must be mad! That's what it is!"

"Tell the Governor I am much obliged to him, but I would rather stay where I am."

"Don't be silly—you must go!"

"I don't want to."

"Why, I tell you the new place is a palace compared to this. Why, it's quite light!"

"I don't care."

"Now, look here! I don't take you to be a fool—that is, for a woman—and I can't believe you're going to be unreasonable. You must go."

"I shan't."

"Oh, you won't, eh?"

"No."

"Why?"

"I'll see the Governor first."

"What for?"

"Because he'll let me stop."

"Now, just look here! You're not always going to be appealing to the Governor, so I can tell you; so if you don't walk quietly when I tell you, I'll carry you, that's all."

She saw that it was perfectly useless, and she rose to go.

"I am ready," said she.

"Just catch hold of your work, then; I'll carry your chair."

She did as she was told

"Now, let me go first," said he; and he led the way.

They went, by several passages, into a distant part of the building, but still close to the roof

At last he opened the door of quite a spacious apartment compared to the last, with a large window, commanding a distant view of the city, in the middle of which the prison stood, and of a broad river, running at the prison's base upon this side.

"I have brought your victuals here, you see," said he, pointing to some food. "I'll go back, now, and fetch your table and your bed."

Her bed!

It was all over with her now!

She gave herself up to despair before this, though. She was capable of no stronger emotion.

She was not frightened very much by any thought of consequences.

She was desperate.

Supposing he had come to set her free, and then they had found out the hole she had made, perhaps they would have kept her still a prisoner.

Most likely. She would then have been worse off than she was now.

She yet had her spike.

She kept it usually concealed about her.

When he had left the room, the idea occurred to her that she might be searched, and she hastily sprang from her seat.

Then, with a spoon, made a hole in the loaf, and buried the iron in the crumb.

"That is safe!" said she.

And she sat down in her chair, and waited.

She was not frightened at all. She even smiled a little when she thought what sort of a face the gaoler would make upon discovery of the hole.

"I would give a trifle to see him," she thought to herself.

Then she remembered that she would see him before long, and she waited as patiently as she could.

But when the time passed away—an hour, two hours, three hours even, without his return—she began to grow uneasy.

What could cause all this delay?

Had he summoned the Governor to inspect her handiwork? Were they consulting together as to what kind of punishment should be meted out to her?

She had everything to fear, and the more and more she thought upon her situation, the more uneasy did she become.

She had heard a great deal from time to time, through her companion, the gaoler, respecting the way in which refractory prisoners were treated in Saint Lazarus's prison, and other French gaols.

Often they were branded with hot irons, and cruelly maimed.

The women were frequently stripped naked in the presence of the other prisoners, both male and female, most barbarously and cruelly flogged, and treated with indignities too shocking to mention.

Some were locked up in dungeons beneath the level of the river, and perhaps this fate was the most terrific.

Loathsome places were these dungeons, in which the miserable prisoner was compelled to remain all day upon a bench, unless he chose to stand almost up to his knees in water.

Upon this bench his bed is placed, and when he is asleep he is in danger of falling over, and getting drenched to the skin.

Sickening reptiles and rats in any number creep into these horrible cells; and if the prisoner does not fight a hard battle with them, he won't get very much of his food.

Yet in these cells prisoners had passed many years. Could such a fate be reserved for her?

She would die rather than remain there, she thought. If it came to that, she would murder the gaoler, and so leave the prison for the guillotine.

At length, when she thought that she could endure the suspense no longer, the gaoler returned.

He was in a tremendous passion.

He came straight into the cell, shut the door behind him, and leaning against it, shook his fist at her.

She looked at him contemptuously, and was silent.

"Why," he roared, "you don't suppose I haven't seen it, do you?"

She made no answer.

"Where is your axe and saw?" he asked at last.

"I haven't got any."

"None of your lies!"

She did not argue with him any further, and treated his oaths and fist-shakings with silent contempt.

"Give them up!" he roared Give them up!"

As she made no answer, he stamped up and down the room, looking to the right and to the left.

He pulled her work to pieces.

Finding nothing.

He examined her work-box.

With the same result.

He ordered her to get out of her chair, and looked at it, feeling the bottom and sides.

Nothing there!

"Damnation!" he roared, in a frenzy.

Then, mad with rage, he seized and shook her.

"Have you anything in your pockets?" he said.

"Look for yourself."

He roughly searched her, but found nothing.

"Curse you!" he roared, as he pushed her from him with such violence that she almost fell to the ground; "I'll be even with you yet!"

"Ha! ha!" laughed the woman, insultingly.

The gaoler gnashed his teeth, and could only mutter "D—n you!"

"Ha! ha!" laughed the prisoner.

"Now, look here," he said, in a tone of concentrated passion—"I'm not going to be played the fool with!"

"Ain't you?"

"If you answer me like that, I'll dash your teeth down your throat!"

Ruth showed her bright ivories with an insulting smile, keeping the while her eyes fixed very steadily upon his.

"Do it," she thought; "and I'll soon show you where the spike is!"

"Come now," said the gaoler; "I tell you I want to know where you have hidden the tools?"

She looked harder at him than before, but made no reply.

"Do you hear?"

"I'm not deaf."

"Will you tell me?"

"No."

"You won't?"

"No."

"Oh, very well! I've tried fair means."

"Fair means, you call it?"

"Yes. I've tried fair means, and now I'll have to try foul. We shall see what the Governor will say to your games, young lady! We shall see—we shall see!"

"Are you going to tell the Governor?"

"Yes; I should rather think I was."

"That will be very simple."

"What do you mean by simple?"

"It will put you in rather an awkward position."

"What the devil do you mean by that?"

"What I say."

"What do you mean, I ask you?"

"Suppose I have made a hole in the floor?"

"Suppose, indeed! Of course you have."

"Well, I have. I don't deny it."

"Listen to that! There never was such a devil, I do believe—even for a woman!"

"Well," said Ruth, without taking any notice of the remark which the gaoler addressed to the winds—"well, if I did make the hole, and you told the Governor, do you know what I should do?"

"No."

"I should be obliged to do it, although it would go against my feelings"

"Devil doubt you! What is it?"

"I should at once inform the Governor that it was you——"

"That it was I——"

"Who supplied me with the tools."

"Supplied you with the tools?"

"Yes."

"Now may I sleep uneasy in my grave, if you don't beat anything on the face of the blessed earth of impudence and insolence! But here——"

"Yes."

"Who do you suppose would believe you?"

"The Governor."

"He wouldn't."

"He would."

"He wouldn't, I say"

"He would, I tell you; and I'll tell you why."

"Why, then?"

"Because I would tell him that I gave the tools back to you."

"I should deny it."

"He wouldn't believe you."

"He would."

"I should call on you to produce them."

"I shall find them."

"Do so; and then I shan't think you quite such a fool as I do now."

The gaoler stamped up and down the cell, and cursed and swore, Ruth laughing at him.

At length he stopped, and, in quite an altered tone, said, "Look here—let's be friends!"

"Willingly," she answered.

"Tell us where the tools are?"

"I have none"

"What's the good of playing the fool? The matter's over now. I own myself beaten. Tell us what you've done with them."

"I have no tools."

"How did you do it then?"

"With my teeth"

"Don't talk nonsense!"

"I don't."

"How could you have done it with your teeth?"

"You don't know what a woman can do till she tries. Look how white and regular they are, and feel how sharp!"

"Damn it!—leave go! That hurts!"

"They cut, don't they?"

"I'd like to draw them all."

"No, you wouldn't, they're so pretty. Don't you wish you had them?"

"No."

"Don't you think they're pretty?"

"No!"

"You don't? Don't you think I'm pretty?"

"I don't care a curse for you or your prettiness either."

"You're a stupid old fool, or else you'd try, instead of bullying, to make me fall in love with you, and then I should tell you all my secrets without having to be coaxed. But you're a stupid old man, and I never shall love you, and I hate you instead, and if ever I get away from here I'll come back and kill you."

CHAPTER XCV.

THE PRISONER UPON THE OTHER SIDE OF THE WALL

WAR was declared.

A terrible feud raged between the gaoler and the prisoner.

The old man grew so spiteful at the thought that this woman—nothing but a woman, too—should treat him with such contempt, that he did not know how sufficiently to vent his ill-nature.

He resorted to numerous little mean acts of tyranny.

Many too paltry to mention, but, nevertheless, extremely galling and exasperating to the prisoner.

He did not bring her her food at the regular time. He kept the window shut, which she could not open without his assistance, and did not allow her a breath of air during the most suffocatingly hot weather.

She could not sleep a wink, and he supplied her with a bolster "as hard as nails."

The meat he brought her was almost putrid; the bread like a stone, and the water dirty.

It made her feel sick to look at her food, and at first she starved herself, but then she thought that it would be wisest to keep up her strength, so that she could, if needs be, struggle with her gaoler.

She made up her mind to murder him, and told him so repeatedly, at which he laughed.

"I will, by heaven!" she said. "I will to-morrow!"

Perhaps he was frightened.

Perhaps he relented towards her.

He opened the door a chink in the morning, and called out, "I'm afraid to come in, but here's something for you."

Instead of her usual food, he had brought her

some warm milk, some eating chocolate, white bread, cutlets, and a water melon.

In spite of herself, she could not help expressing her pleasure.

"Who sent it?" she asked.

"A friend of yours," he replied.

"Who?"

"Don't ask questions."

"I will know."

"Eat it first."

"I won't eat it at all, unless you tell me."

"Was there ever such a devil!"

"Tell me, you old fool!"

"You see, they were complimentary."

"I shan't!"

"You shall!"

"Well, then, I bought 'em for you."

"You—you stupid! Why?"

"Now curse me——"

"No, I won't; I'm much obliged to you. But I say! What made you do it?"

"Because I took a fancy into my head. What's that to you?"

"Everything. I'll tell you what!"

"What?"

"I've made a discovery."

"What discovery?"

"I've found out something about you!"

"And that is——"

"That you're a greater old noodle than I took you for!"

The gaoler turned crimson for a moment; but it appeared, somehow, as though the more insulting the prisoner was to him, the more affable he became.

After having broken the ice, as it were, by this present of fruit, he, upon several other occasions, brought her little presents; and, indeed, he rarely supplied her with her daily food without adding some little delicacy, though it must be owned that a couple of very dry Brazil nuts, a shrivelled walnut or two, a sour apple of the crab family, and an attenuated fig, were not fruits of a highly enticing nature.

"What's he mean by it?" she asked herself.

And she came to the conclusion that, according to the great rule of contrary which guides love affairs in general, now she had left off courting him, he had begun to court her.

But she did not encourage him.

First of all, had not all hope of escape vanished? And even if any hope remained, and escape could only be made by aid of a warder, it was very certain that, however strong the old man's partiality might lately have grown for her, there could be no foundation for hope, even in the most sanguine mind, that he would assist her.

She had, besides, taken a worse dislike to him than ever; and she could scarcely endure his presence, or behave to him with the faintest semblance of politeness, in spite of his numerous presents, cheap fruit, and sweetmeats.

Then, again, had she been inclined to change her manner towards him through any feeling of kindness, would not experience have warned her that kind treatment was not appreciated?

No; most decidedly the best course for her was to continue to snub him, if she wished him to continue to love her.

One thing must not be forgotten, by the by; and that was that the gaoler, although decidedly evincing amatory predilections, was extremely particular in his examination of Ruth's cell every morning.

With an iron bar he tapped the walls all round; and he tried every plank of the floor, particularly the part under her bed.

One place only he omitted to examine or tap; and she noticed this before long.

It was the ceiling.

"That's the way I must get out, if I go," she thought.

But the chance did not appear to be very near at hand.

"I must wait and see what turns up," she thought, after having turned every possible and impossible event over in her mind; and, consequently, she waited for a long while without anything wonderful turning up.

One day Ruth asked the gaoler whether he could not procure her some novels to read.

A Testament and a Mass book were lying in the cell, and the same books were to be found in all the other cells, for the use of those prisoners who chose to avail themselves of religious instruction; but Mrs. Ruth possessing very lax notions about these matters, and being, as the reader well knows, an extremely unprincipled and improper young female, she desired, as she profanely remarked, "something more exciting."

"Well," said the gaoler, after she had put the question to him several times, "perhaps I can."

"Have you any novels at home?" she asked.

"No, but I can get some, perhaps."

When she inquired from what source he intended to procure them, he told her that all the prisoners in the building were not forbidden to have works of that character, and that there was a State prisoner, a young French author, upon the same landing as herself, who had a large quantity of that sort of trash.

Would he lend some to her?

The gaoler would inquire.

The result of the inquiry was so far satisfactory, that a small volume, termed "The Loves of a Fly," being a poem, in the French language, of a highly incorrect character, was brought to her by the gaoler, with the compliments of her fellow-prisoner.

Seeing the nature of the work, Mrs. Ruth was going to refuse it with much indignation, supposing that the gaoler had brought it with the intention of insulting her; but she soon discovered that the old man, although he talked about his school-days at some length, was not able to read.

"What made you bring me this?" she asked indignantly, throwing it down again.

"Well, I never!" said the old man, picking it up again, and staring at her in amazement. "What's the matter with it?"

"You ask me, do you?"

"Is there any wonder that I should, when you behave in that extraordinary fashion?"

Then she saw plainly, by the expression of his face, as he stood puzzling over the title-page, that it was so much Greek to him.

She, therefore, refrained from making any further remark upon the subject; and, much as I may regret to have to record such reprehensible conduct on her part, a strict adherence to truth compels me to say that she read the whole work through with great care and attention.

When she had finished the poem she returned it to the gaoler, with instructions to give the book back to its owner, and to thank him very much for his politeness; though, at the same time, to suggest that she would be still more obliged if he would give her a list of his books, that she might choose one from them more to her taste.

In the course of the day the gaoler returned, bringing a list in which several novels were named, and at the end of it the French gentleman expressed his sincere regret that he should have sent such a work, but that the gaoler had not informed him that it was a lady who did him the honour to request the loan of one of his books.

Returning the list, with one of the books marked with a cross, which she made with a pin, for she had no pencil, nor would the gaoler supply her with one, she scratched at the end "Many thanks."

The book she had chosen came back, and turning to the title-page she found a slip of paper, on which was written—

"Fair unknown and fellow-sufferer, kindly lighten the weary hours of a captive who feels deeply interested in your welfare, by telling me your trouble."

But, most unfortunately, that paper happened to catch the gaoler's eye, and he made a snap at it.

"What's this?" said he.

"Another list of books he had forgotten to name in his last list," said Ruth very glibly.

"It's an infernal lie!" roared the gaoler, who did not mince matters usually.

And he tore the piece of paper to atoms.

"Look here!" said he; "I won't have any of that, you know, or else you'll not have another book. It's against the rules to let you have the books, and I should get into the devil's own row if it were found out. I tell you what! I won't have you two conniving together; and I tell you——"

"It was only a list," said Ruth.

"I won't have any lists, then."

"Very well; I don't want any."

There the matter luckily ended.

But Ruth determined upon corresponding with her friend, only she intended to do it with great caution.

Therefore, on the last page of the book, when she returned it, she scratched with a pin—

"Don't send any more slips of paper. Be cautious! Correspond in this way!"

The gaoler having carefully shaken the book, to see that there was no paper between the leaves, returned it to the Frenchman, and informed him that he must write no more.

However, when the next book came back, there was a good deal of pencilling on the margin.

In this way a regular postal communication was opened between the two cells, and the unconscious gaoler before long was carrying backwards and forwards the most treasonable matter, without the least suspicion of what he was doing.

"Is there any way we can see one another?" asked the Frenchman.

"Have you the courage to attempt an escape?" asked the Englishwoman.

"For your sake, beautiful unknown, I would face death," said the Frenchman.

"He's a fool!" said the lady, when she read his reply. "However, he'll do in lieu of another."

Then, having obtained from him a solemn written promise to do exactly as she bade him, she began to inform him, always with the aid of a pin, on the title-pages of his books, how he ought to do to effect his escape.

"He had no tools fit for prison-breaking work," he said; and she then told him of her spike, with which he could break through the roof of his cell, then break through the roof of her cell, by climbing along in the loft over-head.

As she had ascertained that the Frenchman was, besides being an author, also a bit of an artist, and was fond of drawing huge heads in black chalk, which he stuck about the walls, she saw that he might very easily cover the hole in the ceiling with one of these, should it take him more than one day to make the opening.

Not very much to her surprise, though, it must be owned, somewhat to her disgust, the Frenchman asked her why she did not make the hole herself, and come through to him.

But she told him that the reason she did not do so was because the gaoler suspected her.

"If I were sure of being able to do the work in one day," said she, "I would."

"But," said the Frenchman, "when I have broken through into your cell, what are we to do? We shall still be in prison."

"The wretched idiot!" cried Ruth, stamping her feet with rage.

But I don't think the Frenchman was such a fool, after all. And, to tell the truth, Ruth had not the vaguest notion what they were going to do when they had broken through the roof; only that, being together, they could do something towards forcing a way out—more than one could do, anyhow.

The great difficulty to begin with was how to get the spike conveyed into the Frenchman's cell.

How on earth could it be done?

The Frenchman's idea was that he should send his dressing-gown in for her to mend the sleeves which he had torn, and that when she had mended it she should return the gown folded up, with the spike inside.

But Ruth was terrified lest the gaoler should unfold it; she therefore sent back the dressing-gown, but did not send the spike.

As she had expected, the gaoler undid the gown, and you can imagine the agony of mind the Frenchman was in when he saw the gown returned without the weapon.

"All is lost!" said he, in the next book.

"What is the matter?" said she, unable to forbear tormenting him.

"The tyrant has the spike!"

"No, he hasn't. I did not send it."

"Thank God for that!"

Very soon Ruth thought of a dodge.

The Frenchman had money, and was, consequently, able to purchase what food he chose, in the same way that she had done when first she came into St. Lazarus's prison.

She proposed that he should send a present of a tureen full of thick soup, and that he should make it taste very nasty with salt.

Also, that he should conceal at the bottom of the tureen a paper weight, or some such object, for the purpose of making it feel heavy.

Her reasons for this she explained.

The soup was prepared by the Frenchman, and given to the gaoler to carry; and he was directed to carry it very carefully, for fear he should slop the soup over the sides—it being very full.

Ruth receiving it, pretended to be surprised and delighted; and having had the tureen placed upon the table, waited until the gaoler left the room before she tasted it.

The moment he began to draw the door to, Ruth began to act.

Instantly she plunged her hand into the soup, took out the paper-weight, and replaced it by the spike.

Then called back the gaoler.

He had not had time to put in the last bolt, so quick had she been.

When he entered the room again, she was standing with a spoonful of soup in her hand, making a wry face.

"What's the matter?" asked the gaoler.

"Have you tasted this?" she asked.

"I?—no?"

"Do so."

The gaoler took a spoonful, and spat it out.

"What do you think of it?"

"Beastly!"

"What makes him send me such a mess?"

"Hanged if I know!"

"It's to insult me!"

"Can't be that."

"What shall I do with it?"

"Throw it away! Here, let me!"

"No, no; don't do that! Take it back to him!"

"Very well."

"Give him my compliments, and say I won't rob him!"

"Ha! ha! that'll wake him up."

The gaoler was very much delighted with his message, but he thought the author a conceited fool, and liked to see him taken down a peg or two.

"She's sent it back," said he.

"Why?" cried the author, pretending to be surprised.

"Says she won't rob you."

"She's not robbing me."

"She thinks she is."

"Why?"

"She says, perhaps you've got a pig, and it may come in handy."

"The impudent creature!"

"Take a plateful yourself, sir," said the gaoler.

The Frenchman gulped down a spoonful, and pretended to like it, though it almost made him sick.

"Well?" said the gaoler.

"Splendid!" said the author.

"Glad you like it."

"You have some, old fellow," said the other.

"No, thank you; I don't seem to care about it."

"I do!" said the other, and continued to gulp down the mess till the other left the room, when he took out the spike, and was very quietly sick in a corner.

The work now began in real earnest.

The Frenchman wrote her word next morning, telling her how he was getting on.

It was much easier after the first beginning, he said; and the next morning after, when she was reading, and endeavouring not to be impatient, she was suddenly startled into the most intense joy by hearing a tap upon the floor above her.

A loud tap, followed, after a brief pause, by another, and then another.

It was the Frenchman's signal.

He was in the attic above.

During the day she heard him at work, and gradually, as she fancied that the sounds grew near her, she became more and more joyful.

She had told him to be very careful not to be at work when the gaoler came up to take her for her accustomed walk on the roof; and as the time drew near—for she could hear a clock strike from her new cell—she got into a fever of anxiety, lest he should chance to be hammering when the gaoler came.

But the Frenchman was on his guard, and half an hour before the gaoler's time arrived he desisted from work, and beat a retreat into his own cell.

She got a communication from her accomplice that afternoon.

"I have broken through to the lath and plaster. We will try our luck to-night."

She got the gaoler to take back a book, and it contained her answer.

"I am ready."

When the gaoler had departed for the day, and there was no fear of any further interruption, the Frenchman went to work again.

Ruth waited impatiently.

Soon the end of the spike appeared through the plaster.

Then the Frenchman began to smash it all away with his feet.

Next moment he dropped lightly down on to the floor, and stood face to face with the woman whom he had so long been in correspondence with, but whose face, until now, he had not seen.

It must be owned that he was pleasantly surprised by the beauty of his fair companion, although, at first sight, he was rather doubtful as to her sex, for she had converted his serge skirt into a pair of trousers, and wore a coarse blue shirt.

"But I am a woman!" said she, with a laugh.

"A beauty, too!"

"You can be complimentary when we get outside the walls," said she. "We've no time for that sort of thing just now."

"What do you propose now?"

"Breaking through the roof."

"And then?"

"We shall see."

She did not know herself, and they clambered back through the hole by the end of her table and chair, without either of them being over certain what was in store for them.

CHAPTER XCVI.

AT LAST.

The time had come, then.

This time, the attempt must either end in death or liberty.

There was no other course, no other alternative.

While the Frenchman had been employed in breaking through the ceiling of her cell, she had also been busy at work in another way.

She had been cutting up the mattress and counterpane, and making it into ropes.

Together, then, they swung upon it with all their weight, and tested its strength and durability in every way in their power.

So far, all had gone well; but, as yet, the great difficulties of the undertaking had still to be overcome.

And the greatest difficulty of all she soon found to be in her companion.

After they had taken out some of the tiles on the roof, so as to take an observation, the Frenchman, not at all fancying the appearance outside, began to show the white feather to a very great extent.

"Do you see your way?" he asked, ruefully.

"Yes, yes!" she replied, though she did nothing of the sort.

"It makes my head turn—I can't face it."

"Nonsense!"

"We shall be dashed to pieces."

The increasing difficulty of the situation made her furious.

"I must have his help, curse him!" she muttered. "I suspected all along that he was a cur!"

There was very little doubt about that; and through the remainder of the adventure his cowardice threw so many obstacles in the way, that there were many times that she could have brained him in her savage fury, though at the same time she was obliged to put a fair face upon the matter, and pretend to be good friends with him, and humour him to the utmost, for fear that he might desert her, and that his assistance would become absolutely necessary at some juncture which might yet arrive.

It would not be of any use thinking of starting upon their perilous expedition before nightfall.

It was now twilight, and as Ruth had prepared

the rope by this time, and there was nothing for the Frenchman to occupy himself with except staring through the hole that had been made in the roof, from which a giddy and brain-turning view of the awful distance below could be obtained, she induced him to go back into his cell and occupy himself in packing up certain articles of his personal property, which he seemed to think he could not sacrifice, however much inconvenience their transportation from the prison might cause him.

Ruth, however, while inwardly feeling a great contempt for her companion, did not dare to say anything that would offend him, for, in her heart, she felt very certain that an exceedingly small amount of provocation would cause him to abandon the scheme altogether.

Gradually the twilight thickened into darkness, and the moon, rising slowly in the clear blue-black sky, shone coldly down upon the prison roof, a dark and frowning object in the middle of the busy city surrounding it.

A damp fog had been for some time rising from the river beneath, and as Ruth laid her hand upon the tiles without, she thought with a shudder of the slippery and dangerous path which lay before them.

By this time, after a great deal of grumbling and groaning over his bundles, which, considering the hazardous climbing in store for them, were of most absurd dimensions, the Frenchman came and found her at the spot, where she stood silent against the blue sky, watching the far-off lights upon the opposite side of the river.

"You seem loaded," said she, looking at her companion with a smile which was slightly contemptuous. "Are you going to bring all that rubbish with you?"

"Rubbish!" he repeated, in an injured tone.

"There's a great deal of it!" she remarked.

"A great deal!" he retorted, peevishly. "It is not more than a half of what I ought to bring."

"Not more than half, eh?"

"No; I am leaving all the most valuable behind."

"That seems silly."

"What do you mean?"

"Why do you bring the least valuable away with you?"

"Oh, bah! you know what I mean."

"I don't."

"Well, of course, I did not intend you to take what I said in quite such a literal sense as that."

"Oh! you have brought the most valuable with you, after all?"

"I don't say that, either; only I can't bring all I want away, of course, and——There, it does not signify!"

Ruth laughed shortly, and the dialogue thus terminated.

It would not, however, have required any person gifted with a prophetic intelligence of at all an unusual character to have foretold that the connexion of these two prisoners, the present moment of peril over, did their expedition arrive at a happy termination, would terminate very briefly.

This Frenchman, truly, was a very paltry fellow.

From the very first, without any respect or consideration for the difference in their sexes, he voted Ruth the leader in the expedition, and appealed to her in everything.

He could not move without her, except, indeed, when every now and then he forced himself forward, and, with a pig-headed obstinacy which threatened to bring the business at once to a fatal termination, persisted in having his own way.

"Are you ready?" asked Ruth, in a voice rendered strangely hoarse by half-suppressed emotion—"are you ready?"

"Yes."

"Come, then."

"But, I say——"

She was climbing through the hole she had made in the roof, to take a last look round, and decide upon the course that they must adopt.

"I say—I say!" the Frenchman cried.

"Well?" she returned, sharply twisting round, and facing him.

"What are we going to do?—going out of the roof?"

"Yes."

"But—but——"

"But what?"

"It's frightfully slippery, isn't it?"

"It *is* very slippery."

"We shall never be able to keep our footing."

"I think *we* can."

"*I* don't."

"It is our only chance."

The Frenchman grumbled to himself, as though he thought she caused all the difficulty, and that he was a victim, whose case should be deeply commiserated.

"The roof's as slippery as so much glass," he said, feeling it with his hand. "How the devil are we to manage?"

"I think we can go pretty safely barefoot."

As she spoke, she began to pull off her slippers and stockings, without, it must be confessed, any particular respect for such feelings of modesty which the French gentleman might possess.

When she was prepared, she bade him somewhat imperiously to follow her example, without taking much notice of the remarkably long face that he pulled upon receiving the order.

"What the deuce am I to do with them?" he asked, in a whining tone.

"Do with them?" she repeated.

"Yes."

"Do what you like with them, I don't care."

"I can't carry them."

"Leave them behind, then."

"How you talk! How can I leave them behind?"

"Why not?"

"I can't walk about the streets barefoot, when I get there, can I?"

"Well, carry them, then?"

"But I can't, with all these bundles."

"Leave the bundles, then."

"How can I?"

"Why can't you?"

"I never knew any one to equal you. Why, they're of the greatest value, some of these books."

"Oh, very well; I can't help you."

"You might if you liked."

"How, pray?"

"By carrying one of these bundles."

Ruth felt very wroth at this request, but she thought it best not to show her temper; and, therefore, swallowing her anger with a mighty gulp, she offered to take one of his bundles if he would carry the cords which she had made to assist them in their descent.

He agreed to this, after a good deal of grumbling, and they commenced the ascent.

It was time now that they set off.

The moon was at its full. The gaol seemed very quiet. The river stretched out black at their feet. The distant murmur of the busy traffic in the streets below was wafted, now and then, in their direction—occasionally, some shrill cry of a street seller of fruit, or such like, reaching them with a vivid distinctness which at first almost startled them.

Ruth went first, very cautiously—crept out of the opening—turned her face towards the tilt in the roof, and began to creep, and creep, steadying herself as much as possible by driving the spike which she held in her right hand into a beam of wood which formed an ornamental portion of the roof, and separated two rows of slates.

The Frenchman, following—with many groans and much lamentation at the hardness of his fate—clung to her waistband with one hand, while he clutched at the beam with the other.

The consequence was that she was obliged to bear a great deal of his weight besides her own.

Slowly they crept along.

Slowly, slowly.

When they had performed about three quarters of the journey towards the ridge, the Frenchman cried out.

"What is it?"

"I've dropped a bundle!"

It is not at all probable that a lady would use strong language upon any occasion, is it? Consequently, it is not at all likely that what Ruth's words sounded most like could really have been the words she uttered.

She must have said, "Bless your bundle!" only decidedly it did not sound much like it.

She was very much exasperated, there is not a doubt.

If she had consulted her first instincts, she would have given monsieur a kick in the face, and sent him sprawling backwards into eternity.

But she reflected again, that probably she would require his help; she therefore moderated her rage, and asked, "What bundle have you dropped?"

"The smallest."

"Bother the smallest, and the largest, too! Can't you answer intelligibly? What was in it?"

"Some most valuable articles."

"Not the ropes?"

"No."

"You have them safe?"

"Quite safe."

"Try and keep them so."

"But about these things?"

"You must leave them; we cannot risk our lives by turning back."

The Frenchman grumbled.

"I think we might manage to get hold of them?"

"Come on, idiot!"

She would listen to no more, and dragged him onwards.

Then they climbed on silently.

It was a frightful journey, and when they at length reached the tilt, and, sitting astride upon it, looked back at what they had done, it made their blood run cold, and their flesh fairly creep upon their bones.

The effect of the backward glance was almost too much for Ruth's companion, and he groaned aloud.

"I can't bear that sort of thing," he said. "It makes my head spin round. Oh, heavens! I feel so frightened!"

"Feel frightened!" she cried. "Are you not ashamed of making such an acknowledgment in the presence of a woman?"

"I never came across such a woman as you are," he grumbled. "You're a regular termagant. You seem neither to fear God nor devil."

"My head isn't so weak as yours seems to be."

"It's not my fault, is it?"

"I should think not."

"I can't help it, can I? I was always like this on high places. I wish to heaven I had never come. Oh, dear! I feel such a dizziness coming over me!"

"Try and conquer it, you wretched fool!" she cried, fiercely, for her companion began to sway about in such an awful manner, that she expected every moment to see him roll over on one side and slide helplessly down the slippery slates;—"try and hold up."

But he made such a dreadful lurch backwards upon one occasion, that had she not possessed the strength and courage of a young lioness, he would have fallen, and been dashed to atoms in the street beneath.

As it was, he dropped his hat and one shoe, at which loss he complained very bitterly.

Oh, how she longed to murder him, so disgusted was she at his weakness; but again she conquered her feelings.

"Lie flat on your stomach, and cling to the ridge," she said, "and keep your eyes shut—then you will be all right. Whatever you do, don't look down."

"What are you going to do?"

"I'm going to reconnoitre."

"What! and leave me?"

"Suppose you go yourself, then?"

"Oh, Lord! oh, Lord! I haven't the head for it. I can't stir yet awhile."

"Stop where you are, then."

"I only know one thing."

"Well?"

"If I had known what we had to do, I should never have placed myself in this frightful position."

"Oh, indeed!"

"You told me it would be quite easy when we got upon the roof."

"So it will be, directly—when we get down," she answered, laughing.

"Oh, Lord! I shall be killed, I know that, very well! I wish I had never come!"

"You'd rather rot in prison?"

"I was not going to remain there all my life, I don't suppose; and I wasn't so very badly off, either."

"I was."

"Yes, you were; and so you tempted me on to this risk, just to escape yourself."

"If you are not satisfied, you can go back," she retorted.

"Go back?" he repeated, looking ruefully down the slope—"that's worse than going forward."

"Then hold your stupid tongue, and sit quietly till I return."

"You won't be long?"

"No."

"I say, though——"

"What? For God's sake, come back!"

"Of course I shall!"

"You wouldn't betray me?"

"Do you suppose I have such a cur's heart as yours?" she retorted; and without another word left him.

The journey she had set out upon was anything but a pleasant one, as the reader can easily suppose.

After taking a comprehensive glance of the roof from the place where they sat, she began slowly to creep along upon the tiles, assisting herself as well as she could with the spike which she still retained in her right hand, and keeping astride upon the ridge as the safest position which she could possibly assume.

She was gone a very long while, although she made all the haste that lay in her power; and the Frenchman waiting for her uttered curses both loud and deep.

She took the rope with her, and she was engaged in searching for some place to which it could be fastened.

But her search was in vain.

The further she wandered the more unlikely the roof appeared; and she looked despairingly round for a chimney, but could find one nowhere.

The fact is, that the prison was warmed by hot-water pipes, and the fires used to heat the water were at the other extremity of the building, near the chapel and Governor's house.

It was to that part of the building that Ruth was anxious to direct her course; for even had she been able to find something that she could have secured the rope to at the place where they had come up, it would have been of no use, because she did not want to make a descent into the river on one side of the roof, and on the other she had no particular fancy for coming down in the court-yard of the prison.

As she crept slowly onwards in the dim uncertain light, gazing now and then with a dread which she could not conquer down the deep, black, yawning chasms gaping upon every side as though ready to receive her lifeless corpse, her heart began to sink within her.

Should she, after all, be obliged to give up the scheme and return to captivity?

No, she would rather die than that.

She had thought before she came up upon the roof, that if it came to the worst, and she was discovered, she would rather fling herself off than fall again into the hands of the prison authorities, but it would be a frightful death, she thought, now.

What would be her fate, though, she asked herself. if she were unlucky enough to be retaken?

She had got over her last trouble very easily.

Ah! but she could not hope to be as lucky this time.

No, the gaoler had hushed up the last business to save himself from trouble, but if this attempt at escape were discovered, secrecy would be impossible.

No, all must be known; and then, if what the old man had told her was true—and why should she doubt him?—the fate which was reserved for her was very little better than death itself.

Climbing on and on, she came at last to a part of the building which she judged must be the Governor's house; and here, in a corner, at length she discovered a break in the regularity of the slope.

It was a window, the roof of which projected from the other roof.

With the greatest caution, and very slowly, she now began to descend the slanting roof to get to the top of the window.

But when, after a journey, the terrors of which were indescribable—for every movement she made she expected to slip and slide down so fast that she should be carried over the parapet before she could hope to save herself—she arrived safely upon the top of the window, she was still at a loss what to do.

Creeping to the edge. she stretched her arm over, hoping that the window might be open.

But it was not.

She had to lie on her face to feel for it. It was a great distance to reach, and at the extreme limit that she dare stretch, she could only just manage to touch the glass with the points of her fingers.

One of the panes she found was broken.

Was the room, then, uninhabited? She fancied and trusted that this might be the case.

But how was she to get in?

How could she get round to the front?

It was impossible—absolutely impossible.

In recovering an upright position again, after leaning over to feel the window panels, Ruth almost lost her balance, owing to one of the tiles being loose.

The fright was so great that she sat down for some moments, clutching the roof on either side of her, and trembling too violently to be able to trust herself to move again.

But she soon recovered her courage, when the thought occurred to her that here was the way to get over the difficulty which had hitherto been perplexing her.

The way into the room would be through the roof.

Without losing any more time, then, she set about removing the loose tile.

That having been taken away, she found that the work she had proposed was really not very difficult.

One tile being taken out seemed to loosen the next, and she had very soon taken off a sufficient number to allow the passage of her arm.

Then she worked away, briskly smashing up the morter and laths.

Up the middle of the roof of the window, however, was not a beam, as she expected to find one, and there was nothing that she could fasten the rope to; and, indeed, working on, she found that it would be impossible to make a hole large enough to step through with her body.

No, that could not be managed, but she would be able through the hole, that she could squeeze her arm into, to open the window from the inside, for the bolt was high up.

When the window was open, she could manage to creep round, because there was now some places among the broken tiles to cling to.

"This will do," she said.

And she was going to jump down into the room, when, suddenly, a thought saved her.

"How far was she from the floor?"

She tied a broken tile to the rope, and let it down inside, to sound the distance.

The rope ran through her hands, for, as well as she could judge, nearly thirty feet.

"Thank God I did not go!" she inwardly ejaculated. "Who ever could have anticipated that it would have been such a distance?"

However, thus far, all was satisfactory, and now she thought she would go back and look for the Frenchman.

She naturally supposed that this gentleman would have been glad to see her, and would have expressed some satisfaction at her return, but such was not, however, the case.

"Well, so you've managed to come back at last," he cried, in a most injured tone.

"Yes," she said innocently.

"I'm surprised, I am sure!"

"Did you think I had been long?"

"I thought you was never coming back at all."

"I told you I should."

"Oh, oh! you told me; I know that very well."

"I have not broken my word, you see."

"No, for a wonder. I can't say I expected to see any more of you after the first half-hour."

"What did you suppose had become of me?"

"I thought there was an end of you."

"Did you think that I had deserted you?"

"Well, not so much as that."

"What then?"

"I thought that you had tumbled over——"

"Oh, and this is the welcome you give me, is it?"

"Well, you would not like to be played the fool with, I guess."

"Who has been playing the fool with you, you contemptible fellow. Just come and see what I have done."

"You've been long enough, I'm sure, whatever it is. I'm as cold as a stone."

She could not trust herself to make any answer to his taunts, but she bade him again to follow her, and crept forward in the direction from which she had just come.

The Frenchman, grumbling to himself, and shaking with cold and fright, followed in her wake.

On her way, Ruth explained what she had been about, and asked him how he proposed that they should get down into the room.

"I can let you down very well," said she; "but there is no way of fastening the rope, even if we could afford to lose it thus. So how can I descend afterwards?"

"You let me down first, anyhow," said the disinterested young gentleman, "and then you can think about it afterwards."

"I've a good mind to throw you head over heels," she said, between her teeth.

"What do you say?" he asked.

"Come down after me, and take care you don't slip, because I shan't try to catch you."

The Frenchman found the descent down the roof to the top of the window, and the subsequent journey round the corner, very little to his taste, and he appeared several times to hesitate whether or not he should venture any further, only that the way back was almost as bad as the way lying before him.

When they had managed to get down to the window ledge, the extremely unchivalrous young Frenchman allowed her to adjust the cord round his waist and lower him down.

"Mind you hold tight," said he.

"Have no fear," she replied, and the descent began.

The distance to the floor of the room which this window lighted, was, if anything, greater than she had supposed.

"What am I to do now?" she said, when at length he had safely reached the floor.

"Chuck us down the ropes," he made reply.

But Ruth did not agree to this mild request.

"I will see you —— further first," said Ruth, with a brief pause between the *you* and the *further*, which was, to say the least of it, rather ominous.

Without taking any more notice of him, or of a plaintive inquiry on his part as to what he should do now, she again ascended to the top of the roof, casting her eyes inquiringly upon all sides of her, in the hope of finding something or other that might prove of assistance to her in the difficult position in which she found herself placed.

All at once, to her amazement, and as though some magician's hand had placed it there for her especial accommodation, she perceived a ladder lashed tightly on to some hooks in a dark corner where the tilts of two roofs met behind a round tower.

Without much difficulty she succeeded in unfastening the ladder; and then attaching it to her own person with the rope she carried, she dragged it for some little distance in the direction she wanted to go.

But then she undid the knots of the ropes, for it occurred to her that if the ladder was to slip it would overbalance her to a certainty, and to an equal certainty cause her death.

The enormous trouble, and the great fatigue and anxiety which she had suffered in getting the ladder as far as the roof of the window, made her savage to think that she should have allowed the Frenchman to escape so very easily at the time when he might have been of some assistance.

At last, after much laborious pulling and panting, she had pushed the ladder into such a position that one end of it hung over the gutter while the other touched the window.

Climbing on to the roof of the window, she then dragged the ladder a little upon one side, and contrived to fasten the rope to its sixth round.

After that, she let it down on a level with the window, and swung it to and fro, using all her endeavours to get it to enter into the apartment.

But this was not an easy task, she very soon discovered.

Somehow, the ceiling of the window stopped it.

The only way it could be managed was to cock up the lower end, and then its own weight would cause it to descend into the room.

She did not want to leave one end of the ladder sticking up out of the window, or else she saw a way that it might have been managed, with a little trouble.

But it would never have done to have left an end poking out, because if the gaolers were to have come upon the roof in the morning before they had left the room into which she was getting, and where, for aught she could tell, she might be detained for some time, the ladder would act as a kind of sign-post, indicating clearly the direction in which the fugitives had gone.

She determined, therefore, if possible, to get the ladder bodily into the room.

As she had no one to assist her, she was compelled to creep down to the gutter to lift the ladder up.

She could let go of the ladder, because the gutter supported it to some extent.

But she was obliged to climb down quite close to the edge of the roof, supporting herself as well as she could by the aid of her spike, and lying on her face, with such an awfully small stone ridge to save her from slipping over altogether, that it makes one shudder to realize the terror of the frightful situation.

In this dreadful position, though, she was able to effect her purpose.

She could raise the ladder, and could push it upwards.

At last, she got in about a foot.

Another foot would do, and then she might manage all the rest very well from a safer place.

She was so eager, though, about the work upon which she was engaged, that she did not pay

particular attention to the position she was in herself.

She had climbed up upon her knees, and in that way accomplished what she desired; but pushing at the ladder, she pushed herself too far backwards.

Like lightning she slipped over the parapet.

Her body was over it. Her legs dangled in the air.

God only knows how her elbows caught upon the stone, and how in some miraculous way she managed to support herself.

Or how she managed to retain sufficient presence to sway forward with all her might, and keep her balance.

But somehow she did contrive to do so, pressing her chest down upon the roof, and clawing at everything within her reach that would offer anything like a surface to lay hold of.

Slowly she drew up one leg and then the other, got her knees upon the edge, got safely on

altogether, crept up to the window and down the ladder, and was at last in the room in which the Frenchman was waiting for her impatiently.

"What a while you have been, leaving me all alone!" said he.

She could forbear no longer.

Without a word, she fell upon and shook him until he had scarcely a gasp of breath left in his insignificant little body.

CHAPTER XCVII.

THE TWO PRISONERS BREAK OUT OF THE PRISON, AND INTO THE CHAPEL WHERE A STRANGE ADVENTURE IS YET RESERVED FOR THEM.

They were not free yet. Were they ever to be free again?

So long and tedious had been her labours, that

Ruth had many a time despaired of ever again breathing the sweet air of liberty.

But surely she was now near to the long looked for end, and she must not despair now.

What was it, then, which at this period weighed so heavily upon her spirits, and seemed at once to deprive her of all power of motion, and of all activity, both physical and mental?

An overwhelming fatigue had gained possession of her faculties, and after vainly struggling against it, without being able to overcome its fast encroaching influence, she informed her companion that it was imperatively necessary that for a short time she should repose her already overtaxed energies—in short, that she should go to sleep for half an hour.

"Good heavens!" cried the Frenchman, "you don't mean to say that you're going to sleep?"

"Yes, I must for half an hour."

"Why, it will be our ruin!"

"I don't see why."

"I do."

"Why, then?

"Oh, what's the good of asking such stupid questions as that? You ought to know why, I am sure. It stands to reason, at such a time as this, one ought to be particularly wakeful"

"If it ends in my ruin, I cannot help it."

"That's a very considerate speech to make, I must say! *Your* ruin! That's all you seem to think about."

She made no answer to this observation. She had shaken him as much as she desired for the present, and therefore allowed him to go on accumulating reasons why he should be shaken for the future.

Meanwhile she made the best pillow she could out of the cords, and without a word, laid down and prepared to fall asleep.

The Frenchman kept on "nagging" at her.

"How you can sleep surprises me!"

"Hold your tongue!"

"Oh, very well, do as you like. If it is the cause of both our deaths, you won't care."

"No, I shan't."

He grumbled for a long time—probably long after she had ceased to listen to him—for she very soon fell asleep, and slept as soundly as some condemned criminals are said to sleep upon the fatal morning when the gaoler wakes them up to say that breakfast and Jack Ketch are waiting.

She probably slept for little more than half an hour, at the end of which time the Frenchman awakened her, telling her that for the life of him he could not endure any longer to remain there in the silence and the dark, listening to distant sounds, and trembling at every breath of air sighing through the window above.

"For heaven's sake let us get out of this!" said he: "I can't bear it any longer."

She offered no objection, although she yet felt weighed down with fatigue.

Rising to her feet, she exerted herself to the utmost to rouse herself from this depression; and bidding her companion give her his hand, so that they might not get separated from each other, and in case of one stumbling and falling down any unexpected opening, the other would be able to hold him or her up.

It was a very extensive room in which they found themselves, but it was quite empty.

They, however, by dint of feeling the walls all round with a great deal of care, discovered a door, which was closed but not locked.

The door led into another room, where there were some benches and stools and a table, but which was otherwise unfurnished.

On the table was a jug with some liquid in it, which Ruth eagerly carried to her lips.

But she put it down again directly with an exclamation of disgust, for it was very weak table beer—very flat.

The Frenchman not being so particular, gulped it down rapaciously, and wished there had been more.

In this room they found windows by dint of much groping and clawing at the walls, but the view of high walls opposite to them was not very encouraging.

By dint of much rummaging and fumbling, they discovered a door.

This led into a long passage, down which they bent their steps, walking as noiselessly as possible, and pausing more than once to hear whether there was anybody stirring in the adjacent apartments.

They looked into one or two rooms as they passed along, but most of them were empty.

Upon a table in one, however, they discovered, glistening in the moonlight, a sharp-pointed knife, which they eagerly appropriated.

In time they came to a staircase, at the bottom of which they found a room that appeared to be a kind of office.

Here, on the mantelpiece, to their great joy, the prison-breakers discovered some lucifer matches.

Striking one of these, Ruth ignited the wick in a small oil lamp doubtlessly used for the purpose of sealing letters, and they then carefully examined the apartment.

As there was nothing of a very valuable character lying about, they broke open several cupboards and desks, but found them only to contain letters and papers, but no other valuables.

In one of the desks, however, they discovered a small tin money-box, but it was so enormously strong that they could not for the lives of them force it open.

The Frenchman, though, spent a long while poking the contents about with a pen; and at length, after an immensity of trouble and wasted ingenuity, managed to extract one coin.

It was a penny.

As this was the accountant's office which they had forced their way into, there is no doubt that there was money in some part of the room, but they could not find it; and after spending more then an hour in the search, they continued their voyage of discovery with many regrets

Which way should they go now? Down stairs, decidedly.

Unfortunately for them, though, they found a door which terminated the flight, locked.

They strove in vain to pick the lock, and after a brief consultation, came to the conclusion that they must force a way through one of the panels if they went at all.

"We must go," said the Frenchman, "because it is my opinion that this door leads out into the open air."

"I don't think that," said Ruth, "from the position it is in; though, to tell the truth, it is rather difficult to judge positions with these winding staircases."

"This staircase is the only one from the passage above, isn't."

"I think so."

"I saw no other"

"Let us set to work, then."

"Hold the light up."

Holding up the light was about all that Monsieur

was capable of, so he held it whilst she examined the panels of the door, to see which one contained the fewest knots.

Finding the place which she judged to be the best suited for her purpose, she after a desperate struggle managed to split it with the trusty spike.

The noise of the cracking wood was little short of the noise that would have been made by the discharge of a small pocket pistol

"Oh, lord!" cried Monsieur; "we shall be heard."

"It cannot be helped; we must run the risk."

Again she forced in the spike, with a similar result.

C-r-r-rack!

"Oh, lord! we shall be discovered."

Crack—c-r-rack!

"We shall be ruined!"

C-r-r-r-rack! This one louder than all the others had been.

"I hear some one coming. I am sure I do. It is all over with us. Oh, lord! oh, lord! How could you be such a fool?"

His fears, however, proved to be groundless.

The noise they had made appeared to have alarmed nobody, and in the course of half an hour they had made a hole large enough to get through.

But the process was rather difficult.

The hole in the door was in one of the upper panels, and the Frenchman, adopting the extremely gallant style of proceeding which had hitherto characterized all his conduct throughout the escape, voted that he should go first.

Ruth consenting with anything but a flattering remark, he climbed through head first, she pushing his legs, and every now and then clearing him of the nails and jagged pieces of wood which barred his progress.

When he was through, however, she discovered to her cost that he had had the best of the bargain, for there remained nobody behind to clear her of the jagged edges or perform the friendly services which she had done for him.

Besides, as the Frenchman was of an extremely lithe, not to say lath-like figure, the hole she had made allowed for the passage of his body with comparative ease, whereas for her it was a remarkably tight fit.

"Well, anyhow, I must go," she very naturally remarked; "and it is not the fear of a few scratches that will keep me back, after all I have gone through."

She therefore, with the aid of a stool which she fetched from the office above, climbed into the aperture, and then bade the Frenchman pull her through.

As she expected, the sharp pieces of wood and the rusty nails seized upon her at all points, and penetrating the thin linen sailor-like suit she wore, cruely lacerated her soft flesh.

But she endured the agony bravely and like a martyr.

She uttered not a cry.

And as he continued to pull, and she to struggle, the misery at length came to an end, and they found themselves safely upon the floor of a passage, into which the door led.

"After all," said the Frenchman, "it don't lead out of doors."

"No, it seems not. Let us get on."

"Why, you're all bleeding!"

"Yes, I am rather torn by the nails. There, it does not matter."

"I hope to goodness you won't go fainting—it will be so awkward!"

She made no observation in answer to this remark.

"Oh, my young gentleman," she thought, "I will serve you out for all this, some day or other, I expect. We shall see—we shall see!"

The passage in which they found themselves terminated in a flight of six steps, leading up to another door.

But this one was unlocked, and, with a sigh of relief at the discovery, they passed through, into a great, gloomy building, smelling very cold and damp, which they had not much difficulty in discovering was a church, for, right in front of them, a tall, white figure of the Virgin Mary startled them upon their entrance.

Yes, they were now in the chapel, and in one of the aisles.

They carefully locked and barred the door through which they had entered, finding that they could do so from the side on which they stood, and then looked round them.

"It won't be difficult to get out of here," said Ruth.

"No, not after what we have done already."

"What *we* have done, you said!"

"Well?"

"Oh, never mind! I feel very faint, though. I wish we had some good wine."

"There's wine enough kept in some of these places by the old priests, I'll wager a crown, if one only knew where to drop upon it."

"Would you rob a church?"

"Why not? I feel, after what I have done, that I should stick at nothing.

"I should very much like a glass of wine—just one little one!"

"Come on, then; let's look for it!"

She did not require much persuasion, and they therefore, for the present, abandoned all idea of finding the way out, until they had discovered the "priests' peculiar."

Little did they dream what would be the result of this delay!

CHAPTER XCVIII.

OF THE STRANGE OCCURRENCES WHICH TOOK PLACE IN THE ROMAN CATHOLIC CHAPEL.

"I DARESAY they keep the wine locked up, but we can open the door easily enough," said the Frenchman.

"As easily as you opened the other?"

"Easier, a great deal!"

"That's all right!"

He had not the least idea that she was making fun of him, the young booby.

He was outrageously self-conceited and obtuse One idea could never have been got into his head by any amount of surgical operations—and that was, that he was a fool.

He possessed sufficient intelligence, however, for what was now required of him.

He could point out where the priests kept the wine.

When he was a boy he was educated, as the generality of boys belonging to well-to-do parents are in France, at a public school. There, he had been one of the choir, singing on Sundays and fete days in the college chapel, assisting at public ceremonies, carrying the incense, &c.

He, therefore, knew a good deal of what he profanely termed "the life behind the scenes" He knew where to lay his hand upon the priests' robes; he could make a shrewd guess as to where the little holy-water whisks were to be found; and, above all, whereabouts was hidden the sacramental wine.

Carrying the lamp in his hand, and giving himself an air of great importance—for the idea that he was at last taking the lead, and that his companion was dependent upon his superior intelligence, made him as vain as a peacock—he conducted her round the chapel, and at last stopped before a small door at the back of the principal altar.

"Is this it?"

"This is where it is kept, if there is any."

"The door is locked, I suppose?"

"I suppose so; and it's a good strong one—— But, no! by all that's lucky, it is not fastened—only pulled to!"

This proved to be the case, and they entered, without farther delay, an oblong stone chamber, out of which another opened, with a strong black oak door.

The Frenchman glanced anxiously round the first apartment. There was in it a high desk and a stool, a heavy inkstand, some pens, and a piece of blotting paper; also, a large iron safe, very strong and solid-looking.

"The wine's kept in the next place," said the Frenchman, after inspecting all these objects carefully.

"What's in the safe, do you think?" asked Ruth.

"The registers, I expect."

"Not money?"

"No; it's not likely they keep any money in here."

"Is there any in the church, do you suppose?"

"All there is, must be in the money-box at the door, and I don't expect that is much."

"We ought to have something, you know. I haven't a halfpenny!"

"Don't bother about that. If I can communicate with my friends, I shall be all right. It's the wine we want now!"

"Yes, the wine!"

The Frenchman now was examining the door communicating between the apartments

"We have the devil's own luck! This door is open, too!

"Open, too?"

"It is, and by all that's wonderful——"

"What now?"

"There is a key in it!"

"How on earth could that have occurred?"

"I can't imagine, without one of the priests, or the beadle, or sacristan must have forgot en to lock the place up this afternoon. But it is very extraordinary!"

"Well, I hope one thing——"

"That they're not coming back?"

"Yes"

"I hope not. We'd better get at the wine at once, and make our escape while the coast's clear."

"I think so"

Ruth's companion discovered the place where the liquor was kept which they were in search of, without much difficulty.

It was kept in a hamper, and there were at least a couple of dozen bottles.

"Rare tipple this, I'll wager my head!" said Monsieur.

There were upon a shelf hard by, all ready to their hand, a corkscrew and a couple of glasses

The Frenchman, without more ado, drew the cork of a bottle and filled two bumpers.

"Your health, madame."

"Thank you"

"Here's success to our enterprise."

"With all my heart"

"To our better acquaintance."

She did not respond quite so heartily to this, but she drank it with a good grace, and with it swallowed her third glass.

"Have another?" said the Frenchman, who seemed inclined to be jovial.

"No, thank you; I've had enough."

"One more won't hurt you."

"I'd rather not. I think you've had sufficient also We've got some work to do yet."

"Pooh! nonsense! Do you suppose my head's so weak that it will be knocked over by two or three glasses of Burgundy?"

"I should advise you to drink no more."

"Why, my dear creature, I've often enough made four bottles look foolish, with nobody else to help me!"

"I won't contradict you," retorted Ruth, "although I don't believe you. But whatever you may have done when you were in the daily habit of drinking wine is very different to what you should do now, when you have been kept so long upon low diet and restricted from all use of strong drinks."

"I shall have another glass, anyhow."

"Do what you choose."

She turned away from him with an impatient gesture while he filled himself a brimming bumper, and poured it slowly down his throat with an appearance of great relish

"I'm positive his weak head can't stand it," she thought to herself. "Mine feels a little confused; and it's made of stronger stuff than his, I'll warrant me."

She took the lamp meanwhile, and began to examine the room in which they found themselves. There was a cupboard, in which was some lumber of different kinds, a few broken bottles, and a quantity of waste paper. It was a cupboard large enough for a person to stand upright in. She noticed this casually, her thoughts running upon the chance of the gaoler's coming to seek them there in the chapel, for she was very anxious to be going.

There were two long black robes hanging upon pegs in one corner of the room, which had so much the appearance, at first sight, of priests without heads, that she had started when they met her eyes.

In another corner of the room was a large iron box, the lid of which she found was fast when she tried it.

"What's this got under it?" she asked her companion.

"The church plate, candlesticks, and so on."

"Are they worth much, do you suppose?"

"I should think so. Why?"

"I was thinking that if we were only able to help ourselves!"

"Good heavens! what a dreadful character you are!" said her companion, who was quietly filling himself another bumper, following her meanwhile with his eyes.

"The lock's a strong one!" Ruth remarked, more to herself than to the Frenchman "It would take a long while to break!"

"I'm deuced glad it would! A joke's a joke;

but that's a trifle too serious I don't mind helping myself to a glass of Burgundy, when I want one so badly. I don't see any particular harm in that! But the church plate! No, no! I say, that's really too bad!"

"Hush, you fool!" said Ruth, suddenly bending down her head to listen. "Did you hear anything?"

"No, I heard nothing."

"Listen!"

The Frenchman leant his head on one side in imitation of Ruth, and assumed an expression of drunken gravity; for drunk he was gradually becoming, there was very little doubt.

"I don't hear anything," he said, thickly: "it's your im-im-imagination."

"Come, then, at once; we will waste no more time here. We may have ruined all, as it is, by delaying so long Come, come!"

"All right; don't jerk me off my legs. I can go quietly enough. Hush! what a row you're making."

"It is you, you idiot!"

"You're very fast calling bad names. I would have you to understand, madame——"

"Hold your tongue!"

"I don't want to talk."

"Hush, then!"

He was silent at last, and they both listened.

There could be no doubt about it.

There was a footstep in the chapel.

"Great God!" said Ruth, in a hoarse whisper, "we are lost!"

"Let's get somewhere."

"Where? Ah, the cupboard!—that will do for you. Quick!"

"Which cupboard do you mean? What are you doing? You've put the light out."

"Hush! Hide yourself, or you're a dead man."

"I can't find the way the door opens."

"Make haste."

"Oh, lord! oh, lord! it's stuck fast—it's locked!"

"No, it isn't; pull it. I hear them coming."

"So do I! We're ruined."

"Have you done it!"

"Yes, thank God! I'd got my foot against it."

"Go in, then, and keep quiet if you can."

"It's awfully mouldy."

"Hush!"

Ruth listening intently, distinctly heard footsteps approaching.

She had already selected her hiding-place.

She had crept behind one of the black robes hanging up in the corner to which allusion has been made.

She had also pushed to the door of the inner room, hoping that if the person coming towards them were to go into the other room, they might not be tempted to come into this after they had locked the door, for it was probably for that purpose they were coming.

Her quick ear had told her that the footsteps she heard were approaching from the opposite part of the chapel by which she and the Frenchman had made their entrance a short time since.

She was fearful that they might be locked in their new prison, but of course they would much rather that this fate befel them than that they should be discovered

Besides, she had brought away the box of matches from the office. She could light the lamp, and, after all, it would not be such a hard job to force their way out again from the inside of this cell when they should be left to themselves.

Peeping from behind the robes which partly concealed her, and through a chink in the door, she could see a light slowly travelling along through the gloom of the vast building, with much the appearance of a glowworm.

Gradually and slowly it approached in the direction of the cell where the two fugitives lay concealed.

Ruth waited anxiously for it to come nearer, for she could not altogether, although her reason assured her that the fear was groundless, banish the dread of seeing the familiar face of her old gaoler.

The person, though, who carried the lamp held it purposely, as it appeared to her, in such a manner that while it threw all the light it was capable of throwing upon the path of him who held it, it kept his face in deep shadow.

Slowly the light drew near, Ruth never removing her eyes from the dark figure creeping towards her place of concealment.

Several times upon the way the lamp-bearer came to a halt, as though to listen.

"For what?" she asked herself. Could he have heard the half-whispered conversation between her and the young Frenchman?

Could he have heard the scuffle of their feet?

Decidedly he had not seen the glimmer of Ruth's lamp, nor had he been able, supposing he had heard anything of their movements, to decide from what part of the building the sound proceeded.

But one thing struck Ruth, whoever the person might be who was thus approaching them, he was not the possessor of any large amount of animal courage.

He was a coward, in fact.

The way she knew this was the case was, because hearing, or fancying he heard, some slight noise behind him, he started violently; and, for some time afterwards, as he stood there peering fearfully over either shoulder, she could see the lamp trembling between his fingers like a leaf.

Then, as he still continued to approach in the direction in which he had hitherto been wending his steps, he paused again and again to look behind him, and listen, apparently in the greatest trepidation.

"What does he fancy he hears, I wonder?" thought Ruth to herself. "He can't be looking for us; because, to judge from his movements, he must hear some noise behind him, and it is very certain that he does not attempt to go after the noise. What is he about?"

CHAPTER XCIX.

OF OTHER AND STRANGER EVENTS WHICH TOOK PLACE IN THE ROMAN CATHOLIC CHAPEL, AND HOW RUTH FELL INTO THE HANDS OF THE PRIEST.

What was he about?

That he was about no good, there could be very little doubt, even in the most guileless and innocent of minds.

In the mind of Mrs. Ruth Trail, *alias* Mrs. Belinda Belvidere, who was by no means innocent, and not at all guileless, there was no doubt at all.

"That man's a scoundrel!" she said to herself, before she had even seen his face.

When she saw his face, the opinion she had already formed was strengthened into a positive conviction

Yes, he was a scoundrel.

He was handsome, though.

His features were well-formed and regular; he was young, and tall, and gracefully built, as well as could be discerned, for he wore the hideous dress in which Roman Catholic priests are usually habited.

In spite of all this, there could be no doubt that he was a scoundrel.

There was a certain sneaking, hang-dog, rascally look about his small, deep-set grey eyes.

There was a something about his sharply-chiselled mouth and his thin, tightly-pressed lips, which seemed to betoken meanness, cruelty, and cunning.

Yes, the eyes and the lips betrayed him to be the villain that he certainly was; although, had he been in conversation, and animated and interested by the topic under discussion, you would not have noticed the evil expression which these features wore when in repose.

No; it was when silent that he looked his worst.

He looked his worst, too, undoubtedly at this present moment.

Creeping forward, with terrified, backward glances, and a blanched and quivering face, he had all the appearance of a detected thief.

Was he a thief?

In a few moments she was to see.

The young priest, having paused upon the threshold of the outer room to listen for the last time, now sneaked, rather than walked, into the room, and putting down the lamp which he carried threw a hurried and suspicious glance around, before betaking himself to the performance of the business which had brought him there.

Apparently satisfied that the coast was clear, and that he was unobserved, he drew a key from his breast with a trembling hand.

Then, again, he paused and listened, and then, with a deep-drawn sigh, he put it into the lock of the iron safe which Ruth had observed, and which her companion had given it as his opinion contained the registers

The wards of the lock appeared to be very rusty, and the key to turn with great difficulty, for the priest used both hands to force it round.

When at length it did turn, it was with a jarring sound, like a small shriek, half stifled.

The noise caused the trembling wretch the most violent agitation, and, desisting from his work, he stole out to the door again, to listen.

Returning, after the absence of a few moments, he pulled open the door and lifted out a large book, very old and worn, but bound in a strong parchment cover, which in several places had been repaired.

Carrying the book to the desk, he laid it upon it, and placing his lamp in such a position as to throw a strong light upon what he was about, began very carefully to turn over the leaves.

For a long while he turned slowly, without any manifestation of impatience, as though he expected every moment to light upon the object of which he was in search; but gradually his pace became a more hurried one, and from time to time an angry ejaculation escaped him.

"I saw it here this morning," he muttered aloud, in a tone which was sufficiently distinct to reach the ear of the attentive listener where she stood. "What has become of it?"

That he was searching for some entry in the register was sufficiently evident.

But for what purpose?

The mystery was soon to be unravelled.

"Ah!" he cried suddenly. "It is here!"

A sinister smile passed over his pale face as he opened the book at the spot which he had been so long searching for in vain.

But this sign of his gratification did not long endure.

Again glancing all round him, and again seemingly satisfied that his acts were unknown to all but the One whose wrath he defied, but whose punishment was much more certain to reach him than that of man, he set about the perpetration of the act of villany he had come there to commit.

Producing a small black case, he took from it a sharp penknife.

Then lifting the book down upon his knees, he pulled it open as far as he could in the place where he had been reading, bending back the covers on either side, so as to lay bare the stitches which fastened in the leaves.

When he had done this, he very carefully ran his knife along the page close to the stitches, and cut out the leaf that he wanted.

Then shutting to the book again, he pressed it together with all his might, and fluttering over the leaves several times, endeavoured to ascertain whether it opened more readily at the spot from which the leaf had been abstracted than at any other.

Finding, to his mortification, that it did, in spite of all his pressing and squeezing, he adopted another plan.

That is, he forced it open at another place not very far from the first; and then, not pressing it together any more, it opened without any provocation at the second place, from which no leaf had been cut out.

"That will do!" he said aloud. "That's settled."

He folded up carefully the leaf that he had extracted, and put it away in his breast with the knife that he had used to cut it out.

Then he put away the register in the round safe, and raised the lamp which had lighted him thither from the top of the desk.

"I don't know what he wants it for, but he wants that leaf for no good purpose," thought Ruth.

And then another idea occurred to her.

"After all, I am glad I happened to come in here, and that I chanced to be here while he did this. I don't know that the knowledge may be of any service to me, but still it may. That kind of knowledge is always worth the learning."

While these thoughts were passing the woman's mind, the priest, who had been moving away in the direction of the outer door, suddenly turned round, an idea seeming to strike him.

"I had forgotten the key," he said. "What a fool I am! That would have been utter ruin!"

He drew near to the door communicating between the two rooms as he spoke.

His hand was on the key, and he appeared to be just in the act of pulling the door to, when a thought seemed to strike him.

"I'll look at it again!" said he.

Then he stood still and half-irresolute, as though arguing with himself.

"Why not?" he said abruptly. "I will!"

It was curious to hear him talking thus; and Ruth could scarcely help fancying that he was not quite right in his head.

But another solution to the strangeness of his manner was presently to be found.

He had been drinking. He was now under the influence of drink; and when he had entered the second room, he walked straight up to the hamper which contained the wine.

Arrived at it, he paused, and seemed rather astonished.

"I left the lid open," she heard him presently mutter. "What did I do with the bottle? Oh, here it is! Hilloa!"

Ruth was afraid to peep out from behind the robe. What had he found now? She was dying to know.

"I didn't think I used both the glasses!" she heard him say. "What a cowardly beggar I am till the drink's in me! I don't know what I am doing!"

She heard him uncork a bottle. Then she heard the cluck! cluck! of the wine.

He was filling himself a glass.

"I am very glad I looked in here again to set things a little straight. It would never have done to have left them like this. There! That's put a little heart into me! Now, to put the bottle and glasses away!"

He made a great jingling in doing so. His hand was as unsteady as ever, in spite of the stimulant which he had taken to keep his courage up to the sticking place.

When he had put away the things, he stood quite still and silent for so long, that Ruth was terrified, and longed to look out.

However, she refrained from doing so with a great effort of self-command.

After awhile, he moved, and spoke again.

"I'll look at it!" he said

He went up to the other end of the room, and knelt down by the side of the iron chest.

Then taking out from his breast the key with which he had opened the safe in the adjoining apartment, he applied it again to the lock. It turned, apparently, with less difficulty than it had shown before.

He raised the lid, and next moment was engaged in silent and covetous contemplation of the objects it contained.

"I wish they were mine!' he muttered, with a deep sigh. "Oh, I wish they were mine!"

For awhile, he was silent; and from the jingling she heard, he was apparently engaged in handling coins.

"Yes," he said, as though answering some argument with himself; "I may have to come to it some day. But not yet! not yet! No; I have not fallen as low as that——"

There was a slight pause, in which he remained motionless, in silent contemplation of the tempting treasure before him.

Then he continued aloud.

"They would find it out directly, and I should be suspected. Whom else? Am not I the black sheep of the flock?"

He muttered something which sounded very much like a curse, and after a brief pause, pursued in the same tone as before.

"Even if I ran for it, I should not be able to get away. They would set all the bloodhounds upon me. I should be tracked, and scented out, and hunted down. I should never be able to get out of the country. No, no! Already they have a spite against me. I am the black sheep—the black sheep!"

There followed a strange sound, then, as though the man were sobbing.

His voice during the utterance of the last few sentences had grown thick and husky. Sobs now burst from his labouring chest.

The young priest wept.

Ruth now ventured to look cautiously forth from her place of concealment.

"Are they the maudlin tears of drunkenness," she asked herself, "or is he really suffering from remorse?"

Then she began to wonder what sins he had committed. They were easy enough to guess, she thought.

He had, no doubt, robbed the good institution to which he belonged. He had been suspected—perhaps, proved to be guilty of some petty larcenies and thefts; and he was under a ban, as it were, and marked out as the black sheep of the flock.

By some means or other, he had obtained the key of the strong box and iron safe where some of the treasures of the brethren were kept, and he was contemplating a robbery.

The scene was interesting, and she could not help feeling curious about the history of this man, into whose secrets she had obtained so great an insight, without having in the slightest degree put herself out of the way to do so.

But, at the same time, she felt weary and impatient at this long delay.

How long was he going to remain there at the box? Would he never go? Was she never to be released from her place of confinement?

While she was asking herself these questions, with increasing anger and irritation, the priest, with his face buried in his hands, remained kneeling by the side of the box sobbing bitterly.

By degrees, though, he grew somewhat calmer. This passionate burst of grief had done him good.

He wiped away the traces of his tears from his pale cheeks, and prepared to rise to his feet.

But while he was doing so—while he was in the act of assuming an upright position—a sound from the cupboard containing the young Frenchman struck him suddenly as motionless as a statue.

At the same time the same sound sent a convulsive shiver through the frame of the female prisoner.

"That wretched fool!" she thought to herself. "What is he doing?"

It was a peculiar noise.

A creaking, squeaking sort of sound. Something like a mouse, only decidedly not a mouse.

Ruth listened to it with consternation

She knew very well from whence it came. Her quick ear told her in a moment that her French friend was the culprit.

Presently her reason supplied her with a solution to the difficulty.

A thought flashed through her brain. She knew what he was doing.

He had taken a bottle with him into the cupboard. He was drawing the cork.

When he had sought his place of concealment, he had hastily pushed the cork into the bottle he took in with him. He had been waiting, probably, with great impatience, as long as he possibly could.

An opportunity now offered, he had thought. Or perhaps he had fancied that with great care the cork might be extracted noiselessly. Anyhow, he had made the effort

He had given it a twist. It had given a squeak, and he had desisted.

Could she have seen him, she might almost have been tempted into a smile, so ludicrous was the expression of intense terror which his features wore.

The priest, however, not being acquainted with the fact of any person being concealed in the cupboard, nor of that person's being in possession of a bottle with a cork in it, never for a moment imagined that the sound which had startled him was the cork aforesaid being drawn.

Without moving a muscle, but concentrating all his faculties into the act of listening, the guilty priest stood motionless.

Then, as all was perfectly silent in the cupboard, and the Frenchman, alarmed by the noise he had made, desisted from the stupid act that had caused it, the priest slowly turned his eyes round the room, wondering from what quarter the sound could have proceeded.

Being deceived as to its nature, and fancying that it had been made by a mouse, he naturally directed his gaze towards the ground.

He slowly carried his eyes round the room, following the skirting board, and following it in the direction of the door which led into the adjoining apartment.

Travelling thus, it became necessary that his eyes should pass the bottom of the robe, behind which Ruth had taken shelter.

The robe was very full, and very long; but yet not quite long enough to reach the floor.

Between the bottom of the robe and the floor a white object attracted the priest's observation.

It was a naked foot.

CHAPTER C.

SHOWS WHAT HAPPENED TO RUTH AFTER SHE FELL INTO THE HANDS OF THE PRIEST AND HOW SHE TOOK HOLY ORDERS, AND BECAME A REVEREND BROTHER OF THE ORDER OF ST LAZARUS, WITH OTHER MATTERS MORE OR LESS SURPRISING.

Do you remember that delightful scene in the admirable novel of "Robert Macaire," where the raw-boned valet of the famous French thief hides himself in the cupboard, and the lady's-maid, rummaging there for something or another, catches sight of the creature's boots, and finds, upon inspection, that the boots have live legs in them?

What an awful moment it must have been to the girl when she made the discovery! But how much more awful to the hiding thief, as the gown behind which he had taken shelter was gradually turned higher and higher up, and the cold air creeping in to his legs, apprized him of the terrible fact that he had been discovered!

It would have been very difficult to have decided which was the most terrified, Ruth or the priest.

The priest, when he first caught sight of the naked foot?

Ruth, when she first felt a hand laid upon the robe which concealed her, dragging it slowly and cautiously from off her form?

The terror which the first sight of the woman's naked foot caused the felonious priest was so intense, that he staggered back, and letting fall the lid of the iron box into which he had been prying with a loud noise, sank down upon the top of it, and trembled like one in an ague fit.

But recovering the use of his limbs, of which the first shock of fright appeared to have almost entirely deprived him, he staggered forward towards the object that his eyes had never been removed from since first they had alighted upon it, in mute horror and consternation.

Advancing towards it, yet shrinking from it, the coward at length reached the robe.

Then, with chattering teeth and tottering knees, while his hair bristled on his head, and large drops of perspiration coursed each other down his pallid brow, he clutched at the dark robe which concealed Ruth from his gaze, and slowly drew it on one side.

To say that, when she first became conscious of this movement and its object, Ruth was not intensely frightened, would be as untrue as it would be absurd to suppose that any person, similarly situated, would not have been similarly alarmed.

But the slowness of the priest's movements, and the anticipation of the shock which it would be when, the robe drawn away altogether, they should confront one another face to face, was too much to bear.

Rather, she thought, would she anticipate the dreadful moment.

And with this idea, darting suddenly on one side, she sprang out and upon him.

With a shriek of terror, the cowardly priest dropped down upon his knees, gazing upon her with wildly dilated eyes.

"Mercy!" he babbled almost inarticulately, for his fright was so great as nearly to deprive him of utterance. "Mercy!—mercy!"

"Get up," said Ruth, after regarding him for a moment, with an expression of contempt she did not care to disguise. "What were you doing at that box?"

"I—I—I was doing nothing."

"You are a thief!"

"Who says so?" the priest cried, with a ghastly face, and trembling so that he could hardly stand. "I defy you to prove it."

"I saw you, I say."

"What did you see? I have not touched a penny piece! I was only counting it. I did not displace a penny piece."

"You meant to do so."

"No, I did not—I swear I did not! You cannot prove that I did."

"It looks rather suspicious, that's all I have got to say about the matter."

"It is because you are not acquainted with the circumstances of the case, that you think so."

"Oh, is that it?"

"Yes."

"Ah, that did not occur to me."

There was something, however, in Ruth's tone which was anything but convincing.

He did not feel satisfied, evidently: and he was very anxious to excuse himself, and satisfactorily account for the very suspicious position in which he had been discovered.

In his endeavours to set himself right with her, he became in his excuses childish and puerile in the extreme.

It was quite pitiful to see the way in which the poor wretch stuttered and stammered, contradicting himself at every other sentence.

But the person whom he addressed was very far from being actuated by any such feeling.

She was incapable of pity; and, besides, she was anxious that this man should not slip easily through her fingers, now that she had once got him into her power.

He might be useful; and, until she had made use of him, he must not be allowed to escape.

At last, after floundering about like a big fish in shallow water, he said, as a clincher, "If you suppose you have got any hold on me, you are mistaken."

She turned upon him fiercely.

"What do you say?"

"Did you not hear?"

"I hardly understood. But please let me understand. Do you mean that as a defiance?"

"Take it any way you think fit."

"Any way I think fit?"

"For what I care!"

"Suppose I take it as a defiance, then?"

"You are at liberty to do so."

"In that case, war is declared between us."

The priest shrugged his shoulders.

He had locked up the iron box by now, and put the key into his pocket.

"As you like," said he.

"And if you are reported to the heads of your establishment, you will be able satisfactorily to account for your conduct?"

"Certainly."

"You say you have a perfect right to visit that strong box?"

"Yes."

"That the key now in your possession has not been surreptitiously obtained?"

"Yes."

"And that the hour at which you are visiting it has nothing irregular about it?"

"Yes."

"That, in fact, there is nothing at all out of the ordinary course of events that you should be here at this time with the key, and looking in that box?"

"I say so."

"Well, we shall try that!"

"When you choose; and at the same time, young man, you will perhaps be able to account for your presence here at this moment; who you are, and what you are; and how you come to be so very near to the strong-box after the chapel has been locked for the night?"

"With the greatest ease. I have been sent here as a spy upon you."

The priest started, and staggered.

But his alarm was only of momentary duration.

It was a bold stroke, this, of Mrs. Ruth's, but yet rather a weak proceeding. It might have been very successful, it is true, if it had answered; as it missed fire, it was the worst thing she could have done.

For this reason: that as he happened to see through the falseness of her statement, the discovery gave him confidence; and, plucking up what little bit of courage he possessed—a very little bit it was—he determined to resist her attempt to get him under her thumb, as it were, and make a harvest out of the secret which chance had put into her possession.

"If that is the case," said he, "I thank you sincerely for your consideration, because you have put me upon my guard, and by acknowledging that you are employed as a spy upon my actions you give me the chance of preparing my best defence, before I shall be summoned before the Superior to give an explanation of my conduct."

"What! Then," cried Ruth, fiercely, "you want to invent some lies, do you?"

"I did not say so."

"No; but I understand, perfectly. The lies you told me would do very well, you thought, to put a novice off the scent, but the Superior will have to be more delicately dealt with. However, I intend to reserve the gravest of my charges until we are confronted before the authorities."

"The—gravest—of—your—charges?" gasped the priest, a deadly pallor stealing over his cheeks.

"Yes," cried Ruth.

And, as she spoke, she made a sudden dart forward in his direction; and, before he could make an effort to guard against the act, possessed herself of a piece of parchment, the end of which was visible between the folds of his dress at the breast.

It was the page which he had cut out of the register.

When he saw what was her object, he struggled vainly to regain possession of the page, which, however, she already held firmly in her grasp.

His efforts were fruitless, and in another moment she had secured it in her own breast.

"What do you want with that?" the priest asked fiercely, but still in trembling accents.

He had evidently a great mind to close with her, and wrest the coveted document from her grasp. But, at that moment, he was encumbered with the lamp, which he seemed anxious should not be overthrown in the struggle.

"Give me that paper back!" he said at last, struggling hard to appear calm and unconcerned. "Give me that paper back!"

"Not at all!" replied Ruth. "Now I have gained possession of it, I intend to keep it!"

"To keep it?" gasped the priest.

"Exactly."

"But—but what do you intend to do with it?"

"To restore it to the Superior."

"It's a lie! You are only pursuing this course for the purpose of intimidating me."

"You are perfectly correct—that is my motive."

"Well, then, what on earth is your motive? What do you require at my hands?"

"I want you, first of all, to accompany me to some place outside this building——"

"What! to the chapel?"

"No; beyond the walls of the building altogether. Some place in the town."

"Can you take me there?"

"No; you must take me."

"But the doors are all locked!"

"Have not you a key?"

"No; that I have not."

"You can procure one?"

"Not if my life depended on it."

"Do you mean seriously to tell me that you do not possess the means of obtaining egress from this place into the streets?"

"Candidly, then, I do. Until daylight, there is no chance of getting beyond the walls. Then the doors will be open."

"Then it will be too late. Is there no window that I could easily climb out of? No way that you know of for getting out, without having to pass the doorkeeper?"

The priest seemed to cast about in his own mind for some place where such an exit could be easily performed.

"Yes," he said, after a mute pause; "I think that I do. But tell me," he added quickly, "what earthly reason have you for acting thus? Why do not you go the way you came?"

"Because I came through the prison."

"You astonish me! The prison doors are usually kept strictly locked."

"They were locked."

"Then how——"

"We needn't waste time in fencing words," said Ruth, impatiently. "I was a prisoner in the gaol, and I have so far effected my escape. Without your aid I should have endeavoured to have forced a way through one of the windows or doors of the chapel into the street; as, however, I have been lucky enough to meet with you, without that trouble, I hope to escape with your assistance."

"Well, and if I help you to the best of my ability, in return——"

"I will keep your secret as securely as the grave would keep it. In token of my good faith, take back this parchment sheet."

"I will help you; and if you consent to a plan I shall propose, I can also, perhaps, put something good in your way."

"What is that?"

"It altogether depends whether you have any scruples——"

"Do you mean that we should share the treasure in that chest?" said Ruth, who quickly enough could carry out any scheme of villany, were but an odd word given to her as a cue.

"Yes," said the priest, sinking his voice, and casting a suspicious glance around.

"But the suspicion will fall upon you."

"Not if we leave traces of your having been here behind us."

"True!" said Ruth, a smile lighting up her face as a thought occurred to her. "Where is the place from which I am to escape?"

"It is one of the windows in the chapel through which we can easily force a way."

"Very good. But, in the first place, you must lend me a suit of your clothes, so that I can walk about without attracting any notice. You see what I am wearing is torn all to rags, and my feet are bare."

"If I do that, I shall be obliged to go back into the monastery to my cell. The delay may be dangerous."

"Shall we be likely to meet anybody?"

"No, no! I have no fear of that; only I shall not rest easy until you are gone."

"We shan't be long. I shall waste no time, only I can't go through the town in the dress that I am without creating notice and suspicion."

"Very well, then; if you must have the dress, come. Only we must make the greatest possible haste and the least possible noise."

"Trust to me."

"Wait for a moment, till I peep out. That's right—the coast is clear. Now let us come."

While the priest was peering out into the gloomy chapel to make quite certain that no one was spying their movements, Ruth hastily returned towards the door of the cupboard, which contained the Frenchman.

Then quick as thought, and unseen by the priest, she turned the key and locked her last companion in.

"Now I am ready," said she.

"This way then, my young noviciate," said the priest, with a smile. "The Superiors of the Order of Saint Lazarus little dream that another brother is this night being added to their number, and such a brother!"

Ruth looked quickly at him.

She was not quite certain what could be the priest's motives for these words. But she saw that it was not the one which she had at first suspected.

Then she chuckled inwardly, and followed him quickly.

"And so," said she to herself, "I am going to turn priest now. What next, I wonder?"

CHAPTER CI.

IN WHICH IT IS SHOWN HOW VERY AWKWARD RUTH THOUGHT IT WAS THAT SHE HAD NOT BEEN BORN OF THE OPPOSITE SEX.

Ruth followed her guide across the chapel and into the adjoining monastery, through a small door of communication which he unlocked with a key he carried.

Had he turned round to look at the expression of her face as they journied onwards, he might have been surprised at the smile which played about her lips and sparkled brightly in her blue eyes.

What were the thoughts which thus amused her?

I will explain.

In the first place, she could not help thinking that it was rather droll that this priest should not have been able to see through the disguise which she wore.

She had never intended that it should be a disguise which was to deceive any close observer.

She had not fashioned the coarse check shirt and trousers with any such idea.

On the contrary they had been made by her merely because such a dress was likely to be much more convenient for prison breaking purposes than her ordinary female attire would have been.

After she had stood talking to the young priest for some time, she felt convinced in her own mind that he had fathomed the little mystery about her sex.

She had noticed his eyes more than once wandering over her form.

She felt certain that he knew she was a woman.

But, after all, it seemed that he did not. No. She felt equally convinced now, that he was ignorant of the fact.

In all good faith he had called her "young man," and he had not the faintest idea that she was one of the softer sex.

"Poor innocent!" she said to herself with a chuckle. "How surprised he will be when I tell him!"

When she came to reflect upon the business, though, it was not so very extraordinary that he should not see through her disguise, however transparent.

The reasons are obvious.

First of all, young monks do not, or at any rate should not, mix much in female society, and are anything but ladies' men.

His thoughts not running then upon the charms of the opposite sex, he was not likely to connect the graceful outlines of Ruth's rounded form, and the undoubted beauty of her face, with the attributes of the other sex.

He thought her only a handsome boy of about eighteen or nineteen, rather effeminate in appearance as he was himself.

Another reason was, that he was in such a fright at being discovered in the manner with which we are already acquainted, that he had not been able to think of anything else than his own safety.

There was one other cause for Ruth's mirth, not connected with the young priest.

The idea that she had locked up the selfish Frenchman in the cupboard, and that he would be kept a prisoner there until she returned, afforded her an almost unspeakable amount of gratification.

She had suffered a good deal already at the hands of this person. But she had now a reason for being more indignant than ever.

During her interview with the priest she had every moment been expecting he would come out of the cupboard and show himself, but instead of doing so, he had remained as quiet as a mouse.

At first she had been at a loss to account for this singular behaviour, but a little reflection gave her a clue to it.

The disinterested gentleman expecting that she had got into very hot water, intended to leave her in it, but to take precious good care to keep out himself.

In short, he would have allowed her to be taken into custody, and again committed to prison without stirring a finger in her behalf.

She was quite positive of this, and she resolved to be revenged upon him.

Her first idea was to lock him up in the cupboard and leave him there altogether, so that if the cupboard were too strong for him to break out of, and he found himself dying for want of air, he would roar out for help, and when he had attracted the authorities by the noise he made, be dragged back to limbo.

Afterwards, though, she thought she might yet assist him, for he might be of service to her when free of the prison walls, but at any rate she would lock him up and frighten him a little. There could be no harm in that.

Besides, the very safest place to leave him was under lock and key.

If he were at liberty he was sure to be making a fool of himself some way or another, and for what she knew, most probably jeopardizing her safety as well as his own.

"When I have my dress," she thought, "I will decide whether or not I take him with me. He doesn't deserve it. That's certain."

And I am sure that Ruth was right.

While, however, these thoughts were occupying her mind, the young priest was very cautiously leading the way through a series of gloomy and winding passages towards his cell, which was apparently situated at a considerable distance from the chapel.

Upon the way he several times exhorted her in an earnest whisper to be very cautious that she did not make a noise.

"If we are heard I am ruined," he said. "For heaven's sake be careful."

"Have no fear. I can walk like a cat."

What she said was true enough.

Her bare feet fell noiselessly upon the flagstones, and so very silent was her progress behind him, that more than once the priest turned hastily round to look for her, uncertain whether or not she was following him, or had stolen away round one of the many corners they passed upon their way.

But there was no fear of such an occurrence. She was far too eager to get the clothes which she had asked for, because she felt pretty certain that the feeble disguise which she wore would not impose upon any one else as easily as it had done upon this raw and inexperienced young priest.

She in her turn felt a little suspicious of the fair dealing of her conductor.

She was afraid at first that he might be taking her by a circuitous course round to the prison from which she had escaped, with the intention of giving her up again to the safe keeping of her gaolers.

But, after all, when she came to think of it, such a proceeding was extremely improbable.

Therefore, after a little mutual suspicion, they began to have more confidence in each other.

"This is the cell," said the priest, stopping before the low door, which he unlocked.

Ruth started at the word.

"What is the matter?" he asked.

"Nothing," she replied. "I've had so much of cells, that's all. I don't like the word."

"For my sake, you must not remain long here," said the priest.

Ruth eyed him suspiciously again.

"Why?" she inquired.

"Because, if any one were to find you here, I should have some difficulty in accounting for your presence."

"May not you receive visitors?"

"Oh, yes. Of course, there's no harm in that; only they would wonder that they had not seen you during the afternoon, or in the evening, at supper-time."

It was quite evident, from the way he spoke, that he had not the least suspicion that he was talking to a woman.

"It is very awkward!" thought Ruth to herself, with something of a blush. "I wish to goodness I was a man! It is dreadfully awkward! However can I break the awful intelligence to my clerical friend?"

CHAPTER CII.

THE PRIEST'S CONFESSION.

"My wardrobe is not large," said the priest, as he entered into the cell, and closed the door behind them with a great deal of care, so that the latch should not make more noise than possible.

"Anything will do for me," replied Ruth, who wished herself a hundred miles away, with all her heart. "Anything will do. Only, as quick as you like."

While he was sorting the desired clothing from a very limited stock contained in a black box, Ruth had time to cast her eyes round the apartment, and take a survey of its contents.

It was very barely furnished, as may be supposed.

The floor was bare. A tiny window, high up from the ground, and traversed by four strong iron bars, admitted, during the day, all the light which illuminated what must have been at best a grim obscurity.

A miserable mattress and blanket, lying upon the floor in one corner, was the only attempt at a bed. There was not the ghost of a bedstead.

There was a hall-table, or rather desk, on which lay a prayer-book. A small shelf against the wall held three or four other books.

There were no chairs; and the only thing to sit down upon, besides the bed, which would have been a very low seat, was the black box, where the young priest kept his small stock of clothing.

When I have mentioned a black wooden cross, and two scriptural prints hanging upon the otherwise bare whitewashed walls, I have enumerated all the articles which the cell contained.

The young priest paused in his search when he had collected a certain number of articles together.

"These things will fit you, I think," he said. "We are about the same size."

"Ye-es, I think so."

"You ought to be obliged to me, you know."

"I am."

"I mean when you know that I am giving you my best suit. I have only two."

"You will be able to buy another with the contents of that box in the chapel," said Ruth, with a smile.

"Yes, yes," the young priest answered. "If everything goes off safely, I shall be rich."

"Is there much money in the box?"

"No, there is not much, either; but there is enough to enable me to get away from here—to get free from this cursed place, in which I have been shut up all my life. It will enable me to see the world."

"Why not let us escape together? Come with me to England."

"I wish I could," the young priest answered, with a deep-drawn sigh. "England is the place, above all others, that I am most anxious to visit."

"What prevents you, then, from accompanying me?"

"I must not go yet—not until after the discovery has been made."

"You want them to think I have robbed the church?"

"Yes, the suspicion will fall upon you. It can do you no harm, you know, because, as it is, by escaping from prison you have subjected yourself to a severe punishment. You will be imprisoned for life if you are recaptured. No worse can happen to you if you are thought to be guilty of sacrilege. And then, again, if you are not caught, see what a sum you will possess; there is there at least a hundred pounds!"

Ruth made a wry face at the size of the sum.

She thought there had been more than that, a good deal, by the way he talked.

"He is a very innocent person for a villain!" she said to herself; and she felt anxious to know how he could be the black sheep of his flock.

She asked him to tell her what he had done, and after a little hesitation he told her his history.

"My tale is not a long one," said the young priest, "but it is a sad one."

"I wish you would tell it to me."

"If I thought you would believe me!"

"Believe you?"

"Yes. It may seem strange that I should say so; but all through my life it has been the custom of those who have known me to doubt my truth, and to make me out a villain; and though I swear before God that what I say is true in every respect, and that I conceal no single particular, I have never yet been able to induce any one to place credence in my statement."

"Upon my word," said Ruth, "your prefatory remarks cause me to feel extremely anxious to know what the circumstances of your story can be, that they are so difficult to believe."

"It is not a long story, as I have said before; and as you first saw me in so suspicious a position, and have since heard me make a proposition which must stamp me at once in your eyes as a hardened scoundrel, I should dearly like to have an opportunity of setting myself right—or at least to some extent causing you to form a different opinion of me."

"Pray tell me, then, at once, and we can make up for the time we lose afterwards."

To tell the truth, Ruth was by no means averse to a short rest after the dreadful fatigues she had undergone, and she thought she might just as well sit and listen to the young priest's tale, which certainly promised to be a curious one.

She felt quite safe, too, in the cell, for did the gaolers discover her flight and come to seek her as far as the chapel, it was not at all likely that they would follow her into the monastery, the door communicating with which bore no marks of violence, and was always kept carefully locked.

Even did they penetrate into the monastery, she felt quite safe in the young priest's cell, for she had an inward conviction that for his own sake he would not dare to betray her.

"Come," said she, seeing that he still hesitated; "I am all attention."

"I have been brought up from a child in this monastery," said the young priest. "My father once held a very responsible position under Government; but an unfortunate taste for drink, which he had acquired among the loose company of a gay capital, caused him to neglect his duties, muddle his accounts, and at length, after many warnings and humiliating excuses, he was dismissed with disgrace."

Here the young priest paused to reach down a flat bottle, which stood behind the books on the shelf already alluded to; and after offering it to Ruth, who refused to partake of the liquor which it contained, he took a deep gulp himself, and put the bottle away in his pocket.

Ruth could not forbear, however, from indulging in a faint smile.

This was the man who began a story about his father's intemperance, and washed down the recital of his parent's enormity with mouthfuls of raw spirits.

The priest himself did not appear to notice any inconsistency in his behaviour, if Ruth did; and presently continued his narrative, with a deep sigh and a shake of the head at the thought of his father's folly and vice, and the painful results of the same as to himself.

"When my father was discharged from his situation, having no private means of his own, his wife and family were at once plunged into the greatest distress; and though my poor mother struggled bitterly to turn her accomplishments to account, and support my father and their two baby children by giving lessons in music and singing, her health was not strong enough to bear up against the necessary toil and hardship that a woman of delicacy and refinement must suffer in such an avocation. And after vainly striving to contend against them, she slowly sank and sank, and without a murmur or a breath of complaint, gave up that spirit which in life had been ever misunderstood, oppressed, and trodden on by an unappreciative husband.

"When she died, my father, who had drank himself into *delirium tremens*, was lying in a hospital. To such a depth of misery had he sunk, and so lost, morally and physically, had he become under the influence of the vile demon which held him his slave, that he did not recollect that he had children, nor did he care what became of them.

"There were two—a boy and girl. Cold and neglect soon carried the latter upon the same journey which her poor mother had taken a short time before her. The latter being stronger and luckier—or unluckier, perhaps I ought to say—weathered the storm, fell into the hands of a kind-hearted old priest, the head of this convent, and was reared by his charity within the walls of this hateful place."

There was a tone of savage ill-nature, discontent, and ingratitude about the last few words—which certainly were somewhat out of character with the remainder of the speech—which made Ruth look at her companion with a little surprise.

Was he a hypocrite? she asked herself. She had very strong doubts of his sincerity.

But, after all, what did it matter whether he told truth or lies?

She would hear him out. She wanted to hear him out, and see how he could possibly make his thief's character one to be commiserated rather than despised.

"I was brought up out of charity," said the priest. "Such bringing up, you may be sure, is not the most desirable. I was clothed and fed. It is true, my back was kept warm and my belly well filled; but I was many a time made to feel my position; and many a time have I shed bitter tears at the humiliations which I have been forced to suffer at the hands of those who, because I was poor and friendless, thought themselves at liberty to drive me to and fro, as they might have driven some houseless cur, accompanying each scrap of victuals with an unkind word and a cruel kick.

"Well, I survived it, so it does not matter. I was always a favourite with the Superior; and though there were some who strove hard, and worked night and day, with evil speaking, lying, and slandering, to do me an injury with my master, they were, thank heaven, unsuccessful.

"But to get on to the part of my story where my great misfortune befel me—for we have not much time to spare, and I want us to set about our work. I was made a clerk in the accountant's office in the adjoining prison, one of the elder monks being the accountant over me. I worked very hard to please them, and gave so much satisfaction that I was thought to be quite competent to conduct the business by myself, during the absence of the old man. He fell ill, and I was upon one occasion left quite alone for some weeks. It was at this period that my great misfortune befel me.

"This was the return of my father. He had not been seen or heard of in the town for years; but at last he came back—from whence, nobody could tell. He came back woe-begone, dirty, ragged, and miserable—a most disreputable old man—and he called upon me one day at my office.

"I was alone in the room when he entered. I did not know him, but he pretended to know me, and claimed acquaintance.

"What would you have had a child do, thus finding its long-lost father? Would you have had it set its face against the poor old man, and disbelieve the story that he told? I confess that I was weak, and listened, and believed. Well, I had a soft heart. To that I owe my ruin!

"The old man stayed with me for some time. He told me all that he had suffered for many years wandering about the world. He told me that it was alone the desire to see me, his darling child, that had brought him back to his native land. He said that he had given up a situation where he was earning a poor but sufficient salary to keep him, because he could not rest happy without having seen his child. I believed all this, and more.

"Then he asked me scores of questions, about myself, my past life, my present avocation. He took a great interest in the details connected with the office, and asked me where the money was kept, and whether there were ever large sums there at any time. His questions aroused no suspicion in my mind, and I willingly told him everything he desired to know.

"He asked me whether I was paid any salary for my trouble, and when I told him that I had not, he said that the monks' treatment was shameful, as indeed it was.

"When he went away he told me that I was to take care not to mention anything of his visit to the Superior or the brotherhood, and without asking for a reason I obeyed his command.

"From that day he very frequently paid me visits, and he came in better attire, for he had got some employment in the town. My first trouble about him arose from my being obliged, upon one or two occasions, when he was noticed in my office, to tell an untruth upon his account, and to say that he was a porter sent from some place or other, and awaiting an answer of some kind.

"But he generally timed his visits so well that nobody met him or saw him either entering or leaving my room.

"Alas! after a time I had another trouble, even more serious to contend against.

"Before long I began to get wrong in my balance. It was my habit to count over my money every night before leaving the office. Once or twice my father was there at the time, and assisted me. I missed sums of money upon each occasion.

"I was distressed beyond measure. I could not account for the deficiency, for I never for a moment suspected that my own father was the robber.

"I thought that I must have made mistakes, and paid away wrong sums; but such a thing had never before occurred to me, and I had always been so very cautious.

"The first time that it happened I was unable to sleep all night, I was in such agony of mind.

"The first thing next morning I told the Superior, and he kindly forgave me upon account of my previous unerring accuracy, but bade me be more careful for the future.

"The second time that I missed the money I did not know what to think, though even then I did not think the truth.

"I was afraid to tell of my loss again. I did not know what to do. With tears in my eyes I consulted my father, and he advised me to make a clean breast of it, but at the same time bade me be more careful.

"I must say that I thought his advice was very unkind. I could not bear to be told that I had been careless, because I was really so careful. I spent another sleepless night, praying to God to relieve me from such misery.

"After a long delay, not daring to do so before, I at last told the Superior of my second loss

"He was very angry, and said that if such a thing occurred again I must no longer be allowed to retain the situation of trust, which my hitherto steady conduct had caused him to feel justified in allowing me to occupy.

"A very short time afterwards a third and more serious loss than the others threw me into an agony of terror. I could not conceive what had come to me—that I had fallen under a ban—that the evil one had gained possession over me.

"I told my father of my third loss, and he said that I might anticipate very serious and unpleasant results to arise from it. He said, to my infinite terror and dismay, that it was his opinion that the Superior was going to give me into custody on a charge of felony, and that I should be incarcerated in the adjoining prison.

"Terrified beyond measure by this suggestion. I conjured him to tell me what I should do—what course I could pursue to escape detection.

"Then he suggested a plan. The only way, he said, by which I could escape the suspicion of felony, was in reality to commit the felony which I should be suspected of.

"He did not put it in these terms. I forget what he said, but he reasoned so well that, fool that I was, he easily convinced me that what he suggested was the wisest and best course to pursue.

"He made me cook the accounts, and showed me how it was done. I followed his advice, and escaped detection for a time.

"But, strange to say, although I was now ten times more careful than ever, the losses increased. On counting my balance now two or three times a week, I found sums were missing which I could by no means account for.

"What could I do? I could only do what I had done before. My accounts were again cooked, but the losses were so frequent my books became dreadfully confused.

"I will not weary you with unnecessary details, but, passing over some time, a time of dreadful mental agony to me, I will come at once to the most dreadful part of my story.

"One night, after I had left the office, as usual, and retired to my cell, I was disturbed by an idea, for which I can give no earthly reason, that all was not as it should be in the place that I had just left.

"I had been asleep, and I had had a dreadful dream, from which I awoke, screaming with terror. I dreamt that my father was the thief, and that, in the dead of the night, I surprised him breaking into the cash-box.

"Unable to resist a temptation which took possession of me and was stronger than my will, I rose from my bed, took my key, and bent my steps towards the office.

"As I approached the door, my blood froze in my veins, for I heard a noise within.

"A grating noise, as though of a key turning in a lock. I listened. Then I heard the chinking of coin.

"Feeling certain that the counting-house was being robbed, I flung open the door, and rushed in.

"There stood the robber!

"It was my father!"

The priest paused here, and took another long drink from the flat bottle.

Then he continued his narrative.

"The rest is soon told. I was accused of stealing the prison moneys. I would not betray my father, protested my innocence, and suffered.

"It was only when I found that nobody believed me to be anything else than a thief, that I told the truth.

"No one believed me now.

"I was asked to produce my father. I could not. I did not know where he had gone to.

"He had disappeared upon the night of the last robbery.

"I did not know where he had lived when in the town.

"I was then asked to give the name of any person who had seen him. I gave the name of those people who had met him in the office. They none of them could recollect the circumstance. One denied positively that it had ever occurred. Nobody believed me.

"I should have been publicly tried, ruined, and disgraced, had not the Superior, from his own private purse, repaid the money—the stolen money; and though I was not allowed any longer to remain in the position of trust which I had hitherto filled, I was allowed to stop in the monastery, where I was compelled to occupy a menial position, and to bear more gibes, and insults, and humiliation than ever.

"Alas! mine was a hard fate, but I submitted to it, and have been, with God's assistance, able to support its hardships uncomplainingly. And that is all."

"Well," said Ruth, at last, seeing that he stopped here, "that is, indeed, a curious tale."

"And you do not believe it?"

"I did not say that I did not."

"No; but by the expression of your face, I fancy that you do not."

"I only want to know how it is, supposing you are such a very virtuous character, that you happen to be wanting to steal the monastery's money just now, and suggesting that I should help you?"

"It is because I have struggled all my life against my fate. I have been honest, and I have been thought guilty."

"And so you don't see the force of being called bad names and not deserving them?"

"No."

"Very praiseworthy, I must say."

"I am determined to leave this place, which has seen so much of my misery, and which I so detest."

"By the way, what were you doing with that page out of the register, if I may make so bold as to inquire?"

"I am going to sell it. I can get any price for it."

"I don't exactly see what good it can be of to anybody."

"It is a lawyer in the town who will buy it. I believe it is his intention, by having that destroyed, to prove the illegitimacy of some person entitled to a large property, and to put forward some other claimant in their stead."

"Ah! a very creditable affair, certainly. However, it is nothing to me, I am sure; and now we will set about this business."

"The first thing to do is for you to change your clothes to these."

"Yes, I know; and the only drawback——"

"Well?"

"The only drawback to my doing so is that—that——"

But she somehow was a long while giving expression to her reason.

Whether or not, under ordinary circumstances, she would have been much longer, is a question that it is rather difficult to answer.

Just at this moment, however, there was a knock at the door.

The young priest turned pale, and sprang to his feet.

Ruth hastily whispered, "On your life, do not betray me!"

"No."

"If you do, your life pays the forfeit."

The priest nodded his head, to signify that he would keep good faith with her, and then, without another word, approached the door, at which there had been, by this time, another summons, louder than the first.

CHAPTER CIII.

A VERY DISTRESSING POSITION FOR A YOUNG LADY TO BE PLACED IN.

"JAMES," said a voice from the outside; "James, I want to speak to you"

"Yes, father," replied the young priest, and hurried out.

Ruth stood for a moment, wondering whether or not he would return.

But, to her great relief, she heard the sound of their footsteps retreating down the passage.

Now, then, was the time, if it were ever to come, when she should change her apparel.

The change must necessarily be a complete one, therefore she had hesitated hitherto, uncertain how she should proceed.

The young priest evidently had no idea of beating a retreat while she effected the necessary alteration in costume.

Not knowing that it was a question of a lady's toliet, he, of course, saw little impropriety in remaining where he was while the stranger undressed.

As may be supposed, though, Ruth's opinion upon the subject was a contrary one.

She was not, perhaps, the most bashful of young ladies, and her opinions upon some matters were, to say the least of them, extremely liberal; but, upon this occasion, there was a much greater amount of difficulty in the way of her donning the priest's dress than may be at first understood.

If the young priest had only been aware of the

sex of his visitor, a great deal of the difficulty would have been overcome.

But he did not—no, she was quite certain he did not. And, then, how on earth could the dreadful truth be broken to him?

In spite of the young man's villany in other respects—in spite of the strong conviction on her mind that the story of his father's defalcations was a base fabrication, and had no foundation in fact, she still was as much impressed as ever with the notion that she had at first entertained respecting his innocence.

He was not a libertine, though he might be a thief.

She could read human nature, and knew a great deal of its bad side, and a little of its good; and she knew well enough that the worst have their good points—they're not all bad.

There are some people who, talking of that class of females truly called "unfortunate," assert that they are capable of any crime if capable of frailty.

That is an opinion which, in my humble judgment, exhibits a very limited knowledge of human nature.

Ruth, on the contrary, believed that this man, who proposed a theft without blushing, would have been overwhelmed with confusion and horror at the idea of being associated with a woman of abandoned character, such as it was only reasonable to suppose was the person who had broken out of the prison of St. Lazarus, who adopted male attire, and appeared to possess so little of that modesty and diffidence which one is apt to associate with the softer sex.

"My only chance," said Ruth to herself, "is to change my clothes while he is gone."

There was no knowing how long, or, more properly speaking, how short a time he would be absent, and so "sharp" was the word.

At once, then, with a series of violent rents and jerks, she dragged the clothes from her back, and in the space of a very few moments had as little wearing apparel upon her graceful person as had the goddess of love herself, when she rose from the sea.

But when thus situated, and in the very act of selecting the first article of dress which it was necessary to assume, she heard footsteps again in the passage.

To say that she was horror-stricken would be to use a wild term to express the young lady's terror and dismay.

The footsteps rapidly approached. They were the footsteps of two persons.

Who was coming? The priest and the person he had called "Father," or the gaolers?

What could she do? There was no place to conceal herself.

The only place that she could get into, she got into at once; and that was the bed.

She had barely time to jump in, and pull the bed-clothes—one blanket—up to her chin, when the door opened, and the young priest and an old man, also in a monastic garb, entered the cell.

CHAPTER CIV.

CONFUSION.

To describe Ruth's feelings of shame and terror at this juncture, would be impossible.

She could not have made a remark to have saved her life

She lay in bed, clutching the clothes with the energy of despair, her teeth chattering in her head.

The expression of the young priest's countenance also indicated considerable alarm when first her eyes alighted upon it; but in spite of her own fright, she could not help noticing that when he saw where she was, an expression of satisfaction passed over his features, as though her act had corroborated some statement which he had made concerning her.

This she soon found to be the case.

Meanwhile the old priest approached the bed, and, taking a seat upon the box, sat for a few moments silently contemplating the stranger's face.

Ruth blushed crimson.

"Poor young man," said the old priest, after a long pause,—"poor young man! Do you suffer much?"

"Not so much now," replied Ruth, very truly, though, at the same time, she would very much have liked to have known what was the particular ailment that she was supposed to be troubled with.

"You ought to have told me of this sooner, James," said the old man. "It was very wrong of you."

"I only brought him here after you had gone out, father."

"Ah!—to be sure. But you might have informed some of the brotherhood. They could have assisted you, and given you advice."

"I have done all that was necessary."

"Still I do not think that your knowledge of the healing art is so good as that of others in the house. Indeed, as you are young, and have had no opportunity of acquiring any experience, it is not at all likely that it should be."

"I intended to tell you as soon as you came home, father."

"Very well—very well. And what have you applied?"

"The usual remedies."

Ruth was too frightened to laugh, although the scene was comical enough.

In spite of her fright, though, she could not help whispering to herself, "What the dickens is the matter with me?"

Her doubts as to her supposed ailment were, however, very shortly to be dispersed under circumstances that were very far from agreeable.

"Let me look at your arm, my poor fellow!" said the old man.

Now the young priest had noticed blood upon Ruth's sleeve, and he had come to the conclusion that she had hurt her arm.

But this was not really the case.

The blood had flowed from a very ugly cut that a nail in the door through which the reader may remember she had been pulled by the Frenchman had made in her leg; and it was only the mark of her fingers, wiped upon her sleeve, that the young priest had seen.

When he had been summoned to the door of the cell by his Superior, the latter had inquired, after having requested his services in fastening one of the windows which the old man had found open in the passage, whom it was he had heard him talking to.

At his wits' end for an excuse, the young priest had stammered out that it was a young man whom he had found in the chapel, who had remained after the doors had been shut for the night, and who had fainted in one of the pews,

probably from loss of blood, from a bad wound in his arm.

The old man, being of a very credulous nature, believed the story at once, and, eager to be of service, accompanied the young priest into his cell.

Therefore, you see, when the younger man found Ruth in the bed, he was delighted by the circumstance, because it lent truth to his story. But when the old man wanted to see the lady's arm, he (the younger) had no notion how very embarrassing the affair was becoming.

Certainly it appeared to him—for he had not noticed very closely—that Ruth's arm was bandaged up. If she exhibited the bandage, then, all would be right.

But she did not respond to the invitation.

Then it occurred to the young priest that, perhaps, she might not know whether or not she should do as she was asked; and so, to reassure her, he also added his request to the old man's.

"Show your arm, there's a good fellow!"

"Perhaps," said the old man, "it pains him to raise it?"

"Yes!" gasped Ruth.

"Poor fellow!" said the old man. "Let me turn down the blanket, then! Is it this arm?"

"Don't move it!" cried Ruth, in an agony.—"you hurt me intolerably!"

"Poor fellow! I'll be very gentle!"

What on earth was to be done? The old man continued to tug at the blanket. Ruth continued to clutch it tightly to her chin

She had no idea what state her arm was supposed to be in, though. Why should she not show it as far as her elbow?

She could manage that, she thought, if she were careful.

"Leave go, then, please," said she.

And the old man relinquished his hold. She began to push her arm out from under the blanket in compliance with his wish; but, unhappily for the success of the young priest's scheme, and to the utter confusion and terror of all the three persons concerned in this extraordinary adventure, the blanket somehow fell off her left shoulder, and neck and bosom of snowy whiteness were for one moment, in spite of her efforts to prevent so fatal a catastrophe, exposed to the awe-struck gaze of the two priests, old and young!

CHAPTER CV.

IN WHICH THE TWO PRIESTS GET THEMSELVES INTO "A BIT OF A FIX."

To have said which of the two was the most frightened by the result of this very unfortunate occurrence, would have been extremely difficult; and to have told which of the two priests was the most astonished, would likewise have been a riddle that was very far from easy of solution.

There are many circumstances under which one may suppose that a person is more than usually astonished. I should think that some young gentleman, of strong aquatic propensities, but limited nautical experience, who, pulling along in all the glory of spotless flannels and gorgeous Guernsey, and believing himself the pride and admiration of admiring crowds, comes suddenly, with a fearful smash, against the wood-work of Putney Bridge—is, to say the least of it, knocked considerably out of time.

I should think that the doting parent who has laid out a fabulous amount of money in purchasing an outfit for his hopeful son, and who has, to the best of his belief, taken a long farewell of him for years to come, but accidentally encounters him in the gallery of the National Assembly Rooms in High Holborn, or the body of the hall at Mr. Weston's establishment, or "on the jury" at Baron Nicholson's mock trials, must also be considerably astonished.

These, and many other instances, one might imagine, when astonishment would in all probability really reach the climax of intensity; but I somehow hardly think that the amazement felt by the two priests upon discovering the sex of their visitor far surpassed anything in the way of wonderment which it is possible to realize in the length of a long summer's day.

They were considerably surprised, there is no doubt of that. But the surprise of the elder very shortly gave way to a feeling of intense indignation and wrath.

He had been deceived by the young priest, in whom he had been fool enough to place confidence, though experience ought to have told him that he was anything but trustworthy.

He had been expressing sympathy for the sham sufferer, and making himself look extremely ridiculous.

He had been cheated into holding conversation for upwards of ten minutes with an abandoned female.

He had discovered the same in the cell of a priest.

In fact, he had many reasons for being indignant. He did not know how sufficiently to show his wrath.

He turned scarlet and livid, and shook like a leaf.

"How—how — how dare you?" he found breath enough to gasp out at last.

"F—f—father!" gasped the young priest, who had not much more breath than his companion.

"How dare you, sir?"

"I assure you——"

"Don't assure me, sir!"

"I swear——"

"Don't swear at me, sir!"

"Upon my honour——"

"Honour—a fiddlestick!"

"Upon my soul——"

"Silence, or I'll crush you!"

"I will speak!" roared the young priest, at last. "I will speak! I had no idea—I hadn't the least idea—that—that——"

"That I should find you out."

"No; I don't mean that."

"What do you mean?"

"I mean that I did not know that this young—this person was a—was a——"

"Silence, sir!" cried the old man, perfectly blue with suppressed indignation. "Do you suppose I'm a born fool?"

"No, sir."

"Then, do you want me to suppose that you are?"

The young priest had not another word to say for himself.

He was dumbfounded, flabbergastered, knocked in a heap.

But Ruth, whose fears had given way under the influence of the ludicrous scene now enacting before her at this moment, burst into an uncontrollable fit of laughter.

The effect of this unseemly merriment was too much for the elder priest, who perfectly reeled under the blow that it was to him.

There is no doubt that if providence had not placed the black box in a convenient position for receiving the most ignoble part of his reverend anatomy, he would have gone down flat on his back.

As it was, the effects of the shock mentally, and the hard box physically, knocked every bit of breath out of the poor old gentleman's body.

"Ha! ha! ha!" laughed Ruth.

"Scandalous!" ejaculated the old priest.

"Ha! ha! ha!" laughed Ruth.

"Outrageous!" gasped the old gentleman.

Ruth, however, laughed louder than ever.

"What are you doing here?" cried the old priest.

"I'm waiting for you to go."

"Get up, and leave the house directly!"

"There's nothing would suit me better."

"Go, then!"

"Certainly!"

But the audacious young woman making a feint of being about to get out of bed, the old gentleman, in great perturbation, rushed headlong towards the door, almost upsetting the young priest upon the way.

"Stop a moment, if you please," said Ruth, assuming a serious countenance with a great deal of difficulty. "I cannot allow you to go away with the idea that that young gentleman has committed the heinous offence of being a party to the introduction of a lady to this establishment. I solemnly assure you that his statement is a correct one, and he believed when he gave me shelter that I was a man."

"But—but," stammered the priest, with some

hesitation—"but he said you had hurt your arm."

"Well?"

"Well, have you?"

"No, not in the least; but I deceived him."

"If I could only believe this!"

"I assure you you may."

"But, tell me, what is your motive for acting in this way?"

"Ah, you gentlemen know very little about ladies!"

"No. Heaven forbid!"

"I don't see that. It is you who are the losers."

"I won't argue the point."

"I don't want you to do so. I was only going to say that if you knew a little more about ladies, you would never ask for their motives."

"What do you mean? Had you no motive for coming here?"

"Yes, I had. I came here out of curiosity."

"Extraordinary! And you run all this risk out of idle curiosity?"

"There isn't much risk with such good old gentlemen as you are——"

"There, there!" cried the old man; "let this conversation cease! Dress yourself and leave the building."

"If you will kindly retire, I shall be dressed in a few minutes."

"There is one question I want to ask you, and that is, how came you to get into that bed in a state of—of——without being suitably attired, in short?"

"What! Do you go to bed with your clothes on?" cried Ruth, laughing.

The old man staggered back, and clenched his fist.

"I see you are utterly incorrigible, shameless, and lost!"

"The fact is," said Ruth, "I was profiting by the absence of that young man to change my dress; and if you had not come in when you did, in another five minutes I should have done so without causing this very unpleasant scene; for though it does not appear to strike you in the same light, I can assure you it has been every bit as disagreeable to me as it has to you, if not more so."

"I will no longer stand in the way," said the old priest.

"I shall feel obliged to you if you won't."

"Shall you be long in performing your toilet?"

"Only a few minutes."

"I will return, then, in a quarter of an hour."

"That time will be ample."

"In the meanwhile, you, I trust, will pardon me, if——"

"If what?"

"If I lock you in."

"Why are you going to do that?"

"Only because I should feel more easy in my mind if I had a lady, whose curiosity tempts her on to the performance of such eccentricity, safe under lock and key."

"You are at perfect liberty to do what you choose, sir; my only desire is to be allowed to depart quietly."

"As that opinion directly coincides with my own, madam, I can assure you that I shall not detain you a moment after the time that you deem it necessary to prepare yourself for the road."

Having thus expressed himself with an amount of polished courtesy which, to speak the truth, was not altogether guiltless of a tendency towards burlesque, the old man bowed himself out, and shut the cell door to after him.

When he was outside he turned upon his companion, and asked in a tone which showed the perturbation of his mind, "What, in the name of all that is disastrous, do you propose to do next?"

"I—I—haven't the least idea," replied the other, gloomily.

"Having got me and yourself into this dreadful mess, I ask you how you propose to get us out of it?"

"I trust, sir, that you believe that I innocently caused this most unfortunate scene?"

"Well—well! We won't enter into that," said the old man, testily. "I'll try to believe you. There, I do believe you, if you like that better."

"I thank you, father, from my heart."

"Don't take my hand. I—I'm rather out of temper. I ask you how to get rid of this woman?"

"We must let her out quietly."

"Certainly we must."

"Shall we let her out through the chapel?"

"To be sure. The very way. It did not occur to me."

"That way there will be no chance of any discovery."

"No, that way we shall be safe; but, mind sir, I have looked over much in you as it is. This fault or folly, whichever you may choose to call it, shall be your last."

"But, father!"

"Hold your tongue. I won't hear a word of explanation. And please to remember that it is not any consideration for you which causes me to act as I do, but solely my dread of this shameful affair becoming public. It is one of the first and foremost rules of our order, as you know, that the credit of our order be kept up, and that the sins of an erring brother be kept from the knowledge of our enemies. It is upon that account only that I spare you. But mark my words! I have borne much, and will bear no more upon your account."

The old man trembled with rage as he spoke, and his listener deemed it advisable to keep a silent tongue in his head.

Therefore, he said no word, but waited for the Superior to address him again.

Presently the old man turned to him, after a few moments of silence, and said, "A fresh difficulty occurs to me."

"What is that, father?"

"How are we to secure this woman's silence?"

"I should not think that she is likely to divulge the secrets of this visit."

"How do you know that the visit is a secret?"

"I—I don't know," stammered the other; for he had almost divulged the truth, and revealed to his elder the fact that Ruth had broken out of prison, and consequently was not at all likely to allude to her exploits in the monastery.

"It is my opinion," said the old man, without noticing his companion's confusion, "that she is not a person who would keep this affair to herself."

"You think not?"

"I feel sure of it. I think she will boast of it."

"Boast of it?"

"Yes."

"But I should have thought that she would have been ashamed——"

"She appears to me to be a person totally devoid of that quality. She is, without doubt, one of that fearful class whose trade is debauchery, and she will probably recount all the particulars of this business to her dissolute companions, who will make merry over our humiliation and dishonour."

"I hope your estimate of her character is a wrong one."

"I doubt it very much."

"She is dressed by now, I suppose. Will you have an interview with her?"

"It will be better, perhaps, if I do."

"Will you see her alone?"

"No—yes, that will be best; I will then let her out by the chapel door. You wait here."

Thus saying, the old man approached the door of the cell.

But when upon the point of turning the key, another idea struck him

"What are you to do in the meantime? You cannot wait in the passage. Somebody may come out of his cell and see you"

"What do you propose, father?"

"I had better see her in my own cell."

"Will you take her?"

"Well, no; I think it will be better if you bring her."

There was some small amount of artfulness in this answer of the old man.

The fact is, he was very much afraid that some one of the priests might come out and find him walking along with the strange lady.

This was an idea that he did not over relish.

"No; it must not be that," he thought. "If anybody was to come to disgrace in the matter, it would be best for the real culprit to suffer"

Not he himself, an innocent old gentleman, who had given up his whole life to the pursuit of godliness, and was as free from vice as his reputation was spotless, and his name honoured among his brethren.

No; he had suffered a good deal already upon account of this black sheep, whose misdeeds he had screened. He would suffer no more.

As there was a risk to be run, let him run it.

"Bring the woman to my cell," said he; "it is on the way to the chapel. Whatever you do, be cautious. Tread upon your tip-toes, and, for your life, make no noise!"

CHAPTER CVI.

RUTH METAMORPHOSED.—THE OLD PRIEST STAGGERED BY HER BEAUTY.—A MOMENT OF TEMPTATION.—A CROSS-EXAMINATION.—A DISCOVERY.—MYSTERY.—AMAZEMENT.

The priest knew very well that, by the course which he pursued, he gave the black sheep an opportunity of arranging some talk with the strange woman, and putting her on her guard against betraying herself in the interview which was to take place.

But it was better, the old man thought, to run this risk than the other.

He did not believe that the young man was as guiltless as he represented; but the principal consideration was to get rid of the woman at once, without publicity, after he had threatened or bribed her into silence.

Leaving the young priest, then, who entered the cell, and in a few hasty words acquainted Ruth with what had happened, and informed her that the scheme which he had concocted for the robbery of the strong box must not be abandoned,—the old man, making the best of his way, as quickly and as quietly as possible, to his cell, awaited her coming.

He had not to wait many minutes.

A low tap presently apprized him of her arrival.

"Come in," he said.

The door opened, and she entered alone, and closing the portal behind her, turned and faced him.

It certainly seemed that the reverend father was this evening doomed to be shocked and astonished out of all bounds. If he were not exactly shocked at the present moment—and he was shocked a little, too—he was so surprised that, for a moment or two, he could not find his tongue.

Although he had supposed that Ruth would be clad in male attire, he had no knowledge of the arrangement which had taken place between her and the young priest respecting Ruth's assuming his clerical garb.

Therefore, when the old man's eyes alighted on the lithe and graceful form of the adventuress, attired like a young priest, though, somehow, setting off the clothes in a fashion that he had never yet noticed them to possess upon another wearer, he was surprised beyond the power of addressing her, and could only stare and gape like some ploughboy might do in the presence of a fairy.

"You wish to see me?" said Ruth, donning her hat with a graceful bow.

"Ye-es."

"What do you want with me?"

She was not in the least disconcerted in the company of the reverend father, who had not a word to say for himself.

"Take a seat," he gasped, at last.

Ruth elevated her eyebrows slightly, and smiled a little.

"You're not a lady's man, father?" she said.

"N-n-no; I am not," he stammered.

"If you had been, you'd have handed me a chair!"

There are times when the most self-possessed and dignified of persons lose their confidence and dignity.

This old man, in whose presence it was the habit of all to uncover and bow low, was quite confused and abashed by the rebuke the impudent young hussy addressed to him.

Hardly knowing whether he was standing on his head or his heels, and without having the vaguest idea what he was doing or saying, he made a plunge forward, and tried to reach a chair.

However, Ruth was beforehand with him, and helped herself to one, sat down opposite to him, and assumed an attitude in which the natural grace of her *pose* could not help attracting the notice of even one so unused to turn his attention to such matters as the old priest, who was watching her.

She sat in such a way that the light from a lamp close at hand fell full upon her face.

It was no longer the face which in prison had been so pallid, pinched, and sickly.

The exercise which latterly she had been allowed to enjoy upon the roof of the prison, under the eye of the gaoler—the increased size and airiness of the cell in which she had been incarcerated—and the improvement in her food, which the tender interest of the smitten gaoler had procured for her—had all tended to increase her personal looks, and gradually and by slow degrees she had assumed a great deal of that old beauty which had once been so dazzling, bewildering, unapproachable.

She would never again probably acquire a certain delicacy of complexion, which was a blending of the rose and lily.

She would never again, it was to be supposed, regain the rich luxuriance of golden silk-like hair which once had crowned her lovely head, like a halo of mellow glory.

No, that was past and gone, it is true, never to return; but now, as she sat there, the light playing upon her dark eyes and white teeth, and her cheeks for the time rosy with the unwonted exertions through which she had lately passed, she did indeed look lovely.

The old priest could not, for the life of him, turn his eyes away from the fair prospect which her smiling face offered to him.

What thoughts were, for the first moment or two, coursing each other through his bald noddle, it would be impertinent and improper, I think, for us to endeavour to guess at.

Perhaps he thought, for just one moment, that if the young priest had sinned, there might be more excuse for him than, a few moments ago, he would have believed to be possible.

Perhaps he thought that there might, after all, be some truth in what the enemies of his Church said about the celibacy of its priests.

That it was, to some extent, absurd and unnatural to shut oneself out from the society of that finer portion of creation which brightens life with its smiles and love, its bright eyes, pouting lips, and melting kisses.

That there was, after all, some excuse for Saint Anthony, whom the syren tempted.

Did he think thus? Did any of these ideas float through his mind? Did he picture to himself what he might have done, had such a lovely woman come in his way, had he been thirty years younger, and a profligate, instead of a pious old priest, who had forsworn the devil and all his works?

Perhaps he did; but, as I said just now, I think it is rather impertinent and improper to speculate about the matter, when we cannot say for positive whether we are right or not.

Still I must say that I fancy some such ideas passed through the old man's mind, and that the sigh with which he dismissed them indicated that the struggle with the evil one in days gone by had been a bitter and hard struggle to bear.

But if any such thoughts agitated him, he dismissed them, as I say, with a sigh, and sternly and resolutely set about the work that he had proposed to himself.

Namely, to get rid of the unwelcome visitor to the monastic establishment.

Ruth waited for him to begin, and after waiting some time, he thus opened the conversation.

"Will you allow me to ask you a few questions?"

She answered cautiously.

"Do you expect me to answer them?"

"You are, of course, at liberty to answer, or refuse to answer, as it may seem best to you. One stipulation alone do I make."

"And that?"

"I beg of you, that in the answers you think fit to make to my questions you will tell me the truth alone."

"I agree."

"I will not ask you any questions that I think are likely to tempt you to falsehood. I will not question you with respect to your knowledge of the man in whose cell I found you just now. Let all that pass. It is not with reference to your doings in this place that I wish to question you."

He paused here, as though he expected that she would make some reply.

She, however, said no word, and he resumed after a few moments.

"Pray, then, tell me, do you possess a large circle of acquaintances in this town?"

"I know no one."

"Do you possess independent means?"

"No."

"Do you work for your living?"

"No."

"How do you live?"

"As I can."

"By your wits?"

"When I find that a paying game."

"You own yourself, then, not over honest?"

"Nothing to swear by."

"You belong to that class of women—who—who——"

"I understand you perfectly; you need not distress yourself by endeavouring to make your meaning intelligible."

"Am I right, then, in my conjecture?"

"You are altogether wrong."

"Do you then mean to say that you lead a virtuous life?"

"As virtuous as yours!"

The old priest stared very hard and somewhat incredulously at his companion; but presently he seemed to make up his mind to believe her.

"Well," said he, "I will ask you another question, then."

"A dozen, if you think fit."

"If you do not possess independent means, you may yet possess a sufficient sum of money to keep you for some short period?"

"I do not possess a halfpenny."

"If you have no money and no friends, and do not work, and do not earn your subsistence by immoral practices, how do you manage to subsist?"

"How I shall subsist for the future I have not the least idea. How I have subsisted for some time past, I refuse to inform you."

"Where do you live?"

"I have at present no abode."

"Where have you been living hitherto?"

"I cannot answer you."

"Was it in the town?"

"No."

"In the neighbourhood?"

"I cannot tell you."

"From the way you talk, although your language is fluent, it seems to me that you are not a native of this country?"

"No."

"You are not a Frenchwoman?"

"No."

"What countrywoman are you?"

"I am English."

"What part of England do you come from?"

"From London."

"In what religion were you reared?"

"When I was very young and went to a place of worship, it was to a Roman Catholic chapel."

"What is your name?"

"My surname?"

"Yes."

"Hardcastle."

At the utterance of this word the priest started as though he had been shot, and leaning forward, with his hand resting upon the arms of the chair in which he sat, repeated it slowly, syllable by syllable, while he stared at the woman's face as though he were intent upon getting every feature by heart.

Ruth was somewhat astonished, it is true, but her amazement increased considerably at his subsequent behaviour.

He rose from his seat after taking a long, silent stare at her, and crossing the room, unlocked an old secretary.

Ruth followed his movements with her eyes.

From this he took out a small parcel, carefully wrapped up in paper.

Laying the parcel upon the table, he unfolded it and took from the inside two smaller parcels which he unfolded likewise.

The first of the two was a brooch which contained a portrait that was only visible by touching a spring that opened the back, where it was hidden.

Touching the spring now, the priest held it near to the light, all the time carefully comparing the face which it contained with the face before him.

Ruth sat silently observing him, and not without some degree of apprehension and agitation.

What did his conduct mean?

What was going to occur?

She could form no conjecture as to the probable meaning and result of this strange behaviour on his part.

She could only wait with all the patience she could summon to her aid.

After a long and silent contemplation of the portrait, however, the old priest, with a face in which excitement was plainly visible, laid it down and took up the object contained in the other parcel.

This was a small, square, black leather book, on which was printed, in gold, one word—"Journal."

"Do you know this book?" said the old priest, handing it to her.

Ruth took it in her hand, and turned it over.

"No," she answered.

"Are you sure?"

"Yes."

"Look inside."

"It seems to be a diary."

"Do you know the writing?"

"No."

"Can you read it?"

"Of course I can! It is English."

"Did you write it?"

"I? No; of course I did not!"

"Look at that portrait."

Ruth took the brooch in her hand.

But, as her eye fell upon it, she uttered an exclamation of astonishment.

"Do you know it?"

"Yes, yes! Good heavens! Where did you get it?"

"Is it your portrait?"

"Mine? No! It is——"

"Whose?"

"My mother's!"

"And your name, then, is——"

"Ruth!"

"Ruth?" repeated the priest. "To be sure! You are, then, her sister?"

"Whose sister?" asked Ruth, wondering more and more.

"The writer of the diary!"

"Who was that, then?"

"Cecily Hardcastle, a nun in the Convent of Saint Sorebones, in London!"

CHAPTER CVII.

THE JESUITS' PLOT.

For some time Ruth's heart was too full to allow her to give utterance to the many questions which she longed to ask.

At last, however, she spoke.

"Where did you obtain these things?" she said.

"Well," replied the old priest, "I became possessed of them under very peculiar circumstances."

As he paused here, and appeared to be quite lost in a brown study, she urged him to continue.

But he waved his hand as a token that she should remain silent, and slowly paced the floor of the cell from side to side.

At last, suddenly, he paused in front of her.

"By what you said just now," the priest remarked, slowly and deliberately, as though he were weighing the meaning of each word which he uttered, and deliberating upon its application,—"by what you said, you led me to believe that you were in desperate circumstances."

"That is my position."

"You are, then, in need of money?"

"I am!"

"Are you willing to earn it?"

"How?"

"The means will not be very creditable: have you any objection to the proposition so far?"

"Not the slightest!"

"Will you swear solemnly not to divulge to a living soul what I am now going to propose to you."

"There is no occasion for me to swear—I give you my promise."

"You must know, then, that there is at present residing in your native city of London, a clergyman, of the Protestant faith, of the name of Vivian."

"I have heard of him."

"Everybody has, I should think, who lives in that city, for he is the most popular and fashionable of preachers; he is also, as you may be aware, one of the most violent enemies to our Church."

"I was not aware of the circumstance."

"Probably, also, you were not aware that at one period of his life, he formed a strong attachment for a person in our Church."

"No!"

"Well, then, such was the case, and so great was her influence over him, that he was almost upon the point of abandoning wealth, position, name, honour—religion, even, for her sake."

"Who was she?"

"A nun."

"A nun!"

"Yes; well may you be shocked. Such, however, was the case."

"Was their attachment, then, criminal?"

"Fortunately, no. Ere they fell, they had strength of mind sufficient to throw their folly on one side, and to part."

"And this nun—who was she?—not——"

"Yes, you are right; she was Cecily Hardcastle, your sister."

Ruth was silent for a while; then she asked, "What has this story to do with the plan you were going to propose? I am, as yet, at a loss to understand you."

"You shall shortly. That diary, as I have told you, belonged to Cecily Hardcastle."

"Well?"

"In it is written an account of the mad passion which I have described."

"Well?"

"It was by its aid that I discovered the one weak point in the character of the man who, hitherto, I had supposed to be without a weakness. By its aid, also, I made a most important discovery."

"And what was it?"

"That the flame is not yet extinguished."

"Does she love him still?"

"She? Yes, clearly. And he——"

"Has forgotten her?"

"On the contrary, he loves her as much, if not more, than ever; and it is that discovery which I mean to turn to account, with your aid."

"How, with my aid?"

"You shall represent your sister."

"I shall!" cried Ruth, in indignant amazement.

"If you consent to do so, of course."

"But if I do not?"

"Then I rely on you to keep the promise which you gave me."

"I think it would have been wiser had you selected some one else, if you wish to do my sister any harm."

"But I don't wish to do so," cried the old priest eagerly. "You mistake my motive. With your sister I have nothing to do. Could I have found her, I feel certain that she could have been induced to forward our views."

"I thought you said that she was a nun in the Convent of St. Sorebones?"

"She was."

"Is she there no longer?"

"No. For a year past she has not been seen. She has disappeared from London, and she ran away from the convent."

"She perhaps sought shelter with this Mr. Vivian?"

"No, she did not; and he has not seen her for eighteen months, at least."

"But how could I pass myself off as my sister without his knowing the difference?"

"It is not impossible. I have reason to believe that there must be a most extraordinary likeness between you."

"Why?"

"Because you so exactly resemble your mother."

"What does that prove?"

"Everything. Your sister, in her diary, states that she resembled her mother to an extraordinary extent in every respect but the colour of her hair, which, in your sister's case, was darker."

"And so you imply from that that we must resemble each other?"

"Except in the colour of the hair."

"What am I to do, then, according to your plans?"

"Exercise such influence over this man as a woman best knows how to manage, and draw him from his heresy to the true Church."

"Well, and my reward?"

"Shall be a large one."

"What?"

"It would be impossible to limit your reward to any sum, for you may be a long while before you can effect the object you have in view; but it is not a hundred pounds or so that will stand in the way of the Church when it has set its heart upon the attainment of an object so dear to it as the conversion of this stubborn unbeliever."

Ruth considered for some time. The plan proposed would enable her to go back to England. Did she want to go?

She had been so eager to get away from London. Should she now return? Would it be wise.

A thought struck her.

"Where is this Vivian?" she asked.

"He has recently got a living about fifty miles from the metropolis. He is the Rector of Shenstone."

"I accept, then. What am I to do?"

"You shall proceed at once to England."

"Yes!"

"Obtain an interview with him—renew the acquaintance."

"Yes!"

"Renew the old passion, which slumbers in his heart."

"Is he married?"

"No, single. Although he might to-morrow, if he chose, wed the wealthiest and most beautiful in the land, he refuses. And why?"

"Why, pray?"

"Because he has never yet overcome the passion which he conceived for your sister. That is why."

"He must indeed have loved her, and I fear it will be hopeless to endeavour to deceive him."

"I must leave that to you. This book will give you every particular of the acquaintance. It is your sister's own story. As to her personal appearance, I will give you a letter to the Abbess of the Convent of Saint Sorebones, who will be able to describe exactly in what your sister did not resemble you, if there really existed any difference, a fact that I very much doubt."

"With the Abbess's advice, it is true that I may be able to change my appearance somewhat."

"I place every faith in your powers in that respect."

"And in that of being able to fascinate him?"

"I—I have no experience," stammered the priest.

"Have you any doubt?" asked the mischievous beauty, bringing the battery of those melting orbs of blue, which had so often before been so effectively used in a like case, to bear upon the poor old gentleman, who absolutely quivered beneath their influence.

But he was a wise old man. He did not care to set his heart against the syren's power.

"No, no," he said, rising hastily to his feet, and getting as far away from the influence of those bright eyes which shone upon him as he possibly could,—"I am quite content with supposing that you are capable of the duty allotted to you. You need not give us any example of your accomplishments."

Some arrangements were then entered into with respect to the contemplated journey. She was to start next morning, about ten o'clock, by a boat which left the town for England. She was to have some money given to her for her immediate expenses of travelling, &c. Upon her arrival she was to proceed direct to the Convent of Saint Sorebones, and deliver a letter, with which she would be provided, to the Lady Superior, who would then give her full instructions as to her future conduct.

I, however, think it is necessary to more fully explain the scheme for the reader's better understanding, as, by the foregoing conversation, it is impossible to obtain more than a very shadowy notion of the plot which the fiendish ingenuity of certain crafty Jesuits devised for effecting the ruin of one of the most talented and popular of Protestant clergyman, with what success will be hereafter shown.

Altogether, so crafty and deep-laid a scheme seems, at first hearing, to be utterly impossible. The writer begs to state that it is very far from being the romance that the reader may suppose; and he will now, without any fear of the threats of those whose interest it would be to bury such dreadful details in unfathomable darkness, describe with as much boldness, and as little dread of consequences, the shameful details of this damnable conspiracy, as he described in the beginning of his work the inner mysteries of a certain London nunnery—a subject to which he also intends shortly to return, for the purpose of making further and, if possible, more startling disclosures.

The old Jesuit priest, who had proposed the forthcoming journey to London to our volatile heroine, had, while in the English metropolis, accidentally become possessed of the diary of an escaped nun.

This nun's name was Cecily Hardcastle.

In it he discovered an account of a love affair, which, at the same time, astounded and delighted him; for the hero of it was the man of all others in the world that he, and all the well-wishers of his sect, feared at the bottom of their hearts.

He was the popular preacher before alluded to—a man whose morality was spoken of by all—who was believed to be beyond all suspicion of frailty—to be incorruptible, a good and holy man.

Great was the chuckling over this discovery.

Intense the delight of the crafty Jesuits at the thought that here was a chance of wreaking a terrible vengeance upon the man who so often, so loudly, so fiercely, and so vehemently had denounced them and their faith from his pulpit.

The old priest was almost frantic with joy at the grand discovery he had made. Here was a chance of showing how devoted he was to the interests of his sect—how sharp his eyes were, how he watched over his brethren's welfare, and with what lynx eyes he watched for the weaknesses of the enemy, that he might pounce upon and expose them.

Upon making the discovery he lost no time in calling together a meeting of some brother priests, and they consulted together as to what would be the best method of setting to work to effect the downfall of the preacher.

That his downfall and disgrace were to be effected immediately, they were all determined upon.

The only question that required any consideration whatever was simply "How?"

It is very sad to think that all these good people plotting and scheming, of course, alone for the welfare of the holy religion of which they were such distinguished ornaments, should have committed the very popular error of counting their chickens previous to the successful incubation, or before they were hatched.

The meeting was called together, as I have said.

The old priest, and another who had been taken into the old priest's confidence, entered into a lengthy discussion as to the way and the time, how and when, the preacher should be shown up.

Somebody then asked for a history of the affair. The priest discussed the awful discovery he had made, dilating upon the frailty of the nun and the hideous depravity of the preacher—drawing a fearful picture of the future torments awaiting both seducer and seduced.

Somebody then requested to look at the written evidence of all this sin and infamy.

The old priest, with a triumphant air, produced the diary, and bade them read for themselves.

Now, the old priest was a Frenchman, not very well acquainted with the English language.

The handwriting in which the diary was kept was none of the plainest.

It is not very extraordinary that he should have made a mistake. Indeed, he might have made a much worse mistake than he had done, for he might very easily have mistaken the person who was the hero of this love affair, and taken some one else for the preacher.

He had not done this, though the mistake which he had committed was a most provoking one, and subjected him to an enormous amount of banter and ridicule.

He had discovered a love affair certainly; but, unfortunately for the Jesuits, it appeared upon the showing of this diary, which they had unanimously agreed to receive as evidence, that the love-making was all on one side.

Most unfortunately, that side was the lady's.

Again, which was worse than all, it appeared that the love affair was of the most platonic character.

At least, this was the depressing impression which the perusal of the commencement of the diary left upon the minds of the hearers. However, when they went deeper into the matter, they came to the conclusion that the preacher had loved this nun, but still that he had never profited by the influence which he possessed over her too susceptible heart.

He had loved her; but their love had been pure—virtuous—spotless.

What could be done? What could be made out of this discovery, which at first the old priest had been tempted to believe was going to turn out of so promising a character?

He was at the outset overwhelmed with contempt and derision.

It was only when the old man, worked into a perfect fury by the gibes and taunts which his companions hurled at his devoted head, was upon the point of rushing madly out of the room, that they called him back, and one of the most crafty and calculating of the party suggested that the information which they had acquired, although small, should still be turned to some account.

The account to which he proposed that it should be turned was the extortion of a large sum of money from the preacher.

The old priest, however, would not listen to this.

He said that they had thought fit to underrate the benefit that he was about to bestow upon his order. He would therefore leave them. He would not solicit their aid any further.

He would work in the affair single-handed; and the time would come, perhaps, when they would be sorry for the way in which they had treated him.

With this, he seized his precious volume and beat an angry retreat, in spite of all their efforts to detain him.

No, he would listen to no one. He would allow no one to look at the book. He would work out his plans unaided and alone.

This was what he said himself; but it must be confessed that his plans were none of the clearest.

He took his book home, and read and re-read it with infinite labour, until he not only entirely mastered all in the volume that before appeared to

him somewhat vague and ambiguous, but he acquired an extensive knowledge of the English language which served him greatly hereafter.

The result of his study of the book—the conclusion at which he arrived—was that the first step was to discover the hiding-place of this Cecily.

To gain this end he employed the detective police, though without success. He also searched himself, and was indefatigable in his inquiries, though with the same unfortunate result.

At last, convinced that his search was hopeless, and that he was only wasting time and money to no purpose, he gave the affair up as a bad job, and returned to France again without attaining his object.

Bitterly mortified and humiliated by his failure, it may easily be imagined how intensely delighted he was at the unexpected meeting with Ruth.

The scheme he now proposed, and the expense of which, for the most part, he proposed to defray out of his own private purse—for he was enormously rich, and did not, either, despair of getting the greater part of the money back again in the long run—was that Ruth should go at once to London, and should straightway repair to the Convent of St. Sorehouses, where the Lady Abbess would be able to give her a great deal of very necessary information respecting the personal appearance of her sister, her way of talking, manners, deportment, &c.

The diary which he gave to her would inform her pretty well all that occurred in this love affair. What it did not explain—namely, how far the intrigue had gone—he left to sense and cunning to discover.

Then she was to make herself as much as possible to resemble her sister, which would indeed be no very difficult task, surely; as without any disguise or alteration she was so strikingly like the portrait of the mother, to whom Cecily, in her diary, said that she herself bore such a strong resemblance, that the old priest at first could not believe that he was looking upon anything else than Ruth's portrait, on comparing Ruth's face with the face contained in the brooch.

Having effected the necessary alterations in her personal appearance, she was to go down to the country place of which Mr. Vivian had been recently made vicar, and after obtaining an introduction to him by some means or other, she was to resume the influence over him which her sister had undoubtedly possessed.

This done, she was to effect his ruin.

She was, if possible, to induce him to forsake his faith and embrace the Roman Catholic religion; if not, she was to beguile him from the paths of rectitude and honour.

It mattered not much how his fall was effected, or into what depths he fell, as long as he did fall, and his ruin, dishonour, and disgrace were certain.

The priest could scarcely have selected a better instrument for his purpose than Ruth, as far as her powers of seduction were concerned; but whether or not she would keep good faith with him, the reader and I may perhaps have our doubts, knowing as we do what sort of a young lady she was.

If he had been as well acquainted with her character as we are, it is probable that he would have hesitated for some time before he placed himself in her hands.

He was, however, what vulgar people would term a very green old man, although he was the originator of a scheme of villany worthy of a much blacker scoundrel than he could ever boast of being.

The idea was not altogether his own.

He adopted it, and he proposed it to Ruth; though had he been in her place he would not have had the remotest notion how to set about putting it into execution.

She had. She saw at the first glimpse he gave her of the scheme, that it was one by which she would profit considerably if she only played her cards well.

The only objection to going back to England was her fear of again falling into the hands of some of her enemies.

But that fear was overcome when she heard that she was not expected to go to London.

Without any hesitation, she expressed herself willing, and he supplied her at once with some money to take her safely to England, at the same time handing her the book.

"By the way," said Ruth, as she took it into her hand, "you did not tell me how you got this diary."

"Well, it is almost more than I can tell you," replied the priest, with a smile.

"More than you can tell me?"

"Yes."

CHAPTER CVIII.

THE OLD MAN DESCRIBES, AT LENGTH, CERTAIN TERRIBLE OCCURRENCES WHICH TOOK PLACE IN A LONDON HOTEL; SHOWS HOW HE WAS ROBBED OF HIS BED-CLOTHES RAN AFTER THE THIEF, AND DIDN'T CATCH HIM; AND HOW HE FOUND HIMSELF, INSTEAD, VERY UNPLEASANTLY SITUATED WITH RESPECT TO A CERTAIN ELDERLY LADY.

"What on earth do you mean?" asked Ruth.

"Well, it was a most extraordinary affair, as you shall hear."

"I am extremely anxious."

"I was staying, then, at an hotel in the West End of London; and one night I went to bed at the time I was in the habit of retiring to rest, though, upon this occasion, I neglected to lock the door—a precaution which, I believe, is not unnecessary in London, a great, but sinful, city."

"It is a precaution that it is not usual to omit in any hotel, I should think, either in England or any other country. But I interrupt you."

"I had come to London only that morning, and I had had a great deal of business to transact of one sort and another; the consequence was that I was dreadfully fatigued. I had been dining with Cardinal Benetoi, at that time staying in London, and with whom I had some business. There were a great many people at his house, and it was very late before I could get away, for I was obliged to stay until the last guest had departed in the hope of obtaining an hour's private conversation with the Cardinal.

"I was, indeed, so profoundly weary in mind and body when I got into the cab which one of his Grace's servants procured for me, that I fell fast asleep almost as soon as the cab started; and I did not wake up until the sound of the cab door being opened aroused me in front of the door of the hotel.

"It was an hotel to which I had been recommended by a brother priest. Those of my order whom business took occasionally to London were in the habit of frequenting it. It was very clean and comfortable, though rather expensive.

"Perhaps, if you could have made a complaint, it was that the waiters were rather too attentive, and forced their offers of service upon one until their anxiety to do something for one became rather a bore. But waiters are always so to elderly gentlemen, who, they suppose, will be liberal when the bill is settled.

"I have said that I was dreadfully tired. I could scarcely keep my eyes open when I got into the hotel, and I was exasperated beyond endurance by the peristent inquiries of three or four waiters, who would, in spite of my constant refusals, continue to ask whether I would like to take any refreshment, whether they could show me to the coffee-room, whether they should conduct me to the smoking-room; and one impudent rascal had the audacity to ask if I were looking for the billiard-room!

"The fact is, that upon entering the hotel, the porter had given me a letter, and I was reading it in the passage, foolishly enough, instead of taking it to my room. But the reason why I did it was because I had no pen and ink up-stairs, and I was not certain whether or not I should require to send an answer.

"After reading the letter twice, however, I decided that an answer was necessary, and went into the coffee-room to write one.

"I was a long while performing my task, for I was too tired to think; and you may judge of my intense annoyance when, just as I was completing the epistle, the waiter announced a visitor—the person who had written to me.

"The object of his visit had no reference to the story that I am telling; I only allude to this circumstance, the Cardinal's dinner, and the letter, to show you how fatigued I was likely to be.

"To make a long story short, then, I retired to bed at length, more dead than alive; and, pulling off my clothes as hastily as possible, after I had said my prayers, I scrambled into bed, and quite forgot to fasten the door of the bed-room.

"I certainly returned thanks to heaven for the welcome rest, and I closed my eyes with a hope that I might never again pass such a day, but that, if I did, I should have as comfortable a couch to repose in at its close.

"That I was somewhat hasty in designating the bed 'comfortable,' you will soon have an opportunity of judging.

"Although I had never been so tired in all my life, I found that I could not possibly obtain a wink of sleep. To say, under the circumstances, that one cannot close his eyes, is absurd, for I closed mine, and kept them resolutely shut, but without any effect.

"Occasionally, I managed to doze off for a few moments, but it was only to wake up in a cold perspiration, trembling at some fearful vision which had appeared to me in my half-slumbering state.

"It was once that waking up like this, I felt a human hand upon my head.

"The hand was as cold as the hand of a corpse. It was perfectly quiet. I felt its clammy fingers grasping my bald head, and leaning heavily upon it.

"I cannot explain to you exactly how, awaking suddenly from a state of semi-consciousness, I knew at once that the weight resting upon my head was that of a hand, but I did know it in a moment.

"The first thought that occurred to me, as my mind slowly recovered itself from the supernatural terrors that had in sleep oppressed it, was to think that the visitor to my bedroom was the denizen of another world.

"Reflection and reason, however, soon forced me to another and more probable solution of the occurrence.

"It was a thief!

"I knew not what to do—whether to make a sudden spring at my assailant—whether to be perfectly still—whether to scream loudly for help

"The last course, I decided, would not be a very wise proceeding, but which of the others would be better it would be extremely difficult to determine.

"I suppose that in such cases it generally is.

"However the intruder, whoever he was, saved me the trouble

"Leaving go of my head, his hand travelled rapidly down my breast.

"I made sure that he was feeling for my heart, and that in another moment he would plunge a knife into me.

"I strove to shriek out now, but could not.

"I felt him grapple the bedclothes.

"He was pulling them down, I supposed, so that they might not interfere with the blow, or ward off the fatal stroke.

"I could not, not to have saved my life, have opened my lips. I only lay and trembled. Next moment, the bedclothes were violently jerked off, and the intruder made towards the door.

"Then the spell-bound state in which I had remained hitherto tongue-tied deserted me, and I rushed madly in pursuit.

"When I found that the thief, whoever he was, did not want my life, my courage returned. They were most extraordinary things to steal, a man's bedclothes. I could not understand it; but there was no time to reason about the matter. While I was asking myself what could be his motive, the vagabond was getting away

"I must catch him first, catechise him afterwards.

"I am not a fast runner, and the thief was as rapid as a greyhound. He soon managed to distance me. I scampered up-stairs, along passages, and through corridors, like a madman.

"I had ever so many falls, and hurt myself very much against sharp corners and hard walls I did not expect to find in my path.

"The end of it all was, that while I was sprawling upon the ground, after an awkwarder tumble than usual, he escaped; and though I crept along the passages, and listened attentively at all the doors I passed, I could hear nothing of him.

"What was to be done now? What could be done?

"In the very strange condition in which I found myself, I had absolutely nothing on but an extremely short under garment.

"It was perfectly impossible, and altogether out of the question, that I should dream of raising an alarm.

"No; before I could do that, I must get back to my room, and resume my apparel.

"But where was my room? In that wilderness of an hotel I had been running wildly, harum-scarum, I knew not whither.

"When I came to think the matter over, I had not the remotest notion which way to turn, or in what direction to bend my steps.

"As well as I could judge, however, my bedroom must be upon some floor lower down than the one upon which I then found myself, for I had continued to mount for some time higher and higher, while chasing the impudent vagabond who purloined my blankets.

"I set off in search of my apartment with as little delay as possible; and as there was no other way of arriving at the object of my search, I felt the handle of every door I came to, to ascertain whether it was unfastened.

"'In this way,' I thought to myself, 'I shall be able to find my room; only the Lord guard me from going accidentally into the wrong place.'

"I wandered along in this fashion, trying the doors, though without success; and in time I arrived in the third passage, which I had not investigated.

"I had my hand upon the handle of the first door, when, suddenly, I paused, stood perfectly motionless, and listened.

"I had heard a rustling sound coming up-stairs.

"I heard the creaking of the steps, the sound of breathing.

"Who was it? Who could it be but the miscreant in search of whom I had run half over the house?

"'This time he shan't escape me,' I muttered to myself.

"But I thought I would not make a hasty rush, or he might again lead me on a wild-goose chase. No, this time I would follow him to his destination.

"He passed me by without perceiving me. I crept after him. He felt his way cautiously down the passage.

"'If this is the passage in which my bedroom is situated,' thought I — 'and I have very strong reason for thinking that it is—the wretch is returning to my room for the purpose of still further plundering me.'

"I followed in his track like an Indian savage, stealthily, noiselessly, gloating over the vengeance I would have.

"He opened the door of a room, and passed in. He left the door open behind him.

"I glided in after him, and shutting it noiselessly, turned the key in the lock.

"The sound, though slight, alarmed him, and he cried, 'Who's there?'

"It was a weak voice — the voice of an effeminate man—in my opinion, a man possessing very little physical force.

"'I should soon be able to overcome him,' I thought to myself, with a smile

"I, however, made no answer, and the thief, evidently in alarm, sought for a box of matches and hastily struck a light.

"As the sulphur glared I obtained my first view of the enemy, and if I live to be a hundred, I shall never forget my sensations.

The enemy wore a frilled night-cap. The enemy was not of the male sex.

"The person I had followed into her bedroom was an elderly female of severe aspect.

"She could not be the person who had stolen my bed-clothes. No, there was not the slightest reason for so believing.

"She was a wrong person altogether. I had made an awful mistake, and now what on earth was I to do?

CHAPTER CIX.

CONTINUES THE OLD GENTLEMAN'S STORY, AND SHOWS WHAT THE ELDERLY LADY SAID AND DID AND WHAT AGONY THE OLD GENTLEMAN SUFFERED

"The situation was truly awful.

"I trust that I shall never be placed in a similar position, for it makes my blood run cold now when I think of it. I give you my word of honour, it does."

And the poor old gentleman wiped his head at the recollection of what he had suffered.

"You're laughing," said the old priest, suddenly, happening to turn his eyes towards Ruth's face.

"Oh, no!" cried that young lady, energetically.

"Are not you?" asked the old gentleman, doubtfully.

"No."

"I thought you were."

"You were mistaken."

"Because there does not seem to me to be much to laugh at."

"Oh, no—quite the contrary."

"Well, don't laugh, that's all, or I shan't tell you."

"I wouldn't do so for the world"

"But in spite of the promise she made, it was extremely difficult to refrain from doing so, because not only did the narration of the old gentleman's misfortunes appear to her to be extremely ludicrous, but it also brought very vividly to her recollection a certain narration which Captain Charley Crockford had obliged her with.

Yes, Captain Charley had been the thief, as the reader will remember. He it was who had entered the hotel by the balcony, and left it again by the chimney, stealing, on the way, the blankets, and sheets, and counterpane belonging to the poor old priest, and leaving in their place the brooch and diary, which he had purloined from Sister Cecily's cell.

"Won't Charley laugh," Ruth thought to herself, "if ever I meet him again, and tell him the priest's version of the adventure?"

She looked as serious as possible, however, for fear of offending the old gentleman; and entreated him, as a great favour, to continue his narrative.

And, after a little pressing, he did so.

"For some time," said he, "the elderly lady did not look in my direction, because she was too much occupied with the wick of the candle, which, having been squeezed into the tallow—it had fallen down out of the candlestick, and that was how she came to be walking about in the dark — obstinately refused to stand up to be lighted.

"She, however, mastered it at last; and then she turned her eyes slowly round, until they alighted upon my countenance, with an expression of wild terror, the recollection of which will not very easily desert me.

"'Good heaven!' cried she, 'who's that?'

"'Madam,' said I, 'don't be alarmed.'

"'Great heaven!' cried she, 'it's a man!'

"'I regret to say it is,' said I.

"'How did you come?'

"'I can't say'

"'What are you going to do?'

"'Get out again, as quickly as possible, if you will allow me?'

"With that intention I rose, and made for the door, for up to now I had been crouching down upon the ground, endeavouring to lend a little additional length to my shirt tails.

"Perhaps it was only when I rose that she became conscious of the extreme scantiness and impropriety of my apparel; or, perhaps, she did not understand my motive in rising, for she uttered a piercing scream.

"'For mercy's sake!' I cried, in terror; 'don't do that, you will alarm the whole house!'

"'Horrible man!' she replied; 'that is what I intend to do!'

"'If you carry out your intention I shall be ruined!'

"'And if I do not, I shall be so, perhaps!'

"'I assure you, upon my word of honour, no harm shall befall you.'

"'How can I believe you?'

"'I am sure you will, if you will listen to my story. Somebody burst into my bedroom, and stole my bedclothes. I rushed after them They eluded my pursuit in the dark. I mistook you for them. I followed you in here!'

"'But what made you lock the door?'

"'To secure the thief, as I supposed, of course.

"'Do you know what you have done?'

"'No!'

"'You've fastened us in the room together!'

"'Of course; but if you will allow me, I will——'

"'What?'

"'Open the door!'

"'You can't!'

"'I can't?'

"'No!'

"'Why not?'

"'Because the lock sticks fast! That is why I did not lock it myself!'

"'Good heavens! But do you really mean ——'

"'I do——Try to open it. No; stop where you are. Let me try. Please not to move. Don't stir, or I'll scream!'

"'Madam,' said I, 'I have no wish to do so!'

"The elderly lady, pursing up her lips and avoiding me with her eyes, a circumstance for which I can assure you I was extremely thankful—for, being painfully conscious of the dreadfully indecent figure I was cutting, I was crouching as low down and as close to the wall as I could possibly get—proceeded to the door of the room.

"The elderly lady certainly did struggle manfully with the lock of the door, but without success. What could have been the matter with the lock I cannot imagine, but it had managed somehow or other to stick fast, and no effort of which she was capable would move it.

"After I had watched her for some time vainly struggling, I mildly interposed.

"'Madam,' said I, if you would allow me——'

"'What the plague do you sit there for then, gaping like an owl?'

"'But, my dear madam—if you would be so kind——'

"'So kind as what?'

"As to retire to the other end of the room while I make an effort. You haven't got such a thing as a dressing gown?'

"'Do you suppose I would lend it, sir?'

"'Don't put yourself out of the way on my account, I beg; I can make a dress out of these towels.'

"Don't stir, then, till I get behind the curtains.'

"So saying, the lady hastily retired, and with the greatest haste that I was capable of, I manufactured a kind of robe with the aid of the towels upon a horse standing by my side, and some pins which happened to be on a pincushion on the dressing table.

"When I had done this I devoted myself to the task of mastering the lock.

"It was anything but an easy task, though, let me assure you; and it was a task that overcame my efforts, and defeated me entirely.

"How it was that it had stuck fast in this abominably absurd and ridiculously exasperating fashion I have not the vaguest idea. But it had stuck fast, and it would not open, and I struggled in vain.

"Hearing me cease, the elderly lady called out from behind the curtain where she had taken refuge, 'Can you manage it?'

"'I can't,' said I.

"'What is to be done?' said she.

"'I haven't the least idea,' said I.

"'But you surely don't imagine that you can remain all night in my apartment, do you?'

"'You know well enough that nothing would please me more than to get out of it.'

"'This dreadful scene will be the death of me.'

"'Fiddlestick, ma'am!' cried I in a rage; 'it will much likelier be the death of me, for I shall catch my death of cold!'

"'Think of the scandal!' said she.

"'Think of these wet towels!' said I.

"'Think of my reputation!'

"'Think of rheumatism!'

"We abused each other for a good half-hour, I should think, and only left off doing so to talk more reasonably, owing to the elderly lady being out of breath.

"'Drat the man!' said she, at last. 'Can't you make a suggestion?'

"What suggestion?' asked I in despair.

"'You know you can't stop here,' said she. 'That's settled'

"'Is it?' said I. 'I wish it was.'

"'Can't you jump out of window?'

"'No.'

"'Why?'

"'Because it's a great deal too high.'

"'Can you climb up the chimney?'

"'No.'

"'Why?'

"'Because I'm a great deal too big.'

"'You can get up if you try.'

"'No I can't.'

"'Why not?'

"'I shall stick fast.'

"'Never mind that'

"'Thank you.'

"Then we began to abuse one another again.

"'Gracious heavens!' cried the lady, suddenly.

"'What now?'

"'The candle's going out.'

"'What of that?'

"'What of that, you monster! Do you suppose that I could remain in the dark with you?'

"'I don't think you can help yourself.'

"'I shall faint!'

"'Do as you please.'

"'I shall scream!'

"'If you do, ma'am, I'll murder you!'

"The fact was, I was getting desperate. My situation grew every moment more alarming.

"In short, there was no more time to waste in folly of any kind. I boldly laid the matter before her Here was I, shut up, much against my will, in the bed-chamber of an antiquated maiden lady, who, according to her own account, had a reputation to lose.

"I did not dispute that proposition. All I said was that I had also a reputation, and, if I lost it, the loss would be very serious, for with it would come the most entire shame and disgrace.

"There was no way of getting out of the room until the morning, that I could see, because by this time the inmates of the hotel had in all probability retired to rest; and under what pretext could she disturb them?

"Until the morning, then, I must remain where I was; and how I was to escape then and retire to my own room, was more than I could tell. However, I could only wait for daylight, and pray for a safe delivery from the awful situation into which I had fallen.

"Even if I had been allowed to remain, wrapped up in the damp towels, and seated upon a hard chair by the door, the situation would have been none of the pleasantest, as you may suppose; but it was the pleasure of this inexorable and preposterous old woman that I should be locked up in a small closet usually set apart as a receptacle for dirty linen.

"And here, squatted upon the ground, in an awfully cramped and uncomfortable position, I passed the weary night away, in my soul believing that I should have given up the ghost before the happy hour of release arrived.

"But morning did come at last; and the old lady, ringing the bell, obtained assistance.

"The door was very easily opened, and she very easily obtained her freedom; but how I was to obtain mine, was quite another question.

"When the lady was alone, she came to my door, and having tapped, asked whether I was ready to go.

"'I am,' I said, 'but I can't.'

"'Why, not, in heaven's name?'

"'Because I don't know the number of my room.'

"'You had better go out and look for it.'

"'What! in this state?'

"'Well, what else do you propose?'

"'I can't remain here.'

"'Certainly not! Go!'

"'First find out the number of my room.'

"'How am I to do it?'

"I gave her my name, and instructions how she was to proceed—namely, that she was to go down stairs and inquire of the landlord, under the pretext that she wanted to send a message up to me; and then, having ascertained the number, to change her mind, and presently come up-stairs herself and impart the requisite information.

"Would you believe it? the monster in human form had her baggage conveyed down stairs, got into a coach which she had ordered, and departed without helping me in the least.

"I remained in the cupboard for several hours, suffering a martyrdom, and seeing no hope of release.

"At last, unable any longer to bear the misery I was enduring, I disclosed myself to a chambermaid, who came into the room to make the bed.

"To her I told my story, and though she was at first inclined to summon assistance, and have me given into the custody of the police as a burglar, upon my promising her a five-pound note she found out my bedroom, brought me my clothes, and enabled me to escape."

"And that," said Ruth, who had been scarcely able to keep serious throughout the priest's story, "was the end of your troubles?"

"Not quite," said the old man. "The impudent young hussy pretended not to believe a word of my story, and affected to think that I had been engaged in some disgraceful intrigue. The consequence was, that during my whole stay in London she pursued me remorselessly, and with threats of exposing me, contrived to extort a series of bribes, which, in the end, amounted to an almost fabulous sum."

"Good gracious!"

"You may well say so; and even to this day she every now and then writes to me for another small trifle 'on account.'"

"I hope no other misofrtunes befel you at the time?"

"Nothing worth relating," said the old man. "I had suffered enough, surely. I thanked heaven, though, when I turned my back upon it for good, I can assure you."*

"But," said Ruth, after a pause, "you did not tell me, af er all, how you obtained possession of the diary and the brooch?"

"To be sure! I forgot to say I found them in a livery coat which had been left in my bedroom by the person who had stolen the bedclothes. And now take care you lose neither of them; and if you are ready, I will conduct you to the door——"

But just as the old man was rising to his feet for that purpose, a loud tapping at the door startled him.

He hastily advanced towards it, and inquired of the young priest, whom he found shivering and shaking outside, what was the matter.

"They—they are coming!" stammered the younger man.

"Who?" asked the other, eagerly.

"The—the gaolers!"

"What do you mean?"

"They say some one has escaped," said the young man; "and they think he has come in here."

And as he spoke, the sound of footsteps was heard approaching, and loud voices were heard, talking in excited tones.

* To those who are cu ious to know what other adventure happened to this unfortunate old gentleman, I respectfully refer them to the adventures of "The Short Man," in Chapter XXXVIII of Ruth's history.

"Well," said the old priest, "what does that matter? Let them search."

"But if they do, they—they——"

"They what?"

"They will find her!"

"Well, they won't know she is a woman."

"They may recognise her face."

"Recognise! Why what do you mean? Is she——"

"Yes—I believe——"

"He is right!" cried Ruth, breaking in here upon the conference. "I have escaped from the prison; you must shelter me."

"I—I shall not be able to do so."

"Why not?"

"There is no hiding place"

Ruth looked round the cell.

There were no curtains, no cupboards, no place to conceal her.

"No time to be lost," she said in a low tone. "I must hide in the bed."

"No, no, in the name of all the saints, don't do that," cried the old man, in terror.

But ere he could interpose, the bold adventuress had plunged under the blanket, pulling it up over her head.

The young priest could not refrain from indulging in a mild snigger at the old gentleman's expense.

It seemed to him something like retributive justice that he should be in a bit of a fix.

"Poor dear old man!" thought Ruth to herself. "He is a regular victim to the ladies. And to think that he is so pious through it all! Well, I shall live to see him go wrong through the force of circumstances, I do believe. He's rather old to begin, but there's no knowing. They say old gentlemen are worse than young ones once they take a fancy, and that an old man in love is sillier than any lad."

And she laughed to such an extent that the bed shook.

"For heaven's sake, be quiet!" cried the old priest. "Here they are!"

CHAPTER CX.

THE FRENCHMAN'S FRIGHTFUL DEATH.

We left the Frenchman locked up in the cupboard.

Let us now return to him.

Through his agency was it that alarm had arisen. His indiscretion had led to a discovery of the two prisoners' flight. To his own folly was his dreadful doom to be attributed, as we shall see.

The poor coward remained screwed up into the smallest possible space, and trembling in every limb, until he heard the last sound of the footsteps of Ruth and the young priest die away in the distance.

Then, when they were out of earshot, he began to breathe more freely.

"He! he!" he sniggered to himself "What a fool she was to go with him! I wouldn't have trusted him."

He was a little tipsy, as I have already stated, and like other tipsy people, he thought himself extremely cunning; so he stood there chuckling at his own astonishing sagacity, till he remembered all at once that he felt thirsty, and he continued the uncorking of the bottle, the noise of which, when he before had attempted it, had led to Ruth's discovery.

But he was alone now, and there was no fear of the noise being heard; so he drew the cork fearlessly, and took a deep gulp at the contents of the bottle.

Suddenly a bright idea penetrated his gnat's brain.

He snapped his fingers and kicked up his heels at the thought of it.

"A glorious idea! a splendid idea! a magnificent idea!" he cried ecstatically.

And what was it, do you think?

While the priest and Ruth were absent, he would break into the box himself, and break out of the chapel, and make his escape.

By following this course, don't you see what a pull he had over his companions?

If he waited for them, and shared the money with them, his share would only be a third. If he took it himself without their help, he could take it all.

You must know that previous to his incarceration, this young gentleman had not possessed any thievish propensities, as you might be led to suppose by his conduct now.

He had been an author, and had made what money he had made—that is, enough to starve upon genteelly—by composing words for music, writing small poems in miscellanies, and scurrilous articles upon the leading men of the day.

After a fashion, then, as the world goes, you see, his life had been an honest one.

It was only since he had broken out of prison that he had become a hardened criminal. Perhaps it was owing to his association with that arch corrupter of innocence and good manners, Mistress Ruth. Or perhaps he reasoned with himself upon the principle of in for a penny, in for a pound.

"Perhaps," he said to himself, "if I have the misfortune to get caught, I shall catch it pretty hot. If I can help it, I mustn't get caught. How am I to avoid it, though? I have no money to keep me on my road. Here is money; why shouldn't I take it? I shan't be punished much worse for having done so, than I should if I left it alone. I will take it."

There were several difficulties to be overcome before he could carry out his plan.

The first was to break open the door, which was locked upon him.

This was not a very difficult job, though. And he managed it this way.

He placed his back against the wall and his feet against the door, and he pushed with all his might.

It was a capital plan, as far as opening the door was concerned, and had only one drawback, which some people might be inclined to look upon as a trifle.

When the door gave way, the support for his feet of course gave way with it, and he came down with a run upon the back of his head, with a concussion which, to say the least of, surprised him very considerably.

He picked himself up, and rubbed his head and other parts of him, which had been somewhat damaged by the fall, and swore all the oaths he could think of.

Then he began to grope about for the light, which Ruth had extinguished, as the reader may remember, when the couple were first alarmed by the approach of the young priest.

He found it without much difficulty, and a match, and struck a light.

"Now for the money," said he.

And he approached the box.

"How is it to be opened? It looks awfully strong."

He laid hold of the lid, not because he thought for a moment that he would be able to lift it; and as he did so, he uttered an exclamation of joy.

The box was unlocked.

The next instant he flung wide open the lid.

The next, he was gazing down upon the treasure within.

"There's lots of it," he said. "There's more than I can carry, I believe. What a nuisance!"

He knelt down by the side of the box to examine its contents.

There were two canvass bags.

One full of gold, and one full of five franc pieces.

Besides that, there were a quantity of massive silver candlesticks, dishes, plates, &c.

"I can't carry it all, curse it!" he muttered.

And he felt quite savage.

Ind ed, the idea that he would be obliged to leave some behind exasperated him to that extent, he felt for a moment inclined to leave it all.

But he did not remain long in that mind, as you may imagine, and he soon began to think what would be the best way of carrying what he could carry.

He gave up the idea of the plate and candlesticks as a bad job.

Then about the bags?

They were very heavy.

One was as much as he could conveniently get along with; but then the idea of leaving the other behind!

Such an idea could not be endured.

So he must take both. It was extremely annoying to think that the stupid old fools could not have kept their money in a smaller compass, and had it all in gold, instead of these lumbering silver pieces.

But now that could not be remedied.

He must put up with the money as he could get it and be thankful.

His was not exactly a nature to be thankful, though. He would have grumbled if it had been two sacks of diamonds, I really believe.

After a great deal of consideration and deliberation, to which was added occasional imprecation, he decided upon emptying the gold out of the bag into his pockets, and slinging the silver to his waist.

He very soon effected this arrangement, and then he was ready to be off.

And surely he had already wasted as much time as he safely could.

Yes, he must be off.

He took the light in one hand, and shading his eyes with the other, came stealthily out into the chapel, and gazed around through the uncertain gloom which surrounded him.

Crossing the chapel floor, and passing the benches and chairs upon which, during service, the congregation were wont to be seated, he approached the principal door communicating with the street without.

It was locked, as he had anticipated.

The way then left to him was to keep close to the wall, and examine the doors and windows as he came to them, to see where an egress could be anywhere effected.

The result was not satisfactory.

It then occurred to him that from the vaults an escape could probably be made.

If he could escape at all, that must be the way.

He had heard the young priest say that there was a way in which it could be managed.

Perhaps the way he alluded to lay through the monastery.

In that case he was sold, for the monastery door was locked.

He had just tried it, and found such to be the case

He was not long, however, in finding a door and a flight of stairs communicating with the vaults below.

The vaults were extensive, and he spent a considerable time in searching through them, with a hope of discovering an outlet.

One only could he see.

This was a small window or grating, through which he could, with some difficulty, squeeze himself.

When he had squeezed himself through, he stood upon a narrow ledge of stonework a little more than half a foot broad, and about eight feet from the river, which crept sluggishly past the prison wall below.

This projecting ledge ran along for about twenty or thirty yards.

It terminated at a flight of steps.

At the bottom of the steps there was moored a boat.

The Frenchman took all these things in at a rapid glance. He saw his way to freedom.

He saw how it was to be done; and now only one difficulty remained—doing it!

If he had been Blondin, there would not have been much cause for further hesitation Eight feet was a very trifling distance, you will say; and had flagstones lain beneath his feet, instead of water, in all probability the fall, if he had fallen, would not have hurt him much.

Probabilities are, that he would not have broken many bones.

Had he been a swimmer, twenty yards, you may say, would not have been very far to swim.

But there were two reasons why, under the circumstances, the Frenchman did not feel inclined to face the water.

One was, that he could not swim any more than a stone.

The other was that even if he could have swam under other circumstances, the weight of gold in his pockets, and the weight of silver slung to his waist, would, most certainly, have sunk him.

The risk must be made.

He must keep his balance as well as he could—keep as close as possible to the wall, and creep along until he reached the stairs.

He had already let himself out of the window, as I have said.

He hesitated for some minutes before he finally left go of the bar by which he was supporting himself.

But he did leave go at last, and started upon his perilous journey.

He thought that he would be better able to keep his balance if he stepped boldly forward, and no doubt he was right, but, unfortunately, he did not start fair.

He had made a great mistake, and he did not find his mistake out until he had got too far to remedy it.

He had got at least three yards from the window before he made the fatal discovery.

Then he discovered, to his horror and dismay, that he had hung the bag of silver on the wrong side of him.

Upon the side of him nearest to the water.

The result may, of course, be easily imagined.

He lost his balance.

Vainly and fruitlessly he struggled to maintain it.

He saw that it was hopeless.

He saw that he was doomed.

That a watery grave awaited him in the black and sluggish waters beneath.

He knew that he must fall, and the only chance for his life would have been to have got as near as possible to the steps, so that he might have scrambled into the boat.

By those means there would have been a chance of saving himself.

If he had only had the presence of mind to make a rush forward.

But he lost heart and courage.

He knew that he could not swim. He knew that the weight of the cursed money he had about him would take him down, and hold him down.

That he would be drowned—that he had been his own murderer—that his avarice and cupidity had slain him.

He knew also that close beneath the prison walls the water was many feet deep. That when he sank he would go straight to the bottom.

He knew also that it would be useless to scream for help.

That no help could reach him.

That even had it been possible for help to have come, it would not have come, and that to attract attention was to covet death.

Yet, knowing this, he could not refrain from screaming aloud.

"Help!—help!—help!" he shrieked.

He struggled vainly and frantically to hold on by the smooth, slippery wall.

Poor fool! his efforts were unavailing.

He clawed, and clung, and wept, and screamed.

There was nothing to claw at—nothing to cling to—nothing to keep him from the yawning grave beneath.

"Oh, heaven! Help!—help!—help!"

The money-bag dragged him down.

He tottered.

He staggered.

He fell.

His piercing shriek rent the air, but no help came to him

The cold, black waters closed over his head.

They gurgled in his ears and mouth. They bubbled and frothed over the spot where his body had sank.

But only for a few brief moments.

Then all was still.

Day was breaking. No boats or vessels were visible upon the smooth surface of the water.

Only one living soul had been witness of the Frenchman's dreadful death.

This was a sentinel upon the ramparts.

He shouted aloud, and called for help.

Another sentinel came up.

"A man has fallen out of a window into the water."

"Where is he?"

"He's drowned."

"Shall we give the alarm?"

"Yes, perhaps it's a prisoner."

"They won't be able to catch him, if it is."

"That won't matter. It will look as if we were zealous after duty."

"Perhaps we shall get promoted."

"No doubt of it."

"I'm very glad it happened."

"So am I. I dreamed I was going to be lucky last night; but I never thought I should have been as lucky as this."

"So you see it's an ill wind that blows nobody any good."

The soldiers were pleased, if the Frenchman wasn't.

The young priest, who meant to have stolen the money, was rather vexed.

Ruth did not care twopence about the matter, as she had given up the idea of participating in the robbery.

I do not exactly like to state it as my opinion that she would have pushed the Frenchman into the water, but, supposing he had been in the water. I don't mind taking my oath that she would not have stretched out her hand to pull him out.

CHAPTER CXI.

COMING TO CLOSE QUARTERS.—THE CHASE GETS HOT.

"I say!" exclaimed Ruth, suddenly popping her head out of the bed.

"For heaven's sake, lie still!" cried the terrified old priest.

"No but, I say——"

"Do lie still!"

"Don't you think I had better ——"

"Yes, yes—you had much better be quiet."

"I don't mean that. I want to know whethre I had not better take off my coat and boots?"

"Why, in the name of St Peter?"

"Because they are sure to see there is somebody in bed"

"No, they won't, if you lie flat."

"I can't lie flat enough to escape notice."

"We are ruined, if they catch sight of you."

"Not if you do as I tell you."

"What do you propose, then?"

"That I should take off my boots and coat, and you should say I am a young priest from another monastery, and a friend of yours."

"Quick!—quick, then!"

"I won't be a moment."

"We have not a moment to lose."

Ruth sprang from the bed, and with lightning rapidity divested herself of her upper garment and her shoes.

She was proceeding, also, to take off her stockings, but the old priest stopped her in terror.

"You will be caught!—you will be caught! What will become of us?"

"Bless me!" cried Ruth, with a laugh; "what an old bungler you are, to be sure! Leave me alone; I shall not be a second, if you don't worry me."

The old priest thought it best to leave her to do what she chose.

Indeed, he could not offer any resistance, for he was absolutely at his wits' end.

It was a spectacle at which one would hardly have known whether it was correct to laugh or cry, that of the poor old man, trotting backwards and forwards in the cell, wringing his hands and smiting his breast, and calling himself the unluckiest and unhappiest wretch upon the face of the earth.

Meanwhile, the footsteps of the gaolers drew nearer and nearer.

The young priest keeping guard at the door, reported that they were close at hand.

In another moment they would reach the cell which sheltered the fugitive and the two priests who were conniving at her escape.

Before they had reached the door, however, greatly to the old gentleman's relief, Ruth had hidden herself in the bed, and was lying so flat in the bed that it was with the greatest difficulty that even those who were well aware of her presence therein could detect the faintest outline of her form.

The old priest had pulled his young companion by the arm and forced him to come back inside the cell, for he weakly enough entertained some sort of faint and feeble hope that the party in search of Ruth might pass his door without trying it.

The question was, were they examining the cells as they came along?

No, their approach had been too rapid.

They were advancing straight towards the old priest's cell, intending, no doubt, as head of the establishment, to consult him respecting the steps they should take for examining the monastery.

The old priest and his companion stood listening at the door, with palpitating hearts, to the footsteps, which drew nearer and nearer.

At last, they paused in front of the very door.

Then, suddenly, upon one of the upper panels, fell one single blow, loud and sharp.

The old priest's knees knocked together under him.

He looked towards his companion in mute terror.

The countenance of the younger man was the colour of paste. He was supporting himself against the wall, and shaking like a leaf.

"D-d-d-don't t-t-tremble so, you c-c-coward," stammered the old man.

"I'm not t-t-trembling," replied the other, indignantly.

"I t-t-thought you w-w-ere."

"N-n-no, I'm not."

Again a blow fell upon the oaken panel.

It would not do to delay longer before they opened to the gaolers. Even the short delay that had occurred already might be thought to be suspicious by those waiting without for admission.

The old man laid his hand upon the lock of the door, with the intention of throwing it open, when his companion stopped him.

"Father!"

"What is it?"

"Ought we—don't you think that we had better——"

"Well, what—speak?"

"Don't you think we ought to pretend to be doing something?"

"Doing something?"

"To be employed, I mean, in writing or reading?"

"Yes, yes; we ought to be so"

"Shall I get out some books?"

"No, no; there is no time."

Indeed, there was not. Time enough had elapsed already.

A loud thumping was heard without, at the door, and the voices of the gaolers consulting.

"Is any one inside?"

"Yes, there's a light."

"He must have gone to sleep."

"No, I heard voices."

"Break the door open!"

"Not yet. Here, let me knock. I'll take my oath I'll wake him."

The old priest saw that he could trifle with them no longer, and he immediately opened the door.

Then he found himself facing a dozen or more men.

The governor of the gaol, two gaolers, and some soldiers.

The old priest stood motionless, eyeing the company with well-affected astonishment.

"I thought you were dead!" said the Governor.

CHAPTER CXII.

THE CHASE GROWS HOTTER STILL.—THE OLD PRIEST FINDS HIMSELF IN A WORSE PICKLE THAN EVER, AND HIS REPUTATION BEGINS TO SUFFER CONSIDERABLY.—ANOTHER EXAMPLE OF THE OLD PROVERB, THAT TELLS US WE SHOULD LOOK BEFORE WE LEAP.

"Dead?" repeated the old man, pretending not to understand his meaning.

"Yes, dead! that's what I said," exclaimed the other irritably.

"Why?"

"Why, what on earth made you so hard of hearing?"

The old man, however, replied only by a glance of haughty disdain, as though he thought the other's question and manner to be offensive.

"What do you want with me?" he asked coldly.

"Two prisoners have broken out of the gaol!"

"Well?"

"One has fallen into the river, and has either been drowned, or has swam away and made his escape!"

"Well?"

"We suspect that to be a man. A man and woman have escaped together!"

"Well?"

"The woman we have traced as far as the monastery door, leading into the chapel."

"Well?"

"She is, therefore, we presume, within these walls."

"Impossible!"

"It is, however, very probably the case."

"Where is she, then?"

"That's what we want you to tell us."

"Want me to tell you? What do you mean?"

"I mean, rather, that we want you to aid us in finding out the hiding-place."

"Do you mean to tell me that you believe a person of the other sex to be concealed in this establishment?"

"Exactly!"

"Are you aware that you are bringing a charge against my holy order, which is one of the most horrible that could possibly be conceived?"

"Well, I don't know exactly that I look upon the matter in the same light that you do; but, at the same time, I am well aware that, if any person is wilfully and knowingly giving shelter to the prisoner, they are rendering themselves amenable to a law which is seldom inclined to show much mercy for such an offence."

The Governor chuckled slightly as he said this. The old priest was no favourite of his He was not sorry to be able to give him a quiet slap in the face.

He was highly delighted, indeed, to throw a little mud at the monk's reputation.

He was not an admirer of the order, and he liked to get a chance of ridiculing their much-vaunted chastity.

Besides, there is always a great deal of jealousy betwixt heads of departments.

The Governor, as head of the gaol, thought very little of the old priest as head of the monastery; and though they had to be polite to each other officially, they were neither of them very sorry when an opportunity arose for a little polite slanging and a gentlemanly cuff or two.

If the Governor could only find out that any one of the priests was concealing Ruth in his cell, would not that be nuts to crack for him (the Governor) and all the rest of the scoffers and unbelievers?

Even if he could not succeed in discovering Ruth, it would be a matter of great self-congratulation, because he would be able to disturb the old man to such an awful extent.

He had a perfect right to do so upon such an occasion, and he intended to exercise his power to the utmost.

"Would you have any objection to a search being made?" said the Governor, with affected politeness.

"Of course, I have no objection," replied the priest. "Of course, you can go where you like. The entire establishment is at your disposal."

"I am deeply sensible of your courtesy," replied the Governor, with a bow. "We will, with your permission, commence the search at once."

Had the Governor only at this moment happened to have looked at the old priest's face, it is probable that the search would have been of very short duration.

Surely never in the world was "guilty" written in the face of a trembling prisoner at the bar more than it was written in the old priest's pallid countenance.

The old gentleman rolled his eyes round the cell, and his knees trembled under him.

It cannot exactly be said that he felt a quaking at the heart, because the greatest amount of agitation was in his stomach.

He felt dreadfully faint and sick, and his legs were much too weak to hold his weight; so that, if he had not held on by the door-post, he felt as though he must have fallen head first forward into the Governor's waistcoat.

As for the young priest, his state of terror was perfectly abject. His legs he could place no dependence in, so he had very wisely taken a seat.

He had chosen the edge of the bed, not with any idea of sheltering the person in it, because he had not a sufficient amount of wits about him to think of anything of the kind, and it was Ruth's sheer good luck that he should have chosen that spot.

It was very fortunate, because his body, and the shadow from his body, concealed Ruth's figure effectually.

The Governor glanced carelessly round the room, and saw nothing.

He had not the slightest expectation of finding anything in the old priest's room, for he had no suspicion that the head of the monastery himself would be concerned in the concealment of the notorious malefactor he was in search of.

"Shall we begin?" said the Governor, presently, after waiting for the priest to lead the way.

"Y-y-yes," stammered the poor old gentleman, almost dead with fright, for he expected discovery and disgrace were coming every moment.

"Will you precede us, then?" said the Governor.

"What—what?"

"Will you lead the way?"

Oh, the relief that those words brought to him!

He motioned to the Governor to go first, then called out the young priest, and closed the door of his cell.

The party then proceeded down the passage.

But he had not gone far when an idea occurred to the old gentleman.

He would go back, and give Ruth the key of the chapel, and tell her to escape.

Perhaps she might be able to do so, and perhaps she mightn't. Anyhow, he would get rid of her out of his cell.

"I will join you again in a moment," said he, to the Governor. "Proceed forward, and examine the cloisters; our brother here will show you the way."

Having thus spoken, he hastily retraced his steps, and next moment was standing by Ruth's bedside.

"It's all right," he whispered; "they are gone!"

But she made no answer.

"It's all right!" he said again, shaking her.

Still no reply.

"Good heaven! perhaps she has fainted," thought the old man. "Perhaps she is suffocated—perhaps she is dead!"

It seemed very much like it.

"What *will* become of me?" groaned the poor old gentleman.

He pulled the blanket off her head, expecting to see a corpse.

Miss Ruth lifted up a very red face and towzled head of hair, and yawned.

"I've been asleep," said she.

"Asleep!" cried the old man, aghast. "Is it possible that you can sleep at such a time as this? I don't feel myself as if I shall ever be able to rest any more, except it is in my grave."

"I'll bet you a napoleon, old fellow, that you'd sleep fast enough, if you were as tired as I am, though you knew you were going to be hanged the moment you awoke."

"Come, come, then; let us waste no more time. Will you make an effort to escape?"

"How?"

"Here is the key of the chapel; the gaolers have gone in the other direction."

"What's the good of that? There is no way out of the chapel when I get there."

"Yes, there is; you will find a window in a vault underneath the chapel, looking on to the river."

"What do you expect me to do?"

"Can you swim?"

"I don't mean to try."

"But you can't stop here."

"Why not?"

"Because I shall be ruined if you are found in my cell."

"Well, then, don't let them find me."

"How can I help it, if they insist on searching the cell?"

"My dear sir, that's not my affair. Let me advise you to go back to them, or they will suspect you Come, now, run along, there's a dear old gentleman, and you will make me love you."

The old priest saw it was useless arguing with her; he left the cell with a groan.

"What evil have I ever done, that I should be punished in this way?"

The poor old gentleman was nearly bent double. The blow was a hard one, and a person at his time of life feels being put out of his way more severely than a young man, as you may suppose.

He shut the cell door after him, and then locked it.

He had no hope now of Ruth making herself scarce during his absence His only care, therefore, was to prevent anybody coming in while he was away, and discovering the awful contents of his cell.

He found the Governor and his party prosecuting the search with astonishing vigour and perseverance.

Not a hole or corner escaped them.

Every monk's cell was in turn visited, and subjected to a strict investigation; and it would have been a study for an artist to have seen the faces of the frightened monks, when they woke up, with the light of the lanterns which the gaolers carried falling full upon them, dazzling and bewildering them.

Nothing, however, resulted from the investigation, and in about an hour's time there remained no place unsearched.

The gaolers and soldiers began to murmur among themselves, "Where has she got to? where on earth has she gone to?"

"Is there anywhere else where we can look?" asked the Governor.

"I know of none," replied the old priest.

"I think we have looked everywhere?"

"I believe so."

"I think we had better go," said the Governor at last, speaking in rather a rueful tone

"That is the only thing left for you to do, I fancy," replied the old priest, with a grim smile.

It was a great triumph for him. was it not!

As for the Governor, he felt very crestfallen. He would willingly have given a week of his life if he could have found the missing prisoner in one of the cells. He could then have had the laugh of his friend; but, as it was, the laugh was all against him.

"By the way," said the old priest, "you have not told me what reason you had for supposing that this woman had taken refuge here?"

"We found some footmarks."

"Footmarks!"

"Yes, leading to the door of the monastery."

"Indeed!"

The old man looked rather incredulous. To tell the truth, he hardly believed this statement of the Governor; nor, indeed, was there any reason why he should do so, if we come to look into the matter closely.

Some footsteps! The marks of naked feet had been discovered upon some thinly scattered sand, close to the doorway leading to the monastery; and the Governor had jumped at the conclusion that these footmarks belonged to Ruth.

It might be the case, and it might not. He, at any rate, thought the circumstance gave him sufficient excuse for stirring up his friend, the old priest; and he did so, as we have seen.

He had a faint hope that he might have found her; and now, as he had not, he felt rather small.

"Well," said the Governor, with a sigh, "I suppose we must look elsewhere;" and he bade his men to follow him.

Arriving at his cell door, which they were obliged to pass upon their way back to the chapel, the old priest paused to say "Good night" to them, rather ironically.

He turned the key in the lock, and prepared to enter.

The gaolers and soldiers walked forward, and the Governor appeared as though he were about to follow his men, when suddenly he changed his mind, and retraced his steps.

By this time the old priest had entered his cell, and was about to turn to shut the door.

The Governor stopped him, entered the cell, and shut the door behind him.

The old priest was too terrified to speak, and was too terrified to trust himself to look towards the bed.

Only in his heart he prayed to heaven that she had not gone to sleep again, with her head under the bed-clothes.

He managed also to keep between the Governor and the bed, and he fixed his eyes upon the Governor's face, hoping in that way to prevent his gaze from wandering round the room.

"I want you to lend me pen, ink, and paper," said the Governor. "I must write a message to be sent by the telegraph round the coast. We don't intend the young lady to slip through our fingers easily!"

"Do you think you will catch her?"

"Certain to!"

"What will you do to her?"

"Military law—she'll be flogged and shot!"

The old priest shuddered.

If she were caught, not only would he be disgraced and ruined, he thought, but he would have this woman's blood upon his head!

"Will you oblige me with a pen and ink?"

"Yes, yes—certainly. Sit here, please."

And the old man placed a chair so that the Governor had his back towards the bed.

The Governor, however, being of a very restless

and impetuous nature, was not to be got over quite so easily as could have been wished.

The consequence was, that he seemed inclined to sit down anywhere but in the place chosen for him, and after striding up and down the cell for a few moments, to the old priest's intense horror, he plunged himself down upon the bed.

Is it to be wondered at if the old gentleman should have dropped the inkstand with a smash upon the floor, after jerking the greater part of its contents up in his own face?

It is a wonder how he summoned up sufficient presence of mind to say, "Please, don't sit upon my bed; I don't like anybody to touch my bed."

The remark certainly had the effect of making the Governor jump up; but it had another effect which the old man had not anticipated.

It also caused the Governor to look round upon the bed, to see whether he had disarranged it.

It was rather dark in that corner of the room, and hitherto he had noticed nothing.

"Why, there is somebody in it!"

"What do you say?" gasped the old priest, feeling ready to give up the ghost.

"I say there is somebody in it!" cried the Governor, and he endeavoured to pull down the clothes.

But the old man sprang towards him, and with a strength of which an hour ago he would not have believed himself capable of, he forced the Governor away from the bed.

"You shall not see he person who is there," said the old man; "it is not the one you are looking for."

"Well," said the Governor, "who is it?"

"It is—it is a young priest whom I am hiding here. I will tell you the whole story another time, and I trust to your honour not to reveal the circumstance to any one."

"Well," said the Governor, chuckling to himself, "if you are sure it's a man——"

"Of course, I'm sure—sure it's a man! It's a young priest, I tell you!"

"And you object to showing me his face?"

"I strongly object!"

"You can have no objection to showing me the crown of his head. If he is shaved, I am satisfied."

"I cannot allow you to do so."

"Well, but my dear sir," said the Governor, with a smile, "I must insist upon doing my duty."

"You must kill me first, then," said the old man, setting his teeth.

"We won't have to proceed to such extremities, I trust," said the Governor, sarcastically; "and so I'll tell you what we'll do."

"What?"

"I'll meet you half-way."

"How do you mean?"

"I'll be content if I see the young priest's feet and ankles."

What excuse could the old gentleman make?

None.

He only thanked his stars that Ruth had taken off her stockings.

He therefore gently turned back the clothes for about half a yard, and disclosed as pretty a pair of feet and ankles as could well be imagined.

The Governor burst out laughing.

"I'm afraid you're a wicked old man!" said he.

The old priest was, as well he might be, purple with indignation.

"Never mind," said the Governor, presently, digging the old gentleman in the ribs, and winking at him in a way which filled the pious old priest's soul with horror.

CHAPTER CXIII.

ALL'S WELL THAT ENDS WELL.

"What do you intend to insinuate?" the old gentleman inquired, when he could find his tongue to speak.

"Ha! ha! ha!"

"How dare you——"

"Ho! ho! ho!"

"I pause for a reply."

"He! he! he!"

"I demand an explanation."

"Come, I say," said the Governor, "I think I ought to demand an explanation. Who is that in bed?"

"Who do you suppose it is?" asked the old man, who really did not know what he was saying.

"Well," replied the Governor, "I know very well it isn't the party I'm looking for."

The priest opened his eyes.

Did he hear aright?

To be sure he did. The Governor did not suspect him of harbouring Ruth.

When you come to look at it, it is so very unlikely that a person in his position would have done such a thing.

The poor old gentleman had been obliged to tell so many falsehoods during the last half-hour, that he thought one more would not much signify.

By one more he might save this woman's life.

One more—it was a dreadful cracker; and, in telling it, he ever afterwards put himself into the power of the Governor, who he knew would not scruple to profit by it.

The priest took his companion on one side, close to the door, and nudging him as he himself had been nudged, and winking at him as he himself had been winked at, he said, "You won't let this go any further. I can't gratify you with a sight of the lady's face, and I am sure you are too gallant a man to wish, for the mere sake of gratifying an idle curiosity, to cause pain to one whose reputation, I feel certain, is in the hands of a man of honour."

"Of course not," said the Governor, who, however, was dying to know who the lady was: "I would not think of being so indiscreet She is, doubtless, a resident of this city?" he added, presently.

"Yes," said the priest, who thought he might as well say yes as no, under the circumstances

"The wife of some wealthy townsman, I should not wonder?"

"Exactly," said the priest; and then he began to think what a lot of penance he would have to perform, to wipe away the guilt of this awful night.

"The ink's all spilt," said the Governor; "but never mind, I'll go to my own room. Good night; you may rely upon my silence."

He walked to the door, then paused a moment, looked hard at the old gentleman, and burst out laughing.

"I shouldn't have thought it of you! You are a dreadful old hypocrite, I must say. Only to think how you have taken us all in!"

And he walked away, cracking his sides.

The old priest stood for a while, perfectly paralysed with shame and wrath, and a score of other conflicting emotions warring in his heart.

Miss Ruth meanwhile sat up in bed.

"Well, I'm glad that's over," said she. "You're an artful old gentleman, I must say, to have thought of a tale like that. Any one can see you're an old hand."

"Look here!" said the old man, trembling with rage. "The wealth of the Indies would not repay me for what I have suffered upon your account. It is over now. The past cannot be recalled. The work of a lifetime is scattered to the winds; my character is gone. I'm disgraced—broken-hearted. The only way that you can repay me is by instantly leaving this place, which your presence has defiled."

The last word was an unlucky one. The woman he addressed was a moment before looking at him with some self-reproach and pity.

She responded to his appeal now with a fiercely defiant scowl and a toss of the head.

"I have no wish to stay," she said. "You speak as though I had intentionally placed you in this unpleasant position!"

"Well, well," responded the old man, with a deep sigh, "I don't upbraid you! It was a matter of life and death with you, and your life is more valuable than my good name. Only, for heaven's sake, do not delay any longer, but, now the danger is over, pray leave me!"

"How you talk!" said Ruth, impatiently; "the danger is by no means over yet! Listen there!"

As she spoke, she held up her hand to command silence; and the old man, listening, heard the sound of cannon, the ringing of bells, and the beating of drums.

"The whole town will be alarmed soon," he muttered to himself, wringing his hands in terror; "then what will become of you?"

"You may well ask that!" retorted Ruth, "it is just what I want you to tell me!"

"I am sure I cannot tell you!"

"Let me offer a suggestion, then!"

"What is it?"

"It is that I remain here until the morning."

"It is morning now."

"Yes; but I mean until it is late enough for me to go out without attracting attention."

"What then?"

"What I propose is, that you accompany beyond the walls of the monastery."

"But I cannot be seen walking out with a female!"

"You forget that I am clad in male attire!"

"Yes, yes; it is true—I had forgotten!"

"You can, therefore, have no objection?"

"N-no!"

"You must conduct me, then, to some place of safety, and procure me a passage by the first vessel to England."

The old priest reflected for some moments in silence.

It appeared to him very plain that the young lady had not yet been disposed of.

Perhaps she would yet cause him some considerable trouble and anxiety.

But he must go through with it now that he had begun.

He resolved that he would assist her to the utmost that it lay in his power to do.

"If she does not escape it will not be my fault," he said to himself.

Then he added, aloud, "I will do what you suggest. It is now nearly five o'clock. I never leave the building before ten. Until then you must remain here quietly."

"Trust me; I won't make any noise!"

"At five o'clock, the bell rings for getting up; at six, for prayers; and at half-past seven, for breakfast. I usually read prayers, but I cannot do so to-day, as, perhaps, you can understand. I also, as a rule, take the head of the table at the morning meal, but, to-day, will depute another to fill my place."

"Don't you think they will fancy it strange if you remain away?"

"I don't know, but I dare not leave you here alone."

"Why?"

"In the first place, the Governor might return."

"Well, but what if you lock the door?"

"All the doors are very easily opened from the outside, and there is no fastening upon the inside, as you may have observed."

"What a curious arrangement!"

"Yes, this cell is like the rest. It is so ordered that the Superior may at any moment enter any monk's cell without any impediment. There is no privacy allowed—no locks and keys—no place of concealment."

"But when the Governor and gaolers demanded admittance a short time since, they did not enter at once."

"They could have done so; but some of them did not know that the door was without a bolt. You might have heard one suggest that the door should be broken."

"Yes, I did."

"To that the Governor objected. It would have been a great breach of etiquette had he allowed them to do so. He is always officially correct in what he does, and he would not for the world have ventured upon such a proceeding under ordinary circumstances."

"Well, will he now?"

"Now that I am in his power it is a different matter. He would not hesitate now about opening my door in my absence, or forcing it if needs were, because he knows that fear of exposure would compel me to remain silent and submit to the outrage without daring to make any complaint."

"There is nothing, then, left for it but for you to bear me company for five hours."

"No, I am afraid not."

"That's polite!" said Ruth, laughing.

"Eh?" said the old priest, who did not understand her.

"What a stupid old dunce!" the young lady thought to herself. "I wish I felt sleepy, I'd go to sleep; that would pass the time away; but what on earth I am to do else I can't imagine. I can't converse with such an old dummy as that. I don't know what to say to him. I'd make love to him if it wasn't too fatiguing."

Just then, a bell in the monastery began to toll loudly.

"That is for the monks to get up," said the old man. "It is now five o'clock, and we have five hours to wait. Five hours! Will they ever go?"

CHAPTER CXIV.

A DAY-DREAM—THE RECOLLECTION OF A MIS-SPENT LIFE—A GLIMPSE OF RUTH'S CHILD-HOOD — THE GIN-PALACE AND THE NIGHT-HOUSE—THE OLD PRIEST'S INNOCENCE — A CURIOUS SITUATION.

RUTH thought that it would be advisable were she to resume those articles of attire of which, previous to her concealment, she had deemed it necessary to divest herself.

She did so, without holding any converse with, or even looking towards, the old priest.

He, on his side, kept his eyes steadily averted from that part of the cell where the fair fugitive was, and made believe to be deeply engrossed in the study of a black-lettered volume which he held in his hand; though, I dare say, if the truth were known, Ruth occupied his thoughts quite as much as he occupied hers.

In about half an hour's time a low tap was heard at the door, and the old priest hastening to respond to it, found the young man who had admitted Ruth into the monastery. He came to see whether he could be of any service, and whether Ruth was still hidden in the Superior's apartment.

The old man bade him inform one of the elder of the monks that he was engaged upon some important business, and that he must read the prayers and preside at breakfast in his stead.

When he was gone, he resumed his study as before.

Ruth meanwhile sat alone and silent at the other side of the apartment, occupied by her own thoughts, and occasionally eyeing her companion in a furtive manner, half-dreading to attract his attention, although, at the same time, she was anxious to do so.

Presently she bethought her of the diary she had got in her pocket, and she took it out and began to read.

She read with growing interest page after page, and when she raised her eyes from the book they were wet with tears.

Tears! Was it sympathy for her sister's sorrows, think you? or was it the record of that sorrow which brought her own misfortunes more vividly before her?

Perhaps it was more to the latter than the former cause that her emotion must be attributed; yet, though her grief was selfish, it was not altogether without a certain soft and chastening influence upon her bad, hard heart.

The story of her sister's love here written brought back to her recollection the only one of her loves which, throughout her wicked life, had not been entirely selfish or mercenary—which had not been a horrible mockery, an ugly make-belief and sham.

It brought back to her recollection her love for Crockford.

Love! Yes; for it was love which she had felt for the young Guardsman. He alone, of all her countless admirers, had inspired her with an approach to the tender passion.

Yes, she had loved him, although she had basely plotted his ruin to serve her own wicked ends. She loved him, although she could wrong him, for her love for him was not so strong, after all, as her love for herself.

Since that night, when carried away by passion and desire, the rash young man had accepted the bill of exchange, with the proceeds of which Ruth had intended to fly from the country, she had more than once repented bitterly of her part in the villanous scheme.

More than once during those long, weary weeks in the prison, when she lay sick and suffering, did she think with bitter shame and remorse upon her conduct to this man, who had been so devotedly attached to her, and, to serve her, would have laid down his life.

Now her thoughts turned into the same sad subject, and falling into a deep reverie, dead to all outward things, she pictured to herself what her life might have been, what it was, and what it promised to be.

But it was surely a strange blindness and infatuation which caused this woman who, in other matters, could trace out effect from cause clearly and logically enough in all conscience—in this particular matter to be so blind as not to see that it was to herself alone that all the misery and misfortune which had befallen her were attributable.

But no. She somehow fancied herself a child of destiny. She fancied that she had been urged on by circumstances over which she had no control, to grow worse and worse, to sink deeper and deeper in infamy and sin.

Surely, her conscience must have given her the lie, and pointed out to her instance after instance where her cold-blooded heartlessness, her black treachery, griping avarice and cupidity, had led her to betray her dearest friends for the sake of gain?

But no! I think that the deepest-dyed and most atrocious scoundrel is capable of finding some sort of excuse for his villanies—a poor excuse, perhaps, but good enough for its purpose to satisfy himself.

In like fashion, then, did this wretched woman endeavour to think herself a martyr, and her memory carried her back to the days of her infancy—those days spent in the noisome alleys and squalid courts in the vilest and filthiest of Whitechapel purlieus!

Again, to her hideous childhood—a childhood of precocious infamy, debauchery, and prostitution!

Again, to a girlhood spent among thieves and vagabonds, among hellish revelries in the damnable haunts of the lowest and grossest vice and profligacy!

The glare of the gin-palace—the sodden drunken orgies of the shameless night-house—the nameless horrors of her street life—came back to her recollection, confusedly mixed up with the splendours of that after time when, earning the wages of a spy, she flaunted luxuriously and revelled unthinkingly in countless extravagances, sowing bright, golden guineas broad cast, in sheer and wilful wantonness.

Sadly did she ponder over the misspent time—not because she thought it misspent, because, probably, had she had the chance she would have acted again in the same manner; but she was savage when she looked back at all she had done and all she had gone through, to think what a little advance she had made.

That she was here penniless, as far as her own efforts were concerned; that she was about to begin life again, to enter upon a dangerous, hazardous, and difficult undertaking, which certainly might turn out well, but which at the same time might not.

In any case, the life before her must again be a

weary life of scheming and contriving, plotting, and planning.

Was there ever to be any rest for her in the world?

What would be the end of it all? When this business was over, when the aim had been gained, what next?

What would become of her, the tool of this Jesuit plot? What would be the reward? How would they treat her? Would not she be cast off like an old shoe, to rot and die upon the nearest dung-heap? For what else would she be worth?

She thought long and pondered deeply.

Hour after hour passed, and she sat there immoveable, her head resting upon her hand, her elbow resting upon the arm of the roomy and old-fashioned chair in which she reclined in a careless attitude, which was full of an ease and grace that seemed inseparable from this strange woman's person, when either active or passive.

She fell asleep, and the scenes which had so lately occupied her thoughts passed again through her brain.

A gentle smile played about her pouting crimson lips, and for a moment a bright gleam of tiny pearl-like teeth lit up the oval face which was lovely yet, though the first bloom of youth had departed, and here and there were left undoubted traces of misery and suffering passed through, and the once gentle, even angelic expression of innocence and purity, had given way to a kind of hardy boldness that was almost audacity.

The old priest, seeing that she slept, laid down the book, over the pages of which he had been pausing so long and earnestly; not, it must be owned, because its contents in any way enlisted his attention, but, in truth, because by pretending to be so occupied, he hoped to avoid entering into conversation with the woman who had caused him so much pain and misery, and whose very presence was distressing to him.

He laid the volume on one side, however, when he saw that she was slumbering, and, in his turn, resting his head upon his hand, studied her phisiognomy with a strange interest.

The situation was a curious one.

Here was an old man, who had passed close upon seventy years of his life in prayer, in self-communing, silent meditation, and seclusion. An old man, whose hair was snowy with the work of Time, whose foot was in the grave, and who yet knew absolutely nothing of the world that he was about so soon to leave.

It is true that he often enough passed beyond the walls of the monastery; but his visits in the outer world were only to churches—to similar institutions to that to which he belonged, and occasionally to the bedside of some rich man, who, dying, called for his spiritual aid.

But what was this? He knew absolutely nothing of the fierce struggles, the daily battles going on without. To him the trials and temptations of the world were but names.

He was even ignorant of the very existence of the wild intoxication, the mad delights, and bitter miseries of those who revelled in guilty passions unknown to him.

There are priests who, after a life of sin and profligacy, seek the seclusion of the monastic walls, to find, in prayer and godly works, a forgetfulness of passed wickedness, of which they had wearied and sickened, as years began to tell on them; but this old man had never been exposed to temptation—had never sinned, even in thought.

The vows of chastity and celibacy had never been broken by him. He had, all his life, been accustomed to hear the gross and sensual pleasures of the outer world spoken of with such horror and abhorrence by the stern old priests of the establishment in which he spent his days, that he, with no knowledge of what he spoke of, had in time come to look upon with the same eyes, and speak of in the same terms, the lusts of the flesh, which could only be indulged in at the risk of damnation to the immortal soul.

As to his knowledge of the opposite sex, he had rarely ever been placed in such a position as to necessitate his exchanging half a dozen words with them.

The solitary instance which he had described to Ruth, when ill-luck had brought him into the society of that terrible spinster lady, was, in truth, the only one when he had passed so long a time in a woman's company. And then it must be allowed it was under such extremely unpleasant circumstances, that it is not much to be wondered at if he carried away with him anything but a favourable opinion of that particular lady's powers of fascination.

The housemaid into whose mercenary clutches the poor old gentleman had subsequently fallen, had not, it must be confessed, increased his good opinion of the sex.

This, then, was the third instance of his ever having any conversation with a female upon any secular subject.

This was the first time in his life that the old man had ever had the opportunity of studying a woman's face without, in his turn, being subjected to an unpleasant scrutiny.

If he had ever ventured before to cast his eyes upon a pretty face he had encountered in the street, and its owner had looked back at him, no timid maiden of blushing sixteen could have averted her gaze in greater confusion than the reverend father.

He would probably never have such another chance, he thought, if he neglected this.

"She's fast asleep," said he. "If I could only take a peep at her, without awakening her! I wonder whether I could!"

CHAPTER CXV.

THE OLD PRIEST WONDERS WHETHER HIS HEART WOULD EVER BECOME SUSCEPTIBLE TO THE TENDER PASSION, AND DETERMINES THAT IT WOULD NOT; CIRCUMSTANCES, HOWEVER, CAUSE HIM TO ALTER HIS OPINION.

He made up his mind to try, after much hesitation, trepidation, and calculation.

He approached her on tip-toes, trembling as he went.

What a dreadful position for him to be placed in, though, if by any fatal chance she were to start suddenly from her slumbers, and confront him!

Would he be able to survive such a disastrous occurrence?

No; he was sure that it would be the death of him. However, the temptation was so strong, that he could not resist it.

He approached her upon tip-toe. He took a full minute to make each step; and you may be sure, in consequence, made twice as much noise as he would had he walked boldly forward.

At last, however, the distance was accomplished

in safety, and without having aroused the sleeping beauty from her slumbers

He stood before her, gazing upon her.

She, meanwhile, slept on, unconscious of his scrutiny—as unconscious as she would, in all probability, have been unmindful had she been awake.

The old man mused as he gazed upon her.

"She is what is called beautiful," he thought to himself. "She is more beautiful than the picture of the Madonna, hanging in our church. She is much more beautiful than any woman I have ever seen. But then, to be sure, I have seen none—at least, that I have been able to look at fairly."

He rubbed his chin, thoughtfully, as these ideas passed through his head, and presently a grim smile lit up his face.

"I have chosen well, I think," he muttered to himself. "I could scarcely have found so good an instrument for the purpose I have in hand. It is true that the passions of men are unknown to me, and what the ungodly and sinful term love is an enigma, which it is impossible for me to read; but if what I have heard is true, this woman's power must be great."

A doubt, however, entered his brain, as he thus reflected.

"If this heretic Vivian is as inaccessible to the bewitchment of this syren as I should be myself, what then? Suppose, at the very outset, he should spurn her advances with the same horror that I should myself? What then? Will she be able to overcome the repugnance with which he, like I, may look upon one so shameless, so depraved and lost?"

It was a knotty point, and one which, to a poor old gentleman of such extremely limited experience in these matters, was very difficult to decide.

As he puzzled his head over it, a curious idea occurred to him.

If he could only have an opportunity of judging what were her powers.

But how could he do so?

Whom was she to practise her wiles upon? Whom was she to lure into her nets, to subject to the deadly influence of her meretricious smiles?

There was no one but he himself that she could exercise her arts upon, and dare he undergo the ordeal?

The bare notion of anything so very dreadful, and so opposed to all his previous ideas of right and wrong, turned the old gentleman's blood cold.

"The Lord forbid!" he piously exclaimed. "Not that I would ever fall. That is impossible, if I know myself; and, surely, at my time of life, I ought to know myself pretty well! But no, the idea is absurd, ridiculous, impossible!"

He was thus thinking when the sleeping beauty, prompted by some dream agitating her breast, heaved a deep sigh, and from her slightly parted lips a low murmur, as though of loving endearment, escaped.

The old man, eager to hear the words, approached his head nearer to her—alas! too near, as it proved; for, carried away by a transport of tender passion for the loved object of the vision ravishing her fancy, the seductive syren, stretching forth her arms, encircled the neck of the astonished and terrified priest, and drew him towards her, in spite of his efforts to free himself; and, indeed, almost before he could summon to his aid sufficient presence of mind to make the necessary effort, glued her warm, moist lips to his, and kissed him passionately.

To be thus clasped in her arms, to feel the hot breath upon his face, the soft contour of her voluptuous form coming in contact with his body, and, more than all (for at this moment she awoke), the languishing and tender glances which her eyes, full of a pent-up and smouldering passion, poured out upon him, would, indeed, have been a trial for the virtue of the most cold-blooded and passionless.

But upon this poor old priest, totally unused to be exposed to or to resist the influence of such temptation, the effect was as painful as it was strange and unprecedented.

For one brief moment the surprise was so great that he could not tear himself from her embrace.

A thrill of powerful emotion vibrated through his frame, and sent his blood rushing furiously through all his veins.

Then, with a powerful effort, he regained the use of his senses, which had well-nigh deserted him, and retreated from her, covering his face with his hands in shame and fright.

"God help me!" he muttered to himself. "How weak I am! And I was thinking that this Vivian could withstand the influence of her charms as well as I could. I hope he may be able to do so no better. That is all the harm I wish him."

Just then the monastery clock struck nine.

"I will remain alone with the woman no longer," said the old priest to himself.

Then he added aloud—

"Come, now, are you ready? We will go out together."

Ruth was hardly yet awake, and she was asking herself how it was that, upon opening her eyes, the old gentleman's head had been so near to hers. Perhaps the gallant Guardsman might have acted a part in the dream which had awakened her. It is very sure that the old gentleman had had no share in the ideal, though he had, much against his will, in the real. She, however, forbore questioning him upon so delicate a subject, and, expressing herself ready to accompany him, they left the cell together.

CHAPTER CXVI.

PASSING THE GATES—FRESH DANGERS TO ENCOUNTER—THE INQUISITIVE BUMPKIN.—THE SUSPICIOUS GAOLER—THE DRAWBRIDGE—RUTH'S ARTFULNESS.—A MOUTHFUL OF SNUFF.

THE old priest suggested that when they had passed through the outer door of the monastery chapel, leading into the town, she should pretend to be using her pocket-handkerchief, and hold it as much over her face as possible; and, at the same time, keep it there until she had passed by a sentinel, who usually was stationed at a short distance from the door.

There might also chance to be some other soldiers, and some gaolers perhaps, hanging round and about the door of a small canteen which they would have to pass, and it would be safest to adopt the same precautions in passing there also.

Ruth herself felt that the disguise she wore would prove a great security against discovery; for, as the reader is well aware, this was by no means the first time that she had assumed male attire; and, although, as a general rule, both on and off the stage, the sex of a woman so disguised is very easily detected, in this case it was not so, which circumstance may be thus accounted for. In the case of actresses upon the stage, the assumption of male attire is not usually accompanied by any desire on the lady's part that her sex should remain a secret—therefore, does it not unfrequently happen that no effort has been made to conceal the tones of the voice and the graceful contour of the shape. But in Ruth's case, practising the trade of a spy, an informer, and a detective, it had many a time been a matter of life and death with her that her sex should be unknown, even unsuspected.

With a view to success, then, she had carefully studied, and striven hard to imitate, the style of carriage and the fashion of walking peculiar to men; and, also, by an artful adjustment of her clothing, she contrived so effectually to hide all trace of the magnificently developed bust and the gracefully-rounded form of which she was the possessor, that there would have been as great a difficulty in deciding whether she was man or woman, when she swaggered along attired in male costume, as there was to determine the sex of the famous Chevalier D'Eon, in times gone by.

As it turned out, her estimation of the strength of her disguise was a correct one; and it was very lucky that it was so—for although she adopted the plan proposed by the old priest of keeping her handkerchief up to her face as much as possible, circumstances occurred which rendered a strict adherence to this scheme impossible.

As luck would have it, the sentinel on duty outside the chapel was being pestered, by some country bumpkin intent upon sight-seeing, for information respecting the wonders of the chapel and the monastery adjoining, and was inquiring whether the same were to viewed gratuitously or how, and from whom, he was to obtain permission to see them.

Wearied by his importunities, and seeing the old man coming that way, the sentinel referred the sight-seer to the old priest, and though beyond measure annoyed and disconcerted by so ill-timed an application, the latter was nevertheless compelled to give the desired information, and even to repeat some portions of it, before he could effect his escape.

All this time the priest and Ruth were standing within four feet of the sentinel's box, with the man's eyes fixed upon them; and it was therefore impossible for the woman to conceal her face in the way the old gentleman had suggested, during the whole conversation taking place between his reverence and the bumpkin.

At length, however, the countryman was satisfied, the information desired had been imparted, and they were at liberty to go on again.

The danger, however, had not yet been overcome.

They approached the canteen which the old priest had spoken of. The excitement prevailing among the gaolers and soldiers respecting the attempted escape of the preceding evening had caused a larger number of gaol officials than was customary to assemble at the canteen, to talk the news over among themselves, and discuss the probabilities of Ruth again being captured, together with the reason of her incarceration, about which some slight mystery existed, &c., &c.

The priest, in a whisper, as they drew near the canteen-house, informed his companion that several of the gaolers were standing round about the door.

"For God's sake, keep your face covered!" he whispered eagerly; "and walk steadily."

"All right!"

"How you're trembling!"

"What do you say, father?"

"I say, how you're trembling!"

"No, I am not."

"What do you mean? Why, I can scarcely keep you upright!"

Ruth could not refrain from tittering slightly, in spite of the danger.

"It is you, father," said she, "not I, who shake so."

"Well, well; I wish you wouldn't!" retorted the old man. "I—I'm sure there's n-nothing to be f-frightened about!"

The poor old gentleman was shaking in every limb, and his knees could scarcely support his weight.

On the other hand, the brazen hussy for whom he trembled was as she always was, as cool as a cucumber.

Some people, I daresay, may exist who admire such courage as this in a woman. I confess that, for my part, I do not. I see nothing womanly in her conduct, as there is nothing womanly in any of the qualities, bad and good, which this creature possessed. Surely, if there were ever a woman in the world who ought to have been a man, this young lady was an instance. As a man, she might, perhaps, have distinguished herself in some way or other; as it was, her every act was awfully unnatural—almost revolting. Her face and form were a woman's, but her heart was that of a fiend. Were it not I had also to record in the concluding chapters of my story her downfall and punishment, I should be inclined to regret that I had ever elected myself biographer to such a monster. But the time of retribution, humiliation, and grief, and anguish, is drawing near. Bear with her, then, a little longer, gentle reader.

As I have said, the old priest, trembling with apprehension, led on his fair companion until they arrived in front of the canteen, or garrison public-house, on the steps of which some dozen gaolers and soldiers were standing in earnest conversation, gesticulating violently, after the manner of Frenchmen, when excited.

As they drew near, the priest and the fugitive increased their pace, and endeavoured to pass by unmolested.

This, however, was not to be effected.

As they came up level with the canteen, one of the men stepped out from the crowd and approached the couple.

The old priest communicated the alarming fact to his companion.

Ruth glanced in the direction indicated, and involuntarily tightened her grasp upon the old man's arm.

He looked towards her eagerly, and saw that she had changed colour.

"What is it?" he whispered.

"It is my gaoler!" she replied.

"The gaoler who attended on you?"

"Yes!"

"He knows you well?"

"Perfectly!"

"What is to be done?"

"Let us walk faster."

"No; he is here!"

"We are lost, then!"

"Be calm, and cover your face."

The gaoler approached, bowing low.

"Oh, if you please, your reverence——"

"I will talk to you another time," replied the old priest. "I am in a hurry, and have no time to spare."

"If I might say a few words——"

"Yes; but another time."

"I won't detain you long, sir."

"Come to me at noon."

"If I might speak now——"

"I can't wait, I tell you!"

"A minute only?"

"No!"

"Half a minute?"

"Not a second!"

"If I might walk by your side, sir ——"

"No! I tell you, no!"

All this time the old priest was walking on as fast as his legs would carry him, pulling Ruth along with him; or, perhaps, I ought to say, she was pulling him, for she was decidedly ahead of her companion.

The gaoler, I ought to say, desired to request the old priest to intercede with the Governor in his behalf, as he had just been discharged from his situation, in consequence of the escape of the two prisoners under his charge.

As it was absolutely necessary that, if the old priest did speak, he should speak at once, the gaoler determined not to be driven from his purpose; but knowing the old gentleman to be an easy-going, tender-hearted creature, he thought that if he only stuck to him, and worried him, he would at length, by dint of sheer badgering, induce him to hear his prayer and grant his request.

Therefore, in spite of the old man's energetic refusals again and again reiterated, the gaoler ran first at his side and then at Ruth's, endeavouring to get a word in edgeways, and filling both their hearts with terror and dismay.

So long did this persecution continue, that allthough Ruth, as it was, had kept the handkerchief an unreasonable length of time to her face, she felt that she could not continue to do so much longer without arousing the gaoler's suspicion.

As it was, being unacquainted with the man's motive for following them, she supposed that he did already suspect her, and was following him thus far for the sole object of getting a view of her features.

This idea was shared by her companion, and you can, therefore, imagine what their state of mind must have been when they found the gaoler so persistent in his attentions, and that in spite of the old man's rebuffs, he could not be shaken off.

Indeed, though at first no such idea had entered the gaoler's head, when he at last perceived that the younger of the two persons seemed to be endeavouring to avoid him, which intention there could be no mistake about, he did begin to have some faint suspicion that all was not right.

He certainly had no idea what was the motive of the priest's companion for concealing her face, only he could hardly help thinking, as indeed no person using their reasoning faculties could, that she had some motive in wishing to avoid his gaze.

Never for a moment did the thought occur to him that this person was Ruth.

How could it?

Even if he had noticed anything about her appearance or gait to lead him to suppose that it was a woman, he would never have dreamt that it was the woman who had made her escape, because he could not have believed it possible that the old priest would have been found in her company, and that he would not only have winked at her escape, but even lent her his assistance to effect the same.

Who the deuce, then, could the mysterious person be who was so anxious the gaoler should not obtain a glimpse of her?

The desire to find out who it was almost overcame his desire to speak to the priest about the business which had just made him follow the old man.

He now kept entirely upon Ruth's side, and kept dodging backwards and forwards trying to get a sight of her.

But Ruth effectually kept him at bay with her pocket handkerchief.

"He'll think I've an awful cold in the head, won't he?" said Ruth to her companion, with a chuckle

"He'll think your nose is bleeding."

"Ah, to be sure!"

"He shan't do me, though," thought the gaoler. "My time will come."

The time did come immediately.

He saw a way in which he could oblige her either to show her face or speak to him.

The way was this.

They were approaching a drawbridge. The path across it was only for foot passengers, and it was extremely narrow.

The gaoler got before the priest and Ruth, and took up his station at the beginning of the bridge, standing in a sort of alcove, but in such a position that they would have to squeeze past.

Ruth, ever watchful, saw his manœuvre, judged what his motive was, and determined to defeat it.

"I saw you using a snuffbox a little while ago," she said to her companion, "did I not?"

"Yes. What makes you ask?"

"Give it to me."

"Do you want a pinch?"

"Give it me, if you please. I'll show you why I want it."

"Here it is."

"Thank you. Will you go first?"

"Yes."

The old man obeyed, wondering what on earth was going to happen.

Ruth put away her handkerchief, pulled her hat as much as possible over her eyes, opened the snuffbox, and held it upon the side on which the gaoler stood.

Then walked forward.

As she approached him, then, she screwed up her pretty face into a score of wrinkles, and put on a Dundreary expression as though she were going to sneeze.

The gaoler poked his head forward easier to see her features, but owing to the ingeniously distorted expression she had assumed, he was unable to recognise her.

She waited till he was close to her, and then, when she was quite certain of her aim, she made believe to be taken suddenly with a sneezing fit, and jerked the whole contents of the snuffbox into the miserable man's face

He uttered a howl of agony, and fell flat on his back.

"What's the matter?" cried the old priest, turning suddenly.

"Nothing," said Ruth, "only we must run for it."

"I can't run."

"You must."

"Come on, then."

CHAPTER CXVII.

SHOWS HOW RUTH FOUND HERSELF IN A VERY EXTRAORDINARY AND UNPLEASANT POSITION, AND HOW VERY UNCOMFORTABLE SHE FELT.

The drawbridge was, fortunately for the fair fugitive, hidden from the sight of the soldiers and gaolers standing outside the canteen, by a high wall, which served as one of the fortifications of the town.

The persons there assembled could not, therefore, see what had happened—the great snuff trick, the fall of the gaoler, and so on—or there is every reason to believe that Ruth's farther progress would then and there have been arrested.

As, however, it fortunately happened no one saw them, and, taking to their heels, they cleared the bridge, and entered the town.

Arrived in the street, the priest hastily led the way through a number of narrow and crooked turnings, winding and doubling in such a way that it would have been extremely difficult, even had they been pursued, for the pursuers to have followed them with the start that they had got.

After walking rapidly for some time they emerged again into a broad, leading thoroughfare, and the priest led the way straight into a shop, which was close to the entrance of the alley they had just quitted.

It was a hosier's shop, and over the door was the name of Duval.

The priest glanced hastily to the right and to the left, to see whether anybody was observing him, and having satisfied himself to the contrary, made a sudden dart into the shop, and called to Ruth to follow him.

There were two persons behind the counter: one was a pale, thin young woman; the other a stout, red-faced woman, of forty, or thereabouts.

On seeing the priest, both these women made a low curtsey, but he took no heed of them, but rushed through the shop into the parlour behind it.

"Bless me!" said the stout lady to the thin. "What can that mean?"

"I haven't the least idea!" replied the thin lady to the stout.

As she could get no information otherwise, the stout lady thought she had better go and ask the priest himself. She therefore followed him into the back parlour, and closed the door behind her.

The woman behind the counter followed in her wake, but instead of entering also, applied her ear to the keyhole.

"Madam," said the priest, directly she entered, "is Monsieur Duval at home?"

"No, sir."

"When do you expect him?"

"Not until to-morrow."

The old priest pulled a long face. He was evidently disappointed.

"Can I be of any service to you?"

The priest hesitated. It was most extraordinary how he had broken the ice—how he was forced into ladies' society.

"Yes," he said, "you can be of the greatest service if you will."

"I shall be very happy."

"If your husband had been at home I had intended to have asked him. You know that he has on several occasions expressed a desire to serve me?"

"And not without a cause, for did you not save him from ruin by your kind loan?"

"Well, well, never mind that; that was nothing. He can repay me now, or you can, by doing what I ask."

"Name it, sir."

"I have here, then, a young—a young gentleman, who is under a cloud. I want you to give him shelter to-night, and smuggle him on board the boat bound for England, which leaves, I believe, to-morrow morning. Will you do so?"

"You may depend upon my using every exertion to carry out that end."

"I must further beg of you to procure some disguise in which he could pass the Custom House and police-officers without fear of being recognised."

"To be sure I will!" cried the lady. "He is a very pretty young gentleman. Suppose——"

"Suppose what?"

"I have a capital idea!"

"What is it?"

"Suppose we dress him as a girl?"

"Well, no—I——" stammered the old gentleman, appealing to Ruth,—"Do you think that would do?"

"I am afraid I should be too awkward!" said Ruth.

"Nonsense!" cried the lady,—"you'd make a capital woman!"

"You can talk that over," said the priest, with a smile. "I must bid you good-bye; and allow me, madam to thank you for your kindness"

The old gentleman was so delighted with the chance of getting rid of Miss Ruth, that he would not stay to hear any more, but at once beat a hasty retreat.

Ruth and Madame Duval were left face to face, and it must be owned that both the ladies looked a little bashfully at one another.

She was a stout lady, was Madame Duval, as I have already told you. She was one of those elderly juvenile ladies, very sentimental and sensitive.

She was decidedly good-looking, and there was a certain roguish twinkle in her grey eye which might have meant devilry, might have meant fun—decidedly meant mischief

There was a languishing expression about her eye, and her pouting lips seemed to say, as plain as lips could speak, without giving utterance to words, "Come, kiss me!"

She had a very soft heart, this lady; and it was a heart that could feel for another, particularly when that other was a handsome young man.

The state of the case in the present instance was very apparent.

She was decidedly smitten with the appearance of the pretty young priest.

Miss Ruth's confusion, when she made the discovery, was overwhelming.

She never before had found herself in such a position She was quite confounded, and stood there fiddling her hat in her hand, wishing herself anywhere in the world but where she was; of course, with the exception of the prison out of which she had just broken.

For some time both were silent. Ruth didn't know what to say; the other lady did not know how to say what she wanted to.

Madame Duval was the first to break the silence, which began to grow rather awkward for both parties.

"You look fatigued," she said; "will you take a seat? and will you allow me to offer you some refreshment?"

Ruth was not sorry to embrace both proposals; for as yet, as the reader is aware, she had not broken her fast that day.

She therefore accepted willingly; and the lady rang the bell, and gave orders to the servant to bring up a bottle of wine and a cold fowl.

Then, setting a chair for her guest, the most comfortable one which the room contained, and fixing it in the most comfortable position away from draughts, and also out of sight of the shop, should any customer chance to come in, Madame Duval entreated Ruth to make herself at home, and to make a hearty meal.

In both respects, it must be owned, the young lady did her utmost to comply with the hostess's request.

It was her custom to make herself at home under any circumstances, and she was, besides, ravenously hungry.

Madame having assisted her guest to two or three glasses of wine, and again and again replenished her plate with wings, and legs, and slices off the breast, began to think that it was high time to leave off eating and begin talking.

"Have you come far to-day?" she asked.

"Yes," replied Ruth, with her mouth full.

"From the country, I suppose?"

"Yes, from the country."

"By the railroad?"

"Yes."

"The Paris line, I dare say?"

"Exactly."

"He is very taciturn," thought Madame Duval. "Perhaps he is afraid to tell much."

But the good lady was not to be put off in that sort of way.

"And you are going to London?" she added, aloud.

"Yes."

"A beautiful city."

"So they tell me."

"A lovely place—but one full of snares and pitfalls."

"Indeed!"

"A dreadful place for a young man to live in alone!"

"Is it?"

"Oh, horrible!" cried Madame Duval, throwing up her hands and eyebrows. "Shocking—too dreadful to talk about!"

"You frighten me, madame!"

"Ah, my dear young gentleman!"—laying her hand upon Ruth's shoulder—"it is not for one so good and virtuous as you are that it has so much danger!"

"What makes you think me what you say?" asked Ruth.

"I am quite certain that I read you aright!" replied her companion, who, however, to read her as she said, appeared to find it necessary to approach her face very near indeed to that of the supposed young priest, and to look fixedly into her eyes.

Miss Ruth, feeling uncommonly awkward, and not knowing what to say, took refuge in the cold fowl, and pegged away vigorously.

"No," continued Madame, after a brief pause, "I feel sure that you would not be led away by the snares which might be thrown in your path by those wretches who they say infest the metropolis—those rouged and ringletted creatures who, with their evil smiles and artful wiles, beguile the unsuspecting youth to his destruction!"

"I hope not, ma'am," said Ruth, who felt that she ought to say something, although she did not exactly know what; "I hope not, madame. You know that those who wear my cloth have forsworn the temptations of which you speak, and to listen to the voice of love is to us a crime for which there is no pardon."

"Ah, me!" sighed Madame, with her eyes fixed languishingly upon the young priest, while her hand rested upon his; "what you say is true, but the flesh is weak, and we are all sinners, aren't we?"

"I hope not, ma'am," said Ruth, rising hastily from the table, for the conversation was taking a turn she by no means fancied. "I hope not, I'm sure!"

"He's a stupid young fool!" muttered the lady to herself, and the pale woman coming to tell her that her presence was required in the shop, she left the parlour to speak to them, and to Ruth's great relief, left that young lady to herself.

The customer who had come in was a very difficult one to serve, and he kept Madame Duval for a great length of time engaged in conversation.

Ruth was exceedingly rejoiced, and stretching herself upon a sofa, felt so very cosy and comfortable after the hearty meal that she had eaten, that closing her eyes as she thought, for a moment, she fell fast asleep.

She awoke as suddenly, and it was to find the thin, pale young woman bending over her.

Ruth opened her eyes wide and stared at her. She felt very much relieved that it was not the other, but her satisfaction very shortly changed to a much less pleasurable sensation when she noticed the expression of the young woman's face.

It was a curious expression, in which a variety of emotions were strangely blended. There were confusion and shame at detection; there were sympathy and love.

No, there could be no mistake about it—the unhappy young woman in priest's attire had somehow contrived to inspire a warm affection in the hearts of both mistress and servant.

The stout lady, and the thin young woman—Madame Duval and Mademoiselle Virginie, her shopwoman.

"What in the name of heaven will come of it all?" Ruth asked herself, despairingly. "It's absolutely dreadful to contemplate. One such love affair was quite enough, but two are out of all reason."

Miss Virginie caught the hand of the supposed young priest in hers, and then, before the indignant Ruth could prevent her, hugged it to her bosom and impressed upon it a passionate kiss.

"Promise me one thing," she said.

"What's that?"

"That you won't betray me."

"No, no!"

"Have no fear, then, that harm shall befall you here, but do not trust her more than you can help."

"Trust whom?"

"Her," replied Virginie, pointing in the direction of the shop.

"Madame Duval?"

"Hush! The same."

"You do not think that she would betray me, do you?"

"I say nothing. She is a false, bad woman. All I say is, do not trust her."

"I won't."

"Where she places her affection she can show kindness; when she sets her heart upon the attainment of an object, that object she will attain let the cost be what it may. She hates all who thwart her. I have thwarted her, and she hates me."

Ruth began to think Miss Virginie was rather cracked, but she said nothing more than "Oh!" which she thought, under the circumstances, to be the most appropriate remark she could give utterance to.

At that moment there was a sound of approaching footsteps.

The thin young lady clutched Ruth's hand.

Then, in an impressive whisper, she said, "Now will you remember what I have said?"

"Yes," replied Ruth.

"You will be careful?"

"Yes."

"You will not betray me?"

"No."

"I am your friend, then."

"Thank you."

Virginie squeezed Ruth's hand once more, pressed her lips to Ruth's forehead, and hastily retreated from the room into the shop.

It was, as it turned out, a false alarm. Madame Duval was not coming back, for fresh customers arrived, and she was obliged to remain in the shop, and attend to them. Virginie kept her company.

Ruth, thus left to her own resources, amused herself as best she could, by turning over the leaves of Madame Duval's album, and in examining some book shelves, which stood in one corner of the room.

To look through the library, and to read the titles of the various works, was quite sufficient to convince anybody, even unacquainted with their owner, that Madame Duval must be a very romantic and sentimental lady.

The books were every one of them love stories of a very romantic and improper description. In fact, without fear of exaggeration, I think I may say that they were some of them grossly indecent, and such as we should only, in England, expect to find at the shops of the most infamous venders of obscene literature, in some of the courts and alleys about Drury Lane and the surrounding neighbourhood, where a few of the miserable wretches whom the police have routed out of their dens in Holywell Street have taken refuge.

It may be strange to some that such books should have been found in the parlour of a respectable tradesman's wife, and those unacquainted with the habits and customs of our volatile neighbours may be inclined to believe either that this woman was a most improper character, and openly outraged the laws of decency, or that the picture I am drawing is much over-coloured and altogether unnatural.

Such, however—as those who know French life intimately will own with me—is not the case.

Morality in France is a very different thing to morality in England. Books are openly read and approved of there by decent women, which here would have no audience but among the shameless and depraved. Until within two or three years, prints of a scandalous character, and photographs of revolting indecency, were exposed in shop windows to be gazed upon by women and children. There is even now in the public street in Brussels a statue of so infamous a character, that a description of it is impossible. I might easily quote other instances of the depraved taste, but the subject is an unpleasant one, and had better be quickly dismissed to the oblivion it deserves.

Ruth not being the chastest and most refined young lady in the world, was not much offended and shocked by the contents of the library; but she turned over the leaves of the various books, looked at the pictures, read the text in front of those that most struck her fancy, and in fact, spent the time she was left to herself very pleasantly.

Madame Duval did not return for more than an hour from the time that Ruth awoke; and when she did, it was only for a few moments at a time —for, as luck would have it, the customers kept dropping in every ten minutes throughout the day, making such frequent calls upon her time and attention, that she found it impossible to be with her young guest for long together.

At about four in the afternoon, the servant entered the room to lay the cloth for dinner; and shortly afterwards, Ruth and the two ladies sat down to dinner.

In the presence of both, our heroine felt a great deal more at her ease than she had done before, when alone with either; and she chatted and talked, to the great gratification of the two ladies and her own amusement likewise.

"If they would only both stop, it would be all right," Ruth thought. "I'm not like Captain Macheath, who said, 'How happy could I be with either, were t'other fair charmer away.' My case is somewhat peculiar; and, contrary to the old saying, I can't help thinking that three are company, and two are none."

A duet it was, however, doomed to be, as Ruth soon found to her horror.

Shortly after tea, Madame Duval said to Miss Virginie, "Those things which were ordered by Monsieur Perrin, this morning, must be taken home by you this evening."

"Taken home, madame!" cried the shopwoman. "Why, it is twelve miles off!"

"What of that? Is there not the rail?"

"But there will be no train to return by tonight!"

"You can return by the first train to-morrow."

"But the expense?"

"You can sleep at my sister's. Besides, they are such good customers, that, whatever it costs, they must be obliged."

"Won't the morning do?"

"Of course not. What do you mean? Do you suppose I should send you, if I could help it?"

Miss Virginie was silent. She had her own opinion.

"What do you think I should send you for?" said Madame Duval indignantly.

"To get rid of me," thought Virginie.

But she did not say so

There could be little doubt, too, that such was the lady's intention

She threw a languishing glance at Ruth, as the other woman rose from the table, and her foot resting upon Ruth's shoe, gave it a gentle squeeze.

Ruth drew her foot hastily away, and blushed crimson.

She was determined she would make her escape That was the only course left for her, unless she were to ruin the old priest's reputation, more than she had already done, by divulging the secret of her sex.

Left to herself, after dinner, she pondered how she could effect her object, but without arriving at any definite conclusion.

She took tea alone with Madame Duval, after the other woman was gone; and the mistaken old lady, as before, made furious love to her

Eight o'clock, the time for shutting up the shop, arrived without Ruth's having come to any conclusion.

The shop was shut up.

At ten the servants retired to bed

The unfortunate Miss Ruth found herself in a more perplexing position than ever, for she found herself alone with the amorous old lady, without any fear of friendly interruption from a third party.

Ruth never in her life felt so awkward, and never in her life before had been so at her wit's end for a plan to escape, as she was now that she wished to escape from her present dilemma.

CHAPTER CXVIII.

RELATES HOW THIS EXTRAORDINARY LOVE AFFAIR PROGRESSED, AND HOW RUTH THOUGHT HERSELF OUT OF THE SCRAPE WHEN SHE WAS NOT.

"THE stupid old fool!" Ruth muttered to herself, eyeing the old lady with an extremely unloving expression of countenance. "What the dickens has made her take a fancy to me?"

She, however, felt so very indignant upon the subject that she determined to break the truth to the old lady without any delay.

"Bother the old man!" she said, thinking of the priest; "I can't—I don't see why I should be annoyed like this upon his account. Bother his reputation! What is it to me, I should like to know?"

What, indeed, Mrs. Ruth?

He had saved your life—that was all; but that is nothing, perhaps.

He deserved some consideration at your hands, some people might have perhaps supposed; but Miss Ruth had never been remarkable for any display of that very vulgar virtue called gratitude.

The question she had asked herself with respect to the reason of the old lady's being smitten by her personal appearance, she answered in the most satisfactory manner, by going to a looking-glass and making a long and careful inspection of her own face.

It was decidedly a pretty face. Not as pretty as it had been, as I have told you before, but yet very pretty. She looked an extraordinarily good-looking young gentleman—rather effeminate, perhaps, but that was a matter of taste. That the old lady was decidedly smitten by her there could be no doubt.

And that brings us back again to the point from which we started. Ruth could not for the life of her devise a plan of escape from the awkward dilemma in which she found herself placed.

The stout Madame Duval very shortly made her appearance, after the place had been carefully secured for the night.

She brought in with her, from the cellar to which she had just paid a visit, a bottle of champagne. The table was already laid out with a few delicacies, intended for supper; and Madame Duval, with a gracious smile, requested the young priest to join her.

The young priest—who, at the moment that the lady spoke, was sitting in an arm-chair in front of the fire, with her back turned towards the speaker—affected not to hear the request, and to be fast asleep.

The stout lady, after repeating her words twice, the second time in a louder tone than the first approached upon tip-toe to where the other sat, and leaning over the sleeper, gazed down earnestly into her face.

"Poor dear!" she said to herself; "he is fast asleep."

Then she added in a playful tone, at the same time giving Miss Ruth a gentle shake, "If he don't wake up, I shall win a pair of gloves of him—that I shall!"

As, however, the supposed young gentleman made no reply, and showed no signs of awakening from her sleep, the old lady began to grow rather indignant.

Throughout the day, except at meal times when both ladies (Madame Duval's shopwoman as well as herself) were present, the young priest had been very backward and reserved in his manners; his backwardness and reserve, indeed, amounting to a degree of clumsy awkwardness, and even boorishness, which had exasperated the good lady more than once almost beyond the limits of patience.

"A stupid young fool!" she said to herself: "if he were a little older, he would not throw such a chance away, I'll stake my life on it."

But it is questionable whether the good lady was right, as a general rule, for it is ordinarily only very young men who fall in love with elderly women.

Mind you, this Madame Duval was a very bewitching creature, there can be no doubt of that—a rosy and voluptuous goddess, bordering on fat, but none the worse for that, in my opinion; and had Ruth only been the young man she pretended to be, there is but little doubt that she would easily have effected the conquest she desired over his young and susceptible heart.

As it was, however, unfortunately, all the graces of her mind and the beauties of her person were thrown away upon the object upon whom they were so profusely lavished.

Finding that the young priest continued to sleep, and that, indeed, he had the impudence even to begin to snore, she grasped the pretended young gentleman by the shoulders, and shook her so, that Ruth was obliged to open her eyes, and make believe to wake up.

"You've been asleep!" said Madame, with a smile, but in a tone which was bitterly sarcastic.

"Have I?"

"Yes."

"Long?"

"I haven't been watching you all the time."

"Ah, I'm very tired!"

"I should have thought that a gentleman, however tired he was, would have made an effort to keep awake in the presence of a lady."

"But I'm so very tired!"

"Perhaps if it had been a young and beautiful creature——"

"No, madam, I think I should have gone to sleep even in the company of the Abbot himself, I am so dead beat."

The lady bit her lip, but renewed the attack, after a pause.

"I was wrong," she said, in a low and plaintively melancholy tone, as though she were communing with her own thoughts, rather than addressing her companion,—"I was wrong in thinking that female beauty could have an influence upon you."

The young priest yawned, as much as to say that it had not.

The lady continued, however, without appearing to notice the rudeness.

"I have often thought," continued the lady, "that it is a hard sacrifice for a young man, in the very pride and flower of his youth, to voluntarily immure himself within the gloomy walls of a monastery."

Another yawn.

"To separate himself from all the busy interests of life—to forego for ever the magnetic influence of female beauty—to repudiate as unrighteous and sinful that passion which a divine wisdom has made so powerful, that for its sake crowns have been cast aside, kingdoms have been overthrown, wars raged, countless crimes committed—that great and all absorbing passion—love!"

As she spoke, she had drawn her chair nearer and nearer to that of the supposed young priest; a deep emotion seemed to thrill in her sweet voice, her eyes brimmed over with a languishing desire, her soft white hand sought that of her companion, and pressed it warmly in her feverish grasp

Ruth sprang to her feet.

"Excuse me," she said, "I'm so dreadfully sleepy, madame; can I have my bed candle, if you please?"

Madame gasped for a moment.

The young gentleman's remark fairly took her breath away.

She blushed crimson, then turned as white as a sheet.

Then rose softly, as though she had no bend in her back, and made her guest a low bow.

"Your candle is upon the side-table, awaiting your pleasure," she said coldly.

Ruth, however, feigned utter unconsciousness of the intense severity of her manner, and taking

the candle indicated, lit it, and made her hostess a low bow in return.

Madame Duval, as the other reached the candle, appeared, however, to relent.

"Won't you have some supper?" she asked.

"No, thank you," replied Ruth.

"Not even a glass of wine?"

"No, thank you."

"How very abstemious you are!"

"I have got a bad headache."

"Poor fellow! Go to bed, then."

Ruth moved towards the door, only too happy to escape.

"Won't you shake hands?" said Madame Duval.

She blocked up the doorway, and prevented the other from passing out, as she was only too anxious to do.

Ruth pretended not to hear her.

But the lady was not to be put off.

"Won't you say good night?"

"Good night, Madame!"

"Won't you shake hands?"

"With pleasure!"

"Won't you—won't you——"

"What, madam?"

"Won't you let me kiss you?"

"Kiss me?"

"Bless the boy, how he blushes!"

"I—I——"

"Why how you tremble!"

"I—I——"

"What do you say?"

"I'd—I'd rather not."

"Well, I'm ashamed of you! You're the first young man I ever came across who said such a thing."

"Am I?"

"It isn't every young man that is asked by a pretty woman to kiss her. Do you suppose it is?"

"I—I hope not"

"What do you mean?"

"N—nothing."

"I should think you didn't! You don't seem very sensible. Refuse to give me a kiss, indeed! I never came across such a milksop in all my born days! Why, am I not old enough to be your mother, you noodle?"

"Well," said Ruth, with a great affectation of innocence, "I did not think of that; but of course there can't be any harm in my kissing my grandmother."

"Grandmother!" ejaculated Madame Duval

"Didn't you say grandmother, ma'am?"

"I said mother; but even that is an exaggeration."

"How old are you, then?"

"That's a very rude question, young gentleman. But, if you must know, I'm forty."

"Are you?" replied Ruth, with a stare. "No more than that? I took you for fifty-five, at the very least."

And leaving the good lady dumbfoundered, she walked out of the room.

I am sure, after such scandalous treatment, it is a wonder that Madame was kind enough to take the trouble to show the ungrateful young rascal to his bedroom.

As it was, she merely went to the top of the first flight and pointed out the door, immediately retracing her steps without another word, for she was awfully indignant.

Awfully indignant, and well she might be.

I suppose there is no way in the world so certain of making a woman your enemy for life, as to reject her love when she offers it to you.

When she has her heart trampled upon, is it not apt to make her turn round and snap at you? Only some women will bear such a lot of trampling under foot before they rise.

That was the case with Madame, perhaps.

When she came down again alone into the parlour, and slammed the door to after her, she was thoroughly determined that the young priest should suffer for his rudeness.

His conduct was infamous! It was scandalous!

No punishment was too bad for him!

She snapped a pair of scissors spitefully, as she thought so.

If the young priest had been small enough, and close handy at the moment, and there had been no penalty for so doing, I am not so sure that his head would not have been snipped off there and then.

Luckily for that ungrateful young person, Ruth was now in her bedroom, where, having safely locked the door after her, she threw herself into an easy-chair, and burst into a hearty fit of laughter.

"If I were really a young man, there would be no chance for me," cried the gay young lady aloud; "or if Madame was of the opposite sex, and had taken the same violent fancy for me in the character of a helpless maiden, I am afraid my case would be equally hopeless. Well, I have had to defend myself against my lovers before this, and I'll try and do so again. Ha, ha! poor old lady!"

But Miss Ruth was by no means as safe as she supposed; nor had she got out of the scrape quite so easily as she fancied.

She little thought what trouble was in store for her, or she would not now have retired to bed in such capital spirits, nor slept there so soundly, when she laid her pretty head upon the pillow.

CHAPTER CXIX.

SHOWS HOW THE HUSBAND CAME HOME, AND WHAT AWFUL THINGS HAPPENED UPON HIS ARRIVAL.

I AM afraid that the kind and indulgent reader, who has thus far followed the story of "Ruth the Betrayer," must have grown somewhat impatient at my curiously neglectful behaviour respecting the other characters in the tale, and have thought that my narrative of Ruth's personal adventures is slightly prolix.

But, reader, I must take the opportunity of assuring you that everything shall be shortly cleared up in the most satisfactory manner, and that I am making the greatest possible haste to get on with as little delay as possible, and that I am now only describing the most important events which happened in Ruth's life, so eager am I to get on to that time coming when shall be enacted one of the most thrilling and extraordinary dramas which ever was acted, and which far surpasses anything that my poor pen has hitherto achieved.

So bear with me a little while longer, kind reader, for I am certain that if you have been at all amused hitherto, what is coming will afford you much more gratification than what has gone before

And now let us return to Madame.

In the first place, I must beg of you to suppose that the night has passed away, and that it is seven o'clock next morning.

Have Ruth's slumbers been disturbed? Not in the least

How has Madame slept? She has not slept a wink.

It is a well-known fact that love destroys its victim's appetite, and deprives its victims of rest. Being, then, the victim of a most unfortunate and hopeless passion, the poor lady passed a sleepless night, and arose unrefreshed in the morning.

She arose, however, with one settled determination—a determination to be revenged upon the young priest for his insulting treatment of her.

She quitted the room after a hasty toilet, and a neighbouring clock was striking eight as she proceeded along the landing upon her way to the top of the stairs.

Upon her way she had to pass the room in which Ruth had slept.

The door was open.

Madame, supposing that the young priest had completed his toilet, and gone down stairs, was about to enter the room when she was arrested by the hum of voices in the shop below.

One was a strange voice, and she went to the stair-head to listen, fancying for the moment that it resembled the voice of the young priest.

But half a dozen words proved that this was not the case, because she heard that the person was a sweep boy who had been ordered to come early that morning, though at first Madame had forgotten the circumstance

Indeed, the circumstance may at first appear to the reader to be so trivial as to cause some surprise at my having mentioned it; but my reason for so doing is to call your attention to the fact of the shop below being already open at this early hour, and to explain the reason of what was a very unusual event in this household.

Having satisfied herself upon the point about which she had been doubtful, Madame now re-returned to Ruth's apartment.

That eccentric young lady had not quitted it, however, as her hostess supposed.

She was of late, since her sojourn in the French prison, rather an early riser, and she had already descended to the floor below, when she recollected that she had left that famous diary of her sister's lying upon the table of a small inner room, where over-night she had been reading it

When up here, in the inner room, which was a sort of boudoir leading out of the bedroom, having put the book safely away in her pocket, she naturally paused for a moment to adjust her tresses.

While thus engaged, Madame, innocent of her presence, entered the outer room.

She walked forward, therefore, past the bed, and reached the door of the boudoir before she made the discovery.

A slight scream, to which she gave utterance in her first surprise and alarm, caused Ruth to turn hastily.

"I beg your pardon!" the lady exclaimed, retreating towards the bedroom door; "I did not know you were here!"

As she spoke, she had her hand upon the door-handle.

She paused in terror.

Outside, upon the landing, she heard the rustle of a silk dress, the sound of a footstep. She recognised a short, dry cough she knew in a moment

Outside, upon the landing, she heard Miss Virginie.

The question was, had Miss Virginie heard her?

She stood motionless, with her hand still upon upon the door handle

She heard Virginie's footsteps retreating up the passage, in the direction of her (Virginie's) bedroom.

Madame thought, if she could only get out of the young priest's room before her shopwoman returned, she would be all right.

But before she could open the door, Virginie did return; and she came direct to the door, upon the other side of which Madame was standing.

The fact was, that this was properly Madame's own bedroom; but she had given it up to the visitor, as it was the best bedroom in the house.

Virginie, not being aware of this arrangement, thought the young priest had slept in a spare room, and came knocking at the door, calling for her mistress. At the same moment, Madame's husband was heard calling out loudly below stairs.

Madame was at her wits' end.

She could not hope to escape discovery.

She could not avoid their finding out that she was there locked in with the priest.

A thought struck her.

As she could not avoid discovery, why not turn the discovery to good account?

Why not make it the means of vengeance?

Her plan was formed in a moment.

She began to shake the door violently, and shriek for help at the top of her voice.

"Help! Murder! Fire!" &c.

The husband rushed up the stairs, and he and Miss Virginie began to shake the door violently, whilst Madame called loudly for help.

Ruth was at first dumbfounded by these extraordinary proceedings.

She was at first quite at a loss to conceive the motive Madame could have for so behaving.

But presently, among the "murders" and "fires," she mentioned another calamity, which was supposed either to have befallen, or about to befall her; and Ruth, in spite of the extremely unpleasant position in which she was placed, could not refrain from a slight smile.

Much further concealment, it was very certain, could not exist.

She felt inclined then and there to reveal the secret of her sex; but one idea prevented her.

"I'll pay my lady out," she thought, "in a way she don't expect!"

With this idea, Miss Ruth took a seat, and looked as calm and unconcerned as she could.

Madame, without noticing her, continued to scream, and shake the door.

Virginie, on the outside, shrieked also; and Duval strove, with all his might and main, to rescue his wife.

At length, in spite of the poor dear victim's efforts, the door of the room was forced open.

Then the interesting lady flung herself a dead weight into her husband's arms.

Miss Virginie, catching sight of the young priest, became hysterical.

The unfortunate husband, catching sight of the same object, allowed his wife to fall, and sprawl upon the ground in anything but a graceful position.

"Monster!" cried Miss Virginie, alluding to Ruth.

"Scoundrel!" cried Mr. Duval, also referring to the same young lady.

"Wretch!" cried Madame Duval, meaning her husband.

The Frenchman—he was a a little, podgy man, very red in the face upon all occasions, but perfectly crimson upon this—rushed into the bedroom, and up to Ruth, in whose face he shook his fist.

"Sir!" he screamed, when he could speak at all, for his wrath, at first, almost choked him,—"sir!"

"Well?" replied Ruth, with her accustomed coolness.

"Well!" shrieked the outraged husband. "How dare you sit there, calmly, when you have done me the greatest wrong which it is possible for one man to do another?"

"If I have done you any wrong——"

"If?"

"Exactly! If I have wronged you, I am willing to give you every satisfaction."

"Why, you infamous villain, do you mean to say——"

"I said nothing. What satisfaction do you require?"

"Satisfaction, sir?—the satisfaction of a gentleman, sir! Immediate satisfaction! Deadly satisfaction! We must fight, sir, at once!"

"I'm quite willing. How?"

"With pistols, if agreeable."

"With red-hot pokers, if you choose," replied Ruth, laughing.

The Frenchman was furious.

"Do not think that you are going to treat this affair as a joke," cried the little Frenchman, foaming with passion. "Stay where you are a moment, and I will bring the pistols with me."

So saying, he rushed out of the room, and made for his own private apartment, where he kept his duelling pistols.

Returning with these in his hand, in a few moments, and looking very murderous indeed, Miss Virginie flung herself in the way, and endeavoured to bar the passage.

"Spare his life!" she sobbed.

"He or I die!" replied the Frenchman sternly.

"Oh, spare him! As you hope to be spared yourself, spare him!"

"If you have any respect for me, kill him!" cried Madame.

"You and I must have some conversation presently," said the Frenchman, sternly; "but first this affair must be settled!"

And he waved Madame off with an imperious gesture.

However, his wife was not at all the sort of a woman to quietly put up with such treatment, and she planted herself before him with her arms akimbo.

"Monsieur Duval!"

"Madame!"

"Do you intend, sir, to insinuate that I am to blame in this matter?"

"I have said that we will discuss that question presently."

"With your leave, on the contrary, we will discuss it now!"

"Madame, this interruption is, to say the least of it, indecent!"

"Sir, your conduct, to say the best of it, is absurd!"

Here the husband shook his fist, and the wife snapped her fingers.

Ruth, in the meantime, stood laughing at them both.

"Are you ready, sir?" cried the indignant Frenchman over his wife's head.

"Perfectly, when you are!" replied Ruth.

The husband waxed so awfully indignant at the unexpected way in which his supposed wronger treated him, that he thrust his wife violently upon one side, and rushed past her into the room where Ruth was waiting for him.

Arrived inside, he locked the door; then laid the pistols upon the table.

"Are they loaded?" asked Ruth.

"Yes. We will unload them, and reload again, if you like?"

"Oh, no! the loading will do very well, I daresay."

"Choose one, then."

"First of all, I must ask a question."

"Very well, sir: I await your pleasure."

"What are we fighting for?"

"Fighting for?" shouted the Frenchman. "Why do you persist in this absurdity? Come, sir, take your pistols, or I'll shoot you down like a dog!"

"My dear sir," replied Ruth, with a quiet smile, "allow me, first of all, to make a trifling explanation; after which, we will fight as long as you choose."

CHAPTER CXX.

AN UNSATISFACTORY EXPLANATION LEADS TO A SATISFACTORY TERMINATION OF THE MATRIMONIAL SQUABBLE—RUTH TURNS HER FACE AGAIN TOWARDS ENGLAND, IN THE TEETH OF A GALE AND UNDER A LOWERING SKY.

"Madame," cried the Frenchman, bouncing out of the room about twenty minutes afterwards, "your conduct is scandalous!"

"Have you listened to what that scoundrel was said about me?"

"I have."

"And you believe him, in preference to your wife?"

"When I have told you what his explanation is, you will believe him also."

Then the husband told the wife something in a whisper, which caused the lady to go off, without a moment's notice, into a fit of hysterics, from which she did not recover all the rest of the day.

Towards the evening, however, matters were settled in a much more satisfactory manner than one would at first have supposed to be possible.

The circumstance which led to this alteration in the state of affairs was the discovery by Miss Virginie of Mr. Duval making violent love to Miss Ruth in the back parlour, while his wife was fainting up-stairs.

Madame having, upon receipt of this intelligence, instantaneously recovered from a fainting fit, which had previously laid her prostrate for rather more than an hour and a half, rushed down stairs, and pouncing upon the perfidious pair, surprised Monsieur kissing Ruth's hand.

Nothing, strange to say, could have conduced to a more satisfactory conclusion than this discovery; for now, the lady having an equal cause of complaint to her husband—for that shameful wretch was now as much bewitched by the fair-haired syren as his wife had been when she supposed Ruth to be a pretty young priest—a tremendous row ensued, and then a general reconciliation and general forgiveness; and Monsieur and Madame concluded by loving each other rather more than ever they had done.

But at the same time it must be confessed when the hour arrived for the boat to start for England, which was to carry away Miss Ruth, Madame Duval was by no means sorry.

The boat did not start as soon as they had supposed, for during the night an awful gale had sprung up, and the captain deemed it unwise to leave the harbour.

Several times during the day, Ruth, whose anxiety momentarily increased with the delay, induced Mr. Duval to go down to the pier to ask when the boat would be likely to start.

But upon each occasion he returned only to say that the gale had increased in fury, and that the prospect of leaving France grew more and more vague.

"Is there any way of going overland to some other port?" Ruth asked.

It appeared that there was not; and towards the close of the day, Monsieur Duval brought back the melancholy intelligence that the Captain had decided his boat should not start at all till the next day.

The delay would be fatal, for this reason.

Telegraphic messages had been sent, at the first alarm of Ruth's escape, to all the ports, but a full description of her person had not been forwarded. By this time probably such had been the case—or, at any rate, it very soon would be.

Upon consideration, it was decided that the safest place to start from would be the port of this town, which was the most unlikely one that she would start from, as it was to be supposed that one port would be watched so carefully.

Ruth, however, was of a contrary opinion. By the evening she thought it extremely likely that the prison authorities for the most part would have worn themselves out talking the matter over, and would have given her up for lost.

Anyhow, she determined to risk it. Only, now, what was she to do, since the boat, after all, did not start?

At last, to her great joy, M. Duval came back with the intelligence, which, hitherto, he had stupidly enough neglected—namely, that the mail boat left the harbour that evening, fine weather or foul. She, therefore, determined to go by that boat if she could get safely on board, and safely out of the harbour.

The mail packet was to start at midnight. It was then eleven o'clock, p.m., for the day had somehow or other dragged heavily away.

If she were to go, she must go at once, now—without further delay or procrastination.

Duval agreed to accompany her; Madame and Virginie were also to go; and they had expected that the old priest would have joined the party, but for some unexplained cause he absented himself. Perhaps he thought that the secret of Ruth's sex had, in all probability, by this time been disclosed, and he was ashamed of showing his head.

When the little party left the shop, and set out upon their hazardous adventure, it was, in the sailors' parlance, "blowing great guns."

The bitter wind, driving a drenching sleet before it, swept through the almost deserted streets, the intense cold appearing to gnaw its way into the very marrow of their bones.

Few people were likely to be abroad in such inclement weather, and few people they met.

In French towns one does not meet with the poor outcast beggars crouching in doorways and dark corners, where they can obtain a slight shelter from the wintry blast, such as no pedestrian accustomed to thread the vast labyrinth of bricks and mortar we call London, can have failed many times to observe when the weather has been so bad, one has almost thought it too bad for a dog to be turned out of doors in.

There were no beggars, such as there are in the town where this scene of our story is taking place. The only persons to be met with, and these only at long intervals, were a solitary fisherman or sailor, tacking unsteadily before the wind, returning from the public-house where they had been imbibing rather more freely than was their wont—perhaps rendered desperate and reckless by the unfavourable appearance of things without—and a police or custom-house officer creeping round a corner with that wary, not to say sneaking manner, in which foreign officials are so proficient.

Luckily for our friends, none of these persons whom they encountered upon their way seemed to entertain any suspicion of the loyalty of their designs, and with the exception of a good hard stare, allowed them to pass without appearing to notice anything remarkable in the fact of their being out so late.

Very soon they made the journey between the shop and the harbour

When they had left the streets behind them, all the objects ahead of them seemed enveloped in a pitchy darkness, which was so intense as to appear to them almost as though it possessed a palpable consistency.

Only at one spot was any light visible. A large lamp swinging to and fro with each gust of wind, and every instant threatening to swing altogether off the hook to which it seemed to be attached, and shiver to a thousand atoms upon the ground beneath, indicated the position of the custom-house.

As they drew near to it, Ruth fancied that she could discern in the dim outline of a man standing within, and close to the door, the uniform of one of the officers of the prison.

"I must not go in there," she whispered to her companions.

"But you must get a permission to embark."

Such a passport it is always necessary that a native of France should obtain before he will be allowed to leave the country; and until lately it was also necessary for English people to observe the same formality.

"Cannot you get me one?" asked Ruth.

"No; I am too well known. I cannot ask for it fo myself with a feigned name, and if I did, the description would not do when compared with your personal appearance."

"Cannot you ask for one for me?"

"No; it is necessary that the applicant should apply personally."

"Very well; come on."

A very sharp-eyed man, whose eyes were rendered even sharper than they would otherwise have been by a pair of spectacles which he wore upon the end of his nose, and which he looked over and under, and upon either side of, and indeed every way but right through—a very sharp-eyed man sat at a high desk, with a pen behind his ear, which he took into his hand at their approach, dipped into the ink, and prepared to write with upon a sheet of paper lying ready before him.

"A permission to embark?" he said interrogatively.

"Yes."

"Name?"

"Jerome Ducange."

"Age?"

"Twenty."

"Hem!—ha! Not much beard. Profession?"

"Priest."

"From whence?"

"From the Monastery of St.——, in this town."

"Where to?'

"To England."

"Passport?"

"None."

The man filled up these particulars, eyeing the person he addressed suspiciously from time to time, as though he had no faith in the truth of the statements she was making.

But when the former had been filled up to the writer's satisfaction, he handed it over to Ruth without any further remark; and she, scarcely believing in the reality of her escape, moved towards the door, passed the threshold, and plunged into the darkness without, followed by her friends, unchallenged.

So far, so good. The distance from the custom-house to the boat was but trifling, and they had soon reached it.

When she had got safely on board, her friends bade her good-bye, without delaying the parting moment any longer.

To tell the truth, they were not too sorry to get rid of their companion, for the companionship was rather dangerous. Their fair fame in the little seaport town had hitherto been untainted, and they had no wish to get into a scrape for the sake of this woman, who, as it was, had already caused quite sufficient discord in their small circle.

I am not quite certain, mind, whether that rascal Duval did not endeavour in a quiet underhand sort of way to hang behind, and have a quiet leave-taking of his fair friend, unseen by Madame, but Mrs D. was much too sharp for him, and in spite of his tricks, lugged my gentleman off the boat without giving the smallest opportunity of effecting his scandalous purpose.

Nor did she afterwards for a single moment relinquish her hold of him until she had him safely in her own home, and under lock and key.

Meanwhile, Ruth paced the deck alone, watching the lights quivering in the water, and the water itself, protected in the harbour from the violence of the wind without, gurgling and moaning restlessly between the piles, and the lighters, and the small fishing craft moored alongside the mail packet

There is ever, I fancy, a strange repose about a large steamer, starting in the dead of the night, if visited an hour or so before the time of starting.

Everything on board appears to be asleep. Even the wheel, in its occasional movements, as the rudder creaks in the water below, has the unmeaning motion of a restless dreamer.

Men lie about, like bales of goods, in the most comfortless positions on deck, and you tumble over their legs wherever you go.

There is a faint light through the bulls'-eyes, and down below, in the cabin, the steward is asleep, with his head on the table; while some of the passengers who have come early, and yet not early enough, to secure berths, endeavour to knock up uneasy beds of hard carpet-bags and hat-boxes, which seem full of sharp edges turn them where you will, upon narrow, hard shelves of horsehair.

Now and then the clank of irons and furnace-doors is heard below, and by the light from the glowing engine-room, streaming up through the bars and rails, a thin column of vapour is seen rising from the steam-funnel.

All else is still.

A far different state of things is this, though, to that when, an hour or so hence, plunging, rolling, and madly beating away the black and lashing waves, with every fibre creaking and straining, every glass gingling, and every door chattering, throbbing from the mighty pulsations of its huge, boiling heart, the great monster soars across the dark and leaping wilderness of angry waters.

Ruth had not been very long on board before the police-officers paid their visit on board to make sure that nobody was about to start without a permission such as Ruth had obtained from the custom-house.

She was on the deck, in the shadow of the funnel, and standing in a position that she could not easily have been noticed, even had any one been looking for her.

The captain, passing close by her, did not see her—nor did the police-officers, who met him; and they entered into a conversation within a few feet of the spot where she stood, of which she soon found that she herself was the subject.

You may be sure she did not feel inclined to make her presence known, and that she listened attentively to all they said.

"Well, captain?"

"Well, gentlemen?"

"Many passengers on board?"

"Not many, I fancy. I haven't seen many."

"How many?"

"I've seen two only."

"French or English?"

"One of each."

"Oh, indeed! What sort of a person is the English passenger?"

"Young man—curious sort of fellow—rather light-headed, I fancy."

"Saloon passenger?"

"Yes."

"And the other?"

"A young French priest."

"Ah, to be sure! He came into the office a little while ago for a permission. We don't want him. But we'll look at the other."

They marched off after this, and presently Ruth, taking a turn upon the deck above, and happening to pause at the top of the steps leading to the saloon, was tempted to pause a moment and enlist.

Some one in a weak and effeminate voice, and in extremely bad French, was remonstrating indignantly with the police-officers.

"What the devil do you mean?" the voice demanded in a shrill tone.

"Where's your permission?"

"Well, here it is; and there's my name, if you can read. Now, will that satisfy you?"

"Have you got a passport besides?"

"Well, if I have, it's at the bottom of my portmanteau."

"Don't you know whether you have or not?"

"Yes, I do Do you want to see it?"

"Yes, we do want to see it."

"What the deuce do you suspect me of? Who do you suppose I am?"

"Show us your passport."

"Well, there it is; is that satisfactory?"

"It seems so."

"Seems so? It's curious if it isn't satisfactory, for I'm sure it's been signed and countersigned by every big wig in every town I passed through."

"We must do our duty, sir. We can't help it if we annoy you; we've got orders to examine carefully all who leave this port"

"Well, I've left it before half a dozen times in my life, and I never was a quarter so much annoyed."

"Well, we must do our duty."

"But what's the reason for it?"

"Well, you see, there's a female broke out of one of our prisons."

"Well, what of that?"

"She's an Englishwoman."

"What of that?"

"We expect she's disguised as a man."

"I'll be hanged if I see what that has got to do with me!"

"Well, sir, you see——"

"But, I don't see!"

"We fancied—though now we think otherwise—we fancied you were the party."

A tremendous volley of oaths in French and English concluded the dialogue, and the police officers returned again to the deck.

Ruth avoided them carefully, and very soon she had the satisfaction of seeing them go ashore.

A great scuffling, and shouting, and banging, and bumping, such as attends the departure of a vessel upon most occasions, now ensued, and very soon they were ploughing their way through the tempestuous water, bound for England—the land of liberty.

It would be difficult to imagine, or even to realize, the intense delight with which Ruth watched the fast increasing distance between herself and the shore of the hateful country she was leaving behind her.

England, dear England—if it had been possible for her to be sentimental on any theme, I believe that she really would upon this occasion have been induced to display it. Poor fool! she fancied that her troubles were at an end, and that the land of liberty she was bound for would be a land of liberty to her, and not a land of slavery and bondage.

She little thought of the dreadful future in store for her. She looked out upon the bleak, black prospect ahead, and descried therein bright and hopeful visions—alas! too soon to be blotted out by the dread reality.

While she was meditating smilingly upon the career which she supposed to be in store for her, a voice behind aroused her from her reverie.

Ruth turned quickly, and found herself face to face with a remarkably weak-looking young man, with wide open eyes and straggling locks of hair, the colour of hay.

"Oh, you're the priest I saw come on board a little while ago, ain't you?"

"Yes."

"You heard those policemen tackling me just now, that took me for a woman. Did you ever know such a thing?"

"It was very complimentary to the lady."

"I should have thought they might have known who I was," the young gentleman continued. "Almost everybody in the town knows me, and I am sure everybody does in England."

"Indeed, sir! You must be famous!"

"I am famous—don't you know me?"

"I am ashamed to confess."

"Well, there—I'll tell you, then. My name is Kid."

"Cadbury Kid?"

"The same."

"Then I know you, also, by hearsay," replied Ruth; "and I am extremely happy to make your acquaintance!"

"I'm not sorry to make yours, for you are rather a good-looking young fellow, for a priest. But don't you speak English?"

"Pretty well."

"I should fancy you were English, by the look of you. I only wish you were that Englishwoman in disguise that they talk about."

"Why so?"

"Because, if you were, and you wanted any assistance, I'm the man that would give it you, for I hate the police, and all belonging to them!"

"Ha, ha! Suppose I really were the person, and were to take you at your word, how surprised you'd be, and how soon you would cry off the bargain!"

"I give you my word and honour I wouldn't. I was always a tender-hearted fellow, and I never would see a woman in distress."

"We'll shake hands upon that," said Ruth.

And it was thus that Ruth the Betrayer made the acquaintance of Mr. Cadbury Kid, who was the same extraordinary young gentleman, the reader may remember, I introduced to his notice in Chapter VI in this eventful history.

Very strange adventures were these two doomed to meet with in each other's company, as you shall see.

CHAPTER CXXI.

NIGHT IN LONDON. — THE OUTCASTS IN THE STREETS — WATERLOO BRIDGE. — WANTED, A HALFPENNY — THE SYMPATHISING HEART — JUST IN TIME — DOES SHE MEDITATE SELF-MURDER? — HOMELESS. — LOST!

It is the same night upon which Ruth made her escape from France.

We are in London, and it is night—a pouring, wet night!

Very few people are about in the streets; and those who are compelled to face the storm hurry along with up-turned collars, and do their best to reach the longed-for shelter.

A few beggars are huddled up in the warmest corners, and a few forlorn and wretched-looking women, with but scanty rags to cover their nakedness, hang about up dark archways, leering out, like witches, upon the passers by.

Upon Waterloo Bridge the wind is so high, that it is with the greatest difficulty that anybody can keep their legs at all, as they struggle onward in its teeth.

One woe-begone and miserable female so struggled, hugging her tattered garments closely round her poverty-pinched and emaciated form.

Half-way over the bridge she paused, and mounting into one of the recesses, looked over mournfully into the black depth below. She leant her chin upon her hand, and looked down with a gloomy, hopeless expression, and seemed to be lost in thought.

Then she made a movement, as though she were about to mount upon the seat.

Good heavens! she surely did not intend to commit suicide. Was she contemplating self-murder?

Had she determined upon her own death, and was she about to take the fatal spring?

"Stop! stop! for heaven's sake!"

It was a young man who thus addressed her, and who, rushing forward to the spot where she stood, clutched her suddenly by the skirt.

The woman turned round towards him, and stared him hard in the face.

She was a young, and even beautiful woman.

Her face was deadly pale, and a stray lock of hair hung across her forehead, giving her a wild and haggard look.

Her cheeks were pinched, and her features sharpened by want, but she was beautiful yet, and in her dark eyes there was a depth of pensive melancholy which gave her the expression of an angel.

As she met the young man's gaze those eyes fell, and a faint blush tinged her pallid cheek.

She was not, then, one of the fallen sisterhood, as he at first supposed. Such modesty could not be found among the class that he had thought she belonged to, nor could she have preserved that expression of gentle, innocent, almost angelic sweetness, through a life of shamelessness and crime.

But who was she?

Five minutes ago, when she had been standing chatting with the toll-keeper at the Strand entrance to the bridge, the same miserable creature had crept sadly up, and after fumbling among her rags for a halfpenny, not finding one, had turned away again with a heavy sigh, and appeared as though about to retrace her steps in the direction from which she had just come.

Just then, however, he had called her back, and asked her whether she wanted to go through the gate.

At first she seemed not to understand his question.

She was half dazed and dreamy, as though she had but recently recovered from the influence of some narcotic draught.

But when he had repeated his words she understood them, and replied, "I was going across the bridge, but I have no money."

"I'll pay for you."

"No, thank you"

"Why not?"

"I can walk round by Westminster."

"No, no! I insist on paying!"

"And I insist on refusing!"

"The bridge is paid, at any rate," said he, flinging down a halfpenny "You can avail yourself of it or not, as you think fit!"

The woman looked at him for a moment, as though she fancied that he was mad; and then, thanking him coldly, passed through the wicket

"Strange woman, that!" he remarked to the toll-keeper, when the darkness had swallowed her up

"Not very thankful, was she?"

"Not very," said the other, laughing. "Poor thing! She does not seem accustomed to receive any kindness, when a halfpennyworth knocks her off her perch!"

"What do you take her for, now?" he asked, after a slight pause, during which he had been trying to make up his own mind upon the point.

"Same as the others," replied the tollman, shortly.

"Same as what others?"

"The other women that walks the streets up at this part."

"I think you're wrong. She does not seem to be that sort of thing at all. I fancied so myself, at first."

"And now you don't?"

"No!"

"What do you think, then?"

"Can't quite make her out. She's an honest woman, though—I'll stake my like on it; and she has had a hard struggle to keep body and soul together. To tell the truth, do you know, I don't quite like the look of her—I mean the expression of her face!"

"Why?"

"I fancy, somehow, she means mischief There is a sort of determination and desperation, which looks to me as though she had made up her mind, and screwed up her courage, to do some desperate act!"

"Good heavens!"

"What is the matter, sir?"

"I suppose she intends to fling herself off the bridge?"

"Likely enough."

"You do not mean to say so, surely? I may be in time to save her, perhaps."

"I should stop where I was, sir, if I was you. If she means killing herself, she'll do it, in spite of all you can do to help her"

"Ah, I suppose you are right. Poor creature! I have only a few pence in my pocket, if she is in want of assistance."

"You'd have quite enough to do, sir, I expect, if you were to try and rescue every poor wretch that creeps past my gate in the course of the week, from starvation, or the workhouse, or suicide, or whatever end they are hurrying to."

"Are there many suicides from the bridge now? I thought the practice had been abandoned some time ago."

"There's a tidyish few yet, if we were to count 'em, I daresay. For my part, I've something else to do. Pay here, please!"

A party of men and women, half tipsy and very noisy, came skylarking up to the toll-gate, offering to toss the toll-man double or quits.

The young gentleman who had been talking to him, appearing to be anxious, the new-comers bade the man hastily "good night," and hurried on.

He came up just in time, as he supposed, to save the girl's life; and though when he laid hold of her dress she made no effort to drag it from his grasp he yet maintained a tight hold upon it, fearing that she would presently make another attempt at self-destruction.

"Thank God!" he said, as she came down to the pavement away from the tempting parapet —"thank God, I came in time!"

"Came in time!" she repeated after him, with a look of surprise.

"Yes, in time to save you!"

"From what?"

"From killing yourself!"

"I was not going to try," she said. "There is no fear. At the same time, you were very kind to try and stop me"

"Well," said the young gentleman, doubtfully, "I daresay what you say is true, only ——"

"Only what?"

"Only don't do it again, will you?"

"No, I promise you I won't."

"I'd rather see you safely off the bridge, and then I should be satisfied."

"Well, if you like. Only remember, it was you yourself who paid for me to come on."

"To be sure I was a fool for doing it. I might have known why you wanted to come."

"Indeed, sir, you are wrong."

"I hope so."

"If it will be any consolation to you, though, you shall see me safely over to the other side."

"I should like to Walk under my umbrella. Do you live anywhere hereabouts?"

"I don't live anywhere I have no home"

"Good heavens! What will you do, then?"

"Do?"

"Yes. You cannot mean to——"

"Mean to——"

"To sleep out in the streets on such a night as this?"

"I shall not sleep"

"What will you do?"

"I'll walk about until morning"

"You'll get your death of cold."

"Oh, no, I shall not, thank you."

"But I am sure you will."

"And I am sure I shall not."

"You look almost worn to death now. How cold you are, and how you shiver!"

"Nonsense; it is nothing."

"You are very ill!"

"No, I am not"

"You say you do not live anywhere. Do you work? What is your occupation?"

"I have none."

"You do not mean to say that you—you are —— I mean to say——"

"No, I am not!" she answered, drawing herself up with an indignant flash of her dark eyes. "I am obliged to you, sir, for your kindness, and I will wish you good night."

"Stay a moment."

But she broke from him, and ran, sobbing, down the steps close to the Feathers Tavern

He called after her twice and thrice, and was at first almost inclined to follow in pursuit.

But, upon reflection, he decided that such a course of conduct would be absurd and he allowed her to depart without making any further effort to detain her.

In a few more moments she was lost in the darkness.

LADY FLORENCE.

She had descended in to the labyrinths of filthy alleys and vile back slums below, where vice and poverty had their dwelling places.

CHAPTER CXXII.

A STRANGE MEETING.

It was a horrible neighbourhood into which she was penetrating. And one who knew it well has described it somewhat after this fashion.

Stacks of wretched houses, the dwellings of the wicked, the unfortunate, the furtive, the blighted, and the damned, are huddled together in mean design, one unblushing hot-bed of mental and physical decomposition.

These warrens for the burrowing and multiplying of wretched and depraved materialism adjoining the Waterloo-road—one, perhaps, further back in the world of morals and the bill of health than any other slums in the suburbs of the metropolis.

Dirty and slip-shod improvident wives of improvident mechanics loiter and gossip in gin-shop doorways, with females in figured finery, whose nameless occupation is betokened by the unmistakable evidences of stale carmine and a shameless arrangement of dress antagonistic to decorum, and in defiance of every known order in the architecture of female cost me.

Children—squalid, in-kneed, bandy, and bow-legged—fester in the fetid air of leprous exhalations, crying "Whoop!" at nightfall from hollow jaws and morbid lungs.

Into this choice locality the young woman

hurried with hasty steps, glad to get away from the young man, whose questions annoyed her, and whose sympathy, though kindly expressed, was more painful to bear than the misery which called it forth.

She was very glad when she found that she was again alone, and that he had not followed her.

Then she slackened her pace, for she was going nowhere, and had lots of time to spare.

Indeed, she soon fell into a creeping pace, dragging her feet slowly after her, in the way that outcast women wander along the streets.

And creeping on in this fashion, she came presently to a spot where there was a dark doorstep nicely shaded from the wind and rain.

Into this place she thought she would stow herself away, and rest awhile. Perhaps she might even be able to go to sleep for a while, and so cheat the weariness of the long dreary hours of darkness which had got to be yet through somehow.

Delighted at finding such a nook, the woman steps forward to enter the doorway.

But suddenly she started back, for she fancied in the darkness that she could discern the outline of a female figure, crouching.

She was right.

The exclamation she uttered in her first surprise caused the other outcast wanderer, who at the moment was dosing uneasily, with her head resting against the wall, and her face turned up wards, to start and open her eyes.

Then the two women, staring at each other fixedly and earnestly, uttered a sort of half-smothered cry of recognition, and stood still again, watching one another.

At last they spoke.

"Cecily!"

"Alice!"

"What are you doing here?" asked the woman who had been called Cecily, and who was the same that we have followed across the bridge.

The other looked at her silently—then made a gesture, as though to invite her companion to take a seat beside her.

The other repeated her question.

"What are *you* doing?" Alice asked.

"I am dying, I think; that is all."

"Not as bad as that, dear sister; don't say it is as bad as that."

"Why should I not? Do you care to live longer? I don't. I'm weary of this existence, and I shall not care how soon the grave closes over me."

"How have you fared since we parted? Have you been able to get any work?"

"None."

"Nor have I. But if we persevere——"

"Persevere! I am weary of persevering. There is only one way of getting our living—I am convinced of that; and rather than take to it I will take to the river flowing yonder."

"Yes, yes, Cicely," the other said, stealing her arm round her sister's waist, and pressing her gently against her own heart. "You are right, dear love. Better death than that—better death than that!"

"But what else is there for us?"

"I know of nothing."

"Just now, upon the bridge yonder, I was standing looking down into the black water beneath, thinking how quiet and calm it seemed, and how peacefully I might sleep, with icy arms around my heart, when a man caught me by the skirts——"

"A man!" cried the other, in alarm. "Not—not——"

"No one that we know. It was a stranger."

"Thank God for that!"

"What do you mean, Alice? What makes you tremble so?"

"Oh, dear sister, twice to-night, in this neighbourhood, have I seen that horrid man who persecuted me so cruelly."

"What, Eneas Earthworm?"

"Yes. I was fearful, when first you spoke, that you had met him also, and that he had recognised you."

"No. Did he recognise you?"

"Yes; he followed me for a long time. I managed at last to give him the slip; and worn out with fatigue, for I had been running to avoid him——"

"Did he speak to you?"

"Yes, he claimed my acquaintance up there in the Waterloo Road. He came upon me suddenly, and clutched me all at once by the wrist. I was dreadfully terrified, and cried out to the passers by for protection."

"Will he never cease his persecutions of you?"

"I fear not!" said Alice, with a sigh. "If we could only have got away from this hateful town; but, as you say, Cecily, I see no chance of doing so."

"Have you been equally unfortunate?"

"I have tried high and low for employment."

"And have found none?"

"None that I could take."

"Have you heard of anything at all?"

"I was asked to day if I would mind being a model to an artist."

"What is that?"

"I was to sit to a class of young artists in Berners Street, and I was to receive two guineas a week, but——"

"But what?"

"I was to remain every day for a couple of hours in a state of perfect nudity in the presence of a room full of men. Of course I declined."

"And you found nothing else?"

"I had also an offer from a photographic establishment, where the services I was to render were of such a shameful and horrible nature, that I shudder at the bare recollection of their recital."

"Poor Alice! it is, as I said—there is no way open to us of earning an honest living."

"Have you, too, tried and failed?"

"God knows I have! I applied at a public-house, where I saw a paper in the window stating that the services of a *pianiste* were required within, at a small concert. The man serving behind the bar asked whether I could sing as well, and if I had a good voice. And when I told him I could, he asked if I would mind singing a song that was a bit spicy, as that was the kind that pleased his customers."

"What did he mean?"

"I did not know myself, and so I asked him whether he had any such songs as he meant, and whether he would allow me to see them?"

"Well?"

"Then he went into the room behind the bar, and looked in a drawer, returning presently with a piece of tissue-paper, on which some verses were printed. One side was "Home, sweet home," and the other was a song that had no name. I read the first one through, and said that it was the old one that I knew, and I told him so, and that I was also acquainted with the air. But he burst out laughing, and told me to spell through the the other, and see if I knew that."

"Well?"

"Oh, dear Alice! at first I could not understand the meaning of the strange expressions and the slang terms in which it was written; but I did not remain long in ignorance of the revolting nature of the atrocious composition. With the blood rushing in a torrent to my face and neck, covered with confusion, and indignant beyond the power of words, I flung down the filthy paper, and rushed out into the street."

"What infamy!"

"Alas, such is not the only insult I have suffered!"

The other sister grasped Cecily's hand, and held it sympathetically in hers, while Cecily pursued the theme in a thoughtful and abstracted mood, much as though she were unconscious of giving utterance to her thoughts in words, but was pursuing the course of her reflections silently, and to herself, for her own gratification.

"I have been refused at drapers' shops," she said, "because ladies prefer to be waited on and ogled by members of the opposite sex, just as men prefer pretty waiting girls to serve them to men-waiters. I might have got a place as serving girl at a coffee-house in the Haymarket, only that the landlady gave me plainly to understand that I must suffer the most shameful insults and liberties from the gentlemen customers, even did I not altogether yield to their passions."

"Dreadful!"

"One advertisement that I was rash enough to answer, and which intimated that several young females of pleasing manners and attractive personal appearance were required for some light business, where a good salary would be given, I found was only a snare to catch unprotected young creatures, and effect their ruin in a dreadful house in the neighbourhood of Pall Mall. In short, I have tried hard, and I have failed; there is only one life left for us, I see—only one frightful alternative!"

CHAPTER CXXIII.

THE LAST RESOURCE.

WHILE they were thus talking together, two or three miserable draggle-tailed women, so worn and woe-begone that, saving their raiment, there was nothing else womanly left about them, came creeping up to the doorway where the sisters sat.

They did not observe Alice and Cecily, hidden as they were in the deep shadow of the wall, and they began to shiver and grumble over their griefs and sorrows among themselves, without noticing that they had any listener to their lamentations.

They were talking of the dreadful trade they were for dear life compelled to ply in this stony-hearted city.

One of them, when she got work to do, made mantles at three-halfpence each—another went out washing.

They were poor pinched up, haggard, and miserable creatures—mere bags of bones. Heaven only knows among what class of men they could have sought out brutes willing to profit by the misery and desperation which prompted them to seek such a means of existence.

While they were talking together, complaining of their bad luck, the hardness of the times, the iniquities of the poor-law, the brutality of the police, and the high price of intoxicating liquors, another woman came up, neatly dressed, who paused for a moment in front of them, fancying perhaps, that she knew one of the group; but finding that she did not, hastened on again in some confusion.

"Who's she?" one woman said.

"I know her face, though I don't know her name."

"What lay's she on?"

"The same as ours, I reckon."

"Do you mean it?"

"Why not?"

"She looks so precious quiet!"

"Ah! and modest, too."

"A lot of that, I guess!"

"She's as bad as the rest of us, I suppose, only she has better luck?"

"That's it; but we had better be stirring."

"I think so; it will be daylight soon, and I've earned nothing"

"And I've three empty mouths at home, that will be crying for their breakfast."

"How the wind cuts one—don't it? I'm fainting for a drop of drink."

"Ours is a sad lot. God help us, but one can't starve!"

They shuffled and shambled away with this, and were soon lost in the gloom.

The sisters looked after them with heavy hearts, and sighed deeply.

And that, perhaps, they thought, was the frightful end to which they were journeying.

And what beyond?

In the distance between the houses, a glimpse was obtainable of the dark and silent stream flowing on and towards the open sea.

What was to follow? And then?

* * * * *

"Alice!"

"Cecily!"

"Let us pray together!"

And two innocent angel faces look up towards the dark blue heaven above them, full of gentle resignation, hope, and faith. The storm has abated in its fury, and the rain has ceased. The moon creeps out from behind the angry clouds, which hitherto has hidden its placid beauty, and beams down upon these tender lambs, cast helpless upon a wicked wilderness of bricks and mortar, peopled by hungry wolves and beasts of prey, savage and pitiless, with nothing to defend them but their own spotless purity and innocence.

* * * * *

The same young woman who had come up a little time back, when the other unfortunate creatures were talking together, returned presently, pacing wearily along, and looking for a moment covetously at the shaded doorway, stopped before it, and would have entered also, when she caught sight of the sisters within.

Then she would suddenly have hurried away, but Cecily called to her.

"Come in."

"No, thank you."

"There is plenty of room."

"Never mind."

"But do come in."

The young woman just urged, after some trifling hesitation, consented.

But she screwed herself up to the smallest possible compass.

She seemed, indeed, to be desirous of keeping

aloof from the other two, at whom she did not even look.

"It's very cold where you are sitting," said Cecily. "Come further in."

"But do you feel the cold?"

"I am cold."

"Well, then——"

"It does not matter!"

"What do you mean by it does not matter?"

"Oh, leave me alone!" the other cried, bursting suddenly into tears—"leave me alone! I'm very wretched!"

They said nothing to the poor thing for some time, but allowed her to weep to her heart's content.

Presently, though, she grew calmer; and then, yielding to the kind words with which the sisters greeted her, and the sympathizing manner in which they professed a desire to hear her sorrows, she told them her story

It was, indeed, a wretched one, but too long to be narrated in these pages.

She had been shamefully betrayed, and brutally deserted, like many others.

She had taken to the streets as the one means of earning her daily bread, and her life now was one of struggle and privation, starvation and misery.

But perhaps the most dreadful part of her tale was this.

She had a father, a poor, grey-headed, doting old man, who lived far away in the country—whom a paralytic attack had rendered incapable of work.

This poor old gentleman never in his life having been to London until now, and having had his fare paid by some generous person in the country, came up to see his daughter.

He found her, as he supposed, earning her living by millinery.

She, however, obtained a holiday from her shop, she said, to show him the sights of London.

She took him to St Paul's, and to the Monument, the British Museum, and the National Gallery.

He was delighted, as you may suppose; but how do you think she obtained the money necessary for the treat?

After she had passed the day in taking him from place to place—when the good old man had read his Bible and said his prayers, and gone peacefully to his slumber—she put on her bonnet and shawl, and stealing on tip-toe down the stairs, and into the streets, there to play the fearful trade by which she lived.

The old gentleman, meanwhile, happily unconscious of the sacrifices that the miserable girl was compelled to make upon his account, snored away the night happily enough, and, come morning, was, as usual, ready for his breakfast, and more sight-seeing.

"And are you not afraid that he will find you out?"

"I fear for my life that he will."

"And then?"

"And then——"

She paused, and covered her face with her two hands, through the fingers of which her scalding tears gushed forth.

She rocked herself to and fro, in bitter anguish.

"Oh, my God!—oh, my God!" she murmured, in a tone that was scarcely audible. "He would curse me!"

The sisters endeavoured to comfort her, but in vain.

After awhile she rose to her feet, saying that she must be gone—that she was in a hurry—that the night was wearing away.

They would have detained her, but she resisted their advances, and listened not to their kind words.

Only she grasped tightly a hand that was held out to her, and, murmuring "God bless you!" sped away.

The sisters remained silent for some time. Then Alice, rising to her feet, asked the other whether she did not think it was time that they, too, should be going.

"Where?" asked Cecily, abruptly.

"I do not know."

"Nor I."

"But we cannot stay here."

"We might as well stay here as go elsewhere. We can only wander in the miserable streets if we leave here; and to what end?"

"I know not."

"You would not have us take to the course of life that that poor outcast pursues?"

"No, no!"

"For my part, I would rather die first."

"Yes, yes; far rather, sister."

"Why not, then?"

"What?"

"Why not, I say? Yonder lies the river, cold and peaceful. Come, what say you?"

But Alice hung back, and trembled violently.

"No, no!" she said; "I dare not do that!—do not ask me to do that! Let us try once more—let us have one more trial! We are very young to die, Cecily—and by our own hands! No, no! God will not forgive us!"

"One more chance!" said the other girl, bitterly. "I am weary, and sick unto death! I see no hope of aught else in store for us. There are but two things to choose from—dishonour or death. Which say you?"

"Don't talk like that, my pretty little dears!" an old man's cackling voice at this moment broke in upon them.

The girls looked up in terror, and saw a dark form standing at the bottom of the steps.

"Don't talk like that, my pretty little dears! How snug you are in there, for all the world like two turtle doves! Oh, I have had such a trouble looking for you, pretty Alice!—and only to think that I should have the good luck to catch pretty Cecily at the same time!"

At his first advent the sisters had been so occupied by what they themselves were saying, that they had not been able to recognise the person who had thus unceremoniously mixed himself up in the conversation.

Now recognising him, Alice uttered a shrill scream.

"Eneas Earthworm!" she cried.

The old man replied with a hideous leer.

"Exactly so, my little dear," said he; "the very same."

"Oh, we are lost!" Alice cried, shrinking as far back as possible from the odious wretch who stretched out his claw like hand to clutch her.

"Not lost," retorted Earthworm—"only found. I shan't lose either of you again, my pretty pets, I can assure you."

And as he spoke, a smile passed over his hideous features which was perfectly satanic.

The hearts of the two defenceless victims sunk within them.

CHAPTER CXXIV.

WHICH SHOWS THAT OUR OLD FRIEND, MR. ENEAS EARTHWORM, HAD BY NO MEANS IMPROVED, EITHER MENTALLY OR PHYSICALLY, SINCE WE LAST HAD THE PLEASURE OF SEEING HIM; AND SHOWS ALSO HOW HE TREATED THE TWO POOR CREATURES HE HAD GOT INTO HIS CLUTCHES.

MR. EARTHWORM was no beauty when we saw him last.

That was a year ago.

A year had by no means improved him. Indeed, I don't mind going as far as to say, quite the contrary.

A year had increased his wrinkles, deepened his crow's-feet, and diminished his then scanty stock, and bared more than ever his ill-shaped head. He was really and truly as ugly as sin.

To have been compelled to dine opposite to such an ugly monster, would surely have been sufficient to damage the appetite of any sensitive man's digestion.

But to be the unfortunate object of the creature's love—to be obliged to submit to his hideous caresses, to become the victim of his hateful and sensual devices—such a fate was too horrible to calmly contemplate.

Yet such a fate was threatening the unhappy girls. Both had he most unmercifully persecuted, and though they over and over again repelled him with hatred and loathing, he persevered in his nefarious schemes with the same assiduity and merciless ferocity as ever.

Although, however, poor Alice, shrinking and trembling with terror and disgust, such as his presence never failed to inspire her with, felt inclined to swoon away with terror,—Cecily, on the other hand, was not of a nature to be so easily overcome, and she determined not to yield the superiority to their vile persecutor without a struggle.

Therefore, bidding her sister not to be afraid, she made a step forward, as though she would have forced her way past the old man, down the steps.

He, however, spread out his arms to bar the passage.

"Not so," he said with a fiendish grin. "Not quite so quick, my pretty, if you please."

"Let me pass."

"Oh!"

"You heard me, I suppose?"

"Yes, I heard you."

"Move on one side, then."

"I think not."

"What do you say?"

"I said I thought not."

"How dare you?"

"Dare, you say! Ha! ha!"

"Move on one side, or I'll make you repent this conduct."

"You talk very fiercely, but I like you the better for it," said the horrid old man, leering at her lasciviously. "I'm not very strong myself, as you know, but I've brought some one else to help me."

As he spoke, he pointed to a littl distance off, where two ruffianly-looking men were standing.

"Those are my friends," he said, "who won't stick at anything."

And to show that he spoke the truth, he called them.

They were not far off.

They were waiting just round the corner, ready to come if wanted.

Earthworm called to the men by name, and they approached at a rapid pace. When, however, they were close at hand he called to them to stop.

"Not yet," he said.

"Aren't you ready?"

"No, not quite."

"Are we to wait here?"

"One of you wait; the other look after the cab."

"All right."

"Keep a sharp look-out."

"Never fear."

"Be ready to come when I call."

"You shan't have to call twice."

They were awfully savage and uncouth ruffians, and, to look at, not at all the sort of men likely to be influenced by a defenceless woman's prayers and entreaties.

There was not much need for the old wretch into whose clutches the unhappy girls had fallen, to tell them that they had no chance of escape.

They felt that without his assurance of the fact.

But nevertheless he did tell them with a devilish chuckle.

"You see, my pretty birds, I don't do things by halves."

They made no reply to him.

"I've got you tight—tight—tight; and I mean to keep you so. I do—do—do! Ain't I a funny old man?"

"You are a monster," said Cecily, candidly.

"Do you think so?" cried Earthworm, with a smile, as though it were a compliment. "I'm not a beauty, am I? But what of that? It is not the handsomest men who are most successful in their love affairs. Handsome men want the women to make love to them. It is us ugly devils that know how to make ourselves so agreeable to the ladies."

The girls shrank back from him with horror; but the old wretch only seemed the more delighted the more evident was their hatred for his frightful advances.

"Bless you," he cried with apparent ecstacy, "there never was a more fortunate man than myself in these little affairs of the heart. The proudest and most beautiful women in London have given themselves up to me—have flung their lovely persons into my arms without a struggle. I've had more beauties for my mistresses than other men ever saw. Oh, I'm a lucky old dog!"

"Wretch!" cried Cecily, with an indignant fury which she could not repress. "I hate you! What would you have with us? What fiendish purpose can prompt you to pursue us thus? As there are so many others who, by your own shewing, would willingly give themselves up to you, why, then, waste your fascinations upon us? But you shall never succeed in your evil designs, —no, if we rather seek protection from you in death."

There was desperate determination in the force and attitude with which she accompanied these words, and it struck awe even into the heart of the hardened villain who addressed her. He was silent for a moment, and looked a little as though he was ashamed of himself. But it was not for long. Very soon he managed to overcome such a weak sentiment; and then assuming a tone of dogged sullenness, like a man who had set his mind upon the accomplishment of a design from which no power in heaven or on earth should turn him.

"Look here!" he said, in a stern voice. "Let us talk calmly if we can. I should like to ask you a question."

"Well?"

"From what you know hitherto of my conduct, do you suppose that I am a person likely to be easily thwarted in any scheme that I had set my heart upon carrying out?"

Although the trembling girls made no reply to this question, yet it was very evident to their minds, from what they knew of the person now addressing them, that what he said was correct, and their hearts, in mute terror, beat responsively in the affirmative.

The old man continued, after a pause.

"I need not remind you, Mrs. Trevellyan," said Earthworm, addressing Alice, "of the old times when first I made your acquaintance—when you were living with the husband for whose murder you were afterwards tried at Newgate—except it is to recall to your recollection the vows I then made, when you rejected my love with contempt, that if I lived you should be mine, and that your seduction should be my vengeance."

Alice covered her face, and sobbed, but made no answer.

"Since then," continued the old man, "my mind has remained unchanged—my resolve unaltered. When you lay in prison awaiting your trial, I came to you, and told you that I could prove your innocence, and obtain your acquittal, if you would be mine. You refused, like a fool. I came again I offered you another chance, which you again refused. I would have taken by force what your accursed prudery withheld, had not the gaolers come to your rescue at the moment; but I vowed then, as I vowed before, that you should be my mistress. You were tried, found guilty, and condemned to death. You would have been hanged if it had not been for me. Do you not believe that to be the case?"

"Yes. I know not what strange influence you possess, but you do seem to be able to carry all before you when you exert your power."

She murmured these words in a low tone—more as though she were speaking to herself than to the man addressing her; but his sharp ears caught what she said, and he replied, with a triumphant smile.

"I am glad to find that you acknowledge the truth of what I say," he remarked; "because you cannot then disbelieve any further statement that I shall make. You allow that I might have saved you twice had you acceded to my desires. You know also that it was entirely owing to my exertions, and in consequence of the bribes by which I corrupted the gaolers of your prison, that you and your sister made your escape?"

"I know that."

"Yes: you received a letter from me, telling you where you were to go when you got outside the prison walls. What was your return for my kindness? Nothing else but what I expected that it would be. You guessed whom it would be that you would have to meet—you guessed the price that you would have to pay for your liberty—and you determined to play me false—to have the best of me, and to slip through my clutches."

He paused for them to deny his statement, but they were silent, and he continued.

"Poor fools!" he said, bitterly; "to think that you could deceive me! By some chance you got out of the gaol, and at an earlier hour than I was informed that you would have made your escape. Consequently, I was not on the spot; but you surely might have known me well enough to know that I should provide for such an accident. I left an agent to watch you, and I tracked you both from place to place. Had I so chosen, I might at any moment have put my hand upon you, and delivered you over to justice. But that was not my plan. To-night, when I spoke to you, Alice, in the Waterloo Road, you might have come to terms with me. At that time the bills, offering a reward for your apprehension, had not been given into the hands of the bill-posters. Since then they have; and to-morrow morning every dead wall in London will bear your description—a full and accurate description supplied by me! There is now no escape for you—you must be mine!"

The two terrified girls had silently listened to the villain's words, too frightened to make any reply; and now Alice, sobbing, hid her face in her sister's bosom.

But Cecily was not so easily daunted, and with a glitter of defiance in her eyes, she said, "If such is the case, then, we will give ourselves into the custody of the police. By those means we shall, at least, preserve our honour."

"Not so," cried the old man, with a hellish laugh—"not so. You shall not escape me, I tell you. But listen to what I propose."

"We can readily imagine what your proposition will be."

"No, no, you cannot. Not so readily as you think. I do not propose that you should forfeit this virtue, upon which you set so much store. On the contrary, I will find you a home and employment."

"How can we believe you?"

"You might as well, because you must agree to my terms. The work I shall set you at is easy; you will be well fed and well clothed; you will live in the strictest privacy, and there will be no fear of your being discovered and dragged to the scaffold, from which you have had such a narrow escape."

"But if we refuse?"

"I should not advise you to do so."

"But if we do?"

"If you do, I will carry you away to my house, with the assistance of the men waiting there to receive my orders."

"And then?"

"And then I need hardly inform you what will be your fate. In my power, helpless and defenceless, I think that you will find it would have been much better had you at once yielded to my power. Nor by yielding then shall you escape an ignominious death; for when you are dragged upon the scaffold you will have the consoling thought to cheer you, that you die the cast-off mistress of the man you once affected to repel and despise."

"But how are we to know that such will not be our fate, even if we agree to the terms which you propose, and accept this employment?"

"You can do nothing but trust me!" the old man said with a sneer. "I should advise you to do that!"

And then, without waiting for further opposition, he stepped back into the road and called to his companions.

In another moment a cab was heard approaching round the corner.

The sisters hastily consulted together.

"What shall we do?" asked Alice.

"We will not go!"

"But if we scream, we shall be given into custody!"

"Let us try it!"

"Don't you believe what he says?"

"No!"

"But if ——"

"Well?"

"But if it should be true?"

"Then, surely, death were preferable to the fate in store for us."

"Yes, yes; I was weak and sinful."

"Come with me, then, and scream your loudest!"

They instantly made a rush out.

They ran full butt against the old villain, who attempted to stay their progress, and sent him flat upon his back.

But one of the men rushed up and grappled with them.

"Help! help! help!" they screamed.

The cab rapidly approached

It was driven by the other villain

"Help! help!" they shrieked frantically.

But their cries were in vain.

The ruffians easily overpowered the poor, weak, fainting girls.

They were forced roughly into the vehicle.

The old man got in with them, and pulled down the blinds, the horse was lashed into a gallop, and in another moment they were far away from the spot.

In vain they struggled now to make their voices heard.

One of the ruffians who had accompanied the old man into the cab brutally forced a gag into their mouths, which kept them mute.

CHAPTER CXXV.

THE CAB PROCEEDS ON ITS WAY.—THE MAIDENS' DESPAIR.—THE VIGLIANT "BOBBY."—THE DESERTED HOUSE.—IS IT HAUNTED?—THE CHLOROFORM.—THE TWO SCOUNDRELS.—BAFFLED CURIOSITY.—A MYSTERY NOT EASILY SOLVED

NOT content with gagging the unfortunate captives at the suggestion of the old man, the ruffian in his pay bound their wrists and ankles so that they were perfectly helpless.

With such merciless violence, too, was this done, that the cruel cord cut into the unhappy girls' soft flesh, and caused them intense pain.

They were unable to complain, however; and had they been able, it is not probable that they would have addressed a prayer for mercy to such scoundrels as these into whose hands they had had the misfortune to fall

They remained where they had been placed, or I should rather say flung, on the back seat of the cab, and silently turned over in their minds the probable fate in store for them, and the nature of the occupation to which the old man had alluded.

Was there any truth in it?

When they reflected upon the subject, though, they could hardly arrive at any other conclusion than that Earthworm had told them some gross falsehood in the hope of tempting them to come away quietly.

What end, then, was to be gained by speculating upon the probable termination of the adventure?

What could they look for but ruin and death?

They sank into a state of stupefied grief—almost a kind of torpor—in which they took no account of the time as it passed away.

Meanwhile, the cab continued upon its course, and keeping along the York Road, turned off down the Westminster Road to the left, and passed Bedlam.

They travelled on for about half-an-hour, and then came to a sudden halt

"Hallo!" said the old man, glancing round him through the window at the back; "are we here already?"

"We oughtn't to be yet!" said his companion.

"What's the matter?"

"Something up, I should say?"

While they were wondering, the door opened, and the driver put in his head.

"Why are you stopping?"

"A Bobby at the end of the street, hanging about to see what he can catch."

"Oh, that's it, is it?"

"I mustn't go up to the house while he's looking on, must I?"

"Of course not—take a turn along the road"

"He's moving on now; I shall be able to square it directly."

"Don't be too hasty. Wait till he's out of sight."

The driver went back to his perch, and the vehicle moved on slowly.

It would seem that the "Bobby" alluded to was one of the most vigilant of his class, and kept a sharp look-out, for the cab dawdled backwards and forwards for some time, and then went off at a brisk pace in a directly opposite direction to that which the driver intended to proceed when he thought himself free from the policeman's observation.

After making a good round by some back streets, he returned, however, to the spot from which he had started, and pulled up short.

The cab door then was opened

"Is it all right?" asked Earthworm.

"Yes, all is still!"

"The policeman is not looking?"

"No, he's gone off to the other end of his beat."

"You don't think he noticed you?"

"No; I took good care that he shouldn't have any suspicion of my intention"

"I will go and open the door; then you two fellows bring in the women when I whistle."

The old man got out of the cab and searched in his pocket for a latch-key, which having been found without much difficulty, he opened a street door and whistled to the men to follow; first, however, pausing for a moment to listen whether he could hear in the far distance to the right and left the sound of approaching footsteps.

But all was quiet.

It was a gloomy and deserted street, and the house into which he had stealthily admitted himself had all the appearance of being uninhabited.

It looked, indeed, very much like a house that had fallen into Chancery, and was being allowed to go to decay.

The lower windows were all boarded up, but all the panes of glass had long ago been broken by the vagabond boys of the neighbourhood, who found a cheap kind of excitement, without much fear of the result, in this mode of destruction.

In the same way, some one, a shade more daring than the rest, had stolen the door-knocker.

Dishonest persons had, from time to time, made

inroads upon the premises, and had carried away such trifles as the door handles, the scraper, and the bell-pull.

Any stray piece of iron about the front of the house that could be easily wrenched off and carried away, had been taken; and it appeared even as though, in some instances, desperate efforts had been made to wrench down the iron railings that protected what had once been the garden, while the gate had been carried away altogether.

Nobody could possibly have imagined that this house had any inhabitant from the appearances without.

It was lonely and deserted in the extreme, and looked a complete wreck and ruin.

Some of the superstitious old ladies of the neighbourhood said it was haunted, and there were rumours of strange noises heard within in the dead of night, but nobody had ever seen any ghost, or had noticed anybody going in or out.

Yet people did go in and out sometimes, and Mr. Earthworm, to whom the house belonged, frequently.

As we have seen, though, these visits were made with a great deal of caution, and hitherto so well had they been managed, that nobody was any the wiser.

When the old man whistled, his two accomplices carried the women into the house.

At his direction, they set them down in the passage, and he then sent one of the men back to drive away the cab immediately, so that it might not be seen loitering about in front of the house.

The old man closed the street door directly after his departure, and bade his companion to wait his return for a few minutes in the passage, and keep guard over the captives, while he fetched a light.

The passage was pitch dark, but Earthworm appeared to be well acquainted with its construction, for he rapidly felt his way along, descended some steps and entered a room at the back of the house.

Very shortly afterwards he appeared with a lighted candle, and called to the man to bring the captives forward.

As he was an immensely muscular and brawny ruffian, and the poor creatures were tied hand and foot, he easily managed to carry them both at once.

He bore them along in his arms, and entering the room at the door of which Earthworm was standing, placed them upon the dilapidated sofa which the room contained, without any other article of furniture.

When he had done this, the old man closed the room door carefully.

He then unlocked the door of a small cupboard, and took out a black bottle and glass.

"Will you have something?" he said.

The man nodded assent, and then gulped down some raw gin which Earthworm poured out for him.

This disposed of, the old man drew from his pocket a small phial with a glass stopper.

"Is that something extra good?" asked his companion. "Your own private tipple—eh?"

"Can you read?" asked Earthworm.

"I can spell a bit!" replied the other.

"Spell that, then!"

And the man spelt "C-h-l-o-r-o-f-o-r-m!"

He looked surprised when he had read it; and the other, with a smile, poured some of the contents of the bottle out upon a pocket handkerchief.

Then, while the ruffian in his pay held the unfortunate captives in such a position as to render their struggling impossible, Earthworm placed the saturated handkerchief over their mouths, and, closing their nostrils with his finger and thumb, forced them to inhale the insidious spirit.

In a few moments they were insensible

They lay there close together, as pale, as still as though death had laid its icy hand upon them; yet they lived.

Far better, perhaps, would it have been had they really been dead than lying there helpless, in the power of that atrocious miscreant.

The man who had assisted Earthworm looked at him, as though in some curiosity as to what was coming next But his curiosity with respect to the fate of the two unhappy maidens was doomed to disappointment.

Earthworm took up the candle from the mantelpiece on which he had placed it, and, opening the room door, led the way into the passage.

Here he paused to feel in his pocket, took out some gold, and placed it in the man's hand.

"There is more than I promised you!" he said. "Are you satisfied?"

"Quite satisfied!"

"Good night to you, then!"

"Don't you want me any more?"

"No!"

"Oh!"

He looked into Earthworm's face with a cunning leer, but his employer was perfectly serious; and though he would, perhaps, have liked to have known a little more of what was the meaning of the strange scene he had taken a part in, he did not think there was much chance of obtaining any satisfactory information in this quarter.

The old man having first carefully examined the prospect without, to see that no spies were hanging about in the neighbourhood, shaded the candle in such a way that it threw no light without, and opened the street door.

The man passed through, descended the steps in front of the door, and crossed to the opposite side of the road.

The door through which he had made his exit, was carefully closed and bolted.

The house was pitch dark as before, and as silent as the grave.

"What can the old scoundrel be up to?" the man muttered, as he walked away. "I think I could guess."

But though he did make several guesses, he guessed wrong—as you would, too, reader, I am inclined to think, unless you read my next chapter.

CHAPTER. CXXVI.

THE POOR GIRLS IN EARTHWORM'S POWER—HELPLESS AND UNCONSCIOUS.—THE MONSTER'S REVERIE.—THE INTERRUPTION.—FATHER DRAKE AGAIN—THE MYSTERIOUS UNDERGROUND STOREY—THE BASE COIN—THE TREAT

THE wicked old man paused and listened

After he had fastened the door again upon his late companion, he stood upon the inside with his head bent down and his hand placed behind his right ear, listening intently.

He listened until the footsteps of his brother scoundrel paused upon the other side of the street.

Yet then did he remain listening patiently

until the footsteps were again audible, as their owner plodded heavily away in the direction of the street corner.

It was not until the sound had altogether died away, and the old man, still straining his ears, felt certain that no other spy was hanging about in the quiet street without, that he moved away from the spot where he had hitherto been standing.

"He's gone!" he muttered. "Now for it!"

With a smile flitting over his grim features, which was perfectly hellish in its ferocious exultation, the old wretch took up his light and crept again down the passage towards the room from which he had just issued.

The two unhappy creatures still lay there as he had left them, bereft of consciousness.

They lay there pale as death, but surpassingly beautiful.

They lay there helpless and at his mercy.

His mercy! What mercy could they hope for from this most diabolical, treacherous, lecherous old villain.

He held the light above his he d, and waved it to and fro, shading his eyes with his hand.

The light fell full upon the faces of the sleeping beauties. So pure and innocent did they look, that no one but a demon could have meditated evil against them.

But was it not a demon who now glanced at them, with its wolfish eyes full of devilish malice and gloating lust?

He watched there for some moments silently, then burst out into a fiendish cackle, which sounded more like the noise made by an angry gander than any human laughter.

"Mine, mine, mine!" he cried aloud, placing the candle upon the mantel-piece, that he might rub his lank claw-like hands together in his goblin mirth, and caper to his heart's content. "Mine! mine at last! With no one to protect them, and nowhere to escape! What should keep me now from the perpetration of the grossest outrage, did I feel so inclined? And shall I not? We shall see; but not yet—not yet!"

He approached closer still to the inanimate forms of the unconscious girls, and bent down his head until his hot breath fanned the peach-like cheeks of those over whom he stooped.

Then, seemingly unable to restrain the violence of his desires, he pressed his hot lips upon the red, moist lips of the sleeping girls, and kissed them again and again with greedy eagerness.

But just then, when it was to be feared that the fury of his evil passions might have urged him on to the perpetration of some damnable outrage upon his powerless victims, a creaking sound upon the floor below startled him.

"Fool that I am to trifle in this way!" he said. "As though there were not time enough to revel in all themad enjoyments of love when I shall have them thoroughly in my power—when they have gone too far to retract—when their delicate hands are steeped in crime—when they are my slaves, in soul as well as in body!"

The creaking noise without, which had at first been very feeble, gradually increased. There a footstep might have been heard very cautiously ascending the stairs, and a hand was laid upon the handle of the door.

"Come in," said the old man, sharply turning round to face the intruder.

At the sound of his voice, the person without, whoever he might be, and who appeared to have been hesitating in fear whether he should enter, now thrust open the door and showed himself boldly.

He was a villanous scoundrel, you could see by the first glance at him—a sneaking, crafty-looking dog, with beetling brows; and he was no other than that Father Drake, who, upon the night when Cecily had escaped from the convent, had brutally striven to effect her dishonour, and who the young nun had stabbed with her sharp-pointed scissors.

"It is you, then!" said Drake, peering in at the old man. "That's well!"

"Who did you suppose it was, you fool?" the old man retorted fiercely. "Do you mean to say that you were idiot enough to show yourself, without first making certain that the coast was clear?"

"No, I don't mean to say anything of the kind, Mr. Earthworm. There's no occasion to be so violent!" said Drake, in a conciliatory and cringing tone. "I peeped at you, when you first came, through the peep-holes; and as you had said that you were coming, why I knew that it was all right, of course. But you did not tell me, when you mentioned the matter, whether or not the parties helping you knew of the secrets of this place. That was why I waited until they had gone away. Then I thought that perhaps one of them was coming back again ——"

"If you thought that, what made you come now?"

"I heard you shut the door. I knew that they could not come back suddenly. I thought you might want me."

"Shouldn't I have called if I had?"

"I did not know what had happened. I thought I had better come up and see!"

"You brought up a life-preserver with you, I see!"

"Yes, I thought I might want it if I had made a mistake!"

"Look here, now, Drake!—don't you make a mistake, that's all!" growled the old man savagely; "because, if you do, it will go badly with you, mind that! If my secrets get known, and the hiding place and implements discovered through any fault or bungling of yours, I swear to God your life's not worth a brass farthing!"

The other man was silent, scowling darkly.

"You wretched idiot!" continued Earthworm; "I have told you a score of times that you have no caution, no care, no sense. You act like a maniac, and not like a reasoning creature. Take care what you are about!"

"There's no need to bully so!"

"Isn't there? I think there is. I think it is useful sometimes to remind you who you are, and who I am, and how we come to stand in the position we do stand in towards one another."

"I know it well enough, without any such reminder. I know that I lie hiding here to escape from justice!"

"That if you were caught ——"

"I should be transported for life, perhaps ——"

"Worse than that, you know as well as I!"

"How worse?"

"You know that being a priest, were your order to discover your retreat, you would be secretly murdered, rather than that the story of your infamy should become public!"

"Would they not rather endeavour to prove me innocent of the crime imputed to me?"

"They could not, and should not, do that. The head of your brotherhood invested me with the office of investigating your case and discovering your hiding-place. I did my work conscientiously and thoroughly. I brought all the damning proofs home to you. I collected evidence to convict you twice over, if needs were. And more than that, I traced you to your lair and dragged you out."

"And thrust me into this vile dungeon, instead of one at Newgate!"

"Exactly. I saw how useful you could be to me. I thought what a pity it would be to lose your valuable services; and so, instead of giving you up to death, I kept you here and saved your life, for which I cannot say you are over grateful."

"There isn't much occasion for gratitude, I think," replied the other, bitterly.

"Well, we won't discuss the matter," said the old man. "You're here now, and safe. When you are tired, tell me, and we will make some other arrangement."

"What other arrangement?" asked the man, sharply.

Earthworm smiled darkly.

"I will tell you in good time."

He seemed inclined to prolong the conversation no farther, but with an imperious gesture motioned Drake to approach the spot where the poor girls yet lay insensible.

Hitherto, in the spot where he stood, Drake had not been able to see their faces.

When, however, he approached near enough to do so, and his eyes fell upon the sweet face of Cecily lying pale and motionless before him, he uttered a loud exclamation of surprise.

"What now?" asked the old man, gruffly

"I—I—I thought ——"

"Thought what?"

"That I knew——"

"You know that woman, if you mean that.

She was one of the nuns at St. Starvers Convent—one whom you treacherously assaulted. Don't repeat the experiment, that's all, or—or you will vex me."

"What am I to do?"

"I want you to help me to carry them down below. We will put them in the same place together, but apart from the man. By the way, how has he gone on lately?"

"He's rather restless."

"Keep a sharp look-out upon him, will you?"

"I have done."

"If he gets so restless that he's dangerous, we had better put a knife into him. He will be quite as well out of the way, I think."

Between them, they carried the young girls one at a time down the kitchen staircase, across the ruined kitchen, and through a door which was artfully concealed in the worm-eaten and damp, discoloured panelling.

Then down a dark and narrow passage, the ceiling of which was so low that they were compelled to bow their heads as they went along, and at length into a close-smelling but not altogether comfortless room, in which were a bed and sofa, table and arm-chairs.

Having brought them thus far, the old man dipped a cloth in cold water and wiped it over the faces of the poor girls.

This operation, repeated once or twice, had the desired effect, and they began to open their eyes and return to consciousness.

Slowly, but surely, their senses came back to them; but when, at last, they became aware of outward objects, and saw in whose hands they were, they uttered terrified screams, and, falling into each other's arms, sobbed bitterly.

"What have you brought us here for?" asked Cecily, in accents of bitter rage.

But poor Alice, clinging to her, entreated her sister not to provoke the monster who held them prisoners.

"What need to ask?" she said, sadly,—"what need to ask? Oh, we are lost!—we are lost!"

"I have brought you here," replied the old man, "for the purpose that I told you The employment which you will have is by no means a laborious one. It is almost ladylike, only I don't think young ladies do it. It is, in point of fact, polishing sovereigns!"

The two girls stared in astonishment.

They could not understand what he said. His words were an enigma.

The old man gave Drake some directions in a whisper, and sent him out of the room.

The poor girls waited in terror for his return, feeling that some new danger was in store for them.

Presently Drake returned with a bag, a file, some washleather, and other matters.

He then emptied the contents of the bag upon the table.

It had contained about thirty sovereigns.

The old man took one of them up, and showed it to them.

"You see," said he, "that the edge isn't quite perfect. You have got to mark it with this file in the way that my friend here will show you. You will spoil one or two to begin with, perhaps, but I daresay you will soon get into it."

The sisters looked at each other anxiously: then back, in terror, to the old man.

"Merciful heavens!" exclaimed Cecily; "they are bad ones!"

"Not at all," said Earthworm, with a laugh; "I am sure they are very good, considering how cheaply we make 'em!"

"But they are base coin! It is felony!"

"Exactly!"

"And would you compel us to assist you in this dreadful work?"

"Yes; we mean to do so!"

"But we will not do this," cried Cecily, with desperate energy,—"not if you even kill us!"

"We shall see," cried Earthworm; "there is plenty of time for you to change your mind, so we will leave you for a while by yourselves to think it over!"

Thus saying, he left the room with his companion, locking the door upon the unfortunate sisters.

Arrived outside, the two men held a brief consultation.

"Look here, Drake," said the old man, sternly; "are you listening?"

"Yes—well?"

"Let there be no misunderstanding between us!"

"There is no occasion for any!"

"You will keep a strict watch upon these girls!"

"Yes."

"You will treat them with kindness, and endeavour to reconcile them to their situation!"

"Yes."

"You will not insult them by word or look!"

"No."

"Remember this, above all: do not come between me and them, because it will be bad for you if I find that you have tried to become my rival!"

Drake made no reply.

"I wonder," thought he "which of us they hate the most, him or me?"

CHAPTER CXXVII.

SOME OF THE SECRETS OF THE SUBTERRANEAN.

Left to themselves, the girls consulted together upon the best course of conduct left for them to pursue.

The question for their consideration was simply this—should they submit, or should they resist?

If they resisted, to what end would their efforts bring them? What effect would their resistance have against these desperate ruffians?

If they tamely submitted, what would be their fate?

They felt that it was too horrible to think upon, yet how was it possible that they should banish the dreadful subject from their minds?

What could they do? Alice could not grapple with the difficulty, as it seemed, and could only weep and bewail her miserable fate.

The whole conduct of the affair, then fell, upon her sister.

"Alice," she said, "at any risk we must make an attempt at escape, but we must not be too hasty. To night they probably are keeping a close watch upon us. If we pass over to-night and to-morrow quietly, giving them no cause for alarm, they may slightly relinquish their vigilance. Then our time will come."

The room was lighted by a gas-lamp fixed in the side of the wall, and they were able thus to examine the apartment in which they found themselves prisoners.

The fact of this secret underground hiding-place being supplied with gas may at first appear rather strange, but it is easily to be accounted for.

A pipe had been attached to the main pipe supplying the lamps in the street, and the gas thus abstracted, without the company being able to discover where and how the robbery was being committed upon them, although of course they had some suspicion that such was the case, somehow and somewhere.

But great artfulness had been used in effecting this fraud, and so well had the time been chosen, that to take the requisite steps for discovery of the precise locality in which the gas-pipe had been inserted would have put the company to a great expense.

The reason for this was simply that the offending parties had chosen a time when the roads had only just been repaired, and the gas-pipes investigated, so that it was reasonable to suppose that, in the ordinary state of affairs, a considerable period of time would be allowed to elapse before they were again disturbed.

As I have already shown, the greatest caution was adopted by the coiners to render their underground residence an impenetrable secret.

In the first place, the secret door leading thereto from the uninhabited house above was so well concealed, that it would have been next to impossible for any person not previously aware of its existence to have discovered its whereabouts.

In the second place, no noise could reach the upper surface except through the old house itself, in which no spies were ever listening, for the simple reason that the home was always jealously locked up, and no strangers ever gained admittance under any pretext whatever.

In the third place, nobody had any suspicion of the existence of any such hiding-place—or, indeed, any such desperate gang of outlaws being stowed away anywhere.

The greatest danger which persons in a similar position can be supposed to run, must surely lie in the fact of smoke being seen to come from their chimney-pots.

But this danger they artfully avoided in this way.

Next door their lived a cobbler who had been admitted into the secret, and through his chimney passed the smoke made by the industrious moles below the surface

When he wanted to have his chimney swept, which was very rarely, you may be sure he swept it very quietly himself, and said nothing to any body.

And thus it was, as the coiners took care to make no noise to alarm the neighbourhood, and were extremely careful not to be caught going in or out of the uninhabited house over the subterranean, nobody was any the wiser, and they continued their nefarious career with the greatest possible impunity.

Cecily and Alice rose to examine the room in which they were detained prisoners, without feeling very sanguine of discovering any outlet, because they had heard the key grate in the lock when Earthworm and his companion left the cell; and they knew, alas! by bitter experience, what kind of person they had to deal with.

They rose, however, and examined the room.

They found that it was, as I have said already, furnished with some regard to comfort.

The bed on which they had been just now lying was by no means a hard one.

The sofa, too, was tolerably easy, and one could sit in the chair without much agony.

There was a small case in one corner of the room, upon the shelves of which lay some well-thumbed and well-read volumes.

Out of curiosity, Alice took down one of these.

But the first glance at its contents suffused her face with blushes.

She laid it down again with a shudder, and forbore to examine the remainder.

Indeed, the discovery of the infamous nature of the small library filled the hearts of the two young girls with alarm.

They could not help thinking that the books had been placed there with the devilish purpose of corrupting their minds, and filling their inmost hearts with the filthy images on which the writer's morbid mind appeared to have delighted to revel in

But, after a further search among the contents of the room, they made a discovery which tended in some measure to alter their opinion, as we shall presently see.

They first of all noticed, however, one remarkable peculiarity about the room, which was that that there was no window.

No; not a trace of one. They thought, perhaps, that the head of the bed might have been placed in front of it; but, moving it away for a few inches by their united strength, they discovered, much to their mortification, that the plain brick wall only lay behind.

It was, then, very easy to account for the closeness of the apartment, which had struck them as they recovered from the effects of the chloroform, and which had caused them, half suffocated, to gasp for breath.

They were surprised that, under the circumstances, there should even be as much air as there was.

But, continuing a careful investigation of the room, they at length discovered that there was a tiny grating in the ceiling, which was concealed by a beam in such a fashion that they had not before noticed its existence.

Standing upon a chair, and looking up, Cecily found that she was able to see a light above.

It was the light of the sky—the light of breaking day.

At the same time a soft air played down upon her fevered brow, which was delightfully refreshing.

Still directing her eyes upwards towards the grating, she discovered that the entrance above was blocked up by a luxuriance of rank weeds growing over it, which led her to imagine that it must open into a garden.

Probably the weeds above, and the beam below, shading the light from it, made it appear, from the top, to be quite dark; but Cecily could not help thinking that here lay some faint hope of communication with the outer world, should she watch for the opportunity.

In the meantime, would it not be better to direct her attention to other parts of the apartment?

A cry of amazement from Alice caused her to look round in alarm

"What is the matter?"

"Look here!"

Under the bed she had found a small black trunk, the lid of which she could open.

They pulled it out, and began to examine the contents.

There was a quantity of female apparel of very good quality, and they bore the name of "Emma Smith."

Continuing their search, they discovered some

dirty linen under the bed; and this, too, bore the same name.

Was this, then, the name of the person who had last occupied the room in which they were now prisoners?

If so, how long had she been gone? What had become of her?

Had she escaped, or had she been put out of the way to make room for them?

These thoughts filled the bosoms of the young girls with terror.

They had no positive grounds for supposing that she had been murdered; but still they could not get the notion out of their heads, do what they would.

They pictured a pale and slender girl, pining away in this wretched place, daily forced to submit to most cruel insults at the hands of her ruffianly gaolers, and unable to defend herself in her lonely weakness.

They pictured her to themselves, brutally outraged and murdered—her body buried—all traces of the crime removed, and none the wiser save the Great Judge who sits above, and sees and knows all, and from whom no secrets are hid.

This was their opinion at first, but Cecily, taking down another of the books from its place in the book-case, and turning to the fly-leaf, found scrawled upon it, in a female hand, this same name of "Emma Smith."

It was a volume of vile ribaldry, in the shape of songs—a disgraceful work, which no honest woman could have read; and they began to change their opinion with respect to the supposed martyrdom of this woman, and to think that, after all, she might not be dead, as they supposed, but still living down in the subterranean—one of the villanous gang into whose hands they had fallen.

This discovery was far from making them easy in their minds; and though at last, worn out and wearied with fatigue, they lay down, clasped in each other's arms, and tried to rest their aching heads in slumber, sleep refused to visit their couch, and they lay anxiously waiting for, but dreading, the approach of their gaolers.

CHAPTER CXXVIII

NO WORK—NO FOOD.

When at last worn out with watching and waiting, and yet unable to get to sleep, they determined to rise from their uneasy bed, and wait for the coming of the wretches into whose power they had fallen, and who, they supposed, would, in all probability, pay them an early visit. It must have been broad day out of doors; yet, had the gas-light in their cell not been burning, they would have been in profound darkness, for none of the sun's rays were able to penetrate so far.

They could form no idea respecting the time, as they had no watch, and the church clocks without were inaudible.

Their heads ached dreadfully, and they felt sick and faint, which might have been the result of the chloroform, or perhaps of the stifling atmosphere of their horrible prison.

They would have been heartily thankful for some slight refreshment, such as a cup of tea. A drink of pure water would have been an unspeakable boon, but such water as was in the room was in a stone pitcher, and appeared to have been standing there for many days, until it was quite stagnant.

They waited and waited for somebody to come, until they could scarcely bear the intolerable thirst which devoured them; and at last, when they heard the key grate again in the lock of the door, although they knew that it did so but to admit an enemy, they were intensely thankful that he had come, hoping that he would bring them relief.

It was Drake who entered, with a tray in his hands, on which were two cups, a tea-pot, and some bacon and eggs.

As he put these things down on the table, he glanced at the gold and the implements which had been left there over night

They lay in the same position as when he left them.

"Hilloa!" said he; "what's the meaning of this?"

The girls looked at him inquiringly, but were silent.

"What's your game?"

They answered not.

"Why, you haven't done a stroke at them!"

He gathered up some of the coins in his hands, and turned them over, examining them.

"Not a stroke!" said he; "why haven't you?"

As they still remained silent, he scowled at them fiercely, and took up the tray again.

Then, with the breakfast things in his hand, moved towards the door.

Perhaps the despondent expression of poor Alice's face to some extent elicited the ruffian's pity.

He paused and retraced his steps.

"Perhaps you were very tired?"

"Ye-es," answered Alice.

"And haven't long been up?"

"N-no," she said piteously.

"Well, in that case, perhaps I'd better leave the things. You feel faint, may be, and will be able to get on better when you've had your meal."

He put down the tray again, very much to the relief of the young ladies, and moved towards the door.

But at it, he turned and said, "Mind, when you have had your breakfast, you must set to work without any more foolery!"

He passed through the door, and closed it after him.

Then again opened it, and looked in.

"I don't want to say anything harsh, you know, but I must say one thing"

He waited to catch their eyes, and then added with emphasis—"And that is, if you don't get your work done, you won't have any food! Mind that!"

He shut the door, and retired, leaving them to think the matter over.

"Shall we do it?" asked Alice of her sister.

Cecily replied with a look which was almost indignant.

"Never!" she cried.

"But—but——"

"But what?"

"If we resist, we shall be killed!"

"Better so than to sin!"

"Oh, sister! placed as we are, do you not think that we had better yield—that we had better pretend to agree to what they propose, and be willing to obey their bidding."

"I shall not!" replied Cecily.

And poor Alice's heart sank within her.

She was not intended to be a heroine.

CHAPTER CXXIX.

THE CAPTIVES CONTINUE TO SUFFER.—CECILY IS RESOLUTE BUT ALICE GIVES WAY.—STARVING BY INCHES.—THE GAOLER'S TERMS.—HOLDING OUT.—HOW MUCH LONGER?

THEY were very young to be buried alive.

They were very young to be doomed to perpetual imprisonment in a dark and dreary, bone-smelling dungeon—damp and noisome, badly ventilated, and aguish.

Yet for what other fate were they preserved?

If for any other, for a fate that was worse than death!

At Cecily's suggestion, they had held out at first, and refused to do any of the villanous work which Drake would have employed them upon.

But soon they found that resistance was useless, and that if they must live, they must work.

They held out bravely the first day, and though poor little Alice's heart sunk within her when a hot and savoury dinner was brought in and taken away again upon the discovery that they had not as yet begun upon the coins, yet she did not grumble in the least, and went to bed very hungry, but very courageous, determined to hold out.

Cecily proposed that they should wait, after it got dark, for a sufficient time to elapse for it to be bed-time, and then go to bed for an hour or two, until it was to be supposed that the gaoler had gone to sleep, when they were to attempt an escape.

It was a very fine scheme, but everybody in the world has not the pluck and daring of our friend Miss Ruth Hardcastle; and though she managed to break out of a much stronger gaol than that which held these two poor girls prisoners, they could not manage to get the door open.

The door was a massive one: the lock a ponderous piece of ironmongery.

It could not be managed, and after several hours' hard and painful work in the dark—for the gaoler had turned off the gas by some artful contrivance—they crept into bed again, and cried themselves to sleep

They woke up in the morning many hours before anybody came to call them, and sat in a grim obscurity, getting as much light as possible from the small grating I have before mentioned, but yet sitting almost in the dark.

"Oh, Cecily," said poor little Alice, as the hours rolled slowly away, "I feel so ill!"

"So do I!"

"You have much more courage than I have!"

"Do you want to give in?"

"N-no!"

"Cannot you hold out any longer?"

"A little while longer, I think!"

"Let us try!"

Then they waited again.

Then, as before, Alice broke the silence.

"Cecily!"

"Yes?"

"Do you——"

"Do I what?"

"Do you—do you think——"

"Think what!"

"Do you think that starving is such a very—that is, I mean, is not such a very painful death?"

"After the first few pangs, a kind of stupor will come over us, that will numb all pain, and we shall feel nothing."

Alice remained quiet for a long while, until she could bear it no longer.

"Oh, dear! oh, dear!" she cried at last; "I wish *that* time was come!"

"What do you mean?" asked Cicily, almost angrily.

"Oh, dear! oh, dear! I am so hungry!"

The door opened almost before she had done speaking, and Drake made his appearance with a tray.

"Will you take any refreshment, ladies?"

They made no reply, but Alice could not help looking longingly towards the eatables.

As before, they had a wonderfully savoury odour. It was surely the most provoking thing in the world to see them come in and go out again in that kind of way; and it was more than anybody but a right-down regular first-class heroine in a penny story could have endured.

Alice fairly broke down, and began to sob.

Cecily sat pale, but resolute.

Drake looked from one to the other with a slight grin. He saw how the wind blew.

"Won't you come to terms, young ladies?" he asked.

"No," replied Cecily.

"Oh, do come to terms!" he continued persuasively.

"What terms?" asked Alice.

"You know them already. Do some work, and you shall have something to eat."

"Do you intend to starve us?"

"If you don't work, we do."

"You wretch, you shall not treat us so!"

"How can you help yourselves?"

That was the question.

They felt that they were helpless.

Drake moved away towards the door, which he was about to close after him, when Alice called to him to stop.

"May not we have a light?"

"Not without you work."

The door was then shut to.

Alice went on crying. Cecily sat silently.

After a short interval the door opened again.

Mr. Drake came in and lit the gas.

"I shall give you one more chance," he said. "If you don't set to work directly it will be the worse for you. I shall come back in half an hour's time, and if I find you have not commenced, you will be separated and put apart in the dark, to starve at your leisure."

CHAPTER CXXX.

THE YOUNG LADIES GIVE IN.—ARE THEY BETTER OFF NOW, OR WORSE?

How could they hold out any longer?

They were quite helpless.

The ruffians into whose power they had fallen would mercilessly murder them if they continued to resist.

Indeed, even worse than that was to be expected did they provoke the ruffians much longer.

Exasperated by their obstinacy, it was very probable that the villains would torture them past all power of endurance, and that at last they would be compelled to yield

After they had endured their sufferings a long while and the time which Drake had given them nearly expired, they held a consultation together.

"What shall we do?"

"If it depended only on me," said Cecily, "I should hold out."

"But, Cecily!"

"Well?"

"Do you want me to do so?"

"I do not ask you to."

"But you want me?"

"No."

"Oh, Cicely, I may be wrong! I know I am a poor, weak, foolish creature compared to you, but I don't think there would be much sin in doing this work, pressed as we are."

"I have already made up my mind that there would not be any sin in it; and that if we are to hope to effect our escape, we had better pretend to obey these wretches with implicit obedience."

Alice was truly delighted to hear her sister speak in this way, and she set about the work with great eagerness, while Cecily presently followed her example. They had not filed many of the coins before Drake again made his appearance. He appeared to be pleased at seeing them thus employed.

He evidently did not expect that they would have given way.

Cecily was savage with herself to think that she had been so weak; but the deed was done now, and they could not very well retract.

"Is there anything you would like, ladies?" he asked.

Then, as they made no choice, he suggested breakfast; and shortly afterwards he made his appearance with a teapot, some rolls and eggs, and a beautiful roast chicken.

As soon as the door was closed upon him, the poor young creatures began their much-wanted meal, and surely never in their lives had they tasted any so much to their fancy.

They worked hard after breakfast, and finished their task.

It was not a very hard one, and they did not take a very long time to complete it.

When the man came in with a very nice little dinner and some wine, he said that he would not think of troubling them any more that day, and retired again.

He came back later, bringing with him a very plentiful tea, and then wished them good night, leaving behind him a pint bottle of pale brandy.

There was no lack of food now; and to tell the truth, they had much more than they could eat already.

Next morning he brought in a bag of coins with breakfast, and said that that would be their day's work. It was not by any means a hard day's work, and they had finished it by dinner-time; but he brought them no more, saying that they could employ themselves in any way they thought fit.

In a similar manner to that which I have described, the next three or four days passed away.

No event of any kind that is at all noteworthy occurred to break the monotony of their existence They were well supplied with food, and wine, and beer and spirits: they had very little work, and a great deal of leisure.

Perhaps you might at first be inclined to think that, after all, it was not such a bad kind of life, and that they were not, all things considered, so badly treated.

You might be led to suppose that their gaolers thus treated them because they only required them to do the work assigned to them, and that the business upon which they were employed was of so profitable a nature that they could afford to feed them with lavish profusion, and did so to make them contented with their lot.

It is true that as they paid the girls no wages, and they did not participate in the profits, which were undoubtedly very large, they surely could afford to buy them good food, and plenty of it.

But there was, perhaps, another motive which prompted the villains thus to behave; and what was that?

It is difficult to believe such cold-blooded and deliberate atrocity as to suppose that the course of conduct pursued by the wretch Drake, at the instigation of the elder scoundrel who employed him, was gradually to corrupt the virtue of these two unhappy women.

By keeping them in this well-fed idleness, with so much leisure time, and with no earthly occupation to beguile their time was it not the way to prompt them to fly for refuge to the hideous books which were contained in the book-case?

Once induced to seek amusement in this filthy corruption, what hope could there be for the preservation of their virtue? How could they read such stuff, and retain unspotted the purity of their minds?

Alas, poor victims! was their fate not sealed as they approached the shelves upon which the treacherous abominations lured, lying, as it were, in wait for them?"

Poor things! Poor things!

CHAPTER CXXXI.

THE CAPTIVES HEAR STRANGE SOUNDS.—SOME ONE BREAKING THROUGH THE WALL — A DREADFUL UNCERTAINTY.

THE days passed slowly away, dragging their weary course.

Without a clock, and kept ever in a gloomy obscurity, it was impossible to note the progress of time.

It was, indeed, a weary, weary life, and it was impossible to tell how and when it would end.

More than once the captives made some abortive efforts to escape by the door, but the door was of such a strong nature, and the lock such a massive one, that it effectually resisted all the puny efforts to force it open.

Not only, however, did they desist from their endeavours, because in trying the lock Cecily broke her file, and having to acquaint Drake with the fact, he very easily arrived at a conclusion respecting the manner in which the accident had occurred.

"Ha, ha!" said he, with a grin—"ha, ha! This is how it is, is it?"

And he examined the door with a critical eye.

"And so my little birds have been pecking at their wires, have they?"

He found the end of the file broken lying down by the door-post, where he had kicked it when he came in.

"Oh, you naughty little birds!" he said with ferocious playfulness: "we shall have to cut your claws if you go on this way."

But he said no more upon the subject upon this occasion.

Only every day he peeped and spied about the room when he paid his morning's visit, and carefully examined the lock of the door, and the framework of the small grating behind the beam, which communicated with the garden above.

They consequently relinquished all attempts at prison-breaking for the present, and all hope of escape subsided in their breasts.

Not having anything to amuse themselves with, as I have said, it is not to be wondered at if they should have spent a good deal of their time in speculating upon the size and nature of the extraordinary subterranean establishment, of which they found themselves unwilling inmates.

Were there any other captives except themselves, and where were they?

For some time after they had arrived at their prison house, although they frequently listened at the door of the cell in which they were confined, they could never detect the slightest sound from the cell without, unless it was occasionally the sound of footsteps approaching towards their door, upon which occasions it always turned out to be their gaoler, Drake, coming on his rounds.

And thus it was that in time they came to believe that they alone were prisoners in this horrible place.

However, after they had been in the subterranean about a fortnight, circumstances occurred which caused them to alter their opinion

In the first place, one day they were alarmed by loud shrieking, and the sound of smashing woodwork, followed by the sound of hasty footsteps running in that direction, and the voice of Drake and another man, unknown to them, shouting loudly to know what was the matter, and pouring volleys of foul oaths and curses upon the head of some offending party.

Then followed the noise as of a scuffle, and heavy blows appeared to be dealt plentifully on all sides.

Then followed deep groans, and the sound of a heavy body being dragged along the passage.

Then all was still again.

What did it mean?

What else but murder?

They listened all that day at intervals, but heard nothing else at all of an unusual character, disturbing the ordinarily monotonous character of the silence which reigned in the underground prison.

Towards night, though, about a couple of hours after they had retired to rest, they heard a faint scratching noise upon the other side of the wall, close to their heads.

Alice heard it first, and starting up in bed, awakened her sister.

They both listened to it, in rapt attention.

"I think it is a rat," said Cecily.

"Oh, no, it cannot be!"

"What do you think it is?"

"I cannot think, but I am very much frightened!"

"Don't be silly, but go to sleep!"

If it really was only a rat, he must have been a very indefatigable party, for he pecked away steadily until daybreak, and then the noise suddenly subsided.

Next night about the same time he came again, and worked as before, only his teeth made more noise than they did upon the previous night.

It was very clear to the two girls, who listened with palpitating hearts, that the noise was made by some one breaking through the wall.

Who was it, then, and for what purpose were they coming?

As the person, whoever it was, only worked at night, it was to be supposed that he feared interruption.

In that case it must be a fellow-prisoner; and in that case the sound was hopeful to the two poor girls, for it might be the means of their escaping also.

Still, how was it that the captive, if captive it were, should break into their cell? Surely that was not the quickest road to liberty?

Whoever it was, there was nothing left for them to do but to wait and hope for the best

Meanwhile, the scratching grew louder and louder, and nearer and nearer.

CHAPTER CXXXII.

MORE VICTIMS.—OLD FRIENDS WITH NEW FACES —THE HORROR OF THE VAULT —THE DEATH STRUGGLE.—THE FATE OF THE DUMB ASTROLOGER

INSTEAD of waiting, however, until the mysterious captive has broken through the wall, let us peep into some of the other cells which the mysterious underground residence contains

Let us go back awhile, though, and look into this strange place upon a certain night, some six or seven months before the night on which the sisters were first brought hither captives by Earthworm and his minions.

In a gloomy cellar, crowding over a small fire, sat two gaunt, ragged, and miserable-looking men.

They were sitting silently, and to all appearances buried in thought.

They rested their heads upon their hands and their elbows upon their knees.

The fire-light reflected their pinched and haggard features and their wasted forms.

They were both deadly pale. They bore upon their worn faces the traces of much sickness and suffering.

They were, indeed, two as miserable objects as you could well have wished to look at

It was difficult to tell at first sight which was the most miserable of the two. They looked equally woe-begone, equally dirty and squalid, when you first looked at them, and equally repulsive in feature; but, if one took a second look at them, there certainly was a difference.

There were traces of much manly beauty in the face of one, who appeared to be the junior by about twenty or thirty years. It appeared to have been such a very long time since he had washed his face, that there was hardly any telling what his complexion could have been below the begrimed surface.

His hair hung wildly over his shoulders in straggling, uncombed locks.

His beard had grown to a most unnatural length, and hid all the lower part of the face.

His bushy eyebrows threw his deep-set eyes beneath into dark shadow; and when by chance the fire-light fell upon them, gleamed out with an expression that was savage and almost maniacal

When we find them thus brooding over the fire, we find them silent and thoughtful, and they had thus sat opposite to one another for several hours They had no topic for conversation with which to while away the time. There seemed to exist between them a silent hatred that found vent only in a low, guttural growl—a half-uttered curse.

The elder man was on this occasion the first to change his place, and break the silence.

Looking over stealthily towards his companion, apparently for the purpose of discovering whether he was awake, and after a silent contemplation of him for a few moments, the elder man appeared to

come to the conclusion that his comrade was sleeping.

Then he rose to his feet, and began slowly to pace to and fro from end to end of the cellar.

And as he walked, or rather crept along, he wrung his hands, and groaned, and beat his breast, as though in bitter mental anguish.

It was strange agony this, which convulsed the frame of the miserable man—an agony that seemed too great for words; and as he wandered purposelessly and at random, the contortions of his pallid face were perfectly hideous, and he tore the shirt away from his neck, as though it were choking him past endurance.

It was a curious sound, too, that his misery elicited from him, which was more like the whining of a lashed hound, than the lamentations of a human being.

And gradually increasing his speed, as it appeared, unconscious of the act, he soon reached a running pace resembling that of a wild beast in a cage.

Suddenly the younger man, starting to his feet, roared out to him to stop

"Lie down, you cursed idiot!" he said,—"lie down, will you; or I'll smash you, I will, with this bar!"

He clutched a heavy bar of iron as he spoke, which had laid until then under the grate, and served the purpose of a poker.

The elder man cowed and trembled before the other, and crept back to his seat, holding out his hand to ward off the blow.

"Lie down!" roared the younger man, still brandishing the bar, and making as though he would have struck the other to the earth—"lie down!"

The poor creature that he threatened made no

intelligible reply, but gabbled some queer kind of gibberish that appeared totally unlike any known language.

"Hold your noise!" said the other with a stamp of his foot, and retired to his own place.

Then, resting his head upon his hands, and his elbows on his knees, in the attitude from which he had just been disturbed, he again subsided into silence.

And thus the time passed on, each again buried in thought—busy with the recollection of a miserable past—hopelessly looking forward to a dreary and hopeless future, dark and impenetrable.

Let us pierce through the mystery which enshrouds the offsprings of their busy brains; let us see what they are thinking about; and we may be able to recognise these two miserable men as old acquaintances of the reader, whom the course of our strange story has compelled us for a while to neglect.

First, let us deal with the younger man. Whither were his thoughts leading him? Was it thus?

Was he thinking of a time long, long ago, when he, a struggling poet, toiling laboriously for his daily bread, battled with disappointments and ill-luck, and strove to fight his way into a place in public estimation, which he was doomed never to obtain?

Was he thinking of the little wife with the brown, glossy curls, and pink and white baby's face, who watched him returning of a night, and ran out to meet him, all smiles and roses—alas! but too often to find, by his downcast looks and sullen frown, that he had come back from a fresh defeat, farther than ever off that goal which he was struggling to reach?

Was he thinking of those awful days when things got to their worst; when his friends turned their back upon him; when those to whom, at the last extremity, he appealed, refused to assist him, and sent him home with despair gnawing at his heart?

And did he recollect the time when the crisis had arrived?

When that fearful night arrived upon which he had resolved to do that deed for which there is no repentance—when he had made up his mind to commit self-murder?

Again, did he remember how he had written his wife a letter, bidding her farewell, and had gone out with his loaded pistols in his pockets, to find a place where he could die in peace?

And after this, did he remember that strange scene in the park—comic in its grotesque horrors—when he and a half-mad creature, calling himself Cadbury Kid, had attempted to kill themselves, and how they had been interrupted by Kid's servant; how a struggle had ensued—a pistol had been discharged—a man lay weltering in his blood—and he, Ernest Trevellyan, had fled from the spot, blood-stained and terror-stricken, with the crime of murder upon his soul?

Did he recollect into what strange hands he had fallen—how he became a victim to the fascinations of a lovely syren, a blue-eyed she-devil, bent upon his ruin—and how, under the influence of her snake-like fascinations, he had in his heart turned false to the poor wife whom he had deserted? But if he remembered thus far, there at this period arose, as it were, a dark cloud, blotting out his life for some weeks.

At this period he must have lain dreadfully sick—at death's door—insensible to all outward signs and sounds, unconscious of what befel him.

And when he awoke what had happened to him? He knew not. Where was he? All that he could understand was that he was in the house of a grey-headed villain, whose slave he must remain until the day of his death.

Yes, he had been carried hither—to this hideous underground abode.

He had been plunged into everlasting darkness.

He was doomed to work at the manufacture of base coin, and the produce of his labours went to swell the ungodly wealth of the old villain whose tool he was. Yes, that was the state of the case.

He was in Earthworm's power, and he dare not rebel against his authority.

Did he do so, the old man would have caused him to be apprehended and tried for the murder which circumstances had, as it seemed, caused him to commit, whether he would or not.

Thus was it, then, that he had skulked and hidden, cursing his life, but fearing to lose it, the abject slave of the old wretch who kept him there to serve his own ends.

When first he had been brought there he was alone, and saw no human face save his own and that of the old man, when he came to visit him and bring him food.

But after awhile, and just when he was beginning to think the perpetual darkness and silence of the dreadful hole in which he passed his days would have shaken his reason from its throne, and driven him raving mad, the old man found him companionship.

He brought a woman there of the name of Smith.

A wild, half-savage beauty, through whose veins ran gipsy blood.

An impetuous, passionate, sensual creature, with fiercely-animal propensities, who could love, and hate as easily.

And she, too, was doomed to this unnatural life.

She, too, was in Earthworm's power.

Her hands were also stained with the blood of a fellow-creature, and she was compelled to lurk in secret, and work for the old man, who knew her secret, and threatened her with its consequences.

Between this woman, then, and Trevellyan, there sprung up an attachment which cannot be called love, it was so brutal, so depraved, so shamefully licentious an amour; but it was sufficiently strong and lasting to reconcile him with his lot, and he worked on without repining.

But after a while another man came there—a dumb fortune-teller—a miserably-deformed monstrosity called Jeer, who was skulking away from the police, and whom Earthworm had also laid his claw upon.

This man, then, had been brought into the cellar to live with Trevellyan and his mistress, and a gaoler was placed over them all, to watch them, and to guard against any attempt at escape.

The reader, who knows the character of the scoundrel for whose ruffianly deed poor Cecily had so long suffered — the miscreant who had previously vilely abused and murdered a poor girl who fell into his clutches—can imagine what his conduct was likely to be when brought within reach of a lovely woman, even though a jealous rival should be there to watch and guard her.

It was not long before he contrived, during the progress of one of the drunken orgies, which were of but too frequent an occurrence, to make overtures of a scandalous nature to his companion's mistress.

I need not tell the ugly story.

How this woman listened to him.

How quarrels and bloodshed followed.

How an unlucky blow, dealt in the heat of passion, stretched her dead, and Trevellyan was again a murderer.

That time was past now; and he and the wretch who had urged him on to the deed were left to share the horrors of this frightful prison-house.

And thus we find them.

Rebuked by Trevellyan, who appeared to have the upper hand of his companion by right of might, the dumb man sat mumbling for a time to himself in his corner, afraid to move.

But it was not long that he thus remained.

He soon grew weary of the silence, and his limbs were cramped by keeping in the same attitude.

Quietly, as before, he crept out of his place, and began to pace to and fro

Trevellyan started up.

"Keep quiet, as I told you!" he roared; "or I will make you!"

This time the other man replied only by an angry scowl, but did not desist from taking the forbidden exercise.

"Sit down!"

Still he kept on.

"Sit down!" roared his master.

The dumb man, with flashing eyes, waved his hand as though in defiance, and continued his promenade.

Trevellyan again clutched the iron bar, and rose from his seat.

At sight of him advancing, the other backed into a corner, and glared at him like a wild beast.

"Keep off," his eyes seemed to say,—"keep off, if you value your life. I'm dangerous!"

But Trevellyan heeded not the warning.

He laughed contemptuously for a moment.

Then, ceasing suddenly pointed to the corner which the dumb man had just left, and bade him go back to it.

The dumb man did not stir.

"Go back!"

The dumb man showed his teeth with the grin of an enraged ape.

But he did not move.

"Go back, I say!"

Still he did not move.

"Do you hear?"

Still motionless.

"Very well, then; you will have it."

Trevellyan flung down the iron bar again, and turned up his sleeves.

The dumb man was watching him eagerly.

The expression of his face was horrible to contemplate.

If ever there was a face that meant mischief, that face was here now.

If ever there was a face which plainly said that its owner was a man to be dreaded and avoided, that face was now before him; and yet the other feared it not, nor took the warning.

He only prepared himself for the coming struggle silently and sternly.

Suddenly, with a howl like that of a wild beast, the dumb man rushed out at him full butt.

Next moment they were locked in each other's arms.

Struggling fiercely and silently.

A frightful struggle it was, in which they panted, and wrestled, and beat each other's heads furiously against the walls and floor of the cellar, while the sound of the dumb man's discordant howling made a din that was devilish to listen to.

It was a hard struggle, and for a long while an even one, in which it was impossible to say who would be the master; but suddenly the door was flung open, and Drake and another man rushed in upon the combatants and strove to separate them.

Trevellyan, seeing whom it was, and being yet to some extent a reasoning creature, desisted from the brutal conflict, and then relinquished his hold of his antagonist.

But the dumb man was yet furious.

Nothing would suit him but the life of the man who had provoked him

They dragged him away, but he foamed at the mouth and clenched his teeth in blind fury.

In spite of their efforts to keep him back, he tore himself from their grasp and rushed madly in at his foe.

But Trevellyan met him with a fearful blow in his face, which sent him staggering to the other end of the cellar, where, falling to the ground, he lay covered with blood.

But it was not for long that he thus remained.

Shaking himself together, he scrambled to his feet.

Drake and the other man who had come in, threw themselves between him and Trevellyan.

The dumb man rushed upon them, and was again repulsed.

He uttered a fearful howl, and rushed at the fire.

The men stood still, wondering what he was going to do.

Trevellyan, however, shouted to them that he would get the iron bar, and he started forward to prevent him.

But it was not the iron bar that the dumb man was in search of.

He did not stoop down as they had expected, but suddenly, before they had any notice that such was his design, he had clutched with both hands an iron pot which stood upon the fire.

The two men ran out of the cell with a howl of terror.

It was a pot full of boiling hot metal.

Did he mean to hurl its contents at them?

Trevellyan was not, however, able to follow in their track, for the last one through pulled the door to after him.

Even had he not done so, he could not have hoped to have escaped.

No, his only chance was to close with the monster, and stay him in the perpetration of his hellish design.

Quick as thought he was upon his antagonist.

Then, catching at the pot, he endeavoured to prevent the dumb man from carrying his fiendish design into execution.

The pot itself, like the metal within, was of a boiling heat.

But he grasped the pot side, in spite of the injury which the touch of it caused him, and endeavoured to wrench it away

The dumb man, on his side, was equally determined to gain possession of it

At last, in the struggle, by some unlucky chance, Trevellyan slipped his foot, and suddenly relinquished his hold of the iron vessel.

The dumb man, thrown off his balance, staggered back.

The pot was flung up into the air.

The boiling liquid poured down upon the miserable wretch's face, and he fell to the earth with an appalling shriek of agony.

To his cries at that moment were added those of Trevellyan, who, paralyzed with horror at the fearful sight, staggered back against the wall upon the opposite side of the cellar.

Alarmed by these sounds, Drake and his companion then came running into the cellar.

The shrieks and writhings of the tortured wretch were too horrible to be described.

That his case was hopeless there could be no doubt. That there was no way of saving him was equally certain.

Trevellyan saw this, and seizing the iron bar as the miserable creature lay there beating his scalded head against the earth, he battered out his brains.

And then the three men having dragged away the corpse, and flung it into another cellar, to lie there till they could come to some decision as to the best way to dispose of it, Trevellyan came back to the fire-side, and burying his head again in his hands and resting his elbows on his knees in his old attitude, again became absorbed in thought, ruminating mournfully over his crimes and misery.

The unredeemable past.

The hopeless future.

CHAPTER CXXXIII.

TREVELLYAN LEFT ALONE—A SAD CHANGE.—THE GAOLER'S FEARS.—IS HE MAD?—A CALM BEFORE A STORM—THE CALMNESS OF DESPAIR.

When they went away the last thing at night, they left the man, Trevellyan, still sitting brooding over the fast dying fire. When they returned to the cellar in the morning they still found him there.

They found him in much the same attitude as that in which they had left him.

The fire had gone out—a most unusual occurrence, for the wretched men who inhabited this dreadful cellar were ordinarily such light sleepers, that they rarely allowed the ashes in the grate to grow cold, but rose many times during the night to heap on coals and stir up a blaze.

Now the fire was stone dead, the grate cold, and the wind whistled down the chimney; but the sad lonely man still sat over it, having his head in his hands—still sat in moody meditation.

They thought at first that he was asleep.

Then, seeing how still and motionless he sat, Drake, who entered first, walked up to him, and, in some fear, laid his hand upon Trevellyan's shoulder, half fearing to find him dead.

He might have been dead for all the notice he took of the man's touch or the loud voice in which he called to him to wake up.

But presently, when Drake had shaken him roughly, he raised his head, and turned his eyes slowly towards his gaoler's face.

"What's the matter?" asked Drake.

But he did not seem to heed him.

"What's the matter?"

His face had undergone a strange change since Drake last saw him

He scarcely could recognise him for the same person.

"Good heaven! what is the matter?"

The miserable man seemed to be in a kind of torpor—to be hardly conscious of what was going on round him.

It seemed as though he had prematurely aged. His hair was streaked with white, and Drake looking at it, wondered whether this had all happened during the course of the night, or whether it could have been so for a long while and he, in his carelessness, had not noticed it.

Trevellyan stared into his face with a dreamy, stony stare, and then slowly turned away his eyes again, and allowed his face, as before, to fall down into his hands; and once more be became apparently unconscious of the course of time or of the events occurring around him.

Drake drew back from him, and stood at a few paces distant in a corner of the cellar, conversing in an under-tone with his companion

Thay spoke almost in a whisper, anxious that Trevellyan should not hear what they were saying; though the precaution was quite unnecessary, for it was very certain that he was utterly unconscious of their presence.

"What do you think ails him?" whispered Drake.

"Is he drunk, do you think?"

"How can he be? He had no drink last night, had he?"

"I have not given him any lately, since Earthworm forbid it."

"He had the delirium tremens, had he not?"

"Yes, that was why we were obliged to cut off the supplies."

"He was dangerous, then?"

"He was like a wild beast when he had his fits on him. That was why Earthworm got you here to keep me company."

"You couldn't have managed, then, by yourself?"

"I should have had a hard job of it with him, and that dumb fellow, and those two perverse minxes in the next cellar."

"Do you know, something strikes me?"

"What's that?

"Hush! He's listening, I think."

"No, no! He is taking no heed of us."

"I wouldn't for the world he found out what suspicion I had of him. Come outside, and I'll talk to you."

Drake's companion led him out of earshot into the passage outside, and then continued his communication.

He still spoke, though in a low tone, and still wore an anxious, and half-terrified expression.

"What the deuce is the matter?" asked Drake, growing very much alarmed.

"I can tell you now," said the other—"now we are out of his hearing."

"What is it?"

"Haven't you noticed something about his manner very strange?"

"I? Why, of course I have. What makes you ask that?"

"But I mean something very strange indeed?"

"I don't know what you are driving at!"

"Didn't you notice just the same manner about the other one?"

"Which other?"

"The dumb man, I mean!"

"There was something amiss with him, all day yesterday and the day before, that I couldn't quite make out!"

"That you couldn't quite make out?"

"No!"

"I made it out, though. I saw that it was a sign!"

"A sign?"

"Of what came afterwards?"

"How so?"

"I saw that he was going mad!"

"And do you think ——"

"Yes, I am certain of it; this man is going mad also!"

"Good God! He'll be a rough customer to manage if he grows violent!"

"You're right. What are we to do?"

"I can't think that that should cause it, for my part!"

"I think it is owing to your having cut them off from their drink. The change has been too much for them. It has turned their heads. It often is the case."

"Had we better give them the drink again, do you think?"

"I am sure I cannot say—we must wait for Earthworm's advice. He will come to-day, I suppose. If he doesn't, one of us must creep out to-night, and try and find him."

"I daren't show myself in the streets," said Drake; "and you too, I suppose, are not over-anxious to do so either. However, I hope there will be no occasion."

"Let's give him a little gin to try how it suits him. Shall we?"

"Yes."

They lost no time in fetching a bottle of spirits from their stores, and Drake, filling a glass with the liquor, took it in to the prisoner.

He had as much difficulty as before in causing him to raise his head, but he did raise it at last, and when he saw what had been brought to him, his eyes lit up with an eager sparkle.

"Give it me!—give it me!" he cried, clutching at it, and scowling fiercely at Drake, as though he fancied that the man intended to try to take it away again. "Give it me!"

"Well, there," said Drake, "take it, and may it do you good!"

Trevellyan gulped it down, and flung the glass with a great crash upon the floor.

Drake fell back several paces in alarm.

"Hilloa!" he said; "what the devil are you doing that for?"

But the other man made no answer.

He rose to his feet and stretched himself, and took a turn up and down the cell.

It seemed as though the spirits had given him new life.

He laughed aloud and held his head erect.

"I feel better for that!" he cried in a loud voice. "I feel more of a man. Get my breakfast, will you, and I'll get to work."

"That's right!" said Drake, much relieved at the change. "I thought it was a little drop of something cheery you wanted, and Jones here said the same. I'm glad to see that it has done you so much good—that I am!"

The gaolers then departed, but presently returned with the materials for Trevellyan's breakfast.

When they came back they found that he had lighted the fire, and was warming himself at it.

He had also got out implements of his trade, and appeared to be prepared for work.

They left him eating his meal, and apparently quite calm and resigned to his daily lot.

But it was a calm preceding a storm.

A fearful hurricane about to rage within that cellar's walls.

He was calm with the calmness of despair—of concentrated fury; but soon he would burst forth, and then it would not be safe to stand in his way or try to thwart him in his fell design.

We shall see!

Meanwhile, his poor wife, on the other side of the wall, little dreamt how near he was, or how soon they were to meet.

Little dreamt what would be the result of their meeting.

CHAPTER CXXXIV.

IN WHICH TREVELLYAN MAKES A HOLE IN THE WALL, AND FINDS SOMETHING WHICH HE WAS FAR FROM EXPECTING TO FIND UPON THE OTHER SIDE.

When he was left to himself, Trevellyan rose from his seat and quitted his breakfast, scarcely touched.

Then he paced to and fro the length of his cellar, muttering to himself.

As suddenly he ceased again, and returned to his meal.

"Nothing can be done by violence," he said. "At least, nothing is gained. I will take my measures and not be too hasty. Surely to God I can bear with this misery a little longer, after having borne with it so long!"

He finished his breakfast without any return of the agitation which had shaken him awhile ago; and when he had finished, he put the things away in their usual corner to await the return of Drake to carry them away, as it was his habit to do.

Then he set about his daily work—put the kettle containing the metal upon the fire, and prepared the moulds.

When Drake came in again, he found him at work, and apparently quite as calm as before

But Trevellyan had determined upon making his escape.

He fancied that if he were to have exerted his strength, it would not have been impossible to have fought his way out into the street, even though Drake and his companion had done their best to hinder him.

But he knew that this could not be effected without a great noise and clamour.

He was well aware that a noise during the day-time would be highly dangerous, did it attract the notice of the police, for how did he know but that they might force an entrance into the house?

In which case it was very sure that a discovery of the coining implements would quickly follow.

And then how could he hope to disconnect him self with the rest of the gang?

No, it would be best to attempt an escape at night, when his gaolers slept—when there would be no one to hinder him.

He knew very well that the men whom Earthworm had left in charge would not allow him to escape if they could possibly prevent him.

He was not aware that they had almost as great a fear of the daylight and the open streets as he had himself; and he supposed that they had the instructions of Earthworm to give him into custody if he became too troublesome, just in the same way that Earthworm himself had threatened to do, when he first gave him a shelter from the blood-hounds of the law, then howling upon his track.

He determined to wait for night, and to work quietly, and as much as possible with his usual behaviour, so that they might have no suspicion that he intended to take any extraordinary steps towards effecting his object.

Indeed, he wished them to be kept in entire

ignorance of the fact of his having any object save that which he had always had hitherto—namely, of getting through the day, and sleeping, and eating, and banishing all thought of the life he had once led in the happy days gone, never to return.

Drake, it is true, watched him narrowly whenever he had occasion to come into the cellar; and though Trevellyan was perfectly unconscious of his scrutiny, nothing in his manner prompted the gaoler to suppose that anything was wrong.

The day passed wearily away, and at the customary time Drake bade the captive "Good night."

As soon as he had allowed what he deemed a sufficient length of time to elapse, Trevellyan set about his work.

He had a crowbar and a strong knife at his disposal.

Upon what part of the cellar should he employ them?

Not upon the door. Like the door of the cell where Alice and Cecily were confined, it was too strong to be easily broken open.

He might have shattered the lock with his crowbar, but that would have made too much noise.

There was no window. The only ventilation which the inhabitants of the cellar could obtain, was obtainable by the chimney.

Should he go up the chimney?

No, that was too narrow.

But he had thought the matter over before, and he had come to a determination upon which he now would act.

He would break through the wall at the back of a cupboard, in a spot which he had every reason for believing would bring him out into one of the cellars of the old house, under which the subteranean hiding-place was situated.

He found that it was a difficult job to get the bricks out, and a very slow process.

Indeed, after he had worked for two or three hours, he had only made a very little hole; and he found that he was so dreadfully worn out and weary, owing to the sleepless night that he had passed after the dumb man's death, he thought he would lie down awhile.

He had the forethought to replace the bricks loosely, and close again the cupboard door.

It was fortunate that he did so, because he had hardly lain down before he fell fast asleep.

When he awoke again it was broad day.

He was exasperated beyond measure at the discovery, but there was nothing for it but to get through the day the best way he could, and wait for night.

To provide against a like accident again occurring, Trevellyan slept the greater portion of the day; and as an excuse for so doing, informed Drake that he was suffering from a violent headache.

Next night, when again left to himself, he resumed his work.

He was, however, interrupted by the unexpected entrance of Drake, who had been troubled with the nightmare, he said, and fancied that he had heard Trevellyan calling for help.

By a lucky chance the man was only half awake, and made so much noise opening the door, that Trevellyan had plenty of time to shut the cupboard up again and fling himself down full-length upon the mattrass, which, spread out in a corner of the cellar, usually served him as a couch.

The same reason prevented Drake from noticing anything curious or suspicious in the captive's manner, and so the affair passed off smoothly enough, luckily for Mr. Drake.

I say luckily enough, because it had been Trevellyan's intention, should he be discovered, to knock his gaoler's brains out.

But though he did not resort to such violent measures, he deemed it wise not to continue his work any longer just then, but to delay his escape for another day.

I will not however weary the reader by a minute description of the work. It was done, and that is enough. Upon the third night, after an hour's toil, he had made a hole large enough to thrust his head and shoulders through.

He lighted an old tar link that lay in a corner of his cellar and thrust it through into the cavity beyond, waving it about, so that he could get a good notion of the place into which he was effecting an entrance.

The first glimpse of the interior of the cellar into which he had broken caused him to draw back his head with a deep curse.

He had, somehow, miserably miscalculated the distance, and had broken into the next cell, after having contrived very artfully to miss the cellar, he wanted to get outside the subterranean by about half a foot.

He drew back the torch precipitately, for the light showed him the drapery of a bed, at a short distance from his face, and the first thought that ran through his head was, that perhaps he might disturb some person sleeping in the room.

But a moment's reflection showed him that this supposition was quite an absurd one, because he had already made quite noise enough, in making the hole through the wall, to have awakened the soundest of sound sleepers.

He again thrust his torch and his head into the room, and took another survey of the apartment.

This time an expression of grief and terror crossed his features, and a pang of remorse shot through his heart.

He recognized the room and its furniture.

He recognised it as the place which, a short time ago he had occupied with the guilty woman, who had died from the effects of his drunken violence.

A shudder ran through his frame when he made this discovery, and at first he was almost inclined to withdraw again from a scene fraught with such painfully degrading and humiliating recollections.

But then, he all at once remembered the grating, about which I have already several times spoken.

It was through that that he might make his escape.

Yes, he must persevere.

He felt certain that there was nobody in the room to stop his progress, and, withdrawing his head again from the aperture, he redoubled his efforts to tear away the wall.

It was enormously thick and strong, and the mortar had hardened, till it was almost as difficult to cut away as the bricks themselves, between which it lay.

But he knew that he had very little time before him, and he worked away with desperate energy.

It was not long before he contrived to force his body through, and effect an entrance.

He had left his torch in the cellar, upon the side from which he had come, and when he had safely landed in the cellar, containing the two poor, trembling girls, who had watched his entrance in dread anxiety, he turned round again to reach his torch and crowbar.

Then turning again, and holding the torch high above his head, he found himself suddenly face to face with a ghost!

CHAPTER CXXXV.

WHAT HAPPENED IN THE CELLARS.—A STRUGGLE FOR LIFE.

Yes, it must have been a ghost!

There, deadly pale before him, stood the likeness of a dead woman he had once loved passionately.

It was not the miserable creature whose guilty embraces he had found in this subterranean den of infamy, but the young and virtuous woman whom he had deserted when he intended to have committed suicide—the young, fair creature whom he supposed had met with her death upon the scaffold for a crime of which he alone was guilty.

He uttered a howl of terror, and shrieked out her name.

She could scarcely have recognised in that emaciated and sickly creature before her, with hollow cheeks, wild eyes, and savage beard, the husband she had loved.

But she recognised the voice, and, with a hollow groan, sank senseless into the arms which her sister spread out to receive her.

For several instants of time the miserable husband stood spell-bound.

The torch fell from his hand, and it was only when its flame began to wrap itself round the woodwork of an old-fashioned secretary, at the feet of which it had fallen, that the imminent peril which threatened them recalled him to his senses.

He trampled out the fire almost mechanically, and without noticing whether or not all the sparks were extinguished.

His eyes were riveted upon his wife's face—heavy tear-drops coursed each other slowly down his cheeks—his bosom heaved with convulsive sobs—but, as yet, he could not recover the power of speech, which seemed to have totally deserted him

Cecily, meanwhile, laying the inanimate form of the fainting girl upon the bed, bent over her in anxious solicitude.

Beating her hands, and sprinkling her pale face with cold water, she called upon her again and again to listen to her—to speak to her—to tell her what was the matter.

"Oh, you have killed her!" she cried, pushing Trevellyan angrily away, as he pressed forward eagerly to gaze into that face which lay so still and colourless, as though the light of life had faded away from it for ever.

But Trevellyan made no answer, and his hollow sobs alone broke the death-like silence.

Slowly, then, did the colour revisit the ashy face of the insensible wife, and presently, with a deep sigh and an expression of intense pain, she reopened her eyes.

"Is he there?" she murmured.

"Of whom do you speak?" asked Cicely, still bending over her.

"Oh, sister, sister!"

"What alarms you, dearest?"

"Is he there?"

"Calm yourself, dearest."

At this moment her eyes travelling slowly round they alighted upon her husband's face.

She started up in a sitting posture.

She stretched out her arms

Her eyes dilated wildly.

She recognised him, in spite of the dreadful change which time, and misery, and sickness had made in him.

Yes; it was he!

It was her husband!

"Ernest—Ernest!" she cried, in a fainting voice choked with sobs.

In another instant they were locked in each other's arms.

"Oh, Alice! Oh, my wife! Can you forgive me?"

"Forgive you, dearest?" she repeated, in surprise.

"What! you do not know?"

"Know what? Great heavens, what have you to tell me?"

She looked at him in wild terror. What did he mean? She understood nothing.

She had thought him dead.

Now finding that he had come to life again, she could only rejoice wildly at her great happiness.

But he persisted in his questioning.

He spoke in a faint, despairing voice.

He hid his head upon her shoulder.

"Have you not heard that—that I am a murderer?"

She replied by clasping him to her heart more eagerly than before.

Straining him frantically to her breast.

Kissing him passionately!

"It is false!" she cried, "I know that is false! I care not what they say of you! I will believe none but you!"

"But will you believe me?"

"Yes."

"When I tell you——"

"Tell me what—go on."

"Tell you—no, no, I cannot."

"What makes you hesitate?"

"God have mercy upon me!"

"What mean you, Ernest? What am I to understand from these words?"

"You must understand that I am—alas!"

"That you are what?"

"What they say I am—a murderer."

"No—no; I am sure that it cannot be the truth. You say it but to try me."

"It is the truth—I swear it."

"No, no! Why they accused me of your murder—accused me, who love you more than my own life."

"What I tell you is the truth, Alice. I solemnly assure you that it is, and more——"

"And more—what more?"

"I am unworthy of you."

"You speak in riddles."

"I must be plain, then. I must avow my guilt."

"Oh, heaven, what would you do?"

"Here, at your feet, I kneel and pray for your forgiveness."

"Rise—rise, dear husband, you terrify me."

"No, no! I am a wretch, a monster—I have been unfaithful to you."

"Ernest!"

"The partner of my guilt, I have slain."

"Merciful powers!"

"Her blood is on my hands—the damning guilt is on my soul."

The unhappy young wife covered her face with

her hands, and sank back upon the bed, sobbing convulsively.

The miserable sinner, sinking upon his knees lay with his head at her feet, as though bereft of life.

Cecily appalled by what she had seen, stood by the bedside motionless—awestruck.

While they were in this position the door opened and the hideous face of old Earthworm glared in upon them.

It was a devilish face—was it the face of a demon gloating over his work?

No.

Rather was it the face of some baffled fiend furious at the thought that his victims were slipping out of his clutches.

"Aha!" he cried; "so you are all there together, eh? What is this little plot you are concocting?"

"Wretch!" cried Trevellyan, starting to his feet. "Leave us, or your life is forfeited."

As he spoke, Trevellyan caught up the crowbar, with which, a while ago, be had forced an entrance into this cellar from his own.

Brandishing this formidable weapon, he rushed forward towards the door.

But Earthworm was beforehand with him.

He pulled the door to suddenly, and locked it upon the outside.

Trevellyan rushed at it, though, with the fury of a mad bull, and battered at it desperately, shivering the wood-work.

A few more blows would have sufficed to have opened a way of escape in that direction, but the sound of the voices of Drake and Jones in the passage without, caused him to hesitate and pause in his mad career. What would he gain by forcing a way in this direction?

Could he hope to gain the day against such unfair odds?

No. It would be wisest to block up that entrance and force his way out by the grating of which he had at first thought.

Therefore, suddenly abandoning his original design, he rushed across the room, seized the heavy old-fashioned secretary, and, with a strength that was almost superhuman, dragged it to the door, and flung it against it to bar the entrance.

Then he heaped all the remainder of the furniture against it, and springing through the hole he had made into the other cellar, flung in a score and more of bricks to use as missiles.

Then thrusting the mattress into the hole he had made, he left the two women to guard these two entrances; he again clutched his iron bar, and fell about his work with redoubled energy.

It was a difficult matter to direct his blows against the ceiling in a way that would cause any effect, but he soon found out which would be the best way to manage the business.

He must prize the grating out in the first instance.

The crowbar had a pointed end, which he contrived to force in between the brickwork.

He strained his utmost.

He struggled and panted furiously.

Finding that his efforts to prize out the grating were fruitless, he fell upon it again, and beat and smashed at it like a madman.

The dust flew in all directions, mingled with splintered fragments of brickwork.

Harder and harder he worked, and with more and more effect.

He was almost blinded with the dust.

He was cut and bruised cruelly with the falling bricks; but he worked on, and soon the sky began to peep through a small crevice he had made.

Now for another struggle, and freedom was his.

Again he prized.

The grating gave way, and with a fearful crash fell into the room.

In its fall it had wounded him severely on the shoulder.

He thought at first that his shoulder blade was fractured, and the blood trickled down his arm.

But he recovered himself with a struggle, and called to the women to come quickly. By this time the door of the cell had been completely smashed to pieces by men without, and they were now doing their best to throw upon one side the furniture which had been heaped in front of it.

At the same time Drake made his appearance at the hole in the wall.

He had a pistol in his hand, and appeared to take an aim at Trevellyan.

But Cecily saw his design, and was in time to prevent it.

Suddenly, clutching one of the brickbats lying on the floor, she hurled it with all her strength at the man's head.

He staggered back with a groan.

Then fell to the earth covered with blood.

Trevellyan, deserting his work for a moment, rushed to Cecily's assistance, and replaced the mattress in the hole in the wall, so as to cause a delay of a few moments, should any one else follow Drake's example in attempting to force an entrance at this point.

Having made the place as secure as he could at this hole, he caught Alice in his arms, and raised her up to the hole, from which he had torn away the grating.

With his assistance, she easily contrived to force her way through into the garden above.

Then Trevellyan, in the same way helping up her sister, they together turned to assist their deliverer in effecting his own escape.

But alas! too much time had been expended in doing what had been done hitherto. No longer could the gaolers be kept at bay. Simultaneously with Cicely's reaching the ground above, the door of the cellar, from which she had just escaped, was dashed open, and Earthworm and his man Jones rushed in upon Trevellyan.

They hurled on one side, with a prodigious effort, the heavy piece of furniture with which the doorway had been blocked up.

Jones was the first, and was armed with a formidable cutlass, which gleamed naked and terrible in his hand.

Trevellyan saw at a glance that he had not time left to help himself through the grating, by which the two sisters had, with his assistance, just effected their escape.

The only chance open to him was to turn and face his enemies.

He did not despair of gaining the victory, because, although there were two of them, Earthworm was but a weak old man, quite incapable of making any serious resistance.

To his great relief, too, Trevellyan observed that neither of them carried firearms, the reason for which was that Earthworm was anxious to settle the matter without alarming the neighbourhood—not because he was unprovided with weapons—they, indeed, both he and Jones, carried pistols, which they determined only to use at the last extremity.

CECILY.

Through ignorance of this fact was it, doubtless, which lent Trevellyan a courage he would not otherwise have possessed.

He grasped his crowbar with both hands, and rushed upon his assailants.

Jones, ducking his head, avoided the coming blow, which, however, descended with stunning violence upon Earthworm's shoulder; and though the force of the stroke was diminished, to a great extent, by the end of the bar's scraping the wall-side in its progress, it nevertheless fell heavily enough to send the old man flat upon his face.

And thus upon the ground he lay, groaning, thinking himself dead, and feeling as though all the bones in his body had been broken up into little pieces.

Luckily for Trevellyan, the old man's falling threw Jones slightly off his balance, so that he could not take advantage of the unprotected state in which he was left for a moment after he had struck out with the iron bar.

Recovering, themselves, however, after a momentary hesitation, the two men now rushed together, and were soon engaged in a deadly strife.

With the ferocity of savage animals they struggled together.

For a while Trevellyan warded off the blows of Jones's cutlass, until at length a fiercer blow than usual of the crowbar struck the murderous weapon out of the man's hand, and sent it suddenly to the other end of the cellar.

Then Jones, making a sudden dart, flew at Trevellyan's throat like a bull-dog, and, clutching his windpipe in his powerful grasp, strove, with all his strength, to strangle his antagonist.

But Trevellyan, flinging himself forwards, instead of backwards, when they fell, brought Jones's head with stunning violence upon the floor, knocking all the sense out of him for the moment. Then, hastily scrambling to his feet, he seized the crowbar, and dealt him a fearful blow which shattered his skull.

Escape now seemed again to be possible.

He ran towards the grating, but found himself face to face with Earthworm, who had risen to his feet, and who stood waiting for him with a loaded pistol.

Trevellyan had dropped his crowbar to the ground after dealing the fearful deathblow which had sent the ruffian before his Maker.

Had he still retained his hold of the murderous weapon, he might, perchance, have been able to save himself.

Now his fate was sealed.

He could not avoid the death which faced him.

If he stooped to pick up the bar he would surely be shot.

There was no time to hesitate—to think what he ought to do.

There was no time for anything.

His only chance lay in a rush.

He rushed, therefore, upon his enemy.

At the same time, Earthworm discharged his pistol!

* * * * *

Outside, in the garden, they listened and waited.

Listened and waited.

Listened in terror.

Waited with throbbing hearts.

They heard the sound of struggling below.

They heard the panting breath of the combatants, and the shuffling of their feet.

She heard a crushing, sickening blow, which was the fall of the crowbar upon the skull of the dying man, which caused them to draw back, shivering with terror, from the grating.

Presently they heard the report of a pistol.

And then dead silence.

Silence which was awful in its unbroken terorr.

They listened and waited, and waited and listenened.

Every moment seemed an age.

The time dragged its weary course, and they waited breathlessly.

Below, there was a dull red light, sombre and horrible; but, although they bent down low, and peered eagerly into the cellar, they could discern nothing of the scene which was taking place within.

The silence was yet unbroken.

Yet did they wait and listen.

But as they still peeped in through the hole, it seemed to the frightened girls that the light within was of a lurid, savage hue, like unto the flames of the bottomless pit. Then as they still peeped in a thick volume of smoke, slowly creeping through the cellar in search of an outlet, found at last through the aperture over which they hung in silent terror and drove them back, half choked.

At the same moment a shrill scream arose within and the sound of footsteps hurrying across the the cellar floor.

Alice called loudly the name of her husband but no one replied.

No sound was to be heard now, save the roaring a furnace.

The thick black smoke poured out in volumes growing every moment more intense.

Myriads of sparks shot up as though uncertain what course to pursue, and whither to bend their steps.

What had been Trevellyan's fate? They knew not. They dared not hazard a guess.

What fate could it be? He was either murdered or he lay there below in a state of insensibility, and would soon fall a victim to the devouring element which there raged so fiercely.

"Oh, Cecily," whispered her sister, "he is dead."

The other could find no words of consolation to utter.

"Let us go away," she said at last.

"Oh no—no!"

"We can do no good here."

"But I cannot leave him."

"Perhaps that was he whom we heard returning from the cellar?"

"No; I think not."

"You think not?"

"I fear not."

"But you do not know?"

"My heart tells me that I must not hope!"

"But you have no proof that he is dead?"

"I do not think that the voice we heard was his."

"Are you sure?"

"Yes; I am sure. He is dead!"

"Come, then!—let us get away from this dreadful scene!"

"Oh, Cecily, I feel no power left in my limbs to carry me hence! Oh, what a fate is mine! To have him whom I loved more than life restored to me but for a moment, and then to leave him for evermore!"

"But, dearest, I do not believe that that man was ever worthy of your love"

"Hush, Cecily! Do you think that I placed any credence in those dreadful words that he uttered? No, no! He was delirious—mad!"

Cecily did not attempt to reason with the poor, heart-broken creature.

It would have been a cruel task to have undeceived her, even had it been possible to have convinced that fond, trusting nature of the falseness of the one whom she had loved.

Her sister led her away across the garden, seeking for some outlet by which they might make their escape into the streets.

It was with difficulty that she induced poor Alice to desert her post. But, yielding at length to her sister's earnest entreaties, she tottered slowly away through the rank weeds and long grass with which the deserted garden was overgrown.

Hardly had they gone ten yards, though, before the flames began to pour out of the cellar mouth with a violence which must shortly attract the notice of the neighbours.

It would not be safe for them to remain there much longer; for, if anybody came, they would surely be questioned, and they might get into trouble.

Cecily, who had the most presence of mind, looked round to see what could be done, and soon decided.

On one side of the garden the wall was weaker than in other places.

She found that she could climb up it with a little difficulty.

She did so, and looked over.

There was, on the other side, a narrow lane.

No one was about. They might drop down, unobserved, and make off

Alice would have delayed even longer at the juncture. Perhaps she had still some lingering hope that her husband might come to her through the flames?

But Cecily pulled her onwards

And, as they neared the wall, a low cry arose behind them of—

"Fire! fire! fire!"

CHAPTER CXXXVI.

THE FIRST FALSE STEP.—THE COURSE OF CRIME.

"Fire! fire! fire!"

It was some one who had flung open a window in the back of one of the houses looking upon the garden in which they stood who shouted out these words.

The alarm had begun. Very soon the women knew that it would spread far and near, and that thousands of voices would swell the chorus.

Cecily climbed on to the wall, and pulled her sister after her.

Alice was so weak and feeble from the strong emotions which had agitated her, that she had scarcely power enough to help herself.

But the danger of their situation leant the other sister strength enough for both.

They had soon scaled the wall

Then they dropped quietly down into the lane beyond.

Then huried away.

It was a long, narrow lane, with high buildings upon either side, after they had left the wall over which they had just scaled, about twenty yards behind them

Taking advantage of the first turning they came to, they plunged down it, and found themselves in a sort of mews.

Out of this they came into another lane, and then a court, and an alley.

They hurried on however, as fast as they could go, nor did they once pause until they were quite out of breath and exhausted by their violent exertions.

Then, in a dark archway, they sat down to rest.

No one was about. It was very early morning. They could here converse together, unheard and unobserved, upon their future plans.

"Alice?"

"Cecily?"

"What shall we do?"

"We are just in the same position that we were before we fell into that old villain's clutches."

"Almost."

"Exactly!"

"We have no way of earning a virtuous living open to us; no friends whose assistance we can seek?"

"There is only the two alternatives that there were before—death or degradation!"

It was what the other had been thinking herself.

They were both silent for a while, nursing their own sad reflections.

Daylight was breaking. The light fell full upon a house opposite to them, upon which the eyes of both the women happened to be resting.

Suddenly Cecily uttered a low exclammation of surprise, and pointed.

"Look!" she said.

"What is it?"

"Do you not see?"

"That name over the shop?"

"Yes; it is an office for obtaining situations."

"Well?"

"Well, do you not think that there is a Providence which has guided our steps hither at this time?"

"Why?"

"Because it seems to me that there is a way by which we might obtain a situation."

"And that is——"

"By applying there."

"How you talk, Cecily! We could not get a place without we had a character to refer to—you know that?"

"Suppose we write one ourselves?"

"Cecily!"

"Yes, yes; I know what you are going to say. I know that it would be wicked, but what are we to do? Society is against us; the world has no mercy upon those who need it?"

"But—but supposing we did do this?—we have no money even to buy the necessary materials!"

"Why not?"

"What do you mean?" asked Alice, looking at her sister in terror.

Cecily made no answer, but pulled from her pocket a handful of bright, glittering coins.

"Oh, Cecily, can it be possible? Where did you get them?"

"Where do you suppose?"

"I cannot imagine!"

"Why, have we not been polishing them for weeks past?"

"Are those, then, bad ones?"

"I have every reason to believe so."

"But we cannot hope to be able to pass one off without being discovered."

"Why not?"

"I should be afraid!"

"I should not. I have every confidence in them. See how beautiful they are—there is not a flaw in them."

"But—but—don't you think we should be caught?"

"I don't see why. If they were so difficult to get rid of, why should these men go on making them every day in the large numbers that they do? They must find that it pays, or else they could never have afforded to keep up that subterranean establishment."

"But *if* we should be caught?"

"If we should, I suppose we should be taken to prison. I see nothing else for it. It would be our last chance. But——"

"But what?"

"It is by no means probable that we shall be taken. I tell you I am determined to try, and I will try!"

"But, Cecily, by doing this shall we not be wronging some one? Perhaps the person upon whom we pass the base coin may be in needy circumstances. How can we tell what injury it may do them?"

"It is true what you say; but our circumstances are desperate, and I am desperate, too!"

"Oh, Cecily, shall we do it?"

"Yes; I tell you yes. We will do all we can to make the consequences of our crime as light as possible. We will choose a good shop—a shop where we may suppose the proprietor is rich."

"Yes, that will be best"

"Then, if we are lucky enough to obtain a situation, we can repay the amount anonymously. Can there really be so much sin in such a fraud as this?"

"There does not seem to be; but it is in this way that so many persons have argued when they have sinned."

"Alice!" said the other, almost fiercely, "why should we argue the matter any longer? It shall be done!"

"Be it so, then."

"That is right. The next question, then, is how we are to do it?"

"Let us run equal risks."

"No, that is unnecessary."

"I shall not consent for you to have all the danger, which is what you would propose, I know full well."

"You know that I could not trust a poor timid little thing like you."

"I am sure I've got courage enough, if you will only trust me."

"But there is no occasion."

"What do you mean to do?"

"I mean to pass the money."

"What am I to do?"

"Stop here."

"But why?"

"Because I wish you to take care of the remainder."

"What is that for?"

"So that, if they have any suspicion of the coin I have passed being a bad one, and give me into custody, they will not be able to find any more of the same sort about me."

"How ever could you have thought of all this?"

"It is time that we thought of something, in the state that we are in."

"Indeed it is, but I cannot think how you could have got such experience?"

"It does not require much experience to know what are the simplest and most natural steps to take, in such a case."

"But still——"

"Besides, when I was in the power of that dumb fortune teller, of whom I have told you, and was a prisoner in his house, I have heard some of the men who came there, talking of their feats in this way."

It was not possible to commence operations yet. They must wait until the day was further advanced, before they could do anything. They thought it best too, to move away from the place where they were, as the people in the office opposite might by chance observe them, and then should they decide upon returning there, their appearance would naturally cause suspicion.

They wandered away, therefore, to try and spend the time, until the shops were opened.

They were not long, before they found a shop which they thought would be a good one to try.

It was a milliner's, and the reason why they selected it, was that their first and most pressing necessity was for bonnets, as they were now without any covering to their heads.

Leaving Alice in charge of the surplus coin, Cicily took the brightest and best of the counterfeit sovereigns, and entered the shop.

Her heart beat violently.

She trembled, and could hardly walk straight, so great was her agitation, but she contrived with a strong effort to calm herself sufficiently to ask for what she wanted.

One of the young ladies came forward to serve her.

She took Cicely for a servant from some neighbouring house. Perhaps, had she studied the matter deeply, she could not have chosen any character so likely to disarm suspicion.

"What can I serve you with, miss?"

"I want to look at some of those bonnets you have in the window, about seven or eight shillings."

"Here are some. We have pretty ones a little dearer."

"These will do very well, thank you. I will take two of them."

She chose them without much hesitation.

The shop girl put them up in paper.

"Any thing else to-day, miss?"

"No thank you!"

"Shall I send them?"

"No, no! I won't trouble you."

Cicely laid down the sovereign.

The girl rang it, and looked in the till, but appeared not to find sufficient change.

Then she took the coin up again, and walked with it to the other end of the shop.

Cicely clutched at a chair back, to save herself from falling.

She watched the girl take the coin up to an elderly woman, who looked at it and rang it.

Cicely felt half inclined to rush out of the shop and run away as fast as her legs would carry her.

But she could not have moved, to have saved her life.

She stood rooted to the spot.

What was to be her fate? Was her crime discovered? Would she be given up to the police?

Presently, though, the girl returned with the change, and Cecily walked away unmolested.

It was her first crime, and it had been successful!

She found Alice waiting for her in the greatest anxiety.

What a while she had been gone! Her sister had never expected to see her return.

And had she—done it?

Yes, it was done! But, alas, one crime was was not sufficient! It must be repeated several times before they could hope to be able to get a sufficient quantity of decent apparel to make a good appearance at the agent's office

It is surprising, after the first step has been taken, how easy is the downward course They went next into a quiet coffee-house, and had breakfast, changing another of the coins, this time more courageously, for they had money enough to pay for the breakfast, even had the spurious nature of the sovereign which they tendered been discovered.

After breakfast, Cicely went round to several places to make other purchases, leaving Alice in the immediate neighbourhood to await her return, and take charge of the other money.

This precaution they never failed to take, and when they had both entered the coffee-house together, Cecily had insisted that Alice should leave the house before she offered to pay for the breakfast. She would not allow her sister to run any risk.

And so it appeared that crime could go on swimmingly, and now that they had departed from the path of virtue, it was easy enough to get a living.

But we shall see. Perhaps, after all, the passing of base coin has its drawbacks.

It was not until she came to the last shop upon which she had intended to practise the fraud that Cicely got into trouble, and then it was in this way.

CHAPTER CXXXVII.

SHOWS WHAT BEFEL CECILY IN THE HANDS OF A JEWISH GENTLEMAN.

The last shop she tried was a glove shop.

By this time the sisters had completed all the necessary purchases, nothing more was required to enable them to present themselves in a decent way at the office where they hoped to be able to get some employment.

They had been so successful in the frauds which they had committed, that the recklessness which is ever attendant upon such a state of things ensued in this case as in every other.

Cecily no longer entered the shop where she intended to pass bad money in fear and trembling

She walked in boldly, and in a firm voice asked for the article which was to be the pretext for changing the sovereign.

She went into a glove shop, as I have said.

A very polite gentleman, with very crisp, curly hair, and a great quantity of jewellery, came up smiling, to serve her.

He was probably a Jewish gentleman.

He had a very large nose, and very dark eyes.

He had a sensual-looking mouth, with great thick lips, not much unlike a negro's.

He was not at all a nice-looking gentleman, and decidedly not the sort of person for whose moral character one would have been anxious to have surety.

If she had only been wise she would have had as little as possible to say to this polite tradesman. She would have made her purchase, paid her money, and beaten a retreat with the greatest possible celerity.

But, unfortunately, she had no notion of the danger which threatened her. She came like a lamb to the slaughter—never dreaming with what a wolf she had to deal.

She asked to look at some gloves. He brought her a box, and she chose a couple of pairs.

He politely stretched the fingers, sprinkled the insides with powder, and begged to be allowed to assist her to put on a pair.

She had grown so daring, so reckless, that she consented.

He took her hand tenderly in his, and caressed it with almost a loving gentleness.

He was extremely respectful, but still his dark eyes seemed to say that he thought her hand a very pretty one, and its owner a very beautiful woman. And he was not wrong, perhaps.

At last she laid down the money.

The Jewish gentleman took the coin up in his fingers, and looked at it quite carelessly, as it appeared, but he continued to look at it, particularly at the edge.

Then he turned it over in his hand, and looked back at Cecily; not carelessly this time, but intently, suspiciously, accusingly.

Somehow she could not bear those dark eyes thus fixed upon her.

She had never, for a moment, anticipated such a situation.

She was quite unprepared for such an event.

She turned deadly pale, and quailed beneath his glance.

The Jewish gentleman leant across the counter, and brought his face close to hers.

" You knew that this was bad!" he hissed into her ear.

She tried to look indignant, and failed.

She tried to speak, and failed.

She trembled a moment, and then made an effort to spring towards the door.

The polite gentleman—polite no longer—seized her by the wrist.

She tried to wrench her hand away, but he held on to her with an iron grip.

It was impossible for her to get away, and she ceased struggling, after the first violent effort was over.

She ceased to struggle, not only because she thought that her struggling was useless, but because she saw that these efforts to get away but only made her appear more guilty than ever, in the eyes of the man who now suspected her.

As this thought struck her, she sank back into her chair, and sat motionless: her eyes fixed upon the dark eyes which were fixed on hers.

The Jewish gentleman, without removing his eyes from her face, or relinquishing his hold of her wrist, said in a low tone—

" What would you do?"

" Nothing!" she gasped, after a pause.

" No," he said. " Why should you struggle? How weak it is of you. You know you are in my power until I let you go!"

" Oh, for heaven's sake, let me go!"—and the girl, bursting into a passionate flood of tears, ejaculated, " Oh, forgive me this once!"

" Why!" retorted the man. " I don't see why I should!"

" I—I never did such a thing before to day!" stammered the terrified girl.

" No," replied the man, with a laugh. " I don't suppose you're a very old hand, or you wouldn't be so precious clumsy. Still you've a good deal of cheek, too, for a beginner!"

" Oh, sir!—oh, sir!" said Cecily, in an agony of terror.

But the man only laughed.

The miserable guilty girl sank upon her knees, and implored him to spare her.

The Jewish gentleman seemed to hesitate for a moment upon the course which he should pursue.

Then relinquishing his hold of her wrist, he vaulted lightly over the counter, and bolted the shop door.

" I'm not afraid of you running away," he said, quietly, " because I don't suppose you are such a fool to do something that would cause your shame to be public. If you were to run out of the shop, I should run after you, calling 'Stop thief!' with all the strength of my lungs. What would be the consequence? You would be caught by a policeman, and dragged back here through the mire, with a blackguard mob at your heels. No, it would be better for you to be given quietly into custody, and dealt with, with as little noise as possible!"

Cecily made no reply. She sobbed silently in an agony of grief and remorse.

The Jewish gentleman contemplated her, without speaking, for some time.

Then taking her again by the wrist, he bade her rise.

" Come with me!" he said.

" Where?" she asked, in a fright.

" In the back parlour. I cannot have you crying here. Somebody might come in!"

She rose, without attempting to offer any further resistance.

He led her to the back of the shop, and opened the door into a little drawing-room, elegantly furnished.

"Take off your bonnet and shawl," he said.

She obeyed him.

He took a seat by her side, and looked long and earnestly into her face.

She turned her face away in shame, but he ordered her peremptorily to turn back again.

"You are very young!" he said. "How old?"

"Nineteen, sir!"

"Who are you?"

"Oh, do not ask me, sir!"

"Well, you may well be ashamed of yourself! Are you married?"

"No, sir!"

"Oh! Do you lead an improper life!"

She answered him, with a flush of anger through her tears, "No, indeed!"

"No, indeed!" said he, mocking her; "and so, I suppose you call it a proper life to pass bad money?"

"I didn't mean — that is, I thought you meant——"

"Yes, yes!—exactly! But you think that is more wicked, I suppose?"

"To be sure! But there's less risk about it, isn't there? You know best, of course. But I should say you couldn't hope to pass many of these things without being discovered; and with a pretty face like yours, you ought to make your fortune!"

"Oh, no, sir! Oh, spare me!"

"Well, suppose I do—suppose I have pity on you, and give you back your bad money, and don't give you into custody——"

As he spoke he approached nearer to her on the sofa, and took her hand in his.

She trembled violently with a new alarm.

"What do you say?" he said.

"Oh, sir, what am I so say?"

"What you like!" he replied, with an ugly smile. "You know best. You can imagine my terms!"

It was not difficult to read the villain's meaning in his flushed face, and his eyes glittering with the fire of unlawful passion.

She strove to speak, but her tongue clove to the roof of her mouth.

What could she do?

Should she yield to this ruffian, who had so artfully ensnared her?

If she did not do so, she must certainly be taken back to prison.

How could she hope to fall into the hands of the police without their discovering who she was?

And then, if she should be recognised, what awaited her?

A felon's death!—naught else!

But no, no—she could not now yield tamely to the degradation—the shame which she had striven so hard to avoid!

She struggled.

She fell upon her knees, and poured out wild prayers and entreaties for mercy.

Oh, if he would but spare her!

He knew not what was her motive for committing this crime.

Had he no pity? Was his heart made of stone?

What was there in her face to awaken desire? Were there not hundreds more, more beautiful, who would willingly yield to him? Oh, why, why must he demand this sacrifice of her?

But the Jew grew angry.

"Hold your noise, you fool!" he said fiercely, through his clenched teeth. "Why are you now such an infernal simpleton?"

He took her in his arms, but while he was endeavouring to silence the cries which burst from her in her wild terror, a low rattling at the door communicating with the shop from the street, alarmed him.

He let her fall with a savage curse, and strode to the door.

He pulled the blind on one side, and looked into the shop.

As he did so, the person shaking at the outer door shook it open.

The bolt was but a feeble one, and it had yielded under his hand.

And who was this person, do you suppose, of all people in the world?

None other than a policeman, who had innocently enough come into the shop to make a small purchase in perfumery for his favourite cook.

If it had been the Jew's intention to have given the girl into custody, such an arrival at the moment, would have been still more astonishing, as every one knows how extremely difficult it is to obtain a "man in blue" when he is wanted.

Under the present circumstances, though, our Israelitish friend felt anything but comfortable.

It is true he might have given the girl into custody, but he did not want to.

And then, again, supposing she were respectably connected, as by her manners and appearance he was almost inclined to believe, might she not make out a case against him and make him pay rather dearly for his amorous endeavours?

The Jew hastily closed the door behind him, and walked quickly forward to meet the policeman.

But the moment she was let to herself, Cecily sprang to her feet.

The key was on the inside of the door.

She saw that at a glance, and availed herself of the circumstance.

She turned the key in the lock, and then ran to the other door communicating with the house.

She thought she might be stopped this way, and returning, looked out of the window.

The window was close to the ground.

She saw that she could jump out, and that it would be no difficult matter to climb the wall into the next garden.

She hardly conceived the idea before she put it into execution.

There was a servant beating carpets in the back yard of the next house.

Cecily begged to be allowed to pass through the house, as the Jewish gentleman had behaved rudely to her, and she had just escaped from him.

The simple servant-maid, taking the tale for Gospel truth, readily acquiesced, and in a few moments more Cecily was in the street.

Then she walked away as rapidly as her feet would take her, without once turning her head, nor did she stop until she reached her sister.

"How long you've been!" said Alice.

"Oh, dear, if you only knew!"

"What has happened?"

But Cecily could not tell her.

She burst into a fit of violent sobbing.

At last, when she grew a little calmer, she said that what had occurred had been a warning to her, and that nothing in the world should again induce her to commit such crimes as she had committed that day.

She proposed, then, that they should at once

seek out the office which they had seen in the early morning, and apply for the situations.

She felt confident that they would be able to obtain them if they managed manners properly, and then——

"Then," said Alice, "we shall be able to pay all these poor people back whom we have so cruelly wronged."

It was strange that Cecily did not respond so warmly to this idea, though at first she had herself proposed that such should be the case.

She began to feel a little doubtful now, whether they would be able to find out the shops again if they were to look for them.

Besides, they had changed ten of their sham sovereigns. What a long while it would take to make up such a sum as this out of the salaries they might receive as governesses, or teachers, or lady's-maids.

As they walked along the streets upon the way to the office, Cecily's thoughts involuntarily strayed to a certain popular preacher, whom once she had loved, and she wondered whether she should be able to find him if she tried.

She little knew that Ruth the Betrayer had found him in her stead, and with what result.

CHAPTER CXXXVIII.

THE UNIVERSAL FEMALE EMPLOYMENT OFFICE—A SKELETON'S HEAD IN SPECTACLES—LAMBS GOING TO SLAUGHTER

By some ill-luck they could not for the life of them find the office they were in search of.

At last, in despair, they went into a stationer's shop, and asked to be allowed to look at the post-office directory.

Searching in it, their ill-luck caused them to light upon the name of another office close at hand. This was termed "The Universal Female Employment Agency." This one would do as well as any other.

They set off for it at once, and were not long in discovering its whereabouts, although it was hidden, by a way up a quiet street, in such an out-of-the-way corner, that any person not seeking for it might have passed it by, a score of times, without even noticing its existence.

Perhaps it might have appeared curious to a reflecting mind that the Female Employment Agency should hide itself away like this.

Would it not have been well had the philanthropic promoters of this benevolent scheme chosen a place where it might have attracted more of the public notice? Perhaps not. When the reader has heard all that I have to tell about it, he may feel inclined to believe that the quieter the office is kept the better for its well-being.

Murder does not court publicity, crime hides its head and skulks, licentious outrage cannot be practised in broad daylight in the open streets.

The poor girls, little dreaming what was in store for them approached the door.

The outside of the house had a most respectable appearance. The brass doorplate was highly polished. The window-blinds were snowy white.

The gilt letters upon the front of the house stood out in bold relief.

It was evidently a thriving concern, this Agency for Female Employment.

There was an air of heavy respectability about it, that was extremely imposing. The very office, of all others, that an unprotected female in search of employment would have pitched upon.

Cecily and Alice looked up and down the exterior of the house and hesitated for a moment. But it was only for a moment, and then they stepped across the threshold of the door and entered the office.

A very bright and clean office in a great state of polish.

Perhaps a little gloomy, with a smell as though of old ledgers, but the gloom was so much relieved by the brightness of the brass nails, and the general glitter of the highly-polished mahogany desks that everything seemed to twinkle and blink, as it were, with the reflection of a cozy little fire blazing in the grate in the back room, a view of which, warmly carpeted and handsomely furnished, could be obtained through the door of the office standing ajar.

Cecily approached the desk, at which an elderly gentleman, clad in the newest of black suits, and with the whitest of white neckties, was seated writing.

He wore blue spectacles and a light flaxen wig, and there was not very much of his face to be discerned in consequence.

At the moment that the girls entered, there was less than usual, for he was deeply engaged with the book before him, and he appeared not to hear the approach, although the door from the street in opening rang the bell.

At last he did look up, and smiled upon the sister's, blandly.

"Well, young ladies."

"Oh, if you please——" said Cecily, with some slight trepidation in her tone

The old gentleman blandly waved his hands towards a couple of chairs.

"Pray be seated."

The young girls sat down, but still hesitated as though uncertain what they should ask for.

The old gentleman smiled more kindly than before, and said "Situations as governesses no doubt—or lady's companions."

"If you have a situation vacant for the latter," said Cicely.

"Most luckily, as it happened," said the old gentleman, "I believe I have two vacancies at the present moment upon my books"

The girls were delighted, and showed it in their looks

"Before, however, we say that the matter is settled," continued the old gentleman, "it will be necessary for me to ask you a few questions."

The hearts of the applicants began to flutter with alarm, but they endeavoured to bow in token of acquiescence.

"Is this your first situation?" asked the old gentleman.

Cecily paused undecided for a moment what reply to make, and the old gentleman, after a sharp and scrutinizing glance at the faces, continued rather hastily.

"It does not matter," he said. "In this case I am happy to be able to tell you it does not matter, although, as a rule, as you have no doubt heard it is extremely difficult to obtain any employment, unless you can bring a recommendation as to your ability and experience."

"Certainly, sir," said the young woman, faintly.

"You can, of course, bring some sort of recommendation?"

"Yes, sir."

"You have a good wardrobe?"

"Ye—es, sir."

"That is well. Have you any relations?"

"N-no!"

"None alive?"

"None alive."

"May I ask who recommended you to come here?"

"We saw the name of the office, by accident, in the Directory."

"Did you not hear of it from any one—any one who has obtained a situation by our aid?"

"No."

"And you asked no questions about the office?"

"None; why?"

It was Cecily who asked this question, with some amount of abruptness.

The old gentleman looked at her hard over his spectacles for a moment, rubbing his chin with his hand.

"Well," said he,—"of course it is not for me to say anything against this office, which I honestly believe to be one of the most successful that has ever been established; but, at the same time, I like to see young ladies behave prudently. You might have fallen into bad hands. I thank heaven that you have not."

The old gentleman opened his book and entered the names which the girls gave him.

"If you come here again to-morrow evening, at this time, and bring your written recommendations with you, I shall have been able to see the ladies who are in want of your services," said he. "If the result of my negotiations is satisfactory, I may, perhaps, be able to engage you directly. In that case, when can you go to the situations?"

"Immediately, if we are wanted."

"You may be wanted to go even as early as to-morrow night. The ladies are desirous of obtaining some one directly; and, to tell the truth," he continued, in a confidential tone, "they have made application to a rival office, which, I have no doubt, will be only too eager to supply them."

After a little more conversation, the young girls rose to depart.

The old gentleman conducted them to the door, and wished them politely "Good night!"

Then watched the retreating forms as they walked away in the twilight, with an expression that was anything but benevolent.

When they had turned the corner of the street, Alice said to Cecily, "What do you think of our chance?"

"Of what?" the other asked, raising her head as though she had been in a brown study.

"Of what?" repeated Alice, in amazement. "Of getting the situation, of course!"

"Oh, of that? Yes; I suppose our chance is good enough?"

"What did you suppose I meant?"

"Nothing! I was only thinking!"

"What? How strange your manner is, Cecily!"

"I was thinking where I could have seen that man before."

"What man?"

"He to whom we were speaking."

"At the office?"

"To be sure!"

"But do you know him?"

"No; I can't say that I do; yet I feel certain I have met him somewhere, under some disagreable circumstances, and I fancied——"

"Yes?"

"I fancied that he also recognised me!"

"I did not notice that he showed any sign of recognition."

"Well, perhaps so."

"You intend us to go to-morrow evening at the time he appoints?"

"Oh, yes, we will go; no harm can come of it that I see."

"We must have some clothes?"

"Yes; we ought to——"

"But how are we to get them?"

"There is only one way!"

"Oh, Cecily, do you mean the way we have been doing?"

"I see nothing else for it!"

"Oh, heaven help us!"

"It is always so, I suppose. When once we begin a course like this, there is no turning back!"

"Can you think of no plan by which we might get over this difficulty?"

Cecily was silent for a few moments.

Then she spoke with a bright smile.

"I think we can avoid further crime by an innocent fraud—by a *ruse*, if you like it better!"

"And that is——"

"If we buy a couple of boxes, and fill them with some heavy substance—to appear like clothes——"

"But when we get to our places, what shall we do?"

"*When* we get there will be time enough to think of that!"

Then they walked away, turning the matter over in their minds.

Alice was delighted with the prospect before them; and her sister seemed joyful too, though in a less degree; for she still, somehow, felt uneasy about the likeness which the old gentleman in the blue spectacles bore to some person she had seen before, under some unpleasant circumstances.

But where?—where?

* * * * *

Had they been able to see the face of the old gentleman himself, they would have come to the conclusion that he also was puzzling his brains.

Yes; he too was wondering where he had seen Cecily, and whom she was like.

After he had stood for a while watching their retreating forms until the darkness swallowed them up, he returned to the office shaking his head.

"Where was it I saw her?" said he to himself. "Who is she? The deuce take me, if I can tell!"

He looked up at the clock as he spoke.

"Hallo!" said he,—"its shutting up time! Nobody else is expected to night, so I won't keep open any longer."

It was rather curious, in such a highly respectable office, that nobody should have been kept to do such work; but certain it is that the old gentleman was obliged to shut the shutters and bar the door with his own hands.

"It's cursed lonely without Stone," he observed; "but I'll brew myself a stiff glass of grog when I've had my tea. Where could I have seen that woman before! By heavens, I have it!—and yet——No; that isn't it, either! But then, if it isn't, it's the other one! To be sure!—what a fool I was!"

He burst out laughing as he spoke, and pulled off his wig and blue spectacles.

Then, retiring into the parlour behind, took off

his coat, turned up his sleeves, and set to work cooking a red herring.

"It isn't Ruth the Betrayer," said he; "though at first I fancied it was; and it isn't Lady D'Arcy though I half thought it might have been. It's that girl that was at old Jeer's—that's who it is. What a rum start! Won't Jacob grin when I tell him! Perhaps I shouldn't, by rights, have had anything to say to her; but then I don't see why? Why shouldn't we settle her like the rest, if she has a bit of money, or a rig out of clothes? Who's the other one, I wonder? I couldn't see her face through her veil. That couldn't have been Ruth, though! By the Lord, I shouldn't like to have to tackle Ruth!"

While he was talking, he was kneeling down in front of the fire, cooking his herring. The firelight fell full upon his face, and lighted up his features

He was not a good looking man, this clerk in the employ of universal agency.

He had a head very much like a skull—a death's head, in fact.

And were we not inclined to believe that he was a respectable person of a blandly benevolent turn, one would be half inclined to think he was a certain murderous wretch called Skeleton Key, an accomplice of another unmitigated scoundrel, whose name was Jacob Stone.

If so, perhaps the reader may remember a certain conversation overheard by Jack Rafferty.

A damnably atrocious scheme—of murder and theft — the result of which we have yet to record.

And it was into the clutches of these monsters that the two unhappy girls had fallen, or about to fall

What was to be their fate now? A far worse

fate, may be, than that from which they had escaped.

There was time to escape from this, you will will say.

But it was not to be.

No, their doom was sealed.

They were drawing to an end, as is also this history.

Yet a little while, and my tale will be told.

CHAPTER CXXXIX

SHOWS HOW RUTH CAME TO TOWN AND FOUND AN OLD FRIEND

When we left Ruth she was setting out on a stormy night, upon the mail boat bound for England.

She was disguised as a young Roman Catholic priest.

Her companion was a gentleman of property, of the name of Cadbury Kid.

When the reader heard the name, it is probable that he recollected a person who was going to hang himself in Saint James's Park, owing to the unfortunate termination of his love affairs. If he recollected this much, it is also probable that he may remember the name of the lady for whom he had suffered so much—and that that name was Belvidere.

You may suppose, then, how our fair friend smiled, when she recognised her former admirer.

She was by no means anxious that he should discover who she was just yet.

But there was not much chance of that, for he could hardly have imagined it possible that he should have met her there, dressed in such a garb. It was dark, too, and he did not get a good look at her. Besides, the weather was extremely rough.

This last was no doubt the real reason why he was safe, for poor Mr. Kid had scarcely left the harbour before he began to feel very unwell indeed.

He began by smoking a cigar with a great deal of bravado, when the boat first set out on its journey across the stormy waters, but he very soon relinquished his weed, and muttering something about a slight headache that he had been troubled with, he walked away and leant over the side of the boat.

He had been rather chatty at first, but he soon grew silent—before long, he said he felt that he was rather chilly, and that he thought he would go down below.

Half an hour afterwards he was awfully ill.

Ruth was a pretty good sailor, but she was so weary and worn out by the anxious day through which she had passed, that she was glad enough to go to her berth, and falling asleep in spite of the violent rocking and tossing of the storm-driven vessel, she was soon in the land of dreams.

Next morning, when she awoke, the boat was steaming rapidly up the Thames, and not very far from the Custom House.

She felt rather timid of showing her face to Mr. Kid in the broad daylight—but there was nothing for it; and though he stared at her very hard when they met, she had quite sufficient command of countenance, as those who know her can readily believe, to bear his scrutiny without flinching, and affect to be unconscious of it.

Not that he paid a great deal of attention to her, for he was so dreadfully weak from the effects of his illness that he could hardly stand upon his legs; and what few wits he had remaining were required to invent some artful scheme for escaping the vigilance of the Custom House officers, owing to his being intent on smuggling on shore a most preposterous quantity of contraband articles, such as brandy, cigars, scent, gloves, &c.

Taking his friend, the young priest, into a quiet corner, Mr. Kid stated the case to him.

"What on earth am I to do?"

"Can I be of any assistance?"

"I don't like to ask you!"

"Nonsense, my dear fellow, if I can get anything through I shall only be too happy!"

She spoke the truth, for she saw that this would be a means of prolonging the acquaintance for a short time longer; and when they got on shore she had made up her mind to disclose the secret of her sex.

Mr. Kid, who though extremely rich, was like many other rich people, extremely mean, and he would have preferred to suffer any amount of inconvenience himself, or cause any amount of inconvenience to his friends, rather than pay the few shillings duty which would have taken his property through the Custom House with safety.

He was, therefore, in raptures when he heard the young priest offer to assist him.

"Catch hold of this, please," said he, handing a bottle; "and this one," handing another. "Can you put these gloves in your pocket? That's all right. Here's some scent, too," cramming it in. "It doesn't stick out much behind. Can you carry any more?"

"Well, I think I'm pretty well loaded."

"Havn't you room for this square box of bonbons?"

"I don't see where!"

"Couldn't you jam it into the crown of your hat—or, no—suppose you take it under your arm, and carry a bottle in each hand? That's capital! I wish we had time, we might regularly have padded you!"

Perhaps Ruth was not sorry that he had not.

As it was, she very narrowly escaped detection in passing through. But it was done, and Mr. Kid was in raptures.

"I say," says he, "didn't we manage capitally."

"Pretty well, I think!"

"First rate! I don't know what I could have done without you!"

"You flatter me!"

"You're not a bad sort, you know you are not! I shouldn't have thought one of you priests was up to a trick like that!"

"We're up to a good deal, at times!"

"The devil doubt you! You're awful rascals after the petticoats, they say! I shouldn't like to trust you along with a pretty girl, that I shouldn't!"

"I think you might do so, though, with perfect safety."

"Ah, you don't kiss and tell, I can see."

"No, I don't."

"By the way, will you have breakfast with me? Where are you going?"

"I don't know, hardly. Where are you?"

"I'm going to an hotel in the Haymarket. I'm going to have a bath, though, somewhere, first. Will you come?"

"No, no, thank you. By the way, will you breakfast at my rooms? I live near the Haymarket."

"Well, yes, with pleasure."

Ruth gave the number of a house in Panton Street; and promising to meet again in a couple of hours time, they parted

Ruth then called a hansom, and diving into it as quickly as possible, to avoid the grins and stares of the loafers, who were inclined to crack their jokes and pass their remarks in no under-tone or measured terms upon her strange dress, she bade the driver take her as quickly as possible to the address which she had given to Mr. Kid.

Arrived at the door, she desired the cabman to knock at it for her, and after some slight delay it was opened.

Then she called from the cab, "Does Mrs. Mortimer live here?"

"Yes."

"Is she in?"

"Yes."

Ruth alighted, discharged the cabman, and entered the house.

It was not exactly a private house, for there was something that looked a little like a shop upon the ground floor, only the blinds were drawn, and nothing whatever could be seen of the interior; so that it was rather difficult to say in what mercantile commodity its owner was supposed to deal.

Ruth appeared to be well acquainted with the place; and passing by the servant, who had opened the door, and who regarded the clerical appearance of the stranger with the most intense astonishment, she walked up-stairs.

Before she had reached the first floor, however, the girl called to her.

"Hollo!" she cried, "where are you going to?"

"Up-stairs."

"What for?"

"To see Mrs. Mortimer"

"What do you want with Mrs. Mortimer?"

"That's my business, I think."

"But, I say——"

"Well?"

"I don't think she's up yet."

"It does not signify."

"What do you mean? I say, sir, if you please—come back, I say!"

But Ruth paid no attention to these commands. She walked forward, and opened the door of a room on the first floor.

"This is the place, I expect," said she to herself.

And she walked in.

It was a bed-room, handsomely furnished, and a woman lay asleep in bed.

She woke up at the sound of Ruth's footsteps, and started up in alarm when she saw Ruth's dress.

"Good Lord! what do you want?"

Ruth, in reply, burst out laughing, and threw her hat upon the bed.

"Lor', don't you know me?"

"Eh—what?"

"Don't you know me?"

"You don't mean to say——"

"Yes, I do."

"You're not——"

"Yes, I am?"

"Ruth?"

"The same"

"God bless me! Where have you come from? I thought you were dead and buried!"

"So I have been"

"Good gracious!"

"But, look here," said Ruth, staying her enthusiasm. "I want to know if I can have a room to have breakfast in, and if any one can go and order some breakfast for me. I expect a gentleman here directly. I want the loan of a handsome dress, too, Can you manage it? Yes or no, and quickly, for we have no time to spare"

"Yes, yes, only please explain."

"I'll explain all directly; only let us give the orders first. Ring for your servant."

The servant did not require to be rung for.

She was just outside the door, probably listening.

CHAPTER CXL.

ONCE MORE RUTH PLAYS THE PART OF A SYREN, AND ANOTHER VICTIM IS ADDED TO HER LIST.

Mr. Cadbury Kid was not behind his time.

He arrived to the minute. He inquired for the Abbe Duval. The servant, who had washed her face in the meantime, and had put on a very sedate and serious expression, with her clean apron, showed him up-stairs, to the first floor front, where the breakfast-table was laid for two.

The room was very handsomely furnished Some hothouse flowers stood in a vase, in the centre of the table. The breakfast service was very choice. The window was open. Everything was very fresh and pleasant.

Mr. Cadbury Kid looked round him with a smile.

"My friend, the priest," said he, "seems to do it up here uncommonly brown. He's a man of taste—of singular taste, for a clerical gent"

While he was talking, he was examining the pictures upon the walls, and this accounted for the termination of the sentence.

There were several oil paintings decorating the walls—evidently expensive pictures, and painted by good artists—probably French, to judge by the subjects.

Lucretia struggling in the arms of her brutal ravisher, half naked, with the violence of the fearful conflict in which she had vainly striven to defend her honour from his savage lust.

Messalina lying in her bath; the limpid waters playing round the rich contours of her voluptuous form.

The elders surprising the chaste Susannah at her toilet, and gloating their eyes upon the virgin charms which she vainly endeavoured to conceal from their sight.

Leda's amour with the God Jupiter, who, as a swan, wooed and won the coy nymph. And lastly, Potiphar, the very perfection of female loveliness, with bare bosom, and limbs round and white, parted lips moist and red, and eyes brimming over with the hot fires of unholy desires, clinging to the shrinking youth, who fled in terror from her dangerous presence.

No prudery had stayed the artist's pencil when he produced these shameful pictures. His design was but too manifest.

To provoke the passions of the beholder, to corrupt the mind, and excite desire.

Such a vile motive had spurred him on, and it must be owned that he had so well succeeded. that it would have been almost impossible for the purest and most virtuous to have gazed upon these licentious scenes without a certain amount of corruption.

Mr. Cadbury Kid, however, was not a young man troubled with any particular squeamishness on the score of morality. He examined all the pictures with the greatest attention and considerable gratification, and when he had looked at them all, he was exceedingly sorry that there were not some more to follow.

When he had done with the pictures, he turned over the leaves of a few books lying about, which were of a grossly indelicate character, and was so pleasantly occupied, that he had hardly noticed what a long time his friend, the priest, was keeping him waiting.

At last, however, the door opened.

Mr. Kid shut up his book in some haste and confusion, and rose to meet the young clerical gentleman.

But, in his place, instead, he saw a beautiful woman, spendidly attired in a velvet dress, very low at the neck, and exposing a bosom of snowy whiteness, on which rested a gorgeous necklace, while on her plump, fair arms glittered a variety of bracelets.

Perhaps Mr. Kid might have been justified in feeling surprised to see a lady thus attired at this early period of the day; but he had another reason for astonishment, for the lady before him was none other than his old love.

None other than the woman for whom he had suffered so bitterly in times past—the beautiful Belinda Belvidere, alias Ruth Trail, or Ruth Hardcastle, as the reader is better accustomed to hear her called.

Yes, it was the enchantress, herself. It was the woman who had been wont, in times past, to exercise so potent a spell over him, and in whose presence, now, he felt returning much of the old feeling of half love, half fear with which she used to inspire him.

"Good heavens!" he cried, starting to his feet. "Good heavens, Mrs. Belvidere, is it you, indeed?"

"To be sure it is," she answered, smiling.

"But—but—do you live here?"

"No, I don't."

"Lodge here, I meant to say?"

"No."

"I beg your pardon, but perhaps you are a friend of the Abbe's?"

"Oh, to be sure I am."

"Is—is he a relation?"

"A very near one."

Mr. Kid looked thoroughly mystified, and Ruth came at last to his release, and condescended to offer a little explanation.

"The fact is this——" said she.

But as it was anything but facts which she now began to relate, it is hardly necessary to state the story she told. Suffice it, then, to say that the tale was a wonderful one, and though we have it upon the best authority that truth is stranger than fiction, yet it must certainly have been very strange indeed to have beaten the fiction which this playful lady invented for Mr. Kid's edification.

He was quite satisfied, though, by her explanation; and glad to find that she and the priest were one, and the same person, and that their *tete a-tete* was not likely to be interrupted by the arrival of any third person.

After a little explanation, Miss Ruth declaring that she was dying of hunger, rang the bell and ordered breakfast.

A really sumptuous repast was then brought in, with both wine and coffee, and Mr. Kid and his friend sat down with a very good will, intent upon doing it justice.

They had both had the precaution to take a cup of tea before the meal, to prevent them from having a headache, which would very probably have been the case had they not very wisely adopted that course. As it was, they sat down with tremendous appetites, and certainly did make the delicacies provided for them look very foolish indeed, before they had done with them.

But when the hard work was over, and they had time to play with their knives and forks, Ruth called upon her companion to open a bottle of champagne.

Mr. Kid had been drinking rather heavily, and was growing a little noisy. He struggled with the wire, and then could not draw the cork.

"Shall I knock the neck off?" he asked.

"Yes."

He took up his knife and dealt the neck of the bottle a sharp blow. The cork, and the glass surrounding it, fell to the ground with a crash. The wine bubbled up, and flowed frothing over his hand.

"Quick—quick," cried Ruth, "fill my glass!"

She leant forward towards him, and stretched forth her bare white arm. He leant over her, and poured the wine into the goblet she held in her hand.

Her scented hair brushed against his cheek. The low dress she wore revealed the matchless symmetry of her voluptuous bosom, to which his greedy eyes wandered involuntarily.

She poured the wine down her throat, tilting up the glass, so as to allow the last drops to trickle over her red, moist lips

He tried to take her in his arms, and she resisted, but weakly laughing, as she did so, a sly, noiseless laugh, full of amorous desire.

"Oh, how I love you!" he said.

"Nonsense."

"You know well all that I have suffered for you; but you do not know half of what I would suffer willingly—if——"

"If what?"

Her eyes looked full into his, so fixedly, that he timidly shrank before their lecherous gaze.

"If—you—will—be—mine!" he stammered.

"Do you really love me?" she asked, in a low, hoarse whisper.

CHAPTER CXLI.

RUTH SHOWS A LITTLE TEMPER.

"And how many ladies have you said the same thing to?" Ruth asked about a quarter of an hour after breakfast was finished, as she and her companion stood at the window looking down into the street. "How many foolish women have you beguiled into the belief that you were dying for them?"

"How you go on," said Kid, with a silly laugh. "You want to make me out a regular bad 'un!"

"Are you not? I was told you were an awful rake, and had squandered away all your money in wine and wickedness."

"You were told wrong," said Cadbury, grinning in a foolish way, which he intended to be very sly indeed.

"How so?" asked Ruth.

"Ha! ha!"

"Won't you tell me?"

"Instead of having squandered away all my money," observed Mr. Kid, "I've got a precious sight more than ever I had."

"Oh!"

"I have come into some property lately, and though all my relations have tried hard to bring me in mad, they haven't succeeded."

"The idea of accusing you of being mad!"

"Ridiculous, isn't it? But as I was saying about my money——"

"Yes—yes!"

"Well, instead of wasting it, I have been setting my wits to work to think of a plan by which I may double it."

"And have you found one to your satisfaction?"

"I have, and I fancy you'll think it rather a good one, too."

"I am sure I shall. What is it?"

"I am going to run a horse for the Derby."

Whatever Ruth's opinion might have been upon the subject, she did not give utterance to it, all at once. She looked rather blankly at her companion, but she said nothing for the space of a full minute, and then gave vent to long, "Oh!"

"Don't you think that that's the way to pull it off?" asked Mr. Kid.

"It's the way to lose money as well as to win."

"Lor' bless you, with my horse, it's a dead certainty!"

"A what?"

"I'm safe to come in first. Mine is the favourite, you know. Why, she's at three to one this minute."

"Well—yes—I don't understand."

"No, you don't seem to. But you needn't be uneasy. I'm all right enough. The fact is, I have dipped into my tin rather deeply, and I must do something to set myself straight."

"Oh, you're not so well off, then, after all."

"I've enough left, for the matter of that, and I shall pull through. In fact, if my horse wins—and everybody says it will—I shall make my fortune again—and, by heaven, we'll spend it together to the last farthing."

Ruth smiled; but her face, as it turned away from him, was overcast with a shadow of what might have been rage, or regret. She had heard nothing of this young man's extravagance. She believed him to be enormously rich. Had she given herself up to a beggar? Was she about to become the mistress of an adventurer—a betting man—a leg?"

Mr Kid did not notice her preoccupation. He went on with his remarks, speaking more to himself than to her.

"Ah!" said he,—"there's not much fear of my going very wrong. I reckon I know a thing or two to beat that. You may take your oath I shan't go to the bad, like that fool Crockford!"

Ruth turned hastily at the sound of the familiar name

"What of him?" she asked.

"Do you know him?"

"Only slightly. Where is he now?"

"Well, if you must know, he's languishing at the present moment in Horsemonger Lane, where he has been locked up for felony!"

"Felony?" Ruth exclaimed, involuntarily.

"Well, if he hadn't been a fool, he wouldn't have been there."

"How so?"

"It was all through some woman he got locked up."

"Indeed!"

"Yes; he stuck his name on a bill for her for some enormous amount—— At least, not exactly that; but the name he wrote was not his own, but his elder brother's."

Ruth was silent for a while. She was thinking of her treacherous conduct to the poor young officer who had loved her so deeply.

Presently she asked, in a voice that appeared rather husky, as though she had suddenly caught a cold from the open window at which she and her companion were standing—

"What will he be done to?"

"The trial has not come on yet."

"Do you think it will go hard with him?"

"I should think there was little doubt of it."

"Oh"

"How serious you've grown all at once!" said Mr. Kid, in a playful tone.

And as he spoke, he made as though he would have put his arm round her waist.

But she turned from his grasp, and sent at him an angry flash of her dark eyes, which was enough to warn him that she was in no humour to be played with.

Mr. Kid did not appear to understand her, however.

"You've been crying!" said he, in astonishment, noticing that her cheeks were moist with tears.

"What's that to you?"

"To me? Oh, nothing!"

"Leave me alone, then!"

"I only wanted——"

"Leave me alone!"

She spoke in such a threatening tone, at the same time clutching a knife from the table, and holding it aloft with such a murderous gesture, that her lover fell back in terror, stretching out his hands to ward off the blow which he thought was coming.

But she laid the knife down again, with a short laugh.

"Don't be alarmed!" she said.

"N-n-no!" stammered Mr. Kid.

"I did not intend to kill you! If I killed anybody, I should kill myself! But not yet—not yet!"

She walked back to the window, muttering to herself—heeding not his presence

Kid looked after her uneasily.

"She's a beauty!" he thought; "but a queer temper; a difficult one to manage, I expect; a devil of a one if she got in a rage with a fellow! But a fellow could love her in spite of it all, if she would only let a fellow do so without flying out at him!"

CHAPTER CXLII.

RUTH RESOLVES TO MAKE HER FORTUNE.

A MONTH after the scene which I have just described, Mrs. Cadbury Kid occupied a beautiful little villa at St. John's Wood, was the proprietress of a handsome brougham and pair, had a couple of men-servants and a couple of maids in her employ, and, to all outward appearances, was prosperous and highly respectable.

I am not quite sure that she was looked up to by the neighbours, or that her virtue was believed in, to any great extent, by the tradesmen who supplied her with their goods; and I am very well certain that the parson of the parish did not leave a card at her house when she made her first appearance.

I do'nt think that the servants either quite believed that there had been any marriage ceremony performed between Mr. Cadbury and his beautiful companion; and the extremely riotous character of one or two supper parties which took place at the villa did not tend to increase the fair fame of the lady of the house.

From the reader, then, why should I endeavour to conceal the fact that Ruth was living under the protection of Mr. Kid? In a very short time she had acquired such an influence over his weak mind, that he was now a perfect slave to her will

She was not long in discovering that he was not so poor as he tried to make out; and even though the greater part of his property might have been squandered away, his credit was yet at its best. Under these circumstances, there was very little difficulty about "raising the wind;" and raised it was to a truly alarming extent.

As one of Mr. Kid's principal failings was a great partiality for intoxicating drinks, he was hardly ever sober enough to look his position fairly in the face, and the consequence was, that as long as he could get easily through any little embarrassment that harassed him at the moment, he didn't worry his weak head about the future Now and then, it is true, that in a sober moment, with the help of pencil and paper, he struggled for a while with his accounts, and tried to see exactly how he stood; but upon these occasions the result was always so very unsatisfactory, that it was a long time before he ventured upon any more arithmetic.

"D—n it!" he said sometimes. "If I don't pull off well over this race, I shall jolly well go to smash. But then I'm certain to pull off; for isn't my horse the favourite? and isn't it the best horse entered? and does not everybody, who knows anything about it, say that it is a dead certainty?"

When these remarks were made in Ruth's presence, she offered no observation, but secretly made up her mind upon the course which she intended to pursue.

While the money lasted she intended to feather her nest; and when credit became bad, and nobody would do any more bills for Mr. Cadbury Kid, she would be prepared to shift for herself.

It was difficult to say how long the sunshine would last, and she made hay as quickly as she could. Supposing Mr. Kid's horse won the race, he would certainly make an enormous sum of money. He had backed it right and left.

He had sold, and begged, and borrowed, and he had laid every obtainable halfpenny upon the race. More than once he had grumbled at Ruth's lavish expenditure, because otherwise he could have increased his stakes; and for no one else in the world would he have wasted so much money; but Ruth, as I have said, had him completely in her power, and could have twisted him round her little finger, had she so chosen.

But Ruth was by no means so positive that Mr Kid's horse would come in first. Hearing so much talk about horse-racing, a subject which hitherto had not occupied her attention in the least, and being a shrewd, sensible woman, she began to think the matter over—to make inquiries where she could obtain any information, and to "coach" herself in the subject as though she were about to undergo an examination.

The result was that she ascertained that it was by no means the rule for the favourite to win the Derby; and although the horse which Mr. Kid owned was undoubtedly the best horse entered for the race, by some mischance another and inferior horse might come in before it.

The question then arose—How could she make herself safe?

She had quietly appropriated a large sum of money, and laid it by in a bank. With this, should she back the favourite?

If she did, and the horse lost, she would lose all her money.

But if she "hedged" her money, as they say in sporting circles—if she backed the horse, and bet against it at the same time, could she make anything? No; the odds were too short for that. No; nothing could be made that way.

Long did this artful woman puzzle her brains upon the subject; and it was at last by chance that she hit upon an idea, and determined, by the exercise of that treachery and devilish cunning which she had often used before, to make her fortune by the ruin of the man under whose protection she lived.

Think not that when the time did come any recollection of past kindness would stay her hand.

Pity and compassion were unknown to the hard and callous heart of this inhuman woman.

Is it likely that she who had caused the ruin of the only man for whom, in the course of her long career of heartless enormity, she had felt any affection—namely, Captain Charles Crockford—that she would spare any one else.

No; she was determined, if the opportunity came in her way, to sacrifice her lover, and grasp the wealth for which she had so long struggled fruitlessly.

The opportunity did come, as we shall see, and this most treacherous of fair-faced friends gained her end by the use of means more bold and devilishly cunning than any which I have before recorded.

CHAPTER CXLIII.

OUT SHOPPING.—THE COQUETTE.—THE RAGGED YOUNG MAN.—RUTH'S TERROR.—THE SPY.—THE GARDEN WALL.—THE VILLANOUS SUGGESTION.—MORE PLOTS AND PLANS.

Yes, she gained her end.

She grasped the coveted wealth.

She came one step nearer to the end—oh, what an end! Heaven knows, had she dreamt what fate was in store for her, she would have strangled, or poisoned, or drowned herself now, while there was yet time to escape from it.

But no such knowledge was granted to her, and she kept steadily forward upon her way, as she had ever been beautiful, crafty, treacherous, and lewd. A fiend in an angel's form.

One morning, about a fortnight before the race, Ruth was sitting in her brougham outside a shop in Regent Street, whither she had accompanied a lady friend. The friend had gone into a shop, and was making some purchases, which delayed her, as is not uncommonly the case with ladies, a much greater length of time than she had at first contemplated, when she left her companion to await her return in the carriage.

Ruth, who had very little taste for shopping, or,

indeed, for most of those occupations which the softer sex were wont to take delight in, preferred to await her arrival, and was amusing herself with a novel, when she became conscious of some person passing and repassing the window of her brougham, and hanging about upon the pavement in front of it, with the evident purpose of attracting her attention.

At first she had taken very little notice of the circumstance, because she was so much in the habit of attracting attention wherever she went, in consequence of the extreme beauty of her face, and the magnificence of her toilet.

She was not so beautiful as she was when first we made her acquaintance, it is true; but yet, with the aid of a little rouge and violet powder, she was very lovely, and one could scarcely see her without being struck with her appearance, even were not her dress of so gorgeous a character as to invite attention from its very costliness.

She had not noticed this person, then, at first; or rather, though conscious of somebody's presence, she supposed it to be some admiring dandy in raptures with her pretty face.

She had some idea of lifting up her eyes to see who it was; but, with a spirit of coquetry which even so strong-minded a female did not altogether despise, she resolved instead upon reading her book harder than ever, and continued turning over the pages with a wrapt attention which must have been extremely aggravating to the feelings of the love-sick swain endeavouring to catch her eye—that is, of course, supposing it should be a love-sick swain, and to catch her eye was his desire.

However, it was not quite the sort of person she supposed. It was a shabby person. A man—yet not exactly a man, and, at the same time, not quite a lad. A hobbledehoy is, I think, the correct description of a person at his time of life

He was a person with a singularly old face upon young shoulders, a wrinkled and haggard face, covered with red blotches of an unsightly character, and ornamented with a pair of small, evil-looking eyes, which blinked horribly.

It was at first a difficult question to decide, whether he was a very old man, or a very young old man; but, after a careful examination, one was inclined to lean to the former opinion. He was a youthful scoundrel, who had lived hard and gone the pace.

He was very ragged and woe-begone, and looked half-starved. He was evidently in want, and it is to be supposed that he had arrived at this condition in consequence of his own wickedness.

After dodging about, in the way I have described, for some time, he at length summoned courage, and approached the carriage.

He stared in hard at the occupant's face.

His shadow falling upon her book aroused her from her study, and raising her eyes languidly she uttered a slight scream, when she saw such an ugly object was contemplating her.

The next moment she would have called to the coachman for assistance; but the young man arrested the movement, by clutching her suddenly by the wrist.

"What would you do?" he asked.

"What do you want?"

"Ain't your name Belvidere?"

"No."

"It used to be."

She made no effort to cry out now; she could not have done so, to have saved her life.

She turned deadly pale, and trembled violently.

She was silent, and waited for him to speak again, glancing nervously towards the coachman, to see whether they were observed.

But the coachman was dozing upon the box, and had noticed nothing. The man at the window looked in the same direction, and then continued, in a low voice—"I've been looking for you everywhere. They said you had gone out of England, and they told me you were dead; but I didn't think so."

"Who are you? I don't know you."

"You know Earthworm's office?"

"Well?"

"Don't you recollect his clerk?"

"Are you he?"

"Yes."

"You've altered very much."

"So they say. Improved, haven't I? and grown."

"What do you want with me?"

"I'm hard up."

"Ah! I supposed that was it."

As she spoke, she took a little purse from her bag, and opened it

The young man's hungry eyes greedily devoured the contents.

"How rich you are!" he muttered, hardly above his breath.

"No, I am not," she retorted; "I am poor, instead."

"Ah, I wish I never was no poorer."

"Here is a sovereign for you."

"Bless you for it."

"But mind——"

"Yes."

"Mind you don't bother me again, for you shall never have any more. Get away—here's my friend coming!"

She waved him away, as she saw her friend approach; and he crept into the rear, with a savage expression upon his countenance, which, had she seen, she might not have relished over much.

"That's the way she thinks she's going to settle me," he said to himself, with a grin. "I think not, though—I reyther think not, if I may be allowed to have an opinion."

Ruth gave her coachman orders to drive on, and, as the shopping was over, bade him conduct them home.

The ragged young man did not catch the words, although he did his best to do so; but he was determined not to lose sight of the vehicle, if he could help it.

Therefore, when the brougham set off on its way, he jumped nimbly up behind.

The spikes afforded at best but a very uncomfortable seat, and the advice of some disinterested street-boy brought the driver's whip tingling about his ears; but he held on like grim Death, "tucked in his twopenny," and accompanied the carriage upon its way.

All the way to St. John's Wood they rode thus; and having seen Ruth and her companion alight, the ragged young man rode round to the stable without being discovered, and dropped off at the gate, having made quite sure that he had arrived at the journey's end.

The question now was, did Ruth live at the house where she had alighted, and was this her brougham?

With money in his pocket, he found it no very difficult matter to learn all particulars, and he soon made up his mind what he should do next.

That night, when Ruth was walking alone in her garden—while Cadbury Kid and a male friend were yet dawdling over their wine and cigars in the dining-room—the same ragged young man who had appeared so unexpectedly in the morning appeared again now, suddenly poking his ugly head over the garden wall.

Ruth was passing by the spot at that moment. She started, and looked up.

"Who's that?"

"Only me."

"Who are you?"

"Only the poor young man you was so good to this morning."

"I told you I wouldn't do any more for you. How dare you come here, after what I said?"

"I don't want you to do anything."

"I suppose you followed my carriage?"

"Yes, Mrs. Kid."

"And what do you expect to get, now you have come?"

"Expect to get?"

"Don't you hear me?"

"Nothing, Mrs. Kid. I'm only too grateful for what you have done for me already."

"What has brought you here, then?"

"I couldn't forbear from following after you, to see where you lived. I was so happy, to think that you were alive and well, after I had thought you dead, and that you was in such easy circumstances."

"I tell you that I am not well off!"

"But you're married?"

Ruth made no answer.

"Married to one of the richest gentlemen in England, if what the world says is true; and to the owner of the favourite of the Derby?"

Still she was silent.

"Might I ask Mrs. Kid, if it is not taking too great a liberty, and making too free, if it's going to run to win?"

"What do you mean?" Ruth asked, looking up in astonishment.

The young man sunk his voice.

"Being old friends, so to speak," he said, "I make so bold as to inquire; because, though a humble person, I do a little in the sporting line myself, and I might make a trifle, if you gave me a tip."

"I do not understand you!"

"Oh, lor', how downy you are! But then you always was! I never did know such a leary one! Of course I don't mean to intimate that Mr. Kid would sell the race; but, if he didn't run to win, what an awful pot I might make, to be sure!"

"Would he make more by losing than winning?"

"Wouldn't he, just, if he kept it dark, and laid against himself!"

Just then Ruth heard footsteps approaching.

"Go away!" she said, hastily; "and come here to-morrow at noon; I want to talk to you."

Then she walked back to the house herself, in deep thought.

"Why shouldn't I do it?" she muttered beneath her breath. "I see now how it can be managed! Kid would not sell the race himself. I know that well enough; for all his hopes are bent upon his horse winning. But why should not I sell it? It is my only chance of making money! If I don't do that, I must do what the priest has paid me for doing! And why should I run more risks by stopping longer in this hateful country to carry out their plans? Let them find some one else! I will not waste my time over such a business? No!—my scheme is a better one than that, and I will carry it out! And as for the Jesuits, I snap my fingers at them all!"

But Jesuits are not people to be defied with impunity, as pretty Mrs. Ruth found to her cost, in a way to be hereafter related.

CHAPTER CXLIV.

THE LONELY WATCHER.

At length arrived the night before the Derby.

All London was getting ready to go to the race. All London was packing up hampers, ordering salad, negotiating for carriages and horses, and laying in dozens of bottled beer and fabulous quantities of alcoholic fluids against the national holiday.

All the sporting world was in a state of feverish anxiety, respecting the results which to-morrow might bring forth. The half million of people who had "money on" were thirsting for latest intelligence, respecting the odds, and the "arrivals," and the "scratchings."

"Has anybody heard anything about 'Ginger Brandy?'" "Who said that 'Little Benjamin' is lame?" "You take my advice, and back 'Bullfrog,' if you want to pull it off to any tune. Safe to win? I should think so. Why, it's a moral!"

Everybody was talking about it—everybody was thinking of it; in fact, nobody was talking or thinking about anything else.

The evening papers, you may be sure, were in great request at all the sporting "pubs; and the "stable mouse's squeaks," and the "tips" from "Hotspur," and "Harkaway," and the other authorities, were ever so much more believable than Gospel this evening.

In the sporting "pubs," too, the most wonderful information was to be had for the asking. In the most mysterious stage-whispers, hints were thrown out which ought to have been worth their weight in gold if they had only been true. Here young men from the country, very far gone in gin-and-water, were put up to a thing or two—heard what horses they ought to back, and what horses they ought to leave alone—and how they were to "hedge" their money, to make all square; only that, somehow or other, to-morrow, in spite of it all, they didn't come off the winners they expected.

But the excitement in the coming race was not confined to sporting public-houses. You could hardly have gone anywhere that evening without hearing the name of Mr Kid's horse, and stray observations about the "field" and the "odds."

In the House of Commons the all-engrossing topic occupied much more of the members' attention than the Bill nominally under discussion; and at last one member gets up, and suggests that the house may be counted out, with an expression which seems to say—much more plainly than words could do so—"Hang it all! Let us cut this, and talk about 'Bullfrog.'"

Again, was much more attention being devoted to 'Bullfrog" than to Guiglini, at Her Majesty's Theatre; and the curtain having fallen upon the "Porter's Knot," or the "Dead Heart," everybody straightway forgot all about the drama, and began to talk about the never-ending "odds."

Meanwhile, Mr. Kid's horse, quite unconscious of the commotion it was causing in the "little

village," was comfortably stalled in his training-stable, not far from Epsom Downs. Wonderfully was he muffled up in warm cloths and wrappers; and when Mr. Kid looked in the last thing at night, to see how he was getting on, he expressed himself highly satisfied with Bull-frog's appearance.

"Well, Bob," said Mr. Kid, as he walked towards the door, "what do you think about tomorrow?"

"Safe as the Bank, sir!"

"We shall win easy, you think?"

"From all I can hear, we shall walk over. There's no other horse that is going to run that can touch us."

"He seems in good condition."

"Couldn't be in better."

"Heaven grant what you say may prove true! Every farthing I have in the world is on it."

"You may depend upon me, sir, doing my best."

"I am sure of that, Bob."

"Nobody shall tamper with the horse while he's in my charge."

"I am sure of that, Bob."

"There's only one way that they can get near enough to physic him."

"How is that?"

"Over my dead body."

Mr. Kid smiled, and shaking the jockey warmly by the hand, quitted the stable.

A dog-cart waited for him outside, and, getting into it, he galloped off in the direction of the Spread Eagle, where a hot supper and the beautiful Mrs Kid were expecting his arrival.

But hardly had the sound of the wheels died away in the distance, when a dark figure crept out from behind a low wall which had hitherto hidden it from observation, and the features of Mr. Earthworm's late clerk were turned up towards the moon with a grin of impish cunning.

Bob, the jockey, did not notice the figure any more than Mr. Kid and his groom. He stood at the door listening to the sound of the wheels for a few minutes, and then entered the stable.

The stable contained three stalls, in the centre one of which the favourite stood. In each of the other two stalls was chained up a large savage bull-dog, which followed the jockey's movements with a glare of savage suspicion.

A candle in a dirty lantern was all the light which the stable contained, and it would have been only with difficulty that any person unaccustomed to the dim obscurity could have traced the outline of surrounding objects.

In one corner of the stable was a ladder leading to a loft above, where the jockey slept at night,—for night or day he never quitted his charge; and, carefully ascending the steps, he brought down his saddle and bridle, and began to clean up the chains and buckles with a rag and some wet sand.

This done, he subjected Bull-frog to a lengthy examination, carefully and tenderly passing his hand over its limbs.

Satisfied with the condition in which he found the noble animal, and confident that there was no appearance of stiffness or swelling, he drew a long breath, and, seating himself upon an inverted bucket, took out his pipe and began to smoke.

But just now the dog nearest the door began to growl and sniff the air.

Bob looked up uneasily.

"Halloa, Spot!" said he. "What's the matter?"

The dog was straining at its chain and sniffing fiercely at the air.

"What's the matter, Spot?" asked the jockey again.

The canine guardian growled in reply, and seemed to intimate that he did not think all was right.

The jockey eyed him uneasily, and glanced towards the door.

It was locked and bolted securely. No one could intrude that way.

Bob approached the window, and, shading his eyes, peered anxiously out.

Perhaps somebody might be lurking about, he thought.

But he could hear nothing when he listened. Everything was very still and dark without.

Presently, he left the window, and, with great caution, unfastened the door.

Peeping out cautiously first, he stepped across the threshold, and looked round, listening as before.

No; he could hear nothing.

He lingered for a short time, though, turning at the slightest sound; and, at last, convinced that there was nothing to be alarmed at, returned to the stable, and locked and bolted the door behind him.

The wind moaned drearily over the bare downs, and rustled the leaves upon the trees surrounding the stable.

A distant clock chimed the midnight hour.

The lights in all the houses in the neighbouring village had long since been extinguished, and all good folks were abed and s[illegible]ting.

Far away over the downs a very faint red light was discernible—the light of the gipsies' fire—a faint buzzing noise in the air arose from the voices of those hanging about the scene of the race, getting ready the booths for to-morrow.

No other sign of life was visible.

"It was most likely some tramp who had lost his way," muttered the jockey to himself; and, lighting his pipe, he fell into a pleasant train of thought over his betting-book.

He felt a little sleepy, but he had determined not to close his eyes all night, and so stuck to his pipe and calculations, and worked hard at them both.

Between the hours of one and two the same stealthy figure crept out from the shadow of the wall, under which it had laid hidden so long, and, turning its cunning face towards the village, appeared to be watching and listening eagerly.

Presently, the faint sound of footsteps was heard approaching.

"She's here at last!" the clerk whispered to himself. "She's been long enough!"

He advanced in the direction from which the sound came, and met a woman, dressed in a cloak, and wearing a thick veil.

It was Ruth.

"Well?" she said.

"Well?" he answered.

"Is it all right?"

"All right!"

"Is he alone?"

"Yes."

"Are you sure?"

"Certain."

"You have not left your post?"

"Not a moment all night."

"And no one has been here since Mr. Kid?"

"No one."

"Do you think he is armed?"

"I don't know; but I should think it probable."

"And he has the two dogs with him?"

"Yes"

"Did you bring any arms?"

The man showed, by way of answer, a small pocket-pistol.

"Have you?" he asked.

"I have a knife!" she replied, smiling grimly.

"But we won't use them, if we can help it?"

"Of course not; but if he won't listen to reason?"

"Then we must. But let us use the pistol. I can't bear blood. It makes me sick."

"Nonsense!" the woman answered with a sneer. "I am not so squeamish. A pistol will make too much noise. But come! We must make haste!"

And then silently these two wretches crept towards the stable-door.

CHAPTER CXLV.

MR. CADBURY KID MAKES UP HIS MIND TO GET DRUNK, AND DOES SO WITH A VENGEANCE.

MR. CADBURY KID was so sure that his fortune was made, that he could not see any reason why he should not make merry beforehand.

He had made up his mind to make a night of it after the race, and pray why should not he make a night of it before the race also?

"I shall get drunk," said Mr. Kid, as he sat down to supper,—"I shall get drunk to-night, if ever I did."

And having expressed this highly laudable intention, Mr. Kid took a great gulp of champagne and laughed boisterously at the intense facetiousness of his own remark.

Ruth looked quietly at him from the other side of the table, and echoed his mirth with a low, inward laugh peculiar to her

"Why not put off your drunk till to-morrow?" she asked.

"Because I feel in the humour for it now."

"Very well."

"I can get drunk again to-morrow, if I like, I suppose?"

"I daresay you will, whether you win or lose."

The words were uttered in a calm and thoughtful tone, which appeared to strike her companion for a moment like an electric shock.

He put down a wine-glass, which at the moment he was raising to his lips, and gazed across the table at her uneasily.

"W-what did you say?"

"Eh?"

"What did you say about losing?"

"I said that I supposed you would get drunk, whether you won or lost."

There's no fear of my not winning. What the devil put such an idea into your head?"

"I don't know, I'm sure!"

"I should think you didn't! Who the devil dares to say I'm not going to win? I must win! I shall be a beggar, if I don't! I will win! I will, by G—— !"

Again that noiseless laugh, and a sly smile, half concealed in a cambric handkerchief with a deep border of costly lace, which Ruth spread before her pretty face to hide it.

Mr. Kid did not notice her.

He was helping himself to the contents of a dish before him

He took a small quantity upon his plate, and tasted it, then pushed it away, and helped himself to something else.

But he could not find his appetite.

"Curse it!" said he; "I'm too much worried to feel hungry. Here, waiter, I don't care for champagne; bring me some brandy—or, stop, can you make punch?—make me a bowl of punch."

"A bowl, sir?"

"Yes; don't you hear? What makes you ask? Let me have a bowl, and bring it up all on fire! And look sharp, for I'm dying of thirst."

Pretty Mrs Ruth looked prettier than ever this evening. She apparently had a capital appetite, and nibbled away at the wing of a fowl with extraordinary relish.

Evidently she was not anxious about to-morrow's race The result to her was a certainty.

Meanwhile her companion grew more and more inebriated, and more and more noisy.

By the time the bowl of punch arrived he was already drunk, for he had been helping himself profusely to port and sherry.

Now staggering to his feet, he insisted upon the landlord coming up-stairs and drinking success to Bull-frog in a bowl of punch. The waiter also joined in the festivities.

Ruth sat looking on at the drunken orgie in silence.

She had flung herself luxuriously upon the soft cushions of a sofa, and was gazing earnestly at her companions.

A bitter, scornful smile, which welled up from the bottom of her heart, curled her lip with a writhing contempt for the poor tipsy idiot, making merry there in the full confidence of coming success.

"Ruth, old girl!" he cried, with a drunken hiccup, and swaying over, so that he fell with one hand in the punch-bowl, "won't you drink success to Bull-frog?"

She rose, with a loud, reckless laugh strangely harsh and discordant.

"Here's to Bull-frog, the winner of the Derby!" said she, and drained her glass.

"Hooray!" yelled the drunken fool draining his glass also, and then dashing it through the window with a loud smash. "Hooray!—hoo—ray—ay!"

But in the middle of his cheering, his knees gave way, and he sank down a limp senseless mass, and was presently carried away to bed, there to be violently sick, and otherwise objectionable.

Ruth, after watching the waiters carry him away, ordered her bed-candle, and retired to another bed-room to rest.

Or so the inmates of the house supposed. But if they had peeped into her apartment in the still, dark hours, they would have found her sitting and watching by the open window which looked down into the garden but a few feet below.

Watching and waiting until all should be still, that she might creep forth and do the treacherous work that was to ruin the unhappy fool she had ensnared into her net, and bring her that wealth for which she had so long struggled in vain.

"Only this one crime more!" she muttered to herself; "and then I will fly this hateful country for ever, and find some spot far away over the seas where I may rest in peace!"

CHAPTER CXLVI.

THE JOCKEY AND THE TEMPTER.—THE REJECTED BRIBE.—THE DRUGGED HORSE.—A FOUL AND TREACHEROUS MURDER.

Bob, the jockey, must have fallen asleep for a moment or two, in spite of all his precautions.

There was no doubt about it He had fallen asleep; for if he hadn't, how could he have woke up. And he certainly did wake up, conscious of three things.

The first was a smell of burnt hair, for his head was hanging over the round holes in the top of the lantern.

The second was the loud growling of the bull-dogs.

The third was a sound of knocking at the door

Bob sat bolt upright and listened intently.

The sound was repeated.

The dogs answered it with a volley of fierce barking

"Hilloa!" cried the jockey, starting to his feet "Who's there? I say, who's there?"

But the voice that replied to him was by no means a ferocious one—on the contrary, it was low, and sweet and melodious.

"Mrs. Sedley!" it said. "I want to come in."

"Who is it?"

"Why don't you know me?"

"Why, it's Mrs Kid."

"Yes, open the door, if you please."

The jockey did not hesitate any longer, but withdrew the bolts, and admitted his visitor.

"What's she come here for, I wonder," he said to himself; and as she entered he stood twitching a lock of his hair, and smirking and shambling awkwardly before her.

"Shut the door!" she said, and he obeyed her.

Then, without addressing him again, she took up the lantern and approached the racer standing in its stall.

She stood silently, and examined the horse for several minutes, then turned round to the jockey.

"What do you think of to morrow's business?" she asked abruptly.

"A certainty, ma'am," replied Bob, again twitching at his forelock."

"And Bull-fog is sure to win."

"Safe."

"Unless something happened to him."

"Nothing can happen easily, ma'am."

"Unless he were doctored."

"D—doctored?"

"Yes."

The jockey stared at her hand, and then laughed.

"I don't see how that can be."

"You wouldn't do it, I suppose!"

"Me do it, ma'am! I'd rather my hand rotted off. I've been a jock, ma'am, man and boy, these thirty years, and I never fouled a race. No by heaven, I've not! Me doctor him! Why, damn me——"

"You're a poor man, are you not?"

"Poor enough, God knows, but I can be honest, for all that, I hope."

Ruth laughed.

"After all, honesty's a poor game, Bob, if you can make anything by a safe little swindle."

Bob looked at her doubtfully. He did not quite understand.

"Have you anything on the race?" she asked.

"A few pounds."

"Could you afford to lose them?"

"Well, yes. It would be rather awkward if I did. But there's no chance of that, I hope. I don't think there's much chance of that, or I should not have laid 'em on it."

"You're growing oldish for a jockey, ain't you?"

"I'm getting on."

"Have you made money enough to retire?"

"Well, not quite. I haven't been lucky. No. Perhaps I may make enough during this season, if I have a little luck. But I haven't yet."

"You won't win enough on this race, I suppose, to enable you to do so?"

"Oh, not—not on this race alone."

"Perhaps you expect Mr. Kid to pension you?"

"No, that I don't. I don't think he's quite the sort."

Ruth laughed savagely.

"You're right," said she, "he's not. He does not care a fig what becomes of those who serve him, when he has got all he cares to get out of them. But look here, Bob; suppose I pension you?"

"You, ma'am? God bless your pretty face! Why should you take such an interest in a poor old fool like me?"

"I will tell you the conditions on which you may earn my pension," said she, in a calm, clear voice. "I will pension you if that horse does *not* win."

"Does *not*?"

"No."

"B—but he's sure to!"

"Unless he's doctored."

Bob tumbled back against the wall of the stable and stared at her open-mouthed.

"I—I—don't understand."

"I will try to explain, then, if *you* are so dull of apprehension. I have backed the field heavily against the favourite, and the field must win."

"But the favourite is your husband's horse!"

"I have bet against my husband's horse."

"And you want me——"

"To make Bull-frog safe."

For a few minutes the jockey seemed to be dumbfounded by what he had heard.

He could not understand.

He could not believe that he had heard aright.

But when at last the full meaning of the words dawned upon him, he replied, with indignation—

"If you have come here to try and tempt me to play my master false, you've made a great mistake. If you've come here just to see the stuff I was made of, and test my honesty—well, I've only to say that I think it a dirty trick, and I shouldn't have believed it of you. But if you really mean what you say, although you are a woman, by God! I've a good mind to give you a damned——No—only please to get out of this place as quickly as you can."

He spoke with such determination, and looked so savage, that it was quite evident that it would have been waste of time to endeavour to argue the point with him.

No, she must go.

Had she then, failed?

Was she going thus to give up the project without a struggle?

If she were, it did not sound much like the Ruth we have seen so much of.

Anyhow, she meekly approached the stable-door without a word of remonstrance.

The jockey held the door wide open for her to pass out, and himself stood on one side.

She, however, did not pass through, as he expected.

On the contrary, somebody rushed in. It was the clerk.

In another moment Joe was hurled to the ground, and Ruth's accomplice, kneeling upon his breast, pressed the cold muzzle of a pistol to his forehead, moist with the sweat of terror.

While the clerk was thus occupied, Ruth closed the door, and bolted it as before.

All this while the bull-dogs were barking fiercely, but Ruth, taking up an iron bar which lay in a corner of the stable, dealt each a violent blow upon the head, repeating it again and again until their skulls were shattered, and their brains protruded in a way that was ghastly to behold.

During this operation, the racer, too, began to prick up its ears most restively, as though it knew its enemies were close at hand.

Ruth approached it cautiously, passed into the stall, and soothed and caressed it by word and motion, until she reached its head.

Then suddenly she grasped the horse's jaws with a grip of iron.

The horse, in a fright, flung back its head, but it could not shake off the woman's hold, and she clung to it like a leech.

Ruth drew from her breast a small phial, and, drawing out the cork, flung it upon one side.

After that, she clutched at, and violently wrenched open, the horse's jaws.

At the same moment that the teeth unloosed, then she dashed between them the contents of the little bottle.

The horse flung up its head, rolled its eyes, and

strove to shake her off, but she still clung to her hold.

For a few seconds the struggle was a desperate one.

The racer snorted and plunged.

Ruth clung round its neck, and her bright eyes flashed fiercely into those of the infuriated horse.

In spite of her efforts, she was dashed upwards and downwards, as the racer wildly strove to shake her off and kicked and plunged.

But the struggle was not of long duration.

All of a sudden, the horse, with a deep-drawn sigh and a shiver, sank upon its knees, then rolled over and lay motionless.

Ruth stood looking at it a moment

Then she raised its head, which fell again from her hand to the ground with a dull thud.

"Dead?" said her accomplice in a low voice.

"Yes, dead."

But at this word the jockey began to struggle furiously to get up.

"You shall pay for this, by God—you shall pay for this!" he cried.

Ruth approached him, brandishing her knife.

"You old fool!" she hissed betwixt her teeth, "shall we murder you?"

"You can if you like, but if I have my life, by heavens——"

"Well?"

"You shall cross the herring pond for this."

"You mean what you say?"

"I do."

"Die then, idiot, and your blood be on your own head."

Quick as lightning she plunged the glittering blade into the jockey's breast, and drew it forth again, red with gore,

Once more the cruel steel descended, and his life's blood gushed in torrents from the wound.

The jockey half-started to his feet, then fell back heavily—a corpse.

"Come," whisper Ruth to her companion who who looked on in mute horror—"come; we must away."

As she spoke, she undid the door, for the clerk was too terrified to lend any assistance, and blowing out the lantern, they stole out into the night with the brand of Cain upon their souls.

Thus they left the scene of blood and horror.

CHAPTER CXLVII.

WHAT HAPPENED ON THE DERBY DAY.

DERBY DAY had arrived; all the world had gone to the races. There had been the same scene of battle and confusion upon the road—the upsets—collisions—crashed panels—slaughtered horses, and fights at the turnpikes, which have been so often described, and will probably be described again every year until Derby Days come to an end

Yes, everybody had gone down, and everybody—except that famous van-full which is always too late, and that family gig which always breaks down half-way to Epsom—had arrived on the Downs

The same company of beautiful ladies were to be found on the "hill" The same ragged vagabonds with "correct cards." The same gipsies, singing the same improper songs to the old tune, "Lilla's a Lady." The same "knock'em-downs" were attracting the same heavy swells and aspiring snobs, and the same dashing damsels with brocaded silks and bad language.

Yes, everybody had come down, and everybody appeared to be bent upon enjoying themselves in the manner of enjoyment peculiar to Derby Day.

And yet it cannot be denied that some amount of uneasiness was discernible upon the faces of certain persons among the crowd; but there were not exactly holiday-makers. They were for the most part "horsey" looking men, with tight fitting trousers and cut-away coats, among whom a habit of chewing straws and wisps of hay was curiously prevalent

Some exciting topic moved the gentlemen to discourse together in angry tones, and the words "swindle" and "sold," coupled with Mr. Kid's name, might have been heard every moment upon every side of you in the quarter where the sporting gents were mostly congregated.

Over, over, and over again did some such conversation as the following take place.

"Well, what do you think of this?"

"What, you've heard it have you?"

"Heard of it! I should rather think so! Who hasn't?"

"Is it true, do you suppose?"

"There's not a doubt of it."

"What, the horse is dead?"

"Dead as a door-nail."

"Who did it, do you think?"

"Some say it was Kid."

"I don't believe that, though."

"Why?"

"Because he's backed it too heavily to have meant any caper of that kind."

"But then you haven't heard?"

"Heard what?"

"That the woman he lived with has been laying against it."

"The deuce she has!"

"It's a fact."

"But who says so?"

"Everybody."

"And where is she?"

"That's what everybody wants to know."

* * * * *

Frequent visitors to Epsom races must be acquainted with the existence of a tavern at some short distance across the Downs, at the back of the Grand Stand.

In the parlour of this inn sat a young man, or rather youth, habited in a half nautical costume, smoking a cigar and sipping from time to time the contents of a large tumbler standing upon the table before him.

He sat in a corner, the darkest corner in the room, which the youth had evidently selected upon that account—and from his place he peered anxiously out of the half opened door at the appearance of each new comer.

It was very evident that the young man expected somebody and was very anxious that that person should come, for every five minutes, or so, he consulted his watch with an ejaculation of impatience, and once more stared eagerly out into the passage, and again and again scanned the appearance of the men drinking round the bar, as though he was inclined to believe that the person he expected might, after all, have escaped his recognition.

At length, however, the person so long waited for made his appearance. A sporting gentleman evidently, with bushy black whiskers, a large moustache and some very showy jewellery.

Anybody, to look at him carefully, would hardly

have suspected that this person and Mr. Earthworm's ex-clerk were one and the same person.

It would also have taken a very shrewd individual to have discovered the sex of the youth in the corner.

The reader, though, on being told that it was a woman, can easily guess that it was Mrs. Ruth.

"Well," she said impatiently "What a while you have been!"

"Have I?"

"Yes. You are at least an hour later than the time you promised to be here, and that time was unnecessarily late."

"I wanted to stop till after the race was run."

"Why?"

"I thought I might make a pound or two."

"A pound or two," repeated his companion, in a tone of contempt. "Haven't we made enough?"

"Well—yes, I don't grumble."

"Come, then," and she stretched out her hand eagerly. "Where's the money."

"The money?" the man replied, slowly averting his eyes as he spoke.

"Yes—yes—my share."

"I haven't got it with me."

"What do you mean?"

"I haven't brought it."

"I told you to do so."

"Why won't to-night do?"

"Why didn't you bring it?"

"I haven't seen Jackson. I waited for him ever so long and he hasn't come. I——"

He paused suddenly, for the woman had clutched his arm—clutched it with a grip as though she strove to bury her nails in his flesh.

His eyes turned towards hers, and fell beneath the savage glare which gleamed from them.

"Has he played us false?" she hissed, between her clenched teeth."

"I don't know."

"You *must* know. You shall tell me! Speak!"

"Perhaps he has bolted——"

"And then?"

"And then we're both sold."

"And you believe this to be possible?"

"I think it's probable."

"And you sit calmly there and tell me so!"

"What can I do?"

"Look here; if he has played me false—I—I'll—have his life; I'll murder him as we murdered that man last night—you and I."

"Hush! hush! For God's sake, not so loud."

"Bah! nobody's listening to us. Do you heed what I say?"

"Yes, yes."

"Take care, then, and hearken to this, too. If *you* play me false you shall not escape me, hide yourself as you will; while you are above the earth I'll hunt you out and have your life."

The man looked up at her uneasily, and slunk back against the wall.

"You needn't set on me," he said, "I've acted fair enough."

"I don't doubt you. But mind, you must find this man and bring me the money here, in an hour's time."

"But if I can't find him. If he hasn't come?"

"You lie! he has! I have seen him here."

The man stared, then turned quickly on her.

"Oh!" he said after a pause, "of course, if you know he's here, you know it—only I don't."

"Find him, and bring me the money."

"But if he hasn't got the money?"

"Bring him here in any case; and return in an hour's time."

"Whether I find him or not?"

"Yes, in any case."

* * * * *

The time passed slowly enough, while Ruth waited for the return of her accomplice.

The last race had been run; the course began to clear.

The hour she had fixed for the villain's return had long since gone by. She left the room where she had sat so long, and paced to and fro in front of the public-house.

Oh, why had she been such a fool as to allow him to depart? Why had she not gone away with him—followed him—kept in his company, and not let him slip through her fingers until she had got her share of the money?

Her share! Should she ever see a penny of it? Her share, for which she had committed a foul and treacherous murder—for which she had betrayed the poor fool who had been idiot enough to fall in love with her.

What should she do? What could she do?

Why had she ever embarked in such a mad scheme as this? Why had she ever allied herself to such a treacherous scoundrel as that thievish ex-clerk of old Earthworm's? Having allied herself with him, however, she could not do otherwise than trust him; because, without his aid and the aid of another villain—Paul Jackson—she would not have been able to make those bets which she had calculated were to make her fortune and ruin Kid.

Besides, although, at first sight, it may seem strange that a woman so scheming and calculating, and with such a knowledge of everything that was vile and vicious, treacherous and base, should have believed that these two scoundrels would not have played her false; yet, when we look at similar cases in every-day life, do not we find that it is always the case with these knowing ones, and that they who believe all the world to be made up of rogues, still fancy that the particular rogue who goes partners with them in their little swindle, is the last person in the world to take them in?

Ruth waited until the course was quite empty, and the last drunken roysterer was staggering off homewards.

Then she thought she would go herself. Where to? She soon decided she would go up to London, and search among the low public-houses which she knew the two men to frequent. Who could say? Perhaps, after all, they meant to act fair by her.

Yes, she would go to London. But when she felt in her pocket, she found she had no money left.

She had had a sovereign and some silver a little while ago. Somebody in the public-house must have robbed her. It was probable enough, for there are plenty of bad characters go down to the races.

She determined, after a little thought, to go back and get some money from Kid, whom she had left at the public-house where he had slept the night before. When the discovery had been made of the death of his horse and the murder of the groom, he had gone almost out of his wits.

Since that time he had been drinking furiously, raving and singing and conducting himself like a maniac. She had left him in the disguise we have seen for the purpose of finding out what was doing on the course, and had promised to return shortly. She had not, however, been near the unfortunate gentleman since the morning; and indeed, never intended to have gone back at all had it not been that she now wanted a little ready money to enable her to commence her search after her two accomplices.

She would have felt no remorse in robbing him of his last penny, the poor creature she had already so bitterly wronged, had she thought that by so doing she could have benefited herself in the least.

She now turned her face in the direction of the inn where she had left poor Mr. Kid, and walked rapidly across the downs.

"I'll get some money, and then I'll go to town. I'll find out these wretches and get my share of the money, or I'll know the reason why? Ha! ha! I am not so easily to be foiled, as they shall know to their cost. I have put all on this last stake, and I must not lose. No—no! the end has not yet arrived!"

The end was not far distant, though, and this poor, plotting, scheming wretch was going quickly towards the awful fate which awaited her, and from which she might even now have escaped, had she but known—had she but possessed one friend in the world to whisper to her a word of warning.

* * * * *

Meanwhile her late accomplices were hurrying away towards London, chuckling to themselves.

"We've sold her."

"As dead as nails!"

"We'd better cut our lucky, though, without waste of time. We mustn't let her ferret us out, for she's a very devil when her temper's up."

"Lord bless you, there's no fear. She'll be in the hands of the police before many days are over—you may take your oath of that."

"You think they're sure to trace it to her."

"Lord bless you, yes! I've managed that all right."

"Do you think they'll find her knife that you dropped at the stable?"

"Yes; and the bracelet too. They've got the knife already."

"It'll be a case with her if they only catch her."

"If she goes back to see Kid, they're sure to; and as we didn't let her have any money, she's pretty certain to go back."

"It was an awful knowing dodge of you, to think of getting rid of her in that way."

"We wanted to get rid of her, and I think without we knocked her on the head ourselves, the next best way would be to have her hanged by our friend, the Secretary of State."

CHAPTER CXLVIII.

MORE BLOODSHED —AGAIN A PRISONER.—DEGRADATION —FLIGHT.

It was with something less than her usual assurance that Ruth returned to the tavern, in which she had left her unfortunate lover.

She had never intended to have come back at all, and she scarcely relished meeting the man whom she had so cruelly wronged.

The excuse which she had made to Mr. Kid when she made her escape in the morning, was but a poor one. She had said that she would learn what was the public opinion concerning the death of the favourite, and at the very outside would return again in an hour's time.

It was much more than an hour now. It was more than six hours since she had quitted him. What could she say? What excuse could she make? She could think of none.

And yet it was necessary to concentrate her thoughts—to put a good face upon the matter—to regain this man's confidence should it be weakening.

Bah! Why should she feel afraid? Had she not overcome a ten times greater difficulty in her time? Could she not play false, and smile prettily before any one? Why, that, all her life through, had been her trade—nothing else.

She never dreamt, either, that her accomplice in the foul and treacherous murder which had been committed, had turned against her. She never dreamt that the wretch had acted as falsely as he had—that he had put the police upon her track for the sole purpose of escaping from her himself, and that the nearer she approached to the inn, whither she was wending her steps, the nearer she was getting towards death.

When she reached the inn she found several people hanging about the bar. Two men were talking eagerly with the landlord.

She heard one say, "She won't come back." Then the other replied, "We'll wait and see;" but the landlord at that moment interrupted them with a "Hark, will you—she's here."

"Who was there?" Ruth asked herself. They could mean none other but her. She half-turned for a moment, and stared at them with a frown. Why should they talk about her? But then came the thought—what would be more natural than that they should feel interested in the beautiful companion of the unfortunate gentleman who had lost so much money? Therefore, she paid but very little attention to their nods, and winks, and whispered conference, but hastily ascended the stairs to the room where she had left her companion

It was a sitting room, out of which a bedroom opened. The sitting-room, when she opened the door, was plunged in darkness. A faint light, glimmering through the half-closed folding-doors, and a sound of moving told her that some one was in the room beyond. As she drew near to it hollow sobs struck upon her ear, and she paused for a moment to peep in.

Before the glass, with a face that was unearthly in its ghastly pallor, stood the miserable victim of her treachery. He held an open razor in his hand.

His shirt neck was laid open, and his throat bared. Was he going to kill himself? Her first impulse was to run forwards and stay his hand—to call to him to desist.

Then a devilish thought flitted through the brain of this arch-fiend. Why should she do so? If he killed himself, would it not save her some trouble, for then there would be no explanation between them. She could appropriate his effects without any one to interfere with her. "No—let him die!" she thought, and stood back quietly waiting until he should have effected his fearful purpose.

Poor wretch! it seemed, though, that however he died, he was doomed not to die by his own hand! Just as he was about to draw the razor across his throat he caught sight of Ruth in the glass.

With a shrill cry he turned upon her. She was too much startled by the suddenness of the movement to draw back. She stood still where she had stood at first, as motionless as a statue. Kid, with one bound, was at her side, and the next moment had clutched her arm.

There was a wild look about his eyes. She thought him mad, and strove to free herself from his grasp, but he held her tight

"Oh, Belinda!" he cried, in a hasty voice, "you have come back, then, at last They said that you had forsaken me. They said that now you had ruined me, you had left me to die alone!"

"I ruined you?"

"Yes. But how could you be so cruel—so unnatural? What made you do it? Did you kill the man as well as the horse?"

The woman started and shivered, and drew back from him.

"What do you mean?" she asked in a hoarse whisper. "Who says I did it? Are you mad?"

"No, not yet, though I am not far off it, I think. They say down stairs that I have lost my wits."

"What do they say about me?" she asked, impatiently.

"They say you did it. The police are looking for you. Great heavens! you know not what risk you run in coming here!"

"Are you raving?"

"No, I am speaking the truth. They are looking for you everywhere. The constables are below at this moment?"

"What am I to do?"

"You must escape; though, how, I don't know. Yes, this way, by the window."

As he spoke, he ran to the window and dragged it open, but hardly had he done so, when a burly, red-faced man, and the landlord, came running into the room. They looked round, eagerly. Then the landlord pointed to Ruth.

"That's the woman!" he said.

"You are my prisoner!" cried the burly man, advancing towards her.

But she retreated before him. Very silent and very pale she looked, but with an ugly twinkle in her eyes. The constable seemed to know instinctively that she meant mischief; and as she drew forth a pistol, and levelled it at him, he sprang upon her and pushed aside the muzzle ere she could fire. As he did so it exploded. A piercing cry rent the air, and poor Cadbury Kid fell forward upon his face, struggled for a moment, and lay still and dead.

"Bring her away!" said the landlord, with a shudder. "Take that weapon away from her, for God's sake! She has shed blood enough, surely!"

It would have been useless to have struggled, had she endeavoured to have done so, in the hands of the strong man who held her prisoner. She passively submitted to the operation of putting on the handcuffs, and followed him down stairs

A crowd of persons filled the passage below, anxious to catch a sight of her; and the faces she saw around her upon all sides expressed loathing and disgust. Some hissed and some hooted; and when they got outside the tavern door, some women, hanging about, appeared as though they would have liked to have handled her roughly. But the constable interposed his huge carcass between her and them, and dragged her along, clearing a way for himself and his captive by the aid of a knob-stick he carried in his hand and flourished vigorously.

It was to the village lock-up and round-house that he was conveying her; and here, having locked her up, and left her in charge of a trustworthy person, he set off as fast as he could to the house of the nearest magistrate. Left alone, the caged murderess could hear the murmur of the mob without—an angry murmur, which frightened her much more than the thought of the prison and the gallows that threatened her. But after awhile the sound of the voices without was hushed. The village people had gone to bed, determining to muster in great force to see her brought out in the morning. She was left alone with her own thoughts and the gaoler—pretty companions both of them. He sat upon a stone bench silently smoking his pipe, with his back against the wall, at one side of the cell. She sat upon another bench upon the opposite side A lantern revealed the ugliness of his face and the uncouth deformity of his person. He was a humpbacked man, very much knock-kneed, with huge hands and feet. He squinted a little, and between his great blubbery lips, in a gash that served him for a mouth, she saw his hideous fangs, black and broken. As the light fell upon him she fancied that she never in her life had seen anybody more repulsively ugly. A perfect monster was he—more like some horrible hobgoblin than a human being. What mercy could she expect from him? How could she hope to elicit the sympathy of such a brute as this? And yet she must do so if she were to gain her liberty.

She hardly knew how to begin, but she must begin, and she had to entice him into conversation. She asked if he were a constable, and he told her that he did a little in that and a many other ways. He was a sexton by trade, he said, and a cobbler, and he had, in his time, served as a hangman Was he married? No! Had he been? No! He was not a favourite with the ladies. Why not? He didn't think he was much of a beauty, did she? She laughed. Women take strange fancies sometimes The most beautiful women have before now fallen in love with the ugliest men. The horrible monster chuckled as she talked, gave up his pipe, and sidled closer towards his interesting captive. She was the most beautiful woman he had ever seen in all his life, he told her. He did not believe hardly that there was such beauty upon earth. He did not know whether there were any more beautiful than she was, but he did not think such a thing possible. He was sure of one thing, though—there was no body in the world uglier than himself. "Would it make him happy if such a woman fell in love with him?" she asked. Would he think the possession of such a woman worth any sacrifice on his part. The monster eyed her stupidly, and when her meaning dawned upon his mind, an apeish grin lit up his hideous face. He thought, he said, that such happiness was almost worth getting "scragged" for, and that he would feel inclined to risk it if he had the chance.

"Open the door for me, then," she whispered in his ear, and her arms wound themselves round the monster's neck. "Open the door for me, and let me escape. You say I am beautiful You would not have the heart to see me dragged out, and hanged like a dog. No, no! You will have pity on me! Look at me—see how young I am, and how fair! Oh, you will not let them kill me! No! If you want money, I can get it for you when I escape. Let us escape together! I will make your fortune! I will be your mistress! I will work for you I will sell myself for you! You shall have as much gold as you can desire! Come, come—you cannot refuse me!"

She twined her arms round him—she pressed her luxurious lips to his lips, to his horrible mouth Her golden curls fell upon his face. Her

soft voluptuous form was in his arms—her heart throbbed against his heart. How was it possible that the contact of this hateful wretch did not fill her with loathing? How could she take her life at such a price as this most hideous and sickening degradation, this revolting prostitution of body and soul? But in the monster's arms, and while devoured by brutal lust, the misshapen wretch strained her frantically to his heart, her lithe and thievish fingers had glided unseen and unfelt into his pocket, and had clutched his pocket knife.

The lantern had been overthrown. The ruffian, intent only upon satisfying his passions, was unconscious of all else. But she had opened the blade stealthily with her teeth, and made good her aim Then the blow is struck again and again. The would-be lover writhes in his death-agony, and the betrayer is rifling his pocket for the keys

And now the door is unlocked. She has slipped off her handcuffs. She is free once more, and flying from the spot with the speed of a hunted deer.

Again she is free! But for how long?

CHAPTER CXLIX.

RUTH PLAYS THE SPY, AND HEARS SOMETHING GREATLY TO HER DISADVANTAGE. — TWO FASHIONABLE LADIES SHOW, BY THEIR CONVERSATION, THAT THEY ARE NO BETTER THAN THEY OUGHT TO BE.

She set out upon her travels without a farthing in her pocket.

Had the man whom she had murdered been in

possession of any money, she would have appropriated it before she quitted the body. But she could find nothing, when she searched the blood-saturated garments of her victim.

The only way to escape with her life was to fly at once. She must hesitate no longer. With or without money, she must get up to town.

She drew the door to behind her, and peeped round suspiciously. No one was about—no one watching her.

Then she moved away as fast as her legs would carry her.

The village where the round-house was situated was further away from London than the race-course. The lights of the gipsies' fires upon the downs served to guide her footsteps at first, and she soon found her way back to the course. To find her way thence to London was a more difficult job.

She saw nobody about, whom she could ask. She made some timid inquiries of a tramp, whom she came across, skulking round the tents, evidently with felonious intent; but he eyed her with suspicion, and she could get no satisfactory information from him upon the subject.

The result may be easily imagined. She lost her way, and wandered miles and miles from the road. She had no notion of the time, and possessed no means of ascertaining what o'clock it was, for her watch had been taken from her when she was locked up. She grew, at length, so utterly weary and worn out, that she felt utterly incapable of going any further, and was considering whether she should pass the night out of doors, under a haystack, which was close at hand, when she caught sight of a red light gleaming through the curtain of an inn parlour window.

It was at no great distance down a lane, and when she arrived at it, she found that there were lights burning in all the windows, and no signs of the house having shut up for the night.

She had no money in her pocket; but that fact was not an insurmountable difficulty to a woman accustomed to live by her wits. She had a wedding-ring on her finger, and that was sufficient, if nothing else turned up, to pay the price of a bed.

But when she came to make inquiries, the landlady informed her that there was not a bed to be had. Every room was occupied. In some cases two or three strangers were sleeping in the same apartment. Ruth persisted. Was there not a sofa? No. Nor a table? No. Could she not be accommodated anyhow? The landlady could think of nothing.

"Stay; there was a sofa—a very short one, and rather a hard one, which was in a room—that was to say, not exactly a room, but a kind of closet or passage, which, if it wasn't for it being rather draughty, and there being no window in it, and no ventilation except the draught, wasn't such a bad place under the circumstances."

Ruth accepted the accommodation thankfully, and having partaken of some refreshment, asked to be showed to the room where she was to sleep. The landlady, lighting a candle, preceded her, begging Ruth at the same time to be kind enough to tread as lightly as possible, for fear of making a noise.

"There are two ladies sleeping in the next room, and you must'nt let them hear you, whatever you do," the landlady said. "They're perfect ladies—ladies of fashion—tip-top people."

"How is it they're stopping here to night?"

"Their carriage broke down, and they were obliged to put up here for the night, not being able to get another vehicle until the morning, when they will probably go to London by the first train. But hush! here we are."

"Who are they?"

"I forget their names. I only just heard it. One is Lady—Lady Florence—Florence D'Arcy—that's it; and the other one—I can't think of the other's name. Here's your candle, sir. Good night. Now mind you're quiet."

The landlady closed the door upon Ruth, and left her in a little slip of passage, in which there was a tiny sofa and a couple of blankets by way of bedding. Ruth sat down upon the side of the sofa to meditate. She sat there silently for some minutes, biting her under lip. She could hear voices in the next room, and rustling sounds of dresses. The ladies had not completed their toilets yet for the night."

Ruth extinguished her candle, approached the keyhole, and peeped into the bed room. Lady Florence Darcy was sitting in an arm-chair, by the side of a dressing table, at which another lady was arranging her hair for the night. When Ruth first peeped in at them, they were both silent. Presently, however, the lady who was brushing her hair, in a peevish tone spoke.

"How extremely disagreeable it is to be left here to shift for oneself in this way."

"Yes," said the other, in a low tone, and without raising her eyes from the ground.

"I wish we had never come down to this stupid race, and then we should not have been obliged to sleep in such a pigstye as this."

"I hope we shall never be obliged to sleep in worse."

"Goodness gracious! I hope we shall never sleep in as bad any more! How you do talk, Florence! I've really no patience with you!"

The other made no reply, but sighed deeply.

"There you are again! What is the matter with you? I do believe you are thinking of that—that man again!"

"Of your brother-in-law?"

"Of my brother-in-law, indeed! I will no longer acknowledge such a person. I wonder how you can think of him."

"I shall continue to think of Captain Crockford until I die. I shall do more than that—I shall continue to love him!"

Ruth started at the name, and clenched her fingers fiercely.

"Lady Darcy!" said the other lady in an indignant tone, "I am ashamed of you! I am astonished at you! Are you so utterly lost and careless of what the world may think of you that you openly acknowledge the guilty passion which you entertain for that lost young man?"

"Don't talk nonsense. You knew long ago that I loved him and hated my husband. Pray is there anything unusual or unfashionable in such a state of things? It is as yet a secret to the world——"

"I am afraid, Florence, that it is not so great a secret as you suppose, and that it is as well known as your intrigue with the rich speculator, Mr. John Rafferty."

"Or yours with the opera singer, and the young clergyman, at Saint——"

"Florence, who dares?"

"No matter, my dear, we won't quarrel. We are neither of us the most virtuous of our sex, and there are many poor wretches walking the London streets who have not sinned more heavily; only we are rich ladies, and ladies of fashion, and our reputations are very elastic."

The other lady was silent for awhile. When she again spoke it was in an altered tone.

"What do you want me to do, Florence?"

"I want you to persuade your husband to save Crockford's life."

"But you know very well that I possess no influence over my husband."

"Oh, yes, you do. You are beautiful, and you can be seductive when you like. You must fascinate the poor old gentleman, and make him exert his influence!"

"Crockford was a fool not to beg his brother's pardon for what he had done, and appeal to him for help. I fear now that he has let matters go too far."

"No—no! I am sure that there is plenty of time if you will only try."

"How Crockford could have disgraced himself in such a way is more than I can imagine."

"I suppose it is not the first time in the world that such a thing has occurred."

"He was led away by some disgraceful woman."

"He was in want of money to pay his debts."

"I am sure there was some woman in the case."

"If there was, you may be sure that the subject is not a very pleasant one for *me* to talk about. There certainly was a low, wretched creature, into whose clutches he fell, and who stole the bill of exchange from him, which has caused all this misery."

"And the connexion has now ceased?"

"To be sure it has."

"Don't be too sure."

"What do you mean?" asked Lady Florence, indignantly. "You never knew me to be incredulous. But I swear to you that the passion was only one-sided—that he did not love, but pitied her. I swear to you, also, that he has promised to find out her hiding-place, if she is yet alive, and punish her for her treachery."

"But will he do so?"

"Yes"

"Very well."

"You doubt me, I see. But I swear that what I say is true. I myself have reason for wishing this woman shall meet with her deserts; and if there is a God above us, I will track her to her lair—and she shall not escape me even if she does him!"

"Do you know her, then?"

"Yes. I could find her without Crockford's help; but I will have his help, because I know that she will feel her punishment more acutely when she knows that the man she loved has assisted to bring it about."

It was, perhaps, as well that the ladies could not see the face of the person listening upon the other side of the door to this conversation. Perhaps the sight of it might have destroyed the placidity of their slumbers.

It might have haunted their dreams, had they been able to sleep at all, after the terror with which that white, vengeful countenance would have filled their hearts.

Ruth listened to them as long as they continued to talk together; watched them into bed, and waited until they put out the light.

Then, cautiously, she opened her room door.

The inn was very still. All the weary travellers had gone to bed, and were by this time, most of them, fast asleep.

Carrying her boots in her hand, Ruth stole down stairs.

Then, with some little difficulty, and as little noise as possible, undoing the street door, she crept out of the house and turned her face towards London.

CHAPTER CL.

A WICKED OLD LORD—A GALLANT VALET—RUTH'S DEGRADATION.—TRUTH AND FALSEHOOD.—MORE TREACHERY.—THE SISTERS MEET AGAIN.

THE noble lord who had the misfortune of being the brother of Captain Charley Crockford, occupied, at the time of our story, a very influential post in the Government. It matters very little what; nor do I think it all necessary at this time of day, when my history is so near its close, to distress the reader with an elaborate introduction of himself and his belongings.

He was and is an old man, possessing a highly venerable appearance, and a scandalous notoriety for the licentiousness of his conduct. He was and is a great statesman, and a disgracefully grey-headed old scoundrel, who has broken as many laws as he has made, and ruined so many poor miserable girls, that it is a wonder he is not weary of his own atrocious villany.

One day when, the business of the morning being over, he was dawdling over a cup of tea, previous to going down to the House, his valet entered the room to tell him that a lady wished to speak to him.

"Who is she?" he asked.

"I don't know, my lord. She came when you were at Downing Street this morning. She has been there twice, she says, and could not obtain admittance. Now she has called here again."

"What's her name?"

"She would not give it, my lord."

"What's she like?"

"Very beautiful, my lord."

"Show her in, then, directly."

"Yes, my lord."

"Stop a minute—I'm in a great hurry; perhaps she had better come some other time. Is she very beautiful, do you say? What does she look like? as if she had come to ask a favour?"

"Yes, my lord; she seems very anxious to see you. She has taken a great deal of trouble to obtain an interview, and evidently would *make any sacrifice* to gain her end."

The old man chuckled like a satyr. The valet knew exactly how to manage him. He knew that the old villain exacted a bitter sacrifice from any poor creature who required aught at his hands. The valet himself was in his small way as lascivious a wretch as his master—as unscrupulous a villain where female virtue was concerned.

Leaving the old man's presence, he returned to the ante-room, where he had left Mrs. Ruth Trail awaiting his return. She was magnificently dressed. Her hair was soft and silky, and arranged with consummate tact. There was perhaps a slight suspicion of rouge upon her cheeks, but it was very slight. Her teeth were as bright as ever; her eyes wore their softest and most languishing expression; her well-made dress showed the shape of her magnificent bust. As she slightly raised her dress to walk up the stairs, a sly peep was obtainable of a neatly made kid boot, a tightly fitting pink silk stocking, and a delicious ankle.

"I am afraid his lordship cannot see you, madam," said the valet, coming out after the conversation I have just recorded.

"Not for a moment?"

"I am afraid not."

"Not if you exert your influence?"

She looked at him in her most bewitching way, and drawing out a long purse, offered him a golden piece. The valet, though, was a gallant man. He pushed back her hand very gently. She would have doubled it, but he smiled, and shook his head.

"Will nothing tempt you?" she said, looking at him in her most fascinating style, and thrilling him with her sleepy eyes.

"Perhaps I might be tempted," the low-born knave responded, taking her hand in his, and returning her gaze with interest.

She felt inclined at the moment to smite him in his monkey's face. Her blood boiled at the insult she felt in this lackey's disgusting advances. But it was of vital interest to her that she should have an interview with his master. To do this the valet must be propitiated. She must degrade herself body and soul with this ill-mannered spawn of a scullery wench. Her pollution must be physical as well as mental.

His lordship wondered why she was so long coming, and grew impatient at the delay; but she came at last, looking as fair and beautiful as ever.

"What an angel's face!" his lordship thought to himself as his flunkey's courtezan seated herself before him, and gracefully arranged her rich satin robe in such a way that a glimpse was obtainable of the tiny foot in the dainty kid boot, and the edge of the delicate drapery beneath her gown.

But she had no intention of captivating the old nobleman. A far different reason had brought her thither, and she opened the business at once, heedless of the lears and grimaces of the old fool opposite to her, who thus strove to render himself fascinating.

"I have called respecting Captain Crockford."

The old man started, and the smile fading from his wrinkled face, he glared at his visitor uneasily.

"What about him?" he said, at last.

"I can easily imagine that the name of one who has so disgraced his family cannot be very agreeable to your lordship."

"You are right. The subject is a disagreeable one."

"It is a wonder to me that your lordship could ever have allowed the matter to become public."

"I could not help it. A scoundrel, of the name of Earthworm, into whose hands the forged bill had fallen, forced the publicity upon me; because, in the first instance, he named a most outrageous and exorbitant sum as a bribe, which, however, I would have paid had he remained silent, mind you; but the villain, supposing I would not, overreached himself by giving my brother into custody."

"And now it is too late to take any steps to obtain his release."

"May I ask how you come to be interested in his welfare?"

Ruth smiled.

"I am not!" she said.

"What do you mean?" cried the old man, in astonishment. "What, then, has brought you here?"

"I have come here to beg of you to leave him where he is."

"For what reason?"

"Because, although he has already shamefully disgraced you, if you are instrumental in effecting his release he will disgrace you even more."

"How? What do you mean?"

"I mean that he was carrying on an intrigue with your wife, which he will renew if he is liberated."

The old man opened his eyes and mouth to their widest.

"It is false!" he cried. "It is monstrous. He is the lover of another lady, I know——"

"Lady Darcy?"

"Oh! you, too, have heard the scandal. But as for my wife, why, she hates him. She has always disliked him from the moment I married her, and predicted Crockford's ruin and disgrace. No! no! I cannot believe a word of it."

"She has deceived you, I say. She trusted that you would effect his release without her interference. Knowing now that you think his escape is hopeless, you will find that she will herself beg and implore of you to redouble your efforts."

"I do not—I cannot believe it."

"It is only natural that you should believe in the virtue of a lady whose reputation is so unblemished!"

"Silence!"

"Whose amours with opera singers and Puseyite parsons are so notorious!"

"Silence, I say!" cried the old man; and then he added, "I cannot believe it!"

"I do not ask you to believe anything without proof. Mark my words; the lady will come to you before the day is out, imploring your assistance in Crockford's deliverance from gaol."

"But I know Crockford is incapable of such a base action."

"You would, a year ago, have thought him incapable of forgery!"

"True—true! But then he is my brother, He——"

"He is not."

"What?"

"I possess the secret of his birth. He was but the fruits of some gross amour of your mother's nurse, changed for your brother, whose death the nurse had caused by her drunkenness and neglect!"

"It seems like a dream—I cannot believe it."

"It is, nevertheless, true. Although I have had no time to-day to produce proofs in confirmation of my statements, I will bring them to-morrow, or the next day, at latest. Until then, take no steps in effecting the escape of the man you suppose to be related to you."

"But if I do not, it will then be too late!"

"When you see the proofs I have to bring forward, you will only be too happy I came in time."

"And you—you have some motive for hating this man?"

"Yes, I have!"

"And who are you?"

"I am nobody worth your sympathy: only a poor adventuress—a cast-off mistress of the man who lies in gaol—a rival of your wife's!"

The old man paced the room in agitation. Presently he stopped short.

"It may be too late to prevent his escape should he be the wrong man."

"How so?"

"Because — because I have already taken steps ——"

He was silent again for a time. Then he said, "Will you bring me the proofs to-morrow?"

"To-morrow evening!"

She turned to leave the room as she spoke, watching him with a faint smile of triumph. She felt certain that her fiendish plan of vengeance had succeeded. She chuckled to herself at the thought that her sister's plan would be defeated—that her lover would languish hopelessly in gaol. The statements she had made contained a strange mixture of truth and falsehood. Of course, there was not a word of truth in the statement she had made about the supposed intrigue between Crockford and his lordship's wife; but with regard to Crockford's not being his lordship's brother, the statement was correct.

From Earthworm's clerk she had learnt the particulars of a secret which Rafferty had brought back with him from Australia. Out in the bush he had met with a man who had been a lover of the nurse Ruth had spoken of, and who had assisted in disposing of the body of the dead child, and substituting of the nurse's bastard in its place. Arriving in England, Rafferty had employed Earthworm to scrape together all the necessary evidence, and after much labour the chain was completed. But in the meantime, Rafferty had made Crockford's acquaintance, and the dissolute but warm-hearted young Guardsman had so captivated him, that he had done all in his power to rebury the secret he had so carefully unearthed. Earthworm, who had obtained possession of the forged bill of exchange, which had been discovered on the body of the villain who had stolen it from Ruth, was, as may be supposed, interested in keeping the secret dark, in the hope of preying upon Crockford's friends. And had it not been for the treachery of the clerk, who revealed the secret to Ruth, no one in all probability would have ever been any the wiser. Ruth, delighted at the discovery, soon availed herself of it to effect the ruin of the man whom she already had so bitterly wronged.

She turned now to leave the room, and as she did so, she heard the street door open down below. She attached no consequence to the circumstance, but walked on. On the stairs, however, she encountered Lady Darcy and her friend. Ruth quickly drew down her veil, but not before the former had caught a glimpse of her face. The veil was a very thin one, and did not afford much concealment. Ruth crumpled it in her hand, and contrived to arrange it in such a way that the folds fell across her face as thickly as possible. Lady Darcy, however, with a suspicion of who it was, stopped opposite to her, and stared hard at the Spy, who shrank back beneath her gaze, and dragged the veil more closely together. At last an unhappy twitch of the veil dragged it off altogether, and Ruth and Florence stood face to face.

CHAPTER CLI.

THE SPY IN THE HANDS OF THE SERVANTS.—THE PRIEST AND JACK RAFFERTY.—RUTH IN THE DARK

Escape was out of the question.

Ruth well saw, by the angry glare in her sister's eyes, that the person against whom Lady Darcy had vowed a vow of deadly vengeance should not easily slip through her fingers.

"Ah!" she cried with an accent of fiendish delight; "I have caught you, have I!"

"Let me pass!"

"Never! Here, help! help!"

The footmen from the hall came flocking upstairs in a body, and ran forward to seize her; but the Spy, with a mighty effort, tore herself from her sister's grasp, and flung Lady Darcy violently back against the wall.

"Let me pass!" she cried; "what do you want with me?"

"Hold her fast!" cried Lady Darcy: "she is a thief—a murderess. Hold her until the police can be sent for!"

Then, again, the servants made a rush upon her. Tearing herself from their hands, Ruth rushed widly up the stairs, but she was overtaken and overpowered almost immediately. They took her in their arms, and, in spite of her cries and struggles, dragged her down towards the hall. With the fury and spite of a wild cat, she struggled, and fought, and kicked, and bit, and scratched. But they managed to retain their hold of her, and bore her away, with all her garments torn to rags and tatters, and in such rents and shreds that when she was finally overcome, she was almost naked in the hands of the panting flunkeys.

In the middle of the struggle the door was flung open, and two men entered the house. Ruth was at that moment struggling frantically, but at sight of their faces, however, she became in a moment as still as death; she was struck speechless and motionless, as though with some great terror and dread, with which the appearance of the new comers had inspired her. Yet was there nothing of an alarming character in the outward looks or bearing of either. One was an old Roman Catholic priest, dressed in the habiliments of his order; the other was a gentlemanly-looking person, with a large beard, and dressed in the height of fashion. But though a casual observer might not have seen any reason for Ruth's alarm, yet we who know more of her history may easily understand the cause of it, when we learn that one of the men was the priest who had assisted her to escape from the French prison; the other, her enemy, Jack Rafferty.

Finding that her resistance had suddenly ceased, the servants lost no time in locking up the desperate woman in a stone room, upon the ground-floor, where she could remain in perfect security, and without a chance of escape, until the arrival of the police. So very short a time, therefore elapsed from the appearance of Rafferty and the priest, and Ruth's disposal in her place of captivity, that it might have been supposed she would escape recognition. Such, however, was not the case; both men knew her again in a moment; and the hasty glance which she obtained of their faces, before the servants dragged her away, showed her that she was known, and set her soul quaking with terror at the fate in store for her

Neither the priest nor Rafferty, though, it must be said, had any idea that they both knew the woman; and as that moment was not exactly the one best suited for the settling of their accounts with the betrayer, they mastered their emotions as quickly as possible, and walked up stairs towards the spot where the master of the house was standing with his wife and Lady Darcy. Approaching his lordship, Rafferty hastily whispered in his ear, "We have succeeded."

"Has he escaped?" asked his lordship anxiously, speaking in a low tone.

"Yes. We did it last night. I have just left him in a place of safety, and have come here to tell you of the happy event"

The other's brow was for a moment clouded, as though the intelligence which Rafferty brought him was by no means the most welcome. But, after a slight pause, his face brightened up again, and he replied, "It is well! I have received news, since I saw you, of a character which may cause me somewhat to alter my plans with respect to Captain Crockford. If I had known yesterday what I know to-day, I might, perhaps, have been tempted to have left him in prison." Then, without heeding Rafferty's look of amazement, his lordship turned towards Lady Darcy. "You will be happy to learn that Captain Crockford is free!" he said, in a low tone.

Lady Darcy uttered an exclamation of delighted surprise.

"How did it happen? When? Where is he?"

"I and our friend here," said his lordship, "had concocted together a plan of escape, which we have effected by a bribe to his gaolers."

"And you never said anything to your wife or to me about it!"

"It was necessary to keep it a profound secret; and I wished to surprise you, and feared that I might not succeed; and by telling you beforehand, only raise hopes which were destined to be crushed."

At this moment a bustle in the hall below announced the arrival of the police; but his lordship, without consulting the rest, hastily descended, and dismissed the officers, and returning up-stairs, begged of the priest to accompany him into his private room, where they had a long and deeply interesting conference.

* * * * *

The shades of night gathered over the city and the house where the captive Spy, hugging in her bosom her own evil thoughts, sat waiting in silent terror for the worst.

The darkness falling on the city fell upon the rich man's mansion, and intensified to a pitchy blackness in the stone room, which contained the caged tigress, weaving out her wicked brain with new plots and schemes of blood and horror.

CHAPTER CLII.

RUTH LISTENS TO REASON.—THE PLOT FOR THE RUIN OF THE CLERGYMAN.—JACK RAFFERTY UPON THE TRACK OF THE BETRAYER.

LATE in the night, when the servants had all retired to rest, with the exception of the old deaf hall porter, who slept in his comfortable chair, unconscious of all outward events, and dreaming happily, a cautious footstep might have been heard descending the staircase; and presently the old priest, shading a light, which he carried in his hand, might have been seen creeping carefully downwards, pausing every now and then to make sure that he was not observed. But nobody appeared to be about—no one about to watch his movements, and the old man crept down cautiously, and arriving at last in front of the door of the strong room in which Ruth was confined, with as little noise as possible unlocked the door.

At the sound of the click of the key in the lock, and at the first sight of the first ray of light penetrating into the strong room, the captive started to her feet, and retreated to the farthest end of the apartment, where she stood trembling with terror, awaiting the appearance of her enemy—for she thought that it was Rafferty who had thus come to see her. But when she saw that it was the priest, her terror immediately subsided, although her confusion at the meeting was very evident.

The old man carefully closed the door behind him, then motioning her to take a seat by his side. When she had complied, he addressed her in a calm and determined tone, which, however, was not altogether free from kindness

"Ruth," he said, "you have not kept your faith with me!"

"I could not!"

"Why not?"

"I—I met with an old friend. I could not get rid of him. I lost the money you advanced to me, and I was ashamed of writing for more——"

"There—there! Do not trouble yourself to invent any more excuses!" said the old man, quietly. "You spent the money, perhaps. You thought, perhaps, that you could do better than carry out the plans I had formed. Let that be as it may, I want to ask you a simple question. Where do you intend for the future to obtain your means of living?"

"I do not know!"

"Since you have been in London, I must inform you that you have been carefully watched. All the particulars of your connexion with Kid are known to me; also your speculations upon the turf, and the atrocious means which you adopted to ruin your lover and enrich yourself. All this is known, I say, and at any time I might have ruined you, had I so chosen. I wished, however, to learn all I could about you—to get you into my power; and then, should an appeal to your good feelings prove useless, I could force you to comply with my wishes."

"What do you require of me?"

"Nothing that is unreasonable. I wish you to carry out the compact that we formed together. I wish you to entice into your arms—lure from the path of virtue, the Protestant clergyman who was once your sister's lover. I will not punish or blame you for what has passed; but if you at once set about carrying our plans into execution, you shall have the money at first promised you. You are a fool if you do not consent!"

"Well, I consent. I was a fool not to do at first as you directed me. I have gained nothing by my own schemes and plots. What shall I do, and when shall I begin?"

"I can contrive an interview between the clergyman and yourself to-morrow night. He is going to a dinner party, at which I shall be present. I will take care that he partakes plentifully of the generous wines provided. I will then have a letter purporting to be from the young nun, your sister, given to him; and, with his blood fired by the wine which he has drunk, he shall come to find you in the full plenitude of your charms; and I leave to you to manage the rest."

"Well, I accept But," added Ruth, hastily, and with a white, shuddering terror in her face and voice, "you shall take me away from here at once. You will let me escape from these people?"

"I have no desire to detain you—you shall go at once. To show you that I can trust you, I will give you an address, and see you into a cab; then leave you to go there by yourself, and wait for me. Do you agree?"

"Yes," said Ruth, eagerly. "I am ready this moment."

The old priest opened the door and peeped out. All was quiet. He led Ruth from her place of captivity. They passed by the slumbering porter without any difficulty, and the old priest let his companion out into the street. A cab was passing at the moment. The old man hailed it, and then he gave Ruth the address he had spoken about, and promised to come and call upon her early next day. But as he was turning to re-enter the house, he seemed to bethink him that he would like the cabman's ticket, and having obtained this, he shut the door.

Hardly, however, had he entered the passage, when he found himself face to face with Jack Rafferty. He was coming out of the room which had contained Ruth He was very pale, and appeared to be greatly agitated. Upon catching sight of the priest, he ran towards him and seized him fiercely by the collar.

"Where is she?" he cried. "Where is she gone? Have you assisted her to escape? Speak, I say—speak!"

"I know nothing about it. Of what are you talking?"

"I heard a cab go away from the door just as I came up. She was in it. Where has she gone? Ah!"

His eyes fell upon the cabman's ticket, which the old priest held in his hand. Rafferty, without another word, snatched it from him, and rushed bareheaded into the street.

"By means of this I will find her!" he cried, waving it aloft above his head, and fairly screaming aloud in his wild excitement. "I will find her! This time she shall not escape me! This time my vow shall be fulfilled, and my vengeance shall crush her to the earth!"

CHAPTER CLIII.

RUTH PREPARES FOR CONQUEST—BEAUTY UNVEILED—THE INTERRUPTION.—RAFFERTY AT LAST.—A FATAL LEAP. A HORRIBLE PROSPECT.

UPON the evening of the day upon which Ruth made her escape from his lordship's, she was waiting, a little before midnight, for the arrival of the young clergyman who was to be subjected to the power of her charms. She had taken those apartments in which she had effected the conquest of the unfortunate Mr. Kid. They were magnificently furnished in a style of great luxury. The drawing-room was decorated with the choicest flowers, which shed a soft and delicious perfume around. The bed-room beyond looked like a fairy bower, and its occupant more like some stray angel wandering upon earth than aught else to which one could readily compare her.

To imagine her the guilty wretch she really was would have been impossible To have declared her to be the black-hearted, treacherous murderess that we know her to be, would have been certain to have subjected a person sufficiently courageous to unlimited ridicule and derision. That any one could have imagined her life devoted to aught else but the pleasures of love was impossible. To see her now issuing like Venus from her rose-water bath, her lovely form revealed in all its magnificent voluptuousness, her silken tresses falling in rippling waves from her head almost to her knees, half hiding her swelling bosom, and shining in the candle-light like so much molten gold; to see her thus, had any one been there to see, were provocative of the wildest and maddest desires. Alas! how could the young clergyman, who was to be subjected to such temptations, possibly resist their intoxicating influence?

She stood before the mirror, in which her whole form was reflected, and gazed upon the matchless charms of her loveliness with triumphant delight She threw herself into bewitching attitudes, full of voluptuous languor; and, stretching herself upon a soft crimson velvet ottoman, which set off with ravishing effect the milky whiteness of her flesh, sank into a delicious reverie. in which her hot imagination plunged her into the wildest and most delicious enjoyments.

But of a sudden she was startled by hearing a cab stop in front of the door, a loud knock, and a heavy footstep upon the stairs. She sprang to her feet, and hastily enveloped herself in a robe of half transparent material, and listened intently. Perhaps it was her expected victim, who had arrived before the appointed time; but that was impossible. The old priest had assured her that he would not come before a certain hour—and that hour had not nearly arrived. Then the loud knock—the unceremonious rush up-stairs—what did it all mean?

All these thoughts occupied scarcely a moment's time to run through her brain. She was not doomed to remain much longer in suspense, for the door communicating with the drawing room was flung violently open, and Jack Rafferty appeared before her.

To describe the frantic terror of the miserable woman at the sight of the new comer would be impossible. She saw, from the look of concentrated hate upon her former lover's face, that if she fell into his hands her doom was sealed.

What that doom was to be she had no idea; but she knew that she had bitterly wronged him. She felt in her heart that his vengeance would be terrible. She must escape—anyhow and anywhere. Death by any other means were preferable to death at the hands of him whom she so dreaded.

He advanced towards her with his teeth set. She flew round the other side of the bath. He followed. She slipped through the door into the drawing-room.

She rushed towards the window, shrieking. He was close upon her. She dragged the window open. He clutched at her gauzy garments. They tore like paper in his hands, and she left them in his grasp She was outside the window. He tried to gripe her round the waist Her soft flesh glided through his fingers without him being able to retain his hold upon her. She slipped through his fingers like an eel. She had taken a spring; but somehow her foot caught at the last moment. Her spring was broken.

She fell with a heavy thud upon the pavement—she came down with a sickening, smashing blow, and lay there quivering, naked and bloody—in one moment horribly changed, and utterly unlike what she had been a moment before.

Some drunken night-brawlers, vomited forth from a low den of debauchery next door, who had been attracted by her nudity, came crowding round to jeer, and to laugh at her, but the sight of her blood sickened them, and they stood staring at her in dull, passive horror.

Then a cab drove up, and the old priest forced his way through the crowd, and she was raised, a horrible mass of broken bones, and carried groaning frightfully, into the house from the window of which she had just taken the fearful spring.

They took her up-stairs and laid her upon the bed. All around were the costly preparations for the licentious scene she would have acted. Rich wines and rare flowers upon every side. The walls hung, as of old, with the shameless pictures I have already described.

A doctor was summoned presently; and, amidst the patient's low groans of agony, passed his hands over her limbs, and endeavoured to see what damage had been done. She had fractured her right hip-bone and broken her right arm. Her face was horribly bruised and disfigured by its contact with the kerb-stone. She might live, the doctor said, but he did not think it likely. The old priest turned away from the bed-side with a deep sigh. It was thus that his wicked plans had come to an end.

"God forgive me! God forgive me!" he muttered, wringing his hands; but, looking up, he saw a stern face, with piercing eyes fixed upon him with an expression of intense hatred, which made him shudder.

"Were you a lover of that woman?" asked Rafferty, in a fierce whisper.

"Heaven forbid!" replied the old priest, piously crossing himself.

"What makes you grieve for her?"

"Is it not enough to make any Christian man grieve to see one so young and beautiful, but so wicked, and so unprepared for death, upon the brink of the grave?"

"She was a fiend incarnate!" replied Rafferty, fiercely. "She betrayed every one with whom she came in contact—me among the number! Why, man, I came here to-night intending to take her life, and I should have done so had she not saved me the job!"

"She will not recover, I am afraid!"

"If she does, she will have none of the old good looks with which she worked such damnable mischief."

"No. She will be a miserable cripple, at best, for the remainder of her life."

"I will take care of her."

"Nay," said the priest, "surely your vengeance is complete. Leave her now to the Church, whose secrets she holds. Leave her to me, and I will find an abode for her, where her sins shall trouble the world no more."

CHAPTER CLIV.

IN A LONDON CONVENT.

The notorious convent which I have called that of Saint Sorebones, during the course of this history, is, as I have said before, still flourishing, and has a large number of devout women within its walls. Some of these are willing inmates of the gloomy cells, while the residence of some others is compulsory.

Numerous proofs of a long career of shameless profligacy, coupled with suspicions of a more dark and damnable crime, having been brought against Lady Florence Darcy, by her unhappy husband, he and his family consulted together respecting the best method to be adopted with respect to the abandoned woman's safe keeping for the future, and decided upon immuring her for the remainder of her life in the cell of a convent. Knowing that she must choose between this or suicide, or a felon's death, Florence submitted to her fate, and the convent doors closed upon her for ever. As may be supposed, she soon found the life irksome and tedious—she soon began to long again for freedom. Her hot and ungovernable passions obtained a complete mastery over her, and when her fits were on her, she became a perfect fiend. But there was no escape—no chance of breaking out of her prison-house; and after awhile, when the fit was over, she sank into a despondent state of gloomy despair, from which, for days, and almost weeks together, nothing could arouse her.

And thus she lives and lived.

When Rafferty, during the course of his nocturnal wandering among the vilest slums in the metropolis, searching for Ruth, whom he expected to find in some low haunt of vice and debauchery, fell, as the reader may remember, into the hands of Jacob Stone and his gang, he accidentally overheard the diabolical plot which those scoundrels concocted for the robbing and murdering of servant girls. Knowing that he had money to pay, they allowed Rafferty to regain his liberty upon the payment of a heavy ransom, little dreaming that he knew anything of their schemes. When set free, however, Rafferty resolved to watch the villains and save their victims. Unfortunately, however, he could prove nothing against them, and could trace no crime to their door; and for a long time it is supposed these atrocious wretches carried on their bloody work unmolested, committing acts of the most inhuman cruelty and sickening horror upon the bodies of their unhappy victims before they deprived them of life. At last, however, it so happened that Rafferty, attracted by Cecily's extraordinary likeness to her sister Ruth (a likeness which was shared by Lady Florence, and had led to the intrigue between her and Rafferty), followed them to the door of the famous Agency Office, saw them enter with their luggage, and watched in vain for their coming forth again. Certain, from what he knew of the plot, that they were going to be murdered, he obtained the aid of the police, and forced an entrance into the house after much difficulty. His suspicions were but too sadly verified. He arrived only just in time to save the lives of the unhappy women the scoundrels had brutally ill-treated, and had only desisted after robbing them of that which they had deemed more valuable than life itself—their purity.

The miscreants subsequently met with the fate which they so richly merited, and were hanged for murder in the north of England, whither they had flown for security, and where they endeavoured to resume their hellish trade of wholesale butchery. The question was what was to become of the two unhappy sisters? Rafferty, consulting with the old priest, and it becoming known that Cecily had already been an inmate of the convent, he advised that they should be placed there in safety; and their sad experience of the miseries they had suffered outside its walls, caused them, upon receiving a promise that they would be treated kindly, to agree to a life of seclusion without much resistance. Unlike Lady Florence, they were not the victims of unruly passions and licentious imaginations. They soon became reconciled to their lot, and passed their lives not unhappily, working hard with their needles, reading pious books, and asking forgiveness of God for the sins they had committed. So one day resembled another; and thus they lived a changeless monotonous life without repining.

Ruth, as the reader may have been inclined to suppose, knowing what that lady could live through, did not die from the effects of her accident.

Although it was impossible that she should rise from her bed otherwise than as a cripple, she did rise, and slowly recovered her health and strength.

But her beauty was gone for ever.

Her mind was shattered.

She was not insane or idiotic, but she no longer retained that gigantic power of scheming and plotting which through life had urged her on to commit God only knows what black crimes and damnable acts of treacherous baseness.

It was only by watching her closely that the signs of weakness were observable in her intellectual powers; but that there was weakness was very certain.

She rose at length from her bed, after a weary and painful illness, a complete wreck of what she had once been.

She was a cripple, and was doomed, the remainder of her existence, to totter along with the aid of a crutch—to writhe through life tortuously, with a crab-like circumlocution.

Seeing her crouching before the fire in the sick room, warming her skinny hands at the flame, Jack Rafferty's long cherished wrath died away within his breast.

What more did he want of her now?

Was not the sight of her like this sufficient vengeance?

He who had known her in her peerless beauty—in the hey-day of her youth.

When she was young, rich, happy—idolized by all.

He tried to recall the recollection of all he had suffered, as he stood there looking at her.

How she had falsely striven to swear away his life

How, to obtain entire possession of money which he had stolen for her benefit more than his own, she had betrayed him to the police, worked hard to have him hanged, and succeeded at length in having him transported for life.

He thought of her, while he was languishing in chains and captivity, living a luxurious life at his expense, and laughing at his mad folly in ever having loved her and put himself into her power.

And while these thoughts passed through his brain he clenched his teeth and shook his fist at the wretch who had so treated him.

And she, in her weak terror, shivered at the sight of his lowering brow and flashing eyes, full of scorn and anger.

"Oh, Jack! oh, spare me! Oh, dear Jack—you would not hurt me! You would not have the heart to hurt me—a poor crippled thing like me!"

She made a trade out of her lameness, as she had once done out of her beauty.

She whined like a whipped dog, and crawled round him, her piteously supplicating face turned up towards his.

The rage, still smouldering within his heart, died at the sight of her.

Anger gave way to loathing and contempt.

"I don't want to hurt you," he said.

Then, wrenching himself loose from her grasp, he left the room.

He turned upon the threshold, however, and said, "I forgive you, Ruth!"

"You want to kill me!"

"No, I don't. I never want to see you more"

"I'm sure you hate me!"

"I *have* hated you as I have loved you in my

time; but that is all past. I forgive you all the wrong you have done me. May God be merciful on your soul!"

He quitted the room with these words, and Ruth and he never met again on earth.

It was determined by the old priest that she should be taken away to the convent of Saint Sorebones, and there immured for the remainder of her life.

His wicked scheme for the temptation of the Protestant preacher he abandoned from that time forth; but he deemed Ruth to be in the possession of dangerous secrets, which, if revealed, might cast discredit upon the faith which he professed.

Therefore he had come to a determination respecting her.

She should be locked up for the remainder of her life.

He never knew a half—no, nor a quarter of the crimes which this dreadful woman had committed; but he knew enough to be certain that had he chosen, he could have easily consigned her to an ignominious death at the hands of the common hangman.

And he practised upon this knowledge to induce Ruth quietly to submit to the proposed incarceration

Once within the convent walls, he determined that she should find escape impossible.

And such was the case.

Neither he nor anybody ever learnt all the secrets of this miserable sinner's life.

Frightful secrets they were, no doubt, but closely locked up within her own breast

Never to be revealed.

I, her historian, can give no detailed account of her doings.

In the annals of Scotland Yard are some ugly pages of her story, should you inquire for them under the proper name.

When quite a child she had run away from the people who had charge of her, and, who, it is true, as she told Earthworm, beat and ill-treated her to some extent.

Though it would appear that her precocious viciousness and perversity warranted the chastisements she received.

When little better than a baby, then, she ran away from her friends, and turned thief.

A year afterwards, when she was not more than ten years old, we find her living as the mistress of a boy thief, in some vile lodging-house in Kent Street.

Not long after that, the youthful lover falls into the hands of the police. His "widow" appears in handsome clothes, and living in squalid splendour, and a rumour gets about that she had given information to the police, has been rewarded, and has possessed herself of his property.

A similar connexion between her and another boy ensues, with a similar result.

Then she falls into the hands of the police herself, and is sent to a reformatory.

Soon after, she has escaped, is again the mistress of a thief, and again sells him to the police.

For awhile she disappears.

Then appears again in the company of Rafferty, who is a banker's clerk.

It is not long before he robs his employers, and is transported; his mistress appearing as a witness against him, and endeavouring, though unsuccessfully, to implicate him in another robbery, to which also a murder is attached.

Popular indignation rises high against pretty

Miss Ruth, with her child-like face, and yellow curls and innocent simper.

The judge expresses his horror of her, and the crowd outside hoot her, and would have used her roughly, did not a certain Earthworm — a low attorney, informer, and false swearer generally—come to her rescue and protect her from the mob's violence.

From this time she forsakes her old haunts, and is heard of only as a regular spy and informer, and the kept mistress of the scoundrel who has taken a fancy to her.

A certain needy adventurer—prince in his own country—skulking away from the police, and living a scampish life in London, attracted by the beauty of the female spy, proposed that she should accept of his protection.

Being of an artful turn, she, with the advice of Earthworm, refused, upon any other condition than that of marriage.

Just at this time, an old general, seventy years old, and in his dotage, made her an offer of his hand, which she accepted, and she became one of the queens of fast, fashionable London society.

Very soon after her marriage the husband died.

His relations disputed the will, which left her the whole of the old man's money, but she was victorious.

It was then that the Prince again besought her to listen to his love, and this time he also offered marriage. She accepted, and they were legally married.

The Prince was at that time in the poorest circumstances, over head and ears in debt—a vagabond and adventurer.

No one among his friends ever believed that he would have risen to a better position than the one in which he was living.

But it seems that he thought so; and, perhaps, the woman who had married him was of a similar opinion.

Anyhow, it was agreed between them that their marriage, for the present, should be a secret one.

Together, they took a house in Belgravia, which they opened as a first-class "hell;" and many thousands of pounds did they make out of the rich young good-for-nothings of this wicked city.

In conjunction with Earthworm, she, however, at the same time launched into a scheme for the wholesale passing of bad money; and the manufacturers of the base coin, after acting for a while as their tools, were, if they showed any signs of resistance, served in the way that Jacob Stone had been served, or Trevellyan—down in the mysterious subterranean.

As for the remainder of her career, we know it pretty well. We know how she acted as a decoy at the gambling house, and how, sometimes, she returned to her old trade of spy

How she wished to get Crockford into her power, for her own ends; how she excited the Prince's jealousy, he not being in the secret, and how furious at her conduct, and being at the same time desirous that the connexion should cease, he resolved upon her destruction.

It was at the time that his power was returning to him in his own country; and it is supposed that he wished Ruth to be put out of the way, so that there might be no possibility of her claiming a share of the crown which now he wears.

* * * * *

She was taken to the convent, believing it to be a refuge from her enemies, and a haven of peace and rest.

But very soon she wearied of the monotonous life therein led.

Very soon she began to pine for freedom.

She endeavoured to wheedle the Lady Superior to allow her to go out

Finding this to fail, she endeavoured to escape.

Finding escape hopeless, she gave herself up to despair.

She became unmanageable.

She appeared to lose all command over herself.

To lose all power of reason.

She was like a mad woman

Very often she flew like a wild cat at any one rash enough to enter her cell

She strove to murder all who came in her way.

Failing in this, she endeavoured to take her own life.

She was for ever engaged in some horrible act of self-mutilation.

She swallowed broken glass, and brought on spitting of blood.

She cut and wounded herself; and was found time after time, in her bed, weltering in her gore.

Sometimes she refused to leave her bed for days together.

Sometimes she lay and shrieked all night in an awful manner that broke the rest of the whole convent.

Very often, in her fits of rage, she tore her bedclothes and wearing-apparel all to pieces; and was sometimes discovered dancing frantically in her cell, naked and blood-besmeared

Nothing would cure her of these fits.

She was reasoned with without effect.

Starved without effect.

Scourged without effect.

She was incorrigible.

At such times her blasphemy was appalling—her obscenity revolting.

The nuns fled in terror from her hateful presence, and she was obliged to be kept by herself, out of sight and out of hearing of all.

Then the fits subsiding she would be penitent and sorry for what she had done.

Then she would have a pious turn, and say her prayers with great zeal for a day or two

She would wheedle and coax the Lady Superior to let her have brandy and tobacco.

Sometimes she wanted opium, and it was occasionally given to her to keep her quiet.

She would pretend to want to see the priest, that she might confess her sins to him, and, when alone together in her cell, strive to act her old part of syren and enchantress.

But her beauty had all gone long ago. She was truly horrible to look at, and the scared priest would shrink back from her lascivious advances with loathing and disgust.

It is more than probable that had it not been for the old man who watched over her welfare, she would have been quietly put out of the way by the Lady Superior, who hated her bitterly.

At last she appeared to lose all the little stock of wits which yet remained to her and went raving mad, beyond all hope of recovery

* * * * *

A horrible, mouthing, jabbering, savagely unearthly creature, with a scarred and distorted face, a wild, ragged head of hair, and a form crippled and crooked to an extent which was hideously grotesque—a perfectly idiotic, brutish, and obscene monster, unlike anything human—crafty, treacherous, cruel, dangerous—totally unmanageable, incurably filthy and shameless — a dirty squalid, unkempt, mangy-looking animal, more ape than woman, whom it was impossible to imagine had ever been Ruth, yet the wreck of Ruth it was! No longer did the fiend hide itself in an angel's form. Now was inside and outside alike hideous. She had risen from her sick bed an incurable cripple. She had risen with a face which had been rendered absolutely hideous by her accident. Perhaps it was the horror at her altered self which turned her brain, or it may have been that her busy, scheming brain had overworked itself. She went mad, at any rate; and when the convent gates closed upon her, they shut out for ever from the world the sight of this most treacherous and heartless of women—no longer a goddess of loveliness, before whom all men alike bowed the knee, but the dreadful, unclean, witless, jabbering idiot I have described.

And at this moment that I write she lives this life in the cell of the London convent, and her lovers have almost forgotten her. Perhaps Crockford and Rafferty, out at their farm in Australia, may think of her sometimes, and of the strange events of her life; but they do not talk together upon the subject, and her name never passes their lips

The Prince, who caused her to be taken abroad and confined in the French prison from which she escaped, has other matters to occupy his attention, for he has now a kingdom to look after, and a wife and a child, and a great but troublesome nation to take care of.

A miserable old villain, of the name of Earthworm, who is now a prisoner in the hulks, may think sometimes of the woman whose fortune he made, as he terms it, and whom he really loved more than anybody else, next to himself, in the world. The old man has plenty of time to think of her if he chooses, over his daily labour. But does any one in the world, looking back to any act of her life, think of her with pity and compassion?

CHAPTER THE LAST.

Once, in the height of her splendour, she gave a little ragged beggar-boy, whom she found crying with hunger on a doorstep, half-a-crown—not because she pitied him, but because she wanted to see his surprise at her munificence. Poor little wretch! he never had seen so much money in his life, and he never had seen so beautiful a lady. He spent the half-crown, and treasured her memory. Being a pious little boy, though very ragged and empty in a general way, he said a few prayers the last thing at night, before going to sleep on his favourite flag-stone; and he asked God, in his artless fashion, to bless her and send her to him with another half-crown.

I honestly believe that in all this Christian universe there exists no other living soul who ever knew her and thought of her with a blessing in his prayers.

THE END.

Milton Keynes UK
Ingram Content Group UK Ltd.
UKHW052334070624
443893UK00011B/461